# CLASSIC RABINDRANATH TAGORE



Rabindranath Tagore

PENGUIN BOOKS
An imprint of Penguin Random House

PENGUIN BOOKS

USA | Canada | UK | Ireland | Australia
New Zealand | India | South Africa | China | Singapore

Penguin Books is part of the Penguin Random House group of companies
whose addresses can be found at global.penguinrandomhouse.com

Published by Penguin Random House India Pvt. Ltd
4th Floor, Capital Tower 1, MG Road,
Gurugram 122 002, Haryana, India

Penguin
Random House
India

First published by Penguin Books India 2011



10 9 8 7 6 5 4 3 2

ISBN 9780143416326

Typeset in Sabon by Mantra Virtual Services, Gurgaon
Printed at Manipal Technologies Limited, India



www.penguin.co.in

MIX
Paper | Supporting responsible forestry
FSC® C043100
FSC www.fsc.org

This is a legitimate digitally printed version of the book and therefore might not have certain extra finishing on the cover.

# CONTENTS

PENGUIN BOOKS

CLASSIC RABINDRANATH TAGORE

Born in 1861, Rabindranath Tagore was a key figure of the Bengal Renaissance. He started writing at an early age, and by the turn of the century had become a household name in Bengal as a poet, a songwriter, a playwright, an essayist, a short story writer and a novelist. In 1913 he was awarded the Nobel Prize for Literature and his verse collection *Gitanjali* came to be known internationally. At about the same time he founded Visva Bharati, a university located in Santiniketan, near Kolkata. Called the 'Great Sentinel' of modern India by Mahatma Gandhi, Tagore steered clear of active politics but is famous for returning his knighthood as a gesture of protest against the Jallianwala Bagh massacre in 1919.

Tagore was a pioneering literary figure, renowned for his ceaseless innovations in poetry, prose, drama, music and painting, which he took up late in life. His works include novels; plays; essays on religious, social and literary topics; some sixty collections of verse; over a hundred short stories; and more than 2500 songs, including the national anthems of India and Bangladesh.

Rabindranath Tagore died in 1941. His eminence as India's greatest modern poet remains unchallenged to this day.

Sreejata Guha has an MA in comparative literature from State University of New York at Stony Brook. Apart from Tagore, she has translated works by Bankimchandra Chattopadhyay, Saratchandra Chattopadhyay, Saradindu Bandopadhyay and Taslima Nasrin for Penguin.

*

Sunanda Krishnamurty is a literary translator and a teacher. She has worked as a college lecturer in Delhi and has published articles in professional journals. She has co-authored *Dictionary of South and Southeast Asian Art*, and has translated into English a collection of Tagore's short stories entitled *Monihara and Other Stories*.

*

Radha Chakravarty teaches English literature in Gargi College, University of Delhi. She has co-edited *The Essential Tagore* for Harvard and *Visva Bharati*, and is the author of *Feminism and Contemporary Women Writers* (Routledge, 2008). She has translated several of Tagore's works including *Gora*, *Boyhood Days*, *Chokher Bali*, *Farewell Song: Shesher Kabita* and *The Land of Cards: Stories, Poems and Plays for Children*. Other works in translation include Bankimchandra Chattopadhyay's *Kapalkundala*, *In the Name of the Mother* by Mahasweta Devi and *Crossings: Stories from Bangladesh and India*. She has edited *Bodymaps: Stories by South Asian Women* and co-edited *Writing Feminism: South Asian Voices* and *Writing Freedom: South Asian Voices*.

*

Kaiser Haq is a poet, translator and essayist who was educated at the universities of Dhaka and Warwick. He has been a Commonwealth Scholar in the UK and a Senior Fulbright Scholar and Visa Fellow in the USA. He is professor of English at Dhaka University, where he has taught since 1975.

*

Hiten Bhaya, a former member of the Planning Commission, was also chairman, Hindustan Steel, and director, Indian Institute of Management. Apart from *Yogayog*, he has translated Tagore's writings on language and linguistics into English.

*

Malosree Sandel completed her doctorate and has worked in a premier college of Kolkata as a senior lecturer. She has translated Tagore for a hospice in the USA and is currently based in Manchester.

# A Grain of Sand
## (Chokher Bali)

*Translated by Sreejata Guha*

# 1

Binodini's mother, Harimati, came to Mahendra's mother, Rajlakshmi with an appeal. They were childhood friends from the same village.

That same day, Rajlakshmi broached the topic with her son, Mahendra. 'Mahin, we must do something for this poor girl. I've heard she is very beautiful and she's even had lessons from a British woman—I'm sure she'll appeal to your modern tastes.'

Mahendra said, 'Mother, there are plenty of other boys who have modern tastes.'

'Mahin, this is the problem with you: you always shy away from the subject of marriage.'

'Mother, we can talk about other things, can't we? This unwillingness is not really such a great flaw in my character.'

Mahendra had lost his father as a child. His relationship with his mother was therefore rather unique. He was twenty-two; after completing his MA, he was now studying medicine. Yet, not a day passed when he didn't have a playful tiff with his mother and then patched up ceremoniously. Figuratively speaking, just as a kangaroo cub is most comfortable in its mother's pouch it was second nature for Mahendra to stay in his mother's sheltering shadow. He could not dream of eating, sleeping, or even lifting a finger without his mother's constant ministering.

When his mother began to bring up Binodini as part of every conversation, he said, 'Fine, I will go and see this girl.'

On the appointed day he grumbled, 'What's the point of seeing her! I would only be marrying at your insistence; so it's a waste of time trying to figure out if I like her or not.'

There was a trace of resentment in the words, but his mother was sure that when he finally saw the girl at the time of the wedding, her son would approve of her choice and his ruffled feathers would be smoothed.

Rajlakshmi began to prepare for the wedding with great enthusiasm. But as the day drew nearer, Mahendra grew more and more restless. Eventually, a few days before the wedding he blurted out, 'No Mother, I cannot go through with this.'

From the day he was born, Mahendra had been indulged by the gods and men alike; hence his desires were uncontrolled. He was completely incapable of respecting the desires of others. So, the fact that he was bound by his mother's request and his own promise to her made him very hostile towards the whole proposition of marriage; he now refused point blank.

Behari was a very dear friend of Mahendra's. He addressed Mahendra as Dada and Rajlakshmi as Mother. The latter looked upon him as a mere towboat trawling behind the ship that was Mahendra, a necessary attachment for her son, and as such she felt quite kindly towards him. She said to him, 'Behari, you will have to marry her now; otherwise the unfortunate girl—'

Behari folded his hands and said, 'Mother, forgive me, but I cannot do that. When Mahin da wastes a sweet because he doesn't like the taste of it, I've finished it off at your request often enough. But that's not going to work where a bride is concerned.'

Rajlakshmi thought, 'Behari and marriage? He dotes on Mahin so much that the thought of marriage probably never crosses his mind!' This only served to increase her compassionate regard for Behari.

Binodini's father was not a wealthy man. But he had taken great pains to get his only daughter educated and trained in domestic work by a British missionary lady. It had not occurred to him that the girl was growing past the marriageable age. After his death, his widow began to look for a match desperately. They had no money and the girl was now in danger of remaining a spinster.

Finally Rajlakshmi came to their aid and fixed Binodini's marriage to the son of someone she knew from her native village near Barasat. Soon after her marriage, Binodini was widowed.

Mahendra laughed as he said, 'Thank heavens I didn't marry her. With a widowed wife where would I be?'

Three years later, mother and son were having the following conversation:

'Son, people are talking, and I am the one they're blaming.'

'Why Mother, what harm have you done them?'

'They say that I am not getting you married for fear that you'll forget me when your wife comes.'

Mahendra said, 'Well, that fear is justified. If I were a mother I would never dare get my son married. I would much rather take all the criticism that people dish out without a murmur of protest.'

Rajlakshmi laughed. 'Just listen to yourself.'

Mahendra said, 'But it is a fact that when a wife comes in, she gets all of the son's sympathies. The mother who loved and nurtured him for so many years suddenly grows distant. Even if you can take that, I cannot.'

Secretly thrilled, Rajlakshmi called out to her widowed sister-in-law, Annapurna, who was passing by. 'Just listen to my son, Mejo-bou. He doesn't want to marry for fear that his wife would oust me from his affections. Have you ever heard such nonsense in your life?'

Annapurna said, 'My son, that is going a little too far. There's a time for everything in life. This is the time for you to leave your mother's lap and build a life for yourself with your wife beside you. Such childish behaviour at this age is unbecoming.'

These words did not please Rajlakshmi at all. The words she spoke in response may have been forthright, but they certainly weren't pleasant. She said, 'Mejo-bou, why does it distress you if my son loves his mother more than most other sons? If you had a son you would know what it means to a mother.'

Rajlakshmi felt that the empty womb was envious of the proud provider of the male scion.

Annapurna said, 'I said that only because you broached the subject of Mahin's marriage. Otherwise, what right do I have to speak?'

Rajlakshmi said, 'Why should it trouble you if my son refuses to bring home a bride? Actually, if I have been able to bring up my son and care for him all these years, I can carry on doing so for the rest of my life—I don't need anyone else.'

Annapurna shed some silent tears as she walked away. Mahendra felt upset over this fallout; when he came back from his college he went straight to his aunt's room.

He knew that his aunt had only spoken out of affection for him. He was also aware that his aunt had an orphaned niece and that the childless widow would like to see her married to Mahendra so that she could have her close at hand. Although Mahendra was opposed to marriage, he thought this little wish of his aunt's was a very natural one and he empathized with it.

When Mahendra walked into the room, the light was already failing. Annapurna was resting her head on the bars of the window and staring out despondently. Her lunch lay covered and untouched on a table.

Mahendra was given to tears easily. This vision of his aunt made his eyes moist; he went closer and said, 'Aunty.'

Annapurna tried to smile. 'Mahin, come, sit.'

Mahendra said, 'I am very hungry and I'd love to have some leftovers from your lunch.'

Annapurna understood that he was trying to comfort her and checked her tears with great difficulty. She ate her lunch and fed him at the same time.

Mahendra's heart overflowed with pity and affection. At the end of his meal, just to cheer up his aunt, he spoke on impulse, 'Aunty, remember that niece of yours you'd mentioned—won't you show her to me?' The minute the words were out, he wished he hadn't said them.

Annapurna laughed and said, 'Are you thinking of marriage now?'

Mahendra spoke quickly, 'No, no, not for me. I think I might get Behari to agree. You must arrange for us to see her once.'

Annapurna said, 'The poor girl, will fate be so kind to her? If only she is lucky enough to have Behari for a husband.'

Mahendra turned to leave; at the door he bumped into his mother. 'What were you two discussing all this while?' she asked.

Mahendra said, 'No discussion, I just came for a paan.'

Rajlakshmi said, 'But your paan is ready in my room.'

Mahendra went away without speaking. Rajlakshmi entered the room, took one look at Annapurna's tear-stained face and her imagination ran wild. 'Well, well, Mejo-bou, carrying tales to my son, were we?' she hissed as she turned and left without waiting for an answer.

## 2

Mahendra had almost forgotten his promise to see the girl, but Annapurna hadn't. She wrote to the girl's relatives (on her father's side) in Shyambazar and arranged a date for her to be seen. When Mahendra heard that a date was fixed he said, 'Why did you rush things so much, Aunty? I haven't even spoken to Behari yet.'

Annapurna said, 'But Mahin, now if you don't go to see her, it won't look good.'

Mahendra sent for Behari and explained everything. He said, 'Let's go and see her at least; then if you don't like her, no one will force you.'

Behari said, 'I am not so sure of that. I won't be able to reject a girl who happens to be Aunty's niece.'

Mahendra said, 'Well, that settles it then.'

Behari said, 'But this was a very rash thing to do, Mahin da. You cannot go around putting loads on other people's shoulders when you have kept yours conveniently free. Now it will be very difficult for me to do anything that'll hurt Aunty.'

Mahendra looked a little shamefaced. Then he said somewhat irritatedly, 'So what do you want to do now?'

Behari said, 'Since you have raised her hopes in my name, I will marry the girl—but all this show of going to see her is not necessary.'

To Behari, Annapurna was nothing less than divine. She sent for Behari and said, 'This is not right, son—you cannot get married without seeing her. And promise me that you will say no if you do not like her.'

Behari had to agree.

On the appointed day Mahendra came back from college and said to Rajlakshmi, 'Mother, could I have that silk kurta and my Dhaka-cotton dhoti?'

Mother asked, 'Why? Where are you going?'

Mahendra said, 'Just give it now—I'll explain later.'

Mahendra couldn't resist dressing up a bit. Though he was going to see a girl for someone else, the very occasion was cause enough for a youth to pat his hair down and spray some essence.

The two friends set out for Shyambazar.

Anukulbabu was the girl's paternal uncle. His three-storeyed house surrounded by gardens, built with his own hard-earned money, towered over the neighbourhood. When his indigent brother died, he had brought his orphaned niece to stay with him. Her aunt, Annapurna, had offered to take her in but although that would have relieved him of additional expenses, he had refused for fear of compromising his reputation. In fact, he was so fastidious about his status that he seldom ever sent the girl to meet her aunt.

Soon, it was time to look for a match for the girl. But where preparations for the girl's wedding were concerned, Anukulbabu was unable to keep up his ostentatious ways. His intentions may have been grand, but the lack of money prevented them from being executed. Whenever the question of dowry came up, Anukulbabu said, 'I have daughters of my own; how can I pay for all this?' Thus the days passed. It was at such a time that Mahendra made his appearance with his friend, dressed to kill and reeking of essence.

It was early April; the sun was about to set. At one end of the first-floor veranda, decorated with painted ceramic tiles, arrangements were made for the two friends, with silver trays laden with fruits and sweets and icy liquids that condensed into a latticework of glistening dew upon the silver glasses. Mahendra and Behari sat down to partake of the offerings diffidently. Down in the garden the gardener watered the plants. As the scent of wet earth wafted on the cool April breeze, it also swayed and tugged at Mahendra's shawl. Through the doors and windows around them they could hear slight murmurs, gentle sounds of laughter and the tinkling of bangles.

When they had finished eating, Anukulbabu glanced into the interior of the house and called, 'Chuni, please get us some paan here.'

A little later a door behind them opened hesitantly and a young girl, shrouded in an invisible cloak of shyness, came and stood beside Anukulbabu, holding a tray of paan in her hands.

Anukulbabu said, 'Don't be shy, my child. Keep the tray in front of them.'

The girl bent low and placed the tray on the floor beside them with shaking hands. The rays of the setting sun touched her blushing face. Mahendra caught a quick glimpse of her tremulous expression. She made as if to run away but Anukulbabu said, 'Wait a minute, Chuni. Beharibabu, this is my younger brother Apurva's daughter. He is no more and I am all she has in this world.' He heaved a sigh.

Mahendra felt a bolt of pity strike through his heart. He glanced at the orphan girl once more.

No one had mentioned her age clearly. Close relatives always said, 'She'd be around twelve or thirteen,' which meant that she was perhaps closer to fourteen or fifteen. But her blossoming youth seemed caught up in a faltering timidity, perhaps because she was aware of her obligations as a dependent.

Mahendra's heart overflowed with sympathy as he asked, 'What is your name?'

Anukulbabu gave her encouragement, 'Tell him, child, tell him your name.'

The girl answered in her habitually obedient manner, 'My name is Ashalata.'

Asha! Mahendra felt the very name was poignant and the voice very mellow. Asha, the orphan! Asha, the hopeful!

The two friends came out on the streets, let the carriage go and started walking. Mahendra said, 'Behari, don't let go of this girl.'

Behari avoided a direct answer and said, 'The girl reminded me of her aunt; perhaps she'd be just as charming and good-natured.'

Mahendra said, 'So, perhaps now the load I placed on your shoulders doesn't seem quite so heavy?'

Behari said, 'No, it seems bearable.'

Mahendra said, 'But I don't want to put you to any trouble. Let me relieve you of your burden—what do you say?'

Behari cast a solemn glance at Mahendra and said, 'Mahin da, are you serious? There's still time. If you marry her, Aunty will be the happiest. She would then have the girl close to her all the time.'

Mahendra said, 'Are you mad? If that were possible, it would have happened long ago.'

Behari didn't raise any further objections and went his way. Mahendra took a long-winded route home and walked back slowly. Rajlakshmi was busy frying puris and Annapurna had not yet returned from her niece's.

Mahendra went up to the terrace all by himself and lay down on a mat. The half moon was casting its own silent, unique spells upon the concrete skyscape of Kolkata. When Rajlakshmi came to call him for dinner, Mahendra replied lazily, 'I don't feel like getting up.'

Rajlakshmi said, 'Let me send it up here then?'

Mahendra said, 'I don't want dinner tonight. I have already eaten.'

Rajlakshmi asked, 'Where did you eat?'

Mahendra said, 'That's a long story. I'll tell you later.'

Rajlakshmi was miffed at her son's inexplicable behaviour and made as if to leave. But Mahendra composed himself in a minute and spoke out repentantly, 'Mother, please send my meal up here.'

Mother answered, 'What's the point if you are not hungry?'

A small emotional scene ensued between mother and son following which Mahendra had to sit down to eat again.

## 3

That night Mahendra didn't sleep well. early the next morning he landed up at Behari's house and said, 'Behari, I gave it a lot of thought and finally came to the conclusion that Aunty wishes me to marry her niece.'

Behari said, 'She has made that wish known to you many times in many ways—there was no need to give it fresh thought.'

Mahendra said, 'Yes, well, that's why I feel that if I don't marry Asha she will be a little hurt.'

Behari said, 'It's possible.'

Mahendra said, 'I feel that would be very wrong of me.'

Behari spoke up with a trace of unnatural enthusiasm, 'Great news, that is wonderful—if you say yes, there's nothing more to be said. It would have been even better if you had woken up to your duty yesterday.'

Mahendra said, 'Well, better late than never.'

The moment Mahendra let the thought of marriage take hold of his mind it was difficult for him to show even the slightest patience. He felt that the deed should be done without any further ado.

He went to Rajlakshmi and said, 'Mother, I am agreeable to your wish—I'm ready for marriage.'

Rajlakshmi said to herself, 'Now I know why Mejo-bou rushed off to see her niece the other day and why Mahendra dressed up and left too.'

She felt angry at the entire universe; in spite of her repeated requests, it was Annapurna's plan that had succeeded! She said, 'Let me look for a good match for you.'

Mahendra said, 'Oh, that has been arranged.' He told Rajlakshmi about Asha.

Rajlakshmi said, 'Let me tell you, child, that girl will not do.'

Mahendra controlled his feelings and spoke mildly, 'Why Mother, isn't she a nice girl?'

Rajlakshmi said, 'She has no one to call her own. If I bring her in, I will have no relatives and family to look to from her side.'

Mahendra said, 'I wouldn't mind that, but Mother, I rather liked the girl.'

Rajlakshmi's heart grew harder at the sight of her son's persistence. She went to Annapurna and said, 'You want to get that orphaned, unlucky girl married to my only son so that you can control him, don't you? What audacity, what treachery!'

Annapurna wailed, 'There's no talk of Mahin marrying her; I do not know what he has felt prompted to tell you.'

Rajlakshmi didn't believe her one bit. Annapurna sent for Behari and implored him with tears in her eyes, 'Wasn't everything arranged with you? Why did you turn it all around? You will have to give your consent once again. If you don't help me, I will be greatly embarrassed. The girl is very nice, she won't be unworthy of you.'

Behari said, 'Aunty, you don't have to tell me that. Since she is your niece, there is no question of my disapproval. But Mahin da . . .'

Annapurna said, 'No, my child, there is no way she can marry Mahin. Let me be very honest with you—I'll be happiest if she marries you. I wouldn't consent to a match between her and Mahin.'

Behari said, 'Aunty, if you don't give your consent, the matter is settled.' He went to Rajlakshmi and said, 'Mother, Aunty's niece's wedding is fixed with me. There are no women in my family and so I had to be shameless enough to come and give you the news myself.'

Rajlakshmi said, 'Really, Behari? This makes me very happy. She is a very good girl. Don't let her go.'

Behari said, 'Why would I? Mahin da himself went and fixed this match for me.'

All this got Mahendra well and truly worked up. He was so upset with his mother and aunt that he left home and took up a room in a students' hostel. Rajlakshmi went to Annapurna in tears. 'Mejo-bou, it looks like my son is about to leave the house in misery. Please do something.'

Annapurna said, 'Didi, please be patient; his anger will evaporate in a few days.'

Rajlakshmi said, 'You don't know him. He can go to any extent if he doesn't get what he wants. You must do whatever you can and get him married to your niece.'

Annapurna said, 'Didi, how can I do that? I have given my word to Behari.'

Rajlakshmi said, 'That word can be taken back.' She sent for Behari and said, 'Son, I will find you a better match—you'll have to let this girl go. She isn't worthy of you.'

Behari said, 'No, Mother, that's not possible. It is all fixed.'

So Rajlakshmi went to Annapurna again and said, 'I beg of you, Mejo-bou, please help me. If you tell Behari, he'll do it.'

Annapurna said to Behari, 'Son, I hate to say this to you and I don't know how to say it. I would have been happiest if Asha were to marry you. But you know all that is happening—'

Behari said, 'I understand, Aunty. I will do as you say. But never, ever again will you request me to marry anyone.'

Behari left. Annapurna's eyes filled with tears. But she brushed them away for fear of bringing ill luck on Mahendra. She told herself again and again that whatever happened was for the best.

Thus the day of the wedding drew close, even as a silent, cruel battle of emotions raged between Rajlakshmi, Annapurna and Mahendra. The lights came on, the music played loudly and there was feasting and merry-making all around.

Asha stepped into her new home, decked in bridal finery, swathed in fetching shyness. Her gentle, trembling heart did not envision even a single thorn lining the fabric of her cosy haven. On the contrary, she was filled with joy that she was coming home to her aunt Annapurna, the closest thing to a mother that she had ever known.

After the wedding, Rajlakshmi called Mahendra and said, 'I think Bou-ma should go and stay with her uncle for a while now.'

Mahendra asked, 'Why, Mother?'

Rajlakshmi said, 'Your exams are coming up and you may not be able to concentrate.'

Mahendra said, 'I am not a child. I know how to look after myself.'

Rajlakshmi said, 'May be. But it's only a matter of another year.'

Mahendra said, 'If she had her parents, I wouldn't mind sending her to them. But I refuse to send her away to her uncle's house.'

Rajlakshmi muttered to herself, 'My, my, we are devoted, aren't we? Mother-in-law has no say in the matter! Married for a day and already tied to her apron strings. In our days when our husbands married us, such shameless fawning was unheard of.'

Mahendra said confidently, 'Don't worry, Mother! My exams will be fine.'

# 4

Rajlakshmi began to teach her new daughter-in-law the household duties with untold enthusiasm. Asha's days were spent in the store-room, kitchen and puja room. At night Rajlakshmi took her in to sleep in her own room, so that the young girl wouldn't miss her relatives too much.

After much deliberation Annapurna decided to keep her distance from her niece.

Mahendra's state was like that of the greedy child who watches the adult chewing the sugarcane stick dry, unable to do a thing about it. He could barely tolerate the vision of his newly wedded young wife being crushed under the wheels of household duties.

He went to Annapurna and said, 'Aunty, I cannot stand the way mother is working the new bride half to death.'

Annapurna knew that Rajlakshmi was overdoing things. But she said, 'Why Mahin, it's a good thing to teach the bride some household chores. It's better than her reading novels, sewing or sitting around doing nothing like these modern girls.'

Mahendra got worked up and said, 'A modern girl will be a modern girl, be it good or bad. If my wife can read a novel and appreciate it like me, I don't see what's wrong with it.'

Rajlakshmi heard her son in Annapurna's room, dropped whatever she was doing and rushed in. She asked sharply, 'What are you two discussing?'

Excited beyond words, Mahendra replied, 'Nothing, Mother, I just can't stand by and watch my wife working like a slave.'

Rajlakshmi controlled the burning spikes that jabbed within and answered in her most acerbic voice, 'And what, pray, should her ladyship do?'

Mahendra said, 'I will teach her to read.'

Rajlakshmi left the room without a word and a moment later she returned, pulling Asha by the hand. 'Here, take your bride and teach her to read.'

She then turned to Annapurna and bowed in mock obeisance, 'Forgive me, Mejo-bou, I didn't realize the true worth of your niece. I have stained her soft hands with turmeric in the kitchen; now you can wash them out carefully and hand her over to Mahin—she can put her feet up and study. I am always there to do the slave-work.' Rajlakshmi stomped into her room, slammed the door shut and bolted it noisily. Annapurna sank to the floor under the weight of her misery. Asha failed to get the full implications of this unexpected family spat; but she turned pale with shame, fear and wretchedness. Mahendra felt very angry as he thought to himself, 'Enough is enough. I must take my wife's life in my own hands, or it won't be right.'

These newly emerged feelings of duty fanned the flames of desire like a friendly breeze which bore away his college-work, exams, friends, social sense and all else. Mahendra was fired by the enthusiasm to teach his wife and he went into his room and shut the door, paying no heed to work or people.

A piqued Rajlakshmi thought, 'If Mahendra and his bride come and bang on my door, I will not answer. Let me see how he manages without his mother.'

Days passed and no repentant footfall sounded by the door.

Rajlakshmi decided that if he came to beg forgiveness, she'd forgive him, or he would be too hurt. But there were no entreaties for mercy.

Then Rajlakshmi decided to go to Mahendra's room and say that she had forgiven him. Just because the son was upset, the mother didn't have to be the same way.

Mahendra had a small room all to himself on the second-floor terrace, where he studied and slept. All these days Rajlakshmi had totally neglected cleaning his room, making the bed, putting his clothes away. Her heart was in turmoil since she had not performed her usual motherly duties. One afternoon she decided to go upstairs and tidy up his room while he was away in college; the minute he walked in, he'd know his mother had been there.

Rajlakshmi mounted the stairs. The door to Mahendra's room lay open and when she stood before it, she felt shock ripple through her. Mahendra was lying on the mattress on the floor, sleeping, and Asha sat with her back to the door, caressing his feet. Rajlakshmi was revolted at this blatant display of conjugal affections in broad daylight, with the door ajar. She went downstairs silently.

## 5

When long-famished mustard crops receive a sudden burst of rain, they make up for lost time and flourish in leaps and bounds, laying spontaneous claims to the earth around them. That is how it was with Asha. She had never truly felt that she belonged in the household to which she was related by blood. But after she came into this unfamiliar house, suddenly an intimate relationship, involving total trust, was hers for the asking; when her husband crowned the hitherto neglected orphan with his own hands, she didn't hesitate to rise to the occasion and take what was offered. She brushed aside the hesitant shyness of the new bride and took her rightful place at her husband's feet with artless pride and joy.

That afternoon, when Rajlakshmi spotted this newly arrived stranger-girl occupying her pride of place with such unconscious, easy grace, she came downstairs fuming and fretting indignantly. Since she was burning up with wrath, she went to singe Annapurna too. She said, 'Mejo-bou, just go and have a look at the royal heritage, the kind of thing your ladyship has learnt in her family. If only the elder men of this house were alive—'

Annapurna moaned in agonized distress, 'Didi, she is your daughter-in-law and you must scold her and teach her as you please. Why drag me into it?'

Like a strung bow, Rajlakshmi shrilled, 'My daughter-in-law? As long as you are ministering to her, would she even heed me?'

Annapurna went up to the couple's room, making a lot of noise, startling the pair of them. She looked at Asha. 'Is this how you are going to humiliate me, you stupid girl? Have you no shame, no sense of time or day, that you are resting here while your mother-in-law works herself to the bone? Serves me right for bringing you into this house!' The tears fell from her eyes as she spoke. Asha stood shocked in a corner, picking at her sari, tears streaming down her face.

Mahendra said, 'Aunty, why do you scold her? I am the one who holds her back.'

Annapurna said, 'And is that a good thing you're doing? She is young, an orphan, she has never been trained by her mother in the ways of this world. What are you teaching her?'

Mahendra said, 'Look, I have bought a slate, books and pen-and-paper for her. I am going to teach her to read, even if the world points fingers at me or all of you get angry.'

Annapurna said, 'But do you have to teach her all day long? An hour or so in the evenings would be quite enough.'

Mahendra said, 'It's not so simple, Aunty. Education is time consuming.'

Irked, Annapurna left the room. Asha took slow and hesitant footsteps to follow her. But Mahendra blocked her way, not heeding the pleading in her sad, lustrous eyes. He said, 'Wait, we have to make up for the time I lost sleeping.'

There may be earnest fools who might presume that Mahendra had indeed slept and wasted precious study-time; it is solely for their information that one needs to mention that Mahendra's educational methods would not be endorsed by any school inspector.

Asha trusted her husband. She truly believed that learning did not come easily to her and yet she must pursue it as a duty to her husband. For this precise reason, she did her best to collect her thoughts which ran helter-skelter.

She sat on a corner of the mattress on the floor, pored over her books fervently and began to learn them by rote, swaying to the rhythm. At the other end of the bedroom, her teacher sat at a small table with his medical books open. Every once in a while he cast an oblique glance at his student, apparently to measure her concentration. Suddenly, at some point, he would slam his books shut and call Asha by her pet name, 'Chuni!' Startled, Asha would look up. Mahendra would say, 'Bring the book to me—let me see what you are reading.'

Asha was scared she'd be tested. There was little chance of her passing the test. Her unruly mind was seldom equal to the task of acquiring knowledge from the book of alphabets. The more she tried to learn about the bumblebee, the more the letters swam before her eyes like a pile of mustard seeds. At her teacher's command Asha would guiltily bring the book and stand beside Mahendra's desk. One of his arms would snake round her waist and imprison her to his side firmly; he would hold the book in the other hand and ask, 'How much have you read today?'

Asha would point to the lines she had read.

Mahendra would sound forlorn. 'Ooh, that much? Want to see how much I have read?' He would point to the chapter heading in his medical text. Asha would widen her eyes. 'So what were you doing all this while?' Mahendra would caress her chin and say, 'I was lost in somebody's thoughts—a heartless person who was in turn lost in the life and times of the bumblebee.' Asha could have responded to this unfair accusation. But alas, modesty compelled her to accept this iniquitous defeat in the battle of love.

This will be proof enough that Mahendra's little school did not follow any private or public schooling methods.

If on a certain day Asha tried to concentrate on her books while Mahendra was away, he'd sneak up from behind her and cover her eyes. Then he'd snatch away her books and say, 'You are so cruel, you don't think of me when I am gone?'

Asha would say, 'Do you want me to remain illiterate?'

Mahendra would reply, 'Well, thanks to you I am not very literate myself these days.'

The words sounded harsh to Asha. She would make as if to leave and say, 'How have I stopped you from studying?'

Mahendra would grab her hand and say, 'How would you know that? I can't pore over books when you are gone as easily as you can in my absence.'

A serious accusation! This would naturally be followed by a sudden burst of tears, like an autumnal shower, and soon enough it would disappear to reveal the sunshine of love, leaving behind a golden glow.

If the teacher is the greatest barrier in the path of knowledge, the helpless student can scarcely make her way through the wilderness. Sometimes Asha recollected her aunt's scornful rebuke and felt ashamed. She was aware that her studies were only an excuse for togetherness. Every time she met her mother-in-law she felt mortified. But Rajlakshmi never asked her to do any chores, never had a word of advice for her. If Asha volunteered to lend a hand in the kitchen, she immediately restrained her saying, 'Oh no, no, you go to the bedroom—or your studies will suffer.'

Eventually, Annapurna said to Asha one day, 'Your education, or the lack thereof, is quite apparent to me. But are you going to let Mahin fail his exams too?'

Asha hardened her mind with great resolve and said to Mahendra, 'Your exam preparations are suffering. From now on I shall stay in Aunty's room downstairs.'

Such severe penance at this tender age! Exiled from the bedroom all the way to Aunty's room! Even as she uttered these harsh words Asha's eyes grew heavy with tears, her truant lips trembled and her voice held a tremor.

Mahendra said, 'Fine, let's go to Aunty's room. But then she'd have to come upstairs and take our room.'

Asha felt angry when her solemn, magnanimous gesture was laughed at. Mahendra said, 'Better still, why don't you guard me day and night and see for yourself if I am studying for my exams or not?'

The matter was settled very easily that day. Details of the intimate guarding that took place are needless. Suffice it to say that Mahendra failed his exams that year and despite the elaborate descriptions in her book, Asha's knowledge of the habits of the bumblebee remained meagre.

But it would be wrong to say that such fascinating educational exchanges were conducted uninterrupted. Sometimes Behari dropped in and caused a major disturbance. He'd herald his arrival shouting, 'Mahin da, Mahin da.' He wouldn't rest till he'd dragged Mahendra from his hibernating nest of the bedroom. He chided Mahendra severely for neglecting his studies. To Asha he'd say, 'Bouthan, you can't gulp your food and digest it; you have to chew it. Now you are gulping down the rice greedily—later you'll be hunting for digestive tablets!'

Mahendra would reply, 'Chuni, don't listen to him. He's jealous of our happiness.'

Behari would say, 'Since you hold your happiness in your own hands, consume it in a way that doesn't make others jealous.'

Mahendra would say, 'But it's fun to make others jealous. Chuni, you know, the ass that I am, I had nearly handed you over to Behari.'

Behari would blush and mutter, 'Enough, Mahin da.'

Such exchanges did not endear Behari to Asha. She felt quite hostile towards him, perhaps because at one time her marriage had been fixed with him. Behari knew this, and Mahendra liked to make fun at his expense.

Rajlakshmi often complained to Behari. He said, 'Mother, the silkworm weaving the thread isn't as scary as the moth that cuts the bonds and flies away. Who could tell he'd break away from you thus?'

When Rajlakshmi heard that Mahendra had failed his exams she went up in flames like a forest fire in summer. But it was Annapurna who bore the true consequences of his failure. She gave up food and sleep.

## 6

One cloudy evening, when the land was flooded with the first shower of the season, Mahendra entered his bedroom cheerfully, with a perfume-sprayed shawl on his shoulder and a fragrant garland around his neck. He tiptoed in, meaning to surprise Asha. But as he peeped in he found the window on the eastern corner open wide, the rain lashing in through it; the strong wind had snuffed out the lamp. Asha lay on the mattress, weeping her heart out.

Mahendra took quick steps into the room and asked, 'What's the matter?'

The young girl wept afresh. Many minutes passed before Mahendra finally got an answer: Annapurna couldn't take it any more and had gone away to her cousin's house.

Mahendra thought irately, 'If she had to go, why did she have to go today and spoil this nice, rainy evening for me!' But eventually all his wrath turned towards his mother. She was at the root of this. Mahendra said, 'Let us go and stay with Aunty—I'll see with whom Mother bickers.'

He kicked up a great fuss, began to pack his things and sent for bearers. Rajlakshmi understood what was afoot. She came up to Mahendra slowly and spoke to him calmly, 'Where are you going?'

At first he didn't answer. When she asked a few more times, he said, 'I am going to stay with Aunty.'

Rajlakshmi said, 'You don't have to go anywhere. I will go and fetch your aunt.'

She got into a palki and left for Annapurna's new home. Once there, she bowed low and said, 'Please don't be angry, Mejo-bou, and forgive me.'

Utterly embarrassed, Annapurna rushed to touch her feet as she wailed, 'Didi, why do you put me in the wrong thus? I'll do whatever you say.'

Rajlakshmi said, 'My son and daughter-in-law are leaving the house because you went away.' As she spoke, she burst into tears, tears of anger and humiliation.

The two sisters-in-law came back home. It was still raining. Asha had almost stopped weeping and Mahendra was doing his best to get her to smile. It appeared as if the rainy evening could be salvaged still.

Annapurna said, 'Chuni, you don't let me stay in this house, and you won't let go if I go away! Don't I deserve some peace?'

Asha looked up, startled like the wounded gazelle.

Mahendra was immensely irked as he said, 'Why Aunty, what has Chuni done to you?'

Annapurna said, 'I went away because I couldn't stand a new bride going about so brazenly. Why, you wretched girl, did you have to make your mother-in-law cry and fetch me back?'

Mahendra had not known that mothers and aunts were such a great hindrance to the poetry of one's life.

The next day Rajlakshmi sent for Behari. 'Son, please tell Mahin that I want to go to our ancestral home in Barasat—I haven't gone there in ages.'

Behari said, 'If you haven't gone there in ages, you need not go now. Anyway, I'll tell Mahin da, but I don't think he will agree to it.'

Mahendra said, 'Well, one does wish to see one's birthplace. But Mother shouldn't stay there for too long—the place gets uncomfortable when the rains come.'

Behari was annoyed to see Mahendra agreeing so easily. But he smiled and said, 'If Mother goes alone, there'll be no one to look after her. Why don't you send Bouthan with her?'

Mahendra sensed the covert criticism in Behari's words and disconcerted, he said, 'Of course I could do that.' But the matter didn't go any further than that. Behari only succeeded in alienating Asha's sympathies once again; the knowledge of that fact seemed to give him a wry pleasure.

Needless to say, Rajlakshmi wasn't all that keen to see her birthplace in Barasat. When the river runs dry in summer, the boatman drops the oar every now and then to check how deep the water runs. At such times of emotional rift between mother and son, Rajlakshmi too was plunging the oar here and there from time to time, checking on the depth of the emotions. She had not expected that her proposal of going away to Barasat would be accepted so easily. She said to herself, 'There's a difference between Annapurna leaving the house and my going away. She is a spell-casting witch and I am just a mother. It's better that I leave.'

Annapurna understood the workings of her mind and she said to Mahendra, 'If Didi leaves, I will go with her.'

Mahendra said, 'Did you hear that, Mother? If you go, Aunty will go with you and then how will our household run?'

Consumed with hatred, Rajlakshmi said, 'You will come, Mejo-bou? That's impossible—without you the household cannot run. You have to stay.'

Rajlakshmi couldn't wait any longer. The following afternoon she was ready to leave. Everyone including Behari had assumed that Mahendra would escort her. But when the time came it turned out that Mahendra had arranged for a bearer and a guard to accompany his mother.

Behari said, 'Mahin da, you are not dressed yet?'

A little shamefaced, Mahendra said, 'I have college—'

Behari said, 'Fine, you stay. I'll go with Mother.'

Mahendra was offended. When they were alone, he said to Asha, 'Really, Behari is going too far. He wants to prove that he is more concerned about Mother than I am.'

Annapurna was forced to stay back. But she shrank into her shell from shame, grief and exasperation. Mahendra was angry at this distant behaviour from his aunt; Asha too, felt hurt.

## 7

Rajlakshmi arrived at the barasat house. Behari was supposed to drop her off there and return at once. But when he saw how things were, he stayed back.

There were only a few very old widows living in Rajlakshmi's ancestral home. Thick forests of bamboo and foliage ran wild all around, the water in the pond was a deep, mossy green and jackals howled nearby all day long. Rajlakshmi was quite distressed.

Behari said, 'Mother, it may be your motherland, but "more glorious than all else" it is not. Let's go back to Kolkata. It'd be a sin to leave you alone here.'

Rajlakshmi was close to giving up and returning. But at this point Binodini arrived, seeking shelter with Rajlakshmi and at the same time providing her with loving care. Binodini needs no fresh introduction. At one time her marriage had been fixed first to Mahendra and later to Behari. But the husband that fate had ordained for her, had a spleen disorder that proved fatal very soon. Ever since his death, Binodini had spent her days alone in the cheerless household, like a lone flowering plant in the barren wilderness. Today the orphaned girl came and bowed respectfully, touched her aunt-in-law Rajlakshmi's feet and placed herself at her service. And it was service worthy of its name. There was not a moment's rest for her. Every chore was executed perfectly, meals were cooked to perfection and there was such lovely, gracious conversation.

Rajlakshmi would say, 'It's late my child, why don't you go and have some lunch?'

Binodini wouldn't hear of it. She didn't leave before she fanned her aunt to sleep.

Rajlakshmi said, 'But you'll fall ill, my child.'

But Binodini showed the least concern for her own health and said, 'Unfortunate souls like us don't fall ill, Aunty. You have come to your home after so many years—I have nothing here with which to care for you properly.'

Behari, meanwhile, became the local expert in a couple of days. Some came to consult him for their illnesses while others came to seek his advice on legal matters. If someone sought him out to find a good job for his son, someone else brought an application for him to fill out. He mingled with everyone with his intuitive curiosity and concern, be it the geriatric band of card players or the drinking group of the lower castes. No one resented him and he was welcome everywhere.

Binodini did her best to lighten the burden on this city-bred youth who was unfortunate enough to have landed in this godforsaken place. Every time Behari came back from his rounds, he found his room cleaned up, a bunch of flowers placed by his bed in a brass tumbler and Bankim and Dinabandhu's works neatly placed on his bedside table. On the inside covers of the books Binodini's name was inscribed in a feminine but firm hand.

There was a distinction between this kind of solicitude and the kind one normally encountered in a village. When Behari mentioned this to Rajlakshmi she said, 'And this is the girl both of you turned down.'

Behari laughed and said, 'It wasn't wise, Mother, we have been fools. But it's better to be fooled by not marrying than to be fooled by marrying.'

The thought churning in Rajlakshmi's mind was, 'This girl could have been my daughter-in-law. Why didn't it happen?'

If Rajlakshmi so much as mentioned going back to Kolkata, Binodini's eyes brimmed with tears and she said, 'Aunty, why did you have to come for a couple of days? When I didn't know you, my days passed somehow or other. Now, how will I live without you?'

Overwhelmed with emotion, Rajlakshmi blurted out, 'Child, why didn't you come into my house as a bride—I would have kept you so close to my heart!' These words made Binodini blush and run away.

Rajlakshmi was waiting for a letter from Kolkata, begging her to return. Her Mahin had never been away from his mother for so long in his entire life. He must be missing her terribly by now. Rajlakshmi was waiting eagerly for that letter from her son, bearing all his hurt feelings, tantrums and yearning for her.

Instead, Behari got a letter from Mahendra: 'Perhaps Mother is very happy to be back in her birthplace after so many years.'

Rajlakshmi thought, 'Dear me, Mahin must be very hurt. Happy! How could his wretched mother be happy anywhere without her Mahin!' 'O Behari, do read what more Mahin has written,' she said.

Behari said, 'There's nothing after that, Mother.' He crumpled up the letter, stuffed it into a book and dumped it in a corner of the room.

Rajlakshmi could scarcely contain herself. Mahin must have written such angry words that Behari couldn't read them out to his mother! Sometimes the calf butts against the cow's udder and procures both milk and maternal love. Rajlakshmi felt a similar surge of love for her son at the thought of his wrath. She forgave Mahendra readily and said to herself, 'If Mahin is happy with his bride, let him be. At any cost, he must be happy. I'll not trouble him any more. Poor thing, how angry he must be when his mother, who has never been away from him, has left him and come away.' Her tears overflowed at the very thought.

That day Rajlakshmi went again and again to Behari and hustled him, 'Go and have your bath, son; it's getting late.'

But Behari seemed to have lost interest in bathing or eating. He said, 'Mother, a little indiscipline is good for a hopeless wretch like me.'

Rajlakshmi coaxed him firmly, 'No, son, go and have your bath.'

After such continual badgering Behari went into the bathroom. The minute he left the room, Rajlakshmi rescued the crumpled letter from within the book, gave it to Binodini and said, 'Child, read out to me what Mahin has written to Behari.'

Binodini began to read. At first he had written about his mother, but that was very little. Not much more than what Behari had read out to her earlier. Then he had spoken of Asha. It was as if Mahendra was delirious with joy, mirth and a strange intoxication. Binodini read a little bit, blushed and stopped short, 'Aunty, what do you want to hear all this for?'

Rajlakshmi's yearning, loving face turned to stone in a moment. She was silent for a while and then she said, 'Stop.' She walked away without taking the letter back.

Binodini went into her room holding the letter. She bolted the door from within, sat on her bed and began to read again. Only she could say what she gleaned from that letter. But it certainly wasn't amusement. As she read it over and over again, her eyes began to burn like the desert sands at noon and her breath became as fiery as the desert winds. Her mind was awhirl with thoughts of Mahendra, Asha and their passionate romance. She held the letter on her lap, leant against the wall, stretched her legs out in front and sat still for a long time.

Behari couldn't find Mahendra's letter ever again.

That same afternoon, all of a sudden, Annapurna arrived in Barasat. Rajlakshmi paled at the thought of some bad news. She didn't dare ask anything and just looked at Annapurna with an ashen face.

Annapurna said at once, 'Didi, everything's fine in Kolkata.'

Rajlakshmi said, 'Then why are you here?'

Annapurna said, 'Didi, please take over your household. I have lost interest in these chores. I have set off to go to Kashi. I came here to take your blessings before I go. I may have wronged you, with or without intention, many a times. Please forgive me. And your daughter-in-law,' her eyes filled with tears, 'she is a child, she is motherless. Whether she is guilty or innocent, she is still yours.' She could speak no further.

Rajlakshmi got busy arranging for her bath and meal. Behari came running from Gadai Ghosh's gathering when he heard the news. He touched Annapurna's feet and said, 'Aunty, this is not possible; you cannot be so heartless as to leave us.'

Annapurna checked her tears and said, 'Don't try to hold me back, Behari—all of you be happy; nothing will stop on my account.'

Behari was silent. Then he said, 'Mahin da is very heartless to have bade you goodbye.'

Annapurna looked shaken. 'Don't say that—I am not angry with Mahin. But no good will come to the family unless I leave.'

Behari looked into the distance and sat there in silence. Annapurna undid the knot in her sari and took out a pair of gold bracelets. 'Son, keep these bracelets—give them to your wife with my blessings, when she comes.'

Behari touched them to his forehead and went into the next room to hide his tears.

As she left, Annapurna said, 'Behari, look after my Mahin and my Asha.'

She handed a piece of paper to Rajlakshmi and said, 'This is a deed whereby I give to Mahin my share in the ancestral property. Just send me fifteen rupees every month.'

She bent to the ground and took Rajlakshmi's blessings before she set off on her pilgrimage.

## 8

Asha was very scared. what on earth was going on! Rajlakshmi had gone away, and Annapurna followed suit. Mahendra's and her pleasure seemed to drive everyone away. It would end up driving her away. Their newly-wed love games struck her as a little incongruous amidst the vacant, deserted household.

If the flower of romance is plucked from the tree of life, it cannot sustain itself. Asha could also gradually see that there was a weariness, an ennui in their never-ending romance. It seemed to wilt every now and then—it was difficult sustaining it without the firm and liberal support of household life surrounding it. If romance has no link with other activities, play alone cannot bring out its true colours.

Mahendra tried to rebel against his family, lit all the lamps of his love-life all at once and tried to play out his grand romance amidst the gloom of his deserted household. He tried a dig at Asha, 'Chuni, what's the matter with you these days? Why are you so upset over your aunt's departure? Isn't our love enough to make up for all the loves in the world?'

Asha was miserable as she thought, 'Then there must be a lack in my love. I think of my aunt so often; I am so upset that Mother has left us.' She then tried her best to compensate for this lack in the extent of her love.

The household chores remained half done these days. The servants made hay and work was neglected. One day the maid claimed to be sick and was absent, the next day the cook was too drunk to come in to work. Mahendra said to Asha, 'That's great. Today we shall cook our own meals.'

Mahendra drove down to New Market to shop. He had no idea of what to buy and how much—he just picked up a lot of things and came home happy. Asha didn't have a clue either about what was to be done with the horde that he had brought home. Trial and error drove the clock hands past three o'clock and Mahendra was amused by the end result—a variety of inedible dishes. Asha failed to join him in his mirth—her own ignorance and incompetence shamed her.

Everything was scattered about so untidily in all the rooms that it was difficult to find anything when it was needed. One day, Mahendra's scalpel was used to cut vegetables and it took permanent refuge in the pile of debris. His notes were used to stoke the kitchen fire, whereupon they gave up the ghost on the ashen bed of the stove.

These and many other disasters gave Mahendra much cause for mirth while Asha continued to feel more and more upset. To the young girl such abandoned drifting of the household on the waves of confusion and waste was nothing less than a nightmare.

One evening the two were sitting on a bed they'd made on the covered veranda. Before them stretched the open terrace. After a spurt of rain the skyline of Kolkata was awash with moonlight on the horizon. Asha had gathered rain-drenched bakul flowers from the garden; she now sat with her head bent, weaving them into a garland. Mahendra was pulling at it, hindering her, criticizing and generally trying to pick a mock squabble. If Asha opened her mouth to chide him for such misdeeds, he immediately silenced her by a contrived move and nipped the reproach in the bud.

At this point the neighbour's koel called out from its cage. Immediately, Asha and Mahendra looked up at the cage that hung over their heads. Their koel never let the neighbour's koel go unanswered. Why was it silent today?

Asha was worried. 'What's wrong with the bird?'

Mahendra said, 'It's heard your voice and is too shy to open its beak.'

Asha pleaded, 'No, seriously, please have a look.'

Mahendra brought the cage off the hook. He opened its doors and found the bird had died. After Annapurna left, the bearer had gone on leave. No one had looked after the bird.

Asha's face turned ashen. Her fingers stilled over the flowers piled on her lap. Mahendra was saddened too; but he was more afraid of the mood being spoilt and so he tried to laugh it off, 'Actually it's all for the best. When I go to college the damned bird cried its heart out and disturbed you.' Mahendra reached for Asha and tried to hold her close.

Asha disentangled herself slowly and emptied her sari of the bakul flowers. 'No more,' she said. 'Shame on us! Please go quickly and bring Mother back.'

## 9

At that very moment there was a shout of 'Mahin da, Mahin da' from below. Mahendra replied, 'Hello there, come on up.' Behari's voice actually lifted Mahendra's spirits. Since their marriage Behari had often come between them as a barrier—but today that very barrier seemed welcome and imperative. Asha too felt relieved at Behari's arrival. When she drew the sari over her head and made as if to rise, Mahendra said, 'Where are you off to? It's only Behari.'

Asha said, 'Let me arrange for Thakurpo's tea.'

Asha's dejection lifted a little at this opportunity to do something. She wanted to hear about her mother-in-law and so she stood there awhile. She still never addressed Behari directly.

As he walked in Behari said, 'Oh no, I seem to have run headlong into intense poesy. Don't worry, Bouthan, you sit down and I'll be on my way.'

Asha glanced at Mahendra, who asked, 'Behari, how is Mother?'

Behari said, 'Don't bring up Mother and Aunty today, my friend, there's time yet for all that. Such a night was not made for sleep, nor for mothers and aunts.'

Behari was about to turn back when Mahendra dragged him back by force and made him sit down. Behari said, 'Look Bouthan, it's not my fault—he held me back by force—it's Mahin da's sin and the curse shouldn't come upon me!' Such bantering always irked Asha because she could never respond. Behari did this on purpose.

Behari said, 'Well, the house is a sight. Isn't it time yet for you to fetch Mother?'

Mahendra said, 'Certainly! In fact we are waiting for her.'

Behari said, 'It won't cost much of your time to write that to her and it'll give her immense joy. Bouthan, I appeal to you: please spare Mahin da for a few minutes so that he can write the note.'

Asha stomped away in anger—she had tears in her eyes.

Mahendra said, 'What a moment it was when you two set eyes upon one another—your squabbles never seem to end.'

Behari said, 'You have been spoilt by your mother and now your wife is doing the same. I find it so appalling that I protest ever so often.'

Mahendra asked, 'And what's the upshot of all this?'

Behari replied, 'None where you are concerned but there is some for me.'

## 10

Behari made Mahendra write the letter to Rajlakshmi and took it with him the next day, meaning to bring her back. Rajlakshmi could tell the letter was written as a result of Behari's coercion, but she couldn't stay away any longer. She brought Binodini along with her.

When she returned and found the house in utter disarray and chaos, Rajlakshmi felt even more hostile towards Asha. But what a change there was in Asha! She followed Rajlakshmi around like a shadow now, trying to lend a hand everywhere even without being told. Rajlakshmi exclaimed anxiously, 'Let it be, you'll ruin it! Why do you try to do what you don't know anything about?'

She reached the conclusion that this change in Asha was brought about by Annapurna's departure. But she felt Mahendra should not think that when Annapurna was around he could spend his days freely with Asha and now under his mother's regimen he had lost his wife. He would perceive his aunt as his well-wisher and his mother as an enemy. What was the point?

These days, if Mahendra called her in the day, Asha hesitated to go up. But Rajlakshmi reprimanded her, 'Can't you hear, Mahin is calling you? Can't you answer him? Too much love has gone to your head. Go on, you don't have to do the vegetables now.'

It was back to the mockery of the slate, pencil and the alphabets, blaming each other for the alleged paucity of love, pointless squabbles over who loved whom the most, turning gloomy days into nights and moonlit nights into sunny days, staving off ennui and boredom by sheer force. It was a kind of deadly grip on each other, where even when togetherness yielded no great joy, there was morbid fear in letting go of one another for even a single second—the pleasure of mating turned to ashes and yet, one couldn't move away from it, fearing a vacuum elsewhere. Such was the terrible curse of over-indulgence that although the pleasure wasn't long-standing, the bonds were lethally binding.

Then one day, Binodini came and twined her arms about Asha's neck and said, 'My friend, may your happiness last forever, but don't you think you could spare this hapless soul a mere glance sometimes?'

Asha had a natural reserve in front of strangers, having grown up in another's home. She feared rejection. When Binodini had arrived with her arched brows and sharp glance, her flawless face and her pristine, youthful beauty, Asha hadn't dared approach her to make her acquaintance. She noticed that Binodini was perfectly natural in Rajlakshmi's presence. Rajlakshmi also took pleasure in praising Binodini in Asha's presence, giving her more than her due share of importance. Asha perceived that Binodini was adept at all the household chores and supervision came naturally to her. She never hesitated to set the maids to work, scolding them and ordering them about. All this made Asha feel very small beside Binodini. But when that epitome of perfection, Binodini herself came to seek Asha's friendship, her pleasure drowned her hesitation and flooded her heart with joy. As if a magician had waved his wand somewhere, their friendship grew, blossomed and flourished in the space of a single day.

Asha said, 'Come, let's give our friendship a name—let's be something to each other.'

Binodini laughed. 'Like what?'

Asha suggested many pretty names like flower and bee, Ganga and Yamuna. But Binodini said, 'All those are outdated; an affectionate name is no longer worthy of love.'

Asha said, 'What would you like us to be?'

Binodini laughed and said, 'A grain of sand in the eye. Chokher Bali.'

Asha was more inclined towards the sweeter names, but she took Binodini's advice and settled for the affectionate invective of Chokher Bali—a grain of sand in the eye that drew pearly tears. She hugged Binodini and said, 'Chokher Bali,' and rolled to the floor, giggling.

## 11

Asha was badly in need of a companion. even a romance is incomplete if there are just two players—extra ears are needed to spread the words of love around. A famished Binodini drank up the details of the new bride's new-found romance like a drunkard swigging at a bottle. Her ears reddened as she listened and her blood fairly simmered in her veins.

In the muted afternoons, when Rajlakshmi was asleep, the servants disappeared into the rooms downstairs to rest and Mahendra went to college after much cajoling from Behari, when the faint cries of the kite could be heard from the far end of the blistering horizon, Asha lay flat on the bed with her hair spread out on the pillow and Binodini pulled up another pillow under her breast as she lay on her stomach; the two of them were lost in whispered tales—Binodini's face became flushed and her breath quickened. She always asked eager questions and got the tiniest details, heard the same stories over and over again and once they were told, she took recourse to her imagination and asked, 'What if things happened like this or like that?' Asha too enjoyed dragging the discussions onto those uncharted paths of what-if.

Binodini asked, 'Tell me, Chokher Bali, what would you do if you'd been married to Beharibabu instead?'

Asha said, 'Oh no, don't ever say that—oh God, I feel so embarrassed. But you would have suited him well; there was some talk once, wasn't there?'

Binodini said, 'Oh, there were talks about so many men for me. It's good it didn't happen—I am fine the way I am.'

Asha protested. How could she accept Binodini was happier than she was? 'Just think for a moment, Bali, if you'd got married to my husband! It nearly happened, too!'

Of course it had nearly happened. Why didn't it? Once this bed of Asha's was waiting for her. Binodini glanced around at this well-decorated room and simply couldn't push the thought out of her mind. Today she was a mere guest in this room, here today and gone tomorrow.

In the evening Binodini often took it upon herself to tie Asha's hair in a fancy hairdo and send her to greet her husband. Her imagination, veiled and hidden, crept behind this bedecked bride and entered the isolated room for a tryst with the spellbound young man. On some other days she refused to let Asha go. 'Oh come on, sit a little longer. Your husband won't run away. He's not the fleet-footed buck of the woods, he's the tame deer tethered at your threshold.' She would try to hold Asha back with such comments.

Mahendra got impatient and said, 'Your friend never seems to want to leave—when will she go back home?'

Asha rose to Binodini's defence zealously. 'No, you shan't be angry at my Chokher Bali. You'll be surprised to know that she loves hearing about you—she dresses me up so tenderly with her own hands and sends me to meet you.'

Rajlakshmi didn't let Asha do any household work. Binodini took Asha's side and let her in on some of the chores. Binodini was busy all day long with a variety of housework and now she wanted Asha at her side as well. She had woven a chain of household tasks so skillfully that it was impossible for Asha to find even a few minutes to steal away to Mahendra. Binodini laughed a cruel, jagged smile to herself when she thought of Asha's husband sitting in a corner of that lonely room on the terrace, bursting with impatience and thwarted passion. Concerned and anxious, Asha would remark, 'I'll be off now, Bali dear, or he'll be very angry.'

Quickly Binodini would say, 'Oh wait, just finish this bit and go—it won't take long.'

A little later Asha would grow restless again. 'No my friend, he'll be really angry now—let me go.'

Binodini would say, 'Oh dear, and I suppose that would be so terrible? There's no fun in romance if there isn't a bit of provocation sprinkled on the love—it's like the spice in the curry, it brings the flavour out.'

Actually, only Binodini knew the taste of this spice, but in her life the vegetables were missing from the curry. The blood flamed in her veins; wherever she glanced, her eyes showered sparks of burning embers: 'Such a happy household, such a loving husband—I could have made it a home fit for royalty and turned him into my devoted slave. This home then wouldn't be in this sorry state, and this man would have turned heads. But in my place rules this child of a girl, this infantile doll!' She hugged Asha and said, 'Dear Bali, please tell me what happened last night, won't you? Did you say all that I taught you to say? When I hear of your love, I lose both sleep and hunger.'

## 12

One day Mahendra grew annoyed and said to Rajlakshmi, 'do you think this is a good idea? Why do we have to take on the responsibility of a young widow from another family? I am not for this at all—you never know what troubles may lurk around the corner.'

Rajlakshmi said, 'But she is my Bipin's wife—I think of her as family.'

Mahendra said, 'No, Mother, this is not right. I would advice you to send her back.'

Rajlakshmi was well aware that Mahendra's wish couldn't be ignored easily. She sent for Behari and said, 'Behari, why don't you speak to Mahin? I am able to get a bit of rest in this old age simply because Bipin's wife is here. Call her whatever you like, but I have never got such loyal service from any of my own.'

Behari didn't answer Rajlakshmi, but he did go to Mahendra and say, 'Mahin da, have you thought about Binodini?'

Mahendra laughed and said, 'I am losing sleep over her. Why don't you ask your bouthan—Binodini is all I think about these days.'

Asha chided him silently from behind her anchal raised over her head.

Behari said, 'Well, well, we have a situation rivalling Bankim's *The Poison Tree* on our hands!'

Mahendra said, 'Exactly. Now Chuni is hell-bent on sending her away.'

From behind the veil, Asha's eyes seethed with silent rebuke.

Behari said, 'But it won't take long for her to come right back. I suggest you marry off this widow—that'll take care of her for good.'

Mahendra laughed. 'Kunda in *The Poison Tree* was married off too.'

Behari said, 'Fine, let that analogy be for now. I think of Binodini sometimes. She cannot possibly stay here forever. But sending her back to that godforsaken place is also a severe punishment.'

Binodini had not come face to face with Mahendra yet. But Behari had seen her and realized that she was worthy of more than the wilderness that passed for a home in Barasat. However, he was also wary of the fact that the flame that burned beautifully in an oil-lamp could as well set a house on fire.

Mahendra teased Behari about Binodini in various ways and Behari stood up to the test valiantly. But he stood firm in his belief that this woman shouldn't be toyed with and neither should she be ignored.

Rajlakshmi threw a word of caution at Binodini. 'Be careful my child, don't cling to Asha like that. You are used to the usual customs of a village household and know nothing of the modern ways. You are intelligent, you will know what I mean; just watch what you do.'

Following this, Binodini began to keep Asha at arm's length with great ceremony. She said, 'Oh, who am I? People like me should know their place and stay there or you never know what may happen.'

Asha wept and pleaded, but Binodini stood firm. Asha was fairly bursting with confidences unuttered, but Binodini paid no heed.

Meanwhile, the fervour of Mahendra's embraces slackened somewhat and his fascinated gaze on Asha grew rather weary. The foibles and oddities in Asha that had seemed amusing to him at first now irked him no end. He was piqued every moment by Asha's incompetence around the house, but he never spoke his mind. Even so, Asha could sense that familiarity had taken the sparkle out of the romance. Mahendra's lovemaking struck the wrong chords—some of it seemed excessive and some self-deceptive. At such times, escape was the only route, separation the only remedy. In the naturally intuitive fashion of women, Asha tried to leave Mahendra alone more often these days. But she had nowhere to go, except to Binodini.

Coming back to earth from the dizzy clouds of romance, Mahendra opened his eyes slowly and cast them at last on his studies, and other household chores. He began to retrieve his medical textbooks from all kinds of impossible places, wiped the dust off them and attempted to air out his college clothes.

# 13

When Binodini refused to acquiesce, asha tried another ploy. she said to Binodini, 'Dear Bali, why don't you ever come before my husband? Why do you always run and hide?'

Binodini's answer was brief and snappy, 'Shame!'

Asha said, 'Why? I have heard from Mother that you are related to us.'

Solemnly, Binodini replied, 'In this world, there are no fixed rules for telling who is a relative and who a stranger. Whoever you feel close to is your relative; and whoever perceives you as an intruder, may well be a relative but is still a stranger.'

Asha felt this remark could not be countered. It was a fact that her husband had wronged Binodini; he had thought of her as an intruder and often felt quite irked by her presence.

That same evening Asha pleaded with Mahendra, 'You must have a meeting with my Chokher Bali.'

Mahendra laughed. 'That's a grave risk you're taking.'

Asha said, 'Why, what's there to fear?'

Mahendra said, 'The kind of beauty you have described your friend to be, it's no safe haven for a man to venture into.'

Asha said, 'Oh, I can handle that. Please be serious—say you will meet her?'

It wasn't as though Mahendra wasn't curious to see Binodini; in fact, lately he'd even felt an urge to see her. But he felt this unwarranted impatience was somehow unethical. In matters of the heart, Mahendra's beliefs on what was ethical and what wasn't were a little more stringent than most people's. In the past he had not heeded the idea of marriage for fear that after marriage his mother's place wouldn't stay the same. These days he wanted to hold his relationship with Asha so sacred that he wouldn't let even the slightest curiosity about another woman tarry in his heart. He prided himself on the fact that his love was fastidious and pure. Similarly, he never wanted to acknowledge anyone else as his friend since that position was already given to Behari. If anyone ever felt attached to him and tried to further their acquaintance, Mahendra would go out of his way to be rude to them; he took pleasure in deriding them to Behari, and declaring himself absolutely indifferent to the average men around him. If Behari protested, Mahendra said, 'You can do that Behari—wherever you go, you make plenty of friends. But I'm afraid I don't feel like making friends with every Tom, Dick and Harry.'

Thus, when Mahendra's heart lurched with inevitable eagerness and curiosity at the thought of meeting this unfamiliar woman, he felt he was letting down his own ideals. Eventually, he had lost his patience and gone to Rajlakshmi, requesting her to send Binodini away from their home.

He now said to Asha, 'No, Chuni, I don't have the time to meet your friend. I have my studies to attend to and you are there: where is the space for another friend?'

Asha said, 'It's all right, I won't take up your study time; I'll give my share of the time to Bali.'

Mahendra said, 'You may well want to give it, but why would I let you do that?'

Mahendra claimed that Asha's love for Binodini was eating into her love for her husband. With great pride he would say, 'Your love is not as constant and steadfast as mine.' This often caused the pair to squabble. Asha wouldn't accept it—she'd cry and fight but never was she able to win the argument.

Mahendra grew to take pride in the fact that he was unwilling to let Binodini have even a hair's space between the two of them. Asha hated this pride, but one day she bowed before it humbly and said, 'All right then, will you please meet my Bali for my sake? Just once?'

Mahendra, after establishing the supremacy of his love over Asha's, finally agreed to meet Binodini as a favour to his wife. But he made it clear, 'That doesn't mean she'll be free to disturb me every now and then!'

The following morning Asha went into Binodini's room and woke her up with a hug. Binodini said, 'Wonder of wonders, the sunflower has left the sun and turned to the clouds today!'

Asha said, 'I'm no good at all that poetic stuff, my dear, so don't waste your breath. Why don't you go and say all this to the one who'd appreciate it most?'

Binodini said, 'And who is this poetic genius?'

Asha said, 'Your brother-in-law, my husband! No really, I'm not joking—he's very keen to meet you.

Binodini said to herself, 'Your wife has begged you to and so you've sent for me—if you think I'll come running, you couldn't be more wrong.'

Binodini refused doggedly. Asha lost face before her husband.

Mahendra was also very angry. How dare she refuse to come before him! Did she think he was like any other man? Others may have tried to find some excuse in all these days to talk to Binodini, to see her face. The fact that Mahendra never tried any such tricks should be enough for Binodini to realize that he was different. If she ever came to know him well, she'd surely see how extraordinary he was.

A couple of days ago Binodini had also felt quite upset. 'I've been in this house for so long and Mahendra has never once tried to catch a glimpse of me. When I am in his mother's room he never ever cooks up an excuse to come and speak to his mother. Why all the indifference? I am not a piece of furniture, I am a person, I'm a woman! If he ever got to know me well, he'd know the difference between me and his cherished Chuni!'

Asha came to her husband with an idea. 'I'll go and fetch my Chokher Bali to our room saying you have gone to college. And then you'll come in suddenly and confound her totally.'

Mahendra asked, 'What has she done to merit such a harsh sentence?'

Asha said, 'No, really, I am very angry indeed. She has refused to meet you! I'll break her tenacity or my name is not Asha.'

Mahendra said, 'I am not exactly dying to meet your bosom friend. I refuse to meet her like that, by stealth.'

Asha held his hand and begged, 'Please do this for me, just this once? I want to shatter her pride somehow, on this one occasion; thereafter you two are free to do what you like.'

Mahendra did not reply. Asha pleaded, 'Please dear, for my sake?'

Mahendra was actually getting more and more fired up—and so, with a great show of indifference, he conceded.

It was a sheer, silent autumn afternoon. Binodini was seated in Mahendra's room, teaching Asha how to knit a woollen shoe. Asha was restive, looking at the door every now and then, dropping stitches frequently and revealing her own incompetence to Binodini.

Finally, Binodini lost her temper, snatched the knitting from her hands and said, 'Oh, you are no good at this; I have work to do—I'm going.'

Asha said, 'Sit for a little longer; let me try again—I won't go wrong this time.' She went back to the knitting diligently.

Meanwhile, Mahendra came up soundlessly and stood at the door behind Binodini; Asha smiled without looking up from her knitting.

Binodini asked, 'Now what is making you smile?'

Asha couldn't check her laughter; she burst into giggles and flung the knitting over Binodini's head, saying, 'You're right my dear, this is not for me.' She threw her arms around her friend and went on giggling.

Binodini had understood everything right at the start. Asha's restlessness and gestures had revealed all. She was well aware that Mahendra had come and stood at the door. But she let herself fall into Asha's transparent trap, like a simple, naïve fool.

Mahendra stepped into the room saying, 'Pray share the joke with this hapless soul?'

Startled, Binodini tried to raise her anchal over her head. Asha caught her wrist.

Mahendra laughed. 'Either you sit and I leave, or we both have a seat.'

Binodini didn't go in for a great show of embarrassment, tugging her hands away from Asha's grip and clamouring to leave, like most women would have. She spoke naturally and easily, 'I shall sit because you've asked me to. But please don't curse me and speak ill of me when I am gone.'

Mahendra said, 'I'll curse you so that you lose the power to move for a long time.'

Binodini said, 'Oh, I am not afraid of that curse because your "long time" won't be too long—it's already over probably.'

She tried to get up again and Asha pressed her, 'Please, please do sit a little longer.'

## 14

Asha asked, 'Tell me honestly, what did you think of my Chokher Bali?'

Mahendra said, 'Not bad.'

Asha was a little hurt. 'You never really like anyone.'

Mahendra said, 'Except for one person.'

Asha said, 'All right, I'll know if you've liked her or not once the two of you get to know each other a little better.'

Mahendra said, 'Better than this! So this will happen frequently from now on?'

Asha said, 'Even courtesy demands that you further your acquaintance with some people. If you stop meeting her after just one conversation, what would she think? You are so strange. Anyone else would have been dying to meet such a girl as often as possible—but for you it seems like a great burden.'

Mahendra was happy to have this difference with other people reiterated. He said, 'All right, don't get upset. I have nowhere to run away and your friend shows no signs of leaving—so we'll certainly meet every now and then. And never fear, when we do, your husband has the social graces to be polite and cordial.'

Mahendra was under the impression that Binodini would find excuses and keep running into him from now on. He was wrong. Binodini never came anywhere near him and he never bumped into her accidentally, ever.

Mahendra couldn't bring up the subject with Asha for fear of even a hint of eagerness showing through. His efforts at suppressing the occasional wish to meet and talk to Binodini only served to stoke his desire. And Binodini's seeming indifference turned it into a blazing fire.

The day after he met Binodini, Mahendra asked Asha with carefully arranged airiness and laughter, 'How did your Chokher Bali like this unworthy husband of yours?'

Mahendra had hoped he'd get a gurgling, detailed report from Asha on this subject without his having to ask. But when he waited for it and it didn't come, he playfully brought up the question himself.

Asha felt very awkward. Binodini hadn't said a word on the subject and Asha was quite miffed with her because of this. She said to her husband, 'Be patient, let her get to know you better; how can she say anything on the basis of yesterday's short conversation?'

Mahendra felt crestfallen at this response and it grew even more difficult for him to feign indifference towards Binodini. But before he could ask any more questions, Behari walked in and asked, 'Mahin da, what are you two arguing about today?'

Mahendra said, 'Just listen to this: your bouthan has gone and become a hair-band or fish-bone or something to a Kumudini or Promodini or someone; good for her, I suppose. But now if I too have to be cigar's ash or match-stick to that lady, it's really going too far!'

Behind her veil Asha showed signs of a storm gathering perilously. Behari glanced at Mahendra and laughed silently; then he said, 'Bouthan, this is not a good sign. These are mere smokescreens. I have seen your Chokher Bali and I can swear that if I see her more often I wouldn't call it my bad luck. But if Mahin da protests too much, I do see a cause for concern.'

This was fresh proof to Asha that Mahendra was very different from Behari.

All of a sudden Mahendra developed a desire for photography. Once long ago he had started learning photography and then given it up. Now he got his camera fixed, bought some film and began to take pictures of everything and everybody. He didn't even spare the servants and bearers of the house.

Asha was very keen that he take a picture of her friend.

Mahendra said brusquely, 'Fine.'

But Binodini's answer was even more brusque. 'No.'

Asha had to resort to another ruse and once again, it was obvious to Binodini from the very start. The plan was that Asha would somehow get Binodini to come up to her room in the afternoon and put her to sleep. Mahendra would take her picture as she slept and that would serve her adamant friend right indeed! The strange thing was that Binodini never took a nap in the afternoon. But that day when she came into Asha's room, for some reason her eyes drooped at once. Draped in a red shawl and facing the window, she rested her head on her arm and fell asleep in such a lovely posture that Mahendra said, 'She seems to have posed for a picture even in her sleep.'

Mahendra tiptoed around and fetched his camera. In order to decide on the best angle, he had to look at her from all sides. For art's sake he even had to brush away a few strands of hair from her forehead—and when he didn't like the effect, he had to correct it again. He whispered to Asha, 'Just move the shawl a little to the left near her feet.'

The inept Asha whispered back, 'I can't do it, she'll surely wake up. You do it.'

Mahendra did the needful.

Eventually, just when he had loaded the plate into the camera, Binodini seemed to sense the sound, sighed, turned her head and woke up with a start. Asha chortled in delight.

Binodini was extremely angry. Her sparkling eyes showered wrath upon Mahendra as she exclaimed, 'This isn't right!'

Mahendra said, 'I agree with you. But how can I bear it if after all my stealth I'm not even able to bring home the loot? Pray let me finish my crime and then punish me as you please.'

Asha begged and pleaded with Binodini. The picture was taken. But this first picture was spoilt. So the photographer insisted on taking another one the following day. Finally, Binodini couldn't say no to the proposal of taking one picture with both girls in it as a symbol of their everlasting friendship. But she said, 'This will be the last one.'

So Mahendra deliberately spoilt that one. And then, over pictures and more pictures the acquaintance and camaraderie between them progressed in leaps and bounds.

## 15

Dying embers get a fresh lease of life if the fire is stoked from without. The slight breach that had come about in the newly-weds' romance soon healed itself and their passion burned afresh after the introduction of a third party in their midst. Asha lacked the capacity to laugh and make witty conversation. But Binodini could provide that in abundance; and so Asha found a safe haven behind Binodini's strong persona. She no longer had to try so hard at keeping Mahendra entertained and amused all the time.

Within the short span of a few months, Asha and Mahendra had almost poured themselves out to each other—their song of love had started on the highest possible note—it was as if they were intent on eating up the principal instead of living off the interest. How were they to translate this deluge of recklessness into the mundane simplicity of daily life? How could Asha provide the fresh stimulation that Mahendra looked for every time tedium gripped him after traversing the heights of intoxication? It was then that Binodini brought in a colourful goblet filled with the fresh and the new—and Asha was relieved to see her husband in good humour again.

Now she no longer tried so hard herself. When Mahendra and Binodini laughed and joked, she simply laughed along joyfully. When Mahendra tried to cheat her at card games, she appealed to Binodini for justice. If Mahendra teased her or spoke out of turn, she expected Binodini to take her side and protest. In this fashion the threesome got accustomed to one another.

But this didn't stop Binodini from tending to her household chores. She only joined in the fun after she had finished cooking, cleaning, supervising the servants and taken proper care of Rajlakshmi. Mahendra would get impatient. 'You're going to spoil the servants by doing everything yourself.' Binodini would answer, 'That's better than spoiling yourself by not doing a thing. Go on, you had better go to college.'

Mahendra would say, 'It's a nice cloudy day—'

Binodini would reply, 'Oh no, you don't get away with that—the carriage is ready—you must go to college.'

Mahendra would argue, 'But I cancelled the carriage.'

Binodini would retort, 'I called it back.'

She would bring his clothes for college and stand before him.

Mahendra would say, 'You should have been born in a Rajput household—you'd have had fun placing the armour on your loved one when he went to war.'

Binodini did not like the idea of dropping out of classes or skipping studies for fun. Under her strict regulation the practice of lounging about and having fun at any time of the day became a thing of the past in the household. And hence the evening sessions turned into an oasis of pleasure for Mahendra. His days yearned for themselves to end.

Earlier, when his meals weren't ready on time, Mahendra gladly used this as a pretext to stay back home. These days Binodini took care to see that his meal was ready first thing in the morning and the minute he finished it, he was told that the carriage was waiting for him. Earlier, he seldom found his clothes neatly folded and laid out for him: on the contrary, they usually languished in a forgotten corner of some cupboard instead of going to the laundry and turned up many days later when one was searching for something quite different.

At first Binodini often chided Asha playfully in front of Mahendra, for these and other muddles. Mahendra too smiled indulgently at Asha's helpless ineptitude. But soon, out of affection for her friend, Binodini relieved Asha of her duties. Everything in the household had a changed look since then. If a shirt button broke and Asha stood gazing at it helplessly, Binodini snatched the garment from her nerveless fingers and stitched it up in no time. One day a cat got to Mahendra's plate of rice first and had a few mouthfuls. Asha was worried sick; Binodini went into the kitchen immediately, looked into various pots and pans and deftly rustled up another plate of food. Asha was dumbfounded at her proficiency.

Mahendra felt Binodini's caring touch in his clothing and food, at work and leisure. The woollen shoes on his feet and the woollen scarf around his neck—made by Binodini—felt like a tangible emotional contact. These days Asha came to Mahendra, neat, tidy and all decked up by her friend: she felt like she was partly herself and partly someone else; she and Binodini seemed to have united like the Ganga and the Yamuna.

Behari was no longer as welcome as he was before—he was rarely sent for. Once Behari wrote to Mahendra to say that he'd like to come the next day at noon, a Sunday, and taste his mother's cooking. Mahendra felt the Sunday would go waste. So he quickly wrote back that the next day he had some work and would have to go out. But Behari dropped by in any case to look them up after lunch. The bearer informed him that Mahendra had not left the house. Behari yelled out 'Mahin da,' as he bounded up the stairs and went straight into Mahendra's room. Caught unawares, Mahendra said he had a headache and lay down facing the wall. Asha grew nervous when she saw the complexion of Mahendra's mood. She glanced at Binodini hopefully. Binodini was well aware that it wasn't a serious matter; but she said anxiously, 'You've been sitting up for too long, why don't you lie down. I'll get some eau-de-cologne.'

Mahendra said, 'It's all right, don't bother.'

Binodini paid no heed and quickly fetched some eau-de-cologne mixed with cool water. She handed the wet towel to Asha and said, 'Put this on Mahendrababu's temple.'

Mahendra went on saying, 'It's all right.'

Behari checked his laughter as he watched this performance. Mahendra felt smug that Behari could witness how precious he was to the two women.

Shyness in Behari's presence caused Asha's fingers to tremble and she wasn't very deft with the towel; a few drops of eau-de-cologne sloshed into Mahendra's eyes. Binodini took the towel from her hands and applied it skillfully; she then wet another piece of cloth with the liquid and wrung it out over the towel. Asha veiled her head and fanned her husband quietly.

Binodini asked in soothing tones, 'Mahendrababu, do you feel better?'

Having spoken such honeyed words, Binodini shot an oblique glance at Behari's face. She found his eyes twinkling in merriment. The whole thing was a farce to him. Binodini realized this man couldn't be fooled easily—nothing escaped him.

Behari laughed. 'Binod-bouthan, with therapy like this the ailment is likely to intensify rather than subside.'

Binodini said, 'How would I know that, we are only ignorant women. Is that what they say in your medical textbooks?'

Behari said, 'Of course. This kind of treatment is making my own head throb. But my head had better get all right on its own. Mahin da's head carries a far greater weight.'

Binodini dropped the wet cloth and said, 'Forget it then; let the friend treat his comrade.'

Behari was growing quite impatient with what he saw. He had been busy with his books and wasn't aware of just how complicated a relationship this trio had cooked up in the meantime. Today he observed Binodini carefully and she too took her measure of him.

Behari spoke a trifle harshly this time, 'Fair enough. A friend must indeed care for his friend. I brought on the headache and now I shall leave with it. Don't waste the eau-de-cologne.' He glanced at Asha. 'Bouthan, prevention is better than cure.'

## 16

Behari thought, 'I can't stay away any longer. Somehow, I must make my place among these people. None of them will want it, but it must be done.'

So he began to infiltrate Mahendra's circle without waiting to be invited. He said to Binodini, 'Binod-bouthan, this man has been spoilt by his mother, by his friend and then by his wife; I beg of you, don't spoil him further; show him a different path instead.'

Mahendra said, 'Meaning—'

Behari said, 'Meaning that a man like me, whom nobody spares a second glance—'

'Should be spoilt instead?' Mahendra quipped. 'It's not that easy; simply putting in an application is not enough.'

Binodini laughed. 'One has to have the capacity to be spoilt, Beharibabu.'

Behari said, 'That depends on who is doing the spoiling. Why don't you give it a try?'

Binodini said, 'It doesn't work if you are forewarned and forearmed; unawares is how it has to catch you, isn't it, dear Chokher Bali? Why don't you take on this brother-in-law of yours?'

Asha lifted two fingers and pushed her away. Behari also refrained from joining in the joke. It had not escaped Binodini that Behari wouldn't stand any nonsense where Asha was concerned. It hurt her that Behari idolized Asha but wanted to pull her down a peg or two. She looked at Asha again and said, 'This poor brother of yours is actually begging your love, though he addresses me—so give him some, dear friend.'

Asha was very cross. Behari blushed for an instant and in the next he laughed and said, 'So when it's my turn you pass the plea on to others but when it's Mahin da you take the matter in your own hands, do you, and deal in cash?'

It was obvious to Binodini that Behari was intent on upsetting her applecart; she'd have to be careful where he was concerned. Mahendra was annoyed—all this straight talk rang a false note in the melody. He addressed Behari a trifle harshly, 'Behari, your Mahin da doesn't need to go into any deals; he's happy with what he has.'

Behari said, 'He may not need to go into it, but if fate ordains it, a succession of such deals will come and crash on his doorstep like as many waves.'

Binodini said, 'You have nothing in hand at the moment; but where are your waves crashing right now?' She laughed at Asha and poked her in jest. Incensed, Asha got up and walked away. Behari held his tongue in thwarted rage; as he made to rise, Binodini said, 'Don't go away unhappy, Beharibabu. I'll go and send my Chokher Bali to you right away.'

When Binodini left, Mahendra was displeased that the gathering had broken up. His disgruntled face set Behari's nerves on edge and he burst forth, 'Mahin da, you are free to court disaster for yourself—it's something you have always done. But please don't ruin the simple, pious woman who has sought refuge with you. I beg of you, don't ruin her life.' Behari choked on the last words.

Mahendra shouted in righteous anger, 'Behari, I don't understand what you are saying. Don't speak in riddles; clearly say what you want to.'

Behari said, 'I'll do that then. Binodini is leading you astray on purpose and you are stepping on to the forbidden path like a fool.'

Mahendra roared, 'Lies! If you dare to make such false accusations about a lady from a respected family, you should be barred from the inner chambers.'

At this point Binodini walked in with a plate of sweets and smiling, placed it before Behari. He said, 'What's all this? I am not hungry.'

Binodini said, 'Well, that's how it is. You cannot go without eating some of this.'

Behari laughed, 'Does this mean that my application has been accepted and my "spoiling" has begun?'

Binodini smiled coyly and said, 'Since you are a younger brother-in-law, you have a right; why beg where you can demand? You may choose to seize affection if you wish, isn't that so, Mahendrababu?'

Mahendra was lost for words.

Binodini said, 'Beharibabu, is it modesty or anger that makes you refrain from touching the sweets? Must I call someone else here?'

Behari said, 'There's no need for that; what I have here is more than enough.'

Binodini said, 'Mockery? You are incorrigible. Even sweets cannot silence you.'

That night Asha condemned Behari to Mahendra and he supported her unconditionally, unlike other days when he would laugh and brush aside her complaints against his friend.

The next morning Mahendra visited Behari and said, 'Behari, all said and done, Binodini is not really a member of the family and in your presence she seems to feel a bit uncomfortable.'

Behari said, 'Is that so? That's a pity. Well, if it bothers her I guess I should stay away.'

Mahendra was relieved. He hadn't expected this unpleasant task to be accomplished so easily. He was a little scared of Behari.

The same day Behari strolled into Mahendra's inner chambers and said, 'Binod-bouthan, I beg your pardon.'

Binodini asked, 'But why?'

Behari said, 'I heard from Mahin da that my presence in the inner chambers offends you. So I shall beg your pardon and take my leave.'

Binodini said, 'Oh, that's not right, Beharibabu; I am here today and gone tomorrow. Why should you leave on my account? Had I known there would be such trouble I would never have come here.' Binodini's face fell and she looked as though she was holding back her tears as she walked away.

In that instant Behari felt, 'My suspicions were wrong—I have wrongly accused Binodini.'

That evening Rajlakshmi came to Mahendra in despair and said, 'Mahin, Bipin's wife is determined to leave us.'

Mahendra asked, 'Why Mother, what's troubling her here?'

Rajlakshmi said, 'Nothing. But she says if a young widow like her stays on in another's house for too long, tongues will wag.'

Mahendra was angry. 'This is not exactly "another's house", is it!'

Behari was sitting there and Mahendra threw him an incensed look.

Repentant, Behari mused silently, 'Yesterday I was perhaps too critical of Binodini and she's upset about it.'

Both husband and wife felt offended with Binodini.

One said, 'So you think we are "others"?' and the other said, 'After so long you still don't think of us as your own.'

Binodini said, 'But really, did you think you could keep me here forever?'

Mahendra said, 'Oh no, we wouldn't dare to presume any such thing!'

Asha said, 'Why did you steal our hearts like this if you meant to go away?'

That day nothing was decided. Binodini said to Asha, 'No, my friend, let me go. It's best to leave before the tie grows stronger.' She threw a poignant look at Mahendra as she said this.

The next day Behari came and said, 'Binod-bouthan, why do you speak of going? Have we offended you—is this a penalty we have to pay?'

Binodini turned her face slightly and said, 'Why would you offend me—my own fate is at fault.'

Behari said, 'But if you leave I can't help feeling it would be my fault.'

Binodini raised her eyes full of pleading and asked of Behari, 'You tell me, is it right for me to stay?'

Behari was put in a spot. How could he answer in the affirmative? He said, 'Of course, you must leave at some point; but why don't you stay a while longer?'

Binodini lowered her eyes and said, 'All of you are begging me to stay—it is rather difficult for me to override the requests—but this is really very wrong of you.' As she spoke, the tears fell thick and fast through the dense curtain of her long lashes.

Behari was unnerved by this silent, severe deluge of tears and exclaimed, 'In the short while that you've been here, you have won the hearts of everyone around you. And that is why no one wants to let you go. Please don't take it to heart Binod-bouthan, but who would want to be separated from such grace and charm?'

Asha sat in a corner with her sari pulled over her head, and wiped her eyes repeatedly. After this incident, Binodini never spoke of leaving again.

## 17

In an effort to wipe out the memory of this unpleasantness, Mahendra proposed a picnic in the farmhouse at Dumdum the following Sunday. Asha welcomed the idea but Binodini refused. Both Mahendra and Asha were crestfallen at her refusal. They thought, 'Binodini is trying to distance herself from us these days.'

That evening, the minute Behari arrived, Binodini said, 'Beharibabu, listen to this, Mahinbabu wants to go to the farmhouse at Dumdum for a picnic and because I refused to go, the two of them have been sulking all day.'

Behari said, 'I can't blame them. If you don't go, the bedlam that'll pass for a picnic can't be wished upon one's worst enemies, let alone on these two.'

Binodini said, 'Why don't you come along, Beharibabu? If you come, I'm willing to go.'

Behari said, 'Brilliant suggestion. But it awaits the master's approval—what does the master say?'

Both the master and her ladyship were miffed at this predilection on Binodini's part towards Behari. Hearing the proposal, Mahendra's eagerness for the outing dwindled. He was keen on persuading Behari that the latter's presence was distasteful to Binodini at all times. But now it would be difficult to hold him back.

Mahendra said, 'That's fine, sounds good. But Behari, you always kick up a ruckus wherever you go—perhaps you'll invite a whole bunch of local children there or stir up a fight with a whiteskin, one never knows what to expect with you.'

Behari understood why Mahendra was dragging his feet and he smiled quietly to himself as he said, 'But that's the fun of life—one never knows what's to come, what will happen next. Binod-bouthan, we'll have to leave at the crack of dawn. I'll be here on time.'

At the appointed time two carriages pulled up in front of the house: an ordinary one for luggage and bearers and a deluxe carriage for the gentlemen and ladies. Behari arrived early with a huge box. Mahendra said, 'What is that? There's no room in the servants' carriage.'

Behari said, 'Don't worry, Mahin da, I'll take care of everything.'

Binodini and Asha got into the carriage. Mahendra hesitated, wondering what he should do about Behari. But Behari hauled the box on top of the carriage and jumped into the coachbox beside the coachman.

Mahendra heaved a sigh of relief. He was afraid Behari would want to sit inside the carriage and then there was no telling what he would do. Binodini was concerned. 'Beharibabu, isn't that rather unsafe?'

Behari answered her, 'Don't worry, my role in the performance doesn't include "falls to the ground and bites the dust".'

As soon as the carriage rolled away, Mahendra said, 'Why don't I go and sit out there and send Behari inside?'

Asha didn't like this. 'No, you won't sit there.'

Binodini said, 'Please don't. You are not used to it; you may fall.'

Mahendra got worked up. 'Fall indeed! Not on your life!' He made to open the door and get off.

Binodini said, 'You may well blame Beharibabu, but you take the cake in kicking up a fuss.'

Mahendra was in a huff. 'Fine then,' he said, 'let me hire a second carriage and go in that and let Behari come in and sit here.'

Asha said, 'If you do that, I'll come with you.'

Binodini said, 'And I suppose I should jump off the carriage?' The conversation ended amidst this hullabaloo. But all the way to Dumdum, Mahendra sulked and frowned.

The carriage finally reached the farmhouse. The servants' carriage had left long before theirs, but there was still no sign of it.

Autumn mornings could be very pleasant. The sun had risen high by now and dried up the dew; the trees glistened in the fresh morning light. The compound walls were lined with shefali trees, the earth below them was strewn with fallen flowers and the air redolent with fragrance.

Freed from the concrete jungle of Kolkata and let loose in a garden, Asha ran about excitedly like a wild fawn. She dragged Binodini along, picked up heaps of flowers, plucked ripe custard apples off the trees and ate them raw, and then the two friends had a long and leisurely bath in the pond. Between the two of them, they filled the shade of the trees, the light off the branches, the water in the pond and the flowers in the garden with a sense of sheer delight.

After their bath, the two friends came back to find that the servants' carriage had still not turned up. Mahendra was sitting on a stool on the veranda, looking quite forlorn and reading an advertisement of a foreign store.

Binodini asked, 'Where is Beharibabu?'

Mahendra answered curtly, 'I don't know.'

Binodini said, 'Come on, let's look for him.'

Mahendra said, 'I don't think anyone will steal him away. He'll turn up even without our looking.'

Binodini said, 'But he may be worried sick about you, for fear that he might lose his precious jewel. Let's go and comfort him.'

Near the pond there was a mammoth banyan tree with a cemented bench around its girth. At that spot Behari had opened up his box, taken out a kerosene stove, lit it and started heating some water. The minute everyone arrived, he welcomed them, made them sit on the bench and served them cups of steaming tea and little plates laden with sweets and snacks. Binodini repeated again and again, 'Thank goodness Beharibabu came so well prepared; or else I shudder to think what would have happened to Mahendrababu without his cup of tea.'

Mahendra was greatly relieved to have his tea, but he still protested, 'Behari takes things too far. It's a picnic and it takes the fun out of it if one comes so well prepared.'

Behari said, 'Very well my friend, please hand back that cup of tea. You are most welcome to stay unfed and enjoy the true spirit of the picnic.'

The day wore on and there was still no sign of the servants. Behari's box now began to yield all the necessary food items: rice, dal, vegetables and even tiny jars of ground spices. Binodini was stunned and said, 'Beharibabu, you amaze me. Considering you do not have a wife at home, how did you learn to be so methodical?'

Behari said, 'Necessity has forced me to this—I have to look after myself, you see.'

Behari spoke in jest but Binodini was solemn as she looked at him with eyes full of sympathy.

Behari and Binodini went about setting things up for cooking lunch. Asha offered to help, albeit very hesitantly, but Behari stopped her. Mahendra, inept as he was, did not even proffer his services. He leaned against the tree trunk, hoisted one leg over the other and immersed himself in watching the play of light on the trembling leaves of the banyan tree.

When lunch was nearly ready, Binodini said, 'Mahinbabu, you won't ever finish counting those leaves. Go and have your bath.'

By now the bunch of servants had arrived with their cargo. Their carriage had broken down on the way.

After lunch a game of cards under the tree was proposed. Mahendra refused to join in and by and by he drifted off to sleep in the shade. Asha went indoors, shut the door and planned to have a lie-in.

Binodini raised her sari a little over her head and said, 'In that case let me go inside too.'

Behari said, 'Where are you off to? Sit for a while and chat. Tell me about your home.'

Every now and then the warm afternoon breeze shivered through the leaves and branches, a koel twittered through the thick foliage of the berry tree beside the pond. Binodini spoke of her childhood, her parents, her playmates. As she spoke, the sari slipped off her head. The brightness of her sharply etched beauty was softened by the shadows of childhood memories. The mocking, knife-edge flash of her eyes, that had made Behari feel much concern heretofore, settled into a calm and serene look as she spoke, and Behari glimpsed a different person altogether. The tender heart that was at the centre of her flashing radiance was still full of gentle affection and the burning embers of unquenched desires and all her sharp banter had not yet succeeded in withering the woman in her. Never before had Behari been able to visualize Binodini tending to her husband as a shy, homely wife or holding her child in her arms like a loving mother—but today, all of a sudden, the performing stage that he always seemed to see her on, vanished before his eyes, and he could envisage her in a happy home. He said to himself, 'Binodini may appear to be a teasing, coy temptress, but deep in her heart a chaste woman rests in silent prayer.' He heaved a sigh as he thought, 'One doesn't know one's own true self completely; that is only known to God. The self that emerges circumstantially is the one that the world takes for real.' Behari didn't let the conversation drift. He badgered Binodini with questions and kept her talking; she had never before found a listener like this and never had she so forgotten herself, spoken so much about herself to a strange man. Today, the endless torrent of words spoken so simply and from the heart made her entire self feel drenched, as though cleansed by the first rain shower, tranquil and at peace.

Mahendra woke up at five, still tired from having woken up early that morning. Quite irritated, he said, 'Let's start getting back now.'

Binodini said, 'What's the harm in staying a little while longer?'

Mahendra said, 'Oh no, then we'd run into drunken white men on the way back.'

By the time they finished packing and were ready to leave it was nearly dark. At this point a servant came and informed them that the rented carriage was nowhere to be seen. It had been left waiting outside the gates. Two white men had bullied the coachman and taken it off to the station. The servant was despatched to go and fetch another carriage. Mahendra was thoroughly put out as he thought, 'The day has been an utter waste.' He could scarcely conceal his impatience.

Gradually, the full moon disentangled itself from the web of boughs and branches, and rose high in the sky. The silent, still grounds were etched with shadows. This evening, in this charming, magical world Binodini felt her own identity defined as never before. Today, when she went and put her arms around Asha in the forested grove, her affection was entirely genuine. Asha saw that Binodini's cheeks were wet with tears. Concerned, she asked, 'What's this, Chokher Bali, why are you crying?'

Binodini said, 'Oh it's nothing, my dear; I am fine. It's just that I had a wonderful day.'

Asha asked, 'What was so great about it?'

Binodini replied, 'I feel as if I have died and come to heaven, as if I can get everything here.'

A dumbstruck Asha could make neither head nor tail of this. But she didn't like all this talk of dying and said, 'Shame, my darling Bali, don't talk that way.'

Another carriage was found. Behari took the seat in the coachbox once again. Binodini gazed out of the window in utter silence. The rows of trees, petrified in moonlight, rushed past like a dense shadow-fall in motion. Asha slept in one corner of the carriage. Mahendra sat in forlorn silence all the way back.

## 18

Ever since the debacle of the picnic, mahendra was eager to re-establish his hold over Binodini. But the very next day Rajlakshmi contracted the flu. It wasn't serious, but she was weak enough to be confined to bed. Binodini took it upon herself to look after her and was at Rajlakshmi's side all day and night.

Mahendra said, 'If you work yourself so hard, you will fall sick very soon. Let me hire a servant to look after Mother.'

Behari said, 'Mahin da, don't get so worked up. If Binod-bouthan wants to nurse her, let her do it. This is not something a servant can do.'

Mahendra began to frequent the sickroom. The diligent Binodini found it intolerable that a person who wasn't doing anything, was always underfoot when there was work to be done. Irritated, she did mention a few times, 'Mahinbabu, you are not doing anyone any good by sitting here—don't absent yourself from your classes needlessly.'

Secretly, of course, Binodini was proud and thrilled that Mahendra was following her around. But at the same time she was impatient with this supplication, this 'waiting with a starving heart' even at his sick mother's bedside—she found it somewhat revolting. When Binodini took on a responsibility, she lost sight of everything else. No one could ever find her inattentive as long as there were household chores to be done, a patient to be fed, washed and helped—she was also intolerant of frivolity at moments of greater need.

Behari came sometimes to ask after Rajlakshmi. These were short visits. The moment he entered the room, he'd sense what needed to be done, what was missing—within minutes he'd set things right and then take his leave. Binodini was well aware that Behari approved of the way she was taking care of the patient. And hence Behari's visits were like a special reward for her efforts.

A feeling of indignity forced Mahendra to leave for college every day on time. His temper was already frayed and to add to that—what a change had come over his daily routine! Food was never ready on time, the driver would disappear, the ladders in his socks kept inching higher and higher. Such aberrations no longer charmed him. In the last few weeks he had grown accustomed to having his every need anticipated and looked after. Now, the absence of that attentiveness and Asha's bungling incompetence failed to amuse him.

'Chuni, how many times have I told you to keep my clothes pressed and ready before I go for my bath? It never happens that way. After my bath I have to spend two hours hunting for my clothes and sewing on buttons,' he exploded one day.

This was like a crack of thunder for Asha. She had never received such a dressing down. She could not summon up a suitable reply such as, 'It was you who stopped me from learning anything useful.' She was entirely unaware of the fact that competence in housework was all about practice and experience. She believed, 'I am unable to do a single thing properly because I am inept and stupid.' When Mahendra forgot himself and slighted her with an unfair comparison to Binodini, Asha accepted it humbly and without resentment.

Asha often hovered around her mother-in-law's room—sometimes she even stepped in tentatively. She would have liked very much to make herself indispensable to the household, she wanted to show everyone her willingness to work, but no one seemed to want it. She did not know how to take control of the household, how to run it in her own way. Her diffidence about her own incompetence kept her always outside the circle. A sense of deep misery festered in her heart, growing every day, but she was unable to articulate it, to give this formless agony a name. She perceived that she was not being able to do anything about the household falling apart all around her; but she didn't know how it had all taken shape, why it was eroding away and what would bring it back to life. She wanted to bawl her heart out every now and then, crying, 'I am really quite hopeless and incompetent; my stupidity is unparalleled.'

Earlier, Asha and Mahendra had often spent hours in a corner of the house, sometimes talking and sometimes not but perfectly happy in each other's company. These days, in Binodini's absence, when Mahendra was alone with Asha he seemed lost for words. And he wasn't comfortable not saying anything either.

One day Mahendra saw a bearer carrying a letter and asked, 'Who is that letter for?'

'It's for Beharibabu.'

'Who gave it?'

'Bou-thakurani.'

'Let me see,' Mahendra took the letter. He was tempted to tear it open and read what Binodini might have written to Behari. He turned the letter over and over in his hands a few times and then hurled it back at the bearer.

If he'd opened it, he'd have found this: 'Aunty is refusing to eat gruel and barley water, may I give her a lentil soup today?' Binodini never consulted Mahendra on any medical matters. On such issues she trusted Behari implicitly.

Mahendra paced the veranda for some time, then entered his room and noticed that a picture hung crookedly on the wall—the string holding it was threadbare. He scolded Asha roundly, 'You never seem to notice anything; this is how everything gets spoiled.' The bunch of flowers that Binodini had brought back from the farmhouse in Dumdum and placed in a vase, was still in the same place, withered and dry. Mahendra usually didn't notice these things. But today his glance fell on it and he said, 'These will never be thrown away unless Binodini comes and does it.' He hurled the vase, flowers and all, out of the room and it bumped down the stairs with a metallic thud. 'Why can't Asha be what I want, why can't she work the way I like, why is her innate lassitude and feebleness making me so restless instead of binding me to the path of domesticity?' The words roared through Mahendra's head as he turned and realized that Asha was standing by the bed, holding one of the four-poster pillars, ashen-faced and lips trembling—then she turned away and dashed out of the room.

Mahendra took measured steps and picked up the discarded vase. His desk stood in a corner of the room. He sat at the desk with his head in his arms as the minutes ticked away.

After dark someone brought in the lamps, but there was no sign of Asha. Mahendra paced the terrace with impatient steps. The clock struck nine and the lonely house grew silent as the depths of the night—but Asha still did not come. Mahendra sent for her. Asha came up diffidently and stood by the terrace doorway. Mahendra approached her and drew her in to his heart. In an instant Asha's tears flooded her husband's bosom; she couldn't stop, her tears were ceaseless, her sobs threatened to tear away from her throat. Mahendra held her tight and kissed her hair—from the mute sky the stars looked down at them in mute silence.

Mahendra sat on the bed that night and said, 'I have too many night shifts to work in college. So I guess I should stay at a place near my college for some time now.'

Asha thought, 'Is he still angry? Is he moving away because he's upset with me? Am I so useless that I am pushing my husband out of his home? Death would have been a better fate.'

But Mahendra didn't show any signs of anger. He was silent as he held Asha's head on his chest and played with her hair, running his fingers through it repeatedly so that her hairdo came undone. In the early days of their romance he often did something like this and Asha protested vehemently. But today, far from protesting, she lay there in quiet contentment. Suddenly, she felt a teardrop on her temple, Mahendra raised her face to him and called in a voice choked with emotion, 'Chuni.' Asha did not respond in words. She merely held him closer with her gentle hands. Mahendra said, 'I was wrong, please forgive me.'

Asha pressed her petal-smooth palm to his mouth and said, 'Oh no, don't say that. You haven't done any wrong, it's all my fault. Please take me to task like a truant servant and make me worthy of a place at your feet.'

On the morning of his departure, before he left the bed Mahendra said, 'Chuni, my precious, I shall hold you the highest in my heart, no one can take away that place.'

Reassured thus, Asha steeled herself for all kinds of sacrifices and placed before him her only and slight demand: 'Will you write to me every day?'

Mahendra said, 'I will, if you promise to reply.'

Asha said, 'I wish I could write well.'

Mahendra pulled a few strands of hair tucked behind her ears and said, 'You write better than Akshaykumar Dutta—you could write the Charu-path!'

Asha said, 'Go on, stop teasing me.'

Before he left, Asha took it upon herself to pack his portmanteau. Folding and packing Mahendra's winter clothes were difficult. Between the two of them, they pushed and stuffed all the things into two suitcases where perhaps one would have sufficed. The things that got left out went on to form an array of discrete bundles. Although Asha was shamed by this, yet the squabbling, tugging at things, jesting and hurling reproofs at one another brought back memories of happier days. For a while Asha forgot that all this was in aid of imminent parting. The coachman sent word to Mahendra at least ten times saying that the carriage was ready. Irritated, he finally said, 'Tell him to unharness it.'

Gradually, the morning wore into afternoon and then dusk. Finally, the two of them cautioned one another once again to take care of themselves, promised to write frequently and with a heavy heart, parted company.

Rajlakshmi's fever had abated and she had been sitting up the last couple of days. At dusk she wrapped herself in a thick shawl and sat playing cards with Binodini. She was feeling quite fresh and fit today. Mahendra stepped in and without glancing at Binodini said to Rajlakshmi, 'Mother, I have to work nights in the college and it's difficult living here.

I have rented a place near the college. I am going there today.'

Rajlakshmi felt deeply wounded but only said, 'Go ahead. Naturally, you must do what's good for your studies.'

Although she was now in good health, the minute she heard Mahendra's plan to leave, she felt very ill indeed. She said to Binodini, 'Child, could you please hand me that pillow?' She lowered her head on the pillow as Binodini massaged her head and arms gently.

Mahendra felt his mother's temple, took her pulse. Rajlakshmi pulled her wrist away and said, 'As if the pulse tells you everything. Don't you worry, I'll be fine.' She turned away feebly.

Mahendra touched her feet and walked away, without so much as a word to Binodini.

## 19

Binodini was wondering, 'What is the real reason—wounded ego, wrath or fear? Does he want to prove to me that I don't matter to him? So he'll go and stay in a rented house, will he? Let me see how long this lasts.'

But Binodini herself was affected by Mahendra's departure and felt quite restive.

She had been keen on teaching Mahendra a lesson, throwing barbs at him; now that this didn't occupy her day, she felt time hanging heavy on her hands. All her interest in the household vanished. Asha, without Mahendra at her side, was bland fare indeed. Mahendra's affection, caresses and love towards Asha had always kept Binodini's heart astir. The intense awareness of pain their togetherness roused in Binodini's grief-stricken imagination, was cause for a compelling excitement. She could not figure out whether she loved the man or despised him, whether she should penalize him or give her heart to him; it was the same Mahendra who had deprived her of all fulfilment in life that was due to her, the same Mahendra who had rejected a gem of a woman like her and instead embraced a weak, feeble-minded child like Asha. He had succeeded in lighting a fire within her and she couldn't figure out if it was love, hate or a mixture of both. She would smile bleakly to herself and say, 'Is there another woman with a fate like mine? I cannot even understand if I wish to slay or to be slain.' But either way, whether to be burned by or to set fire to, Mahendra was indispensable to her. Where else would she shoot her poisoned arrows?

Binodini's breath came thick and fast as she muttered, 'Where can he go? He will be back. He is mine.'

Asha was in Mahendra's room, fiddling with his books, pictures, papers on the desk, his chair, on the pretext of tidying up. Her evening of separation was being spent in touching his belongings, picking them up, dusting one, putting another away. Binodini approached her slowly; Asha felt a trifle sheepish to be caught in the act—she stopped what she was doing and pretended to be hunting for something. Solemnly, Binodini asked, 'So, what are you doing, my friend?'

Asha drew up a small smile and said, 'Nothing much.'

Binodini wound her arms around Asha's neck and asked, 'Bali dear, why did Thakurpo take off like that?'

Binodini's question threw Asha into deep quandary and anxiety as she replied, 'As you probably know—he had some college work and so he had to leave.'

Binodini raised Asha's chin with her right hand, silently staring at her with a mixture of pity and concern as she heaved a great sigh.

Asha's heart sank. She considered herself to be stupid and Binodini to be clever. This expression on her friend's face turned her world upside down. She didn't dare to ask Binodini the question. Instead, she sat down on a sofa by the wall. Binodini sat beside her and drew her into her arms tightly. Held in the embrace of her friend, Asha couldn't check her tears as they flowed from her eyes unrestrained. Outside the house the blind beggar twanged his fiddle and sang, 'Give me the shelter of your feet, O mother Tara.'

Behari came looking for Mahendra and from the door he saw Asha weeping and Binodini holding her to her heart as she wiped away the tears. He stepped aside, went into the adjoining room which was dark and sat down. He gripped his head in his hands and began to wonder why Asha should be weeping. Who could be heartless enough to bring tears to the eyes of the girl who was innately incapable of doing wrong to anyone? He recalled the image of Binodini consoling Asha and said to himself, 'I really misjudged Binodini. In her nursing, comforting, and unselfish love for her friend, she is nothing less than a goddess on earth.'

Behari sat there in the dark for a long time. Once the blind beggar had stopped singing, Behari made a lot of noise, shuffled his feet, coughed and walked towards Mahendra's room. Before he reached the doorway, Asha veiled her head and scuttled towards the inner chambers.

The moment he stepped into the room Binodini exclaimed, 'Beharibabu, are you unwell?'

He said, 'Not at all.'

Binodini asked, 'Why are your eyes red?'

Behari avoided answering that as he asked, 'Binod-bouthan, where is Mahendra?'

Binodini grew sombre. 'I've heard that he has work at the college and so he has taken up a room near there. Beharibabu, please step aside and let me pass.'

Behari had been barring her way to the door absentmindedly. He stepped aside quickly as he realized this. Suddenly he remembered that if he were found talking to Binodini alone in a darkened room at dusk, people could take it amiss. As she left, Behari quickly spoke up, 'Binod-bouthan, please look after Asha. She is naïve, she doesn't know how to wound others or to defend herself from hurt.'

In the dark, Behari could not see Binodini's face—or he would have seen the resentment sparked in it. She had realized the minute she set her eyes on Behari today that he was overwhelmed with concern for Asha. Binodini herself didn't matter in the least! She seemed to be born to protect Asha, to free Asha's path of thorns, to fulfil every wish she ever had! Since Mahendrababu wished to wed Asha, Binodini had to be exiled to the wilderness of Barasat and married off to an uncouth ape. Since His Highness Beharibabu couldn't bear to see tears in dear Asha's eyes, Binodini must keep her shoulders ready at all times for her to weep on. Just once, Binodini wanted to smite this Mahendra, this Behari down to the dust at her feet and make them understand the difference between Asha and Binodini! Her helplessness at the injustice of fate, that had prevented her from planting a victory-flag in any man's heart, burned like wildfire inside Binodini and her very soul became combative.

As she left, she spoke to Behari in honeyed tones, 'You can rest assured Beharibabu, and don't worry yourself to death on account of my Chokher Bali.'

## 20

Soon after, Mahendra received a letter in a familiar hand, written to his new address. He didn't open it in the bustle of the day's work—but kept it safe in his pocket, near his heart. As he sat through his classes in college, or did the rounds at the hospital, he felt the bird of romance nestling in its nest next to his heart. If he woke it, his heart would be filled at once with its twittering and chattering.

In the evening he switched on the lamp in his room and leaned back comfortably in a chair. He fished out the letter from his pocket, warmed now by his body-heat. He scrutinized the address on the envelope for a long time, without opening it. He knew that the letter itself wouldn't have much to say. There was scant possibility that Asha would be able to articulate her feelings lucidly. He would have to read between the crooked lines of childlike scrawls to be able to reach her heartfelt thoughts. His own name spelt out in Asha's inept hand struck up a melodious note in Mahendra's mind—it was a pure love song from the concealed depths of a chaste woman's heart.

In the few days of absence from home, all vestiges of the ire of familiarity had vanished from Mahendra's heart and was replaced by his old love for his new bride. In his last few days at home, the mundane, quotidian details had upset and irritated him. All traces of that disappeared now, only to be replaced by an abstract, unadulterated romantic light, which illuminated Asha's image in his mind.

Mahendra opened the envelope very slowly and brushed it across his forehead and cheeks. The scent of the perfume he had gifted to Asha once wafted from the notepaper and pierced his heart like a wayward sigh.

Mahendra unfolded the letter and read it. But what a surprise! The lines were crooked all right, but the language was by no means youthful. The letters were formed in a raw hand, but the words were scarcely so. It said:

Dearest,

Why should I bring to your mind the one you went away to forget? When you have ripped away the creeper and tossed it to the ground, she should be ashamed to try and creep up on you again. She should ideally sink through the earth.

But just this little bit should do you no harm, my heart. Let the memories come for just a few seconds. Will it hurt you terribly? Your dismissal has lodged itself in my heart like a thorn. All day, all night, in whatever I do or think, wherever I turn, I feel the knife twist cruelly. Please tell me how to empty my mind of your thoughts, the way you seem to have done with mine.

Dearest, was it my fault that you loved me? Did I, ever in my dreams, think I would hold such happiness in my hands? I am a nobody from nowhere in particular. If you never looked at me twice, if I had to be a serf without wages in your household, I would still not grudge my fate. I do not know what you saw in me, my heart, and why you raised me to the pinnacle of joy. And today, if lightning had to strike, why did it have to leave me charred, why couldn't it strike me dead instead?

In the past two days, I have been very patient and thought things over at great length—but I couldn't make sense of one thing: couldn't you have pushed me away without leaving home? Did you have to go away to distance yourself from me—do I take up so much room in your life? If you had cast me away to a corner of the room or even out of the door, would I ever have drawn your eyes to myself? Why did you leave? Isn't there someplace I could have gone instead? I came from nowhere and I could have gone the same way.

What a letter! It was very obvious to Mahendra whose language this was. He sat there, stupefied, like someone who has been wounded without warning. He felt as if his mind had been running along a rail track as its own pace when it had been hit from the opposite direction so suddenly, that all his thoughts had skidded off track and lay crumpled in a heap by the wayside.

He was deep in thought for a long time and then he read the letter again, twice, thrice. What had been, for quite some time, a vague notion began to take shape before his eyes. The comet that had hovered like a mere shadow on his horizon now rushed to occupy the whole sky, its massive tail blazing with a glowing light.

This letter had to be from Binodini. The naïve Asha had presumed it to be hers and written it all down. As she wrote down the words dictated by Binodini, thoughts that had never crossed her mind began to take root in her head. Notions that were not her own took her fancy and became part of her thoughts; Asha could never have expressed in so eloquent a language the new pathos that surfaced. She wondered, 'How on earth did Bali know my mind so well? How did she say the exact words that were on my mind?' Asha clung to her bosom friend more ardently now, because the language of expression for the pain that was in her heart was in Binodini's hands—she was completely helpless.

Mahendra stood up, frowned and tried his best to be angry on Binodini. But instead, his anger fell on Asha. 'Just look at this girl's foolishness, how could she subject her husband to such nonsense?' he thought. As if to vindicate himself, he flopped onto the chair and read the letter yet again. As he read it, he felt a secret thrill course through his body. He tried and tried to read the letter as if Asha had written it. But these expressions could never come from the unpretentious Asha. A couple of lines into the letter, a stimulating suspicion bubbled through his mind, like fizzy, overflowing wine. This mark of romance, covert yet uttered, forbidden yet intimate, poisonous yet honeyed, proffered yet retracted, made him feel quite inebriated. He wanted to slash his hands or legs or do some harm to himself to take his mind off this matter. He brought his fist down on the desk with a bang, jumped off his chair and exclaimed, 'Off with you, let me burn this letter.' He held it close to the lamp. But instead of burning it, he read it all over again. The next morning the servant did clear the table of a pile of ashes, but those weren't from Asha's letter. Mahendra had set fire to the many replies that he had tried to write.

## 21

Meanwhile another letter arrived:

> You haven't answered my letter. It's a good thing actually. The truth can hardly be penned down on paper; I have perceived your answers deep in my heart. When the devotee prays to her lord, He seldom gives an answer to her face. But I suppose this poor soul's devout offering has found a place at your feet.
>
> But if the devotee's prayers wrack your concentration, please don't take it amiss, lord of my heart! Whether you grant her wish or not, whether you turn your eyes to her or not, whether you come to know of her or not, this devotee has no option but to offer you her heart. Hence I write these lines today—O my stone-hearted god, stay steadfast on your course.

Once again, Mahendra tried to write a reply. But in the attempt to write to Asha it was a response to Binodini that flew swiftly to his pen. He could not write covertly like Binodini had, naming one but meaning the other. Many attempts and many torn sheets later he did manage to write something, but when he put it into the envelope and was about to address it to Asha he felt a whiplash on his back. A voice whispered, 'You brute, is this how you betray the trust of a credulous girl?' Mahendra tore up the letter into tiny bits and spent the rest of the night sitting at his desk, hiding his face in his hands as if to shield it from his own gaze.

The third letter arrived:

> Can someone who is incapable of indignation ever be a true lover? How will I give you my love if it is received with slights and rebuffs?
>
> Perhaps I have not read your mind right, and hence this impudence. When you left me behind, I felt prompted to write the first letter; when you didn't answer, I still poured my heart out to you. If I have misread you, is it entirely my fault? Just try to look back on the past and tell me if I haven't understood what you wanted me to understand?
>
> Anyway, whether it was truth or illusion, what I have written cannot be erased and what I have given cannot be withdrawn—that is my only regret. Oh, that my fate had to bring me such shame! But let this not assure you that the one who gives her love is also willing to drag it through the mud at all times. If you do not want my letters, then I must stop. If you do not reply, then this must be the end . . .

Mahendra couldn't stay still after this. He thought, 'I will have to go back home, however angry it makes me. Binodini is under the impression that I have left home in order to forget her!' Mahendra decided to return to his home simply to disprove this defiant misreading on Binodini's part.

Even as he reached the decision, Behari walked into the room. Mahendra was very pleased to see him. Earlier, his doubts and suspicions had made him feel jealous of Behari and the friendship had worn a little thin. But after reading the letters, Mahendra's jealousy had disappeared and he welcomed Behari with open arms and extravagant cheer. He got up and slapped Behari on the back, pulled him by the hand and offered him a seat.

But Behari looked crestfallen. Mahendra thought the poor wretch must have gone to meet Binodini and she must have snubbed him. He asked, 'Behari, have you gone to the house in the last few days?'

With a grave face Behari replied, 'I am coming from there right now.'

Mahendra speculated on Behari's anguish and felt quite amused. He thought, 'Poor, unfortunate Behari! He is really unlucky in love.' And he stroked his pocket once, where the three letters rustled noisily.

He asked, 'And how is everyone there?'

Behari didn't answer him and asked instead, 'What are you doing here away from home?'

Mahendra said, 'I often have to work nights these days—it's inconvenient from home.'

Behari said, 'You have had night-shifts in the past as well, I have never seen you leaving home.'

Mahendra laughed. 'Are you doubting me?'

Behari said, 'I'm serious. Come home with me right now.'

Mahendra was mentally prepared to go back home. But Behari's request made him dig in his heels. He said, 'How can I do that, Behari? My entire year's work will be ruined.'

Behari said, 'Look here Mahin da, I have known you since you were this high. Don't try to fool me. What you are doing is not right.'

Mahendra said, 'And who, my lord, am I subjecting to this injustice?'

Upset, Behari said, 'You have always bragged about your big-heartedness. Where is your heart right now?'

'These days, at the college hospital,' Mahendra answered.

Behari said, 'Stop, Mahin da, stop. Here you are laughing and joking at our expense and over there Bouthan is weeping her heart out, sometimes in the living room and sometimes in the inner rooms.'

This news of Asha's tears was a bolt from the blue for Mahendra. His new obsession had driven all thoughts of anyone else from his mind. Startled out of his reverie, he asked, 'Why is Asha weeping?'

Behari was impatient. 'Am I supposed to know that or are you?'

Mahendra said, 'If you must be angry because your Mahin da is not omniscient, I think you must direct the wrath at his maker, not at him.'

Behari then told Mahendra all that he had seen. As he spoke, he remembered Asha's tearful face burrowed into Binodini's bosom and his voice nearly choked with emotion. Mahendra was astounded by this display of intense affection. As far as he knew, Behari didn't have a heart to call his own—this was a new development! Did it start the day they had first gone to see Asha? Oh, poor, poor Behari! Mahendra did think him a poor soul, but the thought tickled him rather than making him feel sorry. He was very sure where Asha's loyalties lay. His heart swelled a little with pride as he thought, 'Those who for others are unattainable stars to be wished on, have actually come within my reach of their own accord.'

He said to Behari, 'All right then, let's go. But do send for a carriage first.'

## 22

The moment Mahendra came into the house, Asha took one look at his face and all her complaints were forgotten, like the lifting of a fleeting mist. Thoughts of the letters she had sent made her cringe coyly and she could scarcely look him in the eye. Mahendra rebuked her, 'How could you accuse me of such things?'

He fished out the three oft-perused letters from his pocket. Asha wailed vigorously, 'Please, I beg of you, destroy those letters.' She made to snatch them from his hands. But he held them away from her and put them back in his pocket saying, 'I left on the call of duty and you thought I was running away? You actually doubted me?'

Asha's eyes filled with tears. 'Please forgive me, just this once? This will never happen again.'

Mahendra said, 'Never?'

Asha said, 'Never.'

Mahendra drew her to him and kissed her. Asha said, 'Give me those letters—I'll tear them up.'

Mahendra said, 'No, let them be.'

Asha humbly thought, 'He has kept them to punish me.'

On the issue of these letters, Asha felt a trifle displeased with Binodini. She didn't go to her friend with the good news of her husband's return home—instead she avoided her. Binodini noticed this and on the pretext of work, she too didn't stray that way.

Mahendra thought, 'That's strange! I had imagined Binodini would be far more visible now. But this is quite the reverse! So what was the meaning of those letters?'

Mahendra had hardened his heart and decided to abstain from all attempts at penetrating the mysteries of the female heart. He had decided that even if Binodini tried to come closer, he'd stay away from her. But now he changed his mind. 'This is not right. It's as if there is really something between us. I must laugh, talk and joke with Binodini naturally and brush away these niggling doubts.'

Mahendra said to Asha, 'It looks like I have now become the grain of sand in your friend's eye. She is nowhere to be seen these days.'

Asha was indifferent. 'I don't know what's wrong with her.'

Meanwhile, Rajlakshmi came to Mahendra in tears. 'Bipin's wife is really determined to leave us.'

Mahendra concealed his surprise and asked, 'What's the matter, Mother?'

Rajlakshmi said, 'I don't know, son, she is quite determined to go home now. You really don't know how to make someone feel welcome. She's a genteel woman, living in a strange home—how can she stay unless you treat her as one of your own and make her feel at home?'

Binodini was darning a bedcover in her bedroom. Mahendra stepped into the room and said, 'Bali.'

Binodini looked up and asked, 'What is it, Mahendrababu?'

Mahendra said, 'Oh dear, since when did Mahendra become babu again?'

Binodini lowered her eyes and fixed them on her darning. 'What should I call you then?'

Mahendra said, 'What you call your friend, Chokher Bali.'

Binodini didn't give a mocking reply as she usually did—she continued silently with her sewing.

Mahendra said, 'Has that become our true relationship now, and so it cannot be played at any more?'

Binodini paused, bit off some extra thread from her sewing and said, 'I don't know, you would know better.'

She turned very grave and stopped whatever Mahendra would have said, by asking, 'Why did you suddenly decide to come back home from college?'

Mahendra said, 'How long can you keep dissecting cadavers?'

Binodini bit off some more thread with her teeth and without looking up, she asked, 'Do you need live people to cut up now?'

Mahendra had decided he would really liven up the evening by chatting and laughing with Binodini in the most friendly fashion. But he was taken aback by her acute seriousness and the light and friendly responses did not come readily to him. Whenever Mahendra found Binodini maintaining a harsh distance, his entire being just rushed towards her blindly—he was sorely tempted to shake the wall raised by her between them and to raze it to the ground. He didn't reply to the last of Binodini's taunts. Instead, he went up to her, sat beside her and asked, 'Why do you want to leave us and go away? What have we done?'

Binodini moved away a little, looked up from her sewing and fixed her large, bright eyes on Mahendra's face. 'Everyone has duties to perform. When you went away to college, leaving everything, was it because of someone doing something wrong? Don't I have to go? Don't I have duties to perform there?'

Mahendra thought hard but failed to come up with a good response. After a pause he said, 'What are the duties that are forcing you to leave?'

Threading the needle with great concentration Binodini said, 'My heart knows what my duties are. I can hardly give you a list of them.'

Mahendra sat in silence, looking grave and concerned, and gazed at a coconut palm outside the window. Binodini continued with her sewing wordlessly. There was complete silence in the room for a while. Then suddenly Mahendra spoke up. At the abrupt shattering of the silence, Binodini pricked her finger with the needle.

Mahendra said, 'Can we say nothing to hold you back?'

Binodini sucked the drop of blood from her finger and said, 'Why would you say anything? How does it matter whether I stay or go? Does it matter to you at all?' Her voice seemed to choke as she spoke. She bent low over her work and it felt as if her lowered eyelashes were checking a trace of tears that threatened to spill over. It was that time of the day when the winter afternoon was poised to surrender itself to the darkness of dusk.

In a flash Mahendra gripped Binodini's hands and said, 'And if it does indeed matter to me, would you stay?'

Binodini drew back her hands swiftly and moved aside. The spell broke for Mahendra. His own words of a minute ago kept ringing in his ears like a huge travesty. He bit down on his culpable tongue and spoke no more.

At this point Asha stepped into the room echoing with silences. Immediately, Binodini laughed and spoke as if in response to something Mahendra had said earlier, 'Since you all have placed me in such high regard, it's my duty to heed your request at least once. I'll stay until you send me away.'

Asha was thrilled at her husband's success and threw her arms about her friend. She said, 'Then that is the last word. Promise me that you will never leave as long as we don't send you away!'

Binodini promised. Asha said, 'Dear Bali, when you were going to stay back, why did you make us beg and plead so? Finally you had to bow your head before my husband, didn't you?'

Binodini laughed. 'Thakurpo, who was it that had to bow down, you or me?'

Mahendra was speechless all this time. He was feeling that the room resounded with his culpability, and shame was lashing away at him. How would he speak to Asha normally? How could he turn his uncouth rashness into a smiling jest at a moment's notice? This web of deceit was beyond his reach. He answered quietly, 'Of course, it was I who had to bow down,' and walked out of the room.

He came back in there immediately and said to Binodini, 'Please forgive me.'

Binodini asked, 'And what are you guilty of, Thakurpo?'

Mahendra said, 'We don't have the right to keep you here under compulsion.'

Binodini laughed and said, 'But where is the compulsion—I don't see it anywhere. You spoke out of kindness and concern and asked me to stay. Is that called coercion? You tell me, dear Bali, can love and coercion ever be the same?'

Asha agreed with her entirely. 'Never.'

Binodini said, 'Thakurpo, that you would like me to stay, that you'll be sorry to see me leave, is an honour in itself. Isn't that so, dear Bali? After all, how often does one find such a well-wisher? If fate is so kind as to hand me such a friend in need, a comrade in sorrows and joys, why would I be so keen to brush aside the friendly hand and leave?'

Asha was distressed to see her husband defeated and silenced and she said, 'Oh, you can never be beaten at words. My husband has laid down his arms, now you should stop.'

Mahendra rushed out of the room once again. At the same time Behari came looking for him, after having spent a few minutes talking to Rajlakshmi. Mahendra ran into him at the door and exclaimed, 'Oh Behari, I am the biggest scoundrel on this earth.' The force of his words carried them into the room.

Immediately, the summons came from within, 'Behari-thakurpo!'

Behari said, 'Just a minute, Binod-bouthan.'

Binodini said, 'Please come and listen to this.'

As he stepped into the room Behari shot a quick glance at Asha's face. The little that could be seen behind the anchal held no trace of sorrow or pain. Asha tried to leave, but Binodini held her back and said, 'Tell me Behari-thakurpo, are you so repugnant to my Chokher Bali? Why does she want to run away the minute she sees you?'

Embarrassed, Asha poked at Binodini.

Behari laughed as he responded with, 'It's probably because my maker has not fashioned me to please the eye.'

Binodini said, 'Did you see that Bali dear, Behari-thakurpo knows the art of defence; he blamed his maker instead of your taste. You are so unlucky—you have such a gem of a brother-in-law and you don't know his worth.'

Behari said, 'If you are convinced of that Binod-bouthan, I have no regrets.'

Binodini said, 'Oh, the ocean stretches to the horizon, but the mariner thirsts for a drop of water.'

Asha could no longer be checked. She snatched her hand from Binodini's grip and ran out of the room. Behari also made to rise. Binodini asked, 'Thakurpo, can you tell me what's wrong with Mahendrababu?'

Startled, Behari stopped in his tracks and said, 'I don't really know; is something wrong?'

Binodini said, 'I don't know, Thakurpo, it doesn't bode well.'

Concerned, Behari sat down on a chair. He looked expectantly at Binodini, eager to hear the whole thing. Binodini continued with her darning without saying another word.

After some time, Behari asked, 'Has something about Mahin da struck you as odd?'

Binodini replied very casually, 'I don't know, Thakurpo, it doesn't look good to me. I just feel terribly concerned for my Chokher Bali.' She sighed, put her sewing away and made as if to get up.

Behari said, 'Bouthan, wait a minute.'

Binodini opened all the doors and windows of the room, stoked up the lamp light, picked up her sewing again and took a seat on the far corner of the bed. She said, 'Thakurpo, I cannot stay here forever. But when I am gone, please look after my Chokher Bali, see that no harm comes to her.' She turned away as if to hide an imminent onslaught of tears.

Behari spoke up impetuously, 'Bouthan, you cannot leave. You don't have anyone to call your own—you must take it upon yourself to safeguard this simple, innocent girl at all times. If you leave her and go, I don't see a way out.'

Binodini said, 'Thakurpo, you know the world as well as I do. If I stayed here forever, what would people say?'

Behari said, 'Oh, let them say what they will. You mustn't pay attention to that. You are divine—it is your responsibility to protect the helpless girl from all the stones and pellets hurled by the world. Bouthan, I misjudged you at first; please forgive me for that. Just like the narrow-minded, common man on the street, I did you injustice when I first met you. Once, I even felt that you envied Asha her happiness, that—anyway, it's a sin even to speak such thoughts aloud. Since then I have glimpsed your divine soul and because I have a deep respect for you, I felt I had to confess all my sins today.'

A stream of pleasure coursed through Binodini. Though her own show of concern was an act, she couldn't refuse this homage from Behari even in her own heart of hearts. She had never received such a gift from anyone. For an instant she truly believed she was chaste, noble—a vague sense of pity for Asha brought tears to her eyes. She didn't hide these tears from Behari—they gave her the illusion that she was indeed worthy of homage.

When Behari saw Binodini weeping, he was close to tears himself. He controlled himself somehow and went into Mahendra's room. Behari had no inkling why Mahendra had declared himself a scoundrel. On reaching his room he found that Mahendra wasn't there. He was told that Mahendra had gone for a walk. In the past Mahendra seldom left his room without reason. Away from his familiar people and places, he felt uncomfortable and fatigued. Behari started homewards, deep in thought.

Binodini fetched Asha to her own room, drew her into her bosom and with tear-filled eyes said, 'Dear Bali, I am very unfortunate, very ill-starred.'

Hurt and puzzled, Asha returned her embrace and said, 'Why, my dear, why do you say that?'

Binodini hid her face in Asha's bosom like a child close to sobbing and said, 'Wherever I go, bad things happen. Let go, my friend, let go of me—I will go back to my wilderness.'

Asha raised up Binodini's face by the chin and said, 'My sweet friend, don't talk like that. I cannot live without you. Why did these thoughts of leaving come to you today?'

Meanwhile Behari, having missed Mahendra, decided to go to back to Binodini on some pretext and thresh out the matter of Asha's and Mahendra's differences at greater length. He made up an excuse of requesting Binodini to ask Mahendra if he could have lunch with Behari the next day, and turned back to the house. From outside the room he called out, 'Binod-bouthan,' and immediately spotted, in the light of the kerosene lamp, the two teary-eyed women holding each other tight. His steps slowed to a halt. Asha noticed his hesitation; suddenly the thought crossed her mind that Behari may have said something unfair or unjust to Binodini and that was why she talked of going away thus. This was very wrong of Behari—he wasn't a good soul, she thought. Annoyed, Asha walked out of the room. Behari too left, with his heart overflowing with respect for Binodini.

That night Mahendra said to Asha, 'Chuni, I am leaving for Kashi by the morning train tomorrow.'

Asha's heart skipped a beat. She asked, 'But why?'

Mahendra said, 'It's been ages since I saw Aunty.'

At this, Asha felt mortified: she should have thought of this before. Filled with self-loathing she felt she was indeed hard-hearted to have forgotten her loving aunt in the midst of the ebb and flow of life, while

Mahendra had recalled that loving soul living in a far-off land.

Mahendra said, 'She had left, entrusting her most precious jewel to my care—I cannot rest if I don't see her once.' Mahendra's voice quivered with unshed tears and his right palm stroked Asha's temple repeatedly in a gesture of silent blessing and unspoken good wishes. Asha couldn't make sense of this sudden onslaught of tenderness, but she felt overcome by emotion, and tears ran down her cheeks. She recalled Binodini's words of exaggerated affection earlier that evening. She didn't know if there was a link between these two incidents. But she did perceive that this was a watershed in her life. She couldn't figure out if it was benevolent or malevolent.

Distraught, she embraced Mahendra vigorously. He sensed her unspoken terrors and said, 'Chuni, you have the blessings of your devout Aunty, you have nothing to fear, nothing at all. She has sacrificed everything and gone away, for your good alone. No harm can ever come to you.'

Asha pushed away all her fears with determination and gathered her husband's blessings to her heart like a protective talisman. In her mind she touched her aunt's feet again and again and prayed fervently, 'Mother, may your blessings protect my husband at all times.'

The next day Mahendra went away without a word to Binodini. She said to herself, 'You make the mistake and then you take it out on me! What an impostor. These pretences won't last long.'

## 23

Annapurna was naturally delighted to see Mahendra after such a long time. But at the same time she feared that he had again fought with his mother over Asha and had come to Annapurna for sympathy. Even as a child, Mahendra had always run to his aunt in times of trouble. When he was hurt, Annapurna would console him, and when he was angry, she would advise him to deal with the situation calmly. But she was incapable of consoling him, let alone solving his problems, since his marriage. When she became certain that whatever she tried to do to help him would only serve to aggravate the domestic strife in Mahendra's life, she had walked out of the house. She had gone away like the helpless mother who goes to the next room when the sick child weeps for water and the doctor forbids it. In this far-off exile, away from the concerns of the house, busy with her religious duties and pious endeavours, she had forgotten the family to some extent. Now she feared that Mahendra had arrived with the intent of bringing up all those conflicts once again and upsetting her peace of mind.

But Mahendra said nothing about any friction with his mother about Asha. Now Annapurna feared other things: why would that same

Mahendra, who was once incapable of leaving Asha long enough to go to college, suddenly come so far away to be with his aunt? Were the bonds of love between them wearing thin? Consumed with anxiety, Annapurna asked Mahendra, 'Tell me honestly, my son, I beg of you, how is Chuni?'

Mahendra said, 'She is fine, Aunty.'

'What does she do these days, Mahin? Are you two still as childish as ever or have you begun to take on some household duties?'

Mahendra said, 'No—the childlishness has stopped. Remember that alphabet book—the root of all evil? I don't know where it has vanished, but it simply cannot be found. If you were there, you'd be happy to see that Chuni is faithfully fulfilling the duties of a woman, in so far as it is advisable for a woman to neglect her education.'

'Mahin, what is Behari up to?'

Mahendra said, 'Everything but his own work. His finances are managed by his clerks and employees—I don't know with what intent. That is Behari for you. His own matters will be managed by others while he handles the affairs of others.'

Annapurna asked, 'Mahin, won't he get married?'

Mahendra smiled at that. 'I don't see any signs of it.'

This jolted Annapurna deep in her heart. She was aware that Behari had once agreed to get married, after seeing her niece and that enthusiastic desire had then been crushed unfairly. Behari had said, 'Aunty, please don't ask me to get married ever again.' Those words, full of hurt and anger, were still ringing in Annapurna's ears. She had left her much-loved and trusted Behari heartbroken and she hadn't even been able to offer him much consolation. With great trepidation and distress Annapurna wondered if Behari still yearned for Asha!

Mahendra brought her up to date on much of the news of their daily lives, with great wit and humour. But he did not mention Binodini at all.

Mahendra's college was in session and there was no reason for him to stay in Kashi for too long. But his visit to Annapurna was giving him the kind of pleasure that one gets while convalescing in healthy environs after a nerve-wracking and tedious illness. And so the days slipped by in quick succession. The conflict with his own self that he had been unable to resolve, disappeared gradually. The few days he spent in the company of the pious and loving Annapurna, made him so attuned to the duties and responsibilities of life, that his earlier fears began to seem almost ludicrous. He began to feel that Binodini was of no consequence. So much so that he could not recall her face clearly now. Eventually, with great force, Mahendra said to himself, 'I cannot see anyone on the horizon who has the power to dislodge Asha from her place in my heart.'

One day he said to Annapurna, 'Aunty, I have to go back to college—so I'll take your leave for now. Although you have cut yourself off from family ties, please allow me to come and visit you from time to time.'

Mahendra came back home and gave Asha the box of sindoor and the little pot made of white stone and glitter that were sent by her aunt with love. Asha wept copiously and when she recalled her aunt's unconditional love for them and the many ways in which all of them including Rajlakshmi had tormented her, she felt very unhappy indeed. She said to Mahendra, 'I really wish I could go to my aunt just once, touch her feet and beg forgiveness. Is that not possible?'

Mahendra understood her misery and he wasn't unwilling to let her go to spend a few days with Annapurna in Kashi. But he really didn't see how he could take leave from college once again, so soon after his previous trip.

Asha said, 'I believe my uncle's wife will go to Kashi shortly. Is it all right if I go with her?'

Mahendra went to Rajlakshmi, 'Mother, Asha wants to go to Kashi to visit Aunty.'

Rajlakshmi replied scathingly, 'Certainly, if her ladyship wants to go, she must go. Why don't you take her?'

She wasn't happy that Mahendra had re-established contact with Annapurna; at this request of Asha going there as well, she was quite displeased.

Mahendra said, 'I cannot go; I have classes. She can go with Anukulbabu.'

Rajlakshmi said, 'Oh, that's wonderful. They are rich people; their paths seldom cross ours, poor as we are. It would be an honour for her to go with them.'

Mahendra was sorely put out by this repeated derision from his mother. He hardened his heart and walked away, silently determined to send Asha to Kashi.

When Behari came to meet Rajlakshmi, she said, 'O Behari, have you heard—our daughter-in-law wants to go to Kashi!'

Behari said, 'What! Mahin da will take leave again to go with her?'

Rajlakshmi said, 'Oh no, why would Mahin do that! It wouldn't be the height of fashion, would it? Mahin will stay here and she will go with her uncle. Everyone is so modern these days.'

Behari felt concerned—not with the emerging signs of 'modernity' though; he wondered, 'What is going on—when Mahin da went to Kashi, Asha was here; now that she wants to go, he is staying back. Something must be seriously wrong between them. How long will this go on? As friends, can't we do something about this—should we just keep our distance?'

Mahendra was sitting in his room, thoroughly exasperated by his mother's rudeness. Binodini had not met him since he returned. Asha was pleading with her in the next room to come and meet him.

At this point Behari walked in and said, 'Is Asha-bouthan's trip to Kashi all fixed?'

Mahendra said, 'Why wouldn't it be fixed? What's the difficulty?'

Behari said, 'Who said anything about difficulty? But what's behind this sudden idea?'

Mahendra said, 'Oh—wish to see her aunt—yearning for one's loved ones who are far away—it is not uncommon to human nature.'

Behari asked, 'Are you going with her?'

Behari's question made Mahendra feel that he had come to suggest that it wouldn't be right to send Asha with her uncle. He didn't want to flare up at Behari and so he answered brusquely, 'No.'

Behari knew Mahendra fairly well. He was fully aware that Mahendra was annoyed. He also knew that once Mahendra's mind was made up, there would be no way of bringing him around. So he didn't bring up the topic of Mahendra's going again. He found himself thinking, 'If poor Asha is stressed out over something and wants to leave with a burden on her heart, it'd help if Binodini accompanied her.' So he said very slowly, 'Wouldn't it be nice if Binod-bouthan went along with her?'

Mahendra roared in anger, 'Behari, why don't you say what's really troubling you? I don't see the need to beat about the bush with me. I am aware that you suspect I have fallen in love with Binodini. It's a lie. I haven't. You do not have to go about guarding me in order to protect me. Please protect yourself instead. If you were a genuine friend, you'd have told me the truth about your feelings long ago and kept yourself far away from your friend's inner chambers. I can say this to your face—you are in love with Asha.'

A speechless Behari stood up, ashen-faced, and advanced on Mahendra. He looked like he was about to lash out without a thought, like someone who had been wounded deliberately in his weakest spot. He stopped short just in time and spoke with great difficulty, 'May God forgive you—I must be gone.' He walked out unsteadily.

Binodini rushed out of the next room and called, 'Behari-thakurpo!'

Behari leaned on the wall and tried to smile. 'What is it, Binod-bouthan?'

Binodini said, 'Thakurpo, I will also go to Kashi along with my Chokher Bali.'

Behari said, 'No, no, Bouthan, that's impossible, absolutely impossible. I beg of you—don't do anything that I have said; I am nobody here, I do not want to interfere, the consequences won't be good. You are a virtuous soul—you must do what you think is right. I must go.'

Behari folded his hands and saluted Binodini politely as he left. Binodini muttered, 'I am no saint, Thakurpo—listen to me. If you leave, no one will be happy. Don't blame me then.'

Behari left. Mahendra sat there, stupefied. Binodini hurled him an angry look, spitting fire like a bolt of lightning, as she walked into the next room where Asha sat in utter mortification and shame. She couldn't bring herself to look up, after she had heard Mahendra say that Behari loved her. But Binodini felt no sympathy for her. If Asha had indeed looked up then, she'd have felt terrified. Binodini was livid, furious with the whole world. Lies indeed! Of course, no one loved Binodini! Everyone only loved this bashful, dainty china doll.

Ever since Mahendra had exclaimed to Behari, 'I am a scoundrel,' he had felt diffident in Behari's presence, ashamed of his confession, especially after his blood had stopped boiling. He felt that his heart lay exposed before his friend. He didn't love Binodini, but Behari felt that he did—this thought was eating away at Mahendra. After that day whenever he came face to face with Behari, he felt his friend was poking at him with amused interest. An irritation was piling up inside and today at the slightest provocation he had given vent to it.

But the manner in which Binodini rushed out of the adjoining room, begging and pleading with Behari to stay and agreeing to obey his wishes by accompanying Asha to Kashi, left Mahendra feeling shattered. He had claimed that he did not love Binodini; but what he saw and heard didn't give him a moment's peace—it taunted him in every way. And above all he felt deeply regretful that Binodini had heard him say he did not love her.

## 24

Mahendra kept thinking, 'I have uttered a lie, that I do not love Binodini. It was a harsh thing to say. While it may not be true that I love her, it is very cruel to say that I do not love her. Is there a woman in this world who wouldn't be hurt by this? How and when can I get a chance to retract what I said? I can't really go and tell her that I love her; but I must convey to her in a more mild and gentle way that I don't. I can't let Binodini go on believing something so wrong.' And so saying, Mahendra brought out the three letters from his box and read them over again. He thought, 'Without a doubt, Binodini is in love with me. But why did she plead that way with Behari? Was it just for my benefit? When I declared in so many words that I don't love her, I suppose she had to decline her love for me in some way in my presence. My rejection may even result in her falling in love with Behari on the rebound.'

Mahendra felt such deep remorse that his agitation worried and surprised himself. So, perhaps Binodini had heard Mahendra saying he did not love her—what was wrong with that? Perhaps this would lead to the indignant Binodini taking her affections elsewhere—would that be so terrible? Unable to make sense of his inner turmoil, Mahendra clung to Asha the way a wayward dinghy latches on to its anchor in a storm.

That night he held Asha's head on his bosom and asked her, 'Chuni, tell me how much do you love me?'

Asha thought, 'What kind of a question is that? Does he doubt me now that all those ugly words have been said with respect to Behari-thakurpo?' She felt she would die of mortification and said, 'For shame, why do you ask me that today of all days? I beg of you, tell me what's on your mind—have you felt anything lacking in my love for you?'

Mahendra enjoyed seeing her so tormented and said, 'Why do you wish to go to Kashi then?'

Asha said, 'I shan't go to Kashi, I shan't go anywhere.'

He said, 'But you did want to go earlier.'

Vexed, Asha said, 'You know why I wanted to go.'

Mahendra said, 'Perhaps you'll find greater happiness with your aunt, if you leave me and go.'

Asha said, 'Never. I didn't want to go for my pleasure.'

Mahendra said, 'I truly believe, Chuni, you'd have been much happier married to someone else.'

Asha jerked away from Mahendra's grasp, dug her face into the pillow and lay there like a wooden doll—an instant later her tears were evident. Mahendra tried to pull her close to him in an effort to console her. But she refused to budge from the pillow. Mahendra felt wracked with guilt but at the same time he was filled with joy and pride at this evidence of his chaste wife's righteous anger.

This sudden articulation of a lot of things that had been running deep in their hearts threw everyone a little off balance. Binodini felt, 'Why didn't Behari protest against such blatant accusations?' She would have been happier had he put up even a token protest, however false. As it was, she felt he had got his just desserts from Mahendra. Why would a noble soul like Behari devote his heart to Asha? Binodini felt a sense of relief that this accusation had thrown Behari into confusion and removed him from the scenario.

But his face—Behari had looked ashen-faced and mortally wounded—began to haunt Binodini wherever she went. The nurturing woman within her heart wept at the remembered vision of anguish. She carried that image of suffering in her heart the way a mother carries about a sick child on her bosom. Binodini felt an impatient eagerness to nurse the image back to health, to see the signs of rejuvenation.

After a few days of this unmindful preoccupation, Binodini could hold still no longer. She wrote a consolatory letter that said:

Thakurpo,

Ever since I saw your anguished face that day I have prayed that you recover soon, and be your old self; when will I see that spontaneous smile again, hear those noble thoughts again? How are you? Drop me a line and let me know.

Your Binod-bouthan

Binodini dispatched the letter through the bearer.

Behari had never imagined in his wildest dream that Mahendra would be able to say such harsh words—that Behari loved Asha—he had never uttered such thoughts quite so clearly even to himself. At first he was thunderstruck. Then he stomped about in anger and hatred as he repeated to himself, 'Criminal, improper, baseless.'

But once the words had been uttered, their effect could not be erased completely. The grain of truth contained in them germinated and took shape in his mind. The face of that shy child-woman, whom he had glanced at just once in the falling light of the evening, as a fragrant breeze drifted in from the garden, haunted him now, and something seemed to grip his heart tightly even as a harsh pain rose all the way to his throat and threatened to choke him. He spent many nights lying on the terrace and many daytime hours pacing the path in front of his house. Gradually, what was hitherto implicit became a truth in his mind. What was repressed became uncontrolled. Mahendra's statement gave flesh and blood to an idea that had been formless henceforth and filled Behari inside out.

He perceived his own culpability and thought, 'It doesn't become me to be resentful. I must beg Mahin da's pardon and take leave of him. The other day I had stormed out as if he was guilty and I was sitting in judgement on him. I must accept that I was to blame.'

Behari knew that Asha had left for Kashi. One evening he approached Mahendra's room with hesitant steps. He met Rajlakshmi's distant uncle, Sadhucharan, and asked him, 'Sadhu da, I couldn't come earlier. Is everything all right here?' Sadhucharan informed him of everybody's well-being and Behari asked, 'When did Bouthan leave for Kashi?' Sadhucharan said, 'She hasn't gone to Kashi; that trip has been cancelled.' In spite of all that had happened, Behari yearned to rush indoors. He knew that he could no longer bound up the familiar stairs, make pleasant conversation with everyone without a thought, now it was all alien and forbidden to him—yet his heart craved for that very thing. He yearned to go inside, just once, like the member of the family that he once had been and speak a few words to Rajlakshmi, a few to Asha behind the veil, and call her bouthan. Sadhucharan said, 'Why are you standing here in the dark? Come inside.'

Behari took a few hurried steps towards the inner chambers, turned back and said to Sadhucharan, 'I have some work—I must go.' He left hurriedly.

The same night Behari undertook a journey. The bearer meanwhile took Binodini's letter to Behari and finding him gone, brought it back home. Mahendra was strolling in the garden. He asked, 'Whose letter is that?' The bearer told him everything. Mahendra took the letter from him. He was tempted to go and give it to Binodini—see her face turn red with shame—and come away without another word. He had no doubt that the contents of the letter would put Binodini to shame. He remembered that once before too such a letter had gone from Binodini to Behari. Mahendra could not rest without knowing the contents of the letter. He tried to tell himself that Binodini was living under his roof and as such he was responsible for her. Hence it was his duty to intercept such letters and read them, since Binodini should not be allowed to ruin herself.

Mahendra opened the short letter and read it. Written in simple language, the writer's genuine concern was quite palpable in it. He read it again and again and pondered on it but could not figure out which way Binodini's thoughts flowed. He couldn't help feeling that Binodini was now trying to transfer her affections elsewhere because he—Mahendra—had declared that he did not love her. Angry with him, she had given up all hopes of ever gaining his affections.

Such thoughts made it very difficult for Mahendra to hold himself in check. The possibility that Binodini—who had once come to surrender herself to him—would slip from his hands for all time to come, thanks to a momentary lapse, drove him wild. Mahendra thought, 'If Binodini has feelings for me, it is good for her—her feelings would not be disrespected. I know myself, I shall never do anything to cause her harm. She can be quite safe in loving me. I am in love with Asha and Binodini will be safe from my attentions. But if she gives her heart to someone else, who knows what can come of it!' Mahendra decided he must get back Binodini's affections, without surrendering himself.

He stepped into the inner chambers and found Binodini standing in the corridor with an anxious look on her face, apparently waiting for something. Mahendra was instantly gripped by vicious jealousy. He said, 'You know, you wait in vain; he will not come. Here is your letter—it's come back.'

Binodini said, 'But it's open.'

Mahendra went away without answering her. Binodini assumed that Behari had opened the letter, read it and sent it back without a reply—and she went up in flames. She sent for the bearer who had carried the letter. He was busy elsewhere and so he didn't come. Behind closed doors, Binodini's tears fell from her burning eyes the way molten wax drips from a candle. She tore her letter to tiny bits and still wasn't satisfied—was there no way to erase those few lines from the past and the present, to nullify all of it? The irate bee stings whoever crosses its path; a thwarted Binodini was now ready to set fire to everything around her. Was she to lose everything that she ever desired? Could success never be hers? Since happiness was not to be hers, she decided she'd rest in peace only when she had dragged to the ground all the people who had hindered her happiness, posed an obstacle to her success and had deprived her of all possible joy.

## 25

That evening, as the first breeze of spring drifted through the air, Asha laid out a mat on the terrace and sat there after ages. In the falling light, she was reading a serialized novel in a monthly magazine. The hero of the story was on his way back home after a whole year and was attacked on the way by robbers, setting Asha's heart aflutter; meanwhile, the unfortunate heroine had woken up at that very moment from a terrible nightmare. Asha could scarcely hold back her tears. She was a generous reader of Bengali literature and she liked nearly everything that she read. She'd call Binodini and say, 'Dear Bali, I beg you to read this one—it's really good. I cried my heart out.' But Binodini would pick faults with the story and tear it to bits, leaving Asha crestfallen.

Today she decided she would make Mahendra read this story, as she shut the magazine, dewy-eyed. It was at this point that Mahendra appeared on the terrace. The look on his face made Asha tense, although he tried to affect an air of bonhomie and asked, 'Who is the fortunate soul you are thinking of, alone on the terrace?'

Asha forgot the travails of her hero and heroine completely and asked, 'Aren't you feeling too well today?'

Mahendra said, 'I feel just fine.'

Asha said, 'But you are lost in some thought, please tell me what it is.'

Mahendra picked up a paan from Asha's box, put it in his mouth and said, 'I was thinking that it's been ages since your aunt saw you. If you could go and visit her all of a sudden, she'd be so happy.'

Asha gazed at his face wordlessly; she failed to understand why this subject was being revived.

Seeing Asha silent, Mahendra asked, 'Don't you feel like going?'

This was difficult. Asha did want to visit Annapurna but she didn't feel like leaving Mahendra. She said, 'When your college closes, we can both go.'

Mahendra said, 'When my college closes, I won't be able to go. I'll have to prepare for my exams.'

Asha said, 'In that case, let it be—I don't have to go now.'

Mahendra replied, 'But why? Since you wanted to go, I think you should.'

Asha said, 'No, I don't want to go.'

Mahendra asked, 'Just the other day you wanted it and now you don't?'

Asha looked down silently. Mahendra wanted an unfettered space to claim his truce with Binodini and he felt impatience tugging at him. When Asha fell silent, he felt an unprovoked surge of anger. He said, 'Are you, by any chance, not sure of me? Do you want to guard me and keep me under surveillance?'

Suddenly, Asha's innate timidity, softness and uncomplaining nature struck him as unbearable. He thought, 'If you want to go to Aunty, you should say, yes I want to go, please arrange it somehow. Instead, it's yes, no, I don't know and then silence—what is all this?'

Asha was taken aback by this sudden, harsh outburst from Mahendra. She tried to think of an answer but nothing came to mind. She was at a loss as to why Mahendra was so affectionate at times and so cruel at others. But the more incomprehensible he grew to her, the harder Asha clung to him, with all the fears and affections of her trembling little heart.

Asha was suspicious of Mahendra and so she wanted to guard him day and night! What a cruel joke, what misplaced sarcasm. Should she take an oath and protest or should she brush it off in jest?

When a confused Asha remained speechless, Mahendra lost his patience, got up and stormed away. The hero and the heroine of the monthly magazine weren't given another thought. The last rays of the setting sun disappeared, the mild spring breeze of the early evening was replaced by a chilly nip in the air—Asha lay still on the mat.

Late that night Asha stepped into the bedroom and found Mahendra had already gone to bed without even calling her. She felt that Mahendra was repulsed by her indifference to her doting aunt. Asha got into bed, took Mahendra's feet in her hands, buried her face in them and lay still. Mahendra was overcome by pity and tried to pull Asha to him. But she refused to budge. She said, 'If I have done any wrong, please forgive me.'

Deeply affected, Mahendra said, 'You have done no wrong, Chuni. I am a great scoundrel to have hurt you so wickedly.'

Asha's tears drenched Mahendra's feet. He got up, held her in his arms and made her sit down beside him. Once her tears stopped flowing, she said, 'Do you think I don't want to visit Aunty? But I don't feel like leaving you and going away. That's why I didn't want to go—please don't be angry.'

Mahendra stroked her damp forehead gently and said, 'How can I be angry about this, Chuni? How can I be angry because you do not want to leave me and go anywhere? You don't have to go anywhere.'

Asha said, 'No, I shall go to Kashi.'

Mahendra said, 'But why?'

Asha said, 'Since the thought that I do not leave you because I don't trust you has crossed your mind, I must go away, even if for a few days.'

Mahendra said, 'But that was my sin, why should you pay for it?'

Asha replied, 'I don't know all that—but I must have sinned too, somewhere, somehow, or such impossible doubts would not have come to your mind. Why would I have to hear things that I cannot imagine in my wildest dreams?'

Mahendra said quietly, 'That is because you cannot imagine, even in your wildest dreams, what an appalling person I am.'

Asha was distressed. 'Not again! Don't say that. But my mind is made up—I will go to Kashi.'

Mahendra laughed. 'All right then, go. But what will you do if I fall to my ruin in your absence?'

Asha said,'Don't you threaten me like that—as though I am quaking in my boots!'

Mahendra said, 'But it needs to be given a thought. If you allow such a great husband of yours to get ruined, who will you blame for it?'

Asha replied, 'I won't blame you, don't you worry.'

Mahendra said, 'Will you accept your part in it?'

Asha said, 'Most certainly.'

Mahendra said, 'All right. Then I'll go tomorrow, speak to Anukulbabu and make the arrangements.'

He added, 'It's very late now,' and turned over to sleep.

A little later he turned to her again and suddenly said, 'Chuni, forget it, don't go.'

Asha was desolate. 'Why are you saying this again? If I don't go just this once, your accusation will stare me in the face. Even if it's for a couple of days, please send me away.'

Mahendra said, 'Fine.' He turned over and went to sleep.

The day before she left for Kashi, Asha hugged Binodini and said,

'Bali, promise me one thing.'

Binodini pinched her cheeks and said, 'What is it, my sweet? You know I'd keep my word to you.'

Asha said, 'I'm not so sure, you have changed these days. You refuse to come in front of my husband.'

Binodini replied, 'Don't you know the reason for that? You heard what Mahendrababu said to Beharibabu the other day. After such words are spoken, do you think I should stand before him ever again—you tell me?'

Asha was aware that Binodini had a point. She herself had recently had a taste of how embarrassing such words could be. Still she said, 'Words come and go; if you cannot rise above them, what's love all about, my dear? You must forget all that.'

Binodini said, 'As you wish—I'll forget it.'

Asha said, 'Look, I leave for Kashi tomorrow. You must keep an eye on what my husband needs and see that he doesn't miss anything. You cannot hide from him the way you've been doing.'

Binodini was silent. Asha held her hands and said, 'For my sake, dear Bali, you must promise me this.'

Binodini said, 'Yes, I promise.'

## 26

When the moon sets, the sun rises. Asha had left, but Mahendra still could not catch sight of Binodini. He walked around aimlessly, sometimes stepping into his mother's room on a slight pretext—but Binodini managed to give him the slip every time. From Mahendra's desolate, forlorn air Rajlakshmi thought, 'Now that his wife is away, Mahin doesn't seem to like being in this house any more.' She felt hurt that nowadays Mahendra's wife was more indispensable to his well-being than his mother. And yet, his lost and despondent air disturbed her. She sent for Binodini, 'Ever since that attack of flu I have developed asthmatic tendencies. I can't go up and down the stairs as easily as before. Child, you must look after Mahin yourself, whether he's eating properly or not. All his life he's been used to being pampered. Ever since Asha left, he's looking so lost. And speaking of the girl—I don't know how she could go, leaving him like this!'

Binodini curled her lip and scratched at the bedcovers. Rajlakshmi said, 'What is it, child, what are you thinking? There's nothing to think about; whatever anyone may say, you are no stranger to us.'

Binodini said, 'Aunty, let it be.'

Rajlakshmi said, 'Fine, let it go. Let me see what I can do myself.' She made as if to get up and climb the stairs to Mahendra's room on the second floor. Binodini hastily stopped her, 'You are unwell, you mustn't go. I'll go. Please forgive me, Aunty, your wish will be my command.'

Rajlakshmi never paid heed to what people said. Ever since her husband's death, with the exception of Mahendra nobody had meant anything to her. She didn't like Binodini hinting at social criticism where Mahendra was concerned. She had known him all his life—there wasn't a better man to be found anywhere! Criticism about her Mahin! If anyone dared to criticize him, may their tongue fall off! Rajlakshmi had a natural tendency to defy the entire world where something that she considered good was concerned.

That day Mahendra came back from college, went into his room and looked around in stunned disbelief. The minute he opened the door the scent of sandalwood and incense had filled his senses. The mosquito nets were adorned with pink tassels. The mattress on the floor glimmered with fresh sheets, and instead of the old cushions on it there were foreign-made, square cushions with embroidered silk and wool covers. The embroidery was the outcome of Binodini's hard labour of many months. Asha had often asked her, 'Who are you making these for?'

Binodini had laughed and said, 'For my deathbed. Death is my only intimate now.'

There were coloured yarns twisted decoratively into knots at the four corners of Mahendra's photo-frame and beneath it, on the floor on either side of a teapoy, were a pair of vases with fresh flowers, as though Mahendra's likeness had been worshipped by an unknown devotee. All in all, the room was transformed. The bed was shifted slightly from its old position; it was screened by the clothes rack and the clothes that hung on it, thereby dividing the room into two discrete spaces. The curio-cabinet which held all the little assortments, dolls and things that Asha held dear, was decorated with scrunched-up red fabric stuck on the inside of the glass panels, so that nothing within it was visible now. The deft touch of a new pair of hands had shrouded all that was reminiscent of the room's past.

Weary from his day's work, Mahendra lay down on the mattress and rested his head on the new cushions. Immediately, an aroma assailed his senses—the stuffing in the pillows were generously mixed with a fragrant pollen and some essence.

Mahendra's eyes drifted shut. He perceived the touch of the hands, light as a feather, that had done such subtle work on the pillows. Now the maid brought in fruits and sweets on a silver plate and iced pineapple juice in a glass tumbler. All this was different from the way things were done earlier. There was great attention to detail and novelty in every gesture. Mahendra's senses were dulled by this onslaught of freshness in every smell, every touch and every sight.

He finished his meal with great satisfaction. Binodini stepped into the room slowly with paan and mouth-freshner in a silver box. She laughed and said, 'Thakurpo, forgive me for not being present all these days, tending to your meals. For my sake, I beg of you, do not tell my Chokher Bali that you have been neglected. I try to do my best—but I have to look into all the household chores, you see.'

Binodini held the box of paan before Mahendra. Today the paan was scented differently—a new kind of lime paste had been used.

Mahendra said, 'It's good to slip up sometimes, even while tending so assiduously.'

Binodini asked, 'And why is that?'

Mahendra replied, 'Then later it can be held against you and greater penalties exacted.'

'So, Mr Shylock, what has the interest come to?'

Mahendra said, 'You weren't present when I had my meal. Now, after the event, you must stay longer and make up for it.'

Binodini laughed, 'Oh dear, you are so particular with the accounts that woe betide anyone who falls into your trap.'

Mahendra said, 'Whatever the accounts say, have I succeeded in exacting payment?'

Binodini said, 'What is there to exact? You hold me a prisoner as it is.' She turned the jest into mock-seriousness by heaving a slight sigh.

Mahendra too grew sombre. 'Bali, is this a prison for you then?'

The bearer interrupted them, coming in to place the lamp on the teapoy.

Binodini shielded her face from the sudden glare of the lamp and answered with lowered eyes, 'I don't know. Who can beat you at wordplay? I must go now, there's work to be done.'

Mahendra grabbed her hand and said, 'Since you've admitted to being captive, where do you want to run?'

Binodini said, 'Oh for pity's sake, let me go—why try to imprison one who has nowhere to escape?'

She snatched away her hand and rushed out of the room.

Mahendra lay there on the scented pillows. The blood roared in his veins. The silent dusk, a room to themselves, spring in the air and Binodini's heart just within his reach—Mahendra felt he could hardly bear the intoxicating thrill of it all. Quickly, he blew out the lamp, bolted the door and went to bed long before his usual time.

It wasn't his old, familiar bed. A few extra mattresses had made it softer than before. Yet another aroma, he couldn't quite name the ingredient. Mahendra tossed and turned; he wanted to discover at least one marker of the past and cling to it. But nothing came to hand.

At nine o'clock there was a knock on his door. Binodini spoke from outside, 'Thakurpo, I have brought you dinner. Open the door.'

Mahendra sat up with a start and reached for the bolt. But he didn't open the door. He dropped down on the floor and said, 'Oh no, I am not hungry. I shan't have dinner.'

Binodini sounded concerned, 'Are you unwell? Shall I get you some water? What would you like to have?'

Mahendra said, 'I don't want anything, I don't need anything.'

Binodini said, 'For God's sake, don't play the fool. All right, even if you're not sick, just open the door.'

Mahendra shook his head vehemently. 'No, I won't, never. Go away.'

He got into the bed hastily. In that empty bed and in his restless state, he desperately groped for memories of the absent Asha.

When sleep eluded him till late at night, he lit the lamp again, sat at his desk and wrote to Asha.

> Asha, please don't leave me alone for too long now. You are the goddess of my heart. When you are gone, I scarcely know how all my instincts run away with me and lead me astray. Where is the light that would light my way—it rests in the loving gaze of your eyes brimming with trust. Please come back soon, my innocence, my eternal, my only one. Make me strong, save me, fulfil my heart. Retrieve me from this nightmare of forgetting you for even an instant, of committing the blunder of sinning against you.

Thus Mahendra wrote, long into the night, goading himself towards Asha. Several clocks on church towers in the distance struck three. The roads of Kolkata were silent, devoid of traffic. At one end of the lane, a singer, invited to a house, had struck up a melody that had also now subsided into silence and slumber. Mahendra felt greatly relieved after meditating on Asha and pouring his heart out in a long letter. He lay his head on the pillow and was immediately claimed by sleep.

When he woke up, it was late in the day and sunlight was streaming into the room. Mahendra sat up with a start. A good night's sleep put the events of the night before in better perspective in his mind. He left the bed and looked at the letter on his desk, written to Asha the previous night. He read it over and thought, 'What have I done! Thank goodness I haven't sent it yet. What would Asha think if she reads this? She wouldn't be able to make sense of this.' Mahendra was embarrassed by the excess of his emotions the previous night; he tore the letter into tiny bits. Then he wrote another letter to Asha in simpler language—'Will you be away for much longer? If Anukulbabu has plans to stay longer, drop me a line; I shall go and fetch you. I don't like it here all alone.'

## 27

When Asha arrived in Kashi soon after Mahendra had left, Annapurna was truly concerned. She began to interrogate Asha, 'Chuni, didn't you tell me that this Chokher Bali of yours is the most talented and competent girl in the whole world?'

'It's true, Aunty, I am not exaggerating. She is as smart as she is pretty and efficient.'

'Well, she's your friend and so you're bound to feel that way about her. But what does everyone else in the house feel about her?'

'Mother is extremely fond of her. If she so much as mentions going back, Mother gets all worked up. There's no one like her when it comes to nursing someone. Even if a maid or a servant is sick, she nurses them like a member of the family.'

'What does Mahendra feel about her?'

'You know him well, Aunty. He doesn't take to anyone unless they are truly near and dear. Everyone is fond of my Chokher Bali; but he doesn't get on too well with her.'

'Why?'

'I worked so hard on getting them to meet. But now they hardly speak a word to each other. You know how reserved your nephew is—people think he's arrogant; but Aunty, except for a handful, he really doesn't like too many people.' The last few words had slipped out inadvertently and suddenly Asha was embarrassed. Her cheeks turned red. Annapurna was relieved and said, 'So that's the reason why Mahin didn't say a word about your Bali when he was here.'

Asha was miffed. 'That's the problem with him. If he doesn't love someone, she doesn't exist for him. He behaves as if he is not aware of their existence.'

Annapurna smiled serenely. 'But when he does love someone, it's as if he has eyes only for her, doesn't he?'

Asha didn't answer. She looked at the ground and smiled. Annapurna asked, 'Chuni, tell me about Behari. Won't he ever get married?'

Asha's face fell in an instant. She didn't know what to say.

Asha's silence worried Annapurna and she asked, 'Tell me honestly, Chuni, is he in good health or is he unwell?'

For this childless woman with a golden heart, Behari had the honoured position of an ideal son. That she had left Kolkata without seeing him settled with a family bothered Annapurna every day in this far-off land. Her meagre demands from life had been fulfilled. The only thought that broke her concentration and stopped her from surrendering herself completely to an ascetic life, was of Behari, unsettled and drifting.

Asha said, 'Aunty, don't ask me anything about Behari-thakurpo.'

Taken aback, Annapurna asked, 'But why?'

Asha said, 'Oh, I cannot tell you that.' She left the room.

Annapurna sat in silence, thinking, 'How could that gem of a boy, Behari, change so much in this short while that the very mention of his name makes Chuni leave the room? It is destiny. If only his wedding hadn't been fixed with Chuni and if only Mahin hadn't snatched her away from him!'

After many months, Annapurna's eyes filled with tears again. She said to herself, 'If my Behari has done anything unworthy of him, he has done it from a lot of pain; he wouldn't do that unless pushed to it.' She imagined his pain, his sorrow and felt misery welling up in her heart.

In the evening, when Annapurna was at her prayers, a carriage came to a stop at the door. The coachman called out to open the door, and thumped on it loudly. Annapurna called out from the puja room, 'Oh dear, it had slipped my mind entirely—Kunja's mother-in-law and her two nieces were supposed to come here from Allahabad today. That must be them now. Chuni, could you please take the lamp and open the door?'

Asha held the lantern up and opened the door. She found Behari standing there. He said, 'Bouthan! But I was told you weren't coming to Kashi!'

Asha dropped the lantern in confusion. She ran upstairs as if she'd seen a ghost, and pleaded with Annapurna, 'Aunty, please tell him to go away.'

Annapurna started as she looked up from her puja, and asked, 'Who is it, Chuni?'

Asha said, 'Behari-thakurpo has come here too.' She rushed to the next room and slammed the door shut.

Behari had heard everything from the bottom of the stairs. He wanted to rush out immediately—but when Annapurna finished her puja and came downstairs, she found him sitting on the doorstep, ashen-faced and very stiff.

Annapurna hadn't brought the light. In the dark she couldn't see Behari's face and neither could he see her.

She called out, 'Behari.'

Alas, gone was that caring, mellow tone of the past. This voice held the thunder of judgement and punishment. Mother Annapurna, on whom were you raising your sword of justice? In this darkness, the unfortunate Behari was here to lay his weary head on your compassionate feet.

Behari started as if he had been whipped. He raised his numb body and said, 'Aunty, no more—don't say another word. I am leaving.'

Behari bent to the ground and bowed to her without touching her feet. Annapurna set him adrift into the dark night, the way unfortunate mothers cast their children into the Ganga; she didn't call him back. The carriage disappeared from sight.

The same night Asha wrote to Mahendra, 'Behari-thakurpo was here all of a sudden this evening. I don't know when my uncle plans to go back home—please come soon and take me away from here.'

## 28

After staying up half the night, Mahendra was gripped by a strange lassitude the next morning. It was early March and the days were beginning to get warmer. On other days Mahendra sat with his books in a corner of his room. But today he leaned back on the pillows and lay flat on the mattress. The day wore on and he didn't go for his bath. The street-vendors called out as they peddled their wares in the street. The road echoed with sounds of traffic, of the people rushing to office. A neighbour was adding a new floor to his house—the artisans struck up a monotonous tune as they hammered away at their work. The delicate, warm breeze cast a languorous spell on Mahendra's senses. No harsh vows, intricate endeavours, or battles with the mind seemed worthy of this slack, lethargic spring day.

'Thakurpo, what's wrong with you—won't you have your bath? Your meal is ready. Why are you in bed still—are you unwell? Do you have a headache?' Binodini walked up to him and touched his forehead.

Mahendra answered in slurred mumbles, 'I don't feel too well today; I think I'll skip the bath.'

Binodini said, 'All right then, have a bite to eat.' She pleaded with him and dragged him downstairs where she personally attended to his meal with great concern and compassion. After the meal, when Mahendra returned to his mattress and lay down, Binodini sat by his side and pressed his head with gentle fingers. Eyes shut, Mahendra said, 'Bali, you haven't had lunch—why don't you go and eat.'

Binodini refused to go. On that lazy afternoon, the curtains flapped in the warm breeze and sounds of the meaningless fluttering of the coconut palm by the compound wall floated into the room. Mahendra's heart beat faster and faster and Binodini's balmy breath kept pace as it gently stirred the locks that lay across his temple. Not a single word emerged from either of them. Mahendra's thoughts went thus—we float through the endless river of life; how does it matter to anyone if the boat stops here or there? Even if it does matter, how long will it last?

As she sat by him, gently stroking his forehead, Binodini's head bent lower and lower, weighted down by the cumbersome, bemused passions of youth. Eventually, the loose strands of her hair rested on Mahendra's brow. The gentle brush of her hair as they stirred on his brow shook Mahendra's entire body and his breath caught at his chest, nearly choking him. He sat up with a start and said, 'No-o, I must go to college.' He stood up without looking at Binodini.

Binodini said, 'Relax—I'll get you fresh clothes.' She brought out the clothes he usually wore to college.

Mahendra went off to college in a rush. But he was restless. After many vain attempts at concentrating on his books, he came back home earlier than usual.

He stepped into the room and found Binodini lying on her stomach, upon his mattress, reading a book. Her jet-black hair was strewn over her back. Perhaps she hadn't heard his footsteps. Mahendra tiptoed into the room and stood beside her. He heard her heave a great sigh as she read.

Mahendra said, 'Oh mother of all sad souls, don't squander your heart on fictitious characters. What are you reading?'

Startled, Binodini sat up straight and concealed the book in the folds of her sari. Mahendra tried to seize it by force. After many minutes of this game of catch, Mahendra managed to retrieve the book from a vanquished Binodini's hands—it was Bankim's *The Poison Tree*. Binodini turned away and sulked, even as her breath came faster from the just-lost tussle.

Mahendra's heart was clamouring in his breast. He tried to laugh and said, 'Shame on you, this is a comedown. I had expected something very clandestine and after all this effort I find it's only *The Poison Tree*.'

Binodini said, 'Pray tell me what can be clandestine about me?'

Before Mahendra could stop himself, the words had slipped out, 'Say for example, if it was a letter from Behari?'

In an instant, lightning flashed through Binodini's eyes. The cupid that was cavorting around in the room was turned to ashes in a second. Binodini stood up, flaring like a flame that had been fanned. Mahendra gripped her hands. 'Forgive me, I spoke in jest.'

Binodini snatched away her hands. 'Whom do you mock? If you were worthy of his friendship I would have endured your mockery of him. You have a small mind; you are not strong enough to be a friend and you talk of jest.'

As she was about to leave, Mahendra reached out with both hands and grabbed at her feet. At the same instant a shadow fell across the doorway. Mahendra let go of Binodini's feet and looked up—it was Behari.

It was as if Behari's steady, withering gaze burned up the two of them in turn. When he spoke, his voice was neutral and toneless, 'I'm afraid I have come at an inconvenient moment, but I shan't stay for long. I came to say one thing—I had gone to Kashi. I didn't know Bouthan was there. With no intent to do so, I have wronged her; there was no time to beg her pardon. So I have come to say sorry to you instead. I have one request to you—if I have ever sinned, even in thought, consciously or unconsciously, let that not result in any suffering for her.'

Mahendra felt helplessly angry because Behari had witnessed his moment of weakness. This wasn't the time for generosity. With a little laugh he said, 'You are like the proverbial man with the guilty conscience. I haven't asked you to beg pardon; why have you come to say sorry and act the martyr?'

Behari stood there like a wooden puppet for a few moments. When his lips trembled in an effort to speak, Binodini said, 'Behari-thakurpo, don't bother to answer him. Don't say a word. What this man has just said, taints only him—it doesn't touch you in any way.'

It wasn't clear if Binodini's words fell on Behari's ears—he turned away like one in a trance and walked out of Mahendra's room. Binodini ran after him and said, 'Behari-thakurpo, do you have nothing to say to me? If you want to reprimand me, please do so.'

Behari continued to walk away without saying a word. Binodini barred his way and gripped his right hand. Behari pushed her away with palpable revulsion. He didn't even notice that Binodini had lost her balance and fallen.

At the sound of Binodini's fall Mahendra came running. He found Binodini's left elbow had a bruise that was bleeding. He said, 'Oh no, that looks bad.' In an instant he ripped off a strip of his thin shirt and made as if to tie a bandage around the wound. Binodini drew away her arm and said, 'No, please don't. Let the blood flow.'

Mahendra said, 'Let me tie it up and I'll give you medication—that'll take away the pain and heal the wound quickly.'

Binodini moved aside. 'I don't want the pain to go—let this wound stay.'

Mahendra said, 'I lost my patience today and insulted you. Can you bring yourself to forgive me?'

Binodini said, 'Forgive you for what? You did nothing wrong; I am not afraid of people. I don't care about anyone. After all, what are they to me if they can hurt me and walk away? Instead, those who touch my feet and draw me towards them, should mean more to me.'

Ecstatic, Mahendra spoke fervently, 'Binodini, you will not reject my love then?'

Binodini said, 'I shall hold it to my heart. Since the day I was born, I have never experienced such an abundance of love that I can ever reject it.'

Mahendra held her hands in his and said, 'In that case, come to my room. I have wounded you today and you have returned the hurt. As long as that is not wiped away, I shall have no peace.'

Binodini said, 'Not today—let me go now. If I have hurt you, please forgive me.'

Mahendra said, 'And you will pardon me as well, or I shall not sleep a wink tonight.'

Binodini said, 'I forgive you.'

Mahendra impetuously wanted to receive a distinct sign of Binodini's forgiveness, right then and there. But he took a look at Binodini's face and stopped short. She ran down the stairs. Mahendra climbed the stairs back to the terrace and began to stroll there. He felt a sense of release in the fact that his feelings were exposed to Behari. The ignominy of smokescreens and camouflages was dispelled by this revelation to one person alone. Mahendra thought, 'No more grand delusions about myself—I am in love, I love and that is not a lie.' The new-found admittance of love made him conceited enough to feel proud of his own fall from grace. He cast a glance of scornful disdain at the entire universe, bedecked with the silent stellar constellations in the tranquil evening light, and said, 'The world may call me whatever they wish, but I am in love.' And he covered the whole world, the endless sky and all sense of duty with an image of Binodini that his mind conjured up. Behari's sudden arrival had acted as a force that upset the ink-bottle, uncorked it and spilled its contents all over—by and by, Binodini's black eyes and inky black hair fanned out and mussed up all the white sheets, and all that was ever written before.

## 29

The next morning, as soon as he opened his eyes, Mahendra's heart was flooded with a sweet sensation. The morning sun spread a veneer of gold on all his thoughts and desires. What a lovely world, what a beautiful sky—the breeze seemed to lift his soul like pollen dust and set it adrift.

The Vaishnav mendicants played their one-string lute and sang on the street below. The watchman was about to shoo them off when Mahendra stopped him and found himself giving them one whole rupee. The bearer dropped the kerosene lamp as he was putting it away right in front of Mahendra. But the master smiled pleasantly and said, 'Hey you, see that you sweep it clean—bits of glass can pierce someone's feet.' Today, nothing angered him, no harm seemed too great.

Romance had been hidden behind a veil all these days. Today, the veil had been ripped away. It was as if a cover had been lifted off the face of a brave new world. Every banal detail of daily life had disappeared. The trees, birds, people on the streets, sounds of the city—they all seemed to look and sound new today. Where had this novelty been all this time?

Mahendra decided that today he would not meet Binodini in the usual way. It was a day fit for poetry and music. He wanted to turn this day into something out of the Arabian Nights, full of sumptuousness and beauty, unconnected to life and the mundane. It would be real and yet a dream, it would be devoid of material realism, duties, rules and norms of everyday living.

Mahendra was restless that morning; he couldn't go to college. There was no telling when the auspicious moment would arrive for that fateful union. All through the day Binodini's voice floated to his ears, sometimes from the kitchen, sometimes from the store room; she was busy with her household chores. He didn't like that—on this day he would have liked Binodini to be far beyond the reach of household duties.

Time hung heavy on Mahendra's hands. He had his bath and ate his meal. Finally, all household chores ground to a halt as the silence of the afternoon extended itself around him. But there was still no sign of Binodini. Mahendra was high-strung with sorrow and anticipated pleasure, impatience and hope.

*The Poison Tree*, rescued from the scuffle of the previous afternoon, lay on the mattress. Mahendra's eyes fell upon it and he felt a thrill coursing through his body as he remembered the tussle. He pulled out the pillow on which Binodini had lain, and laid his head upon it; he picked up the book and began to turn the pages. Mahendra wasn't aware when he lost himself in the book and the clock struck five.

Binodini entered the room with fruits and sweets on a plate and a bowl of iced melons with powdered sugar sprinkled on it. She placed it before Mahendra and said, 'What's wrong with you Thakurpo, it's past five o'clock and you still haven't freshened up or changed?'

Mahendra got a harsh jolt. Did she have to ask what was wrong with him? She should have known the answer to that. Was this day like every other day? Mahendra didn't dare to make any demands by harking back to the day before, for fear that he'd have to face something contrary to his expectations.

He sat down to eat. Binodini went to the terrace, gathered the clothes that were drying on the line and brought them in. She began to fold them deftly and arranged them in Mahendra's cupboard.

Mahendra said, 'Wait a minute. Let me finish eating and I'll lend you a hand.'

Binodini folded her hands and said, 'Oh pray do not try to help me, whatever else you may do.'

Mahendra finished eating as he said, 'Really! So you think I am hopeless with household chores? All right, let this be a test of my abilities.' He tried to fold the clothes, in vain.

Binodini snatched them from his hands and said, 'My dear sir, do let go. You will only pile up more work for me.'

Mahendra said, 'In that case, you carry on with your work while I watch and learn.' He sat down in front of the cupboard, beside Binodini. She began to air out the clothes on his back with a swish, before she folded them and put them on the shelf.

Thus began the first meeting of the day, without a hint of the exclusivity that Mahendra had visualized and fantasized about all day long. Such a meeting did not befit poetry, music or even prose. But it did not upset Mahendra. In fact he felt a little relieved. He hadn't been able to decide how he would go about actualizing his fantasy, what to say, what to do and how to keep all predictability at a distance. The fun and jest that was native to this airing of clothes and folding them away, set him free of a self-induced, impossible ideal—and he breathed easier.

At this point Rajlakshmi walked into the room. She said to Mahendra, 'Mahin, Binodini is folding the clothes—but what are *you* doing there on the floor?'

Binodini said, 'You tell him, Aunty! He is teasing me and getting in my way.'

Mahendra said, 'Is that so! And here I thought I was lending you a hand.'

Rajlakshmi said, 'Rubbish! You and lend her a hand! Binodini, Mahin has always been that way. Always pampered by his mother and aunt, he has never learnt to do a thing for himself.' So saying, the mother cast a loving look upon her inept son. She felt all she had in common with Binodini was the concern that this adult, incompetent mother's boy should have all possible comfort. On the issue of tending to her son, being able to lean on Binodini gave Rajlakshmi great relief, great pleasure. She was also pleased by the fact that lately Mahendra seemed to understand Binodini's worth and worked towards making her feel at home. She made sure Mahendra was listening as she said, 'Binodini, today you've aired out Mahin's warm clothes. Tomorrow you must embroider his initials on his handkerchiefs. Ever since I brought you with me, I haven't been able to pamper you, child; I've only worked you harder and harder.'

Binodini said, 'Aunty, if you talk that way, I will feel that you are creating a distance between us.'

Indulgently Rajlakshmi said, 'Oh dear, who is dearer to me than you, my child?'

When Binodini had finished putting the clothes away, Rajlakshmi asked, 'Shall we start making the sugar syrup now or do you have other things to do?'

Binodini said, 'Oh no, I've finished everything. Let's go and make the sweets now.'

Mahendra said, 'Mother, you were just saying how hard you work her and again you are dragging her off to the kitchen?'

Rajlakshmi pinched Binodini's chin affectionately and said, 'This good little girl of mine loves to work.'

Mahendra said, 'I have nothing to do this evening. I'd planned to read a book with Chokher Bali.'

Binodini said, 'That's fine, Aunty. Let's both of us come and hear Thakurpo read?'

Rajlakshmi said to herself, 'My poor Mahin is feeling really lonely and we must all do our best to entertain him.' So she said, 'Why not! We shall come back later and hear him read, after we've finished cooking Mahin's meal. How about that, Mahin?'

Binodini threw an oblique glance at Mahendra's face. He said, 'Fine.' But his enthusiasm waned. Binodini left the room along with Rajlakshmi.

Mahendra muttered in frustration, 'I shall go out this evening and come back late.' He changed his clothes at once. But having done that, he didn't execute his plan. He paced about on the terrace for many minutes, glanced towards the stairway a million times and finally came and sat in the room. He thought, 'I shall refuse to touch the sweets today and convey the message to Mother that if you boil the sugar syrup for too long, it loses its sweetness.'

At dinner time Binodini brought Rajlakshmi along. The latter was afraid to climb stairs these days, due to her asthma. Binodini's requests brought her upstairs today. Mahendra sat down to his meal with a very glum look.

Binodini said, 'Thakurpo, why are you pecking at your food today?'

Rajlakshmi was immediately concerned, 'Are you not well, my child?'

Binodini said, 'We worked so hard on the sweets, you must have some of it. Hasn't it turned out well? Oh, then leave it. No, no, don't eat it just because we asked you to—that means nothing. Leave it then.'

Mahendra said, 'Will you stop that! I liked the sweets the best and that's what I want to have—why should I listen to you?'

Mahendra finished the two sweets in their entirety; not a scrap, not a crumb was left on the plate. After the meal the three of them came into his room and sat down. Mahendra did not bring up the topic of reading. Rajlakshmi said, 'Didn't you say something about reading something?'

Mahendra said, 'Oh, but what I have doesn't have anything about gods or goddesses in it. You wouldn't like it.'

Not like it! Rajlakshmi was determined to like it, come hell or high water. Even if Mahendra read something in Turkish, she would have to like it! Poor, dear Mahin—with his wife away in Kashi, he was so lonely; Mother must, absolutely must like whatever he liked.

Binodini said, 'Thakurpo, why don't you put your books aside and read some of the holy books that are there in Aunty's room? She would also like that and the evening would pass nicely.'

Mahendra threw a dismal look at Binodini. At this point the maid came with the news that the neighbour's wife had come visiting. This was a close friend of Rajlakshmi's and the latter loved talking to her in the evenings. Yet she said to the maid, 'Tell her I am busy in Mahin's room today and she should come back tomorrow.'

Mahendra spoke hastily, 'But why Mother, certainly you can go and meet her now?'

Binodini said, 'Oh no, Aunty, why don't you stay here and I'll go and talk to her.'

Rajlakshmi gave in to the temptation and said, 'No, you stay here—let me see if I can go and get rid of her. The two of you start reading, don't wait for me.'

The moment Rajlakshmi was out of the room, Mahendra burst out, 'Why do you torture me like this?'

Binodini seemingly didn't know what he was talking about. 'What! When did I torture you? Was I wrong to come into your room then? Fair enough, let me leave.' She made as if to get up with a crestfallen expression.

Mahendra grabbed her wrist and said, 'This is precisely how you torment me.'

Binodini said, 'Really! I didn't know I had so much power. You are not too bad yourself; obviously you can take a lot. You don't look like you've been burnt at the stake.'

Mahendra said, 'Looks cannot tell you the whole story.' He grabbed her hand forcefully and pressed it to his heart.

Binodini screeched in pain and immediately he let go, saying, 'Did I hurt you?'

He saw that Binodini's wound from the previous day was bleeding once again. In abject apology he said, 'I was careless—how remiss of me. But now you must let me tie it and apply some ointment—please don't stop me today.'

Binodini said, 'No, it's nothing. I shall not put medication on it.'

Mahendra said, 'Why not?'

Binodini said, 'What do you mean "why not"! Don't put on your medical airs with me; let it be.'

Mahendra grew solemn and thought, 'Beyond me entirely—a woman's mind!'

Binodini rose to leave. Piqued, Mahendra didn't stop her this time. He merely asked, 'Where are you going?'

Binodini said, 'I have work to do.' She walked out slowly.

A few seconds later Mahendra got up, meaning to go and call her back. But he turned back from the stairway and began to walk about on the terrace instead.

Binodini drew him to her continuously, and yet she never let him get really close to her. Mahendra had recently surrendered the conceit that no one could have complete power over him. But would he also have to give up the conceit that he could have complete power over anyone if he so desired? Today he had to concede defeat as he failed to overpower Binodini. In matters of the heart Mahendra held his head very high indeed. He didn't consider anyone his equal. But today he had to lose that pride as well. And he didn't gain anything in return. Like a beggar he stood empty-handed at dusk, in front of a closed door.

In the months of March and April, Behari's farmlands yielded honey from the mustard flowers. Every year he sent some to Rajlakshmi and this year was no different.

Binodini took the pot of honey to Rajlakshmi and said, 'Aunty, Behari-thakurpo has sent honey.'

Rajlakshmi asked her to put it away in the store room. Binodini did as she was told and then came and sat beside Rajlakshmi. She said, 'Behari-thakurpo never fails to do his bit for you. I suppose because he doesn't have a mother, he sees her in you, doesn't he?'

Rajlakshmi was so used to seeing Behari as Mahendra's shadow that she never gave him much thought. He was an unpaid, uncared for, unthought of, loyal friend to the family. When Binodini mentioned Behari as a motherless boy and sited Rajlakshmi as his guardian, a tender, maternal spot was touched in the latter's heart. Suddenly Rajlakshmi thought, 'That's true. Behari is motherless and he sees me as his mother.' She recalled how Behari had always looked after her in sickness and in health, without being sent for and without any pretentiousness; Rajlakshmi had taken it all for granted, just like the air she breathed. She had never considered being grateful for it. But did anyone ever reciprocate any concern for Behari? When Annapurna was around, she had looked after him. Rajlakshmi had thought that she put on a great show of affection to keep Behari tied to her apron-strings.

Today Rajlakshmi heaved a great sigh and said, 'True, Behari is just like a son to me.'

As she said it, she realized that Behari did more for her than her own son; he was devoted to her even without the promise of any returns. This thought provoked another sigh from the depths of her heart.

Binodini said, 'Behari-thakurpo really loves to eat food cooked by you!'

Rajlakshmi was full of maternal pride as she said, 'He doesn't like fish curry made by anyone else.' As she said it, she realized that Behari hadn't come around for many days. She asked, 'Why doesn't Behari come around these days?'

Binodini said, 'I was wondering about that myself. But then your son has been so busy with his wife ever since he got married—why would friends come round any more?'

Rajlakshmi felt the criticism was justified. For the sake of his wife, Mahendra had distanced all his near and dear ones. Behari was right in feeling hurt—why should he visit them? Rajlakshmi felt sympathy welling up for Behari once she saw him as neglected by Mahendra as she was. She began to narrate to Binodini, in great detail, how much Behari had done for Mahendra since their childhood days, how much he had sacrificed. Through this narration she rationalized all her own grievances against her son. Mahendra had done a grave injustice by alienating his childhood friend for the sake of a new wife!

Binodini said, 'Tomorrow, Sunday, why don't you send for Behari-thakurpo and cook for him? He'd be delighted.'

Rajlakshmi said, 'You are right. Let me send for Mahin and he can go and invite Behari.'

Binodini said, 'Oh no, Aunty, you invite him personally.'

Rajlakshmi said, 'I don't know to read and write, like all you youngsters.'

Binodini said, 'That's nothing—I can write the letter on your behalf.'

Binodini wrote out an invitation on behalf of Rajlakshmi and sent it off.

Sunday was eagerly anticipated by Mahendra. His fantasies went wild from the night before, although till that point nothing had really gone according to his fantasies. Yet, the morning sun seemed to pour honey on his eyes as Sunday dawned. The sounds of the city awakening were like a melodious tune to his ears.

But what was this—did his mother have a religious vow today or something? She wasn't resting like other days, leaving the household chores to Binodini. Today she was busy cooking in the kitchen.

Amidst all the hustle and bustle it was ten o'clock soon. In all that time Mahendra couldn't snatch a moment alone with Binodini. He tried to read but couldn't concentrate. His eyes were glued to an inconsequential advertisement in the newspaper for fifteen whole minutes. Finally he could take it no longer. He went downstairs and found his mother busy cooking in a corner of the veranda near her room. Binodini had her sari tucked firmly into her waist as she went about assisting Rajlakshmi.

Mahendra asked, 'So what are you two doing today? Why all these elaborate arrangements?'

Rajlakshmi said, 'Hasn't Binodini told you? I have invited Behari to lunch today.'

Behari invited to lunch! Mahendra felt vicious anger rise up to his throat. Immediately he said, 'But Mother, I shall not be here.'

Rajlakshmi asked, 'Why?'

Mahendra said briefly, 'I must go out.'

Rajlakshmi said, 'Go out after lunch—it won't take long.'

Mahendra said, 'But I have an invitation for lunch.'

Binodini threw a quick, veiled look at Mahendra's face and said, 'Aunty, if he does have an invitation, let him go. Let Behari-thakurpo have lunch alone today.'

But how could Rajlakshmi bear it if Mahin did not eat all that she was cooking with such great care? But the more she pleaded, the harsher was Mahendra's refusal: 'Very important lunch invitation, simply cannot refuse, you should have asked me before inviting Behari,' etc. etc.

This was Mahendra's way of punishing his mother. It had its effect. Rajlakshmi lost all interest in cooking. She felt like dropping everything and walking away. Binodini said, 'Aunty, don't you worry—Thakurpo may say all this; but he is going nowhere today.'

Rajlakshmi shook her head. 'No my child, you don't know my Mahin.

Once his mind is made up, nothing can stop him.'

But apparently Binodini knew Mahendra no less than Rajlakshmi. Mahendra realized that Binodini was instrumental in this invitation to Behari. The more he burnt in envy at this revelation, the harder it grew for him to walk away. How could he go without seeing what Behari and Binodini were up to? It would be torture, but he had to see it.

After many days, Behari came into the inner chambers today as an invited guest. For an instant he stopped short at the doorway of the room where he had been a regular since his youth, where he had got up to all kinds of mischief as a child. A wave of emotion swelled in his heart, threatening to rise and crash with all its might. He suppressed it and walked in with a smile. Rajlakshmi had just finished her bath when Behari came in and touched her feet. When Behari used to come in almost daily, such a manner of greeting wasn't customary between them. Today it felt as though he was home after a long trip abroad. Rajlakshmi blessed him lovingly.

Rajlakshmi was full of affection and concern for Behari, out of a sense of heartfelt empathy. She said, 'O Behari, where were you all these days? Every day I felt sure you would come, but there was no sign of you.'

Behari laughed. 'If I came here every day, would you have spared me another thought, Mother? Where is Mahin da?'

Rajlakshmi replied glumly, 'Mahin had a lunch invitation; he couldn't stay here today.'

Behari's face fell. So this was the consequence of a lifelong friendship? Behari heaved a sigh, strove to drive away the dejection for the moment and asked, 'What's for lunch today?' He asked after his favourite dishes. Whenever Rajlakshmi cooked, Behari showed himself to be a little more eager and hungry. That was his way of stealing the love from the maternal Rajlakshmi's heart. On this day too, Rajlakshmi enjoyed Behari's eager craving for her food and reassured him with a laugh.

Suddenly, Mahendra arrived and greeted Behari in the most polite tones, 'Hello there, how are you, Behari?'

Rajlakshmi said, 'Mahin, didn't you go to your lunch invitation?'

Mahendra tried to mask his embarrassment as he said, 'Oh no, I was able to cancel it.'

When Binodini walked in, bathed and changed, Behari was lost for words at first. The scene he had witnessed between Mahendra and Binodini was still engraved on his mind. He couldn't bring himself to greet her.

Binodini stood quite close to Behari and spoke in low tones, 'Thakurpo, don't you know me at all?'

Behari replied, 'It's hard to really know someone.'

Binodini said, 'Not if you have good judgement.' She turned to Rajlakshmi, 'Aunty, lunch is ready.'

Behari and Mahendra sat down to eat; Rajlakshmi sat close by and tended to them while Binodini served the food.

Mahendra wasn't interested in the food. He noticed the special favours in the serving more keenly. He began to feel that Binodini was deriving a special kind of satisfaction while serving food to Behari. The fact that Behari got the largest piece of fish and the bigger portion of curds could easily be rationalized thus—Mahendra was family and Behari was the guest. But Mahendra burned with agonized spite simply because there was no cause to vocalize his complaint. A certain variety of delicious fish had been fetched specially from the market—it was unusual for this time of the year. One was stuffed full of roe and Binodini tried to serve it to Behari. He protested, 'No, no, give that to Mahin da; he loves it.'

Full of righteous indignation, Mahendra said, 'Oh no, I don't want it.'

Binodini didn't ask him a second time; she merely dropped it onto Behari's plate.

At the end of the meal the two friends came outside; Binodini came up to them and said, 'Behari-thakurpo, don't go home just yet. Let's go upstairs and sit and talk.'

Behari asked, 'Won't you have lunch?'

Binodini said, 'No, it's ekadasi, the three-quarter moon—the day we widows fast.'

A smile of cruel mockery touched Behari's lips; so even the fast must be kept! All rituals were adhered to!

That faint smile did not escape Binodini's notice. But she bore it the same way she had borne the gash on her arm. She pleaded, 'Please come and sit down for a while.'

Suddenly, Mahendra lost his temper and spoke out of turn, 'What's wrong with you all—drop everything you were doing, whether you like it or not, please come and sit for a while! I don't get the meaning of such excessive fondness.'

Binodini laughed out loud, 'Behari-thakurpo, just listen to your Mahin da talk. Fondness means just that, affection. The dictionary doesn't give another meaning.' She turned to Mahendra, 'I must say, Thakurpo, going by your childhood days there is no one who understands the meaning of excessive fondness better than you.'

Behari said, 'Mahin da, I have something to say. Could I talk to you alone for a moment?' Behari walked out with Mahendra without a backward glance at Binodini. She stood on the veranda, clinging to the railings, and stared into the void of the empty courtyard.

Behari came outside and said, 'Mahin da, I want to know—is this where our friendship ends?'

Mahendra was burning up with envy; Binodini's mocking repartee was splitting his head from end to end, like a searing bolt of lightning. He said, 'I suppose if we patch up, it will be to your benefit. But I do not see anything in it for me. I do not wish to admit strangers into my life, and I'd like to keep the inner chambers secluded from the world at large.'

Behari walked away without another word.

Green with envy, Mahendra vowed never to see Binodini again. Soon afterwards he restlessly paced the stairway and every room of the house in the hope of meeting her by chance.

# 30

One day Asha asked Annapurna, 'Aunty, do you ever think of uncle?'

Annapurna said, 'I was widowed at the age of eleven. My husband is like a shadowy memory to me.'

Asha asked, 'Aunty, who do you think of then?'

Annapurna smiled. 'I think of Him who is now the keeper of my husband—of God.'

Asha asked, 'Does that bring you joy?'

Annapurna stroked her head lovingly and said, 'Child, what would you know of the matters of my mind? It is known only to me and to Him on whom my heart is fixed.'

Asha mulled over this as she thought, 'Does he know my heart—the one I think of day and night? Just because I cannot write well, why has he given up writing to me?'

It was a while since Asha had got a letter from Mahendra. She sighed and thought, 'If only Chokher Bali were with me, she'd have been able to pen down my thoughts faithfully.'

Asha couldn't ever bring herself to write to her husband for fear that her badly written prose would not be appreciated by him. The harder she tried, the more her scrawls went awry. The more she tried to express herself concisely, the further her thoughts scattered themselves. If only she could write the first 'Dearest' and then sign her name, such that an omniscient Mahendra would read between the lines all that she meant to write, Asha would have completed her letters with great success. Fate had gifted her with a great capacity to love but with little verbal skills.

That evening Asha came back from the temple after the aarti, sat down at Annapurna's feet and began to stroke them gently. After many minutes of silence she said, 'Aunty, you always say that a husband should be worshipped and served like a god. But what can a wife do, if she is stupid, slow-witted and doesn't know how to serve him?'

Annapurna gazed at Asha's face for a few seconds and a covert sigh excaped her as she said, 'Child, I too am stupid, and yet I serve my God.'

Asha said, 'But He knows your heart and so He is pleased. But what if the husband is not satisfied with the dumb woman's devotion?'

Annapurna said, 'Not everyone has the capacity to satisfy everyone, my child. If the wife serves her husband and his family with the utmost devotion and genuine dedication, then even if the husband throws her service away as worthless, the Lord of the Universe will pick it up and treasure it.'

Asha sat in wordless silence. She tried very hard to take heart from these words spoken by her aunt. But she simply couldn't accept that a woman discarded by her husband can derive any solace even from the

Lord of the Universe Himself. She sat with her head bent and continued to stroke her aunt's feet.

Annapurna held her hand and drew her closer. She kissed the top of her head. With great effort she cleared her choked voice and said, 'Chuni, the trials and tribulations of life are a great teacher—mere advice can't take their place. At your age, I had struck a give-and-take relationship with life. Just like you, I too thought that I should get recognition from whoever I served. But at every step I found that my expectation wasn't realistic. Eventually one day, I could take it no longer. I felt all that I had done had been in vain. The same day I left home. But today I find nothing has been in vain. My child, He who is the chief of this business called life, with Whom we have a constant give-and-take relationship, has been taking everything I have ever given. Today He rests in my heart and admits my worth. If only I knew it then! If I worked through life seeing it as work done for Him, if I poured my heart into life as if I was pouring it into Him, who would ever have had the capacity to hurt me?'

Asha lay in bed thinking hard, going back to Annapurna's words, although she couldn't make proper sense of them all. But she had immense respect for her pious aunt and in spite of not understanding all that she had said Asha gave credence to most of it. She sat up in bed, folded her hands and sent up a prayer in the direction of that God to whom her aunt had given her heart. She said, 'I am a child, I do not know You. All I know is my husband; please don't blame me for that. Dear God, please tell my husband to accept the devotion that I place at his feet. If he chooses to reject it, I shall surely die. I am not as devout as my aunt; shelter at your feet alone cannot be my salvation.' Asha bowed again and again and prayed fervently before she got into bed.

It was time for Anukulbabu to go back home. The evening before Asha left, Annapurna sat her down by her side and said, 'Chuni, my child, I do not have the power to protect you from the sorrows, travails and hardships of life at all times. This is my advice to you: however anyone may hurt you, keep your faith, your piety intact; may your integrity always be uncompromised.'

Asha touched her feet and said, 'Bless me, Aunty, so that I can do that.'

## 31

Asha returned home. Binodini reproached her petulantly, 'Bali, you didn't write me a single letter in all these days!'

Asha said, 'As if you showered me with letters!'

Binodini said, 'Why should I write? You were supposed to write first.'

Asha hugged her and conceded defeat. She said, 'You know I cannot express myself too well. Especially writing to a learned person like you really makes me shy.'

Gradually, the two friends put aside their mutual complaints and went back to their affectionate selves.

Binodini said, 'You have truly spoilt your husband by keeping him company day and night. He must have someone by his side at all times!'

Asha said, 'The precise reason why I left him in your care! You are better at keeping him company.'

Binodini said, 'In the day I'd be spared by sending him off to college; but the evenings were harder to escape—chat with him, read to him, endless demands!'

Asha said, 'Serves you right! Why would people spare you when you can entertain them so well?'

Binodini said, 'Watch out, my friend. The way Thakurpo behaves at times, I wonder if I have mesmeric powers!'

Asha laughed, 'You'd have to be the one! If only I had even an ounce of your charm.'

Binodini said, 'Why, who do you wish to ruin? Work on guarding the one you have—don't go after strangers; it's not worth the bother.'

Asha chided her with a push and said, 'Oh dear, what nonsense!'

The moment Mahendra met Asha for the first time after her return from Kashi, he said, 'I can see you've put on weight—the trip seems to have done you good.'

Asha felt mortified. She should not have looked so healthy—but nothing ever went right for poor Asha. Even while she was so miserable, her silly body had put on weight. On the one hand she didn't have the words to express herself, and on the other her body played truant.

Asha murmured, 'How have you been?'

In the past, Mahendra would have said, with mock sorrow and some genuine emotion, 'I was only half alive.' But now he couldn't be playful; the words stuck at his throat. He said, 'I've been fine, not bad at all.'

Asha gazed at him and found he had lost weight—his face had a pallor and a bright flame burned in his eyes. A deep-seated hunger seemed to be licking away at his insides. Asha felt upset. 'My poor husband hasn't been well at all. Why did I leave him and go to Kashi?' She was outraged indeed, at her own health, at the fact that her husband had lost weight while she put it on.

Mahendra wondered what he should talk about next and slowly stumbled out with, 'I suppose Aunty is keeping well?'

He was reassured to that effect and thereafter he was lost for things to say. A tattered, old newspaper lay close by. He pulled it close and glanced through it absentmindedly. Asha stood there looking down as she thought, 'We meet after so long and he's not talking to me properly; he hasn't even looked at my face. Is he angry because I didn't write to him the last few days, or is he upset that I stayed back longer in Kashi at Aunty's request?' Desolate and miserable, Asha pondered over the possible sources of her own culpability.

Mahendra went to college and returned later in the day. While he had his snacks, Rajlakshmi waited on him and Asha stood at a distance with her anchal drawn over her head. But no one else was present.

Rajlakshmi asked with a concerned frown, 'Are you unwell today, Mahin?'

The question annoyed Mahendra. 'No Mother, why should I be unwell?'

Rajlakshmi said, 'But you have hardly eaten anything.'

Mahendra snapped back, 'I am eating, am I not?'

It was a summer evening. Mahendra wrapped himself in a light shawl and began to pace the terrace. He had great hopes that the regular reading session (with Binodini) would take place as usual. They were nearly through with Bankim's Anandamath, with just a couple of chapters to go. Binodini may be heartless, but she would surely come and read those out to him today! But the evening wore on, the hands of the clock moved on and Mahendra had to go to bed with a heavy heart.

Asha came into the bedroom, bashful and dressed up. She found Mahendra lying in bed. She didn't know what to do next. A long separation brought with it some coyness—both parties expected a fresh greeting from each other before they could become intimate with each other like before. How could Asha re-enter her old, familiar, pleasure-seat without being asked? She waited at the door for a few long minutes, but Mahendra did not say anything. She stepped into the room, one step at a time. If a bangle or an anklet made a sudden sound, she nearly died of shame. With heart aflutter she went up to the bed and realized that Mahendra was asleep. In that instant, all her finery seemed to strangle her and mock her cruelly. She wanted to hurl everything from her body and rush from the room, go anywhere else.

Asha got into bed as stealthily as possible. Yet, there were enough sounds and movement so as to wake Mahendra if he had truly been asleep. But tonight his eyes stayed shut because Mahendra wasn't asleep. He lay at one end of the bed and so Asha lay still beside him. It was clear to Mahendra, even with his back to her, that Asha was weeping silent tears in the dark. His own cruelty to her was tormenting him. But he simply did not know what to say, how to hold her or love her. He hurled abuses at himself and lacerated himself mentally—it hurt badly but didn't resolve anything. He thought, 'In the morning I won't be able to pretend I'm asleep—what shall I say to Asha then?'

But Asha took care of his concern. At the crack of dawn she left the bed in her affronted finery; she couldn't face him either.

## 32

Asha wondered, 'Why did this happen? What have I done wrong?' But she never considered the obvious. The very idea that Mahendra was in love with Binodini never crossed her mind. Asha was very naïve in worldly matters. Besides, she could never imagine that Mahendra could be anything other than the person she had known forever, ever since their marriage.

Mahendra left for college earlier than usual. As he left, Asha always came and stood at the window. Mahendra would glance up just once before he got into the carriage. This had been a routine with them for the longest time. Thus habituated, Asha drifted to the window mechanically the minute she heard the sounds of the carriage drawing up. Possibly by habit, Mahendra too shot a glance at the window. He found Asha standing there—she hadn't yet bathed, or changed her clothes; her face was pallid. Instantly Mahendra lowered his gaze and looked down at the books on his lap. Alas for that silent greeting as their eyes met, or that meaningful smile!

The carriage went its way; Asha dropped to the floor. The whole world turned to dust before her eyes. In the streets of Kolkata it was business as usual—carriages headed for offices, trams were chasing other trams—this lone, solitary, pained heart in a distant corner of the city was a misfit amidst the hustle and bustle of life.

Suddenly Asha saw the light. 'I know—he has heard that Thakurpo went to Kashi and he is upset about that. Nothing else has happened in the meantime that could cause him any displeasure. But—why blame me for that?'

As she mulled over this for a few seconds, Asha's heart skipped a beat. Suddenly she was gripped by the fear that Mahendra was under the misconception that Asha and Behari had colluded in his sudden arrival in Kashi. A conspiracy. Oh, shame! Such mistrust! It was bad enough that her name was linked to Behari, causing her such trauma; if Mahendra doubted her in this manner now, she'd surely die. But if there was really such a misgiving, if Mahendra felt she'd really gone wrong, why didn't he confront her with it? He should judge her and punish her to his satisfaction. She felt he was avoiding her without tackling the issue head-on. Asha was convinced that Mahendra was suffering from some misconception that he knew was intrinsically false and he was ashamed to admit it even to Asha. Why else would he walk around looking so guilty? The censorious husband would hardly look like this!

All day long Mahendra was haunted by that melancholy expression on Asha's face that he had glimpsed in an instant in the morning. Through the lectures in college, amidst the hordes of students, he could only see Asha, wan and dishevelled, her clothes in disarray, her eyes pained and aggrieved.

After college he went for a stroll around the circular lake. As he strolled, dusk drew close; he couldn't decide what he should do about Asha—sympathetic duplicity or harsh honesty—which did she deserve? Not once did he even consider letting Binodini go. He only wondered how he could honour both his loves at the same time.

Mahendra consoled himself with the thought that the love he still felt for Asha was rare in most women's lives. Asha should be grateful for that love and generosity. Mahendra's heart was large enough to carry both Asha and Binodini in it. His nuptial relationship wouldn't be affected in the least by the platonic, noble romance he had with Binodini.

Having thus convinced himself, Mahendra felt a weight lifting from his shoulders. He grew cheerful at the thought of spending his entire life like a planet with two moons, with both Binodini and Asha being where they belonged in his life. He decided to go to bed early that night and to caress and stroke away all the doubts that Asha was facing. Reassured by his own decision, he walked home hurriedly.

Asha was absent when he had his dinner. But he went to bed thinking that she'd have to come to the bedroom at some point. But in the silent room, in that empty bed, which were the reminiscences that flooded his heart? Were they the ones of the first days of his romance with Asha? No. All those memories had faded away from his mind the way moonshine melts before sunlight. A razor-sharp, accomplished young woman outshone the image of the naïve child-woman cloaked in shyness. Mahendra recollected his scuffle with Binodini over *The Poison Tree*. In the evenings, as Binodini had read out Bankim's Kapalakundala to him, the night crept up and the household fell asleep. In that solitary room, in that still silence, Binodini's voice grew softer and nearly disappeared as she read on. Suddenly, she came back to her senses, dropped the book and stood up to leave. Mahendra said, 'Let me come with you till the bottom of the stairs.' Mahendra reminisced about those evenings and felt thrilled anew. The night wore on and Mahendra began to dread Asha's arrival. But Asha did not come. Mahendra thought, 'I was ready to do my duty, but if Asha takes exception without reason and refuses to come here, what can I do?' And he gave himself up to more pleasurable meditations on Binodini and brought back even more of her.

When the clock struck one, Mahendra could hold still no longer. He went out to the terrace and found the mellow moonlight flooding the night. The mammoth silence of Kolkata felt as tangible as the waves in a speechless ocean—the breeze ambled casually amidst the row of edifices, shrouding them in thick layers of sleep.

Mahendra could not contain his craving: ever since Asha returned from Kashi, Binodini hadn't met him. The lonely night enchanted by moonlight propelled him relentlessly towards Binodini. Mahendra went down the stairs. He stood before Binodini's door and realized that it wasn't locked yet. He stepped into the room and saw that the bed was made, but there was no one in it yet. At the sound of footsteps, Binodini called out from the balcony to the south, 'Who's there?'

Mahendra replied in a voice drenched in emotion, 'Binod, it's me.' He walked straight out onto the balcony.

On this warm summer night Rajlakshmi happened to be lying there, on a mat, along with Binodini. She said, 'Mahin, what are you doing here so late at night?'

Binodini cast an angry, thunderous glance at him from under her thick, dark brows. Mahendra walked away without another word.

## 33

The following morning was cloudy and gloomy. The sky was laden with rain-clouds after days of scorching heat. Mahendra left early for his classes. His discarded clothes lay scattered on the floor. Asha counted them up as she handed them out to the washerman.

Mahendra was absentminded by nature. Hence Asha had instructions to check his pockets before handing his clothes over to the laundry. She fished into a pocket of his discarded shirt and came up with a letter.

If only that letter had turned into a poisonous snake and stung Asha's fingers before she could read it! If a potent poison spreads in the body, it can yield results in five minutes. But a poisoned mind only brings mortal torment, not death.

Asha fished out the open letter and saw it was written by Binodini. Asha's face turned ashen. She took the letter into the next room and began to read—

> After what you did last night, I'd have thought you'll come to your senses. Why did you send me a clandestine note through Khemi, the maid? Shame on you! What must she think! Are you going to make it impossible for me to show my face to anyone in the world?
>
> What do you want from me? Love? Why do you beg? You have received love since the day you were born, but still you crave for it.
>
> In this world, I have no one to love and no one to love me. Hence I play at games of love and satisfy my craving for it. When you had the time to spare, you joined in the game. But all games must end some day. You have summons from the house—why do you still peep into the playroom? Shake off the dust and go back home now. I have no home. So I'll sit in a corner and play games in my head. I shall not call you.
>
> You wrote that you love me. That may have worked while we were playing games—but if you want me to take it for the truth, I do not believe it. At one point in time you believed you love Asha—that was a lie too. Now you think you love me, this too is a lie. The only one you love is yourself.
>
> Thirst for love has parched my heart and soul. You do not have the capacity to quench my thirst—I know that for a fact. As I keep telling you, let go of me, don't come after me. Don't be so shameless as to shame me. My desire for games has ended. Now, if you call me, I shall not answer. You have called me heartless in your note. That may be true. But I also have a soul and hence today I take pity on you and renounce you. If you dare answer

this letter I shall be sure that the only way to escape you is to leave this house.

As she finished reading the letter, everything came tumbling around Asha. Her nerves gave way, she could scarcely breathe and the sun stole away the light from her eyes. Asha tried to hold on to the wall, then the cupboard and finally the chair as she crumpled to the floor. A little later she came back to her senses and tried to read the letter once again. But her shattered mind could hardly take it in. The black letters danced before her eyes. How did this happen? What was all this! What a terrible, earth-shattering disaster! Asha couldn't think of where to go, whom to call and what to do. Her heart fluttered like the fish that was hauled out of water and gasped for breath. Just as the drowning man reached up and groped for the sky over his head, deep down in her heart Asha desperately tried to get a hold of something firm, and finally she sobbed out, 'Aunty!'

The minute she took the name of her beloved aunt, tears sprang to her eyes and flowed relentlessly. She sat on the floor and wept her heart out. When the weeping subsided, she thought, 'What shall I do with this letter?' She cringed as she imagined Mahendra's severe embarrassment if he discovered that Asha had read the letter. She decided to put the letter back in the pocket of his shirt and hang it up on the shelf instead of sending it to the laundry.

With this thought she came back into her room. Meanwhile, the washerman had leaned back on his bundle of clothes and gone to sleep. Asha picked up the shirt and tried to put the letter back in its pocket when she suddenly heard, 'Bali dear!'

She dropped the shirt and the letter hastily on the bed and sat on it. Binodini came into the room and said, 'These days the washerman has been mixing up clothes. Let me take back the ones that haven't been marked yet.'

Asha couldn't bring herself to look at Binodini. She turned away and looked out of the window for fear that her face would give her away. She bit down hard on her lips so that the tears wouldn't escape her eyes.

Binodini stopped short and took stock of Asha's expression. She said to herself, 'I get it—so now you know all about last night. And I suppose I am the only one to blame!'

Binodini did not make any effort to speak to Asha. She just picked out a few clothes and walked away.

Asha was stung by the shame of having been friends with Binodini so naïvely for all these days. She wanted to compare the cruel letter just once more to the ideal of a friend that she carried in her heart.

She was opening the letter once again when Mahendra burst into the room. Apparently, he had rushed out in the middle of a lecture and run home for some reason.

Asha hid the letter in the folds of her sari. Mahendra also stopped short when he found Asha in the room. Then he cast anxious looks all over the room. Asha knew what he was looking for; but she couldn't think of a way to slip the letter back in its place and make good her escape from the room.

Mahendra picked up each discarded item and hunted through it. Asha couldn't bear to watch his pitiful attempts any longer. She hurled the shirt and the letter on the floor, gripped the bedpost with one hand and buried her face in the other. Mahendra picked up the letter in a flash. For a second he gazed at Asha. Then the sounds of his footsteps running down the stairs fell on Asha's ears. The washerman was saying, 'Ma, how much longer for you to give all the clothes? It's getting late and I live far away.'

## 34

Since morning Rajlakshmi had not sent for Binodini. when Binodini went into the storeroom as usual, Rajlakshmi did not even look up.

This did not escape Binodini's notice. She said, 'Aunty, are you unwell? I don't blame you, after what Thakurpo did last night. He just barged in like a madman! I could hardly sleep after that.'

Rajlakshmi merely sulked and didn't say a word.

Binodini said, 'He must have had a minor tiff with Chokher Bali and that was that! He must drag me there to resolve it or to hear them out. He couldn't wait for the morning. I must say this, Aunty, and don't you blame me, your son may have many qualities, but patience isn't one of them. That's what all our spats are about.'

Rajlakshmi said, 'You are blabbering in vain—I am not in the mood to listen to anything today.'

Binodini said, 'Neither am I, Aunty. If I criticized your son I was afraid you'd be hurt and so I tried to pull the wool over your eyes with a bunch of lies. But a time has come when that's no longer possible.'

Rajlakshmi said, 'I know the good and the bad in my son—but I didn't know what a temptress you could be.'

Binodini opened her mouth to say something and then closed it again. She said, 'That's true, Aunty—no one really knows anyone. One doesn't even know oneself. Wasn't it you who once wanted to tempt your son with this temptress, simply to avenge yourself on your daughter-in-law? Think about that and then answer me.'

Rajlakshmi flared up like a forest-fire, 'You wretched woman, shame on you for making such allegations about a mother where her son is concerned. May your tongue drop off for sinning so blatantly.'

Binodini replied calmly, 'Aunty, you know better than me whether I am a seductress or not and what enchantment I possess. Just so, I know the spell that you tried to cast, though you might deny it. But it must've been there or this wouldn't have happened. Both you and I lay the trap with some wilfulness and some ignorance. That's the way our breed goes—we are enchantresses.'

Rajlakshmi was so incensed that she could barely speak. She left the room in a huff.

Binodini stood a while in the empty room; her eyes burned with fire.

Once the morning chores were done, Rajlakshmi sent for Mahendra. He knew that the subject of last night's events would come up. He was already disconsolate with Binodini's response to his letter. As a consequence, his wayward heart was focused entirely on Binodini. A confrontation with his mother was beyond him right now. Mahendra knew that if his mother brought up Binodini and rebuked him, in defence he would be impelled to blurt out the truth; this would lead to terrible domestic strife. Hence it was imperative to leave the house for the moment, sit in solitude and sort out his thoughts. He instructed the servant, 'Go and tell Mother that I have urgent work at college today and I have to leave now. I shall talk to her when I come back.' He changed his clothes and scuttled away like a truant child without even eating. The terrible reply from Binodini that he had carried with him all morning and perused several times, stayed back in his discarded shirt pocket.

After a heavy shower, the sky remained overcast. Binodini was very distraught. Whenever she felt upset, she was given to working harder. So she had decided to gather all the clothes in the house and to mark them for the washerman. When she had gone to collect clothes from Asha and seen the latter's expression, her irritation knew no bounds. If she had to be held responsible for what had happened the previous night, why should she only get the humiliation and none of the pleasures of her crime?

The rain clattered away outside. Binodini sat on the floor in her room. The clothes lay in a heap in front of her. Khemi, the maid, was handing them to her one by one as Binodini stamped the initials onto them. Suddenly Mahendra barged into the room without warning. Khemi dropped her work, pulled the sari over her head and dashed away.

Binodini dropped the clothes she had in her hands, stood up in a flash and said, 'Go away, leave my room immediately.'

Mahendra said, 'Why? What have I done?'

Binodini said, 'What have you done! Coward! What can you do? You can neither love nor do your duty. Why must you drag my name into the mud?'

Mahendra tried to reason with her, 'How can you say I do not love you?'

Binodini said in a scathing voice, 'That's exactly what I say. Stealth, camouflage, indecision—I am repulsed by your knavery. I hate it. Go away.'

Mahendra was miserable. 'You are repulsed by me, Binod?'

Binodini said, 'Yes.'

Mahendra said, 'There's still time for repentence, Binod. If I stop dithering and leave everything behind, will you come with me?'

Mahendra grabbed her with both hands and pulled her to him. Binodini said, 'Let me go, you are hurting me.'

Mahendra said, 'It doesn't matter. Tell me, will you come with me?'

Binodini said, 'No, never, not on your life!'

Mahendra said, 'But why? You were the one to ruin me—today you cannot turn your back on me. You have to come.'

Mahendra drew her to him forcefully and held her close. He said, 'Even your hatred cannot turn me away. I will take you along and somehow I shall make you love me.'

Binodini freed herself with a jerk.

Mahendra said, 'You have set fire all around you; now you cannot put it out and try to escape.'

Mahendra's voice rose as he shouted, 'Why did you play such games, Binod? Now you can't brush it all off as a game and get away. You and I have no choice but to die together.'

Rajlakshmi stepped into the room and said, 'Mahin, what do you think you are doing?'

Mahendra's delirious gaze turned just once at his mother and came back to rest on Binodini as he said, 'I am leaving everything and going away. Tell me, will you come with me?'

Binodini looked at the infuriated Rajlakshmi. Then she stepped forward, took Mahendra's hand and said, 'I will.'

Mahendra said, 'In that case, wait just one more day. I am leaving this house. From tomorrow, you will be all I have left with me.'

Mahendra went away.

At this point the washerman came and said to Binodini, 'Ma, I cannot wait any longer. If you do not have the time today, I can come back tomorrow for the clothes.'

Khemi came and said, 'Bou-thakurun, the coachman says he's run out of hay.'

Binodini used to weigh out a week's feed and send it off to the stables. She would stand at the window watching as the horses ate.

Gopal, the servant, came and said, 'Bou-thakurun, the bearer has had a tiff with Sadhubabu. He says if you take the accounts for the kerosene from him, he will go to the head clerk, work out his pay and leave.'

Life went on as usual.

# 35

Behari was in medical college all this while. But he dropped out of college right before the exams. If anyone asked, he said, 'There's time enough to care for other people's health; I must look after my own first.'

As a matter of fact, Behari had immense energy. He needed to be intensely involved with something at all times; but he did not need to work, to earn a living; nor did he seek fame. After he graduated from college, he'd gone to Shibpur first, to study engineering. He acquired as much knowledge as he wished, and as much skill as he thought was necessary, and left to join medical college. Mahendra had joined medical college a year before him. Among the students in college, their friendship was legendary. They teased them by calling them the Siamese twins. The previous year, when Mahendra failed his exams, the two landed up in the same year. But no one could understand why the pair broke up at this point. Behari couldn't bring himself to go to class where he was bound to run into Mahendra but not meet him in the proper sense of the word. Everyone knew that Behari would pass the exams with flying colours, and win awards and prizes. But Behari didn't sit for the exams.

Behari's neighbour was a poor Brahmin, Rajendra Chakravarty. He worked in a printing press as a compositor and brought home twelve rupees a month. Behari said to him, 'Let your son live in my house, I shall teach him.'

The Brahmin heaved a sigh of relief. With a happy heart he surrendered his eight-year-old son, Vasant, into Behari's care.

Behari began to teach him in his own fashion. He said, 'I shall not give him a book to read before he's ten years old; I'll teach him orally until then.' Behari spent his days playing with the child, taking him to the park, the museum, the zoo and farmlands. Behari's entire day was taken up by teaching him English orally, telling him stories from history, testing his intelligence with various quizzes and games and riddles. He didn't have a moment to spare.

One evening, there was no way they could go out. Since noon, the rain had halted just once and had now begun again. Behari sat in his room upstairs with Vasant and played at a new game he had invented.

'Vasant, quick, tell me how many beams there are in this room—no, you cannot count them now.'

Vasant said, 'Twenty.'

Behari said, 'Wrong—it's eighteen.'

Suddenly he reached out, fingered the blinds and asked, 'How many rows in this blind?'

'Six.'

'Right. How long is this bench? What's the weight of this book?' In this way Behari was sharpening the boy's reflexes when the bearer walked in and said, 'Babuji, a woman—'

Before he had finished speaking, Binodini walked into the room.

Taken aback, Behari exclaimed, 'What is it, Bouthan?'

Binodini said, 'Do you have any female relatives who live here with you?'

Behari said, 'No relatives, no strangers, nobody. My aunt lives in the village.'

Binodini said, 'In that case, take me to your village and leave me there.'

Behari said, 'And what will be my excuse?'

Binodini said, 'Say that I am your maid. I shall do the housework there.'

Behari said, 'My aunt will be a trifle surprised. She has not complained to me about a shortage of maids. First you must tell me how you came up with this idea. Vasant, go to bed now, child.'

Vasant left the room. Binodini said, 'If I tell you the events, you will not really understand what happened.'

Behari said, 'What's the harm—even if I misunderstand?'

'Fine, then misunderstand if you want to—Mahendra is in love with me.'

Behari said, 'That's not news and neither is it something that one would like to hear again and again.'

Binodini said, 'I have no wish to utter it again and again. That's the reason I have come to you—to seek refuge.'

Behari said acidly, 'You have no wish? And who, pray, caused this to happen? Who dragged Mahendra on to the path he now treads?'

Binodini said, 'I did. I cannot lie to you—this is my handiwork. I may be bad, or wrong, but do try to see things from my point of view just this once and understand me. The fire that burned in my heart caused me to set fire to Mahendra's home. Once, I did think that I loved Mahendra, but I was wrong.'

Behari said, 'If you loved him, would you have wreaked havoc like this?'

Binodini said, 'Thakurpo, these are sentiments straight out of your books. I am not yet ready to hear such sermons. Set aside your textbooks and peer into my heart just this once, free from your predisposed notions. Today I have come to tell you everything about me.'

Behari said, 'The books are there for a reason, Bouthan. I leave it to God to comprehend the heart by its own rules. I must stick to the rules set out in the books or I will be lost.'

Binodini went on, 'Thakurpo, I will be shameless enough to admit to you—if you had wanted to, you could've pulled me back. Mahendra may be in love with me, but he is blind, he doesn't know me at all. Once, I did feel that you understand me; once upon a time you felt respect for me. Tell me the truth, don't hold back today!'

Behari said, 'It's true, I felt respect for you.'

Binodini said, 'You weren't wrong, Thakurpo. But if you did understand me, respect me, why did you stop there? Why couldn't you love me? I have abandoned shame and come to you, and so I say this to you—why didn't you love me too? It's my bad luck—you too had to lose your heart to Asha. Oh no, Thakurpo, you can't be angry. Sit down. I shall not hold back today. I knew that you loved Asha even when you didn't know it yourself. But I fail to understand what all of you see in Asha. Good or bad—what is there in that girl? Hasn't God given an ounce of insight to the male gaze? How little, and what stuff does it take to mesmerize you men! Fools, blind men!'

Behari stood up and said, 'I shall listen to everything you have to say today; but I beg of you, don't say that which must not be said.'

Binodini gave a wry smile and said, 'Thakurpo, I know exactly where it's pinching you. But please be patient and spare a thought for me—just think of the extreme agony that has dragged me here tonight, shedding all shame and fear, to appeal to the person who once respected me and whose love would have turned my life around. I can tell you very honestly, if you weren't in love with Asha, I wouldn't have wreaked such havoc on her life tonight.'

Behari turned pale. 'What has happened to Asha? What have you done to her?'

Binodini said, 'Mahendra has committed to going away with me tomorrow, leaving his family and everything behind.'

Behari suddenly snarled, 'That's impossible, this cannot happen!'

Binodini said, 'Impossible? And who is going to stop Mahendra today?'

Behari said, 'You can.'

Binodini was silent for a few minutes. Then she fixed her gaze on Behari and said, 'Why shall I stop him? For your Asha's sake? And I suppose I have no dreams and desires of my own? I am not so pious that I'd wipe out all my wishes from this life, for the sake of your Asha's well-being, for the sake of Mahendra's family—I have not studied the holy books so faithfully. If I give something up, what do I get in return?'

Gradually, the lines on Behari's face hardened as he said, 'You have tried to speak honestly, now let me be frank for a change. What you have done today, and the words you speak now, are all derived from the literature you're so fond of reading. Three-fourths of it is the language of dramas and novels.'

Binodini said, 'Dramas! Novels!'

Behari repeated, 'Yes, dramas and novels. And not of a very high standard, mind you. You believe this is all original—it's not. They are mere echoes of the printing press in your story. Had you been a silly, stupid, bumbling child, you'd still have got some sympathy from this world. But the heroine of the play is only fit for the stage, not the home.'

Where was Binodini's cutting sharpness, her famous pride? In response to Behari's words she bowed down in silence like the spellbound snake. Many minutes later she spoke calmly, without looking at Behari, 'What do you want me to do?'

Behari said, 'Don't try to work wonders. Let an ordinary woman's good sense prevail. Go back to your village.'

Binodini said, 'How can I go?'

Behari said, 'I can board you into the ladies' compartment and escort you to your destination.'

Binodini said quietly, 'Let me stay the night here then?'

Behari replied, 'No! Even I do not have so much faith in myself.'

Binodini slipped off the chair, dropped to the ground, held Behari's feet to her breast and said, 'Thakurpo, don't wipe out that tiny bit of weakness that you have! Don't be purer than the driven snow. Love the vile and be a little vile yourself.' She kissed his feet again and again. For an instant Behari lost control at this unexpected reaction from Binodini. His senses slackened their hold on sanity. Binodini sensed his moment of weakness and she let go of his feet; she raised herself on both knees and wound her arms around Behari who was seated on a chair and said, 'My dearest life, I know you are not mine forever; but do love me even if it's for this moment. After that I shall vanish into the forest where you cast me, I won't ask anyone for anything again. Give me something that can last me till my death.' She closed her eyes and offered her lips to him. For one second the two of them were still and the room seemed to hold its breath. Then, Behari heaved a sigh and unwound her arms from around his neck. He moved away to another chair and spoke in a voice that was nearly inaudible, 'There is a passenger train at one in the night.'

Binodini was mute for a few minutes and then she murmured, 'I shall take that train.'

Vasant walked into the room barefoot, bare-bodied and fair as the day; he stood by Behari's chair and stared solemnly at Binodini.

Behari asked, 'Didn't you go to sleep?'

Vasant didn't answer him and continued to stand there, looking grave.

Binodini stretched out her arms. Vasant hesitated a little and then went up to her slowly. She held him close to her heart as the tears flowed freely from her eyes.

## 36

The impossible can become possible at times and the unbearable can indeed be borne, or that night and the following day wouldn't have passed in Mahendra's house. After instructing Binodini to be prepared, that same night Mahendra mailed a letter to his house. This letter reached the following day. Asha was in bed. The bearer came to her with the letter and said, 'Ma, letter for you.'

Asha's heart leaped in her breast. In the flash of a heartbeat a thousand hopes and worries resonated in her mind. She picked up the letter hastily and found it was in Mahendra's hand, addressed to Binodini. Her head lolled back on the pillow instantly and she handed the letter back to the bearer mutely. He asked, 'To whom should I give this letter?'

Asha said, 'I don't know.'

It was around eight in the evening when Mahendra arrived at Binodini's room, charging in like a maelstrom. He found the room in darkness. He fished out a matchbox from his pocket, struck a match and found that the room was empty. Binodini wasn't there and neither were her things. He went into the balcony to the south and called out, 'Binod!' The balcony was empty and there was no answer.

'Fool! I'm a fool. I should've taken her with me. I'm sure Mother spoke such harsh words to her that Binodini was impelled to walk out,' Mahendra thought.

The moment the thought entered his head he was convinced of its veracity. He strode into Rajlakshmi's room impatiently. That room lay in darkness too, but Rajlakshmi was lying in bed; he could see even in the dark. In an angry tone, Mahendra asked, 'Mother, what have you said to Binodini?'

Rajlakshmi said, 'Nothing.'

Mahendra persisted, 'So where has she gone?'

Rajlakshmi said, 'How would I know?'

Mahendra was sceptical, 'You don't know? Fine, I am going to look for her. I shall find her, wherever she may be.'

Mahendra walked away. Rajlakshmi left the bed and tried to follow him, crying, 'Mahin, don't go, please Mahin, come back. Listen to me.'

Mahendra left the house like a madman. But he came back a moment later and asked the watchman, 'Where has Bou-thakurun gone?'

The watchman said, 'She did not tell us—we do not know.'

Mahendra roared in anger, 'You don't know!'

The watchman folded his hands and bowed low, 'No sire, we don't know.'

Mahendra decided his mother must have tutored them to supply these answers. He said, 'Fair enough!'

On the streets of the metropolis dusk had fallen; the ice-candy man was hawking his ice-candy and the fish seller was yelling out the names of the kinds of fish he carried. Mahendra waded into the throng of noisy people and disappeared in their midst.

## 37

Behari had never sat down to meditate upon himself. He had never turned himself into a subject of analysis for his own mind. Books, chores and friends had kept him busy. He was happy to give the whole world around him more attention than he gave himself. But all of a sudden, one day, everything had crashed to pieces around him. Amidst the darkness and the destruction, he had found himself standing alone on the peak of the colossal mountain of anguish. Ever since, he had feared his own company; he had drowned himself in work and more work so that this unwanted companion of his, his own shadow self, wouldn't have access to him.

But on this particular day, Behari was powerless in keeping his inner self at bay. The previous night he had taken Binodini to her village. Since then, wherever he was and whatever he tried to keep himself busy with, he felt his agonized heart pointing him to his own immeasurable loneliness.

Behari felt defeated by fatigue and heartache. It was around nine at night; the south-facing terrace adjacent to Behari's room was aflutter with a summer breeze. Behari sat alone on the terrace, under a moonless sky. He hadn't been able to teach Vasant that evening; he'd sent him to bed early. His heart wept for the days of his old, familiar past like a motherless child; arms outstretched, it searched for something in the dark of the universe, yearned for consolation, for solace of some sort. His determination, his control over himself, had all washed away. He felt like running to the same people that he had once vowed never to think of again. There was no way of controlling his emotional turbulence.

Like a map marked in different colours for land, water, hills and rivers, the various images of his long friendship with Mahendra and its unfortunate conclusion unfolded before Behari's eyes. He mulled over the precise moment at which his world had come crashing down and all that he held dear to him had been lost forever. Who had been the first to break the charmed circle? The bashful face of Asha, coloured by the rays of the setting sun, etched itself in the twilight. The blowing of the conch shell, auguring good omens at dusk, rang in his ears at the same time. Asha, Behari thought, was something of a benevolent planet that had made its place between the two friends, casting her influence on both. She had brought with her a little conflict, and a strange kind of pain that could neither be spoken of nor nurtured in the heart. And yet, this conflict, this pain were covered in a pleasant light, full of love and affection.

But then had come the malevolent planet and that had ripped apart the friendship, the romance, the peace and purity of the family. Behari tried to push away Binodini's image with great revulsion. But wonders never cease! The push was no more than a gentle thrust, barely touching her. That incredibly beautiful mirage with her dark eyes brimming with inscrutable mystery, stood still before him in the dense dark of the night. The fulsome breeze of the summer night touched him like her breath. Gradually, her still, steady gaze wavered; the dry, intense eyes overflowed with tears as emotion overcame them; like a flash the mirage dropped at his feet and grasped his knees to her breast with all her might. And then she wove herself around him like a human creeper and raised a pair of lips as fragrant as a flower, up to his own. Behari closed his eyes and tried with all his might to banish the image from his mind. But he felt powerless to hurt her in any way—an incomplete, fervent kiss hung on his lips, and he was suffused with a strange exhilaration.

Behari could no longer stay in the solitary darkness of the terrace. He rushed into his lamp-lit room in order to distract himself. In one corner, on a teapoy, was a framed photograph covered with a silk scarf. Behari uncovered it and sat down to gaze at it under the bright light.

It had been taken soon after Mahendra and Asha's wedding, with the couple smiling happily. Behind the photograph Mahendra had written his name and Asha had added hers in her childish scrawl. The sweetness of new-found romance still hung over the photo. Mahendra sat on a chair looking very pleased with his newly married status. Asha stood beside him shyly. The photographer had insisted on her dropping her veil, but he couldn't rid her of her shyness. Today, this same Mahendra was about to leave Asha in tears and go far away. But the Mahendra of the photograph still looked as much in love with her as ever—his emotions were frozen in time, ignorant of the irony of fate that time would unfold.

Behari tried to cast Binodini far away by hurling abuse at her, with the photograph on his lap. But those loving, youthful arms of hers still held on to his knees, strong as ever. Behari said, 'You went and destroyed such a loving, happy relationship!' But Binodini's face, raised for his kiss, silently told him, 'I have loved you. From all the men in this whole wide world I have chosen you.'

But was that an answer! Could these words obscure the pained shriek that arose from a household torn asunder? What a witch!

Witch! Was this only a rebuke or was there some indulgence mixed in the word? When Behari was left standing like a beggar, robbed of all the love he had ever counted on in his life, was he in a position to reject, from the bottom of his heart, such an outpouring of love that came unwarranted and unasked for? In comparison, what had he ever got? He had sacrificed his entire life in search of some crumbs of love. But when the goddess of love had sent him a golden plate replete with her blessings, how could he have the strength to turn his back on the feast?

He sat there with the photograph on his lap, lost in his thoughts. Suddenly a sound beside him made him look up—Mahendra stood at his side. Startled, Behari stood up in a rush and the photo dropped to the floor—he didn't even notice.

Mahendra asked without any preamble, 'Where is Binodini?'

Behari stepped closer to Mahendra, took his hand and said, 'Mahin da, do have a seat. We can discuss everything by and by.'

Mahendra said, 'I don't have the time to sit and discuss things. Tell me, where is Binodini?'

Behari said, 'Your question cannot be answered quite so simply. You must calm down and have a seat.'

Mahendra said, 'Sermonizing, are we? Spare me the trouble. I have read the holy books when I was a child.'

Behari said quietly, 'I have neither the power nor the right to sermonize.'

Mahendra said, 'Perhaps it's reproach, then? I know I am a scoundrel, the worst kind, and whatever else you may choose to call me. But the point is, do you know where Binodini is?'

Behari replied, 'I do.'

Mahendra said, 'And you won't tell me?'

Behari said, 'No.'

Mahendra yelled, 'You have to. You have stolen her away and hidden her. She is mine; give her back to me.'

Behari stood in stunned silence for a while. Then he spoke with firm determination, 'She is not yours. I have not stolen her away; she came to me of her own free will.'

Mahendra barked, 'Liar!' He turned and banged on the closed door of the next room. 'Binod, Binod!' he yelled.

The sounds of weeping from inside the room made him say, 'Don't be afraid, Binod! It's me, Mahin. I shall rescue you—no one can keep you locked away.'

Mahendra pushed hard and the door gave way. He rushed inside and found the room in darkness. He noticed a shadowy figure on the bed sobbing in fear and pressing the pillow to its chest. Behari stepped in hurriedly, picked Vasant up in his arms and consoled him gently, 'Don't worry Vasant, it's all right, everything's all right.'

Mahendra rushed out and searched all the rooms in the house. When he was back, Vasant was still crying out in fear even as he slept. Behari had the lights on in his room and was trying to stroke him gently to sleep.

Mahendra came and asked, 'Where have you kept Binodini?'

Behari said, 'Mahin da, do be quiet. You have needlessly terrified this child so much that he may be sick. I assure you, you needn't concern yourself with Binodini's whereabouts.'

Mahendra said, 'Brilliant! A saint! Spare me your homilies, you impostor. Which god were you meditating on, with my wife's photograph on your lap at this time of the night?' Mahendra hurled the photo to the floor and stamped on it with his boots. The glass shattered into tiny shards. He picked up the photograph, tore it into tiny bits and hurled it at Behari. His crazed behaviour made Vasant wail with fear again. Behari could barely speak as he pointed to the door and said, 'Leave!'

Mahendra ran out like a mad man.

## 38

The green farmlands and tree-lined villages flashed by Binodini's window as she sat in a deserted train compartment. The sights brought back memories of the peaceful village life for her. She felt she'd be able to sit under the shade of those trees with her favourite books and have some respite from all the anger, sorrow and anguish of her sojourn in the city. As she took in the sun setting beyond the expanse of the barren fields of summer, she felt life was complete. She wished to drown in this green stillness and close its eyes, to take the boat away from the crashing waves of life, towards the shore, under the shelter of a banyan tree, and stay there, wishing for nothing else. The scent of green mango blossoms wafted in as the train hurtled on, and her heart came to terms with itself. She thought, 'This is for the best; I cannot tug and pull at myself any more. Now I'll forget, now I'll sleep. I shall be one with the village, live a quiet, rural life and spend my days peacefully and in joy.'

Binodini walked into her tiny home with a heart parched for peace and quiet. But alas for that rare commodity—emptiness and poverty were all she could find. Everything around her was worn, dirty and faded. She choked on the vapid air inside, the house not having been aired for many months. The little furniture that the room held was nearly ruined by dust, termites and rats. The house that evening was joyless and dark. Binodini managed to light an oil lamp and in that meagre light the dismal condition of the house was sadly exposed. All the things that hadn't bothered her before seemed to choke the very life out of her now and she muttered forcefully, 'This won't do for a single day.' A few old books and magazines were gathering dust on the shelf. But she didn't feel like touching them. Outside, in the still air the mosquitoes and insects struck up a dialogue that echoed through the night.

Binodini had an old aunt-in-law living with her earlier. She had gone to a distant village to visit her daughter, having locked up the house. Binodini went to visit her neighbours. They seemed to jump out of their skins when they saw her. My, my! Binodini's complexion had really cleared up, her clothes were well turned out, almost like a lady's. They nudged each other and gestured towards Binodini as they muttered among themselves: as though the rumours they'd heard were now confirmed.

At every step Binodini felt anew how distant she had become from her own village. She was exiled in her own home: there was not a moment's peace for her anywhere.

The old postman knew her since she was a child. The next morning when Binodini was about to go to the pond for a bath, she saw him walking up the street with his bag of letters and she couldn't control herself. She dropped her towel, rushed up to him and asked, 'Panchu-dada, any letters for me?'

The old man said, 'No.'

An anxious Binodini persisted, 'There may be one; will you please check?'

She took the five or six letters he had for that area and leafed through them carefully; not one was for her. When she returned to the pond looking glum, a friend spoke with mock curiosity, 'Bindi, why the rush for this letter?'

Another chatterbox butted in, 'Oh, this is good; how many of us are lucky enough to get letters by mail? We have husbands, brothers and brothers-in-law working in far-off places, but the mailman never has pity on us.'

Thus the conversation took off, the words got more blunt and the jibes sharper. Binodini had pleaded with Behari that he should write to her at least twice a week, if not daily, even if it was just a few lines. She couldn't really expect to have a letter from him so soon. But her craving was so strong that she couldn't let go of the hope, the distant possibility. She felt she'd left Kolkata many months ago.

Thanks to friends and foes, Binodini was left in no doubt as to how her name was being bandied about in every household in the village, linked to Mahendra's of course. Where was the peace!

She tried to distance herself from the people in the village. But the villagers took offence at that. They didn't want to be deprived of the pleasure of mocking and loathing the sinful woman.

In vain did Binodini attempt to hide herself from the public eye in that tiny rural community. There was no space here to nurse her wounded heart in a dark, lonely niche; curious glances poked and pried at her all the time and worsened the wound. The more she thrashed about like a fish in captivity, the more she lacerated herself by smashing against the narrow confines of her prison. There was no space to even indulge in one's own misery here.

On the second day, after the postman had gone his way again, Binodini shut the door to her room and sat down to write:

Thakurpo, don't worry—this is not a love letter. You are my judge and I bow before you. For my sins you have awarded me a harsh sentence. I have accepted it with full humility; my only regret is that you cannot see just how harsh the punishment is on me. I have been deprived of the pity you'd have surely felt, if only you could see my condition, or know of it. With your memories and with my head bowed at your feet, I shall take this in my stride. But my lord, even the prisoner deserves two square meals a day. Not fancy meals—but the bare minimum that is needed to survive. A few lines written by you would be a feast for me in this exile. Deprived of them, this isn't merely an exile; it's a life-sentence. Please do not test me so cruelly, my lord. My sinful heart was full of arrogance—I never thought I would have to bow before anyone so humbly. You have won, my lord. I shall not rebel. But please have mercy on me—grant me life. Give me the meagre bit necessary to survive this exile. It will give me the strength to stay on the path charted by you. This is my only request to you. The other things that my heart is prompting me to tell you, I have vowed never to speak of again. I shall keep my vow.

Your Binod-bouthan

Binodini mailed the letter. Her neighbours continued their slander: 'She shuts the door of her house, writes letters, attacks the postman for letters she expects—this is how one is ruined if one spends a few days in Kolkata!'

The next day went without a letter as well. Binodini was silent all day long and the lines on her face grew harsh. The torment and agony from within and without turned her defences—from the depths of the darkness in her heart—into a violent force that threatened to erupt. Binodini perceived the advent of that merciless brutality with fear and shut the doors to her house.

She had nothing of Behari—not a photograph, not a few lines on paper, nothing! She began to hunt for something in that barrenness. She wanted to hold something of his to her heart and bring tears to her arid eyes. She wanted to melt away the viciousness with her tears and place Behari's sentence on the throne of love, on the gentlest spot in her heart. But her heart continued to smoulder like the parched sky at noon; there was no sign of a single droplet in the distant horizon.

Binodini had once heard that if you contemplate on someone with all your heart and soul, he had to come. So she folded her hands, closed her eyes and called on Behari, 'My life is empty, my heart is empty, there is emptiness all around me—come unto this emptiness, even if for an instant, you have to come, I won't let go of you.'

She said these words over and over and began to feel heartened. She felt that the power of this love, this pleading, could not go in vain. But such tender bleeding of the heart at the roots of despair, such fierce concentration, made it weak and feeble. Still she felt stronger inside after this relentless meditation. She felt that her powerful yearning, neglecting all other worldly thoughts, by sheer will power alone could draw the desired one closer like a magnet.

When her lampless, dark room was suffused with thoughts of Behari, when the whole world, her village, her life and the entire universe lay in shambles before her, Binodini suddenly heard a hammering on her door. She stood up hastily, rushed to the door with heartfelt faith and trust, and opened it exclaiming, 'You have come!' She was convinced that no one other than Behari could stand on the other side of her door at that precise moment.

Mahendra replied, 'Yes, I've come, Binod.'

Binodini shouted with revulsion and distaste, 'Go. Go away from here. Leave right now.'

Mahendra stood there in stunned disbelief.

An elderly neighbour walked up to her door saying, 'Bindi dear, if your aunt-in-law comes back tomorrow—' As her glance fell on Mahendra, she stopped short, drew her anchal over her head and beat a hasty retreat.

## 39

There was an uproar in the village. The elders sat around the temple courtyard and said, 'This cannot be tolerated. It's possible to ignore whatever happened in Kolkata. But she has the audacity to ply him with letters, bring him into her house here and be so brazen about it all! We cannot allow such a fallen woman to stay in the village.'

Today Binodini was sure Behari would write to her. But no letters came. Binodini thought, 'What right does Behari have over me? Why should I obey him? Why did I give him the impression that I shall take his orders humbly and follow his instructions? All he cares about is saving his beloved Asha—he doesn't really care about me. I have no rights, no demands over him—not even two lines in a note—am I so insignificant, such an object of hatred?' The fumes of humiliation and hostility threatened to choke her; she said to herself, 'I would have taken this pain for anybody else but not for Asha. Why do I have to tolerate this poverty, exile, denigration and this continuous denial of all my desires, merely for Asha's sake? Why did I have to accept such a farce? I should have stayed and fulfilled my promise of vengeance. Fool, I am a fool! Why did I have to love Behari?'

As Binodini sat in the room, still as a petrified statuette, her aunt-in-law returned from her trip, walked into the house and said, 'You wretch, what is all this I have heard!'

Binodini said, 'All that you have heard is true.'

Her aunt-in-law said, 'Why did you have to bring your shame into the house, why did you come back?'

Binodini was silent from suppressed misery. The old lady said, 'Child, let me tell you clearly, you cannot stay here. I am still living, even after fate has snatched away all my dear ones from me. I cannot tolerate this. Shame on you—you've disgraced us. Leave the house immediately.'

Binodini said, 'I shall go right now.'

At this moment Mahendra arrived again, unshaved, dishevelled. He looked wan and his eyes were bloodshot from lack of sleep. Earlier, he'd intended to try one last time at dawn, and make Binodini go with him; but Binodini's rudeness and vitriolic response the previous day had given rise to a host of doubts in his mind. Then, as the sun rose and the morning wore on, Mahendra saw that it was time for the train's arrival. He pushed aside all doubts and arguments in his mind, left the station, got into a carriage and arrived straight at Binodini's doorstep. When a person casts away all shame and embarks blatantly on a daring venture, he is imbued with a certain audacious strength; that power lent an abandoned thrill to Mahendra, sweeping away his earlier doubts and dithering. In his feral gaze the curious village folk looked like inanimate dolls in the dust. Mahendra didn't spare a second glance to any of them, walked right up to Binodini and said, 'Binod, I am not such a coward that I'll desert you in the face of public outrage. By hook or by crook, I must take you from here. After that, if you wish to cast me off, do so. I shall not stop you. I can swear by you on this day that nothing will happen without your wish or consent—if you wish to be with me, I shall be grateful. If you don't, I'll go far away from your life. I know I haven't been a model of trust, but please do not distrust me today. We are standing on the brink of devastation and this isn't the time for games.'

Binodini spoke naturally and without emotion, 'Take me with you. Do you have a carriage?'

Mahendra said, 'I do.'

Binodini's aunt-in-law came out of her room and said, 'Mahendra, you may not know me, but we are related. Your mother, Rajlakshmi, is from my village and in that sense I am your aunt. Let me ask you: what kind of behaviour is this? You have a wife at home, a mother, and you walk the streets in this half-crazed, brazen fashion! How can you show your face in civil society?'

Mahendra's world of impassioned madness got a severe jolt at these words. He had a mother, a wife and there was such a thing as civil society! This simple fact came home to him anew. There was a time when he would have trouble imagining that one day he'd have to hear these words from a stranger in an unknown, faraway village. It was a strange chapter in his life, indeed, that in broad daylight Mahendra was taking a virtuous widow by the hand and leading her away from her home. And yet, he had a wife, a mother and there was such a thing as civil society!

As Mahendra stood there dumbstruck, the old woman said, 'If you must leave, go right away. Don't dally at my doorstep—go away, right now!'

She walked into her room, slammed the door shut and bolted it from within. Binodini clambered onto the carriage, dishevelled, squalid, empty-handed and hungry. As Mahendra was about to board the carriage she stopped him, 'No, the station isn't far; you can walk.'

Mahendra said, 'But then everyone in the village will stare at me.'

Binodini said, 'Do you have a drop of honour left here to protect?' She shut the door of the carriage and instructed the coachman, 'To the station.'

The man asked, 'Isn't the gentleman coming?'

Mahendra hesitated a little and then decided to step back. The carriage drove off. Mahendra left the village road and took a roundabout route through the field as he headed for the station, head lowered and eyes to the ground. The village women had finished their bath and lunch; only a few hardworking old housewives, who got off work late, were walking through the mango-groves headed for the cool waters of the pond with their bowls of oil and towels.

## 40

Rajlakshmi was losing sleep and hunger, worrying about Mahendra. Sadhucharan had hunted high and low for him but without any luck. Then, one day, Mahendra returned to Kolkata with Binodini. He dropped her off at his flat in Patoldanga and came home late at night.

Mahendra stepped into his mother's room and found it in darkness; the kerosene lamp was shaded so as to shield the glare of the flame. Rajlakshmi lay on the bed, looking ill; Asha sat at her feet, stroking them gently. At long last, the bride of the house had her place at the mother-in-law's feet. At Mahendra's advent, Asha looked up in surprise and left the room hurriedly. Mahendra cast away his diffidence forcefully and said, 'Mother, I cannot attend to my studies from here; I have rented a flat near college; I'll stay there.'

Rajlakshmi pointed to a corner of the bed and said, 'Mahin, sit down.'

Mahendra sat down awkwardly. Rajlakshmi said, 'Mahin, you are free to stay where you wish, but please, I beg of you, don't make my daughter-in-law suffer.'

Mahendra was silent. Rajlakshmi continued, 'I am so unlucky that I didn't know the worth of my darling daughter all these days.' Her voice broke as she spoke. 'But you have known her for so long, loved her so much; how could you cast her into such misery?' She began to weep openly.

Mahendra desperately wished to get up and leave, but something stopped him from doing so. He sat still in the dark, on one corner of his mother's bed.

Much later, Rajlakshmi said, 'Are you staying here tonight at least?'

Mahendra said, 'No.'

She asked, 'When will you leave?'

Mahendra said, 'Right now.'

Rajlakshmi sat up with great difficulty and said, 'Right now? Don't you wish to meet your wife just once and speak to her properly?'

Mahendra was silent. Rajlakshmi said, 'Can't you even guess how she has spent the last few days? Oh you shameless wretch, it breaks my heart to see just how cruel you can be.' Rajlakshmi fell back on the bed like a felled branch.

Mahendra rose and walked out. He tiptoed stealthily up the stairs towards his bedroom. He had no wish to run into Asha. But there she was, lying down on the covered terrace adjacent to his room. She hadn't heard his footsteps. When he stood in front of her, she sat up in confusion and began to arrange her clothes hurriedly. At that moment if he had called out just once, 'Chuni,' she would have taken his transgression upon her own head, fallen at his feet in remorse and guilt, and wept all the tears she could ever weep. But Mahendra couldn't bring himself to utter that beloved name. However hard he tried and wished with all his might that he could be intimate with her again, though he felt sorrier than ever, he couldn't forget that caressing Asha today would be nothing but an empty gesture on his part. What would be the use of consoling her, when he had closed out all options of renouncing Binodini?

Meanwhile, Asha was flooded with shame as she sat there. She was too embarrassed to stand up, walk away or try to move in any way at all. Mahendra began to pace the floor slowly without uttering a single word. The sky was moonless tonight. In a corner of the terrace a tuberose plant yielded two stems of flowers in an earthen pot. In the dark sky overhead, the same stars that had once been witness to many scenes of impassioned love being enacted between these two, now twinkled mutely.

Mahendra wished he could wipe out the devastating events of the last few days in the dark of the night, and take his accustomed place beside Asha on the mat, on that terrace. No questions, no explanations, just the same trust, the same love and that pure, simple joy. But alas, there was no way of going back to that space ever again. On this terrace, that little space beside Asha upon the mat was lost to Mahendra forever. Until now, his relationship with Binodini had no ties. There was the unfettered pleasure of loving but none of its ancillary bindings. But now that he had ripped her apart from society with his own hands—now that there was no place to keep her, or to send her back to, Mahendra was her sole recourse. Now, whether he liked it or not, he was bound to shoulder all responsibility for her. This thought weighed heavy on him. All of a sudden, he found great solace in this room on the terrace, in the memory of the peace, the sweet romancing of lovers at night that came with it. But this solace, to which he had full rights once, was out of his reach today. Not even for a day would he be allowed to put aside the burden he had promised to shoulder all his life and catch a moment's peace for himself.

Mahendra heaved a sigh and glanced at Asha. She sat in still silence, holding back her mute tears. The dark of the night shielded her mortification and pain, like a protective mother.

Mahendra paused in his pacing and walked up to her, as if to say something. Asha's blood roared in her veins and she closed her eyes. Mahendra lost track of what he had wanted to say and couldn't figure out what he should do. But he couldn't step back without saying something at least. So he asked, 'Where are the keys?'

They were under the mattress. Asha got up and went into the room—Mahendra followed her. Asha took the bunch of keys from under the mattress and placed them on the bed. Mahendra picked them up and began to insert them one by one, to unlock his clothes-cupboard. Asha couldn't check herself; she spoke softly, 'Those keys are not with me.'

She couldn't bring herself to say who had those keys, but Mahendra understood. Asha left the room in a hurry, fearing she'd be unable to hold back her tears any longer. In the dark, she stood in one corner of the terrace and sobbed her heart out, trying very hard to keep the noise down.

But she didn't have much time in hand. Suddenly she remembered it was time for Mahendra's dinner. Quickly, she ran downstairs.

Rajlakshmi asked her, 'Bou-ma, where is Mahin?'

Asha said, 'He is upstairs.'

Rajlakshmi said, 'Then why have you come down?'

Asha lowered her eyes. 'His dinner—'

Rajlakshmi said, 'I will take care of that. Why don't you freshen up, Bou-ma. Wear your new sari from Dhaka and come to my room—I shall do your hair.'

Asha couldn't refute Rajlakshmi's affection, but all this talk of dressing up made her wish she could sink through the floor. She bore Rajlakshmi's ministration patiently, in tortured silence.

Decked up to the full, Asha went upstairs slowly. She peeped in and saw that Mahendra was not on the terrace. Quietly, she walked up to the room and found it empty. His dinner lay untouched.

Having given up on the keys, Mahendra had wrenched open his cupboard, taken some essential clothing and medical textbooks, and left.

The following day was ekadasi, the three-quarter moon fast; Rajlakshmi lay on her bed, weak and fatigued. Outside, the wind blew fiercely, brewing up for a storm. Asha stepped into the room gently. She sat at Rajlakshmi's feet, stroked them softly and said, 'I have brought you milk and fruits; come and eat.'

Rajlakshmi's parched eyes flooded with tears at this diffident attempt at nursing by her sad-eyed bride. She sat up, drew Asha to her heart, kissed her tear-soaked temple and asked, 'Bou-ma, what is Mahin doing?'

Asha felt embarrassed as she said softly, 'He has gone.'

Rajlakshmi said, 'When did he leave—I wasn't even told?'

Asha bowed her head as she replied, 'He went away last night.'

Immediately, all trace of gentleness vanished from Rajlakshmi's face and her touch lost its tenderness. Asha sensed a silent rebuke, and walked away slowly with her head bowed.

## 41

When Mahendra had gone home on that first night, Binodini sat alone in the Patoldanga flat in the midst of the ceaseless commotion of Kolkata, thinking about herself. She had never been blessed with a lot of spaces to turn to; but there had always been enough room to turn over and lie on the other side, if the bed felt too uncomfortable. But today the space left to her was very restricted indeed. Her boat would pitch her straight into the water if it so much as tilted a little to one side. Hence, she had to steer it very carefully now—there was no room for a single error or even a little bit of dithering. It was a daunting prospect for any woman. Where was the space, in these narrow confines, for those little hide-and-seek games so necessary to keep a male mind in thrall? She'd have to spend all her life face-to-face with Mahendra, without any veils. The difference was that if the boat did overturn he had the means to scramble to the shore, but she had none.

As Binodini's vulnerable position became very clear to her, she began to gather strength within herself. She had to find a way out—this wouldn't work for her.

The day she had admitted her love for Behari, she had reached the end of her tether. The lips that she had raised for his kiss, and had been forced to draw back, were suspended in an incompleteness of desire—unable to find their place in this world and carried from place to place like the flowers preordained for a certain deity but never used in worship. Binodini's heart was unfamiliar with the concept of despondency—under no circumstances did she usually let go of hope. Her heart still claimed, every minute of every day, with great vehemence, 'Behari will have to accept my appeal one day.'

To this unrestrained ardour was added her strong desire for self-defence. Behari was her only way out. Binodini knew Mahendra very well indeed—if she leaned on him, he'd not be able to take the pressure. He could be attained only if he was allowed to go—if he were clung to, he would wish to run. Behari alone was capable of giving her the tranquil, reliable, safe haven that a woman needed. Today, she couldn't let go of Behari at any cost.

The day she left the village, Binodini had made Mahendra go to the post office adjacent to the station and leave firm instructions for all letters in her name to be forwarded to her new address in Kolkata. She couldn't bring herself to accept that Behari wouldn't answer even a single one of her letters. She said to herself, 'I shall be patient and wait for seven days—after that I'll decide what to do.' She then opened the window and sat there in the dark, staring out unmindfully at the streets of Kolkata lit by gaslamps. On this dark night, Behari was somewhere in this very same city—a few roads and lanes lay between her and his house, with the same tiny courtyard that had a tap in it, those stairs, that same well-arranged, brightly lit, secluded room—Behari sitting alone on his armchair, amidst tranquil peace; perhaps Vasant, the fair, healthy and handsome boy with large eyes, sat beside him turning the pages of his book. As she conjured up this image bit by bit, Binodini's heart was flooded with love and affection. If she wanted to, she could go there immediately. Binodini's heart picked up this thread of thought and played with it; in the past she would have rushed to fulfil her desires. But now she had to think before taking such steps. Now it was no longer about fulfilling a desire but about accomplishing a mission. Binodini said, 'Let me first see how Behari responds and then I can decide on my course of action.' She did not dare to go and disturb Behari without first understanding his reactions.

As she sat lost in her thoughts, the clock struck ten and Mahendra returned. The last few sleepless nights and fitful days had taken their toll on him; now, when he was finally successful in bringing Binodini to his home, he seemed overwhelmed by fatigue and exhaustion. He had no strength left to fight with himself or with his state in life. Today, he was bent low with the unwieldy burden of his future life.

Mahendra was too embarrassed to stand before the closed door and bang on it. Where now was that ardour that had helped him to overlook the entire world? Even the eyes of a complete stranger on the road were enough to make him cringe in shame.

The new servant was fast asleep inside. It took a while to get the door opened. As he stepped inside an unfamiliar, new home in the dark, Mahendra's heart plummeted. The apple of his mother's eye, Mahendra was used to certain comforts, hand-pulled fans and decorative furniture, and the lack of it all struck him anew this particular evening. Mahendra would have to fill in the requirements himself, he had the sole responsibility of this household. He had never given much thought to someone else's comforts. But from this day, the burden of a new, unfinished household with all its minute details, rested on his shoulders alone. A kerosene lamp on the staircase emitted smoke continually—it needed to be replaced by a proper lamp. The area between the corridor and the stairway was damp and soggy from its proximity to the tap. He must call the mason and get it fixed. He would have to fight with the landlord about the two shops in the front of the house that were occupied by shoe sellers who were yet to vacate the property. In a flash he realized that each of these things could only be done by him, and it merely served to increase the weight of his burdensome fatigue.

Mahendra stood below the stairs for some time, trying to compose himself. He tried to stoke the embers of the love he felt for Binodini. He tried to tell himself that eventually he had got the person he had wanted above all else in the world; today nothing stood between the two of them—it was a day of great joy for Mahendra. But perhaps the fact that nothing stood between them was the greatest barrier—today Mahendra was his own hurdle.

Binodini, spotting Mahendra at the door, left her meditative pose, got up and lit a lamp. She picked up her sewing, lowered her eyes and immersed herself in the needlework. This sewing was her shield, she felt safe behind it.

Mahendra stepped into the room and said, 'Binod, you must be terribly uncomfortable here.'

Binodini carried on with her sewing as she said, 'Not at all.'

Mahendra said, 'I'll arrange for all the furniture to be delivered within the next couple of days; but until then you must bear with the discomfort.'

Binodini said, 'Oh no, you cannot do that—you will not bring in another piece of furniture into this house. The ones that are there are already excessive.'

Mahendra said, 'And am I included in that list?'

Binodini said, 'It's good to have some humility—don't think of yourself as "excessive".'

As he gazed at Binodini, lost in her work with her head bent low, in that furtive lamplight Mahendra felt the thrill of the romance course through his veins once again.

If he had been at home, he would have thrown himself at her feet—but this was not home and so he couldn't do that. Binodini was vulnerable, very much within his reach and if he did not restrain himself now, it would be the worst kind of baseness.

Binodini said, 'Why have you brought your books and clothes here?'

Mahendra said, 'I happen to consider them essentials—they don't exactly belong to the category of "excessive".'

Binodini said, 'I know, but why here?'

Mahendra said, 'You're right—essential things are a misfit here. Binod, if you throw the books out on the street, I shan't say a word. But please don't throw me out as well.' He used this pretext to move a little closer to Binodini and place the bundle of books at her feet.

Binodini didn't look up from her sewing as she replied gravely, 'Thakurpo, you cannot stay in this house.'

Mahendra grew impatient as his renewed enthusiasm was thwarted; he spoke ardently, 'Why Binod, why do you wish to push me away? I have left everything for you and is this what I get?'

Binodini said, 'I will not allow you to leave everything for my sake.'

Mahendra exclaimed, 'Now it is no longer in your hands—my life, my family have gone away from me—only you remain, Binod! Binod—Binod—' Mahendra lay flat on the ground, gripped her feet and covered them with innumerable kisses.

Binodini snatched her feet away and stood up as she said, 'Mahendra, don't you remember your promise?'

Mahendra exerted immense will power and checked himself. 'I remember. I promised I shall only do as you wish and never cross your wishes. I shall keep my word. Tell me, what should I do?'

Binodini said, 'You must go and stay in your own home.'

Mahendra said, 'Am I the only surplus object here, Binod? If that is so, why did you drag me here? What is the point of hunting that prey which you do not like to devour? Tell me honestly—have I surrendered to you of my own free will or have you hunted me down at your will? Why should I endure you playing such games with me? Yet, I shall keep my word—I will go back and stay in that house where I have crushed my own place underfoot so callously.'

Binodini sat on the floor and carried on with her sewing without saying a word.

Mahendra fixed her face in an unwavering glance for a while and said, 'Heartless, Binod, you are heartless. I am unfortunate indeed to have loved you so.'

Binodini made a wrong stitch, held it up to the lamp and began to undo it with great care. At that moment, Mahendra wanted to grab her pitiless heart in his callused fist and crush it to death. He wanted to confront this silent cruelty and unyielding disregard with sheer brute force and bring it to heel.

He walked out of the room and came back immediately to say, 'If I go away, who will look after you, all alone here?'

Binodini said, 'Don't worry about that. Aunty has sacked Khemi, the maid, and she has joined me here today. The two of us will lock the door and be quite safe inside.'

With his anger, Mahendra's attraction for Binodini intensified. He longed to crush her body to his bosom with all his might and wreak havoc on it. In order to escape this terrible urge, Mahendra rushed out of the house.

As he walked the streets, Mahendra vowed to retaliate with equal disregard against Binodini's indifference. Even at her most vulnerable, when Mahendra was her sole recourse, she chose to show him such patent indifference so coolly and fearlessly—such humiliation was perhaps seldom meted out to a man. Mahendra's pride lay shattered and yet it refused to die; it only continued to feel tormented and battered. Mahendra said, 'Am I so pathetic? How dare she treat me thus! Who does she have to call her own, except me?'

Suddenly he remembered—Behari. In the flash of a second his passion turned to ashes. So Binodini had placed all her faith in Behari! He was just a pretext, he was the stepping-stone on which she placed her feet, only to crush it underfoot every single moment. That was what gave her the strength to insult him! Mahendra became convinced that Binodini was in touch with Behari through letters and had received his reassurance.

So, he set off for Behari's house. When he finally banged on Behari's door, the night was all but over. After much banging and shouting the bearer opened the door and announced that his master was not at home.

Mahendra was shell-shocked. He thought, 'All the time that I was walking the streets like a madman, Behari was with Binodini. This is the reason why Binodini humiliated me so heartlessly and I, fool that I am, stormed out in a huff and left her alone, just as she wished.'

Mahendra asked of the old, familiar bearer, 'Bhoju, when did your master leave the house?'

Bhoju replied, 'Oh, about four or five days ago; he has gone somewhere to the west.'

Relief flooded through Mahendra and he thought, 'Now I must lie down and rest a bit—I am too tired to walk any more.' He walked up the stairs, went into Behari's room, lay upon the couch and promptly fell into a deep sleep.

The same night that Mahendra had come and kicked up a ruckus in Behari's house asking after Binodini, Behari had decided to leave for the west without having a particular destination in mind. He felt that if he stayed on, his conflicts with his old friend would take such an ugly turn that he would regret it all his life.

The next day when Mahendra woke up, it was nearly eleven. His glance fell upon the teapoy before him and he saw that a note to Behari, addressed in Binodini's hand, lay on it, a marble paperweight holding it in place. He picked the note up hastily and saw that it was unopened. It was awaiting Behari's return. Mahendra opened it with trembling hands and read the letter. This was the same letter that Binodini had written to Behari from her village, to which she hadn't received a reply.

Every alphabet in the letter bared its teeth at Mahendra. Ever since their childhood, Behari had always stood in Mahendra's shadow. In terms of love and affection, he only received the stale leftovers from the godly Mahendra's plate. Today, Mahendra himself was the seeker and Behari was indifferent; and yet, Binodini had pushed Mahendra aside and chosen this undeserving oaf of a Behari over him! Mahendra had also got a few letters from Binodini. But compared to this letter to Behari, those were mere artifice, a vain and vacuous attempt to pacify the gormless.

Mahendra recalled Binodini's eagerness to send him to the post office to update her present address there, and he now knew why. Binodini was waiting for a reply from Behari, with her heart and soul fixed upon it.

In keeping with the past, Bhoju brought him tea and breakfast from the shop around the corner despite his master being absent. Mahendra forgot all about his bath. His eyes drifted over Binodini's inciting letter with compulsive haste, just as the traveller covers the flaming hot desert sands in hurried steps. Mahendra made promises to never set eyes upon Binodini again. But he realized that if a few more days passed without a response, Binodini would arrive at Behari's house and she would be relieved to know the truth of the matter. That prospect was anathema to him.

So Mahendra pocketed the letter and just before dusk he arrived at the flat in Patoldanga.

Binodini took pity on Mahendra's deplorable condition. She realized that he must have spent the night walking the streets, without a wink of sleep. She asked, 'Didn't you go home last night?'

Mahendra said, 'No.'

Binodini got worked up. 'Haven't you eaten all day?' The nurturing heart in Binodini prompted her to go and arrange a meal for him.

Mahendra said, 'Forget it—I have already eaten.'

Binodini pressed him, 'Where have you eaten?'

Mahendra said, 'At Behari's.'

In an instant Binodini's face turned pallid. After a moment's pause she controlled her emotions and asked, 'Is everything all right with Behari-thakurpo?'

Mahendra said, 'Quite so. He has gone west.' The way he said it implied that Behari had left that very day.

Binodini's face fell once again. But she composed herself valiantly and said, 'I have never seen such a restless soul before. Has he heard all about us? Is Thakurpo very angry?'

Mahendra said, 'Why else would someone go away to the west in this desperate heat?'

Binodini asked, 'Did he say anything about me?'

Mahendra said, 'What is there to say? Here's the letter.'

Mahendra handed the letter to Binodini and began to scan her face with eagle eyes for every reaction.

Binodini took the letter hastily and found that the envelope was open and the writing on the envelope was hers, addressed to Behari. She took it out of the envelope and found that it was her letter. She turned it this way and that and failed to find even a line of reply from Behari.

After a few moments' silence Binodini asked Mahendra, 'Have you read the letter?'

The look on her face frightened Mahendra and the lie slipped out easily, 'No.'

Binodini tore the letter into tiny bits and threw it out of the window.

Mahendra said, 'I am going home.'

Binodini did not answer him.

Mahendra said, 'I shall do exactly as you wish. I will stay at home for seven days. On my way to college every day I'll look into the matters here and leave the rest in Khemi's hands. I shall not disturb you by seeking an audience.'

It was hard to tell if Binodini heard a single word Mahendra spoke; there was no answer. She stared out of the open window, into the dark sky.

Mahendra collected his things and left the house.

Binodini sat in the deserted house, alone and immovable—until finally, perhaps to revive her senses forcibly, she tore off her sari and began to whip herself with it ruthlessly. Khemi heard the sounds and came running, 'Bou-thakurun, what are you doing?'

Binodini snarled, 'You get out of here,' and shooed Khemi out of the room. Then she slammed the door noisily, bunched up her fists, threw herself on the ground and howled like a wounded animal. Eventually, she wore herself out and lay in a faint under the open window all night long.

When the sun rose the next morning, she was gripped by suspicion: suppose Behari hadn't left the city and Mahendra had said that to her merely to delude her? Binodini summoned Khemi immediately and said, 'Khemi, go to Behari-thakurpo's house immediately and find out how they are doing.'

Khemi returned an hour later and said, 'All the doors and windows of Beharibabu's house are firmly shut. When I banged on the door the bearer said from within that the master wasn't at home—he had gone west.'

Now Binodini's doubts were laid to rest.

## 42

When Rajlakshmi heard that mahendra had left home that same night, she was displeased with her daughter-in-law. Rajlakshmi thought Asha's condemnation must have driven her son away. So she asked Asha, 'Why did Mahendra go away last night?'

Asha looked at the floor as she said, 'I don't know, Mother.'

Rajlakshmi thought this was merely Asha's wounded ego speaking. Disgruntled, she said, 'If you don't know, who would? Did you say anything to him?'

Asha merely said, 'No.'

Rajlakshmi didn't believe her. This was impossible. She asked, 'What time did Mahin leave last night?'

Asha cringed in discomfiture and said, 'I don't know.'

Rajlakshmi was furious. 'You don't know anything! My little china doll! Very smart, aren't you?'

Rajlakshmi blamed Asha's behaviour and inadequate personality for Mahendra's actions and spoke her mind vehemently. Asha accepted the insult with her head bowed, went away to her room and began to cry. She thought, 'I scarcely know why my husband loved me once upon a time and now that he doesn't, I don't know how to win his love back.' When you were loved, your heart told you how to please him. But how would she know how to win the heart of someone who didn't love her? How on earth was she supposed to make a brazen attempt at winning back the affections of someone who loved another woman instead?

At dusk the family priest and his sister, Acharya-thakurun, came to the house. Rajlakshmi had sent for them in order to conduct some prayers to a favourable constellation for her son. Rajlakshmi requested the priest to read her daughter-in-law's palm, but that was just a pretext for her to present the unfortunate Asha to the priest. The poor girl cringed in shame when her disgrace was being discussed in public. She sat down, palm extended and eyes lowered. Suddenly, Rajlakshmi heard the soft tread of shoes outside the room, along the dark veranda. Someone was trying to sneak past the door. Rajlakshmi called out, 'Who is it?'

At first there was no response. When she called out again, 'Who goes there?' Mahendra stepped in silently.

Far from being thrilled, Asha's heart brimmed over with sadness for Mahendra. He now had to walk into his own house in stealth. Asha was all the more embarrassed because the priest and his sister were seated there. For her, the censorious gaze of the whole world actually seemed greater than her own personal sorrow. Rajlakshmi murmured to Asha, 'Bou-ma, tell Parvati to bring Mahin's dinner upstairs.' Asha replied, 'I'll get it, Mother.' She wanted to shield Mahendra even from the gaze of the servants.

Meanwhile, Mahendra was quite upset when he found the family priest and his sister in the room. He couldn't bear the thought that his mother and his wife were conniving with these illiterate oafs in order to control him by occult methods. To add to it, when Acharya-thakurun asked him in a honeyed voice, 'How are you, my son,' Mahendra was hard put to sit there any longer. He didn't respond to the question and spoke to Rajlakshmi, 'Mother, I'm going upstairs.'

Rajlakshmi thought he wanted to go up and have a few words in private with his wife. Delighted at the prospect, she rushed to the kitchen and said to Asha, 'Go on, go upstairs quickly—I believe Mahin wants something.'

Asha went upstairs with a beating heart and faltering steps. From what Rajlakshmi had said, Asha had thought that Mahendra had sent for her. But she simply couldn't walk into the room uninvited. Instead she stood at the threshold, in the dark, and gazed at Mahendra.

He was lying on the mattress upon the floor, staring desolately at the beams on the ceiling. This was the same Mahendra she had known, everything about him was the same, yet what a change there was! There was a time when Mahendra had turned this tiny room into heaven for Asha. Why then was he insulting the same room, drenched as it was in happy memories? If you are so sad, so restless, and so piqued, please do not sit upon that bed, Mahendra! If you do not remember those fulfilling, profound nights, the intense afternoons, the fancy-free monsoon days, the overpowering spring evenings swept by a mild breeze, the endless, unlimited, countless conversations that you have had in this room, there are many other rooms to choose from in this house—but do not tarry here a moment longer.

The longer Asha stood there staring at Mahendra, the more she felt that he had just come from Binodini's arms—her touch clung to his body, his eyes held her image, her voice rang in his ears and his heart was filled with desire for her. How could Asha gift her chaste devotion to this Mahendra, how could she say, 'Come unto my steadfast heart, come and place your feet upon the spotless lilies of my chaste wifely devotion'? She couldn't bring herself to follow her aunt's advice, the words of the holy texts and religious sermons. She no longer perceived this Mahendra—dispossessed of conjugal loyalties—as her god. Today, Asha immersed her deity and let go of her devotion in Binodini's oceans muddied by sin; in the dark of that loveless night, the drums of farewell echoed in solemn and sombre tones in her ears, in her heart and mind, in her veins, all around her, in the stars of her sky, in her very own terrace, in her own room, on her own bed.

Binodini's Mahendra was like a strange man for Asha, or something even worse—even with a stranger she wouldn't feel such terrible shame. She simply couldn't bring herself to enter the room.

At one point Mahendra's careless eyes slid down from the ceiling and came to rest on the wall in front of him. Asha followed his gaze and found her own photograph adorning the wall, right beside Mahendra's. She wanted to cover it, tear it off the wall and take it away. She began to curse herself for not noticing it earlier; she should have thrown it away. Asha felt Mahendra was laughing at it and along with him, the image of Binodini that he held in his heart, was also casting an oblique glance at the photograph through her arched brows and smiling in cruel mockery.

Finally, Mahendra's gaze dropped from the wall and roamed around the room. These days whenever Asha had the time to spare from attending to her mother-in-law, she studied until late in the night, wishing to rid herself of her ignorance. Her textbooks and notebooks were neatly arranged in a corner of the room. Suddenly, Mahendra picked out one idly and began to glance through it. Asha wanted to scream and snatch it away from him violently. She could barely stand still as she visualized Mahendra's contemptuous gaze taking in her childish scrawls. Quickly she walked towards the stairs, without making any attempt to hide her presence.

Mahendra's dinner was ready. Rajlakshmi was under the impression that he was busy talking to Asha and so she didn't feel like disturbing him by calling him for his meal. But when she saw Asha coming downstairs, she laid out the dinner and sent word to Mahendra. The minute he went down to eat, Asha ran into the bedroom, tore her own photograph into bits and threw it over the terrace wall, picked up her books and took them away with her.

After the meal Mahendra went and sat in his room again. Rajlakshmi couldn't find Asha anywhere. Eventually, she went down to the kitchen and found Asha boiling the milk for Rajlakshmi. There was no need for this because the maid who usually did this chore stood close by, protesting at this undue interest from Asha. The maid was quite upset about losing her chance of stealing the little bit of milk that she replaced every night with water.

Rajlakshmi said, 'Bou-ma, what's this! Go upstairs.'

Asha went upstairs and took refuge in Rajlakshmi's room. Rajlakshmi was vexed at this behaviour as she thought, 'If Mahendra has come home for a short while, disentangling himself from that siren's clutches, Asha will send him back to her with tantrums and ego tussles like this. After all, it was Asha's fault that Mahendra was caught in Binodini's snares. A man, by nature, is bound to go astray. It is the wife's duty to keep him on the straight and narrow path, by fair means or foul.'

Rajlakshmi spoke to Asha in harsh and unsparing tones, 'What kind of behaviour is this, Bou-ma? You're fortunate enough that your husband has come home; why are you skulking around corners with a sullen face?'

Asha felt she was really at fault and so she ran upstairs in deep distress; without giving herself a chance to think twice, she took a deep breath and stepped into the bedroom. It was past ten o'clock now. Mahendra was standing in front of the bed with a thoughtful expression on his face, dusting the mosquito net slowly. He was beset by a strong sense of indignation against Binodini as he thought, 'Does she take me for such a worthless knave that she didn't feel a moment's fear when she sent me to Asha? From this day on if I revert to abiding by my duties towards Asha, who in this world will be there for Binodini to lean on? Am I such an oaf that this course of action is unthinkable for me? Is that how Binodini sees me? I have lost her respect, failed to win her heart—and been humbled by her.' As he stood before the bed, Mahendra vowed to protest against this disregard from Binodini—by hook or by crook; he'd incline his heart towards Asha once again and take his revenge on Binodini.

When Asha stepped into the room, Mahendra's careless dusting of the mosquito net came to an abrupt halt. He was faced with the insurmountable problem of finding something to say to Asha.

Mahendra tried to smile, failed miserably and said the first thing that came to his mind, 'I see that you have also taken to studies, like me. Where are the books that I saw here some time back?'

The words were not merely out of place, but they also seemed like a whiplash to Asha. The fact that the illiterate Asha was trying to educate herself, was a matter she was very sensitive about. Asha was convinced that it was a laughable thing to do. And if there was one person whose derision and mockery she was determined to shield this matter from, it was Mahendra. When Mahendra, after all these days, chose to begin his conversation with a reference to that very subject, Asha cringed in pain like a small child cringes before the cruel lashes of the schoolteacher's cane. She didn't say a word as she looked away and stood there holding on to the edge of the teapoy.

Mahendra too realized, the minute the words were out, that it wasn't the most apt and opportune thing to bring up. But he simply couldn't think of anything else to say under the circumstances. After the hurricane that had swept their lives, simple words from the past would sound awkward; the heart too was silent, unprepared with new words to say. Mahendra thought, 'If we get into bed, it may be easier to find words within that enclosed, confined intimacy.' With that notion Mahendra began to dust the outside of the mosquito net once again. He began to go over his dialogue and his performance in the manner of a new actor standing in the wings and nervously memorizing his lines just before he has to walk on to the stage. Suddenly, a mild sound made him turn around, and he found Asha had left the room.

## 43

The following morning Mahendra said to Rajlakshmi, 'Mother, I need a room of my own for my studies. I'd like to stay in Aunty's old room.'

Rajlakshmi was thrilled as she thought, 'So then, Mahin will stay at home now. He must have resolved everything with Bou-ma. How could he possibly neglect my darling daughter-in-law for too long? And how long can one be spellbound by that siren, neglecting such a chaste wife?'

She replied in haste, 'Why, certainly Mahin!' She unlocked the room and set about dusting it and cleaning it with great ceremony. 'Bou, oh Bou, where is Bou?' she kept enquiring. After hunting high and low, a tentative Asha was dragged out of a corner of the house. 'Lay a fresh mattress here. There is no desk here—bring one and put it here. This lamp will not do; send the one from upstairs.' In this manner, between the two of them, they prepared a princely seat for the monarch of the house in Annapurna's old room. Mahendra didn't spare a second glance at his willing slaves, moved into the room with his books and notes, and without wasting a single moment, sat down to study.

In the evening, after his dinner, he went back to his books. No one could tell if he would go up to his bedroom to sleep or if he'd sleep in his room downstairs. Rajlakshmi decked a stiff, doll-like Asha in all her finery and said, 'Go on, Bou-ma, ask Mahin if his bed should be made upstairs?'

Asha's feet refused to budge. She stood in silence with her head bent low. An irate Rajlakshmi began to hurl cruel accusations at her. Asha dragged her feet up to the door but simply couldn't go any further. Rajlakshmi looked at Asha from a corner of the corridor and gestured wildly for her to go on inside.

In desperation, Asha walked into the room. Mahendra heard her footsteps behind him and spoke without turning his head, 'I'll be here for some more time—tomorrow I have to wake up early to study—I shall sleep here tonight.'

Oh, the shame of it! Was Asha here to persuade Mahendra to go and sleep upstairs?

As she stepped out of the room, Rajlakshmi asked her eagerly, 'What's the matter, what happened?'

Asha said, 'He is studying, he'll sleep downstairs.' She went into her own dishonoured bedroom. There was no peace to be had anywhere—every little inch of this earth flamed like the desert under an afternoon sun.

A little late in the night there was a banging on Asha's closed door. 'Bou, Bou, open the door.'

Quickly, Asha held the door open. Rajlakshmi had braved the stairs despite her asthma and now she stood there gasping for breath. She tumbled into the room and flopped down on the bed. When she recovered her breath, she spoke in hoarse tones, 'Bou, what are you up to? Why have you come up and shut the door? Is this a time for petty tantrums? Your misery should teach you a few lessons! Go on, go downstairs.'

Asha spoke softly, 'He wishes to be alone.'

Rajlakshmi said, 'And that is that? He may have spoken in anger, without thinking twice, but you don't have to take him up on his word. You cannot afford to be so arrogant. Go now, go quickly.'

In times of trouble, the mother-in-law had no secrets from the daughter-in-law. She wanted to use the only weapons she had to bind Mahendra irrevocably.

As she spoke fervently, Rajlakshmi again had trouble breathing. She calmed herself a bit and rose. Without a word Asha held her and walked downstairs with her. She took Rajlakshmi into her bedroom, sat her down on the bed and began to plump up the pillows and cushions behind her. Rajlakshmi said, 'Let it be for now, Bou-ma. Send Sudho, the maid, to me. You go on, don't linger here.'

This time Asha did not hesitate. She walked out of her mother-in-law's room and headed straight for Mahendra's room. The book lay open in front of Mahendra—he sat with his feet hoisted on the desk and his head resting on the backrest, thinking intently. When he heard her footsteps, he looked up in surprise and turned his head, as if wishing the fleeting appearance of the one in whose thoughts he was lost. When he saw Asha he composed himself, put his feet down and pulled his book to him.

Mahendra was quite stunned today. Usually Asha never appeared before him thus, so boldly. If their paths ever happened to cross, she moved away immediately. But today, at this late hour, her sudden entry into his room was really quite incredible. Without lifting his head from his book, Mahendra sensed that Asha showed no signs of leaving. She came and stood in front of him, still and silent. Now he could no longer pretend to go on reading. He looked up. Asha spoke in clear, ringing tones, 'Mother's had an asthma attack. Could you please take a look at her?'

Mahendra asked, 'Where is she?'

Asha said, 'In her bedroom; she's not able to sleep.'

Mahendra said, 'Come on then, let me go and take a look.'

After ages, this tiny communion with Asha made Mahendra feel very buoyant. Silence had stood between them like an impregnable fortress. Mahendra had no weapons to tear the barrier down. Asha had suddenly opened a door to the fort with her own hands.

Asha waited outside Rajlakshmi's room, while Mahendra went in. Rajlakshmi viewed this inopportune arrival of Mahendra with anxiety—she feared he had sparred with Asha once again and was ready to leave the house. She said, 'Mahin, haven't you gone to bed yet?'

Mahendra said, 'Mother, is your asthma troubling you?'

This question, long awaited and coming so late, piqued the mother deeply. She realized that Mahin had come to ask after her health today only at Asha's insistence. This anxious agony only augmented her trouble and she spoke with difficulty, 'Go on, go to bed—my asthma is nothing.'

Mahendra said, 'No, Mother, it's best to do a check-up; this isn't something one should ignore.'

Mahendra knew that his mother had a weak heart and the look on her face was not too reassuring—he was anxious.

Rajlakshmi said, 'There's no need for a check-up; my ailment is beyond cure.'

Mahendra said, 'All right, let me get you a sleeping pill for tonight and tomorrow we shall examine you thoroughly.'

Rajlakshmi said, 'I've had enough of pills; they don't work on me. Go on, Mahin, it's very late—you go and sleep.'

Mahendra replied, 'I'll go as soon as you feel a little better.'

Miffed and hurt, Rajlakshmi addressed Asha, concealed behind the door, and said, 'Bou, why did you bother Mahin so late at night and fetch him here?' As she spoke she could scarcely breathe.

Asha stepped into the room now and addressed Mahendra in soft yet firm tones, 'Go on, you go to sleep. I'll stay with Mother.'

Mahendra called Asha out of the room and said to her, 'I am sending for some medicine; there'll be two doses in the bottle. Give her one dose first and if she still cannot sleep, administer the second dose after an hour. If it gets worse in the night, don't forget to send for me.'

Mahendra went back to his room. This new face of Asha was a novelty to him. This Asha had no diffidence, no inadequacy; this Asha was confident of what she was doing and she wasn't begging for protection from him. Mahendra may have rejected his wife, but he felt a growing respect for the daughter-in-law of the house.

Rajlakshmi was secretly pleased that Asha had fetched Mahendra out of concern for her health. What she said, however, was, 'Bou-ma, I sent you to sleep—why did you drag Mahendra here?'

Asha didn't answer her and simply began to fan her as she sat behind her on the bed.

Rajlakshmi said, 'Go to bed, Bou-ma.'

Asha spoke softly, 'He has asked me to stay here.' Asha knew that Rajlakshmi would be pleased to hear that Mahendra had instructed her to serve his mother.

## 44

When it became obvious to Rajlakshmi that Asha wasn't able to hold on to Mahendra, she felt, 'If my illness is the pretext needed to hold Mahin back, so be it.' She was afraid that she might be completely cured soon. She began to pull the wool over Asha's eyes and to throw her medication away.

Mahendra, in his preoccupation, didn't notice anything. But Asha perceived clearly that Rajlakshmi's ailment had worsened. She thought that perhaps Mahendra wasn't giving enough thought to his choice of drugs and treatment; so lost was he in his own confusions that even his mother's illness couldn't prod him out of his daze. Asha couldn't help feeling disgusted at the extent of Mahendra's downfall. If a man was ruined in one way, did he have to let everything go in this manner?

One evening, as she was in the throes of pain, Rajlakshmi suddenly recalled Behari. It was ages since he had visited them. She asked Asha, 'Bou-ma, do you know where Behari is right now?' Asha realized that it was Behari who had always nursed Rajlakshmi when she was sick and that's why she was thinking of him now. But Behari, once the bulwark of the household, had also been thrown out. Had he been here, Asha thought, Rajlakshmi would have received proper treatment—he wasn't as heartless as Mahendra. She heaved a sigh.

Rajlakshmi said, 'Has Mahin had a fight with Behari? That's very wrong, Bou-ma. Mahin doesn't have a greater well-wisher, a better friend than him.' As she spoke tears gathered in her eyes.

Many memories flitted slowly through Asha's mind. She recalled how many times, in various ways, Behari had tried to warn the stupid and unseeing Asha, thereby earning her displeasure; today she cursed herself for it. Why should fate spare a foolish woman who had hurled abuses at her true ally and drawn to her bosom her one and only foe? The poignant sighs that Behari had heaved as he left the house were bound to echo between the walls and have an effect someday.

Rajlakshmi was silent and thoughtful for a while before she spoke again, 'Bou-ma, if Behari had been here, he could have saved us in these times of trouble—things wouldn't have gone so wrong.'

Asha sat mutely, lost in her thoughts. Rajlakshmi sighed and said again, 'If he hears I am sick, he won't be able to stop himself from coming over.'

Asha realized that Rajlakshmi wanted this news to reach Behari. She was evidently feeling quite helpless in his absence.

Mahendra was standing by the moonlit window in silence, with the room in darkness. He was tired of studying. The house did not provide him any happiness. When you are estranged from your closest ones, it is not possible to discard them like strangers; neither can you draw them to your bosom comfortably. This weighs heavy on the heart and constricts one's breath. Mahendra hesitated nowadays before going to his mother; if she ever saw him approach, she looked at his face with such anxious panic that he felt wounded. If Asha ever came anywhere close to him, he had trouble finding words to say; but the silence between them was equally troubling. His days had turned into a living nightmare. Mahendra had vowed that he wouldn't set eyes on Binodini for at least seven days. Two days were left for the week to be over—how would he endure those two days?

Mahendra was lost in these thoughts when he heard footsteps behind him. He knew Asha had entered the room. He stood still, pretending not to have heard her. Asha realized his pretense, but she didn't leave the room. She stood behind him and said, 'There's something I have to say—I'll finish saying it and then I'll leave.'

Mahendra turned around and said, 'You don't have to leave—why don't you sit for a while?'

Asha paid no heed to this courteous offer and continued, 'Behari-thakurpo needs to be told about Mother's illness.'

The very mention of Behari was like adding insult to injury for Mahendra. He composed himself and said, 'But why? Don't you have faith in my treatment?'

Asha was already too upset at the thought that Mahendra wasn't working hard enough on his mother's treatment and so she blurted out, 'Well, Mother's ailment hasn't abated one bit! It seems to get worse every day.'

The covert criticism cloaked in this simple statement of fact hit Mahendra hard. Never before had Asha hurled such masked allegations at him. His ego was wounded and he spoke in bemused derision, 'I suppose now I'll have to take medical lessons from you.'

Asha's deep feeling of hurt got a fresh jolt at this disparagement. The room was in darkness; the ever-silent Asha gathered her courage and spoke with resolute vigour, 'Perhaps not medical lessons, but you can surely take lessons on caring for your mother.'

Such a riposte from Asha left Mahendra gasping for words. The unfamiliar harshness of Asha's words made Mahendra turn vicious and he said, 'You are well aware why I have forbidden your Behari-thakurpo to enter this house—I suppose you've begun to miss him again!'

Asha stormed out of the room. She felt impelled to leave because of an onrush of shame. The shame wasn't for herself. How could the person who was himself neck-deep in culpability utter such baseless allegations? Such brazenness could not be covered over even by mountains of mortification.

The moment Asha left, Mahendra perceived his total defeat. He had never imagined that Asha would, in any situation, ever be capable of reprimanding him thus. He realized that his status had now been dragged down from the throne to the ground. He was suddenly gripped by a fear lest Asha's anguish turned into disgust.

Meanwhile, the very mention of Behari filled him with anxious qualms about Binodini. He didn't know whether Behari was back from his trip. In the meantime, Binodini may have found him and the two may even have met up. Mahendra could scarcely honour his vow now.

That night Rajlakshmi's ailment took a turn for the worse and she sent for Mahendra. She spoke with great difficulty, 'Mahin, I would dearly love to see Behari—he hasn't come around for ages now.'

Asha was fanning her mother-in-law as she sat with her eyes lowered to the ground. Mahendra said, 'He is not here; he left on a trip to the west or somewhere.'

Rajlakshmi said, 'I feel certain he is right here and he's just staying away because he is upset with you. For pity's sake, please go and look him up tomorrow.'

Mahendra said, 'All right, I will.'

Today everyone was reaching out for Behari. Mahendra felt that no one in the whole wide world wanted or desired him.

# 45

The very next morning Mahendra landed up at Behari's house. He found the servants at the gate, loading furniture onto several bullock carts. Mahendra asked Bhoju, 'What's up?'

Bhoju said, 'The master has acquired a farmhouse by the river Ganga in Bally and everything is being moved there.'

Mahendra asked, 'Is the master at home?'

Bhoju said, 'He spent just two days in Kolkata and yesterday he went back to Bally.'

Mahendra's heart sank. He was sure that Binodini and Behari had met in his absence. In his mind's eye he could see a similar queue of bullock carts at Binodini's door, and furniture being loaded onto them. He felt certain that for this very reason Binodini had made him, the senseless fool, stay away from her house.

Without a second's delay, Mahendra leaped onto his carriage and barked orders at the coachman. He swore continuously at the coachman for the tardiness of the horses. Once inside the lane at Patoldanga, he found that there were no preparations for a move or transfer. He was afraid that it had all been accomplished already. He banged on the door loudly. The minute the old servant opened the door, Mahendra asked, 'Is everything all right?' He replied, 'Yes sir, everything's fine.'

Mahendra went upstairs. Binodini was in the bathroom. Mahendra stepped into her bedroom and threw himself on Binodini's unmade bed. He gripped the soft mattress with both hands, buried his face in the pillow and took in the scent with a deep breath as he said, 'Heartless! Heartless!'

Thus he emptied his heart of its turbulent emotions, left the bed and began to wait impatiently for Binodini. As he paced the floor he noticed a Bangla daily lying open upon the mattress on the floor. He picked it up casually to pass his time. But from the first spot on which glance fell, Behari's name leaped out at him. In an instant his whole being was concentrated on the newspaper. A report said that Behari had acquired a property in Bally, beside the Ganga, where he proposed to provide free treatment to poor and needy gentlefolk—the clinic could accommodate five people at a time, etc. etc.

Binodini had obviously seen this piece of news. What did she feel? Mahendra felt sure that Binodini yearned to go away to Bally. He was further agitated at the thought that this new step taken by Behari would only enhance Binodini's respect for him. As for himself, Mahendra labelled Behari a 'humbug' and his new venture a 'vagary'; he thought, 'Behari has always had a penchant of making a show of doing good.' As opposed to Behari, Mahendra tried to laud himself as a very spontaneous and genuine person, thinking, 'I abhor the attempt to con simple folk under the guise of philanthropy and altruism.' But alas, perhaps people, and one person in particular, would not really appreciate the worth of his sincerity and lack of subterfuge. Mahendra began to feel this was another way in which Behari had unfairly scored over him.

As he heard Binodini's footsteps, Mahendra folded up the newspaper and sat upon it. When a freshly bathed Binodini entered the room Mahendra looked up at her—and reeled in shock. What a change had come over her—she seemed to have endured austere penance through fire in the last few days. She had grown thin and a strange glow emanated from behind her pallid face.

Binodini had given up all hopes of hearing from Behari. Imagining Behari's obvious indifference towards her, she had suffered in silence every minute of the day. She knew no ways of liberating herself from this torment. She felt Behari had gone away after rejecting her and she had no way of reaching him any more. Binodini, who loved to do the housework to perfection, felt stifled in the walled confines of this house where she had nothing to do—all her energies turned inwards and lacerated her instead. When she imagined her entire future within the confines of this loveless, joyless, activity-less house, when she contemplated this narrow lane and thoughts of living there forever, her rebellious nature made vain attempts at battering away at the sky in mute frustration against providence. Binodini felt relentless hatred and disgust for Mahendra, the senseless fool who had closed out all her escape routes and constricted her life thus. She realized that she would no longer be able to keep Mahendra at arm's length. In this tiny house, Mahendra would inch relentlessly closer to her—every day he'd edge closer, propelled by an invisible attraction; she knew that disgusting battles would be fought within this black hole, on this grimy bed of an immoral life, between hatred and attraction. How could she protect herself from the deadly whiplash of the dragon's tail when she had dug out with her own hands, this drooling, lusting, filthy beast from the depths of Mahendra's heart? On the one hand was her anguished heart, on the other was her entrapment in this tiny house and added to that the waves of Mahendra's desire crashing away at the door—Binodini's soul recoiled in fear. Where would all this end? When would she be free of it all?

The sight of Binodini's gaunt, pallid face lit the fires of jealousy in Mahendra's heart. Did he have any powers by which he could, forcefully, uproot all thoughts of Behari from this woman's heart? The eagle flies down and snatches away the lamb in one fell swoop and flies back to its nest atop the insurmountable mountain. Wasn't there one such spot, shrouded in the clouds and beyond all memories, where a lone Mahendra could hold his gentle, pretty captive to his bosom? The heat of envy augmented the force of his desire. Now he could no longer let Binodini go out of his sight, even for an instant. He must keep the nightmare of Behari at bay; he didn't dare to give Behari even an inch of opportunity hereafter.

Mahendra had read in Sanskrit poetry that the anguish of separation lent a softness to a woman's beauty. Today, the more he looked at Binodini he realized the truth of it, and his heart was astir with a cavernous sorrow tinged with pleasure.

After a few moments of silence Binodini asked Mahendra, 'Have you had tea?'

Mahendra said, 'I may have, but please don't let that stop you from making me another cup with your hands—fill my cup, oh beloved!'

Perhaps quite deliberately, Binodini chose to cruelly lash out at this burst of passion from Mahendra, asking abruptly, 'Do you happen to know where Behari-thakurpo is right now?'

Mahendra lost colour in an instant as he replied, 'He is not in Kolkata now.'

Binodini said, 'What is his new address?'

Mahendra replied, 'He doesn't wish to disclose that to anyone.'

Binodini said, 'Is it possible to look for him and locate it?'

Mahendra said, 'I have no urgent need to do that.'

Binodini said, 'Need is not everything. Isn't a friendship as old as this worth something?'

Mahendra said, 'Behari may be a very old friend of mine, but you have known him for a very short while—yet I sense that you have a greater urgency to find out where he is.'

Binodini retorted, 'That should tell you something; hasn't a friend like that taught you the meaning of the word friendship?'

Mahendra replied, 'No, and that's no great loss to me. But if I had learnt the art of stealing a woman's heart by deception, it would have stood me in good stead now.'

Binodini said, 'That particular art requires skill and not just intent.'

Mahendra said mockingly, 'If you know the guru's whereabouts please divulge it to me—at this age I'm ready to go and take tuitions from him. Then we shall see about skill.'

Binodini said, 'If you fail to locate your friend's address, do not utter words of love to me. After the way you have treated Behari-thakurpo, who can trust you?'

Mahendra said, 'If you didn't trust me totally, you would not have humiliated me thus. If only you hadn't been supremely confident of my love, I would have suffered less today. Behari knows the art of not-being-tamed and if he had taught me that art, he'd have been a true friend indeed.'

'Behari-thakurpo is human and hence he cannot be tamed,' Binodini said as she stood by the window as before, her black tresses snaking down her back. Suddenly, Mahendra stood up, bunched up his fists and shouted in fury, 'How do you have the nerve to humiliate me like this time and again? Is it your belief in my goodness or your superiority that makes you so sure I won't retaliate? If you truly believe I am sub-human, know me to be a brute indeed. I am not so unmanly as to be unable to inflict a wound when I'm hurt.' He gazed at Binodini's face for a few silent seconds. Then he said, 'Binod, let's go away from here. Let's begin our journey—be it the west or the mountains, wherever you wish to go. This is no place to live—it's killing me.'

Binodini said, 'Let's go right away then—let's go towards the west.'

Mahendra said, 'Where in the west?'

Binodini said, 'Nowhere in particular; we shan't stay in the same place for more than two days, we'll keep moving.'

Mahendra said, 'That's good; let's leave tonight.'

Binodini agreed and went away to cook Mahendra's meal.

Mahendra understood that the news item about Behari had escaped Binodini's notice. She no longer had the powers of deliberation necessary to concentrate on a newspaper. He spent the whole day on edge, lest that particular news reached Binodini somehow.

## 46

Mahendra's lunch was prepared at home, in the hope that he'd come back after looking up Behari. When he didn't return, an ailing Rajlakshmi grew anxious. Lack of sleep the night before had already weakened her and worrying over Mahendra did her no good at this stage. Asha went to check and found that Mahendra's carriage had returned. The coachman informed her that from Behari's house Mahendra had gone to the flat in Patoldanga. At this news, Rajlakshmi turned her face to the wall and lay still. Asha sat by her head, her face turned to stone, and fanned her. On other days Rajlakshmi always urged Asha to go and have her meal on time. Today she didn't say anything. If, even after seeing how ill she was the night before, Mahendra felt drawn towards Binodini today, Rajlakshmi had nothing left to live for. She was well aware that Mahendra was not taking her ailment seriously; he was secure in the knowledge that this time too, as on every other occasion, her illness was a temporary malady, curable in a few days. And this casual complacence struck Rajlakshmi as very cruel indeed. In the throes of passion, Mahendra refused to acknowledge any anxiety or any concern and hence he was making light of his mother's pain; he rushed to Binodini at every brazen opportunity lest he found himself bound to his ailing mother's bedside. Rajlakshmi lost all interest in recovery—in a fit of sorrow, she wanted to prove to Mahendra how unfounded his complacence was.

At two in the afternoon Asha said, 'Mother, it's time for your medication.' Rajlakshmi didn't respond. When Asha rose to go and fetch the medicine, she said, 'There's no need for medicines, Bou-ma. You may go.'

Asha could fathom Rajlakshmi's pain and when its ripples touched her own heart, she could hold still no longer. She tried to stifle her sobs, but they broke forth nonetheless. Rajlakshmi half-turned on her side, took Asha's hands in her own and stroked them with gentle compassion as she said, 'Bou-ma, you are very young, there's time yet for you to find happiness. But don't work so hard on my account, my dear—I have lived long enough; there's no point in going on.'

Asha's sobs only increased at these words and she pressed her anchal over her lips.

In this way, the cheerless day dragged on. In spite of their misery and hurt, both Rajlakshmi and Asha hoped in their heart of hearts that Mahendra would arrive at any moment. Both of them realized that they were sitting up at every little sound that came to their ears. Gradually, twilight cast its shadow into the inner chambers of the house—it held neither the joy of light nor the comfort of darkness. It made sorrow weigh heavier and despondency tearless; it stole away the power to work or hope and yet, didn't bring the peace of respite or liberation. In that withered, graceless dusk of the sick house Asha rose, lit a lamp and brought it into the room. Rajlakshmi said, 'Bou-ma, the light bothers me. Keep it outside.'

Asha took the lamp outside and came back to sit by Rajlakshmi's side. When the darkness grew thicker and brought the endless night from the outside into the tiny room, Asha asked in gentle tones, 'Mother, should I send word to him?'

Rajlakshmi answered firmly, 'No Bou-ma, this is my order to you—do not inform Mahendra.'

Asha stood there speechless. She didn't even have the strength to weep.

Outside, the bearer said, 'The master has sent a letter.'

In that instant Rajlakshmi thought that perhaps Mahendra was suddenly afflicted by some ailment and so he couldn't come; hence he had sent the letter. Contrite and concerned, she said, 'Go and take a look Bou-ma—see what Mahin has said.'

Asha held the letter with trembling fingers and read it in the light of the lamp outside the door. Mahendra wrote that he wasn't keeping too well lately and so he was off to the west. There was no need to worry overmuch about Rajlakshmi's health; he had instructed Nabin-doctor to check up on her regularly. He had left instructions for bouts of insomnia or headaches and along with the letter had sent two bottles of light and nutritious tonics that he'd fetched from the chemist's. In the postscript there was a request to be kept posted on his mother's health at an address in Giridih for the moment.

Asha stood there dumbfounded after she finished reading this letter. Her sorrow was overtaken by a terrible sense of guilt—how was she to convey this brutal news to Rajlakshmi?

Seeing the delay in Asha's return Rajlakshmi grew more concerned. She called out, 'Bou-ma, come here and tell me what Mahin has written.' In her eagerness she sat up on the bed.

So Asha came in and read out the letter slowly. Rajlakshmi said,

'What has he said about his health—just read that bit once again.'

Asha reiterated, 'I haven't been feeling too well lately and so I—'

Rajlakshmi said, 'That's enough, stop—how could he feel well! The old mother refuses to die and only bothers him with her sickness! Why did you have to tell him of my illness? At least he was at home; he sat in a corner with his books and didn't meddle in anybody's business. But you had to go and drag him into his mother's troubles and where has that got you—he has left the house! If I had died in one corner of the house, would that have been too bad? Even after all this, you haven't learnt a thing, Bou-ma.' Rajlakshmi lay back on the pillows, panting.

Outside, there was the sound of boots. The bearer said, 'The doctor is here.'

The doctor cleared his throat and stepped into the room. Asha quickly pulled her anchal over her head and moved to the side of the bed. The doctor asked Rajlakshmi, 'Could you tell me what your complaints are?'

Rajlakshmi roared angrily, 'What complaints! Won't you let a woman die in peace? If I have your medication, will I live forever?'

The doctor spoke placatingly, 'You may not live forever, but at least I can reduce the pain—'

Rajlakshmi exclaimed, 'A true remedy for anguish was available to widows who jumped into their husband's pyres. Now, it's only a matter of prolonging the agony. Doctor, please go away—don't bother me; I want to be alone.'

Apprehensively the doctor said, 'May I check your pulse—'

Rajlakshmi spoke irately, 'I'm telling you to leave. My pulse is fine—there's no hope of it giving way in the near future.'

The doctor had no choice but to leave the room. From the door he sent for Asha. He quizzed her in detail about the symptoms of the ailment. After he had heard her out, he re-entered the room with a grave expression and said, 'Look here, Mahendra has entrusted a responsibility to me. If you refuse to let me treat you, he'd be hurt.'

Mahendra feeling hurt sounded like a joke to Rajlakshmi. She said, 'Don't worry too much about Mahin. Everyone is hurt some time in his life. This hurt will not kill Mahin. Please go now, doctor. Let me sleep a little.'

Nabin-doctor realized it was best not to disturb the patient further. He walked out slowly and gave explicit instructions to Asha about what had to be done.

When Asha came back Rajlakshmi said, 'Child, you go on and take some rest—you've been at my bedside all day long. Send the old maid here—she can sit in the next room while I rest.'

Asha knew Rajlakshmi well. This wasn't an affectionate request—it was a command that had to be obeyed. She sent Haru's mother, went into her own room and lay down upon the cool floor in the dark. The day-long fast and privation had left her feeling very weak. The wedding band was playing in some neighbour's house. Now the shehnai struck up again. The notes of the tune echoed in the dark of the night and reverberated everywhere, wounding Asha continually. Upon the dreamscape of the night unfolded every minute incident of her own wedding night: the lights, the chaos, the people, the garlands, the sandal paste, the smell of new clothes and the fumes of the holy fire, the timid, shy, joyous trembling of her new bride's heart; the more the memories took shape and embraced her, the more her sorrow took root and the more her heartache grew. Just as the hungry child, in the midst of a terrible famine, strikes out at his mother, demanding food, these animated memories of past joys looked to Asha's heart for nourishment and struck out at it vehemently when they found no response. A weary Asha could scarcely be quietly supine. She brought her palms together to pray to God; as she did so, the image of the only god she ever knew, that of her chaste and loving aunt, appeared within her tearful soul. Asha had vowed not to drag that saintly figure back into the murk and gloom of mundane lives ever again. But today she could see no way out for herself—the thick, dense anguish surrounding her did not permit even a tiny crack of hope. So Asha lit a lamp, pulled a notepad onto her lap and wrote a letter as she wiped away the tears that streamed from her eyes:

My respected Aunty,

You are all I have left in this world; please come over just this once and draw this unfortunate soul into your bosom. Or else I'll surely die. I do not know what else to write. I place a hundred thousand salutations at your venerable feet.

Affectionately yours,
Chuni

## 47

Annapurna returned from Kashi, walked into Rajlakshmi's room slowly and touched her feet with respect. Despite the intervening tiffs and rows, the sight of Annapurna gave Rajlakshmi a new lease of life. Only after Annapurna's arrival did Rajlakshmi realize that she'd been seeking her all this while, reaching out to her, unknown even to her own self. In an instant she recognized that much of her distress, much of the ennui of the past few weeks were due to Annapurna's absence. In one single moment she became her old self. Rajlakshmi was flooded with memories of the old camaraderie between the two sisters-in-law, which had been there even before Mahendra's birth—from the day they had entered this house as new brides and accepted the good and bad in it as their own, in festivals, in death and sorrow—when they had pulled the vehicle of this household together as one, with one destination in mind. The dearest friend of her youth, with whom she had once begun her journey, had come back to her side after many interludes and interruptions. But the one for whom Rajlakshmi had inflicted such wounds on this friend of hers was now nowhere to be found.

Annapurna sat beside the ailing woman, took her hand in her own and said, 'Didi.'

Rajlakshmi said, 'Mejo-bou,' but she could not say anything more. The tears flowed from her eyes. Asha could no longer check herself; she went into the next room, collapsed on the floor and cried her heart out.

Annapurna did not dare to ask Rajlakshmi or Asha any questions about Mahendra. She called Sadhucharan and asked, 'Uncle, where is Mahin?'

Sadhucharan narrated the entire episode of Mahendra and Binodini. Annapurna asked, 'Where is Behari?'

Sadhucharan replied, 'He hasn't come here for many days now—I don't know his whereabouts.'

Annapurna said, 'Please go to Behari's house and get me news of him.'

Sadhucharan came back to say, 'He is not at home. He is in a farmhouse by the Ganga in Bally.'

Annapurna sent for Nabin-doctor and asked after the patient's health. He said, 'Along with her weak heart, she has now developed dropsy. Death may come suddenly, without warning.'

That evening, when Rajlakshmi's pain worsened, Annapurna asked her, 'Didi, may I send for Nabin-doctor?'

Rajlakshmi said, 'No Mejo-bou, Nabin-doctor won't be able to do anything for me.'

Annapurna said, 'Then tell me who would you like to see?'

Rajlakshmi said, 'It'll be good if you could send word to Behari.'

Annapurna was touched to the quick. One day at dusk, in a far-off land, she had slighted and sent Behari away from her doorstep, and the memory still perturbed her. Behari would never come back to her doorstep again. She had never imagined that in this lifetime she'd get another chance to set right that rebuff.

Annapurna went up to Mahendra's room on the terrace. Once this room had been the one cheerful spot in the house. Today it looked forlorn—the beds were unmade, the décor dishevelled; no one had watered the plants on the terrace and they looked withered.

Asha realized her aunt had gone up to the terrace and she followed her slowly. Annapurna pulled her into her heart and kissed her forehead. Asha went down on her knees, touched Annapurna's feet and laying her head on them said, 'Aunty, bless me, give me strength. I had never imagined that a person could bear such immense heartbreak. Oh Lord, how much longer can I bear this!'

Annapurna sat down on the floor and Asha lay down at her feet. Annapurna picked up her niece's head onto her lap and without saying a word, folded her own hands and meditated in silence.

This silent, loving benediction from Annapurna was like balm to the depths of Asha's soul; after an age she felt at peace. She felt her prayers were nearly answered—the gods may well ignore her, a silly and stupid girl, but they'd surely hear the prayers of her aunt.

With this reassurance and strength in her heart, Asha stood up with a sigh after a while. She said, 'Aunty, please write a letter to Behari-thakurpo.'

Annapurna said, 'No, a letter won't do.'

Asha said, 'But then, how will you send word to him?'

Annapurna said, 'Tomorrow I shall go and meet him in person.'

## 48

While Behari was travelling in the west, he had realized that if he didn't bind himself to a mission, he would know no peace. He resolved to take up the onus of providing treatment to Kolkata's indigent clerks. The life of a low-income, needy clerk living in a shack in a narrow lane, burdened with a family, was like that of a fish in a pond in summer, when it thrashed about helplessly in the mud and gasped for breath as the water around it dried up. For many years Behari had nurtured sympathy for this pallid, emaciated, fretful bunch of gentlefolk. So he wanted to confer upon them the shade of the woods and the breeze of the Ganga.

He bought some land in Bally and with the help of some Chinese artisans started building tiny cottages there. But his heart knew no peace. As the day grew closer for him to inaugurate his mission, his soul rebelled against his chosen vocation. His heart echoed with one thought, 'There is no joy, no pleasure, no beauty in this work—it is nothing but a dreary burden.' Never before had Behari felt so oppressed by the prospect of work.

In the past, Behari had never needed anything. He had always been able to apply himself with ease to the task at hand. But now he felt a strange kind of hunger without appeasing which he couldn't bring himself to feel an interest in anything. In keeping with his old habits he tried his hand at this and that; but in the very next moment he wanted to give it all up and be free of everything.

The yearning of youth which had lain dormant within him and whose existence he had been unaware of had suddenly come alive at Binodini's magic touch. It now began to prowl through the landscape, looking for objects to satisfy its hunger. Behari was unsettled by this hungry animal within himself; what would he do now with the sickly, withered community of clerks from Kolkata!

The Ganga, overflowing in the monsoon, streamed ahead. Every now and then indigo clouds inclined towards each other in intimate embrace over the thick foliage on the other bank. The river sometimes glinted like a steel sword and sometimes it glittered like a flashfire. Every time Behari's glance fell on this festive monsoon scenery, someone emerged from his heart and stood all alone beneath the serene blue glow of the sky; someone with her moist, jet-black tresses cascading in waves over her back—she collected all the scattered rays of the monsoon-laden clouds and directed upon him the unblinking, burning fire of her gaze.

Today, Behari felt that his past, which he had spent in peace and quiet, had actually been a grave loss. Many such overcast evenings and moonlit nights must have come with their untold boon of joys to Behari's empty heart, and gone back unfulfilled—so many melodies had remained unsung, and so many joyous occasions incomplete. Today, Binodini's uplifted face, with the proferred kiss hanging in the air, cast its rosy glow upon all his memories of the past and turned them into wan, insignificant shadows. He had wasted the larger part of his life as Mahendra's bosom friend! What had he gained from it? Behari had been unaware that the pathos of romance could exhume from the very heart of creation such a melodic tune on the flute. How could he now remove from his mind the memories of that woman, who had held him in her arms and elevated him all at once to this unimaginable place of beauty? Her gaze, her desires were everywhere now; her fervent, deep sighs raised waves in Behari's blood and the gentle warmth of her touch embraced Behari again and again and enlivened his heart like a blossoming flower.

And yet, why was Behari so far away from Binodini today? The reason was that he couldn't imagine a relationship that would be as beautiful as the beauty of the emotions with which she had drenched his soul. If you tried to pluck the lotus, the sludge came with it. Where could he place her in the web of relationships so that the exquisite would not be turned into the hideous? Besides, if a tug-of-war ensued with Mahendra, the whole thing would take such an ugly turn that Behari couldn't even bear to think about it. Hence, Behari had come away to this solitary bank of the Ganga, placed his idol on a pedestal and burned his heart like incense at her altar. He did not even write to Binodini or ask after her for fear that he would hear something that would destroy his house of cards.

On this cloudy morning Behari sat pensively in the southern corner of his garden beneath the berry tree. Tiny boats ferried to and fro on the river and he watched them idly. The sun rose higher in the sky. The servant came to ask him if he should get started on lunch. Behari said, 'Not now.' The chief artisan came to him for some urgent consultation and Behari said, 'Later, please.'

Suddenly, Behari was startled to find Annapurna standing before him. He sat up in a rush, held her feet in his firm grasp and bent to the ground, seeking her blessings. Annapurna stroked his head affectionately with her right hand and spoke in a voice laced with tears, 'Behari, why have you grown so thin?'

Behari said, 'So that I could get back your love, Aunty.'

Tears streamed down Annapurna's cheeks. Behari stood up attentively, 'Aunty, have you eaten yet?'

Annapurna said, 'No, it's not time yet.'

Behari said, 'Come then, let me lend you a hand. Today, after all these months I am dying to eat food cooked by you, off your plate after you are finished.'

Behari did not ask a word about Mahendra or Asha. One day, Annapurna had closed her door on Behari's face ruthlessly. With hurt pride, he obeyed her indictment to this day.

After lunch Annapurna said, 'Behari, the boat is ready at the quay—come to Kolkata right away.'

Behari said, 'But I have no work in Kolkata.'

Annapurna said, 'Didi is very ill, she has asked to see you.'

Behari looked up in startled disbelief. He asked, 'Where is Mahin da?'

Annapurna said, 'He is not in Kolkata. He is travelling in the west.'

Behari turned ashen as he heard this. He sat for a while in wordless silence.

Annapurna asked, 'Don't you know everything, Behari?'

Behari said, 'I know some of it but not what has happened recently.'

So Annapurna narrated to him the events leading up to Mahendra's escape to the west with Binodini in tow. In a flash of a second the colour of the earth-sky and water changed before Behari's very eyes; the nectar of his imagination turned bitter all at once: 'So Binodini, the temptress, played with my emotions on that night! The surrender of her heart was a mere illusion! She left her village brazenly with Mahendra and headed westwards! Shame on her, and shame on me—I was a fool to have trusted her even for a moment.'

Alas for the overcast monsoon evening, alas for the rain-soaked full-moon night—where was their magical charm now?

## 49

Behari wondered how he would be able to bring himself to look at the heartbroken Asha. When he stepped into the courtyard, the palpable pathos of the desolate house overwhelmed him. He looked at the servants and on behalf of Mahendra, culpable and absent, he hung his head in shame. He could not bring himself to ask of the familiar old retainers how they were, as he'd always done in the past. On the threshold of the inner chambers, his feet fairly dragged. Mahendra had hurled a vulnerable Asha into a naked humiliation that robbed a woman of all protective mantles and exposed her to the pitying, curious glances of the whole world. How could he bear to gaze upon Asha who would be injured and cringing?

But there was no time for these ruminations and quandaries. The moment he stepped inside, Asha walked up to him quickly and said, 'Thakurpo, please come quickly and take a look at Mother—she is really suffering.'

This was the first time Asha had addressed Behari directly. In times of trouble, masks are ripped away suddenly; people from far and wide are brought together in one lightning stroke and held close.

Asha's forthright fervour struck a chord in Behari. This tiny event told him much about the state in which Mahendra had left his family. The trauma of harsh times robs the household of charm and grace and the woman of the house has no opportunity to shield herself. Trivial shields and barriers come crashing down—no one has time for them.

Behari stepped into Rajlakshmi's room. Rajlakshmi had lost all colour due to a sudden attack of breathlessness—but that passed and she soon composed herself.

Behari touched her feet and sought her blessings. Rajlakshmi indicated for him a seat beside her bed. She spoke slowly, 'How are you, Behari? It's been so long.'

Behari said, 'Mother, why didn't you let me know that you are unwell? I would have rushed to your side immediately.'

Rajlakshmi spoke softly, 'I know that, my child. I may not have given birth to you, but you are all I have left in this world.' Tears coursed down her cheeks as she spoke.

Behari got up hastily and pretended to examine the bottles and jars of medication on the shelf as he controlled his emotions. When he returned to check Rajlakshmi's pulse, she said, 'Leave my pulse alone—let me ask you, why have you grown so thin, Behari?' She reached out her bony fingers and stroked Behari's collarbone.

Behari replied, 'If I don't have fish curry cooked by you, my bones will wither away thus. Get well soon, Mother, and I'll keep everything ready in the kitchen.'

Rajlakshmi smiled wanly and said, 'Behari, you must bring home a bride; there's no one to look after you. O Mejo-bou, all of you must find him a bride now—just look at what he has done to himself.'

Annapurna said, 'Didi, you get well first. This is your duty and you will fulfil it. We shall all join in the fun and enjoy ourselves.'

Rajlakshmi said, 'There's no time left for me to do it, Mejo-bou; I leave Behari in your care—you must make him happy. I could not repay his debts. But God will be merciful to him.' She stroked Behari's head affectionately.

Asha couldn't stay in the room any longer—she went out to cry her heart out. Annapurna gazed lovingly at Behari through her tears.

Suddenly, Rajlakshmi seemed to remember something and she called out, 'Bou-ma, O Bou-ma!'

When Asha re-entered the room she said, 'Have you arranged for Behari's meal?'

Behari said, 'Mother, everyone knows this glutton of a son of yours. The minute I stepped into the courtyard I noticed Bami, the maid, rushing into the kitchen with a large, fresh fish. I knew then that this household still remembers my tastes.' Behari laughed and looked at Asha.

Today, Asha wasn't embarrassed. She smiled sweetly and accepted Behari's banter indulgently. In the past she hadn't known the full weight of Behari's place in this family. Often, she had taken him for an intruder and disregarded him; many a times her exasperation had shown through in her gestures. Today, she regretted it all and it lent a new edge to her respect and sympathy towards Behari.

Rajlakshmi said, 'Mejo-bou, the cook won't be any good—you'll have to take charge of the cooking today. This country lad of ours from the other side of the river needs his food very spicy or he doesn't take to it.'

Behari protested, 'Your mother came from Bikrampur, in East Bengal; and you call a gentleman from West Bengal's Nadia district a country lad from the other side of the river! This I cannot stand for.'

There was a spate of good-humoured exchanges and after many days, the pall of sorrow lifted a little from the house.

But amidst all this conversation, not one person mentioned Mahendra's name. In the past Rajlakshmi only talked of Mahendra to Behari. Mahendra had often teased his mother for this. And today, when the same Rajlakshmi never once mentioned Mahendra, Behari was silently shocked.

When Rajlakshmi seemed to drift into sleep, Behari came out of the room and said to Annapurna, 'Mother's ailment is quite grave.'

Annapurna said, 'That is very obvious.' She sat down by the window in her own room. After many minutes of silence she said, 'Don't you think you should go and fetch Mahin, Behari? We shouldn't wait any longer.'

After a long pause Behari said, 'I shall do as you say. Does anyone have his address?'

Annapurna said, 'Not exactly, you'll have to hunt for it. Behari, let me tell you one more thing. Take a look at Asha. If you cannot salvage Mahendra from Binodini's clutches, she will surely die. If you look at her face you can tell that she has no will left to live.'

Behari laughed at this irony deep in his heart and thought, 'I'm the right choice to go and salvage another—and who, pray, will be my salvation?'

Aloud he said, 'Aunty, do I possess the secret of keeping Mahin da away from Binodini forever? He may come now due to his mother's illness. But how can I promise that he won't go back later?'

At this point Asha walked in slowly with her anchal pulled slightly over her head and sat down at her aunt's feet. She knew that Annapurna was discussing Rajlakshmi's illness with Behari and she was eager to hear about it. When he saw the glow of mute anguish on the chaste Asha's face, Behari was filled with a sense of reverent admiration. This young woman had bathed in the holy waters of sorrow and acquired a divine status like the goddesses of ancient times—she was no longer an ordinary mortal; terrible grief seemed to have made her as old as the acsetic women that the Puranas described.

After Behari discussed Rajlakshmi's diet and medication with Asha and sent her on her way, he heaved a sigh and said to Annapurna, 'I must salvage Mahin da.'

Behari went to Mahendra's bank and found out that the latter had recently begun transactions with their branch in Allahabad.

## 50

At the station Binodini clambered straight into the ladies' coupe in the intermediate class. Mahendra said, 'What are you doing—I'll buy a second-class ticket for you.'

Binodini said, 'But why? I'll be fine here.'

Mahendra was a little surprised. Binodini enjoyed her luxuries. In the past all hint of paucity had been anathema to her. The inherent poverty of her own home had always mortified her. If there was one thing that Mahendra had realized, it was that once Binodini had felt drawn to the comforts of his home, and to its reputation of being richer than average. She had felt restless at the thought that she could very easily have been the mistress of these comforts and the rightful claimant to the household's dignity. But today, when she had a complete hold over Mahendra, when she could easily bring all his wealth to her service, why was she displaying such careless obstinacy and rebelliously welcoming the path of arduous, degrading hardships? The fact was that she wanted to curtail her dependence on Mahendra as far as possible. She didn't want to accept from Mahendra, the man who had dislodged her from her rightful sanctuary forever, anything that could be counted as recompense for her disgrace. When Binodini lived in Mahendra's home, she had never followed the rigid rules of widowhood. But now she had begun to deprive herself of all pleasures. Now she had only one meal a day, wore a coarse sari and her perpetual laughter and banter were things of the past. Now she was so taciturn, masked, so distant and so forbidding that Mahendra didn't dare speak a harsh word to her. In amazement, impatience and fury, Mahendra said to himself, 'Binodini tried so hard to attain me—like the effort one makes to pluck a fruit from a lofty bough; why then did she cast the fruit away without even smelling it?'

Mahendra asked, 'For which place should I buy the tickets?'

Binodini said, 'Anywhere in the west—we can get down wherever the trains halts tomorrow morning.'

This kind of journey didn't appeal to Mahendra. He hated the disruption of his comfortable life. It would be difficult for Mahendra to survive without a proper dwelling in a big city. He wasn't the sort who could fend for himself and go where his fortunes took him. He boarded the train in a very irritable frame of mind. The fear that they were in separate compartments and that Binodini could get off the train without his knowledge made things worse.

In this manner, Binodini spun around on her orbit like a malevolent planet in the skies and she made Mahendra spin likewise—never letting him rest. Binodini had the capacity to make friends easily. Very soon she made friends with the women travelling with her. She gathered information about their desired destinations, put up in the dormitories and went about touring the sights worth seeing with her new friends. Every time Mahendra felt he was superfluous to Binodini, it was like a fresh blow to him. His only task was to buy the tickets from here to there. The rest of the time it was a ceaseless scuffle between him and his desires. At first, he accompanied Binodini on her forays in sightseeing—but gradually he grew tired of it. So he had his meal and tried to sleep while Binodini roamed about all day. No one could have dreamt that Mahendra, the apple of his mother's eye, would one day come out into the streets thus.

One day, the two were waiting for the train at Allahabad station. For some reason the train was late. Meanwhile, Binodini was scanning the faces of the passengers alighting from and boarding other trains. Perhaps she nurtured the hope that since they were in the west, if she looked hard enough, she'd be able to find one particular person. For her, there was a kind of tranquillity in this daily search amidst the chaotic throngs of people; at least it was better than her lonely life, captive in a solitary home, dying each day under the weight of stillness.

At Allahabad station her glance fell upon a glass box on the platform and she got a shock. The postal-department box displayed the letters addressed to all those who could not be located. On one letter carefully arranged inside the box, Binodini spotted Behari's name. The name 'Beharilal' wasn't uncommon and there was no reason to imagine that the Behari whose name was on that letter was the same one that Binodini longed for; yet, his full name spelt out on the letter left her in no doubt that it must indeed be Behari. She memorized the address on the envelope. Mahendra was seated on a bench, wearing a dour expression. Binodini went up to him and said, 'Let us stay here in Allahabad for a few days.'

Mahendra's male ego had felt increasingly slighted and rebellious at the thought that Binodini drove him as per her wishes and never bothered to provide fodder for his hungry, craving heart. At this point he would have been happy to stay longer in Allahabad and get some rest—but he felt like cutting off his nose to spite his face, not wanting to fall in with Binodini's wishes. He spoke irritably, 'Since we have set off we shall continue. I can't go back.'

Binodini said, 'I shall not go.'

Mahendra said, 'You stay alone then, I am off.'

Binodini said, 'That's fine.' She gestured to a porter, picked up her luggage and headed out of the station.

Mahendra with his male ego remained seated on the bench with dark thunderclouds hovering on his face. He could hold still only as long as Binodini was still visible to the eye. When she left the station without once looking back, he quickly summoned a porter, asked him to pick up his luggage and followed her. When he came out of the station he found that Binodini had already hired a carriage. In silence, Mahendra loaded the baggage atop the carriage and jumped into the coachbox. He had no inclination of sitting inside, facing Binodini and his defeated ego.

The carriage went on and on. Nearly an hour later they'd left the city behind and the carriage now rolled over fields and farmlands.

Mahendra was embarrassed to ask questions of the coachman lest he thought that the woman inside was the mistress and she hadn't even bothered to consult this man about their destination. He silently chewed on his wounded ego and sat in the coachbox wordlessly.

The carriage came to a halt in front of a solitary, well-kept farmhouse on the banks of the Yamuna. Mahendra was dumbfounded. Whose farm was this? How had Binodini come upon this address?

The house was shuttered. After much hollering an aged caretaker came out. He said that the owner was a rich man who lived nearby and if his permission was obtained they could stay in the farmhouse. Binodini glanced at Mahendra just once. He was tempted at the sight of this beautiful mansion—the prospect of a few days' relaxation thrilled him no end. He said to Binodini, 'Let us go to this rich man's house. You can stay in the carriage while I go inside and fix the rates.'

Binodini said, 'I am too tired. You go ahead. I'll stay here awhile. I think it's quite safe.'

Mahendra got into the carriage and left. Binodini called the old man to her side and asked after his children—how many there were, where they worked and where his daughters were married and so on. When she heard of his wife's demise she spoke compassionately, 'Oh, it must be hard on you. At this age you are all alone in this world. There's no one to look after you.'

In the course of conversation Binodini asked him, 'Did Beharibabu stay here once?'

He said, 'Well yes, he did for some time. Does madam know him?'

Binodini said, 'He is related to us.'

The description that the old man gave of Behari removed the last traces of doubt from Binodini's mind. She made the old man open up the house, and went into the rooms where Behari had stayed. Since they were locked up after his departure, it felt as if his spirit still lingered in the rooms, the wind had failed to sweep it away. Binodini drew in a deep breath and sucked it into her soul, let the still, silent air touch her all over; but she could not get any information about where Behari had gone. He could come back—nothing was certain. The old man assured Binodini that he'd check with his master and return with the news.

Mahendra paid the advance, meanwhile, and came back with permission for them to stay there.

## 51

The waters that the Himalayas gifted to the Yamuna from its snowy peaks were eternal, as were the torrents of poetry that generations of poets had presented to her. The rippling stream of this river contained sparkling rhythms in its currents and its waves surged with the exuberant emotions of many centuries.

When Mahendra came and sat on its banks at dusk, the sensation of romance conjured up a trance in his eyes, in his breath, in his veins and in his bones. The rays of the setting sun played a golden sitar of secret melodies and tremulous agony. The day cast speckled colours on the expansive banks, and wore to an end. Mahendra sat with half-closed eyes and heard as if from the elegiac dreamworld of Vrindavan the sounds of calves returning home at dusk.

The skies were overcast with monsoon clouds. The darkness was not a mere sheath of pitch-black but also something that echoed with curious mysteries. The bare shapes that were apparent through it in a strange glow spoke in nameless, unspoken languages. The indistinct pallor of the other bank, the inky blackness of the still waters, the huddled stillness of the massive, leafy lime tree at the riverside, the wan, dusty horizon in the distance, all merged together in the dark in various indefinite, indistinct shapes on this rainy evening and embraced Mahendra from all sides.

The rainy trysts of the Vaishnava padabalis came to his mind. The lady has set off on her tryst. She had come to the banks of the Yamuna all by herself and stood at the water's edge. How could she cross the river? 'Please ferry me across,' the cry rang in Mahendra's ears, 'oh please, ferry me to the other side.'

On the opposite bank of the river, in the dark, the lady stood far away—yet Mahendra could see her clearly. She was timeless and ageless, the eternal lover of Krishna and yet, Mahendra recognized her—she was none other than Binodini! She had begun her journey from beyond time with all her anguish, the pangs of separation and the full burden of her youth; her tryst had finally brought her to this river bank today through many melodies and many rhythms—today, the skies above the remote river reverberated with her voice, 'Oh please, ferry me across.' For how many more ages would she stand there thus, waiting for the boatman to ferry her across?

The clouds in a corner of the sky parted, revealing a sickle moon. The elusive magic of the moonlight took the river and its banks, the sky and its horizon far beyond the limits of reality. They were free of all earthly ties. The reins of time snapped, entire histories of the past disappeared, consequences of the future vanished—just this deluge of silvery water on the Yamuna remained—and this moment held Mahendra and Binodini in it, as time and the world stood still.

Mahendra was inebriated. He felt sure that Binodini wouldn't reject him today, she wouldn't refuse to fill this solitary, moonlit paradise with her gracious beauty. He stood up instantly and went towards the house in search of Binodini.

When he reached the bedroom he was overwhelmed by the scent of flowers. Through the open doors and windows the moonlight streamed onto the shimmering bed. Binodini had picked flowers from the garden, threaded them into garlands that she wore in her hair, on her arms and neck—adorned with flowers she lay upon the bed like a creeper in spring, bent under the weight of its blossoms.

Mahendra's yearning intensified. He spoke in a choked voice, 'Binod, I waited on the banks of the Yamuna. The moon in the sky brought me news that you are waiting and here I am.' Mahendra stepped forward and made to sit on the bed.

But Binodini sat up in startled surprise, stretched out her right arm and said, 'Go, go away—you must not sit on this bed.'

The wind went out of the ship's sail and it faltered to a halt—Mahendra stood there, dumbfounded. He couldn't speak for a few minutes. Lest he refused to obey her, Binodini got off the bed and came to stand before him.

Mahendra asked, 'Then why have you dressed up—who are you waiting for?'

Binodini gripped her heart and said, 'The one I wait for is right here, in my soul.'

Mahendra said, 'Who is it? Is it Behari?'

Binodini said, 'Don't you dare utter his name.'

Mahendra said, revelation striking him, 'Is he the reason why you are roaming around in the west?'

Binodini replied, 'Yes, he is.'

Mahendra said, 'And he is the one you are waiting for now?'

Binodini said, 'Yes, he is.'

Mahendra asked, 'Have you found his address?'

Binodini said, 'No, I haven't—but I'll get it somehow.'

Mahendra said, 'I shall not let you find it.'

Binodini said, 'Even if you do that, you cannot take him out of my heart.'

Binodini closed her eyes and perceived Behari within her heart at once.

Thus intensely attracted to and violently rebuffed by this image of a beflowered yet disdainful Binodini, Mahendra suddenly grew fierce—he clenched his fists in rage and said, 'I shall take a dagger, rip your heart out and remove him from it.'

Binodini spoke with unruffled detachment, 'Your dagger will enter my heart more easily than your love.'

Mahendra said in baffled wonder, 'Why are you not afraid of me—who is there to protect you here?'

Binodini said simply, 'You are there—you will protect me even from yourself.'

Mahendra said, 'So there is still this much respect and trust left?'

Binodini said, 'Otherwise, I'd rather have killed myself than set off with you.'

Mahendra said, 'You should have. Why have you hung that slender noose of modest faith around my neck and dragged me around the country? Just think how much good will come of your death!'

Binodini said, 'I know that; but I cannot die as long as my hopes of Behari live.'

Mahendra said, 'As long as you don't die, my aspirations won't die either—I shall not be free. From this day on I shall pray to God with all my heart that you should die. Don't belong to me; don't belong to Behari. Just go. Set me free. My mother weeps, my wife weeps—their tears lacerate me from afar. Unless you die and go beyond my aspirations, I shall not get the chance to wipe away their tears.'

Mahendra rushed out of the room. He ripped away the lacy webs of illusion that Binodini had been weaving in solitude. Binodini stood in silence and gazed out of the window—the skyful of moonlight had disappeared, taking with it the magical nectar. The manicured lawn, the river bed beyond, the inky depths of the water and the obscurity of the other bank—all seemed like a pencil sketch on a large white sheet of paper—quite dreary and hollow.

Today, when she realized afresh just how intensely she'd fascinated Mahendra, how she'd uprooted him like a terrible storm and felled him to the ground, Binodini grew more agitated. She had all these powers. Why then did Behari not come and crash at her feet like the swollen waves on a full-moon night? Why did the powerful memory of a redundant love come sobbing into her meditation every day? An unfamiliar lament continually intruded and stopped her own inner dirge from being fulfilled. What would she do for the rest of her life with this massive upheaval that she had caused? How would she calm it and lay it to rest?

As she realized that the flowers decking her had attracted Mahendra's appreciative gaze, she tore away at them. All her powers, her efforts, her life were in vain—this garden, the moonlight, the river banks, this picturesque world were all in vain.

Such futility—and yet everything stood exactly where it had earlier. Nothing mattered in the least in this world. The sun wouldn't fail to rise tomorrow and life wouldn't forget the tiniest of details. And Behari—impassive and detached—would stay distant as before and teach Vasant a new lesson from his textbook.

Tears welled up in Binodini's eyes. What was this unyielding stone that she was trying to move with all her strength? Her heart knew bloodshed every day, but her fate didn't move an inch from its place!

## 52

Mahendra didn't sleep all night—but towards dawn sleep overcame his tired body. He woke up at around nine and sat up hastily. The anguish from last night had threaded its way into his sleep. The moment he was awake Mahendra felt the pain afresh. Within a few moments the events of the night before came flooding back to him. In the scorching late-morning heat, the fatigue of a fitful night set in and his life appeared quite distasteful to his eyes. Why was he bearing this burden, leaving his family, feeling the guilt of going astray and enduring the discomforts of a nomadic life? In the stark morning light Mahendra suddenly felt he was not in love with Binodini. He glanced at the street and saw the whole world rushing about, people getting on with their work. The stupidity inherent in forfeiting all self-esteem and dedicating his whole, redundant life to the feet of an unwilling woman was suddenly apparent to him. On the heels of a tremendous passion comes terrible fatigue—the weary heart wants to keep away the object of its desire for some time. In these times of waning, when the tide is at an ebb, the sludge and grime of the river bed is clearly visible—the object of desire then provokes revulsion. Today, Mahendra could not understand why he had been dragging himself pointlessly through the mud all these days. He said, 'I am superior to Binodini in every way and yet I endure all kinds of insults and injury and follow her around like a hideous beggar—what kind of a devil put such strange ideas in my head!' Today, Binodini seemed like any other woman and nothing more. When the wonderful glow that had emanated from the world around her and from the poetry and tales involving her vanished suddenly like a mirage, all that was left was an ordinary woman, with nothing to set her apart from the rest.

Mahendra grew impatient, wishing to extricate himself from this insufferable web of illusion and head home at once. The peace, love and affection he had once experienced at home, now seemed like the most sought after elixir to him. He realized that Behari's loyal friendship of many years was the most precious thing in the world. Mahendra said to himself, 'Since it is easy to drown yourself effortlessly into that which is truly profound and eternal, we take it for granted and do not realize its true worth. And since the restless illusion, which brings no pleasure even if you drain it to the dregs, leads us by the nose and makes us dance a merry dance to its tune, we take it to be the most desirable thing.'

He decided, 'I'll go home today—let Binodini stay wherever she wants to stay. I'll make the arrangements and then I'll be free.' As he uttered the words, 'I'll be free', a tremor of delight shook Mahendra's being; he felt the burden of incessant quandary that he had carried around all these days suddenly lifting. For so long, he had been forced to do in one instant what had seemed odious to him a moment ago—he didn't have the power to assert himself; every command that came from his conscience was strangled as he took the other road instead. Today, when he asserted 'I'll be free', his vacillating heart found shelter at least and applauded him.

Mahendra left the bed instantly, washed his face and went to meet Binodini. He found her door closed. He banged on it and asked, 'Are you asleep?'

Binodini said, 'No. Go away now.'

Mahendra said, 'I need to speak to you—it won't take long.'

Binodini said, 'I don't wish to speak to you or hear anything any more—go away, don't bother me now; I wish to be alone.'

At any other time, this rejection would have made Mahendra's heart grow more impassioned. But today he only felt disgust. He thought, 'I have sunk myself so low in this ordinary woman's esteem that she has acquired the right to dismiss me at any time, in any manner! This is not her rightful privilege. It is I who gave it to her and made her think too much of herself.' This rebuff made Mahendra resolute to establish his own superiority to himself. He said, 'I shall win—I'll break her hold over me and I'll go away.'

After lunch Mahendra went to the bank to pick up money. Thereafter he roamed the shops of Allahabad in search of some nice things to buy for Asha and his mother.

Once again, there were knocks on Binodini's door. At first she was irritated and didn't respond. But when the knocking went on, she lost her temper and hurled the door open as she shouted, 'Why must you disturb me again and again?' But her last words hung unspoken in the air. She had seen Behari standing outside.

Behari glanced inside just to check if Mahendra was there. The room was strewn with withered flowers and torn garlands. His heart turned sour in one instant. Away from Binodini, Behari had often been beset by doubts about her, but his imagination was powerful enough to shroud his doubts of immorality and paint a pretty picture over it all. Yet, as he entered the farmhouse, he had shuddered and cringed lest the image in his heart be shattered. Standing at Binodini's door, he received the very jolt he'd dreaded.

From afar, Behari had once imagined that with the power of his love he'd be able to wash away all the grime from Binodini's life. But now, close at hand, he realized it wouldn't be easy—his heart was scarcely filled with compassion! The sudden waves of revulsion that rose within him took him by surprise. He found Binodini looking quite listless.

Behari turned away and called, 'Mahin da, Mahin da.'

Binodini spoke in soft and gentle tones, 'Mahendra is not here, he has gone to the city.'

When Behari made as if to leave, Binodini said, 'Behari-thakurpo, I beg of you, you must sit here awhile.'

Behari had decided he wouldn't give in to any plea and he would remove himself from this hideous scene instantly. But the pathetic pleading in Binodini's tone held him rooted to the spot for a second.

Binodini said, 'If you turn away and leave today, I swear on you that I shall give up my life.'

Behari turned around and asked, 'Why do you try to entangle me in your life? What have I ever done to you? I have never stood in your way or meddled in your joys and sorrows.'

Binodini said, 'I have once told you just how much you mean to me—you did not believe me. Today, faced with your disgust, I shall say the same thing again. You have not given me the time to communicate this wordlessly, or coyly. You have pushed me away and yet, I hold your feet as I say that I—'

Behari interrupted her, 'Don't say those words ever again. There's no way I can believe them now.'

Binodini said, 'Other people may hold their presumptions true, but you too? That's why I have asked you to sit awhile.'

Behari said, 'How does it matter if I believe it or not? Your life will go on as before.'

Binodini said, 'I know it will not make a difference to you. I am so unfortunate that I shall never be able to take my place beside you with honour and esteem. I will have to stay away from you. But my soul wishes to lay just one claim on you—wherever I am, you must think well of me. I know that once you had felt a little respect for me—I shall hold that dear to my heart. That's why you have to hear me out. I beg of you Thakurpo, sit awhile.'

'All right, let's go,' Behari made as if to go someplace else.

Binodini said, 'Thakurpo, it is not what it seems. This room hasn't been touched by dishonour. You had once slept in this room—I have dedicated it to your memory; those flowers were used to worship your thoughts and they lie there now, withered and lifeless. You must sit in this very room.'

Behari felt a secret thrill course through him. He stepped into the room. Binodini silently indicated the bed to him. Behari sat on the bed—Binodini sat on the floor at his feet. At this, he tried to rise in haste and she said, 'Thakurpo, sit down. For my sake, do not get up. I am not even fit to sit at your feet—you are kind enough to give me that space; even if I am far away from you, I shall retain that privilege.'

Binodini was silent for some time. Suddenly, she remembered something and looked up. 'Thakurpo, have you eaten?'

Behari said, 'I ate at the station.'

Binodini said, 'Why did you send back the letter that I'd written to you from the village, through Mahendra?'

Behari said, 'But I did not receive any letter.'

Binodini asked, 'Didn't you and Mahendra meet in Kolkata?'

Behari said, 'I met Mahendra the day after I dropped you off at your village. Soon after that I left for the west and I have never met him since then.'

Binodini inquired again, 'Before that, did you read a letter from me and send it back without an answer once?'

Behari said, 'No, I've never done that.'

Binodini sat there, speechless. Then she heaved a sigh and said, 'Now I know what happened. And now I must tell you everything. If you believe me, I shall consider myself fortunate; if you don't I won't blame you—it is difficult to believe me.'

Behari's heart had melted. He couldn't bring himself to affront the devotion of the pious, devout Binodini. He said, 'Bouthan, you do not have to say anything—I believe you entirely. I am not capable of hating you. Please do not say another word.'

Binodini's tears flowed unchecked as she touched his feet in gratitude. She said, 'I shall die if I don't confess everything to you. You must be patient and hear me out. I surrendered myself to the sentence you meted out to me. In spite of not getting a single letter from you, I would have spent the rest of my life enduring the jibes and taunts of the villagers; I would have gladly settled for your reprimand instead of your love. But fate denied me that too. The sins that I gave birth to, didn't let me remain in exile. Mahendra came to the village, to my door and dishonoured me before everyone. I could no longer stay in the village. I hunted high and low for you, in order to seek your judgement a second time. But I couldn't find you. Mahendra brought back my letter to you, opened, and betrayed my trust. I thought you had given up on me forever. After this, I could have sunk to my doom—but you have untold powers, you can protect one even from afar. I could remain chaste only because I have placed you in my heart. The day you sent me away you revealed your true self, the harsh self, as harsh as pure gold, as harsh as the uncut diamond—it stayed lodged in my heart and made me precious too; my lord, I swear at your feet that its purity has not been defiled.'

Behari sat there in silence. Binodini did not say another word. The afternoon sun had begun to lose its glare. At this point Mahendra returned—and stood stunned seeing Behari. The indifference to Binodini that had taken over his mind was nearly driven out by a sudden force of burning envy. When the slighted Mahendra found Binodini sitting at Behari's feet, his pride was wounded. He was left in no doubt that this meeting was a consequence of prolonged correspondence between Binodini and Behari. All these days Behari had been away; now if he came to her, who could stop Binodini from rushing to him? Today, on seeing Behari, Mahendra realized that he could let go of Binodini, but he couldn't give her up to another man.

In thwarted anger, Mahendra hurled harsh sarcasm at Binodini, 'So now it is exit Mahendra and enter Behari on stage, is it? Quite a pretty scene—one feels like clapping. But I do hope this is the last act. Nothing else can follow this one.'

Binodini's face turned red. Since she had been forced to take Mahendra's help, she had no answer for this slur—she merely cast a fervent glance at Behari.

Behari got up, took a step forward and said, 'Mahin da, you will not insult Binodini like a coward; if your civility doesn't forbid you from doing so, I have the right to forbid you.'

Mahendra laughed. 'Oh, so we have already worked out rights and all, eh? Let us give you a name from this day—Binod-Behari!'

When Behari realized that the invectives were crossing their limits, he gripped Mahendra's hands and said, 'Mahin da, let me inform you that I intend to marry Binodini; from now on do control your language.'

At these words Mahendra went speechless with surprise and Binodini looked up, startled. The blood rushed to her ears.

Behari said, 'I have something else to tell you—your mother is on her deathbed; there's no hope for her. I am leaving tonight. Binodini will come with me.'

Binodini was stunned. 'Aunty is ill?'

Behari said, 'Fatally. Anything can happen at any time.'

Mahendra left the room without saying another word.

Binodini said to Behari, 'How could the words that you just spoke come from your lips! Is it a joke?'

Behari said, 'No, I spoke the truth. I would like to marry you.'

Binodini said, 'So that you can save this sinner?'

Behari said, 'No. It's because I love you and respect you.'

Binodini said, 'This will be my final reward. That you have accepted me is all I could ever hope for. Anything more will not last, and the heavens won't stand for it.'

Behari asked, 'But why not?'

Binodini went red. 'Oh, for shame, even the thought is shameful. I am a widow, I am tarnished—I shall bring dishonour to your name in the eyes of society—no, no, this cannot happen. For pity's sake, never say these words again.'

Behari said, 'Then, you will leave me?'

Binodini replied, 'I do not have the right to leave you. You are involved in beneficial activities for others—give me some duties in one of your missions. I shall perform them all my life and consider myself at your service. But for pity's sake—you cannot marry a widow. Your generosity may have room for anything, but if I do this and ruin your name in society, I shall not be able to hold up my head for the rest of my life.'

Behari said again, 'But Binodini, I love you.'

Binodini said, 'I shall use that privilege today to take just one liberty.'

She knelt on the ground and kissed his feet. She sat at his feet and said, 'I shall pray that I have you in my next birth—in this lifetime I hope for no more, I deserve no more. I have inflicted much misery, received much sorrow, I have learnt a lot. If I had forgotten those lessons, I would have sunk lower by dragging you with me. But since you remain on your pedestal, I am able to hold my head high today—I shall not raze this monument to the ground.'

Behari was silent and grave.

Binodini pleaded with folded hands, 'Don't misunderstand me—you will not be happy marrying me. I, too, will lose my self-esteem. You have always been detached and contented with your lot. Stay that way—I shall serve you from afar. I hope you will be happy and fulfilled.'

## 53

Mahendra was about to enter his mother's room when Asha quickly stepped out and said, 'Don't go in there now.'

Mahendra asked, 'But why?'

Asha said, 'The doctor has said that if Mother gets a sudden shock, of joy or sorrow, the consequences may be grave.'

Mahendra said, 'Let me go and stand by her bedside quietly, just this once—she wouldn't know a thing.'

Asha said, 'The slightest sound is enough to startle her these days—she'll know as soon as you enter the room.'

Mahendra said, 'So what do you suggest?'

Asha said, 'Let Behari-thakurpo come and have a look first—we'll do as he says.'

As she spoke, Behari arrived. Asha had sent for him.

Behari said, 'Bouthan, did you send for me? How is Mother?'

Asha seemed relieved to see Behari. She said, 'After you left, Mother seemed to grow more restless. The first day, when she didn't see you she asked me, "Where is Behari?" I said, "He has gone on some urgent work. He'll be back by Thursday." Ever since then she starts at the slightest sound. She doesn't say anything but she seems to be waiting for someone. When I got your telegram yesterday, I knew that you'll be here today. She heard that and she's arranged a special meal for you today. She sent for all the things that you like to eat; she also arranged for the cooking to be done in the veranda upfront so that she could supervise it from her bed. She refused to obey the doctor's instructions. A little while ago she called me and said, "Bou-ma, you will cook everything with your own hands. I shall sit with him during his meal."'

Behari's eyes grew moist at these words. He asked, 'How is she feeling?'

Asha replied, 'Come and take a look yourself. I feel her condition has worsened.'

Behari stepped into the room. Mahendra stood outside in stunned silence. Asha had taken up the responsibility of the household with ease—how effortlessly she forbade Mahendra from entering the room! There was no hesitation, no hurt. Mahendra's position was so weak today. He was culpable, he stood outside the door silently—he couldn't even enter his mother's room.

It was also surprising how comfortably Asha spoke to Behari! Her entire discussion was with him alone. Behari was the sole guardian of this household today, dear to everyone. He had access everywhere and everyone took his advice. Mahendra had left the space vacant for a while and on his return he found it was no longer there for him to lay claims on.

As Behari approached her bedside, Rajlakshmi laid her grief-stricken eyes on his face and said, 'Behari, you're back!'

Behari said, 'Yes Mother, I am back.'

Rajlakshmi asked, 'Is your work done?'

She looked at him with eager anticipation. Behari smiled cheerfully and said, 'Yes Mother, my mission is accomplished and I have no more worries.' He glanced at the door as he spoke.

Rajlakshmi said, 'Today Bou-ma will cook for you and I shall supervise. The doctors forbid me, but what is the point of all this, my child! Must I leave without once watching you all eat heartily?'

Behari said, 'I don't see why the doctors should object—it won't do if you don't supervise everything. Ever since we were children, we have learnt to love food cooked only by you—Mahin da is heartily sick of the daal and roti they serve in the west—he'd be delighted to have some of your fish curry. Today, we two brothers will compete with each other and eat like old times—let's hope your Bou-ma cooks enough rice.'

Although Rajlakshmi knew that Behari had brought Mahendra along, the very mention of his name made her heart leap and she found it difficult to draw breath. When the feeling passed, Behari said, 'Mahin da's health has improved from the change of air. Today he's a little drawn due to the travails of the journey—nothing that a shower and a proper meal wouldn't put right.'

Rajlakshmi still didn't take her son's name. So Behari said, 'Mother, Mahin da is waiting outside the door. He cannot come in unless you call him in.'

Rajlakshmi glanced at the door mutely. Immediately, Behari called out, 'Mahin da, come in.'

Mahendra stepped into the room slowly. Rajlakshmi couldn't bring herself to look at his face for fear that her heart would suddenly miss a beat and stop entirely. She lowered her eyes. Mahendra looked towards the bed and got the shock of his life—he felt someone had dealt him a mortal wound. He fell at his mother's feet and placed his head on them. Rajlakshmi shuddered as her heart raced with emotion.

A little later Annapurna spoke softly, 'Didi, please ask Mahin to get up or he'll stay there forever.'

Rajlakshmi opened her mouth with difficulty and murmured, 'Mahin, get up.'

As she said his name, after an age, the tears welled up and rolled down her cheeks. They lightened the burden on her heart. Mahendra rose, knelt on the floor and sat close to his mother. Rajlakshmi turned over with difficulty, took his head in both her hands, fondly breathed in the scent of his hair and kissed his forehead.

Mahendra choked with emotion as he said, 'Mother, I have hurt you no end—please forgive me.'

Now much calmer, Rajlakshmi said, 'Don't talk that way Mahin—how can I live without forgiving you? Bou-ma—where's Bou-ma?'

Asha was cooking Rajlakshmi's food in the next room. Annapurna went and fetched her. Rajlakshmi gestured to Mahendra to get off the floor and to sit upon the bed. When he did so, Rajlakshmi indicated the spot beside him and said, 'Bou-ma, you sit here—today I want to make you sit beside each other and take my fill of the sight—that'll ease all my misery. Bou-ma—don't be shy, and cast away your grudges against Mahin—come and sit here, just for once. Let me feast my eyes, child.'

Asha raised her anchal, veiled her head and bashfully, with a trembling heart and a gentle tread, she came and sat beside Mahendra. Rajlakshmi picked up Asha's right hand and pressed it into Mahendra's hand as she said, 'Mahin, I leave this child of mine in your care—mark my words Mahin, you won't find a finer woman anywhere. Mejo-bou, come and bless them; let your virtue prove benevolent for them.'

When Annapurna came forward, the couple was in tears as they bent low and touched her feet. She kissed their foreheads and said, 'May God bless you.'

Rajlakshmi said, 'Behari, come my son, come here and say you forgive Mahin.'

Instantly, Behari came and stood in front of Mahendra, who drew him to his bosom with a firm pull and held him in a tight embrace.

Rajlakshmi said, 'Mahin, I pray to God that Behari stays as close to you as he has been since your childhood—it would be the greatest boon for you.'

Rajlakshmi was tired by now and she fell silent. Behari held a revitalizing drug to her lips, but she pushed it away and said, 'No more medicines, my child. Now let me think of God—He would administer the final cure to release me from all wordly pains. Mahin, you go and rest for a while. Bou-ma, you get started on the cooking.'

That evening, Behari and Mahendra's place was laid in front of Rajlakshmi's bed as they sat down to eat. Rajlakshmi had given Asha the responsibility of serving food and she began to serve them.

Mahendra's heart was surging with tears and he could scarcely eat. Rajlakshmi coaxed him again and again, 'Mahin, why aren't you eating anything? Eat heartily—let me watch and be happy.'

Behari said, 'You know him, Mother, he's always been that way. He can hardly eat anything. Bouthan, you must give me some more of that curry, it's really delicious.'

Rajlakshmi was delighted and she smiled as she said, 'I know Behari loves that curry. Bou-ma, that's not enough, give him some more.'

Behari said, 'This daughter-in-law of yours is so tight-fisted—nothing slips through her fingers.'

Rajlakshmi laughed. 'Look at that Bou-ma—Behari is critiquing you even as he eats your food!'

Asha plied Behari with a ladleful of curry.

Behari said, 'Oh dear me, I suppose I'll have to make do with the curry and all the other delicacies will go to Mahin da!'

Asha chastized him in a whisper, 'The critic's lips can never be sealed.'

Behari replied softly, 'Try some rice pudding and see if it works!'

When the two friends had finished their meal, Rajlakshmi sighed with pleasure and said, 'Bou-ma, you go and have your meal quickly.'

Asha left to do her bidding and Rajlakshmi said to Mahendra, 'Mahin, you go to bed now.'

Mahendra said, 'Why should I go to bed so early?'

He had decided he'd stay up at his mother's bedside that night. But Rajlakshmi wouldn't hear of it. She said, 'Mahin, you are tired, go to bed.'

After her meal, Asha picked up a hand-fan and tried to sit by Rajlakshmi's bed. But the latter conspiratorially whispered to her, 'Bou-ma, just check if Mahin's bed has been made—he is all alone.'

Asha nearly died of shame and made her escape from the room, leaving Behari and Annapurna behind. Rajlakshmi asked Behari, 'Tell me something Behari—do you know what became of Binodini? Where is she now?'

Behari replied, 'Binodini is in Kolkata now.'

In reply to Rajlakshmi's unuttered question, Behari said, 'Mother, don't be afraid of Binodini causing you any more grief.'

'She has caused me a lot of grief, Behari, but deep in my heart I care about her.'

'And she cares about you, Mother.'

'I feel the same, Behari. No one is perfect, but she must have cared about me. No one can fake that kind of tender ministration.'

Behari said, 'She is eager to nurse you again.'

Rajlakshmi sighed and said, 'Mahin and Asha have gone to bed—what's the harm in sending for her in the night?'

Behari said, 'Mother, she is hiding in one of the rooms in this very house. I haven't been able to get her to take even a drop of water through the day—she has vowed that until you send for her and forgive her, she won't have anything to eat or drink.'

Rajlakshmi was concerned. 'Starving the whole day—oh dear, send for her, quick!'

The moment Binodini stepped into her room hesitantly, Rajlakshmi said, 'Shame on you, Binodini, what have you done? You have starved yourself the whole day! Go and eat first and then we'll talk.'

Binodini touched Rajlakshmi's feet and said, 'Aunty, first you must forgive this sinner and only then will I eat.'

Rajlakshmi said, 'I do forgive you, my child—I am no longer angry with anyone.'

She took Binodini's hand in hers and said, 'May you be happy and may no one be harmed by you.'

Binodini said, 'Your blessing won't go in vain, Aunty. I swear at your feet, no harm will befall this household on my account.'

Binodini bowed low and touched Annapurna's feet, too, before she left to have her dinner. When she came back Rajlakshmi looked at her and said, 'Are you leaving now?'

Binodini said, 'Aunty, I will attend to you. As God is my witness, you have nothing to fear from me.'

Rajlakshmi glanced at Behari. He gave it some thought and said, 'Let Bouthan stay, it won't do any harm.'

That night Binodini, Behari and Annapurna nursed Rajlakshmi together.

Meanwhile, Asha woke up very early the next morning, abashed at not having gone into Rajlakshmi's room even once through the night. She left Mahendra still asleep in bed, washed and changed before she came downstairs. The dark of the night still lingered. When she came and stood at Rajlakshmi's door, the sight that greeted her eyes made her wonder if she was dreaming.

Binodini was heating some water over a spirit lamp; it was to make some tea for Behari who hadn't slept all night long. When she saw Asha, Binodini stood up and said, 'Today, with my burden of crimes, I seek refuge from you. No one else can evict me, but if you say "go", I will leave this very minute.'

Asha couldn't say a word—she couldn't even fathom what her heart was saying. She just stood there, overwhelmed.

Binodini said, 'You'll never be able to forgive me—don't even try it. But please, do not fear me any more. Please let me stay here and serve

Aunty as long as she is in need of it. Afterwards, I shall leave.'

The day before, when Rajlakshmi had placed Asha's hand in Mahendra's, Asha had wiped away all traces of hurt and rejection and surrendered herself to Mahendra all over again. But today as Binodini stood before her, the pangs of her rejected love refused to be calmed. The thought that swelled in her bosom was that Mahendra had once loved this woman, and perhaps he still loved her deep in his heart. In a short while Mahendra would wake up, he'd see Binodini—how would he feel? The night before Asha had perceived her whole life to be free of thorns henceforth. But this morning she found the thorny bush planted right at her doorstep. Joy was the most delicate of objects—there was scarcely a place to keep it safe.

With a heavy heart Asha stepped into Rajlakshmi's room and with great mortification she said, 'Aunty, you have stayed up all night—go to sleep now.' Annapurna looked at Asha's face searchingly. Then, instead of going to bed, she took Asha to her room and said, 'Chuni, if you want to be happy, try and forget what happened. The misery of remembering the crimes of others is greater than the pleasure in laying the blame at their door.'

Asha said, 'Aunty, I do not want to remember—I want to forget—but I can't.'

Annapurna said, 'Child, you are right. It's easier said than done. Let me tell you a way of doing it—you must keep the pretense alive that you have forgotten everything. If you succeed outwardly, it'll also take root in your heart. Keep this in mind, Chuni—if you do not forget, you'll keep it alive in others' minds too. If you cannot do it on your own, I command you hereby—behave with Binodini as if she has never done you any harm and neither is she capable of it.'

Asha humbly asked, 'Please tell me what I must do.'

Annapurna said, 'Binodini is making tea for Behari right now. You take the cups, saucers, milk and sugar—work together, the two of you.'

Asha rose to obey her command. Annapurna said, 'This was easy, but I will tell you something much more difficult, which you must do. There will be times when Mahendra will run into Binodini and I know what will pass through your mind—at those times, you must not try to see Mahendra's or Binodini's reaction, even with a covert peep. Even if your heart breaks, you must stay unruffled. Mahendra must come to think that you do not suspect him, you do not grieve, you nurse no fears or worries—things are exactly the same as they were once, before the rift; even the traces of the fissure have vanished. Mahendra, or anyone else for that matter, should not look at you and feel weighed down by guilt. Chuni, this is not a request or advice; this is your aunt's command. When I go back to Kashi you must not forget this for even an instant.'

Asha fetched the teacups and saucers and approached Binodini, 'Is the water ready? I've brought milk for the tea.'

Binodini looked at Asha in amazement and said, 'Behari-thakurpo is sitting on the veranda—you have the tea sent to him while I go and arrange for Aunty to wash her face; she should be waking up any minute.'

Binodini did not take the tea to Behari. She felt embarrassed to claim the rights that he had granted her by admitting her love for him. In order to retain the due respect for privileges, one must use them judiciously. Only the beggar would pull and stretch at his whole booty at once. The true worth of wealth lay in savouring it prudently. Now Binodini couldn't bring herself to go in front of Behari under some pretext, unless he sent for her specifically.

As she finished speaking, Mahendra arrived on the scene. Although Asha's heart missed a beat, she composed herself quickly and addressed him calmly, 'Haven't you woken up early today? I shut the doors and windows lest the sunlight wakes you.'

When Mahendra found Asha speaking to him so normally in Binodini's presence, a burden seemed to lift off his heart. He replied cheerfully, 'I've come to check on Mother—is she still asleep?'

Asha said, 'Yes, she's sleeping—don't go in there now. Behari-thakurpo has said she is much better today. After many days, she slept through the night last night.'

Mahendra was relieved. 'Where is Aunty?'

Asha showed him to Annapurna's room.

Binodini, too, was taken aback to see this calm and controlled Asha.

Mahendra called, 'Aunty!'

Annapurna had finished her bath at the crack of dawn and was about to sit down to her puja, but she called out, 'Come, Mahin, come.'

Mahendra touched her feet and said, 'Aunty, I have sinned and I hate to stand before you thus.'

Annapurna said, 'Oh no, don't talk that way Mahin—the little boy comes to his mother's lap even when he's covered in mud.'

Mahendra said, 'But this mud cannot be washed off.'

Annapurna said, 'A few flicks, a good dusting down and it'll be gone. Mahin, it's all for the best—you were very proud of your ideals, you were too confident in your beliefs—the squall of sins has shattered your arrogance but left you unharmed.'

Mahendra said, 'Aunty, this time we won't let you go—your absence brought all this upon us.'

Annapurna said, 'If the mishap was held at bay by my presence alone, it is better that it has taken its toll. Now you will not need me any more.'

There was another voice at the door, 'Aunty, are you doing your puja?'

Annapurna said, 'No, you may come in.'

Behari stepped into the room. When he found Mahendra awake at this early hour, he said, 'Mahin da, this is perhaps the first time that you are seeing the rising sun!'

Mahendra said, 'Yes Behari, it's my first sunrise. Perhaps you need to discuss something with Aunty—I'll be off then.'

Behari laughed. 'You can be included in the cabinet of ministers. I have never concealed anything from you and if you have no objections, I won't start doing so now.'

Mahendra laughed. 'Objections and me! But of course, I can no longer demand it. If you do not conceal anything from me, I shall be able to respect myself again.'

These days it was rather difficult to say everything in Mahendra's presence. Behari nearly stumbled, but he went on resolutely, 'My marriage to Binodini was a subject broached earlier and I have come to conclude the discussion with Aunty.'

Mahendra shrank away and Annapurna looked up in surprise. 'What's all this, Behari!'

Mahendra made a great effort and shrugged away his qualms. 'Behari, there is no need for this marriage.'

Annapurna asked, 'Is Binodini with you on this talk of marriage?'

Behari said, 'Not one bit.'

Annapurna said, 'Will she agree to this?'

Mahendra spoke up, 'Why wouldn't she agree to it, Aunty? I know that she is devoted to Behari—why would she throw away this chance of a safe haven?'

Behari said, 'Mahin da, I proposed marriage to Binodini—she has turned it down.'

At this Mahendra fell silent.

## 54

For Rajlakshmi, the next two or three days passed somehow, with some good moments and some bad. One morning her face grew contented and all signs of pain vanished. She sent for Mahendra and said, 'I don't have much time—but I die in peace, Mahin, I have no regrets. Today my heart wells with the same kind of joy that I once felt, when you were a child. You are the apple of my eye, my own little boy—I am taking with me all your troubles and that fills me with joy.' Rajlakshmi stroked his face and arms. Mahendra couldn't check his tears as the sobs rose to his throat.

Rajlakshmi said, 'Don't weep, Mahin; the queen of grace is still in your home. Give the household keys to Bou-ma. I have kept everything in order—you two wouldn't lack for anything in the house. One other thing, Mahin, don't tell anyone before I die—there are two thousand rupees in my box that I bequeath to Binodini. She is a widow, all alone in this world—the interest from this money would suffice for her. But Mahin, my request to you is don't keep her within the walls of your own home.'

Rajlakshmi sent for Behari and said, 'Behari my son, Mahin was telling me that you have bought a property where you want to treat impoverished gentlemen. May God grant you a long life to do the poor a good turn. At the time of my marriage my father-in-law had gifted me a village, I bequeath that to you. Use it to serve the poor; it'll bring peace to my father-in-law's soul.'

## 55

When the last rites for Rajlakshmi were concluded, Mahendra said, 'Dear Behari, I have studied medicine—please make me a part of your mission. With the way Chuni has gained control over the household chores, she'd be able to lend you a hand too. We shall all live there.'

Behari said, 'Mahin da, please think this through—would this work satisfy you at all times? Don't take on permanent duties in the throes of a sudden surge of altruism.'

Mahendra said, 'Behari, you think about it too—the life that I have made for myself, can no longer be savoured at leisure. If I do not occupy myself with a worthwhile cause, my restless soul can haul me into the nadir of despair one day. You must make room for me in your mission.'

So it was decided.

When it was time for them to say goodbye, Annapurna and Behari sat immersed in restful sorrow, discussing the days past. Binodini came and stood at the door. 'Aunty, may I sit here for a while?'

Annapurna said, 'Come, come, my child—sit.'

Binodini came in and sat down. Annapurna spoke a few words with her and then under the pretext of making her bed, she went into the veranda.

Binodini asked Behari, 'Tell me what I should do now—what is your command?'

Behari said, 'Bouthan, why don't you tell me what you want to do?'

Binodini said, 'I've heard that you have taken a house by the Ganga to treat poor patients. I'd like to be of some use to you there. If nothing else, I could cook there.'

Behari said, 'Bouthan, I have given this a lot of thought. Through circumstances the webs of our lives are now utterly tangled. The time has come for us to sit in solitude and undo the knots one by one. First, we must clear everything. Now I no longer have the courage to indulge in all that the heart desires. Without laying to rest every upheaval, every tumult that has resulted from the events till now, from all that we have borne, we cannot settle down and anticipate the end of our lives. If our pasts had been different, you are the only one who could have given my life completion—but now I must part from you. Now, it would be a vain effort to strive for happiness. Now we can only repair the damages slowly and surely.'

At this point Annapurna stepped into the room and Binodini said, 'Mother, you must give me shelter at your feet. Please don't push me away as a fallen woman.'

Annapurna said, 'Child, come then, come with me.'

On the day that Annapurna and Binodini were to go to Kashi, Behari sought out Binodini at some point and said, 'Bouthan, I want something from you—a mark—to keep with me always.'

Binodini said, 'What do I have to give, that you can keep as a mark, by your side forever?'

Abashed and diffident, Behari said, 'The English have a custom—they keep a few locks of the dear one's hair as a memento—if you—'

Binodini recoiled, 'Oh no—how shameful! What would you do with my hair? That tainted, dead item means nothing to me, that I would gift it to you. Hapless that I am, I could not be of any use to you—I'd like to gift you something that can help you in my stead. Will you accept it?'

Behari said, 'I will.'

Binodini untied the knot at the end of her anchal, took out two notes of a thousand rupees each and handed them to Behari.

Behari gazed at her steadily, his eyes alight with intense fervour. A little later he said, 'Is there nothing that I can give you?'

Binodini said, 'I have a mark from you, it graces my body—no one can take it away from me. I do not need anything more.' She showed him the scar on her elbow.

Behari was astounded. Binodini said, 'You may not be aware but this was given by you and it is worthy of you. Even you cannot take this back now.'

Despite her aunt's counsel, Asha had not been able to free her mind entirely of vitriol towards Binodini. They had nursed Rajlakshmi together, but every time Asha's eyes had fallen on Binodini, her heart had smarted, the words had dissolved on her tongue and the effort to smile had been painful. She had resented it if she had to accept even the slightest help from Binodini. She had accepted the paan made by Binodini out of courtesy but later thrown it away in distaste. But today, when it was time to take leave, when her aunt was departing from the household a second time, Asha's heart swelled with tears, and she found herself pitying Binodini too. There are few hearts hard enough to be incapable of forgiving the one who is taking leave forever. Asha was sure Binodini loved Mahendra—and why wouldn't she? Asha knew from her own heart just how inevitable it was to feel love for Mahendra. It was the anguish of this love that made her feel compassion for Binodini now. Asha could not wish upon her worst enemy the agony that Binodini was bound to feel as she left Mahendra forever; the very thought brought tears to Asha's eyes. In the past, she had loved Binodini and that love touched her heart again. Slowly she walked up to Binodini and with great compassion, affection and sadness, she said, 'Didi, so you are leaving?'

Binodini held up Asha's chin and said, 'Yes, my sister, it's time for me to leave. Once, in the past, you had loved me—now, in times of joy, set aside a bit of that love for me, my friend—and forget everything else.'

Mahendra came and touched Binodini's feet as he said, 'Bouthan, forgive me.' Two teardrops brimmed over the corners of his eyes and rolled down his cheeks.

Binodini said, 'You forgive me too, Thakurpo. May God grant you two eternal happiness.'

# The Shipwreck
## (Noukadubi)
*Translated by Sunanda Krishnamurty*

# 1

Nobody had any doubt that Ramesh would pass his law examination. The goddess of higher learning always rewarded him with medals and scholarships. He was supposed to go back home after his examinations, but he showed no enthusiasm to pack his cases. To his father's repeated queries he replied that he would come as soon as his results were announced.

Annada babu's son Jogendra was Ramesh's fellow student. He lived next door. Annada babu was a Brahmo. His daughter Hemnalini had taken her FA examination that year. Ramesh used to visit them often, ostensibly to have tea.

Hemnalini would stroll in the terrace after her bath, drying her hair and poring over her books. At the same time Ramesh too would go to the terrace of his house, sit in a corner and study. It was a good place to study, but full of distractions!

No proposal of marriage had come from either side. As far as Annada babu was concerned, there was a reason. He had set his hopes on a young man who had gone to England to become a barrister.

One afternoon there was a debate at the tea table. The gathering included Akshay. He had not passed many examinations, but his thirst for tea and for other things was not less than that of other young men. He was arguing that a man's brain was like an axe: even when blunt it could function well because of its weight. A woman's brain was like a penknife, no matter how sharp, it could not achieve very much. Hemnalini was prepared to ignore Akshay's impudence, but when Jogendra too argued to belittle women, Ramesh was incited and he began to praise womankind.

When Ramesh—in the course of his passionate outburst—had drunk a few more cups of tea than usual, the bearer came in to hand him a letter. It was from his father. He read the letter and stood up hastily in the middle of the debate. When asked what the matter was, he replied that his father was in town. Hemnalini suggested to her brother, 'Why don't you bring Ramesh babu's father here to have tea with us?' Ramesh said, 'Not today, I must leave now.' Akshay commented that Ramesh's father might have objections to eating here.

Ramesh's father Brojomohan babu announced, 'We must leave for home by tomorrow morning's train.' Ramesh asked, 'Is there some important work?' 'Nothing very important,' replied his father. Ramesh wondered and waited for an explanation, but his father did not offer any.

When Brojomohan babu went to visit his friends in the evening, Ramesh decided to write him a letter informing him of his unspoken bond with Hemnalini. But he could not proceed beyond 'Dear father'. He made several drafts, but tore them all up.

Brojomohan had his dinner and went to bed. Ramesh went to the terrace and gazed at his neighbour's house. Akshay left the house at nine o'clock; at nine-thirty the front door was closed; at ten o'clock the light in Annada babu's room was turned off and at ten-thirty all the lights were off and everyone seemed asleep.

Ramesh had to leave the next day by the early morning train. His father was watchful, giving him no opportunity to miss the train.

## 2

Ramesh learnt that he was to be married. Both the bride and the wedding date were fixed. When Brojomohan had not been so well off, his lawyer friend Ishan had helped him. Ishan died before his time, leaving debts, and his wife and daughter in penury. That daughter was now of marriageable age, and Brojomohan had arranged her match with Ramesh. Some so-called well-wishers had objected saying that the girl was not good-looking. Brojomohan had retorted, 'A human being is not like a flower or a butterfly that the question of beauty must be the most important. The girl's mother was a devoted wife, if the girl is like her mother, Ramesh should consider himself lucky.'

Ramesh blanched when he heard about his wedding. He thought of several plans of escape, but none seemed plausible. Finally, overcoming his hesitation, he went to his father and said, 'Father, I cannot agree to this marriage, I am pledged elsewhere.'

Brojomohan remarked, 'Is that so? Are you formally engaged?'

'Not quite a formal engagement, but . . .'

'Have you talked things over with the girl's family?'

'No, not quite, but . . .'

'Since nothing has been said, nothing need be said.'

After a while Ramesh said, 'It would be wrong of me to accept any other girl as my wife.'

'It might be a greater wrong to not do so,' said his father.

Ramesh could not offer any other argument. He could only hope for divine intervention. After the date fixed for his wedding there was no suitable date for the next one year. Ramesh hoped that somehow that day would pass and he would gain a reprieve of one year.

The bride's village was far away and could only be reached by boat. It would take three or four days to cross the rivers. Brojomohan began the journey on an auspicious day, leaving a week's margin to cover for eventualities.

The wind was favourable throughout, and they reached Shimulghata within three days. The girl and her mother were poor. Brojomohan had wished to bring them over to his own village and keep them in comfort, thereby paying back his debt to his dead friend. Earlier, he had hesitated to propose this since he was not related to them. Now, because of the marriage alliance, he could persuade the bride's mother to move. She too raised no objection, because all she had was her daughter and she wished to be near her and be like a mother to her son-in-law. Since they reached Shimulghata a few days before the wedding, Brojomohan started making the arrangements to wind up her establishment. He planned to take her back with them to their village after the wedding.

During the wedding Ramesh did not recite the vows properly, and kept his eyes closed when he was supposed to look at the bride. After the wedding, in the bridal chamber, he kept quiet through the teasing and merrymaking of the womenfolk and at night turned on his side, and slept on the edge of the bed. He left the room early in the morning.

On the return journey, the women got into one boat, the older men, in another and the bridegroom and his friends, in the third. The musicians and servants were in yet another boat, with the musicians playing all kinds of tunes in a haphazard manner.

The heat was unbearable and lasted all day. The sky was cloudless, yet covered in a faded hue, and the lines of trees on the riverbank were colourless. The leaves on the trees were still. The boatmen were covered in sweat. Before dark the boatmen said, 'Master, let us moor the boats by the landing stage of the river here, there is no place to moor ahead.' But Brojomohan babu did not want to delay. He said, 'Not now. The first part of the night can be done by moonlight, and the boats can be moored when we reach Baluhata. You will be rewarded for it.'

The boats went ahead. On one side was the barren sandy bank, on the other, the ragged, high shore. The moon rose in the mist, but was hazy like the eyes of a drunkard.

Suddenly, in that cloudless night they heard a roar. Looking back towards the horizon they saw a huge whirlwind speeding across the sky towards them, sweeping up branches, sticks, twigs, dust and sand in its wake. Within a few seconds, and before anyone could understand what was happening, disaster struck amidst shouts, screams and cries. A twister, speeding along a narrow channel, fiercely uprooted everything in its way and there was no knowing where it took the boats.

## 3

The mist cleared. Moonlight covered the vast stretch of sand like the white sari of a widow. The river had no boats, and no waves. Land and water both were peaceful and still as the peaceful stillness of death following the agony of illness.

Recovering consciousness Ramesh found himself on a sandbank. It took him some time to remember what had happened. It seemed like a nightmare. He walked along the bank in search of his father and other relatives, but saw no sign of anyone.

The small white island between two branches of the river Padma lay facing up like a naked infant. When Ramesh circled one bank and came to the edge of the other, he noticed something like a piece of red cloth at a distance. Rapidly approaching it, he saw that the bride, clad in a red sari, was lying there unconscious.

Ramesh knew the technique of artificial respiration, and applied it. Slowly she started breathing, and then she opened her eyes. Ramesh was extremely tired and sat quietly for a while. He did not even have the energy to ask her anything.

She was not fully conscious yet. Her eyes opened once, but closed immediately. Ramesh found that her breathing was normal. Then, in that deserted frontier between land and water, between life and death, and in the pale moonlight he gazed at her face.

Who said that Susheela was not pretty? Her tender face was small, yet in the moonlight, under the vast sky it had a unique quality, like a flower blooming in glory. Forgetting everything else Ramesh thought, 'I'm glad that I did not see her in the crowded and noisy wedding gathering. I couldn't have seen her in this way anywhere else but here. By bringing her back to life I have endeared her more than by reciting the wedding vows. There I would have received her as my due; here I have received her as a gift of God.'

Regaining consciousness, she sat up and covered her head with the edge of her sari. She asked Ramesh, 'Do you know where the others are?' He shook his head. Then he asked, 'Will you wait here while I look around for them?' She did not reply, but her gesture indicated: please don't leave me here alone.

Ramesh understood. He stood up and looked around. In the vast expanse of white sand there was no sign of anyone. He called out to them, but received no answer. Giving up his futile search he sat down and saw that his bride had covered her face with her hands and was trying to suppress her tears. Ramesh did not say anything to console her but sat close to her and patted her. Her suppressed tears burst out in sobs, Ramesh could not check his own tears either.

The moon had set. In the darkness, the desolate piece of land seemed like a strange dream. The subdued white of the sand was pale like the spirit world. In the dim light of the stars the river surface shimmered like the smooth black skin of a python.

Ramesh held her soft hands and drew her close. The frightened girl did not resist. She wished to be near someone. In that deep darkness, she found comfort and a safe haven in him. It was not the time to be shy. Eagerly she made a place for herself in his arms.

The morning star was disappearing in the light of dawn, and above the line of water the eastern sky turned from pale to bright red. Ramesh was asleep on the sand, and close to him, with her head resting on her arm; the bride too was in deep sleep. When the morning sunlight touched their eyelids, they woke up with a start. They looked around in wonder, then remembered that they were not in their home but had been swept ashore.

## 4

In the morning the river was etched with the white sails of the fishermen's boats. Ramesh called out to them, and with their help he hired a boat. He arranged a search for his relatives by the police, and returned home with his bride.

When his boat came to the village landing, he heard that the police had recovered the bodies of his father, his mother-in-law and a few other relatives and friends from the river. There was no hope of any survivors other than a few boatmen.

Ramesh's old grandmother was at home. When she saw Ramesh with his new bride, she started wailing. They could hear wailing from the houses of neighbours who had accompanied the wedding party. No one blew the conch shell; no one welcomed the bride or took any notice of her.

Ramesh had decided to move away to Kolkata with his wife when the *shraddha* ceremonies were over, but he had to wait to settle property-related matters. The bereaved women of his family wished to go on a pilgrimage, and he had to arrange that too.

Despite all this work, he found time to get to know his bride. Contrary to what they had heard earlier, she was not that young. In fact, the women of the village were making snide remarks about her age. Yet Ramesh, a BA degree holder, did not know how to win his girl-bride's heart; his books had no advice for him. Although his actual experience did not match what little he had read, yet a sweet emotion drew him to this young girl. In his imagination he saw his girl-bride in the future as the woman he would love, and as the mother of his children. Just as a painter or a poet visualizes and nurtures his future painting or poem, Ramesh nurtured the image in his heart; his girl-bride was a symbol.

## 5

After several months the property matters were settled, and the elderly women were ready for the pilgrimage. Meanwhile, a few women of the neighbourhood had got acquainted with the new bride. The bond of affection between Ramesh and his bride got stronger.

In the evening they would spread a mat on the terrace and sit together. Ramesh would often come from behind and cover her eyes with his hands, and hold her head on his chest. If the girl fell asleep early without having her dinner, he would wake her up, and tease her. Irritated, she would scold him.

One evening Ramesh shook her bun and said, 'Susheela, today your hairdo isn't nice.' She asked, 'Why do you people call me Susheela?' Ramesh was surprised; he did not know what she meant. She continued, 'You think that by changing my name, my luck will turn? Since my childhood I have been considered inauspicious; the stigma will remain as long as I live.'

Ramesh's heart missed a beat, he blanched. Something was terribly wrong. He asked, 'Why were you considered unlucky from your childhood?' She replied, 'My father passed away before my birth, and my mother died within six months after I was born. I was very unhappy in my maternal uncle's home. All of a sudden I heard that you had seen me and liked me. The wedding took place within two days, and then came the mishap on the river.'

Ramesh lay down; he was silent. The moonlit night seemed dark to him. He was afraid to ask any more questions, and wished to push away the little he had learnt as though it was a bad dream or a spell of delirium. The southern breeze of summer was blowing like the sigh of a person regaining consciousness. The sleepless cuckoo was singing in the moonlight; from the boats moored on the nearby riverbank, the song of the boatmen resonated in the sky. After some time, not hearing a sound from Ramesh, she touched him lightly and asked, 'Are you sleeping?' He replied, 'No.' He continued to be silent, and at some point she fell asleep. Ramesh sat up and gazed at her. In her beautiful face there was no indication of the strange twist of fate or its inevitable tragic outcome.

## 6

Ramesh realized that she was not his wife. But it was not easy to find out whose wife she was. He posed the question indirectly, 'When you first saw me during the wedding, how did you feel?'

She replied, 'I did not see you, I kept my eyes lowered.'

'Didn't you know my name?'

'I heard that I was to be married, and I was married the next day. I did not hear your name. My aunt was in a hurry to get me married and be rid of me.'

'You can read and write, let me see how you spell your name,' said Ramesh, as though testing her. He brought her a pen and paper. She said, 'As if I can't! It's very easy to spell my name.' Saying this she wrote in large letters: Kamala Devi.

'Write your uncle's name.' She wrote: Shri Tarinicharan Chattopadhyay. She asked, 'Have I made any mistake?' He replied, 'No. Write the name of your village.' She wrote: Dhobapukur.

What he learnt was not much, and not very useful. He thought about what he should do. Her husband had probably drowned. Even if one located her in-laws, they were unlikely to accept her. It would not be fair to send her back to her uncle. If her real position were disclosed, how would society react? She had been living as his wife in his home. Where would she find shelter? Even if her husband were alive, would he wish to, or dare to accept her? Wherever she might go, it would be like drowning in a bottomless ocean.

But he could not keep her with him in any guise other than his wife. There was no other place for her. Yet she could not live with him as his wife. Ramesh had fondly painted a colourful picture of her as the future Lakshmi of his home, but now it must be erased.

Ramesh could not stay on in the village. He left for Kolkata with Kamala, hoping to find a solution there. He rented a house far from where he had lived earlier.

Kamala was extremely eager to see Kolkata. As soon as she set foot in the house she sat by the window. The stream of passers-by filled her with wonder.

Their housemaid worked in the day and went home at night. They could not find a maid who would live in. Ramesh could no longer sleep in the same bed with Kamala, but she could not be expected to sleep alone in a room in the unfamiliar surroundings.

The maid left after dinner. Ramesh said, 'Go to bed, I will sleep after reading this book.' He opened a book and pretended to read. Kamala was tired and soon fell asleep. The next night again he sent Kamala to bed under some pretext. It was a warm night. He spread a mat on the open terrace in front of the bedroom and lay down. Many thoughts drifted through his mind as he fanned himself and finally fell asleep.

Around two or three in the morning, half asleep, he realized that he was not alone, someone was fanning him. Drowsily, he drew her to himself and said, 'Susheela, you don't have to fan me; go to bed.' Being afraid of the dark, she lay down with her arms around him and fell asleep.

When Ramesh woke up in the morning, he was startled to find that Kamala was sleeping next to him with her arms round his neck. She lay close to him claiming him trustingly. He recalled how she had come in the night and fanned him. He sighed, detached her gently, and left.

After a great deal of thought Ramesh decided to admit Kamala to a girls' school as a boarder. This way, he would get a temporary respite from his worry. He asked her, 'Kamala, would you like to study?' She looked at him enquiringly. Ramesh spoke at length about the usefulness of education and the satisfaction it gives, but it was unnecessary. Kamala eagerly said, 'Please teach me.' Ramesh said, 'You must go to school.' Kamala was surprised. 'School! I am too old to go to school.' Ramesh was amused, and pointed out that many of the students were older than her.

She did not say anything further, and went to the school with Ramesh. The building was large and there were many girls, both older and younger than her. When Ramesh was walking away leaving her with the principal, Kamala followed him. He said, 'You must stay here.'

Frightened, she asked him, 'Won't you stay?'

'I am not allowed to stay.'

She clutched his hand and said, 'Then I can't stay either. Take me home.'

Ramesh pushed her hand away and reproached her, 'For shame!'

Kamala stood still as her face fell. Ramesh rushed out, but he couldn't forget her surprised, helpless and frightened expression.

## 7

Ramesh had intended to practise law in the Alipore court, but he was broken-hearted. He didn't have the will to compose himself or to overcome the hurdles in the early stages of the work. He would wander on the bridge over the river and in College Square. He was contemplating travel, when all of a sudden he received a letter from Annada babu.

He had written, 'I saw in the *Gazette* that you have passed your examinations but felt sad that you didn't inform us. We have had no news of you for some time. I will be reassured and pleased if you let me know how you are and when you plan to come to Kolkata.'

It wouldn't be inappropriate to mention here that the young man Annada babu had set his hopes on for his daughter had returned from England and was getting married to an heiress.

After all that had passed, Ramesh couldn't make up his mind whether he should meet Hemnalini. He couldn't disclose the situation regarding Kamala because in spite of being innocent, she might be humiliated by society. Yet, how could he regain his former relationship with Hemnalini unless he explained the situation to her?

Annada babu's letter had to be answered without delay. Ramesh wrote, 'Due to some grave reasons I haven't been able to see you. Please forgive me.' He didn't give his new address in the letter. He posted the letter and the next day donned his lawyer's wig and appeared in Alipore court.

One evening after work he walked some distance and was settling the fare with the driver of a hackney carriage when he heard a familiar voice saying eagerly, 'Father, there's Ramesh babu!'

'Driver, stop, stop!'

The carriage stopped near Ramesh. Annada babu and his daughter were returning from a picnic when they met him unexpectedly.

Ramesh was overcome with emotion at the familiar sight of Hemnalini's pleasant and calm face, her special way of wearing the sari, the way she dressed her hair, the plain, thick gold bangle and the two thin bangles with the star design round her arms.

Annada said, 'Ramesh, we were lucky to spot you by the roadside. You don't write these days, and even when you do, you don't give your address. Where are you going? Do you have any urgent work?'

'No. I am coming from the court.'

'Then come and have tea with us.'

Ramesh was too overwhelmed to hesitate. He got into the carriage. With great effort, he asked Hemnalini, 'How are you?' Without answering him she asked, 'How come you did not inform us of passing the examination?' Unable to find an appropriate reply he said, 'I saw that you have passed too.'

She smiled and said, 'At least you know that.'

Annada asked, 'Where do you live now?'

'In Dorjipara.'

'Why there? Your earlier house in Kolutola wasn't bad.'

Hemnalini looked at him curiously, and this bothered Ramesh. He immediately blurted out, 'I agree. I have decided to return to that house.'

Ramesh realized that he had offended Hemnalini by moving, yet he could not offer an excuse and felt bad about it. No further questions were asked. Hemnalini stared at the road. Ramesh quickly explained. 'One of my relatives lives near Hedua, I moved to Dorjipara to keep in close touch.'

It was not a lie, yet it sounded strange. Kolutola was near enough to keep in touch with a relative. Hemnalini's eyes remained glued to the road. A hapless Ramesh did not know what to say after that. He asked, 'How is Jogen?' Annada replied, 'Having failed his law examinations he is now holidaying in the western provinces!'

When they reached, the familiar rooms and the décor of Hemnalini's home seemed to cast a spell on him. He sighed.

Ramesh was drinking his tea quietly when Annada suddenly asked, 'You spent a long time in your ancestral home; was it for some important work?' Ramesh replied, 'My father passed away.'

'That's terrible! How did it happen?'

'He was returning home by boat on the river Padma, when the boat capsized in a sudden storm and he was drowned.'

This sad news cleared the air like a strong wind clears the sky of dark clouds. Hemnalini thought regretfully, 'I had misunderstood Ramesh babu, he was distracted by the loss of his father. Perhaps that is why he seems so preoccupied. We were blaming him without knowing about his familial concerns.'

Hemnalini became more attentive to the bereaved. She plied him with food although he did not wish to eat. She said, 'You have lost a lot of weight, please don't neglect your health.' She suggested that he should stay to dine with them. Annada concurred.

All of a sudden Akshay arrived. In Ramesh's absence, he had been dominating the tea table meets at Annada's house. When he saw Ramesh, he was taken aback. Taking a hold on himself he smiled and remarked, 'Ramesh babu! What a surprise! We thought you had forgotten us.' Ramesh smiled. Akshay continued, 'Seeing the way you were apprehended by your father, I had feared that he would force you to marry. I hope you managed to free yourself.'

Hemnalini looked at Akshay with distaste. Annada said, 'Ramesh's father has passed away.' Ramesh did not look up. His face was pale. Hemnalini was upset with Akshay for causing Ramesh further pain. She quickly turned towards Ramesh saying, 'You haven't seen our new photo album.' She brought the album and sat near Ramesh talking about the photos. At one point she asked softly, 'Do you live alone in your new house?' Ramesh replied that he did.

'Move into the house next to ours without delay.'

'I will move in this Monday.'

'I had hoped that you would help me with the philosophy coursework for my BA,' said Hemnalini. Ramesh agreed enthusiastically.

## 8

Ramesh soon moved back to his former house. The feeling of distance between Hemnalini and him was now gone. He was like a family member, and his frequent visits were filled with fun and laughter. Earlier Hemnalini had looked fragile, perhaps due to her long hours of study. It seemed as though a strong breeze could break her frame. She spoke little, and one was afraid to talk to her in case it caused offence.

Now, within a few days, there was a remarkable change in her. Her pale cheeks had a glow. Her eyes danced with joy at the slightest pretext. Earlier, she had not paid much attention to her clothes, thinking it frivolous. But now her views changed, although nobody had persuaded her.

Ramesh too had been burdened by his duties, and had looked grim. His preoccupations had slowed him down. Like the stillness of an observatory pointed towards the moving stars and planets, Ramesh too had been silent with his books and his deliberations. What could have lightened his heart? Now, when he could not give a suitable rejoinder to a jest, he laughed loudly. His hair was still unkempt, but his scarf was well washed. He was full of energy.

## 9

Kolkata lacked the ambience that literature requires for lovers. There were no garden with ashok and bakul, no creepers of madhavi blossoms, and no cooing of the cuckoo. Yet, there was the magic of love even in the harsh, modern, ugly and traffic-ridden city.

Both Ramesh and Hemnalini lived in Kolutola. Their rented houses faced a leather shop and were next to a grocery store. Yet in matters of love, they were no less than those living in country houses with gardens. The small tea-stained table in Annada's house was not a lotus pond, but Ramesh did not find anything amiss. Hemnalini's pet cat was certainly no deer cub, yet Ramesh would stroke its neck affectionately. When it arched its back and preened itself, to Ramesh's admiring eye it was no less noble than other animals.

Hemnalini had been too busy with her exams to acquire any skill in needlework. Recently, she had started learning from a friend. To Ramesh, it was an unimportant and superfluous activity. He could discuss literature and philosophy with Hemnalini, but felt left out when she was busy with her needlework. He asked impatiently, 'How can you like stitching? It's only for those who have nothing else to do.' Hemnalini did not reply, but threaded her needle. Akshay commented sharply, 'To Ramesh babu these useful activities are unimportant. Yet even poets and philosophers can't do without these.' Ramesh was prepared for a debate. Hemnalini stopped him saying, 'Ramesh babu, why do you wish to counter every statement?' She then continued with her stitching.

One morning Ramesh found a blotting book with an embroidered velvet cover on his desk. The letter 'R' was embroidered in one corner of the cover, and a lotus flower on another. Ramesh was thrilled. He accepted the importance of needlework, held the book close, and was ready to accept defeat from Akshay. He opened the blotting book, placed a letter paper on it and began to write:

'Had I been a poet I could have reciprocated with a poem, but I don't have that talent. God has not given me the ability to give, but receiving is also an ability. Only God knows the manner in which I have received this unexpected gift. A gift is visible, but the acceptance is hidden in one's heart. I am forever in your debt.'

Hemnalini received the missive. But they did not talk about it.

The monsoons came. In a city rains are a mixed blessing. In vain attempts to keep the rain out, windows are shut, umbrellas are opened and tramcar shutters are closed. In the countryside on the other hand, rivers, hills, forests and fields welcome the rain as a friend.

The rainy season brought with it water pollution and Annada babu suffered from stomach problems. Ramesh and Hemnalini, however, were as merry as ever. The clouds, the thunder, and the sound of rain brought them closer. Ramesh often missed work on the pretext of heavy rain. Some days when the rain was particularly heavy, Hemnalini would ask, 'Ramesh babu, how will you go home in this rain?' Embarrassed, Ramesh would protest that his house was very near. But Hemnalini, concerned about his getting drenched and catching a cold, would persuade him to have his meal in her house. On other days too, when there was just a possibility of rain, Ramesh was invited to have meals and snacks. They seemed to be concerned about his catching a cold but never of his ability to digest all that food!

Days passed this way. Ramesh did not think about where all this would lead. But Annada babu did, as did others in their social circle. Ramesh's common sense did not match his learning, and his infatuation further blurred it. Annada looked at him expectantly every day, but he did not react to it.

## 10

Akshay did not have a good voice, but when he played his violin and sang, non-connoisseurs did not mind. Annada babu could not openly admit that he did not like music, yet he tried to avoid Akshay's singing. If Akshay was requested to sing, he would say, 'It isn't right to trouble him when you know that he can't sing.' Akshay would say humbly, 'It's no trouble.'

The other afternoon dark clouds covered the sky, and the rain did not stop even in the evening. Akshay could not leave. Suggesting that Akshay should sing, Hemnalini played the harmonium. Akshay played on his violin and sang a Hindustani song: 'There is an eastern breeze, yet I am sleepless without my loved one.' It was not necessary to understand every word of the song. When the heart is full of joy, a hint is enough—rain, peacocks, and the longing for each other.

Akshay was trying to express his unspoken love with his music, but the other two hearts touched each other through the music. The world acquired a special significance. Everything was pleasing, and the two hearts trembled with indescribable joy, sorrow and longing. There were no gaps between the clouds, or in the songs. Hemnalini requested Akshay to continue song after song, and his enthusiasm and emotion helped the music to flow out unconstrained. Akshay left very late that evening. When Ramesh said goodbye to Hemnalini he looked at her. No words were spoken yet the music lingered.

Ramesh went home. The rain had stopped for a moment but started again. He could not sleep that night. Hemnalini too sat quietly listening to the sound of the rain. The song kept coming back—'There is an eastern breeze, yet I am sleepless without my loved one.'

Next morning Ramesh thought that he would exchange all his learning for the ability to sing. He decided to learn to play an instrument. Earlier, he had tried to play the violin in a quiet corner in Annada babu's house. But at the sound of the first stroke of the bow he realized that it would be cruelty to others, and gave up the idea. Now he bought a small harmonium. He shut the door and windows of his room, practised playing the instrument and found that the harmonium is more tolerant of mistakes than the violin.

Later Hemnalini remarked that she could hear the sound of a harmonium coming from his house. Ramesh was embarrassed and admitted that he wished to learn. Hemnalini said, 'Instead of wasting your effort in your room, why don't you practise here? I can help you.' Ramesh confessed that he was a novice. Hemnalini replied that she knew just enough to teach a novice.

Ramesh's claim was not exaggerated. In spite of generous help from such a teacher, Ramesh could not acquire a sense of notes and tunes. He had no notion that he was playing off key, could not differentiate between notes and happily violated the rules of music. Whenever Hemnalini interrupted, pointing out his mistakes, Ramesh would rush to cover up one mistake with another. He was diligent and would not give up easily, but he trampled on the scales like a steamroller.

Hemnalini was most amused. Ramesh asked, 'You are laughing at me, but when you first started learning didn't you make mistakes?' She replied that his mistakes were incomparable. Undeterred, Ramesh started all over again. Annada, who knew nothing about music, would listen carefully and commend his progress. When Hemnalini disagreed, he said that with practice Ramesh would play very well.

## 11

In the autumn, during the puja holidays, Annada babu and Hemnalini used to go to Jabalpur to stay with the former's brother-in-law. Annada believed that the change of air improved his health. This year too Annada babu started preparing for their journey.

At the prospect of separation from Hemnalini, Ramesh was even more anxious for his music lessons. Hemnalini said, 'Ramesh babu, I think you too need a change of air. Isn't it so, Father?' Annada thought that it was a good idea in view of Ramesh's recent bereavement. He advised, 'It is a good idea to go somewhere for a holiday, even though the health benefits are only temporary.'

Hemnalini asked Ramesh, 'Have you seen the Narmada falls?' Learning that he had not, Hemnalini said, 'You must see it. Don't you agree, Father?' Annada replied, 'Ramesh should come with us. He can benefit from a change of air and also see the marble rocks,' as if these two things were most essential for him. So Ramesh could not but agree.

Ramesh was ecstatic. He was walking on air. To express his emotions, he closed the door of his room and began playing the harmonium. Oblivious to the rules of music, his fingers on the reeds played havoc with rhythm, but in his joy he let himself go.

Someone knocked on the door. 'What are you doing, Ramesh babu? Please stop.'

Ramesh was terribly embarrassed. He opened the door and Akshay entered. Akshay said, 'I wonder if our Criminal Code covers what you were doing behind closed doors!'

Ramesh laughed. Akshay said, 'If you don't mind, I would like to discuss something important.' Ramesh was curious and waited for Akshay to proceed.

Akshay began. 'By now you must be aware that I am not indifferent towards Hemnalini.' Ramesh did not reply. Akshay continued, 'I am a friend of Annada babu, therefore I have a right to inquire about your intentions regarding her.' Ramesh did not like the way he said it, but it was not in him to be rude. He asked softly, 'Do you have any reason to believe that my intentions are dishonourable?'

Akshay replied, 'You belong to Hindu society, your father was a Hindu. Fearing that you might marry into a Brahmo family, he took you home to persuade you to marry a Hindu girl.' Akshay knew about it because it was he who had planted this idea in Ramesh's father's mind.

Ramesh could not look Akshay in the eye. Akshay said, 'Do you consider yourself free because your father died suddenly? Was it his wish? To . . . ?'

Unable to take it any longer Ramesh interrupted, 'You might believe that you have the right to lecture me on my relationship with others, but you have no right to talk about the relationship between my father and myself.'

'All right, let that be. But you must tell me whether you have the intention and the means to marry Hemnalini.'

Ramesh was upset. He said, 'You might be a friend of Annada babu, but you and I are not close. Please don't say anything more on this subject.'

'Even if I stop, others will talk about it. You can't continue like this without a thought to the future. You seem to be a high-minded person concerned about the condition of the world, yet you don't seem to understand that you will have to answer to outsiders because of the way you are carrying on with this girl from a good family—and it would only ensure that the people you respect would drop in society's esteem.'

'I accept your advice gratefully. Be assured that I will soon decide where my duty lies, and will act accordingly. There is no need to continue this discussion.'

'I am reassured that you will finally see your duty and your course of action. I have no desire to prolong this conversation. I interrupted your music practice, please forgive me. Goodbye.' Saying this Akshay rushed out.

Even Ramesh's off-key music could not be resumed after this. He lay down on his back with his hands under his head. After a long time, when the clock struck five, he got up hurriedly and went to Hemnalini's house.

Hemnalini was concerned and asked, 'Ramesh babu, are you sick?' Ramesh replied that it was nothing. Annada commented that it must be indigestion and recommended the pills that he was taking. There was an argument between father and daughter regarding the efficacy of the pills, when Annada said that Akshay would vouch for their efficacy. Hemnalini kept quiet fearing that Akshay would be called, but Akshay himself arrived soon after and immediately said, 'Annada babu, please give me some of those pills you take. They have really helped me.' Having won the argument, Annada babu looked at his daughter proudly.

# 12

Annada did not want to let Akshay go, nor was Akshay in a hurry to leave. He threw knowing glances at Ramesh, which upset him. Hemnalini was particularly happy that day because they were to leave for their holiday soon. She planned to discuss the itinerary with Ramesh, and wished to make a list of the books that they would read. Ramesh was supposed to come early that day, before Akshay and the others dropped in for tea.

But Ramesh was later than usual, and he seemed preoccupied. Hemnalini's enthusiasm was dampened. When an opportunity arose, she asked him softly, 'How come you are so late today?' Ramesh was quiet for a while and then replied that indeed he was late.

Hemnalini had got ready earlier than usual that day. After tying her hair and changing her sari she kept looking at her watch. Then she thought that the watch was not showing the correct time. When the watch proved to be correct, she had taken a piece of needlework and sat by the window. When Ramesh finally arrived, he looked grave, and gave no excuse for being late as though he had never agreed to come early.

Hemnalini finished her tea somehow. To catch Ramesh's attention, she picked up some books and appeared to leave the room. Ramesh suddenly woke up to this and asked, 'Where are you taking the books? Shouldn't we select some of the books today?' Somehow checking her tears Hemnalini said, 'What is the point of selecting books, let it be.' Saying this she left and threw the books on the floor of her bedroom upstairs.

Ramesh felt lost. Akshay and Annada commented that Ramesh looked unwell. The conversation continued along the lines of health and medication. Akshay suggested that Ramesh should take Annada's medicine and go to bed early. Ramesh replied that he was waiting to discuss something in particular with Annada. Akshay got up commenting that Ramesh should have said so earlier.

After Akshay left, Ramesh said, 'Annada babu, you have treated me like a member of your family and allowed me the freedom of your house. I consider this to be my good fortune and words can't express my gratitude.'

'But of course, you are a friend of Jogen; you are like a son to me.'

After the prologue Ramesh could not think how to proceed. To make it easier for him, Annada said, 'It is my good fortune to have someone like you in our family.' And yet Ramesh could not find the right words to express his thoughts.

Annada continued, 'People have started talking about you and Hemnalini. They say that Hemnalini is of marriageable age, and should be careful about who she befriends. I tell them that I have complete faith in Ramesh, he would never behave dishonourably.'

Ramesh said, 'Annada babu, you know all about me, if you consider me to be suitable, then. . .'

Annada answered, 'It goes without saying. We have made up our minds, but we could not decide on the date because of the tragedy in your family. But it should be delayed no more. There is a great deal of talk about it in our circle, and we must put a stop to that as soon as possible. Don't you think so?'

Ramesh replied, 'I shall do whatever you ask of me. But we must first find out how your daughter feels.'

'I know her wish, tomorrow morning I shall reconfirm it,' said Annada.

Ramesh said, 'It's past your normal bedtime, I should leave.'

'Wait a minute. I think that the wedding should take place before we leave for Jabalpur.'

'But that is too soon.'

'We still have about ten days. If the wedding is held next Sunday, then we will still have a few days to prepare for the journey. I would not have rushed you but for my frail health.'

Ramesh agreed to this, took another dose of the medicine and went home.

## 13

The school holidays were near. Ramesh had arranged with the principal to keep Kamala in the hostel during the holidays.

While walking in the desolate park in the morning, Ramesh decided that he would explain about Kamala to Hemnalini after their marriage. Then he would explain everything to Kamala too. Once things were clear, Kamala would comfortably stay with them as a friend of Hemnalini. Since this might lead to a lot of talk here, they would move to Hazaribag and he would practise law there.

He went to Annada babu's house, and met Hemnalini on the stairs. On other days such a meeting would lead to a chat, but today Hemnalini blushed, and through that blush there was a hint of a smile, like the light of dawn.

Ramesh went home and played the tune that he had learnt from Hemnalini on the harmonium. But one can't play the same tune all day long. He tried reading poetry, but the poems did not capture the depth of his love.

Hemnalini completed her housework and sat down with her needlework. Her face glowed with happiness, and a sense of fulfilment enveloped her. Ramesh left his music and his poems and arrived at their house well before teatime. Usually Hemnalini joined him immediately, but that day he found the downstairs rooms empty. Hemnalini had not come down from her bedroom.

Annada came and sat at the table as usual. Ramesh kept looking at the door expectantly. He heard footsteps, but it was Akshay. Appearing to be friendly, he said, 'Ramesh babu, I had gone to your house.' Ramesh looked concerned. Akshay said, 'Don't be alarmed, I went there not to attack you but to congratulate you, like friends normally do.'

Annada suddenly noticed Hemnalini's absence. He called her, but getting no reply he went upstairs and said, 'How come you are still busy with your stitching? Tea is ready, and Ramesh and Akshay have come.' Hemnalini blushed and replied, 'I want to complete the needlework, please send my tea upstairs.' Annada objected, 'Hem, this is a bad habit of yours. When you get obsessed with one thing, you forget about other things totally. While you were studying, you didn't put your books down. Now that you have taken up needlework, all else has stopped. Come downstairs and have your tea.'

Downstairs, Hemnalini did not glance at the others but busied herself pouring out the tea. Annada said impatiently, 'Why are you adding sugar? I never take sugar in my tea.' Akshay smiled and commented, 'She can't control her generosity today, and she is distributing sweets to everyone.' Ramesh found this comment about Hemnalini repulsive. He decided that after their wedding he would stop all social contact with Akshay. Akshay said, 'Ramesh babu, you must change your name.' Ramesh was further irritated and asked for the reason. Akshay pointed to the newspaper and said, 'See, a student of the same name as yours got someone else to impersonate him at the examination and passed. But he was found out later.'

Hemnalini knew that Ramesh was not good at quick repartee. Whenever Akshay had teased Ramesh, she had replied in his stead. She masked her anger, smiled and said, 'I am sure there are many people named Akshay in the jails.'

'I was only trying to give good advice as a friend. My younger sister studies in Sharat Girls' School. Last evening she said, "Dada, Ramesh babu's wife attends my school." I scolded her. "Are you mad? There are other people with the same name." My sister said, "Whoever he might be, he is unfair to his wife. All the other girls are going home for the holidays, but this man has arranged for his wife to stay on in the hostel. The poor girl is upset and has been crying her heart out." Immediately I realized that others too might make the same mistake.'

Annada laughed. 'Akshay, you are talking rubbish. The wife of some Ramesh has been crying in some school, is that a reason for Ramesh to change his name?' Ramesh turned pale and suddenly dashed out of the room. Akshay followed Ramesh, saying that he had not meant any harm.

Annada was astonished at all this, and Hemnalini started weeping. She said, 'Father, it is wrong of Akshay babu. Why does he humiliate a gentleman in our house?'

'Akshay had said something as a joke, there was no need for Ramesh to get so upset.'

'This kind of joke is intolerable.' Saying this Hemnalini went upstairs.

After returning to Kolkata, Ramesh had tried his best to locate Kamala's husband. He had even located the village called Dhobapukur, and had written to Kamala's uncle, Tarinicharan. The day after that incident at Annada babu's he received a reply. Tarinicharan had written that after the accident he had had no news of Kamala's husband Nalinaksha who was a doctor and had been practising in Rangpur. Tarinicharan had written to that address, but there was no news of him. Ramesh saw no possibility of Nalinaksha being alive.

That morning Ramesh received a few other letters. Some were congratulatory messages on his engagement from his friends. Some demanded a treat; others teased him about keeping it a secret.

A servant from Annada babu's house brought a letter to him. Seeing the handwriting, Ramesh's heart missed a beat. It was from Hemnalini. Ramesh feared that Hemnalini doubted him, and had written to clarify matters. He opened the letter and read, 'It was wrong of Akshay babu to make those remarks. I had hoped to see you this morning. Why didn't you come? Don't take his remarks to heart. You know that I don't give him any importance. Please come early this afternoon, I will keep my needlework aside.'

He was moved by the soothing words that reflected Hemnalini's comprehension of his pain. All this while she had eagerly waited for him, and had finally sent this letter.

Ramesh had come to the conclusion that he must explain the entire matter to Hemnalini without delay. But after the incident of that day it had become doubly difficult. Now it would seem as though he was trying to defend himself after getting caught. It would also give a partial victory to Akshay, who probably believed that some other Ramesh was Kamala's husband. Otherwise he would not have just hinted at it but informed the entire neighbourhood. Something must be done as soon as possible.

There was a letter from the principal of Kamala's school to say that Kamala was so upset that it was not possible to keep her in the hostel during the holidays. The school would close next Saturday, and he must make arrangements to take her home.

But Ramesh was to be married next Saturday!

Akshay entered the room. 'Ramesh babu, please forgive me. I wouldn't have raised it had I known that you would be offended by such a silly joke. People are upset only when there is a grain of truth in a joke, but since there was none, why were you upset? Annada babu has been scolding me; Hemnalini hasn't spoken to me. This morning when I went to their house, she left the room. Did I commit a serious offence?'

Ramesh replied, 'We can discuss this later. Please excuse me; I have an urgent matter to attend to.'

'Are you rushing to place the order for the music for the wedding? I won't keep you from your good work. Goodbye.'

When Akshay left, Ramesh went to Annada's house. At the sight of Ramesh, Hemnalini's face brightened up, but when he asked, 'Where is Annada babu?' she was taken aback. 'He is in his living room. Do you need him immediately? He will come down at teatime.' When Ramesh replied that it was urgent, Hemnalini directed him to Annada babu. She was put out and took up her needlework again.

Annada was dozing with the newspaper covering his face, and woke up with a start when Ramesh entered. He pointed to the paper, 'See Ramesh, so many have died of cholera.' Ramesh said, 'I have some urgent matter to attend to, the wedding must be postponed.'

Annada was astonished. 'How is that possible? Even the invitation cards have been printed.'

'It can be postponed to the Sunday after, and the cards can be corrected accordingly.'

'You surprise me. Is this a court case that you can keep postponing the date of the hearing? What is this urgent work of yours?'

'It is really important and can't be delayed.'

Annada slumped back in his chair like a banana tree felled by a storm. 'Do what you like, take back the invitations. When people ask me, I shall reply that only Ramesh knows why it was postponed, and when it will be convenient for him to marry.' Ramesh sat quietly without answering.

Annada asked if Hemnalini knew. Ramesh said, 'Not yet.'

'But she has a right to know. After all, the wedding is hers too.'

'I thought I would talk to you first.'

Annada called Hemnalini. When she came there he said, 'Ramesh says that he has some important work and does not have the time to get married.' Hemnalini went pale and looked at Ramesh who had not expected that the news would be broken to her in this way.

It was too late to soften the blow. It was true that he had to settle the other matter first, but how could he explain it? Annada said, 'You two must resolve this.' Hemnalini replied that she knew nothing about it, and left the room like the glow of sunset disappearing behind storm clouds. Annada pretended to read the newspaper; Ramesh sat still.

Suddenly Ramesh got up. He found Hemnalini standing quietly by the window in the large living room. The street was full of people like a river in spate. Ramesh hesitated to go to her side, but stood watching her. In autumn's evening light, the still figure at the window etched a picture in his heart. The gentle contour of her cheek, the soft strands of hair falling on the nape of her neck, the glimpse of the gold chain, the sari edge falling over her shoulder, each of these pulled at his heartstrings.

Ramesh came and stood by her. Hemnalini seemed more interested in the people walking by than in him. In a voice choked with emotion he said, 'I have one request.' Hemnalini felt the pain in his voice and turned towards him. Ramesh said, 'Please have faith in me.' He used the familiar form of address for the first time. 'Please promise that you will never distrust me. As God is my witness, I swear that I will never break your faith.' His eyes were wet. Hemnalini lifted her soft and kind eyes and looked at him. Then the tears coursed down her cheeks. No word was said, yet peace and empathy engulfed them, creating a little paradise by the window.

After soaking his heart and mind in the depths of the tear-flooded silence, Ramesh said with a sigh of relief, 'Do you wish to know the reason for postponing the wedding by a week?' Hemnalini shook her head, indicating that she did not wish to know. Ramesh said, 'I will explain everything to you after we are married.'

Earlier that day, when Hemnalini was getting ready for Ramesh's visit, she had imagined scenes of laughter, exchange of confidences, and other joyful moments. Yet she had never imagined the deep peace, the profound joy, and the reassurance of those few minutes when they stood together quietly, when their two hearts exchanged garlands of trust.

She said, 'My father is extremely anxious, please go to him.'

Ramesh left the room prepared to face with a smile the sorrows and the conflicts that life might bring.

## 15

Annada looked anxiously at Ramesh, who said, 'If you give me the list of invitees, I can inform them of the change of date by today's post.'

'Then you have decided to change the date?'

'Yes, there is no other way.'

'I won't be involved; you must do the needful. I don't wish to be a laughing stock. Marriage is a serious matter. If you treat it like a game according to your whim, then an elderly man like me can't have any place in it. Here is the list of invitees. Some of the money I have already spent will be wasted, and I can't afford to waste money like this again.'

Ramesh prepared himself to shoulder all the cost and make all the arrangements.

Annada asked him, 'Have you decided where you will practise after your marriage? Not in Kolkata?'

'No, I am trying to find a suitable town in the western provinces.'

'That's good. Etawah is a nice place; the water is good for digestion. I was there for a month, and my appetite doubled. Hem is my only child. She will be unhappy if I am far from her, and I will worry. So, I would like you to select a healthy place for your practice.'

Annada played on Ramesh's guilt and placed all his major demands to him. Had he asked Ramesh to settle in Gazipur rather than in Etawah, Ramesh would have agreed instantly. Ramesh said, 'If you wish, I shall practise in Etawah.' He took the list and left.

Annada informed Akshay of Ramesh's decision to postpone the wedding. Akshay was astonished and said, 'How can that be? The wedding date is the day after tomorrow!'

'It shouldn't be and it doesn't happen normally. But anything is possible these days.'

Akshay looked grim and appeared to be thinking hard. After some time he said, 'Once you decide that a particular man is eligible, you turn a blind eye to all his faults. You should make inquiries about the person to whom you are entrusting your daughter. One can't be too careful even if he is a god from heaven.'

Annada replied, 'If one must doubt a man like Ramesh, one can't but doubt everyone in the world.'

'Has Ramesh babu given any reason for postponing the date?'

'No, he didn't give any reason; he said that he has some important work'.

Akshay turned his face away and checked a smile. He said, 'Surely he must have explained the reason to your daughter.'

'Perhaps,' said Annada.

'Should we not find out from her?'

Annada called Hemnalini. When she saw Akshay, she stood near her father in such a way that he could not see her face.

Annada asked, 'Has Ramesh explained the reason for postponing the wedding?'

'No.'

'You didn't ask him?'

'No.'

'Strange! He said that he doesn't have the time to get married on that day, and you agreed!'

Taking Hemnalini's side, Akshay said, 'It is obvious that he wishes to keep it a secret. It doesn't seem right to question him about it. Had he wished, he would have given the reason.'

Hemnalini's face went red. She said, 'I don't wish to hear anything about this from outsiders. I have no regret about what has happened.' Saying this she left the room in haste.

Akshay was livid, yet he managed a smile and said, 'I place a high value on friendship. Even at the risk of being reproached or even hated, I believe it is my duty as your friend to doubt Ramesh. I can't sit back when your interests are threatened, and I acknowledge this weakness. Jogen is coming tomorrow; after learning about the situation if he is still sure of his sister's future, I will not say anything further on the subject.'

Annada did understand the need to question Ramesh's behaviour, but his nature was such that he did not wish to cause an uproar by dragging out in the open something that was yet unsaid.

He was displeased with Akshay. He said, 'Akshay, you have a suspicious nature. You don't have any proof, yet why do you . . .'

Akshay was good at concealing his feelings but he lost his patience and said excitedly, 'I have many shortcomings. I am jealous of eligible men, I suspect honest people. I am neither knowledgeable enough to teach philosophy to young women, nor do I aspire to discuss poetry with them. I am an ordinary person, but I am your devoted friend. Compared to Ramesh babu, I fall short on most counts, yet I can say with pride that I have nothing to hide from you. I can admit my failings and beg for your kindness, but I can never take advantage of you. You will comprehend this fully tomorrow.'

## 16

It was night by the time Ramesh finished distributing the letters. He went to bed, but could not sleep. He tossed and turned and finally he got up. He stood by the window and saw that one side of the empty road was covered by shadows of the buildings, and the other side, by moonlight. His entire being seemed to absorb that which was eternal, peaceful and universal. He could perceive that the love between a man and a woman was also part of that eternity.

He climbed up to the terrace and saw that all was quiet in Annada babu's house. Light and shadow created strange shapes on the walls of the house. Wasn't it a wonder, he thought, that of the countless people in this city, he alone would stand beside her by the window in the pale autumn light and experience infinite joy! He strolled on the terrace for a long time. Slowly the moon disappeared behind the house in front; the earth was covered in darkness, and the sky was pale. An unknown dread gripped Ramesh. He remembered that the next day awaited him. He wondered how infinite and eternal peace could coexist with the daily struggle for existence. Which was reality, and which, illusion?

## 17

Next day Jogen arrived by the morning train. It was a Saturday, and Hemnalini's wedding was to have been on the next day, that is, on Sunday. Jogen could not see any sign of festivities. He had imagined that their front door would be decorated with debdaru leaves, but their house looked as drab and plain as the next one.

He feared that someone was ill. Walking in, he found that food was laid out for him on the table, and Annada was reading the newspaper.

Jogendra's first question was to inquire after Hemnalini. Annada replied that she was well.

'What about the wedding?'

'It is postponed to next Sunday.'

'Why?'

'Ask your friend. All Ramesh said was that he has some important work, and the wedding can't be held tomorrow.'

Jogen was irritated by his father and said, 'There's always some problem when I am not here. What important work can Ramesh have? He is independent. He doesn't have any family. Had it been a property-related matter, he needn't have hidden it from us. Why did you let him get away with it?'

'All right, he is still in town, why don't you ask him yourself?'

Jogen drank up his cup of tea and left.

He entered Ramesh's house and rushed up the stairs noisily calling

'Ramesh, Ramesh.' There was no reply. He went from room to room searching, but there was no sign of Ramesh. The servant informed him that his master was not in.

Jogen asked when he had left, and the servant said that he had left early in the morning.

'When will he be back?'

'The master took some clothes with him and said that he might be away for four or five days.' The servant did not know his destination.

Jogendra returned home.

When Annada asked what happened, he got irritated and replied, 'What can happen? The man who is to marry your daughter lives next door to you, yet you don't keep track of his whereabouts.'

'Why? Last night Ramesh was in his house.'

'There seem to be some strange goings-on. You don't know where he was planning to go, and his servant doesn't know where he has gone. I don't like it. Father, how can you be so unconcerned?'

Annada was concerned. He said, 'You are right, it is very strange.'

He went upstairs to find Hemnalini. She was sitting alone in her room. Hearing Jogen's footsteps, she grabbed a book quickly and pretended to read. When he entered, she got up and smilingly asked, 'Dada, when did you arrive? You are not looking well.'

'How can I feel well after hearing all this? This could happen only because I was away. You mustn't worry; leave everything to me. Hem, did Ramesh give any reason for postponing the wedding?'

Any discussion casting aspersions on Ramesh was anathema to Hemnalini. She did not wish to tell Jogen that Ramesh had not offered any reason, yet she could not tell a lie. She said, 'He was ready to explain, I didn't feel it was necessary.'

Interpreting this as hurt pride, Jogen said, 'Don't be anxious, I will soon find out the reason.'

'I have no anxiety, and I don't want you to put any pressure on him.'

'You needn't be concerned about that.' Saying this Jogen stood up to leave.

Hemnalini interrupted him. 'No, you mustn't discuss this matter with him. You may think what you like, but I don't doubt him at all.'

This did not sound like hurt pride to Jogen. His fondness for her was mixed with pity. She was so inexperienced in the ways of the world. She was highly educated but naïve enough to have no doubt when there was enough reason to doubt. This made him even more angry, and more determined to uncover the truth.

As he was about to leave, Hemnalini held his hands and said, 'Dada, you must promise not to bring up this matter with him.'

'I shall see.'

'You must promise. I assure you, there is no reason to be worried, please keep my request.'

'Hem, it is not a question of trust. We must do our duty as the bride's family. You might have an understanding with him, but at this stage it is more important that we have an understanding with him. After the wedding we won't have any say.'

Jogen left in a hurry. As he went out, he met Akshay who said, 'Jogen, you must have heard everything. What do you think of all this?'

'I am concerned, but is there any point in discussing human psychology when it is based on conjecture?'

'I am not interested in it either; I have come to talk about practical matters.'

Jogen was impatient to find Ramesh, and asked if Akshay knew his whereabouts. Akshay replied that he did know but he would rather not say anything at the moment. He offered to take Jogen to meet Ramesh in the afternoon.

Jogen was puzzled by this evasion and insisted that Akshay tell him everything. Akshay agreed and said that he would begin from the beginning since Jogen was ignorant of some of the events.

## 18

Ramesh still had the lease of the house in Dorjipara, although he had not lived there for many months. That morning he got the house cleaned and made arrangements for meals. He was supposed to bring Kamala there after school. While waiting, he thought about the future. He had never been to Etawah, but it was not difficult to imagine a typical town in the western provinces. He imagined a house at the edge of the town, off a road lined with trees; a large field across the road where crops were watered from the well, and occasionally vehicles went by on the road, leaving a trail of dust. He had been concerned about Hemnalini being alone in the bungalow all day, but if Kamala lived there as her friend, Hemnalini would not feel lonely.

He decided not to say anything to Kamala yet. He would leave it to Hemnalini to break it gently to Kamala after they were married. Hemnalini would softly unravel the tangle that was Kamala's life. Later, far away from acquaintances and family, Kamala would find it easy to live with them.

A vehicle stopped at the gate. Kamala returned by the school coach. Ramesh wondered how it would be to meet Kamala after all this time. The servants brought up her luggage, and Kamala followed, but she did not enter the room. Ramesh asked her to come in, and Kamala entered hesitantly. She was upset because Ramesh had wanted her to stay back in the hostel during the holidays. She stood by a window and looked out. Ramesh was surprised to see a great change in her. She was taller and slimmer, and her girlish round face was longer. Her movements were easy, not self-conscious. She was standing by the window with the autumn light on her face. Her head was uncovered, her long plait fell over her back, and a light yellow sari draped her young frame. Kamala's beauty struck him anew. He had not been prepared for it.

He asked Kamala about her school and her studies, to which he received a brief reply. He wondered what to say next. He said, 'Would you like to eat? Your food is ready.' She replied, 'I have already eaten.' 'Have some fruit or sweets,' he said. She shook her head. He gazed at her for some time. She was looking at the pictures in a book. Then he got up suddenly and fetched some fruits on a plate and also a knife. Saying that he was hungry, he tried to peel the apples. Watching his unskilled fingers fumble, she laughed and it lightened the atmosphere. Ramesh felt relieved and asked, 'Let me see if you can do better.' She cut the fruits expertly and placed them on the plate. He requested her to share it with him, but she would not. She promised to have some later, so he put a piece in his mouth. Suddenly he saw Jogen and Akshay standing outside the door. Akshay said, 'Please excuse us, we thought you were alone. We should have sent word. Jogen, let us wait downstairs.' Kamala left the room hurriedly.

Jogendra asked, 'Who is the girl?'

Ramesh answered, 'A relation of mine.'

'How is she related? She is neither an elder, nor of the younger generation. You have talked about all your relatives but not about this one.'

Akshay added, 'Jogen, this is not fair, one might have a secret even from a friend.'

'Ramesh, is it a secret?' asked Jogen.

Ramesh's face was flushed as he answered, 'Yes, it is a secret. I don't wish to discuss her with you.'

Jogen said, 'Unfortunately, I do wish to discuss it because you are to marry my sister. Otherwise there was no need to rake up your relationships with others; your secret could have remained so.'

'I can say this much that I have no relationship with anyone that can be a barrier to my marrying Hemnalini,' said Ramesh.

'You may not think so but Hemnalini's family might. What is the need for this secrecy?'

'If I explain that, it would cease to be a secret. You know me from my childhood; you must trust me implicitly.'

'Isn't her name Kamala?' asked Jogen.

'Yes.'

'Is she known to be your wife?'

'Yes.'

Jogen asked, 'How can we trust you even after this? You would like us to believe that she is not your wife, yet you have told others that she is. It does not speak well for your integrity.'

Akshay added sarcastically, 'Jogen, sometimes it may be necessary to say two different things to two different groups of people. One version is likely to be the truth. Perhaps what Ramesh babu has told us is the truth.'

Ramesh reiterated, 'I wish to say again that it wouldn't be wrong for me to marry Hemnalini. There are strong reasons for not discussing the subject of Kamala even if it leads you to distrust me. Had it been a matter involving only my life or honour, I would have shared it with you, but it would be wrong to do so when someone else is involved.'

Jogen asked, 'Have you explained everything to Hemnalini?'

'No. I have promised to tell her after our wedding. But I can do so even now, if she wants me to.'

'May we ask a few questions of Kamala?'

'Certainly not. No matter what you think of me, I can't ask innocent Kamala to face your questions.'

Jogen said, 'There is no need to prolong this discussion. I have learnt what I came to learn and the evidence is sufficient. Now I must tell you that if you try to enter our house again, you will be humiliated.' Ramesh's face went pale; he sat there in silence.

Jogen added, 'You must not write to Hem, or maintain any contact with her—overt or covert. If someone asks me why the engagement was broken, I shall reply that I didn't give my consent. But if you write or try to contact Hem, I shall reveal everything that you wish to keep secret. Although you have behaved abominably, I am letting you off only because the matter involves Hemnalini. You must not in any manner let it be known that you ever knew Hemnalini. I would have made you swear to this, except that from a liar like you it would have no value.'

Jogen and Akshay left. Ramesh was stunned and sat still as a statue. When he recovered a little he felt like going out for a brisk walk and assessing the situation. But then he remembered Kamala and felt that he could not leave her in the house alone. He found her in the next room sitting by the window with its shutters open. Hearing his footsteps she closed the shutters quickly and turned towards him.

She asked, 'Who were these two men? They were in my school this morning.'

Ramesh was surprised. 'They went to your school?'

'Yes. What were they discussing with you?'

'They wanted to know how you are related to me.'

Kamala blushed slightly. Ramesh continued, 'I told them that we are unrelated.'

Kamala thought that Ramesh was teasing her, so she pretended to be angry. Ramesh wondered how he would explain everything to her.

Suddenly Kamala remembered the cut fruit, and brought it for him. Ramesh asked her to have some but she wanted to wait until he had finished eating. Ramesh found this touching.

Later he said, 'Kamala, tonight we shall go to our village.'

Kamala looked sad and replied that she did not like living there.

'Do you like your school?' he asked.

'No. Please don't send me there again. I feel embarrassed. The girls keep asking me about you.'

'What do you tell them?'

'Nothing much. They asked me why you wanted me to stay on in the hostel during the holidays—but I . . .' She could not complete the sentence. It was a painful subject.

Ramesh asked, 'Why didn't you tell them that we are not related?' Kamala was angry and she frowned at him.

Ramesh was deeply concerned about what he should do with Kamala. He was finding it difficult to suppress his pain of the probable lifelong separation from Hemnalini. How would he bear it? Many questions came to his mind: what was Jogendra saying to Hemnalini; how would he himself ever explain the truth to her, and so on. He did realize that among his friends as well as his critics his relationship with Kamala was now a much-debated topic. The general belief was that Kamala was his wife. He decided that they shouldn't stay a day longer in Kolkata. Kamala interrupted his thoughts by saying, 'If you wish to live in the village, I shall go and live there with you.'

Ramesh remained thoughtful. Kamala asked, 'Are you angry with me because I didn't wish to stay in the hostel for the holidays? Please tell me the truth.'

'Honestly, I am not angry with you, I am angry with myself.' To take his mind off the complexity of the situation he asked her, 'Tell me what you learnt in school.' With great enthusiasm Kamala began an account of all that she had learnt. Recently she had learnt that the world was round, and wished to surprise Ramesh with her knowledge. Ramesh pretended to be suitably surprised. Then Kamala described her fellow students, the teachers, and the daily routine. Ramesh did not pay much attention but made suitable sounds as though he was listening. Finally Kamala got irritated and accused him of not paying any attention. She was about to leave the room when Ramesh said that he was not feeling well and entreated her to stay. She was immediately concerned, but Ramesh shrugged it off. She brought her geography book; there was some more discussion on the roundness of the earth, and how it was shown with two flat pictures, and so on. The evening passed in this way.

## 19

Annada had hoped that Jogen and Akshay would bring good news and all the confusion would be over. He looked at them anxiously when they entered.

Jogen said, 'Father, how could you let things go so far? Had I known I wouldn't have introduced him to you.'

'But you said more than once that you approved of the marriage. Otherwise you should have told me.'

'I hadn't thought of stopping it, but still . . .'

'One can either approve of the match, or disapprove; there are no possible in-between positions.'

'Still, going so far . . .'

Akshay smiled and said, 'There are some things which have their own momentum, they don't need to be pushed. However, what is done is done, no use debating about it. Let us discuss what needs to be done now.'

Annada asked nervously whether they had met Ramesh. Jogen replied, 'Oh yes, we also met his wife!'

Annada was speechless. Then he asked, 'Whose wife did you meet?'

'Ramesh's wife.'

'I don't follow. Which Ramesh?'

'Our Ramesh. When he went home a few months back, it was to get married.'

'But the wedding could not take place because his father died.'

'The wedding took place before his father died.'

Annada sat quietly, stroking his head. After a while he said, 'Hem mustn't marry him.'

'That's what we are saying,' said Jogen.

'You may say that, but all the arrangements for the wedding have been made. Letters have been distributed announcing the change of date to next Sunday. Now we must send another set of letters cancelling the wedding!'

'There is no need to cancel the wedding; just one thing needs to be changed.'

A bewildered Annada babu asked, 'Which one thing?'

'We must find a bridegroom in Ramesh's place, and hold the wedding next Sunday, as planned. Otherwise we won't be able to hold up our heads in society.' Saying this, Jogen glanced at Akshay. Akshay understood the meaning of that look and stood there quietly with his eyes downcast.

'But how can we find a suitable bridegroom at such short notice?' asked Annada.

'Leave that to me,' said Jogen.

'But Hem must agree to it.'

'She will agree when she hears the whole story about Ramesh.'

'Do what you think best. Ramesh is really eligible. He has money and also the potential to earn a good income. Only the day before we were talking about it and he decided to practise law in Etawah. Meanwhile everything has turned upside down.'

Jogen left the room to fetch Hemnalini. When they re-entered, Akshay concealed himself behind a bookshelf.

Annada said, 'Hem, please sit down, I need to talk to you.'

Jogen asked her, 'Don't you find Ramesh's behaviour strange?' She shook her head indicating that she did not.

'He postponed the wedding by a week. What could be the reason that he couldn't disclose even to us?'

Hemnalini replied, 'There must be a good reason.'

'Whatever it may be, isn't it suspicious?'

Hemnalini again shook her head. Jogen continued in a sterner tone, 'You remember that six months ago Ramesh went home with his father. After that, to our surprise, he did not communicate with us. You know full well that the same Ramesh who used to visit us twice a day, and lived next door to us, did not visit us even once after returning to Kolkata. He rented a house somewhere else and avoided us. In spite of all this you trusted him as before and welcomed him back to our house! It couldn't have happened had I been present.'

Hemnalini remained quiet. Jogendra continued, 'Have you found any explanation for Ramesh's behaviour? No questions plagued your mind? I am amazed at your trust in him!' There was no response from Hemnalini.

Jogendra went on. 'You are too gullible, and never distrust anyone. I hope you have some trust in me. I found the school where Ramesh had placed his wife Kamala, and had arranged to keep her during the holidays. Two or three days ago he heard from the principal that they would not keep her during the holidays. The holidays started today, and the school carriage dropped her home. I went to their house, and I saw Kamala peeling apples and Ramesh eating them. I asked Ramesh to explain, but he refused. Had he said just this much that Kamala was not his wife, we could have tried to suppress our doubts, but he neither confirmed nor denied it. Do you still trust him?'

Jogen looked at Hemnalini expecting an answer. Her face had gone pale and she was holding on to the chair with all her strength. Within seconds she fainted and fell down. Annada babu was terribly upset. He held her close and tried to console her. Jogendra lifted her up and placed her on a sofa. He splashed water on her face, and Akshay began fanning her. In a little while, when she opened her eyes, she was startled. She shouted, 'Send Akshay babu away.' Akshay went out and waited behind the door. Annada babu sat by her side, sighed and held her hand.

Hemnalini was crying. Her father said, 'Please don't be distressed. I know Ramesh very well. He will not deceive us. Jogen must be mistaken.' Jogen said impatiently, 'Don't give her false assurances. Give her some time to think.' Hemnalini said, 'I won't believe your allegations until I hear it from him.' She left the room saying that she wished to be alone.

Annada sat in his own room. He remembered his wife who had died when Hem was only six months old. He remembered her patience, and her pleasant nature. He had brought up that little girl by himself, and now he was afraid that she might be hurt. He prayed that she should be happy with a husband whom she loved.

Jogendra's poor opinion of women was further strengthened now. He called Akshay and asked his opinion. Akshay replied, 'Why do you want to involve me? I haven't said anything so far, and you have already put me in a difficult position.'

'We can talk about that later. Now we must find a way of persuading Ramesh to admit his guilt to Hemnalini.'

'How is that possible?'

'You must persuade him.'

Akshay agreed to try.

## 20

That night Ramesh went to Sealdah station with Kamala. He took a long route, and while passing through Kolutala, he gazed at a particular, familiar house. There was no outward change in it.

Ramesh sighed, and Kamala asked, 'What is the matter?'

He replied, 'Nothing,' and sat still in the darkness of the coach. Kamala rested her head in the corner and fell asleep. For a moment Ramesh felt Kamala's presence was unbearable.

They reached the station. He had reserved seats in the second class compartment on the train. He spread her bedding on one bench and said that it was late and she should try to sleep. Kamala sat by the window and watched the people come and go. When the train was about to start, Ramesh caught a glimpse of a familiar face. Kamala laughed suddenly and Ramesh saw a man struggle with a railway guard and get into the moving train. In the struggle, his shawl got left behind with the guard, and now the man was trying to retrieve it. Ramesh recognized the man —it was Akshay. So, Akshay was following them. If Akshay went to his village and inquired there, it would cause a scandal. Ramesh was extremely worried. He stayed awake to see if Akshay got down at any of the stations, but Akshay did not. Late at night Ramesh fell asleep.

Next morning they reached Goalondo. Ramesh saw that Akshay was rushing towards the steamer. There was another one, which was about to start. On inquiry Ramesh found out that it was going westwards, possibly till Kashi. Ramesh decided to take that steamer. He settled Kamala in, and bought some provisions and fruit from the nearby shop.

Akshay had rushed to the other steamer, expecting Ramesh and Kamala to come. He had placed himself on the deck, to watch. But there was no sign of the couple. When the steamer was about to start and still they did not come, Akshay got off. He could not find them anywhere. He suspected that Ramesh had seen him and had taken a train back to Kolkata.

## 21

Akshay took the night train back to Kolkata. He went to Ramesh's house and found it locked. He reported back to Jogendra that he had failed to catch Ramesh. Jogendra was now convinced of his guilt. He pleaded with Akshay to try to find Ramesh and get him to admit everything. There was no other way to convince Hemnalini and Annada babu.

Annada and Hemnalini came in to have tea, but on seeing Akshay there Hemnalini turned back. Jogendra was offended and called Hemnalini to join them. Akshay, however, was a patient man. He asked Jogendra not to put pressure on Hemnalini, and continued to drink his tea.

When Akshay left, Annada asked Hemnalini to join them. Her face was pale, and there were dark circles under her eyes. She kept her eyes lowered and did not glance at Jogendra. Although her love for Ramesh secured her faith in him, she could not ignore the arguments against him. The day before she had made it clear that her trust was unshaken, but a night in her dark bedroom had weakened her conviction. She searched but could not find any reason for Ramesh's behaviour. Doubts were trying to make inroads into her trust. She held on to her trust in him with all her mental strength, like a mother protecting her child from hurt.

Annada's room was next to Hemnalini's. He could hear her tossing and turning in bed, and called out to her asking if she was finding it difficult to sleep. She assured him that she was about to sleep. Next morning Hemnalini was strolling on the terrace. She found all the shutters closed in Ramesh's old house. At dawn, the coming day seemed empty, dry and hopeless. She sat in a corner and wept.

Annada joined her there and persuaded her to come down and have some breakfast. Going downstairs, she heard Jogendra talking to someone. For a moment her heart stopped; was it Ramesh? Who else would come so early? When she saw that it was Akshay again, she rushed out of the room.

When she returned later, the exasperated Jogendra said, 'Father, do you know the latest? Ramesh was taking his wife to his village. They were on the train to Goalondo, when he spotted Akshay; he changed his mind and returned to Kolkata.' Hemnalini's hands shook and some tea spilled. She sat down suddenly. Jogendra observed the effect of his words and continued, 'I can't understand why he had to run away. His earlier behaviour was bad enough, but this cowardice is detestable. I don't know what Hem thinks, but to me this running away is proof enough.' Hem was shaking as she stood up. She said, 'I am not waiting for any proof. If you wish to judge him, go ahead, but I won't judge him.'

'Are we unconnected to the man you are engaged to marry?'

'Who is talking about marriage? If you wish to break the engagement, go ahead. But you will not turn me against him.' Saying this she broke down. Annada gently led her out of the room.

## 22

The steamer started. The first and second class cabins were empty. Ramesh chose one and spread out the bedding. Kamala was gazing at the scenes on the riverbank. Ramesh asked, 'Do you know where we are headed?'

'We are going back to the village.'

'You don't like the village, so we aren't going there.'

'You won't go to the village just to please me?'

'Yes, just for you.'

Kamala was upset. She said, 'But why? I said something without thinking, and you took it to heart? You get angry easily.'

'I am not angry. I didn't wish to return to the village either.'

'Where are we going then?'

'We are going west.'

Kamala was astonished. West! To someone who had spent all her life confined, what did 'west' signify? To her 'west' denoted places of pilgrimage, places where people went for a change of air, legends of kings, beautifully carved temples and stories of chivalry. She was thrilled. She asked where in 'west' were they headed.

Ramesh replied that he had not decided. It could be Monghyr, or Patna, Danapur, Gazipur or Kashi. Any one of these places would do. Kamala's imagination was excited by all these names. She clapped her hands and exclaimed, 'It would be such fun.'

Ramesh said, 'The fun will come later. What shall we do about food? Will you eat food cooked by the sailors?' Kamala declined and said that she would cook herself.

'Can you cook?'

'What do you think? Am I a little girl? I used to cook in my uncle's house.'

Ramesh went to make the arrangements for cooking and found a stove. He also engaged a boy called Umesh to fetch water, wash dishes and do other odd jobs by offering him free passage to Kashi and some money.

He asked Kamala, 'What will you cook today?'

'You have only brought rice and lentils. I will cook khichri today.' Ramesh brought the required spices from the sailors. Kamala laughed at Ramesh's ignorance. She asked, 'How will I powder the spices?'

Ramesh got a mortar and pestle from the sailors. Kamala had never used these, but she was not deterred. They had much fun powdering the spices, and finally she started her cooking in a space enclosed with a bamboo screen. However, there was one more problem. They had no plates. The solution was to use the cover of the earthenware pot that contained sweets.

Ramesh ate well and praised her cooking. When the plate was empty, Kamala gave him another large helping. Ramesh tried to stop her saying that there would not be enough left for her, but she assured him that there was enough. But Kamala had no plate, so Ramesh offered to wash the earthenware lid for her, and Umesh offered to bring some large shal leaves from the vendor on the lower deck. Kamala's housekeeping began in this way.

Ramesh was impressed not only by her cooking but also by the way she kept everything neatly and did all her work without fuss. But he worried about the future. How would he keep her near yet far? Where should he draw the line? Kamala must be told the truth.

## 23

The steamer was stuck in the sand on the riverbank and could not be dislodged. The village women had come to fetch water from the river, and they looked at the steamer curiously. The little village boys were amused at the plight of the boat and made mocking gestures, jumping up and down in joy.

The sun had set. Ramesh stood on the deck and gazed at the glowing western sky. Kamala too came out and stood by the door. She tried to draw his attention by coughing, shaking her key-bunch, etc., but only when the noise was loud did he turn towards her.

'Why didn't you call me,' he asked.

'How should I call you?'

'Why? My parents gave me a name; why not call me by that name?'

'You don't know what you are saying,' she said. 'Come, your food is ready.'

Ramesh was hungry but had not mentioned it so as not to inconvenience Kamala. He felt happy to know that she was concerned about his well-being, yet he was aware that this was based on a false premise. He sighed and entered the room.

Kamala spread a shal leaf and placed luchi and vegetables on it. Ramesh was surprised. 'How did you get the supplies to make luchi?' he asked. Kamala asked, 'Guess how?' He pretended to think hard and said that she must have got the food from the sailors. Kamala vehemently denied that. Ramesh continued to tease her by mentioning various unlikely sources. Finally Kamala disclosed that when the steamer had got stuck in the riverbank, she had sent Umesh to the village and procured some clarified butter and flour.

Umesh had said that the village sweetmeat seller had excellent yogurt. He wanted to buy some flattened rice and have it with the yogurt. But Kamala had no money left. She was hesitant to ask Ramesh. She told Umesh to ask for the money during Ramesh's evening meal. While Ramesh was eating, Umesh came in and very hesitantly asked for some money for grocery. Realizing that Kamala was short of money Ramesh brought his cash box and gave it to Kamala. Kamala took over all the responsibilities of a housewife.

Umesh had a good meal. He had left his home where he was neglected by his stepmother and was on his way to Kashi to be with his grandmother. Now that he was happy to be with Kamala and Ramesh, he wished to stay on with them. He called Kamala 'mother', which touched her heart. She agreed to keep him on.

## 24

The woods on the riverbank etched a dark border on the golden evening, like the black border of a sari. Wild geese were flying back against the glow of the sunset from the marshlands to the ponds by the desolate beach. A single boat was quietly sailing down the golden green waters.

Ramesh drew up a chair on the deck and sat in the light of the crescent moon. The last golden hue disappeared from the western sky. The harsh realities of the world seemed to melt in the magic of the moonlight. Ramesh muttered softly, 'Hem, Hem!' The sweet sound of the name touched his heart. His eyes were damp.

The events of the last two years drifted through his mind. He remembered the day he first met Hemnalini. At that time he had not perceived it as a special day. He was shy by nature. When Jogen took him to his home for tea, he was uncomfortable in the presence of Hemnalini. Slowly he came out of his shyness and reserve, and got used to her company. Having tea in her house and enjoying her company turned into a habit. He thought he was in love and pitied others who had only read about but not experienced love. But it was only after Kamala entered his life and it got entangled in a complex web that his feelings for Hemnalini took shape and became real love.

Resting his head on his palm Ramesh thought of his life ahead, entangled in a crisis. Shouldn't he rip it forcefully? He was determined to do just that when he saw Kamala standing nearby. Kamala had thought that he was asleep, and she apologized for waking him up. Ramesh interrupted her saying that he had been awake, and that he wanted to tell her a story. Kamala was curious, so she drew a chair and sat down. He had decided that he must explain the situation to her, yet he wished to soften the blow. So he started a story.

'Long ago, there was a community of Kshatriyas, and they . . .'

Kamala asked, 'How long ago?'

'Long ago, before you were born.'

'As if you were already born then!'

Ramesh continued, 'Their custom was to send the bridegroom's sword—instead of the bridegroom—to the wedding. After the bride got married to the sword, she came to the bridegroom's house and got married to him.'

'What kind of marriage is that? It's very strange.'

'I don't like it either,' said Ramesh. 'They considered it beneath their dignity to go to the in-laws' house to get married. My story is about a king who belonged to that community. One day he . . .'

Kamala interrupted again. 'What was the name of his kingdom?'

'Madradesh. One day the king . . .'

'What was his name?'

The story was not well prepared. After a pause he said, 'His name was Ranjit Singh. The king heard that another king of his community had a beautiful daughter.'

'Which was his kingdom?'

'Let's say it was Kanchi.'

'Don't you know?'

'He was the king of Kanchi. His name was Amar Singh.'

'And the beautiful daughter?'

'Oh yes, her name was Chandra.'

'You are so forgetful. You forgot even my name.'

In spite of many mistakes, and close scrutiny by Kamala, the story proceeded in this fashion:

'Ranjit Singh, the king of Madradesh, sent an emissary to the king of Kanchi with a proposal of marriage for his daughter. The king of Kanchi agreed happily. Then Ranjit Singh's younger brother, Indrajit Singh, along with many soldiers and with much fanfare, set up camp in the huge garden of the palace. Kanchi was full of festivities.

'The king's astrologer set an auspicious day for the wedding. On the wedding day the town was decorated with flowers and lights.

'Princess Chandra did not know her bridegroom's name. When she was born, a wise astrologer had advised the king that she must not know the name of her bridegroom. Otherwise, she would suffer a misfortune.

'At the auspicious moment the princess got married to the sword. Indrajit Singh brought presents for his new sister-in-law. Her face was covered according to custom, so he did not see her face, nor did she see his.

'Next day the bride sat in a beautifully decorated palanquin, and the wedding party, led by Indrajit Singh, started their journey back to Madradesh. It was a month's journey. On the second night, when they were resting in their tents, they saw torchlights in the forest. It was another wedding party, and they were of the same community. They too were taking their bride back to their home. Since the way was full of danger, they were seeking the protection of Prince Indrajit. The prince agreed to extend his protection. So the other party set up their camp next to his.

'It was a dark moonless night. The tired soldiers were fast asleep, when loud shouts and screams woke them up. They found that someone had cut the ropes that tied the horses, and the horses were running helter-skelter. Some of the tents were on fire, lighting up the dark sky. They knew that bandits had attacked. They fought, but in the dark one could not distinguish between a friend and an enemy. In that chaos, the bandits took their loot and ran away into the forest.

'When all this was over, they couldn't find Princess Chandra. She had come out of her tent, and in the confusion and darkness, mistaken a group of people to be of her own party, and had followed them as they ran away.

'Actually they were from the other wedding party. Not knowing that the bandits had abducted their bride, they thought that Chandra was their bride and took her back with them to their village. They were poor Kshatriyas, and lived near the sea in Kalinga. The bridegroom's name was Chait Singh. His family members were very happy to welcome her.

Everyone said that beauty such as hers was rare.

'Chait Singh adored her and she too was ready to make a success of her marriage. But when he heard her name, he realized that she was not really his bride.'

## 25

Kamala was extremely curious, and asked in a breathless voice, 'Then?'

Ramesh said, 'I know only up to this much, you must tell me the rest.' Kamala protested and entreated him to continue.

Ramesh said, 'The story is being published serially, I don't know when the next chapters will be out.'

Kamala was frustrated. Ramesh pointed out, 'You should be angry with the author, not with me. I would like to know what Chait Singh should do with Chandra.'

Kamala gazed at the river thoughtfully. After a while she said, 'I don't know what he should do—I can't think of a solution.'

'Should Chait Singh disclose the truth to Chandra?' Ramesh asked again.

'How can you doubt it? It would be wrong to let the situation continue. He should tell her everything.'

'That's how it should be,' he agreed. After a while he said, 'Suppose I was Chait Singh and you were Chandra, what . .'

Kamala was upset. She stood up and said, 'Don't say these things; I don't like it at all.'

'I must, otherwise we can't decide what we should do.'

Kamala left the room ignoring the question. She found Umesh and asked, 'Umesh, have you ever seen a ghost?' He replied that he had. She drew up a chair near him and asked him to describe the ghost.

When Kamala left the room, Ramesh did not call her back. The crescent moon disappeared behind the bamboo grove on the riverbank. The sailors were busy preparing their meal downstairs. There were no other passengers in the first and the second classes. The passengers in the third class had gone down to the riverbank to make the arrangements for cooking. He could see the lights of the bazaar in the distance. The steamer was anchored but was swaying in the waves of the river. Ramesh was immersed in the wonders of the unfamiliar scene, and the vast vista, indistinct in the dark. He tried to come to a decision. He must give up either Hemnalini or Kamala. There was no middle way. Hemnalini had her family; in time she might forget Ramesh and marry someone else. But Kamala had nowhere else to go, and no one else to turn to but him.

Ramesh was not consoled by the thought that Hemnalini could lean on others, and might forget him. He was now doubly eager for Hemnalini. He rested his head on his palms and continued to think. When he looked up, he found that Kamala was standing on the deck gripping the railing. He asked, 'It's quite late, aren't you going to bed?'

Kamala asked, 'Aren't you?'

'I shall go soon. My bed is made in the room to the east. You shouldn't stay up any longer.'

Kamala slowly went back to her own room. She could not tell Ramesh that she had heard a ghost story, and that she was afraid to be alone. Ramesh sensed her anxiety, and said, 'Don't be afraid, my room is next to yours, and I shall keep the adjoining door open.' Kamala kept her chin up and denied that she was afraid.

Ramesh went to bed in his room. Since there was no way of leaving Kamala, he had finally resolved to give up Hemnalini. He could feel the pain of a life without Hemnalini acutely. He got up and stood on the deck. Gazing into the dark night he understood that in the larger scheme of things, his problem was insignificant. Infinite time and space were unaffected by his predicament; the river would continue to flow by the villages, groves and sandbanks night after moonlit night, even after his existence was reduced to ashes.

## 26

Kamala woke before dawn. She looked around, but there was no one else in the room. Then she remembered that she was in a steamer. She pushed the door ajar and saw the thin layer of fog over the still water; the darkness was paler, and in the eastern sky, the glow of sunrise was visible over the trees. In a minute the white sails of the fishing boats became visible.

She did not know why she was sad. Why was there no joy in this dew-filled autumn sunrise? Tears, choked inside, were trying to come out. Yesterday, it had not mattered that she had no relatives or friends; she had Ramesh and that was enough. But since then something had made her aware that Ramesh could not be her sole support. She saw her own insignificance in the large world.

She stood holding on to the door for a long time. The river was shining in the sunlight. The sailors had started their work, and the noise of the boats had drawn many children to the riverbank. Ramesh came to inquire after her. Although Kamala's sari was in place, she drew the edge of the sari to cover herself better. Ramesh advised her to wash and get ready before the rush of other people. She was annoyed but went to have her bath.

Ramesh's concern seemed unnecessary and humiliating to her. She had realized that their intimacy only went so far. She did not quite know why, but she felt shy and hesitant with Ramesh.

Her day's work began. She unlocked the portmanteau, and took out the cash box. Earlier, she had derived a sense of pride and independence from the possession of the cash box. Now she felt that it did not belong to her, it was Ramesh's. She was not free to use the money as she liked. It was a burden.

Ramesh entered and asked, 'Why are you staring at the cash box?'

She held it up and said, 'Take it, it's yours.'

'What would I do with it?'

'Please keep it and get me the supplies when needed.'

'Don't you need any money?'

'What use is money to me?'

He smiled and said, 'Very few can make a statement like that. But why should I keep it?'

She placed the box on the floor. He asked, 'Kamala, tell me, are you angry with me for not completing the story that day?'

'I'm not angry.'

'I shall be convinced only if you keep the box.'

'As if!' said Kamala.

'It isn't mine. If I take back what I have given, then I will be a ghost after I die.'

Kamala laughed at this, and the atmosphere got lighter. Then she asked, 'Have you seen a real ghost?'

'I have seen many unreal ones; the real ones are rare!'

'But Umesh says that . . .'

'I must admit that I am not in the same league as Umesh.'

In the meantime, the steamer had started. Suddenly they saw someone with a basket on his head running on the riverbank towards the boat and gesturing to stop it. The ship's captain ignored him, so the man waved to Ramesh and shouted, 'Sir, sir!' Ramesh waved back signalling that he could not stop the boat. Kamala exclaimed, 'That's our Umesh, we can't leave him there, we must pick him up!' Ramesh first requested and finally bribed the captain to stop the boat.

Umesh came aboard, ignored the rebuke of the captain, laughed and placed the basket at Kamala's feet. Kamala scolded him too. Without bothering to answer, Umesh emptied the basket revealing green bananas, and several other vegetables. When asked where he had found these, he gave a confusing account. The day before, on his way to buy yogurt and other things, he had noticed these in the vegetable patches in the village. Early in the morning he had got off from the boat and had collected these items without bothering to ask for permission.

Ramesh was terribly displeased and accused him of theft. Umesh disagreed. He said, 'I didn't steal. There were so many vegetables in the farms, that I just brought a few. No one will notice the loss.'

Ramesh said angrily, 'Take these away. Otherwise, I will throw them in the river.' Umesh looked at Kamala who signalled him to take them away. Umesh gathered them in the basket and left. But he had noticed her slight smile.

Ramesh went back to his room. Kamala saw that Umesh was standing near their makeshift kitchen. She asked if Umesh had thrown away the vegetables. He replied that he had carefully hidden them in the kitchen. Kamala pretended to be angry, warned him not to do this again, and began cooking.

Kamala was aware of the gravity of his offence, yet she understood his need to make a home with them. She was touched by the effort he had made to get the vegetables to please her. She said, 'Umesh, I will let you have the yoghurt left over from yesterday, but you must promise not to steal again.'

'Why didn't you have it?' he asked.

'I'm not that fond of yoghurt. But how can I give my husband a meal without any fish? How do we get some?'

'I can get you some, but I'll need some money,' said Umesh. He had sensed that Kamala did not find it easy to ask Ramesh for money. So he had worked out his plan to get vegetables but not a plan to get fish. Alas, the world was a hard place, his blind adulation for Kamala was not enough, and he needed money to get things for her. He said, 'If you could get a little money from sir, I can find a large rahu.'

Kamala anxiously said, 'I won't allow you to get off the steamer.'

'Why would I? This morning the sailors made a large catch. They might agree to sell one or two.' Kamala brought a rupee and asked him to bring back the change after buying the fish. Umesh brought the fish but not the change. Kamala understood, and commented with a smile, 'From now on we must get some change when the boat is anchored.' Umesh understood what was implied.

At dinner, Ramesh was delighted to find rahu fish on his plate and inquired where they had got it. He enjoyed his dinner. Umesh found the fish curry delicious, and ate so much that Kamala had to stop him by promising to keep the rest of the curry for his dinner.

The day was ending. The ray from the western sky fell on the roof of the boat. The light glittered on the water. The village women were walking towards the river with their water pots. Kamala finished making the paan, tied her hair in a plait, changed her sari and got ready for the evening. By then the sun had set behind the bamboo grove of the village. The steamer was anchored at the riverbank.

Ramesh said that he did not want any dinner because he had eaten too much at lunchtime. So Umesh had all the fried fish and curry.

Ramesh gazed at the small tin-roofed office of the Steamer Company on the riverbank. A clerk was writing in a notebook in the light of a kerosene lamp. Ramesh thought that if only fate had designed his life to be like that man's, narrow yet clear—writing the accounts, working, getting scolded by the boss for mistakes, returning home at night—he could have lived like that. Then the kerosene lamp was turned off. The man locked the room, covered his head with a shawl and walked away through the paddy fields out of sight.

Ramesh had not realized that Kamala was standing behind him, holding the railing. Kamala had hoped that Ramesh would call her. After finishing her work when he still did not call her, she came to the roof of the boat to find him. She saw his face in the moonlight, he seemed far away, completely absorbed in his own thoughts. It seemed to her that the moonlit night was guarding him, and was signalling her to silence.

When Ramesh placed his head on the table, she walked back to her room. She felt herself abandoned and alone in the dark room. Where could she go? Where was her true place? She came out, and something fell, making a noise. Ramesh came rushing and asked, 'Kamala, are you afraid? I'll sleep in the next room and keep the adjoining door open.'

Kamala emphatically denied being scared. She went in, and closed the adjoining door. She threw herself on the bed, covered herself with a sheet. Since she had no one else, she held herself close. How would she live when there was neither dependence nor independence?

The night seemed long. Ramesh was asleep in the next room. Kamala got up and went to the deck. She could see no one on the riverbank. The moon was setting in the west. She gazed at the pathway that led from the riverbank to the village, and she thought, so many women fill their pots in the river and go home walking along this path every day. 'Home', a home was all she wanted, but where was her home? She did not need the vast endless sky that stretched across the horizon, or the vast endless land; she only needed a home.

She noticed someone standing near her. 'It is I, Umesh. It is late, why are not you sleeping, Ma?' he asked. Her tears—held in check for so long—coursed down her cheeks at these caring words from the homeless boy. She turned her face away. She tried to reply, but couldn't.

Umesh did not know how to console her. After a while he said, 'Ma, there are seven annnas left from the rupee you gave me.' Kamala smiled at this and asked him to go to bed.

When Kamala went back to bed, she fell asleep. She was fast asleep when the morning sunlight fell on her door.

## 27

Kamala woke up feeling tired. The sunlight, the flow of the river, and the trees on the riverbank seemed tired like an exhausted traveller. When Umesh offered to help with her housework, she snapped at him: 'Don't bother me.' Umesh explained that he had come to grind the spices. Ramesh was also concerned and asked if she was ill. She shook her head, and showing her displeasure at such unnecessary and inappropriate questions, she went to the kitchen.

Ramesh realized that the situation was getting more complicated every day. A solution must be found soon, but it would be easier to decide after discussing it with Hemnalini. He began a letter to her. He wrote and crossed it out again and again when he heard, 'Sir, may I know your name?' He was surprised to see a middle-aged man with receding hair and a white moustache standing in front of him.

'Are you a Brahmin? Namaskar! I know that you are Ramesh babu, yet I asked out of common courtesy. In case you are offended, as some are, you could reciprocate by asking my name. I will happily tell you not only mine but also my forefathers'.' Ramesh was amused and said, 'Just your name will suffice.'

'I'm Trailokya Chakravarty, known as "uncle". Like Bharata, the *chakravarty* or supreme monarch of India, I am "Chakravarty uncle" in these parts. What is your destination?'

'I haven't decided yet.'

'You take long to decide your destination, yet board the steamer in a hurry!'

'In Goalondo, when I heard the whistle of the steamer, I realized that it wouldn't wait for me to make up my mind. So I had to hurry.'

'I'm all admiration! You are not like us. We are cautious; we decide first and then board. You decided to go but not where to go; remarkable! Are you travelling with your family?'

Ramesh hesitated for a second. Chakravarty said, 'I already know that your wife is with you. I was looking for the kitchen and found her cooking there. I said, "I am Chakravarty uncle, please don't mind me." She is like goddess Annapoorna. I said, "Please include this uncle at your mealtime." She smiled, and I knew that I need not worry about my meals. I consult the almanac before every trip, this time I am particularly lucky. But I won't keep you from your work any longer. If you don't mind, I will go and help her. Please don't get up; I just came to introduce myself.'

Chakravarty went to the kitchen. 'What aroma! I know how tasty the vegetable curry will be even before tasting it. I would like to make the chutney. Don't bother to find the ingredients; I will get some tamarind and spices.' He brought some mustard and tamarind and sent Kamala away saying that since his wife was sickly, he was used to cooking.

Kamala said, 'I will watch and learn how to make chutney.'

'It can't be learnt in a day!' he replied. 'First you must please me by remembering my habits. For example, I like paan, but the betel nuts must be sliced finely. It is not easy to please me, but your smile has done the trick!'

Turning to Umesh he asked his name. Umesh was peeved because he did not want to share Kamala's affection with anyone; so he did not reply. Kamala introduced him. Chakravarty commented, 'He appears to be a nice young man. I know that he isn't pleased to meet me, but I know that we will get along well.'

Kamala forgot her loneliness in Chakravarty's company. Ramesh too was less anxious. His present relation with Kamala was so different from their closeness in the first few months when he had believed her to be his wife, that it could not but hurt her. Chakravarty's arrival diverted Kamala and allowed Ramesh to focus on his own feelings.

Kamala stood by the door, hoping to spend the long idle afternoon chatting with Chakravarty uncle. Chakravarty noticed her shoes and said, 'Ramesh babu, this is not in our tradition. Had Rama made Sita wear Dawson's boots, would Lakshmana have spent fourteen years in the forest? You are laughing. You hear the whistle and board the ship but don't give a thought to your destination.'

'Uncle, why don't you decide for us? Your advice would be better than the steamer's whistle.'

'Although you met me a few hours ago, your mind is much improved already! Well then, come to Gazipur. Will you come to Gazipur, Kamala? It has fields of roses, and your old uncle lives there.'

Ramesh looked at Kamala. She nodded her head in agreement.

Chakravarty and Umesh stayed on to discuss the proposal with Kamala but Ramesh remained outside, and felt left out. The steamer was chugging along. In the autumn sunlight the peaceful yet varied scenes along the riverbanks had a dreamlike quality: paddy fields; moored boats; sandy banks; village cowsheds; tin-roofed shops; and travellers waiting under a banyan tree for the ferry. He heard Kamala laughing and he thought it was all so beautiful, yet so distant; severed from his wretched life by a harsh blow.

## 28

Kamala was young, so doubts and apprehensions did not take root in her. In the last few days she did not have time to think about Ramesh's behaviour that had kept churning in her mind and had blocked the easy flow of her emotions. Now in Chakravarty's company, laughing, chatting, arguing and cooking, she forgot her worries.

Days began in great enthusiasm. Umesh managed to procure a variety of vegetables and his basket was a source of great surprise, curiosity and discussion. Ramesh suspected that Umesh stole from the money for shopping, so he asked for the accounts, but Kamala defended Umesh. The accounts would never tally, but Umesh, unperturbed, would protest, 'If I knew how to tally accounts, I would be the steward of a landlord; would I be in this situation?' Chakravarty too praised Umesh for being enterprising. Ramesh had no support in this matter.

Chakravarty said, 'If you judge him after your meal, it would be a fair judgement. Meanwhile I can't but encourage him. Collecting is an art which few can master. I appreciate the artist.'

'Uncle, you shouldn't encourage him,' said Ramesh.

'The boy is uneducated, and if we don't encourage the ability he has, then he will lose it.' Then Chakravarty gave Umesh instructions on what vegetables to get, and requested Kamala to cook his favourite dishes.

The more Ramesh suspected Umesh, the more Kamala adored the boy. When Chakravarty too took Umesh's side, Ramesh was alone against the three of them. He was like a large ship which has to anchor far from the bank where the smaller boats congregate.

One morning, dark clouds covered the sky. The breeze was blowing helter-skelter; rain and sun alternated. There were few boats on the river, and they appeared hesitant. Women came to fetch water, but did not linger by the riverside. The river water shimmered in the sunlight falling from the gaps in the clouds.

The steamer continued on course, but Kamala found it difficult to cook in that makeshift kitchen. Chakravarty advised her to cook the evening meal too and made the rotis himself. They finished their meal late. The wind was blowing stronger and the river was rough. One could not make out if the sun had set or not. Kamala had once almost drowned, so she was only too aware of the storm. Ramesh reassured her that the steamer was safe, and that she could sleep peacefully because he would be awake in the next room. Chakravarty assured her that the storm would not dare to touch her. Kamala was afraid all the same. She said eagerly, 'Uncle, please come to my room.' Chakravarty was hesitant. He said, 'You two would like to sleep, I better . . .' But entering the room he was surprised at Ramesh's absence. 'Where is Ramesh babu in this weather?'

'Uncle, I am in the next room,' replied Ramesh. Chakravarty went to the next room and found Ramesh semi-reclined, reading a book.

'She is terribly scared. Your book isn't afraid of the storm and can be left alone! Please go to her.'

Kamala, in a fit of emotion, quickly gripped Chakravarty's hand and said, 'No, Uncle, no!' Ramesh did not hear this in the noise of the storm, but Chakravarty was astonished. Ramesh came into her room and asked, 'What is the matter? Kamala is not letting you . . .'

Kamala protested, 'No, no, I called him to tell me a story.' The 'no' could mean: you don't need to reassure me; or it could mean: you don't have to keep me company. The next moment she said, 'Uncle, it is getting late, please go to bed. Just make sure Umesh is all right, he must be scared.'

A voice near the door answered, 'I'm not afraid of anything.' Umesh had covered himself up from the wind and was sitting outside Kamala's room. Kamala was touched. She said, 'Umesh, don't sit there and get wet in the rain, go with Uncle and sleep.' Umesh left with Chakravarty.

Ramesh asked, 'Shall I sit with you and chat until you feel sleepy?'

'No, no, I am very sleepy,' she said. Ramesh understood her feelings, but did not persist. He saw her offended look and slowly went back to his room.

Kamala's state of mind was not such that she could compose herself to sleep. She heard the noise of the swishing wind and water, the shouting of the crew, and the ringing of the captain's bell. In spite of being anchored, the engine was running. She came out on the deck. The rain had stopped for the moment, but the wind, screaming like a wild animal, blew in all directions. In spite of the cloud, the sky was dimly lit and the waxing moon seemed restless and destructive. Neither the river nor the riverbank was clearly visible. Everything far and near, above and below, visible and invisible, was in an inexplicable madness, a blind turmoil, like the fierce black buffalo of the god of death.

Kamala's emotions too were in a turmoil, whether in fear or in joy she could not tell. The unstoppable energy and the boundless freedom embodied in the storm awoke what was asleep in Kamala. She was agitated by the force of nature in protest. Protest against what? Could one get the answer in the roar of the wind? No, because it was mute, like Kamala's emotions. This havoc, this angry cry of the sky and the sea was to tear away the web of a formless and unidentified lie, a dream, and darkness. The wind swept across the land screaming 'no', 'no' in repudiation; but of what?

## 29

Next morning the storm abated, but did not quite stop. The captain could not decide whether to raise anchor, and looked anxiously at the sky. Chakravarty went in search of Ramesh and found him still in bed. Remembering the incident of the previous night, he put two and two together. He asked, 'So, you slept here?' Ramesh avoided answering and said instead, 'Such bad weather! I hope you managed to get some sleep.'

'I may look foolish and perhaps talk foolishly, but in my long life I have thought about many difficult questions, and also found solutions, but I find you most difficult to comprehend.'

Ramesh's face reddened, but he controlled himself and said with a smile, 'It is not wrong to be incomprehensible. A Telugu language primer is difficult but not for a Telugu boy. Don't blame what is incomprehensible. You must know the alphabet to read the language.'

'Please forgive me, Ramesh babu. It was impudent of me to try to understand you. But there are some, like Kamala, with whom one can forge a bond immediately. Even the steamer's captain would agree with me. What is the relevance of the Telugu language in this context? Please don't be angry, but think about it.'

Ramesh said with a sigh, 'It is because I have thought about it that I am not angry. But whether I am angry or not, whether you feel hurt or not, the Telugu language will remain so—such is the cruel law of nature.'

Meanwhile Ramesh was wondering whether they should go to Gazipur. Earlier he had believed that Chakravarty might be useful in an unknown place. But now he saw the disadvantage. If his relation with Kamala became a subject of curiosity and gossip, she might find it unbearable. Instead, it might be better to settle in a place where no one knew them and there was no one to ask questions.

The day before reaching Gazipur he said, 'Uncle, I don't think Gazipur would be good for my practice, so I have decided to go to Kashi.' Ramesh sounded determined.

Chakravarty smiled and said, 'Taking a different decision every time is not a sign of being decisive. Anyhow, for the time being you have decided on Kashi?'

'Yes, I have.'

Chakravarty left without any comment, and began to pack his bags. Kamala asked, 'Uncle, why are you avoiding me since this morning?'

'You are deserting me, and you accuse me of avoiding you?'

Kamala did not respond to that. She said, 'Uncle, let me pack your things.' Chakravarty interpreted this to be indifference on Kamala's part and felt hurt. Then he thought that perhaps this was for the best.

Ramesh came to inform Kamala and said, 'Kamala, we won't go to Gazipur this time. I have decided to practise in Kashi. What do you think?'

Kamala continued with the packing and replied, 'No, I will go to Gazipur.' Ramesh was surprised. 'Will you go alone?'

'Why alone? Uncle will be there.'

Chakravarty, embarrassed, said, 'Kamala, if you show such partiality, Ramesh babu will hate me.'

Kamala reiterated, 'I will go to Gazipur.' It was clear from the way she said it that she did not need anybody's approval.

Ramesh said, 'Uncle, then let it be Gazipur.'

It was a moonlit and clear evening after the storm. Ramesh sat on a deckchair and thought that things could not continue this way. Life would be more and more difficult with Kamala revolting. It was impossible to be so near yet maintain a distance, and it was time to end this. He had accepted Kamala as his wife. He shouldn't hesitate just because the wedding vows weren't said. In that deserted sea beach, the god of death had brought them together. No priest could be his equal.

There was a gulf between Ramesh and Hemnalini. He would stand beside her and hold his head high only when he removed the obstacles of distrust and humiliation. But it was a difficult battle which he did not hope to win. He had no proof, and if he tried to prove his case, it would become public knowledge with terrible consequences for Kamala. He could not allow that. Therefore he must not be indecisive but accept Kamala as his wife. Hemnalini probably despised him, and that would help her accept another eligible man. Ramesh sighed and put an end to his hopes regarding Hemnalini.

## 30

Ramesh asked, 'Where do you think you are going?'

Umesh replied, 'I am going with the mistress.'

'I bought you a ticket for Kashi. This is the landing for Gazipur. We are not going to Kashi.'

'Nor am I.'

Ramesh had not expected him to be a permanent factor in their lives; he was astounded at the confidence of the lad, and asked Kamala, 'Must we take Umesh with us?'

'Where will he go if we don't take him with us?'

'He has relatives in Kashi.'

'No, he wants to come with us. Umesh, stay close to Uncle, otherwise you might get lost in the crowd.'

Kamala seemed to have taken over the responsibility of deciding where to go, and who to take with them. Earlier, she used to accept Ramesh's wishes and decisions without a word, but in the last few days she had passed that stage. So Umesh picked up his bundle and followed them. There was no further discussion.

Chakravarty's small bungalow was between the town and the area where the Englishmen lived. There was a mango grove behind it, a well, a low wall in front, and a vegetable garden which thrived from the water of the well.

Although Chakravarty told people that his wife's health was frail, there was no obvious sign of it; she seemed fit and capable. The slightly greying hair proclaimed she was not young, yet not old either; that old age had staked its claim but had not taken possession. When the couple was young, she had had a bad attack of malaria. With the hope that a change of air would do her good, Chakravarty took a schoolmaster's job and moved to Gazipur. Although she had regained her health, he was not convinced.

Seating his guests in the living room he went inside and called his wife. She was in the courtyard, supervising the servant and keeping various containers with pickles in the sun. Chakravarty immediately remarked, 'It is cold, why don't you have a shawl on?' She replied, 'What rubbish! It's not cold; my back is burning in the sun.'

'That is not good either, sit in the shade.'

'Never mind all that. Why are you so late?'

'That's a long story. I have brought some guests, we must make arrangements.'

She was used to her husband bringing guests unexpectedly, but she was not prepared for a couple. She said, 'We don't have a spare room.'

'Get to know them first, and then think about where to put them up. Where is Shailo?'

'She is bathing the child.'

Chakravarty brought Kamala to his wife, and Kamala touched her feet. She blessed her and said to her husband, 'Her features are like our Bidhu's.' Bidhu was their elder daughter who lived in Kanpur with her husband. Chakravarty smiled to himself because he knew that although Kamala had no resemblance to Bidhu, his wife could never accept that any girl could be superior to her daughters in looks or qualities. Shailo lived with them and might fall short in comparison to Kamala, so his wife compared Kamala with the absent daughter, so that nobody could verify her claim.

Chakravarty's wife's name was Haribhamini. She said, 'I am glad they have come, but our new house is not yet ready, and we ourselves are barely managing; they will find it uncomfortable.'

Their small house in the market area was under repair, but it was meant for a shop. They had no plans to live there, nor was it suitable. Chakravarty chose not to contradict his wife and said instead, 'I know that they can put up with some inconvenience, otherwise I wouldn't have invited them. But you mustn't stay outside; the autumn sun can be harmful.' He went back to Ramesh in the living room.

Haribhamini was curious about Kamala and asked a thousand questions such as: 'Is your husband a lawyer? How long has he been practising? What is his income? Oh, he hasn't begun yet, then how do you manage? Does your father-in-law have property? How come you don't know anything about your in-laws? How much do you get for household expenses? My elder son-in-law gives all his income to my daughter, Bidhu,' and so on. Kamala felt inexperienced and foolish. She realized that her ignorance of her husband's family, work and income appeared strange to outsiders. She never had the opportunity to discuss these matters, and in spite of being Ramesh's wife, she knew very little about him. She was ashamed and felt insignificant.

Haribhamini started again. 'Let me see your bangle. The gold is not of good quality. You didn't get any jewellery from your parents? Your father is no more? Even then, one should have more. Doesn't your husband give you jewellery? My elder son-in-law gets jewellery for Bidhu every other month.'

While all this was going on, Shailaja came in with her two-year-old daughter. Shailaja was dark, with a small face. But her bright eyes and broad forehead gave the impression that she was intelligent, as well as calm and contented. Shailaja's daughter stared at Kamala and said, 'aunty'. She called all women of that age group 'Aunty'. Kamala took the child in her lap.

Haribhamini introduced Kamala. 'Her husband is a lawyer, and wants to set up practice. Your father met them on the steamer and brought them to Gazipur.'

A bond of friendship formed immediately between the two young women. When Haribhamini left, Shailaja took Kamala to her own room. Within a short time they were deep in conversation. It was not obvious that Kamala was the younger of the two. Shailaja was small built while Kamala was not only tall, she also had the ways of an older woman. Since she was married, she had lived free of restrictions and strictures from elders. She held her head up and there was an air of strength and confidence about her.

Shailaja's daughter Uma tried to be the centre of attention, but the two women managed to have a convivial chat. Shailaja had much to say, Kamala, very little. From Shailaja's conversation Kamala caught a glimpse of her married life. She had earlier felt an emptiness, a sense of being deprived, but she did not understand why. When Shailaja spoke of her husband, it was as though music played on her heartstrings. But Kamala had no such music in her heart. What could she say about her husband, when she was not even eager to talk about him? Shailaja's life was full of love, and was running smoothly on course. Kamala's life was empty, and like a boat stuck in the mud, it was not going anywhere.

Shailaja's husband Bipin worked in the opium department. The Chakravartys wished to keep their younger daughter with them, and had married her to a boy from a poor family. Shailaja and her husband lived with her parents.

In the midst of the conversation Shailaja suddenly said, 'Please wait a little, I'll be back soon. My husband is coming in to take his meal before leaving for work.' Kamala asked in surprise, 'How do you know that he is coming?' Shailaja smiled and said, 'As if you don't know how! Don't you recognize the sound of your husband's footsteps?' She laughed and left with her daughter. Kamala did not know that footsteps spoke so clearly. She sat quietly by the window, deep in thought. Outside, a guava tree was in bloom and honeybees were swarming on them.

## 31

They were trying to get a house in a quiet area by the river. Ramesh needed to make a trip to Kolkata to get the required documents to start practising in Gazipur court, and to get some things for the house. He was apprehensive. Even now when he thought of a particular house in a particular street in Kolkata, he felt emotional. He had not disentangled himself completely; yet, a normal married life with Kamala could not be delayed. He kept postponing his date of departure.

Shailaja thought that Kamala would miss her husband terribly, and kept consoling her. Kamala inquired why and Shailaja replied, 'You can't fool me, I know how sad you must be.'

Kamala asked, 'Tell me, if you don't see Bipin babu for two days, do you . . . ?'

Shailaja replied, 'As if he can stay away for two days!' She then talked about Bipin's impatience: when they were young and newly married, how Bipin took recourse to all kinds of deception to catch a glimpse of her without the elders' knowledge; since meeting during daytime was impossible, how they used to see and smile at each other in a mirror in the dining area. Her eyes had a merry glint when she talked about it. Later, when Bipin began working, he would try to avoid leaving for work on any pretext. Once when he was to go to Patna on business, Shailaja asked if he would be able to stay there without her, and Bipin said that of course he would. Shailaja was hurt and she resolved not to show her feelings. But the night before he was supposed to leave, she broke down. Next morning Bipin pretended to be sick, a doctor was called, his trip was cancelled, and the two of them secretly threw away the medicine. Talking about all this, Shailaja would forget that evening had set in, and then hearing her husband's footsteps, she would get up suddenly.

Kamala had experienced a hint of a similar emotion when she and Ramesh were getting acquainted in the early days. Later, when she left the school to stay at home, again a wave of happiness had played beautiful tunes in her heart. Only now she realized the significance. But her experience had no continuity; it was disjointed, not allowed to reach its fullness. Where was the eagerness that drew Shailaja and Bipin together? In spite of not having seen Ramesh for the last few days, she was not restless for him, nor was it likely that Ramesh was searching for an excuse to see her.

Shailaja was embarrassed to spend the entire Sunday with her husband, leaving Kamala all by herself. If she could only get Ramesh and Kamala together, she would not feel guilty. She couldn't consult her father, but he guessed what was on her mind. In the morning he declared loudly that he would go out of town, lock the front door from outside, and that no visitor was expected. He knew that his daughter would take the hint and do the needful.

After Kamala's bath, Shailaja insisted on drying and tying her hair in a beautiful bun. They argued over selecting a sari. Kamala could not understand why she must wear a bright-coloured sari that Shailaja selected. Finally she wore it to please Shailaja.

After the midday meal, Shailaja whispered something to her husband, came to Kamala, and tried to persuade her to go to the living room. Kamala had always gone to Ramesh unhesitatingly. But today she found it impossible. She had understood that Shailaja had a claim on her husband that she herself did not have on Ramesh. How could she demean herself and reach for him? When Kamala could not be persuaded, Shailaja thought that she was upset with Ramesh, and justifiably so because in all these days he had not attempted to try to see her on any pretext.

When her mother went for her afternoon nap, Shailaja asked her husband to send Ramesh inside to Kamala. Although Bipin was reluctant to act as a go-between, he did not want to displease his wife. In the living room, Ramesh was lying down and reading the *Pioneer*. After reading all the articles and not having anything else to read, he was looking at the advertisements when Bipin came in. Although on a normal day Ramesh would not have considered Bipin interesting company, on that long idle afternoon far from home he was happy to have someone to talk to.

Ramesh said, 'Please come in Bipin babu, take a seat.'

Bipin scratched his head and said with some embarrassment, 'She has asked you to come inside the house.'

'Who, Kamala?'

'Yes.'

Ramesh was surprised. He had decided to accept Kamala as his wife, but his vacillating mind sought more time. He was already anticipating his future happiness with Kamala as his wife. But the first step was difficult to take. He had got used to keeping a distance from her, and did not know how to bridge the distance. This is why he was not in any hurry to find a house.

Kamala must have some reason to send for him, probably she needed something. Still he was excited. When he left his magazine and followed Bipin to the inner part of the house, it felt like a lover's tryst.

Bipin pointed to the room and left. Kamala, unaware of all this, sat near the door looking at the garden outside. The leaves of the trees were trembling in the warm breeze, and Kamala's heart too trembled in an unspoken longing. She was startled to hear Ramesh call out: 'Kamala.' Her heart beat faster. She had never felt self-conscious or hesitant in front of Ramesh, but today she could not even lift up her eyes to look at him. She blushed.

Kamala seemed a different person in her beautiful clothes, her coiffeured hair and in her polite manners. Ramesh was overwhelmed. He stood near her and asked softly, 'Did you send for me?'

Kamala denied this with unnecessary vehemence, 'No, no, I didn't. Why should I?'

Ramesh said, 'Even if you did, there is no harm.' Kamala denied it even more forcefully.

'All right, even though you didn't, I have come. Must I go back feeling unwelcome?'

'If the others come to know that you are in the inner part of the house, they will be offended. Please leave. I didn't call you.'

Ramesh held her hand and said, 'Then you come to my room. There is no one there.'

Kamala was trembling. She somehow freed her hand, went to the next room and shut the door.

Ramesh now realized that all this had been planned by one of the women; yet his excitement remained intact. He went back to his room, and again opened the magazine to pore over the advertisements, but he could not concentrate. Emotions drifted through his heart like clouds drifting in the sky.

Shailaja knocked on the locked door to no avail. Then she opened the shutters and somehow pushed her hand in and opened the latch. She found Kamala lying on the floor weeping. Shailaja was surprised. What could have hurt Kamala? She sat beside Kamala and asked what the matter was.

Kamala asked, 'Why did you send for him? It was wrong of you.'

Neither Kamala nor the others could fully understand this flood of emotion. Nobody could know of the accumulated pain over so many months which had never before found expression.

Kamala had imagined a dream world. Had Ramesh entered it naturally, it would have given joy; but by bringing him to her, it was spoilt. She remembered how Ramesh had tried to keep her in the school hostel during the holidays, and his indifference towards her on the journey, and she was terribly upset. She knew that he came when he was asked to and he stood near her, but now she also knew that it did not signify anything. The days spent with Shailaja had taught her that.

But Shailaja could not understand. She could not even imagine that there was a distance between Ramesh and Kamala. She placed Kamala's head on her lap and asked, 'Has Ramesh babu said harsh words to you? Perhaps he was angry because my husband went to call him. Why didn't you explain that it was entirely my fault?'

'No, no, he didn't say anything. But why did you call him here?' Shailaja was subdued and admitted that she shouldn't have. Kamala sat up, gave her a hug and sent her to her husband.

Ramesh got bored of the magazine and tossed it away. Then he decided to leave for Kolkata to arrange his affairs without delay because the more he delayed in accepting Kamala as his wife, the greater would be his guilt. Suddenly his sense of duty overcame all his earlier doubts.

## 32

Ramesh had decided that he would complete his work and return to Gazipur; he would not go anywhere near Kolutola. He stayed in his Dorjipara house. His work occupied little of his time each day, and he did not know how to spend the spare time. He could not meet his former friends, and carefully avoided chance meetings.

But Kolkata brought a change in his feelings for Kamala. In an ambience of peace and quiet, when Kamala appeared in her first flush of youth, he had found her attractive. But in Kolkata his fascination waned. When he imagined Kamala in the Kolkata house, she seemed immature and uneducated instead of a woman to be admired.

The more he tried to forget Hemnalini, the more he remembered her. The determination to forget her only aided his memory of her. Had he been in any hurry, he would have completed his work quickly and left Kolkata. He let his work drag on, until it finally finished.

He was leaving the next day for Allahabad, from where he would go to Gazipur. He thought that as reward for his determination and patience he could surely go to Kolutola to inquire about the family. He wrote a letter explaining about Kamala and the events of the past several months. Also that he planned to accept Kamala as his wedded wife. Having explained the truth, he bade goodbye to Hemnalini. The letter was not addressed to anyone in particular, nor did he write a name on the envelope. His plan was to go to Hemnalini's house after dark, see her from a distance, and send the letter to her through a servant and leave.

In the evening he went there and found the door locked, the windows shut and the house dark. He knocked a few times, a servant opened the door. Ramesh asked, 'Where is your master?'

'He has gone with his daughter to the western provinces.'

'Where exactly?'

'I don't know.'

'Who else is with them?'

'Nalin babu'

'Who is Nalin babu?'

'Sorry, I don't know anything about him.'

After much inquiry Ramesh gleaned that Nalin babu was a young man, and a frequent visitor. Although Ramesh had no hopes regarding Hemnalini, he was not pleased by this information.

'How is Hemnalini?'

'She is quite well.'

'I would like to go to the living room upstairs.'

Ramesh found the room, the furniture, and the arrangement just as they had been earlier, but who was this new factor, Nalin babu? In this world, the space vacated by one is soon filled by another. He had once stood beside Hemnalini by that window at the end of a rainy day, their hearts joined in the light of sunset. When at the same window, someone else wished to stand by her side in the sunset light, would the past bar their way? Would it raise its finger in warning and push them away?

Next day Ramesh went back directly to Gazipur.

## 33

Ramesh had spent a month in Kolkata, and a month was not a short period for Kamala. Her life seemed to be speeding towards a culmination. The woman in her was fully awake, like dawn becoming day. Had she not known Shailaja closely, nor perceived her happiness, the transformation might have taken longer.

Meanwhile seeing that Ramesh was delayed, Shailaja persuaded her father to fix up a house near the river for Kamala and Ramesh. They were getting the house ready and employing servants. So when Ramesh returned, there was no excuse to stay on with the Chakravartys. Kamala set up her own household.

The bungalow had a lot of land, and a road shaded by tall trees led up to the house. A strip of sandy land lay between the house and the river; it had shrunk in winter where the peasants cultivated wheat and planted melon and watermelon. In the southern corner of the compound there was a margosa tree with a paved platform to sit on.

Being vacant for a long time, the house and the garden were neglected. There were hardly any trees, and the rooms were dirty. Yet, Kamala found great joy in being the mistress of the house. She decided how each room would be used, which trees would be planted and—with Chakravarty's advice—how the land would be farmed. She got things fixed to her taste in the kitchen and the storeroom.

Ramesh saw Kamala in the midst of her work, and she seemed like a bird freed from her cage. He was both surprised and happy at her contentment, and her efficiency. Until then he had not seen her in her rightful place, now her beauty acquired a new glory.

He said, 'Kamala, you are doing too much; you will tire yourself.' Kamala smiled and denied that she was tired. His concern was a reward for her. Ramesh asked again, 'Have you had your meal?' 'Of course, long back,' she said. Ramesh knew that she had eaten; nevertheless, he wished to show his concern. Kamala was pleased.

To continue the conversation Ramesh said, 'You are doing so much, give me some work too.'

Efficient people don't trust others to do a job well. Kamala said, 'This is not a man's job.'

Ramesh retorted, 'Because we men are so tolerant you can get away with your poor opinion of us. If we were like you women, we would have made a big fuss. You allow Uncle to help, why not me? Am I so incompetent?'

'That I can't say, but when I think of you cleaning cobwebs in the kitchen, it makes me laugh. Move away from here, it's terribly dusty.'

To prolong the conversation Ramesh said, 'Dust doesn't discriminate between you and me.'

'I tolerate it because I have to work here, why must you suffer?'

Ramesh said softly, 'It's not a question of work. I want to share with you all that you endure.'

Kamala blushed. Without replying, she directed Umesh to clean a particular corner of the kitchen, and then began sweeping it herself in spite of protests from Ramesh.

Chakravarty overheard as he came in and asked, 'Ramesh babu, you had an English education and you preach equality. If sweeping is lowly work, why do we ask the servants to do it?' Then addressing Kamala he said that the grounds were clear and ready for planting and that Kamala must show him where to plant what. Kamala asked him to wait, finished sweeping, and was soon deep in conversation with him about her plan for the vegetable garden.

The day had ended and yet the house was not ready for occupation. To Ramesh's disappointment they had to go back to Chakravarty's house that evening. He had imagined the evening in their own home, where Kamala would light the evening lamp and he would open his heart to her. Since moving was postponed, he went to Allahabad for some work.

Next day Kamala organized a picnic in her garden. Chakravarty was persuaded to take a day's leave, Shailaja joined them, and they cooked the meal under the neem tree in the garden. After the meal Chakravarty went inside to rest, and the two young women sat in the shade and chatted. The riverbank, the winter sun, the shady tree, all seemed incomparably beautiful to Kamala. Like the birds flying in the distant sky, an unknown wish flew out from her heart.

As the afternoon passed Shailaja got restless, it was time for her husband to come home from office. Kamala asked, 'Can't you break the routine even once?' Shailaja smiled, stroked Kamala's face affectionately and went in. She woke her father up and said that she was going home.

Chakravarty asked Kamala to accompany them, but Kamala said that she had some work still, and would return in the evening. Chakravarty left his old servant with Kamala and went to reach his daughter home, and also do some work there.

When Kamala finished tidying and arranging the rooms, the sun had not set yet. She wrapped a shawl and sat under the neem tree. The sun set on the other side of the river behind the large stationary boats with tall masts that were like black scratch marks on the red sky. Umesh came on some pretext and said, 'Ma, I have brought some paan from the other house, you've not had one the whole day.' Realizing that it was getting dark Kamala got up quickly. Umesh said, 'Chakravarty babu has sent the carriage.' Kamala went inside to check the rooms before leaving.

There was a fireplace in the large room. A lighted kerosene lamp stood on the mantelpiece. Kamala placed the packet of paan there and saw a piece of paper with her name written in Ramesh's handwriting. 'Where did you find this paper?' she asked Umesh. 'I found it while sweeping the master's room; it was in a corner on the floor.' Kamala opened the paper and began reading it. It was the letter Ramesh had written to Hemnalini. Ramesh, careless, had not noticed when or where it had slipped from his hand.

Kamala read the letter. Umesh asked, 'Ma, why are you still standing there? It's getting late.' There was no answer. Umesh was alarmed at Kamala's expression. He said, 'Ma, let us go home, it has got dark.' After a while Chakravarty's servant came in and reminded her that the carriage was still waiting.

## 34

Shailaja asked, 'Aren't you feeling well today? Do you have a headache?'

'No. Where is Uncle?' asked Kamala.

'The school is closed for Christmas. Didi is not keeping well, so Ma has sent him to Allahabad.'

'When will he return?'

'Not before a week. You don't look well; you work too hard to get your house ready. Have your meal early and go to bed.'

Kamala would have been only too relieved to confide in Shailaja, but it was not something that one could talk about. She could not possibly tell Shailo of all people that the man who was supposed to be her husband, was actually not.

Kamala closed the door of her bedroom and read the letter again by the light of the oil lamp. There was no name or address on the letter; it was quite clear that it was addressed to a woman, there had been a proposal of marriage between Ramesh and her, and that they broke it off because of Kamala. In the letter, Ramesh did not hide that he loved the nameless addressee with all his heart, and that he must break it off with her out of pity for the helpless Kamala who was thrust on him by cruel fate.

She thought back to their first meeting on the riverbank and all the events that followed, up to their arrival in Gazipur. What was unclear earlier became clear. She was overcome with shame that believing this man to be her husband, she was confidently preparing to set up her home with him. Whereas he knew her to be someone else's wife and must have been extremely worried about what to do with her. Memory of all the daily incidents made her shame unbearable, and she felt that it would never leave her.

She opened the door and went out into the back garden. In the dark winter night, the cloudless black sky seemed cold like a piece of black stone. The stars were clear and shining. The short mango trees stood in front, adding to the darkness. Kamala could not think of a solution. She sat down on the cold grass and was still as a piece of wood, and her eyes were tearless. She might have remained like this for a long time, but she began to shiver in the bitter cold. When late at night the moon rose behind the still palm trees and tore away the darkness, Kamala stood up slowly and went in.

When she opened her eyes in the morning she found Shailo standing by her bedside. Embarrassed for waking up late, Kamala sat up quickly. Shailo said, 'You are unwell; try to sleep for a while longer. There are dark circles under your eyes and you look tired. Please tell me what the matter is.' Saying this, Shailaja sat down next to Kamala and put her arm around her. Kamala burst into tears. Shailo did not say a word but held her close.

Soon Kamala moved Shailo's arm away, stood up, wiped her tears, and laughed aloud. Shailo said, 'You do not have to laugh. I have never seen a girl as uncommunicative as you. You think you can hide it from me? I am not a fool. You are upset because Ramesh babu hasn't written to you since he left for Allahabad. Try to understand that he is there for work, and might not have the time to write. He will be back soon. You shouldn't be angry with him. But I should not be advising you, I would have done the same! Women have to often shed tears for such reasons, but again happiness makes one forget.' She drew Kamala close. 'You feel that you will never forgive Ramesh babu, don't you? Tell me the truth.'

Kamala said, 'Yes.' Shailo said, 'Is that so? Let's bet on it!'

After her conversation with Kamala, Shailo wrote to her father in Allahabad. She wrote, 'Kamala is extremely worried because she has not heard from Ramesh babu. You can imagine her sorrow: she is in a new place; Ramesh babu is away so often and does not write to her. Will his work in Allahabad never finish? Other people also have work, but doesn't he have any free time to write even two lines?'

Chakravarty read out sections of the letter to Ramesh and rebuked him. It was true that Ramesh was attracted to Kamala, but that only worsened his dilemma. Because of this dilemma, he was not returning from Allahabad. He realized from the letter that Kamala had strongly expressed her anxiety for him, only her inhibition prevented her from writing. This realization brought two strands of the dilemma together. Now it was not just a question of Ramesh's own feelings; Kamala loved him. Fate had brought them together on the riverbank, but now it had also joined their hearts. Without any delay Ramesh wrote to Kamala.

Dearest Kamala,

I address you thus not because it is the accepted way of addressing but because to me you are the dearest of all. If you have any doubts, if I have ever hurt your feelings, then may this true address 'dearest' remove all your doubts and unhappiness. How can I elaborate on this? Until now my behaviour might have caused you pain, and if you have resented it, I will not protest or defend myself—I will only say that now you are my dearest, there is none I hold dearer. If this does not redeem my guilt and my unfair conduct, then nothing will.

Kamala, by calling you my dearest I have pushed away our troubled past, and have begun our future of love. I entreat you to believe that you are my dearest. If you can accept it, then you will not need to question me about your doubts.

I don't have the courage to ask if you love me, and I will not ask. No doubt that a favourable answer to my unasked question will quietly touch my heart through yours. I can say this on the strength of my love. I don't proclaim that I deserve it, but why should my endeavour not succeed.

I know that this letter seems forced, perhaps it sounds like an essay. Maybe I should tear it up. But it is impossible to write a satisfying letter at this point. A letter belongs to two; when only one person writes, one cannot write everything in the way one would like to. When you and I get to know each other's feelings completely, only then will I be able to write a letter that is truly a letter. When two doors facing each other are open, only then the breeze flows through freely. Kamala, dearest, when will you fully open your heart to me?

All this will get resolved in due course; there is no point in rushing. I will arrive in Gazipur the day after you receive this letter. My request is that I should see you in our home. We have been homeless for so long. I am now impatient. This time when I enter my home, I wish to see my heart's Lakshmi as the Lakshmi of my home. That moment will be the second auspicious moment of seeing each other. You remember the first time—on that moonlit night, on the deserted and sandy riverbank? There was no roof, no walls, no relatives or neighbours; it was not in a home, but outside. It seems like a dream, as though it never happened. That is why, on another day, in the clear and soft light of the morning, in our home, with true hearts, that auspicious seeing must be completed. I am eagerly awaiting that morning of Paush to impress forever in my heart your innocent, smiling face. Dearest, I wait at the door of your heart, please don't send me away.

Awaiting your favour
Ramesh

## 35

To cheer Kamala up Shailo asked, 'Aren't you going to your bungalow today?'

'No, there is no need.'

'Have you finished decorating the house?'

'Yes, it is done.'

After a while Shailo came again and asked, 'If I give you something, what will you give me in return?'

Kamala said, 'What do I have to give?'

'Are you sure you have nothing?'

'Nothing at all.'

Shailo touched Kamala's cheek and said in jest, 'Is that so? You have given everything away to someone? Guess what this is.' Shailo took out a letter from the folds of her sari.

Seeing Ramesh's handwriting on the envelope, Kamala paled, she turned away her face. Shailo teasingly said, 'Don't pretend to be angry, enough is enough. You are actually dying to snatch the letter from me, but I will give it to you only if you ask for it. Let me see how long you can hold off.'

At this point Uma came pulling a string tied to a matchbox and said, 'Aunty, car.'

Kamala quickly picked up Uma, kissed her and took her to the bedroom. Uma started screaming for the car, Kamala would not let go of her but tried to humour her with all kinds of stories.

Shailo said, 'All right, I admit defeat, you have won. Congratulations. I couldn't have done this. Take your letter.' She left the letter on the bed, took Uma from Kamala and left the room.

Kamala picked up the envelope, observed it for a while, and then opened it. The first few lines made her blush. She threw it away in shame. After the first wave of disgust she controlled herself, picked it up and read the whole letter. She might not have understood it fully, but she felt that she was holding something repulsive. She threw it away again. She was invited to live with a man who was not her husband. Ramesh had knowingly insulted her after all this time. After coming to Gazipur, Kamala's heart had reached out for Ramesh: was it because it was Ramesh or was it because she believed him to be her husband? Ramesh had noticed it, and that was the reason for showing his pity for her through this love letter. Kamala wished to withdraw whatever she had revealed to Ramesh, but how? Why had fate brought so much shame and disgust for her? Was her birth itself a crime? How was she to protect herself from the 'married life' that was advancing and threatening to swallow her up? Could she have imagined a few days earlier that Ramesh would become such a nightmare for her?

Umesh was at the door and coughed to draw her attention, and then he called, 'Ma.' Kamala came to the door. Hesitatingly Umesh said, 'Sidhu babu has brought a jatra troupe from Kolkata as a part of his daughter's wedding festivities.' Kamala readily gave him permission to go. Umesh asked, 'Do you want me to pick some flowers tomorrow morning?' 'No, there's no need.' As Umesh was leaving, she called him back. 'Umesh, you are going to watch a play, keep this money with you.'

Umesh was surprised. Why would he need five rupees to see a play? He asked, 'Do you want me to buy something for you from the town?'

'No, no, I don't need anything. It will come in useful for you.'

As the bewildered Umesh was leaving, she said, 'Are you going to see the play in those old clothes? What will people say?'

Umesh did not think that others expected much of him by way of clothes, and was indifferent to whether his dhoti was white enough or whether or not he had a chaddar over his upper body, so he smiled, but did not say anything.

Kamala brought four of her saris and gave them to Umesh.

Umesh liked the beautiful, broad-bordered saris. He touched Kamala's feet. When Umesh left, Kamala stood near the window. Her eyes were wet.

Shailo came in and asked, 'Kamala, won't you show me your letter?'

Shailo had never kept any secrets from Kamala, so now she could claim Kamala's confidence.

Kamala pointed to the letter which was lying on the floor. Shailo was surprised that Kamala was still angry with Ramesh. She read it and found it strange, although there was much about love. A strange letter to write to one's wife! She asked, 'Does your husband write novels?'

Kamala's body and mind reacted to the word 'husband'. She said, 'I don't know.'

'So, you will go to the bungalow today?'

Kamala nodded in affirmation. Shailo said, 'I could have kept you company, but I am expecting a visitor. Perhaps Mother can go with you.'

Kamala quickly interrupted. 'No, no, what will she do there? There is a servant.'

Meanwhile Uma was scratching every surface with a pencil, blabbering as though she was reading. Shailo took away her pencil, and she started crying. Kamala said, 'Come to me, I have something for you.' She picked her up, hugged and kissed her. Then she opened her jewellery case, took out a pair of gold bracelets and handed them to Uma. The child was very pleased to wear them. Her mother took them away from her, and said, 'Kamala, you must not give the child such things.'

Kamala replied, 'Didi, I am giving these bracelets to Uma.'

'Are you mad?'

'Please, Didi, you mustn't return them to me. Get a gold chain made for her with these.'

Shailo said, 'I have never met anyone as crazy as you.' She wrapped her arm around Kamala who said, 'I am leaving your house today. I was very happy here, happier than I ever was.' She was weeping.

Shailo tried to check her own tears and said, 'As if you are going away very far. You will be happy to have your own household, and wouldn't wish to bother with us.'

When Kamala was leaving, Shailo said that she would visit her the next day. Kamala neither acquiesced nor demurred.

In the bungalow she found Umesh. 'Umesh, didn't you go to see the play?'

'You will be here today, so I . . .'

'Don't worry about me. Bishan will be here; go, don't delay.'

'But there is still a lot of time before the play begins.'

'Never mind that, go and join the festivities.' As he was leaving Kamala said, 'When Uncle comes, you . . . .' She did not complete the sentence. Umesh waited. Kamala thought for a while and resumed, 'Uncle is fond of you. If you need anything ask him.' Even though Umesh could not understand what all this was about, he said, 'Yes, Ma,' and left.

In the afternoon Bishan asked, 'Ma, where are you going?' Kamala replied, 'I am going to bathe in the river.'

'Shall I come with you?'

'No. You watch over the house.' She gave him some money without any good reason and walked towards the river.

## 36

One afternoon Annada went upstairs to ask Hemnalini to join him for a quiet cup of tea. He could not find her in the upstairs sitting room, or in her bedroom. On inquiry the servant said that she had not gone out. Annada became anxious and climbed up to the terrace.

The autumn light was fading over the terraces of the buildings, and a light breeze was blowing. Hemnalini was sitting quietly in the shade of the terrace wall.

She did not notice when her father came and stood behind her quietly. She was startled when he touched her shoulder, and looked embarrassed. He sat beside her, sighed and said, 'Hem, if only your mother were alive now; I am of no use to you.'

Hemnalini was suddenly alert. She looked at his face and saw so much affection, sympathy and pain there. The last few weeks had left their mark. He was facing and fighting the storm that was raging in this household all alone, on her account. He kept coming to her, and when he could not console her, he remembered her mother and was overcome by the pain of his failure. Hemnalini understood this, as though it was revealed by lightning. She was ashamed of herself. She brushed aside the memories that had engulfed her and freed herself. She asked, 'Father, are you feeling well?'

Annada had forgotten about his own health. He replied, 'I am very well. I am anxious about your health. My old body has survived all these years, and is not affected easily. I am concerned about you, because the young are felled easily.' He stroked her back gently.

Hemnalini asked, 'How old was I when Mother died?'

'You were three, you had just started speaking. I remember that you asked me, "Where is Ma?" I said, "She has gone to her father." Your grandfather had passed away before you were born, you did not know him. You did not understand, and pulled me towards her empty room. You believed that I would find a way for you through that emptiness. You thought that your father knew everything, yet he was ignorant and helpless as a child about the most important things. Today I have realized again that we are so helpless, God has given love in the father's heart, yet little power.' He placed his right hand on her head.

She took that trembling hand in hers and said, 'I remember Mother only slightly. I remember that she used to lie down with a book in the afternoons, and I did not like that. I used to try to snatch it away from her.' They talked about her. What she was like, what she did, and so on. The sun was setting and the sky was copper-coloured. All around them was the noise of the busy city, and in the midst of it, the tenderness between father and daughter blossomed in the fading evening light.

They were startled by Jogen's footsteps on the stairs; they stopped their conversation and stood up. Jogen surveyed the scene and remarked, 'Hem's evening assembly is conducted on the terrace these days!' He was impatient. He tried to spend most of his time outside to avoid the ambience of sadness in the house, but his friends kept inquiring about Hem's wedding which made it difficult for him. He was of the opinion that Hemnalini was overreacting, and it was the result of allowing her to read too many English novels. Guided by these novels Hem thought that Ramesh's abandonment should cause her heart to break. So she was making a fuss about her broken heart. Few girls get such a golden opportunity to bear the disappointment of love.

To shield Hem from the harsh sarcasm, Annada quickly said, 'We were having a chat,' as though he had brought her to the terrace for a chat.

Jogen said, 'Why, can't you chat at teatime? Father, even you are encouraging her. If this continues it will be difficult for me to live here.'

Hem was surprised. She asked, 'Father, you haven't had your tea yet?'

'Tea is not the product of a poet's imagination, nor does it pour out of the light of the setting sun! Teacups don't get filled if you sit in a corner of the terrace,' commented Jogen.

To cover her embarrassment Hem said, 'I didn't want any tea today.'

'Father, have you too become an ascetic? What is to become of me? I can't live on air.'

'No, no, I didn't sleep well last night, and thought I might sleep better if I don't drink tea,' said Annada. In fact, he had yearned for a cup but had not wished to get up. After a long time Hem was talking to him normally. He could not remember whether they ever had such a deep and intimate conversation before, but he also realized that elsewhere, the conversation could not be continued; it would have escaped like a startled fawn. So he had ignored his craving for tea. Hemnalini did not believe his story of lack of sleep. She asked him to come and have his tea.

He found Akshay waiting in the room downstairs, and became doubly anxious for Hem. But there was no way of preventing a meeting. Hem followed him into the room. Akshay stood up and said, 'Jogen, let me take my leave.'

Hemnalini asked, 'Akshay babu, are you in a hurry? Have a cup of tea with us.'

They were surprised by this. Akshay sat down again and said, 'I have already had two cups in your absence, but I might be persuaded to have two more.'

'As far as tea is concerned, you have never needed persuasion,' Hem said with a smile.

'God has given me enough sense to not refuse a good thing even when I don't need it,' commented Akshay.

After a long gap there was a lively conversation around the tea table. Usually Hem smiled, but today her laughter could be heard above the conversation. She teased her father saying, 'Akshay babu appears to be doing well without your pills; to show his gratitude he should at least have had a headache!'

'This is called "pill betrayal"!' said Jogen.

Annada laughed. He believed that comments on his pillbox indicated the good health of his family, and he felt relieved. He said, 'You are trying to interfere in people's beliefs and persuading Akshay, the only admirer of my pills, to defect!'

'Don't worry, Annada babu, it is not so easy to persuade Akshay,' said Akshay.

Jogen commented, 'It is like a fake currency note, if you try to get change, it becomes a police case.'

The ambience of Annada's tea table became lighter as though it had ceased to be haunted by a ghost. The gathering broke up when Hemnalini went in to do her hair. Akshay remembered that he had some important work and he left.

Jogen said to his father, 'Start preparing for Hemnalini's wedding without delay.'

Annada was surprised. Jogen continued, 'There is a great deal of talk in our circle about the cancellation of her marriage to Ramesh. I am tired of arguing with them. If I were allowed to disclose the facts it wouldn't have mattered, but because of Hem, I can't. If Hem gets married soon, all the talk would stop, and I wouldn't need to argue with them. Please listen to me and don't delay.'

'Who is she to marry?' asked Annada.

'It would be hard to find a match because of what has happened and because of the gossip. There is only Akshay. He is not deterred by anything. If you ask him to take a pill, he would do so, ask him to marry and he would marry.'

'Are you mad? Hemnalini marry Akshay?' Annada exclaimed.

'I can persuade her if you don't interfere.'

Annada was very agitated and said, 'No, Jogen, no. You don't understand Hem. You will bully her, threaten her, and make her miserable. Let her be. She has suffered enough. There is time enough to marry.'

Jogen said, 'I won't bully her. I shall be careful and gentle, and get her to agree. You seem to think that I can't talk without fighting.'

Jogen was an impatient man. That same evening, when Hemnalini did her hair and came out of her room, Jogen called her. She was alarmed. She followed Jogen into the living room. Jogen said, 'Hem, have you noticed that Father is not keeping well?'

Hem looked anxious but did not reply. 'He will be seriously ill unless we address the problem now,' said Jogen. It was clear to Hem that she was being blamed for her father's ill health. She stood quietly, smoothing the border of her sari.

Jogen continued, 'Let bygones be bygones. The more we think of it, the more ashamed we shall feel. If you wish to remove his mental tension, you must hit at the root of that unpleasant affair.' He then awaited Hemnalini's answer.

Hem was embarrassed and said, 'I will never raise the troublesome topic with Father.'

'You won't, but that won't stop other people from discussing it.'

'What should I do?'

'There is only one way to stop the wagging tongues.'

Hemnalini guessed that Jogen had a scheme. She quickly said, 'Perhaps we should take Father away on a holiday. When we return after a few months, the gossip would have ceased . . . '

'It won't solve the problem completely. Until he is convinced that you have got over the affair, his anxiety will continue, and he won't get well.'

Hemnalini's eyes filled with tears. She wiped her eyes and asked, 'What would you like me to do?'

Jogen replied, 'It might sound harsh, but if you want our well-being, you must get married as soon as possible.'

Hem sat in complete silence. Jogen commented impatiently, 'You make a mountain out of a molehill with your imagination. Many young women experience similar wedding-related problems, but they get over it. If every incident is made into a novel, life would be impossible. You might not be embarrassed to worship the memory of that worthless liar, and live like an ascetic gazing at the sky, but we are greatly embarrassed. Get married into a good family and end this poetic nonsense.'

Hemnalini was fully aware of the embarrassment of it, and was hurt by Jogen's ridicule. She said, 'Have I ever said that I wouldn't marry and that I would live like a hermit?'

'In that case you must marry. But if you don't like anyone short of Indra, the king of gods, then you must follow the way of the ascetic. In life, one rarely gets what one likes, and one must adapt one's mind to suit what one has got. In this lies the true greatness of man.'

Hemnalini was greatly distressed. She asked, 'Why do you make such insinuations? Have I said anything about my likes and dislikes?'

'You haven't, but I have noticed that for no reason or for the wrong reasons you don't hesitate to show your dislike of some of your friends and well-wishers. You must admit that among all your acquaintances, there is one who has been constant through joy and sorrow, and whether or not you regard him well, I admire him for this. If you wish for a husband who would be willing to give up his life for your happiness, then you don't need to search high and low. But if you wish for poetic romance then . . .'

Hemnalini stood up and said, 'Please don't talk to me like this. I shall respect Father's wish and marry who he wishes me to. If I don't, then you may talk about poetic romance.'

Jogen calmed down immediately and said, 'Hem, don't be angry. You know that when I am unhappy, I lose my discretion and can't control my speech. I have known you since childhood, I also know that you are deeply embarrassed by this and how much you love Father.'

Jogen went to Annada's room. Annada was extremely anxious, fearing that Jogen was bullying Hem. Jogen arrived when he was about to get up and intervene in their conversation. He stared at Jogen.

Jogen said, 'Father, Hem has agreed to marry. Don't think that I forced her. If you ask her now she won't raise any objections to marrying Akshay.'

'Must it be me?'

'You can't expect her to say that she wishes to marry Akshay. If you feel hesitant, I can ask on your behalf.'

'No, no, I will talk to her. But what is the great hurry? She should be given some more time.'

'No. There might be other obstacles if we delay. The present situation must not continue.'

Jogen was obstinate. If he made up his mind, he acted on it. Annada was afraid of him. To diffuse the situation, he said that he would talk to Hem.

Jogen insisted, 'Father, now is the right moment. She is waiting for your decision. You must bring it to a conclusion today.'

Annada continued to think. Jogen said, 'Father, this is no time for thoughts. Come and talk to her.'

'Jogen, I wish to see her alone.'

'All right, I shall wait here.'

Annada found that the living room was dark. Someone stood up quickly from the couch and said, 'The light went out. Shall I ask for another one?'

Annada understood why light was unwelcome. He said that there was no need for a light, and sat near her.

Hem said, 'Father, you are not taking care of your health.'

'That is because my health is good, and doesn't require special care. You should look after yourself.'

'That is what all of you tell me. It is unfair. I am just as usual. If you feel that I should take some special care, why don't you tell me? Have I ever disobeyed you?' Her voice was choked with tears.

Annada replied anxiously, 'Never, never. I don't need to tell you anything, you understand me and you have acted according to my wishes. With my heartfelt blessings and with God's grace you will be happy.'

'Father, why won't you keep me with you?'

'Why shouldn't I?'

'I can stay with you at least until Dada marries. Who will look after you if I am not here?'

'Please don't worry about looking after me. I am not worthy of such devotion.'

Hem said, 'Father, it is too dark here. Let me fetch a light.' She brought a lantern from the next room. She said, 'In the confusion of the last few days, I couldn't read aloud the newspaper to you. I'll read it to you this evening.'

Annada said, 'Wait a little, I'll return soon.' He went to Jogen. He had decided to tell him that he could not talk to Hem about her marriage but would do so another day. But when Jogen asked, 'What happened? Did you talk to her about her marriage?' he blurted out, 'Yes I have.' He feared that otherwise Jogen would pester Hem.

Jogen asked, 'She has agreed?'

'Yes, in a way,' replied Annada.

'Let me go and tell Akshay.'

'No, no. Don't tell him anything just yet. If you rush, it might come to nothing. There is no need to tell anyone. We might go on a holiday, and things can be settled after we return.'

Jogen left without replying and went straight to Akshay's house. Akshay was trying to learn bookkeeping from an English accounting book. Jogen took away his book and said, 'This can wait; decide on your wedding date.'

'What are you trying to say?' asked Akshay.

# 37

Next morning when Hemnalini got dressed and went to her father, she found him sitting quietly by the window. The room was relatively bare. There was a bed, a wardrobe in a corner, an old, framed photograph on the wall, and on the opposite wall a woolen wall-hanging made by her. In the cupboard, the arrangement of the curios was the same as always.

Hem stood behind her father. She stroked his head, pretending to pluck his grey hair and said, 'Father, come and have an early tea. Then we will sit in your room and you can tell me about the old days. I love to hear that.'

Annada could understand Hem very well; he realized immediately that since Akshay would soon join them at the tea table, Hem was anxious to avoid his company and sought shelter in his room. He felt terribly sad that his daughter was always afraid, like a doe frightened of the hunter.

Going downstairs they found that the water was not yet boiled. He got angry with the servant who tried to explain that tea had been ordered much earlier that day. Annada commented that the servants had become lazy and that to wake them up from their sleep, more servants were needed. When the tea came, he was in a great hurry to drink it, when normally he took his time over it savouring every sip. Surprised, Hemnalini asked, 'Father, are you in a hurry to go out?' He replied, 'No, no. In winter, if you drink the tea in quick gulps, you perspire and that helps the system.'

But then Jogen arrived with Akshay. The latter had taken special care in dressing that day. He carried a silver-mounted walking stick, wore a pocket watch with a chain, and had a brown-paper-covered book in his hand. He did not take his normal place at the table but pulled up a chair near Hemnalini. He said with a smile, 'Today your watch is running fast.'

Hemnalini did not look at Akshay, nor did she reply. Annada said, 'Hem, let us go upstairs. My woolen clothes need sunning.'

Jogen said, 'Father, the sun is not running away, what's the hurry? Hem, pour some tea for Akshay. I too need a cup, but a guest gets priority.'

Akshay commented, 'Have you ever seen a man make such a sacrifice for the sake of duty? He is another Philip Sidney!'

Hemnalini did not respond. She poured two cups of tea, gave one to her brother, pushed the second one towards Akshay, and looked at her father.

Suddenly agitated, Annada said, 'You are always forcing her. You people insist on forcing your wish on the grief of others. I have tolerated it quietly for long, but it can't go on. Hem, we will take our tea upstairs from tomorrow.'

As he got up to leave the room, she said, 'Let us sit here for a bit longer. You couldn't enjoy your tea today. Akshay babu, may I ask what is in that mysterious packet?'

'You may not only ask but also uncover the mystery.' Akshay handed the packet to her.

Hem opened it and found a volume of Tennyson's poems bound in Moroccan leather. She turned pale. Earlier, she had received the same collection in a similar binding. She had kept it carefully in a drawer in her bedroom.

Jogen remarked with a smile, 'The mystery is not fully unravelled yet.' He opened the first white page for her. On it was written: 'To Miss Hemnalini with infinite regards, from Akshay', thereby he made a pun with his own name. The book dropped to the floor. Not bothering to even look at it, she said, 'Father, let's go.'

They left the room. Jogen's eyes were blazing with anger. 'I can't continue to live here. I'll find a teaching job somewhere and leave.'

Akshay said, 'It is no use being angry. I had suspected that you misunderstood her, but I was moved to consider it because of your repeated assurance. I am sure that Hemnalini will never favour me; so, give up that hope. More importantly, you should help her forget Ramesh.'

'How?' asked Jogen.

'There are other eligible men. You must find someone. Someone—the sight of whom doesn't prompt her to leave immediately to sun the clothes!'

'One can't place an order for an eligible bachelor.'

'Why do you give up so easily? I can suggest someone, but don't spoil it in your hurry. You mustn't bring up the question of marriage in the beginning, thereby causing tension for both the parties. Let them get to know each other slowly, fix the wedding date when the time is ripe.'

'The method is good, but who is the man?'

'You don't know him well, but you have met him. Dr Nalinaksha.'

'Nalinaksha!'

'Why are you surprised? He is the centre of a controversy in the Brahmo Samaj. But does it matter? You can't let go of such an eligible man.'

'Would he be willing to marry?'

'I can't guarantee that he would immediately, but anything is possible given time. He is giving a lecture tomorrow. Take Hem there with you. He is a gifted speaker, and as far as winning the hearts of women goes it is no small ability. Women are fools. They don't know that a husband who listens is far better than a husband who talks.'

'Tell me, what is his background?'

'Jogen, don't be upset if his history has a slight flaw. A small blemish makes a rare thing attainable. I consider it a gain.'

Following was the gist of Akshay's account of Nalinaksha's background:

Nalinaksha's father Rajballav was a minor landlord near Faridpur. He became a Brahmo when he was thirty. His wife, however, did not accept his religion and continued to observe Hindu rites and rituals, thereby distancing herself from her husband. Needless to say, this was a cause of unhappiness for Rajballav. In due course, his son Nalinaksha became well established in the Brahmo community because of his missionary zeal and his oratory. As a doctor in government service he was posted in many different parts of Bengal and through his medical skill, honest nature, and his dedication to do good his reputation spread far and wide.

Meanwhile something strange happened. In his old age Rajballav insisted on marrying a widow. No one could dissuade him. He said that his present wife didn't share his life or his religion, and that it would be wrong not to marry the woman who shared his religion, his beliefs and his heart. In the end, in spite of widespread opposition he finally married her according to Hindu rites.

When Nalinaksha's mother decided to leave her home to go and live in Kashi, Nalinaksha gave up his practice in Rangpur to go and live with her. His mother said, 'Since your ways and mine are different, it would only make you unhappy.'

Nalinaksha replied, 'There won't be any discord.' His mother felt humiliated and abandoned by his father, and he was determined to make her happy. He went with her to Kashi.

'When will you marry?' she asked.

'What is the need? I am fine as I am.'

His mother understood him. He had sacrificed a great deal for her sake, but he was not ready to marry outside the Brahmo community. She felt sad and said, 'You cannot live an ascetic's life because of me. Marry whoever you wish to, I won't raise any objection.'

Thinking over it he said, 'I will marry someone who will be acceptable to you. I will never bring home a wife who might have different ways and cause you grief.'

Nalinaksha came to Bengal in search of a bride. Then there is a gap in the history. Some say that he secretly went to a village and married an orphan, and soon after his wife died. Others doubt it.

Akshay himself believed that he had planned to marry but withdrew at the last moment.

Anyhow, in Akshay's opinion, Nalinaksha's mother would be happy with whoever he married. Where would Nalinaksha find a girl like Hemnalini? Undoubtedly, with her sweet temperament, she would respect her mother-in-law and never cause her any grief. Nalinaksha would soon realize this if he got to know her. Akshay's advice was to get them to meet somehow.

## 38

As soon as Akshay left, Jogen went upstairs and found his father talking to Hemnalini in the upstairs living room. Annada babu was embarrassed because he had lost his normal composure at the tea table that afternoon. To make up for it he welcomed Jogen saying, 'Come in, Jogen, come and take a seat.'

Jogen said, 'Father, you two don't go out anywhere. It is not good to stay indoors all the time.'

'But we have always been like this. It requires a great deal of persuasion to get Hem out of the house.'

Hem said, 'Father, why blame me? Tell me where you wish to go, and I will accompany you.'

Hemnalini wished to prove, even at the cost of going against her nature, that she was not hiding in her home but was eager to know what was happening around.

Jogen suggested, 'Father, there is an interesting meeting tomorrow. Why don't you take Hem there?'

Annada knew Hem's reluctance to go to crowded meetings, so he did not respond to the suggestion.

Unexpectedly, Hem was unusually eager and asked, 'A meeting? Who is the speaker?'

'Dr Nalinaksha. He is an excellent speaker. You would marvel at his life story. Such sacrifice! Such determination! One rarely meets such an extraordinary man!'

Two hours earlier, Jogen knew nothing about Nalinaksha except through hearsay!

Hem enthusiastically suggested that they go to listen to Nalinaksha.

Although Annada did not fully believe her enthusiasm, yet he felt that if she forced herself to go out and socialize, then she would heal sooner. The best medicine for her broken heart would be the company of people. He said, 'Good. Jogen, take us with you to the meeting tomorrow. Meanwhile tell us what you know about Nalinaksha. People say all sorts of things.'

Jogen began by accusing those people. He said, 'Those who give themselves airs for being religious think that they have the God-given right to find fault with others. They are the most narrow-minded.' While saying this, Jogen got more and more excited.

To calm him, Annada said, 'You are right. Discussing other people's shortcomings makes one narrow-minded, suspicious and hard-hearted.

Jogen said, 'Father, are your remarks about me? I am not like those bigots. I praise and also criticize; but I say what I have to say upfront.'

Annada was alarmed and quickly said, 'Why should I remark about you? Don't I know you well?'

Then Jogen narrated Nalinaksha's life story, filling the gaps with a lot of praise. He said, 'Just to please his mother Nalinaksha lives in Kashi and follows orthodox Hindu ways. People may say many things, but I praise him for this. Hem, what do you think?'

Hem replied, 'I too think well of him.'

'I knew that Hem would approve. She seizes any pretext to please Father.'

Annada looked at Hem affectionately. Hem blushed and looked away.

## 39

It was still bright when Annada and Hem returned home from the meeting. While having his tea he remarked, 'I enjoyed the lecture.' He did not say more because his mind was full. Hemnalini went upstairs immediately after tea, but he did not notice.

Nalinaksha, the speaker of that day's meeting, was surprisingly youthful and charming in appearance. Yet, he had an air of solemn spirituality.

The subject of his talk was 'losses'. He said that one who had not suffered loss had not received anything. We don't fully possess what we get without asking; what we get through a sacrifice is truly ours. The human mind is capable of receiving truly only through renunciation. If we could speak of our loss with humility and say, 'I give the gift borne of my sacrifice, my sorrow, my tears', then what is insignificant becomes significant, perishable becomes imperishable, and what is merely for our use abides in the treasure chest of our heart.

These words had touched Hemnalini deeply. She sat still on the terrace under the starlit sky. Her heart was full; the sky and the universe seemed fulfilled.

On their way back from the lecture Jogen remarked to Akshay, 'You have chosen someone strange for Hemnalini. He is an ascetic! I did not follow half of what he said!'

Akshay replied, 'Choose a medicine that suits the disease. Hemnalini is engrossed in meditating upon Ramesh. Only an ascetic can bring her out of it. Did you not notice her expression when the lecture was going on?'

'Of course I did. She was enjoying it. But I don't see why enjoying his lecture would make it any easier to accept him as her husband.'

'Would the same lecture be as enjoyable coming from one of us? Jogen, women are especially drawn to ascetics. Kalidasa has written about Uma's meditation for the ascetic Shiva. I can guarantee that she will compare with Ramesh whoever else you might present to her. No one can win in that comparison. Nalinaksha is not like an ordinary person; she won't think of comparing him. Moreover, if you bring any other man, she will immediately guess your intention and rebel. But if you bring Nalinaksha under some pretext, she won't suspect you. After that it wouldn't be difficult to guide the course from respect to acceptance.'

'I am not good at finding pretexts—force is easier in my case. Whatever you might say, I don't like the man.'

'Jogen, don't spoil it by your cussedness. Everything can't be favourable. Somehow or the other, Hem's mind must be freed from the thought of Ramesh. I don't see any other way. Don't even think that you can accomplish this by force. If you follow my advice, there might be a solution.'

'Nalinaksha is a little too complicated for me. I am afraid of dealing with such men. To fulfil one obligation, I might get caught up in another.'

'You have burnt your fingers through your own mistakes. From the beginning you people were blind about Ramesh: such a man is rare; he doesn't know what deceit is; in philosophy he is a second Shankarachrya; and in literature, the nineteenth-century male version of the goddess Saraswati! I didn't like him from the very beginning. I have, in my time, seen many such high-principled men. But I had no chance to say anything. You believed that an unworthy and undeserving person like me could only be jealous of a high-minded one; that I was capable of nothing else. Now you know that it is easy to respect a high-minded man from a distance but risky to arrange a match with one's sister. However, a thorn must be extracted with another thorn. Since there is no other way, don't fuss about it.'

'Akshay, I can't believe that you had understood Ramesh's nature before any of us did. At that time you disliked him because you were jealous of him; that was not an example of your extraordinary perception. Anyhow, if necessary, you must devise the strategy, I can't do it. On the whole, I don't like Nalinaksha.'

When Jogen and Akshay entered the room where tea was served, Hemnalini was leaving through another door. Akshay realized that she had spotted their arrival from the window. He smiled and sat down near Annada. Pouring a cup for himself he said, 'Nalinaksha speaks from his heart and that is why his words touch ours.'

'He has a gift,' said Annada.

'Not only that, one rarely finds such an honourable person.'

Although Jogen was part of the conspiracy, he could not help remarking, 'Don't tell me about honourable men; may God deliver us from them.' Only the previous day Jogen had praised Nalinaksha's honesty, and denounced those who spoke against him!

Annada babu protested, 'Jogen, I would rather be deceived into believing that those who appear to be good are really good than doubt someone's honesty to prove my cleverness. Nalinaksha doesn't repeat other people's words but expresses his own spiritual experience, and I have learnt something new. An insincere person cannot offer anything of true worth. Like gold, such wisdom cannot be manufactured. I want to go and congratulate him myself.'

'I fear for his health,' said Akshay.

Annada asked anxiously, 'Why, isn't he well?'

'Not likely. He is engrossed in his meditations and his discourses of the scriptures, and neglects his own health.'

'We have no right to neglect our health since we didn't create our bodies. If he were near, I would have suggested some simple rules of health, such as . . .'

Jogen interrupted impatiently, 'Father, don't worry unnecessarily. I found him in good health. Seeing him today, it occurred to me that piety is good for the health. Perhaps I should try it.'

'No, Jogen, Akshay might be right. Many great men in our country die young because they neglect their health, thereby causing a loss for the country. Jogen, you have misunderstood Nalinaksha; he has true good qualities. He must be warned about his health.'

Akshay said, 'I will bring him to you. It would be good if you can convince him. The extract of a root that you gave me before my exam was surprisingly effective. It is the best medicine for someone who exercises his brain all the time. If you could ask Nalinaksha babu . . .'

Jogen stood up and said, 'Akshay, you are overdoing it. I have to go.'

## 40

When Annada was in good health, he took allopathic and ayurvedic pills. But recently he had lost interest in medicines and did not wish to talk about his ill health.

He was sleeping in his easy chair at an unsuitable hour, when Hemnalini heard footsteps on the stairs. She put away her stitching and went near the door to call her brother. She found Nalinaksha being escorted in by him. As she started leaving the room, Jogen said, 'Hem, let me introduce you to Nalinaksha babu.'

She stopped and greeted Nalinaksha without looking at him. Annada babu woke up and called, 'Hem!' She went near him and said softly, 'Nalinaksha babu is here.'

Annada went forward and greeted him eagerly. 'It is my good fortune that you have come to my house. Hem, don't leave. Come and sit here. Nalinaksha babu, this is my daughter Hem. We went to hear you the other day and enjoyed it greatly. What you said—we cannot lose what is genuine, we lose only what is not—has such deep meaning. Hem, don't you agree? The test of what I truly deem to be mine is when it is beyond my reach. Nalinaksha babu, I have a request. If you could come sometimes and have discussions with us, it would be of great help. We don't go out much; when you come you will find my daughter and me in this very room.'

Nalinaksha looked at Hem's slightly flushed face and said, 'Just because I said some high-sounding words at that lecture hall doesn't mean that I am grave by nature. I had agreed to give that lecture because the students were very keen, and I am not good at refusing requests. The students are now saying that they didn't follow much of the talk. Jogen babu, you were present that day, don't think that I didn't feel for you when you kept looking at your watch anxiously!'

Jogen replied, 'Don't let that worry you. If I could not follow, it was because of my feeble mind.'

Annada said, 'Jogen, things can be understood only at the appropriate time.'

'I don't see why we must understand everything,' said Nalinaksha.

Annada said, 'I have something to say to you. God has sent you to this world with a mission, but don't neglect your health because of that. Those who are generous must remember that if one's assets are lost then the ability to give is lost too.'

'When you get to know me better, you will realize that I don't neglect anything. I came to this world with nothing. I have prepared myself through much hardship and with the help of many, and can't afford the luxury of neglecting myself. If one can't build, one doesn't have the right to destroy.'

'Very true. You had said something similar the other day,' said Annada.

Jogen said, 'I have some work and must leave now. But please continue your discussion.'

'Jogen babu, I beg your pardon. I don't wish to inconvenience anyone. I should leave too. I could walk with you part of the way.'

'No, no, please stay. Don't pay any attention to me. I can't sit still for long.'

Annada said, 'Don't mind Jogen. He comes and goes as he pleases. It is difficult to hold him.'

When Jogen left, Annada asked Nalinaksha, 'Where are you putting up?'

'I can't say that I am staying in a particular place. I have several acquaintances that have claims on me, and I don't mind. But one also needs solitude, so Jogen babu has arranged for my stay in the house next to yours. This street is very quiet.'

Annada was very pleased to hear this. But had he noticed he would have found Hemnalini's face blanch in pain. Ramesh used to live next door once upon a time.

Meanwhile the tea was ready and Annada asked Hem to prepare a cup for Nalinaksha. But Nalinaksha declined.

Annada asked, 'But why? Have a cup, or at least some sweets.'

'Please excuse me,' said Nalinaksha.

'You are a doctor, what can I advise you? A few hours after lunch hot water is good for one's digestion. We can give you a cup of very light tea, in case you are not used to it.'

Nalinaksha glanced at Hemnalini and realized that she had found a reason for his refusal to have tea and that she was perturbed as a result. Quickly he said, 'I don't have a dislike for your tea table. I used to drink tea and even now I like its fragrance. You probably don't know that my mother observes many traditional rules and practices. She has no one but me, and I don't wish to have any guilt when I go to her. That is why I don't drink tea. Yet I share the pleasure that you get from it, and would rather not be deprived of your hospitality.'

Earlier Hemnalini was a bit upset by what he had said. She felt that he was not completely candid, and was trying to hide himself behind his words. She did not know that Nalinaksha felt awkward at first meetings, and went against his nature to be voluble. He could not talk about himself naturally without striking a discordant note, and he knew that. So when Jogen lost his patience and left, he felt embarrassed and wished to leave too.

When he talked about his mother, Hemnalini looked at him with great respect, and was touched by his regard and affection for his mother. Annada quickly said, 'Yes, of course! Had I known I wouldn't have asked. Please forgive me.'

Nalinaksha said with a smile, 'I can't accept tea, but why should I be deprived of your warm hospitality?'

After Nalinaksha left, Hem went upstairs with her father, and read out articles from Bengali journals to him. Annada soon fell asleep. It was a symptom of his tiredness.

## 41

Within a few days, they became well acquainted with Nalinaksha. Hem had been under the impression that Nalinaksha could advise only on matters spiritual. She had not imagined that one could talk to him on ordinary mundane matters, since he always maintained a distance.

They were in the middle of a discussion when Jogen came and said in an agitated manner, 'Father, do you know that people are calling us Nalinaksha's disciples? I had a big argument on this with Paresh just now.'

Annada smiled and said, 'I don't see anything to be ashamed of. I am ashamed of joining a group where everyone is a guru, and none a disciple. In the rush to teach, there is no scope for learning.'

Nalinaksha said, 'I am with you. We are all disciples. Wherever there is a possibility of learning, we pack up and move there.'

Jogen said impatiently, 'You can't laugh it off when those close to you are seen only as your disciples, not as friends or relatives. You must give up your strange observances.'

'What are those?'

'I have heard that you practise yogic breathing, stare at the sun in the early morning, observe orthodox rules regarding food—you don't fit in, you are like a sword without its scabbard.'

Hem, hurt by these harsh words, lowered her head. Nalinaksha laughed and asked Jogen, 'Is it wrong to be different? The part of the sword that is inside the scabbard is identical to all other swords. It is only on the handle outside that the artisan displays his art according to his skill and taste. Beyond the common human characteristics that we all have, each individual has the right to have some special, unique qualities. You want to take that away too? I am also astonished at how people have observed my harmless rituals, and why they talk about it.'

'Don't you know? Those who take on the responsibility of reforming the world consider it their duty to be informed about other people's lives. If one does something unusual, it is noticed, even if it is done in privacy. Nobody notices the usual. For example, Hem has noticed your prayer ritual on the terrace, and she has mentioned it to Father. Yet, she hasn't taken the responsibility to reform you.'

When Hemnalini tried to intervene, Nalinaksha said, 'Please don't feel embarrassed. No one can blame you for watching me while strolling on the terrace. You shouldn't be ashamed of having a pair of eyes; besides, we all have this bad habit.'

'Hem has never shown any disapproval of your daily prayers. She asked me about your method of meditation but with respect for it,' said Annada.

Jogen said, 'All this is beyond me. I don't find any problem with the way we ordinary people live our lives. I don't believe that there is any particular benefit from special rituals performed in privacy; on the contrary, it upsets one's mental balance. But you must not be offended. I am a most ordinary person of the middle rank. I can't reach those who occupy the higher echelons unless I throw stones at them. There are many like me; so, if you dwell in an extraordinary plane far from us, many stones will be thrown at you.'

Nalinaksha replied, 'Some stones touch one, some leave their marks. When they say that my actions are crazy, or childish, I don't care. But when they say that I am pretending to be an ascetic, a guru, and trying to gather followers, I can't laugh it off.'

'I must say this again, please don't be upset with me. Who can object to what you do on your terrace? My point is that if you confine yourself to the boundaries of the ordinary, no one will talk. For me, it is good enough to lead life as others are leading; anything more draws people's attention. Whether they rebuke or respect doesn't make any difference to you; but is it comfortable to live like that?' asked Jogen as he was about to leave.

Nalinaksha exclaimed, 'Jogen babu, where are you going? You can't escape now, not after pulling me forcibly down from the rooftop to the paved floor on the ground level!'

'I have had enough for today! I must go out for a while,' answered Jogen.

After Jogen left, Hemnalini looked down and played with the tassels of the tablecloth. No one noticed that her eyelids were damp.

After her discussions with Nalinaksha she had realized the poverty of her soul and had become eager to follow his way. When at a time of great sorrow, she could not find anything to lean on, he had revealed the world anew to her. She was anxious to follow a strict regime of rules, because rules provide support. Moreover, grief likes to manifest itself in austerity. So far Hem had nurtured her pain secretly within herself. Now, following him, she derived a great deal of satisfaction from observing certain rules, and in becoming a vegetarian. She removed the carpet and the floor mat from her room, moved the bed behind a curtain, and kept no other furniture. She would mop the floor every morning, keep some flowers on a platter, and after her bath wear a white sari and sit on the floor of her room. The light from the open window, the sky and the breeze anointed her mind.

Annada could not completely join her in this but was happy to see the glow of satisfaction on her face. Their discussions with Nalinaksha were held in her room.

Jogen protested strongly saying that there was no place for him in this purified environment. Earlier Jogen's sarcasm would hurt her, but now she only smiled. She knew that people found her behaviour strange, but her respect for and faith in Nalinaksha had enveloped her, and she was not embarrassed.

One morning, just as she finished her prayers, Nalinaksha arrived, much earlier than usual. He said, 'I have news from Kashi that my mother is unwell. So I am leaving by the evening train. I have come to say goodbye.'

Annada said, 'I hope she gets well soon. We are deeply indebted to you for your help; we cannot hope to repay it.'

'Please be assured that I too have received a lot from you. You have helped me not only as a neighbour, but your respect for my thoughts and my philosophy has greatly enhanced my own faith. I now understand that spiritual fulfilment is easier to attain with the cooperation of others.'

'When we were in great need of something but didn't know what it was, we found you and realized that we couldn't have managed without you. We don't go out much, but surprisingly we went to hear your lecture that day! It could happen because we really needed you,' said Annada.

'I, in my turn, have never disclosed my deep inner thoughts to anyone but you. The ultimate lesson of truth is to disclose it. I have fulfilled this deep need through you. Please don't forget how much I needed you.'

Hemnalini had remained quiet through this exchange. When it was time for Nalinaksha to leave, she touched his feet and said, 'Please keep us informed about your mother.'

## 42

Akshay had not shown up in the last few days. When Nalinaksha left for Kashi, he turned up with Jogen at Annada babu's tea table. He believed that the hold of Ramesh's memory on Hemnalini could be measured by her show of displeasure towards himself. That day she remained calm at the sight of him. She asked pleasantly, 'We haven't seen you for some time.'

'Are we worth seeing every day?'

Hemnalini answered with a smile, 'If one stops meeting people on account of one's low worth, then many of us should go into hiding.'

Jogen commented, 'Akshay had hoped to get the entire accolade for his humility, but Hem scored over him by her humility on behalf of the whole of mankind. I have something to say here. Ordinary people like us deserve to be seen every day; but it is better to meet the extraordinary only once in a while. They frequent forests, mountains and caves for this very reason. If they were to settle down in human habitation, ordinary mortals like Akshay and Jogen would be forced to leave for forests and mountains.'

Hemnalini felt the sting of Jogen's caustic comments but remained quiet. She prepared three cups of tea and served them. Jogen asked, 'Aren't you having any?' She anticipated a strong reaction from Jogen but firmly said, 'No. I have given up tea.'

'So, you have started your penance! I suppose tea leaves lack spiritual energy, unlike myrobalan, which has it all. Hem, if a mere cup of tea spoils your yoga, meditation and spirituality, then so be it. When even strong things don't last long in this world, how can one live with something so fragile?' Saying this, Jogen made a cup of tea and placed it in front of Hem. Without giving it a glance she asked her father, 'Won't you eat something with your tea?'

Annada babu's voice and hands were shaking. He replied, 'To tell you the truth, I don't feel like taking anything at this table. I have been trying to tolerate Jogen's words without protest. But in my present physical and mental condition I can't always control what I say, and I might say something only to regret it later.'

Hemnalini stood by him and said, 'You mustn't be angry. Dada wants me to drink tea, and there is nothing wrong in that. I wasn't offended. Father, you must eat something. I know that you fall ill if you drink tea on an empty stomach.' She brought a plate in front of him, and he started eating slowly. Then she returned to her chair and picked up the cup of tea that Jogen had offered. Akshay got up quickly and intervened, 'Excuse me, please hand me that cup, mine is empty.'

Jogen took the cup away from Hem and said to his father, 'I was wrong, please forgive me.' Annada did not reply; tears streamed down his face. Jogen and Akshay left the room slowly. Afterwards, Annada held on to Hem's hand and went upstairs on unsteady feet.

The same night Annada suffered an attack of colic. The doctor diagnosed that his liver was affected, although the disease had not progressed very far. He recommended moving to a town in the western parts which had a healthier climate and staying there for six months to a year.

When the doctor left and Annada was feeling better; he said, 'Hem, let us go and live in Kashi.' Hemnalini had the same idea. Since Nalinaksha's departure, she had felt something was lacking in her meditation. His presence gave strength to her prayers. His resolute faith and tranquillity helped her own faith find expression. His absence had cast a pale shadow on it. That day, she had performed all that he had advised with more than her normal care. But it had made her so tired and dejected that she could not check her tears. She had forced herself to be hospitable at the tea table, but her heart was heavy. The sad memories returned with renewed pain; her heart was crying out, homeless and shelterless. So, she agreed to the suggestion of going to Kashi enthusiastically.

When Jogen saw the preparations, he asked what the matter was. Annada replied, 'We are going to the west.'

'Where exactly?'

'We will decide in the course of our travel.' He was hesitant to tell Jogen that they were going to Kashi.

Jogen said, 'I can't accompany you this time. I am waiting for an answer to my application for a headmastership.'

## 43

Ramesh returned to Gazipur early in the morning. There were few people about, and the trees on the edge of the road stood stiff in winter inertia behind the cover of leaves. White fog covered the hutments: still, like a swan incubating her eggs. As his vehicle went along that deserted road, Ramesh's chest heaved with the beat of his heart.

He got down in front of his bungalow hoping that Kamala would hear the sound of the vehicle, and come out on the veranda. He had brought an expensive gold necklace from Allahabad for her, and took the case out of his coat pocket.

He found Bishan, the bearer, fast asleep on the veranda, and the doors of the house closed. He stopped for a moment, and then called Bishan loudly thinking that his call would wake up Kamala too. He himself had been awake half the night in anticipation, and wondered how she could sleep so soundly.

Bishan did not wake up until he was shaken. He stared at Ramesh without comprehending. Ramesh asked if the mistress was in. With sudden realization he answered that she was. Then he tried to go back to sleep.

Ramesh pushed the door and it opened. He went from room to room, but could not see anyone. He called Kamala loudly, but there was no answer. He went outside and looked around, all the way up to the neem tree; he looked in the kitchen, the servants' rooms and the stable but did not find her. By then it was bright, the crows were cawing, and a few women carrying water pots came to fetch water from the well outside. On the other side of the road, a village woman was singing strange tunes as she dehusked wheat.

Returning to the bungalow he found Bishan sleeping soundly. Ramesh shook him; Bishan was reeking of country liquor. The shaking finally woke him and he sat up quickly. Ramesh asked 'Where is your mistress?'

'She is in her room.'

'Where? '

'Inside. She returned here yesterday.'

'Where did she go after that?'

Bishan did not understand. Meanwhile Umesh appeared, red-eyed and wearing a fancy dhoti. Ramesh asked him about Kamala, and he replied that she had moved here the previous day.

'Where were you?' asked Ramesh.

'The mistress allowed me to go and watch the jatra at Sidhu babu's house.'

The coachman came and asked for his fare. Ramesh rushed into the vehicle and went to Chakravarty's house. There he found everyone in a tizzy. He feared that Kamala was ill, but it was not so. Uma was ill, and they had been terribly worried and busy with her treatment. No one had slept last night.

Ramesh thought that they must have brought Kamala here because of Uma's illness. He asked, 'Kamala must be very anxious about Uma?' Bipin did not know whether Kamala had come the previous night, so he replied in agreement, 'Yes, she is so fond of Uma, she must be concerned. However, the doctor said that there is no reason to worry.'

Ramesh was not destined to have the joyful reunion that he had imagined.

Umesh arrived from Ramesh's bungalow, and asked, 'Mashima, where is Ma?'

Shailaja was surprised and said, 'Why? Yesterday you took her home; I was supposed to send Lachchmania to her in the evening, but Uma being unwell, I was too busy.'

Umesh was worried. He said, 'I couldn't find her in that house.'

'How come? Where were you last night?'

'Ma didn't let me stay. As soon as we reached home, she sent me to watch the jatra at Sidhu babu's place.'

'You didn't show much sense! Where was Bishan?'

'Bishan isn't of much help; he drank a lot of country liquor yesterday.'

'Go quickly and call my husband.'

When Bipin came, Shailo said, 'It's a calamity!'

He turned pale with worry and asked, 'Why, what's the matter?'

'Kamala went back to her bungalow yesterday, but they can't find her there.'

'Didn't she come here last night?'

'No. I meant to send someone to her, but there was no one to send. Has Ramesh babu returned?'

'He is here. Not finding Kamala in the bungalow, he thought that she might be here.'

'Go, don't delay. Take him with you and search for her. Uma is asleep now; she is all right.'

Bipin and Ramesh got into the same vehicle and returned to the bungalow. They tried to get some information from Bishan, but all that they could gather was that last evening, Kamala had gone towards the river all by herself. Bishan suggested accompanying her, but she gave him a rupee and turned him back; he sat by the gate, on guard duty, when a man walked by carrying a pot of newly brewed palm liquor—Bishan could not recall what happened after that. He showed them the route that Kamala took to the river.

Ramesh, Bipin and Umesh followed that route through fields wet with dew. Umesh looked around in all directions, keen and anxious like an animal looking for its cub. They stood at the bank of the river by the open land, the sand ashen in the morning sun. They could not see anyone. Umesh called out loudly, 'Ma, where are you, Ma?' It echoed from the high bank across the river; there was no reply.

Umesh saw something white at a distance. Rushing there he found a bunch of keys tied to a handkerchief near the water's edge. Ramesh recognized Kamala's key-bunch. On the damp and soft soil there were deep footprints all the way to the water. At a little distance, something was shimmering in the water. Umesh picked it up. It was a brooch, enamelled on gold—Ramesh's gift to Kamala. When all the indications pointed to the river, Umesh could not control himself. Crying, 'Ma, Ma,' he jumped into the water, dived and searched again and again but in vain. The shallow water turned muddy.

Ramesh stood there as though he had lost his senses. Bipin called Umesh to come out, but Umesh said, 'I won't, I won't. Ma, you can't leave me.'

Bipin was alarmed. But since Umesh could swim like a fish, it was impossible for him to drown. After a lot of searching, he came out tired, flung himself on the sand and wept.

Bipin touched Ramesh and said, 'Let us go back. There is no point in standing here. We must alert the police, and let them do a thorough search.'

In Shailaja's house the only sound was of crying; no one could eat or sleep. The fishermen cast their nets far on the river. The police searched everywhere. They inquired at the station, but no Bengali woman of Kamala's description had boarded the train at night.

Chakravarty returned that evening. After listening to everything, especially Kamala's behaviour in the last few days, he had no doubt that she had committed suicide by drowning.

Ramesh could not cry. He kept thinking, 'Kamala had come to me from the water of the Ganges, and now she has disappeared in the same river, like flower used for worship.'

When the sun was setting, he returned to the riverbank. He stood near the spot where the key-bunch had been, and gazed at the footprints. Then he took off his shoes, hitched up his dhoti, walked some distance in the river, and threw the new necklace that he had brought for Kamala into the water.

No one in the Chakravarty household was in a state to find out when Ramesh left Gazipur.

## 44

Ramesh had no plans for the future. He thought that he would never again take up a job, or settle down anywhere. He pushed away from his mind all thoughts of Hemnalini, and told himself that the terrible events had left him unfit for family life, just as a tree struck by lightning could not hope to find a place in a flower garden.

He set out to travel but did not stay long in any place. He saw the beauty of the riverbanks of Kashi from the boat; climbed to the top of the Qutab Minar in Delhi, and saw the Taj Mahal in the moonlight in Agra. After visiting the gurdwara in Amritsar, he went to Rajasthan to see the temples at Mount Abu. He did not allow himself any rest.

Then his travel-weary heart sought a home. He was troubled both by the memory of a peaceful home in his past and the hope for a happy home in the future. Suddenly his travelling was over; he sighed, bought a ticket for Kolkata, and boarded the train.

In Kolkata, he could not immediately bring himself to enter the particular street in Kolutola. There was no way of knowing what he might see or hear there. He was apprehensive of a major change. Once he went as far as the beginning of the street, and turned back. Next evening, he forced himself to go there. Standing in front of the house, he found the doors and windows shut; there was no indication of anyone being inside. Yet, hoping that Sukhan, the servant, was there to guard the house, he called and knocked on the door a few times. There was no reply. A neighbour, Chandramohan, stood outside his house smoking, and asked, 'Is it Ramesh babu? How are you? There is no one in the house.'

'Do you know where they have gone?'

'I am not sure, but I do know that they have left for a holiday in the western districts.'

'Who have left?'

'Annada babu and his daughter.'

'Are you sure that no one else accompanied them?'

'Of course I am sure. I saw them when they were leaving.'

Losing his patience Ramesh said, 'I heard that someone called Nalinaksha went with them.'

'You were wrongly informed. Nalinaksha babu lived in your former house for a while, then he left for Kashi a few days before these people.'

Ramesh questioned him and got some information about Nalinaksha: his full name was Nalinaksha Chatterjee: it seems that he used to practise medicine in Rangpur, but at present he was living in Kashi with his mother. Ramesh was silent for a while, and then he asked, 'Could you tell me where Jogen is?'

Chandramohan replied that Jogen was in Bishaipur. He was the headmaster of a high school established by a zamindar there. He asked Ramesh, 'We haven't seen you for some time. Where have you been all this while?'

Not having any reason to hide the facts, Ramesh said, 'I was practising in Gazipur.'

'Would you be living there now?'

'No, it wasn't possible to stay on. I haven't yet decided where to live.'

Soon after Ramesh left, Akshay arrived. Jogen had asked him to keep an eye on the house. Akshay never neglected his duties, so he made unannounced visits to check whether at least one of the two servants was always present in the house.

Seeing him, Chandramohan said, 'Ramesh babu left a little while back.'

'Is that so? What was his business here?'

'I don't know. He asked me about Annada babu and his family. It was difficult to recognize him because he has lost a lot of weight. Had he not called the servant, I wouldn't have known him.'

'Did he tell you where he lives?'

'He was living in Gazipur until recently, but now he has left the place. He wasn't sure where he would live.'

Akshay nodded and turned to the work at hand.

Returning home, Ramesh was thinking of the irony of fate, which had brought together Kamala and himself on the one hand, and Hemnalini and Nalinaksha on the other. It was like a bad novel. Like destiny, only a desperate writer would attempt such contradictory matching. A timid writer would not dare to write about such strange events. But now that he was free of the web of problems, he hoped that fate would not end the complex novel of his life with a tragic epilogue.

Jogen lived in a single-storeyed house close to the zamindar's place in Bishaipur. He was reading the newspaper on a Sunday morning when a man from the market gave him a letter. Jogen was surprised by the handwriting on the envelope. The letter was from Ramesh, saying that he was waiting in a shop, and that he had something important to say to Jogen.

Jogen got up hurriedly. Although once he had been forced to insult Ramesh, yet, after such a long time and so far away from home he could not refuse his childhood friend. He was glad as well as curious. Since Hemnalini was not around, Ramesh could do no harm.

He went along with the bearer of the letter, and found Ramesh in a grocery store, sitting quietly on an empty kerosene container. The grocer had offered him a hookah reserved for Brahmins, but Ramesh had refused. The grocer had concluded that the bespectacled young man was one of those peculiar, city-bred people, and did not attempt to converse.

Jogen pulled him up from the seat and said, 'You are incorrigible! Instead of coming straight to my house, you are sitting in a grocery store amidst puffed rice and molasses!'

Ramesh smiled in embarrassment. Jogen talked non-stop on their way home: 'Say what you will, God's intentions are beyond us. He let me grow up in a city, but was that to destroy my soul in this back of beyond village?'

Ramesh looked around and commented, 'Why? It's not so bad.'

'Meaning what?'

'It is quiet.'

'That is why I am so keen to leave and make it even quieter.'

'Whatever you might say, for one's peace of mind . . .'

'Don't say that. After several days of peace of mind, now I am fed up. I have tried my best to disrupt the peace. I almost came to a fist fight with the secretary; and after a dose of my temper the zamindar too is unlikely to interfere. He wanted me to sing his praise in the English newspaper, but I made it very clear that I can't be influenced. That I am still employed is not because of my qualities, but because the joint magistrate likes me. The day I read of his transfer in the newspaper, I would know that my stay in Bishaipur is coming to an end. Meanwhile my dog is my only companion here. Others give me disapproving looks.'

In Jogen's house, as Ramesh was about to sit down, Jogen sent him off to take a bath, promising a round of tea. The day passed in chatting, eating and resting. Jogen did not give Ramesh any opportunity to narrate his story. After the evening meal, in the dim light of an oil lamp, they drew up two easy chairs and sat down. They could hear the jackals nearby, and the dark night resonated with the noise of crickets.

Finally Ramesh said, 'Jogen, you know why I have come to see you. Once you had asked me a question, but the time was inappropriate for an answer. Now there is no reason not to.' He sat still for a while, and then slowly narrated the events. Often, his voice broke or trembled; sometimes he stopped for a few minutes. Jogen listened quietly.

When all was said, Jogen sighed. He said, 'Had you said all this at that time, I wouldn't have believed you.'

'All the reasons for disbelief are just as valid now. That is why I request you to go to the village where I got married, and after that to visit Kamala's maternal uncle.'

'I am not going anywhere. Without moving from this chair, I will believe every word you say. It has always been my habit to believe you. Please forgive me for that one exception.'

Jogen stood in front of Ramesh and the two friends embraced each other. Ramesh cleared his throat and said, 'It was my fate to be caught in a web of untruth, and I could see no other way than to surrender myself completely to it. I am now reborn because I am free, and I have nothing to hide from anyone. I still don't know what information or what emotional state made Kamala end her life, and there is no way of knowing now. Yet, I shudder to think what misery would have engulfed us had death not cut the tight knot. The problem that had emerged suddenly from the jaws of death disappeared as suddenly in the womb of death.'

'You can't be sure that Kamala has killed herself. Anyhow, you are in the clear, I am now thinking about Nalinaksha.' Then Jogen spoke of Nalinaksha. He said, 'I don't understand such people, and I don't like what I don't understand. Yet others think differently; they like the incomprehensible more. I am afraid for Hem. I realized that something was wrong when I noticed that she had given up tea, fish and meat, and when I poked fun at her, instead of being sad, she smiled. But I do know that with your help she can be rescued soon. So, prepare for war, you and me against that ascetic.'

Ramesh said with a smile, 'I am not known for heroism, but I am ready.'

'Wait until my Christmas holidays begin.'

'But that is far off. Why don't I go alone?' asked Ramesh.

'No, that is out of the question. I am responsible for breaking off your marriage, and I myself must remedy that. I won't let you go earlier and steal the show. There are only ten days before vacation.'

'In the meantime I could . . .'

'No, no. I don't wish to hear anything further. You will stay with me for these ten days. I have quarrelled with almost everybody here, now for a change I need a friend, I can't possibly let you go. So far I have only heard the jackals in the evenings. My condition is so pathetic that even your voice sounds like the notes of the veena.'

## 45

When Akshay heard about Ramesh from Chandramohan, several questions arose in his mind. He wondered: 'Ramesh had been practising in Gazipur, and had kept himself concealed; what could have happened in the meantime to make him leave his practice, and dare to reappear in Kolutola? He must have found out that Annada babu and Hemnalini were in Kashi, and would surely go there.' Akshay decided that he would go to Gazipur, get all the information, and then go to Kashi to see Annada babu.

Akshay arrived in Gazipur on an autumn afternoon. He first inquired in the market for the house of the Bengali lawyer Ramesh babu. But they did not know of any such lawyer. Then he went to the court which had just closed for the day. He saw a man wearing the turban of a lawyer getting into a coach, and asked him, 'Sir, a Bengali lawyer named Rameshchandra has recently come to Gazipur. Do you know where he lives?'

He learnt that Ramesh had been living with the Chakravartys until recently, but nobody knew of his whereabouts now. His wife had probably drowned herself. Akshay made for Chakravarty's house. On his way there he concluded that Ramesh's tactics were obvious. Now that his wife was dead, he would try to prove to Hemnalini that he never had a wife. In her present emotional state it would be impossible for Hemnalini to disbelieve him. Akshay told himself that those who make a fuss about morality are dangerous people, and his own self-esteem went up a few notches.

When Akshay inquired about Ramesh and Kamala, Chakravarty was overcome with emotion. He said, 'Since you are a close friend of Ramesh babu, you must have known Kamala well. In spite of my short acquaintance with her, she became as dear to me as my own daughter. I had no idea that after stealing our hearts, she would leave us in this manner; it is like a bolt from the blue.'

Akshay pulled a long face and said, 'I can't understand how this could happen. Ramesh must have ill-treated her.'

'Please don't mind, I couldn't understand your friend Ramesh. He appears to be perfectly normal, but it is impossible to know what goes on in his mind. Otherwise, how could he neglect a wife like Kamala? Kamala was a devoted wife. She and my daughter were close friends, yet she never complained about her husband. My daughter could sense her grief but couldn't persuade her to say anything. You can well imagine what desperation would drive her to such an act. My heart breaks when I think of it. Such is my misfortune that I was in Allahabad at that time. Had I been here, she wouldn't have been able to leave us.'

Next morning Akshay went with Chakravarty and saw Ramesh's bungalow and the riverbank. Later he said, 'I am not as convinced as you are that Kamala has taken her life by drowning.'

'What is your view?'

'I think that she has left home. We should make a thorough search.'

Chakravarty said excitedly, 'You are right. It is quite possible.'

'Kashi, the great centre of pilgrimage isn't far. We have a good friend there. It is possible that Kamala has found shelter with them.'

'But Ramesh babu never mentioned these friends. Had I known, I would have certainly inquired,' said Chakravarty.

'Let us go to Kashi. You know that area well, so it would be easy for you to look for her.'

Chakravarty agreed readily. Akshay knew that Hemnalini would not readily believe his own words, so he took Chakravarty along as a witness.

## 46

Annada babu was living in a rented bungalow in the quiet cantonment area. Soon after arriving they heard that Nalinaksha's mother Khemonkari was sick with pneumonia. Her common cold, cough and slight fever had turned serious because even in winter she had continued her routine of an early morning bath in the river.

After several days of tireless nursing by Hem, the crisis was over, although she continued to be extremely weak. Since she was particular about ritual purity, Hemnalini could not be of much help in preparing her diet. So Nalinaksha took on this responsibility. Khemonkari regretted it and kept saying, 'God has cured me but only to add to your troubles.'

Khemonkari observed strict rules for herself, but she was also particular about the neatness and beauty of her surroundings. Hearing this from Nalinaksha, Hemnalini kept the rooms neat and well decorated, and dressed with care when she came to visit. Every day she brought flowers from their garden, made different arrangements, and placed them at Khemonkari's bedside.

Nalinaksha could not persuade his mother to keep a personal servant. They had servants to fetch water and so on, but she could not bear to get her personal work done by a paid employee. After the death of the woman who had brought her up, she had never allowed any servant to fan her or massage her feet, even when she was sick.

She liked beautiful faces. On her way back after her morning bath in the Ganges, she would offer flowers and water to the Shivalinga, and sometimes she would find a sweet local boy or a pretty Brahmin girl and bring them home. She had befriended a few boys from the neighbourhood with toys, money and food, and they came and played in her house at all odd hours which made her very happy. She had another habit: she could not resist buying beautiful objects, not because these were useful to her, but because she liked to gift these. She stored some of these fancy objects in a large ebony box for her future daughter-in-law. She imagined a beautiful young bride for her son, and spent many a leisure hour thinking of the young girl who would brighten her home, play about, and how she would dress her up in pretty clothes and jewellery.

She herself led an austere life. At the end of the day spent in prayer, she took her only meal consisting of fruit, milk and sweets. Yet, she did not approve of Nalinaksha's austerity. She believed that although the basic religious tenets were important for all, yet rituals and observances were not for men, whom she considered to be big babies and therefore they could not be expected to bear the hardships. Had Nalinaksha been a little inconsiderate and self-centred like other men, yet careful not to enter her prayer room and not touch her at certain times, she would have been pleased.

When she recovered from her illness, she found that Hemnalini—following Nalinaksha's advice—was observing all kinds of rules. Moreover, Annada babu, an old man, was listening to Nalinaksha's words carefully and respectfully as though he were his guru.

Khemonkari was much amused by this. She told Hemnalini, 'You people are giving my son too much encouragement by listening to all that rubbish. You are too young for a life of meditation; you should enjoy life. You might wonder why I observe all this. It is because I grew up in that environment. If I give it up, I won't have any other solace. But you are different. I know about your education and upbringing. If you force yourself to follow these observances, how would you benefit? I believe that one must preserve what one has. Why should you become a vegetarian, and observe penance? Give it up. And since when has Nalinaksha become a guru? What does he know about all this? Until the other day he observed none of these, did what he liked, and reacted strongly to any talk of the scriptures. He began all this to please me, and now I am afraid that he might become an ascetic and leave home. I keep telling him that he should stay with the belief in which he grew up. There was nothing wrong with it, and it would please me. But he smiles in reply. His temperament is to listen quietly, and not protest even when he is abused.'

These discussions took place after five o'clock in the afternoon while she was tying Hemnalini's hair. She did not like the way Hemnalini did her hair. She said, 'You think that I am old-fashioned, that I don't know the modern styles. But I know more ways of doing one's hair than you do. An Englishwoman used to teach me needlework, and I also learnt from her many different ways of dressing my hair. But each day when she left, I had to bathe and change my clothes. What to do, this is the practice; whether it is good or bad, I can't give it up. I make a fuss about ritual pollution even with you, but please don't mind. It is not from repugnance but only from habit. When my husband's beliefs changed and Hindu practices were discarded, I tolerated much without protest. I just said, "Do what you think best, I am only an uneducated woman, I can't give up what I have always believed in."' Saying this, she quickly wiped her tears with the edge of her sari.

She loved to plait Hemnalini's long hair in different styles, and sometimes selected a sari from her ebony box for her. Hemnalini often brought her needlework, and she instructed Hem. She enjoyed reading Bengali books and magazines, so Hemnalini brought the reading material that she had. Hem was surprised by her discussions of the books and articles. She had no idea that such clear and rational thinking was possible without an English education, and found her remarkable. Her preconceived notions were proved wrong.

## 47

Khemonkari fell ill again, but this time the fever was low and did not last. Nalinaksha came in the morning, touched her feet and said, 'Mother, you must observe the regime of convalescence, don't tax your weak body.'

'I will follow a convalescent's regime, and you an ascetic's! It can't go on like this, you must get married, and that's an order.'

Nalinaksha listened quietly. She continued, 'I will not regain my earlier health, but if I see you married I will die in peace. Earlier I thought that a young girl would come as your bride, and I would bring her up, teach and instruct her in household matters, dress her up, and spend my days happily. But the last bout of illness has opened my eyes, and I can't be sure how long I will live. It wouldn't be right to die leaving the responsibility of a young girl on you. Instead, marry someone old enough, from your own society and with similar beliefs. When I had fever, I couldn't sleep at night worrying about it. I won't have any peace of mind until this—my last duty—is fulfilled.'

'But how will I find someone like that who will blend with us?' asked Nalinaksha.

'You needn't worry. Leave it to me.'

Khemonkari had not appeared before Annada so far. That evening when Annada came for a visit, she sent for him to come to the inner part of the house. She said, 'I have grown very fond of your daughter. You know my son well, he can't be faulted. He is also a well-known doctor. Will it be easy to find such a good match for your daughter?'

Annada babu replied enthusiastically, 'I didn't dare to hope for such a match! I would consider myself fortunate if my daughter gets married to Nalinaksha. But will he . . .'

'Nalin won't object. Unlike other young men, he listens to me. Anyway, there is no question of persuasion. Can anyone not like your daughter? Since I don't keep well, I would like to settle this matter soon.'

Annada was most cheerful when he returned home. That very night he told Hem, 'I am old and not in good health. I would like to see you settled. Please don't feel embarrassed discussing this with me because your mother is no more, and I am responsible for you.'

Hemnalini looked at her father anxiously.

Annada babu said, 'I am extremely pleased because a very good proposal has come for you. I hope that no obstacle would come in the way. Today Nalinaksha's mother herself proposed her son's marriage with you.'

Hemnalini was taken aback with embarrassment. She said, 'What are you saying, Father? No, no, it can't be.' She had never thought of the possibility of marrying Nalinaksha. Suddenly hearing of the proposal from her father, she was overcome with hesitation and embarrassment.

'Why isn't it possible?' asked Annada babu.

'Nalinaksha babu! How can that be?' saying this she left the room. Although she did not furnish a reason, it was stronger than a reason.

Annada was greatly disappointed. He had not anticipated such an obstacle. On the contrary, he had thought that Hem would be happy at the prospect of marrying Nalinaksha. Nonplussed, he stared sadly at the light from the oil lamp and ruminated on the unfathomable mystery of women's minds and the sad absence of Hemnalini's mother.

Hem sat in the dark veranda for a long time. When she looked at the room, saw her father's expression of hopelessness, it hurt her. She went in, stood behind his chair, and passing her fingers through his hair said, 'Father, come. Dinner has been long served, it will get cold.'

Annada went to the dinner table mechanically but could not eat much. Thinking that Hemnalini's problems were over, he had been full of hope, but now he felt depressed again. He realized that Hem had not forgotten Ramesh. Breaking his normal habit of going to bed straight after dinner, he sat in a canvas chair deep in thought, staring at the desolate road in front of his garden. Hemnalini said softly, 'It's cold, please go to bed.'

'You go, I will follow soon.'

She stood silently for a little while and again entreated, 'You will catch a chill, why not sit in the living room?' He got up and went to bed, without saying anything.

Hemnalini had not allowed herself to think of Ramesh fearing that it would distress her and interfere with her duties. She had fought many battles with herself, but now the wound became all the more painful. She had not been able to clearly see where her future lay; and in her effort to find something strong and dependable, she had accepted Nalinaksha as her guide and had prepared herself to follow his advice. But when a proposal for marriage tried to free her from the bond that lay in the deepest corner of her heart, she realized how strong that bond was! At the possibility of severance, her anxious heart clung to it with all its might.

## 48

Khemonkari called Nalinaksha to say that she had decided on a suitable bride for him. He smiled and asked, 'You have already decided?'

'What else? Will I live forever? I have decided on Hemnalini, we will never find someone as suitable. She is not very fair, but . . .'

'Please, Mother, I am not bothered about complexion, but how can it be Hemnalini?'

'I don't see any reason why not.'

Nalinaksha found it difficult to give a reason. But Hemnalini—someone he had so freely advised and guided for so long—the idea of marrying her embarrassed him. Finding him silent she said, 'I won't accept any of your objections this time. I can't bear the fact that for my sake you lead an austere life in Kashi at your age. Mark my words, I will not let the next auspicious day go waste.'

After a while Nalinaksha said, 'Let me then tell you something: but you must not get agitated. The event I speak of happened nine or ten months ago, and it is no use being upset about it now. But your nature is such that even when a crisis is over, the fear of it doesn't leave you. I have often thought of telling you but because of this reason I couldn't. You can do what you wish to appease my stars, but please don't distress yourself.'

Khemonkari was very worried. She said, 'I can't guess what you plan to tell me, but I am more disturbed by your introduction. So long as we live, we can't hide under a cover. One doesn't need to look for ill; it comes on its own accord. Whatever it may be, good or ill, tell me.'

'In the month of Maagh, I sold all my belongings in Rangpur, rented out my house, and was on my way back home. When I reached Shanda, don't ask me why, I decided to travel the rest of the journey to Kolkata by boat. I hired a large boat and started. Two days later when the boat was anchored and I was bathing in the river, all of a sudden I saw Bhupen. He was carrying a rifle. He was overjoyed to see me and said that he had come there to hunt. He was the deputy magistrate, on tour, and was camping nearby. Having met me after a long gap, he would not let me leave, and took me with him on his tour.

'He camped in a small village called Dhobapukur one day. In the evening while walking we came to a large farm, and entered a hut enclosed by a wall. The owner of the house welcomed us. A primary school was being held in the courtyard. The house owner's name was Tarini Chatterjee. He asked Bhupen a lot of questions about me. When we returned to the camp, Bhupen said, "You are lucky, you will soon get a proposal for marriage." I asked how come. He said, "That Tarini Chatterjee is a moneylender, and the world's worst miser. He has allowed the school in his house so that he can boast about his generosity to every new magistrate. Actually he just gives the teacher meals and makes him do the accounts until late at night. The teachers' salary comes partly from the government and partly from the students' fees. One of his sisters lost her husband and came to live with him. She was pregnant and died soon after giving birth to a daughter, without receiving any medical help. Another widowed sister did all the housework and saved him the salary of a maid. She took charge of the baby girl but died when the child was small. Since then the child grew up slaving for her aunt and uncle and being harangued constantly. She is of marriageable age, but who would marry an orphan like her? Especially since the people here didn't know her parents, and she was born after her father died, it has caused some talk among the rumour-mongers. They know that the uncle is rich and they want to extract money from him as a price for keeping quiet when she gets married. For the last four years he has said that she is only ten. So she must be at least fourteen. But whatever they might say, the girl is not only Kamala in name but also like the goddess Lakshmi in every way. I have not seen such a beautiful girl. Whenever a young Brahmin arrives here from outside, Tarini begs him to marry the girl. Even if someone agrees to marry, the neighbours say nasty things about the girl and break it off. Now it is your turn."

'I had decided earlier that I would surprise you by marrying a girl from a Hindu family. I knew that if I brought a woman from the Brahmo community into our family it would make everyone unhappy. So without thinking I said, "I will marry this girl."

'Bhupen was surprised, but I said that my mind was made up. He asked, "Are you sure?" I replied, "I am sure."

'That evening Tarini Chatterjee himself came to our camp. He entwined his sacred thread round his fingers and begged me with folded hands, "Please help me. See the girl yourself, and if you don't like her you can withdraw, but please don't listen to the ill-wishers." I replied, "I don't need to see her; decide on a date." Tarini said, "The day after tomorrow is auspicious; let us decide on it." The short notice was an excuse for him to avoid spending much. The wedding took place.'

Khemonkari was startled. 'The wedding took place? What are you saying?'

'Yes. I got into the boat with my bride, and was on my way back. But two hours after sunset that very day, in the unlikely season of Phalgun, before we knew what was happening, all of a sudden a hot whirlwind from nowhere came and capsized our boat.'

Khemonkari exclaimed, 'Madhusudan!'

'After some time when I regained my bearings, I found that I was swimming in the river, but there was no sign of the boat, or the passengers. Later I made inquiries through the police but to no avail.'

Khemonkari's face was pale. She said, 'What has happened has happened. Don't talk to me about it ever again. I get palpitations at the very thought.'

'I wouldn't have said anything to you, but since you insist that I marry, I had to tell you.'

'Will you never marry because of this one unfortunate event?'

'Supposing the girl is still alive?'

'Are you mad? Had she been alive, she would have informed us.'

'What does she know about me? I am the stranger of all strangers to her. She probably never even saw my face. I wrote and gave my Kashi address to Tarini Chatterjee, but he wrote back saying that he didn't have any information of Kamala.'

'Then what else can you do?'

'I have decided to wait for a full year before assuming that she is dead.'

'You overdo everything. Why should you wait till then?'

'The year will be over soon, in just three more months.'

Khemonkari agreed reluctantly. 'All right. But the bride has been chosen; I have given my word to Hemnalini's father.'

'Human beings can only promise, the fulfilment is in God's hands, and we must entrust ourselves in his.'

'That may be so, but I am still trembling in fear.'

'I know that, Mother; it will take time for you to be calm again. That is why I don't tell you about such things.'

'Perhaps you are right. I don't understand what the matter is with me; when I hear of anything bad, the fear doesn't leave me. I am afraid of opening letters lest there be some bad news. In a way I am already dead to this world, why must I suffer more blows?'

## 49

When Kamala reached the bank of the Ganges, the winter sun was about to set in the horizon at the edge of the pale western sky. Facing the impending darkness, she bowed to the setting sun. She sprayed some water on her head, climbed some distance down into the river, poured some water from her cupped palms, and floated some flowers as an offering to the river. She offered her obeisance to her elders with folded hands, and immediately thought of her husband whose face she had never seen.

The one night when she had sat next to him, she had not even looked at his feet; he had talked a little with the other women in the room, but because she had been shy and her face had been covered, she had not heard him clearly. Standing by the river, she tried hard to remember his voice but could not.

Her wedding had been held late at night. Afterwards, extremely tired, she had fallen asleep in a corner of the bed. Next morning a neighbour woman had woken her up laughingly. There had been no one else in the bed. At this critical moment of her life, she had nothing to help her remember him. There was no image, no words, no memento; only darkness. His scarf had been tied to the edge of her red wedding sari. But not realizing the real value of the cheap sari given by her uncle, she had not preserved it carefully.

Kamala had Ramesh's letter to Hemnalini tied to her sari edge. She opened it and read a section of it again in the twilight. That section had some information about her husband. Not much, just that his name was Nalinaksha Chatterjee and that he had earlier practised medicine in Rangpur but presently his whereabouts were unknown. The name was a balm to her. It filled her heart and held her in a formless embrace. She was crying, but her tears allayed her unbearable grief. Her inner self said that it was not all dark or empty, that he was there, he was her own. She told herself, 'If I have been true, then in this very life I will see him and touch his feet; fate will not prevent me. God has kept me alive so that I can serve him.'

She dropped the bunch of keys and noticing the brooch given by Ramesh pinned to her sari, she took it off and dropped it in the water. Then she began walking towards the west. She did not know where she would go or what she would do; she only knew that she must walk on. There was no place for her here.

The winter light at the end of the day disappeared quickly. The white sands were barely visible; the dark night and the steady stars breathed softly on the desolate riverbank.

Kamala could only see infinite darkness ahead of her. But she knew that she must go on, although she did not have the energy to think where she would reach. She had decided to walk along the river because she would not need to ask for direction, and if attacked, she would take shelter in the water of the Ganges. There was no mist. The dense darkness enveloped her, yet she could find her way.

The night progressed. Jackals cried in the fields. After she had walked a long distance, the sand of the riverbank gave way to mud. She noticed a village by the river; the villagers seemed asleep. Trembling with fear, she tried to walk past the village but felt exhausted. Finally she came to a broken bank of the river, and there was no path ahead of her. She lay down under a banyan tree, and fell asleep.

When she opened her eyes before dawn, the light of the waning moon had pierced the darkness. A middle-aged woman was asking her, 'Who are you? Why are you sleeping under a tree on this cold night?'

Kamala was startled, and sat up quickly. She saw two barges moored at the bank. She supposed that the woman had come to bathe before the others woke up.

The woman asked, 'You seem to be a Bengali.'

Kamala replied that she was.

'Why are you in this place?'

'I was going to Kashi. But it got late, and I was sleepy, so I lay down here.'

'How very strange! You were walking to Kashi? Go to that barge, I shall join you after my bath.'

Talking to her later, Kamala learned that she was related to Siddheshwar babu of Gazipur, who had celebrated the grand wedding of his daughter. The woman's name was Nabinkali, and her husband was Mukundalal Dutta. They lived in Kashi and had gone to Gazipur to attend the wedding. But not wishing to eat or stay there, they had travelled by boat.

She asked, 'What is your name?'

'Kamala.'

'I see that you are married. Your husband is alive?'

'My husband left home the day after our wedding.'

'How sad! You are very young.' She gave Kamala a look-over and said that she could not be more than fifteen.

'I don't know for sure, I might be fifteen.'

'Are you a Brahmin's daughter?'

'Yes.'

'Where is your home?'

'I have never been to my in-laws' village, but my father's home is in Bishukhali.' She knew that her father had lived there.

'And your parents?'

'They are both dead.'

'What will you do now?'

'If a respectable family in Kashi allows me to stay with them and give me my meals, I can do their housework. I am a good cook.'

Nabinkali was overjoyed at the prospect of a Brahmin cook willing to work without pay. Yet she said, 'We don't need one because we have our cook and servants with us. We can't manage with any old cook; my husband gets very angry if the food is not up to the mark. I pay the cook fourteen rupees and food and clothes too. Still, you are a Brahmin girl in distress, come and live with us. So many people eat in our house, so much goes waste; one more will make no difference. The work is not heavy. At present there are just the two of us. My daughters are all married into rich families. I have only one son. He is a magistrate, posted in Sirajgunj. Every other month, he gets letters from the viceroy. I asked my husband, "He is lucky to be in a high position, but must he live in that distant place?" My husband said that there are reasons, but being a woman I don't understand. He said, "I didn't ask him to take up a job for money. After all we don't need more. But it is important to have a job. Otherwise a young man might go astray."'

The wind was favourable, so they reached Kashi soon. They went to a double-storeyed house with a small garden, just outside town. Nabinkali fought with the cook and dismissed him without a penny. So Kamala had to do the cooking.

Nabinkali warned Kamala that Kashi was a dangerous place, and since Kamala was young, she shouldn't step out of the house alone. When Nabinkali went to bathe in the Ganges or visit the temple, she would take Kamala with her. She kept a strict watch on Kamala lest she left, and did not give her any free time to meet even other Bengali girls. During the day there was endless work. In the evenings Nabinkali liked to talk about the jewellery, the gold and silver vessels and the brocade and velvet curtains that she had not brought to Kashi for fear of burglary. She said, 'If a few pieces of jewellery get stolen, I can get new ones; but having money doesn't mean that we can suffer loss. Instead, we can live without these for a while. For instance, our house in the village is very large, and we have dozens of servants, but we can't bring them here. My husband suggested that we rent another house nearby, but I said that I couldn't be bothered with looking after so many houses and so many people. I want to relax here.' She talked on in this manner.

## 50

In Nabinkali's house Kamala felt stifled, like a fish in a muddy little pond. She wanted to leave, but where would she find shelter? She had experienced the outside world the other night, and did not dare to repeat the experience.

It was not as though Nabinkali did not care for Kamala; she looked after her well when she was sick. But Kamala found it difficult to be grateful. She did not mind being busy with her work but found the time spent in Nabinkali's company intolerable.

One morning Nabinkali said, 'The master is unwell, so make roti instead of rice, but don't use a lot of ghee. Anyway your cooking is not very good, so I can't understand why you need so much ghee. The Oriya cook was better, he used a lot of ghee, but we could eat it at least.'

Kamala never replied to such talk. She went on with her work as though she had not heard. She was chopping vegetables with a heavy heart thinking that it was a harsh world and that her life was unbearable, when she heard something that startled her. Nabinkali was telling her servant, 'Tulsi, go to the town quickly and bring Dr Nalinaksha. Tell him that the master is very ill.'

Nalinaksha! The sunlight from the window seemed to quiver like the golden strings of a veena. She left the vegetables and stood by the door. She asked Tulsi, 'Where are you going?'

'I am going to fetch Dr Nalinaksha.'

'Who is this doctor?'

'He is a well-known doctor in town.'

'Where does he live?'

'In town, about half a mile from here.'

Kamala used to give extra food to the servants whenever she could in spite of remonstrations from Nabinkali. The mistress was mean about food. Moreover, she and her husband ate quite late, and the servants ate after them. So, whenever they were hungry they came to Kamala, and she could not but give them something to eat. As a result the servants listened to her.

Nabinkali shouted from upstairs, 'What are you two discussing in front of the kitchen? You think I don't have eyes? Tulsi, is the kitchen on your way to the town? This is how things are stolen! And you, Kamala, I brought you home from the street, and you are paying me back in this manner?'

Nabinkali was convinced that they were all thieves. Even when she did not have any proof, she scolded them. She believed that when one threw stones in the dark, at least some hit the target, and the servants realized that she was always vigilant. The rebuke did not hurt Kamala. She was working mechanically, her mind was somewhere else.

She waited for Tulsi by the kitchen door, but he returned alone. She asked, 'Didn't the doctor come?'

'No, he couldn't because his mother is sick.'

'Isn't there someone in his house to take care of his mother?'

'No. He is not married.'

'How do you know that?'

'I hear from his servants that he has no wife.'

'Perhaps she is dead.'

'It is possible. His servant says that when he practised medicine in Rangpur, he didn't have a wife.'

Nabinkali called Tulsi from upstairs. Kamala quickly went inside the kitchen and Tulsi ran upstairs.

Nalinaksha had practised in Rangpur! Kamala had no doubt about his identity now. Later she again asked Tulsi, 'I have a relative with the same name as the doctor. The doctor is a Brahmin, isn't he?'

'Yes, he is. His last name is Chatterjee.'

Kamala went to Nabinkali and said, 'Today after finishing my work I would like to go and bathe in the Ganges.'

'This is most unreasonable! The master is ill; you might be needed for some other work, how can you go out today?'

'I have heard that a close relative is in Kashi, I would like to go and meet him.'

'I don't like all this. I am not a child; I know what is going on. Who informed you of this—Tulsi? I am going to dismiss him. Listen, while you are staying with me, I forbid you to go to the river alone or go to the town in search of some relative. I won't tolerate such conduct.'

She instructed the watchman to throw Tulsi out and not allow him anywhere near the house. The remaining servants avoided Kamala's company now, for fear of their mistress.

Kamala was patient as long as she was not sure about Nalinaksha, but now it was no longer possible. She found it unbearable that her husband was in the same town, and yet she was in someone else's home. As a result she made many mistakes in her work.

Nabinkali asked her, 'What is the matter with you? Are you possessed by an evil spirit? You have stopped eating but must we starve too? Your cooking is so bad that it is inedible.'

Kamala replied, 'I can't work here any longer, please let me go.'

'Is that so? I took pity on you and gave you shelter, and dismissed my excellent cook. I didn't even inquire about your background or whether you really are a Brahmin's daughter, and now you want to leave! If you try to leave I will call the police. My son is a magistrate, and he has sentenced many to death by hanging. You can't escape me. You must have heard that we sent Gada to jail because he talked back to the master. What do you take us for?' It was true that Gada had been falsely accused of stealing a watch, and sent to jail.

Kamala could not find a way out of her present situation. When fulfillment was within reach, her hands were tied. What could be crueller? She could not be absorbed in her work, nor could she stay confined to her room. After finishing her work at night she would wrap a shawl and go into the garden. Standing by the garden wall, she would gaze at the road leading into town. Her young and eager heart traversed the desolate road seeking her unknown home. She would stand still for some time, then kneel and touch her head to the ground in a gesture of obeisance before returning to her room.

But even this much happiness and freedom was not allowed to Kamala for long. One night, when all the work was already done, Nabinkali called Kamala. The servant said that she was not in her room. Suspecting that Kamala had left, Nabinkali took a round of the house but could not find her. Her husband was smoking his hubble-bubble, and hearing that the cook could not be found he told his wife, 'I had warned you not to employ an unknown person. Has she stolen anything?' She replied, 'The shawl that I had given her is missing, but I don't know what else she might have taken.' He decided to call the police.

Meanwhile Kamala came inside and found Nabinkali searching her room. Seeing Kamala she exclaimed, 'What a lot of trouble you have caused! Where were you?'

'I had finished my work, so I went for a stroll in the garden.'

Nabinkali screamed at her, and all the servants gathered near the door of her room. Kamala stood still like a wooden statue. When the tirade was over, she said, 'You are displeased with me; please let me leave.'

Nabinkali said, 'I will get rid of you; I won't waste good money on someone like you. But first I will teach you a lesson.'

Kamala did not dare to go out after that. In her room, behind closed doors, she told herself that she had suffered so much, surely God would help her.

One evening Mukunda babu went for a drive, accompanied by two servants. It was getting dark, and the front door was bolted from inside. Someone called from outside the door, 'Is Mukunda babu at home?' Nabinkali said that it must be Dr Nalinaksha, and called for her servant to open the door. But the servant was nowhere in sight. Then she asked Kamala, 'Go and open the door and tell the doctor that the master has gone out but will be back soon. Request the doctor to wait.' Kamala took the lantern and went downstairs. Her legs were shaking, her heart was throbbing, and her hands were cold. She feared that she might not be able to see him clearly with her anxious eyes. She pulled her sari edge down over her forehead, unbolted the door and stood half hidden by it.

Nalinaksha asked, 'Is Mukunda babu in?'

'No, but please come in.' Nalinaksha entered and sat in the living room. Meanwhile the servant came and explained that the master was out but would return shortly and that he should wait.

Kamala chose a spot in the dark veranda from where she could see Nalinaksha clearly. Her agitated heart and the cold breeze made her shiver. Sitting by the oil lamp, Nalinaksha was deep in thought. From the depths of the darkness Kamala gazed at him. She wiped the tears streaming down from her eyes, and with her gaze seemed to pull him into the innermost corner of her heart. The light fell on his broad forehead and his serene face. It left its imprint in her mind, and she felt that her body was going limp and becoming one with the elements. There was nothing but his face in the entire universe. She too seemed to merge with it.

Kamala did not know whether she was conscious or not. All of a sudden she realized that Nalinaksha had got up and was talking to Mukunda babu. Fearing that they might see her, she left the veranda and went downstairs to the kitchen. The kitchen was at one end of the yard on the way out of the house. She thought of his dignified, calm, bright and pleasant appearance and was thrilled with her good fortune to have such a husband. She thanked God for making her long wait and her suffering worthwhile.

She heard footsteps coming down the stairs, and again stood by the door. The servant held the lamp and showed the way out to Nalinaksha. She addressed him soundlessly, 'You went past me, yet didn't realize that I, your wife, am a servant in someone else's home.'

When Mukunda babu came to the inner part of the house for his meal, Kamala went to the living room. She sat on the floor in front of the chair where Nalinaksha had sat earlier, and kissed the ground. She had no other way to express her devotion.

Next day she learnt that following the doctor's advice for a change of air, they were to move to a healthier climate further west. Preparations for the journey had already begun. Kamala said to Nabinkali, 'I can't possibly leave Kashi.'

'What? If we can, why can't you? You are pretending to be a great devout!

'Whatever you might say, I will stay here.'

'Let me see how you do that.'

'Please have mercy; please don't take me away from here.'

'You are most inconsiderate. How can we find a cook in a hurry just before leaving?'

Kamala's entreaties fell on deaf ears. She closed her door, wept and prayed.

## 51

The same evening, after discussing the proposal of Hemnalini's marriage to Nalinaksha, Annada fell ill. He spent the night in pain. In the morning, when the pain subsided, he sat in the garden in the soft sunlight of the winter morning. Hemnalini was preparing his tea. Annada's face was pale, and there were dark rings under his eyes; it seemed that he had aged overnight.

Whenever Hemnalini looked at him she felt guilty and sad, believing that it was her refusal to marry Nalinaksha that had distressed her father and made him ill. She could not decide on what she should do and how she would console him.

Meanwhile Akshay arrived with Chakravarty. As Hemnalini was about to go inside, Akshay stopped her saying, 'Please don't leave. This is Mr Chakravarty from Gazipur, well known in the western districts. He has some important information.' Akshay and Chakravarty sat down.

Chakravarty said, 'I hear that you know Ramesh babu well; have you any news of his wife?'

Annada babu was surprised and asked, 'Ramesh's wife!?'

Chakravarty replied, 'You probably think that I am old-fashioned and uncivil. But I am here for a reason, and not to force you into a discussion of a third party. I met Ramesh babu on the steamer when he and his wife were travelling west during Dushhera. You might know that Kamala could endear anyone that crossed her path. I am old and hardened by much grief, yet I cannot forget her. Ramesh babu had not decided where they were heading, but Kamala became so fond of me that she persuaded him to stay in my home in Gazipur. There my daughter Shailo cared for her like a sister. I can't comprehend why Kamala left so suddenly, leaving us inconsolable. Since then Shailo hasn't stopped crying.' Chakravarty's own eyes were not dry.

Annada anxiously asked, 'What happened? Where did she go?'

Finding it too distressing, Chakravarty asked Akshay to explain. Akshay narrated the whole story without embellishing it, yet in his narration Ramesh did not show up in good light.

Annada kept repeating, 'We have heard nothing of all this. We have received no letters from him since the day he left Kolkata.' Akshay added, 'Moreover, we didn't know for sure that he had married Kamala. Mr Chakravarty, are you sure that she is Ramesh's wife, and not a sister or a relative?'

'What are you saying, Akshay babu? Of course she is his wife! How many men are lucky enough to have such a good wife?' exclaimed Chakravarty.

'The surprising thing is that the better the wife is, the worse she is treated. God tests good people most severely.' Saying this, Akshay sighed.

Annada passed his fingers through his hair and said, 'No doubt it is terribly sad, but what has happened has happened. No use grieving about it now.'

Akshay said, 'I had a hunch that instead of committing suicide, Kamala may have left home. That is why I came with Mr Chakravarty to search for her in Kashi. Obviously, you have no news of her.'

'Where is Ramesh these days?' asked Annada.

'He left without telling us anything,' said Chakravarty.

Akshay added, 'I didn't meet him but heard from others that he went to Kolkata. Perhaps he would practise in Alipore. After all, one can't mourn forever; especially one as young as he. Mr Chakravarty, let us search the town thoroughly.'

Annada asked, 'Akshay, will you return here?'

Akshay replied, 'I can't be sure. I am very sad about this business. I must spend my time in Kashi searching for her. If she did leave home out of desperation, you can well imagine the difficulty she must be in now. Ramesh babu may be unperturbed but not I.' Akshay left with Chakravarty.

Annada looked at Hemnalini anxiously. She sat there, trying her utmost to control herself. She knew that her father would be anxious. She said, 'Father, call a doctor today and have a thorough check-up. You fall sick too easily, and something must be done about it.'

Annada was greatly relieved that even after such a long and serious discussion about Ramesh, she could be calm enough to talk about his health. At other times he laughed off all discussion of his health, but now he said, 'Good idea. I should have a check-up. Shall I then send for Nalinaksha? What do you think'?

Hemnalini was embarrassed; she could no longer be free with Nalinaksha, especially in front of her father, yet she agreed. And Annada babu, encouraged by her calm, ventured to say, 'What Ramesh has done . . .'

She interrupted him saying, 'Come, let us go in, the sunlight is too strong.' Inside, she made him sit in his easy chair, wrapped a shawl around him, put his glasses on for him, handed him the newspaper, and said, 'Read the newspaper, I will return soon.' Annada could not concentrate on the newspaper because his anxiety for Hemnalini resurfaced. Finally he stopped trying and went in search of her. He found that the door of her room was shut.

Nalinaksha examined Annada and after giving his instructions asked Hemnalini if her father had any special anxiety. She said that it might be so. He suggested, 'I know it is difficult, but his mind needs rest. I face the same difficulty with my mother. She doesn't keep well because she gets agitated about little things. She did not sleep last night worrying about something unimportant. I try to ensure that she stays calm, but it is impossible.'

'You don't look well either,' said Hemnalini.

'No, no, I am perfectly well; it is almost a habit with me! Last night I had to stay up late, which is why I may not look fresh.'

'It would be good to have a woman stay with your mother and look after her. You are busy, how can you manage?' Hemnalini said this easily, and no doubt what she said was right, yet almost immediately she blushed with embarrassment, fearing that he might misunderstand her. Noticing this, Nalinaksha too remembered his mother's proposal.

Hiding her confusion Hemnalini quickly said, 'Shouldn't she have a maid?'

'I have asked her often, but she doesn't agree. Because she is so particular about following the observances, she doesn't like the work of paid employees. Even otherwise, she can't bear it when someone is forced by circumstances to work for her.'

Hemnalini could not say anything more on the subject. After a while she said, 'I try to follow your teaching, but there are setbacks, and then I fear that there is no hope for me. Will my mind never settle down, must it be agitated again and again by adverse events?'

Concerned by her sad appeal, Nalinaksha said, 'Please don't lose heart; obstacles awaken our strength of mind.'

'Could you come tomorrow morning? Your help gives me strength.'

The unwavering peacefulness in his expression and voice was a solace for Hemnalini. He left, but she felt consoled. She stood in the veranda outside her bedroom and looked at the outside world bright in the winter light. Around her in that beautiful afternoon, work and rest, energy and peace, enterprise and renunciation existed side by side. She offered her sad heart to that all-pervading feeling. The sunlight and the bright blue open sky seemed to bless her.

Hemnalini thought about Nalinaksha's mother, and she knew which particular worry and concern kept her awake at night. Hemnalini had overcome the first bout of shock and embarrassment caused by the proposal of her marriage to Nalinaksha. Her respect for him and her dependence on his guidance were getting stronger, but she did not feel love or the sharp pain of love—but did it matter? It did not seem that Nalinaksha, self-assured, would need a woman's love. Yet, he too must need looking after. His mother was old and sickly, who would care for him? His life was precious; perhaps respect was most essential to serve such a man.

She was deeply wounded by what she had heard about Ramesh. Now she gathered all her mental strength to protect herself. She was ashamed to feel any sympathy for Ramesh, yet she did not wish to judge him and pronounce him guilty. After all, millions of people in this world were engaged in deeds good and bad, and yet life went on; she did not have the responsibility of judging them. She did not wish to think about him. But Kamala's suicide sent shivers down her spine. She wondered if it had anything to do with herself, and then shame, disgust and pity would overcome her. She prayed, 'I have not done anything wrong, then why did I get entangled in this? Please remove this bond, sever it with one blow. All I wish for is a normal life.'

Annada was anxious to know Hemnalini's reaction to the subject of Ramesh and Kamala, but he did not dare to ask her directly. In the evening, per the doctor's order, she brought him a glass of milk with some digestive powder mixed in it, and sat near him. Annada asked her to turn the lamp away from his face. When the room was darker, he said, 'The old man who visited us this morning seemed very straightforward.'

Hemnalini kept quiet. Unable to expand on the prologue, he said, 'I am surprised at Ramesh. I had heard many things about him earlier, but I hadn't believed them until today. Now I can no longer . . .'

Hemnalini pleaded, 'Father, let us not talk about it.'

'I don't wish to talk about it, but due to a trick of fate our lives, our happiness and sorrow got involved unexpectedly with this particular man. Now we can't remain indifferent to any aspect of his conduct.'

'Why should we let our lives be tied up with anyone? I am fine as I am. Please don't make me feel ashamed by unduly worrying about me.'

'But I am getting old. I cannot relax until I see you settled down. How can I leave you like this: leading an ascetic's life?'

Hemnalini did not reply. He continued, 'Being disappointed in one thing doesn't mean that one must be indifferent to other things that are precious. Perhaps in your disappointment and regret you don't realize where your happiness and fulfillment lie, but I do. Please don't disregard my suggestion.'

Hemnalini's eyes were damp. She protested, 'Please don't say that. I never disregard your advice. I will accept your wish; I just want to clear my mind and prepare myself.' Annada did not say anything further but placed his hand on her head in a gesture of blessing.

Next morning Akshay came again. Annada looked at him expectantly. Akshay said that they could not find Kamala, and then he sat down with a cup of tea. He brought up the subject gently, saying, 'Some of the belongings of Ramesh and Kamala are in Chakravarty's house, but he doesn't know where to send these. Ramesh babu is sure to get your address and come here, if you could . . .'

Flaring up all of sudden, Annada interrupted, 'Akshay, you have no sense. Why would Ramesh come here, and why should I keep his things?'

'Whether he did something wrong or whether he made a mistake, Ramesh babu must be regretting it. Isn't it the duty of his friends to console him? Must one cut off all association with him?'

'Akshay, you are harping on this subject just to trouble us. I want to make it clear that you must never raise this topic again.'

Hemnalini said softly, 'Father, you mustn't be upset, it will make you ill. Let Akshay babu say what he wants to, what is the harm in it?'

Akshay said, 'No, no. Please forgive my lack of understanding.'

## 52

Mukunda babu decided to leave Kashi and move to Meerut with his family. The luggage was packed and they were to leave the next day. Kamala had hoped against all hope that something would happen in the meantime to prevent their departure. She had also hoped with her whole heart that Nalinaksha would come to examine his patient again. But she was disappointed on both counts.

To prevent any possibility of her running away, Nabinkali kept her near herself and made her do much of the packing.

Kamala wished that she could be violently sick so that it would be impossible to take her along. No doubt she thought of the particular doctor who would treat her. She closed her eyes and imagined that if she were to die of the disease, she would at least have the opportunity to touch his feet before death.

She had to sleep in Nabinkali's room that night, and share the same carriage on their way to the station. Mukunda babu boarded a second class compartment of the train, and Nabinkali and Kamala got into the intermediate class compartment reserved for women.

Finally the train left Kashi station. It roared and tore Kamala away like a rogue elephant tears away a creeper. Kamala longingly stared out of the window. Nabinkali asked for the betel box, and Kamala gave it to her. Opening it, Nabinkali exclaimed, 'Just what I thought! You didn't bring the lime! Unless I supervise, nothing is done properly. You have deliberately done this to harass me. You have been very troublesome lately—no salt in the vegetable one day, burnt smell in the dessert the next—you think I don't know your intention? I will teach you a lesson once we reach Meerut.'

When the train crossed the bridge, Kamala craned her neck to catch a last glimpse of Kashi by the riverside. She did not know where in that town Nalinaksha lived. So, from the speeding train, the riverbank, the houses, the temple roof, and everything that she could see held his presence and touched her heart.

Nabinkali asked, 'What are you trying to see? You are not a bird. You don't have wings that can take you flying!'

Kashi became a blur. She sat still gazing at the sky. The train stopped at Mughalsarai. To Kamala, the noise, and the crowd seemed like a dream. She got down from the train, along with the family, and boarded another one mechanically. When it was time for their train to leave, she suddenly heard a familiar voice calling, 'Ma!' She turned towards the platform and saw Umesh! Her face brightened and she exclaimed, 'Umesh, here?' Umesh opened the door and she got down immediately. He touched her feet and gave a big smile.

The guard shut the door of the compartment. Nabinkali shouted, 'What are you doing? The train is about to start, get in, get in!'

Kamala did not hear her. The whistle blew and the train chugged out of the station.

'Umesh, where are you coming from?' asked Kamala.

'From Gazipur.'

'Are they all well in Gazipur? How is Uncle Chakravarty?'

'He is well.'

'And my Shailo didi, how is she?

'She weeps for you all the time.'

Kamala's eyes filled with tears. 'How is my Uma? Does she remember me?'

Umesh replied, 'She doesn't drink her milk unless the bangles that you gave are put on her. Then she turns her hands and says, 'Aunty has gone,' and her mother cries.

'How come you are here?'

'I didn't like Gazipur any longer, so I came here.'

'Where are you going?'

'I will go with you.'

'But I don't have any money.'

'I have.'

'From where did you get it?'

'I still have the five rupees that you gave me.'

'Then let us go to Kashi. Will you be able to buy the ticket?'

He bought the tickets and helped Kamala into the Kashi-bound train. He said that he would be in the next compartment.

At Kashi station Kamala asked, 'Where should we go now?'

'Don't worry about it; I will take you to the right place.'

'You don't know this town, how will you find the right place?' Umesh assured her that he knew. He hired a carriage, helped Kamala in and got into the coach box. The carriage stopped in front of a house, and they alighted. She followed Umesh into the house. Umesh called, 'Grandfather, are you home?'

Someone replied, 'Is it Umesh? Where have you come from?' In a moment Chakravarty emerged, smoking a hubble-bubble. Astounded, Kamala bent down and touched Chakravarty's feet. Chakravarty was speechless and nonplussed. After a while he held her chin and lifted her bent head. He said, 'My child, you have returned! Come upstairs. Shailo, Shailo, see who is here.'

Shailaja came running to the head of the stairs. Kamala touched her feet, and Shailo held her close and kissed her forehead. Tears streamed down her cheeks. She asked, 'Why did you leave us and make us so unhappy?' Chakravarty said, 'Let us not get into all that. Arrange for her bath and her meal.'

Uma came running with outstretched arms and shouting, 'Aunty, Aunty!' Kamala took her in her arms and kissed her.

Shailaja could not bear to see Kamala's drab sari and her unkempt hair. She gave one of her own saris to her. She asked, 'Didn't you sleep well last night? Your eyes look tired. Rest for some time while I finish my cooking.'

'Let me come with you to the kitchen,' said Kamala. So the two friends cooked the meal together.

Earlier, when Chakravarty had agreed to come to Kashi with Akshay, Shailaja had insisted on accompanying him. He had said, 'How can you? Bipin doesn't have any leave.' But she had insisted, 'It doesn't matter. Mother will be here to look after him.' Shailo had never before agreed to go anywhere without her husband. So he had to agree.

Alighting at Kashi station he found Umesh alighting too. 'Why have you come?' he asked. Umesh was employed in Chakravarty's household, so Chakravarty persuaded Umesh to return to Gazipur. The ensuing events are known already. However, Umesh could not settle in. One day when he was given some money and asked to go to the market, he crossed the river to the station, and took a train to Kashi.

## 53

Chakravarty chose not to tell Akshay about Kamala's return because he had guessed that Akshay did not like Ramesh.

No one in his family asked Kamala why she had left and where she had been. They behaved as though Kamala had come with them to see Kashi.

Shailaja shared her bed with Kamala. She affectionately stroked her forehead. Kamala asked, 'Didi, what did you think of me? Were you angry?'

Shailo said, 'We are not fools. We knew that you wouldn't have taken this extreme step if you had had any other option. In our grief we kept asking why God chose to make your life so difficult. Why must you be punished even though you did nothing wrong?'

'Didi, will you hear my story?'

'Of course I will.'

'I don't know why I couldn't tell you earlier. At that time I didn't have enough time to think it through. It was like a bolt from the blue, and I was too ashamed. I don't have a mother or a sister, but you have filled their place. That is why I want to tell you everything; it isn't something that I can tell anyone else.' Kamala sat up on the bed; so did Shailo. In the darkness, Kamala began narrating the events of her life from her wedding onwards.

When she said that she had not looked at her bridegroom on their wedding night, Shailo said, 'I have never met someone as foolish as you. I got married when I was younger than you, do you think that I was too shy to find an opportune moment to see my husband?'

'It wasn't shyness. I was past the usual marriageable age. When all of a sudden my marriage was fixed, my friends teased me a lot. To show them that getting a husband didn't mean all that much to me, I didn't look at him, nor took any interest in him. Now I am paying the price.'

Kamala sat quietly for a while. Then she continued, 'Earlier I told you about the shipwreck and how we survived. But when I said that, I didn't know that the man I believed to be my husband wasn't my husband.'

Shailo was startled. She put her arm around Kamala and said, 'So that was the reason. Now I understand everything. What terrible misfortune!'

'Didi, had I died in the shipwreck, it would have been the end of all this. Why did God put me in such a difficult situation?'

'Didn't Ramesh babu find out?' asked Shailo.

'Sometime later when he called me Susheela, I said, "My name is Kamala, yet why do you call me Susheela?" I know now that that was when he realized the mistake. But I feel so ashamed to even recall those days.' Kamala was quiet.

Slowly but skilfully Shailo got all the details from Kamala. Finally she said, 'It was most unfortunate, but you were lucky to be with Ramesh babu. I feel sorry for him. It is getting late and you must have some sleep. Tomorrow we must decide what we should do.'

Kamala still had Ramesh's letter to Hemnalini. Next day Shailo showed it to her father. After reading it he asked her what course of action they should take. Shailo said, 'Uma has a bad cold and cough, why don't you send for Dr Nalinaksha. He and his mother are well known in Kashi. Let us see him at least.'

When Nalinaksha came to see the child, Shailo called Kamala excitedly. Although Kamala felt shy, Shailo dragged her near the door. Nalinaksha examined Uma carefully, prescribed a medicine and left.

Shailo said, 'Kamala, you have suffered much, yet you are fortunate. You must be patient for a few days; we have a plan. Meanwhile the doctor will come to see Uma again, so you won't be totally deprived.'

One day Chakravarty deliberately contrived a time to call on Nalinaksha when he was unlikely to be at home. The servant said that the doctor was not in. Chakravarty asked to see Nalinaksha's mother, 'Tell her that an old Brahmin wishes to meet her.'

Chakravarty was asked to go upstairs. He said to Nalinaksha's mother, 'You are well known in Kashi, so I wished to earn merit by seeing you. I came to call your son to come and treat my granddaughter, but he is not in.'

'Why don't you wait for him, he will be back soon. It is past your mealtime; let me get some snacks for you.'

'I knew that you wouldn't let me go without something to eat. Actually I am very fond of food.'

Khemonkari was happy to serve him some snacks, and said, 'You are invited to lunch tomorrow. I wasn't prepared today.'

'I will come whenever you ask me to. My house is near, and I can show it to your servant.' This way Chakravarty became a regular in Nalinaksha's house.

Khemonkari asked Nalinaksha not to accept any fees for treating Chakravarty's granddaughter. Chakravarty laughed and said, 'You don't have to tell him, he never takes any payment from me. Those who are generous recognize the poor.'

One morning, after discussing with Shailo, Chakravarty took Kamala along to the bank of the Ganges, known as Dashashwamedh. He took a different route on the way back and saw an elderly woman wearing a raw silk sari carrying a small pot of Ganges water walking towards them. He brought Kamala forward and asked her to touch the feet of the elderly woman, saying that she was Dr Nalinaksha's mother. Kamala was startled, and then bent down and touched her feet.

Khemonkari exclaimed, 'What beauty, just like goddess Lakshmi! What is your name?' She looked keenly at Kamala.

Before Kamala could reply, Chakravarty said, 'Her name is Haridasi. She is my niece. Her parents are no more, so she is dependent on me.'

Khemonkari invited both of them to her house. Reaching home, she called Nalinaksha, but he was out.

Chakravarty said, 'My niece is most unfortunate. The day after she was married, her husband left home to become an ascetic. She hasn't met him since. She wishes to live in Kashi and lead a life of piety; she can get consolation only from religion. I am a visitor here; I have my work and the responsibility of supporting a family. I can't live here permanently. That is why I have come to you for help. I would be sure of her safety if you keep her with you like a daughter. If you feel inconvenienced, send her back to me in Gazipur. But I can assure you that within a few days you will realize that she is a gem, and then you wouldn't wish to part with her.'

Khemonkari was pleased. 'It's a good idea. Having her with me will be of great help. I often bring home girls I meet on the street, I feed them, give them clothes, but I can't keep them with me. Haridasi can stay with me, and you needn't worry about her. My son Nalinaksha is of excellent character. There is no other family member.'

'Everyone knows of Nalinaksha babu. I am reassured that he lives here with you. I have heard that since his wife died in a shipwreck, he hasn't remarried and lives like an ascetic.'

'Please don't raise that topic. I tremble with fear when I think of it.'

'If you agree, I will leave Haridasi with you now. I will come to see her again. She has an older sister who would like to meet you.'

When Chakravarty left, Khemonkari drew Kamala near and asked her, 'You are very young, your husband must have a heart of stone to leave someone like you. But with my blessings you will get him back. God can't let such beauty be wasted. There is no one of your age here, will you feel lonely?'

Kamala lifted her large eyes and said, 'No, Mother.'

'I wonder how you will spend your days.'

'I will work for you.'

'But there isn't much work here. My only child, Nalinaksha, leads an austere life. I would be so happy if he would tell me that he needs something or wants to eat something special or that he likes something; but he never does. He earns a lot but keeps very little. He spends a great deal on the needy without letting people know. I better warn you that I love talking about my son, so you must be patient with me.'

Kamala was thrilled to hear this. She lowered her eyes.

Khemonkari said, 'I wonder what work I could give you. Do you stitch?'

'Not very well.'

'I will teach you. I suppose you can read?'

'Yes.'

'That's good. I can't read without my glasses, you can read aloud to me.'

'I can cook and do all the housework.'

'Of course you can, you are like goddess Annapurna. I cook for Nalin. When I fall sick, he does his own cooking rather than have food cooked by someone else. Now that you are here, he doesn't need to. And when I become infirm, I can depend on you to cook a little boiled food for me. Come, let me show you my kitchen and my storeroom.'

Kamala found a suitable opportunity and said, 'Please let me cook today.'

Khemonkari smiled. She said, 'A housewife's kingdom is her kitchen and her storeroom. I had to give up many things, but I am still attached to these two. The storeroom is a centre of power. Gradually the responsibility will fall on you, and I will have more time for my prayers. If I cut off all attachments in one go, I will feel unsettled.'

Khemonkari instructed Kamala on what to cook, and went to her prayer room. Kamala's test of household duties began. She made the preparations for cooking with her usual efficiency. Then she tied up her hair, tucked in the sari edge and began cooking.

Usually when Nalinaksha returned home, he went straight to his mother because he was concerned about her health. That day as soon as he entered the house, the sound and smell of cooking assailed him. Thinking that his mother was in the kitchen, he went to the kitchen door.

Kamala heard the footsteps, turned around and their eyes met. She kept the ladle aside, and attempted to cover her head with the sari edge, but by the time she succeeded, Nalinaksha had left. She picked up the ladle with trembling hands.

Having finished her prayers early, Khemonkari went to the kitchen to find that Kamala had not only finished cooking but also washed and cleaned the kitchen thoroughly. She was very pleased and said, 'You are truly a Brahmin's daughter.'

When Nalinaksha sat down for his lunch his mother came to supervise his meal. Kamala stood behind the door, shielded from view. She feared that her cooking might not be good enough. Khemonkari asked, 'Nalin, is the meal well prepared today?' Since Nalinaksha was not a gourmet, she normally did not ask such questions. But today she was curious to know his reaction.

She did not know that he was aware of the change in the cooking arrangements. Earlier he had tried to persuade his mother to keep a cook, but she had not agreed. So he was happy to see someone else doing the cooking. He had not paid much attention to the quality of the cooking, yet he answered enthusiastically, 'The meal is excellent, very well prepared.' Kamala was ecstatic. After his meal Nalinaksha went to study quietly as usual, but he experienced a feeling which he could not quite understand.

In the evening Khemonkari tied Kamala's hair and applied vermilion in her hair parting. She wished she could have a daughter-in-law like this girl. Khemonkari again had fever the same night. Nalinaksha said, 'Mother, I want to take you away from Kashi. This place doesn't suit you.'

Khemonkari did not agree. She said, 'Even if it prolongs my life, I don't wish to leave Kashi and die elsewhere.' She noticed Kamala near the door and said, 'Please don't wait up for me; go to bed. While I am sick, you must take charge. You mustn't stay up.' She then asked her son to leave the room, so that she could talk to Kamala. Kamala massaged her feet. Khemonkari said, 'You must have been my mother in your previous life, otherwise how did I find you? I don't like being served by strangers, but your touch soothes me. I feel as though I have known you from a very long time ago. Now you must go and sleep without any worry because Nalin is in the next room and he doesn't like to hand over his responsibility to anyone else. He is so calm that even when he stays up at night, the strain doesn't show; I am just the opposite. You must be thinking that once I start talking about my son, I go on and on. But I have only that one son, and how many women have such a son! He does so much for me, as though he were my father. I can't do half as much for him. Now you really must leave, otherwise I will go on talking and not get any sleep.'

From the next day Kamala took charge of the household. Nalinaksha had enclosed a section of the eastern veranda. It was his prayer room and he studied there in the afternoons. That morning he found that the room had been mopped, and the brass incense stand was shining like gold. The books on the shelf were well arranged. The morning sunlight further brightened the room and gladdened his heart.

Kamala came to Khemonkari carrying a small pot of Ganges water. Khemonkari was surprised and asked, 'You went alone to bathe in the river? I was wondering who would accompany you since I am sick. But it isn't safe for you to go out alone.'

Kamala said, 'Mother, a servant from my father's house came here last night to see me, I took him along to the river.'

'Your aunt is probably anxious about you and has sent the servant. Let him stay here. He can help you with the housework. Where is he? Call him here.' Umesh came in and touched her feet. She asked what his name was. He replied with a broad grin.

'Umesh, who gave you that colourful dhoti?'

Umesh pointed to Kamala saying, 'Ma has given it to me.'

Khemonkari laughingly said, 'I thought it was a gift from your mother-in-law.'

With Umesh's help, Kamala finished her work early. She cleaned Nalinaksha's room, aired his bedding, washed, dried and folded his clothes carefully. She dusted even those things that did not need cleaning, just so that she could touch them. She opened the wall cupboard behind his bed and found it empty, except for his pair of wooden clogs. She picked them up, touched her head to them, held them to her chest and wiped them with great care.

In the evening Kamala was sitting near Khemonkari and massaging her feet when Hemnalini entered with a basket of flowers, and touched Khemonkari's feet. Khemonkari sat up and said, 'Hem, come and sit here. I hope your father is well?'

'I couldn't come yesterday because he was unwell. Today he is better.'

Introducing Kamala, Khemonkari said, 'I lost my mother in childhood, but she is reborn in the form of this girl whom I met on the street. My mother's name was Haribhamini, but now she has taken the name Haridasi. Have you ever seen someone so like the image of Lakshmi?'

Kamala looked down shyly. Hemnalini and she gradually got to know each other.

Hemnalini asked Khemonkari, 'Ma, how do you feel today?'

Khemonkari replied, 'I am too old to be asked about my health. That I am still alive is enough, and I can't go on avoiding death forever. But I am glad that you have raised the topic because I have been thinking of saying something to you. When I had fever last night, I decided that I shouldn't wait any longer. When I was young, I would have been terribly embarrassed had someone talked about my marriage. But your ways are different. You are educated, and not so very young; I can talk to you frankly. Please don't feel shy, but hasn't your father talked to you about the proposal I made the other day?'

Hemnalini said, 'Yes, he has.'

'Then you must have rejected it. Otherwise your father would have come rushing to tell me. You probably felt that Nalin lives a pious life, engrossed in his meditation and yoga; why should he wish to marry? I don't say this because he is my son, but you would be mistaken to judge him by his outward appearance. It seems as though he can't form any attachments. But I know that he is capable of deep love, and fearing that, he restrains himself. She who breaks the shell of asceticism and captures his heart, will find nectar. Hem, you are mature, educated, and you are taking instruction from Nalin. If I could see you married to him, I would die in peace. I know for sure that he will never marry after I am gone. Just think what his condition would be, he will be rootless. I know that you respect him, then where is the objection?'

Eyes demurely downcast, Hemnalini replied, 'Ma, if you consider me worthy, I have no objection.'

Khemonkari drew her near and kissed her forehead, and did not say anything further on the subject. She said, 'Haridasi, these flowers . . .' and turned towards Kamala, but Kamala had quietly left the room.

Hemnalini was now a little self-conscious with Khemonkari. Khemonkari too felt awkward. Hem said, 'I would like to go home early because Father hasn't been keeping well.' She touched Khemonkari's feet and Khemonkari placed her palm on her head to bless her.

After Hemnalini left, Khemonkari called Nalinaksha and said, 'Nalin, I can't wait any longer.'

'What is the matter?' he asked.

'I spoke frankly to Hemnalini, and she has agreed. I won't listen to any objections from you. I can't be at peace until I see you settled. It keeps me awake at night.'

'All right, I agree. Now please stop worrying, and sleep well.' Later she called Kamala. The room was almost dark, and she could not see Kamala's face clearly. She asked her to arrange the flowers. She kept one rose and handed the rest to Kamala.

Kamala selected a few, arranged them on a platter and kept it in Nalinaksha's prayer room. She arranged a few in a bowl and placed it on a small table in his bedroom. The rest she placed on his clogs in his cupboard and touched them to her forehead. Tears streamed from her eyes. She had only these clogs; she had lost the right to even touch his feet.

Someone entered the room and Kamala stood up in a hurry. She closed the cupboard quickly and saw that it was Nalinaksha. There was no way of escaping. In her embarrassment, she wished to merge into the shadows.

Seeing Kamala, Nalinaksha left the room. Kamala too rushed to her own room. Then he went in again. He was curious as to why she had opened his cupboard, or why she closed it so quickly. He opened it and found the flowers on his clogs He closed the cupboard and stood by the window. The glow of the winter sunset faded and darkness closed in.

## 54

After consenting to marry Nalinaksha, Hemnalini tried to persuade herself that she was indeed fortunate. She told herself again and again, 'I am free of my former ties. The storm clouds that had gathered around my life have passed. I am now free from the ceaseless assaults of my past.'

Repeating this she felt the joy of detachment. After a cremation, life in this world loses its importance and seems like a game, and one's mind seems lighter. Hemnalini was in a similar frame of mind. She derived peace from the closure of one part of her life.

When she returned home she thought, 'If Mother were alive I could have told her everything and shared my happiness with her. But how can I talk as frankly to Father?'

After Annada babu went to bed, she sat at the desk in her quiet bedroom and wrote, 'I was trapped in the web of death and was separated from the world around me. I couldn't believe that God would deliver me from it and give me a new life. I must now prepare myself for my new responsibilities. I don't deserve this good fortune; may God grant me the ability to be worthy. I am certain that the man with whom my life is to be joined will bring me fulfilment. I pray that I may be able to reciprocate it fully.'

She closed her notebook, and paced up and down on the gravel-covered path in the garden in the dark, still and starlit winter night. The infinite sky seemed to chant hymns of peace to her tear-washed heart.

Next afternoon, as Annada was about to leave for Nalinaksha's house with Hemnalini, a carriage stopped by the gate and Khemonkari alighted from it. Annada babu rushed out to welcome her saying that he was honoured by her visit.

Khemonkari said, 'I have come to bless your daughter and to formalize the engagement.' She came in and sat on a sofa. Annada called Hemnalini.

Hemnalini touched her feet and she blessed her saying, 'May you live long and may fortune smile upon you. Please show me your hand.' She slipped a pair of thick gold bangles on Hemnalini's wrists. They were a little loose for her. Hemnalini touched her feet again and she kissed her on the forehead. The blessing and the gesture of affection filled Hemnalini's heart with contentment. Khemonkari invited both of them to lunch the next day.

Next morning, as was their custom, Annada and Hemnalini were having their tea in the garden. His happiness had changed his normal fatigued look overnight. He seemed younger. Looking at Hemnalini's calm and bright face he felt as though his deceased wife's love enveloped her and a hint of tear softened the shine of happiness.

He was anxious that they should be ready on time to go to Khemonkari's house. Hemnalini assured him that it was only eight in the morning and they had plenty of time; but he said that it would take long to bathe and get ready, and that it would be better to reach early rather than late.

All of a sudden, a hired carriage laden with luggage stopped at the gate. Hemnalini exclaimed, 'Dada is here!' and went forward. Jogen alighted and greeted her. Hemnalini asked, 'Is there someone else in the carriage?'

'Of course there is. I have brought a Christmas present for Father.'

Ramesh got down; Hemnalini looked once and then turned back. Jogen called out to her to stop, but she did not heed him. She walked back towards the house very fast, as though running from a ghost.

Ramesh stood still; he could not decide whether to go forward or turn back. Jogen said, 'Come, Ramesh, Father is sitting in the garden.' He pulled Ramesh by the hand and brought him before Annada.

Annada was flabbergasted to see Ramesh. This was a new complication! Ramesh greeted him, and Annada asked him to take a seat. Then turning to Jogen he said, 'You have come at the right time, I was planning to send you a telegram.'

'Why?' asked Jogen

'Hem is engaged to be married to Nalinaksha. Yesterday his mother came to formalize the engagement.'

'What? It is decided already, and you didn't even ask my opinion?'

'Jogen, there is no consistency in what you say. When I didn't even know Nalinaksha, you and your friend were keen on this marriage.'

'At that time I was keen. Anyhow it is not too late yet. There is a lot that needs saying. Hear it first and then decide.'

'Perhaps after a few days; I don't have time for it now, we are going out.'

'Where are you going?'

'Nalinaksha's mother has invited Hem and me. You could eat here.'

'No, no. No need to be concerned about us. Ramesh and I will eat in a restaurant. Will you be back before evening? We will return then.'

Annada babu just could not bring himself to talk to Ramesh. Even looking at him was difficult. Ramesh too remained silent and then folding his palms in a gesture of respect to him, left with Jogen.

## 55

Khemonkari said to Kamala, 'I have invited Hem and her father to lunch tomorrow. What should we prepare? We must feed him very well so that he knows that his daughter won't go hungry in this house! You are such a good cook that I am sure the meal will be excellent. Earlier my son had never commented on the cooking, yet he is full of praise for yours. But you don't look well this morning.' Kamala said that she was fine.

'Perhaps you are missing home. It is only natural, and you shouldn't feel embarrassed about it. You are like a daughter; if you are uncomfortable, or wish to see your family, you must tell me.'

Kamala quickly interrupted, 'No, no. I wish for nothing other than being in your service.'

'Would you like to spend a few days with your uncle and come back when you feel like it?'

Kamala said anxiously, 'When I am with you, I forget all my troubles. Punish me if I have done wrong, but please don't send me away from you.'

Khemonkari stroked Kamala's forehead and said, 'This is why I say that you were my mother in your earlier birth. Otherwise how can we bond so quickly? Tonight you must sleep early; you haven't had any rest.'

Kamala shut the door of her room, extinguished the lamp and sat on the floor in the dark. She thought for a long time, and then told herself, 'I have lost my right due to a trick of faith, and I can't now reclaim it. I must be prepared to give up everything except the opportunity to serve him, which I must find at all cost. Please God, let me serve smilingly, let me not desire anything more. I have suffered much, and now I must be content with what I have received, otherwise I shall lose everything.'

She resolved wholeheartedly, 'From tomorrow I must not allow myself to be unhappy, I must not seem gloomy, must not desire anything that is beyond my reach. I must serve, and not wish for anything more.' She went to bed, turned and tossed for a while and finally fell asleep. She woke up several times at night, and immediately repeated her resolutions. In the early morning she clasped her palms together and addressing her husband she said, 'I will serve you all my life, and not wish for anything more.'

She washed and changed her clothes and went to Nalinaksha's room. She mopped the room, placed the mat on the floor and then went to bathe in the Ganges. After returning Kamala went to Khemonkari, touched her feet and smiled. By then Khemonkari was about to go to bathe in the river. She asked Kamala, 'Why did you bathe so early, we could have gone together.'

'There is a lot of work today. I will chop the vegetables that were bought yesterday and Umesh can go to the market to get the rest of the things.'

'That's a good idea. The food will be ready when Annada babu and Hem arrive.' When Kamala saw Nalinaksha come out, she covered her head with her sari and left the room.

Nalinaksha asked his mother, 'Must you bathe in the river today? Only yesterday you felt a little better.'

'Nalin, don't you practise your medicine on me! Even if I don't bathe in the Ganges in the morning, I won't be immortal. Are you going out? Come back early.'

'Why, Mother?'

'I forgot to tell you that Annada babu is coming to bless you.'

'To bless me? Why should he be especially pleased with me today? I see him every day.'

'I have already pledged you to Hem by giving her a pair of bangles, now it is Annada babu's turn. Anyhow, don't be late. I have invited them to lunch.' Khemonkari went for her bath and Nalinaksha walked out into the street thoughtfully.

## 56

To avoid Ramesh, Hemnalini rushed into her room, shut her door and sat on her bed. Agitation gave way to embarrassment. She asked herself, 'Why couldn't I talk normally to Ramesh babu? Why am I overcome with emotion, even though it is uncalled for? I can't trust anything, nor can I continue in this restless manner.'

She forced herself to open the door and go out. She thought, 'I must not run away, I must overcome this feeling.' She went to meet Ramesh but remembered something and turned back. She took out the bangles given by Khemonkari and wore them. Thus armed, she got hold of herself, and walked towards the garden with her head held high.

Annada asked, 'Hem, where are you going?'

'Aren't Dada and Ramesh babu here?'

'No, they have left.' Hemnalini felt relieved that she would not have to face another test.

Annada said, 'Let us then . . .'

'Yes, Father, I will be ready soon; you can send for a carriage.'

She returned soon, dressed and ready, and finding that the carriage had not arrived, she paced in the garden. Annada sat stroking his head.

When they reached Nalinaksha's house, it was not later than ten-thirty. Nalinaksha had still not returned from work. Khemonkari welcomed them. She asked after his health and about other matters. But whenever she looked at Hemnalini, she wondered why there was no glow of happiness on her face. Why did not the prospect of the happy event brighten her face like the light of dawn before sunrise? Instead, she looked anxious and distracted.

Khemonkari was hurt easily, and felt discouraged by Hemnalini's lacklustre expression. She thought, 'Any girl would consider herself fortunate to marry Nalinaksha. But does this girl, with her intellectual conceit, not consider him to be worthy of her? Why does she worry and hesitate? Perhaps I am to blame. I am old, yet I can't be patient. When I desired the connection, I could wait no longer. I chose a young woman without getting to know her. But alas there is no time to know her better. I have been summoned to quickly complete all my work in this world.'

While she was talking to Annada, all these thoughts kept churning in her mind. She found it hard to continue talking. She said to him, 'Let us not rush the wedding. Both of them are mature, they will think over it and decide. We shouldn't urge them. I don't know Hemnalini's feelings, but I know that Nalin hasn't made up his mind.'

She said this aiming at Hemnalini. Since Hemnalini was obviously worried and unsure, she did not wish to have them think that her son was thrilled at the prospect of marrying her.

Hemnalini had come with a forced cheerfulness, but it had the opposite effect. Momentary excitement turned into deep weariness. When she entered Khemonkari's house, a sudden apprehension gripped her. The new life that she was about to embark on seemed like a long, inaccessible and uphill climb. She felt hurt by her mistrust in herself.

When Khemonkari seemed to withdraw the marriage proposal, Hemnalini was overcome with two contrary feelings. On the one hand, she wished to firm up the proposal so that she could be free of the doubts and hesitation; on the other hand, she felt relieved that it might come to naught.

Khemonkari was displeased to see that Hemnalini was more relaxed now. She thought that her son deserved someone better, and was glad that Nalinaksha was not home yet. She said to Hemnalini, 'Nalinaksha has no sense. He knew that you were expected, yet he is absent! He could have worked a little less today. When I am ill, he leaves all his work and stays home, and it doesn't set him back.'

She then went to find out if the meal was ready. Actually she did not want to continue to converse with Hemnalini and wanted Kamala to talk to her, so that she herself could talk to the harmless old man.

She found that Kamala had kept the cooked rice on low fire to keep it warm, and was sitting in a corner of the kitchen, deep in thought. Kamala was startled to see Khemonkari, and then she stood up and smiled. Khemonkari said, 'I thought you were busy cooking.'

'The meal is ready.'

'Then why are you sitting here alone? Annada babu is an old man; you shouldn't feel shy of him. Hem is here, take her to your room and chat with her. I am old and not fit company for her.'

Kamala was diffident, and said, 'She is highly educated, so how can I converse with her? I am so ignorant.'

'You are no less than anyone. Others might be conceited about their education, but no one else is as deserving of love as you are. Anyone can acquire book knowledge, but how many can be like you? Come with me. But these shabby clothes won't do; you must be dressed appropriately.'

She believed that Hemnalini was too proud and wished to humble her by showing off Kamala's beauty. Kamala had no scope to protest. Khemonkari made her wear a turquoise silk sari, dressed her hair in a novel fashion, and then kissed her forehead and commented that such beauty was suited to a king's palace. She took Kamala with her to the living room saying, 'Don't feel shy, you can hold your head high in any company, and put to shame college-educated women.'

Nalinaksha was there in the living room, talking to the guests. Kamala tried to retreat, but Khemonkari held her hand, 'No need to feel shy, there is no stranger here.' She was proud of Kamala and wished to surprise the others by her beauty. She also hoped to humble Hemnalini in Nalinaksha's presence.

They were amazed. When Hemnalini had first met Kamala, she was in ordinary clothes, and she had sat quietly and humbly in a corner for a few minutes. She had not seen Kamala properly, and was surprised today. She asked the shy Kamala to sit next to her. Khemonkari knew that she had won. Those present admitted to themselves that such beauty was God's rare gift. She said to Kamala, 'Take Hem to your room and chat with her, meanwhile I will see to the food.'

Kamala was concerned that Hemnalini might not like her. Hemnalini would come to this house as a bride and would be the mistress there one day. Kamala needed to be in her good books. She herself was the rightful mistress of the household, but she did not want to think of it, she would not allow herself to be jealous, she had no claims. As she accompanied Hemnalini, her feet were unsteady.

Hemnalini said softly, 'I have heard everything about you from Ma. It made me very sad. You must think of me as a sister. Do you have a sister?'

Kamala was reassured by Hemnalini's sympathy. She answered, 'I don't have a sister, only a cousin. My uncle's daughter.'

'I have no sister. My mother died when I was very young. I have often wished that I had a sister. From childhood I have had no one with whom I could share my thoughts, so I kept my thoughts to myself. Now it has become such a habit that I can't talk freely with anyone. Others think that I am too proud, but you mustn't think that. My mind has become mute.'

The barriers were now broken. Kamala said, 'Didi, I am so ignorant, you won't like me.'

Hemnalini smiled and said, 'When you know me better you will find that I am terribly ignorant. I have only memorized some books, but I don't know anything. I request you that if I join this family, please don't leave me. When I think of having the sole responsibility of the household, I feel scared.'

Kamala said with childlike candour, 'Give me all the responsibility. I have worked hard since my childhood, I am not afraid to take responsibilities. The two of us sisters will run the household; you will keep him happy, and I will serve you both.'

Hemnalini asked, 'You had not seen your husband properly, do you remember him at all?'

Kamala did not give a direct answer but said, 'I didn't know that I should try to remember him. When I came to Uncle Chakravarty's house, and got to know Shailadidi, I saw how well she looked after her husband. Only then did I realize it. I don't know how all my thoughts turned towards my husband whom I had hardly seen. God has rewarded me; now, in my mind, my husband is a real presence. Even though I am not with him, he is mine.'

Hemnalini was moved by this. She sat still for some time and then said, 'I understand what you mean, when we receive in that manner, it endures. When we receive from greed, it doesn't last.'

Perhaps Kamala did not comprehend the meaning fully. She gazed at Hemnalini and said after a while, 'What you say might be true. I don't allow myself to be sad; I am all right. Whatever I have received has enriched me.'

'My teacher says that when sacrifice and gain become one, then it is real attainment. I will consider myself blessed if, like you, I can have the gratification by giving my all.'

Kamala was surprised, 'But Didi, you will attain everything, there will be nothing amiss.'

'May I be happy with that which is of true worth; more than that can be a burden and cause unhappiness. You might be surprised to hear this, sometimes I am surprised myself. Today I came with a heavy heart, but after talking to you it is lighter, and I have found strength. I don't talk much, but somehow you have taken me out of myself.'

# 57

When Hemnalini returned home, she found a large and heavy envelope on her desk. She recognized the handwriting to be Ramesh's. With trembling heart, she closed the door and began reading.

Ramesh had written in detail about the events relating to Kamala. In conclusion he had written:

'The bond between you and me that God had strengthened, has been severed by the events. Your affection is now claimed by another, and I don't blame you for that. Please don't blame me either. Even though I have never treated Kamala like a wife, I cannot deny that she had drawn my heart. I don't quite know what I feel now. Had you not deserted me I could have found solace in you. Distracted, I had run to you with that hope. But when I realized that you have turned away from me in contempt, and have consented to marry someone else, I wavered. I realized that I haven't completely forgotten Kamala. Whether I do or not, it doesn't harm anyone other than me. But does it harm me? I don't have the power to forget the two women whom I have accepted deep in my heart, and to remember them all my life is my supreme gain. This morning, on my return home after the shock of the brief encounter with you, I thought that I am unfortunate. But now I don't feel that way. I bid you goodbye happily and with a steady mind—I am fulfilled—with God's grace I won't feel sad. May you be happy and well. Please don't scorn me; you have no reason to do that.'

Annada was reading a book; he was startled to see Hemnalini and asked, 'Hem, are you ill?'

'No. I have a letter from Ramesh babu. Please read it and return it to me.' She left the room.

Annada read the letter twice. After a great deal of thought he came to the conclusion that it was for the best. Nalinaksha was much more eligible for his daughter than Ramesh. It was good that Ramesh himself had bowed out.

Meanwhile Nalinaksha arrived. Annada was surprised to see him because they had met earlier, the same day. He concluded that Nalinaksha was attracted to Hemnalini.

As he was planning to call Hemnalini and then leaving the two alone on some pretext, Nalinaksha said, 'Annada babu, it has been suggested that I should marry your daughter. Before going any further, I would like to say something. You may not know that I had married earlier.'

'I know, but . . .'

'I am surprised that you know. You probably guessed that she is dead. But one can't be sure; in fact I believe that she is alive.'

'May God grant that it be true.' He called, 'Hem, Hem!' When Hemnalini came in he said, 'If you could show him that part of Ramesh's letter where—'

Hemnalini handed the letter and said, 'He should read the entire letter.'

Nalinaksha read it and sat dazed for a while, and then took leave of Annada. On his way out he noticed Hemnalini in the northern veranda. He felt sad. How could her outward calm hide her heart? There was no way of knowing what she felt at this moment. He could not ask her if she needed him, it would be difficult to answer. He wondered if it was possible to console her. But human beings were separated by such unbreakable barriers! The mind was so terribly lonely!

Nalinaksha made a small detour to pass in front of that veranda in case she wished to ask something, but he found that she had gone into her room. Nalinaksha got into his coach thinking that hearts don't meet easily, and that human relationships were complex.

Jogen arrived after Nalinaksha had left. Annada asked, 'How come you are alone?'

'Who else are you expecting?'

'Why, Ramesh?'

'Wasn't the first day's welcome bad enough? I don't know his whereabouts; for all I know he may have drowned in the Ganges and achieved nirvana. I haven't seen him since yesterday, but he left a note on my desk saying, "I am leaving. Yours, Ramesh." I am not used to such sentimentality, so I too must leave. A headmastership is much better; it involves nothing vague, everything is very clear.'

'Shouldn't we decide something about Hem?'

'Not again! I am fed up of the game of I-decide-and-you-upset-it. Please don't involve me any more. I don't understand all this and it doesn't suit my temperament. Hem's amazing capacity to be inscrutable bothers me. I will leave by the morning train tomorrow; I have some work in Bankipur.'

Annada babu sat silently. The intricacies of life had become more complex.

## 58

Shailaja and her father came for a visit to Nalinaksha's house. Shailaja and Kamala were having a whispered conversation in a corner room, and Chakravarty was talking to Khemonkari.

Chakravarty said, 'My holidays are over, I must leave for Gazipur tomorrow. If Haridasi has annoyed you or if it is difficult for you to . . .'

'What are you saying? Do you want to take your niece away on some pretext?'

'You misunderstand me. Once I give something away, I don't take it back. But if you are even slightly inconvenienced . . .'

'You can't be serious. You know full well that Haridasi is of great help to me.'

'I said it only to hear you praise her! But I have a concern—Nalinaksha babu might think of her as a burden. My niece has her pride; she will feel very bad if she observes even a hint of displeasure.'

'Displeased? Who, Nalin? It is not in his nature.'

'You see, I am very fond of Haridasi, and can't remain complacent about her. It is not enough that Nalinaksha babu remain indifferent to her. Since she is part of his household, he should treat her with affection, like a member of the family. Otherwise she would feel diffident. After all, she is a human being, and not a wall; it is not right if he is neither vexed nor fond of her but only indifferent.'

'Please don't worry. It is easy for Nalin to befriend people. It may not be obvious, but I am sure that Nalin thinks about her comfort and well-being, and unknown to us, he has probably made certain arrangements keeping that in mind.'

'I am reassured. Yet before I leave, I would like to explain this to Nalinaksha babu. Rarely does a man have the ability to take full responsibility of a woman. Since he has that ability, he shouldn't push her away and shouldn't hesitate to treat her like a relative and protect her.'

Moved by Chakravarty's trust in her son, she said, 'Fearing that you might mind, I didn't encourage her to meet Nalinaksha. But I know my son; you can trust him and be free of worry.'

'Then let me be frank with you. I have heard that Nalinaksha babu is to be married, and that his intended bride is not a young girl, and her upbringing and education don't fit into our society. So I thought that for Haridasi it might . . .'

'I understand your concern, but the engagement is off. Nalin was not keen at all; I was the one to insist. However, I have given it up because no good can come in trying to force it. I don't know what God wills; I will probably die without having a daughter-in-law.'

'Please don't say that. What are we here for? I will find him a bride, and claim the reward and the sweets.'

'May it be true. I feel sorry that my son is not marrying because of me. That is why I rushed to arrange this marriage without thinking. You must arrange a suitable match for him soon; I don't have much time left.'

'You will surely live to see your daughter-in-law. I know the kind of girl you wish for your son. She shouldn't be too young, yet respect and obey you. You shouldn't worry; it is predestined. Let me now go to Haridasi and advise her on her duties. I will send Shailo to you. Ever since she met you she is full of your praise.'

'I have some work, why don't the three of you have a chat.'

Chakravarty went to Kamala and Shailo to find that Kamala had been crying. He looked at Shailo inquiringly. Shailo said, 'Father, I told Kamala that she should now talk frankly to Nalinaksha babu, but she doesn't agree.'

Kamala entreated, 'Didi, I just can't do it. It is impossible, please don't ask me again.'

'If you keep quiet, he will marry Hemnalini. From the time of your wedding up until now you have been the victim of adverse circumstances, why do you wish for more complications?'

'Didi, I can't talk about my past. I can bear everything but the shame of it. I am all right the way I am, I have no sorrow. But if you disclose everything, how can I stay a moment longer in this house? How will I continue to live?'

Shailo had no answer, but she could not bear the thought that Kamala would not open her mouth and let Nalinaksha marry Hemnalini.

Chakravarty said, 'With God's grace, that engagement is broken. Kamala, you must not be afraid, righteousness is on your side.'

Kamala could not quite understand, and stared at Chakravarty with wide eyes.

He said, 'That proposal of marriage has fizzled out. Nalinaksha babu was not in favour of it, and now his mother too has seen sense.'

Shailaja was very happy. 'What a relief! I couldn't sleep all last night. Anyhow, how long will Kamala live like a stranger in her own home? When will the matter be clarified?'

Chakravarty cautioned, 'Shailo, don't be in a hurry. When the time comes it will all be clear.'

Kamala said, 'The present situation is simple, and it can't be simpler than this. I am not unhappy. Please, Uncle, don't bring further misfortune by attempting to make me happier. Please, I beg of you both, don't say anything to anyone. Leave me here and forget me. I am fine.' Kamala wept as she said this.

Chakravarty was alarmed; he said quickly, 'Please don't cry, my child. I understand what you are trying to say. We can't possibly disturb the peace that you are experiencing. Providence is working steadily; we can't foolishly interfere and upset things. '

Umesh entered with his usual big smile. 'Umesh, what is the latest?' asked Chakravarty.

'Ramesh babu is downstairs; he wants to see the doctor.'

Kamala turned pale. Chakravarty got up quickly and assured her that he would take care of everything. Downstairs, he asked Ramesh to come for a stroll with him. Ramesh asked, 'Uncle, how come you are here?'

'I am here because of you. I am very glad to see you. Come, let us first discuss the important matter.'

When they were some distance from the house he asked, 'Ramesh babu, why have you come to this house?'

'I came to see Nalinaksha. I should explain Kamala's history to him. I have a feeling that Kamala might be alive.'

'If she is alive, and if you explain everything about her to Nalinaksha, how would that help? If his elderly mother comes to know, would it be good for Kamala?'

'I don't know how society will view it, but Nalinaksha should know that Kamala is blameless. If Kamala is dead, he would at least respect her memory.'

'I don't understand these modern views. If she is dead, I don't see why we must talk about her past. I live in that house that you see there. If you could come tomorrow morning, I would like to tell you everything frankly. Meanwhile please don't meet Nalinaksha.'

Returning to Kamala he said, 'You must come to my house tomorrow and explain your view to Ramesh babu.'

Kamala sat still with her head bent down. Chakravarty continued, 'I am sure that there is no other option. Modern young men don't listen to old men like me. Please don't hesitate. You must not let a third party step into what is your domain. Only you can do this.'

Kamala did not reply. Chakravarty said, 'The matter is getting clearer, now you mustn't hesitate to brush away the remaining small obstacles.'

Hearing footsteps, Kamala looked up to find Nalinaksha at the door, and their eyes met. Earlier, Nalinaksha would quickly look away and leave, but this time he did not. His look seemed to claim something from Kamala. Noticing Shailo, he was about to leave when Chakravarty said, 'Nalinaksha babu, please don't leave. We consider you a member of our family. This is my daughter Shailo, you had treated her daughter.'

They greeted each other and Nalinaksha asked, 'I hope your daughter is well?' Shailo answered that she was well. Chakravarty said, 'You are so busy that we never get to talk to you. Why don't you sit with us for a while?' Then he noticed that Kamala had left the room, perhaps to calm herself. Meanwhile Khemonkari called him to have his meal.

After lunch Chakravarty went to Kamala's room and brought her to Nalinaksha and Khemonkari. He said, 'Nalinaksha babu, please don't consider Haridasi an outsider. I am leaving this unfortunate girl in your house; please think of her as a family member, and grant her the privilege of looking after both of you. You can be sure that she would not do anything wrong knowingly.'

Kamala blushed and sat with her eyes downcast. Khemonkari said, 'She will be here like a daughter. So far I have never had to ask her to do anything. She has herself taken up the responsibilities. She rules the kitchen and the store; the servants no longer consider me to be in charge! I didn't notice how I was dislodged; she has taken my set of keys too! What more would you wish for this robber of a girl? Now if you want to take her from us it would be the biggest robbery of all.'

'Even if I try, will she come? You have so charmed her that she doesn't seem to know anyone else! This is the first time she has found peace in her tragic life. May this peace remain unhindered, may she always please you.' His eyes were wet. Nalinaksha listened quietly. When they left, Nalinaksha went to his room. The winter sunset had cast a reddish glow on his room which touched his heart.

A friend had sent a basket of roses, and Khemonkari had asked Kamala to arrange them. In that quiet evening, the glow of the sunset and the fragrance of the roses mixed together bringing a feeling of restlessness in him. So far his world had had the peace of discipline and the gravity of knowledge, but now, suddenly from somewhere music played out in many tunes, and nature pulsated like the jingling anklets of an unseen dancer! He turned away from the window and spotted the roses in a vase near his bed. They seemed to gaze at him with the eyes of someone, in a silent offering at the door of his heart.

He chose a rose which was yellow, like unbeaten gold; the half-opened petals could not hide the fragrance. The touch of the rose seemed like the touch of someone, and it played music on his nerves. He brushed the soft flower on his face and his eyelids.

Soon the glow of the sunset disappeared from the evening sky. He went near his bed and placed the rose on his pillow. As he turned, he noticed someone sitting huddled in a corner. Kamala had come to keep the flowers and make his bed, but as she was about to leave the room, she heard his footsteps, and in her confusion hid in the corner at the other side of the bed. Now she could neither hide nor leave; she was caught!

To avoid causing further embarrassment, Nalinaksha was about to leave but turned back and stood in front of her. He said, 'You need not be shy with me, please get up.'

## 59

Next morning Kamala came to Chakravarty's house. Finding an opportune moment, she embraced Shailo. Shailo asked, 'What has made you so happy this morning?'

'I don't know, but I feel that my entire burden is lifted.'

'Tell me what happened after we left last evening.'

'Nothing that important, but I feel that at last he is mine, that God is at last pleased with me.'

'However unimportant, please don't hide it from me.'

'I have nothing to hide, or much to say. When I woke up in the morning, I felt that I had found fulfilment; my work seemed lighter, every moment meaningful. I can't believe that every day would be like this and fortune would smile at me.'

'I believe that your fortune will give you much more—all that it owes you.'

'No, no. Nothing is owed to me. I don't blame my destiny, I have no wants.'

Chakravarty came to inform her that Ramesh had arrived and that she must meet him. He had told Ramesh, 'I am aware of the true nature of your life with Kamala. You are now free and my advice is to completely dissociate yourself from the matter. If any knot is still to be untied, leave it to fate, don't intervene.'

Ramesh answered, 'I can't be free until I clarify everything to Nalinaksha. Whether she is alive or not, I must say what I have to before I leave.'

Chakravarty asked him to wait and went to fetch Kamala. Ramesh stared blankly at the flow of people outside. Then he heard footsteps, and saw a woman bowing to touch his feet. He was astounded to see that it was Kamala. Chakravarty said, 'God in his kindness is clearing the mist surrounding Kamala, and turning all her grief into joy. She can't leave without saying goodbye because you had safeguarded her through the crisis and had suffered great distress for her sake. She seeks your blessing.'

After remaining quiet for a few minutes, Ramesh cleared his throat and said, 'I wish you all happiness. Please forgive me if I have wronged you knowingly or unknowingly.' Kamala did not answer but stood still leaning against the wall for support. Ramesh said, 'Let me know if you need me to speak to anyone or clarify anything.'

Kamala answered with folded hands, 'I have this one request—please don't tell anyone about me.'

'For a long time I hadn't spoken about you to anyone, even when I was in a difficult situation. Recently, when I believed that you were beyond any harm, I had disclosed it to a family I know. Even that might work in your favour. Uncle might know Annada babu and his daughter, to whom . . .'

Chakravarty said, 'Yes, of course, Hemnalini. Do they know?'

'Yes. If you wish me to tell them anything else, I can. But I am not keen. I have lost not only time but a great deal more; now I wish to be free. I wish to settle my accounts and go away.'

Chakravarty held Ramesh's hands and said affectionately, 'You don't have to do anything further. You have borne a great burden, but now you are free of it; lead an independent life, and may you be happy and successful.'

Before leaving Ramesh looked at Kamala and said goodbye.

Ramesh walked down the road dreamily as he thought, 'It was good to have met Kamala, otherwise this chapter wouldn't have closed completely. Although I still don't know why she left Gazipur suddenly, it is clear that I am not needed. Now I have only my own life to consider, and I set out in this world accepting the full responsibility for it. I don't have to look back.'

## 60

Kamala returned home to find Hemnalini sitting with Khemonkari. The lady asked Kamala to take Hem to her room, so that she herself could attend to the refreshments.

As soon as they entered Kamala's room, Hemnalini put her arms around her and said, 'Kamala!' Not too surprised, Kamala asked, 'How did you get to know my real name?'

'I heard your life story from someone, and I had no doubt that you were Kamala. I can't explain why.'

'I don't want anyone to know my name. I am ashamed of it.'

'But you must claim what is yours on the strength of it.'

'I have no claims, nor do I wish to use any pressure.'

'But on what grounds can you deprive your husband of your true identity? Would you not wish to offer your all—good and bad—to him? Should you conceal anything from him?'

Kamala turned pale. She could not find an answer and looked helplessly at Hemnalini. She sat down slowly on the floor mat and said, 'God knows that I am innocent, then why does he place me in this embarrassing situation? I have done no wrong, why must I be punished? How will I tell my husband about my past?'

Hemnalini held her hand and said, 'It will not be a punishment but your salvation. As long as you conceal yourself from your husband, you are tied up in a lie. Be determined and tear it off, and God will keep you well.'

'When I fear that I might lose everything again, I have no strength. Yet I agree with what you say. Whatever destiny might hold for me, I can't conceal myself any longer, my husband must know all about me.' Saying this she held her hands together in a tight knot.

Hemnalini felt deeply sympathetic. She asked, 'Would you prefer to have someone else tell him?'

Kamala said with determination, 'No, no. He must not hear it from anyone else. I must tell him myself. I will be able to do so.'

'That is the best. I came here to tell you that we are leaving Kashi. We might not meet again.'

'Where will you go?'

'Kolkata. You have a lot of work, so I won't delay. Goodbye, remember me as a sister.'

Kamala held Hemnalini's hands and asked, 'Won't you write to me?'

'Yes, I will.'

'In your letters, please advise me on my duties. I will derive strength from them.'

Hemnalini smiled and said, 'You will soon have someone who will advise you better than I ever could.'

Hemnalini left, but Kamala felt sorry for her. She saw something in Hemnalini's calm eyes that brought tears to her own. Hemnalini always kept a distance, one hesitated to talk freely to her, or ask her questions. She knew all about Kamala, but left her own feelings unclear. Yet she left behind something unfathomably sad, like the disappearing twilight.

Throughout the day whenever Kamala had a free moment, she thought of Hemnalini's words and her calm but sad look, and it pained her. She did not know much about Hemnalini, only that there had been a proposal of her marrying Nalinaksha, and that it was called off. Hemnalini had brought with her a basket of flowers from her garden. After her evening bath, Kamala was making a garland when Khemonkari came and sat beside her. She sighed and said, 'When Hem said goodbye, I felt so very sad. Such a fine girl; I would have been happy to have her as my daughter-in-law. And it could have happened but for my son. I can't understand why he didn't agree.' Khemonkari did not wish to give any importance to the fact that she herself had changed her mind.

Hearing her son's footsteps outside, Khemonkari called him. Kamala hid the flowers and the garland and covered her head. Khemonkari asked, 'Hem and her father left today; didn't you see them?'

'Yes, I saw them off at the station.'

'Whatever you might say, one rarely finds a girl like Hem.' She said it as though he had always disagreed! Nalinaksha smiled.

She said, 'Why do you smile? I proposed marriage between you two but you upset everything by your cussedness. Don't you regret it now?'

Nalinaksha looked at Kamala and saw her inquiring look. When their eyes met, Kamala quickly lowered hers in embarrassment. He said, 'Mother, your son is not so eligible that just your proposal would be enough. Who would like a dull and grave man like me?'

Kamala looked up again and saw that he was looking at her with his eyes full of humour. She was so embarrassed that she wished to run out of the room. Later, she made a long garland with the flowers, placed it on a basket, sprinkled some water, and kept it in Nalinaksha's prayer room. She felt that Hemnalini had brought the flowers for this reason—to say goodbye.

Then she thought about his expression as he looked at her, and wondered what he thought of her. She had not hidden her feelings from him. It was easier when she did not appear before him, but now she was getting caught at every turn. It was the punishment for concealing her identity. Nalinaksha must think her shameless and wonder where his mother had picked her up from. The thought was intolerable. At night in bed, she made a solemn pledge to reveal her identity to Nalinaksha; she would not worry about the consequence.

Next morning she bathed early. As usual she went to clean Nalinaksha's meditation room but was surprised to find him there. It was most unusual. She turned to go back to her room, and then changed her mind and sat quietly near the door. She did not know what engrossed her, the world seemed like a shadow, and she was unaware of the passage of time. All of a sudden she realized that he was standing in front of her. She bent down and touched his feet, and her long wet hair fell on them. Then she stood still like a stone sculpture. She was unaware that her head was uncovered; she did not see that his gaze was fixed on her face. She was unaware of the external world and—glowing in the light of her inner consciousness—she said in a steady voice, 'I am Kamala.'

As soon as she said that, she seemed to wake up from a trance. She was trembling, her eyes were downcast. She could not move, nor did she have the strength to stand. She had spent all her energy and determination to speak the words 'I am Kamala'. She had exposed herself, now everything depended on his kindness. Nalinaksha gently took her hand and said, 'I know that you are my Kamala. Come into my room.' He took her in, put the garland round her neck and said, 'Come, let us bow together before God.' They knelt on the marble floor together and bowed their heads. The morning sunlight fell on them.

When Kamala stood up, she was free of her unbearable shame. It was not exultation, but an unshakable peace born of a sense of freedom that spread its being into the pure, open, unreserved morning light. Deep devotion filled her heart and her prayer seemed to envelop the world. Unknown to herself, tears streamed down her face, the clouds of her unhappy, orphaned life were washed out in a rain of joy. Without saying anything more, Nalinaksha pushed away the wet strands of hair from her face and left.

Kamala went to his bedroom and wrapped his clogs with her garland and touched them to her head. After that the day's work was like an act of worship for her. Each piece of work gave her joy. Khemonkari asked, 'Are you going to clean the whole house until it looks new?'

In her free time in the evening, instead of doing her needlework, Kamala was sitting still in her room when Nalinaksha came in with some lotus flowers. He said, 'Kamala, sprinkle some water and keep them fresh; this evening we will go to Mother together to seek her blessing.'

Kamala said, 'You haven't heard the full story yet.'

'You don't need to say it; I know.'

She covered her face with her hands in her worry and asked, 'But will Mother . . . ?' She could not complete the sentence.

Nalinaksha held her hand and assured her, 'Throughout her life, Mother has forgiven many wrongs; she will surely forgive what is not wrong.'

GORA

*Translated by Radha Chakravarty*

# 1

The clouds had cleared this Sravan morning, leaving the Kolkata sky filled with pure sunshine. On the streets, traffic moved ceaselessly; hawkers called their wares without pause; baskets of fish and vegetables had been delivered to the homes of those about to leave for office, college or courthouse; and smoke arose from their kitchens as stoves were lit. But still, the golden light streamed through the myriad streets and alleys of this vast, ruthless, workaday city of Kolkata, in a flood of exquisite youthfulness.

On such a morning, at an idle moment, Binoybhushan stood alone on his first-floor balcony, gazing at the movement of people in the street. Having completed his college education long ago, he had not yet entered the world of domesticity. He had immersed himself in organizational and journalistic activities, but they did not entirely satisfy his heart. This morning, at least, a lack of purpose made him restless. On the adjacent rooftop, some crows were cawing raucously over something, and in a corner of his balcony, a pair of nesting sparrows were chirping encouragement to each other. All these incoherent bird-sounds stirred up a vague emotion in Binoy's heart.

Outside a nearby shop, a long-robed baul burst into song:

*In and out the cage, how the unknown bird doth flit;*
*I'd chain it with my heart, if I could but capture it.*

Binoy longed to send for the baul, to write down the lyrics about this unknown bird. But out of languor—just as we shiver at dawn yet lack the energy to reach for the coverlet—the baul was not summoned, and the lyrics remained uninscribed. Only the melody of that unknown bird continued to hum within his heart.

Just then, directly in front of his house, an enormous coach-and-pair rammed into a hackney carriage, smashing one of its wheels, then speeding away heedlessly. The hackney did not overturn but tilted crookedly. Rushing out into the street Binoy found that a girl of about seventeen or eighteen had descended from the carriage. Within was an elderly looking gentleman, preparing to alight. Binoy helped him down.

'You are not hurt, I hope?' he inquired, observing his pallor.

'No, there's nothing the matter with me,' the gentleman replied, forcing a smile; but the smile faded instantly, and he seemed about to faint. Binoy caught him in his arms.

'This is my house,' he said to the agitated girl. 'Let's go inside.'

Once they had helped the elderly man to bed, the girl looked about and noticed a kunjo in a corner of the room. Pouring a tumbler of water from the pitcher, she sprinkled some of it on the old man's face and began to fan him.

'Shouldn't we send for a doctor?' she suggested to Binoy. He sent a bearer to fetch a doctor who lived nearby.

On a table at one end of the room were a mirror, a bottle of hair oil, and some combs and brushes. Standing behind the girl, Binoy gazed at the mirror in silence. Since childhood, Binoy had lived and studied in Kolkata. All he knew about the world had been gleaned entirely from books. Never before had he encountered an unattached woman from a respectable family. Looking in the mirror, he marveled at the beauty of the face reflected in it. His eye was not experienced enough to analyse the individual features of her countenance. But the tender glow that the anxious affection had awakened in that young face appeared to Binoy like a newfound wonder of the world.

Shortly after, the old man slowly opened his eyes and sighed, 'Ma!' The girl's eyes glistened with tears.

'Baba, where are you hurt?' she asked agitatedly, bending her face close to his.

'Where am I?' The old man tried to sit up.

'Don't get up, please!' cried Binoy, coming before him. 'Please take some rest, the doctor is on his way.'

The old man now recalled the entire incident. 'It hurts a little here, on my head,' he said, 'but it is nothing serious.'

At that moment the doctor arrived, his shoes squeaking on the floor. 'It's nothing serious,' he also confirmed. He departed, having prescribed warm milk laced with brandy. At once the old man grew very embarrassed and agitated.

'Baba, why are you so anxious?' said his daughter, sensing his feelings. 'We shall send across the money for the doctor's visit and the medicine.' She glanced at Binoy.

What extraordinary eyes! Whether they were large or small, dark or amber, one did not notice at all. At the very first glance, one felt the unquestionable power of that gaze. There was no coyness in it, no hesitation: it was full of calm strength.

'The doctor's charges are trifling,' Binoy tried to insist. 'So . . . you need not . . . I will . . .' With the girl's eyes fixed on his face, he could not complete his sentence. But there remained no doubt that he must accept the money for the doctor's fee.

'Look, I don't require any brandy . . .' the old man began.

'Why Baba, didn't the doctor prescribe it?' his daughter interrupted.

'Doctors often prescribe such things; it is one of their vices,' the old man replied. 'A little warm milk is enough to dispel any weakness I feel.'

'We'll take your leave now,' he said to Binoy, after the milk had revived him. 'We have caused you a lot of trouble.'

'A carriage . . .' requested the girl, looking at Binoy.

'Why trouble him any further?' protested the old man, embarrassed. 'Our house is quite close after all, we'll walk this little distance.'

'No, Baba, that can't be allowed,' his daughter insisted. The old man did not contradict her. Binoy went personally to summon a cab.

'What is your name?' the old man asked, before mounting it.

'My name is Binoybhushan Chattopadhyay.'

'I am Poreshchandra Bhattacharya,' the old man said. 'I live close by, at number 78. If you ever find the time to drop by, I shall be delighted.'

Raising her eyes to look at Binoy, the girl silently reinforced this request. Binoy was ready to mount the carriage instantly to visit their house, but unsure if such conduct would be proper, he remained standing there. As the cab drove away, the girl joined her hands in a brief namaskar. Utterly unprepared for this gesture, Binoy remained frozen, unable to respond. Back home, he repeatedly cursed himself for this minor lapse. Scrutinizing his own conduct in their company from their first encounter to the moment of parting, he felt his manner throughout had been rather uncivil. He tormented himself with futile thoughts of what he could have said or done at specific moments. Returning to his room, he found on the bed the handkerchief which the girl had used to wipe her father's face. Quickly, he picked it up. The baul's song rang in his ears:

*In and out the cage, how the unknown bird doth flit.*

As the day advanced, the monsoon sun grew harsher, and a stream of office-bound carriages sped through the streets. Binoy could not concentrate on any of his daily tasks. In his whole life, he had never experienced such exquisite joy, mingled with such intense anguish. His tiny apartment and the hideous city of Kolkata that surrounded it now appeared to him like a fantasy kingdom. He seemed adrift in a lawless realm, where the impossible becomes possible, the unthinkable can be accomplished, and transcendent beauty assumes visible form. At this early hour the radiance of the monsoon sun penetrated his mind, coursed through his blood, and descended like a curtain of light, screening his inner being from the paltriness of everyday life. Binoy yearned to express his fulfilment in some extraordinary form, but failing to find the means, his heart began to chafe. He had presented himself to the visitors in an utterly ordinary light. His home was extremely humble, its interior disorderly, the bed none too clean. Some days, he would adorn his room with a bunch of flowers, but as luck would have it, there was not a flower-petal in his room that day! Everyone said it was evident from Binoy's gift for spontaneous public speaking that he would one day become a great orator; but that day he had not uttered a single word that demonstrated his intelligence. 'When that giant carriage was about to crash into their cab,' he repeated to himself, 'if only I had rushed into the street at lightning speed, and effortlessly reined in those wayward horses!' When this heroic fantasy arose in his mind, he could not refrain from glancing at himself in the mirror once.

Just then he noticed a boy of about seven or eight, scanning the number on his building from the street.

'Here, this is the very house you want!' he called from above. He never doubted that his house was indeed the one the boy was trying to locate. Binoy rushed downstairs, sandals flapping noisily. Eagerly leading the boy indoors, he gazed at his face.

'Didi has sent me to you,' the boy said, handing a letter to Binoybhushan.

Taking the letter, Binoy first saw his name inscribed in English on the envelope, in a clear, feminine hand. There was no letter inside, only a few rupee-notes. When the boy prepared to leave, Binoy would not let him go. His arm round the lad's shoulders, he led him to the room upstairs. The boy's complexion was darker than his sister's, but his features resembled hers somewhat. Looking at him, Binoy's heart filled with affection and joy.

The boy was quite quick-witted. Entering the room, he noticed a picture on the wall. 'Who is this?' he inquired.

'A friend of mine.'

'A friend? Who is he?'

'You wouldn't know him,' Binoy smiled. 'He's my friend Gourmohan. We call him Gora. We have been fellow-students since childhood.'

'Are you still a student?'

'No, not anymore.'

'Have you finished studying e-v-e-r-y-thing?'

'Yes, I have,' answered Binoy, unable to resist bragging, even to this young boy. The boy gave a small sigh of surprise. He probably wondered when he too would be done with all this learning.

'What's your name?' Binoy asked him.

'Sri Satishchandra Mukhopadhyay is my name.'

'Mukhopadhyay?' repeated Binoy, in surprise.

Gradually, in bits and pieces, details of the boy's identity emerged. Poreshbabu was not the father of this brother–sister duo but had reared them from infancy. The boy's didi was formerly called Radharani, but Poreshbabu's wife had changed her name to 'Sucharita.' In no time, Binoy and Satish had become fast friends.

'Can you get home on your own?' Binoy asked when Satish prepared to leave.

'I go about alone,' was his proud reply.

'Let me see you home.'

'Why, I can go by myself!' protested Satish, offended at Binoy's lack of faith in his abilities. By way of example, he began to recount several amazing anecdotes about his solitary wanderings. Why Binoy still accompanied him to his doorstep, the lad could not quite fathom.

'Won't you come in?' Satish asked him.

'Another day,' replied Binoy, quelling all his inner urges.

Back home, Binoy extracted from his pocket the envelope with his name on it, and gazed at it for a long time. He memorized the shape and form of every character inscribed on it. Then he lovingly placed the envelope, money and all, inside a box. There remained no possibility of his ever spending that money in some hour of need.

## 2

That rainy evening, the darkness of the sky seemed damp and heavy. Beneath the oppressive silence of those colourless, monotonous clouds, the city of Kolkata lay motionless like a giant despondent dog, curled up with its face tucked under its tail. It had drizzled incessantly since the previous night. The drizzle had turned the streets to mud but lacked the force to wash away the slime. It had not rained since four this afternoon, but the clouds did not augur well. Fear of an impending downpour made it difficult to stay in alone after dark, but there was no comfort outdoors, either. At such a time, occupying cane moras on the damp terrace of a three-storied building, sat two men.

As children, the two friends would run about on this terrace after returning from school; before their examinations, they would pace like maniacs up and down this terrace, reciting their lessons aloud; in summer, back from college, they would dine on this same terrace, then argue sometimes until two in the night; when the sun touched their faces at dawn, they would awaken with a start to discover that they had fallen asleep on the floor-mat at that very place. When there were no further college degrees to be pursued, one friend would preside over the Hindu welfare society's monthly meetings on this terrace, with the other as secretary.

The president's name was Gourmohan; friends and relatives called him Gora. He seemed to have surpassed everyone else, to a disproportionate extent. His college professor had named him the Silver Mountain. His complexion was rather blatantly fair, not softened by the slightest hint of yellow. Almost six feet tall, he was heavy boned, with fists like tiger-paws. His voice was startlingly deep and resonant, enough to give one a fright if heard suddenly. His facial contours were also unduly large and excessively firm, the chin and jawbone resembling strong bolts on a fortress gate. He had virtually no eyebrows, and his brow was wide at the temples. The lips were thin and compressed, his nose suspended above them like a scimitar. The eyes were small but sharp, their arrowlike gaze seemingly fixed on a remote, invisible target, yet capable of turning instantaneously, like lightning, to strike an object close at hand. Though not exactly handsome, Gour was impossible to ignore. He would stand out in a crowd.

And his friend Binoy, like the average educated Bengali bhadralok, was gentle but bright. His gracious nature, combined with his sharpness of intellect, had lent his countenance a distinctive air. In college he had always earned high marks and scholarships; Gora could never keep up with him. Gora felt little attraction for academic subjects; he lacked Binoy's quick comprehension and powers of retention. It was Binoy who had borne him like a vehicle through the sequence of college examinations.

'Listen,' Gora was saying, 'Abinash's denigration of the Brahmos is a sign of the man's good health. Why did it suddenly infuriate you?'

'How extraordinary! I could not have imagined that such things were open to question.'

'Then you have lost your reason. It's not natural for members of a society to adopt a calm, rational stance towards a group of people who violate social restrictions to act in a contrary fashion in all matters. Society is bound to misunderstand them, ascribing perverse motives to their straightforward actions, viewing as evil whatever they regard as good. So it should be. It is one of the penalties to be paid for deliberately breaking social laws.'

'I can't say that the natural alone is good.'

'I have no use for goodness!' exclaimed Gora, heatedly. 'If there are a few good people in the world, let them be, but may all others remain natural. Otherwise, work can't go on, nor can the soul survive. Those who fancy the heroism of becoming Brahmo must endure the minor pain of having all their actions misunderstood and denounced by non-Brahmos. That they should strut about puffed up with pride, while their opponents trail behind applauding them, is not the way of the world; and if it were so, the world would not benefit.'

'I'm not referring to criticism of the group. It is personal . . .'

'Criticism of the group is no criticism at all! It is a weighing of opinions. It's personal criticism we want. Tell me, O saintly one, did you never criticize anybody?'

'I did. Excessively. But I am ashamed of it.'

'No, Binoy, that won't do!' cried Gora, clenching his right fist. 'Not at all.'

'Why, what is the matter?' Binoy asked, after a short pause. 'What are you afraid of?'

'I see clearly that you are weakening.'

'Weak!' exclaimed Binoy, in some agitation. 'Do you know, I can visit their house this very moment if I wish? They had even invited me, but I did not go!'

'But you are unable to forget that you didn't go there. Day and night, you remind yourself: I didn't go, didn't go, didn't go to their house. Better to have gone there, indeed!'

'So you insist that I go?'

'No, I don't insist!' cried Gora, slapping his thigh. 'I can give it to you in writing that the day you go there, you will be well and truly gone. From the very next day, you will start dining at their house, and having enrolled with the Brahmo Samaj, you'll become a world-famous preacher.'

'What do you say! And then?'

'And then? Curse you! Son of a Brahman, you will end up in the dumping ground for dead cattle, with no way to preserve your purity, lost like a sailor with a broken compass. You will imagine then that docking your ship at port is a narrow-minded malpractice, that merely to drift without purpose is true navigation. But I have no patience with such prattle. I say you should go. Why keep us in suspense too, with one foot over the precipice?'

'When doctors give up, patients don't always die,' laughed Binoy. 'I see no signs that my end is near.'

'You don't?'

'No.'

'Don't you feel your pulse grow faint?'

'No, it feels as strong as ever.'

'Don't you feel that, if served by those gracious hands, even the outcaste's food can become a feast for the gods?'

'Enough, Gora!' cried Binoy, highly embarrassed. 'Stop now.'

'Why, there is nothing improper in what I say. It's not as if those gracious hands are screened from public view. If you can't tolerate even the bare mention of those pure, petal-like hands, hands that often exchange handshakes with men, that means you are as good as dead!'

'Look, Gora, I honour the female sex. Even in our holy texts the shastras . . .'

'Don't quote the shastras to defend your way of honouring the female sex! That is not honour; if I called it by the right name, you'd assault me.'

'You say this with brute force.'

'*Pujarha grihadiptayah*: so our shastras describe women. Women should be worshipped, for they light up our homes. It is best not to use the word 'worship' for the kind of respect English culture accords to women when they light up the hearts of men.'

'Should you so despise a noble emotion, just because it sometimes assumes a distorted form?'

'Binu,' urged Gora impatiently, 'Now you have lost your reason, you may as well accept my advice. In the English scriptures, all that hyperbole about women conceals one inner motive, sexual desire. We should worship the female sex at the mother's chamber and the virtuous housewife's holy shrine; when women are worshipped elsewhere, such adoration conceals an element of degradation. "Love" is the English word for what makes your heart circle Pareshbabu's house like a moth around a flame. But may you not ape the English in becoming obsessed with the frivolous notion that this "love" must be revered as life's ultimate goal!'

'Oh, Gora!' Binoy winced like a restive horse under the lash. 'Let it be, that's enough!'

'Enough? By no means. It is because we have not learned to regard men and women normally, in their own proper places, that we have conjured up a cluster of poetic notions about them.'

'Very well, granted that our passions impel us to and falsify the ideal situation where man-woman relationships could be normalized; but is the foreign culture entirely to blame? If the claims of English poetry are false, so is our excessive insistence on renouncing the lure of women and gold. To protect human nature from easy distractions some people poeticize the beautiful aspects of love, ignoring its darker side, while others exaggerate the evils of love, prescribing renunciation. These are merely two different modes adopted by two kinds of people. If you blame one, you cannot absolve the other.'

'No, I must admit I had misunderstood you. You are not in such bad shape, after all. Since your mind still has room for philosophy, you can fearlessly indulge in "love". But pull yourself back in time. That's a well-meant, friendly request.'

'Are you crazy?' exclaimed Binoy, in agitation. 'Me, and "love"? But I must admit, from whatever I've seen of Poreshbabu and the rest, and whatever I've heard about them, I've developed considerable respect for them. Perhaps that explains my urge to see their lifestyle at home.'

'Excellent! That's the very attraction you must resist. Let their life-cycle remain an undiscovered chapter, especially since they are predatory creatures. In your attempt to explore their private lives, you might ultimately delve so deep as to disappear altogether.'

'Look, this is one of your faults. You imagine that you alone are empowered by Ishwar our Lord, while the rest of us are weaklings.'

Gora seemed to be struck by the novelty of this. 'Right you are!' he cried, slapping Binoy on the back. 'That is indeed my fault. A grave fault it is.'

'Oh, you have another major fault. You are utterly incapable of gauging the severity of the heaviest blow a person's spine can bear.'

At this point, Gora's elder step-brother Mahim came upstairs, his heaviness making him pant. 'Gora!' he called.

'Yes, sir!' responded Gora, rising quickly.

'I've come to see if the rumbling rain-clouds have descended upon our terrace. What's the matter tonight? Have you dispatched the English halfway across the Indian Ocean, by now? No loss to the English it seems, but all this roaring might inconvenience Boro Bou, who's nursing a headache in bed downstairs.'

Mahim went back downstairs. Gora stood there, overcome by shame. Along with shame, a degree of rage also began to smoulder within him, whether directed at himself or others, it was hard to say. 'In every matter, I end up applying more force than necessary,' he said slowly after a while, as if to himself. 'I fail to remember how intolerable that must be for others.'

Coming close, Binoy grasped Gour's hand affectionately.

## 3

As Gora and Binoy were preparing to leave the terrace, Gora's mother arrived there. Binoy touched her feet respectfully.

From her appearance, it would not seem that Anandamoyi was Gora's mother. She was very slim, with a compact figure; if she had any grey hair, it could not be seen; at first glance she appeared to be under forty.

Her lineaments were extremely graceful, as if someone had painstakingly used a lathe to carve the lines of her lips, chin and forehead. Her body was shorn of all excess; her face always bore an expression of clear, alert intelligence. Her complexion was dark, in no way comparable with Gora's. There was one thing about her that everyone immediately noticed: she wore a chemise with her sari. At that time, though women of the modern set had begun to adopt the blouse or chemise, elderly housewives continued to dismiss the trend as a flagrant Khristani custom, a Christian practice. Anandamoyi's husband, Krishnadayal Babu, worked at the Commissariat. Since childhood, Anandamoyi had lived with him in the western parts of the country. Hence she did not harbour the superstitious notion that it was shameful or ludicrous to cover one's body properly. Even after scrubbing the house, polishing, washing and mopping, cooking and serving, sewing, counting, keeping accounts, dusting, airing, enquiring after neighbours and relatives, time still hung heavy on her hands. If she fell ill, she would never want to take it seriously, saying, 'Falling ill can do me no harm. Without work, how will I stay alive?'

'Whenever Gora's voice can be heard from downstairs, we know that Binu must have come,' said Gora's mother. 'The house was absolutely quiet these last few days. Tell me, son, what's the matter? Why haven't you been coming? You haven't been ill, have you?'

'No, Ma, not ill,' replied Binoy, diffidently. 'It's been raining so.'

'Indeed!' cried Gora. 'When the rains end, Binoy will say it's too sunny. After all, when you blame the gods, they don't answer back. Only the omniscient One knows what's really on his mind.'

'What nonsense, Gora!' Binoy expostulated.

'Truly son, you shouldn't say such things,' Anandamoyi agreed. 'Men's minds are sometimes cheerful, sometimes sad; moods don't always stay the same! To make an issue of it amounts to harassment. So Binu, come along to my room. I have arranged some refreshments for you.'

'No, Ma, that's not allowed!' Gora intervened, vehemently shaking his head. 'I shan't let Binoy eat in your room.'

'Is that so indeed!' said Anandamoyi. 'Why bapu, I never ask you to eat with me, after all. Meanwhile your father's grown so fanatical about purity, he refuses to eat anything but self-cooked food. This Binu of mine is a good boy, not a fanatic like you. You always try to keep him away by force.'

'You're right, I will force him to stay away,' Gora asserted. 'We can't have meals in your room until you dismiss Lachhmia, that Khristani maid of yours.'

'Oh Gora, don't say such things!' protested Anadamoyi. 'She has always fed you by hand, reared you since you were a child. Until just the other day, you wouldn't relish your food without her chutney. I'll never forget the way Lachhmia nursed you back to health when you contracted smallpox as a child.'

'Give her a pension, buy her land, build her a house, whatever you please. But she can't continue here, Ma'

'Gora, do you think money can settle all debts!' Anandamoyi expostulated. 'She wants neither land nor a house. She'll die if she can't see you.'

'Then keep her on if you please,' said Gora, 'but Binu can't dine in your room. We must follow restrictions, there is no getting away from them. Ma, you belong to such a distinguished professor's family: for you not to follow traditional restrictions . . .'

'Oh your mother used to follow traditional custom, once,' Anandamoyi assured him. 'I had to shed many a tear on that account. And where were you then? Every day, I would set up a clay Shiva and prepare to pray, but your father would come and fling it away. Those days, I'd even shrink from tasting rice cooked by any Brahman I didn't know. The railway network was not extensive then; how many days I spent fasting, on bullock carts, postal carriages, palkis or camelback! Was it easy for your father to break my orthodoxy? His saheb-masters would applaud him for having his wife accompany him everywhere. He even got a pay-rise. For that very reason, they'd keep him in the same post for extended periods, often reluctant to let him move. Now in old age, having relinquished his job and acuired heaps of money, he has suddenly done an about-face, becoming very fastidious about purity. But I can't do that. The superstitious ideas I had inherited from my ancestors have been uprooted, one by one. Can they now be retrieved at anyone's bidding?'

'Achchha, forget your ancestors,' urged Gora. 'They won't raise any objections, after all. But for our sake, there are a few rules you must observe. You may not honour the shastras, but your son's honour must surely be preserved?'

'O, why reason with me at such length! I alone know what goes on in my mind. If I hindered my husband and my son at every step, wherein would my happiness lie? But do you know that I threw orthodoxy to the winds when you were still a babe in arms? The moment you clasp an infant to your heart, you realize that nobody is born into a caste. Ever since I realized that, I knew for sure that if I despised someone for being a Christian or a lowcaste person, Ishwar would snatch you away from me as well. May you continue to occupy my lap, light up my home, and I'll accept drinking water from every caste in the world!'

Anandamoyi's words suddenly roused a hint of doubt in Binoy's mind. He glanced at Anandamoyi, then at Gora but at once dismissed any wish to argue.

'Ma, your logic is not clear,' Gora protested. 'Boys survive even in the homes of those who are discriminating enough to obey the shastras. What gave you the idea that Ishwar might apply special rules in your case?'

'He who gave me a son like you also gave me such ideas. So, what am I to do? I have no hand in this. O you crazy boy, I don't know whether to laugh or cry at your lunacy. Anyway, let such things be. So, can't Binoy dine in my room?'

'He's so greedy he'd rush there at once, given the opportunity,' said

Gora. 'But, Ma, I shan't let him. With a mere handful of sweetmeats, we can't delude him into forgetting he is a Brahman's son. He must sacrifice a lot, control his passions, only then can he preserve the glory of his high birth. But please don't be angry, Ma. I bow at your feet.'

'Me, angry? How can you say that!' Anandamoyi exclaimed. 'You are acting in ignorance, I tell you. I must privately bear the pain of knowing that although I brought you up, you still . . . Anyway, I can't practice the dharma you preach. Never mind if you don't let me feed you in my room, but at least I get to see you in the evenings, and for me that's enough. Binoy, don't look so miserable, baap. You have a soft heart and feel I must be hurt, but it's nothing really, baap. I shall invite you some other time, and serve you food prepared by an expert Brahman cook, not to worry! But as for me, bachha, I shall accept water from Lachhmia: let me make that clear to everyone.' Gora's mother went downstairs.

'Gora, things have gone too far!' said Binoy slowly, after a brief silence.

'On whose part?'

'Yours.'

'Not in the least. I want to protect each person's boundaries. Once you begin to yield the slightest ground on some pretext, you're ultimately left with nothing.'

'But she's your mother!'

'I know what it means to have a mother. As if you need to remind me of it! How many people have a mother like mine? But if I don't begin to obey orthodox restrictions, I may one day cease to obey my mother as well. Look Binoy, let me tell you something: remember that the heart is a wonderful thing, but not above all else.'

'Listen Gora, Ma's words have created strange stirrings in my heart today,' Binoy ventured hesitantly, after a while. 'I feel Ma has something on her mind that she can't explain to us, and that is tormenting her.'

'Oh, Binoy, don't let your imagination run wild!' cried Gora impatiently. 'It's a mere waste of time, and quite futile.'

'Because you never look closely at anything in this world, you dismiss as fanciful whatever escapes your notice. But I tell you I've often observed that Ma seems to nurse a certain anxiety about something, as if there is something amiss that she can't put right, which causes some hidden pain in her domestic life. Gora, listen closely to what she says.'

'I listen as closely as possible. If I try any harder, I'm likely to misconstrue her words, so I don't even try.'

## 4

An idea that sounds definite when aired as an opinion may not always appear so certain when applied to human beings. At least, not to Binoy, who had very strong sensibilities. During an argument he might vociferously defend an opinion, but in practice, he could not help respecting human beings more than opinions. In fact it was doubtful whether Binoy had accepted Gora's public views out of conviction, or his deep love for Gora. Emerging from Gora's house, as he slowly picked his way through the slush that wet evening, his mind wrestled with the dual claims of ideas and human beings.

Binoy had readily embraced Gora's stated conviction that to protect itself from various direct and indirect attacks, society must now remain especially alert about purity of touch and taste. He had engaged in sharp debates with those who opposed this view, arguing that when a fortress is besieged from all sides, there is nothing narrow-minded about guarding it with one's life, sealing every pathway, every door and window, even the tiniest aperture. But when Gora forbade him to dine in Anandamoyi's room, he was now inwardly tormented with pain.

Binoy was fatherless, and had also lost his mother at an early age. His khuro, his father's younger brother, lived in the countryside. Since childhood, for the sake of his education, Binoy had grown up alone in the Kolkata house. Ever since he got to know Anandamoyi through his friendship with Gora, he had regarded her as his mother. How often had he visited her room to harass her for food, eagerly snatching at the morsels! How often had he feigned envy, accusing Anandamoyi of partiality to Gora in serving their portions of food! How anxious Anandamoyi became if she did not see Binoy for a few days, how often she would eagerly wait for their society-meetings to end so she could personally supervise his meal, Binoy was well aware. Could Anandamoyi bear it if that very same Binoy, out of communal hostility, refused to dine in her room tonight? Could Binoy bear it?

'From now on, Ma will offer me food prepared by a good Brahman cook. She'll never cook for me again. She said it cheerfully, but what a heart-rending thought!' Binoy made way his home, turning this thought over and over in his mind.

The room was dark and empty. Books and papers lay scattered everywhere. Striking a match, Binoy lit the sej. The oil lamp's glass chimney was smudged with the bearer's fingerprints. The white cloth on the writing table was stained in places with ink and grease. The room felt stifling. The absence of human company and affection seemed to choke his heart. Saving the nation, protecting the community—try as he might, he could not see these duties as real or true. Truer by far was that unknown bird, which had approached the cage one bright, beautiful Sravan morning, then flown away again. But Binoy must not dwell on memories of that unknown bird. Certainly not. So his mind sought refuge in drawing a mental picture of Anandamoyi's room, from which Gora had banished him.

The bright parquet floor, sparkling clean; at one end, a spotless, soft bed resembling white swan-wings; beside it, on a small stool, a castor-oil lamp would have been lit by now; leaning towards the light, Ma would be embroidering a kantha using skeins of many-coloured thread, with Lachhmia on the floor, prattling away in her broken Bengali; Ma would ignore most of what she said. Whenever Ma felt hurt, she would take up her embroidery. Binoy fixed his mind's eye on the image of her quiet, work-absorbed countenance. 'May the glow of affection on this face save me from all perplexity,' wished Binoy. 'Let this very face become my image of the motherland; may it inspire me and keep me steadfast in my devotion to duty.' In his heart, he invoked her once as 'Ma!' and declared: 'No shastra can convince me that your rice is not my heavenly nectar, my amrita!'

In the silent chamber, the large clock ticked away. Binoy could not bear to remain in the room. After gazing for a while at a lizard hunting an insect near the light on the wall, he rose and went out, carrying an umbrella. He was not sure why. Perhaps it was his inner purpose to return to Anandamoyi. But it occurred to him presently that as it was Sunday, he could attend Keshabbabu's lecture at the Brahmo gathering. Immediately discarding all his hesitation, Binoy strode ahead. He knew there was not much time left for the lecture to end, but that did not deter him.

Arriving at the venue, he saw the devotees emerging. Umbrella aloft, he stood at the corner of the street. That very moment, Poresh Babu came out of the temple, his face calm and serene. He was accompanied by a few relatives. For an instant, in the light of the gas streetlamps, Binoy glimpsed a youthful face among them. Then, to the sound of rolling carriage-wheels, the scene vanished like a bubble in the ocean of darkness.

Binoy had read many English novels, but how could he relinquish the beliefs of a genteel Bengali family? That it was dishonourable for the woman and degrading for him to seek her out so eagerly, was a notion that no argument could drive from his mind. So a terrible sense of shame mingled with the joy that filled Binoy's heart. 'I seem to be heading for a moral downfall!' he thought. Although he had argued with Gora about this, his lifelong inhibitions would not let him regard a woman in a romantic light if society did not sanction it.

Binoy did not make it to Gora's house. He went home, his mind in turmoil about many things. The following afternoon, when he arrived at Gora's place after leaving his house and wandering here and there, the shadows were deepening at the end of a long, rainy day. Gora had lit the lamp and settled down to write.

'So Binoy, which way does the wind blow now?' he inquired, without raising his head.

'Gora, let me ask you something,' said Binoy, ignoring his words. 'Does Bharatvarsha, the idea of India, appear very real to you? Very clear? You think of it day and night, but in what form?'

Gora stopped writing and fixed his penetrating gaze briefly on Binoy's face. Then, laying down his pen, he leaned back on the chowki and said: 'I think of Bharatvarsha, like the ship's captain who constantly bears in mind the port at the other end of the sea, whether he is feasting or reveling, at work or at rest.'

'Where is this Bharatvarsha of yours?'

'Where the compass here points, day and night,' replied Gora, touching his heart, 'not in your Marshman saheb's *History of India*.'

'Where your compass points, does something exist?'

'Indeed it does!' cried Gora, indignantly. 'I may lose my way, or even drown, but my treasured port remains. It is my Bharatvarsha in all its glory, replete with wealth, knowledge, spiritual faith. To say that this Bharatvarsha does not exist! That only the falsehood around us is real! This Kolkata of yours, with its offices, its courthouses and its few brick-and-wood bubbles! How disgusting!' Gora gazed intently at Binoy for a while. Lost in thought, Binoy made no reply.

'Here, reading and writing, running after jobs, slaving away from ten to five without any sense of purpose, this false, illusory Bharatvarsha is what we have taken for the truth,' declared Gora. 'That is why we rush about dementedly day and night, all twenty-five crores of us, mistaking false prestige for honour, futile labour for accomplishment. Caught in this delusion, can we ever find the impulse to strive for a new life! That is why, day by day, we are fading away. There is a real Bharatvarsha—a complete India. Unless we establish ourselves there, we can't absorb its true living essence into our minds and hearts. Therefore I say, forgetting all else, discarding book-learning, the lure of prestige, and the temptation of odd profits, we must set sail for that very port, whether we drown or perish. No wonder I can never forget the true, complete image of Bharatvarsha!'

'Aren't these merely words spoken in the heat of emotion? Do you mean what you say?'

'Indeed I do!' thundered Gora.

'What about those who don't see your point?'

'We must show them the way!' cried Gora, clenching his fists. 'That is our duty. If they cannot clearly discern the image of truth, will the people not surrender to some false idea? Hold up Bharatvarsha's complete image to the public, and they will go berserk. Must we then go from door to door, seeking subscriptions? People would vie with each other to lay down their lives!'

'Either show me that image, or let me remain all at sea, like everyone else.'

'Strive for it. If you are a believer, you will find happiness in sincere effort. Because they have no real convictions, all our fine patriots cannot place any strong demands either on themselves or on anyone else. Even if the god of wealth, Kuber himself, were to offer them a boon, they probably wouldn't dare ask for anything beyond the gilt badge sported by a governor's peon. They have no belief, and therefore, no self-assurance.'

'Gora, everyone's nature is not alike. Because you have found your convictions within yourself and can take refuge in your own strength, you fail to realize the predicament of others. Assign me any task you please, I tell you; let me labour day and night. Otherwise, though I have a sense of achievement while I am in your company, I have nothing to cling to when I move away.'

'Do you speak of tasks? Our sole task now is to express unhesitating, undoubted, complete respect for everything swadeshi, to generate the same respect in the hearts of the unpatriotic. Ashamed of our country for so long, we have weakened ourselves with the poison of slavery. If each of us opposes this by personal example, we can claim a space for future work. Anything we attempt now proves to be a mere imitation, learnt from the schoolbooks of history. Can we ever truly devote ourselves wholeheartedly to such false pursuits? They would only degrade us.'

Just then Mahim sauntered in, hookah in hand. Back home from office, after his evening snack, this was Mahim's hour for smoking tobacco by the roadside with a paan in his mouth and a few more in his betel-box. Soon his neighbourhood friends would arrive, one by one. In the room beside the entrance, they would assemble for a game of primero. As soon as Mahim entered, Gora rose from the chowki.

'You are busy saving your nation Bharat, but meanwhile, please come to your own brother's rescue!' observed Mahim, puffing upon his hookah. Gora stared at him.

'Our new boss at the office has a face like a greyhound. He's a very nasty man,' Mahim declared. 'He calls the clerks baboons. If someone's mother dies, he doesn't want to grant them leave of absence, dismissing it as a lie. Bengalis can never draw their full month's salary, because he riddles their claim with a hundred fines. A newspaper carried a letter about him, and the bastard has concluded it was my doing. He's not entirely wrong either. So unless I publish a rejoinder in my own name, he won't let me survive. As twin gems cast up by churning the ocean of the university, you two must compose this letter properly. It must be littered with phrases such as *even handed justice, never failing generosity* and *kind courteousness*.'

Gora remained silent.

'So many lies in one breath, Dada?' Binoy smiled.

'Let the rogues have a dose of their own medicine,' said Mahim. 'I have associated with them for a long time, and there is nothing I don't know about them. Their knack for supporting falsehoods is admirable. They stop at nothing, if need be. If one of them lies, the rest sing the same tune, like a pack of howling jackals. Unlike us, they don't seek applause by exposing each other. Know this for sure: there's no sin in deceiving them, as long as we don't get caught.' Mahim burst into loud laughter, puffing away at his hookah. Binoy couldn't help laughing, either.

'You wish to embarrass them by confronting them with the truth!' Mahim scoffed. 'If Ishwar hadn't given you such ideas, would the nation be in such a plight? We must realize indeed that those who possess brute force will not bow their heads in shame when we heroically expose their deceit. Instead, they turn their weapons of crime upon us, threatening us like the purest of saints. Tell me if I am wrong.'

'True, indeed,' remarked Binoy.

'Instead, let us grease their feet with drops of free oil wrung from the mill of falsehood, and say: "O saint, Baba Paramhansa, please shake out your holy bag, for even the dust from it will save us!" Then you may retrieve at least a portion of what's rightfully yours, without any fear of disrupting the peace. That's true partriotism, if you like. But my brother here is getting annoyed. Ever since he became a devout Hindu, he has shown me great deference as his elder brother, but I haven't quite spoken as an elder brother in his presence, today. What's to be done bhai, we must be truthful, even about untruths. Binoy, I want that piece of writing from you though. Wait, let me fetch you my notes.' Mahim left the room, puffing on his hookah.

'Binu, please deal with Dada in his own room,' Gora requested. 'Let me complete what I was writing.'

## 5

'Ogo shunchho, do you hear me? I shan't enter your prayer-chamber, don't worry. When you're through with your ahnik ritual, please come to the other room once. I need to talk to you. Now that two new sanyasis have arrived, I know I won't see you for some time; that's why I've come here to speak to you. Don't forget to come there.' With these words, Anandamoyi returned to her household chores.

Krishnadayalbabu was dark and well-built, not very tall. His large eyes were the most prominent feature in a face otherwise largely obscured by a salt-and-pepper moustache and beard. He was always draped in saffron silk, with a brass kamandulu close at hand and wooden kharams on his feet. His hairline was receding; the rest of his long hair was tied in a knot on top of his head.

Formerly, during his soujourn in the west, he had indulged excessively in meat and liquor in the company of white army-men. Those days he thought it manly to deliberately humiliate the priests, holy men, vaishnavas and sanyasis of the land. But now, there was no orthodox rule he would not follow. He would seek training in new devotional modes from every new sanyasi he encountered. There was no limit to his fascination for obscure routes to salvation, and esoteric yogic practices. For some time, Krishnadayal had been receiving guidance in tantrik ways, but of late, news of a Buddhist priest had stirred his mind.

He was twenty-three when his first wife died after giving birth to a son. Blaming her death upon the son, he left the boy with his in-laws, and in a fit of detachment, traveled far west. Within six months, he married the fatherless granddaughter of Shri Sarbabhouma, a resident of Varanasi. In the west, Krishnadayal found himself a job and by various means, gained his employers' esteem. Meanwhile, Sarbabhouma passed away. As she was left with no guardian, Krishnadayal was forced to bring his wife to live with him.

When the sepoy Mutiny broke out, he gained glory as well as property by strategically saving the lives of a few highly-placed Englishmen. Soon after the Mutiny he gave up his job, and spent some time in Varanasi with the newborn Gora. When Gora was about five, Krishnadayal moved to Kolkata, brought his elder son Mahim back from his maternal uncle's house, and raised the boy himself. Now, by the grace of his father's patrons, Mahim was making great headway in the government accounts department.

From his childhood days, Gora would dominate the boys in his neighbourhood and at school. It was his chief aim and source of entertainment to make life hell for the teachers and pundits. When he was a little older, he became the leader of a band of young revolutionaries, by reciting 'Who would wish to live sans freedom' and 'The abode of twenty crore humans' at the students' club, and delivering lectures in English. Eventually, when Gora broke out of the students'-club eggshell to spread his wings in adult gatherings, Krishnadayalbabu was greatly amused at his chirping.

In no time at all, Gora had gained great popularity with people outside his family; but at home, he received scant support from anyone. Mahim was by then a working man. He tried in various ways to dampen Gora's spirit, taunting him as 'Uncle Patriot' or 'Harish Mukhujje the Second.' Often, those days, Gora and his dada would almost come to blows. Privately, Anandamoyi felt very anxious about Gora's hostility towards the British. She would try to pacify him in many ways, but to no avail. Gora thought it glorious to engage in public combat with the British at the slightest opportunity.

Meanwhile, overwhelmed by Keshabbabu's speeches, Gora felt intensely attracted to the Brahmo Samaj. Simultaneously, Krishnadayal became so rigidly orthodox in his ways, he would grow flustered if Gora so much as set foot in his room. He set up his own independent living quarters, occupying two or three rooms in the house. With great pomp, he hung a wooden sign at the door, bearing the incscription *Sadhanashram*, 'Hermitage of Holy Pursuits'.

Gora's heart rebelled at his father's antics. 'I can't stand such idiocy!' he declared. 'It is unbearable.' He was now ready to leave home, severing all ties with his father, but Anandamoyi managed, somehow, to prevent him.

Gora would seize every opportunity to argue with the holy men who visited his father. The encounters were more like fisticuffs than verbal debates. Many of them had limited knowledge and unlimited greed for money. They were no match for Gora, and feared him as if he were a tiger. Only one of them, Harachandra Vidyabagish, earned Gora's respect. Krishnadayal had employed Vidyabagish to discuss the Vedanta. Trying at first to fight him aggressively, Gora found it impossible to provoke him. The man was not only learned but also extraordinarily large-hearted. That mere knowledge of Sanskrit could produce such sharpness and breadth of intellect, was beyond Gora's imagination. Vidyabagish's nature was so calm and patient, so forgiving and serene, that Gora could not but behave with restraint in his presence. Under Harachandra's guidance, he began to study the Vedanta philosophy. For Gora there were no half-measures; he immersed himself completely in philosophical discussions.

At this time, an English missionary happened to publish a newspaper article attacking Hindu religion and society, and challenging the people of the country to a public debate. Gora was incensed. Although he himself denounced the shastras and popular superstitions at the slightest opportunity, harassing his opponents in every possible way, a foreigner's contempt for the Hindu community seemed to wound him like a goad. Gora began his battle through the columns of the newspaper. All his opponent's arguments against Hindu society, he rejected outright. After both parties had exchanged many rejoinders, the editor decreed: 'Henceforth we shall not publish too many letters.' But Gora's blood was up. He began to write an English book titled *Hindooism*.

Sifting all the ideas and scriptural sources at his command, he set about compiling evidence of the unblemished supremacy of the Hindu religion and society. Thus, in his attempt to fight the missionary, Gora was gradually outwitted by his own judicial arguments.

'We shall not allow our own country to be placed in the dock in a foreign court and judged like a criminal by a foreign law!' he declared. 'We shall earn neither shame nor glory in judging ourselves minutely by British ideals. We shall not feel ashamed in the least, either inwardly or before others, of the rituals, beliefs, scriptures and customs of our birthplace. We shall shield our country and ourselves from humiliation, boldly and proudly accepting all that our nation has to offer.'

Gora now took to bathing in the Ganga and performing the sandhya-ahnik rituals at dusk and dawn. He grew an uncut tuft of hair as a tiki on his crown, and began to observe the rules of purity in touch and taste. Every morning, he would respectfully touch his parents' feet. Upon seeing Mahim, whom he formerly addressed unsparingly as 'cad' or 'snob' in English, he would now stand up respectfully or greet him with a pranam. Mahim swore at him for this sudden display of deference, but Gora would not answer back.

By precept and practice, Gora inspired a group of people in the area. 'Whether we are good or bad, civilized or barbaric, we refuse to be answerable to anyone about such things!' they proclaimed in relief, as if rescued from a dilemma. 'We are what we are. We want to fully experience our own selfhood.'

But Krishnadayal did not appear pleased at this new change in Gora. In fact, one day, he summoned Gora and said: 'Look baba, the Hindu shastras are extremely profound. No ordinary person can plumb the depths of the religion our sages had established. In my opinion, it is best not to dabble in such things without understanding them. You are young, educated in English throughout. You were within your rights to develop leanings for the Brahmo Samaj, hence it did not anger me at all; on the contrary, I was rather pleased. But the path you have now adopted does not seem appropriate. It is not the right path for you, at all.'

'How can you say that, Baba!' Gora protested. 'I am a Hindu, after all. If I can't grasp the profound concepts of the Hindu dharma today, I shall master them tomorrow. Even if I never comprehend them, I must still follow this path. Because I could not shed the Hindu connections of my past life, I was born into a Brahman family in my present life. In this way, through a succession of births, it is via the Hindu religion and community that I shall ultimately arrive at the highest stage. If I ever forget myself and tend to follow some other direction, I must return to my faith with redoubled conviction.'

'But, baba, you can't become a Hindu simply by calling yourself one,' said Krishnadayal, shaking his head. 'It is easy to become a Muslim, and anyone can become a Christian, but to become a Hindu? Bas re! That would be difficult, indeed!'

'True,' conceded Gora. 'But being born a Hindu I have already entered the main gate. Now, if I sustain my efforts, I can gradually move ahead.'

'Baba, I can't explain properly by way of argument. But what you say is also correct. One day, by whatever circuitous route, one must return to the fruits of one's karma, one's assigned faith; no one can prevent that. It is the Almighty's will. Is anything within our power? We merely serve His purpose.'

Fruits of karma and divine will, the soul's identity with god and the devotional path of bhakti—Krishandayal accepted all these beliefs in equal measure, without feeling any need for compatibility between them.

## 6

Today, having completed his ahnik, bath and morning repast, Krishnadayal, after many days, placed his woollen mat on the floor of Anandamoyi's room and sat stiffly upright, as if carefully detaching himself from all contact with his surroundings.

'Ogo shunchho, listen to me, you remain lost in meditation without sparing a thought for the household, but I'm constantly anxious about Gora,' Anandamoyi told him.

'Why, what are you anxious about?'

'I can't quite say. But it seems to me that Gora can never adapt to these Hindu ways he has taken up of late. If he tries to follow this path, it will ultimately lead to some calamity. I had advised you at the time against initiating him into Brahmanism with the poité ceremony. But those days, you didn't believe in anything. It makes no difference if we string a thread round his neck, you said. But it's not just a thread, after all! Now there's no stopping him.'

'So! Am I entirely to blame! What about the mistake you made at the very beginning? You refused to give him up under any circumstances. I too was rather headstrong then, quite ignorant about religion and the like. Could I ever take such a step today?'

'Whatever you might say, I can never accept that I broke my faith in any way. You remember don't you, the lengths to which I went, just to have a son! I followed any advice I received, accepted any number of amulets and mantras. One night I dreamt I was at my prayers, a basketful of togor blossoms beside me, when I suddenly opened my eyes to find that the saji contained no flowers but a little boy, fair as a blossom. Ah, how can I describe what my eyes beheld! Eyes streaming with tears, I reached forward to take him in my arms when all at once, I awoke. It was barely ten days later that I received Gora as a gift from my deity. Was he a gift from someone else that I should return him to anyone? In some other birth, I must have suffered greatly when I bore him in my womb; that is why he has come to me now, to call me "Ma". Think of the circumstances in which he came to us. With people fighting, killing each other, all around us, and all of us fearing for our own lives. At such a time, when that white mem sought refuge in our house in the wee hours, you were afraid to even let her in. I hoodwinked you and hid her in the cowshed. That very night she died after giving birth to this boy. Would that orphaned boy have lived if I had not saved him? Not that you cared! You wanted to hand him over to the priest, after all. Why! Why should I give him away to the priest? Was the priest his father or mother? Had he saved the boy's life? To acquire a son in this way—is that any less than carrying him in the womb? Whatever you may say, unless this boy is claimed by the One who gave him to me, I'll die rather than let anyone else take him away!'

'I know that! Well, you can keep your Gora. I have never tried to prevent you in any way. But our community wouldn't accept it if we identified him as our son without performing the poité ceremony. So the sacred thread was obligatory. Now, there are only two concerns. By law, all my property should go to Mahim. Therefore . . .'

'Who wants a share of your property!' Anandamoyi protested. 'Leave all your earnings to Mahim, Gora won't touch a paisa of it. He's a man, and educated; he'll work for his livelihood. Why would he seek a share of someone else's wealth! Let him live, that is all I ask. I have no need for any other property.'

'No, I shall not disown him completely. I'll leave the estate to him. In time, it may yield a thousand rupees a year. Now it's his marriage that poses a problem. Whatever I may have done earlier, I can't let him marry according to Hindu rites into a Brahman family now. Too bad if that makes you unhappy.'

'Alas!' cried Anandamoyi, 'you seem to think, because I don't go about scattering cowdung and spraying holy Ganga-water everywhere, that I have no religious sense whatever. Why would I marry him into a Brahman family, and why should I be unhappy?'

'How can you say that! You, a Brahman's daughter!'

'So what if I'm a Brahman's daughter? I have given up Brahman practices, haven't I? Just recently, at Mahim's wedding, the bride's family had threatened to create trouble about my Khristani ways. So I had deliberately remained aloof, not said a word. The entire world calls me a Christian, and many other things besides, but I accept everything, saying: Aren't Christians human beings, after all! If you are of such high caste and so dear to the Almighty, why does He let you suffer defeat at the hands of Pathans, Mughals and Christians, in turn?'

'That's a long story. You're a woman. Such things are beyond your comprehension. But you do understand don't you, that there is something called a community, which you should respect?'

'I have no need to understand such things. I only understand that having reared Gora as my son, if I now pretend to be orthodox, my faith will certainly be lost, whether the community remains or not. It is out of respect for religion that I have never concealed anything. I let everyone know that I don't follow any restrictions, and suffer everyone's contempt in silence. There's only one thing I've concealed, and for that I live in constant fear of what Thakur might do to me someday. Look, I think we should tell Gora everything. After that, let destiny take its course.'

'No, no, not as long as I live!' cried Krishandayal in agitation. 'You know Gora. There is no saying what he might do if he gets to know. And it will throw our community into a turmoil. And that's not all. There's no saying what the government might do, either. Gora's father died fighting, and I know his mother's dead as well, but we should have informed the magistrate after all that turbulence had subsided. Now, if trouble breaks out over all this, it will put an end to all my prayers and rituals, and who knows what other problems may arise.'

Anandamoyi remained silent, offering no reply. 'As for Gora's marriage, I have thought of a plan,' resumed Krishandayal after a while. 'Poresh Bhattacharya, my former classmate, has recently settled in Kolkata after retiring from his position as school inspector. He is a dedicated Brahmo. And he has several daughters, I'm told. If we can introduce Gora to his family, he might even take a fancy to one of Poresh's daughters in the course of his visits to their house. Then it's up to Prajapati, the god of marriage.'

'How can you suggest that! Gora visit a Brahmo household? He's past all that now.'

As Anandamoyi spoke, Gora entered the room. 'Ma!' he called, in his deep, thundering voice. He was rather surprised to see Krishnadayal there.

'Yes baba, what is it you want?' Anadamoyi asked, quickly rising to go up close to Gora, her eyes shining with affection.

'No, it's nothing important. Let it be for now,' Gora answered, preparing to leave.

'Stay awhile,' said Krishandayal, 'there's something I want to say. A Brahmo friend of mine has recently arrived in Kolkata. He stays at Hedotola.'

'It isn't Poreshbabu is it?'

'How do you know him?'

'Binoy lives close to his house. He has told me about them.'

'I would like you to go and inquire after their well-being.'

'Very well, I'll go there tomorrow itself,' said Gora suddenly, after some consideration. Anandamoyi was rather surprised. Gora paused again to think, then said: 'No, I can't go tomorrow, after all.'

'Why?' asked Krishnadayal.

'I must travel to Triveni tomorrow.'

'Triveni!' exclaimed Krishandayal, in astonishment.

'Tomorrow's solar eclipse calls for a holy bath,' Gora informed him.

'You amaze me, Gora!' said Anandamoyi. 'If you want a holy bath, there's the Ganga in Kolkata. No bath except at Triveni! I must say you have outdone all your countrymen!'

Gora left the room without offering any reply. He had decided to bathe at Triveni because many pilgrims would gather there. Merging with that mass of humanity, he wanted to surrender to the vast current of national life, and to feel the nation's turbulent pulse within his own heart. At the slightest opportunity, Gora wanted to forcefully cast aside all constraints and prejudices, to come down to the level the general public, and declare with all his heart: 'I am yours, and you are mine!'

# 7

Awakening at dawn, Binoy found that the sky had cleared overnight. The morning light had dawned, pure as the smile of a suckling infant. A few white clouds floated aimlessly in the sky. As he stood on the balcony, rapt in the memory of another pure dawn, he saw Poresh walking slowly down the road, grasping a stick in one hand and Satish's hand in the other. Spotting Binoy on the balcony, Satish at once clapped his hands. 'Binoybabu!' he called. Raising his head, Poresh also saw Binoy. As Binoy hurried downstairs, Poresh entered his house, accompanied by Satish.

'Binoybabu, you promised to visit us the other day, but you didn't come!' complained Satish, grasping Binoy's hand. Binoy smiled, patting Satish affectionately on the back.

Carefully propping his stick against the table, Poresh took a chowki. 'Without you, we would have been in deep trouble that day,' he said. 'You did us a great favour.'

'How can you say that! I hardly did anything at all!' said Binoy, flustered.'Tell me, Binoybabu, don't you have a dog?' Satish suddenly inquired.

'A dog?' laughed Binoy. 'No, I don't have a dog.'

'Why?' asked Satish. 'Why haven't you kept a dog?'

'I never thought of keeping a dog.'

'Satish visited you the other day, I'm told,' said Poresh. 'He must have really pestered you. He talks so much, his didi has named him Bakhtiar Khiliji, the Orator.'

'I too have the gift of the gab,' replied Binoy. 'So we've become great friends, the two of us. What do you say, Satishbabu!'

Satish did not reply. But he became anxious not to let his new name lower his dignity in Binoy's eyes. 'Well, why not?' he said. 'Bakhtiar Khiliji is a fine name. Tell me, Binoybabu, Bakhtiar Khiliji was a warrior, wasn't he? Didn't he conquer Bengal?'

'He used to be a warrior once,' answered Binoy with a smile. 'But now he has no need to engage in combat. Now he only delivers speeches. And he still manages to conquer Bengal.'

Thus they conversed for a long time. Poresh spoke least of all, smiling occasionally with a cheerful serenity, and making only a couple of remarks. When it was time to leave, he rose from the chowki and said:

'To get to our House, number 78, you need to keep to the right . . .'

'He knows our house,' Satish interrupted. 'He escorted me all the way to our own doorstep, the other day.'

There was nothing embarrassing about this, yet Binoy felt secretly ashamed, as if he had been caught red-handed somehow.

'You know our house then,' said the old man. 'So, if you ever . . .'

'Of course. Whenever . . .'

'We belong to the same neighbourhood, after all,' Poresh said. 'It's only because this is Kolkata that we haven't yet become acquainted.'

Binoy escorted Poresh down to the street. He lingered at the door for a while. Poresh walked slowly, leaning on his stick, with Satish prattling away by his side. 'I have never seen an old man like Poreshbabu,' Binoy said to himself. 'I feel like bowing at his feet in reverence. And what a wonderful lad Satish is! If he lives, he will be a special person, as bright as he is simple!' However worthy the old man and the boy might have been, such an effusion of admiration and affection could not have occurred under normal circumstances, after so short an acquaintance. But such was Binoy's mental state, he did not wait to get better acquainted.

After this, Binoy began to think: 'For civility's sake, I must visit Poreshbabu's house.' But he seemed to hear Gora's voice warn him on behalf of their own group's version of Bharatvarsha: 'It's not acceptable for you to frequent their house. Watch out!' At every step, Binoy had followed many restrictions imposed by their group's image of Bharatvarsha. He had often hesitated but had obeyed, all the same. Today, his heart rose in rebellion. He began to feel that Bharatvarsha was only a figure of negation.

The servant came to announce the midday meal, but Binoy had not even bathed yet. It was already noon. Suddenly, Binoy shook his head vehemently and declared, 'I shall not eat. Leave me alone, all of you.' So saying he picked up an umbrella and emerged into the street, without even a chador on his shoulder.

He went straight to Gora's house. Binoy knew that an office of the Hindu welfare society had been set up in rented premises on Amherst Street. Gora would go there every day at noon, and write letters to inspire his party members everywhere in Bengal. This was where his devotees came to hear his words of wisdom, and to seek glory in supporting him.

That day as well, Gora had gone to the office for some work. Binoy rushed to Anandamoyi's chamber in the private antahpur of Gora's house. Anandamoyi was at her meal. Lachamiya sat by her side, fanning her.

'Why, Binoy! What's the matter with you?' Anandamoyi exclaimed.

Binoy sat down facing her. 'Ma, I am very hungry,' he said. 'Please give me something to eat.'

'Now you've put me in a fix!' said Anandamoyi, flustered. 'Bamun-thakur, the Brahman cook, has left. Because all of

you . . .'

'As if I've come to taste Bamun-thakur's cooking! Then the Bamun in my own home would have done as well. I want prasad from your own platter—food sanctified by your touch, Ma. Go Lachhmia, fetch me a glass of water!'

Binoy gulped down the water Lachhmia brought him. With loving care, Anandamoyi mashed the rice on her own thala and served portions of it to Binoy on another thala. He began to devour the morsels as if he had been famished for days.

A source of anguish was removed from Anandamoyi's heart. The sight of her cheerful face also made Binoy's heart feel lighter. She settled down to sew a pillowcase. From the adjacent room came the fragrance of keya blossoms, collected to prepare the screwpine-flavoured catechu called keyakhoyer. Binoy reclined at Anandamoyi's feet, head propped on his arm, and prattled on joyfully just as in previous times, forgetting everything else.

## 8

When this dam burst, the new flood in Binoy's heart seemed to grow even more turbulent. Emerging from Anandamoyi's room, he flew down the street as if on winged feet. He wanted to proudly proclaim to everyone the secret feelings that had been making him feel so awkward these last few days. At the very moment when Binoy reached the door of House 78, Poresh also arrived there from the opposite direction.

'Welcome, welcome, Binoybabu! What a pleasure!' With these words, Poresh ushered Binoy into the sitting-room facing the street. On one side of a small table was a bench with a back-rest, and on the other, a chair made of wood and cane. On one wall hung a painting of Jesus Christ, and on the wall opposite, a photograph of Keshabbabu. On the table, under a glass paperweight, lay the folded newspapers of the past few days. Books by Theodore Parker were arranged in rows on the upper shelves of a small almira in the corner. On top of the almira was a globe, covered with cloth. Binoy sat down, his heart racing. What if someone entered the room through the door behind him?

'On Mondays, Sucharita goes to tutor my friend's daughter,' Poresh informed him. 'Satish has also accompanied her, because a boy of his own age lives there. I have just returned after dropping them there. A little more delay, and I would have missed you.'

At this news, Binoy's heart simultaneously felt a pang of disappointment and a sense of relief. He could now chat with Poresh at ease. Poresh learnt all about Binoy in the course of their conversation. Binoy was an orphan. His khuro and khurima lived in the ancestral village and supervised property matters. Their two sons, Binoy's paternal cousins, used to stay with him while they pursued their studies. The elder one became a lawyer and practised in the local district court. The younger brother had died of cholera while still in Kolkata. The khuro wanted his nephew to aim for the district magistrate's post, but Binoy made no effort in that direction, busy instead with all sorts of trivial pursuits.

Almost an hour passed by in this fashion. It would seem uncivil to linger there needlessly any longer.

'It's a pity I didn't get to meet my friend Satish,' said Binoy, rising to his feet. 'Please tell him that I had come.'

'If you had stayed on a little longer you could have met them,' responded Poreshbabu. 'It won't be long before they return.'

Binoy found it embarrassing to change his mind merely at this assurance. A little more persuasion, and he might have stayed on. But Poresh was a man of few words, not given to pressuring anyone, so Binoy had to leave.

'It would be nice if you dropped by now and then,' said Poresh.

Out in the street, Binoy felt no need to go back home. He had nothing to do there. He wrote for the papers. People praised his writings in English, but these last few days, when he sat down to write, no words would come to mind. He felt so restless, it was hard to spend much time at his desk. So he now headed in the opposite direction, for no reason at all.

He had barely walked a few steps when he heard a boyish voice cry: 'Binoybabu, Binoybabu!' Looking up, he saw Satish calling out to him, leaning out of the door of a hired cab. The glimpse of a sari corner and a white blouse-sleeve left him in no doubt about the identity of the passenger within. Constraints of Bengali respectability made it difficult for Binoy to stare at the cab. Meanwhile, Satish dismounted at that very spot, and grasped his hand.

'Come, let's go to our house,' he urged.

'But I've just left your house,' Binoy protested.

'Bah, we weren't there after all, so you must come again.' Binoy could not ignore Satish's importunations.

'Baba, I've brought Binoybabu!' announced Satish loudly, as soon as he had led his prisoner into the house.

'You are in the clutches of a harsh captor,' smiled the old man, emerging from his room. 'You won't escape in a hurry. Satish, send for your didi.'

His heart pounding, Binoy entered the room and took a seat.

'Out of breath, aren't you!' Poresh observed. 'Satish is a very mischievous boy.'

When Satish entered the room with his elder sister, Binoy first felt the whiff of a sweet fragrance. Then he heard Poreshbabu say:

'Radhé, Binoybabu is here. You know him, of course!'

Binoy looked up with a start, to see Sucharita greet him with a namaskar before occupying the chowki opposite his. This time, he did not forget to return her greeting.

'He was walking down the street,' Sucharita explained. 'There was no stopping Satish once he caught sight of him. He got off the cab and dragged him here. Perhaps you were out on some business. I hope this hasn't inconvenienced you?'

Binoy had not even dared to hope that Sucharita would address him directly. Flustered, he quickly blurted out: 'No, I was not out on any business. It was not inconvenient at all.'

'Come on Didi, give me the keys,' begged Satish, tugging at Sucharita's sari. 'Let me fetch our organ for Binoybabu to see.'

'Here we go!' laughed Sucharita. 'For anyone Bakhtiar befriends, there is no respite. He must not only listen to the organ but suffer much worse besides. Binoybabu, this friend of yours is tiny, but his friendship is a heavy burden. I wonder if you can bear it!'

Binoy could not summon up any easy response to Sucharita's unselfconscious conversation. 'No, not at all,' he stammered somehow, despite his firm resolve not to be shy. 'You, he—me—I rather like it!'

Extracting the keys from his didi, Satish fetched the organ and presented it before the company. Inside a square glass cover, on a bed of blue fabric meant to represent ocean waves, rested a toy ship. As soon as Satish wound it up, the ship began to sway to the organ's musical rhythm. Glancing now at the ship, now at Binoy's face, Satish could not contain his excitement. In this way, little by little, Satish's mediation broke down Binoy's restraint. Gradually, Binoy even discovered it was not impossible to meet Sucharita's gaze and exchange a few remarks with her.

'Won't you bring your friend here one day?' asked Satish suddenly, out of the blue.

This led to questions about Binoy's friend. Poreshbabu and his family were new to Kolkata, and knew nothing about Gora. Speaking of his friend, Binoy grew animated. Describing Gora's rare genius, his largeness of heart and unswerving courage, he did not seem to know when to stop. Gora would one day shine above Bharatvarsha's crest like the glory of the midday sun. 'I have no doubt of that,' Binoy declared. As he spoke, his face grew radiant, and all his diffidence seemed to evaporate. In fact, he even exchanged a few arguments with Poreshbabu regarding Gora's opinions.

'If Gora can unhesitatingly accept Hindu culture in its entirety, it's because he regards Bharatvarsha from a very broad perspective,' argued Binoy. 'To him, Bharatvarsha appears in its entirety, all its features, major and minor, merged into a great unity, a vast harmony. Because all of us are not capable of such a vision, we constantly misjudge Bharatvarsha, seeing it in fragments and comparing it with foreign ideals.'

'Do you say caste discrimination is a good thing?' Sucharita asked. She spoke as if there was no scope for argument.

'Caste discrimination is neither good, nor bad,' Binoy declared. 'In other words, it is good in some situations, bad in others. If you asked me whether the hand is a good thing, I would reply that it's best judged in relation to the rest of the body. If you asked, is the hand good for flying?—I would reply in the negative; likewise, wings are not good for grasping things, either.'

'I understand nothing of all this!' exclaimed Sucharita, getting agitated. 'My question is, do you believe in caste distinctions?'

'Yes, I do!' Binoy would have emphatically asserted, had he been arguing with someone else. But now he found it hard to insist, whether from timidity, or whether his heart on this occasion was unwilling to go so far as to declare categorically: 'I believe in caste distinctions', it cannot be said for certain. Lest the argument go too far, Poresh intervened at this point.

'Radhé, send for your mother and all the others,' he said. 'Let me introduce him to them.'

Sucharita left the room, with Satish prancing along by her side as he chattered away. After a while, she returned to say: 'Baba, Ma wants you to come to the terrace upstairs.'

## 9

Upstairs, on the terrace above the portico, chowkis were arranged around a table covered with a white cloth. On the cornice beyond the railing, crotons and flowering plants grew in tiny flowerpots. From the terrace, one could see the rain-washed, glossy foliage of the acacia and gulmohar trees that lined the edges of the street. The sun had not yet vanished; from the western sky, the fading sunshine slanted down upon one end of the balcony.

The terrace was deserted at that hour. Soon, Satish arrived there, accompanied by a small black-and-white dog named Khudé, the tiny one. Satish had the dog display all its tricks for Binoy's benefit. It saluted with one paw, bowed its head to the ground in a pranam, knelt on its hind legs to beg for a biscuit. Satish basked in reflected glory, taking all the credit for Khudé's accomplishments. Khudé had no interest in earning such glory. In fact, the biscuit meant much more to him than fame.

From a room somewhere wafted occasional bursts of female laughter and merriment, accompanied by a single male voice. The sound of such unchecked mirth filled Binoy's heart with exquisite tenderness, mingled with aching envy. Never before in all his life had he heard such joyous female gaiety emanate from a room. The source of this sweet exuberance was so close to him, and yet he was so far removed from it! Binoy found it impossible to focus on what Satish was babbling, close to his ear.

Poreshbabu's wife now appeared on the terrace, accompanied by her three daughters. With them was a young man, a distant relative.

Poreshbabu's wife was called Borodasundari. She was not young but had clearly dressed with special care. Having followed the provincial mode until she grew up, she had suddenly, at one point, become desperate to keep abreast of modern trends. So her silk sari rustled too much, and her high heeled shoes clattered too loudly. She was always extremely alert about the distinctions between what was Brahmo, and what was not. That was why she had changed Radharani's name to Sucharita. One of the elders in her in-laws' family, having returned after a long stint of work abroad, had sent them presents for the Jamaisashthi ritual in honour of sons-in-law. Poreshababu was away on business at the time. Borodasundari had returned all the Jamaisashthi gifts. She regarded such things as social evils, forms of idol-worship. She considered it a part of the Brahmo worldview for women to sport socks or hats when going outdoors. But seeing people use asanas on the floor at a Brahmo family meal, she had voiced the fear that the Brahmo Samaj was now lapsing back into idol-worship.

Labanya was her eldest daughter. She was chubby and jovial, fond of company and conversation. Round of face, with large eyes and a dark, glowing complexion, she was by nature careless about her dress and appearance but had to follow her mother's dictates in such matters. Though uncomfortable in high-heeled shoes, she had no choice but to wear them. When it was time for the evening toilette, her mother personally powdered her face and patted colour on her cheeks. Because she was somewhat plump, Borodasundari had her blouses stitched so tight that Labanya emerged looking like a trussed-up machine-stuffed jute sack.

The second daughter was named Lalita. Taller than her didi, thinner and darker, she could be described as the very opposite of the elder daughter. She said little and followed her own whims, and could be sharp-tongued if she chose. Borodasundari was secretly scared of her, and usually did not dare to provoke her.

The youngest, Leela, was about ten years of age, a tomboy, always engaged in physical tussles with Satish. In particular, the two of them had not yet agreed upon the true ownership of Khudé the dog. Had the dog been consulted, he would probably not have chosen either; but still, between the two, he probably had a slight preference for Satish. For it was not easy for this tiny creature to withstand the force of Leela's caresses. It was relatively easier for him to tolerate the boy's authority rather than the girl's affection.

As soon as Borodasundari appeared, Binoy arose and bent to greet her with a pranam.

'It was at his house, the other day, that we . . .' Poreshbabu explained.

'Oh!' said Boroda. 'You were a great help. Many thanks.'

Binoy was too embarrassed to reply. He was also introduced to the young man named Sudhir who had accompanied the girls. He was in college, studying for his B.A. degree. His appearance was pleasant, his complexion fair; he wore glasses, and had a thin moustache on his upper lip. He seemed extremely restless, unable to sit still for long, always rearing to go. He would constantly joke with the girls and tease them, never allowing them a moment's peace. The girls, too, would keep reprimanding him, yet they could not manage without Sudhir. He was always ready to take them to the circus or the Zoological Gardens, or to buy them something they fancied. Sudhir's easy familiarity with women struck Binoy as a complete novelty, quite amazing. At first he metally condemned such behaviour, but a tinge of envy began to colour this critical attitude.

'I think I have seen you at the Samaj, once or twice,' Borodasundari remarked.

Binoy felt as if he had been caught out in some crime. 'Yes, I go there sometimes, to listen to Keshabbabu's lectures,' he admitted, with unwarranted embarrassment.

'You're a college student I suppose?' Borodasundari inquired.

'No, I am not in college anymore.'

'What is the extent of your college education?'

'I have received my M.A. degree.'

Borodasundari felt a certain respect for this boyish-looking young man. 'If my Monu had been here today, he too would have acquired an M.A. degree by now,' she sighed, glancing at Poresh.

Boroda's first child Monoranjan had died at nine. Whenever she heard of any young man obtaining a major degree, attaining a high professional position, writing a good book, or doing something worthwhile, Boroda would immediately assume that if Monu had lived, he would have accomplished exactly the same things. But since he was no more, it was now one of Borodasundari's special duties to publicize the talents of her three daughters. She made a point of informing Binoy that her daughters were studying very hard. Nor was he left in the dark as to how their white governess, the mem, had praised the daughters' intelligence and accomplishments on various occasions. Binoy was also told of the time when Labanya had been specially selected from among all the girls in her school, to present flowers to the Lieutenant Governor and his wife when they visited the girls' school on prize-distribution day; and of the sweet words of encouragement that the Governor's wife had spoken to Labanya.

'Ma, my little one, fetch your prize-winning piece of embroidery!' Boroda urged Labanya, finally. A parrot, embroidered in silk, had gained considerable fame among relatives and friends of the family. Labanya had created this piece long ago with the mem's assistance; nor did Labanya herself deserve much of the credit for this work of art; but it was taken for granted that every new acquaintance must be shown this creation. Poresh would object at first, but now he no longer resisted, realizing the futility of such protests. As Binoy gazed in wide-eyed amazement at the artistry that had produced the silken parrot, the bearer brought a letter for Poresh.

'Bring Babu upstairs,' Poreshbabu instructed, cheering up as he read the letter.

'Who is it?' Boroda wanted to know.

'My childhood friend Krishnadayal has sent his son to meet us,' Poresh informed her.

Binoy's heart suddenly skipped a beat, and his face grew pale. The next moment, he clenched his fists and stiffened his body, as if bracing himself for a confrontation with some adversary. He seemed already flustered, anticipating that Gora would view this family with disrespect, and pass judgement on them.

## 10

Having arranged tea and snacks on a khunche, Sucharita handed the small tray to the attendant and came up to the terrace. At that moment, Gora also arrived on the scene, escorted by the bearer.

Everyone was wonderstruck at Gora's tall, fair figure and his attire. His forehead was marked with a tilak of sacred Ganga soil. He wore a coarse dhoti, a knotted upper garment and a wrap made of rough fabric. His feet were shod in Cuttack shoes with pointed, curling toes. He was the living image of rebellion against the modern age. Even Binoy had never seen him in such garb.

Gora's heart was indeed aflame with revolt today. He had reason to feel rebellious. The previous day, a steamer-company had set out at dawn with a group of passengers going to Triveni for their ritual holy bath during the eclipse. On the way, hordes of female passengers boarded at each station, accompanied by a few male guardians. The urgency of finding a place caused a great deal of pushing and shoving. With their muddy feet, some lost their balance during the tussle and fell off the boarding plank into the water in an unguarded moment; some were pushed off by the seamen; some managed to clamber on board but were desperate because their companions had been left behind; sometimes, a shower of rain would drench their bodies; their seating area on board was soiled with mud. Their expression was anxious, agitated and pathetic. They were feeble but knew they were so insignificant that nobody, from oarsmen to captain, would offer them the slightest assistance in response to their pleas; hence there was a terrified pathos in their struggles. In this situation, Gora was trying to help the passengers as much as possible. On the first class deck above, an Englishman and a Bengali of the modern breed were leaning on the railing, engaged in good-humoured conversation, watching the entertaining spectacle as they smoked their cigars. From time to time, seeing a passenger suffer some sudden mishap, the Englishman would burst out laughing, and the Bengali would also join in his mirth. Having crossed two or three stations in this fashion,

Gora could bear it no longer. He ascended to the upper deck.

'Shame on you! Aren't you ashamed of yourselves?' he roared in his thunderous voice.

The Englishman glared at Gora, surveying him from head to toe.

'Ashamed?' the Bengali replied. 'One is ashamed of all the idiots in this country, no better than animals!'

'There can be people even more bestial than idiots; they are the ones with no heart!' retorted Gora, his colour high.

'You don't belong here!' cried the Bengali, enraged. 'This place is reserved for first class passengers!'

'No, you and I don't belong together,' replied Gora. 'My place is with those passengers over there. But let me warn you in parting, don't compel me to enter this class of yours again.'

With these words, Gora marched down to the lower level. The Englishman immersed himself in a novel, lounging on the armchair with his legs on the armrests. His Bengali co-passenger made a couple of attempts to revive their conversation but failed to generate much warmth. To prove that he did not belong to the ordinary masses, he sent for the khansama and inquired if any chicken dish was available.

'No, only bread-and-butter with tea,' replied the attendant.

'Their arrangements for our creature comforts are appalling!' complained the Bengali in English, for the Englishman's benefit. The Englishman did not reply. A gust of wind blew his newspaper off the table. The Bengali babu rose to pick it up but received no thanks. While disembarking at Chandannagar, the saheb suddenly went up to Gora and raised his hat.

'I'm sorry about the way I behaved,' he apologized. 'I hope you will forgive me.' He hurried away.

But Gora seethed with indignation at the arrogance of an educated Bengali who could invite a foreigner to join him in mocking at the plight of the masses. Gora's heart seemed to burst with anguish at the deep-seated, nationwide ignorance at the root of his countrymen's submission to all sorts of humiliation and ill-treatment, for even when abused like animals, all of them would accept it as natural and appropriate. But what galled him most was the educated class's indifference towards the nation's constant degradation and misery. Such people could heartlessly remain aloof and bask in glory without any qualms. When he came and stood proudly before the Brahmo family, it was to show his complete disregard for the bookish and imitative ways of the educated class that Gora had applied Ganga-soil to his forehead and bought an odd pair of Cuttack sandals to wear. Binoy privately sensed that Gora had come armed for battle. Uncertain of what Gora might do, Binoy felt a sense of apprehension, mingled with embarrassment and a will to resist.

While Borodasundari was conversing with Binoy, Satish had been obliged to amuse himself, spinning a tin top in a corner of the terrace. When he saw Gora, his top-spinning came to a halt; he crept close to Binoy and stared at Gora. 'Is this your friend?' he whispered to Binoy.

'Yes.'

When Gora arrived on the terrace, he glanced at Binoy's face for a fraction of a second, but after that, seemed not to notice him at all. Greeting Poresh with a namaskar, he dragged a chowki away from the table and seated himself without any embarrassment. He deemed it uncivil to notice the presence of women anywhere on the scene. Borodasundari had almost decided to take her daughters away from this uncouth person's company, when Poresh informed her:

'This is Gourmohan, my friend Krishnadayal's son.'

Gora now turned to greet her with a namaskar. Although Sucharita had already heard about Gora from Binoy, she had not realized that this visitor was indeed Binoy's friend. At very first sight, she resented Gora. It was not in her upbringing or temperament to tolerate such extreme Hindu fanaticism in a person with an English education.

Poresh asked Gora for news of his childhood friend Krishnadayal. Then, speaking of his own student days, he mused: 'We were quite a twosome those days. Great iconoclasts, we believed in nothing. We only considered dining at restaurants a worthwhile duty. How many evenings we'd spend at Goldighi, devouring kababs from a Muslim shop, arguing into the wee hours about ways to reform Hindu society!'

'What does he do now?' Borodasundari wanted to know.

'Now he follows the Hindu code,' Gora informed her.

'Isn't he ashamed of himself?' asked Boroda, aflame with rage.

'Shame is a sign of weakness,' smiled Gora. 'Some people are ashamed of acknowledging their own fathers.'

'Wasn't he a Brahmo earlier?' Boroda inquired.

'Even I was a Brahmo once,' Gora retorted.

'Do you believe in image worship now?'

'I am not superstitious enough to disrespect the concept of embodied form without any reason. Does form diminish if abused? Has anyone penetrated the mystery of form?'

'But form is finite,' Poreshbabu gently pointed out.

'Without finitude, there can be no expression,' Gora argued. 'The infinite takes refuge in the finite only to manifest itself, else how would it find expression? That which remains unexpressed cannot be complete. The formless finds completion in form, just as the idea is fulfilled in words.'

'Would you say that form is more complete than the formless?' exclaimed Boroda, shaking her head.

'Even if I didn't say so, it would make no difference. The status of form in this world does not depend upon what I say. If the formless were truly complete, there would be no place for form at all.'

Sucharita longed for someone to utterly vanquish this high-handed young man in argument, leaving him humiliated. She was secretly angry with Binoy for listening to Gora in silence. Gora spoke so forcefully that Sucharita also felt a powerful inward urge to subdue him.

Just then, the bearer arrived with a kettle of hot water for tea. Sucharita got up and busied herself making tea. Every now and then Binoy shot a quick glance at her face. Although Gora and Binoy did not differ much in their views about forms of worship, Binoy was troubled at the way Gora was unhesitatingly flaunting his contrary views before this Brahmo family, after joining them uninvited. In contrast to Gora's militant behaviour, the elderly Poresh's manner displayed a self-contained calm, a profound grace transcending all argument, which filled Binoy's heart with devotion. 'Opinions don't matter,' he told himself. 'For the mind and soul, wholeness, stability and self-satisfaction are the rarest values of all. Much as we may argue about the truth or falsehood of words, when it comes to attainment, only the truth is real.' In the midst of the conversation, Poresh habitually closed his eyes from time to time, to sound the depths of his own heart. At such moments, Binoy closely observed his self-absorbed, tranquil expression. He was extremely disturbed at Gora's failure to restrain his words in deference to this old man.

Sucharita poured a few cups of tea, and glanced at Poresh, unsure who should receive their hospitality.

'You won't accept anything to eat, will you?' Borodasundari blurted out pointedly, looking at Gora.

'No.'

'Why?' asked Borodasundari. 'Will you lose your caste purity?'

'Yes,' Gora replied.

'Do you believe in caste?' Boroda inquired.

'Is caste of my own making, that I should reject it?' Gora demanded. 'If I believe in my community, I must believe in caste as well.'

'Must you believe in everything the community prescribes?'

'To disbelieve would be to destroy the community.'

'What harm in that?'

'What harm in sawing off the very branch we occupy?'

'Ma, why argue in vain?' protested Sucharita, inwardly disgusted. 'He will not accept any food that we have touched.'

For a moment, Gora rested his sharp gaze upon Sucharita's face.

'Will you . . .?' faltered Sucharita, looking at Binoy.

Binoy never drank tea. Long back, he had also given up bread and biscuits prepared by Muslims. But today he had no choice. 'Yes, indeed, I'll have some,' he forced himself to say, raising his head. He glanced at Gora. A faint sneer appeared on Gora's lips. The tea tasted bitter upon Binoy's tongue, but he swallowed it nevertheless.

'Aha, this Binoy is such a nice boy!' said Borodasundari to herself. She turned her back on Gora and devoted all her attention to Binoy. Noticing this, Poresh drew his chowki close to Gora and began to converse with him in a low voice.

Presently, a hawker came down the street, selling warm, roasted peanuts. Hearing his call, Leela clapped her hands in delight. 'Sudhirda, please send for the peanut-seller!' she pleaded. Satish at once began calling out to the peanut-seller from the terrace.

Meanwhile, another gentleman joined them. Everyone greeted him as Panubabu, but his real name was Haranchandra Nag. Within their circle, he was known for his learning and intellect. Neither side had said anything definite, but the likelihood of his marrying Sucharita was in the air. That Panubabu was attracted to Sucharita was something no one doubted, and the girls never spared a chance to tease Sucharita about it. Panubabu taught at a school. Because he was a mere schoolmaster, Borodasundari did not respect him much. Her manner indicated it was just as well Panubabu had not dared to express a preference for one of *her* daughters. Her future sons-in-law must vow to attain a deputyship, a feat of marksmanship as challenging as the legendary lakshyabheda.

When Sucharita pushed a teacup towards Haran, Labanya smirked at her from afar. That smirk did not escape Binoy's notice. Very quickly, his eye had grown quite sharp and alert in certain matters, though he had not been known earlier for his acuity of vision. Haran and Sudhir had known the girls in this house for so long and were so closely involved in their family history, they had become the subject of secret signals between the sisters. This now struck Binoy as a painful instance of divine injustice.

Meanwhile, Sucharita felt more hopeful, now that Haran had arrived. She could overcome her indignation only if someone curbed Gora's arrogance somehow. Previously, she had often been irritated by Haran's argumentativeness, but now, upon seeing this champion debater, she delightedly plied him with tea and bread.

'Panubabu, meet our . . .' Poresh began.

'I know him very well,' Haran interrupted. 'He was once a very enthusiastic member of our Brahmo Samaj.' With these words, he turned to his cup of tea, making no attempt at conversation with Gora.

At that time, only a couple of Bengalis had come to these parts after entering the civil services. Sudhir spoke of the welcome that one of them had received.

'However successful they may be at passing examinations, Bengalis are incapable of doing any work,' Haran declared. To prove that no Bengali magistrate or judge would be able to discharge his duties after assuming charge of a district, he began to analyse the faults and weaknesses of the Bengali nature.

In no time, Gora's face reddened in fury. 'If that is indeed your opinion, aren't you ashamed to sit at this table, chewing bread?' he demanded, restraining his lion-like roar as far as possible.

'What do you suggest I should do?' asked Haran, raising his eyebrows in surprise.

'Either erase the blot on the Bengali character, or go hang yourself. Is it so easy to declare that our race will forever remain good for nothing? Didn't you choke on your bread, saying such things?'

'Should I not speak the truth?' Haran retorted.

'No offence meant, but if you really took it to be true, you could never have stated it so casually, with such arrogance. It's because you know them to be false that such words could pass your lips. Haranbabu, uttering falsehoods is a sin, making false accusations is a greater sin, and there are few sins to match that of falsely condemning one's own community.'

Haran was beside himself with fury.

'Are you, alone, superior to your entire community?' Gora asked. 'You, alone, have the right to be angry, whilst all of us must tolerate all your remarks on our ancestors' behalf?'

Now it became even harder for Haran to admit defeat. His condemnation of Bengalis grew even more shrill. Referring to sundry Bengali social customs, he declared: 'As long as such things prevail, there is no hope for Bengalis.'

'Your account of social evils is merely learned by rote from English books,' Gora asserted. 'You yourself know nothing of such practices. You should voice your opinions on this subject only when you are capable of expressing a similar contempt for all English malpractices.'

Poresh tried to change the subject, but there was no restraining the incensed Haran. The sun went down. From within the clouds, an exquisite rosy glow lit up the sky. Overriding the babble of argument, a certain melody stirred Binoy's soul. To attend to his evening prayers, Poresh left the terrace for a paved platform beneath the large champa tree at one end of the garden.

While Borodasundari had developed an aversion to Gora, she was also not particularly fond of Haran. When she could no longer bear the argument between them, she called out:

'Come, Binoybabu, let us go indoors.'

Borodasundari's affectionate partiality compelled Binoy to leave the terrace and go indoors. Boroda called the girls to join her. Sensing which way the argument was going, Satish had already vanished with Khudé, on the pretext of getting a small serving of peanuts.

Borodasundari began to sing her daughters' praises to Binoy. 'Why don't you fetch that notebook of yours, for Binoybabu to see?' she proposed to Labanya.

Labanya had grown used to displaying this notebook to all new acquaintances who visited them. In fact, she now looked forward to such occasions. This evening, she had been upset at the argument that had developed. Opening the notebook, Binoy found inscribed in it the poems of Moore and Longfellow. The handwriting was neat and laborious. The titles of the poems and the first letter of every line were etched in Roman characters. The sight of these writings filled Binoy's heart with unfeigned wonder. In those days, it was no mean feat for girls to copy Moore's poems into their notebooks.

Observing that Binoy was suitably impressed, Borodasundari addressed her second daughter: 'Lalita, my angel, that poem of yours . . .'

'No, Ma, I can't,' protested Lalita firmly. 'I don't remember it properly.' She moved to a window at a distance, and gazed at the street.

Borodasundari explained to Binoy that Lalita remembered everything but was too reserved to display her erudition. Recounting a few anecdotes as proof of Lalita's extraordinary learning and wit, she said Lalita had been like this since infancy, unable to shed tears even when she wanted to weep. She commented on the girl's similarity to her father in this respect.

Now it was Leela's turn. As soon as she was asked, she burst into a peal of laughter. Then like a clockwork organ, she rattled off the nursery rhyme *Twinkle twinkle little star*, all in one breath, without understanding a word of it. Realizing it was now time to display their musical talent, Lalita left the room.

Out on the terrace, the argument had gone out of hand. In a fit of rage, Haran was on the verge of abandoning argument for abuse. Embarrassed and annoyed at his lack of restraint, Sucharita had taken Gora' side. Haran did not find this comforting or soothing at all. The sky grew heavy with darkness and rain-clouds. From the street came the call of a hawker selling jasmine garlands. Fireflies twinkled in the clustered foliage of the roadside krishnachura tree opposite the house. A deep blackness descended upon the pond next door. Done with his evening prayers, Poresh appeared on the terrace. Seeing him, both Gora and Haran subsided, feeling embarrassed.

'It's late. I'll take your leave now,' said Gora, rising to his feet.

Binoy, too, made his exit from the room and appeared on the terrace.

'Listen, you must come here whenever you like,' Poresh invited Gora. 'Krishnadayal was like a brother to me. We don't see eye to eye now, nor do we meet or correspond, but childhood friendships remain in the blood. My relationship with Krishnadayal makes me feel very close to you. May the Almighty bring you good fortune.'

At the sound of Poresh's calm, affectionate voice, Gora's heated, argumentative mood seemed to soften. When he first came there, Gora had shown scant respect for Poresh. But while taking leave, he touched Poresh's feet with genuine deference. Gora made no gesture of farewell to Sucharita. He thought it uncivil to make any move acknowledging her presence. Binoy bowed at Poresh's feet, and turning to Sucharita, offered a namaskar before quickly stepping out after Gora.

Avoiding these farewell greetings, Haran went indoors, picked up a book of Brahmosangeet from the table, and began to leaf through the musical score. As soon as Binoy and Gora had left, he hastened to the terrace. 'Sir, I don't like the idea of your introducing the girls to all and sundry,' he told Poresh.

Sucharita was seething inwardly. 'If Baba had followed that rule, we couldn't have met you, either,' she protested, unable to restrain herself.

'It is best to confine introductions to our own circle,' Haran declared.

'You wish to extend the inner quarters of the home, to create an antahpur within society,' smiled Poresh. 'But I believe the girls should mingle with gentlemen of various persuasions, or we'd be deliberately curbing their intellect. I see no cause for anxiety or shame in this.'

'I don't say girls shouldn't mingle with people of diverse views, but these people lack the civility to know how to conduct themselves with girls,' Haran expostulated.

'No, no, how can you say that!' cried Poresh. 'What you call lack of civility is merely an awkwardness that cannot be overcome unless one mingles with the female sex.'

'Listen, Panubabu, during today's argument I felt ashamed at the way members of our own community behaved!' declared Sucharia indignantly.

At this moment, Leela came running to her. 'Didi! Didi!' she cried, and dragged Sucharita indoors by the hand.

## 11

Haran had been particularly keen that day to humiliate Gora, to flaunt his own victory before Sucharita. At first, that was also what Sucharita had wanted. But by a quirk of fate, quite the opposite happened. In religious faith and social perspective, Sucharita differed from Gora. But affinity with her nation and sympathy for her countrymen came naturally to her. Although she did not always involve herself in political issues, Gora's sudden, thundering outburst against criticism of his own people had struck an answering chord in her heart. Never before had she heard anyone speak of the nation so forcefully and with such conviction. Generally, our countrymen like to wax eloquent about our nation and its people, but they don't have a deep, sincere belief in such ideas. However lyrical their patriotic utterances, they have no faith in the nation. But Gora could look beyond all the sorrows, travails and weaknesses of our land to perceive the manifestation of a great truth. That was why, without ignoring its impoverished state, he still cherished such strong reverence for the country. He was so firmly convinced of the nation's intrinsic power, that in his company, listening to the unquestioning patriotism of his utterances, skeptics were compelled to admit defeat. Confronted with Gora's unqualified faith, Haran's contemptuous arguments struck Sucharita as painfully insulting. Throwing decorum to the winds, she could not refrain from protesting indignantly at certain moments. Later in Gora and Binoy's absence, when Haran, in a fit of petty jealousy, accused them of being uncivil, Sucharita felt compelled to take Gora's side against such unfair meanness.

Not that Sucharita's heart had completely ceased to rebel against Gora. Even now, she felt inwardly offended by Gora's rather overstated, flagrant display of Hindu orthodoxy. She could somehow sense that this Hindu fanaticism had a perverse quality; neither natural and peaceful, nor replete with personal devotion but constantly and aggressively militating against others.

That evening, in all her words and actions, at dinnertime, and during Leela's storytime, Sucharita was constantly tormented by some unknown pain in the recesses of her heart. It was a pain she could not dismiss by any means. One can remove a thorn if one knows where it is lodged. That night Sucharita lingered alone on the terrace above the porch, trying to locate the thorn in her heart. With the night's gentle darkness, she tried to wipe away the unwarranted burning sensation within, but to no avail. The indeterminate heaviness in her heart made her want to weep, but no tears came.

That Sucharita should be tormented all this while merely because a young stranger had arrived with a tilak on his forehead, or because he could not be humbled in argument! Nothing could be more ridiculous! She dismissed this reason as utterly impossible. Then she remembered the real reason, and felt very ashamed. For three or four hours that day, Sucharita had sat opposite the young man, and had even supported his arguments from time to time, yet he appeared not to have noticed her at all, seemingly oblivious of her presence even at parting. Doubtless, it was this complete disregard that had stung Sucharita deeply. There was a shy diffidence in the behaviour of someone unaccustomed to mingling with women of other families, an awkwardness apparent in Binoy's conduct. But there was no trace of it in Gora's manner. Why did Sucharita find it impossible now, to either tolerate or dismiss his tremendous, heartless indifference? She wanted to die of shame at her own garrulity for having joined the argument with such lack of restraint, despite this great indifference. Once, when Sucharita reacted strongly to Haran's unfair arguments, Gora had glanced at her face; there was no diffidence in that gaze, but it was also hard to gauge its meaning. Was he saying to himself, 'What a brazen girl!' or 'How arrogant of her, to join a male argument uninvited'? But if that was how he felt, what did it matter? It did not matter at all, yet Sucharita was deeply disturbed. She struggled to forget it all, to erase it from her mind but without any success. She began to resent Gora. She longed fervently to dismiss him as a prejudiced, arrogant young man. But the memory of the self-assured gaze of that towering male figure with his thundering voice made her feel very small. Try as she would, she could not sustain her pride. Sucharita had grown accustomed to being the apple of everyone's eye. Not that she craved such affection, but why then did Gora's indifference feel so intolerable? After much thought, Sucharita concluded it was her keen desire to outwit Gora that made his unshakable indifference so painful to bear.

Thus she wrestled with her own thoughts, until it grew quite late. Everyone at home had gone to bed, putting out the lights. The door at the entrance clanged shut, indicating that the bearer was preparing to retire, having completed his chores. At this moment, Lalita appeared on the terrace, dressed for bed. She walked past Sucharita without a word and leaned on the railing in a corner of the terrace. Sucharita smiled to herself, aware that Lalita was sulking. She had completely forgotten that she was to sleep in Lalita's room that night. But Lalita was not willing to forgive a lapse of memory, for forgetting was the greatest crime of all. She was not a girl to remind one in time about one's promises. Until now, she had remained stiffly in her bed, her petulance increasing as time went by. Ultimately, when it became intolerable, she left her bed and came only to signal silently that she was still awake. Leaving her chowki, Sucharita went slowly up to Lalita and hugged her.

'Bhai Lalita, don't be angry!' she pleaded.

'No, why should I be angry?' protested Lalita, pulling herself away.

'You can stay on here if you like.'

'Come bhai, let's go to bed,' said Sucharita, tugging at her hand.

Lalita remained standing there, making no reply. Finally, Sucharita dragged her to the bedroom by force.

'Why did you take so long?' cried Lalita, in a choking voice. 'It's eleven, do you know? I've been listening to the chiming of the clock. Now you'll doze off at once, of course.'

'Bhai, I have acted wrongly tonight,' said Sucharita, drawing Lalita close.

As soon as she had acknowledged her guilt, Lalita's anger evaporated. 'Who were you thinking of all this while, all by yourself, didi?' she asked, her heart melting. 'Was it Panubabu?'

'What nonsense!' Sucharita rapped her with her forefinger.

Lalita could not stand Panubabu. Unlike her other sisters, she found it impossible to even tease Sucharita about him. It angered her to think that Panubabu wanted to marry Sucharita.

'Tell me, didi, Binoybabu is quite nice, isn't he?' she proposed, after a short silence. It would be hard to say definitely that her question was not intended to probe Sucharita's feelings.

'Yes,' replied Sucharita. 'Binoybabu is nice indeed, quite a decent person . . .' Her words did not strike the expected note.

'But whatever you might say didi,' Lalita persisted, 'I didn't like Gourmohanbabu at all. What a strange, pale colouring, and such a rigid air, as if he doesn't care for anybody in the world. What did you think of him?'

'His Hindu fanaticism is quite excessive,' observed Sucharita.

'No, no,' said Lalita, 'Meshomoshai—our maternal uncle—is a staunch Hindu after all but in a different way. But this seems—rather strange.'

'Strange, indeed!' laughed Sucharita. The memory of Gora's image, with the tilak on his broad white forehead, made her angry. What angered her was that Gora had inscribed the tilak on his forehead as if to proclaim: 'I am different from all of you'. Only by demolishing his tremendous pride in that difference could Sucharita have overcome her indignation.

Discussion over, the two of them eventually fell asleep. At two o'clock, Sucharita woke up to find it raining heavily outside. Flashes of lightning lit up their mosquito net intermittently; the lamp in the corner had gone out. In the dark stillness of the night, listening to the sound of incessant rain, Sucharita began to feel an aching sensation in her heart. Envying Lalita who slept soundly by her side, she tossed and turned, struggling for sleep, but to no avail. Frustrated, she left her bed and stepped out. Standing at the open door, she gazed at the terrace before her. Occasional gusts of wind sprayed her body with rain. Over and over again the evening's events surfaced in her mind, recalled in minutest detail. Clear as a picture, she remembered Gora's animated face as it had appeared in the rosy sunset glow on that terrace above the portico. She recapitulated, from beginning to end, all the arguments that evening, resonant with the timbre of Gora's deep, powerful voice.

'I belong with those you call uneducated!' his voice rang in her ears. 'I believe in the ideas you denounce as superstition. Until you can love your country and join your own countrymen on an equal footing, I shan't tolerate the slightest criticism of the nation from your lips.'

'But in that case how will our nation be reformed?' retorted Panubabu.

'Reform!' thundered Gora. 'Reform must come much later. Love and respect are more important by far. We must unite first; then reform will follow automatically, from within. Remaining separate, you all want to fragment the nation; alleging that the nation is full of social evils, you wish to keep aloof as a band of do-gooders. I tell you, it's my greatest desire not to separate myself from anyone else on the pretext of superiority. Afterwards, when we are one, the nation, and the Maker of its destiny, will decide which customs to retain, and which ones to discard.'

'There are customs and beliefs that prevent the unity of the nation,' countered Panubabu.

'Expecting to uproot those customs and beliefs one by one before uniting the country, is like dredging the ocean before attempting to cross it,' Gora declared. 'With humility and love, banishing contempt and arrogance, surrender yourself wholeheartedly to all, and such love will easily overcome a thousand faults and shortcomings. Every country, every society, has its faults and shortcomings, but as long as the people of a nation are bound together by love for their countrymen, they can deal with the poison. The germs of decay exist in the air. As long as we stay alive, we manage to survive them, but once dead, we succumb to decay. I tell you, we shan't brook any attempts at reform, whether from you or from the missionaries!'

'Why not?' demanded Panubabu.

'There are reasons. One can tolerate reforms imposed by one's own parents, but those imposed by watchguards are humiliating rather than corrective. It is dehumanizing to tolerate such reforms. First join the family, then assume the reformer's role. Otherwise even your well-meant observations will do us harm.'

So, one by one, Sucharita's mind recalled all the things that were said. She was also inwardly tormented by some indeterminate anguish. Exhausted, she returned to bed, and pressing her palms over her eyes, she tried to sleep, pushing her thoughts away. But her face and ears were burning, and fragments of the conversation kept haunting her mind.

## 12

As they emerged from Poresh's house and stepped into the street, Binoy pleaded: 'Gora, please slow down bhai. Your legs are much longer than ours; unless you shorten your stride, we'll get exhausted trying to keep pace.'

'I want to proceed on my own,' Gora replied. 'I have many things on my mind today.' He hurried away at his usual rapid pace.

Binoy was hurt. He had broken his own rule and rebelled against Gora that day. He would have felt better if Gora had reprimanded him for it. A storm would have cleared the air, restoring their old friendship, and he would have felt relieved. There was something else that bothered him. When Gora arrived suddenly at Poresh's house for the first time and saw Binoy present there on such familiar terms, he must have concluded that Binoy was a regular visitor there. Not that there was anything wrong with being a frequent visitor there, of course. Whatever Gora might say, the opportunity of becoming intimately acquainted with Poreshbabu's well-educated family seemed to Binoy a great advantage. If Gora saw anything wrong in mingling with such people, his orthodox attitude was entirely to blame. But since he had previously heard that Binoy was not in the habit of frequenting Poreshbabu's house, Gora might suddenly assume now that this was not true. In particular, it had not eluded Gora's sharp gaze, that Borodasundari had specially invited Binoy indoors, to introduce him to her daughters. Binoy was inwardly proud and delighted at such familiarity with the girls and such intimacy with Borodasundari, but he was also privately troubled at the difference between Gora's reception in this household, and his own. Until now, nobody had hindered the deep friendship between these two classmates. Only once, Gora's enthusiasm about the Brahmo Samaj had cast a temporary shadow upon their friendship; but as I have said before, opinions did not carry much weight with Binoy. For all his arguments over opinions, people mattered more to him. Now, he was apprehensive because people threatened to come between the two of them. Binoy valued his relationship with Poresh's family because he had never before tasted such joy. But Gora's friendship was an organic part of Binoy's existence; he could not imagine life without it.

Until now, Binoy had not allowed any human being to come as close to him as Gora. Until today, he had only read books, argued with Gora, quarreled with Gora, and loved Gora, without the opportunity of paying any attention to anyone else in the world. Though he had no lack of devoted followers, Gora, too, had no other friend save Binoy. There was a solitary streak in Gora's nature. It was not beneath his dignity to mingle with ordinary people, yet he found it impossible to form close relationships with all and sundry. Most people could not help sensing a certain aloofness in him.

Binoy now realized that his heart was profoundly drawn to Poreshababu's family. Yet, he had not known them long. This made him feel guilty, as if he had wronged Gora in some way. He could clearly visualize Gora's contempt at Borodasundari's display of maternal pride to Binoy that evening, when she exhibited her daughters' English handwriting and artistry, and flaunted their prowess at recitation. There was indeed something ridiculous about it, and in a sense, something demeaning too, in Borodasundari's pride at her daughters having a smattering of English, receiving praise from an English mem, and being briefly patronized by the Lieutenant Governor's wife. But even though he understood these things, Binoy could not scorn them in accordance with Gora's ideals. He was rather enjoying the whole affair. That a girl like Labanya—there was no denying that she was quite pretty—should take pride in showing him Moore's poem inscribed in her own hand, was also quite gratifying for Binoy's own self-esteem. Not that Binoy had failed to observe the incongruity of Borodasundari's excessive attempts at being up-to-date when she had not quite acquired the right shade of modernity; but he rather liked her, all the same. The simplicity of her vanity and intolerance had disarmed him. The way these girls filled the room with the sweetness of their laughter, prepared and served tea to visitors, decorated the walls with their own handiwork and relished English poetry—however trivial these things might be, Binoy was captivated by them. Never before in his rather lonely life had Binoy savoured such pleasures. These girls, with their attire and adornments, laughter and conversation, their chores and activities, conjured up countless lovely visions in his mind's eye. Immersed only in books and intellectual debate, this boy who had entered adolescence without being aware of it, now discovered a wonderful new world in Poresh's humble abode! When Gora walked away in a huff, Binoy could not regard his anger as unwarranted. Finally, their long friendship was threatened by a real obstacle.

Clouds began to rumble, causing vibrations in the dark silence of that rainy night. Binoy's heart felt very heavy. It seemed to him that his life had taken a new turn, abandoning the course it had always followed. In this darkness, where had Gora disappeared, and where was Binoy himself going? The prospect of separation makes love more intense. Now, when it had suffered a blow, Binoy realized the magnitude and force of his love for Gora.

Back home, the darkness of the night and the solitariness of his chamber filled Binoy with a heavy feeling of emptiness. He stepped out once, ready to go to Gora's house. But he could not hope, tonight, for a meeting of hearts with Gora. So he went back indoors, and lay down wearily.

When he awakened the next day, his heart felt lighter. At night, his imagination had needlessly exaggerated his own pain. In the light of day, his friendship with Gora did not appear so directly contrary to his intimacy with Poresh's family. Binoy now wanted to laugh at the previous night's agony, dismissing it as not so grave after all!

Throwing a chador over his shoulders, he hurried to Gora's house. Gora was downstairs, reading the newspaper. He had spotted Binoy coming down the street but did not raise his eyes from the paper when his friend arrived. Without a word, Binoy snatched the paper from Gora's hands.

'I think you are making a mistake,' Gora observed. 'I am Gourmohan, a superstitious Hindu.'

'It is you who are mistaken. I am Srijukta Binoy, the superstitious friend of the aforementioned Gourmohan.'

'But Gourmohan is so obdurate, he never feels ashamed of his superstitious nature.'

'Binoy is exactly the same. But he doesn't aggressively attack others with his own convictions.'

In no time at all, the two friends were embroiled in a heated argument. The entire neighbourhood became aware that there was a confrontation between Gora and Binoy.

'Why did you deny the other day, that you were a regular visitor to Poreshbabu's house? What was the need?' Gora demanded.

'It was not from any need but because I am not a regular visitor there that I denied it. After all this while, I finally set foot in their house for the first time yesterday.'

'I suspect that like Abhimanyu, you know only the way in, but not the way out.'

'That's as it may be. Perhaps that is my inborn nature. I can't abandon someone I love or respect. You, too, have encountered this trait in my nature.'

'So, from now on your visits there will continue?'

'Why should I be their only visitor? You are mobile too; it's not as if you are a motionless object.'

'I may come and go, but judging from your symptoms, you seem committed only to going there. So, how did you relish the hot tea?'

'The brew was rather bitter.'

'So?'

'Rejecting it would have felt more bitter still.'

'Is adherence to social norms merely a matter of observing civilities then?'

'Not always. But look here, Gora, where society clashes with matters of the heart, it's difficult for me to . . .'

Impatiently, Gora cut Binoy short.

'Matters of the heart!' he roared. 'It's because you belittle society that your heart feels afflicted at every juncture. If you realized how far the pain travels when you attack the community, you'd be ashamed to mention that heart of yours. It pains you to cause the slightest offence to Poreshbabu's daughters, but it pains me that you should so casually attack the entire nation for so slight a reason.'

'Bhai Gora, let me speak the truth, then. If drinking a cup of tea wounds the entire nation, then the nation must benefit from this assault. If shielded from such a blow, the nation would be enfeebled, like an effeminate babu of the respectable class.'

'I am familiar with all those arguments, mister! Don't think me so obtuse. But these things are not new. When a sick boy refuses his medicine, his mother takes the medicine herself though she is in good health, just to signal that she shares his plight; it is not a rational argument but a show of love. Without such love, despite all the arguments in the world, the mother-son bond would suffer. Then the medicine wouldn't work either. I too wouldn't quibble about that cup of tea, but I can't bear to be alienated from the nation. Easier by far to refuse the tea, for offending

Poreshbabu's daughters is a matter of far less significance. At present, it's our primary duty to unite wholeheartedly in the nation's cause. Once such unity is achieved, all arguments about accepting or refusing tea will be settled in no time.'

'I must wait very long for my second cup of tea, it seems!' Binoy observed.

'No, you need not wait too long. But, Binoy, why continue with me? Along with many other unpleasant features of Hindu society, it's time to discard me, as well. Else, you would offend Poreshbabu's daughters.'

At this moment, Abinash entered the room. He was Gora's disciple. He would broadcast whatever he heard Gora say, demeaned by his own intellect and distorted by his own use of language. Those who could not comprehend Gora's words found it easy to understand and praise what Abinash said. Abinash was extremely jealous of Binoy. Hence, he would foolishly take every opportunity to draw Binoy into an argument. Binoy would lose patience with his idiocy. Then, Gora would take up cudgels on Abinash's behalf and fight Binoy. Abinash would imagine that Gora was acting as his mouthpiece.

Abinash's arrival interrupted Binoy's exchange with Gora on the subject of union. He rose to his feet and went upstairs. Anandamoyi was chopping vegetables on the veranda outside the larder.

'I have been hearing your voices for a long time,' she remarked. 'What brings you here so early? I hope you had a snack before you set out?'

On another occasion, Binoy would have said, 'No, I haven't eaten,' and relished being fed in Anandamoyi's presence. But today, he declared:

'No, Ma, I shan't have anything to eat. I ate before I left home.'

Today, Binoy had no urge to aggravate his guilt in Gora's eyes. He was inwardly troubled at the thought that Gora was keeping him at arm's length, unable to forgive him for socializing with Poreshababu. Taking a knife from his pocket, he busied himself peeling potatoes.

About fifteen minutes later, he went downstairs to find that Gora had left with Abinash. For a long time, Binoy lingered quietly in Gora's room. Then, picking up the newspaper, he glanced through the advertisements absently. Presently, he left with a sigh.

## 13

At noon, Binoy again felt the urge to visit Gora. He had never felt ashamed of bending to Gora's will. But even in the absence of personal pride, the pride born of friendship is hard to withstand. In yielding to Poreshbabu, Binoy had felt guilty indeed, about failing to live up to his long-term loyalty to Gora. But he had expected only that Gora would mock and reprimand him, never imagining that his friend might try to keep him at arm's length in this fashion. Having walked some distance from his house, Binoy turned back, unable to proceed to Gora's house lest his friendship be spurned.

After lunch, Binoy settled down with pen and paper to write to Gora. Needlessly cursing the pen for its bluntness, he began to sharpen it with a knife, slowly, with excessive care, when someone called out to him from downstairs. Flinging down his pen, Binoy hurried downstairs.

'Come, Mahimdada!' he cried. 'Please come upstairs!'

In the room upstairs, Mahim made himself comfortable on Binoy's bed and carefully scrutinized the furnishings.

'Look, Binoy,' he said, 'not that I don't know your house, and occasionally I do feel the urge to look you up, but I know you boys are well-behaved, in the present-day mode. There's no hope of finding any tobacco in your homes, so except for some special purpose . . .'

'If you're thinking of immediately sending for a new hookah from the market for my sake, please give up the idea,' Mahim continued, seeing Binoy rise hastily to his feet. 'I can forgive you for not offering me tobacco, but I can't tolerate tobacco inexpertly stuffed into a new hookah.' With these words, Mahim picked up a fan from the bed and began fanning himself.

'There is a reason why I have come to you, sacrificing my Sunday afternoon nap,' he observed. 'You must do me a favour.'

What was the favour, Binoy wanted to know.

'Give me your word first, then I'll tell you what it is.'

'Only if it's something within my power.'

'Only you have the power. You just have to say "yes", that is all.'

'Why beg me in this fashion? You know I'm one of the family. I can't deny you a favour that is within my means.'

Taking a leaf-wrapped package from his pocket, Mahim extracted a couple of paans which he handed to Binoy before stuffing the remaining three paans into his own mouth.

'You know my Shashimukhi, of course,' he remarked, chewing on the paan. 'She's not bad looking, meaning she hasn't taken after her father. She's almost ten now. It's time to arrange a match for her. I can't sleep nights, worrying about the rascally hands she might fall into.'

'Why worry? There's plenty of time.'

'If you had a daughter of your own, you'd understand my concern. Age advances automatically as the years pass, but prospective grooms don't automatically appear! So, as time passes, the heart grows ever more anxious. Now, if you were to give me some assurance, I could even wait for a while.'

'I don't know too many people,' Binoy responded. 'In Kolkata, I know virtually no family but yours. But still, I shall make enquiries.'

'You know all about Shashimukhi's nature and temperament.'

'Indeed I do. I have known her since childhood. She is such an angel.'

'Then why look far, my boy? I shall place the girl in your hands.'

'How can you say that!' cried Binoy, in agitation.

'Why, have I said something unfair? True, your family is much more highly placed than ours. But Binoy, what use is all your education, if you still insist on caste distinctions?'

'No, no, there's no question of caste distinctions here, but in age, she is so . . .'

'What's this you say! Shashi is hardly young! After all, a Hindu girl is not a mem. One can't afford to ignore the community, can one?'

Mahim was not one to give up easily. He pestered Binoy beyond endurance.

'Please give me some time to think!' Binoy begged, finally.

'I'm not about to fix the wedding date tonight, am I!'

'Still, consulting family members . . .'

'Indeed, that is a must. We must seek their consent, for sure. With your khuromoshai still alive, nothing can be decided against the wishes of your father's elder brother.'

Emptying the contents of the second sachet of paan from his pocket, Mahim took his leave, his manner indicating that the matter was all but clinched.

A few days earlier, Anandamoyi had indirectly hinted at a match between Shashimukhi and Binoy. But Binoy had paid no attention. Even now, it was not as if the proposal struck him as apposite, but at least the matter registered somewhere in his consciousness. Binoy felt that if this marriage were to take place, Gora could never spurn him for relying too much on matters of the heart. So far, he had always derided the idea of a love-marriage as an anglicized fetish, hence marrying Shashimukhi did not seem an impossible prospect. Meanwhile, he was pleased only that he now had a pretext to consult Gora regarding Mahim's proposal. Binoy desired some persuasion from Gora. If he did not readily consent to Mahim's proposal, he had no doubt that Mahim would try to get Gora to convince him. Thinking of these things, Binoy's lethargy evaporated. He set out at once for Gora's house, with his chador draped over his shoulder. He had walked only a short distance before he heard someone call out from behind:

'Binoybabu!' Turning around, he saw Satish. Binoy re-entered his house, accompanied by Satish

'Guess what's inside!' From his pocket, Satish produced a handkerchief knotted into a bundle.

Naming several impossible things, such as a skull or a puppy, Binoy was admonished by Satish's wagging finger. Satish then proceeded to undo the handkerchief, from which he produced four or five blackened fruits.

'Do you know what these are?' he asked.

Binoy attempted some random guesses. When he finally gave up, Satish told him that the fruits were a gift from an uncle in Rangoon to his mother, who in turn had sent five of them as a present for Binoybabu.

Mangosteens from Myanmar were not easily available in Kolkata then. Hence, feeling the fruits, Binoy asked:

'Satishbabu, how are these to be eaten?'

'Watch out! You'd better not bite into them,' laughed Satish, scornful of Binoy's ignorance. 'You're supposed to pare them with a knife.'

Satish himself had just been derided by his relatives for his futile attempts at biting into these fruits. So, he dispelled his agony by laughing knowledgably at Binoy's lack of experience. Subsequently, after these two friends of unequal age had exchanged some banter, Satish declared:

'Binoybabu, Ma says you must drop by if you have the time today—it's Leela's birthday!'

'I have no time today, bhai. I'm going elsewhere.'

'Where?'

'To my friend's place.'

'That friend of yours?'

'Yes.'

That Binoy could visit other friends' houses but not their own seemed irrational to Satish, who had taken a particular dislike to this friend of Binoy's. He seemed harsher than a school headmaster; nobody was likely to earn any glory from playing the organ to him. That Binoy should feel the slightest need to visit such people was not to Satish's liking, at all.

'No, Binoybabu, you must come to our house,' he insisted.

Binoy had boasted to himself that he would go to Gora's house even if Poreshbabu invited him. He had decided that he would not hurt his friend's sentiments, that he would respect his friendship with Gora above all else. But it did not take him long to succumb. With a mind full of doubts and a heart full of objections, he ultimately allowed the boy to lead him by the hand towards House Number 78, as before. It was impossible for Binoy to ignore the sense of kinship expressed in the sharing of rare Myanmar fruits thoughtfully sent to him.

Approaching Poreshbabu's house, Binoy saw Panubabu emerge from within, accompanied by some unknown people. They had been invited to Leela's birthday lunch. Panubabu walked past Binoy, as if he had not noticed him at all. Entering the house, Binoy was greeted with sounds of laughter and running feet. Sudhir had stolen Labanya's keys; not only that, he was threatening devilishly to divulge to the vulgar world the comic details of the would-be-poetess' writings in the notebook within her drawer. The two sides were locked in battle when Binoy entered the arena. Seeing him, Labanya's group vanished at once. Satish ran after them, to take part in their merriment.

After a while, Sucharita came in. 'Ma has requested you to wait awhile,' she said. 'She'll join you in a few moments. Baba has gone to Anathbabu's; he won't be long, either.'

To quell Binoy's awkwardness, Sucharita spoke of Gora. 'I don't suppose he'd ever visit us again!' she smiled.

'Why not?'

'He must have been surprised that we appear before male company. He probably can't respect women if he sees them in any situation but a domestic one.'

Binoy found this hard to refute. He would have liked to contradict it, but how could he lie?

'It is Gora's belief that unless completely absorbed in housework, women lose their devotion to duty,' he replied.

'Then why not let men and women carve up the world into private and public spaces, once and for all?' demanded Sucharita. 'Perhaps it's because men have access into private areas that they fail in their public duties? Do you also subscribe to your friend's views?'

So far, Binoy had indeed supported Gora's views regarding rules for women. He had even published newspaper articles on the subject. But now, he found it hard to declare these views his own.

'In these matters, we are slaves of custom,' he insisted. 'That's why the sight of women venturing out in public makes us uneasy. We merely try to prove by forceful argument that it offends us as something improper, a violation of duty. The argument here is merely a pretext; it's the convention that is real.'

'Such conventions seem firmly ingrained in your friend's mind,' Sucharita observed.

'So it may seem momentarily, if viewed from outside,' Binoy replied. 'But please bear in mind that if he clings to the traditions of our country, it's not because he thinks them the best. It's because we were ready to dismiss all our land's customs out of a blind disrespect for our country, that he has taken it upon himself to stem the tide. He says we must first possess and understand our nation as a whole, through respect and love. Subsequently, the process of reform will begin automatically from within, according to the natural rules of health.'

'If it was automatic, why didn't it happen in all these years?' Sucharita asked.

'It didn't happen because until now, we were unable to perceive our nation or our community as a unified whole. We may not have disrespected our own race then, but we showed them no respect either. In other words, we ignored them, hence their power was not aroused. The patient was neglected once, denied any treatment or medication. Now, he has been taken to the hospital indeed, but apart from amputating his limbs one by one, the doctor is too disdainful to patiently prescribe a long-term course of treatment based on nursing. Now another doctor, this friend of mine, insists: 'I cannot bear to allow my close relative to be utterly destroyed by such treatment. I shall stop these surgical procedures, and by means of a suitably wholesome diet, arouse the life-spirit within the patient's soul. Subsequently, the patient will be able to withstand surgery, or even recover without such procedures.' According to Gora, profound respect is the most potent diet for our nation's present predicament. It is lack of such respect that prevents us from a unified vision of our country, and it is due to lack of such awareness that all our attempts at redressal prove counterproductive. Without loving our nation, we can't have the patience to understand it properly. And without understanding it properly, we cannot benefit the country, despite all our good intentions.'

Unobtrusively, with her probing comments, Sucharita ensured that the discussion about Gora continued. Binoy also presented his defense of Gora in the best manner possible. He had never argued so cogently and with such vivid examples; it is doubtful whether Gora himself could have declared his own views with such clarity and brilliance. Exhilarated by his own cleverness and powers of expression, Binoy began to enjoy himself, and his face glowed with pleasure.

'*Atmanam biddhi*: know thyself, the scriptures say,' he argued. 'There is no other path to liberation. My friend Gora is Bharatvarsha's self-awareness incarnate, I tell you. I cannot take him for an ordinary man. While all our minds are scattered in the external realm, seduced by the petty lure of novelty, this man alone stands firm amidst all this frenzy, chanting in his leonine voice that same ancient mantra: *atmanam biddhi*.'

This discussion could have lasted much longer, and Sucharita too, was listening avidly, but suddenly, from the adjacent room, Satish began to recite in a loud voice:

*Say not in sorrow, without pausing to reflect,*
*That the world's an illusion, and life but a dream.*

Poor Satish never got to display his learning before visitors to the house. Even Leela could arouse the audience with her recitation of English verse, but Borodasundari never sent for Satish. Yet Leela and Satish were great rivals in every matter. It was Satish's foremost pleasure to somehow demolish Leela's pride. The previous day, Leela's talents had been tested in Binoy's presence. Uninvited there, Satish could have made no attempt to outshine her. Even if he had tried, Borodasundari would have quelled him immediately. Today, therefore, he made a show of reciting loudly from the next room, as if to himself. Hearing him, Sucharita could not refrain from mirth.

At this point, Leela came in, tossing her braids. Throwing her arms around Sucharita's neck, she whispered something in her ear. Satish rushed in, close on her heels.

'Tell me, Leela, what does "monojog" mean?' he asked her, referring to the Bengali word for 'attentiveness'.

'I shan't tell you!' Leela replied.

'Ish! Not tell me indeed! Admit you don't know what it means!'

'You tell us what "monojog" means, then,' laughed Binoy, drawing Satish close.

'"Monojog" means "mononibesh,"' answered Satish proudly, head held high.

'And what is "mononibesh?"' Sucharita wanted to know.

Could anyone but a family member cause such embarrassment? Satish bounded out of the room as if he had not heard the question at all.

Today, Binoy had firmly resolved to leave early from Poreshbabu's house to go across to Gora's. Talking about Gora deepened his enthusiasm about visiting him. Hearing the clock strike four, he therefore rose quickly from his chowki.

'Must you leave now?' pleaded Sucharita. 'Ma is preparing some snacks for you. Can't you go a little later?'

For Binoy this was not a question but an order. He at once resumed his place on the chowki.

'Didi, the snacks are ready,' announced Labanya, entering the room, all dressed up, in colourful silk. 'Ma wants us to go up to the terrace.'

On the terrace, Binoy had to accept the refreshments. Borodasundari began to recount the life-stories of all her offspring. Lalita dragged Sucharita indoors. On a chowki, Labanya bent her head over a piece of knitting. Somebody had once told her that when she knitted, the play of her delicate fingers was an exquisite sight; ever since, she had grown used to knitting unnecessarily in the presence of others.

Poresh arrived. It grew dark. As this was Sunday, they were supposed to go to the prayer-temple.

'Would you object to visiting the Samaj in our company?' Borodasundari asked Binoy.

After this, there could be no ifs and buts. They went to the prayer hall, all of them, in two carriages. On the way back, as they mounted the carriages, Sucharita suddenly remarked, in a startled voice:

'Look, there goes Gourmohanbabu!'

There was no doubting that Gora had spotted their group. But he hastened away as if he had not seen them at all. Gora's arrogant uncivility made Binoy cringe in shame before Poreshbabu's family. But privately, he clearly realized that it was the sight of Binoy in the group that had prompted Gora to rush away in such a hostile manner. The glow of pleasure in his heart was utterly extinguished. Sucharita instantly sensed Binoy's mood and its cause. She was again incensed at Gora for misjudging a friend like Binoy, and his unwarranted disrespect for Brahmos. She wished with all her heart that Gora could somehow be vanquished.

## 14

When Gora sat down to his meal at midday, Anandamoyi gently broached the subject:

'Binoy came by this morning. Didn't you meet him?'

'Yes, I did,' answered Gora, without looking up.

'I asked him to wait but he left, looking rather preoccupied,' resumed Anandamoyi, after a long pause.

Gora made no reply.

'Something has hurt him very deeply,' Anandamoyi asserted. 'I've never seen him like this before. I am extremely upset.'

Gora continued to eat in silence. Because she was so fond of him, Anandamoyi was also secretly a little in awe of him. If he did not confide in her, she never pestered him about anything. On any other occasion, she would have desisted at this point. But now, because her heart was aching for Binoy, she persisted:

'Look Gora, let me tell you something. Please don't mind. Ishwar has created innumerable human beings, but he has not made just one path for everyone to follow. Because Binoy loves you with his heart and soul, he tolerates whatever you inflict on him. But if you insist that he must follow your path alone, it will not bode well.'

'Ma, please bring me some more milk,' was Gora's reply.

The conversation ended there. Meal over, Anandamoyi sewed in silence on her bed. After a futile attempt to draw her into a discussion of a particular servant's bad conduct, Lachhmia lay down on the floor and went to sleep.

Gora spent a long time over his correspondence. Amidst all his work, Gora listened for Binoy's footsteps, thinking it impossible that his friend would fail to come and pacify him, after having received a clear signal that morning that Gora was angry with him. The hours passed by, but Binoy did not come. Laying down his pen, Gora was about to rise from his desk when Mahim entered the room.

'What are your thoughts on Shashimukhi's marriage, Gora?' he asked as soon as he was seated.

Never having given the matter a single thought, Gora was forced to maintain a guilty silence. Highlighting the exorbitant price of bridegrooms in the marriage market and his own insolvency, Mahim begged Gora for a solution. When Gora failed to come up with a suggestion, Mahim sought to rescue him from his dilemma by proposing Binoy's name. Such a roundabout approach was not necessary, but whatever he might say, Mahim was privately afraid of Gora. Gora had never dreamt that Binoy's name could be mentioned in such a context. He and Binoy had resolved to remain bachelors, devoting their lives to the service of the nation.

'Why should Binoy marry?' Gora therefore expostulated.

'Is this what your Hindu beliefs are worth! For all your tikis and tilaks, your English ways are ingrained in your very bones. Are you aware that our holy shastras define marriage as an essential ritual for a Brahman boy?'

Mahim neither violated traditional customs like modern youths of today, nor cared much for the scriptures either. He considered dining in hotels to be excessively bold, but he also did not consider it normal to constantly dabble in the shastras like Gora. But one must adopt the customs of the land one's in, as the saying goes. With Gora, he was forced to use the shastras as a pretext.

Even a couple of days earlier, Gora would have dismissed this proposal out of hand. But today, the matter did not strike him as utterly dispensable. The proposal at least provided an excuse for going immediately to Binoy's house.

'Very well, let me find out what Binoy feels about this,' he agreed ultimately.

'There is nothing to find out. He can never reject a suggestion from you. The matter is virtually settled. A word from you is all that's needed.'

That very evening, though it was late, Gora arrived at Binoy's house. Storming into his friend's room, he found it empty. He summoned the bearer, who informed him that Babu had gone to House Number 78. Gora's spirits drooped. Binoy, for whom Gora had fretted all day, now did not even have the time to remember his friend! Gora might fret and fume, but it would not disturb Binoy's peace of mind at all!

Gora's soul rose in bitterness against Poreshbabu's family and the Brahmo Samaj. He rushed to Poreshbabu's house, a tremendous rebellion surging in his heart. He wanted to raise issues that would torment this Brahmo family, and make Binoy uncomfortable as well. Reaching Poreshbabu's place, he was told that no one was home. They had all gone to the prayer hall. For a moment, he doubted that Binoy may have accompanied them. Perhaps, at this very moment, he had gone to Gora's house.

He could not restrain himself. Gora rushed to the prayer-temple at his usual stormy speed. At the entrance, he saw Binoy following Borodasundari into their carriage. In public, he was shamelessly entering a carriage in the company of women from another family! Fool that he was! To let himself be ensnared like this, in serpent-coils! So quickly! So easily! Friendship was no longer worthy of respect, then. Gora rushed away from the scene. And from the darkness of the carriage, Binoy gazed silently at the street.

Imagining that the Acharya's advice was taking effect on his mind, Borodasundari did not utter a word.

## 15

Back home, Gora paced up and down the terrace at night. He was angry with himself. Why had he wasted his Sunday in this fashion? He was not born into this world to get embroiled in one person's love affairs at the expense of all his other duties! To try holding Binoy back from the path he had taken would be a waste of time, and a painful experience as well. So, from now on, he must exclude Binoy from his life. Giving up his only friend, Gora would prove his faith true. With this resolve, Gora gestured violently with his arms, as if pushing away his association with Binoy.

At this moment, Mahim appeared on the terrace, panting.

'Why build a three-storey house when humans don't have wings?' he protested. 'The gods in the heavens don't like it if human beings, creatures of the soil, attempt to inhabit the sky. Did you see Binoy?'

'Binoy cannot marry Shashimukhi,' declared Gora, avoiding a direct reply.

'Why? Is Binoy unwilling?'

'I am unwilling.'

'How extraordinary!' exclaimed Mahim, spreading his hands. 'Here's a new twist, I see! So you are unwilling! May I know why?'

'I see clearly that it will be hard to keep Binoy within our community. We can't let him marry one of our girls.'

'I've seen a lot of Hindu fanaticism but nothing to match this. You surpass even the Hindus of Kashi and Bhatpara! Your rulings are based on future predictions, I find. One of these days, you will prescribe swallowing cowdung to restore my caste purity, just because you've dreamt of my conversion to Christianity!'

After much ranting, Mahim said: 'I can't marry the girl to an illiterate, after all! An educated, intelligent young man is bound to circumvent the shastras sometimes. Argue with him, curse him if you like, but why punish my daughter by preventing his marriage? All your ideas are totally perverse!'

'Ma, please restrain this Gora of yours!' Mahim went downstairs and begged Anandamoyi.

'Why, what's the matter?' asked Anandamoyi anxiously.

'I had almost fixed a match between Shashimukhi and Binoy. I had even got Gora to agree to it. But meanwhile, Gora has understood clearly that Binoy is not Hindu enough, because he deviates occasionally from the views of Manu and Parashar. So Gora has dug his heels in, and you know what he's like when he chooses to be obdurate. In today's depraved world, this Kaliyug of ours, if Janak were to decree that he would offer Sita's hand only to a suitor who could make Gora unbend, I can wager that Shri Rama would have failed. After Manu-Parashar, you are the person Gora respects the most. Now, if you find a way, my girl's future will be assured. Search as we might, another such suitor is not to be found.'

Mahim proceeded to recount all that had passed between him and Gora on the terrace. Sensing the developing hostility between Binoy and Gora, Anandamoyi was distressed. Going upstairs, she found that Gora, having stopped pacing the terrace, was reading on one chowki, his feet propped up on another. Anandamoyi drew up a chowki close to him. Lowering his feet, Gora sat upright and glanced at her face.

'Gora, my boy, you must keep a request of mine,' Anandamoyi pleaded. 'Don't quarrel with Binoy. To me, you two are like brothers. I can't bear the prospect of a split.'

'If a friend wants to sever our ties, I can't waste my time running after him.'

'Baba, I don't know what has occurred between you two. But if you can believe that Binoy wants to sever his ties with you, then what's your friendship worth?'

'Ma, I prefer to be direct. I can't hold with those who equivocate. If it's in a person's nature to have one foot in each boat, he must step off the boat that is mine, even if it hurts me or the person concerned.'

'Tell me what the matter is,' Anandamoyi insisted. 'His only crime is having visited a Brahmo home occasionally, isn't it?'

'It's a long story, Ma.'

'So what? Let me tell you Gora, you are so obstinate in all matters, that no one can divert you from your chosen course. But why are you so detached only where Binoy is concerned? If your Abinash wanted to leave your group, would you let him go so easily? Is it because Binoy is your friend that he means least of all to you?'

Gora lapsed into a thoughtful silence. Anandamoyi's words made him clearly understand his own feelings. He had imagined all this while that he was ready to sacrifice his friendship for duty's sake, but now he realized it was quite the contrary. It was because his pride as a friend had been wounded that he was about to inflict on Binoy the ultimate punishment possible in a friendship. He had assumed that friendship alone would keep Binoy bound to him; any other method would be an insult to their mutual affection.

As soon as Anandamoyi sensed that her words had had some effect on Gora, she gently prepared to rise, without saying more. Gora too, jumped to his feet suddenly, and taking his chador from the alna, he flung it across his shoulder.

'Where are you going, Gora?' Anandamoyi inquired.

'To Binoy's.'

'Your meal is ready. Please dine before you set out.'

'I'll go get Binoy. He'll dine with us too.'

Anandamoyi went downstairs, without saying more. Hearing footsteps on the stairs, she stopped suddenly.

'Here comes Binoy!' she exclaimed.

As she spoke, Binoy arrived on the scene. Anandamoyi's eyes grew moist.

'Binoy, baba, haven't you dined yet?' she asked, patting him tenderly.

'No, Ma.'

'You must dine with us,' Anandamoyi insisted.

Binoy glanced at Gora.

'You'll have a long life, Binoy,' Gora remarked. 'I was just going to your place.'

Anandamoyi's felt light-hearted with relief. She hurried downstairs.

Once the two friends had moved indoors, Gora made a random remark:

'Do you know, I've found a good gymnastics coach for our boys. He's training them quite well.'

Neither of them dared raise the subject closest to their hearts. At dinner, Anandamoyi sensed from their conversation that the veil of constraint had not yet been lifted.

'It's very late, Binoy,' she observed. 'Sleep here tonight. I'll send word to your house.'

'*Bhuktwa rajabadacharet*,' quoted Binoy in Sanskrit, after darting a swift glance at Gora's countenance. 'One should not walk the streets after a meal. So one may as well sleep here tonight.'

After dinner, the two friends went to the terrace and settled on a madur. It was the month of Bhadra; moonlight flooded the sky, for it was the bright quarter of the lunar cycle. Flimsy white clouds floated gently across the sky, blurring the moon occasionally, like short spells of drowsiness. Rows of rooftops of varying shapes and sizes stretched to the horizon in every direction, their outlines sometimes merging with the treetops in the play of light and shade, the scene resembling a vast, needless fantasy. The church clock struck eleven; the ice-seller called out his wares for the last time, and departed. The hum of traffic had dwindled. In Gora's street, there was no sign of wakefulness. There was only the occasional sound of horse hooves on the wooden floor of the neighbour's stable, or every now and then, the barking of dogs.

Both of them were silent for a long time. Then Binoy, after some initial hesitation, ultimately poured out his inner feelings, in full force, without restraint.

'Bhai Gora, my heart is full to bursting. I know you have no taste for such things, but I'll die if I don't unburden myself. I can't tell good from evil anymore, but one thing is certain: no clever strategy will work here. I have read many things in books, and assumed, all these days, that I know everything: like looking at a painting of water and assuming that swimming would be easy, only to discover, once in the water, that staying afloat is no easy feat!'

So Binoy tried fervently to explain this extraordinary insight to Gora. Nowadays, he said, his days and night were too full to allow any space—as if there was no chink in the sky, it was so utterly dense—like a beehive in spring, full to bursting with honey. Formerly, much of the universe had been left out of his life, his gaze fixed only on the small part of it that met his needs. Today, he saw the entire universe, was touched by everything in it, and found everything imbued with a new meaning. He had not realized he loved the world so much, that the sky was so extraordinary, the light so exquisite, even the movement of unknown pedestrians on the street so intensely real. He longed to be of some service to all, to offer all his energy to the world forever, like the sun in the sky.

It was not immediately apparent that Binoy was saying all this with reference to any particular person. He could not bring anyone's name to his lips, embarrassed even to offer a hint, as if he had wronged someone even in discussing such things. It was wrong of him, and an insult, but tonight, by his friend's side, in the solitary darkness, under the silent sky, he found it impossible to avoid this guilty act.

What a face! How exquisitely her spirit glowed on her tender cheeks! How extraordinary her inner radiance that shone forth in her smile! What an intellectual brow! And what deep, unfathomable mysteries lurked in those eyes, beneath the shadow of those dense lashes. And those hands, so eloquently expressive, ready to fulfil with grace the promise of devotion and love! Binoy's heart seemed to swell with the joy of knowing that his life, his youth, were indeed worthwhile. That Binoy should see incarnate the vision that most people would die without ever beholding—what could be more amazing?

But what madness was this? How wrong of him! But, wrong or not, it could be checked no longer. If this tide should wash him up on some shore, all the better; and if it should sweep him away and drown him, there was no preventing it. The problem was, he did not even want to be rescued. As if being carried away, surrendering all long-cherished beliefs, all stability, was life's true fulfilment!

Gora listened in silence. Upon this terrace, on such solitary, drowsy moonlit nights, they had exchanged many thoughts on many other occasions: so many thoughts on literature, human nature, social good, the future course of their lives, so many resolves the two of them had made together. But never had they spoken of such things. Gora had never before been confronted with such truths about the human heart, expressed so cogently, in such a manner. All along, he had dismissed such things as romantic claptrap. But today, he saw them so closely that he could no longer disavow them. Not only that, these emotions jolted his heart, with a thrill that streaked like lightning through his body. Momentarily, the veil was lifted, as in a breeze, from an unseen part of his youth, and the Sharat moonlight entered that long-sealed chamber, suffusing it with magic.

The moon went down, beneath the line of rooftops. From the east came the faintest hint of light, like the smile on a face in sleep. At last, Binoy's heart felt light, and a certain embarrassment crept in.

'All my words must seem very petty to you,' he observed, after a short silence. 'In your heart you probably feel contempt for me. But tell me, what else can I do? I have never concealed anything from you. Today too, I have concealed nothing, whether you understand me or not.'

'Binoy, I can't say I understand these things correctly,' Gora said. 'Just a couple of days ago, you wouldn't have understood them, either. Nor can I deny that, until now, I have found such worldly obsessions to be extremely trivial. But that may not mean they are actually insignificant. They have struck me as insubstantial illusions because I have had no direct experience of their force and intensity. But how can I say this major insight of yours is false? The fact is, a man cannot function unless he belittles all things outside his own field of action as trivial. That is why Ishwar has made distant things appear small to the human eye, instead of placing man in grave trouble by presenting all truths in an equal light. We must choose a particular direction, relinquishing our desire to cling to everything at once, or else we shall never grasp the truth. I cannot transfer myself to your position to salute the image of truth that you have beheld, for that would mean losing what's true for my life. It's either one or the other.'

'Either Binoy, or Gora. I am ready for self-fulfilment, while you prepare for self-sacrifice.'

'Binoy, stop trying to compose a book with your pronouncements,' protested Gora, impatiently. 'I see clearly from your words that you are today confronted with a powerful reality which you cannot evade. Once you recognize a truth, you must surrender to it; there is no holding back. It is my desire that one day, I, too, shall similarly attain the truth of my chosen field. So far, you were satisfied with knowledge of love gleaned from books. I, too, know patriotism only from books. Now that love has revealed itself to you, you have instantly realized how much truer it is than book-learning. It has taken over your whole universe, and you can find no respite from it anywhere. The day patriotism confronts me similarly in its entirety, there will be no saving me either. It will effortlessly draw to itself my life and wealth, my blood, marrow and bones, my sky, and all my light. Listening to your words, I get an inkling of how wonderfully exquisite, how manifestly well-defined is the true image of our own nation swadesh, how tremendously powerful are its joys and sorrows, engulfing life and death in an instant, like a flood. Your experience affects my life, today. I don't know if I'll ever understand what you have found, but through you, I seem to have a foretaste of what I myself wish to achieve.'

As he spoke, Gora rose from the mat and began pacing about on the terrace. The glow of dawn in the east appeared to him like a statement or a message, like a mantra from the Vedas chanted in some ancient meditation-grove. His hair stood on end. For an instant, he stood transfixed, and from his crown, a ray of light seemed to rise like a fine stem, blossoming into a thousand-petalled lotus that filled the whole sky. His entire spirit, consciousness and strength seemed to extinguish themselves in surrendering to this supreme bliss.

'Binoy,' Gora suddenly exclaimed when he was himself again, 'you must transcend this love of yours as well. You can't stop there, I tell you. One day, I shall demonstrate to you how immensely real is the great power that summons me. My heart is overjoyed today. Now I cannot relinquish you to anyone else.'

Rising from the madur on the floor, Binoy came and stood close to Gora, who embraced him with both arms in extraordinary enthusiasm. 'Bhai,' he said, 'if we die, we die together. We two are one. Nobody can separate us, or come between us.'

The force of Gora's passionate enthusiasm rocked Binoy's heart as well. Wordlessly, he surrendered to Gora's magnetism. Side by side they roamed the terrace together, in silence. A rosy hue appeared in the eastern sky.

'Bhai,' said Gora, 'I see my devi, the female deity I worship, not in a beautiful setting, but where there is famine and poverty, pain and humiliation. There, one does not worship with music and flowers but with one's life and blood. To me, that seems the greatest joy. There, no pleasure exists to delude you; by one's own strength, one must awaken fully and give oneself completely. This is no sweetness but an invincible, unbearable manifestation, cruel and terrible. It has a harsh resonance that strikes all seven notes at once, causing the strings of the instrument to snap. The thought of it thrills me. This indeed, is the joy of manhood, I think—the tandava-dance of destruction. It is to see the exquisite image of the new appear above the violent sacrificial flames of the old, that men must strive. In the blood-red sky, I see a free, radiant future—I see it in today's impending dawn. See how my heart vibrates to the rhythm of some unknown tabor!'

As he spoke, Gora pressed Binoy's hand to his heart.

'Bhai Gora, I'm with you,' declared Binoy. 'But never let me hesitate, I tell you. Draw me in your wake, relentless as destiny itself. We are destined for the same path, but the two of us are not equal in strength, after all!'

'Our natures differ, but an immense bliss will merge our disparate temperaments,' Gora asserted. 'A love even greater than our mutual affection will unite us. Until that love materializes, there will be many clashes between us at every step, many conflicts and separations. Then, one day, forgetting everything, our differences and even our friendship, we shall be able to stand together, united in unshakable strength, in a great, magnificent act of self-surrender. That terrible bliss will be our friendship's final outcome.'

'Let it be so!' cried Binoy, grasping Gora's hand.

'But until then, I shall trouble you a lot,' warned Gora. 'You must put up with all the torment, for we can't regard friendship as life's ultimate goal, nor dishonour our friendship by trying to keep it alive at any cost. It can't be helped if our friendship collapses as a result; but should it survive, it will indeed be worthwhile.'

Sudden footsteps startled them. Turning, they saw that Anandamoyi had come up to the terrace.

'Come, it's time to sleep now,' she insisted, dragging them by the hand towards the room.

'We can't sleep now, Ma!' both of them protested.

'You can!' declared Anandamoyi. She forced the two friends to lie in bed side by side, and shutting the door, she sat close to their headstead and began to fan them.

'Ma, we can't sleep if you start fanning us,' Binoy objected.

'We'll see about that,' she said. 'The moment I leave, the two of you will start talking again. We shan't allow it.'

When they had fallen asleep, Anandmoyi tiptoed out of the room. As she descended the stairs, she saw Mahim on his way up.

'Not now,' she told him. 'They didn't sleep at all last night. I have just put them to bed.'

'My goodness, that's called true friendship indeed,' responded Mahim. 'Do you know if they spoke of marriage?'

'I don't know.'

'Perhaps something has been decided. When will they wake up? If the wedding doesn't take place soon, there will be many problems.'

'No problems will arise from their falling asleep,' laughed Anandamoyi. 'They are bound to wake up in the course of the day!'

## 16

'Aren't you going to get Sucharita married?' Borodasundari demanded.

'Where is a groom to be found?' asked Poreshbabu gently, after stroking his beard in his usual quiet, grave manner.

'Why, her marriage to Panubabu is more or less fixed,' replied Borodasundari. 'At least, so we privately assume. Sucharita knows it, too.'

'I don't think Radharani quite fancies Panubabu.'

'Look, I don't like such ideas. I don't distinguish between Sucharita and my own daughters, but we must admit there's nothing very extraordinary about her either! If a learned, devout man like Panubabu fancies her, is that to be taken lightly? Say what you will, my Labanya is much prettier, but I assure you she'll marry the man we choose. She will never say 'no.' If you encourage Sucharita's arrogance, it will be hard to find a match for her.'

Poresh said no more. He never argued with Borodasundari. Especially about Sucharita.

Sucharita was seven when her mother died at Satish's birth. Her father, Ramsharan Haldar, joined the Brahmo Samaj after his wife's demise. Hounded by his neighbours, he left his village and sought refuge in Dhaka. While deployed at the Post Office there, he developed a close friendship with Poresh. Since then, Sucharita had regarded Poresh as a father-figure. Ramsharan had died suddenly. Having bequeathed his savings in equal shares to his son and daughter, he had appointed Poreshbabu executor of his will. Since that time, Satish and Sucharita had become part of Poresh's family.

Borodasundari did not like it if relatives or outsiders showed Sucharita any special affection or attention. Yet Sucharita somehow won everybody's liking and respect. Borodasundari's daughters would fight like rivals for her affection. In particular, the second daughter Lalita seemed to cling to Sucharita day and night, with a jealous, possessive love. Borodasundari desired that her daughters should surpass all the learned women of their time in their reputation for educational prowess. It did not please her that Sucharita, raised along with her own daughters, should equal them in these things. Hence, Sucharita encountered all sorts of obstacles when it was time for school.

Sensing the reason for all these obstacles, Poresh withdrew Sucharita from school and began to tutor her personally at home. Not only that, Sucharita came to be a special companion to him. He discussed many subjects with her, taking her with him wherever he went. When he was forced to be away, he elaborated on many issues in his letters to her. In this way, Sucharita's mind matured far beyond her age and status. Her demeanour developed a gravity that made it impossible for anyone to think of her as a little girl, and though close to her in age, Labanya regarded Sucharita as her senior in every respect. In fact, even Borodasundari could not treat her lightly, even if she wished.

Readers have already realized that Haranbabu was a very enthusiastic Brahmo. As night-school teacher, newspaper editor and secretary of the girls' school, he had a hand in every Brahmo activity. He was utterly indefatigable. Everyone hoped that this young man would one day occupy a very high position in the Brahmo Samaj. Especially concerning his command of English and his philosophical expertise, his fame had spread beyond the Brahmo Samaj through the university student network.

Hence, like all other Brahmos Sucharita too had a very high regard for Haranbabu. When they arrived in Kolkata from Dhaka, she had also been very eager to make Haranbabu's acquaintance. Ultimately, she was not only introduced to the famous Haranbabu, but within a few days, he did not hesitate to express his attraction for Sucharita. Not that he had directly declared his love to her; but he concentrated so intensely on compensating for all her shortcomings, amending her errors, encouraging her interests and improving her personality, that it became obvious to everyone that he wanted to make this girl a suitable companion for himself.

This destroyed Borodasundari's former respect for him, and she tried to dismiss him as a mere schoolmaster. And Sucharita, sensing that she had won the famous Haranbabu's heart, secretly developed towards him a feeling of devotion mixed with triumph.

Although no proposal had been made by the dominant party, when everyone assumed the certainty of Sucharita's marriage to Haranbabu, she too had mentally consented to the match. She had become especially anxious to determine how, through education and endeavour, she could also become worthy of the Brahmo Samaj's benevolent activities, to which Haranbabu had dedicated his life. In her heart, she could not feel that she was marrying a human being; she seemed to be preparing herself to be wedded to the great beneficence of the Brahmo community—a beneficence made highly erudite from extensive book-learning, and excessively profound in its command of philosophy. In her imagination, this marriage appeared like a stone fortress built of fear, deference and overwhelming responsibility—not just a place to live in comfortably but a site for struggle, a space not domestic but historic.

If the wedding had taken place at this stage, the bride's party at least, would have considered it a blessing. But so important to Haranbabu were the responsibilities of his self-created vocation that he considered it unworthy of himself to marry merely on account of a personal attraction. He could not proceed without calculating exactly how much the Brahmo Samaj would benefit from this marriage. Hence, he began to test Sucharita from this perspective. To test others in this way is to submit oneself to similar trials as well. Haranbabu became a familiar visitor to Poreshbabu's house. Here, too, he came to be known as Panubabu, from his family nickname. It was no longer possible to regard him simply as a storehouse of English learning, a source of philosophy and an incarnation of Brahmo altruism. It was primarily as a human being that everyone regarded him. Now, instead of commanding respect and deference alone, he became subject to the likes and dislikes of others.

Strangely, Haranbabu's manner, which had formerly attracted Sucharita's devotion from afar, now began to offend her, when seen up close. As the guardian of all that was true, good and beautiful about the Brahmo Samaj, Haranbabu, in assuming the caretaker's role, seemed incongruously reduced in stature. Man's real relationship with truth is based on devotion: it makes man naturally humble. Where man becomes arrogant and proud instead, his pettiness becomes readily apparent in comparison with that truth. Here Sucharita could not refrain from privately analysing the contrast between Poreshbabu and Haran. Poreshbabu's head seemed always bowed in humility before all that he had received from the Brahmo Samaj. There was no trace of arrogance here; he had immersed his life in those profound depths. Poreshbabu's tranquil face revealed the greatness of the truth that he bore in his heart. But Haranbabu was not the same. His aggressive self-projection as a Brahmo manifested itself in an ugly way, in all he said and did, obscuring all else. This had raised his prestige within the organization; but Sucharita, unable to confine herself to the narrowness of community loyalties, thanks to Poresh's tutelage, found Haranbabu's extreme Brahmoism an assault upon her natural humility. Haranbabu believed that his spiritual pursuits had given him such clarity of vision that he could easily assess people's levels of morality and honesty. Hence, he was always judgemental about everyone else. Worldly folk are also given to criticism and gossip; but those who indulge in these things in religion's name combine a spiritual arrogance with this critical attitude, generating great trouble in the world. Sucharita could not stand this. Not that she took no pride in the Brahmo community; nevertheless, she had grave reservations about Haranbabu's notion that eminent members of the Brahmo Samaj had attained their distinctive status only through the special power of being Brahmo, while morally depraved persons outside the Brahmo Samaj had lost their integrity through the special weakness of not being Brahmo.

For the benefit of the Brahmo Samaj, Haranbabu would not spare even Poreshbabu, judging and condemning him. On such occasions, Sucharita would react instantly with the ferocious intolerance of a wounded female serpent. The Bhagavad Gita was not a subject of discussion among Bengalis educated in English in those days. But Poreshbabu would sometimes read the Gita to Sucharita. He had also read most of Kalisingha's Mahabharata to her. This had displeased Haranbabu. He was in favour of banishing such texts from Brahmo families. He himself had not read these texts. He wanted to segregate the Ramayana–Mahabharata–Bhagavad Gita as Hindu property. The Bible was the only religious text to which he had recourse. It troubled Haranbabu like a thorn in the flesh that Poreshbabu, in studying the scriptures and in other small matters, did not observe the boundaries between Brahmo and non-Brahmo. Sucharita could never tolerate the possibility that anyone should criticise Poreshababu's behaviour in any way, openly or in private. And when his arrogance in this regard became apparent, Haranbabu lost his stature in Sucharita's eyes.

So, for various reasons, Haranbabu was gradually losing his lustre in Poreshbabu's household. Even Borodasundari, though no less enthusiastic than Haranbabu about maintaining the divide between Brahmo and non-Brahmo, and though she too, often felt ashamed of her husband's behaviour, did not regard Haranbabu as an ideal man. She detected a thousand shortcomings in him.

Although Sucharita's secret aversion for Haranbabu increased daily due to his communitarian zeal and narrow-minded dullness, neither of the two questioned or doubted that it was Haranbabu Sucharita would marry. When a man puts a boldly inscribed, highly expensive price tag on himself in the market of the religious community, others too, eventually begin to acknowledge his priceless worth. So once Haranbabu had selected Sucharita after suitably testing her according to his noble vocation, neither he nor anyone else doubted that everyone would bow to this decision. Even Poreshbabu had not mentally dismissed Haranbabu's claims. Everyone regarded Haranbabu as the future hope of the Brahmo Samaj, and he too acquiesced, without any thoughts to the contrary. It was therefore a matter of concern for Haranbabu whether Sucharita would prove adequate to a man like himself. It had not occurred to him to consider how much he might appeal to Sucharita. Just as nobody had deemed it necessary to think of Sucharita's views regarding this marriage proposal, she too had not thought about herself. Like all other members of the Brahmo Samaj, she had also assumed that the day Haranbabu said, 'I am ready to take this girl as my wife,' she would accept this marriage as her noble duty.

So things had continued, up until now. But that day, overhearing the heated tone of Haranbabu and Sucharita's brief argument about Gora, Poresh began to suspect that Sucharita did not respect Haranbabu sufficiently, that perhaps there were reasons why their natures clashed. Hence, when Borodasundari pressed for an early wedding, Poresh could not acquiesce as before. That very day, Borodasundari called Sucharita aside.

'You have caused your father great anxiety!' she declared.

Sucharita was startled. Nothing could pain her more than to give Poreshbabu cause for anxiety, even unintentionally.

'Why, what have I done?' she asked, turning pale.

'I don't know, child! He thinks you don't approve of Panubabu. Everyone in the Brahmo Samaj knows your marriage to Panubabu is more or less fixed. In this situation, if you . . .'

'Why, Ma, I haven't said a word to anyone about this!'

Sucharita had reason to be surprised. True, she was frequently irritated at Haranbabu's behaviour, but she had never nursed any objections to the marriage. Nor had it occurred to her to question whether this marriage would make her happy or unhappy, for she knew only that it was not to be judged in terms of happiness or grief. Then she remembered having clearly expressed her exasperation with Panubabu, in Poreshbabu's presence the other day. Her heart ached to think that this had made Poreshbabu anxious. Indeed, she had never shown such lack of restraint before, and she privately vowed not to do so in future, either.

Meanwhile, Haranbabu also arrived there that very day, not long afterwards. His heart had grown restless too. He had believed until now that Sucharita worshipped him in private; his share of her devotional offerings would have been fuller if Sucharita's blind faith had not made her incongruously devoted to old Poreshababu. Even if the many shortcomings in Poreshbabu's life were pointed out to her, Sucharita still seemed to regard him as a deity. Haranbabu had privately derided this, and also been offended by it, but he had hoped that at a suitable time, he would eventually be able to steer this unwarranted devotion into a single, proper channel.

At any rate, as long as Haranbabu considered himself an object of Sucharita's devotion, he had constantly criticized her minor actions and behaviour, and striven always to mould her personality with his advice, but he had never clearly mentioned marriage. But that day, when he realized from some of Sucharita's remarks that she, too, had begun to judge him, it became difficult to retain his unruffled gravity and composure. Since then, the couple of times he had met Sucharita, he had failed to experience or display his own glory as before. A discordant note had entered his conversation and behaviour with Sucharita. He fussed over her conduct, either without reason or on trivial pretexts. Sucharita still maintained a calm indifference that forced him to privately admit defeat, and back in his own home he regretted his own loss of face.

When Sucharita showed signs of having lost her respect for him, it became hard for Haranbabu to sustain his exalted position as her examiner. Earlier, he never visited Poreshbabu's house very frequently. Lest anyone suspect that love for Sucharita had made him desperate, he visited only once a week, and acted with gravity, as if Sucharita was his pupil. But something had come over him these last few days, for on the smallest pretexts, Haranbabu had been turning up more than once a day, and trying on even flimsier pretexts to engage Sucharita in conversation. This also gave Poreshbabu the opportunity to observe the two of them closely, and his doubts continued to intensify.

When Haranbabu arrived that day, Borodasundari immediately took him aside.

'Tell me, Panubabu,' she demanded, 'everyone says you're going to marry our Sucharita, but we never hear you say a word about it. If you really have such intentions, why don't you declare them clearly?'

Haranbabu could not delay any more. All he wanted now was to somehow secure Sucharita. Her devotion to him and her worthiness of the Brahmo cause could be tested later.

'I didn't mention it because it was so obvious,' he assured Borodasundari. 'I was only waiting for Sucharita to turn eighteen.'

'You are rather extreme, I must say,' she complained. 'We think fourteen is old enough.'

At teatime that evening, Poreshbabu was astonished at Sucharita's manner. She had not attended upon Haranbabu in this way for a very long time. In fact, when Haranbabu prepared to depart, she requested him to stay a little longer, for Labanya to show him one of her new creations. Poreshbabu felt reassured. He had been mistaken, he thought. He was privately a little amused, even. He assumed that the two had been involved in some secret lovers' quarrel, which had now blown over. That day, while taking his leave, Haran placed his marriage proposal before Poreshbabu, saying he did not favour any delay.

'But you say it's wrong to marry off girls before they're eighteen!' protested Poreshbabu, rather surprised. 'You have even published these views in the newspapers!'

'Such views don't apply to Sucharita, for she is mentally more mature than girls who are much older.'

'Be that as it may, Panubabu,' said Poreshbabu with quiet firmness. 'Since there is no particular danger to be feared, it is our duty to abide by your convictions and wait until Radharani comes of age.'

'Indeed it is!' cried Haranbabu, embarrassed that his weakness had been exposed. 'I would only like us to invite everyone to confirm this match in the name of the Almighty, one of these days.'

'That is a wonderful idea,' Poreshbabu declared.

# 17

After sleeping for a few hours, when Gora awakened to find Binoy asleep beside him, his heart brimmed over with joy. It was like dreaming of having lost something precious and then awakening to find that it was not lost, after all. How much abandoning Binoy would cripple his life, Gora realized tonight, when he awoke to see Binoy by his side. Restless with joy, he shook Binoy awake.

'Let's go, there's something we must do,' he announced.

Ritually, every morning, Gora would visit the lower-class homes in his neighbourhood. He went there not to offer charity or advice but to actually meet and mingle with the people. He was scarcely on similar visiting terms with members of the educated class. The poor addressed Gora as their respected elder brother, Dadathakur, and greeted him with shell-adorned hookahs. Gora had forced himself to take to tobacco, just to accept their hospitality.

In this crowd, Gora's chief admirer was Nanda, a carpenter's son. He was twenty-two. He built wooden chests in his father's workshop. No hunter in the marshy rubbish dumps could match him in marksmanship. He was also a matchless bowler in cricket games. In his hunting group and cricket team, Gora had merged these boys, sons of carpenters and cobblers, with trainees from respectable bhadra families. In these mixed groups, Nanda outshone everyone else in every form of sport and physical exercise. Some of the bhadra pupils were jealous of him, but under Gora's discipline, they all had to acknowledge Nanda as their leader.

Wounded in the foot by an accident with a chisel, Nanda had been absent from the playing field for a few days. Depressed about Binoy, Gora had not been able to visit their home these last few days. Today, at the crack of dawn, he arrived at the carpenters' colony, accompanied by Binoy. As soon as they neared the two-storey dwelling where Nanda's family lived, they heard women wailing. Nanda's father was away, and so were all other adult males.

'Nanda died early this morning; they have taken his body for cremation,' the nearby tobacco-shop owner informed them.

Nanda dead! So healthy, so strong, so fiery, so full of warmth, so young—Nanda had died that morning! Gora stood silent and rigid. Nanda was the son of an ordinary carpenter. Few people would notice the shortlived void that his absence had caused. But today, Nanda's death struck Gora as terribly inappropriate and impossible. Gora had seen how spirited he was, after all. So many people were alive, but it was hard to find such abundance of spirit anywhere.

Inquiries about the cause of his death revealed that he had developed tetanus. Nanda's father had suggested sending for a doctor, but the boy's mother had insisted that her son was possessed by some evil spirit. The ojha had spent the entire night scorching and beating the boy and chanting mantras to exorcise the demon. When he fell ill, Nanda had begged that Gora be informed. But, lest Gora demand proper medical treatment, Nanda's mother had not allowed it.

'What stupidity, and what a terrible penalty!' exclaimed Binoy, on their way back.

'Don't console yourself Binoy, that you can distance yourself from this stupidity,' Gora warned him. 'If you could clearly discern the enormity of such stupidity and the magnitude of its repercussions, you wouldn't try to brush it off with a mere expression of regret!'

Gora's pace increased with his agitation. Without answering, Binoy tried to match his speed.

'Our entire breed has sold out to falsehood,' Gora continued. 'There is no end to the things they fear—gods, demons, tetanus, sneezes, Thursdays, the conjunction of three lunar days on one calendar day. How would they understand the boldness with which one must tackle the realities of this world? And you and I imagine that we are not of their party, simply because we have studied a few pages of science! Know this for certain: a select few can never protect themselves with textbook knowledge from the seductions of self-debasement all around them. So long as they fail to recognize the supremacy of tradition in worldly life, so long as they remain bound by false fears, even our educated members cannot escape their influence.'

'And what if educated members were indeed able to escape such influences?' demanded Binoy. 'How many educated people do we have, indeed! Not that others must progress in order to promote the educated. Rather, the glory of the educated lies in using their education for the advancement of others.'

'That's exactly what I want to say!' cried Gora, grasping Binoy's hand. 'But I've repeatedly observed that your respectability and education makes all of you arrogant enough to remain very comfortable with your distance from the masses. That's why I wish to caution you that without freeing the people beneath you, there can be no freedom for yourselves, either! If there's a hole in the hull of a boat, its mast, however high, can never wander free of care!'

Binoy marched beside Gora without replying.

'No, Binoy, I can never accept this easily!' Gora exclaimed suddenly, after walking in silence for a while. 'That ojha who killed my Nanda—his assault wounds me, wounds my entire nation. I cannot view such matters as minor, scattered incidents.'

Binoy still made no reply.

'Binoy, I quite understand what you're thinking!' roared Gora. 'You think there is no remedy for such things, or that the time for such remedies is far away. You think no power on earth can shake the burden of the fear and falsehood, heavy as the Himalayas, oppressing all of Bharatvarsha! But I can't think like that. If I did, I wouldn't survive. There must be a remedy for whatever hurts my country, however massive and strong the assailant might be. And it's because I firmly believe that the remedy lies in our hands, that I can withstand all the sorrows, adversities and humiliations all around me.'

'I lack the courage to sustain my belief in front of this vast, tremendous, nationwide suffering,' confessed Binoy.

'Darkness is vast, the lamp's flame tiny. I have more faith in this tiny flame than in that vast darkness,' Gora asserted. 'I can never believe in the permanence of misery. It's constantly assailed from within and without, by the entire world's powers of knowledge and vitality. However small each of us might be, we shall side with the supporters of this knowledge and vitality. If that kills us, we'll die with the certainty that our side will win. We shall not rest in comfort upon the nation's moribund state, taking it to be supreme and all-powerful. I believe banking on the devil and fearing ghosts are exactly the same, for they leave us with no urge to seek true treatment for our malaise. False fears and false ojhas—both together are out to destroy us. Binoy, I urge you repeatedly, not for a single moment, even in your dreams, to think it impossible that our nation will definitely gain freedom, that it will not always remained shackled by ignorance, and that the merchant ships of the British will not always hold us in tow. Bearing this firmly in mind, we must be ever-ready. You are content, all of you, to bank upon some future date when Bharatvarsha will start fighting for independence. I tell you the fight has already begun, and it rages, every moment. There can be nothing more cowardly than for you to remain complacent at such a time.'

'Look, Gora,' argued Binoy, 'one difference I see between you and the rest of us is that you seem to discover anew, every day, all that occurs daily in the streets and alleys of our nation, things that have been happening for a long time. Like our own breathing process, these things don't draw our attention; they arouse neither hope nor despair in us, neither joy nor sorrow. My days pass in utter emptiness; amidst my surroundings, I feel neither my own presence nor my nation's.'

Suddenly, Gora's face reddened, the veins swelling on his forehead. Fists clenched, he began to run down the middle of the street, chasing a coach and pair. 'Stop the carriage!' he thundered, startling all the pedestrians. With a single backward glance, the babu sporting a heavy watch-chain, who had been driving the carriage at speed, lashed his spirited horses and vanished from sight in an instant.

An elderly Muslim had been carrying on his head a basketful of fruit, vegetables, eggs, bread, butter and other provisions for his English master's kitchen. The babu with the watch-chain had sounded his horn, warning him to move out of the carriage's path. But as the old man did not hear, the carriage almost crushed him. He escaped with his life, but the basket, with all its contents, went tumbling across the street. The incensed babu, turning around in his coach-box, abused him as 'a damned swine,' and lashed him on the face, drawing blood. 'Allah!' sighed the old man, and began to gather some of the still-intact items back into his basket. Gora walked back and began to collect the scattered things, returning them to the basket.

'Why bother, babu, these things are useless now,' protested the Muslim porter, acutely embarrassed at such behaviour from a respectable bhadra pedestrian. Gora understood the futility of his action, and also that it shamed the person being helped; in fact, such efforts meant little in terms of actual assistance. But then the man in the street could not understand that this was one bhadralok's attempt to restore equilibrium by coming down to the level of a common man who had been unjustly insulted by another bhadralok.

'You can't bear this loss,' said Gora, once the basket was full. 'Come home with me and I shall buy everything at its full price. But let me tell you baba, Allah will never forgive you for enduring this insult without a word.'

'Allah will punish the guilty one,' the Muslim declared. 'Why would he penalize me?'

'He who tolerates injustice is also guilty, for he generates injustice in the world. You will not understand my words, but remember still that meekness is not true religion, for it encourages evildoers. Because your Mohammad understood this, he didn't preach in the guise of a meek person.'

Since his own home was not close by, Gora brought the Muslim to Binoy's house.

'Take out some money,' he urged Binoy, standing near his chest of drawers.

'Why so anxious?' Binoy asked. 'You go make yourself comfortable, and I'll get the money.'

Suddenly, he couldn't find the keys. Impatiently, Gora yanked at the fragile drawer, and the lock gave way. As the drawer fell open, a photograph of Poreshbabu's family first caught his eye. Binoy had procured it from his young friend Satish. Having obtained the money, Gora dispatched the Muslim but said nothing about the photograph. Observing Gora's silence, Binoy too was unable to mention it, although exchanging a few remarks about it would have relieved him.

'I'm off,' announced Gora suddenly.

'Wah, how can you go alone!' protested Binoy. 'Ma has invited me to dinner at your place, after all. So I'm off, too.'

They set out together, the two of them. Gora said nothing, the rest of the way. The picture in the drawer had suddenly reminded him once again that a major stream of Binoy's emotional life had taken a course completely unrelated to Gora's. That the main current might eventually flow this way, diverted from their friendship which was its now dwindling source, was a vague fear secretly weighing upon Gora's innermost heart. All these days, the two friends had not differed in their thought and behaviour, but now this was hard to sustain. In one area of his life, Binoy was becoming independent. Binoy realized why Gora had fallen silent but felt embarrassed to break down that wall by force. He, too, felt that Gora's heart had come up against a real obstacle that threatened to separate them.

Arriving at Gora's house, they immediately saw Mahim at the door, gazing at the street.

'What's the matter?' he demanded, seeing the two friends. 'You stayed up all of last night. I wondered whether you two had fallen asleep somewhere on the pavement! It's not early, is it? Go, Binoy, have a bath.'

Having urged Binoy to his bath, Mahim turned to Gora.

'Look, Gora,' he importuned. 'Think about what I said. If you suspect Binoy of being unorthodox, then where in today's market shall we find a Hindu bridegroom? We want not only a Hindu but also an educated one, after all! True, the product of Hindu orthodoxy and education combined is not quite what the Hindu scriptures might decree, but it's not a bad thing either. If you had a daughter, your opinions on this would surely coincide with mine.'

'Very well,' replied Gora, 'Binoy will probably have no objections.'

'Listen to this! Who's afraid of Binoy's objections? It's your objections I fear. Ask Binoy yourself, just once: that's all I want, even if it proves useless.'

'Very well.'

'Now I can go ahead and order sandesh from the sweet shop and yoghurt and kheer from the milkman,' gloated Mahim to himself.

'Dada is really plaguing us about your marriage with Shashimukhi,' Gora said to Binoy when he found the opportunity. 'What do you say?'

'Tell me first what you would desire.'

'Not a bad idea, I'd say!'

'You didn't think it a good idea earlier! It was more or less understood that neither of us would marry.'

'It is now understood that you will marry, but I won't.'

'Why? Why must the same journey yield different outcomes?'

'It's to preclude different outcomes that the present arrangement is intended. Our Maker has created some of us to be easily weighed down, while others remain casually carefree. For two such beings to move in tandem, one must be loaded with some ballast, in order to balance their weight. If you marry and assume some responsibilities, you and I can match our steps.'

'If that is your intention, add extra weight to my side of the scales,' smiled Binoy.

'You have no objection to the weight itself, I hope?'

'For the sake of balance, one can manage with anything at hand. A stone, a clod, anything.'

Why Gora expressed enthusiasm about the marriage proposal, Binoy was left in no doubt. He felt privately amused, guessing that Gora was anxious lest his friend marry into Poreshbabu's family. Not for an instant had the idea or likelihood of such a marriage occurred to Binoy. It was totally impossible. Anyhow, he consented readily to marry Shashimukhi, thinking that such a move would completely uproot such bizarre fears, restoring the health and peace of his friendship with Gora, and removing all cause for embarrassment about his mingling with Poreshbabu's family.

After lunch, they spent the day making up for lost sleep. There was no further discussion between the two friends that day. But as the veil of dusk descended, at the hour when lovers mutually unveil their hearts, Binoy observed, gazing directly at the sky from the terrace:

'Look Gora, I want to say something. I think there is a serious lack in our patriotism. We see only half of Bharatvarsha.'

'Why do you say that?'

'We see Bharatvarsha only as a land of men; we don't notice women at all.'

'So, like the English, would you like to see women everywhere, indoors and out, on earth, in water and in space, at meals, feasts and work, everywhere? As a result, you will notice women rather than men, and it will destroy your balance of vision.'

'No, no, you can't dismiss my words like that. Why ask whether I'll adopt the English point of view? I say it's true that in our own country, we don't give women enough place in our thoughts. About you, I can declare you don't spend a moment's thought on women. You know the nation as a place without women. Such knowledge can never be true.'

'In seeing and knowing my mother, I have simultaneously seen and known all the women of my country.'

'That was just a well-put statement to delude yourself with. When members of a household gaze with long familiarity at women performing domestic chores, they don't really see the women at all. If we could view our nation's women outside our domestic needs, we would perceive our nation in its beauty and wholeness. We would see an image of the nation easy to die for. At least we would never behave mistakenly as if the women of our country are nowhere to be found. I know you will be incensed if I attempt any sort of comparison with English society. That is not what I wish to do. I don't know how and to what extent our women can appear in public without loss of dignity, but we must admit the seclusion of women has reduced swadesh, our own nation, to a half-truth, incapable of infusing our hearts with love and power in their complete forms.'

'How did you make this sudden discovery, so recently?' Gora asked.

'Yes, it's indeed a recent discovery, and a sudden one,' Binoy acknowledged. 'I was blind to such an immense reality, for so long! I count myself fortunate to have discovered it. Because we see the peasant only as farm labour, and the weaver only as fabric producer, we dismiss them as lowly and uncouth, not recognizing them as complete human beings, and this rich-poor divide weakens the nation. For very similar reasons, our entire nation's growth remains stunted because we imprison the women of our country within their routine of cooking and grinding, regarding them reductively as merely the female sex.'

'Just as day and night are the two halves of time, so are men and women the two halves of human society,' Gora asserted. 'In normal social situations, woman remains invisible like the night, all her actions concealed and private. We exclude the night from our work-time. But that doesn't halt any of the night's profound operations. Behind the veil of rest, the night secretly heals our losses, and nurtures us. But in abnormal social situations, night is turned into day, with machines operated by the light of gas-lamps, nightlong revelry by lamplight—but what's the result? The night's natural, private processes are destroyed, fatigue sets in, there's no restoration of injury or loss, and people become overwrought. Similarly, if we drag women into the public workplace, it disrupts their private activities, ruining social health and peace, driving society into a kind of frenzy. This frenzy may be mistaken for power, but it is only the power to destroy. Power has two aspects, one manifest, the other not manifested, one involving effort, the other rest, one productive, the other abstemious. If this balance is destroyed, power grows turbulent, and such turmoil is not beneficial. Man and woman represent two aspects of social power; man is power manifest, but the magnitude of his strength does not lie in its visibility; woman's power remains unexpressed, and to try constantly to express this secret power is to propel society towards swift bankruptcy by expending all its stored-up capital. That is why I say, if we men perform the holy sacrifice while women take charge of the grain-store, the yajna ritual will be successful, despite the women's invisibility. Those who try to expend all forms of power for the same purpose, at the same place and in the same way, must be insane.'

'Gora, I don't want to contradict you. But you, too, have not contradicted what I said. Actually . . .'

'Look, Binoy, if we say much more on this subject, it will be merely for the sake of argument. I admit I'm not as aware of the opposite sex as you have lately become, hence you can never make me feel what you are experiencing. So, why not accept for now that on this subject, our opinions differ?'

Gora dismissed the matter. But seeds, even when blown away, land on the soil, and then there is nothing to stop them from sprouting at a suitable time. Up until now, Gora had completely excluded women from his life's arena; even in his dreams, he had not regarded this as a lack or loss. Today, witnessing Binoy's change of attitude, he had become aware of women's special presence and influence in society. But because he could not determine the place of women or what purpose they served in society, he was reluctant to argue with Binoy about these things. He could neither ignore nor master this subject, hence he wanted to avoid discussing it.

'Binoy, I hear your marriage to Shashimukhi has been fixed?' asked Anandamoyi that night, calling Binoy aside when he was leaving for home.

'Yes Ma, Gora is the go-between in this auspicious matter,' smiled Binoy, embarrassed.

'Shashimukhi is a nice girl, but don't act impulsively, bachha. I know you, Binoy. You are acting in a hurry because you are somewhat doubtful. You still have time to think. You are old enough, baba—don't take such a serious step lightly.'

She gently patted him on the shoulder. Without a word, he walked away slowly.

# 18

On his way home, Binoy reflected upon Anandamoyi's words. Up until now, he had never disregarded anything she said. That night, his heart felt heavy.

Next morning, he awakened to a sense of freedom. He felt he had bought his freedom from Gora's friendship at a very price. In exchange for the lifelong bondage which he had accepted in agreeing to marry Shashimukhi, he had gained the right to loosen his ties in another area of his life. Gora had, very unjustly, suspected Binoy of being tempted to leave his own community to marry into a Brahmo family. Binoy obtained his freedom by offering his marriage to Shashimukhi as a permanent security against this false suspicion. After this, he began to frequent Poresh's house without any constraint.

It was not at all difficult for Binoy to make himself at home where the company was to his liking. Once he had discarded his qualms about Gora, he quickly grew intimate with everyone in Poreshbabu's household, as if he had long been part of the family. Only Lalita, as long as she suspected Sucharita of having developed a weakness for Binoy, seemed to have armed her heart for battle against him. But when she saw clearly that Sucharita was not particularly partial to Binoy, she dropped her resentment with immense relief. Now she had no reason not to regard Binoybabu as a remarkably decent person.

Even Haranbabu was not hostile to Binoy. He seemed rather too eager to acknowledge that Binoy knew all about respectable conduct, implying that Gora lacked this quality. Binoy never raised any topic of debate in Haranbabu's presence, and Sucharita, too, tried to ensure against it, hence Binoy had so far not disrupted the peaceful atmosphere at the tea-table.

But in Haran's absence, Sucharita would herself try to get Binoy to discuss his social views. How educated men like Gora and Binoy could support the ancient social evils of the country was a question that continued to arouse her curiosity. Had she not been acquainted with Gora and Binoy, Sucharita would have had no second thoughts about dismissing anyone who held such views as worthy of contempt. But ever since she met Gora, she had been unable to dismiss him with contempt. Hence, at every opportunity, in her conversations with Binoy, she would somehow raise the subject of Gora's views and lifestyle, and by contradicting every argument, try to stretch the discussion until she had extracted the minutest details. Exposure to the views of every community was the best education for Sucharita, Poresh felt; therefore, he never felt anxious about these arguments, nor tried to prevent them.

'Tell me,' asked Sucharita one day, 'does Gourmohanbabu really believe in caste difference, or is it an exaggerated form of patriotism?'

'Do you believe in the steps on your staircase?' Binoy retorted. 'They, too, are differently placed, some higher, some lower.'

'I recognize them only because I must climb from a lower level to a higher, or there would be no need to heed them. On level ground, stairs become redundant.'

'Quite so! Our society is a stairway, meant to enable mankind's ascent to a particular goal. If we took society or the world for an end in itself, there would be no need for hierarchies; like European societies we could continue snatching and killing, each individual trying to grab more than everyone else, allowing the successful to flourish, and failures to sink into oblivion. Because we want to transcend the world by worldly means, we have not based our duties on desire and competition. We have made worldly endeavour our dharma because through endeavour, we seek no success but liberation. Hence, keeping in mind both worldly activities and their outcome, our society has created caste distinctions and division of labour.'

'I don't understand you clearly, I must confess,' Sucharita said. 'My question is, do you see that the purpose of promoting caste discrimination has been fulfilled?'

'It's hard to encounter fulfilment in this world. Simply because the achievement of the Greek civilization is no longer found in Greece, we can't declare the idea of the Greek civilization to be mistaken or futile. The idea of the Greek civilization continues to bear fruit in different forms within the human world. The caste system, India's answer to the problems of society, has not yet died out. It still remains, for the world to see. Even Europe has not yet found any other answer to the problems of society; there you still find only jostling and wrestling. The answer provided by Bharatvarsha still awaits fulfilment in the human world. Don't expect it to evaporate simply because a small community, out of their blindness to reality, might wish to dismiss it. Our tiny communities will vanish like bubbles in the ocean, but this great solution born of Bharatvarsha's natural genius will survive unmoved, until its task here is accomplished.'

'Please don't mind,' asked Sucharita hesitantly, 'but are you simply echoing Gourmohanbabu's words, or do you believe wholeheartedly in all these things?'

'I have told you truly that my convictions are not as strong as Gora's,' smiled Binoy. 'I often voice my doubts when I observe the mess caused by caste discrimination and the aberrations of society. But Gora says doubts are born when we view great things in a reductive light; it is intolerant to mistake broken branches and dry leaves for the tree's essence. I don't ask you to praise the broken branch, he says, but try to see the tree in its wholeness, and to understand its significance.'

'Even if we overlook the dry leaves, the fruits of the tree must be considered,' Sucharita insisted. 'What are the fruits of caste discrimination, for our country?'

'What you call the fruits of caste discrimination are also the products of a situation, not only of casteism. If it hurts to chew with loose teeth, it's not the teeth that are to blame but their shakiness. Because a variety of causes have damaged and weakened us, we have distorted the idea of Bharatvarsha instead of fulfilling its promise. But that distortion is not intrinsic to the idea. Once we achieve plenitude of energy and health, everything will be set right. That's why Gora insists we must not dismiss the head because we have a headache. Grow healthy, grow strong, he urges us.'

'So, you'd want us to view Brahmans as living deities?' demanded Sucharita. 'Do you really believe that dust from a Brahman's feet can purify people?'

'Many honours in this world are man-made, after all. As long as a monarch is necessary for some reason, men declare him extraordinary. But a monarch is not really extraordinary, is he? Yet, he must transcend his ordinariness to become extraordinary, or he cannot rule. We project a monarch as extraordinary to ensure that we receive proper administration under his rule. The monarch must respect the demands of the honour we bestow on him; he must become extraordinary. Such artificiality affects all human relationships. In fact, it's our idealization of parenthood and not just natural parental love that determines parents' role in society. Why, in a joint family, does an elder brother tolerate and sacrifice so much for his younger brother? Our society, unlike others, has constructed this special image of the dada. If the Brahman's image were also similarly constructed, that would be no mean advantage for our society! We desire a living deity. If our desire for this human deity is really heartfelt and intelligent, then we shall have him. And if ours is a foolish desire, we shall add the world's burdens, increasing the number of anti-gods who indulge in all sorts of wrongdoing and survive by scattering on our heads the dust from their feet.'

'Does your human deity exist?' inquired Sucharita.

'He exists as the tree lives in its seed, in Bharatvarsha's deepest purposes and needs. Other nations want generals like Wellington, scientists like Newton, millionaires like Rothschild, but our nation wants Brahmans. Brahmans who are fearless, who despise avarice, conquer grief, ignore deprivation, who are *param brahmani jojitachittah*, unshakable, calm, and free. That is the kind of Brahman Bharatvarsha wants, and only when he is found can Bhratvarsha really become free. Our society needs Brahmans to constantly provide a song of liberation for every group, every form of labour, not to cook or to sound the prayer bell. We need Brahmans to keep our society's value constantly in view. The greater our ideal of Brahmanism, the more highly we must honour Brahmans. Such honour is greater by far than that accorded to kings, it amounts to honouring the gods. When the Brahmans of our country become truly worthy of such honour, nobody can dishonour our nation. Do we bow to kings, or allow despots to enchain us? We bow to our own fear, entangled in the net of our own avarice, enslaved by our own folly. Let the Brahmans pray; let them liberate us from that fear, avarice and folly. We don't ask them to wage war, engage in trade, or serve any other purpose; let them actualize the pursuit of liberation in our society.'

Poreshbabu had been listening in silence. Now, he spoke up gently: 'I can't say I know Bharatvarsha, and I certainly don't know what Bharatvarsha desired or whether that desire was ever fulfilled. But can we ever return to our bygone days? Our endeavours must focus on present possibilities. What use wasting time in groping for the past?'

'What you say echoes my line of thinking, and what I've often said as well,' Binoy responded. 'Gora says, is the past really over because we dismiss it as such? It does not become obsolete simply because it may be out of sight, screened by the turmoil of the present; it survives in the very marrow of Bharatvarsha's bones. No truth can ever become obsolete. That is why this truth about Bharatvarsha has begun to impinge upon us today. One day, if even one of us recognized and accepted this truth, it would unlock the door to our mine of strength, and the treasures of the past would become the possessions of the present. Do you imagine that a man of such significant destiny has not appeared on Bharatvarsha's horizon?'

'You phrase these things differently from ordinary people,' observed Sucharita. 'Hence one hesitates to accept your views as a reflection of the entire nation.'

'Look, scientists describe sunrise in one way and ordinary people in a different way. That does not harm the sunrise much. But we do gain something from understanding the truth in its proper form. Gora has the amazing capacity to take a unified, coherent view of the truth about our nation, which we regard in scattered, fragmented ways. But would you, therefore, regard Gora's vision as an optical illusion? And is the fragmented vision of others to be taken for the truth?'

Sucharita remained silent.

'Don't count my friend Gora among our ordinary countrymen who pride themselves on being supreme Hindus,' Binoy continued. 'If you knew his father Krishnadayalbabu, you would have perceived the difference between father and son. Krishnadayalbabu is anxious day and night to keep himself pure, constantly changing his clothes, sprinkling Ganga water, studying the holy almanac and the scriptures. Regarding food, he doesn't trust even the best Brahman cook, lest there be some flaw in the man's Brahmanhood. He doesn't let Gora anywhere near his own room. If he ever has reason to visit his wife's quarters in the house, he purifies himself upon his return. His days and nights in this world are spent in extreme detachment, lest he be touched, knowingly or unknowingly, by the minutest impurity arising from a violation of sacred rules. Just like the dandy Ghor Babu, constantly anxious to maintain the radiance of his complexion, the glory of his hair and the neatness of his dress, by avoiding the sun and screening himself from exposure to dust. Gora is not like that at all. He does not disrespect the rules of Hindu orthodoxy, but he can never be so petty and fastidious. He views the Hindu religion from within, and with great regard for its magnitude. He never thinks of the Hindu spirit as something very delicate, shrivelling at the slightest touch, destroyed by the merest contact.'

'But he seems very cautious about observing the purity and impurity of touch!' said Sucharita.

'That caution of his is a strange thing,' Binoy explained. 'If asked, he at once says: "Yes, I believe in all this. That touch can taint our caste purity, that eating certain things is sinful: these are unshakable truths." But I know for sure that these are mere overstatements; the more inappropriate they are, the more loudly he seems to proclaim them for everyone to hear. Gora wants to observe all orthodox rules indiscriminately, lest rejecting minor features of present-day Hinduism should lead other unwise people to disrespect even its major features, and lest this give the detractors of Hinduism a sense of victory. He wouldn't slacken his stance, even before me.'

'There are many such among the Brahmos as well,' remarked Poreshbabu. 'They would indiscriminately reject all contact with Hinduism, lest outsiders mistakenly imagine that they endorse Hindu malpractices as well. Such people can't lead a natural life; they either pretend or exaggerate. Thinking that the truth is weak, they consider it part of their duty to protect it, through either force or strategy. "I don't depend on truth, the truth depends on me": those who believe this become fanatics. Those who believe in the power of truth keep their own aggressiveness under control. If outsiders temporarily misunderstand us, there's not much harm done; far worse is the harm resulting from inability to acknowledge the truth because of petty hesitations. I always pray to the Almighty that, be it a Brahmo prayer hall or a Hindu chandimandap, let me in every situation be able to salute the truth easily, with bowed head, and without resistance. Let no external hindrance restrain me.'

Poreshbabu fell silent, as if briefly immersing himself in introspection. These few words uttered by him in a low voice seemed to lend a certain harmony to the entire discussion, arising not merely from those words, but from the tranquil depths of Poreshbabu's own life. A glow of blissful devotion lit up the faces of Sucharita and Lalita. Binoy remained silent. He, too, was privately aware of a tremendous aggressiveness in Gora's nature. The easy, simple tranquility to be expected in the mind and conduct of purveyors of the truth was lacking in Gora. This fact struck Binoy afresh and more clearly, upon hearing Poreshbabu's words. Of course, Binoy had so far argued with himself in Gora's defence that when one's community is precariously placed and in conflict with the external political atmosphere, soldiers of the truth cannot preserve their natural demeanour. At such times, temporary necessities demand even the fragmentation of truth itself. Today, Poreshbabu's words made Binoy wonder momentarily, that if it was natural for ordinary persons to be tempted to distort the truth in serving their temporary needs, did Gora too belong to that same order of people?

When Sucharita retired for the night, Lalita came and perched at one end of her bed. Sucharita sensed that Lalita was brooding over something. Realizing also that it must be something concerning Binoy, she brought up the subject herself.

'I must say I rather like Binoybabu,' she remarked.

'You like him because he talks about Gourbabu all the time.'

Sucharita grasped the insinuation but ignored it.

'True indeed,' she admitted, feigning innocence. 'I enjoy hearing him speak of Gourbabu. He brings Gourbabu to life.'

'I don't enjoy any of it! It annoys me.'

'Why?' asked Sucharita in surprise.

'It's only Gora, Gora, Gora, day and night!' protested Lalita. 'His friend Gora may be a very eminent man, that's all very well. But Binoy is a person in his own right, too!'

'Indeed he is,' smiled Sucharita, 'but what's the problem?'

'His friend has overshadowed him to such an extent that he is unable to express himself. Like a cockroach captured by a green glass beetle. In such situations, I feel angry with the beetle but can't respect the cockroach either.'

The sharpness of Lalita's tone made Sucharita laugh, though she said nothing.

'You laugh Didi, but let me tell you, if someone tried to suppress me like that, I couldn't tolerate him for a single day!' Lalita declared. 'Take yourself, for instance. Whatever people may think, you don't overshadow me, it's not in your nature. That's why I love you so. Actually, it's what you've learned from Baba: he gives everybody their own space.'

Sucharita and Lalita were Poreshbabu's devoted followers in this family, the very mention of 'Baba' making their hearts swell with pride.

'Baba is beyond compare,' Sucharita agreed. 'But say what you will, Binoybabu has a way with words.'

'It's because the words are not his own that he can utter them with such grace,' Lalita insisted. 'If he spoke his mind, his words would sound quite natural; we wouldn't feel he'd made them up. I'd find that much better than wonderful words.'

'So what makes you angry, my dear? Gourmohan's words *have* become Binoy's own.'

'Then it's a terrible thing. Has the Almighty Ishwar given us brains to elaborate on other people's views, and mouths to utter other people's words in a marvelous way? I have no use for such marvelous words!'

'But why don't you see that Binoybabu loves Gourmohanbabu, that their views truly coincide?'

'No, no, no!' cried Lalita impatiently. 'Their views don't coincide entirely. He has become habituated to following Gourmohanbabu. That is slavery, not love. Yet, he would force himself to believe that their views are exactly similar. That's why he tries so hard to present Gourmohanbabu's views in wonderful terms, to delude others as well as himself. He constantly wants to suppress the doubts and contradictions that arise in his own heart, lest he be compelled to reject Gourmohanbabu's ideas. He lacks the courage to disown Gourmohanbabu. Where there is love, acceptance is possible even where opinions differ; self-surrender is possible even without blindness. But that's not true in his case. He may follow Gourmohanbabu out of love but cannot bring himself to acknowledge it. That's clear from his words. Well, Didi, haven't you realized that? Tell me honestly.'

Sucharita had not considered the matter in this way at all. For she was curious to understand Gora completely but without any urge to regard Binoy separately in his own right.

'Very well, suppose we accept your argument,' she said, not directly answering Lalita's question. 'So what's to be done now?'

'I feel like extricating him from bondage to his friend, to set him free.'

'Why don't you try, bhai?'

'No use my trying. If you put your mind to it, it would work.'

Although Sucharita had privately sensed Binoy's attraction towards her, she tried to laugh off Lalita's suggestion.

'I like him because of the way he comes to surrender himself to you, flouting even Gourmohanbabu's authority,' Lalita asserted. 'Others in his place might write a play condemning Brahmo women, but his love for you and respect for Baba shows his mind is still open. Didi, we must make Binoybabu a person in his own right. I can't bear to see him merely promoting Gourmohanbabu.'

'Didi! Didi!' cried Satish, rushing into the room at this moment. Binoy had taken him to the circus at Gorer Maath. Late though it was, Satish could not contain his excitement at his first visit to the circus.

'I almost dragged Binoybabu to my bed tonight,' he informed them, after describing the circus. 'He entered the house, then left, saying he'll come tomorrow. Didi, I've asked him to take both of you to the circus one day.'

'What did he say to that?' Lalita inquired.

'He said the girls would be frightened by the tigers. I wasn't frightened at all, though.' Satish puffed up his chest in male arrogance.

'Indeed!' said Lalita. 'I can clearly see how brave your friend Binoybabu is! No, bhai Didi, we must take him to the circus!'

'But tomorrow's show is scheduled for the morning,' objected Satish.

'All the better!' Lalita declared. 'We'll go in the morning.'

As soon as Binoy arrived the next day, Lalita cried:

'Here's Binoybabu, just on time. Let's go!'

'Where?' asked Binoy.

'To the circus.'

To the circus! To visit the circus in broad daylight, in the company of women, in full public view! Binoy was dumbfounded.

'It will offend Gourmohanbabu, I suppose?' Lalita demanded.

Binoy was rather startled at Lalita's question.

'Does Gourmohanbabu have an opinion about escorting girls to the circus?' Lalita persisted.

'He certainly does,' answered Binoy.

'Please explain it to us,' Lalita demanded. 'Let me call Didi, so she can hear it too.'

Binoy smiled at her sarcasm.

'Why do you smile Binoybabu! You told Satish yesterday that women are afraid of tigers. Are you afraid of someone, too?'

Binoy took the girls to the circus that day. Perturbed, he wondered again and again how his relationship with Gora might appear to Lalita, and possibly to other women in this family.

'Did you tell Gourmohanbabu about the circus performance that day?' Lalita asked him the next time they met, feigning naïve curiosity.

This pointed question unsettled Binoy profoundly.

'No, I haven't told him yet,' he had to admit, flushing to the tips of his ears.

'Binoybabu, please come with me, will you?' called Labanya, coming in.

'Where?' asked Lalita. 'To the circus?'

'Wah, as if there's a circus performance today! I'm calling him to draw a border along the edges of my handkerchief, for me to embroider,' Labanya told her. 'Binoybabu draws so beautifully!'

Labanya dragged Binoy away.

## 19

In the morning, Gora was busy working when Binoy suddenly arrived on the scene.

'I went to the circus with Poreshbabu's daughters the other day,' he announced very abruptly.

'So I heard,' replied Gora, continuing to write.

'Who told you?' asked Binoy, surprised.

'Abinashbabu. He was also at the circus that day.'

Gora said no more. He scribbled away. From long force of habit, Binoy was terribly embarrassed that Gora should have heard the news already, and that too from Abinash, which meant there would have been no lack of description and detail. He would have been happier if the circus visit, and public knowledge of it, could have been avoided.

He now remembered having stayed awake the previous night, mentally quarreling with Lalita. She thought he was in awe of Gora, deferring to him as a small boy obeys his tutor. How could one human being so unfairly misjudge another! Gora and Binoy were soulmates after all! True, he respected Gora for his uniqueness, but what Lalita imagined was unfair to Gora and Binoy both. Binoy was not a minor, and Gora was not his guardian.

Gora continued to write in silence, and Lolita's pointed questions continued to haunt Binoy. He could not dismiss them easily. But soon, he grew indignant.

'So what if I went to the circus! Who is Abinash to raise the issue with Gora, and why, for that matter, should Gora discuss my activities with that good-for-nothing fellow? Am I under Gora's surveillance, answerable to him for the company I keep, and my movements? This is a grave assault upon our friendship!'

Had he not suddenly recognized his own cowardice, Binoy would not have felt so incensed at Gora and Abinash. He seemed to be privately trying to blame Gora for his own compulsion to conceal something from Gora, even momentarily. If Gora had said a few harsh things to Binoy about the circus visit, their friendship would have remained on an equal footing and Binoy would have felt consoled as well. But when Gora silently ignored Binoy, acting like a grave judge, Lalilta's barbs began to sting Binoy insistently.

At this moment, Mahim entered, hookah in hand. Lifting the damp cloth covering the casket, he handed Binoy a paan.

'Baba Binoy, everything is settled on our front,' he said. 'Now, all we need is a letter from your father's elder brother, to set our hearts at rest. You've written to him haven't you?'

This pressure to marry struck Binoy as deeply offensive at this time, yet he knew Mahim was not to blame, for he had received a promise. But Binoy felt that this promise was inadequate somehow. After all, Anandamoyi had virtually forbidden him, and the idea of marriage did not attract him at all either. So how, amidst all this confusion, had the matter ripened so quickly? Not that Gora had actually urged him to hurry. Nor would he have importuned Binoy if the latter had objected strongly. But still! Still, it was on this account that Lalita's barbed remarks pierced his heart. Behind it lay no particular recent development but a long history of domination. Purely out of affection and simplicity, Binoy had grown accustomed to tolerating Gora's supremacy. Hence, this relationship of dominance had overwhelmed their friendship. Binoy had not felt it all these days, but now it could no longer be denied. Must he marry Shashimukhi, then?

'No, I haven't written to Khuromoshai yet,' he said.

'I'm to blame for that,' Mahim declared. 'It's not a letter you should write. I shall write it. Tell me, what's his full name, baba?'

'Why are you in such a hurry?' asked Binoy. 'The wedding can't happen in the months of Ashwin and Kartik, after all. That leaves only

Agrahayan, but even that is problematic. Long back in our family history, somebody suffered a mishap in Agrahayan. Ever since then, our family has avoided weddings and other auspicious events during that month.'

'Binoy,' said Mahim, propping his hookah against the corner wall, 'does your education amount to mere rote-learning, that you should believe in such things? It's hard enough to find auspicious dates in this wretched country, and then if every family starts following a private almanac, how would our business proceed?'

'Then why do you believe in the inauspiciousness of Bhadra-Ashwin?' Binoy demanded.

'As if I do! Never! What's to be done baba—in these parts, you can manage quite well without believing in God, but unless you believe in Bhadra–Ashwin, the planets Brahaspati–Shani, and what the stars decree, they won't let you survive. Besides, though I may refute these things in theory, violating the almanac in practice makes the mind uneasy. Fear pervades the air of our nation, just like malaria. I can't overcome it.'

'Our family's fear of Agrahayan can't be overcome, either. Khurima, at least, will never agree.'

So Binoy managed to suppress the matter for that day. From his tone, Gora guessed that he had developed some doubts. For a few days, Binoy had not been visible at all. Gora had realized he had started visiting Poreshbabu's house oftener than before. Now this attempt to evade the marriage proposal roused Gora's suspicions. Just as a snake cannot relinquish the victim it has begun to swallow, Gora too was virtually incapable of giving up a resolve or discarding parts of it. Any resistance or slackness on the part of others only aggravated his obstinacy. He became determined, heart and soul, to cling to the wavering Binoy by force.

'Binoy,' said Gora, looking up from his writing, 'having given your word to Dada, why torment him needlessly by keeping him in a state of uncertainty?'

'Did I give him my word, or was a promise hastily extracted from me?' demanded Binoy, suddenly losing patience.

'Who extracted a promise?' asked Gora harshly, surprised at Binoy's sudden show of indignation.

'You did!'

'Me! I'd barely exchanged a few remarks with you on the subject—is that called extracting a promise?'

Indeed, Binoy had no clear evidence to support his claim. Gora was right, they had exchanged very few remarks, hardly involving the kind of urging that could be termed as insistence. But still, it was Gora who had taken Binoy's consent, virtually by force. People are especially resentful about allegations regarding lack of external evidence. Hence Binoy sounded unduly angry when he said:

'It doesn't take many words to extract a promise.'

'Take back what you said!' demanded Gora, rising from the table. 'This promise is not so valuable that I must beg you for it or extort it from you.'

'Dada!' he thundered, calling to Mahim in the adjacent room. 'Dada!' Gora exploded, as soon as the flustered Mahim rushed in, 'didn't I tell you at the outset that Shashimukhi cannot marry Binoy, that I don't approve of the match?'

'Of course you did,' Mahim confirmed. 'No one but you could have said such a thing. Any other brother would have been enthusiastic from the beginning about a marriage proposal for his niece.'

'Why did you make me seek Binoy's consent?' Gora persisted.

'Only because I imagined it would work.'

'I'll have nothing to do with all this,' announced Gora, flushing. 'Matchmaking is not my trade. I have other things to do.'

With these words, Gora marched out of the room. Before the stupefied Mahim could question him on this, Binoy too walked directly out into the street. Retrieving the hookah from the corner, Mahim began to puff away in silence.

Gora and Binoy had quarreled many times previously, but never before had such a sudden, terrible eruption taken place. At first, Binoy was stunned at what he had done. Afterwards, once he was home, pain seared his heart. Thinking of the grievous blow he had inflicted on Gora in so short a time, he could not eat or sleep. He was especially troubled by remorse at the utter unreasonableness of blaming Gora for the present situation.

'It was unjust, unjust, unjust!' he repeated.

At two in the afternoon, when Anandamoyi had just taken up her sewing after lunch, Binoy came and perched close to her. She had heard some news of the morning's developments from Mahim. At lunch, she had also guessed from Gora's expression that there had been a storm.

'Ma, I have acted wrongly!' declared Binoy as soon as he arrived. 'There's no justification for what I said to Gora this morning about my marriage to Shashimukhi.'

'Never mind, Binoy,' Anandamoyi consoled him. 'When we try to suppress something painful, it comes out in this way. This was for the best. A couple of days, and both you and Gora will forget this quarrel.'

'But Ma, I have no objection to marrying Shashimukhi. That's what I've come to say.'

'Bachha, don't get into another mess in your haste to overcome a quarrel. Quarrels last only a couple of days, but marriage is forever.'

Binoy refused to be persuaded. He could not go to Gora immediately with his proposal. He went to inform Mahim that there was nothing to hold up the wedding. It would take place in Magh itself. Binoy would himself ensure that Khuromoshai raised no objections.

'Why not go ahead with the betrothal then?' suggested Mahim.

'Good idea. Please consult Gora first.'

'Consult Gora again?' exclaimed Mahim, flustered.

'No, we can't proceed otherwise,' Binoy insisted.

'Then we have no choice. But . . .' He stuffed a paan in his mouth.

## 20

Mahim said nothing to Gora that day. The next day, he went to his house, anticipating another struggle to persuade Gora again. But when he announced that Binoy had consented to the marriage the previous evening and asked for Gora to be consulted about the betrothal, Gora at once expressed his own approval:

'Very well, let the betrothal take place.'

'Now you say "very well"!' exclaimed Mahim in amazement. 'But you won't throw a spanner in the works again later, will you?'

'If I did, it was by way of a request, and not by posing obstacles,' Gora reminded him.

'Therefore I entreat you to neither pose obstacles nor make requests. I have no use for Narayani sena, Krishna's troops, on the Kaurav side, nor for Narayan, Krishna himself, on the side of the Pandavas. Best to manage with my own resources. I made a mistake. I did not know earlier that even your assistance could be so perverse. Anyway, you wish this betrothal to take place, don't you?'

'Yes I do.'

'Let it remain a wish then; no need to try converting it into action.'

Gora was hot-tempered, no doubt, and capable of anything when incensed; but it was not in his nature to nurse his anger and destroy his own resolve. He wanted to tie Binoy down by any means; this was no time for sulking. Gora was privately pleased at the previous day's episode, realizing that it was in reaction to yesterday's quarrel that the wedding had been finalized, and it was Binoy's rebellion that had confirmed his bondage. Gora wasted no time in restoring the natural relationship between Binoy and himself that had existed all along. But this time, there was a slight deviation from their utterly direct manner towards each other.

Gora had now realized it would be hard to restrain Binoy from afar. He must guard the danger-zones. 'If I visit Poreshbabu's house regularly, I can keep Binoy within proper limits,' he thought.

The very day after their quarrel, Gora arrived at Binoy's house in the late afternoon. Binoy had never imagined Gora would visit him that very day. Hence he was as pleased as he was surprised. Even more surprisingly, Gora raised the subject of Poreshbabu's daughters, yet without any air of hostility. It did not take much to excite Binoy when this subject came up. He began to recount in detail to Gora all the things he had discussed with Sucharita. He tried to enthuse Gora by informing him that Sucharita herself raised these subjects with special eagerness, and that despite all her arguments, she was unconsciously acquiescing, little by little, to Gora's point of view.

'When I recounted what you and I said about Nando's mother sending for the ojha and causing his death,' Binoy said conversationally, 'Sucharita said, "You people think women have fulfilled their duties if they are confined within the home and allowed to cook and clean. On the one hand you stunt their mental growth like this, but on the other, when they send for the ojha, you don't spare them either. Those for whom a couple of families constitute the whole world can never become complete human beings. And if denied their full humanity, they are bound to destroy and retard all major male undertakings, dragging men down to avenge their own plight. The way you have moulded Nando's mother and kept her circumscribed, you couldn't make her see sense even if your life depended on it, because you wouldn't get through to her." I've tried hard to argue about this, but truly, Gora, because I secretly agreed with her, my arguments didn't carry any force. With her, one can at least argue, but I dare not argue with Lalita. When Lalita arched her brows and said—"You think you will serve the world while we serve all of you! That's not possible! Either we, too, must serve the world, or we must remain a burden. If we become a burden, you grow angry and say women are expendable. But if you allowed women to advance, outside or in the home, there'd be no need to discard them!"—her words rendered me speechless. Lalita doesn't open her mouth easily, but when she does, one must respond with care. Whatever you say Gora, I too am deeply convinced that our work will make no progress if our women's development remains stunted like Chinese women's feet.'

'But I've never said women should not be educated!' Gora protested.

'Does Part Three of the primer *Charupath* amount to an education?'

'Very well, from now on we can introduce Part One of *Binoybodh*.'

That evening, the two friends kept returning to the subject of Poreshbabu's daughters, until it grew quite late. On his way home alone, Gora mulled over these things, and once back home in bed, could not drive the thoughts of Poreshbabu's daughters from his mind, until he fell asleep. Such complications had never occurred in Gora's life. He had never spared women a single thought. Now Binoy had proved that this too, was a significant part of life. One could not dismiss it; it called for resistance, not compromise.

The next day, when Binoy proposed, 'Come on, let's go to Pareshbabu's, it's been long since you visited them. He keeps asking after you'—Gora agreed without demurring. Moreover, he was inwardly not as indifferent as before. At first, Gora had been totally detached about the very existence of Sucharita and Poreshbabu's daughters; then, lately, he had developed a contemptuous hostility towards them; but now, a certain curiosity had arisen in his mind. He felt a special urge to understand what it was that had so captivated Binoy.

It was dark when the two of them arrived at Poreshbabu's house. In the room on the first floor, Haran was reading one of his English pieces to Poreshbabu by the glass-shaded light of a sej. Poreshbabu here was just a pretext, actually; Haran's real target was Sucharita. At the far end of the table, shading her eyes from the oil lamp's glare with a palmleaf fan, Sucharita listened in silence. From habitual compliance, she was trying hard to be attentive, but her mind wandered, every now and then. When the attendant announced Gora and Binoy, Sucharita started. As she rose from her chowki, preparing to leave, Poreshbabu stopped her:

'Where are you going Radhé? It's only our own Binoy and Gour.'

Sucharita sat down again, embarrassed. She was relieved that Haran's prolonged reading of his English composition had been interrupted. She was excited no doubt at news of Gora's arrival, but the thought of seeing him there in Haranbabu's presence unsettled her and made her very uneasy. Was it the prospect of a confrontation between the two men, or was there some other reason? It was hard to tell.

The very mention of Gora's name aroused deep hostility in Haranbabu's heart. After somehow returning Gora's namaskar, he remained silent and taciturn. As soon as he saw Haran, Gora's aggressive instincts were aroused.

Borodasundari had been invited out with her three daughters. Poreshbabu was supposed to fetch them in the evening. It was time for him to go. The arrival of Gora and Binoy at this time made things difficult for him. But knowing he should delay no more, he left, whispering to Haran and Sucharita:

'Please keep them company. I'll be back as soon as possible.'

In no time, a terrible argument broke out between Gora and Haranbabu. The quarrel was about Brownlow Saheb, magistrate of a district not far from Kolkata, whom Poreshbabu and his family had met during their stay in Dhaka. Because Poreshbabu's wife and daughters came out of the antahpur to socialize in public, the saheb and his wife showed them special respect. Every year on his birthday, the saheb held an agricultural fair. This time, when she met Brownlow Saheb's wife, Borodasundari spoke of her daughters' expertise in English poetry.

'The Lieutenant Governor and his wife will attend the fair this year,' the memsaheb suddenly observed. 'It would be very nice if your daughters could enact a short English verse drama for their benefit.'

Borodasundari was highly enthused by this proposal. Today, it was for a rehearsal that she had taken the girls to a friend's house. When asked if he could attend the fair, Gora had said 'No!' with unwarranted belligerence. Now Gora and Haran engaged in a violent altercation about Anglo–Bengali relations and the obstacles to mutual social intercourse between them.

'The Bengalis are to blame,' Haran declared. 'With all our social malpractices and evil customs we are not even worthy of social interaction with the British.'

'If that's true,' countered Gora, 'then it is humiliating for us to be tempted by the idea of mingling with the British despite our unworthiness.'

'But those who have made themselves worthy are sufficiently honoured by the British,' insisted Haran. 'Take everyone here, for instance.'

'Where honour for one highlights the dishonour of all others, I count such honour an insult,' Gora retorted.

In no time, Haranbabu flew into a rage, and Gora continued to sting him with a succession of barbed remarks. As they argued in this fashion, Sucharita, at the other end of the table, observed Gora intently from behind her fan.Though within listening range, she paid no attention to what was being said. Had she realized she was staring fixedly at Gora, she would have felt embarrassed; but she seemed to forget herself as she gazed at him. Gora was leaning forward, his powerful arms resting on the table; the lamplight shone on his broad, fair forehead; sometimes a contemptuous smile, sometimes a frown of disgust, would play upon his face; every fluctuating mood expressed proud self-esteem. Not only his voice but his face and entire body seemed to exude the strong conviction that his words expressed not passing thoughts or emotions but attitudes born of long cogitation and practice; his words bore no trace of hesitation, weakness or randomness. Sucharita watched him in wonder, as if, for the first time in all her life, she saw someone as a special human being, a special man. She could no longer compare him with other ordinary persons. In contrast to Gora, Haranbabu now seemed insignificant. His own bodily and facial contours, his expression and mannerisms, even his outfit and chador, seemed to mock Haranbabu. All these days, in her repeated conversations with Binoy regarding Gora's character, Sucharita had taken Gora for an unusual man who belonged to a certain group and held a certain set of beliefs. She had imagined merely that he might serve to accomplish some special goal for the nation's benefit. But today, gazing at him with rapt attention, Sucharita saw Gora as himself alone, independent of all groups, all belief-systems and all goals. Like an ocean that surges in unaccountable turmoil when it sees the moon rise above all everyday needs and actions, Sucharita's heart also filled to overflowing, its flood engulfing everything, all her thoughts and beliefs, her entire life. For the first time, she experienced what it meant to be human, to possess a human soul, and in this exquisite sensation, she forgot herself completely.

Haranbabu had noticed Sucharita's total absorption. This weakened the force of his arguments. Ultimately, he lost his patience, and rising to his feet, he called to Sucharita with an air of deep intimacy:

'Sucharita, step into this room for a moment, there is something I must tell you.'

Sucharita started, as if someone had struck her. Not that Haranbabu's relationship with her precluded his calling her aside in this way. At any other time, she would have thought nothing of it; but today, in the presence of Gora and Binoy, she felt insulted. Gora, in particular, glanced at her with such an expression that she could not forgive Haranbabu. At first she remained silent, as if she had not heard.

'Do you hear me, Sucharita?' demanded Haranbabu, a hint of annoyance in his voice. 'I have something to tell you. We must step into the other room.'

'Let it be for now,' Sucharita answered, without meeting his eyes. 'Let Baba join us first.'

'We should be going,' said Binoy, rising.

'No, Binoybabu, please don't get up!' Sucharita quickly intervened. 'Baba wants you to stay. He'll be here any moment.' There was a desperate plea in her voice, as if they were proposing to abandon a female deer to the hunter's clutches.

'I can't take this anymore! I'll take your leave, then.' With these words, Haranbabu rushed from the room. Having left precipitately in the heat of the moment, he regretted it instantly but could find no other excuse to return.

After Haranbabu's departure, as Sucharita sat with bowed head and flushed countenance in a state of acute embarrassment, Gora found a chance to take a good look at her face. In Sucharita's expression there was no sign of the arrogance and garrulity that Gora mentally expected of educated women. Her face shone with intelligence no doubt, but how gentle it appeared now, softened by modesty and shame! How delicately graceful were the contours of that face! Above those eyebrows, how pure and clear her forehead, like the Sharat sky in early autumn! Those lips were mute, but the sweetness of unspoken words nestled between them like a tender, unopened bud. Never before had Gora noticed the attire of a nabina, a modern young lady, having spurned such things without even having seen them. But today, he saw with special approval the new style in which Sucharita had draped her body in a sari. Her arm rested on the table. To Gora's eyes, that arm, emerging from the folds of her sleeve, seemed like a beneficent message from her tender heart. On this tranquil, lamplit evening, Sucharita's chamber appeared to him as a special, unified vision, encircling her with its light, its picture-embellished walls, its décor and its orderliness. In a single instant, Gora realized that this was a home, adorned by the care, affection and grace of a woman skilled at nurture, the room's atmosphere far exceeding its physical dimensions, its walls, beams and ceiling. Gora sensed the presence of a living spirit in the environment around him, his heart rocked by surging tides of emotion, held captive by a deep intimacy. Never before in his life had he experienced anything so exquisite. As he gazed at her, everything about Sucharita, from the unruly tendrils of hair above her forehead to the sari border at her feet, gradually assumed for him a very special significance. Gora felt simultaneously attracted to Sucharita's personality as a whole, and also to every separate aspect of it.

For a while, all of them were embarrassed, at a loss for words. Then, glancing at Sucharita, Binoy said, to start a topic of conversation:

'As we were saying, the other day . . .' He continued: 'I've told you earlier, I once believed there was no hope for our nation and our society, that we would remain immature forever, the English always deployed as our custodians, that things would remain exactly the same, that we had no means whatsoever of resisting the tremendous power of the British and the moribund state of our own culture. Most of our compatriots share a similar attitude. In such situations, people either immerse themselves in selfish pursuits or live in a state of detachment. That's why middle class folk in our country think of nothing but professional advancement, and the rich feel gratified simply with titles conferred by the government. Our life's journey comes to a halt after just a small distance, so distant goals don't even arise in our imagination, and we deem it unnecessary to equip ourselves for such ventures. I, too, had once decided to get myself a job, with Gora's father as my patron. But then Gora forbade me, saying "No, a government job is not for you".'

'Please don't imagine I made that remark because I was angry with the government,' Gora clarified, seeing a hint of surprise on Sucharita's face. 'Those who serve the government arrogantly mistake the government's power for personal authority, and form a class apart from their fellow-countrymen. With each passing day, this attitude is becoming increasingly evident among us. I know a relative, a deputy in earlier times but now living in retirement after he resigned from the post. The district magistrate had asked him: "Babu, why are so many persons acquitted in the trials you conduct?" "Saheb, there's a reason for that," he had answered. "Those you send to prison are mere animals in your eyes. But those I condemn to imprisonment are my brothers, after all." Those days, one could still find deputies capable of making such a major statement, nor did we lack British magistrates willing to listen. But day by day, the trappings of service are becoming mere decorations, the deputy of today increasingly treating his own countrymen as mere animals. And they are even losing the awareness that, in ascending the professional ladder by such means, they are constantly falling downwards on the moral scale. No good can ever come from condescension born of heights attained with someone else's support, for we immediately start being unjust to those we despise.'

As he spoke, Gora smashed his fist on the table, making the oil lamp tremble.

'Gora, this table doesn't belong to the government,' Binoy reminded him, 'and this sej is Poreshbabu's.'

Gora burst into a loud guffaw. The sound of his laughter filled the entire house. Sucharita was surprised that Gora could respond to sarcasm with such effusive childlike mirth. Privately, she was delighted. She had not known earlier that people who think about grave matters can also be capable of heartfelt merriment. Gora spoke of many things that day. Although Sucharita remained silent, the approval he saw on her face filled his heart with enthusiasm.

'Please remember one thing,' he said in conclusion, as if addressing Sucharita, 'if we mistakenly believe that because the British have assumed power, we too can never become powerful unless we ape them, then the impossible can never become a possibility, and blindly imitating them, we shall be neither here nor there. Know this for sure: Bharat has a special character, a special power, a special reality, and only through a complete flowering of these elements can Bharat be saved, its aims fulfilled. If we have not learned this from studying British history, then all our learning is false. I request you to enter the arena of Bharatvarsha with all its virtues and flaws, and if there are any imperfections, correct them from within. But observe, understand and reflect upon Bharatvarsha, confront it, merge with it. Opposing it from outside, steeped to your very bones in Khristani ways right from your childhood days, you will not understand Bharat at all. You will continue to attack the nation, and will be of no service to it.'

Gora called it a request no doubt, but this was no request, more like an order, too forceful to depend on anyone else's consent! Head bowed,

Sucharita heard him out. These words, specially addressed to her by Gora with such intense urgency, threw her heart into turmoil. She had no time then to analyse the nature of this turmoil. Never, for a single moment, had Sucharita imagined the existence of a vast, ancient entity called Bharatvarsha. Today, listening to Gora's powerful words, Sucharita suddenly realized that this entity, controlling the distant past and remote future, was secretly weaving a strand of distinctive hue, in a distinctive pattern, into the giant web of human destiny. How fine that strand was, how variegated, and how profoundly connected with distant goals! In an instant Sucharita realized how petty we become, and how blind to our surroundings as we pursue our activities, if we do not remain aware that every Indian's life is encompassed and possessed by an entity of such magnitude. Shedding all her inhibitions in that wave of sudden elation, Sucharita confessed with simple humility:

'I had never thought about the nation like this, with such breadth of vision, such verity. But I have a question: what is the connection between dharma or religious duty, and the nation? Isn't religion the nation's past?'

Sucharita's query, voiced so gently, was music to Gora's ears. Reflected in her wide eyes, the question appeared even more exquisite.

'The nation's past, greater by far than the nation itself, manifests itself through the nation,' he replied. 'The Almighty Ishwar has expressed his eternal image in this motley form. Those who claim there is only one truth, and therefore, that only one faith is true, that only one form of faith is true, are believers only in a single truth but unwilling to acknowledge that the truth is infinite. The infinite One manifests itself in an infinite multiplicity: that is the play of realities we encounter in this world. That is why faith acquires diverse forms, offering us manifold routes to sensing the presence of the One who is the monarch of faith. I assure you that you can glimpse the sun through the open windows of Bharatvarsha. For that you need not cross the seas to look out of the window of a Christian church.'

'You suggest that Bharatvarsha's mantra of faith leads us to the Almighty by a distinctive route,' Sucharita said. 'What is distinctive about that route?'

'It's the fact that Brahma, the divinity without attributes, is manifest within the particular and the definable. But there is no end to his special manifestations. Water, land, air, fire, life, intellect, love—all manifest his existence in special ways. He cannot be quantified, for he is infinite, and this has endlessly baffled science. The formless assumes countless forms without end; his eternal flow contains everything within it, large or small, abstract or concrete. The One with infinite attributes is also the One without attributes; the One who assumes infinite forms is also the One without form. Other nations have reduced Ishwar's stature, trying to confine Him to a single particularity. In Bharatvarsha, too, there is an attempt to see Ishwar within the limits of the particular, but Bharatvarsha doesn't count that particularity as the sole or ultimate truth. No devotee in Bharatvarsha would deny that Ishwar, with his infinite attributes, transcends even that particularity.'

'The knowledgeable may not, but what about the ignorant?' Sucharita asked.

'I have already said that the ignorant will distort every truth in every country!'

'But hasn't such distortion gone too far in our country?' Sucharita persisted.

'Perhaps,' conceded Gora. 'But that's because Bharatvarsha wants to fully acknowledge both aspects of religion: concrete and abstract, internal and external, bodily and spiritual. So, those who can't embrace the abstract accept only the concrete, and out of ignorance, they create strange distortions within that material image. But it is unthinkable that we should foolishly dishonour Bharatvarsha's extraordinary, diverse and tremendous effort to apprehend comprehensively, in body, mind and deed, the One who exists in form as well as formlessness, the concrete as well as the abstract, in contemplation as well as in manifest reality. Or that we should, instead, embrace as our sole religion a narrow, dry, featureless eighteenth century European faith, a hybrid mix of theism and atheism. Owing to convictions imbibed since childhood, you will not even understand me properly; this man's English education has proved futile, you will think. But if ever you should develop respect for Bharatvarsha's true nature, its true endeavour, if you can penetrate the deep secret of Bharatvarsha's success in manifesting itself, despite a thousand obstacles and distortions, then—then, what can I say? Having regained the Indianness of your nature and abilities, you will be liberated.'

'Don't take me for a fanatic,' persisted Gora, observing Sucharita's long silence. 'Please don't interpret my arguments as the language of Hindu orthodoxy, especially of those who have suddenly assumed a new orthodoxy. I have glimpsed a vast, profound unity in the many manifestations and multiple endeavours of Bharatvarsha, a unity that drives me wild with joy. Rejoicing at such unity, I have no hesitation in mingling with the most ignorant of Bharatvarsha's inhabitants, taking my place beside them in the dust. Some understand this message of Bharatvarsha, others don't, but never mind—I am one with everyone in Bharatvarsha—they are all my own people—within all of them, I have no doubt, eternal Bharatvarsha's concealed presence is constantly at work.'

The words, uttered in Gora's powerful voice, seemed to vibrate in the walls, tables and all the furniture in the room. Sucharita could not be expected to readily understand such words, but the first, vague stirrings of experience are also extremely powerful. Sucharita was now tormented by the realization that life was indeed not confined to four walls or a single party.

At this juncture, swift female footsteps were heard near the staircase, mingled with sounds of uproarious laughter. Poreshbabu was back with Borodasundari and the girls. The laughter concerned some prank Sudhir had played upon the girls as they mounted the staircase. Entering the room, Labanya, Lalita and Satish composed themselves as soon as they saw Gora. Labanya left the room. Standing beside Binoy's chowki, Satish began a whispered tete-à-tete with him. Drawing up a chowki behind Sucharita, Lalita all but hid herself from view.

'I really got delayed,' apologized Poresh, entering the room. 'Has Panubabu left?'

Sucharita did not reply.

'Yes,' said Binoy. 'He couldn't wait.'

'We'll take leave, as well,' said Gora, rising to his feet.

He bowed deferentially to Poreshbabu, joining his hands in a namaskar.

'I had no time to chat with all of you today,' said Poreshbabu. 'Visit us sometimes, when you have some spare time, baba.'

As Gora and Binoy prepared to leave, Borodasundari arrived on the scene. They greeted her with a namaskar.

'Are you leaving right away?' she asked.

'Yes,' Gora replied.

'But Binoybabu, you can't leave,' she insisted. 'You must dine with us tonight. I have something urgent to discuss with you.'

'Yes Ma, don't let Binoybabu leave!' cried Satish, springing to his feet and grasping Binoy's hand. 'He'll stay with me tonight.'

'Do you want to take Binoybabu away?' Borodasundari asked Gora, seeing that Binoy was too embarrassed to reply. 'Do you need him?'

'No, not at all,' answered Gora. 'Binoy, why don't you stay on? I'll take my leave.' He rushed from the scene.

When Borodasundari asked Gora's permission for Binoy to remain, Binoy could not help stealing a glance at Lalita's face. Lalita turned away with a suppressed smile. Binoy could not counter these small barbs she directed at him, yet they pierced him like thorns. As soon as he came inside, Lalita said:

'Better, Binoybabu, if you had managed to escape tonight.'

'Why?' he wanted to know.

'Ma is conspiring to get you into trouble. They're short of an actor for the performance at the magistrates' fair. Ma has decided you're the right person.'

'What a disaster!' exclaimed Binoy, flustered. 'I can't take it on!'

'I've already said so to Ma,' Lalita assured him with a smile. 'Your friend will never permit you to participate in this performance.'

'Leave my friend alone,' said Binoy, stung. 'I've never acted in my life, not since I was born. Why me?'

'It's not as if we have been actors all our lives either, through all our different births!'

At this moment, Borodasundari entered the room.

'Ma, it's no use your asking Binoybabu to join the performance,' Lalita told her. 'If you can first get his friend to agree . . .'

'This has nothing to do with my friend's consent!' pleaded Binoy. 'Acting isn't child's play. I just don't have the talent.'

'Don't worry about that,' Borodasundari assured him. 'We can train you up. If little girls can act, why can't you?'

There was no way out for Binoy.

## 21

Gora walked home slowly in a preoccupied state, abandoning his usual brisk pace. Instead of taking the direct route to his house, he made a detour via the Ganga shore. At that time, the land and water of the Ganga riverside in Kolkata had not yet been assailed by the hideousness of mercantile greed, the river's edge was not shackled by railway lines, nor the water by bridges. On winter evenings, the city's dark breath did not blacken the sky so intensely. The river carried a message of peace from the lonely peaks of the remote Himalayas into the dust-filled turmoil of Kolkata.

Nature had never found a chance to attract Gora. His mind was constantly in upheaval, caused by his own enthusiasm. He had not even noticed stretches of water, land and sky that were not related to his field of activity.

But today, the sky above the river began to silently stir Gora's heart, insistently, with its darkness steeped in starlight. No ripple disturbed the river. At the ghaat on the Kolkata rivershore some boats twinkled with lights, while others remained unlit and still. In the dense trees on the opposite shore, an inky blackness had congealed. Above them glowed the planet Jupiter, its unblinking gaze piercing the night like the all-knowing god of darkness.

Nature, great and silent, seemed to overwhelm Gora's mind and body tonight. The darkness of the vast night sky began to pulsate to the rhythm of his heart. All this while, Prakriti, the force of Nature, had waited patiently. But now, finding a door to Gora's heart unlocked, it instantly conquered this unguarded fortress. For so long, Gora had remained very independent, engaged with his own intellect, ideas and activities. But what happened tonight? When did he acknowledge Nature's presence! And all at once, how did these deep dark waters, this dense black shore, that great black sky, embrace and welcome him! How did Gora surrender to Prakriti tonight?

From the roadside, the delicate fragrance of some unknown flower wafted across from a foreign vine in the garden surrounding a commercial office, seeming to gently stroke Gora's agonized heart. The river diverted his attention from the tireless workspaces of human habitation, pointing towards some indistinct, far-off place; there, upon the solitary shore, what blossoms those interlocking tree-branches produced! What shadows those trees had cast! There, beneath the pure blue sky, the days resembled someone's wide-eyed gaze, and the nights were like the shade of her bashfully lowered lashes. Never before had Gora experienced anything like the attraction of the unfathomable eternal force that swept him away suddenly, engulfing him in a whirlwind of sweetness. It simultaneously seared his mind with extremes of pain and joy. On this cool Hemanta night, on the rivershore, amidst the city's inarticulate babble and the indistinct starlight, Gora forgot himself as he stood before a veiled enchantress whose presence filled the whole universe. Because he had not previously greeted this empress with bowed head, the magic web of her authority suddenly bound Gora tonight, its multicoloured strands fastening him to land, water and sky. Amazed at himself, Gora sank down to one of the steps of the solitary ghaat. Repeatedly he asked himself what this new apparition signified, and why it was necessary to his life! Where was its place in the resolve by which he had always determined and mentally arranged his life? Was it opposed to such a resolve? Must he struggle to vanquish it? With these thoughts, as Gora clenched his fists, he saw in his mind's eye the questioning gaze of a pair of moist eyes, bright with intelligence, tender with modesty. The fingers of a flawlessly beautiful hand disrupted his reflections with the promise of the untasted heavenly nectar of their touch. Rapture streaked like lightning through Gora's entire body. In the solitary darkness, this profound experience demolished all his questions and hesitations. He began to enjoy this new sensation with all his mind and body, reluctant to relinquish it.

'You're so late baba, your food has gone cold!' Anandamoyi remarked when Gora came home late at night.

'I don't know, Ma, what got into me tonight,' replied Gora. 'I spent a long time at the Ganga ghaat.'

'Binoy was with you, I suppose?' she asked.

'No, I was alone.'

Anandamoyi was secretly rather surprised. Never before had Gora unaccountably lingered at the ghaat so late, lost in his thoughts. It was not his nature, at all, to brood in silence. As he ate absentmindedly, Anandamoyi noticed a strange, animated glow on his face.

'You went to Binoy's house, I suppose?' she asked him gently, after a short silence.

'No, both of us went to Poreshababu's place today,' Gora replied.

Anadamoyi reflected in silence for a while.

'Have you got to know all of them?' she now wanted to know.

'Yes, I have.'

'Their daughters come out to meet everyone, I suppose?'

'Yes, they follow no restrictions.'

Seeing no sign of the intense emotion that would normally have accompanied such an answer, Anandamoyi again lapsed into a thoughtful silence.

When he got up the next morning, Gora did not immediately proceed to wash and dress for work, as on other days. Absently, he opened the bedroom door facing east, and stood there for a while. Their alley opened onto a major road, at the east end of which was a school. Above an ancient jamun tree in the school grounds floated a wisp of white mist, and behind it one could see the rosy haze of approaching dawn. Slowly, as Gora watched in silence, the fragile mist evaporated, bright sunshine penetrating the tree-branches like so many glittering bayonets, and in no time, the streets of Kolkata filled with crowds and babble. Just then, seeing Abinash and some other students approach his house from the corner of the alley, Gora ripped the magic web in a single violent move.

'No, all this means nothing. It won't do, at all!' he told himself, striking a great blow at his own heart.

He rushed out of his bedroom. For Gora's gang to arrive at his house and not find him ready well in time, was unprecedented. This minor lapse struck Gora as utterly contemptible. He privately resolved not to visit Poreshbabu's house anymore, and to try putting a stop to more such discussions by avoiding Binoy for a few days as well.

When he went downstairs, it was determined after mutual consultation that Gora, accompanied by two or three others, would proceed on a walking tour on the Grand Trunk Road. He would carry no funds, accepting the hospitality of homes along the way. Armed with this wonderful resolve, Gora felt a sudden surge of extreme enthusiasm. He was gripped by a powerful exhilaration at the prospect of breaking all bonds to set out on the open road like this. He felt as if the very idea of his setting forth had ripped the web in which his heart had secretly become entangled. Reminding himself resonantly that such emotional obsessions were merely illusory and that duty alone was real, Gora rushed from the ground floor sitting room like a schoolboy after class, to prepare himself for the journey.

At that moment, Krishnadayal was returning from his bath in the Ganga, his small round ghoti filled with Ganga water, shoulders wrapped in a namavali inscribed with the deity's name, chanting the holy mantra to himself. Gora all but collided with him. Embarrassed, Gora hastily greeted him with a pranam. 'Never mind, never mind!' cried Krishandayal, flustered, and hastened away awkwardly. Gora's touch had erased the purifying effect of his bath in the Ganga before his daily puja. Gora did not quite realize it was his touch that Krishnadayal particularly tried to avoid. He thought it was an obsession with purity that made it Krishnadayal's sole aim, always, to avoid all contact with everybody. After all, he spurned Anandamoyi as a non-believer, and Mahim being a working man, Krishnadayal hardly had the opportunity to interact with him. Mahim's daughter Shashimukhi was the only family member he sought out, to teach her Sanskrit stotras and initiate her into the rituals of prayer.

After Krishnadayal had escaped in dismay at Gora having touched his feet, the cause of his embarrassment dawned upon Gora, who felt privately amused. In this manner, his ties to his father had been virtually severed, and for all his criticism of her lack of orthodoxy, Gora worhipped his unconventional mother with full devotion. After his morning meal, Gora came to his mother, carrying a small bundle of clothing on his back as British travelers do.

'Ma, I'm going away for a few days.'

'Where are you going, baba?'

'I can't say for sure.'

'Do you have some task to accomplish?'

'Nothing that would qualify as a task. This journey is a task in itself.' Then, seeing that Anandamoyi was silent, Gora pleaded: 'Please, Ma, you can't forbid me. You know me after all. There is no fear of my becoming a sanyasi. I can't stay away from my mother for long.'

Never before had Gora articulated his love for his mother in this way. As soon as the words were out of his mouth, he felt embarrassed.

'Binoy will go with you, I suppose?' asked Anandamoyi, hastily concealing her delight.

'No, Ma, he won't be going with me,' Gora told her. 'Just look—Ma is immediately worried, wondering who will protect her Gora on the way! If you consider Binoy my bodyguard, that's your blind faith. If I come back safe this time, I'll dispel that false belief of yours.'

'I'll hear from you every now and then, won't I?' Anandamoyi inquired.

'Assume that you won't. Then you'll be pleased if you do hear from me. There's nothing to fear; nobody will snatch away your Gora. Ma, nobody values me as you do. But

if anyone fancies this bundle, I'll hand it to him and come away. I shan't stake my life trying to safeguard it, that's for sure!'

Gora touched Anandamoyi's feet. She stroked his head and kissed the hand with which she had blessed him, without forbidding him in any way. Anandamoyi never forbade anyone anything simply because she herself might suffer, or from any imaginary misgivings. Having overcome many obstacles and mishaps in her own life, the outer world was not unknown to her and fear was alien to her mind. She had not entertained any apprehensions that Gora might come to some harm. But since the previous day, she had been wondering what revolution had taken place in Gora's heart. Today, hearing that Gora was off on a tour for no reason, her anxiety increased.

Gora had barely stepped out into the street, bundle on his back, when he met Binoy, carefully carrying a pair of blood-red Basra rosebuds.

'Binoy, now we can test whether seeing your face augurs well or ill for my journey,' Gora remarked.

'Are you going away?'

'Yes.'

'Where?'

'"Where?" the echo replies.'

'Is there no better answer than an echo?'

'No. Go to Ma, she'll tell you everything. I'm off.'

Gora rushed away.

Entering the interior space of the antahpur, Binoy greeted Anandamoyi with a pranam and placed the roses at her feet.

'Where did you find these, Binoy?' she asked him.

'When one obtains something of value, one's first desire is to offer it to one's mother in devotion,' he replied evasively. Then, settling on Anandamoyi's taktaposh, her wood-plank bed, he observed: 'Ma, I must say you are preoccupied.'

'Why do you say that?'

'You've completely forgotten to offer me the usual paan.'

Embarrassed, Anandamoyi fetched some paan for Binoy. They spent the afternoon chatting, the two of them. Binoy could shed no clear light on Gora's random travels.

'Yesterday you went to Poreshababu's with Gora, I believe?' asked Anandamoyi, conversationally.

Binoy recounted all that had taken place the previous day. Anandamoyi drank in all his words.

'Ma, now my puja is over, may I reverentially carry away the flowers that your feet have blessed?' said Binoy, while taking his leave.

Anandamoyi handed the roses to Binoy with a smile. These roses are valued for more than their beauty, she thought: surely they conceal some truths too deep for botany to define.

In the evening, after Binoy had left, she grew very thoughtful. Again and again she prayed to the Almighty that Gora should not be unhappy, and that nothing should separate him from Binoy.

## 22

Those roses have a history.

The previous night, Gora had come away from Poreshbabu's house, but Binoy had to suffer an ordeal regarding his proposed participation in the performance at the magistrate's house. Not that Lalita was particularly enthusiastic about this performance; rather, she had a distaste for such occasions. But she seemed stubbornly determined to involve Binoy in this performance, somehow. She was bent on making Binoy do things that were against Gora's wishes. Why she found Binoy's devotion to Gora so intolerable, Lalita herself could not understand. As if breaking all bonds to liberate Binoy would bring her great relief.

'Why, sir, what's the harm in acting?' Lalita demanded, tossing her braids.

'There may be no harm in acting,' Binoy replied, 'but the thought of performing at that magistrate's house makes me uneasy.'

'Are those your thoughts, or someone else's?'

'It's not my brief to speak for others and in any case that would be difficult. You may not believe me, but it's my own thoughts I express, sometimes in my own words, sometimes in others'.'

Lalita smiled faintly, offering no reply. 'Your friend Gourbabu probably considers it extremely heroic to ignore the magistrate's invitation, as effective as fighting the British,' she observed after a while.

'My friend may not think so, but I do!' declared Binoy heatedly. 'What is it but a form of battle? If a man treats me with utter disregard, thinking I'd be grateful if he just beckoned me with his little finger, then how can I preserve my self-esteem unless I return his contempt?'

The injured pride in Binoy's words appealed to Lalita, herself proud by nature. But for that very reason, realizing the weakness of her own argument, Lalita began to inflict Binoy with the sharpness of her unwarranted sarcasm at the slightest provocation.

'Look, why are you arguing with me?' Binoy ultimately protested. 'Why don't you say, "I want you to join our performance"? Then I would have the pleasure of sacrificing my own convictions to keep your request.'

'Wah, why should I say any such thing? If you truly have convictions of your own, why should you sacrifice them at my request? But they must be true convictions.'

'Very well, let that be so. I have no true convictions. I agree to perform, not at your request but because you have defeated me in argument.'

At this moment, Borodasundari entered the room. Rising at once, Binoy went up to her.

'Please tell me how I must prepare for the performance,' he said.

'Have no worries on that score,' replied Borodasundari proudly. 'We'll get you into shape. But you must come regularly for practice every day.'

'Very well. I'll take leave of you now.'

'That's out of the question! You must dine with us.'

'Not tonight, let it be.'

'No, no, that's not possible.'

Binoy stayed for dinner but lacked his usual cheerfulness. Sucharita, too, was strangely silent and preoccupied. She had been pacing the veranda while Lalita and Binoy were engaged in their war of words. Tonight, the conversation flagged.

'I failed to please you, even after admitting defeat,' Binoy remarked, observing Lalita's grave expression when it was time for him to leave.

Lalita walked away, without offering any reply. She was not given to weeping, but tonight her eyes were brimming with unshed tears. What was the matter? Why did she provoke Binoybabu repeatedly, hurting her own self? As long as Binoy remained averse to joining the performance, Lalita's obduracy had kept increasing, but as soon as he consented, all her enthusiasm disappeared. All the arguments against his participation in the show now gathered strength in her heart.

'Binoybabu should not have consented like this, just to keep my request!' her heart protested in torment. 'Request! Why must he keep my request? Does he think he's being civil, keeping my request? As if I'm dying to receive this bit of civility from him!'

But was it any use making such tall claims now? She had indeed importuned Binoy continuously, to drag him into the theatre troupe. How could she be angry with Binoy for conceding her request out of sheer politeness? Lalita was overcome with contempt and shame at her own behaviour, emotions acute beyond all reason. On any other day, she would have gone to Sucharita at this moment of inner turmoil. But today she didn't go to her, and why her eyes overflowed with tears that choked her heart, she herself could not fathom.

The next morning, Sudhir had brought Labanya a bouquet. In the bouquet, a pair of ready-to-bloom Basra rosebuds grew on a single stem. Lalita extracted the stem from the bouquet.

'What are you doing?' Labanya demanded.

'It hurts me to see fine blossoms tied into a bundle with a mass of common flowers and leaves,' Lalita told her. 'It is barbaric to forcibly bind everything into a single category, like that.'

With these words, Lalita untied all the flowers and arranged them separately in different parts of the room, reserving only the pair of roses, which she took away.

'Didi, where did you get those flowers?' asked Satish, running up to her.

'Won't you visit your friend today?' Lalita inquired, without answering his question.

Satish had forgotten about Binoy all this while, but at the mention of his name, he jumped up.

'Yes, I will.' He declared, impatient to leave at once.

'What do you do there?' asked Lalita, restraining him.

'We chat,' answered Satish, briefly.

'He gives you so many pictures, why don't you ever give him anything?'

Binoy would cut out all sorts of pictures for Satish, from English papers and other such sources. Satish had begun pasting the pictures into a notebook. He was now so obsessed with filling up the pages that even when he saw a proper book, he would long to cut out pictures from it. He had suffered many reprimands from his sisters on account of this greed.

Today, suddenly confronted with the awareness that acts of kindness must be reciprocated, he became very worried. It was not easy to renounce his attachment to any of the personal belongings stored in his broken tin trunk.

'Never mind,' laughed Lalita, seeing Satish's anxious expression. She pinched his cheek. 'You needn't get so worried. Just give him this pair of roses.'

He brightened at such an easy solution to his problem. Carrying the twin rosebuds, he set off at once to repay the debt of friendship. On the way, he ran into Binoy.

'Binoybabu! Binoybabu!' called Satish from a distance, rushing up to him with the flowers concealed under his clothing. 'Guess what I've brought for you!'

When Binoy admitted defeat, Satish produced the flowers.

'Oh, how wonderful!' exclaimed Binoy. 'But, Satishbabu, these don't belong to you, after all. I hope I won't end up in police custody for harbouring stolen goods?'

Satish was suddenly doubtful whether he could actually describe the flowers as his own property.

'No! Wah, Lalitadidi asked me to give them to you, after all,' he disclosed, after some thought.

The matter ended there, and Binoy dispatched Satish with the assurance that he would come by that evening.

Binoy was unable to forget his pain at Lalita's barbed comments the previous night. As he rarely rubbed anyone the wrong way, he never expected such a sharp onslaught from anybody. Before this, he had merely regarded Lalita as Sucharita's follower. But for some time now, Binoy's feelings for Lalita had resembled the plight of a goaded elephant unable to ignore his keeper, the mahout, even for an instant. It had become Binoy's chief concern to determine how to find peace by pleasing Lalita ever so slightly. When he returned to his lodgings in the evening, Lalita's sarcastic, piercing remarks would resonate in his mind, one by one, keeping him awake.

'Lalita despises me as Gora's shadow, thinking I lack substance of my own, but that is utterly untrue!' He would mentally accumulate all sorts of counter-arguments. But all these arguments were of no use to him, for Lalita had never explicitly charged him with this accusation. In fact, she had not given him a chance to debate the issue at all. Binoy had so many arguments to answer her with, but because he could not articulate them, his inward resentment grew even more intense. Ultimately, seeing no pleasure on Lalita's countenance even after he acknowledged defeat, he felt extremely restless when he came back home. 'Am I really so despicable?' he began to wonder. So, when he learnt from Satish that it was Lalita who had sent the flowers, he felt exhilarated. He thought Lalita had given him the roses as a token of reconciliation because she was pleased at his agreeing to participate in the performance.

'Let's leave these flowers at home,' he thought, at first. Then he reconsidered: 'No, let me purify them with the touch of Ma's feet, because these flowers are a peace offering.'

When Binoy arrived at Poreshbabu's that evening, Satish was reading his school homework aloud to Lalita.

'Red is the colour of war,' said Binoy to Lalita. 'So the flowers of truce should have been white.'

Lalita gazed at him in incomprehension. Binoy drew a bunch of white oleanders from beneath the folds of his chador, and held them out to her. 'Lovely though your flowers might be,' he declared, 'they still retain shades of anger. These flowers of mine can't match them in beauty, but they present themselves to you humbly, in the white hue of peace.'

'My flowers? What are you referring to?' asked Lalita, flushing to the roots of her ears.

'I must have misunderstood, then,' said Binoy, rather taken aback. 'Satishbabu, did you deliver the right flowers to the right person?'

'Why, Lalitadidi asked me to present them, didn't she?' Satish protested loudly.

'Who did she want them given to?' Binoy asked him.

'To you.'

'I've never seen someone so stupid!' exclaimed Lalita, reddening. She rapped Satish on the shoulder. 'Didn't you want to offer flowers to Binoybabu in return for those pictures?'

'Yes, that's true, but wasn't it you who suggested I give them to him?'

asked Satish, stupefied.

In trying to argue with Satish, Lalita found herself entangled even more securely in a web of words. Binoy clearly understood that the flowers were indeed sent by Lalita, but she had intended the gift to be anonymous.

'I relinquish all claims to your flowers,' he said, 'But that doesn't mean there's something wrong with the flowers I've brought. On the auspicious occasion of our reconciliation, these flowers . . .'

'What is our quarrel about, and how is it resolved, for that matter?' asked Lalita, shaking her head.

'Is the whole thing an illusion then, from beginning to end? The quarrel, the flowers, the reconciliation, is everything a lie? Is this merely a case of mistaking an oyster shell for silver, or is the oyster itself an illusion? What about that proposal regarding a performance at the magistrate saheb's?'

'That's no illusion,' said Lalita. 'But why quarrel about it? Why do you imagine that I have stirred up a great dispute just to make you agree to this performance, or that I am gratified at your consent? If you consider acting a sin, why should you agree to it simply at someone else's urging?'

With these words, Lalita left the room. Things had turned out completely contrary to her expectations. Today, Lalita had resolved that she would concede victory to Binoy, and persuade him to withdraw from the performance. But the way the topic was broached, and the way it developed, the outcome was exactly the opposite. Binoy thought Lalita still chafed with the desire to retaliate against his prolonged reluctance to perform. He felt she could not overcome her indignation because Binoy had accepted defeat only outwardly, remaining inwardly negative about the idea. He was full of anguish that the matter had hurt Lalita so deeply. Privately, he resolved never to discuss the matter even in jest, and to perform his promised task with such skill and dedication that nobody could accuse him of indifference.

That morning, in the seclusion of her bedroom, Sucharita had been struggling since dawn to read an English religious text called *Imitations of Christ*. She had not taken up her other routine chores. At times, when her mind wandered from the book, the words on the page seemed to her mere shadows; but the very next moment, angry with herself, she would forcibly concentrate on her book, refusing to give up. Presently, hearing voices from afar, she sensed Binoybabu's arrival. She gave a start, at once feeling the urge to put her book aside and move to the outer room. Then annoyed at her own restlessness, she sank back onto the chowki and took up her book. She tried to block her ears as she read, to shut out all sounds.

At this juncture, Lalita came into her room.

'Tell me, what's the matter with you?' Sucharita asked, glancing at her face.

'Nothing at all!' insisted Lalita, vigorously shaking her head.

'Where were you?'

'Binoybabu is here. I think he wants to chat with you.'

Today, Sucharita could not bring herself to ask if anyone else had accompanied Binoybabu. Had there been another visitor, surely Lalita would have mentioned him, but still, Sucharita could not rest content. Giving up her attempts at self-restraint, she went towards the outer chamber to do her duty by their visitor.

'Won't you come?' she asked Lalita.

'Go ahead, I'll join you later,' replied Lalita rather impatiently.

Entering the outer room, Sucharita found Binoy chatting with Satish. 'Baba has gone out,' said Sucharita. 'He'll be back soon. Ma has taken Labanya and Leela to Mastermoshai's house to help them memorize a poem for that show of ours; but Lalita simply refused to go. Ma has asked us to keep you here when you arrive; today, you will be tested.'

'Are you not involved in all this?' Binoy asked her.

'If everyone became an actor, who on earth would the spectators be?'

Borodasundari excluded Sucharita from such matters, as far as possible. This time, too, Sucharita had not been called upon to display her talents.

On other days, Sucharita and Binoy were never at a loss for words when they met. But today, there were such obstacles on both sides that all their efforts at conversation failed. Sucharita had vowed not to mention Gora. Binoy also could not bring up Gora's name easily, as before. He found it difficult to speak of Gora, imagining that Lalita, and perhaps everyone else in this house, regarded him as Gora's minor satellite.

It had often happened before that Binoy arrived first and Gora joined them later. Imagining that the same might happen today, Sucharita remained restless and alert. She was afraid that Gora might come, yet also tormented by the fear that he may not arrive. After exchanging a few desultory remarks with Binoy, Sucharita found no option but to take up Satish's notebook and discuss it with him. She annoyed Satish, finding fault sometimes with his arrangement of pictures. Highly agitated, Satish began to argue loudly. And Binoy, humiliated and aggrieved at the sight of the rejected oleander-bunch on the table, began to think, 'Lalita should have accepted these flowers of mine, out of civility, if nothing else.'

Startled by a sudden footfall, Sucharita turned around to see Haranbabu entering the room. Because she had started so visibly, she blushed.

'Why, isn't your Gourbabu here?' asked Haranbabu, taking his place on a chowki.

'Why, do you have some need of him?' asked Binoy, annoyed at Haranbabu's needless query.

'You're not often seen without him,' observed Haranbabu. 'That is why I ask.'

Binoy was privately incensed. Lest his anger become apparent, he answered curtly: 'He is not in Kolkata.'

'Has he gone on a preaching tour?' asked Haran.

Binoy's fury increased. He made no reply. Sucharita also rose and left the room without a word. Haranbabu rushed after her but could not catch up.

'Sucharita, I have something to tell you,' he called from a distance.
'I'm not well today,' she replied. As she spoke, the bar slammed down on her bedroom door.

Borodasundari now arrived, and summoned Binoy to another room to rehearse his lines for the show. Not long after, the flowers suddenly vanished from the table. That night, Lalita did not appear at Borodasundari's rehearsal, and Sucharita also stayed up very late, gazing out at the darkness of the night, the *Imitations of Christ* lying folded on her lap, the lamp in her room turned to face the corner. Like a mirage, a strange, exquisite land seemed to arise before her eyes, a terrain somehow utterly divorced from everything she had seen and known until now. Hence the lights burning at the windows there frightened her with their remote mysteriousness, like a garland of stars in the dark night sky. Yet, she felt, 'My life is insignificant, all my long-held certitudes riddled with doubt, my regular daily activities utterly meaningless. Perhaps, in that other place, I shall gain complete knowledge, perform deeds that are noble, and make my life worthwhile. Who has brought me to the unknown gateway of that exquisite, unfamiliar, terrifying land? Why does my heart tremble so? Why are my feet frozen immobile when they try to advance?'

## 23

Binoy came daily for rehearsals. Sucharita would glance at him once, then concentrate on the book in her hands or go away to her own room. Every day she suffered the frustration of seeing Binoy arrive unaccompanied, but she asked no questions. Yet, the longer this state of affairs continued, Sucharita's heart grew ever more reproachful against Gora, with each passing day. As if, on that previous occasion, there had been an understanding that Gora was bound to visit them. Ultimately, learning that Gora had unaccountably gone away to some unknown place for a few days, Sucharita tried to dismiss the matter as a trifling piece of news, but it continued to pierce her heart. While performing her daily chores, she would suddenly remember it. When preoccupied, she would realize suddenly that it was this matter that she had secretly been thinking of.

After her discussion with Gora the other day, Sucharita had never expected him to vanish suddenly like this. Despite the great divide between Gora's views and her own convictions, there had been no contrary currents of resistance in her heart that day. Whether she understood Gora's opinions clearly it is hard to say, but she seemed to have arrived at a certain understanding of Gora as a human being. Whatever Gora's views might be, they had not reduced his human stature, nor rendered him contemptible; rather, they had made his strength of character visible.

This she had felt deeply, that day. She could never have tolerated such words from another person's mouth; she would have been furious, regarded the person as a fool, and her mind would have felt a strong urge to mend his ways by teaching him a thing or two. But that day, with Gora, none of these things happened; combined with Gora's nature, the sharpness of his intellect, the firmness of his unquestioning faith, and the penetrating force of his thunderous voice, his words had acquired a life and a reality of their own. Sucharita herself might not accept all these opinions, but if someone else embraced them like this with all his life and soul, there could be no cause to spurn him. In fact, it was even possible to respect him, beyond one's own reservations. Such was the feeling that had completely overwhelmed Sucharita that day. This state of mind was entirely new to her. She was extremely impatient about differences of opinion; despite the example of Poreshbabu's detached, steady, tranquil lifestyle, she regarded opinions in an exclusive light, because she had been surrounded by communalism since childhood. That day she had for the first time seen ideas in relation to human beings, sensing the mysterious presence of something alive and whole. She had forgotten that day, the divisive vision that saw human society in black and white alone, separating my side from yours. She had been able to regard a person of different views as primarily a human being, so his opinions became secondary.

That day, Sucharita had felt that Gora had enjoyed his discussion with her. Was it merely the joy of expressing his own opinions? Did she contribute nothing to that joy? Perhaps not. Perhaps no human being had any value for Gora, perhaps he had moved far away from everyone else, absorbed in his own ideas and intentions. Perhaps human beings, to him, merely served as occasions for the application of his ideas.

Of late, Sucharita had been concentrating on her prayers. She seemed to be trying, harder than ever, to make Poreshbabu her refuge. One day, when Poreshbabu was reading alone in his room, Sucharita silently came in and joined him.

'What is it, Radhé?' asked Poreshbabu, placing his book on the table.

'Nothing,' she replied. She began to rearrange the books and papers on the table, although they were already arranged quite neatly.

'Baba, why don't you teach me as you used to before?' she blurted out, after a while.

'But my pupil has graduated from my school,' Poreshbabu smiled affectionately. 'Now you can grasp things by reading on your own.'

'No, I can't grasp anything,' declared Sucharita. 'I'll read under your guidance, as before.'

'Very well, I'll tutor you from tomorrow,' Poreshbabu consented.

'Baba,' resumed Sucharita suddenly after a short silence, 'The other day, Binoybabu said a lot of things about caste discrimination. Why don't you explain such matters to me?'

'Ma, you know I have always encouraged all of you to try to think and understand things for yourselves, instead of merely making a habit of parroting my opinions or someone else's. To offer advice on a subject before the question has formed properly in your mind is like offering food before you have developed an appetite: it only creates distaste and indigestion. Whenever you ask me a question, I'll answer as best I can.'

'It's a question I ask you,' Sucharita persisted. 'Why do we condemn caste discrimination?'

'There is no harm in a cat approaching our plate and devouring rice from it, but if a certain human being enters the room, we must throw away the rice. If caste discrimination causes men to treat other men with such humiliation and contempt, how can I call it anything but anti-religion? Those who can treat human beings with such contempt can never attain greatness. They must suffer the contempt of others.'

'There may be many flaws in the malpractices prevalent in our community today,' argued Sucharita, echoing Gora. 'But then such flaws have pervaded all aspects of the community. For that, is the original community itself to blame?'

'If I could locate the original element, I would have an answer,' replied Poreshbabu with his customary tranquility. 'When I see with my own eyes that people in our country are treating other people with intolerable contempt, tearing us apart, how can I in such circumstances console myself with thoughts of an imaginary original element?'

'Tell me,' said Sucharita, echoing Gora's party again, 'It was our nation's ultimate philosophical ideal to regard everyone equally, wasn't it?'

'Equality concerns knowledge, not emotions of the heart. It includes neither love nor contempt, for it is beyond anger and jealousy. The human heart can't sustain such a state, shorn of everything the heart must believe. That is why, in our country, despite such an egalitarian philosophy, low-caste people are not even allowed into temples. If our country does not permit even equality of worship, how does it matter whether such ideas exist in philosophy?'

For a long time, Sucharita mulled over Poreshbabu's words in silence, trying to comprehend them.

'Tell me, Baba,' she finally said, 'Why don't you try explaining these things to Binoybabu and the others?'

'It's not as if Binoybabu and the others lack the intellect to understand these things,' smiled Poreshbabu. 'Rather, it's from an excess of intellect that they don't want to understand, only to explain. When they develop a heartfelt desire to understand all these things from the perspective of religion, the greatest truth of all, they won't have to depend on your Baba's intellect. At present, they are viewing things from a different perspective. My words will be of no use to them now.'

Sucharita had listened to Gora and the others with respect, but their views, clashing with her convictions, had been inwardly troubling her. She could not rest in peace. Today, her conversation with Poreshbabu brought her temporary relief. Sucharita did not want to entertain the slightest possibility that Gora, Binoy, or anyone else, knew more on any subject than Poreshbabu. She could not help being angry with anybody who contradicted Poreshbabu. Of late, since her acquaintance with Gora, it was because she could not completely dismiss his words in anger or contempt, that she suffered such mental agony. That was why she had grown desperate to seek refuge again in Poreshbabu, like his shadow, as in her childhood days. Rising from the chowki, she went to the door, then came back again, and standing behind Poreshbabu, leaning against the back of his chowki, she said:

'Baba, let me join you at your prayers today.'

'Very well.'

Afterwards, going into her bedroom, Sucharita closed the door and tried to remove Gora's words from her mind. But Gora's image, glowing with intelligence and conviction, lingered before her mind's eye. She began to feel that his words were not words alone but Gora himself; those words had a form, a motion, a life of their own, brimming with the strength of his convictions and the pain of his patriotism. They were not mere opinions to be countered; they comprised an entire being, and no ordinary one. It was hard indeed to spurn this being. Caught in an intense inner conflict, Sucharita felt like weeping. Her heart was full to bursting at the thought that someone could cast her into such a major dilemma and then so easily grow remote, like someone utterly detached. Yet there was also no end to her self-castigation at her own agony.

## 24

It had been determined that Binoy would dramatically recite a poem about music by the English poet Dryden, while the girls, appropriately attired, would mime the accompanying actions onstage. In addition, the girls would also recite English poems and sing English songs. Borodasundari had repeatedly assured Binoy that they would somehow groom him for the performance. She herself had only a smattering of English, but she could rely on a couple of experts in her troupe. But when they assembled for rehearsals, Binoy astounded Borodasundari's team of experts with his recitation. Borodasundari was denied the satisfaction of moulding this outsider to their coterie. Those who had formerly treated Binoy with scant respect now could not help privately admiring him. In fact, even Haranbabu requested him to write occasionally for his paper. And Sudhir started pestering Binoy to deliver occasional lectures in English at their students' assembly.

Lalita found herself in a peculiar situation. She felt pleased, yet privately rather dissatisfied, that Binoy did not require any help from anybody. Binoy was not inferior to any of them; rather, he was superior to them all, and secretly aware of his own superiority, he would not expect any guidance from them. This thought tormented her. Regarding Binoy, she herself could not understand what she desired, what might ease her mental discomfort. Meanwhile, her unhappiness constantly expressed itself sharply in trivial ways, always targeting Binoy in the end. Realizing that such conduct towards Binoy was neither fair nor civil, she felt remorseful and tried hard to restrain herself, but she could not understand why, at the slightest pretext, some unwarranted inner anguish would suddenly burst forth, snapping her self-control. She now pestered him to desist from the very activity which she had earlier ceaselessly urged him to join. But now, how was it possible for Binoy to abscond without reason, throwing the entire plan into jeopardy? There was not much time left, either; and having discovered a new skill, he had himself become enthusiastic about it.

'I'm dropping out,' Lalita ultimately told Borodasundari.

'Why?' asked Borodasundari very anxiously, for she knew her second daughter.

'Because I'm not good at it!'

In fact, ever since it became impossible to regard Binoy as a novice, Lalita never wanted to recite or rehearse her role in his presence. 'I'll practice on my own,' she would declare. This would hinder everybody's practice, but Lalita was impossible to handle. Defeated, they ultimately had to manage their rehearsals without Lalita. But finally, when Lalita wanted to opt out altogether, Borodasundari was thunderstruck. Knowing she could not find a solution, she sought Poreshbabu's help. Poreshbabu never interfered in his daughters' minor preferences. But considering that they had made a commitment to the magistrate, that the hosts would also have made arrangements accordingly, and that time was also very short, he sent for Lalita and inquired, stroking her head:

'Lalita, it would be wrong of you to withdraw now.'

'But Baba, I'm not good at it,' answered Lalita, her voice choked with unshed tears. 'I can't.'

'If you can't perform well you won't be to blame, but if you withdraw, it will be wrong on your part.'

Lalita hung her head.

'Ma, my little one, having taken it on, you must complete this undertaking. It's too late now to escape lest your pride suffer a blow. Even if your pride is hurt, you must ignore it to perform your duty. Can't you do that, ma?'

'I can!' declared Lalita, raising her face to her father's.

That very evening, especially for Binoy's benefit, she seemed to set about her task with excessive force and daring, casting aside all inhibitions. Until now, Binoy had never heard her recite. Today, listening to her, he was amazed. Binoy was thrilled beyond his expectations at such clear, spirited pronunciation, no trace of indistinctness anywhere, and such unhesitating power of expression. Her voice continued to ring in his ears long after.

In recitation, a good elocutionist casts a spell on the listener's mind. The poem's emotions lend an aura of glory to the one who recites, blending with her voice, appearance and nature. Like a flower on a tree-branch, the poem blossoms in the speaker's personality, enriching her. Lalita, too, began to appear to Binoy in a poetic light. All these days, she had troubled him continuously by her sharpness. Just as we tend to feel only the sore spots on our body, Binoy, too, had been unable lately to think beyond Lalita's sharp words and pointed mockery. He had been compelled to wonder repeatedly, why Lalita had acted or spoken in a certain way; the more he failed to penetrate the mystery of her displeasure, the more his mind grew obsessed with thoughts of her. Awakening suddenly at dawn, he would be reminded of those thoughts, and every day, on his way to Poreshbabu's, he would wonder what Lalita's mood that day would be. When Lalita showed the slightest sign of pleasure, Binoy would heave a sigh of relief, and wonder how to make the feeling last, but he had failed to find a way.

After the mental turmoil of the last few days, the beauty of Lalita's recitation moved Binoy with particular force. It delighted him so much that he could not find suitable words of praise. He was afraid to say anything, good or bad, directly to Lalita's face, for the general human tendency of being pleased by a compliment may not apply to her. In fact, it may not apply precisely because it was the general rule. Hence, Binoy effusively praised Lalita's talents to Borodasundari. This deepened Borodasundari's respect for Binoy's learning and intellect.

There was another surprising development. As soon as Lalita herself realized that her recitation and acting had been flawless, that she had handled her difficult duty with the ease of a well-built boat riding a wave-crest, her bitterness towards Binoy evaporated. She made no further attempts to discourage him. Her enthusiasm for the task at hand increased, and the rehearsals brought her closer to Binoy. In fact, she had no objections now to seeking Binoy's advice about recitation or any other matter.

This transformation in Lalita removed a load from Binoy's mind. So overjoyed was he, that he began visiting Anandamoyi at odd hours to indulge in playful antics, just like a little boy. He stored up many things to prattle about to Sucharita, but nowadays, he did not get to see her at all. He conversed with Lalita whenever he had the chance, but with her he had to guard his tongue. Because he knew Lalita was sharply judgemental about him and everything he said, his words lacked their spontaneous flow in her company.

'Why do you speak as if your words are taken from a book?' Lalita would ask, sometimes.

'Because I have only read books all these years, my mind now resembles a printed book,' he would reply.

'Please make no effort to say things very gracefully,' she would urge. 'Just utter your own thoughts directly. You speak such fine language, I suspect you are using someone else's words, thoughtfully rearranged.'

So, if his natural talent spontaneously presented him with a finely worded idea, Binoy would have to struggle to shorten and simplify it for Lalita. If ever an ornate phrase rose to his lips, he would feel embarrassed.

Lalita's heart glowed as if a cloud had inexplicably lifted from it. Even Borodasundari was amazed at her transformation. Now Lalita did not resist all suggestions, as before; she would participate enthusiastically in all activities. She drove everyone to distraction, coming up with new ideas every day regarding costumes and other arrangements for the forthcoming event. However enthusiastic Borodasundari might be about such things, she also had an eye on the expenses. Hence, she felt as concerned about Lalita's present enthusiasm as she had been earlier about her aversion to acting. But she did not dare to oppose Lalita's active creative instincts either, for at the slightest hurdle in any task she had enthusiastically undertaken, Lalita would become utterly disheartened, unable to participate at all.

In this effusive mood, Lalita had often rushed eagerly to Sucharita. Sucharita had smiled, indeed, and spoken to her, but Lalita repeatedly came up against some hidden inner obstacle that made her turn away, secretly offended at the rebuff.

One day, she went up to Poreshbabu and said: 'Baba, Suchididi can't be left to read alone in a corner while we go off to perform. She must join us.'

Of late, Poreshbabu had also been feeling that Sucharita was drifting away from her female companions. He feared that this mental state was not healthy for her nature. Lalita's words convinced him that unless Sucharita could participate in the general merriment, this aloofness would grow more pronounced.

'Go speak to your mother,' he instructed Lalita.

'I'll speak to Ma, but you must to take the responsibility of persuading Suchididi,' Lalilta insisted.

When Poreshbabu asked her, Sucharita could not refuse. She set forth to do her duty. As soon as Sucharita emerged from her corner, Binoy tried to engage her in conversation as before, but something had happened in the last few days, for she seemed beyond his reach. In her face, in her glance, was a remoteness that made him hesitate to approach her. Even earlier, Sucharita's social interaction and everyday activities had revealed a certain detachment, but now it had become extremely apparent. Even in joining the rehearsals her independence had not been affected. Immediately after completing the bare requirements of her task, she would go away. At first, Binoy was deeply hurt at this aloofness. Gregarious by nature, he found it hard to accept any resistance from those he found congenial. In this family, it was Sucharita who had so far shown him a special regard; now, spurned without reason, he was deeply wounded. But when he realized that Lalita was also similarly offended at Sucharita's behaviour, he felt comforted and his relationship with Lalita grew more intimate. Without giving Sucharita a chance to avoid him, he forsook her company. In this way, Sucharita soon drifted far away from Binoy.

During Gora's brief absence, Binoy had been able to mingle very freely with Poreshbabu's family in every way. Everyone in Poreshbabu's household felt a special satisfaction at this uninhibited revelation of Binoy's true nature. Binoy, too, felt an unprecedented delight at achieving this unobstructed, natural state of mind. The feeling of being liked by all these people further enhanced his capacity to please. As his personality blossomed, as he sensed his own independent strength, Sucharita drifted away from Binoy. This loss, this blow, would have been intolerable at any other time, but now he could overcome it easily. Surprisingly, Lalita, too, had not expressed any reproach at Sucharita's change of heart, this time. Was it only the enthusiasm for recitation and drama that had completely possessed her soul?

Meanwhile, seeing Sucharita join the performance, Haranbabu suddenly became very enthusiastic. He volunteered to recite an extract from *Paradise Lost*, and to deliver a short lecture on the enchantment of music, as a prelude to the recitation of Dryden's verse. Privately, Borodasundari was extremely annoyed at this. Lalita was also displeased. Haranbabu had already met the magistrate to confirm this plan. When Lalita protested that the magistrate might object prolonging the show like this, Haranbabu silenced her by producing from his pocket a letter of thanks from the magistrate.

Gora had set out on a journey without a mission; nobody knew when he would return. Although Sucharita had decided not to give this matter any place in her thoughts, she hoped in her heart, each day, that Gora might arrive that very day. Her heart could never suppress such thoughts. When she was excruciatingly tormented by Gora's indifference and the unruliness of her own heart, when her soul was desperate to escape this net, Haranbabu requested Poreshbabu once again in the name of the Almighty Ishwar, to confirm his betrothal to Sucharita.

'But the wedding is a long way off,' Poreshbabu demurred. 'Is it a good idea to commit yourselves so soon?'

'I consider it very essential for our maturing sensibilities for both of us to spend some time in this state of commitment before the wedding takes place,' declared Haranbabu. 'Between early acquaintance and the wedding itself, such a spiritual relationship, a bond without worldly responsibilities, would be particularly beneficial.'

'Very well, let me ask Sucharita,' said Poreshbabu.

'She has already given her consent,' Haranbabu reminded him.

Poreshbabu still had doubts about Sucharita's feelings for Haranbabu. So he sent for her and placed Haranbabu's proposal before her. Relieved at the possibility of surrendering her fraught, divided life to some ultimate cause, Sucharita gave her consent so instantly and decisively, that all Poreshbabu's doubts were dispelled. He begged her to consider carefully whether it was advisable for her to be forsworn so long before her marriage. Still, Sucharita raised no objection to this proposal. It was decided that, once Brownlow Saheb's invitation was taken care of, they would invite everyone to the betrothal on a special date.

For a brief moment, Sucharita felt as if she had emerged from the devouring maws of the malign planet Rahu. She privately resolved to harden her heart, preparing herself to marry Haranbabu and join the activities of the Brahmo Samaj. She decided to read some English theological texts with Haranbabu every day, and to follow his guidance. Having vowed to accept what was difficult, even unpleasant for her, she experienced a great sense of elation.

For some time now, she had not read the English paper that Haranbabu edited. Today, she received the paper as soon as it appeared in print. Perhaps Haranbabu had sent it especially for her. Carrying the paper to her room, Sucharita sat motionless and began to read it from the very first line, as if it was her sacred duty. Respectfully, she began to absorb the advice offered in the journal, as if she was a student. The ship in full sail suddenly keeled over when it touched a mountain. In the present issue of the paper, there was an article entitled 'Breathing the air of olden times,' attacking people who remained backward-looking even in the present age. Not that the arguments were unreasonable; in fact, Sucharita had been looking out for such ideas. But as soon as she read the article, she realized that Gora was its target. Yet, there was no mention of his name, nor any reference to any of his published articles. Every line of this essay exuded the vicious joy of spearing live flesh, like the satisfaction of a soldier when every bullet finds its mark.

This article was too much for Sucharita to bear. She longed to shred its every argument to bits. 'Gourmohanbabu could reduce this essay to dust, if he wished,' she thought to herself. The image of Gora's glowing face arose before her mind's eye, and his powerful voice echoed even within the recesses of her heart. So trivial did this essay and its author's meanness appear, in comparison with the extraordinariness of that face and those words, that Sucharita flung the paper to the ground.

After a long time, Sucharita approached Binoy of her own accord. 'Tell me,' she remarked conversationally, 'you had promised to bring me the papers in which you people have published articles. Then why haven't you given them to me?'

Binoy did not tell her that he had not dared to keep his promise, observing Sucharita's change of heart. 'I've put them together,' he said instead. 'I'll get them tomorrow.'

The next day, Binoy brought a bundle of books and papers and left them with Sucharita. Having obtained them, Sucharita put them away in a box without reading them. Because she was dying to read them, she did not do so. Vowing that she would not allow her mind to be diverted under any circumstances, she once again sought consolation in surrendering her rebellious heart to Haranbabu's authority.

# 25

On Sunday morning, Anandamoyi was stuffing rolled up paan with spices. Beside her, Shashimukhi was shredding supari into a tiny heap. At this moment, Binoy came in. Shashimukhi immediately ran from the room, scattering the betelnut gathered in her lap in the corner of her sari aanchal. Anandamoyi suppressed a smile.

Binoy could get along with everybody. So far, he had enjoyed a very friendly relationship with Shashimukhi. They would tease each other a lot. Shashimukhi had invented the strategy of stealing Binoy's shoes in order to extract stories from him. Binoy had invented a couple of tales, highly coloured versions of some trifling events in Shashimukhi's life. If he began recounting one of those stories, Shashimukhi would be outwitted. First she would loudly accuse the narrator of lying; then, admitting defeat, she would flee the room. To counter this, she too had tried to create stories that were distortions of Binoy's biography; but as she could not match Binoy's creativity, she had not achieved much success in this matter. Anyway, whenever Binoy visited this house, Shashimukhi would drop all her work and rush to attack him. Sometimes she troubled him so much that Anandamoyi would scold her, but Shashimukhi was indeed not solely to blame. Binoy would provoke her beyond endurance. When the same Shashimukhi quickly escaped from the room upon catching sight of Binoy, Anandamoyi smiled, but it was not a happy smile.

Binoy, too, was so offended at this trifling matter that he remained speechless for a while. It was apparent from such trivial instances how inappropriate it would be for him to marry Shashimukhi. When consenting to the match, Binoy had thought only of his friendship with Gora; he had not imagined what the experience of marriage might actually be like. Besides, he had taken pride in publishing many newspaper articles about the fact that marriages in our country are primarily family affairs rather than a matter of personal choice. As for himself, he had never entertained any personal likes or dislikes in this matter. Today, when Shashimukhi bit her tongue and ran away upon seeing Binoy because she saw him as her would-be husband, he witnessed an aspect of his future relationship with her. At once, his whole heart rebelled. He felt furious with Gora for forcing him to act in a way so contrary to his own nature. He cursed himself, and recalling that Anandamoyi had been against this marriage from the start, his heart was filled with respect mixed with wonder at the subtlety of her perception.

Anandamoyi sensed Binoy's mood. To divert his mind, she said: 'Binoy, I received a letter from Gora yesterday.'

'What does he say?' asked Binoy, rather absently.

'He doesn't say much about himself. He writes in sorrow about the plight of the lower classes in this country. He recounts the injustices committed by the magistrate at some village called Ghoshpara.'

'Gora only notices what others are doing,' Binoy blurted out impatiently, provoked into opposing Gora. 'And when we ourselves oppress society, straddling its body and stifling its breath, that must always be pardoned, as the holiest task ever undertaken.'

Seeing Binoy suddenly attack Gora in this way, contradicting him in order to establish his own credibility, Anandamoyi smiled to herself.

'You smile, Ma,' said Binoy. 'You wonder why Binoy should suddenly grow so angry. Let me tell you why. The other day, Sudhir had taken me to a friend's garden estate at their Naihati station. As soon as we pulled out of Sealdah, it started raining. When the train stopped at Shodpur station, I saw a Bengali in Western attire, sporting an umbrella, helping his wife off the train. The wife had a baby boy in her arms. Covering the child somehow with her heavy wrap, the poor thing stood at one end of the open platform, huddled in cold and embarrassment, getting drenched. Her husband, carrying the umbrella, attended to the luggage, creating a commotion. I was instantly reminded that, in the whole of Bengal, rain or shine, among the elite or uncultured, no woman carries an umbrella. I saw the husband shamelessly protecting his head with the umbrella while his wife silently got drenched in her wrap, without condemning his own behaviour even in his private thoughts, and nobody at the station found anything wrong with this. I have vowed ever since not to utter poetic falsehoods claiming that we revere our women greatly, regarding them as Lakshmi, as devi, and so on. We call the nation our motherland, but if we don't see the greatness of that female image manifest in our womenfolk, if we don't see our women as mature, spirited, and direct in their intelligence, physical strength, sense of duty and largeness of heart, if we find only weakness, narrowness and immaturity in our homes, then we shall never experience the glory of our nation.'

Suddenly embarrassed at his own fervour, Binoy continued in his normal tone: 'Ma, you are thinking, sometimes Binoy tends to launch into lectures, making tall claims, and today as well he is obsessed with the urge to hold forth. By force of habit, my words begin to sound like lectures, but today, this is no public speech. I had not understood properly, never considered, how far ahead of the nation our nation's women might be. Ma, I won't say more. Because I talk too much, nobody believes my words to be my own. From now on, I'll say less.'

Binoy left without further delay, his heart aflame with enthusiasm.

'Baba,' Anandamoyi sent for Mahim and said, 'Binoy can't marry our Shashimukhi.'

'Why? Do you have any objection?'

'It's because this match won't work in the long run that I am against it. Otherwise, why should I object?'

'Gora is in favour of it, so is Binoy. Why shouldn't it last? Of course if you withhold your consent, Binoy won't proceed. Of that I'm well aware.'

'I know Binoy better than you do.'

'Better even than Gora?'

'Yes, I know him even better than Gora does. That's why, all things considered, I can't give my consent.'

'Very well, let Gora return.'

'Mahim, listen to me. If you are too persistent in this matter, it will ultimately create trouble. I don't want Gora to say anything about this to Binoy.'

'Well, we shall see,' declared Mahim, stuffing a paan in his mouth. He rushed from the room in fury.

## 26

When Gora set out on his journey, he was accompanied by four people: Abinash, Matilal, Basanta and Ramapoti. But they could not keep pace with Gora's relentless enthusiasm. Within four or five days, Abinash and Basanta returned to Kolkata on the pretext of poor health. Purely out of devotion to Gora, Matilal and Ramapoti could not bring themselves to abandon him. But there was no end to their sufferings, for Gora never tired of walking, nor did a sedentary existence exasperate him. However inconvenient the diet and lifestyle, he would spend day after day in the home of any village householder who offered him hospitality out of respect for his Brahmanhood. All the villagers would gather about him to listen to his discourses, reluctant to let him go.

For the first time, Gora saw what our country is like, outside the social worlds of the respectable bhadralok, the educated, and the Kolkata-dwellers. How fragmented, narrow-minded and feeble was this vast, concealed realm of rural Bharatvarsha—how utterly unaware of its own power, how completely ignorant and indifferent about its own interests! How extreme were the social differences between places only five or seven krosh, ten to fifteen miles apart—how many self-created and imaginary obstacles constrained the land from advancing in the world's giant workspace—how much importance it attached to trivialities, how moribund it had grown, clinging to every prejudice and superstition—how somnolent was its mind, how faint its heart, how feeble its efforts! Had he not dwelt among the villagers in this way, Gora could never have imagined all this. During his stay at a village, a fire broke out in one of the localities. Even in the face of such a grave disaster, Gora was amazed to see how poor was their capacity to band together and fight the danger wholeheartedly. They ran about in confusion, all of them, weeping and wailing but unable to do anything in an organized fashion. There was no water-body near that neighbourhood. The women would fetch water from far away to perform their household chores, yet even the more well-to-do villagers had not thought of reducing that daily inconvenience by digging an inexpensive well in their backyard. There had been fires in this locality on earlier occasions as well, but the people passively took them for acts of God, making no effort to arrange some supply of water near at hand. Gora thought it a mockery to discuss the state of the entire nation with people who were mentally so inert, even about their urgent local needs. What amazed him most was that Matilal and Ramapoti felt no consternation at witnessing such scenes; on the contrary, they found Gora's rage inappropriate. This was how poor folks always behaved, such was their mindset. They did not regard these hardships as hardships at all. To imagine that things should be any different for the poor folk was taking things too far, they thought. Gora's heart was tormented day and night because he now realized clearly the terrifying enormity of the burden of such ignorance, stasis and suffering, a burden oppressing the educated and the illiterate, rich and poor, allowing nobody to progress.

Matilal left, claiming he had news of illness in the family; now Gora had only Ramapoti with him. Travelling on, the two of them arrived at a Muslim settlement beside the river. Searching for hospitality, they heard of only one family of Hindu barbers in the entire village. Seeking refuge there, the two Brahmans noticed that the old barber and his wife had adopted a Muslim boy. Ramapoti, very devout, became highly agitated. When Gora reprimanded the barber for his sinful act, he said:

'Thakur, we say Hari and they call Him Allah, but there's no difference.'

The sun beat down upon their heads, the sand-bank was vast, the river far away. Desperate with thirst, Ramapoti asked:

'Where can we find some water for a Hindu to drink?'

There was an unpaved well in the barber's house but unable to drink from a well polluted by such irreligious conduct, Ramapoti felt dejected.

'Is this boy an orphan?' Gora inquired.

'He has parents, but for him, they're as good as dead,' the barber replied.

'How's that?'

The gist of the background narrated by the barber was as follows:

The zamindari they belonged to was leased by sahebs, traders in indigo. There were endless disputes between the tenants and the owners of the factory, the nilkuthi, over the indigo fields on the chors or sandbanks. All the other tenant-farmers had yielded, but the sahebs had not been able to subdue the tenants of this sandbank named Chor-Ghoshpur. All the subjects here were Muslims and their leader, Pharu Sardar, feared no one. He had served a couple of jail sentences for thrashing the police after being harassed by the nilkuthi owners. He was virtually starving now, but giving up was alien to his nature. This season, farming on the zigzag sandbanks of the river, the villagers had managed to grow some boro paddy. But a month ago, the nilkuthi manager had arrived in person to rob his tenant-farmers, accompanied by strongmen armed with staves. During that attack, Pharu Sardar had dealt such a blow to the saheb's right hand that it had to be amputated at the clinic. Never had this area witnessed such a daring feat. Ever since, police torture had spread like wildfire through every neighbourhood. They left nothing intact in the tenant-farmers' homes, and the honour of women in their homes was jeopardized. Pharu Sardar and many others were behind bars; most of the villagers were absconding. Pharu's wife was starving; in fact, her only garment was so tattered that she was ashamed to emerge from her house. Her only son Tamiz used to address the barber's wife as his aunt, as fellow villagers do. Seeing that he was starving, the barber's wife had taken him in. One of the courthouses of the nilkuthi was about a krosh and a half away; the police superintendent was still stationed there with his team. There was no saying when he might show up in the village and what he might do there, in connection with the investigations. The previous day, the police had arrived at the doorstep of old Nazim, the barber's neighbour. A young brother-in-law of Nazim's had come there from another village, to visit his sister. Without any provocation, the superintendent declared: 'I must say this is a strapping young fellow, look at his puffed up chest!' And he attacked him so violently with his stave that the youth began to bleed from the mouth, his teeth smashed. Witnessing such torture, his sister rushed up to him, but the policeman pushed the old woman aside. Formerly, the police would not dare create such trouble in the locality, but now every able-bodied youth in the area was either behind bars or absconding. It was to capture the fugitives that the police still roamed the village. There was no saying when the dominance of this malign planet would end.

Gora showed no inclination to leave, but Ramapoti meanwhile was growing desperate. The barber had barely ended his narrative, when he demanded:

'How far away is the Hindu neighbourhood?'

'You know the nilkuthi courthouse a krosh and a half away? The tehsildar there is a Brahman named Madhab Chatujje,' the barber informed him.

'What's he like?' Gora inquired.

'Like the devil's own messenger,' answered the barber. 'It's hard to find someone so heartless, yet so devious. He'll make us pay for the superintendent's stay with him as his guest, with some profit added too.'

'Let's go,' pleaded Ramapoti. 'That's enough.' Especially when the barber's wife began to bathe the Muslim boy near the well, drawing water from it in her small ghoti, he flew into a rage and lost all desire to linger in this house.

'How is it that you have remained in this locality, amidst all this oppression?' Gora asked the barber while taking his leave. 'Don't you have relatives elsewhere?'

'I've lived here a long time,' the barber told him. 'I have grown attached to these people. I am a Hindu barber. Because I have no landed property to speak of, the nilkuthi folks leave me alone. Among the men in this locality, there is no elderly person left. If I leave, the women will die of apprehension.'

'Very well,' said Gora, 'I'll return after my meal.'

Faced with this prolonged description of the oppressive conduct of the nilkuthi owners, at a time when he was acutely hungry and thirsty, Ramapoti became incensed at the villagers. It seemed to him an extreme instance of the daring and folly of staunch Muslims that these fellows should rise against those in power. He did not doubt that it would be all for the best if their arrogance were to be demolished through appropriate disciplinary action. He considered it customary for the police to oppress such lawless wretches for such things were inevitable, and these people were primarily responsible for them. After all, they could always compromise with the owners. Why create trouble? Where was all their fire and mettle, now? As a matter of fact, Ramapoti privately sympathized with the saheb who owned the nilkuthi.

All the way, traversing the scorching sand under the midday sun, Gora uttered not a word. Ultimately, they spotted the thatched courthouse roof through the foliage, from a distance. Gora suddenly declared:

'Ramapoti, please go ahead and have your meal. I am going to that barber's house.'

'How can you say that!' expostulated Ramapoti. 'Won't you have something to eat? You must proceed on your way after stopping for a meal at Chatujje's.'

'I'll take care of my duties,' responded Gora. 'Now after your meal, please proceed to Kolkata. I might have to stay on at the Ghoshpur Chor for a while. It would be too much for you.'

Ramapoti's hair stood on end. He could not imagine how a devout Hindu like Gora could even propose staying with that infidel. He began to wonder whether Gora had resolved to renounce food and drink, to fast unto death. But this was not the time to ponder; every moment seemed an age to him. He did not need much persuasion to escape to Kolkata, abandoing Gora. Glancing at him briefly, Ramapoti saw the small shadow of Gora's tall frame trudging back alone amidst the desolate, scorching sands, in the heat of the midday sun.

Hunger and thirst had overwhelmed Gora, but the more he thought about having to accept the hospitality of the vile, unjust Madhab Chatujje just to preserve his caste purity, the more intolerable the prospect appeared. His face reddened, his temper flared, and a tremendous sense of rebellion arose in his heart. He thought, 'What a great heresy we are committing in Bharatvarsha, making purity a matter of appearances alone! It would save my caste purity to dine at the home of a man who torments Muslims by creating all sorts of trouble, but I would lose my caste status in the home of a person who accepts such torment to protect a Muslim boy, and is even ready to suffer social condemnation for it. Anyway, I'll reflect later upon the pros and cons of such discriminatory practices, but at present, I have no choice.'

The barber was surprised to see Gora returning alone. When he arrived, Gora first scrubbed the barber's ghoti thoroughly with his own hands, then collected water from the well to drink.

'If there's some rice and dal in the house, please let me have some,' he requested. 'I'll cook for myself.'

Flustered, the barber made arrangements for him to cook.

'I'll stay with you a few days,' Gora informed him, after he had eaten.

Terrified, the barber pleaded with folded hands: 'I cannot be more fortunate than to have you stay with someone as humble as myself. But the police have their eye on us, you see; there's no saying what problems might transpire if you remain here.'

'As long as I am present here, the police won't dare trouble you,' declared Gora. 'If they do, I shall protect you.'

'I beg you,' urged the barber, 'if you try to protect us, we shall have no rescue. Those fellows will think that I have conspired to get you here as a witness against them. I have survived somehow, all these days, but I cannot continue here if that happens. If I, too, am uprooted from here, the village will be trampled underfoot.'

Having grown up in the city, Gora found it hard to even understand the barber's apprehensions. He thought taking a strong stand on behalf of justice was sufficient to combat injustice. His conscience refused to let him abandon an endangered village, leaving it helpless. Now the barber prostrated himself at his feet.

'Look, sir, you are a Brahman,' he pleaded. 'On the strength of my punya, the accumulated virtue of my past lives, you have become our guest. It is wrong of me to ask you to leave. But because I know your sympathy for us, I can tell you that if you stay here and try to prevent police harassment, you would place us all in grave danger.'

Taking the barber's anxieties for baseless cowardice, Gora was rather annoyed. He left their home and set out in the late afternoon. He even began to regret having accepted food and other hospitality at this heretic's dwelling. Physically exhausted and mentally embittered, he arrived at the nilkuthi courthouse in the evening. Ramapoti had wasted no time in setting off for Kolkata after his meal, so there was no sign of him. With a special show of cordiality Madhab Chatujje offered Gora his hospitality.

'I shall not even taste the water in your house,' declared Gora, flying into a rage.

When a surprised Madhab asked him why, Gora abused him for being an unjust oppressor. He remained standing, refusing to take a seat. The police officer was lolling against a bolster, puffing upon his gurguri, the hookah with its long flexible tube.

'Who are you, mister?' he asked belligerently, sitting up. 'Where are you from?'

'Are you the superintendent?' Gora inquired, without answering his question. 'I have learnt all about your assaults on Ghoshpur Chor. If you don't take heed now, . . .'

'Will you send me to the gallows?' laughed the superintendent. 'A fine fellow, I must say. I thought he had come to beg for favours, but he threatens us instead! O Tewari!'

Flustered, Madhab grasped the superintendent's hand. 'Arré, what are you doing?' he said. 'Don't insult him, he's a bhadralok!'

'What sort of bhadralok is he!' fumed the superintendent. 'When he was so rude to you, wasn't that an insult, too?'

'What he said was not untrue,' said Madhab. 'So how can we be angry? We make our living as agents of the nilkuthi sahebs; need we say more? Don't mind Dada, but you're a police superintendent, after all; would it be infamy to call you an agent from hell? It's well understood that the tiger is a man-eater, no vegetarian boshtom ascetic. What's the tiger to do? He must survive, mustn't he?'

No one had seen Madhab angry without reason. When someone might prove useful—or when crossed, what harm they might do—who could tell? Extremely careful about injuring or insulting anybody, he did not waste his destructive powers by making others the target of his wrath.

'Look here baba,' said the superintendent to Gora, 'we are here to serve the government. If you object to that, or make a nuisance of yourself, you'll be in trouble.'

Gora left the room without a word.

'Moshai, what you say is true,' admitted Madhab, rushing after him. 'Our job makes butchers of us, and as for that superintendent, it's a sin even to share the same divan with him. I can't bring myself to mention all the misdeeds I've made him perform. It won't take much longer—if I work for just two or three years more, I'll acquire the means to marry off these daughters of mine, and after that, my wife and I will head for Kashi, renouncing the world. I don't relish all this anymore, moshai; sometimes I want to hang myself. Anyway, where else will you go tonight? Please dine with us and spend the night here. You need not come anywhere near that superintendent fellow. I'll make separate arrangements for you.'

Gora's appetite was above the ordinary, and he had not had a proper meal in the morning, either. But his entire body seemed to be on fire. He could not remain here under any circumstances.

'I have some urgent work,' he declared.

'Wait, then, I'll organize a lantern.'

Gora rushed away without offering any reply.

'Dada, that man is on his way to the headquarters,' said Madhab, returning to his room. 'Send a messenger to the magistrate while there is still time.'

'Why, what must we do?' asked the superintendent.

'Nothing, just let him inform them that a bhadralok has surfaced from somewhere and is at large, trying to subvert witnesses.'

## 27

At sunset, Magistrate Brownlow was walking along the riverside path. With him was Haranbabu. Not far away, his wife, the mem, was savouring the air in the motor car, along with Poreshbabu's daughters.

From time to time, Brownlow Saheb would invite the Bengali bhadraloks to garden parties at his house. It was he who acted as chief guest at prize distribution ceremonies at the district entrance school. If invited to wedding rituals at some well-to-do person's house, he would accept the householder's hospitality. In fact, when invited to a jatragaan performance of songs from indigenous popular theatre, he would recline on a large armchair and for a while, patiently try to listen to the music. During the last puja, he had particularly appreciated the performance of the two lads who had played the bhisti or water-carrier and the methrani or scavenger-woman, in the jatra enacted at the house of the government pleader at his court. At his request, their scene had been replayed for his benefit more than once.

His wife was a missionary's daughter. Sometimes, they hosted a tea for missionary women at their house. He had established a girls' school in the district, and tried very hard to ensure that it had no shortage of students. He always encouraged the educational discussions he had witnessed among the female members of Poreshbabu's house. He would drop them a line every now and then, even when he was far away, and send them religious books for Christmas.

The mela was on. Borodasundari and the girls, accompanied by Haranbabu, Sudhir and Binoy, were present at the occasion, all of them. They had been offered accommodation at the Inspection Bungalow. Poreshbabu had no patience for such noisy events; he had stayed behind in Kolkata, by himself. Sucharita had tried very hard to remain with him, to give him company, but advising her strongly that it was her duty to respect the magistrate's invitation, Poresh sent her away. It had been decided that on the penultimate day, in the presence of the Commissioner Saheb and the Lieutenant Governor and his wife, at the after-dinner party at the magistrate's house, Poreshbabu's daughters would perform and recite. Many of the magistrate's British friends from the district as well as from Kolkata had been invited to the event. A few select Bengali bhadraloks were also to attend. There would even be snacks prepared for them by Brahman cooks in a garden tent, so it was rumoured.

In a very short time, Haranbabu had succeeded in winning the heart of the magistrate saheb by virtue of his lofty conversation. The saheb had been amazed at Haranbabu's extraordinary knowledge of Christian theology, and he had even asked Haranbabu why he had the slightest hesitation in embracing the Christian faith. This afternoon, pacing the riverside path, he was deeply engaged in discussion with Haranbabu about Brahmo and Hindu practices. At this juncture, Gora appeared before him.

'Good evening, sir,' he said.

Trying to meet the magistrate the previous day, he had realized that he must grease the sentry's palm to cross the saheb's threshold. Unwilling to tolerate such subjugation and insult, he had come to meet the saheb during his outing today. During this action, Haranbabu and Gora showed no sign of mutual recognition.

The saheb was rather perplexed when he saw this man. He could not recall having encountered such a person in Bengal, more than six feet tall, heavy boned, sturdy. Even his complexion was unlike that of the ordinary Bengali. Khaki shirt, coarse, faded dhoti, bamboo stave in hand, chador wound around his head like a turban.

'I've just come from Ghoshpur Chor,' Gora told the magistrate.

The magistrate gave a surprised whistle. He had received news the previous day, that an outsider was obstructing the investigations at Ghoshpur. So this was the man!

'What is your caste?' he asked Gora, surveying him once from top to toe.

'I am a Bengali Brahman.'

'Oh! Do you have any connections with the press?'

'No.'

'Then what are you doing at Ghoshpur Chor?'

'I took shelter there during my wanderings. Having witnessed the predicament of the village under police torture, and realizing the likelihood of further trouble, I have come to you to ask for redress.'

'Are you aware that the people at Ghoshpur Chor are utter scoundrels?'

'They're no scoundrels. They're bold and independent, unable to endure unjust oppression in silence.'

The magistrate was incensed. He concluded privately that this new Bengali had learned to parrot some words gleaned from history books. This was insufferable!

'You understand nothing of the present situation!' roared the magistrate.

'You know much less than me about the situation here,' thundered Gora in reply.

'I warn you,' declared the magistrate, 'if you interfere in the Ghoshpur matter in any way, you will not get off easily.'

'Since you have decided not to counter the injustice that is taking place, and since your attitude towards the villagers is predetermined and unshakable, I have no choice but to incite the villagers against the police, by my own efforts.'

'What!' The magistrate stopped suddenly in his tracks. 'How dare you!' he shouted, wheeling about to face Gora.

Gora stalked away slowly, without uttering another word.

'Haranbabu,' said the magistrate, 'what does the behaviour of your countrymen signify?'

'It's due to lack of in-depth study, especially due to the total absence of spiritual and ethical education in our country that all this is happening,' Haranbabu asserted. 'They have not yet earned the right to receive the best of English education. If these ungrateful people are reluctant even now to acknowledge British rule in India as God's decree, it's only because they have merely learned by rote. Their religious sense is extremely underdeveloped.'

'Without embracing Christianity, people's religious sense will never develop to maturity in India,' the magistrate declared.

'In a sense, that is true,' Haranbabu assented. He had then engaged the magistrate in a discussion of his possible conversion to Christianity, making fine distinctions between where his opinions coincided with or differed from a Christian's. So deeply had he kept the magistrate engrossed that when the memsaheb, returning in the carriage after dropping Poreshbabu's daughters at the dak bungalow, called to her husband: 'Harry, we must go home,' the magistrate started, took out his watch and exclaimed: 'By Jove, it's eight twenty!'

Before stepping into the car, he wrung Haranbabu's hand. 'Our discussion has made this evening very enjoyable,' he said, by way of farewell.

Back at the dak bungalow, Haranbabu recounted his interchange with the magistrate in detail. But he made no mention of his encounter with Gora.

## 28

Forty seven accused persons had been condemned to prison without being tried for any crime, just to keep the village under control. After his meeting with the magistrate, Gora set out in search of a lawyer. Someone told him that Satkori Haldar was a good lawyer.

'Wah, it's Gora , isn't it?' exclaimed Satkori, as soon as Gora arrived at his house. 'What brings you here?' It was as Gora had thought: Satkori was his classmate.

'The accused at Ghoshpur must be released on bail and their cases fought in court,' Gora declared.

'Who will stand security for bail?' Satkori asked.

'I will.'

'What resources do you possess, to stand guarantor for forty seven persons on bail?'

'If all the mukhtars, the legal representatives, collectively offer security, I shall pay their fees.'

'It won't be a small amount.'

The next day, they applied for bail at the magistrate's court. Looking askance at the previous day's hero dressed in his faded garments and turban, the magistrate ignored the request. From a fourteen year old boy to an old man of eighty, all the accused were condemned to rot in jail.

Gora requested Satkori to defend their case.

'Where will you find witnesses?' Satkori asked him. 'All potential witnesses are among the accused. Moreover, the people of this area are overwrought due to the investigation into the case of those murdered sahebs. The magistrate is convinced there is a secret bhadralok hand in this whole affair. Who knows, perhaps he even suspects me! The English papers keep saying that if the local people are incited to such daring, the unprotected, helpless British can't survive in the provincial areas any more. Meanwhile, things have reached a stage where our countrymen can't survive in their own land. I know there is oppression, but there's nothing we can do.'

'Why not?' thundered Gora.

'You're exactly as you were in school, I see,' smiled Satkori. 'When I say there's nothing we can do, I mean we have wives and children at home. If we don't earn our daily bread, many will go hungry. There aren't many in this world willing to give up their lives shouldering other people's burdens, especially in a country where the family is not taken lightly. Those with many dependants have no time for the problems of all and sundry.'

'So you'll do nothing for these people?' said Gora. 'If, by a motion in the high court, we . . .'

'Arre, they've killed Englishmen, don't you see!' cried Satkori impatiently. 'Every Englishman is a raja, after all. To murder even an ordinary Englishman amounts to a minor act of treason. I can't let myself fall into the magistrate's bad books in a false bid to achieve something futile.'

Gora set out the next morning, planning to catch the ten-thirty train to Kolkata, to see if he some lawyer there could help him with the case, when he encountered an obstacle. To coincide with the local mela, a cricket tournament had been scheduled, between students from Kolkata and the local students' team. The Kolkata boys were playing amongst themselves, to hone their skills. One of the boys was severely hurt when the cricket ball hit him on the leg. There was a large pond at the end of the field. Carrying the injured boy to the pond's edge, a couple of students shredded a chador, soaked the strips and began to bandage his leg with them. Suddenly, a watchman appeared from nowhere, and shoved a student by the shoulder, abusing him in obscene language. The Kolkata students did not know that it was forbidden to enter this pond because it was reserved for drinking water. Even had they known, they were not used to accepting such sudden humiliation from a watchman. Being physically strong as well, they began to suitably avenge the insult. Witnessing this spectacle, four or five constables rushed to the spot. At that very moment, Gora arrived on the scene. The students recognized Gora, for he had often played cricket with them.

'Don't hit them! I warn you!' cried Gora, unable to bear the sight of the students being beaten and dragged away.

When the watchman's party swore abominably at Gora as well, he created such a commotion, hitting and kicking them, that a crowd collected on the street. Meanwhile, the students quickly formed a cluster. When they attacked the police at Gora's urging and command, the watchman's party at once beat a hasty retreat. Onlookers in the street found this highly amusing. But needless to say, this spectacle did not remain a mere piece of entertainment for Gora.

At around three or four in the afternoon, when Binoy, Haranbabu and the girls were busy rehearsing at the dak bungalow, a couple of students known to Binoy came and reported that Gora and a few students had been arrested by the police and put in the lockup. The following day, the case would come up at the magistrate's very first session in court. Gora in the lockup! Everyone but Haranbabu was dumbfounded. Binoy immediately rushed to their classmate Satkori Haldar and having first told him the whole story, took him along to the lockup. Satkori offered to defend Gora in court, and to try getting him out on bail at once.

'No,' said Gora. 'I won't engage a lawyer, and there's no need to try and get me out on bail either.'

How could he say that!

'Look at this!' expostulated Satkori, turning to Binoy. 'Who would think Gora is out of school! His mindset remains exactly the same.'

'I don't want to be free of lockup and handcuffs simply because I'm fortunate enough to have money and friends,' declared Gora. 'According to our nation's religious law, we know it is the ruler's responsibility to ensure justice; it's the ruler who must be blamed if his subjects suffer injustice. But in this kingdom, if subjects must rot in the lockup and die in jail because they can't afford the lawyer's fee, if even under a king's rule one must go bankrupt trying to buy a fair verdict with money, I wouldn't spend a paisa on such justice.'

'But in the days of the kazis, one had to sell one's soul to afford the bribes,' Satkori pointed out.

'But bribery was not the ruler's decree,' Gora insisted. 'Corrupt kazis would demand bribes, and that continues even in the present regime. But now, to seek justice at the ruler's door, the subject must suffer, be he plaintiff or defendant, guilty or innocent. For the destitute, both victory and defeat spell disaster in their fight for justice. And where the ruler is the plaintiff and the defendant is a man like me, lawyers and barristers would all take his side, and as for me, I'd be lucky to find someone, or else I'm at the mercy of my fate! If a court case doesn't need a lawyer's assistance, why have government lawyers at all? If legal help is necessary, why must the party opposing the government have to find his own lawyer? Does this make the government an enemy of the nation's subjects? What sort of political ideology is this?'

'Bhai, why are you so angry?' asked Satkori. 'Civilization doesn't come cheap. For fine judgement, fine laws must be formulated, and to create fine laws, one must become a trader in law. To run a business you must buy and sell, hence the court of justice called civilization automatically becomes a market where judgements can be bought and sold. And it will remain likely that a person without money will get a raw deal. Tell me, what would you do if you were king?'

'If I created laws impenetrable even for a judge on a salary of a thousand rupees or a thousand-and-a-half, I would employ government-paid lawyers for both unfortunate parties, plaintiff and defendant alike. I wouldn't insult the Pathans and Mughals, vaunting the fairness of my own judgement while forcing my subjects to bear the costs of a well-conducted trial.'

'Good idea,' said Satkori, 'but since that auspicious day has not yet arrived, since you have not become king, since at present you are the defendant in a civilized monarch's court, you must either spend from your own pocket or seek the help of a lawyer friend. The third option would not be pleasant for you.'

'Let my fate be that which comes of making no effort,' said Gora obstinately. 'Let me share the fate of those who are utterly helpless in this kingdom.'

Binoy tried very hard to persuade him, but Gora paid no heed to his pleas.

'How did you suddenly turn up here?' he asked Binoy.

Binoy flushed slightly. Had Gora not been confined in the lockup, Binoy might have explained his presence in defiant terms. But now he could not offer an outspoken reply.

'We'll talk about my affairs later . . .' he demurred. 'Now as for you . . .'

'Today, I am a royal guest,' declared Gora. 'Today, the king himself is concerned about me, so none of you need have any concern.'

Knowing it was impossible to sway Gora, Binoy had to relinquish his efforts to engage a lawyer.

'I know you can't swallow the food here,' he said. 'I'll arrange to have some food sent to you from outside.'

'Binoy, why do you struggle in vain?' cried Gora, losing his patience. 'I don't want anything from outside. I want nothing more than what's meted out to everyone in the lockup.'

Binoy went back to the dak bungalow with a heavy heart. In a bedroom facing the street, Sucharita was awaiting his return, with her door shut and window open. She could not bear the company and conversation of others. Seeing Binoy approach the dak bungalow looking worried and dejected, her heart lurched in fear. Forcing herself to remain calm, she picked up a book and made her way to the drawing room. Lalita did not enjoy needlework, but today she was sewing silently in a corner. Labanya was playing a spelling game with Sudhir, with Leela as her audience. Haranbabu was discussing the next day's festivities with Borodasundari.

Binoy gave them a detailed account of Gora's confrontation with the police early that morning. Sucharita sat frozen still. The sewing fell from Lalita's lap and her face grew flushed.

'Have no fear, Binoybabu,' Borodasundari assured him. 'This evening, I shall personally petition the magistrate saheb and his mem on Gora's behalf.'

'No,' said Binoy, 'please don't do that. If Gora hears of it, he will never forgive me, all his life.'

'But we must make some arrangements for his defense,' Sudhir insisted.

Binoy told them all about Gora's objections to seeking bail or engaging a lawyer.

'This is too much!' exclaimed Haranbabu impatiently.

Whatever Lalita's opinion of Haranbabu, she had shown him deference up until now, and had never argued with him. But now she burst out, shaking her head violently:

'It's not too much at all! Gourbabu has done the right thing. If magistrates entrap us, are we supposed to defend ourselves? Must we provide taxes for them to receive a fat salary, and then pay a lawyer from our own pocket to escape their clutches! Better go to jail than receive such justice.'

Haranbabu had known Lalita since she was very young; he had never dreamt that she had opinions of her own. He was amazed to hear such sharp words from her lips.

'What do you understand of such things?' he admonished her reprovingly. 'You are carried away by the irresponsible, frenzied delirium of those who have just cleared college by learning a few books by rote, those who have no religion, no considered opinions.'

He proceeded to recount Gora's meeting with the magistrate the previous evening, and his own discussion about it with the magistrate. Binoy was unaware of the incident at Ghoshpur Chor. Hearing about it, he was filled with apprehension, realizing that the magistrate would not easily forgive Gora. Haran's purpose in telling this story was completely thwarted. Sucharita was wounded by the secret pettiness of his having kept his meeting with Gora a total secret until now. Haranbabu's personal envy of Gora, evident in every word he uttered, elicited the disrespect of all present, at such a time when Gora was in trouble. Sucharita had remained silent, but now she felt the urge to say something. Controlling herself, she opened her book and began to turn the pages with trembling hands.

'However closely Haranbabu's views might match the magistrate's, the Ghoshpur affair has demonstrated the greatness of Gourmohanbabu!' declared Lalita with pride.

## 29

Because the Lieutenant Governor was expected that day, the magistrate arrived at the courthouse punctually at half past ten, and tried to dispense with the day's legal business as early as possible.

Satkoribabu tried to save his friend by defending the schoolboys. Given the circumstances, he had realized that pleading guilty was the best strategy here. He pleaded for mercy, arguing that boys were naturally mischievous, that they had acted immaturely and foolishly, and so on. The magistrate ordered that the boys be taken to jail, and caned five to twenty times, according to their age and the gravity of their offence. Gora had no lawyer to defend him. In his own defense, he tried to say something about police torture. The magistrate at once silenced him with a sharp reprimand, sentenced him to a month's rigorous imprisonment for obstructing police activities, and acclaimed this light sentence as extremely lenient.

Sudhir and Binoy were present in the courtroom. Binoy could not bear to meet Gora's eyes. Feeling suffocated, he rushed from the courtroom. Sudhir begged him to return to the dak bungalow for his bath and breakfast, but he would not listen. He walked some distance down the path that skirted the field, and collapsed under a tree.

'Go back to the bungalow,' he told Sudhir. 'I'll come after a while.'

Sudhir went away. How long he remained in this state, Binoy had no idea. When the sun that had been directly overhead was declining westwards, a carriage stopped just in front of him. Raising his head, Binoy saw Sudhir and Sucharita dismount and approach him. Quickly, he rose to his feet.

'Come, Binoybabu,' pleaded Sucharita tenderly, coming up close.

Binoy suddenly realized that people on the street were highly entertained at this spectacle. He quickly stepped into the carriage. Nobody said a word, all the way back. Arriving at the dak bungalow, Binoy found that a fight had broken out there. Lalita had stubbornly refused to participate in the magistrate's programme that evening, under any circumstances. Borodasundari was in a grave dilemma. Haranbabu was outraged at such inappropriate rebelliousness in a girl so young. 'How depraved today's youngsters have become!' he kept exclaiming. 'They won't observe any discipline! This is the outcome of discussing all sorts of ideas in the company of all sorts of people.'

'Forgive me Binoybabu,' Lalita blurted out as soon as Binoy arrived. 'I have wronged you greatly. I had not understood any of your words before this. It's due to our total ignorance about the outside world that our notions are so mistaken. Panubabu says it's by God's decree that magistrates rule Bharatvarsha. In that case, it's by the same God's decree that one feels a heartfelt desire to curse this rule.'

'Lalita, you . . .' began Haranbabu angrily.

'Please be quiet!' Lalita interrupted, turning her back on Haranbabu. 'I am not speaking to you. Binoybabu, please ignore all requests. The show cannot be allowed to take place today.'

'Lalilta, you are quite amazing, I must say!' Borodasundari hastily intervened, to silence Lalita's outburst. 'Won't you give Binoybabu a chance to bathe and eat today? It's one-thirty already, do you realize? See how drained he looks!'

'Here we are guests of the magistrate,' declared Binoy. 'I can't bathe or dine in this house.'

Borodasundari pleaded with Binoy, trying hard to persuade him. Observing the girls'silence, she scolded them angrily:

'What's the matter with all of you? Shuchi, why don't you try to explain to Binoybabu? We have given them our word. People have been invited. We must somehow manage this occasion, or what will they think, tell me! We could never face them again.'

Sucharita bowed her head in silence.

Binoy left by steamer from the riverside not far away. The steamer with its passengers would depart for Kolkata in a couple of hours, to arrive there at approximately eight o'clock the next day.

Haranbabu began to criticize Gora and Binoy agitatedly. Quickly rising from her chowki, Sucharita went into the adjacent room and slammed the door. Soon afterwards, Lalita pushed the door open and came in. She saw Sucharita lying on the bed, both hands covering her face. Locking the door from within, Lalita gently sat down beside her, and began to run her fingers through Sucharita's hair. After a long while, when Sucharita had calmed down, Lalita prised away the arms shielding her face, and bent close to whisper in Sucharita's ear:

'Didi, let's go back to Kolkata. After all, we can't go to the magistrate's tonight.'

For a long time, Sucharita offered no answer. When Lalita persisted, she sat up in bed.

'How is that possible my dear?' she said. 'I had no wish to come here. But since Baba has sent me here, I can't leave without completing my undertaking.'

'But Baba knows nothing of what has transpired. Had he known, he would never have asked us to stay on.'

'That I couldn't say, bhai!'

'Didi, can you really bring yourself to do it?' asked Lalita. 'Tell me, how can you go there? And then, we must don our costumes to recite poems on stage! Even if I bit my tongue till it bled, I couldn't utter a word!'

'I know that bon, sister of mine! But even hell must be endured. There's no way out now. I'll never forget this day, all my life!'

Incensed at Sucharita's compliance, Lalita left her room.

'Aren't all of you going, Ma?' she asked.

'Have you lost your mind?' said Borodasundari. 'We're supposed to go there after nine.'

'I'm talking about going to Kolkata.'

'Listen, just listen to this girl!'

'Sudhirda, will you remain here as well?' Lalita demanded.

Sudhir's heart was broken at Gora's conviction, but he lacked the capacity to resist the temptation of displaying his learning before all those powerful sahebs. He uttered something inarticulate, signifying that although he was hesitant, he would stay back, after all.

'With all this confusion, it's already very late,' Borodasundari interrupted. 'We can't delay any longer. Now nobody must arise from bed before five-thirty—you have to rest. Otherwise you'll get tired and look haggard in the evening, and what an ugly sight that would be!'

She firmly propelled everyone to their rooms and to bed. They all went to sleep. Only Sucharita could not sleep, and in another room Lalita remained sitting upright in bed.

The steamer horn sounded, again and again.

As the steamer was preparing to leave and the sailors were about to draw up the gangway, from the upper deck Binoy saw a woman, seemingly from a respectable bhadra family, rushing towards the vessel. From her attire and appearance she looked like Lalita, but Binoy could not immediately believe it. Ultimately, when she came closer, he was left in no doubt. For a moment he thought she had come to take him back, but it was Lalilta after all who had opposed their participation in the magistrate's programme. She boarded the steamer. The sailors pulled up the gangway. Full of foreboding, Binoy descended from the upper deck to face Lalita.

'Take me to the upper deck,' she said.

'But the steamer is about to leave,' protested Binoy.

'I know.'

Without waiting for Binoy she ascended to the upper deck. Sounding its horn, the steamer set out.

Having offered Lalita an armchair on the first class deck, Binoy looked at her questioningly without saying a word.

'I'm going to Kolkata,' she said. 'I found it impossible to stay on.'

'What about all of them?'

'They don't know as yet, any of them. I've left a letter; as soon as they read it, they will know.'

Binoy was astounded at Lalita's daring.

'But . . .' he faltered.

'The steamer has left, so there's no room for ifs and buts!' she interrupted quickly. 'I don't understand why I must bear everything in silence just because I'm born a woman. Even women are capable of distinguishing between just and unjust, possible and impossible. I'd rather kill myself than perform at tonight's event.'

Binoy realized that now the deed was done, it was no use brooding over the pros and cons of having taken such a step.

'Look,' Lalita resumed after a short silence, 'privately, I had gravely misjudged your friend Gourmohanbabu. I don't know why, from the moment I saw him and heard him speak, my heart grew averse to him. He spoke too forcefully, and all of you seemed to comply. This used to make me angry. Such is my nature—if I see anyone use force in their speech and behaviour, I just can't tolerate it. Gourmohanbabu exerts force not only on others, though but also on himself. That is real power. I have never seen such a person.'

Lalita prattled on in this fashion. Not that she was saying all this only from remorse about Gora. Actually, embarrassment at her impulsive act was constantly threatening to make itself felt. She was beginning to doubt whether she had acted wisely. Until now, she had never imagined how awkward it might be to confront Binoy alone on the steamer. But because the slightest expression of shame would at once make the whole affair utterly shameful, she desperately babbled on. Binoy found himself at a loss for words. For one thing there was Gora's misery and humiliation, then the shame of having come here to entertain himself at the magistrate's house, and to top it all, this sudden predicament created by Lalita. All this, taken together, had rendered Binoy speechless.

On earlier occasions, such daring on Lalita's part would have evoked Binoy's disapproval, but today that did not happen at all. In fact, the amazement roused in him was mingled with respect. There was the added satisfaction that, out of their entire group, only Binoy and Lalita had made the slightest attempt to oppose Gora's humiliation. For this, Binoy would not have to suffer too much, but Lalita's act would cause her great torment, for a long time to come. Yet Binoy had always regarded the same Lalita as hostile to Gora. The more he thought about it, the more he began to respect Lalita's courage, so heedless of her actions' outcome, and her extreme contempt for injustice. He could not think of a way to demonstrate or articulate this respect. Binoy was haunted by the feeling that Lalita's disdain for him as a spineless person constantly dependant on others' views, was entirely justified. He could never have forcefully disregarded the approval and disapproval of all relatives and friends, to express his own views on any subject through courageous action in this fashion. Today, secretly acknowledging that he had often avoided following his own instincts for fear of hurting Gora's feelings or appearing weak in Gora's eyes, and that he had often used a web of subtle arguments to delude himself that Gora's ideas were his own, he admitted that Lalita was vastly his superior in her capacity for independent thought. He was ashamed to remember that he had often privately censured Lalita. Indeed, he wanted to apologize to her but could not think of a way. Binoy saw Lalita's graceful feminine figure illumined by such inner glory, that he felt that this revelation of woman's uniqueness had made his own life worthwhile. Today he surrendered all his pride, all his pettiness, to this shakti, this power infused with sweetness.

## 30

Accompanied by Lalita, Binoy arrived at Poreshbabu's house.

Before he boarded the steamer Binoy was unsure about the nature of his feelings for Lalita. His antagonism with Lalita had kept his heart engaged. For some time now, it had become his daily preoccupation to devise some way of making some kind of truce with this irrepressible girl. It was Sucharita, with the pure radiance of her feminine charm, who had first appeared on Binoy's horizon like the evening star. His exquisite joy at her arrival had imparted wholeness to his nature, or so he had privately imagined. But that other stars had also meanwhile appeared, and that the first star having ushered

in the festival of lights had slowly started to fade unnoticed from the horizon, was something Binoy had not clearly realized.

The day the rebellious Lalita came aboard the steamer, Binoy felt: 'Lalita and I are united in our stand against the rest of the world.' He could not dismiss the thought that, ignoring everyone else, it was to him that Lalita had come, seeking his support. Whatever the reason and whatever the purpose, today Lalita did not merely regard Binoy as one in a crowd; he alone was by her side, he was the only one; all her relatives and dear ones were far away, he alone was close. The rapture of this proximity throbbed in his heart like the rumbling of thunder clouds. When Lalita withdrew to the first class cabin Binoy could not tear himself away to retire to his own sleeping quarters. Removing his shoes, he began to silently pace up and down the deck outside that cabin. Lalita was not likely to face any harassment on board the steamer, but tempted to savour his sudden newfound rights to the full, Binoy could not resist exercising them even without need.

The night was intensely dark, the cloudless firmament covered in stars, the treeline on the shore still and silent like the night sky's deep ink-black base, the wide river's powerful current flowing silently beneath. In this setting, Lalita lay sleeping. This lovely, trustful sleep was all she had placed in Binoy's hands today. Binoy had assumed the responsibility of guarding her sleep like a priceless jewel. With neither parents nor siblings near her, Lalita was sleeping peacefully, resting her beautiful form on an unfamiliar bed, her breath rising and falling very gently, as if in rhythm with the poem that was her slumber; not one braid of her skilfully coiled hairknot had come undone; those hands, with their tender feminine grace, lay on the bed in a posture of complete repose; her feet with their lovely flowerlike soles rested on the bed, stilling all her charming restlessness, like music at the end of a festival. This image of tranquil repose filled Binoy's imagination. Like a miniscule pearl within an oyster, Lalita's tiny spell of sleep in the midst of this dark, silent firmament adorned with planets and stars, appeared to Binoy today as his only precious possession. 'I am awake, I am awake!'—like the fearless sound of a conchshell, these words arose from the expanded recesses of Binoy's heart, floating up to the vast, endless sky to merge with the wordless utterance of the ever-watchful, wakeful being who presides over the great universe.

On this night of the moon's dark quarter, another thought continued to torment Binoy. Tonight, Gora was in jail! Until now, Binoy had shared all Gora's joys and sorrows. This was the first time that it had happened otherwise. Binoy knew that for a person like Gora, the constraints of prison were of no consequence; but in this matter, from beginning to end, Binoy had not been involved with Gora at all; this important episode in Gora's life had occurred entirely without Binoy's participation. Once the course of their lives had diverged at this single point, could the two friends fill the gap when they were united again? Wasn't there a breach now in the completeness of their friendship? A friendship so perfect, so rare! Tonight, simultaneously experiencing emptiness on one account and fulfilment on another, having arrived at a moment in his life where the forces of creation and destruction merged, Binoy gazed silently into the darkness.

Had it indeed been purely due to circumstances that Binoy was unable to join Gora in his travels, or to share Gora's travails in prison after he was sentenced, their friendship could not have been damaged. But it was not mere happenstance that Binoy was acting in a show while Gora set forth on his journey. It was because Binoy's entire lifestream had deviated from the course of their former friendship that this outward separation had also become possible after so long. But now there was no denying the truth. It was no longer really possible for Binoy to singlemindedly adopt Gora's unswerving path. But would their lifelong mutual love be altered due to this change of direction alone? This doubt made Binoy's heart tremble. He knew Gora could not proceed without drawing all his friendship, his sense of duty, towards a single goal. How powerful Gora was! How fierce his desire! Fate had granted Gora's nature the royal splendour to draw all his relationships into a victory march in celebration of that single desire.

The hired cab stopped at Poreshbabu's door. Binoy could clearly sense how Lalita's legs trembled as she dismounted and how she braced herself when entering the house. Lalita herself was unable to gauge the extent of her guilt at the step she had impulsively taken. She knew Poreshbabu would not say anything that could be taken for a direct reprimand; for that very reason, it was his silence she feared most of all. Observing

Lalita's hesitation Binoy could not determine exactly what to do in such a situation. To test whether his presence would aggravate Lalita's awkwardness, he said rather doubtfully:

'I'll take my leave then!'

'No,' said Lalita quickly. 'Come, let's go to Baba.'

Binoy was secretly delighted at this desperate plea. Thinking that his duty was not over as soon as he had brought her home after all, that these sudden developments had created a special bond between himself and Lalita, Binoy seemed to stand by her with added confidence. The thought of Lalita's dependence upon him was like a physical touch that electrified his entire body. He imagined Lalita was clutching his right hand. His male breast swelled at this contact with her. He privately expected that Poreshbabu would be incensed at Lalita's stubborn antisocial stance, that he would admonish her, at which point Binoy would take as much of the blame as possible. He would unhesitatingly accept his share of the reprimand and like a suit of armour, try to protect Lalita from every onslaught.

But Binoy had not understood Lalita's actual state of mind. It was not merely because he could protect her from rebuke that she was reluctant to let him go. Truth be told, Lalita was incapable of subterfuge. She seemed to assume that all aspects of her action would be apparent to Poreshbabu and that she must accept the full consequences of her trial. Since that morning, Lalita had been secretly fuming at Binoy. She knew full well that her anger was unwarranted, but precisely for that reason, her fury increased instead of diminishing.

While on the steamer, Lalita's mood had been different. Since childhood, she had always managed to get into unimaginable scrapes, acting sometimes out of anger, sometimes out of stubbornness. But this time it was a serious matter. That Binoy should have been involved with her in this forbidden escapade caused her embarrassment on one hand and deep elation on the other. This elation seemed to be enhanced by its very forbiddenness. The way she had sought refuge with an outsider to her family, coming so close to him without her relatives as a protective barrier between them, could have caused great awkwardness. But Binoy's natural civility had created such a restrained aura of propriety, that in this risky predicament, the knowledge of his fine sense of decency had delighted Lalita. This was surely not the same Binoy who always laughed and joked with everybody in their house, who prattled on without pause, whose familiarity even with the servants was open and free! Binoy had maintained such a distance where he could easily have claimed more time in Lalita's company in the name of watchfulness, that this in itself had increased her secret sense of intimacy with him. At night, in the steamer cabin, all sorts of anxieties had kept her awake. As she tossed and turned, she presently felt sure that dawn must be approaching. Gently opening the cabin door she looked out and saw that the dew-drenched darkness of the late hours still enveloped the open sky above the river and the treeline along its shore. A cool breeze had just aroused gurgling sounds in the river, and below in the engine room there were signs of activity, as if the sailors were about to resume work. As soon as she stepped out of the cabin, Lalita found Binoy asleep on a cane chair not far away, a warm wrap around his shoulders. The sight at once set her heart racing. Binoy had stayed there all night guarding her! So near and yet so far! With trembling footsteps Lalita immediately left the deck and returned to her cabin. Standing at the door on that autumnal Hemanta dawn, she gazed at Binoy's solitary sleeping figure, within that darkness-enshrouded, unfamiliar riverine landscape. To her, the stars on the horizon before her seemed to encircle Binoy's slumber; her whole heart brimmed with an indescribable solemnity and sweetness; why her eyes so swiftly filled with tears she could not understand. The deity she had been taught by her father to worship seemed to bless her today. And on this sleeping rivershore dense with foliage, at the sacred moment of union when the night's darkness first secretly embraces the new light of dawn, at the full assembly of stars in the firmament, a divine melody rang out on the unstirred strings of the vast cosmic mahaveena, like unbearably exquisite pangs of joy. Just then Binoy's hand twitched slightly in his sleep. Lalita quickly shut the cabin door and lay down in her bed. Her palms and soles turned cold. For a long time, she was unable to quell the restlessness of her heart.

The darkness faded. The steamer was on the move. Having washed and dressed, Lalita came out and stood leaning on the railing. Binoy too, having already awakened at the sound of the steamer horn, was ready and waiting to watch the dawn break over the eastern shore. As soon as Lalita emerged, he grew embarrassed and prepared to leave.

'Binoybabu!' she called out at once.

'You probably didn't sleep well at night,' she observed when he came close.

'I didn't sleep too badly.'

After this, neither of them said a word. At the far end of the dew-moist kash fields with their tall feathery reeds, shone the golden radiance of approaching sunrise. Neither of them had ever witnessed such a sunrise before. The light had never touched them in this way. For the first time they realized that the sky was not empty, that it gazed steadfastly at Creation in silent wondrous bliss. Such an intense awareness had awakened in their hearts that they seemed to physically collide with the innermost consciousness of the entire universe. Neither of them uttered a word.

The steamer arrived at Kolkata. Hiring a cab at the ghaat, Binoy settled Lalita within and took his place beside the coachman. Travelling in the carriage on these Kolkata streets in the daytime, why Lalita's thoughts underwent a reversal, who could say! That Binoy was on the steamer at this time of crisis, that Lalita had become involved with him in this way, that he was escorting her home as if he was her guardian—all these things began to torment her. She now found it intolerable that Binoy should have acquired a certain authority over her by force of circumstance. Why should it be so! Why did that music of the night end on such a harsh note when confronted with the daytime workaday world!

So when Binoy came to the door and asked hesitatingly, 'I'll take my leave then?' Lalita was even more annoyed.

'Binoybabu thinks I'm ashamed to face my father in his company,' she thought. To demonstrate emphatically that she had no qualms about this, and to present the complete facts of the case to her father, she was reluctant to let Binoy depart from the doorstep like a culprit. She wanted her relationship with Binoy to revert to its former transparent footing. She did not want to appear to Binoy in a reductive light by allowing any constraint or any hazy fantasy to linger as an obstacle between them.

## 31

As soon as he saw Binoy and Lalita, Satish rushed up, placed himself between them, and held their hands.

'Why, hasn't Borodidi come?' he demanded.

Binoy patted his pocket, looked all around and said: 'Borodidi! Really, what could have happened! She is lost.'

'Ish!' exclaimed Satish, giving Binoy a shove. 'Indeed! I don't believe you! Lalitadidi, please answer me!'

'Borodidi will come tomorrow' said Lalita, and headed for Poreshbabu's room.

'Come and see who is here,' Satish insisted, dragging Binoy and Lalita by the hand.

'It doesn't matter who's here,' said Lalita, pulling her hand away. 'Don't bother us now. We're going to Baba.'

'Baba is out. He'll be back late.'

Hearing this, both Binoy and Lalita felt a temporary sense of relief.

'Who is our visitor?' Lalita wanted to know.

'I shan't tell you. Achchha Binoybabu, can you guess who is here? You can never guess. Never never!'

Binoy began to suggest some preposterously impossible and inappropriate names: Sirajuddaula, Raja Nabokrishna, at one point even Nandokumar. Satish protested loudly, offering irrefutable reasons why such an assembly of guests was utterly impossible.

'True indeed,' conceded Binoy, acknowledging defeat. 'It hadn't occurred to me before that there might be some serious reasons why Sirajuddaula would find it inconvenient to visit this house. Anyway, let your didi investigate the matter first. Then, if necessary, I'll come as soon as you send word.'

'No, both of you must come,' Satish persisted.

'Which room must we go to?' asked Lalita.

'The room on the second floor.'

In a corner of the second floor terrace was a small attic with a jutting tiled roof sloping southwards to keep out the sun and rain. There beneath that sloping sunshade, the duo following in Satish's wake found a bespectacled elderly lady reading Krittivasa's Ramayana on a small mat. The broken end of her spectacle frame was tied with a string, secured behind her ear. She would be about forty-five. The hair had thinned in front, but her fair countenance was still almost perfectly smooth, like a ripe fruit. Between her brows was a tattoo mark. She was in widow's garb, her form unadorned. Spotting Lalita first, she hastily removed her spectacles, and abandoning her book, she gazed at her face with special eagerness. The next moment, seeing Binoy following behind Lalita, she swiftly rose to her feet, pulled her sari aanchal over her head and prepared to retreat into the room. Satish rushed up to hug her.

'Mashima, why are you running away?' he demanded. 'This is our Lalitadidi, and this is Binoybabu. Borodidi will arrive tomorrow.'

This brief introduction to Binoybabu was enough; there had undoubtedly been plenty of discussion about him already. At the slightest opportunity Satish would hold forth on the few subjects in the world he was equipped to speak about, and he kept nothing back. Not understanding who the term 'Mashima' might refer to here, Lalita stood transfixed in amazement. When Binoy touched this elderly woman's feet in a pranam, Lalita followed his example. Mashima hurriedly fetched a mat from the room and spread it out.

'Sit, baba. Please sit down, ma.'

When Binoy and Lalita had settled on the mat, she resumed her place on her own mat with Satish close to her. Embracing Satish firmly with her right arm, she declared:

'You don't know me, all of you. I am Satish's mashi. His mother was my own elder sister.'

This brief introduction did not reveal much, but there was something in Mashima's face and voice that manifested a pure, tear-bright hint of the deep sorrows of her life. When she clasped Satish to her bosom declaring 'I am Satish's mashi,' Binoy's heart ached in sympathy even without knowing anything of this woman's life history.

'You can't be Satish's mashi alone, for then Satish and I will quarrel for the first time in all this while. As it is Satish calls me Binoybabu, not Dada. For him to deprive me of Mashima as well would be utterly unfair.'

It did not take Binoy long to win people over. In no time at all this young man with his charming appearance and pleasing speech had usurped part of Satish's dominion in Mashima's heart.

'Where is your mother, my son?' Mashima asked him.

'I lost my own mother long ago,' Binoy replied, 'but I can't say that I have no mother.'

As he spoke, he remembered Anandamoyi and his eyes instantly grew moist, as if misted over by emotion. The conversation between the two of them became very animated. One could never have guessed that they were new acquaintances. Satish began to interrupt this dialogue with utterly irrelevant opinions of his own. Lalita remained silent.

Lalita seemed to find it difficult to express herself easily, even if she tried. She took very long to break the inhibitions of a first meeting. Besides, she was not in a good mood today. She did not like the way Binoy was effortlessly chatting with this unknown woman; privately, she condemned his frivolity in remaining so free of anxiety, heedless of the gravity of Lalita's predicament. Not that Binoy could have escaped Lalita's displeasure if he had remained morose and silent, with a grave expression; for then, surely, Lalita would have angrily said to herself: 'It is I who must confront my father, but Binoybabu is behaving as if he must shoulder all the blame!' Truth be told, in the broad light of day the impact that had struck a musical note last night now only produced chords of pain. Nothing was as it should be. That was why Lalita was mentally taking Binoy to task at every step. Nothing he did could have prevented this quarrel. The Almighty alone knew the root cause that must be addressed, for the problem to be solved.

Alas, why should women, who deal solely in matters of the heart, be condemned as irrational? If the heart is in the right place to begin with, it functions so easily and beautifully that all rational arguments bow to it in defeat. But should the slightest trouble occur in the beginning, it is beyond the brain's capacity to repair that instrument. It is fruitless then to even try gauging how anger and indifference, laughter and tears, lead from one thing to another.

Meanwhile it was not as if Binoy's heart-machine was functioning quite normally either. If its condition had remained exactly as before, he would have rushed to Anandamoyi this very moment. Who but Binoy could break the news of Gora's jail sentence to his mother? Who else did she have to console her! This painful thought was like a huge weight grinding away constantly at the bottom of his heart. But it had become impossible for him to part from Lalita immediately. He was trying to convince himself that he was now Lalita's sole protector against the whole world, and that if any intervention was required when Lalita faced Poreshbabu, he must discharge those duties before departing. His heart was easily convinced; it had no capacity to resist. However deep his anguish for Gora and Anandamoyi, Lalita's close proximity delighted Binoy so much, made him feel so expansive, made the whole world seem so glorious, gave him such a distinctive sense of identity, that his pain remained buried in the lower reaches of his heart. Today he could not meet Lalita's eyes. Even the tiniest glimpses that caught his eye every now and then—a corner of her clothing, a hand resting quietly on her lap—instantly made him ecstatic.

It grew late, but Poreshbabu did not return. Binoy's heart prompted him with increasing urgency to rise and take his leave. To suppress it, he continued to concentrate on his conversation with Satish's mashi. Ultimately, Lalita could no longer contain her annoyance. Suddenly interrupting Binoy, she blurted out:

'For whose sake must you delay so long? There's no saying when Baba might return. Won't you see Gourbabu's mother once?'

Binoy was startled. He was only too familiar with Lalita's angry tone. Glancing at her face, he instantly sprang upright like a bow when its string is snapped. For whose sake had he delayed his departure? After all, the arrogant assumption that he was urgently needed here had not occurred to Binoy on its own. He had been about to depart from their very doorstep, and it was Lalita who had requested him to accompany her inside. And now, for Lalita to ask him such a question! So suddenly had Binoy sprung up from the mat that Lalita stared at him in surprise. She saw that his natural cheerfulness had been extinguished at a single puff, like a lamp. Never before had she seen such pain on his face, nor such a sudden change of mood. Looking at him, Lalita at once felt the stinging whiplash of acute regret, striking repeatedly at her heart.

Quickly scrambling to his feet, Satish clung to Binoy's arm, pleading: 'Please stay Binoybabu, don't leave just now. Please have dinner with us. Mashima, why don't you ask Binoybabu to stay for dinner! Lalitadidi, why did you tell Binoybabu to leave!'

'Bhai Satish, not today,' Binoy demurred. 'If Mashima remembers, I'll come another day to taste her prasad, food sanctified by her touch. Today it's too late.'

There was nothing extraordinary about his words, but there were tears in his voice. The pathos did not escape Satish's Mashima's ear either. Swiftly glancing at Binoy and then at Lalita, she understood that this was a game of destiny.

Not long after, Lalita got up and went to her room on some slight pretext. How often had she brought herself to tears in this way!

## 32

Binoy at once headed for Anandamoyi's house. He was inwardly tormented by a mixture of shame and pain. Why had he not gone to Ma all this time! What a mistake he had made! He had imagined that Lalita needed him urgently. The Almighty Ishwar had punished him suitably indeed, for not rushing to Anandamoyi as soon as he reached Kolkata, irrespective of all other needs. Ultimately, he was forced to hear such a question from Lalita's lips: 'Won't you see Gourbabu's mother once?' Could such an aberration ever be possible, that Lalita should care more about Gourbabu's mother than Binoy did! After all, Lalita only knew her as Gourbabu's mother, but to Binoy, she was the sole image of motherhood personified.

Anandamoyi had just bathed. Immobile on her floormat, she was probably meditating silently. Binoy rushed to her and fell at her feet.

'Ma!'

'Binoy!' Anandamoyi stroked his bowed head with both her hands.

Was there anyone with a voice such as Ma's! At the very sound of that voice, Binoy's entire body felt the touch of sympathy flow over it. Restraining his tears with difficulty, he murmured:

'Ma, I have come too late!'

'I have heard all about it, Binoy.'

'You've heard all about it!' exclaimed Binoy, startled.

From the lockup itself, Gora had written a letter to Anandamoyi, which he had forwarded through the lawyer. He must have anticipated that he would be sent to prison.

In conclusion, the letter said:

> Imprisonment will not succeed in harming Gora in the least. But it will not do for you to suffer at all. Your sorrow is the only thing that could be my punishment; it is beyond the magistrate's power to inflict any other penalty on me. Don't think of your own son alone, Ma! The sons of many other mothers serve jail sentences for no fault of theirs. I want to share an equal footing with them, for once; if this wish is fulfilled now, please don't grieve for me.
>
> Ma, I don't know if you remember, but the year there was that famine, I had left my money pouch on the table in the room facing the road, and gone into the next room for five minutes. I returned to find the pouch had been stolen. It contained eighty-five rupees I had saved from my scholarship; I had privately resolved to have a silver ghoti made for you to wash your feet if I saved a little more. Finding the money stolen, as I seethed with futile rage against the thief, the Almighty Ishwar suddenly planted a good thought in my mind. I told myself that at this time of famine I had donated the money to the very man who had taken it. As soon as the words were said, all my fruitless indignation subsided. Similarly, I have now made my heart declare that I am going to prison of my own free will. There is no pain in my heart, no anger against anybody. I am going to accept the hospitality offered by the prison. There will be inconveniences with food and amenities; but after all, when I accepted the hospitality of many homes during my recent travels, I did not find there the comforts I was accustomed to or needed. The suffering I accept willingly is not suffering at all; today I shall voluntarily accept the jail as my refuge. Know this for sure: as long as I remain in prison, not for a single day will anyone keep me there by force.
>
> When we remained at home, effortlessly enjoying our food and amusements, we were not conditioned to even feel the tremendous magnitude of our right to move freely in the daylight under the open sky. Until today I had neither thought about nor maintained any contact with the majority of human beings in this world who at that very moment were suffering bondage and humiliation, deprived of their god-given right to the world, deservedly or undeservedly. Now I wish to emerge in public as a marked man like the rest of them. I don't want to preserve my social prestige by joining the falsely virtuous men of this world, most of whom pretend to be civilized bhadralok.
>
> Ma, this time my encounter with the real world has taught me

> a great deal. Ishwar knows that most of those responsible for passing judgement on others are themselves in need of mercy. Prisoners in jail pay for the sins of those who go unpunished while meting out punishments to others; the crime is committed by many, but these people alone are penalized. As for those who enjoy comfort and prestige outside the prison walls, I do not know how, when and where they will atone for their sins. Spurning such comfort and prestige, I shall emerge in public bearing on my breast the mark of mankind's guilt. Ma, please grant me your blessings, don't shed tears for me. Lord Krishna bore the mark of Bhrigu's kick on his chest, forever; in this world, wherever arrogance inflicts injustice, it deepens that scar on the deity's breast. If that mark becomes His ornament, what have I to worry about, and why should you grieve at all?

Upon receiving this letter Anandamoyi had tried to send Mahim to Gora. Mahim replied that he had to go to work, and that his boss, the saheb, would never give him leave. He then proceeded to curse Gora roundly for his arrogance and lack of judgement, declaring that he too might one day lose his job on Gora's account. Anandamoyi deemed it unnecessary to apprise Krishnadayal of this matter. Regarding Gora, she had a deep-seated grievance against her husband, knowing that Krishnadayal had not given Gora the place of a son in his heart. In fact, he was privately hostile to Gora. Like the Vindhya mountain range, Gora stood as an obstacle to the conjugal relations between Anandamoyi and her husband. On one side of the breach was Krishnadayal, isolated by his excessive vigilance about ritual purity; on the other side was Anandamoyi, alone with her outcaste Gora. It was as if the channels of communication were closed, between the only two people in the world who knew Gora's life history. For all these reasons, Anandamoyi's affection for Gora was solely her treasure. She tried as far as possible to make light of Gora's illegitimate presence within this family. It was her daily worry lest someone should say, 'This was your Gora's doing', 'We had to hear such things, thanks to your Gora,' or 'Your Gora has caused us this loss.' After all, she alone was entirely responsible for Gora. And her Gora was no ordinary mischievous child, either! It was not easy, was it, to conceal his existence, wherever he might be? Having spent all these years bringing up her precious, unruly Gora in the midst of this hostile family, managing him day and night until he was now so grown up, she had faced many allegations she could not answer, borne many ordeals she could not share.

Anandamoyi remained at the window, in silence. She saw Krishnadayal enter the house, chanting mantras after his early morning bath, marks of Ganga earth on his forehead, arms and chest. Anandamoyi could not approach him. Forbidden, forbidden, all was forbidden! Finally, with a sigh, she arose and went to Mahim's room. He was reading a newspaper on the floor while his servant gave his body an oil massage before his bath.

'Mahim,' said Anandamoyi, 'give me an escort, let me go and see what has happened to Gora. He has made up his mind to go to prison; if he is imprisoned, can't I visit him once before that?'

Whatever his outward manner, Mahim had a soft spot for Gora. Verbally, he continued to growl:

'Let the wretch go to prison, then. Surprising it hasn't happened before now!'

But having said this, the very next moment he sent for Poran Ghoshal who was beholden to them. He gave him some money for the lawyer's fees and dispatched him immediately. He also decided to travel there himself, if the saheb at the office gave him leave, and if his wife permitted.

Anandamoyi was also aware that Mahim could not rest content without doing something for Gora. Once assured that Mahim had made all the arrangements possible, she returned to her room. She was well aware that at this difficult time, amidst all the public mockery, curiosity and gossip, no one in this family would escort her to Gora's unfamiliar location. Eyes clouded with silent pain, she clenched her lips and remained quiet. When Lachhmia burst into loud sobs she scolded her and banished her to another room. It was her lifelong habit to digest all her anxiety in silence. She calmly accepted both joy and sorrow; only the all-knowing Lord could see the grief in her heart.

Binoy did not know what to say to Anandamoyi. But she never awaited words of consolation from anybody. Her nature shrank from others who tried to talk about her sorrows, which were beyond redress. Preventing any further discussion, she said, 'Binu, I see you have not bathed yet. Go and have a bath quickly, it's very late.'

When Binoy sat down to his meal after a bath, Anandamoyi's heart wept in grief at the sight of Gora's empty place beside him. Gora would have to eat prison food today, food with the bitter taste of heartless discipline, not sweetened by a mother's care. At one point, the very thought compelled Anandamoyi to rush from the room on some pretext.

## 33

When he returned home, as soon as he saw Lalita at this odd hour, Poreshbabu realized that this wild daughter of his had got into some unprecedented scrape. He looked at her inquiringly.

'Baba, I came away,' she blurted out. 'I couldn't remain there under any circumstances.'

'Why, what is the matter?' Poreshbabu asked.

'The magistrate has sent Gourbabu to jail.'

How Gour came into the picture and what exactly had occurred, Poreshbabu could not understand at all. When Lalita told him the whole story, he remained silent for a while. Immediately thinking of Gora's mother, his heart filled with anguish. He thought, 'if only the judge could sense how cruel was the punishment inflicted on several innocent people whenever one man was sent to prison, it could never be such an easy, routine matter to condemn someone to jail.' Only an extreme paralysis of the ethical sense could have generated the barbarity that enabled the magistrate to pronounce with equal ease the same punishment for Gora as for a common thief. The news of Gora's prison sentence made Poreshbabu recognize how much deadlier than other forms of violence was man's tyranny towards man, and also how social power and royal authority had combined to lend tremendous force and magnitude to such tyranny.

'Tell me, Baba, isn't this a terrible injustice?' demanded Lalita, encouraged by Poreshbabu's thoughtful silence.

'I don't quite know the extent and nature of Gour's actions,' replied Poreshbabu with his customary calm. 'But I can say this for sure: Gour may go beyond his rights when carried away by his strong sense of duty, but it is entirely against his nature to commit what the English language calls a crime. Of that I have not the slightest doubt. But what can we do, ma, the sense of justice in our times has not yet attained that level of moral discrimination. Even now, the same punishment is prescribed for mistakes as for crimes; both entail the same prison sentence, the same hard grind. We cannot blame any one person for this state of affairs. For this, all the sins of humanity are to blame.' Then, suddenly dropping the subject, Poreshbabu asked: 'Who did you come with?'

'With Binoybabu,' replied Lalita, drawing herself upright as if by some special effort. Whatever her outward display of strength, inwardly she was vulnerable. Lalita did not find it easy to declare that she had come with Binoybabu. From somewhere, a hint of embarrassment arose within her, and thinking that this embarrassment was visible in her facial expression, she grew even more self-conscious.

Among all his offspring, Poreshbabu loved this capricious, indomitable daughter of his the most. It was because her conduct seemed blameworthy to others that he had developed a special respect for the forthrightness of Lalita's behaviour. He knew that people would specially notice her faults but her virtues, however rare, would go unappreciated. Poreshbabu had carefully nourished her good qualities, all along; in the process of subduing Lalita's unruly nature, he had not wanted to trample upon her inner nobility as well. People acknowledged the beauty of his other two daughters at first sight; their complexion was fair, their facial contours flawless; but Lalita's complexion was darker, and the extent of her facial charm was debatable. Hence Borodasundari constantly expressed anxiety to her husband about finding a match for Lalita. But the beauty Poreshbabu saw in Lalita's face was not that of complexion or of build, it was the profound beauty of the inner self. It had not only grace but also the fire of independence and the firmness of strength, a firmness not everyone would find appealing. It would attract a few special people but repel many others. Realizing that Lalita would not be popular but that she would be genuine, Poreshbabu would draw her to him with a certain tender pain—because he knew that others were unforgiving, he judged her with compassion.

When he heard that Lalita had suddenly come away alone with Binoy, he instantly understood that she would have to undergo intense and prolonged suffering on this account. People would prescribe for her a punishment appropriate for a crime much greater than the minor one she had committed. As he pondered over this in silence for a while, Lalita blurted out:

'Baba, I have done wrong. But I have understood very clearly now that the relationship between the magistrate and our countrymen is such that his hospitality implies no honour for us, only condescension. Ought we to have stayed on, tolerating even this?'

The question did not strike Poreshbabu as an easy one.

'You crazy girl!' he smiled, patting her head with his right hand, avoiding any direct answer.

As Poreshbabu paced outside the house that afternoon, thinking about this episode, Binoy appeared and touched his feet respectfully. Poreshbabu spent a long time discussing Gora's imprisonment with him but did not even mention Binoy's arrival with Lalita on the steamer. 'Come, Binoy, let's go inside,' he proposed when it grew dark.

'No,' said Binoy. 'I'll go home.'

Poreshbabu did not ask him a second time. Casting a swift, lightning glance at the upper storey, Binoy slowly walked away. Lalita had spotted Binoy from upstairs. When Poreshbabu entered alone, she assumed that Binoy would follow him in shortly. But even after a short while, Binoy did not appear. Then, after shuffling about some of the books and paperweights on the table, Lalita left the room. Poreshbabu called her back.

'Lalita, sing a Brahmo song for me,' he requested, looking tenderly at her downcast face.

He turned down the lamp, shading its light.

## 34

The next day, Borodasundari and the rest of her troupe came back. Unable to contain his disapproval of Lalita, Haranbabu accompanied them instead of returning to his own lodgings, and went directly to Poreshbabu. Angry and upset, Borodasundari went straight to her room without glancing at Lalita or saying a word to her. Labanya and Leela had also come back incensed with Lalita. The departure of Lalita and Binoy had so disabled their recitation and acting that their embarrassment was beyond description. Taking no part in Haranbabu's indignation, Borodasundari's tearful laments or Labanya and Leela's awkward indifference, Sucharita had fallen completely silent, mechanically performing her routine chores. Today as well, she followed everyone mechanically into the room. Cringing with shame and remorse, Sudhir went home from Poreshbabu's doorstep itself. Failing in her repeated attempts to invite him in, Labanya vowed not to speak to him anymore.

'Something terribly wrong has happened,' blurted out Haranbabu as soon as he entered Poreshbabu's room.

Lalita was in the adjacent room. As soon as these words entered her ears, she came and stood there, hands clasping the back of her father's chowki, gaze fixed on Haranbabu's face.

'I have heard all about it from Lalita,' said Poreshbabu. 'Now the deed is done, it is no use discussing it.'

Haran regarded the calm, restrained Poresh as extremely weak-natured. Hence he said, rather disdainfully:

'Episodes end once they have occurred, but character remains, after all. That is why even past events must be discussed. What Lalita has done today could never have been possible had she not always been pampered by you. How much you have harmed her will become apparent when you hear all about today's happening.'

Sensing a slight rocking movement at the back of his chowki, Poreshbabu quickly drew Lalita to his side and grasping her hand, he said with a faint smile:

'Panubabu, you will realize in due course that affection, too, is necessary for one's children's upbringing.'

Putting her arm round her father's neck, Lalita bent to whisper in his ear:

'Baba, your water is growing cold. Please go and have your bath.'

'I'll go a little later,' said Poreshbabu in an undertone, glancing at Haran. 'It's not so late.'

'No, Baba, please have your bath,' insisted Lalita tenderly. 'Meanwhile, we shall keep Panubabu company.'

After Poreshbabu had left the room Lalita firmly occupied a chowki and fixing her gaze on Haranbabu's face, she accused him: 'You think you have the right to say anything to anybody!'

Sucharita knew Lalita well. On any other day, the sight of Lalita in her present mood would have secretly aroused her anxiety. But today, she remained on her chowki by the window, staring silently at the open page of a book. By nature and habit, Sucharita was always self-restrained. In the last few days, the more she had felt the accumulated pain of all sorts of afflictions, the quieter she had become. Today, the burden of this silence had become intolerable, so when Lalita took it upon herself to express her views to Haran, it was as if the torrent imprisoned in Sucharita's heart found an opportunity for release.

'Do you think you know better than Baba what his duties towards us should be!' Lalita erupted. 'Are you sole Headmaster of the entire Brahmo Samaj!'

At first Haranbabu was stunned at such arrogance in Lalita. He was about to offer a very harsh reply when she interrupted:

'We have endured your superior airs all these days with great patience, but if you try to surpass Baba as well, nobody in this house will tolerate you—not even our bearer.'

'Lalita, you . . .' Haranbabu began to expostulate.

'Silence!' Lalita interrupted sharply. 'We have been hearing you at length, now listen to what I have to say. If you don't believe me, please ask Sucharita: my Baba is far more noble than you imagine yourself to be. Now you may give us all the advice you wish to offer.'

Haranbabu's face darkened. 'Sucharita!' he cried, rising from his chowki.

Sucharita looked up from her book.

'Can Lalita be allowed to insult me before your very eyes!' said Haranbabu.

'It is not her aim to insult you,' answered Sucharita calmly. 'Lalita wants to say that you should treat Baba with due respect. We don't know anyone more worthy of respect than he.'

For a moment it seemed as if Haranbabu would leave at once, but he did not rise. He remained seated, his face very grave. The more he realized that he was gradually losing respect in this house, the harder he tried to establish his claim. He was becoming unmindful of the fact that the tighter one grasps a worn-out crutch, the faster it tends to crumble. Observing Haranbabu's solemn, offended silence, Lalita arose and went up to Sucharita. She began to chat with her in a low voice as if nothing serious had happened. Meanwhile, Satish came into the room.

'Borodidi, come with me,' he said, tugging at Sucharita's hand.

'Where must we go?' asked Sucharita.

'Just come with me, I'll show you something. Lalitadidi, you haven't told her have you?'

'No,' replied Lalita.

Lalita had promised Satish not to disclose his mashi's presence to Sucharita. She had kept her word. But Sucharita could not abandon their guest.

'I'll come in a little while, bakhtiar,' she said. 'Let Baba join us after his bath.'

Satish began to fret. If it had been within his power to somehow make Haranbabu disappear, he would have left no stone unturned. Being in awe of Haranbabu, he could not say anything to him. Haranbabu had not maintained any form of contact with Satish, apart from occasionally trying to mend his nature.

As soon as Poreshbabu appeared after his bath, Satish dragged his two sisters away.

'About that proposal concerning Sucharita,' declared Haranbabu, 'I wish to delay no further. I would like the ceremony to take place next Sunday itself.'

'I have no objection,' replied Poreshbabu, 'provided Sucharita agrees.'

'But we have already taken her consent.'

'Well then, the matter is decided.'

## 35

That day, after parting from Lalita, Binoy was haunted by a doubt that pierced his heart like a thorn. He began to think:

'I have been visiting Poreshbabu's house regularly without knowing for sure whether anyone likes or dislikes my going there. Perhaps that is not correct. Perhaps I have tested their patience frequently and at odd times. I don't know the ways of their culture, or the extent of my rights of access in this house. Maybe I am stupidly entering spaces forbidden to anyone but relatives.'

Considering these things it seemed to Binoy that Lalita may have seen something in his expression today that had affronted her. Until now, Binoy's own feelings for Lalita had not been clear to him. Today, they were no secret. He could not fathom how to handle these new revelations of his heart's inner state. A thousand times, he debated its links with the external realm, its relations with the world, whether it meant dishonour for Lalita or a betrayal of Poreshbabu. He felt like sinking into the earth, imagining that Lalita was angry at having caught him out. It became impossible for Binoy to go to Poreshbabu's house. The emptiness of his own house also weighed upon him. Early the next morning, he went to Anandamoyi.

'Ma, I'll stay with you for a few days,' he announced.

At heart, he also meant to console Anandamoyi to assuage her grief at separation from Gora. Realizing this, Anandamoyi's heart melted. Without a word, she stroked Binoy affectionately. Binoy made all sorts of demands upon her affection, concerning his meals and the attention he required. He quarreled with her on the false pretext that he was not being looked after properly there. With his diverting chatter he constantly tried to keep both Anandamoyi and himself distracted. In the evening, when it was hard to contain his emotions, he would pester her, dragging her away from all her housework to the mat spread on the veranda before the room. He would make her narrate stories about her childhood in her parents' house, stories about the days when she was an infant, extremely popular with the residential students at her grandfather's tol—his Sanskrit school—a special cause for anxiety for her widowed mother because as a fatherless girl, she was indulged by everyone in every way.

'Ma, I feel surprised to imagine a time when you were not our mother,' Binoy declared. 'I think the students at the tol saw you as a tiny mother, ever so small. As if it was you who had assumed the responsibility of bringing up Dadamoshai.'

One evening, placing his head upon Anandamoyi's outstretched legs upon the mat, Binoy said: 'Ma, I feel like returning all my learning and intellect to the Maker and to seek shelter in your lap as an infant. I wish there would be nothing in the world for me but you alone.'

Binoy's voice expressed such emotional fatigue that Anandamoyi was both moved and surprised. Shifting closer, she began to gently stroke his head. After a long silence she asked:

'Binu, is all well with Poreshbabu's household?'

Her question startled Binoy, making him suddenly embarrassed. 'There is no hiding anything from Ma,' he thought, 'she knows the secrets of my soul.'

'Yes indeed, they are all well,' he faltered.

'I really want to become acquainted with Poreshbabu's daughters. After all, Gora was not favourably disposed towards them at first, but since they have now won him over as well, they must be out of the ordinary.'

'I, too, have often wanted to introduce you to Poreshbabu's daughters somehow,' Binoy responded enthusiastically. 'I never proposed it lest Gora take offence.'

'What is the eldest daughter's name?' Anandamoyi wanted to know.

As introductions proceeded through such questions and answers, Binoy tried to abridge the discussion when Lalita's name came up. But Anandamoyi would brook no obstacle.

'Lalita is very intelligent, I am told,' she observed, privately amused.

'Who told you that?'

'Why, you did.'

There was a time when Binoy had felt no self-consciousness about Lalita. He had completely forgotten that in that unattached state, he had freely discussed Lalita's sharpness of intellect with Anandamoyi. Like a skilled oarsman Anandamoyi steered the conversation about Lalita past all obstacles so that almost all the significant details about the history of her acquaintance with Binoy were revealed. Now he even blurted out the fact that Lalita, anguished at Gora's prison sentence, had escaped alone with Binoy on the steamer. As he spoke, his animation increased; the dejection that had oppressed him in the evening evaporated without trace. He began to feel now that to get to know an extraordinary person like Lalita and to be able to speak of her in such terms was itself a great boon for him. When dinner was announced and the conversation ended, Binoy seemed to suddenly awaken from a dream, realizing that he had recounted to Anandamoyi all the secrets of his heart. Such was Anandamoyi's manner of listening to everything and accepting it, that Binoy did not even feel any cause for embarrassment. Up until today he had nothing to hide from Ma, confiding in her about the most trifling of things. But ever since he was introduced to Poreshbabu's family, a sort of communication block had appeared that was not healthy for Binoy. Now, sensing that his secret feelings for Lalita had been completely disclosed to the subtly perceptive Anandamoyi, Binoy felt overjoyed. Had he been unable to offer up this development in his life to his mother, in all its entirety, it would never have become pure and transparent. It would have continued to taint his thoughts like an inkblot.

At night Anandamoyi had reflected upon this matter for a long time. Thinking that a solution to the increasingly complex problem in Gora's life could be found in Porershbabu's household itself, she began to feel that she must meet the girls once, by any means.

# 36

Mahim and his family had been proceeding on the assumption that Shashimukhi's marriage to Binoy was more or less fixed. In fact, Shashimukhi would not even approach Binoy. Binoy was barely acquainted with Shashimukhi's mother. Not that she was shy, exactly, but she was abnormally secretive. The door to her room was often closed. Her husband apart, everything else in her life was kept under lock and key. The husband did not enjoy much access either: under his wife's discipline, his movements were clearly charted and his sphere of activity was extremely limited. Owing to this natural tendency to circumscribe everything, Shashimukhi's mother Lakshmimoni, had complete control over her own world; entry for outsiders and exit for insiders was not unrestricted. In fact even Gora did not receive much encouragement in Lakshmimoni's domain. In the administration of this kingdom there were no dichotomies. For the lawmaker here was Lakshmimoni and from the lower court to the highest court of appeal, she alone was all in all. Not only were the executive and the judiciary unsegregated, but the legislative was also combined with them. In his conduct towards outsiders, Mahim seemed very firm indeed, but within Lakshmimoni's territory, he had no power to exercise his own wishes. Not even in trivial matters.

Lakshmimoni had seen Binoy from behind the screen, and liked him as well. Since childhood, Mahim had regularly seen Binoy as Gora's friend; it was due to such excessive familiarity that he had been unable to think of Binoy as his daughter's suitor. When Lakshmimoni drew his attention towards Binoy, his respect for his wife's intelligence increased. Lakshmimoni firmly resolved that it was Binoy her daughter would marry. She impressed upon her husband a major advantage in this proposal: Binoy could not claim any dowry from them. For a few days, even when he found Binoy at home, Mahim had been unable to raise the subject of the marriage. He desisted because Binoy was dejected about Gora's imprisonment.

Today was a Sunday. The lady of the house did not allow Mahim to complete his weekly daytime siesta. Binoy was reading aloud to Anandamoyi from Bankim's newly published *Bangadarshan*. Casket of paan in hand, Mahim approached them and slowly lowered himself onto the wooden taktaposh. First offering Binoy a paan, he expressed his annoyance at Gora's reckless stupidity. Then, in the process of discussing how much time remained for Gora's release, he very suddenly remembered that the month of Agrahayan was almost half over already.

'Binoy,' he said, 'It's impractical of you to say that Agrahayan weddings are forbidden in your family. As it is the holy books and almanacs are full of restrictions; to add to that, if you keep inventing family shastras as well, how will we preserve our family line?'

'Binoy has been seeing Shashimukhi ever since she was very tiny,' Anandamoyi interrupted, observing that Binoy was in difficulty. 'The idea of marrying her does not appeal to him, hence this pretext about Agrahayan.'

'He could have told us right at the outset,' complained Mahim.

'It takes time even to know one's own mind, after all,' Anandamoyi replied. 'Is there any shortage of suitors, Mahim? Let Gora come back. He knows many nice young men. He will be able to fix up a match.'

'Hm!' said Mahim, his face like thunder. After a short silence, he said, 'Ma, if you had not discouraged Binoy he would not have objected to this proposal.'

Flustered, Binoy was about to speak, but Anandamoyi interrupted: 'Well, truth be told Mahim, I couldn't bring myself to encourage him. Binoy is young. He might have unwittingly taken a step that would have ultimately led to no good.'

Shielding Binoy, Anandamoyi bore the brunt of Mahim's rage. Realizing this, Binoy was ashamed at his own feebleness. As he was about to clearly announce his rejection of the proposal, Mahim left the room without waiting any longer, telling himself that a stepmother can never truly belong.

Anandamoyi was aware that Mahim was capable of such thoughts, and that as a stepmother she would always be listed as a criminal in the world's law-court. But it was never her habit to let other people's opinion determine her actions. From the day she had adopted Gora she had made herself independent of the ways of the world and the views of other people. Since then, indeed, she had adopted ways that invited public blame. The concealment of a certain fact constantly tormented her at the very core of her being, but it was the blame heaped upon her by society that offered her some relief from that pain. When people called her a Khristan she would clasp Gora in her lap and declare: 'God knows being called a Khristan does not condemn me.' So, gradually, it had become part of her nature to detach her conduct from public opinion in every respect. Even if Mahim secretly or openly humiliated her for this by calling her a stepmother, she would not be diverted from her chosen path.

'Binu, you haven't gone to Poreshbabu's house in a long time,' Anandamoyi remarked.

'A long time, how is that?' asked Binoy.

'You haven't gone there even once since you returned on the steamer.'

That was not long ago. But Binoy knew that his visits to Poreshababu's house had once been so frequent that even Anandamoyi had scarcely got a glimpse of him. By that measure, he had not visited Poreshbabu's house for many days, and it had indeed become noticeable. Shredding a thread pulled from the end of his dhoti, Binoy remained silent.

'Maji, kahanse mayilog aya,' the bearer came and announced in Hindi at this point (Ma, some ladies have come to see you).

Binoy quickly rose to his feet. While he was trying to ascertain who had come and from where, Sucharita and Lalita entered the room. Binoy did not get a chance to leave the room. He stood there, stupefied. Both girls touched Anandamoyi's feet in a pranam. Lalita scarcely looked at

Binoy. Sucharita greeted him with a namaskar.

'How are you?' she asked. 'We have come from Poreshbabu's house,' she added, addressing Anandamoyi.

Receiving them warmly, Anandamoyi said, 'Such introductions are not required. I have not seen the two of you before, ma, but I consider you members of my own household.'

In no time, their conversation grew warm and animated. Observing Binoy's silence Sucharita tried to draw him into the discussion.

'Why haven't you come for so many days?' she asked him in a low voice.

'I am afraid of losing your affection from troubling all of you too frequently,' said Binoy, casting a glance at Lalita.

'Don't you know that affection also waits to be troubled again and again?' asked Sucharita with a faint smile.

'He knows it only too well, ma!' Anandamoyi assured her. 'What can I tell you—with all his whims and fancies, it's a miracle if I get any time to myself all day.' As she spoke, she looked tenderly at Binoy.

'The Almighty Ishwar has granted you patience,' retorted Binoy. 'He is using me to test it.'

'Do you hear that, bhai Lalita?' demanded Sucharita, nudging Lalita. 'Our own test is over, it seems. We couldn't pass the test, I suppose?'

'Now our Binu is putting his own patience to the test,' smiled Anandamoyi, observing that Lalita showed no reaction to this banter. 'Indeed, you have no idea of his high regard for all of you. In the evenings, you are the sole topic of conversation. And he melts at the very mention of Poreshbabu's name.' Anandamoyi kept her eyes on Lalita's face. Making a supreme effort to meet her gaze, Lalita flushed for no reason at all.

'He has sprung to your father's defence against so many people!' Anandamoyi continued. 'The members of his community are on the verge of declaring him an outcaste for becoming a Brahmo. Truly, Binu my boy, such impatience won't do. I see no reason to be ashamed about it either. Ma, what do you say?'

This time, Lalita dropped her gaze as soon as she looked at her.

'We are well aware that Binoybabu thinks of us as family,' said Sucharita. 'But that is not solely to our credit, it owes much to his own ability.'

'That I couldn't say for sure, ma!' replied Anandamoyi. 'After all I have seen him ever since he was little. All these days, my Gora was his only friend. In fact I have noticed that Binoy could not mingle even with the men of his own community. But such has been the effect of his brief acquaintance with all of you that we, too, cannot reach him anymore. I wanted to pick a quarrel with you about this but now I find I must take his side. You people will outdo everyone else.' With these words Anandamoyi touched Lalita's chin, then Sucharita's, and kissed her own fingers in a gesture of affection.

'Binoybabu, Baba is back,' said Sucharita compassionately, noticing Binoy's wretchedness. 'He is talking to Krishnadayalbabu in the outer room.'

At her words, Binoy hastened from the room. Now Anandamoyi began to speak of the rare friendship between Gora and Binoy. She was not unaware that her two listeners were not indifferent to the subject. To these two boys Anandamoyi had given all her devotion, the holy offering of all her mother-love; no one mattered more to her in all the world. Indeed she had moulded them personally like the shivalinga of a young girl's prayers, but they had been the sole recipients of all her devotional efforts. Her narration of the story of these two deities raised in her own lap was so vivid, so saturated with affection, that listening to her, Sucharita and Lalita longed for more. They did not lack respect for Gora and Binoy but through the loving eyes of a mother such as Anandamoyi, they seemed to see the young men in a fresh perspective.

After meeting Anandamoyi, Lalita seemed to grow even more incensed at the magistrate. Anandamoyi smiled at her heated remarks. 'Ma,' she said, 'the all-knowing Lord alone understands my anguish at Gora's imprisonment. But I could not be angry with the saheb. I know Gora after all; he has a total disregard for rules and laws when it comes to his beliefs. If he does not observe the law, the dispensers of justice will of course send him to jail, and why should I blame them? Gora has performed his duty, they have performed theirs; if someone must suffer for this, suffer they will. If you read my Gora's letter, Ma, you will realize that he was not afraid of misery, nor vainly angry with anyone. He had acted with a definite awareness of what the fruits of certain actions might be.'

With these words, she drew Gora's letter, carefully preserved, from her box, and handed it to Sucharita.

'Please read it aloud, ma,' she requested, 'let me hear it once again.'

When Gora's extraordinary letter had been read out the three of them remained silent for a while. Anandamoyi wiped the corner of her eye with her aanchal. Those tears contained not only the pain of a mother's heart but also a mixture of joy and pride. Her Gora was no ordinary person, indeed! Was he the sort to be forgiven and set free by the magistrate! Had he not acknowledged all his guilt and deliberately shouldered the burden of all the sufferings of imprisonment? There was no need to quarrel with anybody about his sufferings. Gora was bearing them unflinchingly, and Anandamoyi, too, could bear the pain.

Lalita gazed at Anandamoyi's face in surprise. The traditions of a Brahmo family were very firmly entrenched in Lalita's mind; she had no respect for women who had not received a modern education, whom she knew as 'daughters of Hindu households.' In their childhood, when Borodasundari scolded them saying 'Even daughters of Hindu households don't do such things,' Lalita would bow her head with a special sense of shame for the misdeed in question. Today, hearing Anandamoyi's words, she was repeatedly overwhelmed with amazement. Anandamoyi's strength was as extraordinary as her calmness and her astonishing soundness of judgement. Compared to this woman, Lalita felt extremely small and humble for her own lack of emotional restraint. Her mind was in turmoil today, hence she had neither glanced at Binoy nor even spoken to him.

But gazing at Anandamoyi's face, graced with affection, tenderness and peace, the heat of rebellion in her heart seemed to subside, easing her relations with everyone around her.

'Having seen you now, I understand where all Gourbabu's strength comes from,' Lalita told Anandamoyi.

'You don't really understand,' Anandamoyi corrected her. 'Had my Gora been like other ordinary boys, where would I have found the strength? Could I have borne the thought of his misery in this way?'

It is necessary to offer a brief history of the cause for Lalita's present state of anguish. These last few days, her first thought upon leaving her bed every morning was that Binoybabu would not visit them today. Yet all day long, not for an instant did her mind cease to await Binoy's arrival. Moment to moment, she constantly imagined that perhaps Binoy had come, perhaps instead of coming upstairs he was talking to Poreshbabu in the room downstairs. There was no saying how many times in the day she needlessly went from room to room, on this account. Finally, when she went to bed at the end of the day, she didn't know how to deal with her own heart. She felt like crying, fit to burst her heart, but at the same time she also felt angry, but with whom, it was hard to say. As if she was angry with herself. 'What's the matter!' she asked herself constantly. 'How will I live! I see no way out. How long can this continue!'

Lalita knew Binoy was a Hindu. There was no possibility of her marrying him. Yet, unable to control her heart by any means, her spirit drooped in shame and fear. That Binoy was not averse to her was something she sensed; it was because she realized this that she now found it hard to contain herself. Hence, while she anxiously awaited Binoy's arrival, she also felt inwardly afraid that Binoy might arrive. Wrestling with her own emotions like this, her patience had collapsed this morning. Her heart seemed to be in constant turmoil at Binoy's failure to arrive, and she felt that if she could only meet him once, her restlessness would disappear. In the morning she dragged Satish to her room. These days, his mashi's presence had made Satish more or less forget about his friendly interchanges with Binoy.

'Have you quarreled with Binoybabu then?' Lalita asked him.

He strongly repudiated this slanderous suggestion.

'What sort of friend is he!' taunted Lalita. 'You keep speaking of Binoybabu, but he doesn't even spare you a glance.'

'Ish! As if that's true!' exclaimed Satish. 'Never!'

As the family's tiniest member, Satish often had to assert himself vociferously in this manner, to establish his prestige. Now, to demonstrate it even more definitely, he rushed to Binoy's house at once. Upon his return he said:

'He's not at home, that's why he couldn't visit us.'

'Why didn't he visit us these last few days?' Lalita wanted to know.

'Because he was away all these days.'

'Didibhai,' Lalita now proposed to Sucharita, 'we ought to visit Gourbabu's mother once.'

'But we don't know them,' Sucharita protested.

'Why, wasn't Gourbabu's father Baba's childhood friend, after all?' Lalita reminded her.

'Yes, indeed he was,' Sucharita now recalled. She too became very enthusiastic.

'Bhai Lalita,' she said, 'go speak to Baba about this.'

'No, I can't talk to him. You go ask him.'

Ultimately it was Sucharita who went to Poreshbabu.

'You're quite right,' he instantly agreed, when she broached the subject. 'We should have visited them long ago.'

After their meal, as soon as their visit had been planned, Lalita's heart rebelled. Petulance and doubt assailed her unaccountably, and began to pull her in a contrary direction.

'Didi, you go with Baba,' she told Sucharita. 'I'm not going.'

'How is that possible!' Sucharita expostulated. 'I can't go alone without you. Bhai, my angel, please let's go, don't make a fuss.'

After a lot of persuasion Lalita accompanied her. But she seethed at the humiliation of this defeat, for she had been outdone by Binoy. He could easily abstain from visiting their house, but here she was, rushing to meet him! In her heart she strove to deny outright that it was the hope of glimpsing Binoy there that had made her so enthusiastic about visiting Anandamoyi's house. Due to that stubborn desire, she neither glanced at Binoy nor returned his namaskar, nor spoke a word to him. Binoy concluded that because Lalita had detected his secret feelings, she was ignoring him like this by way of repudiation. He did not have the self-assurance to imagine that Lalita might actually be in love with him. He came and stood bashfully at the door.

'Poreshbabu wants to go home now,' he announced. 'He has asked me to inform everyone.' He made sure to remain beyond Lalita's range of vision.

'How is that possible!' Anandamoyi protested. 'How can he leave us without tasting some sweets! It won't take long. Wait a little Binoy, let me go and see. Why are you standing outside? Come and join us inside the room.'

Keeping his face averted, Binoy somehow found a place far away from Lalita,.

'Binoybabu,' said Lalita in a natural tone, as if there had been nothing unusual in her conduct towards him before this. 'Are you aware that your friend Satish went to your house this morning to find out whether you've completely abandoned him!'

Binoy jumped in amazement, as people do when they suddenly hear a divine prophecy from the heavens. Embarrassed that he had started so visibly, he failed to summon up a reply with his customary skill.

'Had Satish gone there, then?' he asked, flushing to the tips of his ears. 'But I was not in!'

These casual words from Lalita aroused great elation in Binoy's heart. In an instant, a vast cloud of doubt was lifted from over the whole universe, vanishing like a stifling nightmare. As if this was all he desired in this world. 'I am saved! I am saved!' his heart began to chant. Lalita was not angry, she did not mistrust him at all. In no time, all constraints were removed.

'Binoybabu has suddenly taken us for long-nailed, sharp-toothed, horned, armed demons, or something of the sort,' laughed Sucharita.

'In this world, those who keep quiet, unable to complain openly, are the ones who end up as the accused,' protested Binoy. 'Didi, such words don't become you. You have yourself become so remote, and now you imagine that others have grown distant.'

This was the first time Binoy had addressed Sucharita as Didi, his elder sister. It sounded sweet to her ears. From their very first acquaintance, she had developed a sisterly tenderness for Binoy, a feeling that assumed a concrete, affectionate shape as soon as he addressed her as Didi.

The daylight had almost waned when Poreshbabu took his leave, along with his daughters.

'Ma, I won't let you do any work today,' said Binoy to Anandamoyi. 'Let's go upstairs.'

He was finding it impossible to contain the turbulence in his heart. Taking Anandamoyi to the room upstairs, with his own hands he spread a mat for her on the floor.

'Binu, what is it?' asked Anandamoyi. 'What is it you want to say?'

'I have nothing to say,' he declared. 'You must speak to me.' It was to hear Anandamoyi's opinion of Poreshbabu's daughters that Binoy's heart was yearning so restlessly.

'So, is this why you called me here?' exclaimed Anandamoyi. 'I ask you, is there something you want to say?'

'If I hadn't called you here, you would have missed watching such a sunset,' Binoy replied.

That evening, above the Kolkata rooftops, the Agrahayan sunset looked rather pale. There was nothing unusual in the sun's radiance. In a corner of the sky, the golden glow blended indistinctly with dusty vapours. But even the dullness of this faded dusk had lent a rosy hue to Binoy's mind today. He began to feel that he was closely encircled in every direction, as if the sky was touching him.

'They are good girls, both of them,' remarked Anandamoyi.

Binoy did not let the discussion end there. He kept it alive from diverse perspectives, recalling sundry small incidents from long ago, involving Poreshbabu's daughters. Many of these were insignificant, but on that lonely, fading Agrahayan evening, owing to Binoy's eagerness and Anandamoyi's curiosity, these unknown fragments of minor domestic history were infused with a profound glory. Suddenly, at one point, Anandamoyi sighed.

'I would be very happy if Sucharita were married to Gora,' she blurted out.

'Ma, I've often thought of it,' cried Binoy, jumping up. 'She is just the companion for Gora!'

'But would it be possible?'

'Why not? I don't think Gora dislikes Sucharita.'

Anandamoyi was not unaware that Gora had been attracted by

someone. That the woman in question was Sucharita, she had also gleaned from some of Binoy's remarks.

'But would Sucharita marry into a Hindu household?' Anandamoyi wondered aloud, after remaining silent for a while.

'Tell me, Ma,' said Binoy, 'can't Gora marry into a Brahmo household? Would you not approve?'

'I would approve wholeheartedly.'

'You would?' Binoy asked again.

'Yes indeed, Binu! Marriages are born when two hearts meet; who cares what mantras are chanted on the occasion, baba! As long as you take God's name in some form or other.'

A load seemed to lift from Binoy's mind. 'Ma, I feel very surprised to hear such words from you. Where did you acquire such largeness of heart?'

'From Gora,' smiled Anandamoyi.

'But Gora says the exact opposite!'

'What if he does? All that I know is imbibed from Gora. How real an entity is man, and how false are the causes that prompt men to partisanship, fighting and killing! That's something the Almighty made me realize the day He gave me Gora. Who is a Brahmo, baba, and who is a Hindu, for that matter? The human heart has no caste or creed; it is the site where the Lord brings everyone together and unites with them Himself. Can we afford to spurn Him and depend solely on mantras and opinions to bring about unity?'

Binoy touched Anandamoyi's feet respectfully.

'Ma, your words are music to my ears,' he declared. 'My day has proved worthwhile, indeed.'

## 37

Sucharita's mashi Harimohini posed a serious problem for Poreshbabu's family. Before describing it, an abridged version of Harimohini's self-introductory remarks to Sucharita is offered below:

I was two years older than your mother. The two of us received boundless affection in our parental home. For at that time, only the two of us, both girls, had been born into the family, and there was no other infant in the house. Our kakas pampered us so much, we never felt any hardship.

At the age of eight I was married off into the famous Roychoudhury family of Palsa, as distinguished in lineage as in wealth. But I was not destined to be happy. At the time of my marriage, my father had fallen out with my father-in-law over the wedding expenses and other related matters. For a long time, my in-laws could not forgive my father's family for that offence. 'We'll get our boy married again,' they would all say.

'Let's see the girl's plight then.' It was the sight of my misery that made my father vow never to marry his daughters into a rich family. That was why he had married your mother into a poor household.

Many families lived together in my marital home. At the age of eight or nine, I had to cook for almost fifty or sixty people. After serving everyone else, I had to survive on plain rice, or sometimes with rice and dal. Sometimes I would get to eat at two in the afternoon, sometimes at the very end of the day. As soon as I had eaten, I had to go and cook the evening meal. I could dine only at eleven or twelve at night. There was no clearly designated place for me to sleep. In the private quarters of the antahpur, I would sleep next to anyone, wherever and whenever it suited their convenience! Sometimes I had to place a pinri to sleep on the wooden seat.

The general neglect I faced from everyone in the house could not but affect my husband's attitude. For a long time he kept me at arm's length. When I was seventeen, my daughter Manorama was born. Having given birth to a girl-child, I was subjected to even greater humiliation by my in-laws. Amidst all the neglect and shame that I suffered, it was this girl who became my sole consolation, my only joy. Because Manorama had not received much affection from her father or anyone else, she became the object of my heartfelt love.

Three years later, when I produced a boy, my status began to change. Then I became worthy of being considered the mistress of the household. My mother-in-law was no more, and my father-in-law had also left us just a couple of years after Manorama was born. Immediately after his demise, we were involved in property disputes with my deors, my husband's younger brothers. Ultimately, having squandered much of our property on legal expenses, we broke off from the rest of the family. When Manorama was of marriageable age, fearing that she might be taken far away, that I should never see her again, I married her off into Simulé village, five or six krosh away from Palsa. The boy looked just like the god Kartika, as fair as he was handsome. And they had the means of subsistence as well.

I had suffered great degradation and hardship once, but before misfortune struck, providence had temporarily granted me happiness in equal measure. In his last days, my husband showed me great care and respect, never taking a step without first consulting me. How could I enjoy such an excess of good fortune without paying a price? My son and husband died of cholera, four days apart. Ishwar the Almighty kept me alive just to demonstrate that human beings can tolerate even the sort of pain that is unimaginable.

Gradually, I began to discover my son-in-law's true nature. Who would have imagined that such a venomous serpent could lie hidden within such a beautiful flower? That he had fallen into bad company and become an addict was something even my daughter never told me. My jamai, this son-in-law, would come to me at odd times and ask for money, citing all sorts of needs. I had no need to save for anyone else in the world, so when my jamai asked my indulgence, I rather liked it.

Sometimes my daughter would dissuade me. She would scold me, saying: 'You are spoiling him by giving him money like this; when money comes his way, there's no saying when and how he squanders it.' I would imagine that Manorama was forbidding me to give him money because her in-laws would lose respect if her husband accepted money from me in this fashion.

Then I grew inspired to provide money for my jamai's addictions, unbeknownst to my daughter. When Manorama got to know of this, she came to me one day and wept, telling me all about her husband's scandalous behaviour. Then I struck my forehead in self-reproach. My grief was indescribable. It was one of my deors who had ruined my jamai with his evil company and wicked ideas. When I withdrew my monetary support, my jamai began to suspect that it was my daughter who had forbidden me. The matter could be concealed no longer. Now he began to torment my daughter so extremely, insulting her so publicly, that to prevent it I again started giving him money behind my daughter's back. I knew I was condemning him to hell, but I could not rest in peace when I heard that he was subjecting Manorama to unspeakable torture.

Ultimately, one day—I remember that day so clearly! Towards the end of Magh, the summer having set in early that year, we were saying: 'The trees in our back garden are already laden with mango-blossom!' One afternoon, that Magh, a palki came and stopped at our door. I saw Manorama approach us, smiling; then she came and touched my feet.

'Why Manu,' I asked, 'what news?'

'Can't one visit one's mother just like that, even if there is no news?' laughed Manorama.

My beyan, Manorama's mother-in-law, was not a bad person. She sent me a message that as Bouma, her daughter-in-law, was expecting, she would be better off staying with her mother until the child was born. I took that for the truth. But I had no inkling that my jamai had started assaulting Manorama even in her condition, and that it was from fear of a disaster that my beyan had sent her daughter-in-law to me. Manu and her mother-in-law kept me deluded in this way. If I tried to give my daughter an oil massage and a bath, Manorama would elude me on various pretexts; she did not want to expose the scars on her tender body, even to her mother's eyes.

Occasionally, my jamai would come and create a scene, wanting to take Manorama back with him. Because my daughter was staying with me, it prevented him from seeking my indulgence with requests for money. Gradually, even this obstacle ceased to deter him. He began to pester me for money even in Manorama's presence. 'You must not give him money under any circumstances,' Manorama would stubbornly insist. But I was extremely vulnerable; I could not refrain from giving my jamai some money, lest he become too annoyed with my daughter.

One day, Manorama said: 'Ma, I'll take care of all your money.' She now took charge of my keys, cash box, everything. When my jamai found no further possibility of extracting money from me, and failed to make Manorama unbend by any means, he began to insist: 'I'll take

Mejobou home.' 'Give him, ma, give him some money and get rid of him,' I would urge Manorama, 'or who knows what he might do!' But my Manorama could be as firm as she was tender. 'No,' she would declare, 'he must not be given money under any circumstances.' One day, my jamai came and announced, glaring at us:

'I shall send the palki tomorrow evening. If you don't let Bou go, I warn you of dire consequences.'

'Ma, let's delay no more,' I urged Manorama when the palki arrived before dusk the following day. 'I'll send for you again next week.'

'Not today, let it be,' pleaded Manorama. 'I don't feel like leaving today, Ma. Ask them to return after a couple of days.'

'Ma, will my insane jamai spare us if I turn away the palki?' I persisted. 'Let's not try that, Manu. Please go today itself.'

'No, Ma, not today,' Manu begged. 'My father-in-law is away in Kolkata. He is expected back in mid-Phalgun. I'll go back then.'

Still I said: 'No, ma, we'd best not do that.'

At this, Manorama went to prepare for her departure. I busied myself arranging meals for the attendants and palki-bearers from her in-laws' household. I did not get the opportunity to spend a little time with her before she left, to give her special care that day, to dress her with my own hands, to feed her some favourite dishes before bidding her goodbye. Just before she mounted the palki, she touched my feet and said:

'Ma, I'll take your leave, then.'

How was I to know that she was really leaving me! She had not wanted to go, but I forced her to depart—my heart burns with grief at that thought, even today. Nothing has quenched that fire!

That very night, Manorama died of a miscarriage. Before I received the news, she had already been hastily cremated in secret. You will not understand, any of you, the kind of grief that leaves nothing to be said, nothing to be done, no end to one's thoughts, nor any relief to be found in tears. Such grief is best not understood.

So I lost everything, but my problems did not end there. From the time I lost my husband and son, my deors had been eyeing my property. They knew they were sole heirs to my property after my demise, but they could not bear to wait so long. For this, nobody is to blame; it was truly a crime for a wretch like me to remain alive at all. How could people with diverse worldly needs tolerate it if people like myself, with no needs at all, should unaccountably remain alive, occupying their rightful space?

As long as Manorama was alive, I did not let myself be deluded by any of my deors' arguments. I did my best to defend my property rights against them. I had vowed, as long as I lived, to save money for Manorama and bequeath it to her. It was my effort to save for my daughter that had become intolerable for my deors, who felt it was their wealth I was stealing. Nilkanta, a trusted old retainer of my husband, was my only support. If I tried to arrive at a mutual settlement by surrendering my claim to something that was rightfully mine, he would never agree. 'I'd like to see who touches a single paisa that is ours by right,' he would declare. Amidst this struggle over our rival claims, my daughter passed away. The very next day my deor came to me and advised me to renounce the world.

'Boudi,' he urged, 'Ishwar has placed you in such circumstances now, that it would no longer be appropriate for you to cling to a worldly existence. For the remainder of your life, retire to a place of pilgrimage and turn your mind to holy things. We shall arrange for your upkeep.'

I sent for our Guruthakur, our spiritual guide.

'Thakur,' I begged, 'please tell me how I may escape the clutches of sorrow. Whatever I do, I can find no consolation anywhere. I seem to be trapped in a fence of fire; wherever I go, whichever way I turn, I cannot see the slightest way out of my agony.'

My guru led me to the puja-room and said: 'This deity Gopiballav is your husband, son, daughter, your all in all. In his service alone can you fill the vacuum in your life.'

Day and night I sojourned in the puja-room. I began to try to devote myself wholeheartedly to the deity, but how could I give unless He was willing to receive? He did not accept my offering, did he?

Sending for Nilkanta, I said: 'Niludada, I have decided to sign over all my life's possessions to my deors. They will give me some money every month to take care of my needs.'

'That cannot be allowed under any circumstances,' Nilkanta declared. 'You are a woman; don't involve yourself in such matters.'

'What need have I of property anymore?' I inquired.

'How can you say such a thing?' exclaimed Nilkanta. 'Why should we give up our rights? Don't take such an irrational step.'

In Nilkanta's eyes nothing was greater than one's rights. I was in a quandary. Worldly matters were anathema to me, but Nilkanta was the only person I trusted in this world. How could I hurt him? After all, he had suffered a lot trying to protect those 'rights' of mine. Ultimately one day, unbeknownst to Nilkanta, I signed a document. I had not properly understood what was written there. Why should I be afraid to sign, I had thought; what did I wish to keep that I could not bear to be defrauded of? After all everything belonged to my father-in-law; if it went to his sons, let them have it.

When the legal procedures had been registered, I sent for Nilkanta and said: 'Niludada, don't be angry, I have signed over everything I had. I have no further need of anything.'

'What!' cried Nilkanta in agitation. 'What have you done!'

When he read the document drafted by the agent and realized that I had indeed surrendered all I possessed, Nilkanta's anger knew no bounds. Ever since his master's demise, protecting my 'rights' had become the mainstay of his life. All his thoughts and strength had been tirelessly devoted to this sole purpose. Litigation and court proceedings, trips to the lawyer's house, unearthing relevant legal clauses—he had found pleasure in these things alone. So much so, he did not even have the time to attend to his own personal affairs. When those 'rights' vanished at a single stroke of a woman's pen, Nilkanta could not be pacified.

'That's it, then,' he declared. 'My links with this place are broken. I'll take my leave.'

Was it my ultimate misfortune in my in-laws' home that Niludada would abandon me in such fury? I called him back, pleading:

'Dada, please don't be angry with me. Let me give you these five hundred rupees from my savings. When you acquire a daughter-in-law, give her my blessings and use this money to order some jewellery for her.'

'I have no further need of money,' Nilkanta asserted. 'Now that my employer has lost everything, accepting those five hundred rupees will bring me no happiness. Let it be.' With these words, my husband's last true friend left me and went away.

I took refuge in the prayer room.

'Go and take up lodgings in a holy place,' my deors urged me.

'My father-in-law's ancestral property is a holy place to me,' I declared. 'And where my deity resides, there I shall take refuge.'

But they could not bear to let me occupy any portion of the house. They had already decided who would use the rooms and how, once their belongings had been transferred to our house. Ultimately they said:

'You may carry your deity's image with you, we shall not object.'

'What will you live on if you stay here?' they demanded, when I demurred even at this suggestion.

'Why, the allowance you have assigned me will suffice for my needs,' I replied.

'But there's no mention of any allowance!' they told me.

At this, taking my deity's image with me, exactly thirty-four years after my marriage, I left my marital home and set out on my own one day. Enquiring after Niludada, I heard that he had already departed for Brindavan. I accompanied pilgrims from our village to Kashi. But my sinful heart found no peace anywhere. Daily I would call upon my deity and say, 'Thakur, please become as real for me as my own husband and children had once been!' But he didn't answer my prayers, did he? My heart finds no solace, ceaseless tears wrack my body and soul. Baap re baap, how harsh the human heart can be!

Ever since I entered my marital home at the age of eight, I could not visit my parents even for a day. I had tried very hard to attend your mother's wedding, but to no avail. Afterwards, I received news of your birth in a letter from my father, and news of my sister's death as well. Until now, Ishwar has not given me an opportunity to draw you two motherless children into my lap.

Travelling in holy places, when I found my heart still enslaved by the illusion called maya and my inner thirst for an object of love still unquenched, I began to inquire after all of you. I had heard that your father had abandoned his religion, abandoned his community and broken free. But what could I do about that! Your mother was my sister after all, born of the same womb.

I have come here after a gentleman in Kashi informed me of your whereabouts. Poreshbabu doesn't believe in deities I'm told, but you only have to see his face to realize that Thakur, the almighty Lord, is happy with him. Prayers alone do not melt Thakur's heart, as I know only too well; I shall find out how Poreshbabu won Him over. Anyway, bachha, it is not yet time for me to live in isolation—that is beyond my power. Thakur may grace me with his favour when He pleases, but without having all of you close to my lap, I cannot stay alive.'

## 38

In Borodasundari's absence, Poresh had given shelter to Harimohini. Offering her the secluded room on the terrace, he had made all arrangements to ensure that her observance of orthodox rituals could proceed unimpeded. Upon her return, Borodasundari was aflame with fury at finding such an unimaginable presence in her household.

'I can't accept this,' she protested very sharply to Poresh.

'You can tolerate all of us but not this widow who has no support?' Poresh reproached her.

Borodasundari knew that Poresh had no practical sense; every now and then, he would suddenly do something outrageous, never sparing a thought for matters of worldly advantage. Subsequently, one may rave or rant, scold or weep, but he would remain unmoved as a statue. Who could cope with such a man? Which woman could live with a man who could not even be provoked into a quarrel when necessary!

Sucharita was about the same age as Manorama. Harimohini began to feel that she even resembled Manorama a great deal. She appeared similar in temperament as well, calm but firm by nature. At times, when Sucharita's back was turned, Harimohini's heart would miss a beat, looking at her. When she sometimes wept silently in the evening, if Sucharita approached her, Harimohini would clasp her to her bosom, eyes shut tight, and say:

'Aha, I feel as if it is she herself I have found, here in my heart. She did not want to go but I forced her to leave. Can I ever, under any circumstances, be pardoned! I have suffered the punishment that was my due. Now she is here. Here she is, back with me, back with the same smiling countenance. Here's my ma, my jewel, my treasure!' Saying this, she would stroke Sucharita's face all over, kiss her, shed floods of tears. Tears would stream from Sucharita's eyes as well. Throwing her arms around Harimohini's neck, she would declare:

'Mashi, I too could not enjoy my mother's love for long, but now my lost mother has returned. How often, when things were difficult, when I lacked the strength to pray to Ishwar, when my heart had shrivelled within, I would call out to my Ma! Today, my Ma has come, in response to my call.'

'Don't, please don't say such things,' Harimohini would plead. 'Your words bring me such joy that I feel apprehensive. O Thakur, please spare us from the evil eye! I plan to avoid any further attachments, wanting my heart to turn to stone, but indeed I can't! I'm very weak. Have pity on me, strike me no more. O my Radharani, go, go, go away from me. Don't entangle me further, please don't! O my Gopiballav, Lord of my life, my Gopal, my priceless jewel, what predicament have you placed me in this time!'

'You can't get rid of me by force, Mashi,' Sucharita would reply. 'I'll never let you go—I'm here to stay by your side forever.' Like an infant she would nestle her head in Harimohini's bosom, and fall silent.

In no time, a deep bond evolved between Sucharita and her mashi, not to be measured by the yardstick of time. This too irked Borodasundari. 'Just look at this girl's behaviour. As if we never looked after her, all of us. Where was her mashi all these days, I'd like to know? We raised her right from childhood, and now she swoons at the very mention of her mashi! I've always told my husband, this Sucharita you all laud as such a wonderful person, makes an outward show of decency, but it's impossible to win her heart. All we've done for her all along has indeed proved futile!'

Borodasundari knew Poresh would not understand her agony. Moreover, she also had no doubt that she would lose respect in Poresh's eyes if she expressed her hostility to Harimohini. That infuriated her even more. She began to rally support to prove that whatever Poresh might say, most intelligent people would be in agreement with her. She started discussing the Harimohini affair with all members of their social circle, eminent or otherwise. There was no end to her laments and complaints about Harimohini's orthodox Hindu views, her idol worship, and the bad example she set for youngsters in the family.

Borodasundari not only complained to others but also began to trouble Harimohini in all sorts of ways. She would choose her moment to assign other tasks to the milkman deployed as bearer to draw water for Harimohini's cooking and other chores. If the matter came up she would say, 'Why, Ramdeen is available, isn't he?' Ramdeen being a low caste Dosad, she knew Harimohini would not accept water drawn from the well by him. If anyone pointed this out she would retort: 'If she was so fussy about Brahmanical ways, why come to our Brahmo household? Here, it won't do to be so finicky about caste. I shall never encourage it.' On such issues her sense of duty became very aggressively manifest. The Brahmo Samaj, she felt, had gradually become very slack in matters concerning the community; that was why it could not accomplish enough. She would try her best not to participate in such leniency. No, never. If someone misunderstood her, she was ready to take it; if even her kinfolk turned against her, she would humbly accept that too. She began to remind everyone that all great men of the world who had performed noble deeds had been compelled to tolerate criticism and opposition.

No inconvenience could vanquish Harimohini. She seemed to have vowed to attain the ultimate heights of self-mortification. As if to match the rhythm of the unbearable suffering her heart had inwardly undergone, she seemed to constantly torment herself outwardly with her strict observance of rules. Her endeavour was to voluntarily embrace sorrow, in order to master it through intimacy. When Harimohini faced trouble obtaining water, she gave up cooking altogether. She began to live on milk and fruits that she had dedicated to her deity as holy prasad. Sucharita was extremely distressed at this. Her mashi tried hard to convince her:

'Ma, this has proved a boon for me. This is what I needed. It does not hurt me at all; rather, it brings me joy.'

'Mashi,' said Sucharita, 'if I don't accept food or water from members of other castes, will you let me attend upon you?'

'Why, ma,' expostulated Harimohini, 'please follow the dharma you believe in. There is no need for you to change track on my account. It is a source of joy to me that I have been allowed this proximity to you, to hold you close, to see you every day. Poreshbabu is your guru, and like a father to you. Follow the path he has shown you, and for that alone, the Almighty will bless you.'

Harimohini began to endure all the torment inflicted upon her by Borodasundari as if she was totally unaware of it. In answer to Poreshbabu's daily queries—'How are you? I hope you are not finding things inconvenient?'—she would reply: 'I am very happy.'

But Sucharita was wounded every moment by Borodasundari's unjust behaviour. She was not a girl to complain, and in particular, could never bring herself to speak to Poreshbabu about Borodasundari's conduct. She began to endure everything in silence, too shy to express any unhappiness at this state of affairs. As a result Sucharita gradually drew very close to her mashi. Despite her mashi's repeated remonstrations, she began to follow her aunt's dietary habits completely. Ultimately, observing Sucharita's discomfort, Harimohini was obliged to resume her interest in culinary matters.

'Mashi,' said Sucharita, 'I'll live exactly as you advise me, but I shall personally draw water for your use. I shan't stop that on any account.'

'Don't mind, ma' Harimohini pleaded, 'but the ritual food offering, my Thakur's bhog,, is cooked in that water, after all.'

'Mashi,' argued Sucharita, 'does your Thakur observe caste laws too? Can He also be tainted by sin? Does He also belong to some community?'

Finally, Harimohini had to concede to Sucharita's dedication. She accepted Sucharita's service completely. Imitating his didi, Satish, too, started insisting, 'I'll eat food cooked by mashi.' In this way, the three of them formed a small, separate domestic unit in a corner of Poreshbabu's house. Only Lalita remained as a bridge between the two household units. Borodasundari did not allow any of her other daughters to approach that part of the house, but she lacked the power to forbid Lalita.

# 39

Borodasundari began to invite her female Brahmo friends frequently to her home. Sometimes they would congregate on the terrace. With her natural provincial simplicity, Harimohini would offer these women her hospitality, but she did not fail to realize that they held her in contempt. In fact, Borodasundari would begin criticizing Hindu ritual practices even in Harimohini's presence, and many ladies would join the attack with Harimohini as their special target. Clinging to her mashi's side, Sucharita would silently endure all these onslaughts. She only seemed anxious to demonstrate that she belonged to her mashi's party. On days when refreshments were offered, if invited to help herself, Sucharita would declare:

'No, I don't eat such things.'

'What! Won't you eat with all of us?'

'No.'

'Sucharita is now a staunch Hindu, don't you know?' Borodasundari would say. 'Indeed she will refuse food that we have touched!'

'Sucharita has also become a Hindu! What further blows will Time inflict on us, I wonder.'

'Radharani, ma, please go ahead!' Harimohini would plead in agitation. 'Ma, please go and have something to eat!'

She found it very painful that because of her, Sucharita was suffering such taunts from members of her own community. But Sucharita remained unshakeable. One day, when a Brahmo girl, out of curiosity, was about to enter Harimohini's room with her shoes on, Sucharita blocked her way, saying:

'Don't go into that room.'

'Why not?'

'Her Thakur is there.'

'Thakur! You worship the Thakur every day, do you!'

'Yes ma, I worship Him indeed,' Harimohini asserted.

'Do you feel any devotion for Thakur?'

'Curse my misfortune! Could I attain devotion after all? If I had, I would indeed have been saved!'

Lalita was present on that occasion. Red-faced, she asked the questioner:

'Do you feel any devotion for the One you worship?'

'Wah, how strange, what would I feel but devotion?'

'You feel no devotion at all,' Lalita declared, vigorously shaking her head. 'And what's more, you're not even aware that you feel no devotion.'

Harimohini struggled to ensure that Sucharita should not be alienated from her own group because of the rules she followed, but to no avail. Until now, Haranbabu and Borodasundari had secretly harboured a certain mutual hostility. In the present situation, the two of them found their stances very well matched. Borodasundari pronounced that, whatever others might say, if anyone had an eye to preserving the purity of Brahmo ideals, it was Panubabu. Haranbabu also declared to everyone that Borodasundari's single-minded, sensitive awareness of the need to keep the Brahmo community untainted in all respects was a good example for every Brahmo housewife. His praise for her contained a special barb directed at Poreshbabu.

'You have started taking prasad, food blessed by the deity, I hear,' Haranbabu once asked Sucharita in Poreshbabu's presence. Sucharita flushed, but pretending not to have heard this remark, she started rearranging the pens on the inkstand upon the table.

'Panubabu, whatever we eat is blessed by the Lord, isn't it?' protested Poreshababu, casting a distressed glance at Sucharita's face.

'But Sucharita is all set to reject our Lord,' Haranbabu pointed out.

'Even if that were possible,' Poreshbabu argued, 'would making a fuss prevent it in any way?'

'Must we not even try to haul ashore a person adrift on the tide?' Haranbabu demanded.

'If we all try to stone her on the head, that can't be described as hauling her ashore,' replied Poreshbabu. 'Rest assured, Panubabu, I have observed Sucharita ever since she was little. Had she fallen into deep waters I would have known of it before all of you and I would not have remained indifferent.'

'Sucharita is here,' said Panubabu. 'Why not ask her directly? She doesn't accept food touched by all and sundry, we hear. Isn't that true?'

'Baba knows I don't accept food touched by all and sundry,' responded Sucharita, giving up her unwarranted interest in the inkpot. 'If he could tolerate my behaviour, that is enough. If it displeases all of you, blame me as you please, but why torment Baba? Do you know how forgiving he is about your behaviour? Is this what he receives in return?'

Even Sucharita had learned how to talk back these days, marveled Haranbabu to himself.

Poreshbabu was a peace-loving man. He did not enjoy discussing himself or others at length. So far, he had not accepted a prominent position within any project of the Brahmo Samaj; he had led a secluded life, away from the public eye. Haranbabu took this for detachment and lack of enthusiasm on Poreshbabu's part, and had even taken Poreshbabu to task for this.

'Active and inactive: Ishwar has created substances of both categories,' Poreshbabu had replied. 'I happen to be utterly inactive. Ishwar will extract from me whatever service a person like me can render. It's no use fretting over what's not possible. I am sufficiently advanced in years; my strengths and deficiencies have already been identified. Now it's fruitless to push and prod me.'

Haranbabu believed that he could enthuse even an indifferent heart, that he had the natural ability to push the lethargic towards the path of duty and soften with remorse the lives of the fallen. He was convinced that nobody could withstand for long his extremely powerful and single-mindedly benevolent desires. He held himself chiefly responsible, in some way or other, for all positive changes in the personal character of members of his community. He had no doubt, either, that his invisible influence also had a secret effect. Up until now, whenever someone had specially praised Sucharita in his presence, he had acted as if the credit went entirely to him. Using advice, example and the reflected glory of his company, he had moulded Sucharita's personality so as to present her to society as a living example of his own extraordinary influence. At the deplorable moral decline of this very same Sucharita, his pride in his own abilities remained undiminished. He laid the entire blame on Poreshbabu. People had always praised Poreshbabu, but Haranbabu had never joined them. He hoped everyone would now recognize this as evidence of the extent of his own sagacity.

A man like Haranbabu could tolerate all else, but if those he had especially guided to the moral path used their own judgement to adopt an independent course, he could never forgive such a crime. It was impossible for him to let them off easily; the more he found his advice disregarded, the more obstinate he became, repeatedly renewing his assaults. Like a machine that cannot stop until it winds down completely, he too could not restrain himself. Parroting the same words a thousand times to unwilling ears, he still did not want to give up.

This tormented Sucharita greatly, not on her own account but on Poreshbabu's. Poreshbabu had become the target of criticism among all members of the Brahmo Samaj. How could this distressing situation be overcome? On the other hand, Sucharita's mashi was also growing daily more conscious that the humbler and more self-effacing she tried to be, the more she became a nuisance for this family. Sucharita was constantly haunted by her mashi's intense shame and embarrassment. She could not think of any way out of this predicament. Meanwhile Borodasundari began to pester Poreshbabu to get Sucharita married off quickly.

'We can't take responsibility for Sucharita anymore,' she argued. 'She has now started following her own views. If her wedding is likely to be delayed, I'll go away somewhere else with my daughters. Sucharita's odd example is proving a source of great damage to the girls. You will regret this later, wait and see. Indeed, Lalita was not like this before. Now, when she does outrageous things randomly and willfully, obeying no one, who is at the root of the problem? Her escapade the other day, for which I am dying of shame, do you think Sucharita had no hand in that? I have never protested the fact that you have always loved Sucharita more than your own daughters, but I tell you plainly, we can't let this continue any longer.'

Poreshbabu had grown worried, not about Sucharita but about the discord within his family. He had no doubt that Borodasundari would make a huge fuss, now that she had found a pretext. The more fruitless her agitation, the more obdurate she would become. In the present circumstances, it might doubtless be better for Sucharita's peace of mind as well, if her wedding could be quickly arranged.

'If Panubabu can persuade Sucharita,' he told Borodasundari, 'I shall not oppose the marriage.'

'How many times must she be persuaded?' Borodasundari demanded. 'You surprise me, I must say! And why all this persuasion? Where will her ladyship find a suitor like Panubabu, I ask you! Truth be told, whether you like it or not, Sucharita is not a bride worthy of Panubabu.'

'I haven't clearly understood Sucharita's feelings for Panubabu,' Poreshbabu observed. 'So until they mutually clarify these things, I can't interfere in any way.'

'Haven't understood! At last you admit it! That girl is not easy to understand. She's different on the outside and different within!'

Borodasundari sent for Haranbabu.

That morning, the newspapers carried a critique of the current predicament of the Brahmo Samaj. The article targeted Poreshbabu's family in such a way that even without names being mentioned the real object of the attack was quite apparent to everybody. And from the style, it was not difficult to identify the author. After scanning the paper, Sucharita was tearing it to shreds. Frenziedly she tore the pieces of paper, as if bent upon reducing them to atoms. At this moment, Haranbabu entered the room and pulled up a chair beside her. Sucharita did not look up even once. She continued shredding the paper as before.

'Sucharita, I have a serious matter to discuss with you today,' Haranbabu declared. 'You must listen carefully to what I have to say.'

Sucharita went on tearing the paper. When it became impossible to shred it with her nails, she took scissors from her drawstring pouch and used them instead. Just then, Lalita came in.

'Lalita,' said Haranbabu, 'there is something I must discuss with Sucharita.'

When Lalita made as if to leave, Sucharita clutched at her sari aanchal.

'But you have to discuss something with Panubabu!' protested Lalita.

Without answering, Sucharita clung to Lalita's aanchal. Lalita sat down beside her on the mat. Haranbabu was not one to be deterred by any obstacle. Without any further preamble he went straight to the point.

'I don't think it wise to delay our wedding any longer,' he declared. 'I have spoken to Poreshbabu. He says there will be no further hindrance once we have your consent. I have decided, the Sunday after next . . .'

'No,' said Sucharita, before he could finish.

Hearing this very curt, distinct and haughty 'No' from Sucharita's lips, Haranbabu came up short. He knew Sucharita to be extremely docile. He had not even imagined that she might instantly shoot down his proposal in mid-air with this single arrow, her 'No'.

'No! What is 'No' supposed to mean?' he demanded irritably. 'Do you want to delay even further?'

'No.'

'Then?' he asked, astonished.

'I don't consent to this marriage,' replied Sucharita, head bowed.

'Don't consent?' repeated Haranbabu, as if nonplussed. 'What does that mean?'

'Panubabu,' Lalita jibed, 'have you forgotten your Bengali today?'

'It is easier to admit that one has forgotten the mother tongue, than that one has misunderstood someone whose words one has always respected,' retorted Haranbabu, looking daggers at Lalita.

'It takes time to understand people,' replied Lalita. 'Perhaps that applies to you as well.'

'From the beginning until now, I have never been inconsistent in my words, opinions or behaviour,' declared Haranbabu. 'I can claim with emphasis that I have given no one any cause for misunderstanding, none whatsoever. Let Sucharita herself say whether I am right or wrong.'

Lalita was on the point of retorting again, but Sucharita interrupted: 'You are quite right. I have no desire to blame you.'

'If you won't blame me, why wrong me either?' Haranbabu protested.

'If you call this wrong, then I must wrong you indeed,' declared Sucharita firmly. 'But . . .'

'Didi, are you in?' called a voice from outside.

'Come, Binoybabu, please come in,' Sucharita quickly responded, delighted.

'You're mistaken, Didi, it's not Binoybabu. I'm just Binoy. Please don't embarrass me with such deference,' said Binoy, as he entered. At once he saw Haranbabu and noticed the displeasure on his face. 'Are you angry because I haven't visited, all these days?' he asked.

'I have reason to be angry, indeed,' responded Haranbabu, trying to join in the banter. 'But today you have come at a rather inappropriate time. I was discussing a special matter with Sucharita.'

'There you are,' said Binoy, flustered. 'I still haven't understood when it is inappropriate for me to visit! That's why I don't have the courage to visit at all.' He prepared to leave.

'Binoybabu, please don't go,' pleaded Sucharita. 'Our discussion is over. Please stay on.'

Binoy realized his arrival had rescued Sucharita from some grave danger. Pleased, he took a chowki and said, 'If you encourage me, I can't resist. If you ask me to stay, then stay I will. Such is my nature. So, I humbly request Didi to think before she says such things, or she will find herself in trouble.'

Saying not a word, Haranbabu remained still as a gathering storm. 'Very well,' he seemed to say silently, 'I shall wait. I shall leave only after I have finally had my say.'

Hearing Binoy's voice outside the room, Lalita had felt the blood surge within her heart. She had struggled to sustain her normal manner but without success. When Binoy entered the room she was unable to address him with familiar ease. It became hard to decide where to look, in what posture to place her arm. She tried once to get up and leave but Sucharita would not release her aanchal. Binoy, too, spoke only to Sucharita throughout. It became difficult, expert conversationalist though he was, to start any conversation with Lalita today. So he began chatting with Sucharita with redoubled volubility, allowing no gaps or silences.

But this new awkwardness between Lalita and Binoy did not escape Haranbabu's notice. He smouldered inwardly, observing that the same

Lalita who was so sharply articulate with him these days, became so constrained in Binoy's presence. Considering how Poreshbabu was leading his family on the path to moral ruin by letting his daughters mix freely with men outside the Brahmo Samaj, his disdain for Poreshbabu increased. Like a curse, the desire arose in his heart that Poreshbabu should regret this terribly some day.

After things had continued like this for quite a while, it became clear that Haranbabu would not leave.

'You have not met Mashi for a long time,' Sucharita now pointed out to Binoy. 'She often asks after you. Can't you go and see her once?'

'Please don't make the false allegation that I have forgotten Mashi,' said Binoy, rising to his feet.

When Sucharita had led Binoy away to meet her mashi, Lalita arose and said, 'Panubabu, I don't think there is anything you particularly need to say to me.'

'No,' replied Haranbabu. 'You must be urgently needed elsewhere. You may leave.'

Lalita understood the innuendo. Haughtily raising her head, she at once put the matter into words:

'Binoybabu has come after a long time. I'll go chat with him. Meanwhile, should you wish to read your own article—but oh no! I find Didi has torn the paper to shreds. If you can bear to read the writings of others, you may glance through these.' With these words, she brought Gora's writings from the corner table where they had been carefully preserved, and placing them before Haranbabu, she rushed from the room.

Harimohini was delighted to see Binoy. It was not just out of affection for this good-looking young man, but also because visitors to this house who had met Harimohini had seemed to regard her as a creature of an alien species. Residents of Kolkata, they were better versed in English and Bengali letters than she. Their aloofness and contempt made her feel extremely inadequate. In Binoy she seemed to find a refuge from all this. He too belonged to Kolkata, and Harimohini had heard that his scholarly prowess was not negligible either. Yet he showed her no disrespect, treating her as a member of the family. This shored up her self respect. Especially for this reason, even upon a slight acquaintance, Binoy acquired an intimate place in her affections. She began to feel that he would protect her like a suit of armour from the arrogance of others, that like a cover he would shield her from view since she had become too visible in this house.

Lalita would never have approached Harimohini readily so soon after Binoy had gone there, but now, goaded by Haranbabu's sarcasm, she seemed compelled to go upstairs, tearing aside all her hesitation. She not only went there but also began at once to prattle ceaselessly to Binoy. Their conversation grew so animated, that every now and then, the sound of their laughter reached the ears of Haranbabu, alone in the room on the floor below, piercing him to the heart. Unable to remain by himself for long, he tried to quell his inner bitterness by conversing with

Borodasundari. Upon hearing that Sucharita had rejected Haranbabu's proposal, Borodasundari could hold her patience no longer.

'Panubabu,' she exhorted him, 'you can't afford to behave so decently. She has repeatedly expressed her consent, and the entire Brahmo Samaj is awaiting this marriage. Now we can't let everything be turned topsy-turvy just because she has made a gesture of denial today. You must not relinquish your claims, I tell you. Let's see what she can do!'

Haranbabu needed no incitement in this matter. Stiff and wooden, head held high, he was saying to himself:

'On principle, this claim must not be relinquished. Giving up Sucharita is no great matter for me, but I can't bring embarrassment upon the Brahmo Samaj.'

To cement his intimacy with Harimohini, Binoy had made a childlike demand for food. Flustered, Harimohini had at once offered him soaked chickpeas, cottage cheese, butter, a little sugar and a banana, arranged on a small platter, and some milk in a small brass bowl.

'I thought I would hassle Mashi, demanding food at an odd hour, but I have been outwitted,' smiled Binoy. He now made a great show of settling down to a feast. At this moment, Borodasundari arrived on the scene. Bending as low over his thala as possible, Binoy greeted her with a namaskar and said: 'I was downstairs for a long time but did not get to see you.'

Without answering him, Borodasundari addressed Sucharita: 'So her ladyship is here! Just as I had thought. There's a party going on! She is entertaining herself! Meanwhile poor Haranbabu has been waiting for her since early morning, as if he is merely her gardener. I've reared them from childhood, but bapu, I never saw such behaviour, all these days. I wonder where they are learning such things nowadays. What was unthinkable in our family has started happening now. Indeed, we can't face the members of our Samaj any more. To destroy in a couple of days everything you were always taught! What outrageous conduct!'

'I didn't know someone was waiting downstairs,' Harimohini agitatedly protested to Sucharita. 'We have been very unfair, I must say. Go, ma, please go quickly. I am to blame for this.'

Lalita was instantly about to assert that Harimohini was not at all to blame. Sucharita secretly gripped her hand to silence her, then went away downstairs.

I have already said that Binoy had attracted Borodasundari's affection. She had no doubt that he would eventually join the Brahmo Samaj under the influence of their family. She took a certain pride in moulding Binoy with her own hands, as it were, and had even shared this pride with some of her friends. Seeing this same Binoy now ensconced in the enemy camp, she seethed with indignation, and needless to say, her inner agony was redoubled at the sight of her own daughter Lalita aiding Binoy's second moral downfall.

'Lalita, do you have any business here?' she asked, brusquely.

'Yes,' answered Lalita, 'Binoybabu is here, so . . .'

'The person Binoybabu has come to see will look after him. You come downstairs now. There are things to be done.'

Lalita concluded that Haranbabu must have made some unwarranted remark to her mother concerning Binoy and herself. This surmise hardened her heart. With unnecessary garrulity, she declared: 'Binoybabu is here after so long, I'll come after chatting with him awhile.' From Lalita's tone it became clear to Borodasundari that force would not work here. Lest her defeat be exposed to Harimohini, she said no more and left without any farewell greeting to Binoy. To her mother, Lalita expressed enthusiasm for conversation with Binoy, but once Borodasundari had gone, there was no sign of that eagerness. They felt a certain constraint, all three of them, and soon afterwards, Lalita arose, went to her room and closed the door.

Binoy could clearly sense Harimohini's predicament in this house. He brought up the subject and bit by bit he gleaned all the details of Harimohini's past.

'Baba,' she finally said, 'the world is not a suitable place for an orphaned soul like me. Better if I could have gone to some holy place and devoted myself to my deity's service. I could have managed for a while on the little money I have left, and if I lived longer I could have somehow survived by cooking for others and being fed by them. I saw so many people managing quite well like this in Kashi. But sinner that I am, I could not adapt to those conditions. Whenever I am alone, thoughts of my own grief overwhelm me, keeping all gods and deities at bay. I fear for my sanity. For me, Radharani and Satish are like a raft for a drowning man—I find that the very thought of relinquishing them makes me choke for breath. So day and night, I fear that I must lose them—else why, having once lost all I had, would I again so quickly grow to love them so much? Baba, I have no qualms telling you, ever since I discovered the two of them, I've been able to concentrate wholeheartedly on my prayers to Thakur; if I lose them, my Thakur will instantly harden, turn to stone.'

Harimohini wiped her eyes with the corner of her sari.

## 40

Entering the room downstairs, Sucharita faced Haranbabu.

'Tell me what you have to say,' she said.

'Sit down,' said Haranbabu.

Sucharita did not sit. She stood immobile.

'Sucharita, you are being unjust to me.'

'You, too, are being unjust to me.'

'Why,' protested Haranbabu, 'I have given you my word, and that still . . .'

'Do justice and injustice reside in words alone?' interrupted Sucharita.

'By emphasizing your word, would you torment me in deed? Isn't a single truth larger than a thousand falsehoods? If I have made a hundred mistakes, would you forcibly give them first priority? Now that I have realized I was mistaken, I shall not go by anything I may have said earlier, for it would be unjust of me to do so.'

How Sucharita could be so transformed, Haranbabu failed to comprehend. He had neither the courage nor the humility to infer that he himself might be responsible for her loss of habitual quietness and modesty.

'What was your mistake?' he asked, privately blaming Sucharita's newfound companions.

'Why do you ask?' demanded Sucharita. 'Earlier I had consented, but now I no longer consent—does that not suffice?'

'We are answerable to the Brahmo Samaj after all. What shall we say, either you or I, to members of the Samaj?'

'I shall say nothing at all,' Sucharita declared. 'If you wish to speak, you may tell them that Sucharita is young, lacking brains, inconsistent by nature. Say whatever you please. But between us, this is the end of the matter.'

'It can't be the end. If Poreshbabu . . .'

As he spoke, Poreshbabu arrived on the scene.

'What is it, Panubabu, what were you saying about me?' he asked.

Sucharita was on her way out.

'Don't go, Sucharita,' Haranbabu called out, 'let's discuss the matter with Poreshbabu.' Sucharita turned around. 'Poreshbabu,' Haranbabu continued, 'after all these days, Sucharita now says she does not consent to the marriage. Should she have treated this grave matter so frivolously, for so long? Mustn't you also take responsibility for this ugly development?'

'Ma,' said Poreshbabu gently, stroking Sucharita's head, 'there is no need for you to remain here. You may go.' These simple words instantly brought tears to Sucharita's eyes and she rushed out of the room.

'Because I had long suspected that Sucharita had consented to the match without fully knowing her mind, I could not keep your request that we confirm your betrothal in the presence of Samaj members,' Poreshbabu explained.

'Doesn't it occur to you that Sucharita indeed knew her own mind when she gave her consent, and now declines because she no longer understands herself?'

'Both are possible, but in such a state of doubt, the wedding cannot take place.'

'Will you not give Sucharita good advice, then?'

'I am sure you know that I would never willingly give Sucharita bad advice.'

'If that were true, Sucharita could never have come to such a sorry state. I say this to your face: all the things currently happening in your family are the results of your own lack of judgement.'

'Indeed you are right,' smiled Poreshbabu. 'Who but me can be held responsible for the consequences of my family's actions?'

'You will repent this, I tell you.'

'Repentance is God's will, after all. It is sin I fear Panubabu, not repentance.'

Sucharita came in. 'Baba, it is time for your prayers,' she announced, taking Poreshbabu's hand.

'Panubabu, would you wait a while, then?' Poreshbabu inquired.

'No.'

Haranbabu strode out of the room.

## 41

Sucharita was frightened by the conflict that had broken out simultaneously within herself and with the outer world. Her feelings for Gora had intensified without her knowledge. This had become completely, transparently and irrefutably clear to her ever since he went to jail. What to do about her feelings and where they might lead her, she could not determine. She could not speak of this to anyone else, diffident about it even to herself. She had not even found a secret opportunity to come to terms with herself about this private anguish. Haranbabu was threatening to rouse their entire community at her threshold; even the likelihood of newspaper publicity loomed large. Besides, her mashi's problem had grown so acute that a solution had to be found without a day's delay. Sucharita realized her life had reached a crossroads where it was no longer possible to traverse well-known paths in her habitual contented way.

At this difficult moment, Poreshbabu was her only recourse. She had not sought his counsel or advice. There were many things she could not reveal directly to Poreshbabu, things unfit for disclosure because they were shameful and degrading. Poreshbabu's lifestyle, his company itself, seemed sufficient to make her feel silently drawn into some paternal lap, or maternal bosom.

These days, because it was winter, Poreshbabu did not visit the garden in the evening. In a small chamber on the western side of the house, he would place his mat before an open door and prepare himself for prayer. The glow of the setting sun would fall upon his tranquil face, framed by white locks. At this time, Sucharita would quietly approach him and silently take her place by his side. She seemed to immerse her own unquiet, agonized spirit in the depths of Poresh's prayers. Nowadays, at the end of his prayers, Poresh would often find this daughter, this pupil of his, seated silently beside him. Seeing this girl enveloped in an indescribable spiritual grace, he would quietly bless her with all his heart.

Because he saw union with the sublime as his life's sole target, Poresh's spirit was always inclined towards what was worthiest and truest. Hence worldly life could never assume much importance for him. Because he had thus acquired a certain internal detachment, he could not exert any pressure on others about their opinions or conduct. Dependence on divine beneficence and patience with the world came very naturally to him. So pronounced were these qualities in him, that he was condemned by those who were communal; but he received blame in such a way that it might assault him but not injure him permanently. He would constantly repeat to himself: 'I shall accept nothing from anyone else, receiving everything from Him alone.'

To receive the touch of this deep, silent tranquility at the core of Poresh's life, Sucharita would come to him on a variety of pretexts nowadays. At this inexperienced stage in her life, when her contrary heart and a contrary world made her frantic, she would repeatedly think: 'If only I could prostrate myself, clasping Baba's feet to my head and lie there just awhile, my heart would find peace.' In this way, Sucharita hoped to summon up all her inner strength and to withstand all assaults with unshakeable patience. Ultimately, all hostility would be vanquished automatically. But that was not how things turned out. She found herself compelled to take an uncharted course.

When Borodasundari found it impossible to sway Sucharita by raving and ranting, and saw no hope either of finding an ally in Poreshbabu, her fury against Harimohini reached violent proportions. Harimohini's presence within her household began to torment her every moment. One day, she had invited Binoy to the prayers for her father's death anniversary. The ceremony was scheduled for the evening, but before that, she was decorating the hall where the gathering would take place. Sucharita and the other girls were assisting her.

Suddenly, she spotted Binoy going up to meet Harimohini by the staircase at the side. When the mind is under pressure, even trivial incidents assume major significance. Binoy's going upstairs became instantly so unbearable for her that she abandoned her room-decoration and immediately went to Harimohini. There she saw Binoy on the floormat, chatting familiarly with Harimohini like a member of the family.

'Look here,' Borodasundari blurted out, 'stay here as long as you please, and I shall take good care of you. But I tell you, that deity of yours can't be kept here.'

Harimohini had always led a provincial life. She had imagined that Brahmos represented a particular branch of the Christian faith, and therefore that it was their company one might discriminate against. But in these few days, she had gradually begun to realize that they, too, might hesitate to associate with her. She had been agonizing over what she ought to do, when hearing these words from Borodasundari she understood there was no time left to think. She had to take a decision, somehow. First she thought of taking up residence somewhere in Kolkata, so she could see Sucharita and Satish now and then. But with her limited resources, she could not afford to remain in Kolkata.

After Borodasundari's sudden, stormy entry and exit, Binoy hung his head in silence.

'I want to go on a pilgrimage,' Harimohini announced after a brief pause. 'Could one of you escort me there, baba?'

'Of course we can! But it will take a few days to make arrangements. Come along meanwhile Mashi, come and stay with Ma.'

'Baba, I am a heavy responsibility. I don't know what burden destiny has placed upon my forehead, for it is too much for anyone to bear. I should have realized this when even my in-laws' home failed to take the weight of my burden. But my heart is blind, baba; my bosom is hollow, and to fill the emptiness I wander from place to place, but my wretched destiny tags along. Let it be, baba, I'd best not go to anyone else's house. I shall seek refuge at the lotus-like feet of the One who bears the burden of the entire universe. I can't cope anymore.' She began to wipe her eyes again and again.

'You can't say that, Mashi! My Ma is incomparable. For someone who has surrendered her entire life's burden to the Lord it is no ordeal to bear the burden of others. Take my mother for instance, or Poreshbabu here. I shall brook no arguments. I shall take you first to my place of pilgrimage, and only then shall I visit your holy place.'

'Then we should send word once . . .'

'When we arrive, Ma will know of it. That will be confirmation indeed.'

'Tomorrow morning, then . . .'

'Why? We can go tonight.'

In the evening, Sucharita came to him and said, 'Binoybabu, Ma has sent for you. It is time for the prayer ceremony.'

'I have things to discuss with Mashi. I can't attend tonight.' Actually, Binoy now could not bear to accept Borodasundari's invitation on any account. The whole affair struck him as a farce.

'Baba Binoy, please go,' begged Harimohini, flustered. 'We can discuss things later. Let your ceremonies first be over, then come to me.'

'It would indeed be best for you to join us,' Sucharita suggested.

Binoy realized that if he did not join the gathering, it would further aggravate the revolution taking place within this family. So he went to the prayer venue, but even that did not entirely accomplish the desired results. After prayers, there was food.

'I have no appetite today,' declared Binoy.

'Your appetite is not to blame,' retorted Borodasundari. 'After all, you have already dined upstairs.'

'Yes, such is the fate of the greedy,' smiled Binoy. 'Tempted by the present, one loses the future.' He prepared to leave.

'So you're going upstairs, are you?' Borodasundari inquired.

'Yes,' replied Binoy curtly, and left the scene. Sucharita was at the door.

'Didi,' he murmured in a low voice, 'please go to Mashi once. There's something urgent to be discussed.'

Lalita was busy attending to their guests. At one point, when she came near Haranbabu, he announced for no reason: 'Binoybabu is not here. He has gone upstairs.'

Hearing this, Lalita stood her ground, met his gaze and declared, unabashed: 'I know. He will not depart without seeing me. I shall go upstairs by and by, once my duties here are done.'

Having failed to embarrass Lalita in the least, Haranbabu's inner fury began to grow. It had also not escaped his notice that Binoy had suddenly whispered something to Sucharita, and that she had followed him shortly thereafter. Today, his repeated attempts to find pretexts for conversation with Sucharita had met with no success. A couple of times, she had evaded his explicit invitation in such a way that Haranbabu had felt himself insulted before the entire gathering. So he was not in a wholesome frame of mind.

Going upstairs, Sucharita found Harimohini waiting with all her things packed as if ready to depart immediately for some other place.

'Mashi, what is this?' Sucharita demanded.

Unable to reply, Harimohini burst into tears. 'Where is Satish?' she asked. 'Please send for him just once, ma!'

When Sucharita glanced at Binoy he explained: 'Mashi's presence in this house causes inconvenience to everybody, so I'm taking her to Ma.'

'From there, I have decided to proceed on a pilgrimage!' Harimohini declared. 'It is not appropriate for someone like me to remain in anyone's house. Indeed, why should people tolerate me like this forever?'

Sucharita herself had been thinking the same thing of late. She had sensed that it was humiliating for her mashi to remain in this house. Hence she was at a loss for a suitable reply. In silence she went to her mashi's side. It was late. The lamp in the room was unlit. In the blurred Hemanta sky above Kolkata, the stars were enveloped in a vaporous haze. In the darkness it was impossible to tell who was weeping.

'Mashima!' Satish's high-pitched voice resounded from the stairs.

'What is it, baba? Come, baba,' called out Harimohini, quickly rising to her feet.

'Mashima,' said Sucharita, 'there's no question of your going anywhere tonight. We can arrange everything tomorrow morning. Tell me, how can you depart without bidding proper farewell to Baba? That would be very wrong of you, indeed.'

In his agitation at Borodasundari's humiliation of Harimohini, Binoy had not thought of this. He had decided that Mashi should not spend another night in this house, and to dispel Borodasundari's notion that Harimohini put up with everything just to remain in this house because she had no other refuge, he was reluctant to brook the slightest delay in removing Harimohini from this place. Sucharita's words suddenly reminded Binoy that it was not as if Harimohini's only or primary relationship in this house was with Borodasundari. It was not right, after all, to give more importance to the person who had inflicted an insult, and to forget the one who had been large hearted enough to shelter her like a member of the family.

'True, indeed,' exclaimed Binoy. 'We certainly can't leave without informing Poreshbabu.'

'Mashima,' declared Satish as soon as he arrived, 'do you know that the Russians are coming to attack Bharatvarsha? What fun!'

'Whose side are you on?' Binoy inquired.

'I am for the Russians.'

'In that case the Russians have nothing to fear.'

When Satish had managed to liven up Mashima's circle in this fashion, Sucharita slowly arose and went downstairs. She knew that before retiring to bed, Poreshbabu would read from one of his favourite books. Often, at such times, Sucharita would go to him and at her request, he would read to her as well.

Tonight, too, Poreshbabu had lit the lamp in his secluded chamber, and was reading Emerson's book. Gently, Sucharita drew up a chair and sat by his side. Putting aside his book, Poreshbabu glanced once at her face. Sucharita's resolve wavered. She could not bring up any worldly subject.

'Baba, please read to me,' she said.

Poreshbabu began to read to her, and to explain. At ten in the night, the reading session ended. Even now, Sucharita prepared to leave quietly without saying anything, lest she arouse any distress in Poreshbabu's heart.

'Radhé!' called Poreshbabu, affectionately. She came back.

'Did you come to speak to me about your mashi?' he asked.

'Yes, Baba,' replied Sucharita, surprised that he had read her thoughts. 'But tonight let it be, we'll talk tomorrow morning.'

'Sit down.'

When she had obeyed, he said, 'I have considered the fact that your mashi is finding it difficult here. I had not realized clearly before this that her beliefs and rituals would assault Labanya's mother's convictions so strongly. When it is obviously causing her pain, keeping your mashi here would inhibit her freedom.'

'My mashi is ready to leave,' Sucharita replied.

'I knew she would leave. You two are the only people she can call her own. I'm also aware that you will be unable to abandon her to her fate. So I've been thinking about it, these last few days.'

Sucharita had no idea Poreshbabu had realized her mashi's predicament and was worrying about it. She had proceeded very cautiously all along, lest he sense the true state of affairs and be pained by it. Now, she was amazed to hear Poreshbabu's words. Tears glistened on her lashes.

'I have selected a house for your mashi,' Poreshbabu informed her.

'But she . . .' faltered Sucharita.

'She can't afford the rent,' said Poreshbabu. 'Why should she pay rent? You will pay it.' Sucharita gazed at his face in amazement. 'Let her stay in your own house,' he smiled. 'She won't need to pay rent.' Sucharita was even more amazed.

'Don't you know,' Poreshbabu continued, 'you own two houses in Kolkata, the two of you! One yours, the other Satish's. When he was dying your father left some money with me. Investing the capital to make it grow, I bought two houses in Kolkata. All these days I was receiving rent for them, which was also accumulating. The tenant has vacated your house recently. There will be no inconvenience if your mashi lives there.'

'Can she live there by herself?' Sucharita inquired.

'With you two as her very own relatives, why must she live by herself?'

'That is what I came to discuss with you tonight. Mashi is ready to leave, but I was wondering how I could let her depart alone. So I have come to you for advice. I shall do whatever you say.'

'Do you see this alley here, skirting our house?' asked Poreshbabu. 'Your house is just two or three buildings down this alley. If you stand at that veranda there, you can see the house. If you all live there, you won't remain entirely unprotected. I can look after you.'

Sucharita felt as if a huge boulder had rolled off her chest. She had been ceaselessly worrying, 'how shall I abandon Baba?' But leave she must: that too had become a certainty. Her heart too full for words, Sucharita sat silently beside Poreshababu. He too remained silent, deeply self-absorbed. Sucharita was his disciple, his daughter, his soulmate. She had become a part of his life, even of his devotional path. His prayers seemed to gain a special completeness on days when she came and joined him quietly. Moulding Sucharita's life daily with his benevolent affection, he had been bestowing a certain fulfilment to his own life as well. No-one had come to him before with Sucharita's devotion and utter humility. Like a flower gazing at the sky, she had turned to him, laying bare her entire being. When approached by someone with such single-minded eagerness, the limits of human generosity are extended of their own accord; the heart bows down in its own fullness, like a cloud burdened by its own moisture. There can be nothing more auspicious than the opportunity of daily gifting one's truest and worthiest qualities to a heart that is compatible. Such was the rare opportunity Sucharita had given Poreshbabu. Hence, his relationship with her had grown very intense. Today it was time to sever his outward bond with Sucharita; having ripened the fruit with his own life-sap, he must now free it from him. The pain he felt within at this, he offered up to the all-knowing Ishwar. Sucharita was equipped with resources for her journey; for some time now, Poresh had been observing her preparations for the call to take the path that stretched out ahead, aspiring to new experience on her own strength, arriving at it through joy and sorrow, blows and counter-blows. Privately, he was saying: 'My child, proceed on your journey . . . it is impossible that I should overshadow your entire life with my intelligence and my protection alone. May Ishwar liberate you from me and draw you to the ultimate goal through a diverse range of experiences. May your life find its fulfilment in Him!' With these words he was mentally surrendering Sucharita, so lovingly cherished from her infancy, as an offering to Ishwar. Poresh was not angry with Borodasundari; in his mind, he had not fostered any hostility towards his own family. He knew that a deluge unleashed by the new rains can create a tremendous upheaval in a beach that is narrow; the only solution is to release the waters into an open field. He was aware that sheltering Sucharita had in a short time given rise to unforeseen situations within this small family, disrupting their regular traditions. He also sensed that setting her free, instead of clinging to her, was the only way to restore peace and normalcy, in keeping with her natural tendencies. Realizing this, he was quietly trying to arrange things so that peace and harmony could easily be restored.

As they sat there in silence, the two of them, the clock struck eleven. Rising to his feet, Poreshbabu led Sucharita by the hand to the terrace above the portico. The evening vapours had evaporated, and the stars were shining in the pure darkness. On that silent night, with Sucharita by his side, Poresh uttered a prayer: 'Dispelling all the falsehoods of this world, let the pure image of perfect truth manifest itself in our lives.'

## 42

At dawn the next day, Harimohini knelt to touch Poresh's feet in a pranam.

'What are you doing?' he protested, flustered, moving aside at once.

'I can never repay my debt to you,' Harimohini replied, with tears in her eyes. 'You have found help for someone as helpless as myself. No one but you could have accomplished this. I have seen that nobody can do anything for my benefit, even if they want to. You are deeply blessed by the Lord, that is why you can favour even a person such as me.'

Poreshbabu was acutely embarrassed.

'I have not done anything much,' he insisted. 'All this is Radharani's . . .'

'I know, I know,' Harimohini interrupted. 'But Radharani herself belongs to you; whatever she does is really your doing. When she lost her mother, and her father too was no more, I regarded her as a very unfortunate girl. But how was I to know that the Lord would transform her misfortune into something so gloriously worthwhile? Having met you, after all my wanderings, I now understand clearly that the Lord has been kind to me as well.'

'Mashi, Ma has come to fetch you,' announced Binoy as he arrived.'Where is she?' asked Sucharita, springing to her feet.

'Downstairs, with your mother.'

Sucharita hastened downstairs.

'Let me go and arrange all the things in your house,' said Poreshbabu to Harimohini.

When he had departed, Binoy asked in surprise: 'Mashi, I didn't know about your house!'

'I didn't know about it either, baba! Only Poreshbabu knew. It's our Radharani's house.'

'I had thought Binoy would prove useful to at least one person in the world,' declared Binoy, after listening to the whole story. 'But even that opportunity has eluded me. Until now, I have not been able to do anything for my mother; it is she who does the needful for me. I can't do anything for Mashi either; I shall draw favours from her instead. It is my destiny to take, not to give.'

After a while, Anandamoyi arrived there, accompanied by Lalita and Sucharita.

'When the Lord shows kindness, he does so without stinting,' said Harimohini, advancing towards them. 'Didi, today I get to meet you as well.' She took Anandamoyi's hand and drew her to the madur on the floor.

'Didi,' said Harimohini, 'Binoy speaks of no one but you.'

'That has been his ailment since childhood,' smiled Anandamoyi. 'Once he takes up a subject, he doesn't drop it easily. Very soon it will be Mashi's turn, too.'

'That will happen, let me tell you in advance,' confirmed Binoy. 'I have found Mashi late in life, acquired her by my own efforts. I must find diverse ways to compensate myself for this long deprivation.'

'Our Binoy knows how to acquire what he lacks,' smiled Anandamoyi, glancing at Lalita, 'and having acquired it, he also knows how to cherish it with his heart and soul. Only I know how he perceives all of you—as if he has suddenly glimpsed a vision he could never have imagined possible. Ma, what can I say? How happy I am that he has made your acquaintance! The way Binoy has taken a fancy to this household of yours, it's done him a world of good. He knows it only too well and doesn't hesitate to admit it, either.'

Lalita tried to reply but could not find the words. She began to blush. Observing her distress, Sucharita interposed:

'Binoybabu can detect the inner goodness in everybody, so he gets to enjoy the best in everybody. That is largely due to his special talents.'

'Ma, you assume Binoy is a major subject of discussion but he doesn't enjoy such eminence in this world,' protested Binoy. 'I want to explain this to you every time but, from pure vanity, I fail to do so. But now it won't do anymore. No more of this, Ma, no more talk of Binoy today.'

At this moment Satish came bounding up, clasping his newborn puppy to his breast.

'Baba Satish, my dearest boy, please take the dog away, baba!' cried Harimohini, highly flustered.

'He won't trouble you, Mashi!' Satish assured her. 'He will not go into your room. Just pet him a little, he won't object.'

'No baba, no,' said Harimohini, shrinkng away. 'Take him away.'

At this, Anandamoyi drew Satish to her, dog and all. 'You're Satish, aren't you? Our Binoy's friend?' she asked, as she took the puppy on her lap.

Satish saw nothing incongruous in being identified as Binoy's friend. So he confirmed, without any hesitation:

'Yes.' He gazed expectantly at Anadamoyi.

'I am Binoy's mother,' she informed him. The puppy proceeded to amuse itself by trying to chew upon Anandamoyi's balas, the thick bangles she wore.

'Bakhtiar,' prompted Sucharita, 'touch Ma's feet.'

Awkwardly, Satish somehow performed the task. At this moment, Borodasundari came upstairs.

'Will you join us for something to eat?' she asked Anandamoyi without so much as glancing at Harimohini.

'I don't discriminate about food, touch and so on,' Anandamoyi declared. 'But today, let it be. Let Gora come back, I'll dine with you after that.' She could not bring herself to do something in Gora's absence that would have displeased him.

'So here you are, Binoybabu!' remarked Borodasudari, glancing at Binoy. 'I thought perhaps you had not come.'

'Do you think I would go away without telling you I was here?' Binoy at once retorted.

'Yesterday you avoided the feast to which you were invited,' persisted Borodasundari. 'So today, perhaps, you could join us for a meal uninvited.'

'I find that much more tempting,' Binoy responded. 'Tips are more attractive than a salary.'

Harimohini was privately surprised. Binoy dined at this house, and even Anandamoyi did not observe such restrictions. She was not happy about this.

'Didi,' asked Harimohini diffidently, after Borodasundari had left, 'is your husband . . .'

'My husband is a staunch Hindu.'

Harimohini was dumbfounded. Sensing her thoughts, Anandamoyi said:

'My sister, when the Samaj was greater than all of us, it was the Samaj I followed. But one day, Ishwar visited our home in such a form that He made it impossible for me to follow the Samaj anymore. Once the Lord Himself snatched my caste status away from me, what have I to fear from anyone else?'

'Your husband?' faltered Harimohini, not understanding this explanation.

'My husband is angry with me.'

'And the boys?'

'The boys are not happy either. But must I live to please them alone? My sister, I can't explain my situation to anyone else—only the all-knowing One can understand it.' Anandamoyi folded her hands in reverence.

Harimohini imagined that some missionary's daughter had visited Anandamoyi and filled her mind with Khristani ideas. She now felt an acute sense of constraint.

# 43

Sucharita had felt very reassured when told that she could live close to Poreshbabu's house, constantly under his supervision. But as the time approached for them to move into her new home once it was furnished, she felt a catch in her heart. No matter if they lived close to each other; but now it was time to sever the all-encompassing link between their lives, she felt as if a part of herself would die. Her place within this family, however insignificant, her duties there, even her relationship with each member of their domestic staff, became a source of agony for her.

Upon learning that Sucharita had some resources of her own and that she was comfortably preparing for an independent life on the strength of those resources, Borodasundari repeatedly expressed her approval, indicating her relief at being freed of the burden she had borne so long and so carefully. But inwardly she developed a reproachful attitude, as if it was wrong of Sucharita to break away from them and become self-sufficient. She had often felt sorry for herself, considering Sucharita a burden on her family, imagining themselves to be Sucharita's sole recourse. But upon suddenly learning she would be relieved of Sucharita's burden, she felt no joy within her heart. Anticipating that Sucharita might pride herself on having no urgent need for their protection, that she might feel no obligation to acknowledge her indebtedness to them, Borodasundari condemned her in advance. During this period, she remained especially aloof from Sucharita. Completely dropping her former habit of summoning Sucharita to help with the housework, she now showed her an unnatural degree of respect. Before she left, Sucharita, in her distress, tried to participate even more actively in Borodasundari's household chores, following her around on various pretexts, but Borodasundari kept her at arm's length, as if to ensure Sucharita did not suffer any loss of respect. It pained Sucharita most of all that the one who had reared her like a mother should remain hostile when it was time for her to leave. Labanya, Lalita and Leela began to cling to Sucharita. With great enthusiasm they went to decorate her new home, but even that enthusiasm was suffused with unshed tears.

Up until now Sucharita had performed many small errands for Poreshbabu on a variety of pretexts. Arranging flowers in a vase or books on a table, sunning his bedclothes, reminding him when it was time for his bath—neither of them had attached any importance to these habitual daily tasks. But when it was time to leave, abandoning even these unnecessary chores, these tiny acts of service, which someone else can also easily perform, which even if neglected would not greatly matter—it was these acts that became a source of torment for both parties. Now, when Sucharita came into Poresh's room to perform some trivial task, it would assume great importance in his eyes and he would stifle a sigh. And the thought that this task would shortly be taken over by someone else would bring tears to Sucharita's eyes.

On the appointed day, when Sucharita and the others were to move into the new house after lunch, Poreshbabu entered his secluded room to pray at dawn and found Sucharita waiting for him in a corner. In front of his prayer mat, she had arranged flowers on the floor. Labanya and Leela had also conspired to be present there, but Lalita had prohibited them. Knowing that Sucharita, when she joined in Poreshbabu's solitary prayers, seemed to receive a special share of his bliss as well as his blessings, and that she had a special need to glean those blessings this morning, Lalita had not allowed the solitude of today's prayers to be disrupted. As the prayers ended, tears were flowing from Sucharita's eyes.

'Ma, don't look back,' Poreshbabu advised her. 'Advance on the path that lies ahead, without any hesitation. Set forth joyfully, vowing that whatever happens, whatever situation confronts you, you will use all your power to imbibe the best from it. Surrendering yourself completely to Ishwar, make him your sole support. Then, even through mistakes, errors and loss, you can progress in the right direction. And if you divide yourself in two, dedicating part to Ishwar and part to something else, then everything will become very difficult. May Ishwar ensure that you have no further need of our humble shelter.'

After prayers, the two of them emerged to find Haranbabu awaiting them in the outer chamber. Vowing not to harbour any resentment against anybody on this day, Sucharita greeted him politely with a namaskar. At once assuming a rigid posture on his chair, Haranbabu declared, very severely:

'Sucharita, today you are about to regress from the truth that had sustained you for so long. This is a sad day for us.'

Sucharita offered no reply. But a discordant note entered the music that had filled her heart today with a melodious blend of peace and compassion.

'Only the One who knows our hearts can say who is making progress and who is falling back,' answered Poreshbabu. 'We vainly grow anxious trying to judge things from outside.'

'Do you mean to say that your heart is free of anxiety?' demanded Haranbabu. 'And that you have had no cause for remorse either?'

'Panubabu,' Poreshbabu responded, 'I entertain no imaginary anxieties and I shall only know whether I have cause for remorse when remorse arises in my heart.'

'What about your daughter Lalita arriving alone on the steamer with Binoybabu, is that imaginary too?' retorted Haranbabu.

Sucharita's face grew flushed.

'Panubabu, you are agitated for some reason, so it would be unfair to you to discuss the matter with you now,' Poreshbabu observed.

'I never say anything in the heat of emotion,' declared Haranbabu, head held high. 'I am sufficiently responsible for whatever I say, don't worry. What I say to you is not personal, but spoken on behalf of the Brahmo Samaj, and I speak because it would be wrong to remain silent. Had you not been blind, you would have realized from this one instance of Lalita traveling alone with Binoybabu that this family of yours is about to drift away from its moorings in the Brahmo Samaj. This will not only inflict remorse upon you but also dishonour upon the Brahmo Samaj . . .'

'Blame can be ascribed from outside, but to pass judgement one must penetrate the inner reality of things,' Poreshbabu asserted. 'Please don't condemn people on the basis of incidents alone.'

'Incidents don't occur randomly,' Haranbabu insisted. 'You bring them about through your inner compulsions. You are developing intimate ties with people who wish to take your family away from your own community. Indeed, they have already drawn them away, can't you see?'

'Our perspectives don't coincide,' replied Poreshbabu, rather annoyed.

'Your perspective may not coincide, but I call upon Sucharita to testify. Let her say truthfully whether Lalita's current relationship with Binoy is merely an outward link? Has it not touched their inner selves at all? No Sucharita, you can't leave, you must answer. It's very important.'

'However important, you have no right to discuss it,' Sucharita retorted harshly.

'Had I no right, I would not only have held my tongue but refrained from anxiety as well,' Haranbabu declared. 'You may disregard the Samaj, all of you, but as long as it exists, the Samaj must judge you.'

'If the Samaj has deployed you as a judge, then exile from the Samaj is our best recourse,' pronounced Lalita, storming into the room.

'Lalita, I am glad you are here,' said Haranbabu, rising from his chair. 'The charges against you should be judged in your presence.'

Sucharita's face and eyes were aflame with fury. 'Haranbabu, please go to your own home and summon your court there. We can never accept your right to enter a household and insult a family within their own home. Come bhai Lalita, let's go.'

Lalita would not budge. 'No Didi, I shan't run away,' she insisted. 'I want to leave only after I have heard everything Panubabu has to say. Go ahead, please say what you will!'

Haranbabu was speechless in surprise.

'Ma Lalita,' pleaded Poreshbabu, 'Sucharita is leaving our home today. I cannot permit any disturbance this morning. Haranbabu, however guilty we might be, you must forgive us for today.'

Haran maintained a grave silence. The more Sucharita spurned him, the more determined he became to hold her captive. He firmly believed he was bound to win by the force of his extraordinary moral power. Not that he had given up even now, but he was tormented by the anxiety that if Sucharita moved into a different house with her mashi, his power would suffer constant rebuffs there. Hence, today, he had come armed with his ultimate weapons, properly honed. He was ready to force a very tough compromise that very morning. Indeed he had come there shedding all his hesitations that day, but that his opponents could also cast off their inhibitions in this way, that Lalita and Sucharita would also draw arrows from their quiver to suddenly join the fray, was something he had never imagined. He was convinced that when he began shooting his flaming moral shafts with resplendent force, the enemy would suffer abject defeat. Things did not turn out quite that way, and the opportunity was lost. But Haranbabu would not give up. He told himself that the truth was bound to triumph, in other words, that he, Haranbabu, was bound to win. But victory does not come of its own accord. One must fight. Bracing himself, Haranbabu entered the battlefield.

'Mashi,' said Sucharita, 'I shall eat with everybody today. You must not mind.'

Harimohini remained silent. She had privately assumed that Sucharita was entirely devoted to her. Now that Sucharita was free to live independently on the strength of her own property, Harimohini had thought that no further constraints were necessary, for she could now act entirely as she pleased. Hence, when Sucharita once again disregarded the laws of purity and proposed to eat with everyone else, Harimohini was displeased. She remained silent.

'Thakur will be pleased at this, I can assure you,' Sucharita told her, sensing her attitude. 'The same all-knowing Thakur of mine has ordered me to eat with everybody today. If I don't obey, He will be angry. I fear His anger more than yours.'

As long as Harimohini faced humiliation from Borodasundari, Sucharita had accepted her rituals to share her plight, but now it was time to be free of that humiliation, Sucharita had no hesitation in dissociating herself from restrictions concerning purity. Harimohini had not quite anticipated this. She had not understood Sucharita completely, and it was difficult, indeed, for her to do so. She did not openly forbid Sucharita but privately, she was annoyed. 'Oh ma,' she thought, 'I can't imagine how people might develop such tendencies. She was born into a Brahman home, after all!'

'Let me tell you something, bachha,' she said, 'do as you please, but don't accept water served by that bearer of yours.'

'Why Mashi,' protested Sucharita, 'it's Ramdeen the bearer who milks his own cow to supply you with milk!'

'You amaze me' exclaimed Harimohini, wide-eyed, 'is milk the same as water?'

'Tell me Mashi,' smiled Sucharita, 'let me not drink water touched by Ramdeen today. But if you forbid Satish, he is bound to do exactly the opposite!'

'Satish is a different matter,' said Harimohini.

Harimohini knew that when it came to the male sex, lapses in discipline must be forgiven.

## 44

Haranbabu entered the battlefield.

It was now fifteen days since Lalita had arrived on the steamer with

Binoy. The rumour had reached a few ears, and little by little, it had been trying to gain ground. But in the last two days, the news had spread like wildfire.

Haranbabu had persuaded many people that it was one's duty to curb such misdemeanour to safeguard the morals of the Brahmo family. It was not hard to convince others of such things. When we respond to the 'call of truth' and the 'call of duty' by condemning and punishing the blunders of others, it is not too difficult to meet the demands of truth and duty. Hence when Haranbabu proclaimed the 'bitter' truth to the Brahmo Samaj and proceeded to perform a 'harsh' duty', most people were not averse to joining him enthusiastically, awed by the magnitude of such bitterness and harshness. Well-wishers of the Brahmo Samaj visited each other by hired cab or palki to declare that now such things had begun to happen, the future of the Samaj looked bleak indeed. Alongside, news also spread that Sucharita had become a Hindu, and having taken refuge in her Hindu mashi's house, was devoting her days to sacrificial rituals, meditation, and idol worship.

For a long time, a battle had raged in Lalita's heart. Every night, before going to bed, she would tell herself, 'I shall never admit defeat,' and every morning, when she awoke, she would sit up in bed and declare, 'I shall never admit defeat under any circumstances.' Thoughts of Binoy obsessed her; the awareness that he was chatting with people in the room downstairs would make her heart race; if he failed to visit their house for a couple of days, her heart would seethe with suppressed reproach; every now and then, on various pretexts, she would incite Satish to visit Binoy's house, and when he returned, she would try to extract a detailed account of Binoy's activities and their conversation from Satish. The more unavoidable this became for Lalita, the more she fretted at the degradation of defeat. Sometimes, she was even angry with Poreshbabu, for not opposing her interaction with Binoy and Gora. But she was determined to fight to the end, to die rather than concede victory. As for how she would pass the rest of her life, all sorts of possibilities drifted through her imagination. The biographies she had read, relating the exploits of female welfare workers in Europe, began to appear possible and achievable.

One day she went to Poreshbabu and said: 'Baba, can't I take up a teaching post in some girls' school?'

Glancing at his daughter's face, Poreshbabu saw her eyes, full of the anguish of a yearning heart, gazing at him beseechingly like a destitute. 'Why not, ma?' he replied tenderly. 'But where can we find such a girls' school?'

We speak of a time when schools for girls were scarce; there were only ordinary pathshalas, and women of bhadra families had not yet advanced into the field of education.

'Is there no such school, Baba?' asked Lalita in agitation.

'Indeed I haven't seen one.'

'Tell me, Baba, can't we start a girls' school?'

'It's a very expensive proposition and would require help from many people.'

Lalita knew it was hard to even arouse the will to do benevolent deeds, but she had never imagined accomplishing them might pose so many obstacles. After a short silence she slowly arose and left. What was the source of his favourite daughter's heartache, Poreshbabu wondered thoughtfully. He was reminded, too, of Haranbabu's insinuations about Binoy. Sighing, he asked himself: 'Have I done something unwise?' Had it concerned one of his other daughters, there would be no special cause for worry, Lalita saw her life only too literally; with her, there could be no half-measures; joy and sorrow were not half-truths to her.

How would Lalita live, bearing false condemnation every day of her life? She could see no stability, no positive outcome ahead. It was not in her nature to drift along helplessly like this. That very afternoon, she arrived at Sucharita's house. The house was sparsely decorated. A wall-to-wall mat covered the floor on which Sucharita's bed had been laid out at one end. Harimohini's was at the opposite end. Because Harimohini did not sleep on a bed, Sucharita had also arranged to sleep on the floor, in the same room. On the wall hung a picture of Poreshbabu. In a small adjacent room, Satish's bed had been placed, and beside it, on a small table, ink, pens, notebooks, books and papers lay randomly scattered. Satish was in school. The house was silent.

After their meal, Harimohini prepared to sleep on the madur, and on her own mat, Sucharita sat immersed in her reading, open tresses outspread across her back, a pillow on her lap. A few more books lay in front of her. Seeing Lalita suddenly enter the room, Sucharita first closed her book in apparent embarrassment, then opened it as before, even more embarrassed. She was reading the collected works of Gora.

'Come, come, ma,' called Harimohini, sitting up. 'Come in, Lalita. I know what Sucharita is feeling, having left your house. Whenever she is upset, she takes up those books. Just now, lying here, I was thinking how nice it would be if one of you came by, and here you are. You will have a long life, ma!'

Settling beside Sucharita, Lalita at once broached the subject on her mind. 'Suchididi,' she proposed, 'what if we were to open a school for girls in our neighbourhood?'

'Just listen to her!' exclaimed Harimohini. 'How can you start a school, the two of you?'

'Tell me, how would we accomplish it?' Sucharita asked. 'Who would help us? Have you told Baba?'

'The two of us can teach, after all,' Lalita declared. 'Borodidi might also agree.'

'But it's not simply about teaching after all,' Sucharita reminded her. 'We must formulate rules for the running of the school, locate a building, acquire students, and find the funds. How much of this can the two of us accomplish, as women?'

'Didi, you can't say that!' Lalita protested. 'Just because I was born a woman, must I remain confined at home, dashing my brains against the walls? Can I be of no use to the world?'

The anguish in Lalita's words resonated in Sucharita's heart. She began to think, without offering any reply.

'There are many girls in the neighbourhood, aren't there?' Lalita persisted. 'If we want to teach them free of cost, their parents would actually be pleased. Let it suffice for us to teach as many of them as possible, here in this house of yours. What would it cost us?'

At this proposal to gather innumerable girls from unknown families, to teach them here under this roof, Harimohini grew very agitated. She wanted to remain pure and unsullied, busy with her prayers and holy offerings in seclusion. She began to resist the possibility of disruption.

'Have no fear, Mashi,' Sucharita assured her. 'If we manage to procure pupils we shall deal with them in the rooms downstairs. We shall not disturb you upstairs. So, bhai Lalita, if we can find pupils, I am willing.'

'Very well, let's give it a try,' said Lalita.

'Ma, you can't imitate the Khristans in every respect, can you?' Harimohini protested repeatedly. 'Since my father's times, I have not heard of women from middle class households teaching in schools.'

From Poreshbabu's terrace, conversations took place with women on the neighbouring terraces. One of the thorniest issues in these interchanges was the fact that the women next door often expressed curiosity and surprise that the girls in this house were still unmarried, even at such an advanced age. Hence Lalita tried her best to avoid these rooftop conversations. It was Labanya who was most enthusiastic about spreading friendship from terrace to terrace. There was no limit to her curiosity about the details of life in other homes. Discussions of many matters, significant or otherwise, concerning her neighbours' daily lives, would reach her through these airy channels. Comb in hand, tending her hair, she often enjoyed these afternoon colloquia under the open sky.

Lalita gave Labanya the responsibility of procuring students for her projected school for girls. When Labanya announced this proposal across the rooftops, many girls were fired with enthusiasm. Pleased, Lalita began to prepare the room on Sucharita's ground floor, sweeping, washing the floor, decorating the place. But her schoolroom remained empty. The male heads of households were incensed at the proposal to lure their daughters into a Brahmo house on the pretext of educating them. In fact, when they got to know, in this connection, that their daughters regularly chatted with Poreshbabu's daughters, they considered it their duty, indeed, to put a stop to the practice. Their daughters' freedom to climb up to the terrace was jeopardised, and the men were not very civil in the language in which they voiced their attitude towards the good intentions of the Brahmo girls. Poor Labanya, climbing to the terrace comb in hand at the usual time, found the young, modern nabinas replaced by congregations of mature, old-fashioned prabinas on the neighbouring terraces; and she did not receive a warm greeting from any of them.

Lalita was not daunted even by this. 'Many Brahmo girls find it impossible to go to Bethune School,' she declared. 'It would help if we took up the responsibility of educating them.' She applied herself to the hunt for such female students, and deployed Sudhir as well.

Those days, Poreshbabu's daughters were widely reknowned for their learning. In fact their fame had far exceeded the truth. Hence many parents were pleased to hear that the girls would teach female students free of charge. At the outset, Lalita's school established itself within just a few days, with five or six girls. She did not allow herself a moment of leisure, discussing the school with Poreshbabu, framing the rules by which it would be run, organizing everything. In fact, a proper quarrel broke out between Labanya and Lalita concerning the kind of prizes to be awarded to the girls after the annual examinations. The books that Lalita proposed Labanya did not like, but Labanya's tastes did not match Lalita's either. They even differed somewhat regarding the choice of examiners. Although Labanya detested Haranbabu on the whole, she was overwhelmed by his fame as a scholar. She had no doubt that it would be a matter of pride if Haranbabu were involved in their school, as examiner, teacher, or in some other capacity. But Lalita dismissed the suggestion out of hand—no connection could be allowed between Haranbabu and this school of theirs.

Within two or three days, the number of her students dwindled until the class became empty. Waiting in her vacant classroom, Lalita would start at the sound of footsteps, anticipating the arrival of female students, but no one came. When several hours passed by in this fashion, she realized something was wrong. She visited a pupil who lived nearby.

'Ma won't let me go,' confessed the girl tearfully.

'It's inconvenient,' the mother asserted. It was not clear where the inconvenience lay. Lalita was proud; at the slightest trace of reluctance in others, she could neither insist nor ask the reason why.

'If it's inconvenient, why proceed?' she said. At the next house she visited, she faced some plain speaking.

'Sucharita has become a Hindu nowadays,' they said. 'She observes caste differences. Idols are worshipped at her house,' and so on.

'If that is your objection then we can run the school from our own house,' proposed Lalita. But even this did not allay their doubts. There was something more to it. Instead of visiting any other homes, Lalita sent for Sudhir.

'Sudhir, tell me honestly what the matter is,' she demanded.

'Panubabu is up in arms against this school of yours,' Sudhir replied.

'Why, is it because there is idol worship at Didi's house?' asked Lalita.

'Not just that.'

'What else is it? You may as well tell me!' demanded Lalita impatiently.

'That's a long story.'

'Am I to blame as well?' Lalita wanted to know. Sudhir remained silent.

'This is the price I must pay for that steamer journey!' exclaimed Lalita, flushing. 'Even if I acted thoughtlessly, does our Samaj permit no atonement through good deeds? Does this community forbid me to undertake any benevolent action? Is this the mode of spiritual upliftment all of you have prescribed for me and for our community?'

'Not quite,' said Sudhir, trying to soften the blow. 'They are afraid Binoybabu might eventually become involved with this school.'

'Would that be fearsome, or fortunate?' flamed Lalita. 'How many among them can compare with Binoybabu in personal worth!'

'True indeed!' admitted Sudhir, daunted by Lalita's rage. 'But then, Binoybabu . . .'

'Is not a member of the Brahmo Samaj! Therefore the Brahmo Samaj will punish him. I feel no pride in such a society.'

Observing how the students had vanished, Sucharita had realized what the matter was and who was behind it. Without saying a word about it, she was with Satish in the room upstairs, tutoring him for his approaching examinations.

'Have you heard?' demanded Lalita, going to Sucharita after her conversation with Sudhir.

'I haven't heard,' replied Sucharita with a faint smile, 'but I have understood everything.'

'Must we tolerate all this?'

'There is no humiliation in tolerance,' asserted Sucharita, taking Lalita's hand. 'You've seen, haven't you, how Baba puts up with everything?'

'But Suchididi,' protested Lalita, 'I often feel that tolerance amounts to accepting injustice. Refusing to tolerate injustice is indeed the right way to retaliate.'

'Tell me, bhai, what you would like to do.'

'I haven't thought about it at all,' confessed Lalita. 'I don't even know what I can do about it, but do something we must. Those who are persecuting women like us in such a vile fashion are cowards, regardless of their high opinion of themselves. But I shall never admit defeat at their hands—never! Let them do what they can.' Lalita stamped her foot. Without answering, Sucharita began to stroke her arm gently.

'Bhai Lalita,' she said after a while, 'try speaking to Baba once.'

'I'll go to him straightaway,' declared Lalita, rising to her feet.

Approaching the door to her house, Lalita saw Binoy emerge with bowed head. Seeing Lalita he stopped short for a moment, debating whether or not to exchange a few words with her but restraining himself, he greeted her with a namaskar, eyes averted, and left, still hanging his head. Lalita felt as if a white-hot stake had speared her body. Rushing indoors, she went straight to her mother's room. Her mother was at the table, poring over a long, slim ledger, trying to concentrate on household accounts. Seeing Lalita's expression, Borodasundari was alarmed. She tried to vanish quickly into the depths of her ledger, as if her household would be utterly destroyed if she did not immediately balance a particular account. Lalita drew up a chowki close to the table. Still Borodasundari did not raise her head.

'Ma!'

'Wait, bachha, I just . . .' Borodasundari bent excessively low over her ledger.

'I shall not trouble you for long,' Lalita assured her. 'There is something I want to know. Was Binoybabu here?'

'Yes,' said Borodasundari, without lifting her head from the ledger.

'What did you discuss?'

'That's a long story.'

'Did you speak about me or not?'

Seeing no way out, Borodasundari flung aside her pen, and raised her head. 'Yes we did, bachha,' she admitted. 'I found that things were going too far, with people of our community casting aspersions on us everywhere, so I had to warn him.'

Lalita's face grew red with shame. Her head seemed ablaze with fury.

'Has Baba forbidden him to come here?' she demanded.

'As if he thinks about such things!' responded Borodasundari. 'If he did, all this could have been prevented from the very beginning.'

'Is Panubabu allowed to visit?'

'Just listen to this!' exclaimed Borodasundari, astounded. 'Why should Panubabu not visit us?'

'Why should Binoybabu not visit us, either?'

'Lalita, there's no arguing with you, bapu!' said Borodasundari, drawing the ledger to her once again. 'Go away, don't plague me now. I have a lot to do.'

In the afternoon, while Lalita was away at Sucharita's to work at the school, Borodasundari had taken the opportunity to send for Binoy and give him a piece of her mind. She had imagined Lalita would never get to know. Suddenly caught out in her intrigue, she now sensed danger. She realized that the outcome would not be peaceful, and that the matter would not be easily resolved. All her rage now directed itself against her utterly impractical husband. What an affliction for a woman to be compelled to live with this obtuse man!

Lalita left Borodasundari, carrying a cataclysmic storm in her heart. She went straight to the room downstairs where Poreshbabu was writing letters, and asked him directly:

'Baba, is Binoybabu unfit company for us?'

Her question at once made the situation clear to Poreshbabu. He was not unaware of the recent upheaval within their Samaj regarding his family. It had caused him a great deal of worry, as well. If he did not have doubts about Lalita's feelings for Binoy, he would have paid no attention to outside gossip. But he had repeatedly asked himself what his duty should be, if Lalita had developed romantic feelings for Binoy. After having openly adopted the Brahmo creed, his family now faced another difficult moment. Hence, while he was inwardly tormented by a certain apprehension and pain, simultaneously all his intellectual faculties were also aroused, declaring: 'I passed a difficult test when I adopted the Brahmo faith with my eyes fixed only on Ishwar, my life finding eternal fulfilment in valuing truth above happiness, property, society, everything. If I should now face a similar moment of reckoning, I shall overcome it by looking to Him alone.'

In answer to Lalita's question, Poreshbabu said: 'I know Binoy to be a very good person, in intellect as in character.'

After a short silence, Lalita said: 'Gourbabu's mother came by a couple of times recently. May I visit her today, along with Suchididi?'

For a while, Poreshbabu could not reply. He knew for sure that in the present climate of opinion, such visits would foster even greater social disapproval. But his heart protested: 'As long as it is not wrong, I cannot forbid it.'

'Very well, you may go,' he said. 'I have work to do, or I would have accompanied you myself.'

## 45

Binoy had not dreamt that beneath the terrain he had entered so nonchalantly as a visitor and a friend, smouldered such an active social volcano. When he first started mingling with Poreshbabu's family, he had been quite diffident. Unsure of the extent of his claims upon them, he trod carefully. Gradually, as his fears faded, he had not even suspected there could be the slightest hint of danger from any quarter. Today, when suddenly informed that Lalita had been condemned by members of the Samaj on account of his own behaviour, he was thunderstruck. What disturbed him most was his own awareness that the intensity of his feelings for Lalita had far exceeded the limits of ordinary friendship. In the present instance, given the gulf between their respective communities, he privately considered this excessive intensity an offence. He had often felt that he had not been able to keep to his proper place as a trusted visitor to this family, that he had somehow been dishonest. If his true feelings became known to them, it would be a matter of shame for him.

At this stage, when Borodasundari sent a note to summon Binoy one afternoon, and asked him, 'Binoybabu, you are a Hindu, are you not?'—and upon his answering in the affirmative, when she asked again: 'You can't abandon the Hindu community, can you?'—and upon Binoy's asserting that it would be impossible, when Borodasundari exclaimed, 'Then why are you . . .'—Binoy could find no answer to her query, 'Then why . . .?' He hung his head in silence. He felt he had been caught out, that something he had tried to conceal even from the moon, stars and wind had been publicly exposed here. He kept wondering what Poreshbabu must think, what Lalita must think, and what, indeed, must Sucharita think of him! He had briefly found a place in heaven due to some error on the divine messenger's part, but now he must suffer complete exile, bearing the stigma of unauthorized entry.

Afterwards, glimpsing Lalita as soon as he stepped out of Poreshbabu's door, he thought, 'At this moment of my final parting from Lalita, let me admit that I have brought great shame upon her, so the floodtides of our former acquaintance may subside.' But he could not think of a way. So, without meeting Lalita's gaze, he left with a silent namaskar.

Until very recently, Binoy had been an outsider to Poreshababu's household, and now he was back outside. But what a difference! Why did the outside seem so empty now? Nothing was missing from his former life after all; his Gora, his Anandamoyi, were still there. But still he began to feel like a fish cast ashore: wherever he looked, he found no support to keep him alive. On the crowded main streets of this densely built up city, Binoy began to detect everywhere a pale, shadowy image of the disaster that threatened his life. He was amazed at this all-pervading sense of dry hollowness. Why this happened, or when, or how it became possible, were questions he kept addressing to an unfeeling, unresponsive void.

'Binoybabu! Binoybabu!'

Binoy turned to find Satish behind him.

'What is it, bhai, what's the matter, my friend?' asked Binoy, embracing him. His voice seemed choked with tears. Binoy realized now, as never before, how much sweetness this boy had also added to Poreshbabu's household.

'Why don't you visit us?' demanded Satish. 'Labanyadidi and Lalitadidi are to dine with us tomorrow. Mashi has sent me across to invite you.'

Binoy realized that Mashi had not kept abreast of recent developments. 'Satishbabu,' he said, 'my pranams to Mashi, but I can't come.'

'Why not?' pleaded Satish, clasping Binoy's hand. 'You must come, I shan't take no for an answer.'

There was a special reason for the urgency of Satish's plea. In school he had been asked to compose a piece on 'Behaviour Towards Animals,' on which he had scored forty-two marks out of fifty, a piece he was very keen to show to Binoy. Knowing Binoy to be very learned and wise, he was convinced that such an accomplished man would appreciate the true value of his composition. If Binoy acknowledged the merits of Satish's work, then Leela, who lacked aesthetic sense, would be disgraced if she showed contempt for Satish's talent. It was Satish who had urged Mashi to issue the invitation. He wanted his sisters to be also present when Binoy evaluated his writings.

Learning that Binoy could not attend the social gathering under any circumstances, Satish was extremely disheartened.

'Satishbabu, come home with us,' proposed Binoy, hugging him.

As Satish was carrying that composition in his pocket, he could not ignore Binoy's invitation. The young would-be-poet went to Binoy's house, acknowledging that he was guilty of wasting time when his school examinations were so close. Binoy seemed reluctant to let him go. Not only did he listen to Satish's composition, but his words of praise also did not express a critic's neutral objectivity, and what was more, he fed Satish snacks ordered from the market. Then, escorting Satish almost to his home, he said with unwarranted agitation:

'Satisbabu, I'll take your leave then.'

'No, please come to our house,' begged Satish, tugging at his arm.

This time, such pleas proved futile.

Walking like one in a dream, Binoy arrived at Anandamoyi's house but could not meet her. He entered the empty room on the terrace where Gora used to sleep. How many happy days and nights of their childhood friendship had been spent in this room—such joyful conversation, such resolutions, such profound discussions—such romantic quarrels and such tendersweet reconciliations afterwards! Binoy longed to enter that former life, forgetting himself as before; but the new acquaintances formed in this short interim blocked his access to that same place. Until now, Binoy had not clearly understood when his life's focus had shifted, the route of entry changed; but now with all doubts dispelled, he grew afraid.

When the sun declined in the late afternoon, Anandamoyi came to take in the washing hung out to dry. Seeing Binoy in Gora's room, she was surprised. Quickly going to his side, she patted him and asked: 'Binoy! What's the matter, Binoy? Why do you look so pale?'

Binoy sat up. 'Ma,' he said, 'when I first began to frequent Poreshbabu's house, Gora used to be angry. I then thought his anger unjustified, but that was my foolishness, not his mistake.'

'I don't say you're the brightest of our boys,' replied Anandamoyi with a faint smile, 'but how in this case did the flaws in your intellect manifest themselves?'

'Ma, I had never considered the fact that our community is utterly different. I felt attracted by the sense of joy and advantage that their friendship, behaviour and example gave me. Not for a moment had any other considerations arisen in my mind.'

'They don't arise in my mind even after listening to you.'

'Ma, you have no idea, I have caused a great upheaval within the community regarding their family; people have started casting such slurs that I can no longer go . . .'

'Gora often says something that I find extremely sound,' responded Anandamoyi. 'He says, where there is something wrong within, outward calm is most dangerous. If their community is in a turmoil, I see no cause for remorse on your part. It will be for the better, you will see. As long as your own conduct remains above board, that's enough.'

But that was indeed Binoy's greatest doubt. Try as he might, he could not decide whether his own conduct was blameless. Since Lalita belonged to a different community, and marrying her was not a possibility, it was Binoy's tenderness for her that troubled him like a hidden sin, and he was tormented by the thought that he must now do terrible penance for it.

'Ma,' said Binoy suddenly, 'better if the proposed match between Shashimukhi and myself were finalized. I should somehow be confined to my proper place, so I don't stray from it under any circumstances.'

'In other words,' smiled Anandamoyi, 'you would make Shashimukhi the chain-latch on your door rather than the bride in your home. What a pleasant fate for Shashi!'

At this moment, the attendant announced the arrival of two ladies from Poreshbabu's house. Binoy's heart missed a beat. He thought they had come to complain to Anandamoyi, as a warning to him.

'I'll be off, Ma!' he cried, springing to his feet.

'Don't leave the house, Binoy,' Anandamoyi persuaded him, rising to grasp his hand. 'Wait in the room downstairs.'

'There was no need for this, really,' Binoy kept repeating to himself on his way down. 'What's done is done, but I would not have gone there again even if my life depended on it. Once the punishment for one's sins is under way, the fire refuses to subside even after the sinner is burnt to death.'

As Binoy was about to enter Gora's room on the ground floor overlooking the street, Mahim returned home from work, releasing his expansive paunch from the confinement of his chapkaan buttons.

'Here you are, Binoy! How nice to see you!' he exclaimed, grasping Binoy's hand. 'I've been looking for you.'

He drew Binoy into Gora's chamber and offering him a chowki, seated himself as well. Extracting a box from his pocket, he offered Binoy a paan.

'You there! Fetch us some tobacco!' he roared, then immediately turned to the matter at hand. 'What's the decision about that business? How long, after all . . .'

He found Binoy's attitude much softened. Not that Binoy expressed much enthusiasm, but he also made no evasive attempt to dodge the issue somehow. Mahim wanted to finalize the date and time immediately.

'Why not wait until Gora returns?' Binoy suggested.

'That's just a matter of a few days,' consented Mahim, reassured. 'Binoy, shall I send for some snacks? What do you say? You look very downcast today. You are not ill, I hope?'

When Binoy eluded the pressure to consume snacks, Mahim went inside to appease his own hunger. Pulling a book at random from Gora's table, Binoy began to turn the pages, then flinging the book aside, he began to pace the room from end to end.

'Ma has sent for you,' the attendant came and announced.

'Who has she sent for?' Binoy demanded.

'You, sir.'

'Are all the others there as well?'

'Yes, they are.'

Binoy made his way upstairs like a student heading for the examination hall. Approaching the room, he hesitated a little. At once, Sucharita called out to him in her usual natural, sisterly manner.

'Come, Binoybabu,' she invited him tenderly.

Her tone made Binoy feel that he had chanced upon an unhoped-for treasure. When he entered the room, Sucharita and Lalita were amazed at his appearance. In this very short time, his face already bore signs of the sudden, harsh blow he had suffered. His ever-cheerful countenance now resembled a lush green field suddenly devastated by a plague of locusts. Lalita secretly felt pain and pity but also a hint of joy. On a different occasion, Lalita would not have suddenly launched into a conversation with Binoy. But now, as soon as he entered, she declared:

'Binoybabu, we have something to discuss with you.'

It was as if Binoy's heart had been struck by an arrow of joy that pierced the sound barrier. He was exhilarated. His pale, dejected face instantly lit up.

'We sisters want to jointly start a small school for girls,' Lalita told him.

'It has long been one of my life's resolves to create a school for girls,' cried Binoy enthusiastically.

'You must help us,' Lalita demanded.

'I shall spare no effort to do whatever is in my power,' Binoy assured her. 'Please tell me what I must do.'

'Because we are Brahmo, Hindu guardians don't trust us,' Lalita explained. 'You must try to assist us.'

'Have no fear,' said Binoy, aflame with eagerness. 'I can handle it.'

'Handle it he can,' remarked Anandamoyi. 'When it comes to charming people with words, there is no match for Binoy.'

'You must handle all the work involved in running a school according to proper rules and procedures,' Lalita informed him. 'Forming timetables, allotting classes, prescribing textbooks—you must undertake all these things.'

This, too, was not difficult for Binoy, but he was baffled. Was Lalita utterly unaware that Borodasundari had forbidden him to mingle with her daughters, and that within their community there was a rising tide of hostility against them? Under such circumstances, would it be wrong, and harmful for Lalita, if Binoy agreed to her request? The question began to torment him. On the other hand, when Lalita sought his assistance in some worthwhile project, did Binoy possess the strength to avoid acceding wholeheartedly to her request?

Meanwhile, Sucharita was also amazed. She had not dreamt that Lalita would suddenly ask Binoy to assist with the girls' school, in this fashion. So many complications had already arisen concerning Binoy, and now, what was this new predicament! Seeing that Lalita was deliberately creating this situation, Sucharita felt apprehensive. She realized that Lalita's heart had grown rebellious, but was it right to involve poor Binoy in this turmoil?

'We must consult Baba about this once, mustn't we?' Sucharita blurted out anxiously. 'Let us not immediately arouse Binoybabu's hopes of acquiring the post of the inspector of a girls' school.'

Binoy realized that Sucharita had artfully stalled the proposal. This struck him as odd. Sucharita was obviously aware of the problems that had arisen, hence Lalita could not be in the dark about them either. Then why was Lalita . . .? Nothing was clear.

'Of course we must consult Baba,' Lalita affirmed. 'I shall speak to him as soon as Binoybabu confirms his willingness. Baba would never object. He, too, must be involved in this school of ours. We shan't let you off either,' she added, turning to Anandamoyi.

'I could go sweep your schoolrooms,' smiled Anandamoyi. 'What more would I be capable of?'

'That would be sufficient, Ma!' Binoy declared. 'The school would be completely purified.'

After Sucharita and Lalita had taken their leave, Binoy headed straight for the Eden Gardens on foot.

'I found Binoy much more amenable,' Mahim came to Anandamoyi and said. 'Now it's best to complete the ceremony at the earliest. Who knows when he might change his mind again?'

'What's this!' exclaimed Anandamoyi in astonishment. 'When did Binoy ever agree to the proposal? He hasn't told me anything about it.'

'We have discussed the matter today itself. He says we can fix a date as soon as Gora returns.'

'Mahim,' insisted Anandamoyi shaking her head, 'you have not understood him right, I tell you.'

'Thick-headed I might be, but please rest assured I am old enough to understand simple facts.'

'Bachha, I know you will be angry with me, but I can foresee complications ahead.'

'If you create complications, then complications are bound to occur,' retorted Mahim severely.

'Mahim, I shall tolerate anything all of you may say to me, but for your own good, I refuse to be party to something that may cause trouble.'

'If you leave it to us to decide about our own good, you will be spared unpleasant words, and we, too, might benefit,' Mahim declared harshly. 'Better you should think about our own good once Shashimukhi is married. What do you say?'

Offering no reply, Anandamoyi heaved a sigh. Chewing upon a paan he extracted from the box in his pocket, Mahim walked away.

# 46

'Because we are Brahmo no Hindu girl wants to come to us for tutoring,' Lalita came to Poreshbabu and said. 'So we feel it might facilitate our work if we involve someone from the Hindu community. What do you say, Baba?'

'Where would you find someone from the Hindu community?' Poreshbabu inquired.

Lalita had indeed braced herself for this meeting, but she suddenly found herself embarrassed at the prospect of mentioning Binoy's name.

'Why?' she said, forcibly shedding her awkwardness, 'it's not as if someone can't be found. There's our Binoybabu for instance, or . . .' This 'or' was utterly redundant, merely a grammatical excess. The sentence remained suspended, incomplete.

'Binoy!' exclaimed Poresh. 'Why would Binoy agree?'

Lalita's pride was hurt. Binoybabu not agree! She had realized only too well that it was not beyond her power to make Binoybabu agree.

'Well, he might consent,' she said.

'All things considered, he would never consent,' declared Poreshbabu, after a pause.

Lalita blushed to the roots of her ears. She began toying with the bunch of keys knotted at the end of her aanchal. Observing his daughter's tormented face, Poreshbabu's heart ached, but he could find no way to console her. After a while, Lalita slowly raised her head and said: 'Baba, our school can never be established, then!'

'I can see many hindrances that would prevent it from being established now,' Poreshbabu agreed. 'Any attempt would spark a lot of unpleasant discussion.'

Nothing was more painful for Lalita than the fact that Panubabu would ultimately triumph and that she must silently let injustice win. In this regard she could not have accepted anyone else's authority save her father's, not for a single moment. She did not fear any form of unpleasantness, but how could she tolerate injustice? Slowly she arose and left Poreshbabu's side. Back in her own room she found that a letter had arrived by post, addressed to her. From the handwriting she realized it was from her childhood friend Shailabala, who was married, living with her husband in Bankipur. The letter said:

> I was upset to hear all sorts of rumours about all of you. For many days I have been thinking of writing to inquire about you, but could not find the time. But the day before yesterday, the news I received from somebody (he shall go unnamed) left me thunderstruck. I could never have imagined this possible. But it is also hard to disbelieve the person who wrote to me about it. Apparently you are likely to marry a Hindu boy. If that is true . . .

Lalita's whole being was aflame with fury. She could not wait a single moment. At once she replied:

> What amazes me is the fact that you have sent me a query to verify the news. Is it necessary to verify even the news received from a member of the Brahmo Samaj? Such lack of faith! Next, you are thunderstruck upon hearing that I am likely to marry a Hindu boy; but I can assure you, there is a well-known member of the Brahmo Samaj who is a worthy young man, and yet the prospect of marrying him fills me with a dread as terrible as a thunderbolt. And I know a couple of Hindu boys whose hand in marriage would be a matter of honour for any Brahmo maiden. Beyond this I have nothing more to say to you.

Meanwhile, Poreshbabu's work had come to a standstill for the day. For a long time he was silent, lost in thought. Then, slowly and pensively, he went to Sucharita's room. The sight of Poresh's worried face pained Sucharita's heart. She knew, too, what he was worried about, and she herself had been anxious about the same thing of late. Poreshbabu took Sucharita aside to a secluded chamber and said:

'Ma, it is time for us to worry about Lalita.'

'I know, Baba,' she replied, gazing at him with compassion.

'I am not worrying about social slander,' he explained. 'I am thinking . . . tell me, is Lalita . . .'

Observing his embarrassment, Sucharita took it upon herself to clarify matters.

'Lalita always shares her thoughts with me,' she said. 'But of late she has been rather evasive. I clearly sense . . .'

'Some feelings have been aroused in Lalita's heart, which she does not want to admit even to herself,' Poresh interrupted. 'I can't think what we can do so she . . . Would you say we have done Lalita any harm by allowing Binoy to visit us?'

'Baba, you know there are no flaws in Binoybabu's character. He is pure of nature; one rarely comes across a born bhadralok like him.'

'Quite right, Radhé, quite right,' exclaimed Poreshbabu as if apprised of a new fact. 'It is his goodness of nature that we must take into account. Ishwar, the all-knowing, does the same. I offer him my pranams again and again, that Binoy is a good man, and that I was not mistaken about him.'

Poreshbabu seemed relieved, as if he had broken free of some net that would trap him. He had not sinned before his deity. He had followed the same scales of justice on which Ishwar weighed humans, the scales of daily duty. Because he had not used the false weights created by society to tamper with those scales, his mind was now free of self-blame. He felt surprised he had been so tormented, unable for so long to understand something so simple.

'I have learnt a lesson from you today, ma,' he told Sucharita, patting her head.

At once she touched his feet, protesting, 'No! No! How can you say that, Baba!'

'The community makes us completely forget the simplest thing: our own humanity. Human beings create a complicated maze, questioning whether one is Brahmo or Hindu, making this socially produced issue more important than the truth of the universe. All this time, I was vainly wandering in that maze.'

'Lalita is finding it hard to relinquish her resolve to start a school for girls,' continued Poresh after a short silence. 'She wants my permission to take Binoy's help in the matter.'

'No, Baba, let it wait for a while.'

Poresh's affectionate heart was deeply disturbed at the way Lalita had looked when she left his presence as soon as he forbade her, suppressing the turbulence of her troubled soul. He knew that his spirited daughter was less offended at the unjust harassment inflicted on her by her community than at being thwarted in her struggle against such injustice, especially since the cause of obstruction was her father. He was therefore eager to withdraw the prohibition he had imposed.

'Why Radhé?' he demanded, 'why let it be for now?'

'Or else Ma will be very annoyed.' Thinking about it, Poreshbabu realized she was right.

Satish came in and whispered something in Sucharita's ear.

'No bhai,' Sucharita responded. 'No bakhtiar, not now. Tomorrow.'

'But I have school tomorrow,' protested Satish, downcast.

'What is it Satish, what do you want?' smiled Poresh affectionately.

'He has a . . .' Sucharita began.

'No, no, please don't tell, don't tell!' pleaded Satish in agitation, clamping his hand on Sucharita's mouth.

'If it's a secret, why would Sucharita reveal it?' asked Poreshbabu.

'No Baba, he must be very keen for this secret to reach your ears,' Sucharita informed him.

'Never!' shouted Satish, 'not at all!' He ran off.

He was supposed to show Sucharita the composition that Binoy had praised so highly. Needless to say, Sucharita had correctly surmised why he had reminded her of the matter in Poresh's presence. Poor Satish did not know that such deep, secret motives could be detected so easily.

## 47

Four days later, Haranbabu came to Borodasundari with a letter. He had now given up all expectations of Poreshbabu.

'From the outset I have tried very hard to warn all of you,' declared Haranbabu, handing the letter to Borodasundari. 'That has made me unpopular here as well. Now from this very letter you will realize how far things have secretly advanced.'

Borodasundari read the letter Lalita had written to Shailabala.

'Tell me, how was I to know?' she lamented. 'The unthinkable is happening. But you mustn't blame me for this, I tell you. All of you have collectively turned Sucharita's head, praising her excessively for being such a good girl, as if there is no girl to match her in the Brahmo Samaj. Now you must deal with the handiwork of your ideal Brahmo girl. It is she who has brought Binoy and Gour into this household. Still, I had managed to a great extent to bring Binoy around to our way of thinking. But then she brought a mashi of hers and introduced idol worship into our own household. She even poisoned Binoy's mind, so now he avoids me. This Sucharita of yours is at the root of all that's happening now. I knew all along what that girl was really like, but I never said a word. All along, I have brought her up so nobody could tell she wasn't my own daughter—and now see what rewards I have reaped! It's no use showing me this letter now. Now it's up to all of you.'

Openly acknowledging that he had once misunderstood Borodasundari, Haranbabu apologized very generously. Ultimately,

Poreshbabu was sent for.

'Just look at this!' said Borodasundari, flinging the letter down on the table before him.

'So, what's wrong?' asked Poreshbabu after reading the letter two or three times.

'What's wrong!' exclaimed Borodasundari, outraged. 'What more do you want! Could there be worse to come? Idol worship, caste discrimination, everything has happened already; now it only remains for your daughter to be married off to a Hindu family. After that, you will perform penance and join the Hindu fraternity. But let me tell you . . .'

'You need tell me nothing,' Poreshbabu interrupted with a faint smile. 'At least, not yet. The question is, why have all of you concluded that Lalita's marriage into a Hindu family is already fixed? I see no hint of that in this letter, after all.'

'I have still not understood what might make you see anything clearly,' Borodasundari retorted. 'If you had seen things in time, the present calamity would not have occurred. Tell me, can a letter state things more plainly than this?'

'I think we should show this letter to Lalita and ask her what she intends. If you permit, I could ask her myself.'

At this moment, Lalita stormed in.

'Look, Baba,' she cried, 'we're receiving anonymous letters of this kind from the Brahmo Samaj these days!'

Poresh read the letter. Assuming that Binoy's marriage to Lalita had been secretly fixed, the writer had filled the letter with diverse reprimands and suggestions, along with assertions that Binoy's intentions were suspect, and that he would soon abandon his Brahmo wife to marry again into a Hindu family. After Poresh had finished with the letter, Haran read it through and said:

'Lalita, does this letter make you angry? But aren't you yourself not the cause for such letters to be written? Tell me, how could you write this letter in your very own hand!'

For a moment Lalita stood stock-still. 'So, have you been corresponding with Shaila on this subject!' she demanded.

'Bearing in mind her duty towards the Brahmo Samaj, Shaila felt obliged to return this letter of yours,' responded Haran, without answering her directly.

'Please tell me what the Brahmo Samaj would like to say now,' said Lalita, bracing herself.

'I can't bring myself to believe these current rumours about you and Binoybabu,' declared Haran, 'but still, I want to hear you clearly repudiate them yourself.'

Lalita's eyes began to blaze. Gripping a chair-back with trembling hands she asked:

'Why, can't you believe the rumours at all?'

'Lalita, your mind is not balanced now,' warned Poresh, patting her back. 'You and I can discuss this matter later. Let it be for now.'

'Poreshbabu, don't try to suppress the matter,' Haran interrupted.

'Would Baba try to suppress the matter!' Lalita erupted in fury, once again. 'Unlike the rest of you, Baba does not fear the truth. He places truth above even the Brahmo Samaj. I tell you, I don't consider my marriage to Binoybabu either impossible or sinful.'

'But is he to adopt the Brahmo faith?' Haranbabu demanded.

'Nothing is decided, and who says it is compulsory to adopt the faith?' Lalita retorted.

So far, Borodasudari had said nothing. Secretly she wanted Haranbabu to triumph on this occasion, and Poreshbabu to feel guilty and repentant. She could contain herself no longer.

'Lalita, have you lost your mind!' she blurted out. 'What are you saying!'

'No Ma, these are not the ravings of a lunatic. I speak after much consideration. I cannot bear to be confined like this. I shall break free of this Samaj of Haranbabu's.'

'Do you mistake waywardness for freedom?' Haranbabu asked.

'No,' replied Lalita. 'Liberation from assaults of baseness and enslavement to falsehood—that's what I mean by freedom. Where I see no wrong, no breach of faith, why should the Brahmo Samaj hold me, or try to restrain me?'

'Poreshbabu, see for yourself!' declared Haran ostentatiously. 'I knew a calamity like this was inevitable. I have tried my best to warn you all, but to no avail.'

'Look here Panubabu,' retorted Lalita, 'we have reason to warn you as well. You should not be arrogant enough to caution those who are your superiors in every respect.' With these words she left the room.

'What a mess!' cried Borodasundari. 'Please think, what is to be done now?'

'It is duty that we must observe,' Poreshbabu answered. 'But we cannot identify our duty amidst such confusion. You must excuse me. Please don't discuss this matter with me now. I want to be left alone for a while.'

## 48

What a mess Lalita had created! Sucharita thought. After a short silence, she put her arm around Lalita's neck.

'I must say, bhai, that I feel afraid.'

'What are you afraid of?' Lalita demanded.

'The entire Brahmo Samaj is in turmoil, indeed, but what if Binoybabu turns down our request in the end?'

'He is sure to agree,' Lalita insisted, her head bent low.

'As you know, Panubabu has assured Ma that Binoy would never abandon his community to accept this marriage. Lalita, why did you speak of it to Panubabu without pausing to consider everything!'

'I still don't regret what I said,' Lalita asserted. 'Panubabu imagined that he and his Samaj had pursued me like a hunted animal to the edge of the bottomless ocean, where I must surrender. He doesn't realize I'm not afraid to plunge into this ocean; I fear being hounded into his cage by his pack of hunting dogs.'

'Let's consult Baba once,' Sucharita proposed.

'Baba will never join a hunting party, I can assure you. He had never wanted to shackle us, after all. If we have ever disagreed with his views, has he ever expressed the slightest annoyance? Has he tried to silence us by hounding us in the Brahmo Samaj's name? This has annoyed Ma so often, but Baba only feared we might lose the courage to think for ourselves. Having reared us like this, would he ultimately hand me over to a man like Panubabu, who acts as the community's prison warder?'

'Very well, presuming Baba poses no obstacle, what should we do next?'

'If you people don't do anything, I shall myself . . .'

'No, no,' cried Sucharita in agitation, 'you need not do anything, bhai! I'll find a way.'

Sucharita was preparing to approach Poreshbabu when he came to her himself that evening. Every evening at this hour, Poreshbabu would pace up and down in his garden, head bent low, lost in thought. It was as if he would slowly remove all the scars of the day's work by stroking his heart with the pure darkness of that evening hour, and prepare himself for the night's rest by filling his inner soul with pure tranquility. But tonight, having sacrificed the pleasant tranquillity of that solitary evening meditation, when Poreshbabu came to Sucharita's room with a worried expression on his face, her affectionate heart was moved, like a mother's heart when her usually playful infant falls ill and lies motionless.

'Radhé,' said Poreshbabu, 'you have heard everything, haven't you?'

'Yes, Baba, I have heard everything, but why are you so anxious?'

'I am not anxious about anything, save Lalita's capacity to bear the whole impact of the storm she has raised. Sometimes in the heat of excitement we are driven to blind daring, but when we begin to gradually experience the fruits of such daring, we lose the strength to bear them. Has Lalita carefully weighed all the consequences before determining what is best for herself?'

'I can say with emphasis that no form of social pressure can ever defeat Lalita,' Sucharita declared.

'I want to be completely sure that Lalita is not merely expressing rebellious defiance in a fit of rage.'

'No, Baba,' replied Sucharita, lowering her head, 'if that were so I would have paid no attention to her words. This sudden blow has exposed what lay concealed deep within her heart. If we now try to suppress the matter somehow, it would not be good for a girl like Lalita. Baba, Binoybabu is a wonderful person, after all.'

'Tell me,' asked Poreshbabu, 'would Binoy agree to enter the Brahmo Samaj?'

'I couldn't say for sure. Baba, should I go to Gourbabu's mother once?'

'I was also thinking that it might be a good idea for you to see her.'

## 49

From Anandamoyi's house, Binoy would drop by at his own home once, every morning. That day, he found a letter waiting for him. It bore no signature. It was full of lengthy advice, asserting that marriage to Lalita could never be a happy prospect for Binoy, and that it would prove inauspicious for Lalita. In conclusion it said that if Binoy still did not desist from marrying Lalita, then he must bear in mind that Lalita's lungs were weak, due to suspected tuberculosis.

Binoy was dumbfounded at receiving such a letter. He had never imagined that such things could even be conjured up as falsehoods. For nobody was unaware that Lalita's marriage to Binoy could never take place against the Samaj's wishes. Indeed, that was why he had always considered his weakness for Lalita a crime. But for such a letter to have reached him, the matter had doubtless been widely discussed within the Samaj. He was deeply agitated to imagine the humiliation Lalita must have suffered at the hands of her community members. He felt extremely ashamed and embarrassed that rumours had publicly linked his name with Lalita's. He was haunted by the feeling that Lalita was cursing and repudiating the fact that she knew him. He felt she could never again tolerate the sight of him.

But alas for the human heart! Even amidst this extreme feeling of rejection, a secret, profound, subtle, intense joy shot through Binoy's heart; it was unstoppable, denying all shame, all humiliation. To avoid encouraging that sensation in the least, he began to pace swiftly up and down his veranda, but the morning light sent a heady feeling through his heart. Even the hawker's call from the street aroused a deep restlessness in him. It was as if the tide of public slander had swept Lalita away and deposited her on the shore of Binoy's heart. He could no longer resist this image of Lalita having floated up to him, away from the social realm. 'Lalita is mine, mine alone!' his heart kept repeating. Never before had his heart dared to declare this so forcefully. But now that these words echoed so suddenly in the outer world, Binoy could no longer hush his own heart.

As he restlessly paced up and down the veranda, Binoy saw Haranbabu coming down the street. He realized at once that Haranbabu was coming to meet him, and became certain that there must be a major upheaval underlying that anonymous letter. Binoy did not display his natural loquaciousness as on other occasions. Offering Haranbabu a chowki, he silently waited for him to speak.

'Binoybabu, you're a Hindu, are you not?'

'Yes, indeed I am.'

'Please don't be offended at my question. Very often we act blindly without considering the situation around us, and that becomes a cause of misery. In such circumstances, should someone ask who we are, what are our limits, how far-reaching the consequences of our actions might be, however unpleasant this might seem, you should consider such a person your friend.'

'No need for such long preambles,' responded Binoy, trying to summon up a smile. 'It is not in my nature to react violently in any way out of anger at an unpleasant query. You may safely ask me all sorts of questions.'

'I don't want to accuse you of any deliberate offence. But needless to say, even errors of judgement may have poisonous effects.'

'You could avoid stating the needless,' answered Binoy, inwardly irritated. 'Please come to the point.'

'Since you belong to the Hindu community and since leaving the community is also impossible for you, should you frequent Poreshbabu's household in a way that may encourage rumours in the Samaj concerning his daughters?'

'Look Panubabu, how a community may construe certain facts depends largely on the nature of its members; I cannot take full responsibility for it. If even Poreshbabu's daughters can become targets of gossip within your community, that's a matter of shame for your community rather than for their family.'

'If an unwed girl is encouraged to leave her mother's side to travel in the same boat with a man outside her family, which community could be denied the right to criticize her, I ask you?' Haranbabu demanded.

'If you people also equate external events with internal sins, then why leave the Hindu community to join the Brahmo Samaj? Anyway Panubabu, I see no need to argue about all this. After due consideration I shall determine my appropriate course of action; you can be of no help to me in that regard.'

'I don't have much to say to you,' declared Haranbabu, 'but my last word to you is, you must now keep your distance. It would be very wrong of you to do otherwise. You people have only stirred up trouble by invading Poreshbabu's household; you have no idea how much harm you have done to their family.'

After Haranbabu had departed, Binoy's heart was pierced by a shaft of pain. Straightforward and open minded, how warmly Poreshbabu had welcomed the two of them into his home! Perhaps, unknowingly, Binoy had constantly overstepped the bounds of his rights within this Brahmo family, but still, he had never been denied Poreshbabu's affection and respect for a day. In this family, Binoy's nature had gained a safe haven such as he had not found anywhere else, as if, having got to know them, he had discovered a special aspect of his own identity. And here in this household, where he had received such care, such joy, such a sense of refuge, to think that Binoy's memory would forever prick like a painful thorn! For him to have cast the shadow of indignity over Poreshbabu's daughters! That he should have tainted Lalita's entire future in this way! How could he compensate! Alas, alas! What an immense contradiction this thing called community had generated within the domain of truth! There was no real obstacle against Lalita's union with Binoy; the Lord alone, who lived within both their souls, knew Binoy's readiness to surrender his whole life for Lalita's happiness and well-being. It was He who had brought Binoy so close to Lalita through the attraction of love; His eternal spiritual law had proved no hindrance. Was it some other deity then, worshipped by the Brahmo Samaj, by people like Panubabu? Was this deity not the profoundest arbitrator of the human heart? If some law of prohibition stood between Lalita and Binoy, baring its fangs at them, if it obeyed only the dictates of society and not of the Lord of all humanity, then was such prohibition itself not sinful? But alas, perhaps this prohibition was powerful even in Lalita's eyes! Besides, perhaps Lalita's feelings for Binoy were not . . . So many doubts! How could they be resolved?

## 50

Exactly when Haranbabu arrived at Binoy's house, Abinash had reported to Anandamoyi that Binoy's marriage to Lalita was confirmed.

'This can never be true,' asserted Anandamoyi.

'Why not?' demanded Abinash. 'Is Binoy incapable of it?'

'That I cannot say, but Binoy would never conceal something so important from me.'

Abinash repeated that it was from members of the Brahmo Samaj that he had heard this news and that it was completely believable. He had long known that Binoy was bound to end up in such deplorable circumstances; in fact, he had warned Gora about it. Having apprised Anandamoyi of these facts, Abinash gleefully proceeded downstairs to tell Mahim the news. When Binoy came to her that day, Anandamoyi could tell from his expression that his heart was disturbed by a particular anguish. Having fed him, she called him into her own chamber.

'Tell me Binoy, what is the matter with you?' she asked.

'Ma, read this letter and see for yourself.'

When Anandamoyi had read the letter, Binoy told her: 'This morning Panubabu came to my house. He rebuked me very sharply.'

'Why?'

'He says my conduct has aroused nasty rumours within their community about Poreshbabu's daughters.'

'People say your marriage to Lalita has been finalized. I see no cause for nasty rumours in that.'

'If marriage were possible there would be no cause for slander. But where there is no such possibility, how unjust to spread such rumours! It is particularly cowardly to spread such slander about Lalita.'

'If you have the slightest element of manliness in you Binu, you can easily shield Lalita from such cowardice.'

'How, Ma!' asked Binoy in astonishment.

'How? By marrying Lalita of course!'

'What's this you say Ma! I wonder what you imagine your Binoy to be! You think Binoy just has to say once, "I shall marry," and nobody in the world could contradict him—as if the whole world is awaiting a signal from me.'

'I see no reason for you to worry about so many things. Suffice it for you to do the little bit that is in your power. You could say, "I'm willing to get married."'

'Wouldn't it be humiliating for Lalita if I said something so improper?'

'Why do you call it improper? If there are rumours linking the two of you, surely they have arisen because the idea is proper indeed. You have no cause for hesitation, I tell you.'

'But Ma, we must think about Gora as well.'

'No my dear child, this matter does not involve thinking about Gora at all,' replied Anandamoyi firmly. 'I know he will be angry. I don't want him to be angry with you. But it can't be helped! If you respect Lalita, you can't let society cast a permanent slur upon her name.'

But this was a very difficult proposition indeed. How could Binoy keep such a major blow in store for Gora, whose imprisonment had redoubled Binoy's affection for him! And then there was tradition. It is easy to cross society in theory, but to cross it in practice creates so many tensions, big and small! Terror of the unknown and rejection of the unaccustomed keeps pushing one back, without any rational cause.

'Ma, the more I observe you, the more amazed I feel,' Binoy declared. 'How is your heart so pure? Don't you need to tread on the ground? Has Ishwar given you wings? Is there nothing to confine you, anywhere?'

'Ishwar has left me with nothing to bind me,' smiled Anandamoyi. 'He has swept everything clear.'

'But Ma, whatever I may say outwardly, my heart still poses constraints. For all that I comprehend, read and study, or argue about, I still realize suddenly that my heart has remained uneducated, after all.'

At this point, Mahim entered the room and immediately subjected Binoy to such rude interrogation about Lalita that his heart cringed in humiliaiton. Controlling himself, Binoy hung his head and offered no reply. After making some extremely insulting remarks pointed sharply against all parties concerned, Mahim left the scene. He argued: 'There's a shameless conspiracy afoot in Poreshbabu's family to ensnare Binoy like this and bring about his downfall. Binoy has been caught in such a trap only out of foolishness. Let them ensnare Gora, that will be something. That's difficult, indeed!'

Seeing such signs of humiliation everywhere, Binoy was stupefied.

'Do you know, Binoy, what you should do?' Anandamoyi asked him. He raised his head to look at her.

'You ought to meet Poreshbabu once. A few words with him and everything will become clear.'

## 51

Sucharita was surprised to see Anandamoyi so suddenly.

'I was just getting ready to visit you,' she exclaimed.

'I didn't know that,' smiled Anandamoyi, 'but hearing why you were getting ready, I couldn't wait. I just came along.'

Sucharita was astonished to learn that Anandamoyi had heard the news.

'Ma,' said Anandamoyi, 'I regard Binoy as my own son. Because of that relationship, how often I have mentally blessed you all, even without knowing you! How can I sit still upon being told that you have been wronged? I don't know whether I could be of any benefit to all of you, but I have rushed here because my heart was full of anguish. Ma, has Binoy done anything wrong?'

'Not at all. It is Lalita who is responsible for the matter that is causing such turmoil. Binoybabu had never imagined that Lalita might suddenly leave on the steamer without informing anybody. People are talking as if the two of them had hatched a secret conspiracy. And Lalita is such a spirited girl, she would never contradict the rumours or somehow explain what really took place.'

'We must find a solution,' declared Anandamoyi. 'Ever since all this reached his ears, Binoy has lost all his peace of mind; he has assumed himself to be the culprit.'

'Please tell me, do you think Binoybabu . . .' said Sucharita, lowering her flushed face.

'Look here, bachcha,' interrupted Anandamoyi, not letting the embarrassed Sucharita complete her words, 'I assure you Binoy would do anything you ask, for Lalita's sake. I have known him since he was a child. Once he surrenders himself, he can hold nothing back. That is why I must remain in constant dread, lest he give his heart where there's no hope of his receiving anything in return.'

Sucharita felt a load had been lifted off her mind. 'You need not worry about Lalita's consent,' she affirmed. 'I know her mind. But will Binoybabu agree to leave his community?'

'His community may reject him,' declared Anandamoyi, 'but why should he anticipate that by withdrawing from his community beforehand, ma? Is there any need for that?'

'How can you say that, Ma! Can Binoybabu marry into a Brahmo family while he is still part of the Hindu community?'

'If he is willing, why should all of you object?'

Sucharita found this extremely complicated.

'I can't see how that might be possible,' she confessed.

'To me it seems very simple, ma! Look, I can't follow the restrictions that prevail in my own household, hence many people label me a Khristan. When any rituals are performed, I deliberately remain aloof. You will be amused to know this, ma, but Gora doesn't accept the water served in my room. But why, therefore, should I say, "this is not my room, this community is not my own"? I can't bring myself to say that. Accepting all the abuse heaped upon me, I remain within this home and this community, with no undue hindrance. If the obstacles become too much for me, I shall take the path that Ishwar shows me. But to the end, I shall claim what is mine as my own; if others don't accept me, it is their problem.'

Sucharita was still not certain. She argued, 'The views of the Brahmo Samaj, if Binoybabu doesn't . . .'

'His views are similar too. The views of the Brahmo Samaj are not outlandish after all. He often reads to me the advice published in your journal; I can't see where the difference lies.'

'Suchididi,' called Lalita, entering the room. Seeing Anandamoyi, she immediately flushed in embarrassment. From Sucharita's expression she instantly guessed they had been discussing her. She would have been relieved to escape from the room, but it was too late.

'Come, Lalita ma, come,' cried Anandamoyi. Taking Lalita's hand, she drew her very close, as if they had developed a special intimacy. 'Look ma,' Anandamoyi now said to Sucharita, continuing in her earlier vein, 'it is hardest to combine the good with the bad, yet even that happens in this world, and we pull along somehow with a mixture of joys and sorrows. Not that it only causes harm: for sometimes, even good may come of it. If that too is possible, I fail to understand why a minor difference of opinion should keep two people apart. Are human affinities really a matter of opinions?'

Sucharita hung her head.

'Would your Brahmo Samaj also prevent two human beings from coming together?' Anandamoyi pursued. 'Would your Samaj outwardly divide people whom Ishwar has inwardly united? Ma, is there no community anywhere that would disregard minor differences and bring everyone together in a major union? Will human beings continue forever to oppose Ishwar like this? Were communities created only for that?'

Was Anandamoyi's fervour in pursuing this subject aimed solely at removing the obstacles blocking Lalita's marriage to Binoy? Was there not another motive in her wholehearted attempt to dispel the hint of doubt she sensed in Sucharita? It would not do, indeed, for Sucharita to remain trapped in such traditional ideas. If it was decided that the marriage could not take place unless Binoy converted to Brahmoism, the hopes Anandamoyi had nurtured of late, even in these difficult times, would be reduced to dust! That very day, Binoy had asked her:

'Ma, must I register with the Brahmo Samaj? Must I accept that as well?'

'No, no,' Anandamoyi had insisted, 'I see no need for that.'

'What if they pressurize me?'

'No, pressure would not work in this case,' Anandamoyi had replied, after a long silence.

Sucharita did not participate in Anandamoyi's discussion; she remained quiet. Anandamoyi realized that inwardly Sucharita was still not convinced.

'If my heart has broken free of all social prejudices, it is only because of my affection for Gora,' Anandamoyi thought to herself. 'Is Sucharita not attracted to Gora, then? If she were, this trivial issue would surely not seem so important.'

Anandamoyi felt rather downcast. There were just a couple of days for Gora's release from prison. She had privately imagined that the ground had been prepared for his happiness. Gora must somehow be pinned down this time, else there was no saying what predicament he might get into, or where. But it was not in every girl's power to pin Gora down. It would be wrong, though, to marry Gora to a girl from the Hindu community—hence she had rejected outright the proposals received from various families burdened with daughters. 'I shall not marry!' Gora would declare. People were surprised that as a mother, she never protested even once. But this time, observing some signs in Gora's behaviour, she had felt secretly overjoyed. That was why Sucharita's silent opposition to her views was a great blow to her. But she was not one to give up easily.

'We shall see,' she said to herself.

## 52

'Binoy, I don't want you to take a rash step, to rescue Lalita from a difficult predicament,' Poreshbabu declared. 'Social blame does not mean very much; in a couple of days, nobody will even remember what the fuss was all about.'

Binoy had no doubt that it was only to do his duty by Lalita that he had braced himself for battle. He knew such a marriage would cause awkwardness in the community, and more importantly, that Gora would be furious. But using only his sense of duty as a pretext, he had dismissed such unpleasant thoughts. Now that Poreshbabu suddenly sought to abjure that sense of duty completely, Binoy was loath to let it go.

'I can never repay all of you for your affection,' he responded. 'If I cause the slightest trouble for your family even for a couple of days, that too would be intolerable for me.'

'Binoy, you don't quite understand. I am delighted that you hold us in such high esteem, but if you are ready to marry my daughter only to repay that debt, it would not gain her much respect. That is why I was saying that the predicament is not grave enough to require the slightest sacrifice from you.'

So, Binoy was relieved of the burden of duty. But his heart did not rush out to embrace freedom like a bird that swiftly flaps its wings and flies away upon finding its cage door unbarred. He still did not want to move. For on the pretext of duty, he had demolished the dam of long-imposed self restraint, deeming it unnecessary. Where his mind would earlier advance very timidly and step back in shame like a culprit, it now firmly occupied a large space. Now it was hard to turn him back. When the sense of duty that had led him there now urged him: 'It's needless to remain here any longer bhai, let's turn back!' his heart replied: 'Return if you find it needless, but here I shall remain.'

When Poresh left no more room for subterfuge, Binoy blurted out: 'Don't imagine for a moment that I am ready to accept something painful to answer the call of duty. If all of you consent to it, there could be nothing more fortunate for me. My only fear is, lest . . .'

'Your fears are baseless,' the plainspoken Poreshbabu declared unhesitatingly. 'I have learnt from Sucharita that Lalita is not averse to you.'

Binoy felt a lightning flash of joy in his heart. A deep secret of Lalita's heart had been revealed to Sucharita. When and how had this happened? Binoy was pierced by a sharp, mysterious bliss upon learning that through hints and suggestions, such intimate knowledge had passed between these two women.

'If you all consider me worthy, nothing would bring me greater joy!' cried Binoy.

'Wait a little. I'll just go upstairs once.' He went to seek Borodasundari's consent.

'But Binoy must convert,' she said.

'Indeed he must,' Poreshbabu assented.

'Arrange that first,' she insisted. 'Why don't you send for Binoy?'

'So we must fix a date for the conversion,' Borodasundari said, when Binoy came upstairs.

'Is there any need for conversion?' Binoy asked.

'Any need? How can you say that! How else can you marry into the Brahmo Samaj?'

Binoy remained silent, hanging his head. Upon hearing that Binoy was willing to marry into his family, Poreshbabu had instantly assumed he would convert and join the Brahmo Samaj.

'I have a high regard indeed for the spiritual beliefs of the Brahmo Samaj, and my conduct up until now has not contravened them either,' Binoy pointed out. 'So is formal initiation necessary?'

'If your beliefs are consonant, what harm in seeking initiation?' Borodasundari argued.

'It is impossible for me to declare that I have no connection with the Hindu community,' Binoy replied.

'Then it was wrong of you to bring up the subject at all,' Borodasundari declared. 'Have you consented to marry my daughter out of kindness, in order to help us?'

Binoy was deeply hurt. He realized that his proposal had indeed become humiliating for all of them. It was a while since the law sanctioning civil marriage had been passed. At the time, Gora and Binoy had sharply opposed it. For Binoy to accept civil marriage now and announce himself 'not a Hindu' was also very difficult.

Inwardly, Poresh could not accept the suggestion that Binoy should marry Lalita while still a member of the Hindu community. Sighing, Binoy rose to his feet and joining his hands in a namaskar, he said:

'Please forgive me. I shall not add to my wrongdoings.'

He left the room. Approaching the stairs he glimpsed Lalita alone at a small desk in a corner of the veranda ahead. She was writing a letter. Hearing his footstep, she raised her eyes to look at him. That momentary glance instantly set Binoy's heart in turmoil. His acquaintance with Lalita was not new after all; she had often raised her eyes to his face; but today, what mystery did her gaze unfold to him! Sucharita had learned a secret concealed Lalita's heart. That intimate secret appeared to Binoy's eyes today like a moisture-laden, gentle cloud that had gathered, full of pathos, under the shadow of Lalita's dark lashes. In Binoy's momentary glance, his heart's anguish also flashed across like lightning. With a farewell namaskar in Lalita's direction, he went down the stairs without addressing her.

## 53

When he came out of prison, Gora saw Poreshbabu and Binoy waiting for him at the gate.

A month was not a long time. Earlier, Gora had traveled for more than a month, away from relatives and friends. But seeing Poresh and Binoy as soon as he emerged from a month of separation in jail, he felt he had been reborn into the familiar world of his old friends. On the highway, under the open sky, in the glow of dawn, seeing Poresh's calm, affectionate, naturally dignified face, Gora touched his feet in an unprecedented ecstasy of devotion. Poresh embraced him.

'Binoy, I have shared my entire education with you, right from school,' smiled Gora, taking Binoy's hand. 'But at this school, I have given you the slip and outstripped you.'

Binoy could neither smile nor speak. His friend seemed to have emerged from his mysterious ordeal in prison with a stature far greater than that of a friend. In deep reverence, he stayed silent.

'How is Ma?' Gora enquired.

'Well enough,' Binoy replied.

'Come my dear boy,' said Poreshbabu, 'the carriage is waiting for you.'

As the three of them were about to mount the carriage, Abinash arrived there, panting for breath. He was followed by a crowd of boys. Seeing Abinash, Gora tried to hurry into the carriage, but Abinash blocked his way before he could succeed.

'Please wait a little, Gourmohanbabu,' he said. He had not finished speaking when the boys burst into song at the top of their voices:

*Gone is the night of sorrow, the day has dawned.*
*Broken, broken, are our chains of bondage.*

Gora flushed. 'Quiet!' he roared, in his thunderous voice. The boys were stunned into silence.

'What's all this, Abinash?' Gora demanded.

From the folds of his shawl Abinash produced a thick garland of kunda blossom, wrapped in banana leaf. Taking his cue, a young lad produced a piece of paper printed in gold lettering, and in a voice as shrill as a clockwork organ, started rapidly reading out a message congratulating Gora upon his release from prison.

Forcefully flinging aside Abinash's garland, his voice choked with suppressed rage, Gora exclaimed: 'Is this the first act of your show! Have you been practising all month to make me the clown in your jatra party here at the public roadside today?'

This had been Abinash's long standing plan; he had hoped to create a dazzling impression. Such annoying public spectacles were not current at the time we are speaking of. Greedy to take the entire credit for this extraordinary event, Abinash had not even discussed it with Binoy. In fact he had himself drafted a report for the newspapers, planning to send it off as soon as he got home, after filling in a couple of missing details.

'You are unfair,' protested Abinash, upset at Gora's reprimand. 'We have suffered no less than what you underwent in prison. Every moment, this last month, our ribs have been scorched by the inextinguishable flames of burning husks.'

'You are making a mistake Abinash,' Gora insisted. 'Look carefully and you will see at once that all the husks are still intact, and your ribs have suffered no fatal damage either.'

Abinash was not subdued. 'Those in power have insulted you,' he persisted, 'but today, on behalf of the entire land of Bharat, we offer this garland of honour . . .'

'This is becoming intolerable!' interrupted Gora. 'Poreshbabu, please get into the carriage,' he urged, brushing Abinash and his party aside. Poreshbabu heaved a sigh of relief as he mounted the carriage, followed by Gora and Binoy.

Travelling by steamer, Gora arrived home early the next morning. He saw a large number of his party members assembled in the outer portion of the house. Somehow extricating himself from their clutches he went to

Anandamoyi in the privacy of the antahpur. Having bathed early that morning, she was ready and waiting for him. When Gora came and fell at her feet in obeisance, tears gushed from Anandamoyi's eyes. The tears she had suppressed all these days could not be restrained anymore.

As soon as Krishnadayal returned from his bath in the Ganga, Gora met him, greeting him with a pranam from afar, without touching his feet. Embarrassed, Krishnadayal seated himself at a distance.

'Baba, I want to do penance,' Gora declared.

'But I see no need for that.'

'While in prison, I did not mind any other hardship, but I felt utterly impure. That sense of degradation has not left me yet. I must do penance.'

'No, no,' protested Krishnadayal in agitation. 'There is no need for such an extreme step. Indeed I can't agree to it.'

'Achchha, perhaps I shall consult the pundits about it.'

'No need to consult any pundit. I decree that you need not do penance.'

Gora had never been able to understand why a man like Krishnadayal, so obsessed with rites of purity, refused to accept that Gora should observe any restrictions—for he not only rejected but obdurately resisted any such suggestion.

That day, Anandamoyi had placed Gora directly next to Binoy at mealtime. But Gora insisted:

'Ma, please move Binoy's mat a little further away.'

'Why, what crime has Binoy committed?' demanded Anandamoyi in surprise.

'The fault is not in Binoy but in me. I am unclean.'

'Never mind,' Anandamoyi assured him, 'Binoy is not so fussy about purity.'

'Binoy may not be but I am,' Gora declared.

After their meal, when the two friends went to their secluded room upstairs, both felt rather tongue-tied. Binoy could not think how to broach to Gora the one subject that had assumed the greatest importance for him in this last month. Gora, too, secretly wanted to ask about Poreshbabu's family, but he said nothing at all. He was waiting for Binoy to raise the subject. True, Gora had asked Poreshbabu how all the girls in the family were doing, but that was just a polite query. Privately, he was eager for a more detailed account, beyond the mere assurance that they were all well.

At this point Mahim entered the room, and taking a seat, took some time to recover his breath after the effort of climbing the stairs. Then he said:

'Binoy, we have waited for Gora all these days. Now there is nothing to stop us. Let's fix the date and time now. What do you say, Gora? You understand what we are talking about, don't you?' Gora smiled faintly without saying a word. 'You smile!' exclaimed Mahim. 'Dada has still not forgotten the matter, you are thinking! But the girl is not a figment of the imagination—I see quite clearly that she is made of real stuff—so how can I forget the matter? This is no time to be facetious, Gora. Now let things be finalized somehow.'

'The one who must finalize things is here in person,' Gora pointed out.

'That would be disastrous!' cried Mahim. 'When he is not even sure of his own life, how can he fix anything! Now you're back, the entire responsibility is yours.'

Binoy remained grave and silent on this occasion, making no attempt to say anything even with his customary jocularity. Gora sensed that something was wrong.

'I may undertake to invite people, or to order the sweets, and may even be willing to serve the guests, but I cannot undertake to ensure that Binoy will marry your daughter. I am not well acquainted with the One who ordains such things, having always saluted Him from afar.'

'Don't imagine that He would keep away just because you remain aloof,' Mahim cautioned him. 'There is no saying when He might take you by surprise. I can't say for sure what He intends for you, but regarding Binoy I fear grave complications. If you don't involve yourself instead of leaving things entirely to Prajapati, the god of marriage, we may have cause for regret, I warn you.'

'I'm willing to regret an undertaking for which I am not responsible,' Gora replied, 'but it is harder if one must regret a responsibility after accepting it. I want to save myself from such a predicament.'

'Would you sit back and watch a Brahman's son lose his caste, blood ties and social respect?' Mahim demanded. 'You sacrifice your food and sleep to preserve your countrymen's Hindu beliefs, but if meanwhile your own best friend throws caste purity to the winds to marry into a Brahmo family, you will not be able to face the world. You may be angry, Binoy, but I have spoken to Gora in your presence, while many people might say the same things to him behind your back—they are dying to do so. It is best for everybody to be frank. If the rumours are indeed false, you just have to say so and the matter ends there; but if they are true, we must come to an understanding.' Mahim rose to his feet and left. Still, Binoy did not say a word.

'Why Binoy, what's the matter?' Gora inquired.

'It is very hard,' Binoy replied, 'to explain the situation accurately by merely offering some items of news. That's why I had thought I would gradually clarify the whole matter to you. But in this world, nothing tends to happen unhurriedly, according to one's convenience. Events, too, advance slowly and silently at first like a tiger on the prowl, then suddenly they pounce on you. News of such events also remains initially suppressed like a fire, but when it suddenly bursts into flames afterwards, it can no longer be controlled. That's why sometimes I feel that man's freedom resides in giving up all action and remaining utterly immobile.'

'How can freedom be possible if you alone are static?' smiled Gora. 'Unless the whole world also freezes, why would it let you remain still? On the contrary, it would create another problem. When the world is in action, if you do not act as well, you will be constantly cheated. Hence you must be careful not to let events get the better of your alertness. Let it not happen that you alone are unprepared while all else continues.'

'That's true. It is I who am unprepared. This time also I was not ready. I had no idea what was happening, and how. But when it has happened, one must take responsibility for it. Unpleasant though it is, one cannot now refuse to acknowledge what should not have happened in the first place.'

'Without knowing what happened, it is hard for me to discuss it theoretically.'

Binoy sat bolt upright and blurted out: 'Due to circumstances beyond our control, my relationship with Lalita has reached a stage where she must suffer unjust and baseless social humiliation all her life, unless I marry her.'

'What stage is that, may I know?'

'That's a long story. I shall narrate it to you in due course, but rest assured that the little bit I've told you is true.'

'Very well, suppose I accept it as true. I have this to say: if the event is inevitable, so are its painful consequences. If Lalita must suffer humiliation in the Samaj, there's no help for it.'

'But it is within my power to prevent it,' protested Binoy.

'If so, that is a good thing. But asserting the fact forcefully is not enough, after all. When in need, it is within the power of human beings to steal or even murder, but is that power real? You want to do your duty towards Lalita by marrying her, but is that really your supreme duty? Don't you have a duty towards your community?'

Binoy did not point out that it was his sense of duty towards the community that had made him reject a Brahmo wedding ceremony.

'I think you and I will perhaps differ on this issue,' he argued even more passionately. 'After all I am not opposing society in favour of individuals. I am saying that above both individual and society is something else, a spiritual ethic called dharma, and that must be kept in mind when we act. It is not my supreme duty to protect either a particular individual or my community. It is protecting my dharma that is my supreme duty.'

'A dharma that exists without either individual or society! I have no faith in such a dharma.'

Binoy grew even more obdurate. 'Granted,' he said. 'Dharma is not based on individual and society; rather, both individual and society are based on dharma. To be forced to accept society's wishes as one's dharma would ruin society itself. If society obstructs my legally and spiritually sanctioned freedom, it would be my duty towards society to flout such inappropriate prohibitions. If my marrying Lalita is not wrong but in fact justified, then it would go against my dharma to desist simply because it violated social injunctions.'

'Are questions of justice and injustice confined to you alone? Will you not consider where you are placing your future progeny by agreeing to this marriage?'

'It is through such considerations indeed that people perpetuate social injustices. Why then blame the clerk who accepts lifelong degradation, kicked around by the sahebs who are his masters? After all he, too, has his children's welfare in mind.'

His argument with Gora had brought Binoy to a point he had not reached before. Just a little while earlier, his whole being had shrunk from the prospect of severing his ties with society. He had not mentally debated the issue in any way, and but for this exchange with Gora, Binoy's heart would have followed its own accustomed prejudices and taken him on a course completely contrary to his present stance. But as he argued, his attitude, supported by his sense of duty, began to grow strong.

He and Gora started arguing heatedly. In such discussions Gora often expressed his views very forcefully, without relying on logic. Few could match his assertiveness. Now, he tried to demolish all Binoy's arguments by this aggressive force but found himself thwarted. As long as their ideas alone had clashed, Binoy had always been defeated. But this was a confrontation between two real persons; instead of fending off airy weapons of its own kind, Gora's airborne verbal arrows now encountered a human heart full of pain.

Ultimately Gora said: 'I don't want to engage in a war of words with you. There is nothing much to argue about here; it's a matter for the heart to comprehend. It is your desire to disengage from the common people of the land by marrying a Brahmo girl: that is a source of great distress for me. You are capable of it, but I could never do such a thing. That is where we differ, not in learning or intellect. The target of my love is not the same as yours. You have no sympathy for what you would destroy in order to free yourself. But I have blood-ties with it. I want my Bharatvarsha; blame and curse it if you will, but it is Bharatvarsha I desire. I don't desire myself or any other human being above that. I would not take the slightest step that might create the minutest division between me and my Bharatvarsha.'

'No Binoy, you argue in vain,' Gora insisted when Binoy tried to reply. 'I want to share the degradation of the Bharatvarsha that the world has forsaken and condemned, this Bharatvarsha with its caste discrimination, social evils, idol worship. If you wish to distance yourself from it, you must distance yourself from me as well.'

Gora arose, went out of the room, and began to wander about on the terrace. Binoy remained where he was, silent and motionless. The attendant came to inform Gora that several babus were waiting for him in the outer chamber. Relieved to find an escape route, Gora went away.

Emerging into the outer room, he noticed Abinash among the motley crowd assembled there. Gora had assumed Abinash must be feeling offended. But he saw no signs of anger. In terms even more effusively laudatory, Abinash was recounting to everyone the way Gora had spurned him the previous day.

'My respect for Gourmohanbabu has grown immensely,' he declared. 'All these days I took him for an unusual man, but yesterday I realized that he is great. Yesterday we had gone to honour him, but the way he publicly spurned that honour—how many people in today's world could have done that! Indeed it is no ordinary matter!'

Gora's mind was already overwrought. Now Abinash's effusiveness made him furious. 'Look here Abinash,' he cried, losing his patience. 'It is your devotion that is offensive. If you people want to make me dance like a clown by the roadside, do you think I lack the decorum to refuse? Is this what you call a sign of greatness? Do you consider this land of ours a mere jatra party with everyone dancing about in order to collect the rewards of their performance? Is nobody doing any real work? If you want to join us, or even to pick a quarrel, that is acceptable; but I beg all of you not to laud me in this fashion.'

Abinash's reverence grew even more intense. He beamed at all present, as if to draw their attention to the wonder of Gora's words. 'Give us your blessing,' he pleaded, 'that we may selflessly surrender our lives to protect the eternal glory of Bharatvarsha, just like you.' With these words Abinash reached out to touch Gora's feet in a pranam. Gora at once recoiled. 'Gourmohanbabu,' Abinash declared, 'you will indeed accept no token of honour from us. But you cannot also remain averse to making us happy. We have planned a feast one day, where you will dine with all the rest of us. To this you must agree.'

'Until I have done penance I cannot dine with you,' Gora asserted.

Penance! Abinash's eyes lit up. 'That had never occurred to any of us,' he confessed, 'but no decree of the Hindu dharma can ever escape Gourmohanbabu's notice.'

It was an excellent idea, everyone agreed. The penance ritual itself would provide all of them an occasion to sit down together to a feast. That day they must invite all the great teachers and pundits of the area. The invitation to Gourmohanbabu's penance would make people aware that the Hindu dharma was alive and thriving, even now. The date and venue for the penance ceremony also came up for discussion. Gora declared that this house would not be suitable. A devotee proposed that the ritual be performed at his garden estate beside the Ganga. It was also decided that the group would collectively bear the expenses for the event. When it was time to depart, Abinash rose and addressed everyone, gesturing like an orator:

'This may annoy Gourmohanbabu, but my heart is so full today that I cannot refrain from saying that just as the avatars, divine incarnations, were once born into this sacred land to protect the Vedas, so we have now found this avatar to rescue the Hindu dharma. In this world, our land alone has six seasons; in our land alone, through the ages, have avatars been born, and there are more to come. It is our glory that this truth has now been demonstrated. Come, bhai, let us all cry, 'Victory to Gourmohan!' Swayed by Abinash's eloquence all of them began chanting Gora's praises. Deeply offended, Gora rushed away from the scene.

On this day of his release from prison, a powerful sense of fatigue assailed Gora. In the confines of the jail, he had often imagined that he would work for the nation with renewed enthusiasm. But today he kept asking himself:

'Alas, where is my nation? Is it a nation to me alone! That my childhood friend, with whom I had discussed all my life's resolves, should be willing, after all this time, to ruthlessly abandon his nation's entire past and future, just to marry a woman! And as for those who are generally identified as members of my group, after all I have explained to them all along, that they should now conclude that I was an avatar born only to rescue the Hindu faith! Am I merely the shastras personified? And does Bharatvarsha have no place in their scheme of things? Six seasons! Bharatvarsha has six seasons indeed! If the six seasons have conspired to produce a man like Abinash, we could have done with a few seasons less!'

The bearer came to say that Ma had sent for Gora. Gora started. 'Ma has sent for me!' he exclaimed to himself. The words seemed to assume a new significance. 'Come what may, my mother is there,' he said. 'And it is she who has sent for me. It is she who will unite me with everybody, allowing no separation between people; I shall find my dear ones in her space. In prison, Ma had called me, and had appeared to me in a vision; out of prison, too, Ma is calling me; I shall set forth now to meet her.' With these words Gora gazed out at the wintry afternoon sky. The discordant note struck by Binoy on the one hand and Abinash on the other dwindled and faded away. Bharatvarsha seemed to open its arms to the afternoon sunlight. Before Gora's eyes the rivers, mountains, human habitations of Bharatvarsha lay outspread, extending to the sea; from the eternal realm, a free, pure light seemed to irradiate this Bharatvarsha everywhere. Gora's heart was full. His eyes began to blaze, and no trace of despair remained in any corner of his mind. His nature blissfully readied itself for ceaseless service of Bharatvarsha, with its distant goals. He felt no bitterness that he would not witness in his lifetime the glory of Bharatvarsha that he had seen in his contemplation. Again and again he told himself: 'Ma is calling me. I am on my way to the place where the mother goddess awaits me as Annapurna, as Jagaddhatri—to that distant time, yet at this very moment, to that other shore beyond death, yet within this present lifetime—to that glorious future which has brightened my humble present, making it completely worthwhile—I am on my way to that very place—to that place which is very distant, yet very near, Ma is calling me.' It seemed to Gora that Binoy, and even Abinash, were part of that bliss, that they too were no longer alienated from him. All the petty conflicts of the present were lost in a tremendous sense of achievement.

When Gora entered Anandamoyi's room his face was alight with joy, as if his eyes were gazing at some exquisite image, beyond the material things before him. When he suddenly entered the scene, he seemed not to quite recognize the person who was with his mother. Sucharita arose and greeted Gora with a namaskar.

'So you have arrived! Please make yourself comfortable,' said Gora. He spoke as if Sucharita's arrival was no ordinary event but an extraordinary manifestation.

Gora had once avoided Sucharita's company. As long as he wandered, undergoing many hardships and performing diverse tasks, he had managed to keep thoughts of Sucharita at bay. But in the confines of prison, he had been unable to ward off memories of her. There was once a time when Gora had not even been aware that there were women in Bharatvarsha. At last, he newly discovered this fact in the shape of Sucharita; his nature, so robust, trembled at the impact of the sudden and immediate apprehension of such an important truth, so ancient and so great. In prison, when the sunshine and open breeze outside tormented his mind, he did not view that world as merely his workplace or as a male society. Whatever form of meditation he adopted, he could see only the faces of two founding deities, singled out by the light of sun, moon and stars, enveloped exclusively by the tender blue sky. One was the face of the mother he had known all his life, and the other gentle, lovely face, glowing with intelligence, was that of his new acquaintance.

In the joyless confines of prison, Gora had been unable to fight the memory of this countenance. The rapture of contemplating it brought a sense of the profoundest freedom into his jail cell. The harsh, physical bonds of prison would seem to him a shadowy illusion. From his pulsating heart emanated supranatural waves that penetrated all the prison walls unhindered, merging with the sky, swaying with the flowers and foliage, sporting in the world's workspaces. Imagining there was no reason to fear this fanciful image, Gora had for this last month given full rein to it. He feared only substantial things.

Seeing Poreshbabu as soon as he emerged from prison, Gora had felt overjoyed. His delight was not merely at the sight of Poreshbabu; Gora had not realized at first the extent to which his joy was infused with the magic of that imaginary figure who had lately become his companion. But gradually he understood. Travelling on the steamer he distinctly sensed that his attraction towards Poreshbabu was not on account of the latter's own virtues alone. At last, Gora again braced himself. 'I shall not admit defeat,' he declared. On the steamer he resolved firmly that he would again go somewhere far away, and not allow his mind to be fettered by any bonds, however subtle.

At this juncture he became involved in a debate with Binoy. When the two friends first met after their spell of separation, the argument would not normally have grown so intense. But now, concealed within this argument raged a debate with himself. Through this argument, Gora was clarifying his own premises even to himself. That was why he spoke so vehemently on this occasion, for it was he who particularly needed such vehemence. When this assertiveness aroused Binoy's antagonism, when Binoy mentally countered Gora's statements with his entire soul militating against the unjust fanaticism of Gora's strictures, he had not dreamt that Gora's onslaught might not have been so aggressive if it had not been directed against himself.

After his debate with Binoy, Gora decided: 'I cannot afford to quit the arena. If I abandon Binoy to save my own life, there will be no saving him!'

# 54

At this moment, Gora's mind was in a trance, regarding Sucharita not as an individual but an abstract idea. In the form of Sucharita the image of Indian womanhood manifested itself to him. It was to make the Indian home sweet and pure through virtue, beauty and love that this image had appeared. The goddess Lakshmi who nurtures the infants of India, tends to the sick, comforts the troubled, glorifies even the humble with her love, who has not abandoned or ignored even the poorest of us in times of trouble, who though herself venerable has devotedly worshipped even the unworthiest of us, whose lovely, skilful hands are dedicated to our service, and whose ever-sympathetic, merciful love we have received from the Almighty as an eternal gift—seeing her incarnate here before his very eyes, seated beside his mother, Gora was filled with profound joy. He began to think: 'We had not glanced at this Lakshmi-figure, pushing her completely into the background! There can be no greater sign of our degradation.' He now felt: 'She signifies the land itself, ensconced upon a thousand-petalled lotus in the soul's garden, at the heart of the entire nation Bharatvarsha. We are her servants. The country's plight is her dishonour; it is because we are indifferent to her humiliation that our virility is put to shame.'

Gora was privately astounded. Up until now he had not even realized how incomplete was his understanding of Bharatvarsha, as long as he had remained unaware of Indian womanhood. When the female sex had been an opaque mystery to him, he had felt something missing from his sense of patriotic duty. As if it had strength but no life, muscle but no nerves. In an instant Gora realized: 'The more we have kept women away and belittled them, the more our own virility has dwindled and wasted away.' Hence when Gora said to Sucharita, 'Here you are, you have arrived!' his words were not uttered merely as a customary polite greeting. They were loaded with a newfound joy and wonder.

Gora's body bore some marks of his prison days. He had become much thinner than before. Out of contempt and distaste for prison food, he had virtually fasted through this month-long period. His glowing, fair complexion had also grown somewhat dull. His extremely short-cropped hair made the haggardness of his countenance all the more apparent. It was this leanness that aroused pain and awe in Sucharita's heart. She longed to touch Gora's feet in obeisance. Gora appeared to her like a pure flame that burns so brightly, the wood and smoke become invisible. An intense devotion mingled with sympathy made her heart tremble inwardly. She could not utter a word.

'I now realize what joy a daughter could have brought me, Gora!' said Anandamoyi. 'How can I tell you what solace Sucharita offered me, when you were away! I didn't know their family before, but in times of trouble one discovers many great and good things in this world. I now recognize this glorious aspect of sorrow. We suffer only because we don't always realize where, in how many places, the Almighty Ishwar has left provision for our solace. You are embarrassed, ma, but how can I help mentioning in your presence the joy you have brought me during my difficult days?'

With profound gratitude, Gora glanced once at Sucharita's embarrassed face. 'Ma,' he said to Anandamoyi, 'she came to share your sorrows in your times of trouble, and is here again to enhance your joy in happier circumstances. Only those with largeness of heart are capable of such unwarranted sympathy.'

'Didi, once a thief is caught he is chastised by all concerned,' observed Binoy, noticing Sucharita's awkwardness. 'You are now suffering the result of being captured by all of them. Now there's no escape! I've known you a long time, but I never gave anything away. I have kept very quiet, knowing in my heart that nothing remains hidden for long.'

'You have kept quiet, indeed!' smiled Anandamoyi. 'As if you are the sort of boy to keep quiet! Ever since he met all of you, he has sung your praises continuously, but he can never say enough.'

'Pay heed, didi!' said Binoy. 'Here's direct proof that I appreciate the virtues of others and that I'm not ungrateful.'

'That only indicates your own virtues,' Sucharita retorted.

'But you will learn nothing about my virtues from me,' Binoy replied. 'If that's what you seek, please go to my mother and you will be dumbfounded. When I hear such praise from her lips, I am myself astonished. If Ma were to write my biography, I'd willingly die early.'

'Just listen to this boy!' said Anandamoyi.

'Binoy,' observed Gora, 'your parents indeed gave you a fitting name.'

'It was perhaps because they expected no other virtue of me that they claimed for me the quality of binoy or modesty, else I would have become a laughing-stock for everyone.'

In this way, the constraint of their first encounter melted away.

'Won't you visit our part of the town sometime?' Sucharita asked Binoy while taking her leave.

She invited Binoy but could not bring herself to ask Gora. Unable to quite understand what this meant, Gora was secretly hurt. So far he had never felt the slightest pang at the fact that he could not match Binoy's ability to easily make himself at home in everybody's midst. But today he felt this missing quality as a lack.

## 55

Binoy had realized that it was to discuss his marriage to Lalita that Sucharita had invited him. He may have dispensed with the proposal, but that did not mean the matter had ended there. As long as the issue remained alive, there could be no reprieve for either party.

All these days, Binoy's biggests worry had been, 'How can I hurt Gora's feelings?' By Gora he meant not just the man himself, but his attitude, his faith and the life he had adopted. To always keep in step with this had been Binoy's habit, his source of joy. Opposing it in any way seemed to him like rebelling against his own self. But his initial hesitation about striking that blow had vanished. Now that he had discussed the Lalita affair openly with Gora, Binoy felt heartened. Before his sore was lanced, there had been no end to the patient's fear and apprehension; but once the instruments were applied, he felt pain indeed but also relief, and found the procedure not as terrible as he had imagined.

All this while, Binoy had been unable to argue with himself, but now the doors to internal debate were also opened. Now, in his mind, he exchanged words with Gora. Mentally summoning up all the arguments one might expect from Gora, he began to counter them from diverse angles. If the entire debate with Gora could have taken place verbally, it would have aroused excitement but also quenched it. But Binoy realized Gora would not carry this particular argument to its conclusion. This, too, angered Binoy. 'Gora will neither understand nor explain but only apply force. Force! I cannot submit to force.' 'Whatever happens, I am on the side of Truth,' he declared. With these words, he clutched the word 'Truth' to his heart. It was necessary to set up a very strong opposition to Gora; hence Binoy repeatedly told himself that Truth itself was his final recourse. In fact, he developed tremendous self-respect at having made Truth his refuge. So when Binoy headed for Sucharita's house that afternoon, he held his head high. Whether his strength came from his leanings towards Truth or whether his leanings lay elsewhere, he was in no state to determine.

Harimohini was preparing to cook. There, at the kitchen door, Binoy made her sanction the Brahman's claim to a midday meal, and proceeded upstairs. Fingers busy, eyes on a piece of embroidery, Sucharita raised the topic that was uppermost in their minds.

'Look here, Binoybabu,' she said, 'must external antagonisms matter where there is no internal obstacle?'

In his debate with Gora, Binoy had opposed him. But in his discussion with Sucharita, he again took the opposite side. Who could tell, now, that there was any difference of opinion between Gora and him!

'Didi,' he argued, 'all of you are not minimizing the external obstacles either.'

'There's a reason for that Binoybabu! The obstacles we face are not exactly external. Our Samaj is based on our spiritual faith after all. But in your community, the restrictions are merely social. Hence it would not be as great a loss to you to renounce your community as it would be for Lalita to withdraw from the Brahmo Samaj.'

Binoy began to argue that religion is a personal pursuit, not to be associated with any community. At this juncture Satish entered, carrying a letter and an English newspaper. Seeing Binoy, he became very excited, eager to somehow convert Friday into Sunday. In no time, Binoy and

Satish were deep in conversation. Meanwhile, Sucharita began to read Lalita's letter and the accompanying paper. This Brahmo paper carried the news that there was no longer any fear of a match between an eminent Brahmo family and the Hindu community, because the prospective Hindu groom had declined the proposal. In this connection, the pathetic weakness of the Brahmo family was decried, in contrast to the steadfastness of the aforementioned Hindu boy.

Sucharita privately resolved that Binoy and Lalita must be married, by whatever means. But that could not be accomplished by arguing with this young man. She sent a note to Lalita, inviting her home and mentioning that Binoy was present there. As no almanac offered any provision for turning Friday into Sunday by some planetary conjunction, Satish had to go and get ready for school. Sucharita also went away, saying she needed time to bathe.

Alone in Sucharita's secluded chamber, once the heat of the argument had evaporated, the young man in Binoy was aroused. It was about nine or nine-thirty in the morning. There was no hubbub in the street. A clock was ticking on Sucharita's writing desk. The room exuded an influence that began to overwhelm Binoy. The small decorative items all around him seemed to set up a conversation with him. The neatness of the tabletop, the embroidered cover on the chair, the deerskin rug at the foot of the chair, the few pictures hanging on the wall, the small bookshelf at the back, with its books covered in red fabric—all this struck a profound chord in Binoy's mind. There seemed to be some beautiful mystery tucked away inside this chamber, as if all the intimate confidences shared here between sakhis on lonely afternoons still lingered in the room, scattered here and there. Binoy began to visualize the place and posture of the female companions during their conversations. The words spoken by Poreshbabu the other day—'I have learnt from Sucharita that Lalita is not averse to you'—appeared to his mind's eye in a myriad different ways, with a picture-like clarity. An unutterable anguish haunted his heart like a sad, melancholy melody. Because he lacked the capacity to express in any way the things that inhabit the recesses of one's heart in such secret, profound forms, like wordless hints—in other words, because Binoy was not a poet or painter—his whole inner being grew restless. He began to feel as if there was something that might bring him relief if only he could accomplish it, yet there seemed no way of doing so. The screen that hung before him, very close at hand yet keeping him at a slight distance—did Binoy not have the strength to arise and forcefully rip it apart, this very minute?

Harimohini looked in to ask if Binoy wanted a snack.

'No,' he replied.

Now Harimohini entered the room and sat down. While at Poreshbabu's, she had felt strongly drawn towards Binoy. But ever since she had set up house independently with Sucharita, these visits had become extremely distasteful to her. She had decided these companions were to blame for the fact that Sucharita did not completely follow Harimohini in observing orthodox restrictions nowadays. Though she knew Binoy was not a Brahmo, she clearly sensed that he inwardly lacked any firm convictions about Hindu tradition. So she no longer wasted the deity's prasad by enthusiastically inviting this Brahman's son to taste the consecrated food, as before.

'Tell me, baba, you are a Brahman's son after all, so don't you perform the sandhya prayer ritual, or offer any archana?' she asked Binoy conversationally that day.

'Mashi,' he answered, 'I'm so busy memorizing my lessons all day, I've forgotten gayatri, sandhya, everything.'

'Poreshbabu is also an educated man,' Harimohini protested. 'But he still performs some rituals, morning and evening, according to his faith.'

'Mashi, what he does cannot be accomplished by memorizing mantras alone. If I can ever become like him, I too shall follow his path.'

'Meanwhile,' said Harimohini rather sharply, 'why not follow the path of your forefathers? Is it a good idea to be neither here nor there? A person must have a religious identity after all. Neither Rama nor Ganga—O ma, what sort of conduct is this!'

At this moment Lalita entered the room. She started when she saw Binoy.

'Where is Didi?' she asked Harimohini.

'Radharani has gone for a bath,' Harimohini replied.

'Didi had sent for me,' said Lalita, by way of a needless explanation.

'Why don't you wait, she will join us very soon,' suggested Harimohini.

Harimohini was not favourably disposed towards Lalita either. She now wanted to bring Sucharita completely under her control, freeing her of all her former ties. Poreshbabu's other daughters did not visit here very frequently. Only Lalita would drop by at odd hours to chat with Sucharita, which Harimohini did not like. She often tried to disrupt their conversation, calling Sucharita away on some errand or other, or expressing regret that Sucharita's studies were no longer progressing unhindered as before. Yet when Sucharita applied herself to her studies, Harimohini would also not refrain from pointing out that excessive learning was unnecessary and harmful for women. Truth be told, because she could not succeed in bringing Sucharita as completely under her power as she wished, she would sometimes blame Sucharita's companions and sometimes her education.

Not that it pleased Harimohini to linger there with Lalita and Binoy; but there she remained all the same, because she was angry with both of them. She had sensed a mysterious relationship between Binoy and Lalita. Hence she told herself: 'Whatever the customs of your community, I shall not permit such shameless intermingling, such outrageous Khristani ways, in this house of mine!'

Meanwhile, Lalita's heart also bristled with rebellion. The previous day, she too had resolved to accompany Sucharita to Anandamoyi's house, but she could not force herself to go. Lalita respected Gora immensely, but her hostility towards him was also very intense. She could never dismiss the fact that Gora was opposed to her in every respect.

Indeed, from the day Gora came out of prison, her attitude towards Binoy had also undergone a change. Even a few days earlier, she had arrogantly assumed that she had strong claims upon Binoy. But the very thought that Binoy could never overcome Gora's influence made her brace herself for battle with him.

As soon as he saw Lalita enter the room, Binoy's heart was flung into a turmoil. Try as he might, he could not maintain a natural demeanour towards her. Ever since rumours had spread within their social circle about the likelihood of their getting married, Binoy's heart would tremble at the very sight of Lalita, like a magnet within an electrical field. Seeing Binoy in the room, Lalita was incensed with Sucharita, assuming that Sucharita had been trying her best to persuade the reluctant Binoy and that it was to iron out this problem that she had been summoned here today.

'Please tell Didi I can't wait for her now,' she declared, addressing Harimohini. 'I'll come another time.' With these words, without so much as glancing at Binoy, she rushed from the room. Now that it was pointless for Harimohini to remain with Binoy any longer, she too departed to attend to her housework.

Binoy was not unfamiliar with this smouldering expression on Lalita's face. But he had not seen this look for a long time. He had thought with relief that those bad days were over when Lalita was constantly up in arms against him, but now he found her producing the same fiery arrows from her armoury. The arrows had not rusted at all. Anger could be tolerated, but for someone like Binoy, contempt was hard to bear. He recalled the sharp disdain Lalita had once felt for him, taking him for a mere satellite of Gora. He was tormented to imagine that even now, his hesitation made him appear cowardly in Lalita's eyes. He found it unbearable that though his sense of the constraints of duty may appear cowardly to Lalita, he would not have a chance to say even a few words in self-defense. To be denied the right to argue was a grave punishment for Binoy. For he knew he was a good debater, with an uncommon gift for presenting well-constructed arguments in support of a particular cause. But when Lalita quarreled with him she never gave him the chance to argue, nor would he have such a chance today.

The newspaper lay there still. Gripped by restlessness, Binoy pulled it towards him and suddenly noticed a certain section marked out in pencil. Reading, he realized that the discussion and moralizing there was directed at them both. He clearly understood the extent of the daily humiliation inflicted upon Lalita by the members of her community. Yet Binoy was making no effort to shield her from such dishonour, preoccupied only with fine arguments about social philosophy. Hence it seemed to him appropriate that a spirited woman like Lalita should treat him with disdain. Remembering Lalita's boldness in her complete disregard for society, and comparing himself with this woman ablaze with fury, he began to feel ashamed.

After her bath, having fed Satish and sent him off to school, Sucharita came to Binoy and found him sitting in silence. She did not raise the former subject. Before his meal of rice, Binoy did not perform the gandush ritual of chanting mantras over cupped handfuls of water.

'Tell me, bachha,' said Harimohini, 'you don't observe any Hindu rituals after all, so what harm in becoming a Brahmo?'

Binoy was privately rather offended. 'The day you take Hinduism for mere observance of meaningless purity-rituals, I shall adopt the Brahmo, Christian, Muslim or any other faith you please,' he declared. 'But I still haven't developed such disrespect for Hinduism.'

Binoy emerged from Sucharita's house in an extremely dejected frame of mind, as if he had been buffeted about in all directions and arrived at a void with no refuge. He could not claim his former place by Gora's side, yet Lalita too was keeping him at arm's length. Even with Harimohini, his close relationship was on the verge of rapid dissolution. Borodasundari had once cherished a heartfelt affection for him and Poreshbabu loved him still, but in return for their affection he had brought such turbulence into their home that he had no place there either. Binoy was always hungry for the respect and affection of those he loved, and he also had considerable power to engage their hearts in diverse ways. How he came to be suddenly cast out now from his familiar trajectory of love and friendship, was something he began to privately ask himself. Now that he had left Sucharita's house, he could not think where to go next. Once he could have easily and unthinkingly made his way to Gora's home, but now he no longer had natural access there as before. If he went there he must remain silent in Gora's presence, and such silence was utterly unbearable. Meanwhile, Poreshbabu's home was not easy for him to access, either.

'How did I arrive at such an unnatural situation!' wondered Binoy as he walked slowly down the road with bowed head. When he reached the Hedua pond, he sank beneath a tree. So far, whenever a problem had arisen, large or small, he had solved it by discussing it with his friend, arguing about it. But now that path was not open to him, and he must think for himself.

Binoy did not lack powers of introspection. It was not easy for him to absolve himself by blaming everything on outward events. Hence, thinking in solitude, he concluded that he alone was to blame. 'In this world, I can't afford to be so cunning as to have something without paying its price,' he thought to himself. 'Whenever we seek to choose something, we must renounce something else. A person who can't decide to surrender any option will end up like me, rejected by all. Those who have firmly chosen their path of life are the ones who have found contentment. The unfortunate wretch who loves this path and that one as well, unable to deprive himself of either, is denied the destination itself, and is left wandering like a street dog.'

Diagnosing an ailment is difficult, but it is not as if treatment becomes easy as soon as the diagnosis is made. Binoy's understanding was extremely sharp; it was power of action that he lacked. Hence until now he had depended upon his friend, a person of much firmer resolve. Ultimately, at this very difficult moment, he had suddenly discovered that even if one lacks will-power, one can handle small matters by borrowing from others, but in times of real need, one can never do business by proxy.

As the sun declined, the shade was replaced by sunshine. He now left his shelter beneath the tree and took to the road again. He had not gone far when he suddenly heard someone call:

'Binoybabu! Binoybabu!' The next moment, Satish came and grasped his hand. He was returning home from school after his lessons.

'Come Binoybabu, come home with me,' Satish pleaded.

'How is that possible, Satishbabu?'

'Why not?'

'If I visit so frequently, how would your family members tolerate me?'

'No, come with me,' insisted Satish, deeming Binoy's argument utterly unworthy of any reply.

The boy had no inkling about the immense revolution that had occurred in Binoy's relationship with his family; he just loved Binoy. Realizing this, Binoy felt deeply perturbed. In the paradise that Poreshbabu's family had become for Binoy, it was only in this boy that the quality of bliss had remained complete and unaffected. In these stormy days, no cloud of doubt had shadowed his mind, no social onslaught had tried to destroy his moorings.

'Come bhai,' said Binoy, putting his arm around Satish's neck. 'Let's see you to your doorstep.' Embracing Satish, Binoy seemed to feel the sweet touch of all the love and affection that Satish had received from Sucharita and Lalita since his infancy. All along the way, Satish's unceasing, irrelevant chatter showered honey upon Binoy's ears.

In contact with the boy's simplicity of heart, Binoy could briefly become oblivious to the complicated problems of his life.

They had to cross Poreshbabu's house on their way to Sucharita's. His sitting-room on the ground floor was visible from the road. When they arrived before that room, Binoy could not refrain from raising his head to glance at it once. He saw Poreshbabu at his table, but it was not clear whether he was speaking; and close to his chair on a small cane mora, her back to the street, was Lalita, silent as a pupil. Having no other means of quelling the petulance and wounded pride that had tormented her unbearably since she returned from Sucharita's house, Lalita had crept to Poreshbabu's side. There was such an air of perfect peace within Poreshbabu that the impatient Lalita sometimes came and sat quietly by his side, to control her own restlessness.

'What is it, Lalita?' Poreshbabu would ask.

'Nothing, Baba,' she would reply. 'This room of yours is very cool.'

On this occasion, Poreshbabu clearly sensed that Lalita had come to him with a wounded heart. A feeling of pain had also made him inwardly depressed. Hence he had gently broached a subject that could lighten the burden of trivial personal joys and sorrows.

The sight of this inaudible dialogue between father and daughter brought Binoy to a momentary halt. He did not hear what Satish was saying. The boy was asking him a very complicated question about war strategy. He wondered what the chances of victory might be if one's own side placed a pride of tigers in the frontline after giving them prolonged training. So far their question-and-answer session had proceeded unhindered; now, at this sudden interruption, Satish glanced at Binoy's face. Then, following Binoy's gaze, he looked towards Poreshbabu's room and cried out loudly:

'Lalitadidi, Lalitadidi, look! I have captured Binoybabu from the street!'

Embarrassed, Binoy broke out in a sweat. Within the room, Lalita instantly sprang to her feet. Poreshbabu turned around to look at the street. Altogether, the situation took a dramatically awkward turn. Having dispatched Satish, Binoy stepped into the house. Entering Poreshbabu's room, he found Lalita gone. Imagining that everyone saw him as a disruptive intruder, he awkwardly took a chair. As soon as they had finished exchanging customary polite queries about their mutual welfare, Binoy took the plunge:

'Since I don't respect the restrictions imposed by Hindu society and violate their laws daily, I consider it my duty to seek refuge in the Brahmo Samaj. It is from you I wish to receive my initiation.'

This desire and this resolve had not taken clear shape in Binoy's even fifteen minutes earlier.

'You have considered everything carefully I hope?' asked Poreshbabu after a moment's silence.

'There is nothing left to consider,' Binoy insisted. 'One need only consider the fairness or unfairness of it. That is a very simple matter. Given our education, I certainly cannot honestly accept that mere rituals and restrictions constitute inviolate faith. That is why at every step my conduct shows a lack of decorum; by remaining involved with those who respectfully follow Hindu custom, I only succeed in hurting them. I have no doubt that this is extremely wrong of me. In these circumstances, I must be ready to abjure such wrong conduct, without considering anything else. Otherwise I cannot retain my self-respect.'

There was no need to explain at such length to Poreshbabu, but he said all this only to fortify himself. Declaring that he was caught in a battle between right and wrong and that he must sacrifice everything to ensure victory for what was right, he puffed his chest in pride. After all, he must sustain the dignity of human life.

'In questions of religious faith, your opinions coincide with those of the Brahmo Samaj I hope?' Poreshbabu inquired.

'Truth be told,' confessed Binoy after a short silence, 'I used to believe earlier that I possessed religious faith of some sort, and I even quarreled with a lot of people on these issues. But now I have understood with certainty that in my life, the quality of spiritual faith remains imperfectly developed. This I have realized from observing you. I have never felt a true need for religion in my life and have developed no true belief in dharma. Therefore, all these days, I have used my imagination and debating skills to create fine arguments, reducing our community's religious practices to mere rhetoric. I never need to consider which form of faith is true; the faith that brings victory to me is the one I have propagated. The harder it is to prove, the greater my pride in proving it. Even now, I can't say whether spiritual belief will ever take root in my mind in a perfectly true and natural way, but given favourable circumstances and good example, I'm certainly likely to advance in that direction. At least, I shall be spared the degradation of forever carrying the insignia of something that inwardly perturbs my intellect.'

As he spoke to Poreshbabu, Binoy began to concretize the arguments favouring his own present situation. He spoke with much enthusiasm as if after long debate he had arrived at this firm, definite conclusion. Still Poreshbabu urged him to take some more time to consider. Imagining that Poreshbabu had doubts about the firmness of his resolve, Binoy grew even more obdurate. He reiterated that his thoughts had arrived at a point beyond all doubt, that there was no likelihood of his wavering in the slightest. Neither side mentioned the subject of his marriage to Lalita.

Borodasundari now entered the room to perform some household chore. Completing the task at hand, she prepared to leave the room as if Binoy was not present there. Binoy had expected Poreshbabu to immediately send for Borodasundari to tell her the latest news. But Poreshbabu said nothing at all. Actually, he had not even judged the time ripe for disclosing the matter, still keen to keep it concealed from everyone. But when Borodasundari, exuding contempt and rage against Binoy, was about to leave the room, Binoy could not contain himself. With bent head he touched Borodasundari's feet as she was about to depart, and said:

'I have come to you all today with a request to join the Brahmo Samaj. I'm unworthy, but I depend upon all of you to make me worthy.' Hearing this, the astonished Borodasundari turned around, and slowly came into the room. She looked questioningly at Poreshbabu.

'Binoy requests intitiation,' Poreshabu informed her.

Hearing this, Borodasundari felt the triumph of victory indeed, but why was she not completely happy? Inwardly, she keenly desired that this time, Poreshbabu should really learn a lesson. Having repeatedly and vehemently predicted that her husband would have cause for deep remorse, she was privately losing patience with Poreshbabu for not being sufficiently perturbed at the turmoil within their community. At this point, Borodasundari did not feel unalloyed pleasure in finding all their problems so nicely solved.

'If this proposal had come a few days earlier, all of us would have been spared so much humiliation and suffering!' she pronounced severely.

'Our pain, suffering or humiliation is not the issue here,' Poreshbabu reminded her. 'Binoy wants to be initiated.'

'Initiation, is that all?' Borodasundari demanded.

'The all-knowing One knows that your suffering and humiliation are also entirely mine,' Binoy assured her.

'Look here, Binoy,' cautioned Poreshbabu, 'don't trivialize the fact that you are seeking initiation into dharma. I have told you this once before—don't take any serious step just because you imagine we are caught in a difficult social predicament.'

'True indeed,' assented Borodasundari. 'All the same, it's not his duty either to sit idle after getting us entangled in a net.'

'If one struggles instead of remaining still, the knots in the net grow even tighter,' countered Poreshbabu. 'Not that action is itself a duty; often, our greatest duty is to do nothing at all.'

'That may be true,' said Borodasundari. 'I'm illiterate, not always able to understand everything properly. But I want to know what's been decided at present. I have lots to do.'

'I shall join the faith on Sunday itself, the day after tomorrow,' asserted Binoy. 'I hope Poreshbabu . . .'

'I can't perform an initiation rite where my family may expect to benefit from it,' demurred Poreshbabu. 'You must apply to the Brahmo Samaj.'

Binoy at once grew hesitant. He was in no frame of mind to apply formally to the Brahmo Samaj, particularly when so much had been said by the community about his relationship with Lalita. Did he have the humility, or the words, to write to them? When that letter was published in the Brahmo newsletter, how would he show his face in public? Gora would read that letter, and so would Anandamoyi. There would be no other background information accompanying that letter; it would only publicize the fact that Binoy's soul was suddenly thirsting for initiation into the Brahmo dharma. That was not entirely true after all. Unless this fact was seen in relation to other things, Binoy would be left with no shred of protection from shame. Observing Binoy's silence, Borodasundari grew anxious.

'But he knows nobody in the Brahmo Samaj,' she argued. 'We shall make all the arrangements ourselves. I shall send for Panubabu right away. There's no time left, Sunday is the day after tomorrow.'

Just then they saw Sudhir pass by the room on his way upstairs.

'Sudhir, Binoy will join our Samaj the day after tomorrow,' Borodasundari called out to him.

Sudhir was delighted. Being secretly devoted to Binoy, he was greatly enthused to hear that he would become part of the Brahmo Samaj. Binoy's written English was so fluent, he was so well read and intelligent, that Sudhir used to consider it extremely inappropriate for him not to be a member of the Samaj. Having found proof that a person like Binoy was unable to remain outside the Brahmo Samaj, Sudhir swelled with pride.

'But what can we accomplish by the day after tomorrow?' he protested. 'The news would not have reached many people by then.' Sudhir wanted to proclaim Binoy's conversion to the general public, by way of example.

'No, no, it will be done this very Sunday,' Borodasundari insisted. 'Run along, Sudhir, fetch Panubabu quickly.'

As for the unfortunate wretch whose example Sudhir excitedly wished to publicize as proof of the Brahmo Samaj's invincibility, his heart was by then cringing in acute embarrassment. Seeing the outward appearance of something that he privately regarded as little more than mere rhetoric,

Binoy grew desperate. As soon as Panubabu was sent for, he rose to take his leave.

'Wait a bit,' pleaded Borodasundari. 'Panubabu will be here in no time. He won't take long.'

'No,' insisted Binoy, 'please excuse me.' He was desperate to escape this confinement, for a chance to think things over carefully in private.

As soon as Binoy stood up, Poreshbabu arose as well. 'Binoy, don't do anything in a hurry,' he urged, placing a hand on his shoulder. 'Be calm, be steady, and think over everything. Don't proceed with such an important step in your life without fully understanding your own mind.'

'First, nobody thinks before acting!' protested Borodasundari, secretly very displeased with her husband. 'They create a mess, and then, once the situation becomes suffocating, you say, "sit down and think!" You people may think calmly, but we can't bear it anymore.'

Sudhir accompanied Binoy out into the street. He was restless, like someone longing to taste the food even before sitting down to a meal. He wished he could drag Binoy at once to his own circle of friends, to break the good news and begin the celebrations. But the onslaught of Sudhir's elation disheartened Binoy even further. When Sudhir proposed: 'Binoybabu, why not come with me? Let's go to Panubabu, the two of us together,' Binoy ignored his words and snatching his hand away, he left the scene. He had gone only a short distance when he saw Abinash hurrying somewhere with a couple of members of his group.

'Here you are Binoybabu,' exclaimed Abinash as soon as he saw him. 'Excellent! Come with us please.'

'Where are you going?'

'We are going to prepare the garden estate at Kashipur. A gathering will take place there for Gourmohanbabu's penance.'

'No, I can't get away now,' Binoy demurred.

'How is that possible!' protested Abinash. 'Do you realize, all of you, what a major event this is going to be? Else would Gourmohanbabu have made such a needless proposal? In today's world, the Hindu community must express its might. What an upheaval this penance of Gourmohanbabu's will create in the hearts of our countrymen! We'll invite great learned Brahman sages from all over the world. This will have a major impact on the Hindu community. People will realize that we are still alive. They will understand that the Hindu community is indestructible!'

Evading Abinash's allurements, Binoy went away.

## 56

When Borodasundari sent for Haranbabu and told him everything, he remained gravely silent for a while, then said:

'It is my duty to discuss this with Lalita once.' When Lalita appeared, Haranbabu put on his severest expression and declared: 'Look here Lalita, you have arrived at a moment of great responsibility in your life. Your faith on one side, and your inclinations on the other—between these two, you must choose your path.' Pausing, Haranbabu fixed his gaze on Lalita's face. He was aware that this gaze of his, ablaze with the fire of justice, made cowardice quail and deceit turn to ashes. His radiant spiritual gaze was one of the precious possessions of the Brahmo Samaj.

Lalita said nothing. She remained silent.

'Perhaps you have heard,' Haranbabu continued, 'that either out of concern for your predicament, or for whatever reason, Binoybabu has finally agreed to be initiated into the Brahmo Samaj.'

Lalita had neither heard this news before, nor did she express her feelings upon hearing it. Her eyes lit up. She remained still as a stone statue.

'Doubtless Poreshbabu is delighted at Binoy's compliance,' Haranbabu observed. 'But it is for you to decide whether there is any real cause for rejoicing in this. Therefore on behalf of the Brahmo Samaj I request you now to set aside your own wild inclinations and ask your heart, fixing your gaze only on your dharma—is this any real cause for joy?'

Still Lalita was silent. Haranbabu thought his arguments were working very well. 'Initiation!' he pursued, with redoubled enthusiasm. 'Must I now explain how sacred is the moment of initiation? Would you pollute that very idea of initiation! Seduced by pleasure, convenience or attachment, should we allow the untrue to enter the Brahmo Samaj and invite deceit into our midst with pomp and ceremony! Tell me Lalita, must your life be forever associated with this history of the degradation of the Brahmo Samaj?'

Still Lalita said nothing. Gripping the chair handle, she remained completely still.

'I have often witnessed how weakness attacks human beings invincibly, using attachment as a loophole,' Haranbabu continued. 'And I also know how to forgive human weakness. But you tell me Lalita, can one for a single instant forgive the weakness that attacks not only one's own life, but the very foundation of a hundred thousand lives? Has Ishwar given us the right to forgive such a thing?'

Lalita rose from her chair. 'No, no, Panubabu,' she cried, 'please don't forgive us. People the world over have grown used to your attacks, but your forgiveness I think would be too much for anyone to bear.' With these words Lalita left the room.

Haranbabu's words made Borodasundari very anxious. She could not release Binoy now, under any circumstances. After many futile pleas, she ultimately lost her temper and sent Haranbabu away. Her problem was that she had neither Poreshbabu nor Haranbabu on her side. Nobody could have imagined such an unthinkable situation. It was now time for Borodasundari to change her mind again about Haranbabu.

As long as Binoy remained vague about the prospect of initiation, he had been expressing his resolve very strongly. But when he discovered that he must apply to the Brahmo Samaj and that Haranbabu would be consulted in the matter, he grew extremely perturbed at the threat of such open publicity. He could not think where to go, or whom to consult. It even seemed impossible for him to approach Anandamoyi. Nor had he the strength to roam the streets. So he went to his empty home and lay down on the woodplank bed in the room upstairs.

It was almost dark. When the attendant brought a light into the dark chamber, Binoy was about to forbid him when he heard someone call from downstairs:

'Binoybabu! Binoybabu!'

Binoy heaved a sigh of relief, as if he had found water to quench his thirst in the desert. At this moment, no one but Satish could have brought him solace. Binoy overcame his listlessness.

'What is it, bhai Satish?' he answered, jumping up from the bed and rushing downstairs without even putting on his shoes.

In his tiny courtyard, facing the stairs, he saw Borodasundari standing with Satish. Again the same problems, the same conflict! Flustered, Binoy led Satish and Borodasundari to the room upstairs.

'Satish, go sit in that veranda for a while,' ordered Borodasundari.

Pained at Satish's joyless exile, Binoy took out some picture books for him and settled him in the adjacent room, lighting the lamp there.

'Binoy, you don't know anyone in the Brahmo Samaj. Let me carry a letter from you, which I shall deliver personally to the editor tomorrow morning, to arrange everything so your initiation ceremony takes place this very Sunday, the day after tomorrow. You need have no further worries.'

Borodasundari's proposal left Binoy speechless. Under her directions, he wrote out a letter and handed it to her. He needed to take up some course of action, no matter what, so it would become impossible for him to retract or hesitate.

Borodasundari also left some hints about his marrying Lalita. When she had departed, Binoy began to experience a tremendous feeling of distaste. Even the memory of Lalita struck a rather discordant note in his heart. He began to feel that Lalita too had something to do with this unseemly haste on Borodasundari's part. Along with his own loss of self-esteem, his respect for everyone else seemed to diminish as well.

As soon as she was home, Borodasundari thought she would delight Lalita. That Lalita loved Binoy she had understood for certain. That was why their prospective marriage had stirred up such trouble within the community. At that time she had blamed everyone but herself. For a few days she had more or less stopped speaking to Lalita. So, now that a solution had been found, she was eager to take major credit for it, in order to achieve a reconciliation with Lalita. Lalita's father had virtually ruined everything, after all. Lalita herself had not been able to tackle Binoy. Nor had they got any help from Panubabu. Borodasundari had cut through all the knotty problems, all by herself. Yes, yes indeed! What a woman alone could accomplish was beyond the capacity of five men.

When she came home, Borodasundari was informed that Lalita had retired early tonight, as she was not feeling too well. 'I shall help her recover,' Borodasundari smiled to herself. Lamp in hand, she entered the dark bedchamber to find Lalita not yet in bed but reclining instead in an armchair.

'Ma, where had you gone?' she demanded, sitting up at once. She had heard that Borodasundari had accompanied Satish to Binoy's house.

'I had gone to Binoy's place.'

'Why?'

Why! Borodasundari was privately rather annoyed. 'Lalita imagines that I am always working against her, as her enemy! How ungrateful!' she thought.

'See why!' she said, and held out Binoy's letter, letting it unfold before Lalita's eyes. As she read the letter, Lalita's face grew flushed. To publicize her own achievements, Borodasundari informed her with some exaggeration that extracting this letter from Binoy had been no easy matter. She could claim with confidence that such a feat was beyond the powers of any other human being.

Covering her face with both hands, Lalita fell back into her armchair. Borodasundari imagined she was too shy to express the intensity of her emotions in front of her mother. She left the room.

The next morning, when it was time to carry the letter to the Brahmo Samaj, Borodasundari found that someone had torn it to shreds.

## 57

As Sucharita was getting ready to visit Poreshbabu in the afternoon, the attendant announced a visitor, a babu.

'Which babu? Binoybabu?'

'No, a very fair, tall babu.'

Sucharita started. 'Bring the babu upstairs,' she said.

Until then, she had not even noticed what she was wearing or how she had draped her sari. But now, standing before her mirror, she found she did not like her own attire. There was no time to change. Hands shaking, she tidied her sari aanchal and her hair, then entered the room with a trembling heart. She had completely forgotten that Gora's collected works were lying on her table. Gora sat on a chair directly facing that very table. The books lay shamelessly, in front of his eyes; there was no means of concealing or removing them.

'Mashima has been anxiously waiting for you all these days. Let me send for her.' With these words, Sucharita left the room immediately after entering it. She could not find the strength to converse alone with Gora. After a while she reappeared, accompanied by Harimohini. For some time now, Harimohini had been hearing Binoy's accounts of Gora's convictions, devotion to duty, and way of life. Often, in the afternoon, at her request, Sucharita had been reading Gora's writings to her. Not that Harimohini completely understood those pieces. Actually, they helped her to doze off. Still, she could more or less gather that Gora was fighting in support of the scriptures and social customs, against the present-day disregard for rituals. For a modern, English-educated boy, what could be more extraordinary, or more creditable! When she had first seen Binoy in the midst of a Brahmo family, it was he who had brought her a great deal of comfort. But having gradually grown accustomed to this, when she began to observe Binoy in her own household, what she noticed with great displeasure were the lapses in his observance of restrictions. It was because she had come to depend heavily on Binoy that her rejection of him grew more pronounced with each passing day. That was why she had been so eagerly awaiting Gora's arrival.

As soon as she saw Gora, Harimohini was utterly amazed. Here was a Brahman indeed! Like the sacrificial hom fire personified. Like Lord Shiva with his white body. She felt such a surge of devotion within, that when Gora touched her feet in obeisance, Harimohini was embarrassed to accept his pranam.

'I have heard a lot about you, baba!' Harimohini told him. 'Are you Gour? Gour indeed, so fair! I'm reminded of that kirtan song:

*With moon's ambrosia and sandal paste,*
*O who has polished Gora's form . . .*

Today I see it with my own eyes. How did they have the heart to throw you jail, I wonder!'

'If people like you became magistrates, rats and bats would nest in our prisons,' smiled Gora.

'No baba,' protested Harimohini, 'is there any lack of thieves and scoundrels in this world? Didn't the magistrate have eyes in his head? One only has to glance at your face to see you're no ordinary person, that you're chosen by the Almighty Ishwar. Must you be sent to prison just because prisons exist? Baap re! What sort of justice is this!'

'Magistrates look only at law-books when they apply the law, lest they confront the Almighty's image in the faces of human beings,' Gora replied. 'Otherwise, having condemned human beings to flogging, imprisonment, exile or the noose, could they enjoy sleep or the taste of rice?'

'Whenever I get a chance, I make Radharani read aloud from your books,' Harimohini informed him. 'All these days, I was waiting hopefully for the day I could hear all sorts of wonderful words from your own lips. I am an illiterate woman, and very unfortunate; I don't comprehend everything, nor can I concentrate on all things. But I'm deeply convinced, baba, that I shall learn something from you.'

Gora maintained a polite silence, without contradicting her.

'Baba, you must have a bite before you leave,' Harimohini persisted. 'It's been a long time since I fed a Brahman's son like you. Today, just taste what sweets are at hand, but you are invited to dine properly at my place another day.' When Harimohini went away to arrange some refreshments, Sucharita's heart began to race.

'Did Binoy come here today?' Gora began directly.

'Yes.'

'I have not met Binoy since, but I know why he came here.'

Gora paused. Sucharita also remained silent.

'You people are trying to get Binoy married according to Brahmo customs,' Gora continued. 'Is that a good idea?'

At this jibe, all the constraints of diffidence or shyness vanished from Sucharita's mind.

'Do you expect me to consider a Brahmo wedding improper?' she demanded, lifting her eyes to look at him directly.

'I have no small expectations of you, that's for sure,' Gora retorted. 'I expect much more of you than what may be expected from a member of some community. I can assert with great certainty that you don't belong to the category of labour leaders who care only about swelling the numbers of a particular party. It is my desire that you too should understand yourself properly. Please don't be misled by others into underestimating yourself. You are not merely an ordinary member of some party: this you yourself must realize clearly, within your own heart.'

Sucharita summoned up all her mental strength to remain alert and firm. 'Aren't you a member of some party too?' she asked.

'I am a Hindu. Hindus are not a party after all. Hindus are a community. So immense is this community, it is impossible to express its essence by confining it to any label. Just as the ocean can't be described by its waves, Hindus can't be described as a party either.'

'If Hindus are not a party, why do they resort to party politics?'

'When you try to kill a man, why does he try to defend himself? Because he has a living spirit. Only a lifeless stone would lie passive in the face of all assaults.'

'If Hindus take for an assault what I understand to be my faith, what would you advise me to do?'

'I would urge you that, since what you consider your duty is a painful assault on the great entity called the Hindu community, you must ponder very carefully whether there is some delusion or blindness within yourself, and whether you have contemplated everything from all angles, in every way. It is not proper to cause such a great disruption, taking the customs of one's own party to be the truth, through sheer force of habit or out of laziness. When a rat begins to nibble away at a ship's hull, it goes merely by its own convenience or natural instincts; it does not realize that boring a hole through such a great refuge will cause far greater harm to everyone else than the little bit of ease it will gain for the rat itself. Similarly, you too must consider whether you are thinking only of your own party or of humanity as a whole. Humanity as a whole—do you realize the magnitude of what that signifies? How diverse are the natures, tendencies and needs that it encompasses? All human beings do not occupy the same position on the same trajectory—some confront mountains, some face oceans, others open fields. Yet no one can afford to remain idle; everyone must move on. Do you want to impose your own party's sole authority upon everyone else? Do you wish to turn a blind eye, imagining there's no diversity among human beings, that everyone is born into this world only to enlist with the Brahmo Samaj? Those brigand races who believe it's best for the world if they vanquish all other races to extend their sole empire, who are too arrogant about their own power to admit that the distinctiveness of other races is of priceless benefit to the world, who spread only slavery across the world—how are you people different from them?'

For a moment Sucharita forgot all her arguments. Gora's voice, deep as thunder, swayed her entire soul with an extraordinary force. She forgot Gora was arguing about something, aware only that he was speaking.

'It is not your Samaj alone that has created the twenty crore people of Bharatvarsha,' Gora continued. 'On what grounds do you seek to utterly flatten out this vast Bharatvarsha, by forcibly seizing the responsibility of decreeing which course of action is suitable for these twenty crores, or which beliefs and practices would ensure sustenance and strength for all of them! The greater the hindrances you encounter in your impossible attempt, the more angry and disrespectful you will feel towards your own country, and the more your contempt will alienate the very people you wish to help! Yet, the Lord who made human beings so diverse, who wishes to preserve their diversity, is the very One you imagine that you worship. If all of you truly believe in Him, why are you unable to recognize his decree? Why does pride in your own intelligence and your own party prevent you from accepting its significance?'

Observing that Sucharita was listening in silence without trying to offer any reply, Gora felt sorry for her. He paused, then continued in a gentler tone:

'Perhaps my words strike you as harsh. But don't view me with hostility as a member of the enemy camp. Had I perceived you as an enemy I would not have spoken to you at all. It pains me to see your natural broad-mindedness confined within the limits of a party.'

Sucharita's face grew flushed. 'No, no,' she protested, 'don't worry about me at all. Please continue what you were saying, and I shall try to follow your argument.'

'I have nothing more to say. View Bharatvarsha through your natural intelligence and natural emotions. Love Bharatvarsha. If you see the people of Bharatvarsha as non-Brahmos you will distort their image and regard them with contempt, and constantly misunderstand them. You will never get to see them from the perspective that allows one to see them whole. The Lord has made them human; they think in many different ways, act in many different ways, follow many different beliefs and customs, but underlying all this is a basic humanity; within all this is something that belongs to me, to Bharatvarsha, something that, when viewed from a true perspective, will pierce its outward shell of pettiness and incompleteness to present before us the vision of a great, noble entity. It is infused with the spirit of long endeavour; in it I can see the ancient sacrificial fire still burning amidst all the ashes, and I have no doubt that this fire will transcend its petty location in place and time to cast up its flame at the centre of this earth. The people of this Bharatvarsha have been saying many big things for a very long time; they have accomplished many great tasks; even to imagine that all that has become utterly futile is to show disrespect for the truth, and that itself is atheism.'

Sucharita had been listening with bowed head. Now she raised her head and asked:

'What are you asking me to do?'

'Nothing,' asserted Gora, 'I only say you must understand that the Hindu faith has tried to nurture people of many attitudes, many views; in other words, the Hindu faith alone has acknowledged people as human beings, not as members of some group. The Hindu faith accepts the illiterate as well as the learned—and not just a single facet of learning, but the growth of knowledge in many dimensions. Christians don't wish to acknowledge diversity; they say there's Christianity on one side and limitless destruction on the other, with no shades of difference in between. Because we follow those Christians, we feel ashamed of the diversity of the Hindu dharma, failing to recognize that Hinduism strives to perceive the One through the medium of the many. Unless our minds break free of the fetters of Khristani learning, we cannot claim the glory of understanding the true nature of the Hindu dharma.'

It seemed to Sucharita she was not merely hearing Gora's words but seeing them manifest before her eyes; she felt Gora's contemplative gaze, fixed upon the distant future, merge with his words. Forgetting all shame, forgetting herself, she raised her eyes to Gora's face, which glowed with the intensity of his emotions. In that face Sucharita saw a power that seemed to realize the greatest resolves through its own spiritual energy. She had heard many philosophical discourses from many learned and intelligent members of her community, but Gora's utterance was no mere discourse, it resembled a new creation. It was so tangible that over time it could dominate one's whole mind and body. Today Sucharita beheld Indra, the king of deities, armed with his thunderbolt; as the words forcefully assailed her ears, shaking the very doors of her heart, she felt flashes of lightning dance through her blood from moment to moment. She no longer retained the strength to determine how far her opinions coincided with Gora's.

At this juncture, Satish entered the room. Being in awe of Gora, he avoided him and edged close to his didi. 'Panubabu is here,' he informed her in an undertone.

Sucharita started as if someone had struck her. She grew desperate to somehow push away, remove, suppress or utterly erase the fact of Panubabu's arrival. Imagining that Gora had not heard Satish's murmur, she quickly got to her feet. Rushing downstairs, she confronted Panubabu.

'Please forgive me, but it will not be convenient for me to speak to you today,' she told him directly.

'Why not?'

'If you come to Baba's place tomorrow, you may see me there,' said

Sucharita, without answering his question.

'Do you have visitors today, then?' Haranbabu inquired.

'Today I shall not have the time,' repeated Sucharita, evading this query as well. 'Please excuse me.'

'But I heard Gourmohanbabu's voice from the street,' persisted Haranbabu. 'He is here I suppose?'

Sucharita could not suppress this question. 'Yes he is,' she answered, blushing.

'All the better,' said Haranbabu. 'I needed to talk to him as well. If you are busy with something special, I can chat with Gourmohanbabu in the meantime.'

So saying, without awaiting Sucharita's consent, he began to climb the stairs. Ignoring Haranbabu's presence beside her, Sucharita entered the room and announced to Gora:

'Mashi has gone to prepare some refreshments for you. I'll just go to her.' She rushed from the scene.

Haranbabu solemnly took a chair. 'You seem to have lost some weight,' he observed.

'Yes sir, for some time now I was under treatment to make me lose some weight,' Gora replied.

'Indeed,' remarked Haranbabu, feigning concern. 'You suffered a lot.'

'No more than what's expected.'

'There is something I must discuss with you concerning Binoybabu. Perhaps you have heard that he is preparing to join the Brahmo Samaj next Sunday.'

'No, I had not heard.'

'Do you consent to it?'

'Binoy did not seek my consent after all.'

'Do you think Binoy is willing to receive this initiation out of genuine conviction?'

'Since he has agreed to receive initiation, your question is utterly redundant.'

'When our instincts grow powerful, we have no time to think about our convictions. You know what human nature is like.'

'No,' Gora declared. 'I don't engage in needless discussions on human nature.'

'We don't share the same opinions, or the same community, but I have a high regard for you. I know for sure that whatever you believe in, whether true or false, no temptation can divert you from your convictions. Yet . . .'

'What is the value of that little shred of respect you have retained for me,' interrupted Gora, 'that it would be such a great loss for Binoy to be deprived of it! Indeed there are good and bad things in this world, but while you may evaluate them if you wish according to your respect or disrespect for them, you can't tell the rest of the world to accept your judgement.'

'Very well, we need not resolve this matter immediately. But I ask you—won't you oppose Binoy's attempts to marry into Poreshbabu's family?'

'Haranbabu,' protested Gora, flushing, 'how can I discuss such things about Binoy with you? Given your constant awareness of human nature, you should also have realized that Binoy is my friend, not yours.'

'I brought up the subject because it concerns the Brahmo Samaj, or else . . .'

'But I have nothing to do with the Brahmo Samaj, so what do I care about your anxieties!'

At this moment, Sucharita entered the room.

'Sucharita,' said Haranbabu, 'I have something special to discuss with you.'

Not that he needed to say this. It was only to show Gora his special intimacy with Sucharita that Haranbabu pointedly made this remark. Sucharita made no reply. Gora remained unmoved, showing no signs of getting up to give Haranbabu a chance for private talk.

'Sucharita, come into the next room for a moment,' urged Haranbabu. 'Let me just tell you something.'

'I hope your mother is well?' Sucharita asked Gora, without answering Haranbabu.

'I have never seen Ma unwell,' Gora responded.

'I've seen how easily she finds the strength to remain well,' Sucharita observed. She remembered having met Anandamoyi while Gora was in jail.

At this point, Haranbabu suddenly picked up a book from the table, and opening it, he first glanced at the author's name before turning pages at random and running his eyes over them. Sucharita flushed. Knowing what book it was, Gora smiled faintly to himself.

'Gourmohanbabu,' asked Haranbabu, 'are these your childhood writings?'

'That childhood is not yet over,' smiled Gora. 'For some living beings, infancy is short-lived, but for others it lasts rather long.'

'Gourmohanbabu,' declared Sucharita, 'Your refreshments should be ready by now. Let's go into the other room then. Mashi will not emerge before Panubabu. Maybe she's waiting for you.' This last statement was deliberately directed against Haranbabu. She had borne a lot on this occasion, and could not help retaliating in some measure.

Gora rose to his feet.

'I'll wait, then,' declared Haranbabu, undaunted.

'Why wait in vain?' Sucharita objected. 'After this I won't have the time.'

Still Haranbabu did not arise. Sucharita and Gora left the room. Seeing Gora in this house, and observing Sucharita's behaviour towards him, Haranbabu's heart was up in arms. Would Sucharita lose her footing in the Brahmo Samaj in this fashion! Was there nobody to protect her! This must be prevented, at any cost. Snatching a piece of paper, Haranbabu began composing a letter to Sucharita. He had a few fixed notions, one being that when he reprimanded people in the name of truth, his fiery words could not fail to have effect. He did not even consider that apart from words alone, there was also something called the human heart.

After a long chat with Harimohini at the end of his meal, when Gora entered Sucharita's room to collect his walking stick, it was almost dark. A lamp had been lit on Sucharita's desk. Haranbabu had departed. A letter addressed to Sucharita lay upon the table, prominently visible immediately upon entering the room. The sight of that letter instantly hardened Gora's heart. It was undoubtedly written by Haranbabu. Gora knew Haranbabu had a special claim upon Sucharita; he was unaware that this claim had been eroded in any way. Today, when Satish whispered to Sucharita about Haranbabu's arrival, and the startled Sucharita rushed downstairs to reappear shortly with Haranbabu in tow, Gora's heart had been struck by a very discordant note. Subsequently, when Sucharita left Haranbabu alone in the room and took Gora downstairs for refreshments, her behaviour certainly appeared rude, but thinking that intimacy might permit such conduct, Gora had taken it for the sign of a close relationship. After that, the sight of that letter lying on the table was a heavy blow for Gora. A letter is a very mysterious thing. Because it displays only the name on the outside, concealing everything else within, it can torment a person needlessly.

'I shall come tomorrow,' Gora announced, glancing at Sucharita's face.

'Very well,' replied Sucharita, with downcast eyes.

On the point of leaving, Gora paused suddenly.

'Your place is in the solar system of Bharatvarsha,' he declared. 'You belong to my own country; we can never allow some comet to sweep you away on its tail, whirling you off into empty space! Where you truly belong, there must I place you firmly on a pedestal, only then shall I desist. These people have persuaded you that your notion of truth, your dharma, would forsake you in that place; but I tell you clearly, your notion of truth, your dharma, does not merely consist of opinions or words belonging to you or a few others. It is entangled in every direction with the strands of countless lives; one cannot uproot it from the forest and transplant it into a flowerpot at will. If you wish to keep it sparkling and alive, to bring it to complete fulfilment, then you must assume the position assigned to you long before your birth, at the heart of popular society. You cannot afford to say: "I am unfamiliar with it, unrelated to it in any way." Should you say such a thing, your idea of truth, your dharma, your power, will fade like a shadow. If your opinions drag you away from the position assigned to you by the Almighty, whatever that position may be, I can convince you for sure that your opinions will never triumph. I shall come tomorrow.'

With these words, Gora left the scene. For a long time afterward, the air inside the room seemed to resonate. Sucharita remained motionless as a statue.

# 58

'Look Ma,' Binoy told Anandamoyi, 'Truth be told, whenever I have offered pranam in obeisance to an idol, I have inwardly felt a strange sense of shame, which I have suppressed. On the contrary, I have written wonderful essays in praise of idol worship. But to tell you the truth, when I have bowed at the idol's feet, my inner heart has not acquiesced.'

'As if your heart is so simple!' declared Anandamoyi. 'You cannot take a broad view of anything. In every matter, you look for finer nuances. That is why you can never shed your fussiness.'

'True indeed. Because I have such fineness of perception, I can use hair-splitting arguments to prove even what I don't believe in. I deceive myself as well as others as it suits me. All my arguments about religion so far have been prompted not by faith but by partisanship.'

'That's what happens when one has no real attachment to dharma,' Anandmoyi asserted. 'Then even dharma, like family, social prestige and wealth, becomes a matter of pride.'

'Yes, we no longer perceive it as dharma in general, but as our own personal dharma, fighting our battles for its sake. That's what I too have been doing all these days. Still, it's not as if I can completely deceive myself. Because I pretend faith where belief fails me, I have always felt ashamed of myself.'

'Don't I know that! From the fact that you all go to such extremes, beyond the ordinary, it is clear that you are forced to use many resources to fill the void in your hearts. Where faith comes easy, one need not go to such lengths.'

'That is why I have come to ask you whether it is good to pretend that I believe in something that does not inspire my faith,' said Binoy.

'Just listen to him! What sort of question is that?'

'Ma, I'm going to formally join the Brahmo Samaj the day after tomorrow.'

'What's this you say, Binoy!' Anandamoyi exclaimed. 'Where is the need to seek formal initiation?'

'That need is what I was trying to explain all this while, Ma!'

'Can't you remain within our community and still keep your faith in whatever you believe in?'

'To remain, I would have to resort to deceit.'

'Don't you have the courage to remain with us sans deceit? The members of our community will make you suffer, but can't you withstand that?'

'Ma, if I don't follow the dictates of the Hindu community, then . . .'

'If three hundred and thirty-three crores of opinions can prevail within the Hindu community, why should your opinions not be acceptable too?'

'But Ma, if members of our community were to say, "You are not a Hindu," can I still insist that "I am a Hindu"?'

'People in our community call me a Khristan, after all. In practice, indeed, I don't eat with them. But still, just because they call me a Khristan, I don't assume I must accept what they say. When I know something to be right, I consider it wrong to run away and hide myself on that account.'

Binoy was about to reply, but before he could say anything, Anandamoyi interrupted: 'Binoy, I shan't let you argue; this is no matter for argument. Can you conceal anything from me, after all? I can see you're trying to forcibly delude yourself on the pretext of arguing with me. But don't plan those false tactics in such a grave matter.'

'But Ma,' said Binoy, hanging his head, 'I have promised in writing that I shall accept my initiation tomorrow.'

'That cannot be allowed. If you explain to Poreshbabu, he will never urge you to proceed.'

'Poreshbabu has no enthusiasm for my initiation; he is not participating in the ritual.'

'Then you have nothing to worry about.'

'No Ma, the matter has been decided, and can't be reversed. Never.'

'Have you told Gora?'

'I haven't met Gora.'

'Why not?' asked Anandamoyi. 'Is Gora not at home now?'

'No, I hear he has gone to Sucharita's.'

'But he went there yesterday!' exclaimed Anandamoyi in surprise.

'He has gone there today as well.'

At that moment, they heard palki bearers approach the yard. Expecting the visitor to be some female relative of Anandamoyi's, Binoy went out.

Lalita came in and touched Anandamoyi's feet in a pranam. Anandamoyi had not expected her to come there that day, under any circumstances. Looking at her face in surprise, she at once realized that Lalita had come to her because of some problem concerning Binoy's initiation.

'Ma, I am delighted to see you here,' said Anandamoyi, to give Lalita a chance to raise the subject. 'Binoy was here a moment ago. Tomorrow he is to join your community. That's what we were talking about.'

'Why must he seek initiation?' Lalita burst out. 'Is there any need?'

'Is there no need, Ma?' asked Anandamoyi, astounded.

'I can't think of any.'

Unable to fathom Lalita's intentions, Anandamoyi stared at her in silence.

'It is demeaning for him to suddenly seek initiation in this way,' continued Lalita, hanging her head. 'Why is he accepting such humiliation?'

'Why'! Didn't Lalita know why? Did she have no cause to rejoice?

'Tomorrow is the date set for his initiation. He has given his word,' said Anandamoyi. 'Now it is beyond his power to change it, so Binoy told me.'

'In such matters one's word means nothing,' declared Lalita, fixing her burning gaze on Anandamoyi's face. 'If change is necessary, it must be allowed.'

'Ma, don't be shy with me,' Anandamoyi coaxed her. 'Let me be completely open with you. All this while I was trying to persuade Binoy that whatever his religious beliefs, he should not, and need not, abandon his community. I'm not sure he himself is blind to the fact, whatever he might say. But ma, you are not unaware of his feelings. Surely he knows that he can't be united with you unless he leaves his own society. Don't be shy ma, tell me honestly if that's true?'

'Ma, I shan't be shy with you at all,' said Lalita, raising her head to look at Anandamoyi. 'I tell you I don't believe in all these things. I have thought things over very thoroughly. Whatever a person's religion, faith or community might be, it can never be possible that people can only come together by erasing all those things. In that case, there can be no friendship between Hindus and Christians either. Then we might as well raise high walls and keep each community confined within its own separate fence.'

'Ah, your words make me very happy!' beamed Anandamoyi. 'That's exactly what I say. One person's appearance, talents and nature may not match another's but that doesn't prevent a union between two persons; so why should a difference of opinion stand between them? Ma, you have brought me great relief, for I was very worried about Binoy. I know he has surrendered his whole heart to you people; he could never bear it if his relationship with all of you were affected in any way. The Lord alone knows how it pained me to oppose him. But how fortunate he is! It is no trifling matter that you should so easily dispel such a grave threat to him! Let me ask you a question: have you discussed this matter with Poreshbabu at all?'

'No I haven't,' confessed Lalita, suppressing her embarrassment. 'But I know he will understand everything.'

'If he wasn't capable of that, from where would you have imbibed such intelligence and strength of mind? Ma, let me send for Binoy; you should come to a direct understanding with him. Let me take this opportunity to tell you something ma: I have seen Binoy since he was ever so small. He is the kind of boy about whom I can say emphatically if you all suffer any pain on his account, he will make that suffering entirely worthwhile. How often I have wondered, who is there so fortunate as to gain Binoy's hand! Now and then a proposal has come our way, but I have not liked anyone! But today I see that he is no less fortunate.' With these words, Anandamoyi chucked Lalita under the chin and kissed her own fingers in a gesture of affection. Then she sent for Binoy. Leaving Lachhmia in the room on some pretext, she went away to arrange some refreshments for Lalita.

Now there was no room for embarrassment between Lalita and Binoy. The demands of the difficult situation threatening their lives made them see their mutual relationship in natural and significant terms; no haze of emotion came between them like a coloured screen. Without any discussion, they unhesitatingly accepted, humbly and solemnly, that their hearts were united and that like the rivers Ganga and Yamuna the twin streams of their lives were about to merge at a holy junction. Society had not called upon them to unite; no belief had brought them together; theirs was no artificial bond. Aware of this, they perceived their union as a merging of dharmas, in a faith that was immensely simple, that did not squabble over small things, that could not be obstructed by any panchayat pundit.

'I can't bear the dishonour of your bending and belittling yourself in order to have me,' declared Lalita, her eyes and countenance aglow. 'I want you to stand firm exactly where you are.'

'You too must stand firm in the place where you belong,' Binoy responded. 'There is not the slightest need for you to displace yourself. If affection cannot admit difference, then why should difference exist at all in this world?'

That was the gist of what the two of them said to each other over nearly twenty minutes. They forgot whether they were Hindu or Brahmo. That they were human spirits, both of them, was the sole thought that blazed in their hearts like the steadfast flame of a lamp.

## 59

After his prayers Poreshbabu sat silently in the veranda in front of his room. The sun had just set. At this juncture Binoy arrived there, accompanied by Lalita. Prostrating himself, he touched Poreshbabu's feet in a pranam. Poresh was rather surprised to see the two of them arrive together.

'Come, let's go in,' he said, as there were no chairs at hand.

'No, please don't get up,' Binoy insisted. He sat down on the floor. Lalita, too, placed herself at Poresh's feet, a little way off.

'We have come to you together, the two of us, to seek your blessings,' declared Binoy. 'That will be our real initiation.'

Poreshbabu stared at them in amazement.

'I shall not take my vows in the Samaj in fixed words according to fixed rules,' Binoy continued. 'Your blessing is the initiation that will bend our lives in bondage to truth. It is at your feet that our hearts have prostrated themselves in reverence. It is through your hands that the Lord will grant whatever is best for us.'

For a while Poreshbabu remained speechless and still. Then he asked: 'You won't become a Brahmo then, Binoy?'

'No.'

'Do you want to remain within the Hindu Samaj itself?' Poreshbabu persisted.

'Yes.'

Poreshbabu looked at Lalita.

'Baba,' she said, sensing his feelings, 'I still retain my faith and always will. It may cause me inconvenience, even suffering; but I can never think that it would hinder my faith not to alienate and reject those whose beliefs and habits differ from mine.'

Poreshbabu remained silent.

'Formerly I used to think of the Brahmo Samaj as the only world that existed. Everything beyond it seemed a mere shadow,' Lalita explained. 'As if renouncing the Brahmo Samaj amounted to renouncing all forms of truth. But of late, I have completely lost that feeling.'

Poreshbabu smiled wanly.

'Baba, I can't tell you what a great change of heart I have undergone,' she continued. 'Even if I share their faith, I am in no sense identical with the people I encounter in the Brahmo Samaj. I see no sense, now, in using the name of the Brahmo Samaj to call these people specially my own, keeping everyone else in the world at arm's length.'

'Can one make reliable judgements when one's heart is agitated for personal reasons?' asked Poreshbabu, gently patting his rebellious daughter's back. 'One needs a community to ensure the welfare of one's family line from ancestors to future progeny. That is no artificial need. Will you not think of your community, which bears responsibility for the far-reaching future of your would-be descendants?'

'But there is the Hindu community,' Binoy pointed out.

'What if the Hindu community does not take responsibility for you two, refuses to accept it?' asked Poreshbabu.

'We must take it upon ourselves to make them accept it,' declared Binoy, recalling Anandamoyi's attitude. 'All along, Hindu society has extended shelter to new communities; any religious community can belong to Hindu society.'

'In verbal argument we may represent things in a certain way, but it may not be borne out in practice,' Poreshbabu replied. 'Otherwise, could anyone willingly leave their old social world? To believe in a community that would use outward rituals to shackle people's religious thoughts to the same fixed position, we must become puppets for the rest of our lives.'

'If the Hindu community has indeed become so narrow, we must assume the responsibility of setting it free. If one can let in more light and air into the house simply by multiplying its doors and windows, nobody wants to demolish a well-built structure in a fit of rage.'

'Baba, I understand nothing of all this,' Lalita blurted out. 'I have not resolved to take responsibility for the advancement of any community. But I am so oppressed by injustice from all quarters that my heart feels suffocated. I should never tolerate all this with compliance. I don't even understand what's right or wrong, but, Baba, I can't accept this!'

'Wouldn't it be better to allow yourself more time?' suggested Poreshbabu gently. 'Your mind is restless now.'

'I don't mind taking some more time. But I know for sure that untrue rumours and unjust oppressions will keep on multiplying,' declared Lalita. 'That is why I am terrified lest, if things become intolerable, I end up doing something that might hurt you as well. Don't imagine, Baba, that

I have not given the matter any thought. I have considered everything well, and concluded that given my habits and education, I may have to accept a great many constraints and sufferings once outside the Brahmo Samaj. But my heart does not shrink from that at all; rather, I feel a certain strength arise within me, a certain elation. My only anxiety, Baba, is lest some action of mine should cause you the slightest pain.' With these words Lalita began to gently stroke Poreshbabu's feet.

'Ma,' said Poreshbabu with a faint smile, 'if I depended solely upon my own intellect, I would be hurt by any action that contradicted my desires and beliefs. I can't say with conviction that the passion that possesses both of you now is entirely inauspicious. I too had once left home in revolt, with no thought for pros and cons. The attacks and counter-attacks constantly directed against our community nowadays are clear signs of the Lord's power at work. How do I know what He will create and how, through his process of breaking, making and mending things in various ways? What does the Brahmo Samaj mean to Him, or the Hindu community either? He perceives only the human element in us.' With these words, Poreshbabu closed his eyes for a moment, as if to steady himself inwardly, in the private recesses of his soul.

'Look here Binoy,' he continued after a short silence, 'In our land, society is completely entangled with religious beliefs, hence all our social practices involve religious rituals. Because outsiders to our religion cannot be allowed inside the boundaries of our society under any circumstances, there is no loophole for that purpose. I cannot think how you might circumvent this fact.'

Lalita did not understand him properly, for she had never witnessed the difference between the customs of other communities and her own. She assumed that their customs and rituals did not differ very much, on the whole. As if the relation between different communities resembled that between Binoy and her own family, where differences were not apparent. Actually she was not even aware that the Hindu marriage rites might pose any particular problem for her.

'Are you referring to the fact that our wedding ritual takes place before the holy stone, the shalgram?' Binoy inquired.

'Yes,' replied Poreshbabu, casting a glance at Lalita. 'Can Lalita accept that?'

Binoy looked at Lalita's face. He realized that her whole being was shrinking at the thought. In the heat of passion Lalita had arrived at a point that was unfamiliar and dangerous for her. This aroused extreme compassion in Binoy's heart. He must save her, bearing the whole brunt of the onslaught himself. It was intolerable to allow such a fiery spirit to turn back in defeat, and equally terrible that in her indomitable eagerness for victory she should bare her bosom to these arrows of death. She must be allowed to triumph, but must also be protected.

For a while Lalita sat with drooping head. Then, raising her face once, she looked pitifully at Binoy and asked: 'Do you really believe in the shalgram, with all your heart?'

'No I don't,' responded Binoy at once. 'For me the shalgram is not a deity, merely a social symbol.'

'But what you privately recognize as a symbol must be publicly acknowledged as a deity?' Lalita persisted.

'I shall dispense with the shalgram,' declared Binoy, glancing at Poresh.

'Binoy, you two are not considering everything clearly,' complained Poresh, rising to his feet. 'We are not speaking only of your views or someone else's. Marriage is not just a personal matter after all, it is a social act—how can we afford to forget that? Give yourselves some time to think things over. Don't make up your minds just yet.' With these words Poresh left the room and went out into the garden. He began to pace up and down there, all by himself.

Lalita paused briefly before she too left the room. Her back to Binoy, she said: 'If our desires are not wrong, and if they don't entirely coincide with the laws of a particular community, must we then hang our heads and turn back defeated? This I utterly fail to understand. Is there room for false behaviour in society, but none for conduct that is just?'

Slowly Binoy came up to Lalita. 'I am not afraid of any community,' he declared. 'If we two make truth our refuge, where can a greater community be found than the one we have created?'

Borodasundari stormed into the room. 'Binoy, you will not take initiation, I hear!' she demanded.

'I shall accept initiation from a guru worthy of the name, not from any community,' Binoy informed her.

'What is the meaning of all your conspiracies, all these deceitful acts!' cried Borodasundari, in a rage. 'Think of the mess you have created, fooling me as well as the Brahmo Samaj by pretending these last two days that you will be initiated! Did you not think even once of the disaster you will bring upon Lalita?'

'But all members of your Brahmo Samaj do not approve of Binoybabu's initiation,' protested Lalita. 'You have read the papers, haven't you? What is the need for such an initiation ceremony?'

'Without that how can the marriage take place?' Borodasundari demanded.

'Why not?' countered Lalita.

'Will it take place according to Hindu custom then?' Borodasundari asked.'That may be possible,' said Binoy. 'I shall deal with the minor obstacles that remain.'

Borodasundari was speechless for a while. Then in a choked voice she said:

'Binoy, go away from here. Please leave. Don't come to this house again.'

# 60

Sucharita knew for sure that Gora would visit her that day. Since dawn her heart trembled inwardly. As if the joy of anticipating Gora's arrival was mixed with a certain apprehension. For at every step she was tormented by the conflict between Gora's pull in a certain direction and the direction in which her life had grown since infancy, roots, branches and all. So when Gora had bowed at the idol's feet in Mashi's room the previous day, Sucharita felt as if daggers had pierced her heart. She could by no means comfort her heart by telling herself: so what if Gora offers pranams, so what if such are indeed his beliefs? When she detected anything in Gora's behaviour that contradicted her basic religious beliefs, Sucharita's heart trembled in fear. What sort of battle had Ishwar flung her into!

To offer a good example to Sucharita, the proud novice in their faith, Harimohini led Gora into her prayer room on this occasion as well, and again Gora bent to offer pranams to the deity.

As soon as Gora came into her sitting room downstairs, Sucharita demanded: 'Do you feel any devotion for this thakur?'

'Yes I do indeed,' replied Gora with a little more emphasis than necessary. Hearing this, Sucharita hung her head in silence. Her humble, silent suffering wounded Gora to the heart. 'Look, I'll tell you the truth,' he hastened to clarify. 'I can't say for sure that I feel devoted to the deity, but I am devoted to patriotism. I believe in revering the object of the entire nation's worship through all these ages. I can never regard Him with venom like a Christian missionary.'

Sucharita fixed her gaze on Gora's face, preoccupied with her thoughts.

'I know it is very difficult for you to really understand what I'm saying,' Gora told her. 'For having grown up within a community, you people have lost the ability to view these things in a natural way. When you look at the thakur in your Mashi's room, all you see is the stone, but all I see is your Mashi's tender heart, full of devotion. Seeing that, how can I remain angry or indifferent! Do you think the deity who rules that heart is made of stone?'

'Is it enough to be devoted? Must one not consider the object of one's devotion?' Sucharita demanded.

'In other words you consider it a delusion to worship a finite object as divine! But must finitude be determined only by one's own time and place? Suppose a particular line in the scriptures arouses your devotion when you remember it; would you determine the significance of that line merely by measuring the size of the page on which it is inscribed or counting the letters of the alphabet in its words? After all infinitude of emotion is a much greater thing than infinitude of extent. That tiny little idol is more real for your Mashi than the boundless sky embellished with moon, sun and stars. It is because you quantify your idea of the infinite that you must close your eyes when you think of it; I don't know if that proves effective. But with open eyes one can find the infinitude of the heart in even the smallest things. If that were not accessible, how after losing all her happiness could your Mashi still cling to that idol? Is it possible to fill such a great void in one's heart casually, with a piece of stone! Without infinitude of emotion, one can't fill the emptiness in one's heart.'

Sucharita could not answer such fine arguments, yet nor could she accept them as true. Hence, her heart only resonated with a pain without language, without power of retaliation. Gora had never felt the slightest sympathy when arguing with his opponents. Rather, in such situations, his heart was aggressive as a beast of prey. But now Sucharita's silent defeat began to strangely affect his feelings.

'I don't want to say anything against your religious beliefs,' he assured her, softening his tone. 'All I have to say is, that the deity you attack as a mere idol cannot be known merely by seeing his image; only the person whose heart has found stability, whose soul has been satisfied, whose nature has found a refuge, would know whether this deity is clay or spirit, finite or infinite. I tell you, no devotee in our country worships the finite; the joy of their devotion lies in dispelling all constraints within the limits of the finite.'

'But everyone is not a devotee,' Sucharita pointed out.

'Who cares what someone who is not a devotee may worship!' countered Gora. 'What happens to a member of the Brahmo Samaj who is faithless? All his worship ends up in a bottomless void. No, worse than a void: partisanship is his deity, with pride itself for its priest. Have you never witnessed the worship of this blood-thirsty deity in your own community?'

'Do you speak from your own experience when you say these things about religion?' asked Sucharita, without answering his question.

'In other words,' smiled Gora, 'you want to know whether I have ever sought Ishwar. No, my mind has never been inclined that way.'

His words should not have pleased Sucharita, yet she could not help feeling relieved. She felt rather comforted that Gora had no right to speak assertively in these matters.

'I claim no right to offer religious guidance to anybody,' Gora admitted. 'But I also cannot tolerate it if all of you should mock the beliefs of my countrymen. You call out to our people: "You are foolish, you idol worshippers." But I want to call all of them to announce: "No, you are not foolish, nor idol worshippers, but wise, and devoted!" By professing my respect, I want to awaken the nation's heart to the greatness of our sacred philosophy, the profundity of our devotional tradition. I want to arouse its pride in its own riches. I shall not let the country bow its head in shame, nor make it blind to its own reality by generating self-hatred. That is my vow. That is also why I have come to you today. Ever since we met, a new idea haunts my mind, night and day. I had not thought of it before. I constantly feel that Bharatvarsha cannot be completely represented through the masculine perspective alone. Its existence will be fully realized only when manifest to the eyes of our women. I seem to be consumed by the desire that you and I should jointly keep the nation's image before us. As a man I may strive to death for my Bharatvarsha, but without you, who would ceremonially welcome the nation with a lighted lamp? If you remain distanced from it, the act of serving Bharatvarsha can never acquire beauty.'

Where was Bharatvarsha, alas! And where, far removed from it, was Sucharita! Where did he come from, this worshipper of Bharatvarsha, this delirious ascetic! Why, pushing all others away, did he take his place by her side! Why, ignoring all others, did he call out to her! Without any diffidence, brooking no opposition! Why did he say: 'We can't do without you, I have come to take you away, our yajna, this holy sacrifice, will not be complete without you'? Tears streamed from Sucharita's eyes, but she could not fathom why. Gora glanced at her face. She did not lower her tearful eyes before that glance. Like a dew-bedecked blossom, free of care, her gaze turned itself unselfconsciously upon Gora's face.

Before those unconstrained, undoubting, tear-flooded eyes, Gora's entire being seemed to tremble like a stone palace in the throes of an earthquake. With supreme effort he turned away, looking out of the window to regain self-control. It had grown dark. Where the alleyway narrowed, joining the main road, stars were visible against the stone-black darkness of the open sky. That piece of sky, those few stars, carried Gora's soul away tonight, to a place remote from all worldly demands, far, far away from the mundane routines assigned for this workaday world! Transcending the rise and fall of so many kingdoms and empires, far beyond the efforts and prayers of so many ages, that patch of sky and those few stars were waiting, in complete detachment. Yet when one heart called out to another from within the bottomless abyss, that wordless yearning from the solitary edge of the world seemed to set off a vibration in that remote sky, in those stars so far away. At this moment, the movement of traffic and pedestrians on the busy Kolkata streets appeared shadowy and immaterial to Gora's eyes. The hubbub of the city did not reach him at all. Glancing within his own heart he found that he too was silent, lonely and dark like that sky. There, it seemed, a pair of tear-filled, simple, sorrowful eyes had been gazing at him unblinkingly, from before the beginning of time, towards an eternal future.

'Baba, please taste some sweets before you leave.'

At the sound of Harimohini's voice, Gora started and turned around. 'Not tonight I'm afraid,' he declared hastily. 'You must excuse me tonight. I'm leaving right away.' Gora rushed from the place without waiting for any more words.

Harimohini stared at Sucharita in surprise. Sucharita left the room. What was this astounding situation? Harimohini wondered to herself, shaking her head.

Not long after, Poreshbabu arrived there. Not seeing Sucharita in her room, he went to Harimohini and asked:

'Where is Radharani?'

'How would I know?' responded Harimohini, sounding annoyed.

'She was chatting with Gourmohan in the sitting room all this while. Now I suppose she's walking on the terrace by herself.'

'Walking on the terrace so late at night, in such cold weather?' asked Poresh in surprise.

'Let her cool down a little,' declared Harimohini. 'A bit of cold will not harm these girls of today.'

Because Harimohini was feeling upset that evening, she had not sent for Sucharita at mealtime. Sucharita too had lost all sense of time.

When Poreshbabu himself came up to the terrace, Sucharita felt very embarrassed. 'Come Baba, let's go downstairs,' she insisted. 'You will catch a chill.'

Back in the room, when she saw Poresh's anxious face in the lamplight, Sucharita felt deeply disturbed. Severing all her childhood ties, who was now drawing her away from the man who for so long had been both father and guru to a fatherless girl! Sucharita felt she could never forgive herself. When Poresh sank down on the chowki in fatigue, Sucharita stood behind the chowki to hide her uncontrollable tears, and began to stroke his grey hair.

'Binoy has refused to accept initiation,' Poresh informed her. Sucharita offered no reply.

'I had many doubts about Binoy's initiation,' Poresh continued. 'So I was not greatly upset. But from Lalita's tone, I can sense that she sees no obstacle to her marrying Binoy even without his initiation.'

'No Baba, that cannot happen,' Sucharita suddenly exclaimed, very vehemently. 'Never!' She generally did not speak with such unwarranted urgency. Rather surprised at this sudden emotional force in her voice, Poresh asked:

'What cannot happen?'

'If Binoy does not become a Brahmo, what rites will be followed at the wedding ceremony?'

'Hindu rites,' Poresh declared.

'No, no,' protested Sucharita, vigorously shaking her head. 'What sort of things are we speaking of these days! One should not entertain such ideas at all. That idol worship should take place at Lalita's marriage, ultimately! I can never allow that to happen.'

It was because she felt drawn to Gora that Sucharita showed such unaccustomed agitation at the mention of a Hindu wedding. The fact of the matter, concealed within this agitation, was that she was holding Poreshbabu to a certain position as if saying: 'I shall not let you go. Even now, I shall not, by any means, allow my bonds with your community, your worldview, to be severed.'

'Binoy has agreed to dispense with the shaligram at the wedding ceremony,' Poresh informed her. From her place behind the chowki, Sucharita came forward to take a chowki facing him. 'What do you say to that?' he asked her.

'In that case, Lalita must leave our community,' she replied after a brief pause.

'I have had to think deeply about this,' Poresh told her. 'When a person comes into conflict with society, there are two things to be considered: of the two sides, who is just, and who is more powerful. Since society is undoubtedly more powerful, the rebel must suffer. Lalita assures me repeatedly that she is not only prepared for suffering, but also happy to embrace it. If that is true, how can I stop her unless I perceive something unjust in it?'

'But Baba, what sort of development will this be?'

'I know it will cause some trouble. But since there is nothing wrong in Lalita's marrying Binoy, since in fact it is justified, my heart tells me it is not our duty to accept the objections offered by the community. It can never be true that it is the human being who must always submit to social considerations. It is society that must constantly grow and extend itself for the sake of human beings. Hence I cannot bring myself to blame those who are willing to undergo suffering on this account.'

'Baba, it is you who must suffer the most on this account,' Sucharita reminded him.

'That is not a consideration at all.'

'Baba, have you given your consent?'

'No, not yet. But I must. Given the path Lalita has taken, who but I can offer her blessings and who but Ishwar can come to her aid?'

After Poreshbabu left, Sucharita remained stupefied. She knew how much Poresh privately loved Lalita. She had no illusions about the extent of his distress at the fact that Lalita was abandoning the prescribed path to enter a realm of such great uncertainty. Still, at his age, he was ready to support such a rebellion, and yet, how little bitterness he harboured! He had never displayed his own strength at all, yet how immense was the power that lay easily concealed within him!

Formerly, this aspect of Poreshbabu's nature would not have struck her as unusual, for indeed she had known him since childhood. But because Sucharita's whole inner being had endured Gora's assaults only a little while earlier that day, she could not help feeling, very clearly, the complete contrast between these two types of human nature. How tremendously Gora's own desires mattered to him! And with what overwhelming power he could impose these desires upon others! Anyone who accepted any sort of relationship with Gora must bow to his will. Sucharita had submitted that day, and even derived pleasure from it, feeling she had gained something significant from her self-surrender. But still, when Poresh, his head bent with worry, emerged slowly from the lamplight in her chamber into the darkness outside, it was after contrasting his image with Gora's youthful radiance that Sucharita inwardly offered up her special reverence at Poresh's feet. And for a long time she sat calmly, hands folded in her lap, motionless as a picture.

## 61

That day there was a great to-do in Gora's house, starting from dawn. First Mahim appeared, puffing away at his hookah.

'So Binoy has finally flown the cage, it seems?' he asked Gora.

Gora stared at Mahim in bewilderment.

'What's the point trying to fool us any longer?' said Mahim. 'After all the news about your friend is no secret anymore—it's being drummed all over town. Look here, look at this.'

Mahim handed Gora a Bengali newspaper. It contained a pointed article about the news of Binoy's initiation into the Brahmo Samaj that very day. The writer had deployed a great deal of harsh rhetoric to elaborate upon the fact that while Gora was in jail, some eminent members of the Brahmo Samaj, burdened with marriageable daughters, had secretly tempted this weak-willed young man away from the sacred Hindu community. When Gora denied any knowledge of this news, Mahim refused to believe him at first. Then he repeatedly expressed his amazement at such profound deceit on Binoy's part. Before leaving he added that when Binoy started equivocating even after clearly agreeing to marry Shashimukhi, they should have realized he was already headed for disaster.

'Gourmohanbabu, what a terrible situation!' cried Abinash, who now arrived, breathless and panting. 'This is beyond anything we could have dreamt of! That Binoybabu should ultimately . . .' Abinash could not finish what he was saying. So delighted was he at Binoy's ignominy that it had become hard for him to feign worry or anxiety.

In no time all the prominent members of Gora's group had assembled there. Binoy became the subject of a heated discussion among them. Most of them agreed there was nothing surprising in the present development for they had always noticed signs of vacillation and weakness in Binoy's conduct. In fact, Binoy had never surrendered himself wholeheartedly to their group. Many of them declared that Binoy from the outset had tried to somehow pass himself off as Gora's equal, a tendency they could not tolerate. Where all others, out of deference, had maintained an appropriate distance from Gora, Binoy would go out of his way to show his intimacy with Gora, as if he was different from everyone else, and on an equal footing with Gora. It was because of Gora's affection for Binoy that everyone tolerated such extraordinary brazenness. This sort of unbridled arrogance always led to such deplorable results.

'We are not learned like Binoybabu,' they asserted, 'nor do we boast of great intellect. But bapu, we have always followed a principle. We don't say one thing and believe in another. Call us fools if you like, or idiots, or what you please, but we are incapable of acting one way today and another way tomorrow.'

Gora added not a word to this discussion. He sat silent and motionless.

As the day advanced, after they had all gone away, one by one, Gora saw Binoy going up the staircase at the side without entering his room. 'Binoy!' called Gora, rushing out of his room.

Binoy came down the stairs. As soon as he entered the room, Gora said: 'Binoy, have I unwittingly wronged you in some way? You seem to have abandoned me.'

Having already decided that he and Gora would quarrel today, Binoy had come there with a hardened heart. But now, seeing Gora's dejected expression and sensing an aching tenderness in his voice, his mental defences crumbled instantly.

'Bhai Gora,' he exclaimed, 'please don't misunderstand me. Life brings many changes, and one must give up many things, but why would I give up a friendship?'

'Binoy, have you been initiated into the Brahmo Samaj?' asked Gora after a short silence.

'No Gora, I have not, and I shall not, either. But I don't wish to give the matter any importance.'

'What does that mean?'

'It means I no longer feel there is any need for a great hue and cry about whether I accept the Brahmo path or not.'

'What were your feelings formerly, and what are they at present, may I ask?'

At Gora's tone Binoy again braced himself for battle. 'Formerly,' he declared, 'if I heard of anyone converting to Brahmoism, I would be enraged and wish him to be specially punished for it. But now I no longer feel that way. I feel one can counter opinion with opinion and argument with argument, but to punish an intellectual act with anger is barbaric.'

'You will no longer be enraged at seeing a Hindu become a Brahmo, but seeing a Brahmo perform penance to convert to Hinduism, you will blaze with fury,' asserted Gora. 'That's the difference between your former state and your present one.'

'You say this because you are angry with me; your words are not spoken judiciously.'

'I say this out of respect for you,' Gora insisted. 'Things should indeed have turned out this way. It would have been the same with me. If adopting or rejecting religious beliefs were a superficial matter, no different from the colour changes of a chameleon, there would be no problem at all. But because it was a matter of inner significance, I could not take it lightly. If there were no hindrances, if one did not have to pay a penalty, why would a person use all his intellectual powers when accepting or altering an attitude towards some significant issue? One must prove to people whether one is acknowledging the truth solely because it is true. One must accept the penalty for it. To claim the jewel without paying its price—trading in truth is not such an artful business.'

There was no longer any check on the argument. Words met words like a volley of arrows, clashing in a shower of sparks.

'Gora,' Binoy asserted, finally rising to his feet after a long war of words, 'there's a basic difference between your nature and mine. All this while, it had remained suppressed; whenever it threatened to rear its head, it was I who forced it to subside, aware that you don't know how to compromise where you detect any difference. You just rush on, sword in hand. So to protect our friendship, I have always repressed my own nature. Now I realize that this was not beneficial and can never be.'

'What are you intentions now?' Gora inquired. 'Please tell me frankly.'

'Now I stand alone,' Binoy declared. 'That one must somehow pacify the monster called society by daily sacrificing human beings to him, and bear the yoke of his dominance by whatever means whether it kills one or not, is something I can never accept.'

'So will you set out to kill the stork-headed demon Bakasur with a straw, like the Brahman-infant in the Mahabharata?' taunted Gora.

'I don't know if my straw would destroy Bakasur,' retorted Binoy, 'but I can never accept that he has the right to chew me up, not even while he is chewing me up!'

'You speak in metaphors,' complained Gora. 'All this is hard to understand.'

'It's not hard for you to understand,' countered Binoy, 'accepting it is what you find difficult. You know as well as I do, that where man is independent in nature, independent in his religious beliefs, our society imposes meaningless restrictions even upon his food, sleep and rest. But you want to use force to obey this enforcement. Today I declare that I shall not submit to force from any quarters, in such matters. I shall accept the claims of society as long as it protects my rightful demands. If society does not count me as a human being, if it tries to make me a clockwork toy, I too shall not worship it with flowers and sandalwood. I shall consider it an iron machine, nothing more.'

'So, in short, you will become a Brahmo?' Gora asked.

'No.'

'Will you marry Lalita?'

'Yes.'

'By Hindu rites?'

'Yes.'

'Does Poreshbabu approve?'

'Here is his letter.'

Gora read Poresh's letter twice over. The concluding lines read:

> I shall not mention my own likes and dislikes at all. Nor do I want to discuss your convenience or inconvenience. The nature of my beliefs, and the community to which I belong, are known to both of you. Nor are you unaware of the education Lalita has received since her childhood and the traditions within which she has been brought up. Knowing all this fully well, you have chosen your path. I have nothing more to say. Do not imagine that I have given up hope without thinking about anything or because I can't find a way out. To the best of my ability I have thought about it. I have realized that there is no religious cause to oppose your

union for I have full respect for you. In such a situation you are not obliged to accept any objections raised by society. I just have a small thing to say: if you wish to exceed the limits of society then you must rise above society, be greater than it. Let your love, your conjugal life, not merely signal revolt but also contain elements of creativity and stability. It is not enough to suddenly express a certain daring in this single undertaking; after this you must let the thread of heroism run through all your life's works, or you will become utterly degraded. For society will no longer support you from the outside on an equal footing with the ordinary populace. If you cannot rise above the masses on your own strength, you must descend to a level beneath them. I remain gravely concerned about your future welfare. But I have no right to hold you back because of this concern. For in this world, those who have the courage to solve ever-new problems by the example of their own lives are the ones who raise society to greater heights. Those who merely follow rules only support society, they do not help it advance. Hence I shall not block your path with my timidity and my anxieties. Follow what you have chosen to believe, in the face of all adversities, and may Ishwar support you. Ishwar does not chain Creation to a single state of being; through ever-new transformations, he awakens it to eternal renewal. As the emissaries of that renewal, you two are forging ahead on a difficult path, lighting the way with the flaming torch of your lives, guided by the One who steers the entire universe. I cannot impose upon you the restriction of having always to follow my path alone. At your age, we too had once unmoored our boat and set it afloat in the face of a storm, brooking no prohibitions. I do not regret that to this day. Even if there had been cause for regret, what of it? Human beings must err, be thwarted, suffer pain, but they cannot remain still. They must surrender their lives to what they understand to be right. In this way, the pure stream of this world's river will remain ever-flowing and unpolluted. To dam the flood forever, fearing it might occasionally erode the river banks causing temporary damage, would bring pestilence upon us; that I know for sure. Hence I offer my devoted pranam to the force that draws you at relentless speed beyond the boundaries of happiness, ease and social law, and I leave you in His hands. May He make it all worthwhile, all the shame, humiliation and separation from kin that you have suffered in your lives. It is He who has summoned you to this difficult path, and it is He who will guide you to your destination.

After reading this letter Gora remained silent for a while. Then Binoy urged him:

'Just as Poreshbabu has given his consent, so must you, Gora.'

'Poreshbabu may give his consent, for it is their current that is eroding the rivershore,' Gora countered. 'I cannot give my consent for our stream preserves the shore. On this shore of ours are so many monumental creations, hundreds of thousands of years old, that we can by no means declare that only the laws of nature should apply here. We shall pave our shores with stone, whether you blame us or not. This is our sacred ancient city; from our perspective, it is not desirable that new layers of soil should be deposited upon it every year or that droves of peasants should plough this land, whatever we may stand to lose. This land is for habitation, not farming. Hence we don't feel dire shame when all you people from the agriculture department condemn the hardness of our stone.'

'So, in short, you will not recognize this marriage?'

'Certainly not.'

'And . . .'

'And I shall part company with all of you.'

'What if I had been a Muslim friend of yours?'

'Then it would have been a different matter. When a branch breaks off, severing itself from the tree, the tree can never take it back as its own, as before. But it can offer shelter to a vine that approaches it from outside; in fact, if the vine is cast down in a storm, there is nothing to stop the tree from offering it support once again. When our own dear ones become alien to us we have no choice but to abandon them completely. Hence all the ritual prohibitions, all the desperate attempts to rein us in.'

'That is why the reasons for separation should not have been so flimsy, nor the rules of separation so accessible,' argued Binoy. 'True, an arm once severed cannot be joined again but that's why the arm doesn't break off easily. Its bones are very strong. Will you not consider how hard it is for people to freely pursue their lives in a society where the slightest blow is enough to cause separation and where the separation becomes an eternal fact?'

'Such considerations are not my responsibility. Society is collectively involved in thought processes so vast that I don't even become aware of them. I survive on the belief that for thousands of years it has been thinking, and protecting itself as well. I don't worry about whether the earth is following its proper orbit around the sun or not, whether it deviates from its path or not, and so far I have not been let down despite my oblivion. I feel the same way about society.'

'Bhai Gora,' laughed Binoy, 'I too have been saying just such things in this fashion, all these days. Who could have known that I too would now have to listen to such words? I realize only too well that I must now pay the penalty for all my made-up speeches. But it's no use arguing. For today I have seen something very closely, something I had not observed before. I have understood now that human life flows like a great river; by the force of its own current, in unimaginable ways, it travels in new directions which it had not taken before. That is the extraordinary quality of its movement, and its unforeseen transformations are precisely what the Maker of our destiny intends. It is not a manmade canal, we cannot keep it confined within a fixed channel. Now that I have witnessed this directly within my own self, you can't beguile me with made-up arguments anymore.'

'A moth about to fall into the flame uses the very same argument, so I too shall not try in vain to persuade you now.'

'That's a good idea,' declared Binoy, rising from his chair. 'I'll be off then. Let me go and see Ma.'

After Binoy had left, Mahim slowly entered the room. 'Didn't make much headway, did you?' he asked, chewing on his paan. 'You won't, either. I have been warning you since so long that you should be careful, that there are signs of his going astray, but you ignored my words. If we had somehow forced him into marrying Shashimukhi at that time, these problems wouldn't have arisen at all. But *ka kasya paribedana*! And who am I speaking to? No amount of head-banging would help me convince you of something you fail to understand yourself. Now, isn't it regrettable that a boy like Binoy should defect from your group?'

Gora made no reply.

'So you couldn't make Binoy change his mind?' Mahim persisted. 'Let that go, but the question of his marriage to Shashimukhi has created too many complications. Now we can't afford to delay Shashi's marriage any further. You know the attitudes of our community: if they get after a person they won't rest until they have reduced him to abject misery. So we need a groom—no, have no fear, you won't have to act as go-between. I have taken care of that myself.'

'Who is that prospective groom?'

'Your very own Abinash.'

'Has he consented?'

'As if he wouldn't! He's not like our Binoy is he? No, whatever you might say, in your group, it's that boy Abinash who has proved truly devoted to you. He virtually danced for joy upon hearing that he would acquire a family connection with you. "This is my good fortune, my glory!" he cried. I asked him about money. He at once covered his ears and said: "Forgive me, but please don't mention such things." "Very well," I said, "I shall discuss these matters with your father." I went to his father as well, and found a big difference between father and son. The father didn't block his ears at the mention of money, not at all. Rather, he started saying such things, I almost had to stop my own ears. The son, too, I found to be extremely devoted to his father in these matters—regards his father as absolute divinity—so it will be no use asking him to mediate. This time liquidating my company assets will not suffice. Anyway, you too must discuss a few things with Abinash. A word of encouragement from you . . .'

'That will not reduce the sum of money to be paid,' Gora interrupted.

'I know that. When filial devotion proves useful, it becomes hard to control.'

'Is the wedding fixed?' Gora asked.

'Yes.'

'Have the date and hour been determined?'

'Determined indeed, for the full-moon night in the month of Magh this winter. That's not far away. The father has decreed he has no use for diamonds and gemstones but the gold jewellery must be very heavy. Now I must spend some days consulting the goldsmith on ways of increasing the weight of gold without adding to its price.'

'But why such haste? There's no fear of Abinash joining the Brahmo Samaj in the near future.'

'No indeed, but you people haven't noticed that Baba's health has deteriorated a great deal recently. The more the doctors object, the more rigid he becomes about his ritual restrictions. The sanyasi who now keeps him company makes him bathe three times a day and to add to that, he has started Baba on such a course of hathayoga that his eyes, eyebrows, breath, nerves, are all precariously jumbled up. It would be convenient if Shashi's wedding took place while Baba is still alive; I wouldn't have much to worry about if we could accomplish the act before Baba's pension savings fall into the clutches of Omkarananda Swami. I had even mentioned it to Baba yesterday but found it was no easy matter. I have decided I must ply that rascally sanyasi with ganja for a few days to bring him under control and then get him to perform the rites. Know this for sure: middle class householders, who have the greatest need for money, will never get to enjoy their father's wealth. My problem is that someone else's father pressurizes me with demands for money and my own father takes to meditation at the very mention of money. Must I now drown myself with that eleven year old girl tied to my neck as deadweight?'

## 62

'Radharani, why didn't you eat anything last night?' asked Harimohini.

'Why,' said Sucharita, surprised, 'indeed I did!'

'As if you did!' persisted Harimohini, pointing out the food that still lay covered. 'There's your food, still untouched.'

Sucharita now realized she had indeed forgotten her dinner the previous evening.

'These are not good signs,' declared Harimohini roughly. 'From what I know of your Poreshbabu, I don't think he likes such excesses. He looks so calm and reassuring. Tell me, what would he say if he got to know all about your current inclinations?'

Sucharita was left in no doubt what Harimohini wanted to imply. At first, she felt momentarily embarrassed. She had never imagined that her relationship with Gora could be equated with an utterly ordinary man–woman relationship, bringing such false social aspersions upon them. Hence she was upset at Harimohini's insinuations. But the very next moment, she sat upright, casting aside the chores at hand, and looked Harimohini in the eye. Instantly resolving not to be coy about her relationship with Gora, she asserted:

'Mashi, you know Gourmohanbabu was here last evening. Because I was preoccupied about the subject of our discussion, I had utterly forgotten my dinner. Had you been present there last night, you could have heard us talk of many things.'

The things Gora had said were not quite what Harimohini wanted to hear. She wanted only to hear about devotional matters. But Gora's words did not ring with simple and interesting feelings of devotion. It was as if he was constantly confronting an adversary, against whom he must struggle. He wanted to persuade disbelievers, but what could he preach to the converted, after all? Harimohini was utterly indifferent to the things that enthused Gora. It caused her no inner anxiety if members of the Brahmo Samaj retained their own beliefs instead of merging with the Hindu community. As long as there was no cause for separation from her own dear ones, she was quite content. Hence she had not found her discussion with Gora interesting at all. Subsequently, once Harimohini sensed that it was Gora who had captured Sucharita's heart, she found his conversation seemed even more unappealing. Sucharita was completely independent, both financially and in her opinions, beliefs and conduct. Therefore, Harimohini had been unable to fully control her in any respect; yet Sucharita was Harimohini's sole support in her declining years. It was for this reason that Harimohini felt deeply perturbed if anyone but Poreshbabu asserted any sort of claim over Sucharita. Harimohini was haunted by the feeling that everything about Gora was false, from beginning to end; that his real aim was to attract Sucharita by some ruse. In fact, she even began to imagine that Gora was chiefly tempted by Sucharita's material assets. Identifying him as her prime enemy, Harimohini mentally braced herself to oppose him.

Gora was not expected at Sucharita's house that day, nor had he any reason to visit. But he lacked diffidence by nature. When he chose a course of action, he did not pause to think about it, forging straight ahead like an arrow. Now, when Gora came to Sucharita's room at dawn, Harimohini was at her prayers. Sucharita was tidying the books, notebooks and papers on the table in the sitting room, when Satish came in to announce Gora's arrival. Sucharita was not particularly surprised. It was as if she had expected Gora to visit her that day.

'So Binoy has finally abandoned us,' observed Gora, taking a chair.

'Why? Why would he abandon us?' Sucharita asked. 'He hasn't joined the Brahmo Samaj after all.'

'If he had gone to the Brahmo Samaj he would have been closer to us than he is now,' declared Gora. 'It is by clinging to the Hindu community that he is causing it so much trouble. Better if he had made a clean break.'

'Why do you have such extreme views about society?' demanded Sucharita, inwardly very hurt. 'Is it natural for you to place such excessive faith in the community? Or is it self-coercion, rather?'

'But it's coercion that is natural in the present circumstances,' Gora asserted. 'When treading on shaky ground, one must step more firmly with every stride. Because we are in a hostile environment, our speech and behaviour are somewhat extreme. That is not unnatural.'

'Why do you consider the hostile environment to be entirely unjust and unnecessary? If society obstructs the progress of time, it must suffer.'

'The progress of time is like a series of waves; it keeps eroding the soil. But I don't believe it is the soil's duty to accept such erosion. Don't imagine I have no consideration for the welfare of our community. It's so easy to pass such judgements that today even a boy of sixteen presumes to be a judge. It's harder by far to see everything as whole, and to view it with respect.'

'Does respect always yield the truth? It also leads us to blindly accept falsehoods, after all. Let me ask you a question: is respect for idol worship allowed too? Do you believe such things to be true?'

'I'll try and tell you the exact truth,' answered Gora after a short silence. 'I have from the outset taken these things to be true. I did not hasten to challenge them simply because they contradict European traditions and because some lowly arguments can be deployed against them. I am not committed to any particular religious pursuit. But I cannot blindly parrot the idea that deism and idol worship are identical, or that idol worship does not represent the culmination of devotional philosophy. In art and literature, even in science and history, the human imagination has a place. I do not accept that relgion alone denies a place to the imagination. It is in religion that all human faculties find their ultimate expression. This attempt to fuse imagination with knowledge and devotion in the form of idol worship in our country—hasn't it made religion more completely real for the people of our nation, compared to other nations?'

'Idol worship was practiced in Greece and Rome as well.'

'The human imagination that produced those idols relied more on aesthetic sense than on knowledge and devotion. In our country, the imagination is closely allied with knowledge and devotion. Whether you take our Radha–Krishna or our Hara–Parvati, they are not merely historical objects of worship; they contain elements of eternal human philosophy.That's why the devotion of a Ramaprasad or a Chaitanyadev found expression through all these idols. When did the history of Greece or Rome produce forms of devotion of such a high order?'

'You do not wish to accept any change at all in religious or social practices, in tune with changing times?' Sucharita inquired.

'Why would I not!' protested Gora. 'But change should not become a form of madness. Changes in human life follow a human course: a child grows gradually into an old man, but a human being doesn't suddenly change into a dog or cat, does he? The transformation of Bharatvarsha should follow the path of Bharatvarsha itself; if we suddenly adopt the path of British history, the whole process will be ruined and rendered meaningless. The nation's power and wealth are stored within the nation itself: I have dedicated my life to the task of making all of you aware of this very fact. Do you understand my words?'

'Yes I do. But I have never heard nor thought of such things before. I am like someone who takes time to recognize even the most obvious things when she finds herself in an unfamiliar place. Perhaps because I am a woman, my comprehension is not very strong.'

'Never,' declared Gora. 'I know many men, and have long been discussing these matters with them. Doubtless they have assumed that they understand me only too well. But I tell you for certain, what you see before your mind's eye today is something not one of them has perceived at all. Within you is a depth of vision that I had sensed as soon as I saw you. That is why I have come to confide in you everything my heart has ever wanted to say, all these years. I have laid bare my entire life before you, without the slightest diffidence.'

'When you speak like that I feel very perturbed. What you expect of me, how much of it I can offer you, what tasks I must undertake, how to express the overwhelming emotions arising within me—I can't understand any of these things. I feel afraid all the time, lest your trust in me should one day prove to be utterly misplaced.'

'It is not misplaced at all,' Gora insisted, his voice deep as the rumbling of clouds. 'I shall show you how great is the power within you. Don't be anxious in the least. It is my responsibility to draw out your worth. Depend on me.'

Sucharita said nothing; but wordlessly the signal was conveyed that she was completely ready to depend on him. Gora too was silent. For a long time, there was a total hush in the room. Outside in the alleyway, a hawker selling old utensils passed by their door, his brass vessels clanging.

Having completed her prayer rituals Harimohini was on her way to the kitchen. It had not even occurred to her that there might be any other person in Sucharita's silent chamber. But glancing into the room, when she suddenly saw Sucharita and Gora lost in silent thought without any small talk, she instantly felt anger streak like lightning, to her very head. Then she controlled herself.

'Radharani!' she called from the doorway.

When Sucharita arose and came to her, Harimohini said in a low voice: 'Today is the ekadashi, the eleventh lunar day, but I don't feel well. Go and light the stove in the kitchen. Meanwhile, let me spend some time with Gourbabu.'

Agitated at her Mashi's expression, Sucharita went away to the kitchen. When Harimohini entered the room, Gora touched her feet respectfully. Without a word she took a chowki. Lips pursed, she remained silent for a while. Then she asked:

'Baba, you are not a Brahmo are you?'

'No.'

'Do you believe in our Hindu community?'

'I do indeed.'

'Then what sort of conduct is this?'

Utterly failing to comprehend Harimohini's complaint, Gora gazed at her in silence.

'Radharani has come of age, and you people are not related to her after all. What do you have to say to her at such length? She is a woman and must attend to the housework. What need has she to involve herself in such matters? It distracts her mind. You are a learned man indeed, and across the land, people are all praise for you; but when was such conduct accepted in our country and what place does it have in our scriptures?'

It was as if Gora had suddenly received a great blow. It had not even occurred to him that such comments on Sucharita could arise from any quarters.

'She is a member of the Brahmo Samaj,' he observed after a short silence, 'and I have always seen her mingle in this fashion with everybody; so I thought nothing of it.'

'Very well, so she is a member of the Brahmo Samaj, but you have never supported such conduct after all. Your words are arousing the consciousness of so many people today, but if you behave like this, why should they respect you! You just chatted with her till late evening yesterday, but still you didn't finish what you had to say, and here you are again this very morning! Since morning today, she has entered neither larder nor kitchen. It didn't even occur to her to help me today, though it is the ekadashi. What sort of education is she receiving! There are women in your own households too. Are you giving them the same education, halting all their work? Or do you approve if someone else imparts such training to them?'

Gora had no answer to all these charges. He only said: 'Because she has grown up with this sort of training, I thought nothing of the matter.'

'Whatever her training, as long as she stays with me and as long as I live, such conduct will not do. I have succeeded in turning her around, to a great extent. Even while she was at Poreshbabu's, it was rumoured she had become a Hindu after mingling with me. Later, after moving to this house, I don't know what she began discussing with this Binoy of yours, and everything turned topsy turvy again. He is now going to marry into a Brahmo family. Anyway, I got rid of Binoy with great difficulty. After that, a person called Haranbabu used to visit. Whenever he came, I would take Radharani upstairs to my room, so he didn't find it encouraging. In this way, after much hardship, she seems to have changed her attitudes again, a little. After moving to this house she had again started accepting food touched by all and sundry, but yesterday I found that she had stopped. Yesterday she fetched her own rice from the kitchen and forbade the bearer to bring her water. Now, baba, I beg you with folded hands, please don't ruin her again, all of you. Having lost all my dear ones in this world, she's the only one I have left, and she too has nobody she can exactly call her own, except for me. Please leave her alone, all of you. They have so many other grown girls in their house after all—there's that girl Labanya, and Leela; they too are intelligent, educated. If you have anything to say, go say it to them. Nobody will forbid you.'

Gora was utterly stupefied. After a short silence, Harimohini resumed: 'Think about it: she must marry, she's old enough. Do you suggest she should always remain a spinster like this? A woman needs to perform her domestic duties after all, it is her dharma.'

In a general way, Gora had no doubts about this; indeed, he was of the same opinion. But even in private, he had never tried applying his own opinion to Sucharita. He could not imagine Sucharita as a housewife, busy with domestic chores in the antahpur of some middle-class home. As if she would always remain exactly as she was now.

'Do you have any thoughts about your bonjhi's marriage?' Gora inquired.

'I must think about it indeed. Who will, if I don't?'

'Can she marry into the Hindu community?'

'One must try. If she does not create any more trouble, and conducts herself properly, I can pass her off. I have mentally planned everything, but so far her tendencies were such, I could not summon up the courage to act. Now, these last couple of days, I find her attitude softening again, so I'm hopeful.'

It was not proper to ask too many questions, thought Gora, but he could not refrain from asking:

'Have you thought of a prospective bridegroom?'

'I have. The patra is rather nice—he's my younger deor Kailash, my husband's brother. He lost his wife some time ago. It's because he couldn't find a grown girl he liked that he's waited so long, otherwise could such a boy remain single! He will suit Radharani very well.'

The sharper the sting he felt, the more inquisitively Gora asked about Kailash. Among Harimohini's deors it was Kailash who had, by his own efforts, acquired some education, but about the extent of his education, Harimohini could not say. In the family it was he who was reputed for his learning. When lodging a complaint with the authorities against the village postmaster, it was Kailash who had composed the entire document in such extraordinary English that a senior official from the post office had come there personally to conduct the investigations. At this, all the villagers had been amazed at Kailash's skill. But despite the extent of his scholarship, Kailash's commitment to orthodox restrictions had not flagged.

When Kailash's life-history had been recounted completely, Gora rose, touched Harimohini's feet, and left the room without a word.

As he descended the stairs leading out into the courtyard, Sucharita was busy working in the kitchen across the courtyard. Hearing Gora's footsteps she came and stood near the door. Gora went straight out, without glancing in any direction. Sighing, Sucharita resumed her chores in the kitchen. At the corner of the alley, Gora bumped into Haranbabu.

'Here so early in the day!' remarked Haranbabu with a faint sneer. Gora made no reply.

'You have been there, I suppose?' asked Haranbabu, with another sneer. 'Sucharita is home, I hope?'

'Yes,' replied Gora and quickly strode away.

Going directly into Sucharita's house, Haranbabu glimpsed her through the open kitchen door. Sucharita had no escape route, nor was her mashi nearby.

'I just met Gormohanbabu,' Haranbabu informed her. 'He was here all this while, was he?'

Without answering his question, Sucharita suddenly became very busy with her pots and pans, as if she did not have time to breathe at that moment. But this did not deter Haranbabu. Standing in the courtyard outside the kitchen, he struck up a conversation. Harimohini came to the stairs and coughed two or three times, but that too had no effect. Harimohini could have confronted Haranbabu directly, but she knew for certain that if she emerged but once before him, neither she nor Sucharita would find any refuge in this house to shield themselves from this earnest young man's irrepressible enthusiasm. Hence if she glimpsed the mere shadow of Haranbabu, she would draw her sari aanchal so low over her face that it might have seemed excessive even when she was a young bride,.

'Tell me Sucharita, tell me, what direction have you people taken?' Haranbabu accused her. 'Where will it ultimately lead you? Perhaps you have heard that Lalita and Binoybabu are to marry according to Hindu rites. Are you responsible for that?' Receiving no response from Sucharita, he lowered his voice and asserted severely: 'You are the one responsible.'

Haranbabu had imagined Sucharita would be unable to endure the blow of such a major, terrible accusation. But seeing her wordlessly go about her chores, he adopted an even more severe tone and declared, wagging his finger at her:

'Sucharita, I repeat, you are the one responsible. Can you swear with your right hand upon your heart that the Brahmo Samaj will not hold you guilty?'

Silently Sucharita placed her oil-filled karahi on the stove, and the oil began to splutter.

'It was you who invited Binoybabu and Gourmohanbabu into your household,' Haranbabu continued. 'And you have encouraged them so much that these two have become more important to you people than all your eminent Brahmo friends. Can you see what that has resulted in? Did I not warn you from the start? What has happened today? Who will dissuade Lalita now? You think she alone will bear the consequences and the problem will blow over? Not at all. I have come to caution you today. Now it will be your turn. Today you must be secretly remorseful at Lalita's mishap, but the day is not far when you will not even feel any remorse at your own downfall. But Sucharita, there is still time to turn back. Just think, how once we two had met, in a state of such great and noble optimism; how brightly our life's goal shone ahead, how expansively the future of the Brahmo Samaj stretched before us. How many resolves we made and how much support we garnered, each day! Do you think all that is ruined? Never. The ground of our optimism remains ready for us, as before. Look back but once. Come back, just for once.'

A lot of greens and vegetables were sizzling in the boiling oil, and Sucharita was stirring them with her spatulate khonta as required. When Haranbabu fell silent, waiting to observe the effect of his call, she lifted the karahi off the fire, turned around and declared firmly:

'I am a Hindu.'

'You, a Hindu!' exclaimed Haranbabu, utterly dumbfounded.

'Yes, I am a Hindu.' With these words, Sucharita replaced the karahi on the fire and began to stir violently with her khonta.

It took Haranbabu a short while to regain his balance. Then he demanded sharply: 'Is that why Gourmohanbabu was giving you initiation, night and day?'

'Yes, it is from him I have received my initiation. It is he who is my guru,' Sucharita asserted, without turning her head.

Haranbabu had once considered himself Sucharita's guru. Today, if Sucharita had told him she loved Gora, he would not have felt so hurt. But to hear from her that Gora had wrested from him the right to be her guru was like being pierced through the heart by a stave.

'However great your guru,' he said, 'do you think the Hindu community will accept you?'

'That I don't know, nor do I know the community, but I know I am a Hindu.'

'Do you know that simply for having remained unmarried for so long, you have lost your caste status in Hindu society?'

'Please don't worry about that needlessly. But I tell you I am a Hindu.'

'Will you sacrifice at your new guru's feet even the training in dharma you received from Poreshbabu?'

'As for my dharma, the omniscient One knows what it is. I don't want to discuss it with anybody. But please understand, I am a Hindu.'

'However staunch a Hindu you might be, it will bring you no rewards, I tell you,' cried Haranbabu, now completely losing his patience. 'Your Gourmohanbabu is not like Binoybabu. Even if you declare yourself "a Hindu, a Hindu," until you are hoarse, don't entertain the slightest hope that Gourbabu will accept you. Easy enough to play guru to the disciple, but don't dream that he would therefore take you into his home to set up house.'

'What's all this!' flashed Sucharita, turning around at lightning speed, cooking completely forgotten.

'I say Gourmohanbabu will never marry you.'

'Marry!' exclaimed Sucharita, eyes blazing. 'Didn't I tell you he was my guru?'

'You did indeed. But I also understand what you didn't tell me.'

'Please go away. Don't insult me. From now on, I tell you, I shall never come out in your presence.'

'How can you come out, tell me, now that you are zenana, a woman in seclusion! A Hindu woman! One so pure the sun has never witnessed her beauty! Now Poreshbabu's vessel of sin is full to the brim! At this advanced age, let him taste the fruits of all his actions. I take your leave.'

Slamming the kitchen door, Sucharita sank to the floor and stuffing the end of her aanchal into her mouth, struggled to stifle her uncontrollable sobs. Face dark as thunder, Haranbabu left the house.

Harimohini had heard the entire exchange between the two. What she had heard from Sucharita's lips today was beyond her expectations. Swelling with pride, she said:

'Wouldn't it be so! Could all my heartfelt prayers to the Lord Gopiballav prove futile!' She immediately went to her prayer chamber and prostrated herself before her deity, promising to increase the quantity of food offered in the bhog ritual, from that day. So far, her devotion had been a quiet affair, a consolation for her sorrows. But now, as soon as they took the form of self-service, her prayers became extremely aggressive, fierce and greedy.

## 63

Gora had never spoken to any other person as he had done in Sucharita's presence. All these days, for the benefit of his listeners, he had merely spouted sentences, opinions and advice. But that day, it was his own self he presented before Sucharita, projected from deep within himself. At the joy, and not just the power, of this self-expression, all his views and resolves were filled with a spirit of elation. A feeling of grace enveloped his life, as if the gods had suddenly rained heavenly nectar upon his life's pursuit.

It was in the grip of this exultation that Gora had visited Sucharita every day for a few days, without thinking anything of it. But now, Harimohini's words made him suddenly remember that he had once scolded and taunted Binoy severely for a similar infatuation. Now, realizing he had himself arrived at the same state without his own knowledge, he was startled. Like a person suddenly jolted awake as he sleeps uncovered in an unfamiliar place, Gora summoned up all his strength to become alert. He had always preached that while many powerful races in the world had been utterly destroyed, Bharatvarsha had survived all adversities through all these centuries, only by firmly adhering to its principles. Gora would not permit any slackening of these principles anywhere. According to him, all else in Bharatvarsha was going to the dogs, but it was beyond the power of any oppressive ruler to touch the holy spirit that Bharatvarsha had sustained, permeating all these harsh restrictive practices. As long as we remain under the yoke of an alien race, we must firmly adhere to our principles. This is not the time to think about right and wrong. A person swept away by a lethal current clings to whatever support he finds, without considering whether it is beautiful or ugly. Gora had said this all along, and was expected to say the same thing on that day as well. But when Harimohini cast aspersions on Gora's own conduct, the king elephant was wounded with the proverbial goad.

When Gora reached home, Mahim was inhaling tobacco, barebodied, on a bench he had placed on the street, just in front of the entrance. His office was closed for the day. He followed Gora in.

'Just a minute Gora,' he called, 'I have something to say.'

Taking Gora to his own room, Mahim said: 'Don't be angry bhai, but let me inquire first if you have caught a touch of Binoy's illness? Your visits to that place have grown very frequent, I must say!'

'You have nothing to fear,' declared Gora, flushing.

'From the signs, it's hard to tell. You think it is a morsel to be easily swallowed, before you return home as usual. But within it the fishhook lies concealed, as you would realize from your friend's predicament. Arré, where are you going? I haven't come to the main point yet! Binoy's marriage to a Brahmo girl is completely certain, I hear. But once that happens, we can't have any truck with him, let me inform you beforehand.'

'No indeed,' Gora assented.

'But if Ma creates problems, it won't be easy,' warned Mahim. 'We are simple householders, harried by the burden of marrying off our daughters. If on top of that you install the Brahmo Samaj in our midst, I too will have to uproot myself from this place.'

'No, that will never happen,' Gora declared.

'The marriage proposal for Shashi is taking shape. Our behai, her prospective father-in-law, will not be satisfied without extracting gold worth more than the girl he's taking into his household, for he knows that human beings are perishable goods, while gold lasts much longer. He is more interested in the chaser than in the medicine. Behai is an inadequate name for him, because he is utterly behaya, without shame. It may cost me some money, but from this man I have learnt a lot that will stand me in good stead when I get my son married. I felt very tempted to be reborn into the present age, and using my father as go-between, arrange my own marriage according to the rules, to make one hundred percent capital out of being born a male! That's what manhood is all about! To utterly ruin the bride's father. No mean achievement, is it! Anyway, I can't find the enthusiasm, bhai, to join you night and day in celebrating the Hindu community's triumph. My voice fails me. All this has left me completely exhausted. My Tinkori is only fourteen months old: having produced a daughter at the very outset, my wife has taken very long to rectify her mistake. Anyway, Gora, please keep the Hindu community alive, all of you, until my son is married. After that, whether the people of this country become Muslims or Christians, I'll have nothing to say.'

'That's why I was saying,' Mahim added, when Gora rose to his feet, 'it won't be appropriate to invite your Binoy to Shashi's wedding celebrations. We can't let him create a fuss all over again, about all this. Please caution your mother beforehand.'

Approaching his mother's room, Gora saw Anandamoyi on the floor, with her spectacles on, making some sort of list in an exercise book. Seeing Gora, she removed her glasses, closed the notebook, and said: 'Come and join me.'

When he had found a place to sit, she said: 'I need to consult you on something. You have heard about Binoy's marriage, haven't you?'

Gora remained silent.

'Binoy's kaka, his father's younger brother, is displeased,' Anandamoyi continued. 'None of them will attend. It is also doubtful if this wedding can take place in Poreshbabu's house. Binoy himself must make all the arrangements. So I suggest –since the ground floor of our house, on the northern side, has been rented out and the tenants on the first floor have moved out as well—that if we arrange for the wedding ceremony on that upper floor, it might be convenient.'

'How would it be convenient?' Gora inquired.

'Who will supervise everything if I am not present at the wedding?' Anandamoyi pointed out. 'Binoy will be in a fix. If the wedding takes place there, I can arrange everything from home, without any trouble.'

'That's not possible, Ma!'

'Why not? I have persuaded the one in charge.'

'No Ma, I tell you this wedding cannot take place here. Please believe me.'

'Why, Binoy is not marrying according to their customs after all!'

'Those are mere arguments. You can't use legal arguments with the communnity. Binoy may do as he pleases, but we cannot accept this marriage. There is no dearth of houses in Kolkata. He owns a house himself, after all.'

Houses were there aplenty, as Anandamoyi was aware. But it rankled in her heart that Binoy, abandoned by relatives, friends and everybody else, should somehow undergo the wedding ritual in his own home, like some godforsaken wretch. Therefore she had privately decided to organize the wedding ceremony in the part of their house set aside for renting out. Thus, without opposing their community, she could have enjoyed the satisfaction of arranging the auspicious ritual in their own home.

Seeing that Gora was firmly against the idea, she remarked: 'If all of you are so averse to this suggestion, we must rent other premises. It will put a great strain upon me, though. But never mind, if this option is impossible, what use dwelling upon it!'

'Ma, you ought not to participate in this ceremony,' Gora objected.

'What's this Gora, how can you say such a thing! If I don't participate in our own Binoy's wedding ceremony, then who will!'

'That is simply not possible, Ma!'

'Gora, you and Binoy may not see eye to eye on some things, but must we therefore behave like his enemies?'

'Ma, that is an unfair thing to say!' protested Gora. 'It brings me no joy that I can't join in the merriment of Binoy's wedding. How dear Binoy is to me, you know better than anyone else. But Ma, this is not a question of love; it has nothing to do with friendship or enmity. Binoy has chosen this course, knowing its consequences fully well. We have not deserted him, it is he who has deserted us. Hence the present estrangement will not hurt him beyond his expectations.'

'Gora, it's true Binoy knows he will have no connection with you where this wedding is concerned. But surely he also knows I can never abandon him on this auspicious occasion. If Binoy imagined I would not receive his bride with my blessings, he could never have gone ahead with this wedding, not if it cost him his life. Don't I know Binoy's mind!' Anandamoyi wiped away a tear from the corner of her eye. This stirred up the deep, painful feelings for Binoy that Gora nursed in his heart.

'Ma, you belong to a community and you are indebted to them,' he insisted. 'That's something you must bear in mind.'

'Gora, I have told you repeatedly that my links with the community have long been severed. That is why the community disdains me, and I too keep my distance.'

'Ma, these words of yours wound me most deeply.'

'Bachha, Ishwar knows it is beyond my powers to protect you from the pain of this blow,' replied Anandamoyi, her tender, tearful gaze seeming to caress every part of Gora's body.

'Then let me tell you what I must do,' declared Gora, rising to his feet. 'I shall go to Binoy and tell him not to widen the gulf between you and the community by involving you in his wedding plans. For that would be extremely unfair and selfish on his part.'

'Very well, do what you can,' smiled Anandamoyi. 'Go tell him, and I'll handle what follows.'

After Gora had left, Anandamoyi thought for a long time. Then she slowly arose and went to her husband's quarters. Tonight being ekadashi, there were no arrangements for Krishnadayal to cook for himself. He had found a new Bengali translation of *Gherandasamhita*, which he was reading, seated on a deerskin. Seeing Anandamoyi, he grew agitated. Keeping a suitable distance from him she knelt on the threshold.

'Look, this is very unfair,' she declared.

Krishnadayal was beyond worldly things like fairness or unfairness. So it was with indifference that he asked:

'What is so unfair?'

'We ought not to keep Gora deluded for a single day longer. Things are getting out of hand.'

This had occurred to Krishnadayal the day Gora had spoken of penance. Subsequently, busy with sundry yogic practices, he had not found the time to think about it.

'There is talk of getting Shashimukhi married,' Anandamoyi told him. 'Perhaps it will happen soon, this coming month of Phalgun. Previously, whenever any community ritual has taken place in our house, I have always taken Gora elsewhere on some pretext or other. So far, no major ritual has taken place either. But now that Shashi's wedding is due, tell me what I should do with Gora. The wrong we have done him becomes more serious with each passing day. Every day, morning and evening, I beg the Almighty's forgiveness with folded hands. Let me bear any punishment He wishes to inflict, but I am constantly afraid that we can't hold out any longer, that there will be trouble with Gora. Please give me permission now, let me frankly disclose the whole truth to him, whatever misfortune it may bring upon me.'

What sort of hurdle had Indra, king of gods, cast in Krishnadayal's way, just to disrupt his holy pursuits! These pursuits, too, had grown very intense of late. He was accomplishing impossible feats with his breathing, and his diet had also gradually dwindled to such frugal proportions, it would not be long before he achieved his resolve to flatten his abdomen until his stomach touched his back. What a nuisance all this was, at such a juncture!

'Are you mad?' Krishnadayal demanded. 'If these facts become public now, I shall have to offer all sorts of explanations. My pension will be stopped for sure, and maybe even the police will be after me. Let bygones be bygones. Try to manage as best you can. If you can't, even that won't be too bad.'

Let things take their own course after his death, Krishnadayal had decided. Meanwhile he would remain detached. Then, one could somehow manage by turning a blind eye to what others were doing without his knowledge.

Unable to decide what was to be done, Anandamoyi arose dejectedly and stood in silence for a while. Then she said:

'Can't you see what's happening to your body?'

'My body!' Krishnadayal gave an abrupt guffaw at her stupidity. Their discussion on this subject did not lead to any satisfactory conclusion. Krishnadayal once again immersed himself in the *Gherandasamhita*.

Meanwhile, Mahim was in the outer chamber, discussing lofty spiritual truths with Krishnadayal's sanyasi. Having anxiously inquired, with extreme humility, whether mukti or spiritual liberation was possible for householders, he folded his hands and awaited the reply so attentively, with such excessive devotion and eagerness, it seemed that he had pledged all he possessed to attain mukti. The sanyasi was trying to console Mahim somehow, assuring him that heaven, though not mukti, was available to householders. But Mahim refused to be consoled. His heart was set on mukti, heaven was of no use to him. If he could somehow marry off his daughter, he could devote himself to the pursuit of mukti by serving the sanyasi. Who could deter him? But marrying off a daughter was indeed no easy matter. Not unless the sanyasi baba took pity on him.

## 64

Remembering that he had lately forgotten himself somewhat, Gora became even more rigid than before. He had decided it was due to slackness in his observance of restrictions that he had been overwhelmed by a powerful enchantment, forgetting his own community.

Completing his sandhya rituals in the morning, Gora entered the room and found Poreshbabu there. Lightning seemed to streak through his heart. Even his nerves and blood vessels could not deny Poresh's deep, intimate connection with his own life. Gora found himself bowing to touch Poresh's feet in a pranam.

'You must have heard of Binoy's marriage plans?' Poresh asked him.

'Yes.'

'He is not willing to be married by Brahmo rites.'

'Then this wedding should not take place at all.'

Poresh smiled faintly, without arguing about it. 'No one in our community will participate in this wedding ceremony,' he told Gora. 'Even Binoy's own relatives will not attend, I hear. I am there to represent my daughter's side; on Binoy's side there is perhaps nobody but you. That is why I have come to consult you.'

'What use consulting me on this? I have nothing to do with it.'

Poreshbabu stared at Gora in surprise. 'You have nothing to do with it?' he repeated, after a while.

For a moment, Gora felt a little awkward at Poresh's astonishment. But the very next moment, because he felt this awkwardness, he declared with redoubled firmness: 'How can I be involved in this!'

'I know you are his friend,' persisted Poreshbabu. 'At such a time, doesn't he need his friends most of all?'

'I am his friend, but that's not my only tie in the world, or the most important one.'

'Gour, do you find anything wrong or irreligious in Binoy's conduct?'

'But there are two aspects to dharma,' Gora insisted. 'The eternal aspect, and the everyday one. Where dharma takes the form of social laws it cannot be ignored, for then the world would be devastated.'

'But there are countless laws. Must we take every law for an expression of dharma?'

Poreshbabu had touched the very area of Gora's consciousness that was already in turmoil, where Gora had already drawn a certain conclusion from the churning of his thoughts. So, even before Poreshbabu, he had no reservations in pouring out the words accumulated within. The gist of what he had to say was this: unless we defer completely to society by following its rules, we obstruct its innermost, profoundest purpose; for this purpose lies deep, and every man does not have the capacity to perceive it clearly. Therefore we must have the strength to obey society even by suspending our judgement.

Poreshbabu calmly heard Gora out. When he stopped, rather embarrassed at his own garrulity, Poresh remarked: 'I accept your premise. It is true that the Maker of our destiny has a certain purpose in creating each community. Nor is that purpose clearly evident to everyone. But it is human duty to try and perceive it clearly. There is no fulfilment in following rules blindly, like members of the plant kingdom.'

'What I'm saying is, that only if we first follow our society's dictates in every respect, can we attain a pure awareness of our society's true purpose,' Gora persisted. 'To oppose society is not only to hinder its progress but also to misinterpret it.'

'Without opposition and obstacles, the truth can never be tested,' Poreshbabu countered. 'Not that the truth is tested once by a group of wise men in some ancient age, after which the matter is permanently settled. The truth must be discovered afresh by the people of every era, through obstacles and conflict. Anyway, I don't wish to argue about all this. I believe in the personal freedom of human beings. It is only by attacking the truth with this personal freedom that we can discover what is permanent and what is passing fancy. Upon that knowledge and the pursuit of that knowledge depends the welfare of society.'

With these words Poresh rose to his feet, and Gora, too, arose from his chair. 'I had thought I would have to remain somewhat aloof from this wedding, at the request of the Brahmo Samaj, and that you, as Binoy's friend, would see the whole thing through. That is a friend's advantage over a relative, for he does not have to endure the onslaughts of society. But since you have deemed it your duty to abandon Binoy, the entire responsibility now rests with me. I must accomplish this task alone.'

How alone Poreshbabu felt, Gora did not realize at the time. Borodasundari opposed Poreshbabu, the daughters of the house were not pleased, and fearing Harimohini's objections, Poresh had not even consulted Sucharita about wedding preparations. Meanwhile, everyone in the Brahmo Samaj had taken up cudgels against him, and the couple of letters he had received from Binoy's khudo, his paternal uncle, abused him as an evil, scheming kidnapper.

As soon as Poresh left, Abinash and some other members of Gora's group came in, ready to make fun of Poreshbabu. But Gora objected:

'If you are incapable of respecting someone worthy of it, at least spare yourselves the pettiness of mocking him.'

Once again Gora had to immerse himself in his customary activities involving his group. But how distasteful everything seemed! It was all worthless. This could not be described as work at all. There was no soul in it. Until now, it had never struck Gora so forcibly that merely by saying things on paper, or giving speeches, or forming groups, nothing real was being accomplished; rather, a vast amount of useless effort was being accumulated. Broadened by his newfound powers, his life-stream now demanded a true channel where its current could flow in full force. His present activities no longer pleased him.

Meanwhile, arrangements were under way for the ceremonial penance. Gora had been particularly enthusiastic about these preparations. This penance was not only for the impurity of life in prison, it seemed a way for him to purify himself in every respect, to be reborn into his field of work with a new body. They had obtained instructions about the rites of penance, the date and venue had also been fixed, and invitations were ready for distribution to famous teachers and scholars of East and West Bengal. The affluent among Gora's group had also raised the funds. All members of the group had assumed that the country had at last undertaken a worthwhile task. Abinash had secretly conspired with his group that on this occasion, all the learned men present at the gathering would confer upon Gora the title of 'Hindupradeep,' Light of the Hindu World, along with flowers, sandalwood paste, rice grains, holy durba grass, and sundry other religious offerings. Gora would be gifted a sandalwood box containing some Sanskrit shlokas inscribed in gold and signed by all the learned Brahmans present. Alongside, a volume of Max Mueller's edition of the Rig Veda, bound in priceless Morocco leather, would be presented to him by the seniormost and most eminent professor, as a token of blessing from Bharatvarsha. This would beautifully express the feeling that in the modern era of depravity, it was Gora who was the true guardian of the sacred Vedic faith.

So, unbeknownst to Gora, members of his group conspired daily to make the event extremely appealing and productive.

## 65

Harimohini received a letter from her deor Kailash. He wrote:

> By the grace of the revered One, all is well here. Please relieve us of our anxiety by informing us of your well-being.

Needless to say, ever since Harimohini had left their home, they had been burdened with this anxiety, but had made no effort to address the lack of information about her well-being. After exhausting all the news about Khudi, Potol, Bhajahari and everyone else, Kailash wrote in conclusion:

> Please send us proper details about the paatri, the prospective bride. You inform us she would be about twelve or thirteen years old, but she is a growing girl and looks a little mature—no harm in that. From what you indicate about her claims to property, if you let us know after proper verification whether her ownership is valid for life or permanently, I shall consult our elders about it. I think they would not object. I am relieved to hear that the paatri is committed to the Hindu faith, but we must try to suppress the fact that she was reared in a Brahmo household all this while. Hence you must not divulge this to anyone else. The lunar eclipse on the next full moon is auspicious for a bath in the Ganga. If possible, I shall visit you then to see the girl.

She had somehow remained in Kolkata all these days, but at the faint hope of returning to her in-laws' home, Harimohini lost all patience. Each day of exile now seemed intolerable. 'Let me talk to Sucharita at once and fix a day to complete the task,' she began to wish. But she did not dare make haste. The more closely she observed Sucharita, the more clearly she realized she had not understood her. Harimohini waited for an opportunity, and became even more vigilant about Sucharita's conduct. Now she tended to spend less time at her prayers than before, no longer willing to let Sucharita out of her sight. Sucharita noticed Gora's visits had ceased abruptly. She realized Harimohini must have said something to him.

'Very well,' she resolved, 'let him not come, but it is he who is my guru, my own guru.' An absent guru exerts a much greater influence than one present in the flesh. For then the heart compensates from within for that absence. Where Sucharita would have argued with Gora if he were present, she now read his works and accepted his statements unresistingly. If she did not understand them, she told herself he would surely have explained if he had been there.

But it was not easy, indeed, to quench her hunger for the sight of Gora's radiant image, and to listen to his words, charged with lightning like thunderclouds. Her insatiable inner yearning seemed constantly to erode her physical being. From time to time Sucharita would think, achingly, of the many people who had ready access to Gora, night and day, though they could not understand the value of such a sight.

One afternoon, Lalita came to Sucharita and embraced her.

'Bhai Suchididi!'

'What is it, bhai Lalita?'

'It's all arranged.'

'What date has been fixed?'

'Monday.'

'Where?'

'I don't know about all that. Baba knows.'

'Are you happy, bhai?' asked Sucharita, putting her arm round Lalita's waist.

'Why would I not be happy!'

'Now you've got everything you desired, you have no reason to quarrel with anyone about anything. That makes me fear you might lose your enthusiasm.'

'Why? Why should I lack people to quarrel with? Now I need not look beyond the home.'

'Is that so!' cried Sucharita, rapping Lalita on the cheek. 'Are you plotting such things already! I shall warn Binoy. The poor fellow still has time to put himself on guard.'

'Your poor fellow has no time left to put himself on guard, my dear,' Lalita retorted. 'There is no saving him now. What was destined for him has come true, now he can only smite his forehead in despair, and weep.'

'How can I tell you how pleased I am, Lalita!' said Sucharita gravely. 'I pray that you should prove yourself worthy of a husband like Binoy.'

'Indeed! Is that so! And must nobody prove themselves worthy of me! Just try discussing it with him once. If you hear his opinion once, even you will regret that you failed to appreciate such a wonderful person, all these days. How blind you were!'

'Never mind,' Sucharita responded, 'at last we have found an expert on jewels. No point crying over the price he offers, for now you will no longer need appreciation from ignorant people like us.'

'Shan't I, indeed! Of course I shall,' Lalita insisted. She pinched Sucharita's cheek so hard, she cried out in pain. 'I want your appreciation always. You can't evade that and offer it to someone else.'

'I shall not offer it to anyone else, anyone at all,' Sucharita assured her, placing her cheek against Lalita's.

'Anyone?' Lalita persisted. 'Not to anyone at all?'

Sucharita only shook her head.

'Look bhai Suchididi,' said Lalita, moving away a little. 'You know bhai that I could never tolerate it if you cared for anyone else. I didn't tell you all these days, but I tell you now, when Gourmohanbabu used to visit . . . No, Didi, you can't do that, today I must speak my mind—I've never concealed anything from you, but that's one thing I could never bring myself to tell you, I don't know why, and that has troubled me all along. I can't bid you farewell until I have told you about it. When Gourmohanbabu visited us I used to feel very angry. What made me angry? Did you think I didn't understand anything? I noticed you wouldn't even mention his name to me, and that would infuriate me even more. I found it intolerable that you should love him more than you loved me. No, bhai Didi, you must let me speak—how can I tell you what I suffered on that account? Even now, you

won't discuss that subject with me, I know. But even if you don't, I'm not angry anymore. I would be so delighted, bhai, if your . . .'

'I beg you, bhai Lalita, don't utter those words!' pleaded Sucharita, quickly placing her hand on Lalita's mouth. 'I want to sink into the ground when I hear that suggestion.'

'Why, bhai, is he . . .'

'No, no, no!' cried Sucharita in great agitation. 'Stop saying such crazy things! One must not utter the unthinkable.'

'But this is too much, bhai,' protested Lalita, annoyed at Sucharita's embarrassment. 'I have been watching very closely, and I can tell you for sure . . .'

Breaking free of Lalita's grasp, Sucharita rushed from the room. Lalita ran after her and dragged her back

'Achchha, achchha, I won't mention it again,' she swore.

'Never again!'

'I can't make such a big promise,' Lalita responded. 'I'll mention it if I turn out to be right, not otherwise. That much I promise.'

These few days, Harimohini had hovered close to Sucharita, keeping a strict watch on her. Sucharita had realized it, and Harimohini's wary vigilance weighed heavily upon her mind. Though inwardly desperate, she could not say a word. Now, after Lalita had left, Sucharita wept in exhaustion, head between her hands, elbows on the table. When the attendant came to light the lamp, she forbade him. That was the hour for Harimohini's evening prayers. From the upper floor, having seen

Lalita depart, untimely she came downstairs and entered Sucharita's room.

'Radharani!' she called.

Secretly wiping away her tears, Sucharita quickly rose to her feet.

'What's going on?' Harimohini demanded.

Sucharita offered no reply.

'I fail to understand what's going on here!' declared Harimohini harshly.

'Mashi, why do you watch me like this, day and night?' Sucharita demanded.

'Don't you understand why? All this fasting, all these tears, what do these things mean? Am I a child, not to understand something so simple?'

'I tell you Mashi, you have not understood anything at all. You have misunderstood things so terribly, I'm finding it harder to endure, every moment.'

'So if I have misunderstood, why don't you explain things to me properly?'

'Achchha, let me explain then,' said Sucharita, determinedly subduing all her diffidence. 'From my guru I have learnt something new, something it takes a lot of strength to accept. It is that strength I seem to lack now. I can't cope with the constant need to fight you. But Mashi, you have a distorted view of my relationship with him. You have insulted him and sent him away. Whatever you said to him was wrong, and your view of me is false! You have wronged us! It is beyond your power to degrade a man like him. But why did you torment me so? What have I done to you?' As she spoke, Sucharita's voice became choked. She left the room.

Harimohini was stupefied. 'Never in my whole life have I heard such words!' she said to herself. Allowing Sucharita some time to compose herself, she called her to dinner. Then she said:

'Look Radharani, I am not so young, after all. Since childhood I have followed what the Hindu religion says, and heard a lot about it as well. You know nothing about such things, that is why Gourmohan can beguile you, posing as your guru. I have heard some of the things he says; there is nothing genuinely traditional in his words, those scriptural truths are of his own making. We can detect such things because we have been trained by gurus. I tell you Radharani, you need not follow any of those injunctions. When the time comes, my Guru, who is not so false, will himself offer you the mantra of initiation. Have no fear, I shall get you into the Hindu community. Never mind that you were part of a Brahmo family. Who would ever know? You are indeed a little too mature, but there are so many girls like you, older than required. Who will check your birthchart after all? And since there is money, there will be no hurdles, everything will be accepted. I have myself seen a low-caste kaibarta pass off for a higher-caste kayastha. I shall marry you into such a good Brahman family in the Hindu community that nobody will dare gossip, for the family would themselves be the leaders of the community. For that, you won't have to suffer, worshipping a guru and shedding so many tears.'

While Harimohini was waxing eloquent, Sucharita discovered she had lost her appetite, and her food seemed hard to swallow. But she silently forced herself to eat. For she knew that even her lack of appetite would invite the sort of comment she would not find at all palatable.

Finding Sucharita unresponsive, Harimohini said to herself: 'One must hand it to them! Shedding all these tears in the name of Hinduism, and then ignoring such a great opportunity! No need for penance, no excuses required, just spending a little money here and there to gain easy entry into the community—if even that fails to enthuse her, can she call herself a Hindu!' Harimohini was left in no doubt about the extent of Gora's duplicity. But trying to determine the motive behind such deception, she felt it was Sucharita's wealth that was at the root of all this mischief—that, and Sucharita's youthful beauty. The sooner she could rescue this girl, company documents and all, and confine her in the fortress of her marital home, the better. But without softening her mind a little more, the plan would not work. In the hope of softening Sucharita's mind, she began to constantly sing the praises of her own in-laws' family, for Sucharita's benefit. Using diverse examples, she extolled their extraordinary influence, their impossible achievements in community affairs. How even blameless persons suffered social opprobrium for trying to oppose this family, and how many people supported by this family managed to survive comfortably within the Hindu way of life even after consuming chicken cooked by Muslims—Harimohini authenticated all these anecdotes with names, addresses and detailed descriptions.

Borodasundari made no secret of the fact that she did not want Sucharita to frequent their house, for she prided herself on her bluntness. She often announced this virtue when being unabashedly harsh to others. Hence Sucharita had plainly received the message that she should not expect any warmth in Borodasundari's household. Sucharita also knew that Poresh would have to face tremendous domestic discord if she visited their house regularly, so she did not go there unless strictly necessary. Hence Poresh would drop by at Sucharita's house to see her, once or twice a day.

Poreshbabu had been unable to visit Sucharita for a few days, preoccupied with various concerns and responsibilities. Sucharita had eagerly awaited his arrival, yet privately she too had felt rather uneasy and hurt. She knew for sure that her deepest ties of harmony with Poresh could never be severed, but was tormented by the painful awareness that some major outer strands were threatening to snap. Meanwhile Harimohini had made her life more intolerable by the hour. Hence, braving even Borodasundari's displeasure, Sucharita now arrived at Poresh's house. At that hour, the late afternoon sun had slanted to the back of the three-storied building on the western side, casting a giant shadow. And beneath that shadow, head bowed, Poresh was walking slowly on the garden path, all by himself. Sucharita joined him.

'Baba, how are you?' she asked.

Poreshbabu's trend of thought was suddenly broken. 'I am fine Radhé,' he replied after a brief pause, gazing at her face. The two of them strolled along together.

'Lalita is getting married on Monday,' said Poreshbabu.

Sucharita thought of asking why her advice or assistance had not been sought in organizing this wedding. But she too felt hindered now by a certain constraint. Formerly, indeed, she would not have waited to be asked for help.

Then Poresh raised the very subject that was on her mind. 'I couldn't send for you this time, Radhé,' he said.

'Why Baba?'

Poresh looked at her without offering any reply. Sucharita could bear it no longer.

'You thought I had undergone a change of heart,' she said, lowering her face.

'Yes, that is why I thought I would avoid embarrassing you with any request.'

'Baba, I had planned to tell you everything but I didn't get to see you at all. That is why I have come here today. I don't have the ability to properly communicate my innermost feelings to you. I am afraid I might not manage to convey the exact truth.'

'I know such things are not easy to communicate clearly,' Poreshbabu assured her. 'There is something you have discovered in your heart, through your emotions alone; you feel it, but its nature is not yet known to you.'

'Yes, exactly!' said Sucharita, relieved. 'But my feelings are so strong, how can I describe them to you? As if I have found a new life, a new awareness. I have never viewed myself from such a perspective. All these days, I felt no connection with my nation's past or future, but so powerfully has my heart now recognized the great reality of that connection, I simply cannot drive it from my mind. Look, Baba, to tell you the truth, I could never have declared earlier that I am a Hindu. But now my heart vehemently and unabashedly proclaims: "I am a Hindu." That brings me great joy.'

'Have you considered all aspects, all angles of this matter?'

'Have I the capacity to consider everything as a whole? But I have read a lot on the subject, and discussed it extensively too. Before I learnt to take a large view of the matter, I used to magnify the petty details of what it means to be a Hindu. That made me very contemptuous of the whole business.'

Poreshbabu was surprised at her words. He clearly realized that Sucharita had developed a certain awareness, that she undoubtedly felt she had attained something real. She was not merely adrift on a vague tide of emotion like one entranced, uncomprehending.

'Baba,' persisted Sucharita, 'why should I say I am an insignificant person, divorced from my country and my community? Why can't I say "I am a Hindu"?'

'In other words Ma,' laughed Poreshbabu, 'it is me you are asking, why I don't call myself a Hindu. When one thinks about it, there seems to be no major reason why. One reason is that the Hindus don't acknowledge me as a Hindu, and another is that the people who share my views on religion don't identify themselves as Hindus.'

Sucharita was silent, lost in thought.

'I have already told you,' Poresh continued, 'that these are not major reasons, merely outward ones. One can ignore such obstacles. But there is also an internal, deeper reason. There can be no entry into Hindu society. Or at least, there is no front gate, even if a backdoor exists. This community is not for the whole of humanity, it is only for those who happen to be born as Hindus.'

'But that is true of every community,' Sucharita protested.

'No,' insisted Poreshbabu, 'it is not so with any major community. The gates of the Muslim community are open to the whole of humanity, and the Christian community also welcomes everyone. The same law applies to all communities belonging to the Christian world. If I want to become an Englishman, it would not be entirely impossible: by living in England and obeying their laws, I can gain entry into their society; I need not even become a Christian. Abhimanyu knew how to enter the battletrap but he did not know the way out. With Hindus it is the exact opposite. The way into their community is completely shut, but there are a hundred thousand ways out of it.'

'All the same, Baba, the Hindu community has not declined to this day. It still survives.'

'It takes time to sense the decline of a community,' explained Poresh. 'Before this, the backdoor to Hindu society was open. Non-Aryan people then felt a certain glory in entering the Hindu world. Later, during the days of Muslim rule, the Hindu kings and zamindars exerted considerable influence almost everywhere in the country, hence there was no limit to rules and restrictions against leaving the community easily. Now British rule offers everyone protection under the law, so it is no longer so easy to use such artificial means to guard the doors leading out of the community. That is why for some time we have seen a constant decline in the number of Hindus in Bharatvarsha, while the Muslim population increases. If this continues, the country will gradually develop a Muslim majority. Then it will be unjust to even call it Hindustan.'

'Baba, shouldn't we try to prevent it, all of us?' cried Sucharita in distress. 'Shall we too abandon the Hindu world and aggravate its decline? This is indeed the moment for us to cling to it with all our might.'

'Can we keep someone alive at will, by clinging to him?' said Poreshbabu, affectionately stroking Sucharita's back. 'To gain protection, there is a worldly law to be followed. One who rejects that natural law is naturally rejected in turn by everyone else. Hindu society insults people, excludes people, hence in today's world it is becoming daily more difficult for it to protect itself. For it can no longer remain in seclusion, now that all roads to the world are open, and people from everywhere are coming into contact with the community. Now it cannot dam or fortify itself with the shastra-samhitas, to somehow shield itself from contact with everyone else. If the Hindu community does not foster within itself, even now, the power of conservation rather than the disease of decay, then this unchecked encounter with people from outside will become a lethal blow to its survival.'

'I understand nothing of all this,' declared Sucharita, in agony. 'But if this is indeed true, I cannot bring myself to reject the community today when all of you are ready to abandon it. As its children born in times of need, we must now attend upon its sickbed.'

'Ma, I shall say nothing to contradict the feelings that have arisen in your heart,' Poreshbabu assured her. 'Steady your mind with prayer, and judge everything by the truth, the ideal of greatness, that you carry within. Gradually everything will become clear to you. Don't regard the greatest One as inferior to the nation or to any human being. That will not be beneficial for you or your nation. With this in view, I wish to surrender myself wholeheartedly to Him. Then I can easily remain true to the nation and to every human being.'

At this juncture, someone delivered Poreshbabu a letter.

'I don't have my glasses, and the light has waned,' said Poreshbabu. 'Please see what the letter says.'

Sucharita read the letter to him. It was addressed to him by a Brahmo Samaj committee, bearing the signatures of several Brahmos. In sum, the letter declared that since Poresh had consented to non-Brahmo rites at his daughter's marriage and was prepared to participate in the ceremonies himself, the Brahmo Samaj in such circumstances could by no means count him among the civilized. If he had anything to say in his own defence, the committee must receive a letter to that effect before the coming Sunday. That day the matter would be discussed and resolved according to the views of the majority. Poresh took the letter and put it in his pocket. Gently clasping his right hand, Sucharita silently walked beside him. Gradually, dusk descended and the darkness deepened. In the alley to the south of the garden, a light came on.

'Baba, it is time for your prayers,' said Sucharita softly. 'I want to pray with you this evening.' So saying, Sucharita led him by the hand to the secluded prayer chamber. There, the mat had been spread and a candle lit, as usual. That evening, Poresh meditated silently for a long time. Ultimately after uttering a small prayer, he arose and came away.

As soon as he emerged he saw Lalita and Binoy waiting quietly outside the door. Seeing him, the two of them bent to touch his feet in a pranam. Placing his hands on their heads, he blessed them in his mind.

'Ma,' he said to Sucharita, 'I shall visit your house tomorrow. Let me complete my work tonight.' With these words he went into his room.

Tears were streaming from Sucharita's eyes. Motionless as a statue, she stood silently in the darkness of the verandah. For a long time, Lalita and Binoy also did not utter a word. When Sucharita prepared to leave, Binoy came before her.

'Didi, will you not bless us?' he asked in a low voice.

He and Lalita bowed together at Sucharita's feet. What Sucharita said in a tear-choked voice was audible only to the One who resides in our hearts.

Back in his room, Poreshbabu wrote a letter to the Brahmo Samaj committee:

> I must take charge of Lalita's wedding. If you abandon me for that reason, it will not be unjust of you. At this moment I only pray to Ishwar that he remove me from all social shelter and grant me a place at his own feet.

## 66

Sucharita became desperate to tell Gora what Poresh had said to her. Had Gora not realized that the very Bharatvarsha for whose sake he had expanded his outlook and drawn his heart to a powerful love, was now affected by Time and on the path to decline! Because Bharatvarsha had survived on the strength of its internal organization all these years, its people had not needed to be vigilant. But was there any time left now for such a complacent existence? Could we afford to stay indoors, clinging to old systems as before?

'I too have a duty to perform here,' Sucharita began to think. 'What might it be?' At this point, Gora should have come before her to offer instructions and show her the way. Sucharita said to herself: 'If he could have rescued me from all my constraints and ignorance, and positioned me in my proper place, would the significance of that not have overridden all petty questions of social propriety and malicious gossip?' She was infused with a sense of her own superiority. She asked herself why Gora had not put her to the test, why he did not ask her to accomplish the impossible. Was there a single man in Gora's group, capable like Sucharita of effortlessly surrendering all they possessed? Did Gora see no need for such voluntary self-sacrifice and such strength? Would it not harm the nation at all if this urge was rendered ineffective by the shackles of propriety? Refusing to acknowledge such indifference, Sucharita dismissed it from her thoughts. 'He could never possibly reject me in this fashion. He must come to me, seek me out, giving up all constraints and hesitations. However powerful a man he is, he needs me: he told me so himself, once. How could he forget that now simply due to some meaningless speculations!'

'Didi!' cried Satish, rushing up to stand close to Sucharita's lap.

'So, bhai bakhtiar!' she responded, hugging him.

'Lalitadidi's wedding is on Monday. I stay with Binoybabu for the next few days. He has sent for me.'

'Have you told Mashi?'

'I told her. She got angry and said: "I don't know about that, speak to your didi, she'll decide what's best." Didi, please don't forbid me. My studies will not suffer at all there, I'll study every day. Binoybabu will guide me.'

'You will cause disturbance in a house where everyone will be busy,' Sucharita told him.

'No Didi, I shan't disturb anything,' Satish promised anxiously.

'Will you take your little puppy along, then?'

'Yes, I must take him. Binoybabu has specially asked me to. There was a separate invitation for him printed on red paper. It says he must attend and savour the refreshments, along with his family.'

'And who might his family be?'

'Why, Binoybabu says it's me,' Satish hastened to assure her. 'He has also asked us to bring along that organ, Didi. Please let me have it. I won't break it.'

'But I would be relieved if it were to break. So now it's quite clear—it is to play the organ at his wedding that your friend has invited you? Does he intend to avoid the professional musicians of the rowshan-chowki altogether?'

'No, never!' cried Satish, greatly agitated. 'Binoybabu says he will make me his mitbar, the groom's young double. What is the mitbar's role, Didi?'

'He must fast all day,' Sucharita informed him. Satish was utterly incredulous. Now Sucharita drew him firmly to her lap and asked: 'Tell me bhai bakhtiar, what will you become when you grow up?'

Satish was mentally prepared with his answer. It was his class teacher who stood for his ideal of indomitable power and extraordinary learning. He had already decided to become a mastermoshai, a schoolteacher, when he grew up.

'There's a lot to be done, bhai!' Sucharita told him. 'Brother and sister, we two must perform our duties together. What do you say Satish? We must give our lives to enlarge our nation's stature. Indeed, what is there to enlarge! Is there anything as great as our nation! It is our spirit we must enlarge. Do you know that? Do you understand?'

Satish was not one to readily acknowledge that he had not understood. 'Yes,' he affirmed emphatically.

'You know how immense is our country, our population,' Sucharita declared. 'How would I explain it to you? What an extraordinary nation this is! How many thousands of years the Maker of our destiny has spent, preparing to place this nation on the world's pinnacle; how many people from diverse lands have come here to join in the preparations, how many great men have been born here, how many great wars fought, how many great utterances pronounced, how many great tasks accomplished, how diversely religion has been viewed in this country and how many varied solutions have been found here for life's problems! Such is this Bharatvarsha of ours. Know its greatness bhai, don't ever disdain it even by mistake. What I tell you now you must one day understand. Not that I imagine you have understood nothing of it even today. Bear this in mind—you have been born into a very vast country; you must revere this immense nation with all your heart, and lay down your life in its service.'

'Didi, what will you do?' asked Satish after a short silence.

'I shall do the same,' Sucharita assured him. 'You'll help me, won't you?'

'Yes I shall,' declared Satish, immediately swelling with pride.

There was no one at home to whom Sucharita could confide the thoughts that swelled in her heart. Hence all her emotions overflowed when she found this younger brother close at hand. What she said, and the words in which she said it, were not meant for a young boy's ears, but that did not deter her. She had sensed that only if she gave a complete account of the insight she had gained in her present excitable state, would everyone, young or old, somehow interpret it according to their own levels of comprehension. But if she held things back, trying to explain them in other people's terms, the truth would inevitably become distorted.

Satish's imagination was aroused. 'When I grow up, when I have a lot of money . . .' he began.

'No, no, no!' objected Sucharita. 'Don't talk of money. We two have no need for money, bakhtiar. For our undertaking we need devotion, the commitment of the heart.'

At this moment Anandamoyi entered the room. The blood raced in Sucharita's heart. She bent to touch Anandamoyi's feet. Pranams did not come easy to Satish. Awkwardly, he somehow performed the gesture. Drawing Satish to her lap, Anandamoyi kissed the top of his head and said to Sucharita:

'I came for a bit of consultation with you, ma. I don't see anyone else after all. Binoy was saying, "The wedding will take place at my own house." "That cannot happen under any circumstances," I objected. "As if you are a great nawab, that a daughter of ours should come to your own home for the wedding ceremony!" That can't be allowed. I have located a place, not far from yours. I have just come from there. Please speak to Poreshbabu and convince him.'

'Baba will agree.'

'And then ma, you too must go there. The wedding is on this very Monday. In these few days we must stay there and make all the arrangements. Indeed, we don't have much time. I can handle everything alone, but if you are not involved Binoy will feel very hurt. He can't bring himself to request you directly, in fact he did not mention you even to me, but from that itself I can sense that for him it is a very sensitive issue. You can't afford to remain detached any longer, ma. Lalita too would be deeply hurt.'

'Ma, can you participate in this wedding?' asked Sucharita, rather surprised.

'How can you say that, Sucharita! Participate! Am I an outsider, to merely participate! This is Binoy's wedding after all! It is I who must handle the whole affair. But I have told Binoy, "As far as this wedding is concerned, I'm no relation of yours. I represent the bride's party." He is coming to my house to marry Lalita.'

Anandamoyi's heart was heavy with the sorrow of knowing that despite having a mother, Lalita had been abandoned by her at this auspicious moment. For that very reason, she was trying single-mindedly to ensure that the wedding ceremony did not smack of neglect or disrespect. Taking her mother's place, she would personally adorn Lalita for the ceremony, organize the ceremonial reception of the bridegroom, ensure that there was not the slightest lapse in hospitality if a few invitees should turn up. And she would decorate this new dwelling in such a way that Lalita would regard it as a home. Such was her resolve.

'Will this not create problems for you?' Sucharita asked her.

'Indeed it might, but so what?' responded Anandamoyi, recalling the upheaval Mahim had caused at home. 'There are always some problems, but if we bear them quietly, in time they too disappear.'

Sucharita knew Gora had not participated in the wedding preparations. She was curious to know whether he had made any attempt to dissuade Anandamoyi from participating. But she could not broach the matter directly, and Anandamoyi did not even mention Gora's name.

Harimohini had heard of the developments. Having completed the chores at hand in a leisurely way, she entered the room and asked:

'Didi, I hope you are doing well? We don't see you, nor do you inquire after us.'

'I have come to fetch your bonjhi,' responded Anandamoyi, without answering her complaint. She then proceeded to explain her purpose. Displeased, Harimohini remained silent for a while. Then she said:

'I can't attend, in the middle of all this.'

'No bon, my sister, I don't ask you to attend,' Anandamoyi assured her. 'Don't worry about Sucharita. I shall be with her, after all.'

'Let me tell you, then,' declared Harimohini. 'Radharani has been telling people she is a Hindu. Now she feels inclined towards Hinduism. So if she wants to follow the Hindu ways, she must be careful. As it is it will cause a lot of gossip, but I can counter that. But from now on, she should mind her ways for a while. The first thing people ask is why she isn't married, at such an advanced age. That can somehow be suppressed. Not that one couldn't find a good match for her, if one tried. But if she again takes to her recent ways, how many fronts can I manage, tell me? Daughter of a Hindu family, you understand everything; so how can you say such things either? If you had a daughter of your own, could you have sent her to attend this marriage? You would be compelled to worry about getting your daughter married!'

Anandamoyi glanced in amazement at Sucharita, whose face flamed blood-red.

'I don't want to exert any force,' she explained. 'If Sucharita objects, I . . .'

'I can't fathom what you have in mind, the two of you!' protested Harimohini. 'It is your son who has accepted her according to Hindu tradition, so how can you appear so surprised?'

Where was the Harimohini who in Poreshbabu's house was always afraid of making a mistake, clinging avidly to anyone who showed the slightest signs of being favourably inclined! Now she was poised like a tigress to defend her rights, always on edge, suspicious that adverse forces were at work everywhere, to wrest her very own Sucharita from her possession. Unable to surmise who was her friend, and who her enemy, her mind could not remain at ease. Her spirit could not find equilibrium even in worshipping the deity in whom she had previously sought refuge in desperation, finding the whole world hollow. She was extremely worldly, once; when extreme grief made her indifferent to material things, she could never have imagined that she might some day regain the slightest attachment to money, property or family relationships. But now, as soon as her heart had recovered somewhat from its wounds, the world was again present before her, tugging at her emotions. Once again, all her hopes and desires had reared their heads, fed by her long-time hunger. So strong was the urge to resume what she had renounced, she had not experienced such restlessness even when she had formerly belonged to the everyday world. Anandamoyi was astonished at the unimaginable transformation that had taken place in just a few days, its signs evident in Harimohini's facial expressions, body language and social conversation. Anandamoyi began to feel very sorry for Sucharita in her tender heart. Had she sensed such imminent danger, she would never have come to call Sucharita. Now she found it a problem to protect Sucharita from pain.

When Harimohini made pointed remarks about Gora, Sucharita hung her head and silently walked out of the room.

'Have no fear, bon!' Anandamoyi assured her. 'I was not aware of this. Well, I shall not trouble her with any more requests. Please don't say anything to her either. She has previously been brought up in a certain way. If you suddenly pressurize her too much, she cannot endure it!'

'As if I don't realize that, considering my advanced age!' retorted Harimohini. 'Let her declare in your presence then, if I have ever caused her any pain. She does whatever she pleases, I never say a word. I pray the Lord should protect her, that is all I ask. Such is my misfortune, I can't sleep for fear of what may happen someday.'

When Anandamoyi was on her way out, Sucharita emerged from her room and touched her feet.

'I shall come ma, and bring you all the news,' promised Anandamoyi, patting her tenderly. 'Nothing will hinder you. With Ishwar's blessings, the auspicious event will materialize.'

Sucharita did not say a word.

Early next morning, when Anandamoyi, along with Lachhmia, had unleashed a torrential flood to wash away the long-accumulated dust in their building, Sucharita arrived on the scene. Quickly dropping her broom, Anandamoyi drew her to her bosom. Now there was a great to-do, washing and mopping, moving things about and decorating the place. Poreshbabu had given Sucharita a suitable amount of money for their expenses. With that capital in hand, the two of them made countless lists, and then proceeded to amend them.

Not long after, Poresh himself arrived there with Lalita. Her own home had now become intolerable for Lalita. Nobody dared say anything to her, yet their silence had begun to assault her at every step. Ultimately when Borodasundari's friends began to visit their home in groups, to express their sympathy with her, Poresh judged it better to take Lalita away from this household. When it was time to depart, Lalita went to offer her pranams to Borodasundari. But the latter kept her face averted and started weeping after Lalita had left. Labanya and Leela were quite curious about Lalita's wedding; if they could somehow gain permission, they would not have wasted a moment in rushing to the wedding celebrations. But when Lalita took her leave, they maintained an extremely grave exterior, bearing in mind the harsh requirements of the Brahmo community. At the door, Lalita came face to face with Sudhir for a split second. But as some elderly members of their community were just behind him, she could not speak to him. Mounting her carriage, Lalita spotted a paper-wrapped package tucked into a corner of her seat. Opening it she found a German silver flower vase. Inscribed on it in English were the words: 'May Ishwar bless the happy couple.' Accompanying it was a card bearing only Sudhir's initials. Hardening her heart, Lalita had determined not to shed any tears that day. But as she clasped this sole token of love from their childhood friend at the moment of departure from her paternal home, tears streamed from her eyes. Poreshbabu sat motionless, his eyes closed.

'Come, come, ma, come,' Anandamoyi welcomed her, taking both Lalita's hands and drawing her inside, as if she had been expecting her just then.

Poreshababu sent for Sucharita. 'Lalita has left our house for good,' he told her in a trembling voice.

'She will not lack for care and affection here, Baba,' Sucharita assured him, clasping his hand.

When Poresh was about to leave, Anandamoyi appeared before him, head covered, and greeted him with a namaskar. Flustered, Poresh returned her greeting.

'Please have no worries about Lalita,' said Anandamoyi. 'She will never suffer any pain at the hands of the one to whose care you have surrendered her. And after all this time, the Almighty has filled a gap in my life. I had no daughter, but now I have acquired one. For a long time, I had been waiting in the hope that Binoy's bride would compensate for my lack of a daughter. Well, just as Ishwar has granted my wish at last, He has also brought me unimaginable good fortune in gifting me such a daughter and in such a wonderful way.'

For the first time since the upheaval about Lalita's marriage had begun, Poreshbabu's heart found a glimmer of hope in this world, and felt genuinely comforted.

# 67

After his release from prison so many visitors thronged Gora's house all day, it became impossible for him to remain at home amidst the suffocating verbosity of their prayers and homage, arguments and discussions. So he resumed his travels across the countryside.

He would leave home in the morning after a light repast, and return only at night. Travelling by train, he would alight at some station near Kolkata and enter the village. There, he would seek hospitality from localities where oil-men, blacksmiths, fishermen and others lived. Why this fair-skinned, towering Brahman should wander among their dwellings asking after their wellbeing, the people could not comprehend at all. In fact, all sorts of suspicions arose in their minds. But dismissing all their diffidence and wariness, Gora roamed in their midst. At times he faced hostile comments, but even that did not deter him.

The deeper he penetrated into their world, the more a certain thought began to trouble his mind. He observed that in these rural areas, social restrictions were far more powerful than in educated, cultured society. In every household, food, sleep, rest, work, everything was conducted, day and night, under the unblinking gaze of society. Each individual had a very simple faith in popular traditions, never questioning such things. Yet social restrictions and adherence to custom did not empower them at all in their fields of activity. It was doubtful whether such timid, helpless beings, so incapable of judging what was good for themselves, existed anywhere else in the world. Beyond adherence to tradition, there was no other good that they wholeheartedly acknowledged, or were willing to understand. It was prohibition, enforced through punishment or partisanship, that they regarded as supreme. The awareness of what must not be done entrapped their nature in a net from head to toe at every step, through various forms of discipline. But this was the net of indebtedness, the moneylender's bond, not the bondage imposed by a king. There was no broad unity within them that could draw them all together in good times or bad.

Gora could not help noticing that humans were using these practices as weapons to suck the blood of other human beings, brutally robbing them of their selfhood. How often he had observed that in performing social rituals, nobody showed the slightest compassion for anybody else! One man's father had been ailing for a long time. The poor man had spent all he had on his father's treatment and medication, with no help from any quarters. On the contrary, the people of his village insisted his father do penance for the unknown sin that caused his permanent ill-health. No one was unaware of that unfortunate man's poverty and lack of resources, but there was no forgiveness. It was the same with every ritual. Just as a police investigation was a worse calamity for the village than a robbery, so also was the parents' funeral a greater source of affliction for their offspring than even their parents' death. No one would accept low income or lack of strength as an excuse; the heartless demands of social custom must somehow be fulfilled to the letter. When arranging a marriage, the bridegroom's party would adopt every strategy to make the burden intolerable for the bride's father, without the slightest pity for the wretched man. Gora observed that this society did not help a man in times of need, nor supported him in times of trouble; it only used discipline as a threat to subdue him.

In educated society, Gora had forgotten this, for in that world, the power to unite for the general good operated from the outside. Various attempts at achieving unity had begun to manifest themselves in that social realm. The only cause for anxiety there was lest these collective efforts, being imitations of other societies, should prove fruitless.

But in the total passivity prevalent in the villages, where external pressures did not work in the same way, Gora saw his nation's profoundest weakness completely exposed. The dharma that gave everyone strength, energy and wellbeing in the form of service, love, compassion and self-sacrifice, was nowhere in evidence. The practices that only drew boundaries, divided people and tormented them, that would even deny the intellect and keep love at arm's length, were the ones that constantly hindered everyone in every respect, in every movement and activity. In the rural areas, the harmful effects of this foolish compliance drew Gora's attention so clearly and in so many forms, and he saw it attacking people's health, knowledge, religious sense and activities from so many angles, in so many ways, that it became impossible for him to continue deluding himself with the illusion of abstract thought.

The first thing Gora observed was that, among the lower castes in the villages, either because of a low female population or for some other reason, a large sum was required for obtaining a bride. Many men had to remain bachelors all their lives or until an advanced age. But widow remarriage was strictly forbidden. Owing to this, in every household, the atmosphere had become polluted and every member of society experienced the damaging effects and inconvenience that resulted. Everyone was obliged to tolerate this evil, yet it was not in anyone's power to oppose it. The same Gora who was reluctant to relax any restrictions in educated society, now attacked the restrictions prevalent in this place. He succeeded in influencing their priests but failed to win the consent of community members. Incensed at Gora, they declared:'Very well, when the Brahmans allow their widows to marry, so shall we.' Their main cause of anger was that they imagined Gora regarded them with contempt as a lowly community. They felt Gora had come there to preach that it was appropriate for people like themselves to adopt the meanest of customs.

Roaming in the villages, Gora had also observed that the Muslims possessed the unifying element that could draw them together. He had noticed that in times of trouble or difficulty in the village, the Hindus would not close their ranks to stand by each other like the Muslims. Gora had repeatedly wondered why such a vast gap should exist between these two communities, the closest of neighbours. He did not want to accept the answer that came to mind. It pained his entire being to acknowledge that Muslims were united by their dharma, not merely by their practices. Just as the bonds of tradition had not needlessly restrained all their activities, so also were their bonds of religion extremely close. Together, they had all accepted something that was not merely a 'no' but a 'yes', not impoverishing but enriching, for which human beings could, at a single call and in a single instant, stand together and readily surrender their lives.

In educated society, when Gora wrote, argued or delivered speeches, to persuade others and make them toe his line he had naturally coloured his ideas with the attractive hues of fancy, embellished the concrete with abstract analysis, presented even redundant ruins as enchanting images illumined by the moonlight of emotion. Because a section of his own countrymen were hostile to the country, because they viewed all aspects of their country in a negative light, a strong sense of patriotism had prompted Gora to protect his land from the humiliation of this self-detached view by trying day and night to cover his country's entire image with a dazzling emotional aura. That had become his habit. All was praiseworthy, even what others called a fault was somehow a virtue. Not that Gora tried to prove this like a lawyer; rather, he believed it with all his heart. Even in the most impossible situations he had flaunted this belief boldly like a victory flag, grasping it firmly and holding it aloft as he stood alone, confronting all his jeering adversaries. He had just one thing to say: he must first renew his countrymen's respect for their own land, before he took on any other task.

But when he entered the village, there was no audience to face, no need to prove anything, no longer any need to arouse all his confrontational instincts to subdue the contempt or jealousy of others. Here, therefore, he did not view the truth through any sort of veil or screen. It was the force of his patriotism that added extraordinary sharpness to his vision of the truth.

## 68

Dressed in a tussar jacket with a Chinese collar, chador wrapped around his waist, canvas bag in hand, Kailash came in person to Harimohini and greeted her with a pranam. He was close to thirty-five, of short, compact, sturdy build, his shaven moustache and beard sprouting like fresh grass after a few days minus the shaving blade. Seeing a relative from her husband's side of the family after so long, Harimohini exclaimed: 'What's this, it's Thakurpo is it not! Come, come, sit down!' She hastened to lay out a mat.

'Will you wash your hands and feet?' she asked.

'No, there is no need,' Kailash replied. 'Well, you seem to be in good health.'

'I'm hardly keeping well,' responded Harimohini, sensing that it was culpable to be in good shape. She proceeded to offer a catalogue of her various ailments and added: 'Well, I would be relieved to lay down my wretched body, but death doesn't favour me.'

Kailash objected to this indifferent attitude to life, and to prove that they derived great comfort from Harimohini's being alive even after dada, their elder brother, was no more, he declared:

'Don't you see, it's because you are there that one had reason to visit Kolkata, and found a place to stay, at least.'

After exhaustively recounting all the news about relatives and fellow-villagers, Kailash suddenly inquired, looking all around: 'Does this house belong to him, then?'

'Yes,' replied Harimohini.

'A brick-and-mortar house, I see.'

'Indeed it is,' affirmed Harimohini, fanning his enthusiasm. 'All of it.'

He also noted that the building's beams were made of sturdy sal and that the doors and windows were not built of mango wood. Nor did he fail to observe whether the walls of the house were a brick-and-a-half in thickness, or two. He also found out through interrogation the number of rooms, upstairs and down. Altogether, the whole affair struck him as rather satisfactory. It was hard for him to gauge what the cost of constructing this house might have been, for he did not know the exact price of all these building materials. Thinking it over, jiggling his crossed ankles, he told himself: 'It would have cost ten to fifteen thousand rupees at least.' Verbally reducing his estimate, he asked: 'What do you say Bouthakrun, it might have cost seven or eight thousand, maybe?'

'What's this you say Thakurpo, what is seven or eight thousand?' exclaimed Harimohini, expressing surprise at Kalilash's provincial ignorance. 'It wouldn't have cost a paisa less than twenty thousand rupees.'

With great attention, Kailash began to silently inspect everything around him. He derived a tremendous satisfaction from the thought that at this very moment, at a single nod of the head, he could become the sole master of this brick-built house, complete with sal beams and segun doors and windows.

'This is all very well, but where is the girl?' he asked.

'She has been invited away to her pishi's house,' Harimohini hastily replied. 'She may take three or four days longer.'

'Then how is one to see her?' Kailash said. 'I have another legal case coming up, and must leave by tomorrow.'

'Forget your legal case for the moment,' Harimohini urged him. 'You can't leave until the business here is settled.'

'Well, maybe the court case will be stalled, decreed one-sided. So let it be,' Kailash decided after some thought. After inspecting his surroundings once more, he judged that there were provisions here to compensate him. Suddenly he noticed some water that had collected in a corner of Harimohini's puja room. The room had no drainage, yet

Harimohini constantly washed and cleaned it with water. Hence some water always remained in a corner.

'Bouthakrun, that's not good,' Kailash exclaimed in agitation.

'Why, what is the matter?'

'That water collecting there, it won't do at all.'

'How can I prevent it Thakurpo?'

'No no, that can't be allowed. The roof will be completely damaged. Let me tell you Bouthakrun, we can't let you pour water around in this room.'

Harimohini was forced to remain silent. Kailash then expressed curiosity about the beauty of the prospective bride.

'That you will notice as soon as you see her,' Harimohini assured him. 'I can venture to say that your household has not received such a bride.'

'What! Our Mejobou . . .'

'There's no comparison! As if your Mejobou can match her!' Harimohini was none too pleased that it was Mejobou he named as the ideal of beauty in their family. 'Whatever you may say bapu, I like our No'bou much better than Mejobou!'

Kailash was not enthused at all by this comparison of Mejobou's beauty with No'bou's. In his imagination, he had added elongated eyes and a banshee-like nose to some previously unseen image, unleashing his fancy amidst a mass of ankle-length tresses. Harimohini realized that this matrimonial prospect was full of hope. In fact, she felt that even the bride's significant social shortcomings may not count as insurmountable obstacles in this case.

# 69

Knowing that Gora set out at dawn these days, Binoy arrived early at Gora's house on Monday, while it was still dark. He went straight upstairs to Gora's bedchamber. Not finding him there, he asked a servant and was informed that Gora was in the puja room. He was privately rather surprised. Going to the door of the thakurghor, he found Gora in an attitude of prayer, dressed in a raw-silk dhoti, a raw-silk wrap around his shoulders, but with the greater part of his massive white body uncovered. Seeing Gora at his prayers, Binoy was even more astonished. Hearing his footsteps, Gora turned around and seeing Binoy, he rose to his feet.

'Don't enter this room,' he cried in agitation.

'Don't worry, I won't,' Binoy assured him. 'It was you I had come to see.'

Gora emerged, changed his clothes, and led Binoy to the room on the second floor.

'Bhai Gora, it's Monday,' Binoy reminded him.

'It must be Monday,' Gora responded. 'The almanac might be wrong, but you cannot be mistaken about today's date. At least it's not Tuesday, that's for sure.'

'You may not attend, I know, but on this day, I cannot proceed with this undertaking without asking you once. That is why I have come to you first thing in the morning, immediately upon awakening.' Gora remained motionless, saying nothing. 'So it is decided that you will not be able to attend my wedding celebrations?'

'No Binoy, I can't attend.'

Binoy remained silent.

'So what if I don't attend?' smiled Gora, completely suppressing his inner anguish. 'The victory is yours. You have managed to drag Ma away after all. I tried so hard, but I could not hold her back by any means. Ultimately, even with my own mother, I had to lose to you! Binoy, will you take away everything from me then, one by one—*sab lal ho jayega*? Will I alone be left on the map that I have drawn?'

'Bhai, please don't blame me. I had told her very emphatically: "Ma, you can't attend my wedding under any circumstances." Ma said, "Look here Binu, those who will not attend your wedding would boycott it even if you invited them, and those who will attend it would do so even if you forbade them. Hence I advise you to remain silent: neither invite nor prohibit anyone." Gora, is it to me that you have lost? Your defeat is at your mother's hands, a thousand times over. Can there be another mother like her?'

Although Gora had tried with all his might to restrain Anandamoyi, in his heart of hearts he had not felt hurt that she had gone away to attend Binoy's marriage, disregarding all his restrictions, ignoring his anger and pain. Rather, he had felt a sense of joy. Now he knew for certain that, however wide the gulf between him and Binoy, he could never succeed in depriving Binoy of his share of that deep nectar of affection, that portion of his mother's boundless love to which Binoy had acquired a claim. The knowledge seemed to console and pacify Gora's heart. In all other respects he might drift far apart from Binoy, but at a very profound level, this bond of invincible maternal love would forever bind these two eternal friends in the closest of relationships.

'Bhai, I'll take your leave now,' said Binoy. 'Don't attend if it is utterly impossible for you, but don't harbour displeasure in your heart, Gora! If you can feel within you the tremendous fulfilment my life has attained through this union, you will never be able to banish this marriage of ours from its place in your heart—this I declare with conviction.' Binoy rose to his feet.

'Wait, Binoy! The hour for your wedding ceremony is late at night. What's the hurry so early in the day?'

At Gora's unexpected, affectionate request, Binoy's heart melted and he at once resumed his place. Now after a long time, at this early hour, the two of them engaged in intimate conversation as in old times. Gora struck the very note to which Binoy's heart was tuned these days. Binoy's words did not seem to end. The histories of so many trivial events, which if written in black and white would seem insignificant if not ridiculous, rose to his lips like the taan of a classical song, repeated like a refrain with effusions of new sweetness. In his skilful language, Binoy began to describe, in very fine yet deeply moving terms, the exquisite range of emotions evoked by the wonderful drama currently being played out on the stage of his heart. What an unprecedented experience his life had offered him! Surely the indescribable substance that had filled Binoy's heart was not for everyone! Not everyone had the power to accept it, did they? In the union between men and women generally seen in this world, one rarely heard this supreme harmony. Binoy repeatedly urged Gora not to compare the two of them with all the rest. He doubted that such a thing had ever happened before. If it were so common, society would be surging with the spirit of restless energy, just as a single touch of the spring breeze inspires a rapturous blossoming of new leaves and flowers in every forest and grove. Then people could not have spent their days eating, drinking, sleeping and relaxing in indolent ease. Then all the beauty or power that each person possessed would have blossomed everywhere in different ways, in different forms. This was a magic wand indeed—who could remain inert, ignoring its touch? It transformed even ordinary people into extraordinary individuals. If a human being savoured that extraordinariness even once, he understood what life was really about!

'Gora, I assure you, love is a way to instantly awaken the whole of human nature,' Binoy marveled. 'For some reason love manifests itself very faintly in our lives, so each of us is deprived of complete understanding, remaining ignorant of what we possess, unable to express what is concealed, and not empowered to expend what we have accumulated. That is why there is such joylessness everywhere, such utter joylessness. That is why only a few persons like you recognize that there is any greatness within us. There is no general awareness of it at all, in people's minds.'

When Mahim arose from bed with a noisy yawn and went to wash his face, the sound of his footsteps halted the flood of Binoy's enthusiasm. He took his leave of Gora and went on his way. From the terrace, gazing at the blood-red eastern sky, Gora sighed. For a long time he roamed the terrace. He did not make it to the village that day.

Gora found himself unable to compensate by any means, through any activity, for the longing, the lack he now felt within his heart. Not just his self, but all his endeavours, seemed to reach upward with arms outstretched, begging: 'I need a light—a bright, beautiful light.' As if all the ingredients were ready, as if diamonds, gems, gold and silver were not priceless, and iron, thunder, armour and leather were not scarce, but only the soft, beautiful light, aglow with hope and solace, suffused with the rosy hue of the sun, was missing. It required no effort to augment what was already there, it was only waiting to be rendered more bright, more lovely and more clearly visible.

When Binoy declared that an indescribable wonder arises from the love between man and woman at certain auspicious inaugural moments, Gora could not dismiss the matter as a joke, like before. He privately acknowledged that this was no ordinary union, but complete fulfilment. Everything gained value from contact with it. It gave body to imagination and infused the body with energy. It not only redoubled the soul's vitality and the mind's capacity for reflection but also crowned them with a new rasa, a new flavour.

On this day of their social separation, before he departed, Binoy's heart played a complete, singular melody upon Gora's. Binoy went away, the morning advanced, but that music refused to fade. Like the merging of two oceanbound rivers, the stream of Binoy's love encountered Gora's and the waves began to resonate as they met. What Gora had been trying to conceal from himself by somehow obstructing, suppressing or enfeebling it, now broke its banks and manifested itself in a clear, forceful form. Gora no longer retained the strength to denounce it as illicit, or dismiss it as negligible. The entire day passed in this fashion. Ultimately, as afternoon was fading into dusk, Gora picked up a wrap, flung it over his shoulder and stepped out into the street.

'I shall claim the one who belongs to me,' he declared. 'Otherwise I shall remain unfulfilled on earth, my life will be futile.' Gora remained in no doubt that in the whole world, Sucharita was awaiting his call alone. This very day, this very evening, he must answer this expectation. He rushed through the crowded Kolkata streets. Nobody and nothing seemed to touch him. His mind seemed to outrun his body, advancing single-mindedly, far ahead.

Arriving before Sucharita's house, Gora seemed to suddenly come to his senses. He paused. All these days, he had never found her door closed whenever he came, but today he discovered that it was not open. He pushed, and found it locked on the inside. After pausing briefly to think, he banged on the door a few times. The bearer opened the door and came out. Seeing Gora in the indistinct twilight, he declared, without waiting for any questions: 'Didithakrun is not home.'

'Where is she?'

'She has been busy elsewhere these last few days, organizing Lalitadidi's wedding.'

For a second Gora considered going to Binoy's wedding celebration itself. At this moment, an unknown gentleman emerged from within the house and asked:

'Yes mahashai, what do you want?'

'No, I don't want anything,' replied Gora, inspecting him from head to toe.

'Please come in for a while,' Kailash invited. 'Perhaps you might fancy some tobacco.'

Kailash was at his wits' end for lack of company. If he could only drag someone, anyone, into his room for a chat, he would feel relieved. During the day, he somehow passed his time standing at the corner of the alley, hookah in hand, observing the passers by. But in the evening, confined indoors, he grew desperate. All that he had to discuss with Harimohini had been completely exhausted. Harimohini's capacity for discussion was also extremely limited. Hence Kailash had ensconced himself with his hookah on a wooden divan in a small room next to the outer door on the ground floor, and would occasionally send for the bearer to pass the time chatting with him.

'No,' said Gora, 'I can't stay now.' In the blink of an eye, even as Kailash began to repeat his request, he had already crossed the alley.

Gora had developed the fixed notion that most events in his life were not arbitrary, nor prompted by his personal wishes alone. He had been born to fulfil some purpose of the Maker of his nation's destiny. Hence he tried to attach some special meaning even to the minor events of his life. Today, driven by such a powerful desire, when he suddenly arrived at Sucharita's door and found it locked, and upon the door being opened, discovered that she was not home, he took it to be a significant event manifesting some purpose. The One who guided Gora had chosen this way to forbid him. In this life, Sucharita's door was closed to him, she was not meant for him. A person like Gora could not afford to be obsessed with his own desires, for his own joys and sorrows did not count. He was a Brahman who belonged to Bharatvarsha, he must worship the deity on Bharatvarsha's behalf, his duty it was to meditate upon Bharatvarsha. Attachment and love were not for him. Gora told himself:

'The Maker has clearly shown me what attachment is like. He has demonstrated that it is not fair, not peaceful but red like wine, and pungent like wine. It does not allow the intellect to remain steady, it presents things in a false light. I am a sanyasi, and in my holy endeavour such an emotion has no place.'

## 70

After many days of torment, the comfort Sucharita enjoyed with Anandamoyi was beyond anything she had experienced before. Anadamoyi had drawn her so close so easily, it was impossible for Sucharita to imagine she had ever been unfamiliar or remote. She seemed somehow to have understood Sucharita's heart completely and seemed to offer her a deep solace even without words. Never before had Sucharita uttered the word 'Ma' with all her heart. Even without any need, she would invent various pretexts for addressing Anandamoyi as Ma, and call her by that name. When arrangements for Lalita's wedding were complete, lying tiredly in bed, she was haunted by the thought: how could she now leave Anandamoyi! 'Ma, Ma, Ma!' she repeated, involuntarily. As she spoke, her heart swelled and tears streamed from her eyes. Then she suddenly saw Anandamoyi raise her mosquito net to enter her bed.

'Were you calling me?' asked Anandamoyi, patting Sucharita. Now Sucharita realized she had been calling for 'Ma'. Unable to reply, she hid her face in Anandamoyi's lap and wept. Without a word, Anandamoyi slowly stroked her body. That night she slept by Sucharita's side.

Anandamoyi could not depart as soon as Binoy's wedding was over.

'They are novices, both of them,' she declared. 'How can I go away without organizing their household a little bit?'

'Then I too shall stay here with you these few days, Ma,' Sucharita decided.

Hearing this proposal, Satish rushed up to embrace Sucharita. 'Yes Didi, I'll stay with you all too,' he cried, bouncing up and down.

'But you have your studies, bakhtiar!' Sucharita pointed out.

'Binoybabu will tutor me.'

'Binoybabu can't tutor you now,' said Sucharita.

'I certainly can,' Binoy called from the adjacent room. 'I fail to see how I could have become so infirm in a single day. Nor do I feel a single night has made me forget all I had learned from many nights of study.'

'Will your mashi agree?' Anandamoyi asked Sucharita.

'I'll write to her,' Sucharita proposed.

'Not you,' Anandamoyi said. 'I shall write to her myself.'

Anandamoyi knew Harimohini would feel offended if Sucharita wished to stay there. But if Anandamoyi requested her, she would become the target of any rancour Harimohini might feel, and there was no harm in that. In her letter, Anandamoyi intimated that she must spend some time in Binoy's house, to set up Lalita's new household. She would find it a great help if Sucharita were also permitted to remain with her these few days. Harimohini was not only incensed at Anandamoyi's letter, she also developed a certain suspicion. She thought, since she had forbidden the son to visit the house, the mother was now casting her web of deceit upon Sucharita. She clearly detected a conspiracy between mother and son, also recalling that Anandamoyi's attitude had displeased her from the beginning. She would be relieved to ensure Sucharita's safety by making her a member of the famous Ray family at the earliest, without further delay. How long could Kailash be kept waiting like this, either? The poor fellow was close to blackening the walls of their house from puffing on tobacco day and night.

The very morning after receiving this letter, Harimohini traveled in her palki to Binoy's house in person, accompanied by her bearer. Sucharita, Lalita and Anandamoyi were busy with cooking preparations in the room downstairs. From upstairs, Satish's voice had roused the entire neighbourhood in his attempts to memorize the spellings of English words and their Bengali equivalents. At home, one could scarcely sense his vocal powers, but here he must expend much unnecessary energy on the sound of his voice, to prove beyond doubt that he was not neglecting his studies at all. Anandamoyi welcomed Harimohini with special warmth.

'I have come to fetch Radharani,' Harimohini announced bluntly, ignoring such civilities.

'Very well, so you shall. Please spend a little time with us.'

'No, all my prayers and rituals are unfinished, I haven't even completed my ahnik. I can't linger here now.'

Sucharita was quiet, busy chopping a pumpkin.

'Do you hear me?' Harimohini called to her. 'It's getting late.'

Lalita and Anandamoyi remained silent. Sucharita completed her task and rose to her feet. 'Come, Mashi, let's go,' she said. As Harimohini went towards the palki, Sucharita grasped her hand and said: 'Come, please come inside this room just for a moment.' Leading her into the room, Sucharita firmly declared: 'Since you have come to fetch me, I shall not turn you away immediately in front of everyone. I shall accompany you indeed. But I shall come back here this very afternoon.'

'What a suggestion!' spluttered Harimohini. 'You may as well announce that you will remain here forever!'

'Indeed I can't remain here forever. That is why, as long as I can remain with her, I shall not leave her.'

Harimohini fumed at her words, but did not deem it wise to say anything now.

'Ma, I'll go visit my home once,' smiled Sucharita, going up to Anandamoyi.

'Very well ma, we shall see you again,' Anandamoyi responded, asking no questions.

'I'll be back this afternoon,' Sucharita whispered to Lalita. 'Satish?' she called, waiting near the palki.

'Let Satish stay here,' said Harimohini. Thinking that Satish might prove a hindrance if he went home, she considered it prudent to let him remain away. When the two of them had mounted the palki, Harimohini tried to broach the subject.

'So Lalita is married now,' she began. 'That's a good thing. Poreshbabu can be relieved about one daughter at least.' She then proceeded to explain how great a burden an unwed daughter was upon her family, a cause of such unbearable anxiety. 'What can I tell you, I have no other anxieties. When I chant the Almighty's name, I'm haunted only by that one worry. Truth be told, I can no longer concentrate on my Thakur's service as before. Gopiballav, I pray, after snatching away all I possessed, what is this new trap you have devised for me!'

This was not merely a worldly concern for Harimohini: it was blocking her path to spiritual liberation. But still, even after being told of such a major threat, Sucharita remained silent. Harimohini could not fathom her exact state of mind. She felt it suited her purpose to accept the common saying, silence means consent. She thought Sucharita's heart had softened a little. Harimohini hinted that she had made it extremely easy for a woman like Sucharita to accomplish the immensely difficult feat of joining the Hindu community. She was about to receive such an opportunity, that even at feasts hosted by the most eminent of kulin households, nobody would dare say anything against her dining in their company.

When the preamble had reached this point, the palki reached their house. As they mounted the stairs after alighting at the door and entering the house, Sucharita glimpsed, in the room beside the entrance, a strange man receiving an oil massage from the bearer, to the accompaniment of loud thumps. Seeing her, the man showed no embarrassment. He stared at her with special curiosity.

Once upstairs, Harimohini informed Sucharita of her deor's arrival. Tallying this with Harimohini's preamble, Sucharita correctly surmised the significance of this event. Harimohini tried to reason with her, saying there was a visitor in the house, and it would not be civil of Sucharita to abandon him and depart that very afternoon.

'No Mashi, I must go,' Sucharita insisted, shaking her head vehemently.

'Very well, stay tonight and go tomorrow,' her aunt proposed.

'I shall bathe now, and immediately go to Baba's place for lunch. From there, I'll move to Lalita's house,' Sucharita asserted.

'But he has come to see you,' Harimohini now declared bluntly.

'What is the use?' demanded Sucharita, flushing.

'Just listen to this! Can such events take place without viewing the bride, nowadays? It was the custom, rather, in earlier times. Your mesho had not seen me before the shubhodrishti.' Having uttered these words, Harimohini quickly added a few more remarks to mask the explicitness of her suggestion. She recounted how, when it was time to see the bride before fixing the match, an old family retainer called Anathbandhu and an elderly maidservant named Thakurdasi had been sent by the eminent Ray family, how the two had arrived with a pair of staff-bearing turbaned guards to view the girl in her parental home, how nervous her guardians had become on that occasion, and how their household had been thrown into a frenzy of activity to please these representatives with food and hospitality. Sighing, Harimohini observed that times were different now.

'It'll be no trouble, he'll just see you once for five minutes,' she told Sucharita.

'No,' said Sucharita. So emphatic and clear was her 'no,' that Harimohini had to retreat a little.

'Achchha, let it be. He need not see you after all. But still, Kailash is a modern, educated young man, and like the rest of you he doesn't observe any rules. "I'll see the paatri for myself," he insists. So, since you girls come out in public, I told him, "Seeing her is no problem. I'll arrange a meeting with her some day." But if you feel shy, let the meeting not take place.'

She now waxed eloquent about Kailash's extraordinary learning, how with a single stroke of his pen he had overwhelmed the village postmaster, how no one from the surrounding villages could afford to take a single step without consulting Kailash about handling court cases or writing applications. And as for his moral character, it was needless to elaborate. After his wife's death he had not wanted to remarry under any circumstances; when greatly pressured by his relatives, he had simply bowed to his elders' command. Hadn't Harimohini herself found it so hard to make him agree to the present proposal? As if he was willing to listen! They were of such eminent descent after all. They enjoyed such immense social prestige!

Sucharita utterly refused to damage that prestige. Not under any circumstances. She expressed total disregard for her own honour or self-interest. In fact, she indicated she would remain quite unperturbed even if she were refused a place in Hindu society. The foolish girl failed to realize that Kailash's hard-won consent to this marriage was no mean honour for her. Instead, she found it humiliating. Harimohini was completely stupefied at these perverse attitudes of the modern age. Now she vented her inner rage through repeated insinuations about Gora.

'However much Gora may boast of his Hindu identity, what is his place within the community? Who takes him seriously? If he is tempted into marrying some rich girl from a Brahmo family, by what means will he earn a reprieve from the disciplinary processes of society? He will have to burn up all his money just to stop tongues wagging.' And so on, in the same vein.

'Mashi, why do you say such things?' Sucharita protested. 'You know such remarks are baseless.'

Harimohini retorted that at her age, no one could deceive her with words. She kept her eyes and ears open. She could see, hear and understand everything but was speechless with surprise. She expressed her firm conviction that Gora was conspiring with his mother to seek Sucharita's hand in marriage, that the deeper motive behind this was not a noble one, and that unless she managed to protect Sucharita with the Ray family's help, matters would indeed take this course.

Though patient by nature, Sucharita found this too much to bear. 'I respect the persons you mention,' she objected. 'Since you will never truly understand the nature of my relationship with them, I have no other option but to leave this place at once. When you calm down, when it becomes possible for me to come and live in this house with you alone, I shall return.'

'If you are not partial to Gourmohan, if it is certain that you will never marry him, then what's wrong with this present suitor?' demanded Harimohini. 'You wouldn't remain a spinster, after all.'

'Why not? I shall never marry!'

'Until you are old . . .' spluttered Harimohini, wide-eyed and incredulous.

'Yes, until I die.'

## 71

This blow brought about a change of heart in Gora. He tried to determine why his heart had become vulnerable to Sucharita. He had mingled with these people, and at some stage, unbeknownst to himself, had become involved with them. Where lines of prohibition were drawn, Gora had arrogantly overstepped those limits. This was not the way of our nation. Unless each person safeguards his own boundaries, he not only harms himself intentionally or unintentionally but also loses the unsullied power to do good to others. Through commingling, various strong urges are aroused, polluting one's knowledge, commitment and strength.

Not that he had discovered this truth solely through his interaction with the women of a Brahmo family. When Gora had tried to mingle with the common folk, there too he seemed to have been sucked into a whirlpool, almost losing touch with himself. For at every step he felt pity, and overwhelmed by this emotion, he constantly told himself: that is evil, that is unjust, that must be removed. But did this pity itself not distort one's judgement concerning right and wrong? The stronger our urge to show pity, the more we lose our ability to view the truth objectively. Darkened by pity's smoky vision, what is utterly pale appears to us in very intense hues.

That is why, Gora argued, it has always been customary in our land for the person responsible for the general good to remain unattached. It is baseless to claim that only by closely mingling with his subjects can a ruler look after his people. The kind of knowledge about his subjects that a ruler requires grows tainted through commingling. Therefore the subjects themselves have deliberately kept their king confined to a certain distance. If the ruler becomes their companion, there would no longer be any need for him to rule. A Brahman, too, was similarly remote, similarly unattached. A Brahman must do a lot of good, hence he must be denied close association with many others.

'I am that Brahman of Bharatvarsha,' Gora declared. He did not count among the nation's living substance those Brahmans who were dying of suffocation, having tied the noose of lowcaste Shudra tendencies around their own necks by getting entangled with all and sundry, wallowing the mire of trade, and succumbing to the lure of wealth. Gora considered them inferior to the Shudras, for the Shudra remained alive by virtue of his designated Shudra ways, whereas these Brahmans were virtually dead from having lost their Brahman qualities, and therefore impure. It was because of them that Bharatvarsha today was undergoing such a degraded phase of grieving without purity.

Gora now prepared his mind to practice within himself the Brahman's revival mantra. 'I must be extremely pure and clean,' he resolved. 'I do not occupy the same ground as everyone else. Friendship is not necessary for me. I do not belong to that ordinary category of people who delight in the company of women. And I must completely reject close intimacy with the base commoners of this land. They look up to Brahmans as the earth gazes at the sky in hope of rain. If I come too close, who will save them then?'

Up until now, Gora had never concentrated on idol worship. But ever since his heart had been thrown into turmoil, ever since he became unable to restrain himself, ever since his work began to seem hollow and meaningless and life seemed to be broken in two, crying out in anguish—ever since then, Gora had been trying to concentrate on his prayers.

Seated motionless before the idol, he tried to completely immerse his mind in that image. But he could not arouse his own devotion by any means. He would analyse the deity with his intellect, unable to accept divinity in any but a symbolic form. But one cannot offer devotion to a symbol. One cannot worship a metaphysical explanation. Rather, instead of trying to pray in a temple, when he stayed home and allowed his mind and speech to float away on a tide of emotion while arguing with himself or someone else, he felt the stirrings of bliss and devotion within his heart.

Still Gora did not give up. He sat down to pray regularly, every day, accepting it as a discipline. He persuaded himself that where one could not unite with everyone on an emotional basis, it was the law that preserved such unity everywhere. Whenever Gora had visited a village, he had entered the local temple and after deep meditation had told himself: 'This indeed is my special place. Deity on one side, devotees on the other, and between them the Brahman, a bridge to shore up the union between them.'

Gradually Gora felt that a Brahman had no need for devotion. Devotion was a special commodity meant for the common people. It was knowledge that formed the bridge between devotee and object of devotion. This bridge upheld the union of the two but also protected the boundaries of both. Without pure knowledge to distance devotee from deity, everything became distorted. Hence, overwhelming devotion was not for the Brahman's consumption. Seated upon the pinnacle of knowledge, the Brahman meditates in order to keep this stream of devotion pure for the general public to consume. Just as the Brahman has no comforts to enjoy in his worldly life, so also he has no devotion to relish in his life of prayer. That is the Brahman's glory. For the Brahman, worldly life offers discipline and control, and the pursuit of prayer offers knowledge.

His heart had overpowered him. For this crime, Gora condemned his heart to exile. But who was there to lead it into exile! Where was the army to perform that task!

## 72

Preparations were under way for the ritual penance at the garden estate on the Ganga shore. Abinash felt rather regretful that this ceremony would not draw much public attention because it was taking place outside Kolkata. He knew Gora had no need to perform penance for himself: it was for the sake of his countrymen. For moral effect. Hence this ritual ought to be performed before a crowd.

But Gora would not agree. The interior of Kolkata was not suitable for the massive sacrificial hom fire and the chanting of Veda mantras that were part of his plans for this ceremony. One required a forest grove for meditation. On the secluded Ganga shore, resonant with the chanting of mantras and illuminated by the hom fire, Gora would summon the ancient Bharatvarsha that was the entire world's guru, and having bathed to purify himself, he would accept His initiation into a new life. Gora was not concerned about moral effect.

Abinash now had no other recourse but the newspapers. Without informing Gora, he announced the penance ceremony in all the papers. Not only that, he wrote lengthy pieces in the editorial columns, insisting that no blame could attach to a strong, pure Brahman like Gora, who had nevertheless undertaken this penance on the entire nation's behalf, shouldering all the sins of the depraved Bharatvarsha of today. 'As our nation now frets in the prison of foreign rule owing to its own misdeeds, so too has Gora, in his personal life, accepted the pain of living in that prison,' he wrote. 'Just as he has personally borne his nation's sorrows, so also is he prepared to do penance for the nation's wrongdoings, at this personal ceremony. Hence, bhai Bengalis, you beloved, suffering, hundred thousand children of Bharat, you . . .' and so on.

Reading these pieces, Gora was beside himself with fury. But there was no curbing Abinash. Even if Gora swore at him, he did not mind. Rather, it pleased him. 'My guru inhabits the realm of lofty ideas, he understands nothing of such worldly matters. He is like Narada on the mountain Baikuntha, who created the river Ganga by melting Vishnu's heart with the music of his veena. But bringing that river down to this earth to revive Sagara's offspring from their ashes is a task for the Bhagiraths of this world, not for those who inhabit the heavenly sphere. These two activities are completely separate.' So, when his activities enraged Gora, Abinash was secretly amused, and his devotion to Gora increased. 'Our guru resembles Shiva in appearance,' he told himself, 'and his moods too are similar. He comprehends nothing, has no practical sense, loses his temper at the slightest provocation but doesn't take long to cool down either.'

Abinash's efforts caused a general sensation about Gora's penance. An even larger number thronged Gora's house to see him and talk to him. So many letters started pouring in every day from everywhere, he stopped reading his mail. He began to feel this countrywide discussion had eroded the dispassionate purity of his penance, making it a worldly, passion-based affair. The times they lived in were to blame.

Nowadays Krishnadayal did not touch newspapers, but public rumours penetrated even into his prayer-sanctum. With special pride, Krishnadayal's beneficiaries communicated to him the news that his worthy son Gora was readying himself for penance with great pomp and ceremony, and the hope that following in his father's sacred footsteps he would one day become an enlightened man just like him.

It was hard to say how long it had been since Krishnadayal had last set foot in Gora's chamber. Shedding his silk attire for cotton, he went directly into Gora's room. He did not see Gora there. Upon asking the attendant, he was told that Gora was in the puja room. What! What business had he in the puja room? He was praying there. Rushing in agitation to the puja room, Krishnadayal found that Gora was indeed at his prayers.

'Gora!' he called from outside.

Surprised at his father's arrival, Gora rose to his feet. Krishnadayal had specially installed his own tutelary deity in his prayer-sanctum. Theirs was a Vaishnava family, but having accepted the shakti mantra, Krishnadayal had not had direct contact with their household deity for a long time.

'Come, come,' he called to Gora. 'Come out.' Gora emerged from the room. 'This is outrageous!' spluttered Krishnadayal. 'What are you doing here?' Gora offered no reply. 'There is a Brahman priest to perform the daily puja on the entire household's behalf,' Krishnadayal insisted. 'Why must you come into this!'

'There is nothing wrong in that.'

'Nothing wrong! How can you say that! It's very wrong indeed. What is the need for someone to attempt what he doesn't have the right to do? That is sinful. Not only for you but for all of us in this house.'

'In terms of inner faith, very few people have the right to sit before the deity, indeed. But are you saying I don't even possess the same rights as that Ramahari Thakur of ours, who is entitled to pray here?'

Krishnadayal was suddenly at a loss for a reply. 'Look here,' he said after a short pause, 'performing puja rituals is Ramahari's family trade. Occupational sins don't matter to the deity. Looking for lapses here would put a stop to the trade itself, making it impossible for society to function. But in your case, that excuse doesn't apply. What is the need for you to enter this room?'

It did not seem totally incongruous for a man like Krishnadayal to declare it a sin even for a disciplined, committed Brahman like Gora to enter the prayer chamber. So Gora bore his remarks in silence.

'There's something else I hear, Gora!' Krishnadayal continued. 'You have invited all the pundits to perform a ritual penance, I believe?'

'Yes.'

'I shall never allow it, as long as I live!' cried Krishnadayal in great agitation.

'Why not?' Gora demanded, beginning to feel rebellious.

'Why not indeed! I had told you once before that the penance cannot take place.'

'Indeed you had, but you had not offered any reason.'

'I see no need to offer reasons. We are your elders after all, you owe us respect. There is no law that permits you to perform such religious rituals without our consent. The ritual involves praying for your ancestors' souls, do you know that?'

'Why is that forbidden?' asked Gora in astonishment.

'It is utterly forbidden,' insisted Krisnadayal, in a fury. 'I cannot allow it.'

'Look, sir, this is my personal business,' said Gora, wounded to the quick. 'I have planned this for my own purification. Why torment yourself with futile argument?'

'Look Gora, don't try to argue about everything. These are not matters for argument. There are many such things that remain beyond your comprehension. I tell you again—you imagine you have entered the Hindu faith, but that is a completely mistaken assumption. It is not within your power to do so. Every drop of your blood, from head to toe, is against it. You cannot suddenly become a Hindu, even if you want to! You need the accumulated virtue of many births.'

Gora's face grew flushed. 'I don't know about past births,' he asserted, 'but may I not claim even the right that flows in your ancestral blood?'

'Again you argue! Aren't you ashamed to answer me back! And you call yourself a Hindu! Where will your British arrogance hide itself, after all! Listen to what I say. Stop all those preparations.'

Hanging his head, Gora stood silent. 'Unless I perform the penance, I'm afraid I can't join everybody at Shashimukhi's wedding feast,' he said after a while.

'That is fine,' Krishnadayal responded enthusiastically. 'What's wrong with that? They'll arrange for you to sit separately, then.'

'So I shall have to remain separate within the community.'

'All the better.' Observing Gora's surprise his enthusiasm, Krishnadayal added, 'Take me for instance. I don't dine with anybody, even when invited. What contact do I have with society? Considering the pure, disinterested life you wish to lead, you too should adopt such a path. This will be most beneficial for you, I can see.'

At noon, Krishnadayal sent for Abinash. 'So all of you together have incited Gora, am I right?'

'How can you say that! It is your Gora who incites all of us. In fact he himself is less easily swayed.'

'But I tell you, baba, all your penance and suchlike cannot be permitted. I don't approve of it at all. Stop it at once.'

What sort of obdurate whim had this old fellow developed! Abinash wondered. History offers many instances of famous men's fathers who failed to recognize their sons' greatness. Krishnadayal was a father of that category. If he could have taken a few lessons from his son instead of spending his days and nights in the company of some useless sanyasis, he would have benefited greatly. Abinash was a crafty man, not one to waste words where argument was futile and even moral effect a remote possibility.

'Very well sir,' he said. 'If you don't approve, it will not take place. But now, with all arrangements complete, invitations issued and no time for delay, there's one thing we can still do: let Gora be, it is we who will perform penance on that day. There is no dearth of sins committed by our countrymen, after all.' At Abinash's assurance, Krishnadayal felt relieved.

Gora never had much respect for anything Krishnadayal said. On this occasion, too, he did not privately accept the idea of obeying his orders. In the realm beyond worldly life, Gora did not feel obliged to follow the prohibitions imposed by his parents. But still, a terrible pain now tormented him all day. In his heart arose the indistinct suspicion that some truth lay concealed in all that Krishnadayal had said. He seemed to be haunted by a vague nightmare, which he could not dispel by any means. He felt as if someone was assaulting him from every direction, trying to push him away. Today his own loneliness manifested itself to him in a gigantic form. The field of work before him was vast, and his task was enormous, but no one stood by his side.

# 73

The penance ritual was scheduled for the following day, but Gora was supposed to move into the garden estate the night before. As he was preparing to set out, Harimohini arrived on the scene. Gora was not pleased to see her.

'You have come, but I must leave immediately,' he said. 'Ma has not been home these last few days either. If you need to see her . . .'

'No baba, it is you I have come to see,' Harimohini insisted. 'You must wait a little but not for long.'

Gora waited. Harimohini broached the subject of Sucharita. She observed that Sucharita had benefited greatly from Gora's tutelage. In fact, nowadays she did not accept water from anyone and everyone, and had become more sensible in every way.

'Baba, how worried I was about her! I can't begin to tell you what a great service you have done me by bringing her on to the right track. May the Almighty make you king of kings. Marry a nice girl from a good family, worthy of your eminent lineage; may she light up your home, and may goddess Lakshmi bless you with wealth and male offspring.'

She then observed that Sucharita was of age, and must marry immediately without an instant's delay. Had she belonged to a Hindu family, her lap would have been teeming with infants by now. Gora must surely agree that delaying her marriage had been a grave lapse. After a long period of intolerable anxiety about the problem of Sucharita's marriage, Harimohini, with much pleading and cajoling, had ultimately persuaded her deor Kailash to come to Kolkata. All the major hindrances she had feared had been removed, by Ishwar's grace. Everything had been decided, the groom's party would not take a paisa as pledge money, nor raise any objections about Sucharita's past history—Harimohini had adopted special strategies to solve these problems—but at this juncture, surprisingly, Sucahrita had dug her heels in. What she had in mind, Harimohini did not know. Whether someone had put ideas into her head, whether she was partial to someone else, who could say! . . .

'But bapu, let me say openly that this girl is not worthy of you. If she marries into a provincial family, nobody will get to know the truth about her, and things will somehow be managed. But you people live in the city; if you marry her, you will not be able to show your face to the people here.'

'What are you talking about! Who has told you that I have gone to her with a marriage proposal?'

'How would I know baba! It's out in the papers. I'm dying of shame after hearing of it.'

Gora realized that either Haranbabu or someone of his party had publicized this affair in the papers. 'These are bare lies!' he proclaimed, clenching his fists.

'So I believe too,' said Harimohini, startled by his thunderous tone. 'Now you must keep one request of mine. Just come with me to Radharani.'

'Why?'

'You must explain to her once.'

Gora's heart was instantly ready to approach Sucharita on this pretext. 'Come, let us go and meet her today, one last time,' his heart counseled him. 'Tomorrow is your penance, and after that, you will be a hermit. There is just this one night, and just a small part of it. There is no sin in that. Even if there is, it will be reduced to ashes tomorrow.'

'Please tell me what I must explain to her,' Gora asked, after a short silence.

'Nothing, just that according to Hindu principles, it is the duty of a mature woman like Sucharita to marry without delay and that in the Hindu community, it is an unthinkable blessing for a girl in Sucharita's circumstances to acquire a worthy groom like Kailash.'

Gora was pierced to the heart. Remembering the man he had met at Sucharita's door, he was stung, as if by a scorpion. Gora could not bear to even imagine that this man would possess Sucharita.

'No, this can never be!' his heart thundered in protest.

It was impossible that Sucharita's should unite with anyone else. Her deep, silent heart, full of profound intelligence and emotion, had never revealed itself to any second person but Gora, and could never reveal itself thus to anyone else. How extraordinary that revelation had been! How exquisite! What an indescribable reality had manifested itself, in the innermost chamber of mystery's abode! How often could one behold a human being in this way! The man who by divine grace had seen Sucharita in a dimension so profoundly true, and experienced the vision with his whole being, was the very one to possess her. How could anyone else ever possess her!

'Will Radharani always remain a spinster like this?' demanded Harimohini. 'Can that be possible?'

True, indeed. After all, Gora was about to do penance tomorrow. Then he would be completely purified, a true Brahman. Must Sucharita remain unmarried forever, in that case! Who had the right to impose this lifelong burden upon her! What heavier burden could a woman bear!

Harimohini prattled on. Her words did not reach Gora's ears. He began to think:

'When Baba forbade my penance so strongly, did his admonition have no value? The way I construe my life might be merely a figment of my imagination, not congenial to my nature. That artificial burden would cripple me. Under that relentless weight, I would be unable to accomplish any task with ease. For instance, I find desire permeating my heart. Where shall I move this boulder? Somehow Baba realizes that in my heart of hearts I am not a Brahman, nor an ascetic. That is why he forbade me so strongly.'

'Let me go to him,' Gora thought. 'Now, at once, this very evening, I shall ask him forcibly to disclose what he had seen in me. Why did he say even the path of penance is closed to me? If he can explain, I shall be relieved on that score. So relieved!'

'Please wait a little,' Gora requested Harimohini, 'I'll be right back.' He rushed to his father's quarters. He felt Krishnadayal knew something that could offer him an instant reprieve. The door to the prayer sanctum was closed. He banged on it a couple of times. It did not open, nor did anyone respond. From within, the scent of incense wafted out. Tonight, behind closed doors, Krishnadayal, along with the sanyasi, was practicing an extremely esoteric and difficult mode of yoga. Nobody would be allowed in that night.

## 74

'No,' said Gora, 'my penance is not tomorrow. It has begun this very day. The fire ignited today is far greater than the one to be lit tomorrow. It is because a tremendous sacrificial offering is required of me at the start of my new life that the Almighty has aroused such a powerful desire in my heart. Or else why would such a strange thing happen! Where was I located before this! There was no earthly likelihood of my encountering these people. Nor does such a contrary union generally take place in this world. Nor could anyone have imagined that this union would arouse such a great, invincible desire even in the heart of a detached person like me. This very day, I needed such a desire. So far, whatever I have given my country has been easy to part with, no donation ever caused me pain. I could not fathom why people should be at all miserly about sacrificing anything for the nation. But a major yajna does not require such easy donations. It is pain that this sacrificial ceremony requires. The umbilical cord must be cut for my new life to be born. Tomorrow, at daybreak, I shall perform my earthly penance before the general public. On the very eve of that occasion, Destiny has knocked on my door. Unless I perform the profoundest penance within my heart, how can I achieve purification tomorrow! Only after completely surrendering to my deity the offering that is hardest for me to yield, can

I become utterly, purely dispossessed. Only then shall I become a Brahman.'

'Baba, please come with me once,' exclaimed Harimohini as soon as Gora appeared before her. 'If you come, just a word from you would take care of everything.'

'Why should I go?' Gora protested. 'What have I to do with her? Nothing whatever!'

'But she reveres you like a god, and calls you her guru.'

Like a bolt of lightning, a red-hot pain pierced Gora's heart. 'I see no need to go,' he declared. 'There is no possibility of my ever meeting her again.'

'True indeed,' agreed Harimohini, delighted. 'It is indeed not a good idea to mingle with a girl so mature. But baba, you can't get away without doing me this favour today. After that, see if I ever call upon you again.'

Gora repeatedly shook his head in refusal. No more, never. It was over. He had surrendered to Destiny. He could not allow any blot upon his purity at this stage. He would not go to see her. Realizing from his expression that it would be impossible to budge him, Harimohini said: 'If you truly cannot go there, then please do me this one favour, baba. Write her a letter.' Gora shook his head. There was no question. No letters. 'Very well,' persisted Harimohini, 'write a couple of lines addressed to me. You know all the shastras. I have come to you for a clarification.'

'What clarification?'

'Whether or not it is the greatest duty of a girl from a Hindu family to marry at an appropriate age and obey the laws of domestic life.'

'Look, please don't entangle me in such affairs,' said Gora after a short silence. 'I am not a pundit to offer such clarifications.'

'Then why don't you tell me frankly what you really want?' demanded Harimohini rather sharply. 'It was you who first knotted the noose, and now it's time to undo it, you say, "don't entangle me"! What is that supposed to mean? The fact is, you don't want her mind to be cleared of all doubt.'

At any other time, Gora would have flared up in fury. He could not have tolerated even such an accurate charge. But now his penance had begun, he did not lose his temper. Probing his heart, he found Harimohini was indeed right. He had become ruthless in order to break his major bond with Sucharita, but he still wanted to preserve a fine thread, pretending not to have seen it at all. He had not yet managed to accept giving up his relationship with Sucharita completely. But he must vanquish this miserliness. It would not do to give away with one hand while holding on with the other. Immediately drawing out a sheet of paper, he firmly inscribed, in large letters:

> Marriage is a woman's path to religious pursuits, domesticity her main dharma. Such a marriage is not for wish-fulfilment but for the benefit of all. Whether the home is a happy one or not, to

welcome that home, to remain virtuous, devoted and pure, to preserve the image of dharma within the house—that is the holy pledge of womanhood.

'In a similar vein you could make some small mention of our Kailash, baba!' urged Harimohini.

'No, I don't know him. I can't write about him.'

Having lovingly folded the piece of paper and knotted it into her sari aanchal, Harimohini returned home. Sucharita was still with Anandamoyi at Lalita's house. Fearing it might be difficult to discuss things there and that contrary remarks from Lalita and Anandamoyi might arouse doubts in Sucharita's mind, Harimohini sent word to Sucharita, inviting her to lunch the following day. There were urgent matters to discuss. She could go back the same afternoon.

The next day, Sucharita arrived at noon, having steeled herself for resistance, aware that her mashi would again bring up the same marriage proposal, in some other way. She had resolved to end the matter once and for all with a very strong reply.

'I went to see your guru last evening,' Harimohini remarked, after Sucharita had eaten.

Sucharita's was inwardly distressed. Had Mashi insulted him by bringing up her name!

'Don't worry, Radharani,' Harimohini assured her, 'I did not go there to quarrel with him. I was alone, and thought I would go across to hear a few words of wisdom from him. In the course of our conversation, your name came up. Well, I found he was of the same view. Indeed, he doesn't approve of a woman remaining unmarried for long. He says, according to the shastras, it goes against one's dharma. Such things may prevail in sahebi families but not in Hindu homes. I have also told him frankly about our Kailash. The man was indeed learned, I realized.'

Sucharita cringed in shame and misery.

'You consider him your guru after all,' Harimohini continued. 'You must obey him, mustn't you?' Sucharita remained silent. 'I told him,' Harimohini pursued, '"Baba, please come and explain to her yourself, she doesn't listen to us." He said, "No, it will not be right for me to see her again, it goes against our Hindu social custom." "Then what's the solution?" I asked. Then he wrote down these words for me in his very own hand. Here: why not have a look?'

With these words, Harimohini extracted the piece of paper from her aanchal, unfolded it and held it open. Sucharita read it. Her breath seemed to choke. She sat stiff as a wooden puppet. The words contained nothing that was new or improper. Nor did Sucharita's views differ from the ideas expressed in those words. But the implications of his specially sending her this written missive through Harimohini wounded Sucharita in many ways. Why such a decree from Gora today? Certainly, Sucharita's time would come, and she too would have to marry some day; but what had caused Gora to make such haste on that account? Was Gora completely finished with her? Had she done him any harm?

Had she posed an obstacle in his life? Was there nothing left for her to offer Gora or to expect from him? But she had not felt that, she had still been waiting for him. Sucharita struggled against this intolerable pain within herself but could find no consolation in her heart.

Harimohini gave Sucharita a lot of time to think. She even took her usual daily nap. Upon awakening, she came to Sucharita's room to find her sitting quietly, just as before.

'Tell me Radhu, why do you think so much? What's so worrisome about this matter? Why, has Gourmohanbabu written something wrong?'

'No, what he writes is true indeed,' replied Sucharita quietly.

'Then why delay any more bachha?' cried Harimohini, highly reassured.

'No I don't want to delay things. I'll go across once to Baba's place.'

'Look Radhu, your Baba will never want you to marry into the Hindu community. But the one who is your guru has . . .'

'Mashi, why do you say the same thing again and again?' protested Sucharita impatiently. 'I am not going to Baba to discuss marriage, not at all. I'll go to him once, just like that.'

Poresh's company was indeed Sucharita's source of solace. Going to his house, she found him busy packing his clothes into a wooden trunk.

'Baba, what is this?'

'Ma, I am going for a vacation to the Shimla hills,' Poresh smiled. 'I shall depart by the morning train tomorrow.'

That Poresh's smile encompassed the history of a major rebellion, Sucharita did not fail to realize. His wife and daughters at home and his friends outside were leaving him no room for peace. If he did not go away to some far-off place for a few days at least, he would remain in the eye of a storm at home. He had resolved the day before to travel elsewhere, yet none of his own people came forward to pack his clothes today. He had to perform this task himself, and observing this scene, Sucharita suffered a powerful blow. Forcing Poreshbabu to desist, she first completely emptied his trunk. Then folding the clothes with special care, she began to rearrange them in the trunk, placing his favourite books so even movement would not damage them. While packing the box, she gently inquired:

'Baba, are you going alone?'

'That is no problem for me, Radhé!' replied Poresh, sensing a hint of pain in Sucharita's question.

'No Baba, I shall go with you.' Poresh stared at her. 'Baba, I shan't trouble you at all,' she assured him.

'Why do you say that? Have you ever troubled me Ma?'

'Unless I stay close to you it will not be good for me Baba! There are many things I don't understand. If you don't explain them to me, I shall not find my feet. Baba, you tell me to rely on my wits, but I don't have the intelligence, nor the necessary strength in my heart. Please take me with you Baba!'

She turned away from Poresh and bent low over the clothes in the trunk. Large tear-drops fell from her eyes.

## 75

When Gora handed that piece of writing to Harimohini, he felt he had signed away his relationship with Sucharita. But work does not cease as soon as one signs a document. His heart utterly ignored that document. The document had been signed with a firm hand by Gora's willpower alone, but it did not bear his heart's signature. So his heart remained disobedient. So extreme was this disobedience, it almost sent Gora rushing to Sucharita's house that very night! But at that very moment, the church clock struck ten and Gora came to his senses, realizing that this was no time to visit anyone. Subsequently he heard the church clock strike virtually every hour. For he did not go to the garden estate at Bali that night. He had sent word that he would go there early the next morning.

At dawn he duly went to the estate, but where was the pure, strong frame of mind in which he had resolved to receive his penance?

Many scholars and pundits had arrived there. Many others were expected. Gora asked after everyone and greeted them with civility. They showered praise on Gora for his unwavering commitment to the ascetic dharma. The garden gradually filled with the hubbub of human voices. Gora went about supervising the arrangements. But amidst all the hustle and bustle, a single thought haunted the deepest recesses of his mind. 'You have done something wrong! Something wrong!' someone seemed to accuse him. There was no time to clearly determine what wrong he had committed, but he was unable to silence his innermost heart. Amidst all the elaborate arrangements for the penance ceremony, some internal enemy within his heart was testifying against him: 'The wrong you have done still remains.' That wrong was not a breach of rules or an error in mantra-chanting, or a violation of the shastras. That wrong had occurred within his nature. Therefore, Gora's whole inner being had become averse to the preparations for this ceremony.

The time drew near. Outside, a marquee had been raised on bamboo frames to create a pavilion. After his bath in the Ganga, Gora was changing his attire when he sensed a stir in the crowd. Some agitation seemed to be gradually spreading in all directions.

'They have sent word from your house that Krishnadayalbabu is bleeding at the mouth,' Abinash finally informed him dejectedly. 'He has sent someone with a carriage to fetch you quickly.'

Gora rushed away. Abinash wanted to accompany him. 'No, please remain here to receive everybody,' Gora insisted. 'You can't afford to leave the venue.'

Entering Krishnadayal's chamber, Gora saw him lying in bed, with

Anandamoyi gently stroking his feet. Gora anxiously searched their faces. Krishnadayal signaled to him to take the chowki beside the bed. Gora obeyed.

'How is he now?' he asked his mother.

'A little better now. They have gone to fetch the saheb-doctor.'

Shashimukhi and an attendant were present in the room. Krishnadayal waved them away. After ascertaining that everyone had left, he silently glanced at Anandamoyi, then addressed Gora in a low voice:

'My time has come. Unless I disclose what was concealed from you all along, my soul will not be free.'

Gora's face grew ashen. He remained motionless. For a long time, nobody said a word.

'Gora,' said Krishnadayal, 'I did not believe in anything then, that was why I made such a great mistake. After that, I had no means of correcting my error.' He again fell silent. Gora also remained motionless, asking no questions. 'I had thought it would never become necessary to tell you, that things would go on as before,' Krishanadayal continued. 'But now I realize that is not possible. After my death, how will you perform my sraddha?' Krishnadayal seemed to tremble at the very prospect of such a calamity. Gora became impatient to know the real truth. He glanced at Anandamoyi.

'Ma, you tell me what that means,' he urged. 'Have I no right to perform the sraddha?'

All this time Anandamoyi had been silent, with downcast face. At Gora's question, she raised her head. 'No baba, you don't,' she declared, looking him steadily in the eye.

'Am I not his son?' Gora demanded, startled.

'No,' she replied.

'Ma, are you not my mother?' The words burst from Gora's mouth like flames from a volcano.

Anandamoyi's heart broke. Her voice choked with unshed tears, she said: 'Baba, to me you are the son granted to a childless woman, dearer by far than a child of one's womb, baba!'

'Where did you find me then?' Gora now asked, looking at Krishnadayal.

'During the Mutiny,' Krishnadayal answered. 'We were at Etowah. Your mother had sought refuge in our home one night, fleeing in fear of the sepoys. Your father had died in battle the previous day. His name was . . .'

'No need to name him!' roared Gora. 'I don't want to know his name.'

Krishnadayal stopped abruptly, amazed at Gora's agitation. Then he continued: 'He was an Irishman. That very night, your mother died after giving birth to you. You have been brought up in our own house ever since.'

In a single instant, Gora's felt his entire life become like an extraordinary dream. The foundation of his life, developed over all these years since his very infancy, was utterly destroyed. What he was, where he was, he did not seem to understand. As if behind him there was nothing called a past, and before him, the future, so purposeful and clearly determined for such a long time, had completely vanished. As if he was simply floating like a momentary dewdrop on a lotus leaf. He had no mother, no father, no country, no caste, no name, no family gotra, no deity. All he had was a 'No.' What would he cling to, what would he do, from what point would he begin again, where refix his goals, and from where would he slowly gather, day by day, all the necessary resources for his work! In this strange, directionless void Gora remained transfixed, utterly speechless. Seeing his face, no one dared say another word.

Just then the saheb-doctor arrived, accompanied by their Bengali family physician. While observing the patient, the doctor could not refrain from glancing at Gora as well. 'Who is this?' he wondered. Gora's forehead still bore its tilak of Ganga earth and he had come there still wearing the raw silk fabric he had donned after his bath. He wore no upper garment; through the gaps in his wrap, his massive body could be seen.

Earlier, the very sight of a British doctor would have instinctively aroused Gora's hostility. But now, as the doctor examined his patient, Gora looked at him with special curiosity. 'Is this man my closest relative here?' he began to ask himself, again and again.

'Why, I see no special cause for anxiety,' pronounced the doctor, having completed his examination and asked some questions. 'His pulse is not alarming, nor are his organs malfunctioning. As for the symptoms, if one is careful they can be prevented.'

After the doctor had departed, Gora wordlessly tried to rise from the chowki. Anandamoyi had gone into the adjacent room when the doctor came. She now rushed in and clasped Gora's hand.

'Baba Gora, please don't be angry with me,' she pleaded. 'Otherwise I shall die!'

'Why didn't you tell me, all these days!' Gora demanded. 'It would not have done you any harm.'

Anandamoyi took all the blame upon herself. 'Baap, it was from fear of losing you that I committed such a great sin. If that is what ultimately happens, if you abandon me today, I cannot blame anyone. But it will be a death sentence for me, baap!'

'Ma!' was all Gora could say. Hearing him address her thus, Anandamoyi's suppressed tears burst forth at last.

'Ma, I'll go to Poreshbabu's now,' Gora declared.

A load was lifted from Anandamoyi's heart. 'Go ahead, baba!' she said.

There was no fear of his dying soon, yet the truth had been revealed to Gora! Krishnadayal became extremely alarmed.

'Look here Gora, I see no reason to disclose all this to anyone,' he urged. 'Just act prudently and with caution, and things will continue as before. Nobody will suspect a thing.' Gora walked out without giving an answer. He felt comforted to remember that he was no relation of Krishnadayal's.

Mahim could not suddenly stay away from work. After sending for the doctor and making all the necessary arrangements, he had gone to the office, just to ask the saheb for leave of absence. Just as Gora was emerging from the house, Mahim arrived on the scene. 'Gora, where are you going?' he demanded.

'Good news,' said Gora. 'The doctor was here. He said there's no cause for worry.'

'Thank heavens,' said Mahim, greatly relieved. 'The day after tomorrow is an auspicious date. I shall get Shashimukhi married that very day. Gora, you will have to be a little enterprising, I tell you. And please warn Binoy in advance, not to come there that day. Abinash is a Hindu fanatic: he has specially decreed that such people must not be allowed at his wedding ceremony. Let me tell you something else bhai: I shall invite the big sahebs of my office on that day, but you must not attack them. If you just say "Good evening sir" with a slight nod of the head, no more, it won't pollute your Hindu shastras. Better that you seek the pundits' advice. Do you understand bhai? They are of kingly caste: you won't be demeaned if you curb your arrogance a little in their company.'

Without offering any reply, Gora walked away.

## 76

As Sucharita bent over the trunk, busily arranging clothes in order to hide her tears, they received word that Gourmohanbabu had arrived. Hastily wiping her eyes, Sucharita abandoned her task and rose to her feet. And just then Gora entered the room. He was not even aware that the tilak still marked his forehead. The silk fabric still swathed his body. No one usually came visiting in such attire. Sucharita was reminded of that day when she had first encountered Gora. She knew he had come armed for battle on that occasion; was he in battle-gear today as well?

As soon as he entered, Gora prostrated himself at Poresh's feet in a pranam. Agitated, Poresh drew him up, saying,

'Come, come, baba, join us.'

'Poreshbabu, I have no ties,' Gora blurted out.

'What ties?' asked Poreshbabu in surprise.

'I am not a Hindu.'

'Not a Hindu!'

'No, I am not a Hindu. I was informed today that I am a foundling from the days of the Mutiny. My father is an Irishman. From north to south across the whole of Bharatvarsha, all temple doors are now closed to me. Today, in this whole country, there is no place for me, at any level, to sit down to a meal with others.'

Poresh and Sucharita were dumbfounded. Poresh could not think of what to say to him.

'Today I am free Poreshbabu!' Gora declared. 'I am no longer afraid of becoming a fallen person, or losing my caste status. I need no longer watch the ground at every step for fear of losing my purity.'

Sucharita gazed transfixed at Gora's radiant countenance.

'Poreshbabu,' Gora continued, 'all these days I strove wholeheartedly to realize the idea of Bharatvarsha, and always came up against some obstacle or other. All my life, day and night, I have constantly struggled for a compromise between all those obstacles and my sense of respect. In my effort to strengthen the basis of that respect, I was unable to accomplish any other task; that was my sole endeavour. That is why, when I tried to serve Bharatvarsha while viewing it in the light of truth, I repeatedly turned back in fear. Creating an untroubled, unblemished abstract image of Bharatvarsha, how I battled on all fronts to keep my devotion safe within that impenetrable fortress! Today in a single instant my imaginary fortress has evaporated like a dream. Set completely free, I have suddenly arrived at the heart of a great reality! All Bharatvarsha's virtues and flaws, joys and sorrows, knowledge and ignorance, have come directly close to my heart. Today I have gained the right to true service. The real field of action now lies before me. It is not the arena within my heart, but the actual site for promoting the welfare of those hundred crore people in the world outside.'

Poresh too felt stirred by the force of Gora's tremendous enthusiasm about this newfound insight. Unable to contain himself, he arose from his chowki.

'Do you comprehend my words?' Gora inquired. 'Today I have become what I earlier strove day and night to become but without success. Today I have become an Indian—Bharatvarshia. In me there is no hostility towards any community, Hindu, Muslim or Christian. Today, I belong to every community of this Bharatvarsha, I accept everyone's food as mine. Look, I traveled to many districts of Bengal, accepting the hospitality of even very lowly localities—please do not imagine that I only lectured at city assemblies—but I could never bring myself to sit in the company of all and sundry. All these days, I went about carrying with me an invisible gap, which I could never bridge. Hence there was a great void within my heart. I constantly tried to disown that emptiness by various means; with sundry outward embellishments, I tried to specially beautify this void itself. For Bharatvarsha was dearer to me than my own heart: I could not tolerate the slightest reason to criticize any feature of the partial aspect of Bharatvarsha visible to me. Now, freed of such futile attempts at embellishment, I am relieved, Poreshbabu!'

'When we attain the truth, it satisfies our soul even with all its lack and incompleteness,' assented Poreshbabu. 'One feels no desire to decorate it with false ingredients.'

'Look Poreshbabu, last night I beseeched the Almighty to grant me a new life this morning, a new birth after completely destroying all the falsehoods and impurities that had enveloped me since infancy. Ishwar paid no heed to the imaginary reward I was praying for. Instead, He startled me by delivering His own truth directly into my hands. I did not dream that he would remove my impurity so radically. Today I have become so pure that even in a lowcaste chandal's home I will no longer be afraid of sullying myself. Poreshbabu, at dawn today, with my naked soul, I was born directly into Bharatvarsha's lap. At last I have fully understood what a mother's lap signifies.'

'Gour,' responded Poreshbabu, 'Please lead us also into the mother's lap, to which you have gained the right of entry.'

'Do you know why I have come to you first of all upon attaining my freedom today?' Gora asked him.

'Why?'

'You are the one with the mantra for this freedom. That is why, in our present times, you could not find a place within any community. Make me your disciple. Initiate me today into the mantra of that deity who belongs to everyone, Hindu, Muslim, Christian or Brahmo, whose temple doors are never closed to any community or any individual, who is not merely a deity for Hindus but the deity of Bharatvarsha!'

The profound sweetness of devotion passed its gentle shadow across Poreshbabu's face. He stood in silence, with lowered gaze.

At last, Gora turned to Sucharita. She remained motionless on her chowki. 'Sucharita, I am no longer your guru,' Gora smiled. 'This is my prayer to you: please take my hand and lead me there, to your guru.' With these words Gora advanced towards her, stretching out his right hand. Arising from the chowki, Sucharita placed her hand in his. Taking her with him, Gora bent to offer his pranams at Poresh's feet.

# EPILOGUE

When he came home after dusk, Gora found Anandamoyi waiting silently in the veranda outside her room. He knelt at her feet and drawing them close, bowed his head upon them. With both hands, she raised his head and kissed it.

'Ma, you are my real mother! The mother I sought everywhere was waiting in my own home. You have no caste, no discrimination, no contempt for anyone. You are the very image of goodness! It is you who is my Bharatvarsha! . . .

'Ma, please send for your Lachhmia now. Ask her to fetch me some water.'

In a low, tearful voice, Anandamoyi whispered, close to Gora's ear: 'Gora, let me send for Binoy now.'

# NOTES AND GLOSSARY

**Abhimanyu** Heroic son of Arjuna in the Mahabharata, killed on the battlefield by his Kaurava uncles who trapped him in a circular battle formation.

**Agrahayan** Eighth month of the Bengali calendar, mid-November to mid-December.

**ahnik** A daily Hindu prayer ritual.

**alna** Traditional clothes rack.

**Annapurna** Goddess of bounty; another name for Shiva's consort Parvati, who went from door to door seeking rice to appease the hunger of Shiva when he came to her as a mendicant.

**antahpur** Inner part of the house, where women stay in seclusion.

**asana** Prayer mat.

**Ashwin** Sixth month of Bengali calendar, mid-September to mid-October.

**Baikuntha** Celestial abode of Vishnu.

**Bakasur** Crane-headed demon destroyed by Bhima in the Mahabharata.

**Bakhtiar Khilji** Aide of Qutbuddin Aibaq, he conquered Bihar and Bengal in the early thirteenth century; 'bakhtiar' means 'talkative'.

**bala** Armlet.

***Bangadarshan*** A monthly magazine (1872–1876), founded and edited by Bankimchandra Chatterjee.

**baul** unorthodox religious mendicants, nomads who sing mystical devotional songs.

**behai** Father-in-law of a son or daughter.

**beyan** Mother-in-law of a son or daughter.

**Bhadra** Fifth month of the Bengali calendar, mid-August to mid-September.

**bhadra** Belonging to the respectable class.

**bhadralok** Member of respectable Bengali society.

**Bhagavad Gita** Verses Krishna is said to have uttered as Arjuna's charioteer in the Mahabharata, advocating the path of duty that forms one aspect of Hindu philosophy.

**Bhagirath** King Sagara's great-grandson, he brought the river Ganga down from Heaven to the earth and to the nether regions, to purify the ashes of his 60,000 ancestors.

**bhakti** The path of devotion in Hindu philosophy.

**Bhatpara** Village near Kolkata, a centre of orthodox Brahmanical learning.

**bhog** Food offered to a deity.

**Bhrigu** A sage who kicked Vishnu (Krishna) to awaken him from his pre-creation sleep. Vishnu responded so gently that Bhrigu declared him the only god worthy of worship.

**bon** Sister.

**bonjhi** Sister's daughter.

**boro** Paddy crop harvested in April.

**Brahman** Member of the priestly caste.

**Brahmo Samaj** A monotheistic religious community founded by Raja Rammohun Roy; they advocated social reform.

**Brahmosangeet** Brahmo hymns.

**Brindavan** Holy place for Hindus, associated with Krishna.

**Chaitanyadev** Religious reformer and founder of Vaishnavism in medieval Bengal.

**champa** Variety of magnolia.

**chapkaan** Knee-length upper garment.

**chor** Strip of sandy land arising out of a river-bed.

**churning the ocean** Amrita, heavenly nectar, was cast up when deities and demons churned the ocean.

**crore** Ten million.

**dada** Elder brother.

**deor** Husband's younger brother.

**devi** Female deity.

**didi** Elder sister.

**Dosad** A low caste.

**ekadashi** Eleventh day of the lunar fortnight; widows would fast on this day.

***Gherandasamhita*** Ancient Sanskrit text dealing with the tantrik practices of Shakti devotees.

**Ghor Babu** A dandy.

**ghoti** Small round water pot.

**Goldighi** Another name for College Square in Kolkata.

**Gopiballav** Another name for the deity Krishna.

**Hara-Parvati** The deity Shiva and his consort.

**Harish Mukhujje the second** Harishchandra Mukherjee (1824–61), Brahmo leader and editor of the *Hindu Patriot*.

**hathayoga** Form of abstract meditation involving harsh self-discipline.

**Hemanta** Late autumn to early winter; the months Kartik and Agrahayana of the Bengali calendar.

**Indra** King of the gods.

**Ishwar** The Creator, Lord of the universe.

**Jagaddhatri** Mother goddess who upholds the universe.

**jamai** Son-in-law.

**Jamaisashthi** Annual ritual performed by parents-in-law to bless the son in-law.

**jamun** Blackberry.

**Janak** Sita's father in the Ramayana.

**jatra** A form of indigenous theatre in Bengal.

**jatragaan** Open air performance of jatra.

**kaibarta** A fisherman by caste.

**kaka** Father's younger brother.

**Kalisingha** Kaliprasanna Sinha (1840/1841–1870), who translated the Mahabharata into Bengali.
**Kaliyug** Fourth or last age of creation according to the Hindu Purana; the age of sin.
**kamandulu** An ascetic's water-pot, made of wood or metal.
**kantha** Embroidered coverlet made of layered soft fabric.
**karabi** Oleander.
**karahi** Narrow-bottomed cooking utensil.
**karma** The path of duty or action in Hindu philosophy; the law of karma decrees that one must be rewarded or punished according to one's past deeds.
**Kartika** God of war, son of deities Shiva and Parvati. Also the seventh month of the Bengali calendar, mid-October to mid-November.
**Kashi** Varanasi, sacred to the Hindus.
**Kaurava** The Kuru side in the Mahabharata.
**kazi** A dispenser of justice under the Muslim law.
**kayastha** A Hindu caste.
**Keshabbabu** Keshub Chunder Sen (1838–84), who succeeded Debendranath Tagore, Rabindranath's father, as leader of the Brahmo Samaj.
**kharam** Wooden sandal.
**khansama** An orderly.
**khatanchikhana** Ledger room, where accounts are kept.
**kheer** Milk condensed by boiling, used to prepare sweets.
**khonta** A flat cooking spoon.
**khunche** A small tray.
**khuro** Father's younger brother.
**khurima** Wife of father's younger brother.
**kirtan** A form of devotional music in praise of Radha–Krishna or Kali.
**krishnachura** Gulmohur, a tree with red and yellow flowers.
**Krittivasa** A poet and scholar of Bengal, who wrote the first Bengali Ramayana, probably in the fifteenth century.
**krosh** A measure of distance, a little over two miles.
**Kuber** God of the dead and of wealth.
**kulin** Born of a Brahman family of unblemished caste status; men of such families enjoyed and often misused the privilege of polygamy.
**Lakshmi** Goddess of fortune.
**Lanka** The capital of demon king Ravana in the Ramayana.
**Lakshyabheda** A feat of marksmanship performed by Arjuna to win Draupadi's hand in the Mahabharata.
**madur** Mat.
**Magh** Tenth month of the Bengali calendar, from mid-January to mid-February.
**mahaveena** A string instrument.
**Manu** Father of the human race; the law-code of the Manusmriti

is ascribed to him.
**mashi** Mother's sister.
**mesho** Mother's sister's husband.
**maya** In Hindu philosophy, the illusory material world.
**mela** Fair; exhibition.
**mitbar** A young boy accompanying the bridegroom as his supposed substitute or double.
**mora** low stool made of cane and bamboo.
**Mutiny** The uprising of 1857, termed the 'Sepoy Mutiny' and 'Sipahi Revolt' by British and Indian historians respectively.
**nabina:** Young woman who follows modern ways.
**namavali** A wrap with the deity's name inscribed on it.
**Nandokumar** Raja Nando Kumar, faujdar of Hooghli during the Palashi battle and diwan of Mir Jafar, was hanged for forgery in 1775 at the instigation of Warren Hastings
**Narada** A sage who fomented discord among gods and men.
**Narayan** Another name for Vishnu, or Krishna.
**Narayani Sena** When Krishna (Narayan) asked the Kauravas in the Mahabharata to choose either him or his troops, the Narayani Sena, they chose the troops.
**ojha** Exorcist; one who cures snake bites and other fatal wounds by ritual means.
**palki** Palanquin.
**panchayat** Village council with five or more members.
**Pandavas** The descendants of kind Pandu in the Mahabharata.
**Parashar** Ancient law-giver in the Hindu tradition.
**pathshala** Primary school.
**patra** Prospective bridegroom.
**Phalgun** Eleventh month of the Bengali calendar, from mid-February to mid-March.
**pinri** Low wooden seat.
**pishi** Father's sister.
**poite** Sacred thread; ritual of wearing the sacred thread for the first time.
**prachina** Woman who follows traditional, old-fashioned modes.
**Prajapati** God of marriage.
**Prakriti** Nature; the female principle.
**prasad** Food blessed by a deity or spiritual guide.
**puja** Worship; prayer.
**punya** The virtue that accrues from meritorious deeds.
**Radha–Krishna** Krishna and his consort Radha are the subject of much romantic lore.
**ragini** A musical mode in the Indian classical tradition.
**Rahu** A demon beheaded for trying to drink nectar with the gods, believed to cause eclipses when he attempts to devour the sun and moon; considered a malign planet.
**Rama** Son of Dasharatha, hero of the Ramayana.
**Ramaprasad** Ram Prasad Sen (1720–71), who composed devotional songs

in praise of goddess Kali and other forms of Shakti.

**Rig Veda** The first of the four Vedas, the ancient spiritual hymns that created the first stage of Hindu mythology.

**rowshan-chowki** Orchestra of shehnai and other instruments.

***sab lal ho jayega*** Hindi phrase meaning 'everything will turn red'. Gora is alluding to British rule in India, for British troops wore red uniforms and the territories under their direct control were coloured red in contemporary maps of India.

**Sagara** The 60,000 sons of King Sagara were cursed by sage Kapila, and saved only when Bhagirath brought the river Ganga down from Vishnu's feet onto this earth.

**saji** Round, high-rimmed wicker-basket.

**sal** Tree valued for its timber.

**samhita** Ancient Hindu law-book.

**sandesh** Sweet made of cottage cheese.

**sanyasi** Ascetic.

**segun** Teak.

**sej** Oil lamp with a glass shade.

**shakti mantra** The occult worship of goddesses Kali–Durga–Shakti as embodiments of divine energy.

**shalgram** Sacred stone supposed to represent Vishnu, worshipped by the Vaishnavas.

**sharat** Early autumn, the months Bhadra and Ashwin in the Bengali calendar.

**shastra** Hindu scriptures.

**Shiva** Third god of the Hindu triad

**shivalinga** Phallic image worshipped as Shiva.

**shubhodrishti** Wedding ritual where bride and bridegroom first look at each other.

**Shudra** Fourth or lowest of the Hindu castes.

**Sirajuddaula** Nawab of Bengal, defeated by the British at the Battle of Palashi in 1757.

**Sita** Daughter of Janak and wife of Rama in the Ramayana.

**Sravan** Fourth month of the Bengali calendar, mid-July to mid-August.

**stotra** Hymn of praise.

**supari** Betel nut.

**swadesh** One's own land.

**swadeshi** Of one's own country; phase of Indian National Movement favouring indigeneous elements and boycott of foreign goods

**taan** Combination of notes in a classical melody.

**taktaposh** A plain rectangular bedstead.

**tandava** A frenzied dance of destruction.

**tehsildar** Officer in charge of revenue collection in a demarcated area called a tehsil.

**Tantrik** Follower of the doctrine of the Tantras of Shaktas.

**thakur** A Hindu deity; an idol; a Brahman; a Brahman cook.

**thala** A metal dish.

**tilak** A Hindu sectarian mark on the forehead, usually of sandal paste or sacred clay.
**togor** A small white flower.
**tol** Village school for teaching Sanskrit.
**Triveni** Sacred confluence of rivers Ganga, Yamuna and Saraswati at Allahabad.
**tussar** Coarse silk made from silkworm cocoons.
**vaishnava** Follower of Sri Chaitanya; member of a modern Hindu sect devoted to the deity Vishnu.
**Vedanta** Monistic school of Hindu philosophy that became popular after the Vedic period; their teachings are summarized in the treatise called the first Brahmasutra.
**veena** Musical instrument, usually with seven strings.
**yajna** Sacrificial rite.

# QUARTET
(Chaturanga)

*Translated by Kaiser Haq*

# Uncle

## 1

I came up from the country and entered college in Calcutta. Sachish was studying for his BA then. We were roughly the same age.

In appearance Sachish gives the impression of a celestial being. His eyes glow; his long, slender fingers are like tongues of flame; the colour of his skin is more a luminescence than a colour. As soon as I set eyes on him I seemed to glimpse his inner self; and from that moment I loved him.

Amazingly, many of his classmates harboured deep resentment against him. The fact is, those who are like everyone else arouse no hatred unless there is a reason. But when a resplendent inner self pierces the grossness that envelops it, some, quite irrationally, extend it heartfelt adoration; others, just as irrationally, try heart and soul to insult it.

The students I boarded with realized that I secretly admired Sachish. This became such a thorn in their sides that they didn't let a single day pass without reviling him in my hearing. I knew that if sand gets in the eye rubbing makes things worse; it was best not to respond to unpleasant words. But one day such calumny was poured on Sachish's character that I couldn't keep quiet any more.

I was at a disadvantage because I hadn't yet got to know him. On the other hand some of my opponents came from his neighbourhood, others claimed some sort of distant kinship with him. 'It's absolutely true!' they declared with great vehemence; with even greater vehemence I declared that I didn't believe an iota of it. At which they all belligerently rolled up their sleeves and called me a very impertinent fellow.

Tears welled up in my eyes as I lay in bed that night. Between classes the next day, I went up to Sachish as he reclined with a book on the shaded grass by the circular pond and without a word of introduction launched into an incoherent torrent of words. He closed his book and gazed at me for a while. Those who haven't seen his eyes can never understand what lies in their gaze.

'Those who slander others,' Sachish said, 'do so because they love slander, not because they love truth. It's pointless therefore to struggle to prove that a piece of slander is untrue.'

'But if they're lying . . .'

Sachish stopped me. 'But you see, they're not liars. There's a poor boy in our neighbourhood who has palsy and shakes in every limb. He can't do any work. One winter I gave him an expensive blanket. That day my servant Shibu indignantly complained to me that the illness was a pretence. Those who deny any virtue in me are like Shibu. They believe what they say. An expensive extra blanket has fallen to my lot and all the Shibus in the land have decided I have no right to it. I would find it embarrassing to quarrel with them over this.'

Without responding to that I asked, 'But they say you're an atheist—is it true?'

'Yes, I am an atheist,' Sachish said.

My face fell. I had argued violently with my fellow boarders that Sachish could not be an atheist.

Indeed I suffered two nasty shocks at the very outset of getting to know Sachish. As soon as I saw him I decided he was a Brahmin's son. After all, his face was like a god's image carved out of marble. I had heard that his family name was Mullick; a kulin Brahmin household in our village bore the same name. But I discovered that Sachish was of the goldsmiths' caste. Ours was a devout kaystha family—for the goldsmiths' caste we felt profound contempt. And as for being an atheist, I knew it to be a greater sin than murder, or even eating beef.

I stared speechless at Sachish's face. Still the same luminescence there—as if prayer-lamps were shining in his soul.

No one would have thought I would ever share a meal with one of the goldsmiths' caste and in my fanatical atheism outdo my guru. But with time even this came to pass.

Wilkins was professor of literature at our college. His impressive learning was matched by his contempt for the students. To him teaching literature to Bengali boys in a colonial college was tantamount to menial labour; and so if he came across the word 'cat', even in the course of teaching Milton or Shakespeare, he would gloss it with the explanation, 'a quadruped of the feline species'. But Sachish was excused from taking down such notes. 'Sachish,' he would say, 'I'd like to compensate you for having to sit in this class. Come to my house—there you'll get back your taste for literature.'

The incensed students claimed that the sahib was fond of Sachish because Sachish was light-complexioned and had beguiled him by showing off his atheism. The more cunning students rallied together and went to the sahib to ask to borrow a book on positivism; he dismissed them, saying, 'You won't understand it.' The imputation that they were unfit even to be atheists merely increased their rage against atheism and against Sachish.

## 2

I have listed the aspects of belief and behaviour that provoked condemnation in Sachish's life. Some of these I came to know before my acquaintance with him, some after.

Jagmohan was Sachish's uncle. He was a celebrated atheist of those times. It would be an understatement to say he didn't believe in God; he believed in 'no-God'. A battleship commander's occupation has more to do with sinking ships than with navigation; similarly, Jagmohan's theological enterprise lay in torpedoing manifestations of faith wherever he got a chance. This is how he marshalled his arguments before a believer:

'If God exists, then my intelligence is his creation. My intelligence says there is no God. Therefore God says there is no God. Yet you contradict Him to His face and say that God exists! Thirty-three billion godlings will twist your ears to make you atone for this blasphemy.'

Jagmohan had married when still a boy. His wife died in his youth, but he had read Malthus in the meantime. He never married again.

His younger brother Harimohan was Sachish's father. Harimohan's character was so strikingly antithetical to his elder brother's that if I write about it readers will mistake it for fiction. But it is fiction that must be chary in order to seduce the reader. Since Truth is not under such constraints it doesn't balk at being strange. And so, just as dawn and dusk are opposed in Nature, human society doesn't lack instances of similar opposition between elder and younger brother.

Harimohan had been a sickly child. He had to be protected from harm by all sorts of amulets and charms; rites of exorcism; water sanctified by washing sadhus' matted locks; dust from prominent holy places; food-offerings to deities and the ambrosial water that has washed their feet; and above all, the blessings obtained from priests at great expense.

Harimohan's illnesses left him when he grew up, but the belief that he was very delicate persisted in the family. Nobody wished of him anything more than that he should just stay alive somehow. He didn't disappoint anyone in this regard and went on living quite satisfactorily. But he kept everyone on tenterhooks by pretending that his health was always on the verge of collapse. Taking advantage of the apprehensions roused by his father's early death, he appropriated the doting attentions of his mother and aunts. He was served his meals before anybody else; his diet was specially prepared; he had to work less than others but was entitled to more rest. He never forgot that he was in the special care not only of his mother and aunts but of the gods as well. He extended deference, in proportion to the quantity of favours he might expect in return, not only to the gods but to worldly powers—he held such personages as the OC of the police station, rich neighbours, highly placed civil servants, newspaper editors, not to mention Brahmin priests, in awed reverence.

Jagmohan's apprehensions were of a contrary sort. He avoided the powerful, lest anyone suspect him of currying favour. A similar attitude underlay his defiance of the deity: he simply refused to bow before any power, be it earthly or divine.

In due course, that is to say well before due time, Harimohan's marriage took place. After three daughters and three sons came Sachish. Everyone said he bore a striking resemblance to his uncle. Jagmohan too became deeply attached to the child, as if it were his own son.

At first Harimohan was pleased at the thought of the advantages accruing from this. For Jagmohan had taken on responsibility for the boy's education, and he was well known for his exceptional mastery of English. In the opinion of some he was the Macaulay of Bengal, to others he was Bengal's Dr Johnson. He seemed to be encased within a shell made up of English books. Just as a line of pebbles shows the course of a mountain stream, the parts of the house where he spent his time could be recognized by the English books lining the walls from floor to ceiling.

Harimohan lavished his paternal affection on his eldest son, Purandar. He could never say no to Purandar's demands. His eyes always appeared to brim with sentimental tears for this son; he feared that Purandar would simply cease to live if thwarted in anything. Purandar's education came to nothing. He had married very early, and no one had managed to bind him to his marital vows. When his wife protested vigorously, her father-in-law turned on her angrily and declared that her nagging had driven his son to seek solace elsewhere.

Observing such goings-on, Jagmohan sought to protect Sachish from the hazards of paternal love by never letting him out of sight. It wasn't long before Sachish, still at a very early age, acquired a sound knowledge of English. But he didn't stop there. With his brain cells kindled by Mill and Bentham, his atheism began to glow like a torch.

Jagmohan behaved with Sachish as if he was of the same age. He considered reverence for age an empty convention that confirmed the human mind in its servitude. A young man who had married into the family wrote to him, addressing the letter in traditional style, 'To your auspicious feet'. He replied with the following advice:

> My Dear Naren
>
> What it means to describe the feet as 'auspicious', I do not know; nor do you; it is therefore sheer nonsense. Then again, you have completely ignored me and addressed my feet instead. You ought to know that my feet are a part of my body and cannot be seen as separate from me as long as they are not severed. Further, they are neither hand nor ear; to make an appeal to them is sheer madness. Finally, your choice of the plural number over the dual with reference to my feet may express reverence, given that a certain quadruped is an object of devotion to you, but it bespeaks an ignorance of my zoological identity that should, I feel, be removed.

Things that others sweep under the carpet Jagmohan openly discussed with Sachish. If anyone complained about this he would say, 'If you want to get rid of hornets, break up their nest. In the same way, removing the embarrassment that attaches to certain topics dispels the cause of embarrassment. I am breaking the nest of embarrassment in Sachish's mind.'

## 3

Sachish completed his degree. Harimohan now mounted a campaign to rescue him from his uncle. But the fish had swallowed the bait and was caught on the hook. The more one tried to pull it free the more firmly attached it became. Harimohan's anger at this was directed more at his brother than at his son. He strewed the neighbourhood with colourful slander about him.

Harimohan wouldn't have minded if it was only a question of opinions and beliefs; even eating forbidden chicken was tolerable—it could be passed off as goat. But his brother and son had gone so far in their behaviour that nothing could cover it up. Let me narrate the event that gave most offence.

Service to humanity was an important aspect of Jagmohan's atheistic creed. The chief delight in such altruism lay in the fact that it brought nothing save financial loss—no award or merit, no promise of baksheesh from any scripture—nor did it placate any irate deity. If anyone asked, 'What is there for you in the greatest good of the greatest number?' he would say, 'The greatest thing for me is that there's nothing in it for me.' He would say to Sachish:

'Remember, my boy, our pride in being atheists requires us to be morally impeccable. Because we don't obey anything we ought to have greater strength to be true to ourselves.'

Sachish was his chief disciple in seeking the greatest good of the greatest number. In their neighbourhood there were some hide-merchants' warehouses. The social work of uncle and nephew brought them into such intimacy with the Muslim tanners and traders that Harimohan's caste mark positively blazed, and threatened to turn his brain into an inferno. Knowing that invoking scripture would have the opposite of the desired effect, Harimohan complained instead that Jagmohan was misusing their patrimony. 'Let my expenses reach what you have spent on fat-bellied priests,' Jagmohan replied, 'then I will square accounts with you.'

One day Harimohan's household noticed that preparations were afoot for a huge feast in Jagmohan's part of the house. The cooks and attendants were all Muslim. Beside himself with rage, Harimohan summoned Sachish and said, 'I hear you will treat all your chamar friends to a feast here?'

'I would if I had the means,' Sachish replied, 'but I don't have any money. They're coming as Uncle's guests.'

Stomping about in fury, Purandar threatened, 'I'll see how they dare come to this house to eat.'

When Harimohan protested to his brother, Jagmohan told him, 'I don't say anything about your daily food-offerings to your gods. So why do you object to my making an offering to *my* gods?'

'Your gods?'

'Yes, my gods.'

'Have you become a Brahmo?'

'Brahmos accept a formless deity who is invisible to the eye. You accept idols who cannot be heard. We accept the living who can be seen and heard—it's impossible not to believe in them.'

'What, these Muslim chamars are your gods?'

'Yes, these Muslim chamars are my gods. You will notice that among all deities they are distinguished by a remarkable ability to polish off whatever eatables are placed before them. None of your gods can do that. I love to watch this miracle, so I have invited my gods into my home. If you weren't blind to true divinity you would be pleased at this.'

Purandar went up to his uncle, said many harsh things in a loud voice, and declared that he would do something really drastic that day.

'You monkey,' Jagmohan said with a laugh, 'you have only to lay a finger on my gods to see how potent they are. I won't have to do a thing.'

No matter how boastful he was, Purandar was in reality even more of a coward than his father. He was formidable only with those who spoiled him. He didn't dare enrage his Muslim neighbours. He went instead to Sachish and abused him. Sachish merely raised his exquisite eyes towards his elder brother and didn't utter a word. That day the feast was held undisturbed.

## 4

Harimohan girded his loins now for a campaign against his elder brother. Both of them derived their income from the trusteeship of ancestral property endowed as a religious trust. Harimohan filed a suit in the district court in which he claimed that being an atheist, Jagmohan was ineligible for the trusteeship. Respectable witnesses for the plaintiff were not lacking; virtually the entire neighbourhood was ready to testify.

There was no need to resort to pettifoggery. Jagmohan unequivocally stated in court that he didn't believe in gods and goddesses; didn't care for scriptural restrictions on diet; didn't know from which part of Brahma's anatomy the Muslims had originated; nor saw any objections to dining or mixing socially with them.

The judge found Jagmohan unworthy of the trusteeship. Jagmohan's lawyers assured him that the judgement would be overturned in the High Court. But Jagmohan said, 'I will not appeal. I cannot cheat a god, even one I do not believe in. Only those stupid enough to believe in a god can deceive him in good conscience.'

'How will you live?' his friends asked.

'If I can't get food,' he said, 'I'll live on air.'

Harimohan had no wish to boast of his victory in the law suit. He was apprehensive that his brother might put a curse on him. But Purandar still smarted at having failed to turn the tanners out of the house. Now that it was quite obvious whose gods were more potent, he hired drummers who from dawn on shattered the neighbourhood's peace with their din.

'What's up?' said a friend who called on Jagmohan, ignorant of what had transpired.

'Today my god is being dunked in the water with great pomp, hence the music,' Jagmohan replied.

For two days Brahmins were feasted under Purandar's personal supervision. Everybody declared he was the glory of his family. Following this, the family home in Calcutta was divided between the two brothers by a wall down the middle.

Harimohan had enough confidence in human nature to assume that everybody—no matter what he thought of religion—possessed a natural good sense when it came to practicalities like food and clothing and money. He fully expected his son to abandon the impoverished Jagmohan and, drawn by the aroma of food, slip into the gilded cage. But Sachish had evidently inherited neither the piety nor the worldly wisdom of his father. He remained with his uncle.

Jagmohan had become so accustomed to treating Sachish as one of his own that it didn't strike him as extraordinary when on the day the house was partitioned his nephew fell to his share.

But Harimohan knew his brother only too well. He spread the rumour that Jagmohan was scheming to secure his own livelihood by holding on to Sachish. He put on a look of injured innocence and tearfully complained to everyone, 'I am not heartless enough to deprive my elder brother of food and clothing. But I will never tolerate his diabolical effort to manipulate my son. Let me see how far his cunning goes.'

When friends carried word of these developments to Jagmohan he was stunned. He cursed his own stupidity for not having anticipated them. 'Goodbye, Sachish,' he said to his nephew.

Sachish realized that the anguish with which Jagmohan had bid him farewell forbade any remonstrance. He would now have to end an association that had lasted without interruption through the eighteen years of his life.

When Sachish put his box and bedding-roll on the roof of the hackney carriage and was driven off, Jagmohan went up to his room, bolted the door and collapsed on to the floor. Dusk fell, the old servant knocked to be let in so he could light the lamp, but there was no response.

The greatest good of the greatest number, indeed! The statistical calculations of science do not apply to the mysteries of human nature. The person who is a single unit in a census is beyond the reckoning of statistics in matters of the heart. Sachish could not be categorized in terms of statistical units—one, two, three . . . He rent Jagmohan's heart and pervaded his whole world.

It hadn't occurred to Jagmohan to ask Sachish why he had ordered a carriage and loaded his belongings into it. Instead of moving to his father's half of the house Sachish went to a boarding-house where a friend of his lived. At the thought that one's own son could turn into a total stranger Harimohan shed frequent tears. He *was* very tender-hearted!

Soon after the partitioning, Purandar, out of sheer bloody-mindedness, set up a permanent altar for idol-worship in his father's half of the house and danced for joy at the thought that each morning and evening the noise of the ritual cymbals and conch-shells was driving his uncle to distraction.

Sachish took up tutoring pupils privately, and Jagmohan became headmaster of a high school. Harimohan and Purandar embarked on a mission to rescue the children of respectable families from the clutches of the atheist pedagogue.

## 5

One day not long afterwards Sachish suddenly appeared in Jagmohan's upper-floor study. The custom of making obeisance, or pranam, being alien to them, Jagmohan embraced Sachish and offering him a seat on the bed, asked, 'What news?'

There was indeed some special news.

A widowed girl called Nonibala and her widowed mother had taken refuge in the house of a maternal uncle. She was safe as long as her mother was with her, but the old woman had died not long ago. The girl's cousins were scoundrels. One of their cronies lured Nonibala out of the house and seduced her. After some days he became prey to jealousy, suspected Noni of betraying him, and started heaping insults on her. All this was going on next door to the house where Sachish was employed as tutor to the children. Sachish wanted to rescue the wretched girl. But he had neither money, nor a place where he could take her; hence the visit to Uncle. By now the girl had become pregnant.

Jagmohan flew into a rage. If he could have laid hands on the seducer he would have instantly crushed the fellow's head! He wasn't the sort of person to deliberate calmly on such matters. 'Very well,' he declared. 'My library is empty. I'll put her up there.'

'The library!' Sachish exclaimed in surprise. 'But what about the books?'

During the time that Jagmohan had been looking for a job he supported himself by selling off his books. Those that remained could be easily accommodated in his bedroom.

'Fetch the girl straightaway,' Jagmohan said.

'I've already brought her,' Sachish replied. 'She's waiting downstairs.'

Jagmohan went down and saw the girl cringing like a little bundle of rags on the floor of the room by the staircase. He swept into the room like a gale and said in his deep voice, 'Come, my little mother. Why are you squatting in the dust?'

The girl buried her face in a corner of her sari and broke into sobs.

Tears didn't come easily to Jagmohan's eyes, but they brimmed over now.

'Sachish,' he said, 'the shame this girl has to bear today belongs equally to you and me. Who has forced such a burden on her?'

Then to her, 'Ma, your shyness won't do before me. My schoolmates nicknamed me Jagai the Madcap. I am still the same madcap.'

So saying he unhesitatingly took the girl's two hands and drew her to her feet. Her sari slipped from her head. Such a young and tender face, free of the slightest taint of disgrace! She was lovely as a raintree blossom, and just as dust on a flower cannot destroy its essential purity, so the beauty of her sacred inner being had remained unbesmirched. Her dark eyes were fearful like those of a wounded gazelle, her lissome frame was constricted by a sense of shame, but her frank sorrow revealed no sign of stigma.

Jagmohan took Nonibala upstairs to his room and said, 'Ma, look at the state of my room. The broom hasn't touched it in ages, everything's topsy-turvy, and as for me I eat at no fixed time. Now that you are here, my room will become neat and tidy again, and even Jagai the Madcap will be able to live like a human being.'

Nonibala hadn't known till this day what human beings could mean to each other. She hadn't known it even when her mother was alive, for her mother had come to see her not simply as a daughter but as a widowed daughter, and this defined a relationship that was like a path strewn with the tiny thorns of foreboding. So how could a complete stranger like Jagmohan rend the veil of such judgements and accept her totally?

He engaged an elderly maidservant and did everything to make Nonibala feel at home. Noni had been very apprehensive that Jagmohan wouldn't accept food from her hands—she was a fallen woman, after all. As things turned out, Jagmohan was unwilling to accept food except from her hands; he even swore that unless she cooked his meals and served them herself, he wouldn't eat at all.

Jagmohan knew another round of condemnation was imminent. Noni too knew this and had no end of anxiety on this account. It started in a few days. The maidservant had taken Noni to be Jagmohan's daughter. Then one day she came and after heaping abuse on Noni walked out on her job with a display of great disgust. Noni grew despondent out of solicitude for Jagmohan. He comforted her, saying, 'Ma, the full moon has risen in my house, it's time for the flood-tide of calumny to rise. But however muddy the waves, they can't taint my moonlight.'

An aunt on Jagmohan's father's side walked over from Harimohan's part of the house and said, 'How disgusting, Jagai! Get rid of this sin.'

'You people are religious,' Jagmohan said, 'so you can say such a thing. But if I get rid of the sin, what is to be the fate of the poor sinner?'

A distant cousin of his grandmother came and advised, 'Send the girl to hospital. Harimohan is willing to bear all expenses.'

'But she is a mother,' Jagmohan replied. 'Can I send a mother to hospital for no reason, just because money is available for the purpose? What sort of logic does Harimohan follow?'

'Who do you call a mother?' said the cousin, raising her eyebrows.

'A person who nurtures life in her womb, who risks her own life to give birth to her child. The heartless creature who fathered the child I'll never call a father. That fellow only puts the girl in trouble but doesn't face any trouble himself.'

Harimohan was overcome with disgust, as if his entire body had been soaked in filth. How could one bear the thought that on the other side of the boundary wall of a respectable home, on property that had come down from one's revered ancestors, a fallen woman lived so brazenly?

Harimohan readily believed that Sachish was intimately involved in this heinous sin and was indulged in it by his atheist uncle. Wherever he went he spread this tale with great outrage.

Jagmohan didn't do anything to stem the tide of obloquy.

'The religious scriptures of us atheists decree the hellfire of calumny as the prize for good deeds,' he pronounced.

The more varied and colourful the rumours that spread, the more Jagmohan and Sachish gave themselves up to satiric merriment. To joke with one's nephew over something so sordid was unheard-of by Harimohan or respectable citizens like him.

Purandar hadn't stepped into Jagmohan's part of the house since it was partitioned. But he now swore that his prime task in life was to drive the girl out of the neighbourhood.

Jagmohan, when he went to school, secured all entrances to his house and, whenever during the day he could take some time off, didn't fail to come and check if everything was safe.

One day around noon Purandar placed a ladder against the parapet of the roof on his father's half of the house and descended into Jagmohan's portion. Nonibala had finished her midday meal and dozed off, leaving the door of her room open.

Purandar entered the room and, seeing her, roared in anger and surprise, 'So! You are here!'

Startled out of sleep, Noni's face turned pale at the sight of Purandar. She didn't have the strength to flee or to say anything. Quivering with rage, Purandar called her name, 'Noni!'

Just at that moment Jagmohan entered the room from behind and screamed, 'Get out! Get out of my house!'

Purandar puffed up like an enraged cat.

'If you don't leave at once I'll call the police,' Jagmohan threatened.

Purandar shot a fiery glance at Noni and left. Noni fainted.

Jagmohan understood now. When he asked Sachish he found that

Sachish knew it was Purandar who had ruined the girl's life but had kept the information from Jagmohan lest he became angry and created an uproar. Sachish knew that Noni wouldn't be safe from Purandar's persecution anywhere else in Calcutta; if there was any place where Purandar wouldn't dare intrude it was his uncle's house.

Seized with fear, Noni trembled like a bamboo shoot for several days, then gave birth to a stillborn child.

Purandar had literally kicked Noni out one midnight, and had then, for a long time, looked for her in vain. On discovering her in his uncle's house he burned from top to toe with jealousy. He assumed that Sachish had enticed her away to keep her for his own enjoyment and had put her up in Jagmohan's house in order to add insult to injury. On no account could this be tolerated.

Harimohan came to know of all this. In fact Purandar felt no embarrassment about letting his father find out. Harimohan looked upon his son's misdeeds with something like affectionate indulgence. He considered it highly unnatural and immoral of Sachish to snatch the girl from Purandar. It became his firm resolve that Purandar should avenge the insufferable insult and injustice by retrieving what was rightfully his. He put up money to hire the services of a woman who would pose as Noni's mother and plead with Jagmohan to give back her daughter. But Jagmohan drove the imposter away with such a terrible look on his face that she didn't dare go back.

Noni grew emaciated day by day, till she seemed about to fade away into her shadow. The Christmas holiday had come. Jagmohan didn't leave her alone in the house even for a moment.

One evening he was reading a novel by Scott and retelling the story to Noni in Bengali. Just then Purandar stormed into the room with another youth. When Jagmohan rose with threats to call the police, the youth insisted, 'I am Noni's brother, I have come to take her home.'

Without another word Jagmohan grabbed Purandar by the neck, marched him to the stairs and with one shove sent him clattering on his way. To the youth he thundered, 'Have you no shame? When Noni needs protection you are nowhere around, and when people try to ruin her you join them saying you are her brother!'

The young man backed away quickly, but from a distance he shouted back that he would seek police assistance to rescue his sister. He was indeed Noni's brother; Purandar had asked him along in order to make out that it was Sachish who had brought about Noni's ruin.

Noni prayed silently, 'O Mother Earth, swallow me up.'

Jagmohan called Sachish and said, 'Let me take Noni to some town upcountry. I'll find some sort of a job. The persecution has reached such a pitch that the poor girl won't survive here much longer.'

'When my elder brother is involved the persecution will follow wherever you go,' Sachish replied.

'Then what is to be done?'

'There is a way out. I'll marry Noni.'

'Marry?'

'Yes, according to Civil Law.'

Jagmohan hugged Sachish to his chest. Tears streamed from his eyes. In all his life, he had never shed such tears.

## 6

Since the partition of the house Harimohan hadn't visited Jagmohan even once. One day he turned up suddenly, all dishevelled and distraught. 'Dada,' he said, 'what's this disaster I've been hearing about?'

'Disaster was imminent, but a way has been found to avert it.'

'Dada, Sachish is like a son to you—how can you let him marry that fallen woman?'

'I have brought up Sachish like a son, and my efforts have borne fruit today. He has done something to gladden our hearts.'

'Dada, I'll surrender to you—I'll give up half my income to you—please don't wreak such terrible vengeance on me.'

Jagmohan stood up from the cot on which he was sitting.

'Indeed! You have come to pacify the dog with the leavings on your plate! I'm not a pious man like you, I'm an atheist, remember that. I don't seek revenge in anger, nor do I accept charity.'

Next, Harimohan turned up at Sachish's lodgings. He drew him aside and said, 'What's that I hear? Couldn't you find some other way to ruin your life? How can you dishonour the family like this?'

'I wasn't keen on marriage,' Sachish replied, 'but I'm trying to erase the stain of dishonour from our family.'

'Haven't you any moral sense?' Harimohan said. 'That girl is virtually your Dada's wife, yet you . . .'

'Virtually his wife?' Sachish interrupted in protest. 'Don't you dare say such a thing.'

After that Harimohan hurled at Sachish whatever abuse came to his mind. Sachish made no reply.

Harimohan found himself in dire straits because Purandar was shamelessly telling everybody that he would commit suicide if Sachish married Noni. 'That would end the bother,' Purandar's wife said, 'but you don't have the guts to do it.' Harimohan didn't quite believe Purandar's threat, but neither could he stop worrying about it.

Sachish had avoided Noni's company all these days. He hadn't ever seen her alone, and it was doubtful if he had exchanged even a couple of words with her. When the final arrangements for the marriage had been made Jagmohan told Sachish, 'Before the wedding you ought to have a word with Noni in private. You need to know each other's true feelings.'

Sachish agreed.

Jagmohan set a date. 'Ma,' he said to Noni when the day arrived. 'You must dress up now to my liking.'

Noni lowered her eyes bashfully.

'No, Ma, don't be shy. It's my fond wish to see you fully decked out today. Please satisfy my whim.'

He then handed her a set of clothes he had bought himself—a gilt-embroidered Benares sari, blouse and veil.

Noni reverently bent down to take the dust of his feet. He hastily drew back his feet and said, 'In all these days I've failed to rid you of your reverence for me. I may be older in years, but you, Ma, are greater than I because you are a mother.'

Then kissing the top of her head he said, 'I have an invitation to Bhabatosh's—I may be a little late.'

Noni took his hand. 'Baba,' she said, 'give me your blessing today.'

'Ma, I can see very clearly that you'll turn this old atheist, in his dotage, into a believer. I don't care a straw about blessings, but when I see that face of yours I must confess I do feel like blessing you.'

He took her chin to raise her face and gazed silently at it; tears streamed from her eyes.

That evening messengers hastened to Bhabatosh's to call Jagmohan home. When he came he saw Noni lying in bed in the clothes he had given her, clutching a note in her hand. Sachish was at the head of the bed. Jagmohan opened the note and read:

> Baba,
>
> I can't go on. Please forgive me. All these days I have tried heart and soul for your sake, but I can't forget him even now. A million obeisances on your blessed feet.
>
> The sinner Nonibala

# Sachish

## 1

On his deathbed Jagmohan said to Sachish, 'If you fancy a Sraddha have one for your father but not for your uncle.'

This is how he died. When the plague first came to Calcutta people were more fearful of the uniformed government employees who carted victims off to quarantine than of the disease itself. Harimohan reckoned that the tanners in the neighbourhood would be among the first to catch the disease; and then his family would surely die with those wretches. Before escaping to safety, he approached his brother with an offer. 'Dada,' he said, 'I've found a house in Kalna, on the bank of Ganges. If you . . .'

'Splendid!' Jagmohan said. 'But how can I abandon these people?'

'Who?'

'The tanners.'

Harimohan made a wry face and left. He went to Sachish's lodgings and said, 'Come with us.'

'I have work to do,' Sachish said.

'What, playing undertaker to those tanners?'

'Well, yes, if necessary.'

'Necessary indeed! It seems you might consider it necessary to consign your ancestors to hell, you wicked atheist.'

Harimohan saw ominous signs of apocalypse, and returned home filled with despair. That day, to bring himself luck, he filled a quire of paper with the holy name of Durga in a minuscule hand.

Harimohan left Calcutta. The plague reached the neighbourhood. Victims were reluctant to call in a doctor lest he force them to move into hospital. Jagmohan visited the plague hospitals.

Saying on his return, 'Should the sick be treated like criminals?' he converted his house into a hospital. Sachish and a handful of us were volunteer nurses; a doctor also joined our team.

Our first patient was a Muslim; he died. The second was Jagmohan himself; he didn't survive either. 'The creed I have lived by all my life has given me its parting gift,' he said to Sachish. 'I have no regrets.'

Sachish, who had never made obeisance to Uncle when he was alive, bent down and for the first and last time reverently touched his feet.

When Harimohan next met Sachish he said, 'This is how atheists meet their end.'

'Exactly!' said Sachish with pride.

## 2

Just as the light of a lamp put out by a puff of breath vanishes instantly, after Jagmohan's death Sachish disappeared—we didn't know where.

It's impossible for us to Imagine how much Sachish loved Uncle. Uncle was Sachish's father, friend, and even—in a sense—his son. For he was so absent-minded about himself and so ignorant of wordly affairs, that one of Sachish's prime responsibilities was to keep him out of trouble. Thus it was through Uncle that Sachish acquired what was his own and gave away what he had to contribute of his own.

It is also futile to try to imagine how Sachish was affected by the void left by Uncle's death. Sachish struggled in intolerable anguish to establish that the void could never in fact be so empty, that no emptiness was so absolute that it left no room for truth. For if it wasn't the case that what was 'No' in one sense was also 'Yes' in another, then through the tiny hole of that 'No' the entire universe would vanish into nothingness.

Sachish roamed the countryside for two years, and I had no contact with him. Our group continued with its activities with increased vigour. We became the scourge of those who had any kind of religious belief, and deliberately undertook charitable work of the sort that would not win the approval of our more respectable contemporaries. Sachish had been the flower in our midst; when he stepped aside only our naked thorns were displayed.

We had no news of Sachish for two years. I don't wish to say anything critical about Sachish but I couldn't help thinking then that at the shock of bereavement the note to which he had been tuned had slid down the scale.

'Just as a moneychanger rings a coin to test if it is counterfeit,' Uncle had once remarked on seeing a sannyasi, 'the world tests the quality of man by making him experience loss, bereavement and the lure of salvation. Coins that ring false are discarded as counterfeit; these sannyasis are like those fake coins, useless in life's transactions. Yet they go around saying that they have renounced the world. If one is of any use there's no way one can slip out of the world of samsara. Dry leaves fall from the boughs because the tree shakes them off—they are trash after all.'

Among so many was it going to be Sachish's lot to end up as trash? Had it been inscribed on the dark touchstone of grief that Sachish was worthless in life's marketplace?

Then we heard that Sachish was somewhere in Chittagong. *Our* Sachish was with Swami Lilananda, dancing ecstatically, singing kirtans, playing cymbals, and rousing whole neighbourhoods into a state of excitement.

Once I couldn't imagine how someone like Sachish could be an atheist; now I couldn't understand how Swami Lilananda made Sachish dance to his tune.

Meanwhile how could we not lose face? Our enemies would laugh at us. And they were far from few.

Members of our group turned violently against Sachish. Many claimed to have known all along that there was no real substance to Sachish; he was all empty theory.

I realized now how much I loved Sachish. He had aimed a fatal missile at our group, yet I couldn't bring myself to feel any anger towards him.

I set out in search of Swami Lilananda. I had to cross many rivers, cut across many fields, spend nights in grocers' stalls, before finally catching up with Sachish in a village. It was about two in the afternoon.

I wanted to see him alone, but there was no hope of that. The courtyard of the disciple's house in which the Swami had halted was thick with people. There had been kirtan singing all morning. Arrangements were afoot to provide a meal to those who had come from afar.

As soon as he saw me Sachish rushed forward and hugged me. I was astonished. Sachish had always been restrained in manner; with him, silence evinced depth of feeling. Today it seemed as if he was high on drugs.

The Swami was resting in a room. The door was slightly ajar.

He caught sight of me and called out in a deep voice, 'Who is it?'

'My friend Sribilash,' said Sachish.

My name had begun to get around. A certain Englishman of intellectual repute had observed on hearing me lecture in English, 'The fellow's quite . . .' but let me not make more enemies by going into all that. I had become well known among students and their parents as a formidable atheist who could drive the four-horse carriage of English conversation at twenty or twenty-five miles an hour with amazing finesse.

I believe the Swami was pleased to hear of my arrival. He wished to see me. I entered his room and greeted him with a namaskar. It was a namaskar in which my joined palms rose perpendicularly to my forehead; my head didn't bow at all. We were Uncle's disciples, our namaskar was like an unstrung bow: dispensing with the nama, it stood ramrod straight.

Noticing this, the Swami said, 'Get the hookah ready for me, Sachish.'

Sachish sat down to prepare the hookah. As the tikka lit up I too began to burn. I couldn't decide where to sit. The only furniture was the cot on which the Swami had made his bed. I didn't consider it improper to sit down on one side of it, but I didn't do so I don't know why—I kept standing by the door.

I discovered that the Swamiji knew I had won the Premchand-Raychand scholarship. 'Baba,' he said, 'the diver has to go down to the seabed to look for pearls, but it's fatal to get stuck there, so he comes gasping to the surface to save his life. If you want salvation you must leave the floor of the ocean of knowledge and come to the shore. You have won the Premchand-Raychand scholarship, now look to the Premchand-Raychand renunciationship!'

When the hookah was ready Sachish handed it to him and sat on the floor at his feet. The Swami at once stretched out his legs towards Sachish, who began slowly massaging them.

The sight was so distressing to me that I couldn't remain any longer in the room. I realized it was in order to provoke me that Sachish had been made to prepare the Swami's hookah and massage his legs.

The Swami continued with his rest, the visitors finished their meal of khichuri. At five, kirtan singing resumed and went on till ten at night.

Catching Sachish alone at night I said, 'Sachish, from the moment you were born you have lived in a liberated atmosphere. What strange bondage have you got yourself into now? Can Uncle's death be such a devastating event?'

Partly as an affectionate joke, partly because of my appearance, Sachish used to transpose the first two syllables of my name, Sribilash, and call me Bisri, which means ugly. 'Bisri,' he said, 'when Uncle was alive he gave me freedom in the sphere of life's activities, and this was like the freedom a child enjoys in the playpen. With his death he has set me free in the ocean of ecstasy which offers the freedom a child finds at its mother's breast. Having enjoyed the freedom of daylight, why should I now forgo the freedom of the night world? You may rest assured Uncle has had a hand in both.'

'Whatever you say,' I retorted, 'Uncle's weaknesses didn't extend to making others massage his legs and prepare his hookah. This doesn't look like liberation.'

'Uncle trained my limbs for work and gave me the freedom of the shore,' said Sachish. 'Now I am in the ocean of ecstasy, where a boat's moorings are its guarantee of liberty. That is why the guru has bound me like this to a life of service; by massaging his legs I am making my way across the ocean.'

'The words don't sound unattractive on your lips,' I said, 'but the person who stretches out his legs towards you like that is surely . . .'

'He can do that because he doesn't really need anyone's service. If he did he would feel embarrassed; the need is mine alone.'

I realized that Sachish was in a realm I had never entered. The 'me' whom Sachish had embraced when we met wasn't 'me, Sribilash', it was the Universal Soul that inheres in all beings, it was an Idea.

Such an Idea is like wine; whoever is drunk with it will clasp anyone to his breast and shed tears; it makes no difference whether that one is me or another. But I couldn't share the inebriate's joy; I didn't want to lose my power of discrimination and be a mere ripple in a flood of Sameness—after all, 'I' am 'me'.

I knew it wasn't a question that could be settled through argument. But it was beyond me to abandon Sachish; drawn into the Swami's group because of him, I too drifted from village to village. Gradually the intoxication came to possess me as well; I too embraced everyone, shed unrestrained tears, massaged the guru's legs; and one day in a sudden, ineffable rapture I saw Sachish assume an other-worldly form that could only be that of a god.

## 3

Having roped two formidable English-educated atheists into his fold, Swami Lilananda's fame spread far and wide. His disciples in Calcutta implored him to make his base in the city. So he went.

The Swami once had an extremely devoted disciple named Shibtosh, with whom he would stay whenever he was in Calcutta. The pride and joy of Shibtosh's life was to serve the Swami and his retinue.

Before his death Shibtosh made out a will granting life-rent for his house and other property in Calcutta to his young and childless wife, and ultimate ownership to his guru; it was his wish that in time the house would become the chief place of pilgrimage for his guru's followers. This was where we billeted.

During my delirious wanderings from village to village, I had been in one frame of mind. After coming to Calcutta I found it difficult to sustain my drunkenness. All these days I had been in the realm of ecstasy, where the cosmic Female and the consciousness-pervading Male made love endlessly; the music of that cosmic romance filled the village pastures, the peepul-shade at the river-crossing, leisurely afternoons, and the evenings pulsating with the chirp of crickets. It was like a dream in which I floated without hindrance in the open sky; coming to the tough city my head suffered a knock, I was jostled by crowds—the spell broke. Once in lodgings in this very Calcutta I had devoted myself day and night to study; had met with friends by the Goldighi lake to ponder the nation's future; played the volunteer at political conferences; nearly landed in jail in protesting against police brutality. Responding to Uncle's call, I had vowed to oppose the brigandage of society with my last breath and to liberate the minds of my countrymen from all forms of bondage. From early youth till now I had moved through the city throngs like a sailboat travelling proudly upstream with chest puffed out, derided by stranger and kinsman alike. Now in the same Calcutta, I tried desperately to sustain the trance of lachrymose ecstasy amidst crowds tossed about by hunger and thirst, pleasure and pain, and the baffling problems of good and evil. At times I felt I was too weak, I was straying, my devotions lacked concentration. But turning to Sachish I saw in his face no recognition of the fact that Calcutta had a position in geographical space; to him it was all shadow.

## 4

My friend and I continued to live with our guru in Shibtosh's house. We were his chief disciples and he wanted us to be constantly with him.

Day and night we discoursed with our guru and fellow disciples on the theory of rasa, the essence of ecstasy. Amidst the obscure profundities loud feminine laughter would suddenly reach us from the zenana. Sometimes we would hear a loud summons to the maid, 'Bami!' Seen from the rare heights of abstraction in which our minds were absorbed these were trivialities; but it would suddenly seem as if a shower had pattered down in the middle of a drought. Whenever such small signs of life in the hidden world on the other side of the wall touched us like falling petals, I would be struck by the realization that the desired partner in ecstasy was there—where the rattling bunch of household keys was tied to a corner of Bami's sari, where the smell of cooking rose from the kitchen, where I could hear the sound of sweeping, where all was trivial yet true, where the sweet and the bitter, the crude and the subtle, were inextricably intertwined—there lay the paradise of ecstasy.

The widow's name was Damini. At first we would catch only fleeting glimpses of her, but Sachish and I were so close to the guru that she couldn't keep herself hidden from us for long.

Damini means lightning and Damini was like the lightning in thunderous monsoon clouds. Her outward form brimmed with youthful vitality; and in her soul danced a restless flame.

At one point in his diary Sachish noted:

'In Nonibala I saw one form of the Universal Feminine—the woman who takes upon herself the stigma of sin, who sacrifices her life for a sinner's sake, who in dying adds to the contents of life's cup of ambrosia. In Damini the Universal Feminine assumes another form. She has no truck with death, she is a celebrant of the vital force. Like a spring garden she is always brimming with waves of lovely fragrance. She doesn't want to renounce anything in life; she is unwilling to play host to the *sannyasi*; she has sworn not to pay a paisa in homage to the cold north wind.'

Let me say a few words about Damini's background. Damini's marriage took place at a time when her father Annadaprasad's coffers overflowed with a sudden flood of profit from the jute trade. Till then Shibtosh had only a good pedigree; now fortune smiled on him. Annadaprasad presented his son-in-law with a house in Calcutta and arranged for him an income sufficient to ensure a comfortable life. The dowry also included a large quantity of ornaments.

He tried to train up Shibtosh in his office. But it wasn't in Shibtosh's nature to take an interest in worldly matters. An astrologer once told him that the influence of Jupiter during a certain conjunction would liberate him from earthly attachments. Henceforth, in anticipation of his salvation, he decided to forgo the desire for gold and other precious substances. He had by then become a disciple of Swami Lilananda.

Meanwhile a crosswind in business had overturned the full-sailed pinnace of Annadaprasad's fortune. He had to sell off everything, even his house, and was hard put to provide his family with regular meals.

One evening Shibtosh entered the zenana and told his wife, 'Swamiji is here—he has asked to see you to give some advice.'

'I can't go now. I don't have any time,' Damini said.

No time! Shibtosh drew closer and saw that in the darkened room Damini had taken her jewellery out of its boxes.

'What are you doing?' he asked.

'I am sorting out my jewellery,' Damini replied.

Was that why she had no time? Really! The next day Damini opened the steel chest and found her jewellery gone.

'Where's my jewellery?' she demanded of her husband.

'You have presented it to your guru,' her husband said. 'That was why he had summoned you at that moment, for he is omniscient. He has liberated you now from desire for gold.'

Damini flared up. 'Give me back my jewellery!'

'Why, what for?' her husband asked.

'It was my father's gift,' Damini replied. 'I'll return it to him.'

'It has fallen into better hands,' said Shibtosh. 'Instead of going to feed those with earthly attachments it has been dedicated to the service of religious devotees.'

Thus began the brigandage in the name of spiritual devotion. In order to rid Damini of the spirits of all earthly desires, the exorcist's raids continued apace. While Damini's father and young brothers starved, she cooked daily, with her own hands, for sixty to seventy devotees. She would wilfully put no salt in the curry, she would let the milk go off: such was her brand of asceticism.

Just then her husband died after imposing on her a penalty for her lack of devotion. Together with all his property he placed his wife under the guardianship of the guru.

Throughout the house the tide of devotion rose tirelessly. People thronged from far away to seek the guru's blessing. Yet Damini, who could come close to him without trying, kept this precious opportunity at bay with continuous taunts and insults.

Whenever the guru asked to see her to impart some special advice she would say, 'I have a headache.' If he questioned her about a slip-up in the dinner arrangements she would say, 'I was out at the theatre.' It wasn't true, but it was barbed. The guru's women devotees saw how she behaved and raised their eyebrows in disbelief. To begin with, Damini didn't dress like a widow; then, she would pointedly ignore the guru's instructions; and finally she showed no hint of the radiance of ascetic purity that lights up body and soul through being close to such a great man. Everybody voiced the same opinion: 'Some creature indeed! We have seen a lot, but such a woman—never!'

The Swamiji would laugh and say, 'The Lord loves to wrestle with a strong opponent. When she eventually concedes defeat, she will be struck dumb for ever.'

He began showing excessive forgiveness towards her. This was even more intolerable to Damini, for it was merely a disguised form of punishment. One day when Damini was with a female friend he overheard her mimicking, amidst merry laughter, the exceedingly lenient manner he adopted with her.

He said nonetheless, 'God is using Damini as an agent for bringing about the unexpected. She isn't to blame.'

So far we had seen one side of Damini; now the unexpected did indeed begin.

I don't feel like writing any more; it's also hard to put these things into words. In life the web of suffering that is spun by invisible hands working behind the scene has a pattern that is neither dictated by scripture nor made to anybody's order; that's why inner and outer awkwardness forces us to suffer so many knocks, why life explodes with such sobs.

The brittle armour of rebellion silently shattered and fell off in the light of an unforeseen dawn, and the blossom of self-sacrifice raised its dew-laden head. Damini's service now became so effortlessly splendid that it seemed to spread a rare boon of sweetness over the devotion of the disciples.

When Damini's thunder and lightning had thus mellowed into a steady glow, Sachish began to notice her loveliness. But in my opinion Sachish saw only Damini's beauty, he didn't see Damini herself.

In Sachish's sitting room a photograph of Swami Lilananda in meditation had been placed on a slab of china. One day he found it in splinters on the floor. Sachish thought it was his pet cat's doing. From time to time many such accidents occurred that would be beyond the strength of a wild cat to bring about.

The atmosphere around us became charged with restless energy. Invisible lightning flickered in hidden recesses. I don't know about the others, but my soul throbbed with pain. At times I thought I wouldn't be able to bear the ceaseless play of the waves of ecstasy any longer; I felt like escaping it at a gallop. Those bygone discussions with tanners' children on Bengali conjunct letters, so utterly devoid of ecstasy as they were, seemed preferable.

One winter afternoon, the disciples were tired and the guru was resting in his room. Sachish, who needed to go there for something or the other, stopped short in the doorway. He saw Damini prostrate, with hair let down, repeatedly banging her forehead on the floor and muttering, 'O stone, stone, have mercy, have mercy on me, strike me dead!'

Sachish shivered all over with fright; he withdrew as fast as he could.

## 5

Once a year, in the winter month of Magh, guruji went away to some remote, solitary place. The time had come round again.

'I'll go with you,' Sachish said.

'Me too,' I said. The pursuit of ecstasy had left me with frayed nerves. I badly needed a spell of fatiguing travel and solitary living.

Swamiji called Damini and said, 'Ma, I'm setting off on my travels.

As in the past I will arrange to send you to your aunt for the duration of the trip.'

'I will go with you,' she replied.

'How can you?' Swamiji said. 'It'll be a hard journey.'

'I'll manage,' Damini said. 'You won't have to worry about me.'

The Swami was pleased at Damini's new devotion. In past years this had been the time for Damini's holiday; she would yearn for it all year long. 'What a miracle!' mused the Swami. 'How the divine chemistry of ecstasy softens even stone.'

Damini wasn't to be put off; she came along.

## 6

After walking six hours in the sun that day we reached a promontory jutting into the sea. It was absolutely quiet and deserted; the susurrus of leaves in a coconut grove mingled with the lazy rumble of a nearly still sea.

It seemed to me as if a slumbering earth had stretched a weary arm over the sea. In the hand at the end of that arm stood a blue-green hill. There were ancient rock carvings in a cave on the side of that hill. Whether these were Hindu or Buddhist, whether the figures were of Buddha or Krishna, whether their craftsmanship betrayed Greek influence, these were contentious issues among scholars.

We were supposed to return to human habitation after seeing the cave. But that proved impossible. The sun had nearly set and it was the twelfth day of the dark half of the lunar month.

'We shall have to spend the night in the cave,' Guruji said.

We went and sat on the sandy beach between the sea and the edge of the grove. The sun was on the sea's western rim: the departing day's final bow before the advancing dark. Guruji struck up a song—a modern poet's lyrics, which he sang in his own style:

*Travelling, we meet*
*at day's end.*
*The evening glow*
*vanishes when we go*
*towards it.*

That day the magic in the song was realized. Tears rolled out of Damini's eyes. Swamiji took up the middle stanza:

*Whether or not we meet*
*I shall not grieve,*
*Just pause a moment*

*While I cover your feet in my loosened hair.*

When the Swami ended the song, the silence of the evening, filling sky and sea, swelled from the lingering essence of the tune into a ripe golden fruit. Damini prostrated herself in a pranam before the Swami. For a long while she didn't raise her head; her loosened hair lay piled on the sand.

## 7

An extract from Sachish's diary:

The cave had many chambers. I spread my blanket in one and lay down.

The darkness of the cave was like a black beast—its moist breath seemed to touch my skin. It seemed to me like the first animal to appear in the very first cycle of creation; it had no eye, no ears, only a huge appetite. It had been trapped for eternity in that cave. It didn't have a mind; it knew nothing but pain—it sobbed noiselessly.

Weariness like a heavy weight bore down on my entire body, yet I couldn't sleep. A bird, perhaps a bat, either flew in or went out, travelling from darkness to darkness with a flailing noise from its wings. I broke into gooseflesh at the touch of the air stirred by it.

I thought I would sleep outside the cave. But I had forgotten the way to the entrance. When I crawled forward, in one direction my head touched the ceiling; in another direction I bumped my head; in yet another I slipped into a small ditch filled with water that had seeped through a crack.

Finally I gave up and lay down on the blanket. It seemed the primordial beast had thrust me deep into its saliva-drenched maw; there was no escape. The beast was all dark hunger, it would lick at me slowly and consume me. Its saliva was acidic, it would corrode me.

If only I could sleep; my wakeful mind couldn't bear the close embrace of such colossal, destructive darkness: that was possible for death alone.

After I don't know how long, a thin sheet of numbness spread over my consciousness. At some point in that semi-conscious state I felt the touch of a deep breath close to my feet. That primordial beast!

Then something clasped my feet. At first I thought it was a wild animal. But a wild animal is hairy, this creature wasn't. My entire body shrank at the touch. It seemed to be an unknown snake-like creature. I knew nothing of its anatomy—what its head looked like, or its trunk, or its tail—nor could I imagine how it devoured its victims. It was repulsive because of its very softness, its ravenous mass.

I was speechless with fear and loathing. I began pushing the creature away with both feet. It seemed to place its face on my feet—it was breathing heavily—I didn't know what sort of a face it was. I began to kick at it.

Eventually I came out of my trance. At first I had thought the creature was hairless; but suddenly I felt a mass of hair, as from a mane, fall on my feet.

I got up quickly and sat down.

Somebody seemed to move away in the dark. A strange sound reached my ears: such as stifled sobs!

# Damini

## 1

We returned from the cave. Accommodation had been arranged for us on the upper floor of the house of one of Guruji's disciples, close by the village temple.

We didn't see much of Damini now. She cooked and served our meals but avoided our company as far as possible. She made friends with the village women and spent her time visiting their homes.

This annoyed Guruji somewhat. He felt that worldly life still attracted her more than the celestial realm. She seemed to tire of the nearly religious devotion with which she had been looking after us for some days past. She made mistakes, the natural grace with which she did things wasn't there any longer.

Guruji began to be secretly fearful of Damini once again. Her brows had for some days been darkened by a frown and her temper had become rather unpredictable. Signs of rebellion were noticeable in her lips, the corners of her eyes, the clumsily knotted hair on her neck, and at times in the involuntary motions of her hands.

Guruji once more concentrated on the devotional hymns, he thought their sweetness would draw the errant bee back to the honeycomb. The short winter days frothed and overflowed with the intoxicating brew of music.

But there was no catching Damini. 'God is out hunting,' Guruji observed with a chuckle one day, 'and the doe by leading him a chase is adding zest to the hunt; but die she must.'

When we first got acquainted with Damini she didn't appear among the disciples, but we didn't notice that. Now her absence from our midst became all too conspicuous. Not being able to see her affected us like being blown about by gusts of wind. Since Guruji interpreted her absence as pride, it hurt his pride. As for me, it's hardly necessary to talk about my feelings.

One day Guruji mustered enough resolve to put a mild request to her: 'Damini, if you can make time this afternoon . . .'

'I can't,' she said.

'Why not?'

'I've got to go to the village to help make sweets.'

'Sweets? Why?'

'There's a wedding at the Nandys'.'

'Is it absolutely essential?'

'Yes, I've promised.'

Without another word Damini left like a sudden gust of wind. Sachish was sitting with us; he was astounded. So many eminent, learned, wealthy and wise men had come with bowed heads to his guru; yet where did this slip of a girl acquire such brazen arrogance?

On another day in the evening, when Damini was home, Guruji began a ponderous sermon, speaking especially carefully. After a while he became aware of a certain blankness in our faces. He noticed that we had become inattentive. Turning round he saw that Damini was no longer where she had sat sewing buttons on shirts. He realized that both Sachish and I were filled with the same thought—that Damini had got up and left. The thought that Damini hadn't listened to him, hadn't in fact wanted to listen to his words, rattled in his mind like a tambourine. He lost the thread of his discourse. He couldn't restrain himself any longer but got up and called from outside Damini's room, 'Damini, what are you doing all by yourself? Won't you join us in the other room?'

'No, I'm busy,' Damini replied.

The Guru peeped in and saw a kite inside a cage. A couple of days back the kite had flown into a telegraph wire and fallen to the ground, where it had been set upon by crows. Damini had rescued it—and nursed it ever since.

So much for the kite. Damini had also got hold of a puppy whose appearance and pedigree matched each other perfectly. It was discord personified. At the first sound of our cymbals it raised its muzzle towards heaven and vociferously complained to God. It was a small consolation that God didn't heed the plaint, but those of us who had to hear it on earth were driven to distraction.

One day when Damini was tending some flowering plants grown on the roof in a broken pot Sachish went up to her and asked, 'Why have you stopped attending?'

'Attending what?'

'Guruji's meetings.'

'Why, what use have you people for me?'

'None, but you have some use for us.'

Damini flared up: 'Not at all!'

Sachish stared dumbfounded at her. 'Can't you see,' he said after a while, 'how uneasy you've become? If you want peace . . .'

'*You* give me peace? You've driven yourselves crazy, forever stirring up waves in your minds. Is that peace? I beg you, help me. I used to be at peace, let me live in peace again.'

'You may see waves on the surface,' Sachish said, 'but if you have the patience to dive beneath and look you'll see that all is calm.'

Joining her palms in entreaty Damini said, 'For God's sake don't ask me to dive any more. I'd feel relieved if you gave me up.'

## 2

I didn't have enough experience to know the secrets of the female heart. My superficial observations led me to believe that women are ready to lose their hearts where they are sure to be requited with sorrow. They will string their garland for a brute who will trample it into the horrid slime of lust; or else they will aim it at a man whose head it won't reach because he is so absorbed in a world of abstraction that he has virtually ceased to exist. When they have a chance to choose their mates women shun average men like us, who are a mixture of the crude and the refined, know women as women—in other words, know that women are neither clay dolls nor the vibrations of veena strings. Women avoid us because we offer neither the fatal attraction of murky desire nor the colourful illusion of profound abstractions; we cannot break them through the remorseless torment of lust, nor can we forget them in the heat of abstraction and recast them in the mould of our own fancy. We know them as they really are; that's why even if they like us they won't fall in love with us. We are their true refuge, they can count on our loyalty; but our self-sacrifice comes so readily they forget that it has any value. The only baksheesh we receive from them is that whenever they need us they use us, and perhaps even respect us a little, but . . . enough! These words probably stem from resentment, and probably aren't true. Perhaps it is to our advantage that we get nothing in return; at least we can console ourselves with that thought.

Damini avoided Guruji because she bore him a grudge; she avoided Sachish because she felt exactly the opposite towards him. I was the only one around for whom she felt neither anger nor attraction. For this reason whenever she got a chance Damini would chat with me about her past, her present, what she heard in the neighbourhood—trivial things like that. I never imagined that such an insignificant event as Damini jabbering away as she sat slicing betel-nuts on the little veranda in front of our rooms upstairs would affect Sachish so much in his present mood of abstraction. Well, it might not have been such a trivial event, but I knew that in the realm in which Sachish existed there was no such thing as an event. The divine workings of Hiadini, Sandhini and Jogmaya in that realm were a perennial romance, and therefore beyond historic time. Those who listened to the whistle of the ever-steady breeze that played there on the banks of an ever-flowing Jamuna wouldn't, surely, see or hear anything of the transitory events in the mundane world around them. At any rate, till our return from the cave Sachish's eyes and ears had been pretty inactive.

I myself was partly to blame. I had begun to play truant every now and then from our discussions on mystic ecstasy. Sachish began to notice my absence. Once he came looking for me and found me following Damini with an earthen bowl of milk that I had bought from the local cowherds to feed her pet mongoose. The task would hardly suffice as an excuse for truancy; it could have been easily postponed till the discussion ended; and in fact if the mongoose had been left to forage for its meals the principle of kindness to all creatures wouldn't have been grossly violated and my reputation for decorum would have remained intact. Consequently, I was quite flustered at Sachish's sudden appearance. I set the bowl down at once and tried to retrieve my self-esteem by sneaking away.

But Damini's behaviour was astonishing. She wasn't embarrassed at all, and asked me, 'Where are you going, Sribilashbabu?'

I scratched my head and mumbled, 'Well . . .'

'Guruji's meeting has ended by now,' Damini said, 'so why don't you sit down?'

My ears tingled with embarrassment at hearing such a request in Sachish's presence.

'There's a problem with the mongoose,' Damini said. 'Last night it stole a chicken from a Muslim house. It's not safe to let it loose—I have asked Sribilashbabu to buy a large basket to keep it in.'

Damini seemed rather keen to inform Sachish about Sribilashbabu's submissiveness in the matter of feeding milk to the mongoose or buying a basket for it. I was reminded of the day Guruji had asked Sachish in my presence to prepare the hookah. It was the same thing.

Without a word Sachish walked away quickly. Glancing at Damini's face I saw her eyes cast lightning shafts after Sachish. Inwardly she smiled a cruel smile.

God knows what she made of the incident, but the practical outcome was that she began to seek me out on the flimsiest of pretexts. One day she cooked some sweet dish and insisted on serving it exclusively for me. 'But Sachish . . .' I protested.

'Asking him to eat will only annoy him,' she said.

Sachish came round several times and saw me eating. Among us three, mine was the most difficult position. The two main characters in the drama were thoroughly self-possessed in their performance. I was conspicuous for the sole reason that I was utterly insignificant. At times this made me angry with my lot, but neither could I help my craving for whatever little my auxiliary role brought me. Such dire straits!

## 3

For some days Sachish played his cymbals louder than ever as he danced in the chorus of kirtan singers. Then he came to me one day and said, 'We can't keep Damini among us.'

'Why?' I asked.

'We must sever all connection with Nature.'

'If that is so,' I retorted, 'we must admit there's a grave flaw in our spiritual endeavour.'

Sachish gave me an open-eyed stare.

'What you call Nature is a reality,' I said. 'You may shun it, but you can't leave it out of the human world. If you practise your austerities pretending it isn't there you will only delude yourself; and when the deceit is exposed there will be no escape route.'

'I'm not interested in logical quibbles,' Sachish replied. 'I am being practical. Clearly women are agents of Nature, whose dictates they carry out by adopting varied disguises to beguile the mind. They cannot fulfil their mistress's command till they have completely enslaved the consciousness. So to keep the consciousness clear we have to keep clear of these bawds of Nature.'

I was about to continue but Sachish stopped me: 'My dear Bisri, you can't see Nature's fatal charm because you have already succumbed to it. But the beautiful form with which it has bewitched you will disappear like a mask as soon as she has realized her purpose; when the time comes she will remove this very desire which has clouded your vision and made you see her as greater than anything else in the universe. When the trap of illusion is so clearly laid, why walk straight into it with bravado?'

'I accept all you are saying,' I replied, 'but I'd like to point out that I didn't myself lay this worldwide trap of Nature, and I know no way of evading it. Since we can't deny it, true devotion in my view ought to allow us to accept it and yet enable us to transcend it. Whatever you say, dear Sachish, we are not doing that, and so we are desperately trying to amputate one half of the truth.'

'Could you spell out a little more clearly what sort of spiritual path you wish to follow?' he asked.

'We must row the boat of life in Nature's current,' I said. 'Our problem should not be to stop the current; our problem is to keep the boat from sinking and in motion. For that we need a rudder.'

'Our guru is that rudder,' Sachish retorted, 'but you can't see that because you don't accept him. Do you wish your spiritual development to follow your own whims? The result will be disaster.'

So saying, Sachish retired to the guru's room, sat down at his feet and began massaging them. That day, after preparing the guru's hookah, he raised with him his complaint against Nature.

The question couldn't be resolved over a single smoke. For days the guru pondered the problem from various angles. He had suffered much on account of Damini. Now it appeared that the presence of this one woman had created a whirlpool in the current of his disciples' devotion. But Shibtosh had bequeathed to him the guardianship of Damini together with the house and other property, making it difficult to get rid of her. The problem was compounded by the fact that the guru was afraid of Damini.

Meanwhile, though Sachish continued massaging the guru's feet and preparing his hookah with doubled, even quadrupled enthusiasm and increasing frequency, he couldn't be oblivious of the fact that Sachish's spiritual path had been well and truly obstructed by Nature.

One day a renowned group of kirtan singers from another part of the country were performing at the local Krishna temple. The session seemed set to go on till late. I slipped away soon after the start, thinking my absence wouldn't be noticed amidst the crowd.

That evening Damini laid bare her soul. The things that are hard to say, that stick in the throat even if one wishes to say them, were said by her with a wonderful simplicity. As she spoke she seemed to discover many dark and unfamiliar corners of her own mind. Quite fortuitously she had found an opportunity to come face to face with herself.

We didn't notice when Sachish came up behind us and stood listening. Tears were streaming from Damini's eyes. Not that what she said was very serious, but that day it all seemed to flow from the deep wellspring of her tears.

When Sachish turned up the kirtan session was clearly still a long way from the end. I could see that he had been agitated by something for some time.

Suddenly catching sight of Sachish standing in front of her, Damini hurriedly wiped her tears and made to retreat into the next room. In a quavering voice Sachish asked her to stop. 'Please, Damini, there's something I have to say to you.'

Damini sat down again slowly. I began to fidget, looking for an escape, but Sachish fixed me with such a stare that I didn't dare move.

'You don't share our purpose in following Guruji,' Sachish said.

'No,' Damini replied.

'Then why do you remain with us?'

Damini's eyes flashed. 'Why? Do you think I came willingly? You believers have kept this unbeliever in the fetters of belief. You have left me with no choice.'

'We've decided to pay for you to live with some female relative,' Sachish said.

'*You* have decided?'

'Yes.'

'I haven't.'

'Why, what objections do you have?'

'For some reason or the other one of you decides one thing, while for some other reason another one of you decides another thing; am I to be a pawn caught in the middle?'

Sachish stared in astonishment.

Damini went on. 'I didn't choose to come here to please you. I won't budge just because you are not pleased with me now and wish me to leave.'

As she spoke she pressed the edge of her sari to her face with both hands and burst into tears. She hurried into her room and shut the door.

Sachish didn't return to the kirtan session. He sat quietly on the dusty roof. That day the sound of distant sea waves, swept by the south wind, rose towards the stars like sobs from deep within the earth's breast. I went out and aimlessly wandered the dark deserted village paths.

## 4

The earth had girded up her loins to destroy the paradise of ecstasy in which Guruji had tried to keep us cloistered. All these days he had been pouring the wine of his mystic moods into the cup of metaphor for us to guzzle, but now the clash of a beautiful figure with the figures of speech threatened to tip the cup over and spill its contents on the ground. The signs of impending danger didn't escape the guru.

Sachish had become rather strange lately. He was like a kite whose string had just snapped—still airborne but at any moment liable to go into a spin and plummet to earth. He showed no neglect in the outward forms of devotion—jap, austerities, prayer, discussion—but looking into his eyes one knew that inwardly he was faltering.

And as for me, Damini left nothing to conjecture. The more she realized that Guruji secretly feared her and that Sachish was in secret agony, the more she dragged me around. It got to a point where she would suddenly appear near the door when, for instance, Guruji, Sachish and I were in earnest colloquy, and then vanish after calling out: 'Sribilashbabu, will you please come to me?' She couldn't be bothered to explain why she wanted Sribilashbabu. Guruji would give me a look, Sachish would give me a look, and, deliberating whether to get up or not, I would turn towards the door and suddenly get up and rush out. Even after I had gone an attempt would be made to keep the discussion going, but the effort would be out of all proportion to the things said; then the words would cease altogether. Thus everything became topsy-turvy and threatened to disintegrate; things just wouldn't hold together any more.

Sachish and I were the stalwarts of Guruji's camp—one might say we were to him what the mythic mounts, Airavata the elephant and Ucchaisraba the horse, were to the god Indra—so he couldn't just give up on us. He went to Damini and said, 'Ma, we're going to some remote and inaccessible places now. You must turn back.'

'Where?'

'To your aunt's.'

'I can't.'

'Why?'

'First, because she is only a distant aunt, and second, because she is under no obligation to keep me in her house.'

'It won't cost her anything. We can . . .'

'Is it only a question of cost? It's not her responsibility to look after me and watch over me.'

'Must I take care of you for ever?'

'Is that for me to say?'

'Where will you go if I die?'

'Why should I have to think about that? I only know that I have no mother, no father, no home, no money, I have absolutely nothing, and that's why I am such a great burden. You gladly took the burden on yourself, you can't now shift it to somebody else's shoulder.'

As Damini walked away, Guruji invoked Lord Krishna with a sigh.

One day Damini commanded me to get her some good Bengali books. Needless to say, by good books she didn't mean devotional literature, and she had no qualms about ordering me about. She had come to see that the greatest favour she could show me was to make demands on me. There are some plants that thrive if their branches are kept trimmed: in my relationship with Damini I was like those plants.

The writer whose books I had to procure was thoroughly modern. In his writings the influence of Man was much stronger than that of Manu. The packet of books fell into Guruji's hands. 'What's this, Sribilash?' he said, raising his eyebrows. 'Why have you got these books?'

I remained silent.

Turning over a few pages Guruji said, 'I find no scent of piety in this.'

He didn't like the author at all.

'If you read with a little care you will smell the scent of Truth,' I blurted out.

Truth to tell, rebellion had been brewing in my soul. The intoxication of mystic flights had given me a bad hangover. Pushing Man aside to deliberate day and night on his emotional essence had produced in me an aversion as strong as one can get.

Guruji gazed at my face for a while, then said, 'Very well, I'll read them attentively and see.'

Saying this he put the books under his pillow. I could tell he had no intention of returning them.

Damini in her room must have had an inkling of what had transpired. She came to the door and said to me, 'Those books I had asked you to order—haven't they arrived?'

I kept quiet.

'Those books aren't suitable for you, Ma,' Guruji said.

'How would you know?' she asked.

'And how would *you* know?' Guruji said with furrowed brow.

'I read them once before. I don't suppose you ever have.'

'So why do you need them again?'

'Your needs are never questioned. Am I alone to be denied any needs of my own?'

'You know very well I am a sannyasi.'

'And you know that I am not a sannyasini. I enjoy reading those books. Give them back?'

Guruji took the books from under the pillow and tossed them towards me. I handed them to Damini.

The upshot of this incident was that Damini now summoned me to read out to her the books she used to read in the solitude of her room. Our readings, followed by discussions, took place on the veranda. Sachish would frequently pass by, now in one direction, now in the other, longing to join us but unable to do so unasked.

Once as we came to an amusing episode in a book Damini burst into uncontrollable giggles. There was a fair going on at the temple and we thought Sachish had gone there. But suddenly he came out through the back door and sat down with us.

Damini's merriment ceased instantly. I too felt discomfited. I thought I should say something to Sachish, however trivial it might be but couldn't think of anything, and silently went on turning the pages of the book. Sachish got up and left as suddenly as he had come. After that we couldn't go on with our reading that day. Sachish perhaps didn't realize that while he envied the absence of any barrier between Damini and me, I actually envied the barrier between him and Damini.

The same day Sachish went to Guruji with a request: 'Master, I wish to go alone to the seaside for a few days. I'll be back in about a week.'

'Excellent idea,' said Guruji enthusiastically. 'By all means, go.'

Sachish went away. Damini stopped asking me to read; nor did she need me for anything else. I didn't even see her go to gossip with the village women. She kept to her room, her door shut tight.

A few days went by. One day when Guruji was taking a midday nap and I sat writing a letter on the upper veranda, Sachish suddenly arrived and without a glance at me knocked on Damini's door and called, 'Damini! Damini!'

Damini at once opened the door and came out. How Sachish's face had changed! It gave the impression of a storm-tossed ship with tattered sails and broken masts. A strange look in his eyes, hair awry, face haggard, clothes dirty.

'Damini,' Sachish said, 'it was wrong of me to ask you to leave. Please forgive me.'

'Why are you saying such things?' Damini asked with palms joined submissively.

'No, really, please forgive me. I'll never again entertain for a moment the utterly unjust thought that to preserve our spirituality we can decide to keep you or abandon you, as the whim takes us. But I have a request that you must keep.'

At once bowing and touching his feet Damini said, 'I am yours to command.'

'Come and join us,' Sachish said. 'Don't hold yourself aloof like this.'

'Yes, I will join you,' Damini said. 'I won't break any rules.' She bent down again, touched Sachish's feet in obeisance and repeated, 'I won't break any rules.'

## 5

The rock melted again. Damini's blinding radiance retained its light but lost its heat. A sweet aura pervaded her prayers and acts of kindness. She would never miss the sessions of kirtan singing or discussion, in which Guruji expounded the Bhagavad Gita or the Puranas. Her dress too changed; once again she wore tussore. Whenever one saw her during the day one felt that she had just had a bath.

Damini's greatest trial lay in her behaviour with Guruji. Whenever she bowed to him I would detect a flash of fierce rage in a corner of her eye. I knew that deep in her heart she couldn't abide any of Guruji's commands; but she followed all his injunctions so completely that one day he ventured to put forth his objections to the insufferable writings of that ultra-modern writer she had asked for. The next day he found some flowers beside the bed on which he took his siesta, arranged on pages torn from that fellow's books.

I had often noticed that what Damini found most intolerable was for Guruji to command Sachish to wait on him. She would try to thrust herself forward to take Sachish's task on herself, but it wasn't always possible. So, while Sachish blew on the tobacco-bowl of Guruji's hookah, Damini desperately mumbled to herself, 'I won't break the rules, I won't break the rules . . .'

But things didn't turn out the way Sachish had expected. The last time Damini had humbled herself like this Sachish had seen only the sweetness, not the bee who produced the sweetness. This time Damini herself had become so real to him that she jostled the words of hymns and the teachings of scripture and made her presence felt: there was no way she could be suppressed. Sachish became so aware of her that his mystic trance broke. He could no longer regard her as a metaphor for a transcendental mood. Damini didn't embellish the songs any more; the songs embellished her.

Here I may as well add the simple fact that Damini had no more use for me. Her demands ended suddenly. Of my few companions the kite had died, the mongoose had fled, the puppy had been given away because its unseemly behaviour annoyed Guruji. Unemployed and companionless in this way, I went back to my old place in Guruji's court, even though the songs and the conversation I heard there had become utterly distasteful to me.

## 6

One day while Sachish was brewing a wonderful concoction in the open cauldron of his fancy, compounded of philosophy, science, aesthetics and theology, drawn from the past and the present of both the East and the West, Damini suddenly ran towards us and called, 'Please come quickly!'

I got up hurriedly and asked, 'What's the matter?' 'I think Nabin's wife has swallowed poison,' Damini said. Nabin was related to one of Guruji's disciples. He was a neighbour and sang kirtans with our group. We found when we got there that his wife had died. On enquiry we learned that Nabin's wife had brought her motherless sister to live with her. Theirs was a kulin Brahmin family, so it wasn't easy to find a suitable match for the girl. She was good-looking. Nabin's younger brother chose her for his bride. He was still a college student in Calcutta, and it was understood that after taking his finals, which were due in a few months, he would marry her in the month of Ashar. Just then Nabin's wife discovered that a mutual attraction had developed between her husband and her sister. She asked him to marry her sister. Not much persuasion was necessary. Now that the nuptials were over, Nabin's first wife had committed suicide by swallowing poison.

There was nothing we could do. We came back. The disciples flocking round Guruji began singing kirtans to him; he joined in and began to dance.

The moon had risen in the evening sky. Damini sat quietly in a corner of the roof dappled with light and shade by the overhanging branches of a chalta tree. Sachish slowly paced up and down the covered veranda at the back. Keeping a diary was a weakness of mine; alone in my room I scribbled away.

The cuckoo was sleepless that night. The leaves of trees glittered in the moonlight and at the touch of the southerly breeze seemed to want to burst into speech. At one point, impelled by some notion or the other, Sachish suddenly went and stood behind Damini. She was startled and, drawing the edge of her sari over her head, she rose in a hurry—but before she could leave, Sachish called her name.

She stopped short. With joined palms she beseeched, 'Listen to me a moment, Master.'

Sachish gazed at her face in silence. 'Please explain to me,' Damini said, 'what use to the world are the things that engross you so day in and day out? Who have you succeeded in saving?'

I came out of my room and stood on the veranda. Damini went on: 'Day and night you go on about ecstasy, you talk of nothing else. Today you have seen what ecstasy is, haven't you? It has no regard for morals or a code of conduct, for brother or wife or family pride. It has no mercy, no shame, no sense of propriety. What have you devised to save man from the hell of this cruel, shameless, fatal ecstasy?'

I couldn't restrain myself and blurted out, 'We have planned to drive Woman far from our sphere and then devote ourselves undisturbed to the pursuit of ecstasy.'

Without paying any heed to my words Damini said to Sachish, 'I have got nothing from your guru. He hasn't been able to calm my restless mind even for a moment. Fire cannot put out fire. The path along which your guru has been driving everyone isn't the path of non-attachment or heroism or peace. That woman who died today was killed on the path of ecstasy by the demoness of ecstasy who sucked the blood out of her heart. Haven't you seen how hideous the demoness looks? My Master, I beseech you not to sacrifice me to her. Save me! If anybody can save me it's you.'

All three of us fell silent for a while. It became so still all around that it seemed to me as if with the chirp of crickets a numbness was stealing over the pale sky.

'Tell me what I can do for you,' Sachish said.

'Be my guru,' Damini replied. 'I won't obey any other. Give me a mantra that is above all these things, something that will keep me safe. Don't even let my guardian deity come close to me.'

Standing in a daze Sachish said, 'It will be so.'

Damini made a prolonged pranam with her head touching Sachish's feet. She mumbled over and over, 'You are my guru, you are my guru, save me from all sin, save me, save me . . .'

## Postscript

Once more the rumour went round, and the papers reported in abusive terms that Sachish's opinions had been revised yet again. He had once loudly denied religion and caste; then one day he had just as loudly proclaimed faith in gods and goddesses, yoga and asceticism, purificatory rituals and ancestor worship and taboos—the whole lot. And yet another day he threw overboard the whole freight of beliefs and subsided into peaceful silence—what he believed and what he denied became impossible to determine. One thing was apparent: he had taken up the welfare work he had done once in the past, but the caustic combativeness was no longer in him.

The papers had many taunts and harsh words about another matter: my marriage with Damini. Not everyone will understand the mystery behind this marriage, nor is it necessary that they should.

# Sribilash

## 1

An indigo factory used to stand here. It had fallen into ruins; only a few rooms still stood. Having taken a fancy to the spot I stopped here for some days on my way home after cremating Damini's remains.

The road that led from the river to the factory was lined with sissoo trees. The gateposts of the entrance to the indigo plantation and a bit of its boundary wall still stood, but of the plantation itself nothing was left. The only thing one could see on the plantation lands was, in one corner, the grave of a Muslim steward of the indigo factory. Lushly flowering shrubs of akanda and bhantiphool grew in the cracks in its brickwork; having tweaked the nose of death they seemed to roll with laughter in the southerly breeze, like a groom's sisters-in-law chaffing him in the bridal chamber. The banks of the plantation's large pond had collapsed and the water had dried up. On the dry bed peasants had planted a mixture of coriander and chick-peas. When I would sit of a morning on a mound of mossy bricks in the shade of a sissoo tree, my head would fill with the scent of coriander blossoms.

I sat and mused that the factory which today was no more than a few scattered bones in a charnel house had once brimmed with life. One might have imagined that the waves of happiness and sadness it had set off were a tempest that would never be stilled. The redoubtable sahib who on this very spot had made the blood of thousands of poor peasants run indigo blue would have seen me as just an ordinary Bengali youth. Yet the earth had quietly girdled the edge of her green sari around her waist and with a liberal plastering of clay erased all trace of him and everything of his, his factory included; whatever vestiges of the past were still visible would be totally obliterated by just one more wipe of her hand.

Such philosophizing is old hat and I haven't set out to reiterate it here. My real feeling was this: No, my dear chap, the last word isn't the daily plastering of mud, morning after morning, on the courtyard of time. The planter sahib and the terrible life of his factory have indeed been erased like a marking in the dust—but what about my Damini?

I know no one will accept what I am saying. The demystifying verses of Shankaracharya's *Mohamudgar* spare none. 'This world is illusion,' etc, etc. But Shankaracharya was a sannyasi. He had said such things as, 'Of what avail are wife and child?' but without grasping their significance. I am no sannyasi, so I know in my bones that Damini is not a dewdrop on a lotus leaf.

But I am told even some householders speak in the same world-denying terms. That may be so. They are only householders; they may lose their housewives. Their houses are maya, illusion; and so are their housewives. Both are man-made things, and vanish at the touch of the broom.

I haven't had time to be a householder, and—thank heaven—it's not in my temperament to be a sannyasi. That's why the woman I found as a companion didn't become a housewife; she couldn't be dismissed as maya; she was real. Till the end she remained true to her name, Damini, lightning. Who would dare call her a shadow?

There are many things I wouldn't have written, if I had known Damini merely as a housewife. It is because I have known her in a nobler, truer relationship that I can tell everything frankly, whatever others may say.

If I had been able to turn Damini into a regular housewife and pass my days as others do in this world of maya, I would have had a carefree existence, oiling my body, taking my bath, chewing paan after meals; and after Damini's death I would have said with a sigh, 'Varied is the world of samsara.' And to taste once again its variety I would have respectfully accepted the proposal of a matchmaking aunt. But a smooth entry into samsara, like that of feet entering an old pair of shoes, was not for me. From the start I forswore all hope of happiness. No, that's not quite true—I am human enough not to give up hope of happiness; I must have had some hope of it, but I certainly didn't feel I had a claim on it.

And why not? Because I had to persuade Damini to assent to our marriage. We didn't exchange ritual glances under the corner of a red silk shawl to the accompaniment of Raga Shahana. I had entered marriage in the broad light of day, with full understanding of everything involved.

When we left Swami Lilananda we were faced with the necessity of thinking about food and shelter. Till then, wherever we went we gorged on food-offerings brought to our guru: indigestion was a greater worry than hunger. We had totally forgotten that people in this world had to build houses and maintain them, or at least rent them. All we knew was that people had to sleep in houses. As for our householder host, where he would find some space for himself wasn't our concern; but he had to worry all right about finding a place for us to sprawl luxuriously.

Then I remembered that Uncle had willed his house to Sachish. If the will had been with Sachish it would have sunk like a paper boat in the waves of his ecstatic devotion. But it was with me; I was the executor. My task was to ensure the fulfilment of certain conditions, of which the most important were: that no religious service could be held in the house; that a night school for the children of Muslim tanners had to be set up on the ground floor; after Sachish's death the whole house had to be used for their welfare. Uncle hated piety more than anything else, deeming it more vile than worldliness. The provisions in the will were intended to neutralize the odour of sanctity from next door. Uncle described them—using the English term—as 'sanitary precautions'.

'Let's go back to Uncle's house in Calcutta,' I suggested to Sachish.

'I am not yet ready for that,' Sachish replied.

I couldn't see what he meant. He went on: 'Once I tried to base my life on intelligence and found that it couldn't take life's full weight. Then I tried to build my life on ecstatic devotion and found it bottomless. Intelligence is an aspect of my self, and so is mysticism. It is not possible to balance oneself on oneself. Unless I find some support I can't return to the city.'

'Tell me what to do,' I said.

'You two go ahead,' Sachish said. 'I'll wander alone for a while. I think I can make out the vague outline of a shore. If I lose it now I'll never find it again.'

Damini drew me aside and said, 'That cannot be. If he wanders all by himself who will look after him? He did go away once. I shudder whenever I remember how he looked when he came back.'

Shall I confess the truth? Damini's anxiety roused me into anger like a bee-sting. It irked me. For nearly two years after Uncle's death Sachish had wandered alone; he hadn't died. I couldn't suppress my feelings and I spoke out pungently.

'Sribilashbabu,' Damini said, 'I know people may take long to die. But why should he suffer at all when we are there?'

We! At least half of the first-person plural was this wretched Sribilash. In this world one group of people has to suffer in order to save another group from distress. The world of samsara is made up of these two categories of human beings. Damini well knew to which group I belonged. Still, it was some consolation that she had drawn me into her party.

I went to Sachish and said, 'Very well, we won't go to the city now. We can spend a few days in that ruined house across the river. Since it's rumoured to be haunted, people won't bother you there.'

'And you?' Sachish asked.

'We'll try to remain as unobtrusive as ghosts,' I said.

Sachish glanced once at Damini. Perhaps there was a touch of fear in that glance.

Damini appealed to Sachish with joined palms, 'You are my guru. No matter how greatly I may sin, allow me the right to serve you.'

## 2

Whatever you may say, I couldn't understand Sachish's enthusiasm for spiritual austerities. Once I would have dismissed such things with a laugh; now—whatever else—my laughter had ceased. I was dealing no longer with a will-o'-the-wisp but with a blazing fire. When I saw its flames engulf Sachish I didn't dare behave towards it like a disciple of Uncle's. What phantasmagoric faith gave birth to it and what miraculous faith would ultimately consume it? It was pointless to approach Mr Herbert Spencer to settle such questions. I could clearly see that Sachish was in flames, his life was ablaze from end to end.

Until now he had been in a state of perpetual excitement, singing and dancing, shedding tears of joy, attending on his guru; and in a way he was quite content. His mind was exerted to the utmost at every moment, squandering all his energy. Now that he had gathered himself in stillness, his mind could no longer be kept in check. No more did he wallow in mystic contemplation of ecstatic union with the divine. Such a desperate struggle to attain understanding raged within him that it was terrifying to look upon his face.

Unable to contain myself any longer I said to him one day, 'Look here, Sachish, it seems to me you need a guru who can lend you the support to make your quest easier.'

'O shut up, Bisri, shut up,' Sachish replied with annoyance, 'why take the easy way out? The easy way is a fraud, the truth is hard to attain.'

I said a little nervously, 'It is in order to show the way to the truth that . . .'

Sachish cut me short: 'My dear fellow, this isn't the truth of a geographical description. The God within me will tread my road and none other; the guru's road only leads to his own courtyard.'

Words from Sachish's lips have so often contradicted each other! I, Sribilash, was Uncle's follower no doubt, but if I had ever called him my guru he would have chased me with a stick. Sachish had got me, the selfsame Sribilash, to massage a guru's legs, and now soon after he was giving this lecture to the very same me! Not daring to laugh, I adopted a sombre expression.

Sachish went on. 'Today I have clearly grasped the significance of the saying, "Better die for one's own faith than do such a terrible thing as accept another's." Everything else can be taken from others, but if one's faith isn't one's own it brings damnation instead of salvation. My god can't be doled out to me by someone; if I find him, well and good, otherwise it's better to die.'

I am contentious by nature, not one to let go easily. 'One who is a poet finds poetry in his soul,' I said, 'and one who isn't borrows it from others.'

'I am a poet,' said Sachish brazenly.

Well, that settled it. I came away.

Sachish hardly bothered to eat or sleep and seemed oblivious of his whereabouts. His body seemed to grow as thin as an over-honed blade. Looking at him one would think he wouldn't hold out much longer. Still, I didn't dare interfere. But Damini couldn't bear it and became quite furious with God: frustrated by those who didn't worship him, must He take it out on those who did? With Swami Lilananda she could occasionally vent her rage quite forcefully, but there was no chance of reaching God.

She never, though, slackened her efforts to keep Sachish fed and bathed regularly. To bind this strange man to a routine, she resorted to countless ruses.

For a long time Sachish made no protest against this. Then early one morning he crossed the river to the sand flats on the other side. The sun reached its zenith, then declined to the west, but there was no sign of Sachish. Damini waited for him without eating her meal. When she could no longer bear the wait she took a plate laden with food and waded across the knee-deep water.

Emptiness all around, no sign of life anywhere. The waves of sand were as pitiless as the sun—as if they were sentinels of emptiness, lying in ambush.

Damini's heart sank as she stood in the middle of an unbounded, bleached space where no cry or query drew any response. Everything seemed to have dissolved into primal dry whiteness. There was nothing at her feet save a 'No'—no sound or motion, no trace of the red of blood, the green of plants, the blue of the sky or the brown of earth. Only the wide, lipless grin of a gigantic death's-head. As if under the pitiless blazing sky a huge dry tongue was displaying its thirst like a vast petition.

Damini was wondering which way to turn when she suddenly noticed footprints in the sand. Following them she reached a pond. The wet earth of its edges bore innumerable footprints of birds. Sachish was seated in the shade cast by a sandbank. The water was dazzling blue and on the bank fidgety snipes dipped their tails and flashed their two-tone wings. A little farther off noisy flocks of herons seemed unable to preen themselves to their satisfaction. As soon as Damini appeared on the bank they spread wings and took off with loud squawks.

When he saw her Sachish said, 'Why are you here?'

'I've brought some food,' Damini replied.

'I don't want to eat,' Sachish said.

'It's very late,' said Damini.

Sachish just said, 'No.'

Damini went on. 'Let me wait a little. After a while you . . .'

Sachish cut in. 'Oh, why do you . . .'

But suddenly catching sight of Damini's face he stopped. Without another word Damini got up with the plate and left. The bare sand all around glittered like tigers' eyes at night.

Damini's eyes blazed more readily than they shed tears. But that day I found her squatting with legs carelessly splayed while tears streamed from her eyes. On seeing me, her sobs seemed to burst through a dam. My heart felt uneasy. I sat down beside her.

When she had composed herself somewhat I said, 'Why do you worry so much about Sachish's health?'

'Tell me,' she replied, 'what else can I worry about? He has taken all other worries on himself. Do I understand them or do anything about them?'

'Look,' I said, 'when the mind runs hard into something the body's needs automatically diminish. That's why in a state of great joy or intense grief one feels no hunger or thirst. Sachish's state of mind is such that his body won't suffer if you don't look after it.'

'But I am a woman,' Damini protested. 'It is in our nature to devote ourselves body and soul to caring for the body. This task is entirely the responsibility of women. That's why when we see the body being neglected our hearts cry out.'

'That's why those who are preoccupied with their spirits don't even notice guardians of the body like you,' I said.

Damini retorted warmly, 'Don't they indeed! In fact they take notice in a way that's quite weird.'

'In that case,' I said to myself, 'the longing of your sex for the weird is boundless . . . O Sribilash, earn enough merit in this world so that you can be reborn as one of those weirdos.'

## 3

The outcome of the shock Sachish dealt Damini on the riverbank was that he couldn't erase from his memory her anxious expression as she had gone up to him. For some days after he did penance by paying special attention to Damini. For a long time he hadn't even bothered to speak politely with us; now he would often call Damini for a chat. They talked about the results of his profound meditation.

Damini had not been afraid of Sachish's indifference, but these attentions filled her with dread. She knew they were too good to last, for they came at a price. One day he would look at the balance sheet and see that the expenditure was too high. Then there would be trouble. Damini's heart trembled in apprehension, a strange embarrassment overcame her when Sachish behaved like an obedient child and had his bath and meals at regular hours. She would have felt relieved if he had disobeyed the rules. She said to herself, 'He did right to spurn me that day. But by paying me attention now he is only punishing himself. How can I bear that?' Then she thought: 'Damn it all. It seems that in this place also I'll have to make friends with the local women and spend time hanging around the village.'

One night we were woken up by loud shouts: 'Bisri! Damini!' It was one or two in the morning but Sachish would have no inkling of that. What he might be up to at such an hour I didn't know, but clearly his activities were driving the ghostly denizens of that haunted house to distraction.

We got up in a hurry and went out to find Sachish standing on the cement terrace in front of the house. 'I understand it all,' he shouted. 'There's no more doubt in my mind.'

Slowly Damini sat down on the terrace. Sachish followed her absent-mindedly and sat down. So did I.

'If,' Sachish said, 'I move in the same direction in which He is approaching me I'll only move away from Him, but if I move in the opposite direction we shall meet.'

I stared in silence at his burning eyes. What he had said was correct according to linear geometry, but what was it all about?

Sachish continued. 'He loves form, so He is continuously revealing Himself through form. We can't survive with form alone, so we must pursue the formless. He is free, so he delights in bondage; we are fettered, so our joy is in liberty. Our misery arises because we don't realize this truth.'

Damini and I remained as silent as the stars. 'Damini,' Sachish said, 'don't you understand? The singer progresses from the experience of joy to the musical expression of the raga, the audience in the opposite direction from the raga towards joy. One moves from freedom to bondage, the other from bondage to freedom; hence the concord between them. He sings, we listen. He plays by binding emotion to the raga and as we listen we unravel the emotion from the raga.'

I don't know whether Damini understood what Sachish was saying, but she did understand Sachish. She sat quietly, hands folded in her lap.

'All this while,' Sachish said, 'I've been sitting in a dark corner, listening in silence to the divine maestro's song. As I went on listening I suddenly understood everything. I couldn't contain myself, so I woke you up. All these days I've only fooled myself in trying to make Him in my own image. O my apocalypse, let me forever crush myself against you! I can't cling to any bondage because bondage isn't mine, and because bondage is yours you can never escape the fetters of creation. While you concern yourself with my form I plunge into your formlessness.'

Then saying over and over the words, 'O Infinity, you are mine, you are mine,' Sachish got up and walked through the dark towards the riverbank.

## 4

After that night Sachish reverted to his former ways. There was no knowing when he would bathe or eat. It was impossible to make out when the currents of his soul sought the light, or when they sought darkness. Whoever takes on the responsibility of keeping such a person regularly bathed and fed like a gentleman's son deserves divine assistance.

After a sultry day a violent storm burst at night. The three of us slept in separate rooms fronting a veranda on which a naked kerosene lamp burned. It went out. The river surged, the sky burst into torrents of rain. The thrashing of the waves below and the noise of the rain in the sky mingled to produce the continuous cymbal-crashes of an apocalyptic concert. We could see nothing of the turbulence within the womb of the massed darkness, yet the medley of noises emanating from it turned the entire sky as cold with fright as a blind child. A widowed ghoul seemed to shriek in the bamboo thickets, branches groaned and crashed in the mango grove, intermittently in the distance portions of the riverbank collapsed thunderously into the water, and as the gale repeatedly stabbed our dilapidated house with sharp thrusts through the ribs it howled like a wounded beast.

On a night like this the bolts to the doors and windows of the mind come loose, the storm enters and upsets the carefully arranged furniture, the curtains flap and flutter any which way and there's no catching hold of them. I couldn't sleep. There's no point transcribing the random thoughts that passed through my mind; they have no relevance to the story.

Suddenly I heard Sachish shout from within his dark room:

'Who is it?'

'It's Damini,' came the reply. 'The rain is getting in through your open window. I've come to shut it.'

As she did so she saw Sachish get out of bed. After what appeared to be a momentary hesitation he bolted out of the room. Lightning flashed, followed by a muffled rumble of thunder.

Damini sat for a long time in the doorway of her own room. But nobody came in from the storm. The gusty wind grew more and more impatient.

Unable to restrain herself any longer, Damini went out. It was hard to keep one's balance in the wind. Footmen of the gods hustled her along, as it were, with loud imprecations. The darkness began to stir. The rain tried desperately to fill all the holes and crannies in the sky. If only she herself could have deluged the cosmos like this with her tears.

Suddenly a lightning shaft ripped through the sky from end to end. In the fleeting light Damini spotted Sachish on the riverbank. Mustering all her strength she ran and fell at his feet. Her voice triumphed over the wind's roar as she begged, 'I swear at your feet that I have not wronged you, so why do you punish me like this?'

Sachish stood in silence.

'Kick me into the river if you wish,' Damini said, 'but get out of the storm.'

Sachish turned back. As soon as he got back to the house he said, 'I am seeking a Being whom I need desperately. I don't need anything else. Do me a favour, Damini. Abandon me.'

For a while Damini stood in silence. Then she said, 'Very well, I'll go.'

## 5

Later I heard the whole story from Damini, but that day I knew nothing of it. And so when from my bed I saw the two of them part on the front veranda and walk to their respective rooms, my hopelessness seemed to crush my chest and reach for my throat. I sat up in a panic and couldn't go back to sleep all night.

I was shocked at Damini's appearance the next morning. Last night's storm seemed to have left on her all the footprints of its dance of destruction. Though ignorant of what had transpired I began to feel angry with Sachish.

'Come, Sribilashbabu,' Damini said to me, 'you will have to escort me to Calcutta.'

I knew very well what agony such words were for Damini but I didn't probe her with questions. Even in the midst of anguish I experienced a sense of relief. It was for the best that Damini should leave. She was like a boat that had wrecked itself against a rock.

At the leave-taking Damini bowed to Sachish in a pranam and said, 'I have offended you in many ways. Please forgive me.'

Lowering his gaze to the ground Sachish said, 'I have also done much wrong. I will do penance to obtain forgiveness.'

On the way to Calcutta I saw clearly that Damini was being consumed by an apocalyptic Inferno. And I too—inflamed to fury by its heat—said some harsh things about Sachish. 'Look here,' Damini shot back, 'don't you talk like that about him in my presence. Have you any idea of what he has saved me from? You have eyes for my suffering only. Can't you see how *he* has suffered in order to save me? He tried to destroy Beauty, and in the process the Unbeautiful got a kick in the chest. Just as well. . .just as well . . . it was quite right.' Saying this Damini began violently striking her chest. I caught hold of her wrists.

On reaching Calcutta I took Damini to her aunt's, then went to a boarding-house I knew. On seeing me my acquaintances were startled into exclaiming, 'What on earth's the matter with you? Have you been ill?'

The following day the first post brought a note from Damini: 'Please take me away. I am not wanted here.'

The aunt wouldn't let Damini live with her. The city was apparently buzzing with condemnation of us. Shortly after our desertion of the guru's party the puja specials of the weeklies came out; so the chopping blocks were ready for us, and there was no dearth of bloodshed. The scriptures forbid the sacrifice of female animals, but in the case of human beings sacrificing females gives the greatest satisfaction. Though Damini's name was not explicitly mentioned in the papers care was taken to ensure that there would be no doubt about the target of the slander. Consequently it became totally impossible for Damini to live in her aunt's house.

By now Damini's parents were both dead. Her brothers, however, were still around. I asked her about their whereabouts. 'They are very poor,' she said with a shake of her head.

The fact was she didn't want to put them in a difficult position. She feared that the brothers too would say, 'No room for you here!' The blow would be unbearable. 'So where will you go?' I asked.

'To Swami Lilananda.'

Swami Lilananda! I was struck dumb for a while. Fortune could be so cruelly whimsical!

'Will Swamiji take you back?' I asked.

'Gladly.'

She knew human nature. Those dominated by the herd instinct prefer to find company than to seek truth. It was quite true that there would be no lack of room for Damini at Swami Lilananda's. Still . . .

At this critical moment I said, 'Damini, there's a way out. If you'll permit me I'll explain.'

'Let's hear,' Damini said.

'If it's possible for you to accept a man like me in marriage . . .'

Damini interrupted me. 'What are you saying, Sribilashbabu? Have you gone mad?'

'Let's say I have. When you're mad it becomes easy to solve many difficult problems. Madness is a pair of Arabian Nights shoes; if you put them on you can leap clear of thousands of bogus questions.'

'Bogus questions? What exactly do you mean by bogus?'

'For instance, what will people say? What will happen in future?'

'And the real questions?' Damini asked.

'Let's hear what you understand by real questions.'

'For instance, what will happen to you if you marry me?'

'If that's the real question I'm not worried, because my condition can't get worse. If only I could change it completely. Even turning it over on its side would provide a little relief.'

I refuse to believe that Damini had not already received some sort of telepathic message about my feelings. But till now this information had been of no consequence to her; or at least there had been no need for a reply. Now at last the need had arisen.

Damini pondered the matter in silence. 'Damini,' I said, 'I am one of the most ordinary men in this world. Indeed, I am less than that, I am insignificant. Marrying me or not marrying me will make no difference, so you needn't worry.'

Damini's eyes brimmed over. 'I wouldn't have to consider it at all if you were really ordinary,' she said.

After a little more thought Damini said to me, 'Well, you know me.'

'You know me too,' I said.

That is how I put my proposal. In the exchange between us the unspoken words outnumbered the spoken.

I have already mentioned that I had once conquered many hearts with my orations in English. In the time that had elapsed many had shaken off the spell. But Naren still regarded me as one of God's gifts to the present age. A house he owned was to remain untenanted for a month or so. We took temporary shelter there.

The day I put the question to Damini the wheels of my proposal had buckled and run into such a rut of silence that it seemed it would remain stuck there, beyond the reach of both 'yes' and 'no'. If only with extensive repairs and much hauling and heaving I could get it out! But the situation was unexpectedly saved because the psyche has been created—perhaps as a jest—specially to deceive the psychologist. That spring month of Phalgun, the Creator's merry laughter over this reverberated between the walls of our borrowed quarters.

All these days Damini had not had the time to recognize that I was of any consequence; perhaps a more intense light from another source was entering her eyes. Now her whole world narrowed to a point where I was the sole presence. Consequently there was nothing for her to do but open her eyes wide to see me. How lucky I was that just at this moment Damini seemed to see me for the first time.

I had roamed widely in Damini's company, by the sea and across many hills and rivers, while ecstatic melodies and a tumult of drums and cymbals set the air on fire. The line, 'At your footsteps the noose of love tightens round my soul,' was like a flame showering sparks in all directions. Yet the veil between us didn't catch fire.

But what an extraordinary thing happened in this Calcutta alley! The jostling houses seemed to turn into blossoms of amaranth. Truly, God gave a spectacular demonstration of his powers. Brick and woodwork became notes in his celestial melody. And with the touch of a philosopher's stone of some kind he instantly transformed a nonentity like me into an exceptional being.

When something is concealed behind a screen it seems eternally inaccessible, but when the screen is removed it can be reached in the twinkling of an eye. So we didn't tarry any longer. 'I was living in a dream,' Damini said. 'All I needed was to be jolted awake. A veil of illusion kept us separate. I bow to my guru in gratitude, for he removed the veil.'

'Don't stare at me like that,' I said to Damini. 'When you once before found that this particular divine creation wasn't attractive, I could bear it, but it would be very difficult to bear it now.'

'I'm now finding that same creation to be quite good-looking,' Damini said.

'You'll go down in history,' I said. 'Even the fame of the intrepid man who plants his flag at the North Pole will be nothing compared to yours. You have achieved something not merely difficult but impossible.'

Never before did I have such an absolute realization of the extreme brevity of Phalgun. Only thirty days, and each of them not a minute longer than twenty-four hours. God has all eternity in his hands, and yet such appalling niggardliness! I couldn't see why.

'Since setting yourself on this mad course, have you thought of your family?' Damini asked.

'They wish me well,' I said. 'So now they will disown me completely.'

'And then?'

'You and I will build a new home from scratch. It will be our very own creation.'

'And the housewife in it will have to be trained from scratch. Let her be entirely your own creation, let there be no fragments of the past.'

We set a date for our wedding in the summer month of Chaitra, and made the necessary arrangements. Damini insisted on getting Sachish to come.

'Why?' I asked.

'He will give away the bride.'

But there was no news of the madcap's whereabouts. I wrote letter after letter and got no reply. Probably he was still at that haunted house; otherwise the letters would have come back. But I doubted whether he opened any letter and read it.

'Damini,' I said, 'you'll have to convey the invitation in person. "Please forgive an invitation by post"—that sort of thing won't do here. I could have gone alone, but I am a timid sort of fellow. By now he has probably moved to the other side of the river to supervise the herons at their preening. Only you would have the guts to go there.'

'I promised never to go there again,' Damini said with a laugh.

'You promised not to go there again with food, but what's the harm in taking an invitation to a meal?' I said.

This time there was no hitch. The two of us took Sachish by the hand and marched him back to Calcutta. He was as delighted over our wedding as a child is with a new toy. We wanted to get it over with quietly; Sachish would have none of that. And when Uncle's Muslim following got wind of the event, they gave themselves up to such boisterous revelry that our neighbours thought the Emir of Kabul—or at least the Nizam of Hyderabad—had arrived on a ceremonial visit.

There was even greater excitement in the papers. The next puja specials duly provided the altar for a dual sacrifice. We had no desire to put a curse on anybody, though. Let Durga fill the coffers of the editors and at least this once let readers freely indulge their addiction to human blood, we thought.

'Bisri, I'd like you to use my house,' Sachish said.

'Why don't you join us too, so that we can get to work again?' I replied.

'No, my work lies elsewhere,' Sachish said.

'You can't leave before the bou-bhat ceremony,' Damini insisted.

There weren't too many guests at the bou-bhat. In fact there was only Sachish.

Sachish had blithely invited us to enjoy the use of his property, but what it entailed only we knew. Harimohan had taken possession of it and rented it out. He would have moved in himself, but those who advised him on spiritual matters considered it unwise because some Muslims had died of the plague there. The tenants who lived there would also . . . But they could be kept in the dark.

How we retrieved the house from Harimohan's grip would make for a long tale. Our chief strength lay in the neighbourhood Muslims. I simply gave them a glimpse of Jagmohan's will. After that it was unnecessary to go to any lawyer.

Till now I had always received some help from my family; it stopped. The two of us set up house unaided, but our hardship was our delight. I bore the badge of a Premchand-Raychand scholar, so it was easy to land a lectureship. In addition I put out patent medicines to help students pass examinations: voluminous notes on the text-books. I needn't have gone to such lengths, because our needs were few. But Damini said we must see to it that Sachish didn't have to worry about earning a living. There was another thing Damini didn't ask me to do, nor did I speak to her about it; it had to be done on the quiet. Damini's brothers lacked the means to ensure that her two nieces were married well or her several nephews well educated. They wouldn't let us into their houses—but money has no smell, especially when it merely has to be accepted and needn't be acknowledged.

On top of my other responsibilities I took up the sub-editorship of an English newspaper. Without telling Damini I engaged the services of a servant-boy, a bearer and an indigent Brahmin cook. The next day she dismissed them all without telling me. When I objected she said, 'You are always indulging me for the wrong reasons. How on earth can I do nothing while you are working yourself to the bone?'

My work outside and Damini's work inside the home—the two mingled like the confluence of the Ganges and the Jamuna. Besides, Damini began giving sewing lessons to the Muslim girls of the neighbourhood. She seemed to have vowed not to be outdone by me.

Calcutta became Vrindaban and our daily struggle became the nimble Krishna's flute, but I lack the poetic talent to express this simple truth in the right key. Let me just say that the days that went by didn't walk or run, they danced.

We passed yet another Phalgun. But no more after that. Ever since the return from the cave Damini had been suffering from a pain in the chest that she mentioned to no one. When it began getting worse she said in reply to my anxious queries: 'This pain is my secret glory, my philosopher's stone. It is the dowry that enabled me to come to you, otherwise I wouldn't have deserved you.'

The doctors each diagnosed the ailment differently. None of their prescriptions agreed. Eventually, when like Rama conquering Lanka the blaze of their fees and medicine bills had reduced my savings to cinders, the doctors capped their triumph by pronouncing unanimously that a change of air was necessary. By then my resources had dwindled into thin air.

'Take me to the place by the sea from where I brought the pain,' Damini said. 'There's plenty of air there.'

When the full moon of wintry Magh gave way to Phalgun and the entire sea rose, filled with the aching tears of high tide, Damini took the dust of my feet and said, 'My longings are still with me. I go with the prayer that I may find you again in my next life.'

# GLOSSARY

| | |
|---|---|
| **Airavata** | The white elephant, created by the churning of the ocean; became the mount of the god Indra. |
| **Akanda** | Mauve flower growing on a small tree. |
| **Ashar** | The first of the two months of the rainy season, mid-June to mid-July. |
| **Baba** | Father; also used affectionately for a son or young boy. |
| **Babu** | A gentleman; as a suffix added to a name it is equivalent to 'Mister', e.g. Sribilashbabu. |
| **Bhantiphool** | Sweet-smelling white flower with deep red spots. |
| **Bou-bhat** | Bou means bride, bhat rice. One of the many traditional Hindu wedding feasts, organized by the groom's family to welcome the bride. |
| **Chaitra** | The second of the two spring months in the Bengali calendar, mid-March to mid-April; it is hot and dry. |
| **Chalta** | An evergreen tree bearing large white scented blossoms and an edible fruit. |
| **Chamar** | Traditionally the caste of leather-workers, described as 'untouchable'. |
| **Dada** | Elder brother, grandfather, great-uncle. |
| **Durga** | One of the fierce forms assumed by the great Hindu goddess Devi, when she is the great protectress of humanity. |
| **Haidini, Sandhini and Jogmaya** | All associated with Vaishnava cults based on the ideal love of Radha and Krishna as the path to the realization of the Ultimate Being. Hiadini, identified with Radha, manifest the power of bliss; Sandhini, the power of existence; Jogmaya, identified with Durga, the power of divine diffusion. |
| **Jap** | The silent recitation of prayers and mantras. |
| **Ji** | Suffix added to a name or title as a mark of respect, e.g. Swamiji. |
| **Kayastha** | Important high caste of North India, originally of scribes. |
| **Khichuri** | Dish of rice cooked with dal (pulses). |
| **Kirtan** | Religious songs celebrating the sacred romance of Krishna and Radha. |
| **Kulin** | The highest subcaste of Brahmins, traditionally said to have been created by the twelfth-century Bengal king, Vallal Sena. |
| **Lanka** | Ancient name of Sri Lanka. |
| **Ma** | Mother; used affectionately for a daughter or young woman. |
| **Magh** | The second of the two winter months in the Bengali calendar, mid-January to mid-February. |
| **Manu** | Orthodox Hindu law-giver, probably legendary. |

| | |
|---|---|
| **Maya** | Illusion; the mundane realm, considered illusory in relation to the (transcendental) ultimate reality. |
| **Namaskar** | The Hindu salute, given by bowing (nama) and simultaneously raising joined palms. |
| **Paan** | Betel-leaf filled with various spices, chewed as a digestive. |
| **Phalgun** | The first of the two spring months in the Bengali calendar, mid-February to mid-March. |
| **Pranam** | Obeisance made by kneeling and touching forehead to the floor. |
| **Puja** | Hindu worship; often used as a shorthand for Durga Puja, the chief festival of Bengali Hindus, when magazines and periodicals publish special numbers. |
| **Puranas** | Hindu ancient narratives with a didactic purpose about the birth and deeds of gods and goddesses and mythological characters. |
| **Raga** | Indian musical mode, e.g. Raga Shahana, mentioned in the novella. |
| **Rasa** | Generally translated here as 'ecstasy'. It is a key concept in Sanskrit aesthetics as 'mood', of which there are nine principal ones: erotic, comic, compassionate, heroic, terrible, disgusting, wrathful, wonderful, calm. A work of art evokes one or more. In ordinary parlance it means the sap/essence/juice of life. In colloquial Bengali it can mean the sex drive. |
| **Samsara** | The world of the householder, characterized by worldly attachments. |
| **Sannyasi** | One who has renounced the world; a religious mendicant. |
| **Sanyasini** | Feminine form of sannyasi. |
| **Sissoo** | Large deciduous tree, valuable for its timber. |
| **Sraddha** | Rituals and feast marking the end of the period of mourning among Hindus. |
| **Tikka** | Cake of charcoal paste used as fuel to light the tobacco in the tobacco-bowl of a hookah. |
| **Ucchaisraba** | The horse of the god Indra. |
| **Veena** | Ancient stringed musical instrument, used chiefly in classical music. |

# Home and the World
## (Ghare Baire)
*Translated by Sreejata Guha*

# Bimala

Oh Mother, today I remember the sindoor on your forehead, the red-bordered sari you used to wear, and your eyes—calm, serene and deep. They touched my heart like the first rays of the sun. My life started out with that golden gift. What happened after that? Did the dark clouds come charging like brigands? Did they destroy the gift of light? And yet, that touch of the chaste dawn at the most important moment of one's life may perhaps be clouded by disaster, but it can never be erased completely.

In our land, only the fair-skinned are considered beautiful. But the sky that radiates light is dark. My mother was dark-skinned; her glow came from her inner goodness. Her virtue could put the vanity of beauty to shame. They all said I looked like my mother. As a child, this was my quibble with the mirror. I felt my entire being had been wronged—the colour of my skin was not my own, it was someone else's, a mistake from start to finish.

I was not beautiful. But I prayed to God with all my heart that, like my mother, I would be blessed with the gift of chastity. At the time of my marriage, the astrologer from my in-laws' came to read my palm and said, 'This girl has all the signs of good fortune and she will make a virtuous wife.' All the women said, 'Well, naturally. After all, isn't Bimala the spitting image of her mother?'

I married into an aristocratic family. Their title could be traced back to the days of the Mughals. I had heard fairy tales as a child and created the image of a prince in my mind. An aristocratic prince: his body would be like chameli petals; his face would be shaped as a result of the long and fervent prayers that a young maiden offered to Lord Shiva. Those eyes, that nose! His slim, newly emerged moustache would be as dark and delicate as the wings of a bumble bee.

When I saw my husband, he didn't exactly match this description. Even his skin, I noticed, was just as dark as mine. It did take away some of my regret about my own lack of beauty, but a sigh escaped my lips as well. I could have lived with remorse for my own looks, if only I could have one glimpse of the prince of my dreams!

But perhaps it is best when beauty slips past the sentry of the eyes and secretly shows up in the heart. There, on the banks that are lapped with the swelling waves of reverence, beauty can come unadorned. In my childhood, I have seen how the glow of bhakti turns everything beautiful. Even as a child I felt the caress in my mother's gracious, nurturing hands and the love from my mother's heart that poured out and plunged into a sublime ocean of beauty when she carefully peeled the fruits for my father and arranged his meal on a white marble plate, when she kept aside the paan for him, wrapped in fine cloth sprinkled with keora water, and as she gently fanned him and kept the flies off his plate when he sat down to eat.

Didn't the same strain of reverence run in me? It did. No debate, no deliberations over good or bad—it was just an inexorable strain! An entire lifetime spent playing it like a hymn in praise of the Lord Almighty in a corner of His temple—if that made sense, then that strain of melody heard in the early hours of my life had begun its work.

I remember, when I woke up at dawn and, very cautiously, touched my husband's feet, the sindoor on my forehead seemed to shine brighter than ever. One day he woke up, laughed and asked, 'What's this, Bimal, what are you doing!' I was so embarrassed. Perhaps he felt that I sought his blessings furtively. But no, oh no, it wasn't for the blessings—it was the woman's heart, where love itself seeks to worship.

The family I married into was very orthodox. Here, some rules were as old as the Mughals and some were even older, set by Manu and Parashar. But my husband was very modern in his outlook. He was the first in his family to be highly educated; he had earned an MA. Both his elder brothers died young from intemperance, they had no children. My husband did not drink and he was solemn by nature; this was unusual in this family and not everyone appreciated it. They thought such purity only suited those who were not blessed by the goddess of wealth. Only the expanses of the moon could contain blemishes with ease.

My husband's parents had died a while ago. The household was run by his grandmother. My husband was the jewel in her crown, the apple of her eye. This was the reason he dared to transgress the bounds of conformity. So, when he appointed Miss Gilby as my companion and tutor, tongues started wagging at home and outside, and yet, my husband's will won in the end.

At that time he had completed his BA and was studying for his MA. He had to stay in Calcutta for his classes in college. He wrote me a letter nearly every day. They were short and simple. That rounded, distinct writing from his hand stared back at me serenely.

I stored his letters in a sandalwood box. Every morning I picked some flowers from the garden and covered the box with them. By then my prince of the fairy tales had vanished like the moon on a sunny morning. The true prince of my heart had gained his rightful place. I was his princess and my place was beside him; but it was a greater joy to take my place at his feet.

I am educated. I am acquainted with this day and age in today's language. The words I speak now sound inordinately poetic even to my own ears. If I had never known today's world, I would have found my thoughts and feelings of those bygone days quite commonplace—I'd have thought, just as my being a woman was a fact, it's equally natural that a woman would turn her love into devotion. I wouldn't waste a moment's thought on whether there was any extraordinary kind of poetic beauty in this sentiment or not.

But from those days of my childhood to this day of my youth, I seem to have traversed an entire age. Thoughts, once as natural as breath, have to be constructed as poetic craft. The impassioned poets of today sing loud praises about the incredible beauty in a wife's chastity and a widow's celibacy. It is evident that truth and beauty have parted ways at this juncture of life. So then, can Truth be salvaged only under the guise of beauty?

All women don't think the same way. But this I know for certain—I have that element of my mother in me, the urge to revere. Today, when it is no longer considered natural by society, it is clear to me that it is an innate quality in me.

But woe for my Fate, my husband didn't wish to give me an opportunity to revere him. That was his generosity of spirit: at the holy place, the greedy priest grapples to get worshipped because he doesn't deserve it rightfully. In this world, only the weak demand reverence from their wives as their due. It shames both the worshipper and the worshipped.

But why this abundance of luxury for my benefit? It was as if his affection overflowed and flooded my banks, with maids and material things and creature comforts. How was I to push through all this and find a gap to offer myself up to him? I needed ways to offer more than to take. Love is, after all, reclusive by nature. It will blossom profusely and carelessly on the dust by the roadside. But it can't bloom in all its glory, trapped in a ceramic pot in a sitting room.

My husband couldn't violate all the orthodox rules and customary regulations of the inner chambers of the house. It wasn't possible for me to meet him freely in the mornings or at any odd hour of the day. I knew exactly when he would come in; so we would never meet casually, for no rhyme or reason. Our meeting was like a poem: it came with its own meter and its own rhythm. After the day's work, I freshened up, tied my hair carefully, dotted my forehead with sindoor, wore a freshly creased sari, collected my scattered mind and body from all its domestic concerns and offered myself on a golden tray at a special time to a special person. The time was little, but in itself it was boundless.

My husband always claimed that men and women have equal rights over one another and hence their love is also on an equal footing. I have never argued with him on this. But my heart says that devotion doesn't stop people from being equals. It tries to equalize people by elevating them. Hence, the pleasure of becoming equal is ever-present in it and it never turns into a thing of indifference. On the tray of love, devotion is like the light of the lamp in the ritual of worship—it falls the same way upon the worshipper and the worshipped. Today I know for sure that a woman's love is sanctified only through her own veneration—or else it's worth nothing. When the lamp of our love glows, the flame rises upwards and only the burnt-up oil remains at the bottom.

Dearest, it is your greatness that you refused my invocation, but it would have been best if you'd accepted it. You have loved me by adorning me, by educating me, by granting me what my heart desired and even what it did not desire, your love did not take time out to blink and I have seen the stolen sighs you have spent over your love for me. You have loved my body as if it was a parijata flower from the heavens, my soul you have loved as if it was your good fortune. This makes me proud; I feel that it is the wealth of *my* attributes that have thus drawn you to me. It makes me feel like the rightful occupant of the queen's throne—I sit here and demand homage. The demands increase constantly and can never be met. 'I have the power to conquer a man'—does this thought alone bring joy to a woman or for that matter, is it even good for her? Her salvation lies in the act of setting adrift such thoughts on the currents of reverence. Shiva came to Annapurna in a beggar's guise; but if she hadn't done penance for him, would she have succeeded in thus enduring his empyrean powers?

I can remember how many people used to burn in the slow fire of envy at my good fortune. It was something that warranted envy all right—I came by it as a bonus, without deserving it. But luck doesn't last long. One has to pay the price or Fate does not put up with it. The price of good fortune has to be paid over years, every day and only then can ownership claims be staked. God is quite capable of granting it to us, but we have to receive it on our own merit. Sometimes we are not blessed enough to live with what has been bestowed upon us.

Many a girl's father sighed at my good fortune. It was the talk of many households all over town: how I didn't deserve to be married into this family, since I have no great beauty or qualities to boast of. My grandmother-in-law and mother-in-law were known for their extraordinary beauty. My sisters-in-law were also confirmed beauties. Gradually, when misfortune befell both of them, my grandmother-in-law vowed that she wouldn't look for a beautiful girl for her youngest and favourite grandson. I was able to enter this house solely on the merits of the 'good omens' in my charts.

In this house, amidst such profusion of wealth, very few wives had received the true status and respect that was due to them. But apparently that was the rule; hence, even when all the tears of their life sank beneath the froth of liquor and the tinkle of the courtesans' anklets, they still clung to the pride of being a daughter-in-law of this aristocratic household and managed to keep their heads afloat. Yet, my husband never touched liquor and did not go around depleting his humane qualities seeking female flesh at the doorsteps of the houses of sin; was this, in any way, to my credit? Did Fate gift me with any special charms to control the restless, wild spirits of a man? No, it was pure good fortune and nothing else. In the case of my sisters-in-law, was Fate suddenly so ruthless that every word in store for them turned into warped expressions? Long before nightfall, all the lamps of their joyous lives were extinguished and the flames of their youth continued to burn in vain, through the night in empty ballrooms. No music—just pain.

Both my sisters-in-law pretended that they didn't think much of my husband's masculinity. To think that he steered this great vessel of life solely with the help of the lone sail of his wife's anchal! I have had to bear so many jibes from them, off and on, as if I had stolen my husband's affections, as if I was full of artifice and pretence—the insolent, modern, fashionable woman. My husband dressed me up in contemporary fashions and they would burn in envy when they saw those colourful jackets, saris, blouses, petticoats and all the other accessories. 'Such elaborate adorning when there isn't even any beauty to speak of! It is shameful how you have gone and decked your body up like it's a novelty shop!'

My husband was well aware of all this. But his heart brimmed over with sympathy for women. He would always advise me, 'Don't be upset.' I remember, once I had said to him, 'Women's minds are very crooked, very narrow.' He had replied, 'Just like the feet of Chinese women which are crooked and narrow. The entire society has squashed our women's minds from all sides and made them narrow and crooked. Fate gambles with their lives—their lives depend on the turn of the dice; do they have any powers of their own?'

My sisters-in-law always got whatever they demanded from their brother-in-law. He never stopped to think whether their demands were valid. I fumed silently when I noticed that they didn't feel a shred of gratitude. So much so, that my eldest sister-in-law—who spouted piety so freely with her holier-than-thou chants, pujas, vows and fasts, that there wasn't even an ounce left for her soul—would often quote her brother, a lawyer, that if she were to take her case to the court then my husband . . . oh, it was a lot of rubbish that she'd say! I promised my husband that under no circumstances would I ever retort to anything that either of them said. Hence my misery lay heavier on my shoulders. I felt there was a limit to forbearance and if that limit was crossed it almost made one less of a man. But he said, 'The law or society has not supported my sisters-in-law; it was a great humiliation for them to have to beg and ask for what they once knew to be rightfully theirs, by virtue of their husbands' legacy. To add to that one shouldn't ask for gratitude—how can one get kicked around and also have to shell out a tip for it?' Shall I be honest with you? I often felt that my husband ought to have been more audacious, enough for him to be a little less compassionate.

My second sister-in-law was of a different kind. She was younger and didn't have any saintly pretences. On the contrary, her comments and gestures often carried lewd suggestions. The comings and goings of the young maids she'd hired were questionable to say the least. Nobody, however, raised eyebrows as these things were supposedly customary in this house. I knew that my sister-in-law hated the fact that I was fortunate enough to have a husband who didn't have a vice. Hence, she would find several ways to waylay her brother-in-law. I am ashamed to admit that, even with a husband such as mine, I sometimes felt the slightest twinge of fear. The very air in this place was murky and even the clearest objects appeared distorted. On some days, my second sister-in-law would cook and invite her brother-in-law affectionately. I often wished desperately that he would make some excuse and refuse the invitation. She was wrong to try to trap him, and why should this wrong go unpunished? But instead, when he smiled and accepted the invitation each and every time, a niggling doubt troubled me—it was entirely my fault, but feelings wouldn't heed reason—I felt this indicated the inherent flightiness in men. At these times, however busy I was otherwise, I would find an excuse to go and sit in my sister-in-law's room. She would laugh and exclaim to my husband, 'My goodness, Chhotorani won't let you out of her sight at all—she's the strictest of guards. I must say, even in our heyday, we had never learnt how to guard so carefully.'

My husband could only see their misery and never the flaws. Once I said, 'Fine, let's assume that the fault lies entirely with society; but why do they deserve so much pity? It's all right for people to deal with a little misfortune sometimes.' But he was impossible. Instead of arguing, he just smiled a little. Perhaps he knew about the occasional pangs of doubt I suffered. The main object of my anger was neither society nor anyone else, it was just that—oh well, I won't go into that.

One day he sat me down and explained, 'All these criticisms that they direct at you—if they really thought that you were so blameworthy, would it upset them so much?'

'Then why this unfair resentment?'

'I don't know if you can call it unfair. There is a grain of truth embedded in envy; it is this: whatever brings happiness should ideally be received by every individual.'

'Then one should quarrel with one's Fate, not take it out on me.'

'But Fate isn't close at hand.'

'So then they can just go ahead and take whatever they want—you would never deprive them. Let them wear sari-jacket-jewellery-socks and shoes; if they want a memsahib to tutor them, she comes here already, and even if they want to remarry, you have the resources to be able to cross every barrier just like Vidyasagar did.'

'That is precisely the problem—it isn't always possible to hand them whatever their heart desires.'

'Is that any reason to go on playing such coy games, as if whatever one hasn't got is actually a bad thing so that when someone else gets it, one burns up in envy?'

'When someone is deprived, this is the only way they know to conquer their deprivation—it is their only consolation.'

'I don't care what you say—women are very coy. They never admit the truth and resort to many pretences.'

'That only proves how very deprived they are.'

When he brushed aside every little spiteful barb from the women of this household, I used to get very angry. There was no point discussing what society could have or may have been; but it was impossible to feel sorry for these thorns strewn on the way, the cruel jibes and the artifice.

When he heard this, he said, 'So you have enough sympathy for yourself when your own feelings are bruised, and you have none to spare for those whose lives have been ripped to shreds by the cruel arrows of society? Should the loser be made to pay a fine for losing?'

Oh well! I was narrow-minded. Except me, everyone of course was good. A little miffed, I said, 'You don't even know half of it, since you don't stay indoors—' I tried to divulge some specific information about the other part of the house, but he abruptly got up saying, 'Chandranathbabu has been waiting for me for a while now.'

I sat and wept. How could I bear to look so wretched in my husband's eyes? There was no way I could prove to him that if *I* had been faced with misfortune, I would never have behaved in this manner.

Sometimes I feel that if God grants women a chance to be vain about beauty, they are spared from vanity of other kinds. One could be vain about jewels and baubles, of course; but in a rich household that would be meaningless. I placed my conceit in my chastity. I knew that even my husband would have to bow before it. But every time I spoke to him about some domestic matters, I ended up looking so petty that it tore me up inside. Hence, I wanted to make him look small in turn. I said to myself, 'I'll not let your words make you look good; it is mere naivety. It's not altruism, you are being taken advantage of by others.'

My husband had a great wish that I'd step outside the inner chambers. One day I said to him, 'I don't need the world outside.'

He said, 'The world outside may be in need of you.'

'If it has survived for so long without me, it can continue to do so; it won't die of sorrow.'

'Let it die, I am not bothered. My concerns are for myself.'

'Really? And what are you worried about?'

My husband smiled and didn't reply. I knew his ways and so I said, 'No, you can't fool me by keeping quiet. You must finish your sentence.'

He said, 'Can one sentence be enough to finish the thought? There are so many thoughts that take a lifetime to finish.'

'Please stop your word-games and tell me.'

'I would like you to be mine in the world out there. We need to settle our accounts in that space.'

'Why, what's wrong with our perceptions here, in this room?'

'Over here, your eyes, ears and mouth have been wrapped in me; you don't know who you want and who you've got.'

'I know very well, dearest, I really do.'

'You think you know, but you don't even know if you really do.'

'I just hate it when you talk like this.'

'Which is why I didn't want to bring it up.'

'Your silence is even more unbearable.'

'That is why I wish that I won't have to speak or keep quiet; you should just come out there and comprehend everything by yourself. Neither you nor I were made to play the game of life within this domestic chicanery. Our love will be true only if we really know each other in the midst of truth.'

'Maybe you are yet to know me wholly, but my understanding of you is complete.'

'Fair enough. Then why don't you do it just to complete my understanding?'

We had many different versions of this conversation. He'd say, the glutton who loves the fish curry would cut up the fish, stew it and cook it to his taste, but the man who truly appreciated the fish wouldn't really want to capture it in a bowl—he'd rather try to master it in the water itself, or he'd wait on land. When he returned home, he'd be happy that although he didn't get what he wanted, at least he didn't cut it up and destroy it for his own pleasure. It's best to get all of something and if that is not possible, then it's best to lose it in its entirety.

I never really liked these discussions, but that wasn't the reason why I stayed indoors at the time. My grandmother-in-law was alive then. My husband had gone against her wishes and recast nearly four-fifths of the household by twentieth-century standards, and she had accepted it. If a daughter-in-law of this aristocratic household renounced her purdah and chose to come out, she'd have accepted that too. She knew for a fact that this was bound to happen one day. But I felt, it wasn't so important that she should have to undergo the pain of it. I have read in books that we are all birds in a cage; I could not speak for others, but my cage was so full that I wouldn't find such fullness out there amidst the world. At least that is how I felt at the time.

The primary reason my grandmother-in-law loved me so much was because she thought that I had been able to hold my husband's love solely by the powers of my own qualities or the strengths of my astrological stars. She felt it was the inherent nature of a man to sink into decadence. None of her other granddaughters-in-law, with all their beauty and youth, had been able to lure her grandsons; they were destroyed by the flames of sin and no one could save them. She firmly believed that I was the one who had finally doused those flames singeing the men in this family. So she was very protective of me; my slightest ailment made her tremble with fear. She didn't really like the clothes which my husband bought from foreign stores and dressed me in. But she felt that men were bound to have some such idiosyncrasies that were quite silly and a mere waste. There was no way of restraining them, but it was important to see that it didn't lead them to total destruction. If my Nikhilesh didn't deck up his wife, he'd have done the same to another woman. So, every time a new dress arrived for me, she called my husband and riled and teased him merrily. Gradually her taste changed too. Thanks to this unholy age of modernism, a day came when her evenings would be incomplete unless her granddaughter-in-law read her stories from English books.

After her death, my husband wanted us to go and settle in Calcutta. But I just didn't feel right about it. The family roots were here—our grandmother-in-law had borne so much misery and yet held onto this home for so many years and if I just dropped everything and left, her sighs wouldn't let me rest. This thought haunted me continually—her empty seat stared me in the face. That pious woman came into this house at the age of eight and she died when she was seventy-nine. She didn't have a happy life. Fate had repeatedly shot arrows at her, but each misfortune had only made her stronger. This large household was a memento built on the piety of her tears. How could I leave this and go into the muck of Calcutta?

My husband felt that this was a chance to hand over the charges of this house to my sisters-in-law; that would make them happy and our life would be able to take its own course, in its own space, in Calcutta. But that is what I didn't want to accept. Were they to be rewarded for torturing me all these years and for envying my husband's good fortune and character? Besides, the 'royal' house was right here. All our subjects, our employees, the luckless relatives, the guests, were all strewn around, clinging to this homestead. I did not know who we were in Calcutta where no one knew us. The complete image of our status, power and wealth lay right here. Should I just hand over all this to them and go into exile, like Sita? Only to have them mock me in my absence? Did they know the value of this magnanimity that my husband wanted to show or did they even deserve it? Later when I'd have to return here someday, would I get back my rightful seat? My husband said, 'Why do you need that seat? Life has other things to offer.'

I said to myself, 'Men really don't understand these things very well. They don't know how significant the positions in the inner-chambers are since they live and breathe the air outside. Here they should abide by the advice of women.'

I thought it was most important for one to have some firmness in one's character. It would be a defeat if we went away, handing over everything to those who have only wished us ill. Although my husband was ready to do that, I wasn't. In my heart of hearts, I felt I was speaking from the righteousness of my chastity.

Why didn't my husband force me to leave? I know why. It was because he had the power to do so, that he didn't use it. He has always said to me, 'I wouldn't accept it if you were to always agree with whatever I said and had to put up with every whim of mine. I'd rather wait—if you and I come to a consensus, it'll be great. If not, there's nothing to be done.'

But there is something called firmness of character and that day I'd felt that perhaps on that score I was—no, I can't even utter those words today.

It would be impossible to close the gap between night and day if one were to start doing it slowly, over a period of time. But when the sun rises, night disappears—the lengthy reckoning is resolved in a moment. All at once, the age of swadeshi came upon Bengal; but no one knew how it arrived suddenly. It was as if the passage of time between the age of swadeshi and the one before it just didn't exist. Perhaps that was the reason why the new age swept away all our fears and worries in the blink of an eye, like a deluge. There was no time to consider what had happened and what the future had in store.

When the groom and his party are at the door, with the music playing and the lights glowing, the women of the village stream up to the terrace, scarcely caring to cover their face. Just so, when the music played, signalling the arrival of the groom of the entire country, how could the women stay busy with their household chores? Ululating and blowing on the conch, they peeped out from the door or window nearest to them.

In that moment my sight and mind, hopes and wishes, were coloured by the tempestuous new age. On that day, although the mind didn't break free of the bonds of wishes, desires and pious thoughts within which it had settled itself happily, the world that it had known till then, it did peer over it all and it heard the clarion call from far away; the meaning of that call wasn't clear, but the heart lurched dangerously.

During his college days, my husband was interested in manufacturing all that the land needed within the land itself. There were many date trees in the area and he spent several days trying to figure out how to collect the extract from all the trees at the same spot with the help of a single pipe and boil it to produce sugar. I have heard that a very effective way was indeed discovered, but it required so much more money to be spent than what could be earned, that the business soon folded up. The kinds of crops he reaped from the farmlands, through various experiments, were quite remarkable, but the money that he spent in the process was even more astonishing. He felt that the reason no large-scale industries can be sustained in our country was because there were no banks. At that time he began to teach me political economy. There was no harm in that. But he felt it was imperative to inculcate the habit and the desire to save money in banks among our people. So he started a small bank. The urge to save money in the bank was strong among the villagers because the rate of interest was very high. But for the precise reason for which the people's interest grew, the bank slipped through the high interest chasm and disappeared. His old clerks grew very upset over these eccentricities and his enemies made fun of him. One day my elder sister-in-law saw to it that I was within earshot when she exclaimed that her cousin brother, a renowned lawyer, had told her that if one pleaded the case before a judge, it may still be possible to salvage some of the reputation and wealth of this distinguished family from the hands of a lunatic.

Of all the people in this family, only my grandmother-in-law was unperturbed by all this. She called me and chided me often, saying, 'Why do you all plague him like this? Are you concerned about the fortune? In my days, I have seen this estate go into the hands of the receiver all of three times. Men are not like women. They are restless and they only know how to squander. Granddaughter-in-law, you are lucky that he isn't frittering himself away along with it. Since you have never been hurt that way, you seldom remember that.'

The list of my husband's charities was endless. If someone tried to install a loom or a rice-husking machine or something along those lines he helped him till the project was obviously a failure. He floated a swadeshi company to compete with the British ships that journeyed to Puri. Not a single ship sailed from that, but several company documents were drowned in the process.

I used to be most upset when Sandipbabu extracted money from him, giving some excuse about the country's work. Sandipbabu wanted to run a newspaper, or spread the word about swadeshi, or said that the doctor has advised him to spend a few days in Ootacamund on health grounds—and my husband casually shouldered the cost. Besides, he received a certain amount every month to meet his regular expenses. But the strangest thing was that my husband didn't even agree with him on most principles or ideologies. My husband felt that it was a kind of destitution if one failed to mine the existing resources in one's land properly and in the same way, if we couldn't discover and realize the essential richness in the heart of our land, it was the greatest shame of all. One day I was a little irked and said to him, 'You are being cheated by all these people.' He laughed and said, 'I have no qualities to speak of and yet, just by throwing away some money, I am acquiring some greatness—I am the one who's gaining something treacherously.'

The moment the air of the new age brushed past me, I told my husband to burn all the foreign clothes I owned.

He said, 'Why should you burn it? Instead, stop using them for as long as you wish.'

'How can you say "as long as I wish"; never in my entire life—'

'Fine, don't wear them ever again. Why should you make a display of burning them?'

'Why are you stopping me from doing this?'

'I feel you should devote all your energy to building something instead of wasting even a quarter of it in the excitement of destroying something.'

'But this excitement helps you build something.'

'So you would claim the only way to light up one's home is by setting it on fire? I am ready to go to great lengths to light a lamp, but I don't want to set my house on fire just to get the job done quickly. That only *looks* like exuberance, but in reality it is a weak compromise.' He went on, 'Listen, I can see that my words seem futile to you today, but I suggest you consider them. Just as a mother decks each of her daughters with her own jewels, the day has come when the earth is adorning each of its countries with her own jewellery. Today all our needs are linked to those of the whole world. I believe that this connection is a sign of good fortune for every nation and there is no greatness in rebutting that.'

Then there was another problem. When Miss Gilby first came into the house, there was a furore for some days. Gradually everyone became accustomed to her and there was no further talk about it. But now all those debates surfaced again. I had quite forgotten whether she was a Bengali or British, but the thought crossed my mind again at this time. I said to my husband that she'd have to go. He was silent. That day I spoke to him harshly and he walked away, despondent. I cried my heart out. At night when I was a little more collected after my crying bout, he said, 'I can't look at Miss Gilby in a bad light simply because she is British. So many years of familiarity should be able to break through the barriers of names. She happens to care for you.'

I was a little ashamed and yet, with a shade of my earlier tantrum I said, 'Fine then, let her be. Who wants her to leave?'

Miss Gilby continued to come. One day as she walked to church, a young boy who was a distant relation of ours, hurled a stone at her and insulted her. Until then the boy had lived in my husband's care; after this incident he was promptly thrown out. This caused quite a commotion. People believed whatever that boy went out and said to them. They began to say it was Miss Gilby who had insulted the boy and made up the tale. I too felt that wasn't entirely improbable. The boy didn't have a mother and his uncle pleaded with me. I tried very hard on his behalf, but it was of no avail.

That day, no one could pardon my husband's decision, not even I. In my heart of hearts I criticized him. This time Miss Gilby herself quit. She had tears in her eyes when she left, but I didn't feel a thing. I felt for the boy: poor child, how she had ruined his life. And what a splendid boy! His enthusiasm for swadeshi had robbed him of hunger and sleep.

My husband personally escorted Miss Gilby to the station in his own car. I thought this was taking things a bit too far. I felt he deserved the censure when this incident was blown up and recounted in the local newspaper, which called him all sorts of names.

Until that day, I had suffered many anxieties on account of my husband, but never did I feel ashamed of him. That day I did. I didn't know what crime Naren had committed against Miss Gilby, but in this day and age it was shameful that one could be righteously just and be punished for it. I had no desire to smother those feelings, which made Naren act so rudely towards a British woman. When my husband refused to agree with me on this, I took it as a lack of boldness in his nature. And that made me feel shame. Moreover, what hurt me most was the fact that I had to concede defeat. My resolute nature only served to make me miserable and it couldn't raise my husband from ignominy—it was a humiliation of the power of my chastity.

Yet, it was not that my husband had no interest in matters of swadeshi or that he was opposed to it. But he could never wholly accept the absolute superiority of the 'Vande Mataram' mantra. He said, 'I am willing to serve my country; but the One whom I'll invoke is far above it. If I pray to my country, it will be disastrous for her.'

At this juncture, Sandipbabu arrived at our place with his entourage, to spread the swadeshi message. A meeting was to be held in our temple courtyard that evening. We women waited on one side of the hall, behind the woven screen. As the roars of 'Vande Mataram' drew closer, my heart began to tremble. Suddenly a stream of young men and boys, barefoot, dressed in saffron with turbans on their heads, burst into our immense front yard like the tawny flood of the first monsoon rains along a dry river bed. The place was thronged with people. Cutting through the throng a group of ten or twelve boys held aloft a large stool, on which Sandipbabu was seated, and bore him into the yard on their shoulders. 'Vande Mataram!' 'Vande Mataram!' 'Vande Mataram!' It felt as though the sky would shatter and fall around us in tiny bits.

I had once seen a photograph of Sandipbabu. I can't say I'd really liked his looks then. He wasn't unattractive, in fact quite the opposite. Yet I had somehow felt that although his appearance was bright, it was compounded with much dross: there was something about his eyes and mouth that were not quite genuine. So, when my husband met every one of his demands without so much as a question, I wasn't pleased. I could've put up with the monetary loss, but I felt that as a friend this man was cheating my husband. He scarcely had the air of a hermit or a poor man—he looked quite the babu. Obviously, he liked his creature comforts, and yet—many such thoughts had clamoured in my mind. Today they are stirring again: but let them be.

Yet, on that day when Sandipbabu was making his speech and the heart of that huge gathering swayed and swelled, overflowing its banks, threatening to sweep everything away, I witnessed the compelling aura of the man! At a certain point, when the declining sun peeped below the rooftops and brushed his brow with its golden fingers, it felt as though a god had declared him, before all the men and women present there, to be one of the immortals. Every word of his speech, from beginning to end, seemed to carry the gust of a storm. His boldness knew no limits. The slight obstruction of the screen seemed unbearable to me. I don't remember when, quite unaware of my action, I parted the screen a little, thrust out my face and gazed steadily at him. Not a single person in that assembly had the time to spare me a glance. But at one point, I noticed that Sandipbabu's eyes, bright as Orion in the sky, settled on my face. I was past caring. At that moment I was no longer the daughter-in-law of this aristocratic household: I was the sole representative of all the women in Bengal and he was its hero. The sunbeams from the sky poured down upon his brow: it was no less needful to anoint him from the nation's womanly heart. How else could his expedition be truly propitious?

I sensed very clearly that after he looked at my face, his words took on a new fire. It was as if the divine chariot could no longer be reined in—it was like thunderbolt upon thunderbolt, lightning flash upon lightning flash. My heart said it was the flames in my heart that lit this fire; we aren't merely Lakshmi, we are also Bharati, the goddess of speech.

I returned to my room that day, full of joy and self-exaltation. A storm raging deep inside me dragged me from one state of mind to another in an instant. Like the brave women of Greece, I felt an urge to cut off my knee-length hair and hand it to that gallant warrior for his bowstring. If the ornaments on my body had any link with my heart, my necklace, torque and armlets would have dropped upon that meeting like shooting stars. I needed to do something self-destructive to be able to bear the ecstasy I felt.

When my husband returned that evening, I dreaded that he might say something about the day's speech to strike a false note amidst the blazing symphony or disagree in the slightest over something that offended his sense of integrity. Had he done so, I was quite capable of treating him with open contempt that day.

But he didn't say a word to me. That didn't please me either. He should have said, 'Sandip's words have opened my eyes today: they have cleared my old misconceptions on these matters.' I felt that he was keeping quiet obstinately and expressing disinterest deliberately.

I asked him, 'How long will Sandipbabu stay here?'

'He's leaving for Rangpur tomorrow morning.'

'Tomorrow morning?'

'Yes—he's supposed to give a speech there.'

I was silent for a while. Then I asked again, 'Can he manage to stay a day longer?'

'That won't be possible. But why do you ask?'

'I'd like to ask him to lunch and serve him myself.'

My husband was surprised. He had asked me to come out before his friends many times. I had never agreed. He looked at me fixedly, in a strange way; I couldn't really interpret that look. But I suddenly felt embarrassed and said, 'No, never mind.'

'I don't see why,' he said. 'Let me speak to Sandip. He'll stay back another day if he possibly can.'

It turned out that it was indeed possible.

I will be very honest: that day I wished God had made me beautiful. It was not to steal anyone's heart but because beauty was glory in itself. On this momentous day, the men of this land need to behold the Earth-mother (Jagatdhatri) in its women. But would male eyes be able to perceive the goddess unless there was surface beauty? Would Sandipbabu be able to glimpse in me the life force of the nation? Or would he think of me as an ordinary woman, his friend's wife and the mistress of the house?

Early in the morning I washed my long hair, left it loose and tied it neatly with a red silk ribbon. Sandipbabu was coming to lunch; so there was no time to dry my hair and tie it up. I wore a white Madras sari with a zari border, a matching blouse with short sleeves and zari piping.

I decided that this was a very modest outfit: nothing could be simpler. But suddenly my second sister-in-law came in and subjected me to a head to toe inspection. She gave a sardonic smile and laughed a little. I asked, 'Didi, why are you laughing?'

She said, 'How you have dressed up.'

I felt a little irritated. 'What's so special about my dress?' I asked.

She smiled sarcastically again and simply said, 'Nothing at all, my lady: in fact it's pretty good. But I can't help wondering if that revealing jacket of yours from that foreign shop wouldn't have completed the effort.' She finished the sentence and left, her whole body shaking with suppressed laughter. I was very angry and even considered taking everything off and wearing a simple, coarse, everyday sari instead. I still don't know why I didn't carry out that impulse in the end. I thought, 'If I don't appear decently dressed before Sandipbabu, my husband will be upset—after all, women are supposed to uphold the social prestige of the household.'

I thought I would make my appearance as Sandipbabu sat down to eat. By tending to his meal, I could dispel the embarrassment of our first meeting. But lunch was late today—it was almost one o'clock. So my husband sent for me in order to introduce us. When I first entered the room, I felt too shy to look Sandipbabu in the face. Somehow I managed to brush aside my shyness and said, a little awkwardly, 'Your lunch is a bit late today.'

He walked over quite spontaneously to the seat next to me and said, 'We get our daily rice after a fashion, but the goddess who provides it stays out of sight. Today when Annapurna has deigned to appear, the meal actually becomes insignificant.'

His conduct was as confident as his speeches. There was no hesitation about him: he seemed used to securing his rightful place within minutes in any situation. If he upset someone or even seemed offensive that did not bother him. He assumed the right to come and sit very close to one; if people looked askance, it seemed more their fault than his.

I was afraid Sandipbabu might decide that I am an old-fashioned dullard. The very thought embarrassed me. I had hoped that my speech would turn brilliant and flow smoothly so that each of my responses would fill him with wonder. But that did not happen. I agonized inwardly. Why did I suddenly decide to appear before him?

I was about to make my escape after he finished his meal. But as before, he walked up to the door casually and blocked my way, saying, 'Please don't take me for a glutton. I didn't come here to eat. I was eager to come only because you have invited me. If you run away like this after the meal, you'll be cheating your guest.'

If these remarks hadn't been uttered very frankly and persuasively they could have struck a false chord. But after all, my husband was his dearest friend and I was like a sister-in-law to him. As I was battling my own feelings and trying hard to attain the same level of informal familiarity, my husband sensed my discomfiture and said, 'Why don't you finish your lunch and then join us here again?'

Sandipbabu said, 'But promise me that you will keep your word.'

I smiled a little, 'I'll be back soon.'

'Let me explain why I don't trust you. It's nine years since Nikhilesh married. But you've cheated me of your presence all these nine years. If you disappear now for another nine years, I'll never see you again.'

I reciprocated the familiar tone and replied softly, 'Why will you *never* see me again?'

'My horoscope says I'll die young. Neither my father nor his father lived to be thirty years, and I've just completed twenty-seven.'

He knew this would distress me and so it did. Now my softly spoken words were laced with compassion as I said, 'The blessings of the entire nation will ward off the curse.'

'The nation's blessings are best received from the lips of its goddesses. That's why I'm begging you to return so that the warding off of the curse can begin from this very day.'

Flowing water, however muddy, is still good for a wash. Everything about Sandipbabu was so swift and vigorous that the same words, which may have seemed distasteful from someone else, seemed innocuous coming from him. He laughed as he said, 'Look here, I'm holding your husband hostage. If you don't return, he shan't be released.'

As I was leaving the room he spoke again, 'I have another small request.'

I stopped in my tracks and turned around. 'Don't worry, all I want is a glass of water. You must have noticed that I don't drink water during the meal. I have it some time later.'

At this, I couldn't but ask anxiously, 'Why is that so?'

Then came the history of how he was once afflicted by severe dyspepsia. I also heard how he had suffered for nearly seven months. He described the drudgery of homeopathic and allopathic treatment before being miraculously cured at last by ayurveda. He laughed and said, 'God has fashioned even my illnesses in such a way that they refuse to be cured without Indian-made pills.'

My husband now spoke up after a long time, 'And what about the fact that bottles of allopathic medicine also refuse to leave your side? They take up nearly three shelves in your sitting room—'

'Do you know why? They're like the punitive police. They are not there because they serve a purpose; but the modern dispensation has brought them in and thrust them on us. I keep paying for them as punishment and I get my share of jabs as well.'

My husband abhors exaggeration. But rhetoric, by definition, exaggerates: it was, after all, invented by humans and not by God. Once while trying to justify a fib I had said to my husband, 'It's only trees, animals and birds that are always truthful; the poor things lack the capacity to lie. That's where humans are superior to animals, and women again are superior to men. Women are best embellished with ornaments and fabrications.'

When I came out of the room my second sister-in-law was in the corridor, prising apart one of the window blinds. 'What are you doing here?' I asked.

'I was eavesdropping,' she whispered.

Later, when I returned to the room again, Sandipbabu said sympathetically, 'You couldn't have had much to eat today.'

I was flustered. I was obviously back a little too soon. I hadn't allowed the length of time needed to finish one's meal decently. If one were to calculate, it'd be clear that I couldn't have eaten much that day. But it had hardly occurred to me that anyone might notice.

Perhaps Sandipbabu sensed my discomfiture, which was more disconcerting still. He said, 'You were all set to run away like the wild deer. I'm honoured that you did go to the trouble of keeping your word.'

I couldn't make a suitable reply. Blushing and fretting, I sat on the edge of a sofa. It had been my resolve to present myself before Sandipbabu honourably and confidently as the image of the nation's Shakti and to adorn his brow with victory garlands simply by appearing before him. So far, I had utterly failed.

At this point, Sandipbabu got into an argument with my husband quite deliberately. He must have known that in an argument his razor-sharp mind shone in all its brilliance. Many times later as well, I noticed that in my presence he never let slip the slightest opportunity for a debate.

He was aware of my husband's opinions on the Vande Mataram mantra. Referring to that he said, 'Nikhil, don't you agree that there is a space for the imagination in the act of serving the country?'

'I agree there is a space, but it isn't all of it. I intend to know that thing called "my country" in a more heartfelt, genuine fashion and that's how I'd like to have others know it. I feel quite nervous and ashamed to use some kind of entertaining hocus-pocus mantra in relation to such a profound concept.'

'That thing which you call an entertaining mantra is precisely what I call the Truth. I truly believe my country is my God. I believe God resides in man—He truly reveals Himself through men and their land.'

'If you truly believe this, then you wouldn't discriminate between two men or between two countries.'

'That's true. But I am a man of limited strengths and so I fulfil my duties towards God through the worship of my *own* land.'

'I'd never stop you from worshipping, but if you disregard the presence of God in another land and feel hatred towards it, how will your worship be complete?'

'Hatred is an aspect of puja. Arjuna got his boon only when he fought with Shiva dressed as a kirata. If we are ready to battle God, He will be pleased with us eventually.'

'If that were the case, then those who are ruining the country and those who are serving it are both worshipping it in the same way. So what is the point of going out of your way to spread the message of patriotism?'

'When it comes to one's own country, it's a different matter. On that the heart has clear orders to venerate.'

'In that case, why just one's own country, there are even clearer instructions about one's self. The mantra that dwells in our heart to worship God through man, is the same one that resonates throughout all the lands.'

'Nikhil, all your arguments are based on dry logic. Will you deny the fact that there is something called a heart?'

'Sandip, I'll be honest with you: when you try to pass off misdeeds as duty and irreverence as piety in the name of the nation-god, it pains my heart and I can't keep still. If I steal to satisfy my own needs, isn't it a blow to the true love that I bear for myself? That's why I can't steal. Is it because I am intelligent or because I respect my self?'

I was seething inwardly. I couldn't hold back; I said, 'English, French, German, Russian—is there a civilization that doesn't have a history of stealing for the sake of the country?'

'They will be answerable for those crimes; they're still paying for them. History hasn't yet come to an end.'

Sandipbabu said, 'Fine then, we'll pay up too. First let us stock up our home with the stolen loot and then we'll pay for them slowly over many centuries. But let me ask you, where do you see them paying the price for it as you just mentioned?'

'When Rome paid the price for her sins, there were no witnesses. There's no telling when the day of reckoning will come upon renowned brigand civilizations and when they'll have to pay for their misdeeds and at that time, no outsider will witness it. But aren't you missing something—their bag of politics is full of lies, deception, betrayals, espionage, forfeiting right and Truth for the sake of saving their face; the weight of all these sins can't be a light one. Isn't this draining the blood, drop by drop, from the heart of their civilization every day? I believe that those who don't accept the place of Truth over their land don't respect their land either.'

Never before had I seen my husband argue with an outsider. He argued with me but his tenderness for me made him feel sorry to corner me in an argument. Today I got to see his fencing skills in a debate.

Somewhere my heart refused to agree with my husband's words. I felt that there must be some appropriate rejoinders to his arguments but they wouldn't come to mind just then. The problem was that if you bring up virtue/dharma, one has to keep silent. It's difficult to claim that I don't take dharma to those extremes. I decided to write a fitting retort to this debate and hand it over to Sandipbabu one day. So I quickly noted down today's conversation once I returned to my room.

All of a sudden Sandipbabu turned to me and asked, 'What do you feel about this?'

I said, 'I won't go into subtleties; I'll state my case bluntly—I am human, I am avaricious and I'll be greedy for the sake of my country. When I want something, I'm prepared to snatch it. I feel anger and I'll use it for my land. I need someone to tear into bits, on whom I'll avenge the humiliation I have lived with for so long. I have illusions and I shall be bewitched by my country; I need a tangible form for her—which will be Mother, a goddess or Durga to me—for whom I'll sacrifice an animal and let loose a bloodbath. I am human, I am not a god.'

Sandipbabu jumped up from his seat, raised his right hand high in the air and shouted, 'Hurrah! Hurrah!' The next moment he corrected himself and exclaimed, 'Vande Mataram! Vande Mataram!'

A shadow of pain crossed my husband's face. He spoke very softly, 'Neither am I a god; I too am human and that's why I will not, at any cost, thrust all my imperfections upon the country.'

Sandipbabu replied, 'Look here Nikhil, Truth is something that is innate to womankind, at one with their heart and soul. For us men, Truth is all logic and no shades, emotions or life. The woman's heart is the lotus on which Truth resides and it is not insubstantial like our Reason. That is precisely why it is only the women who can be truly heartless and not men, since rationality weakens them. Women can destroy someone with ease; so can men, but the threads of reason trip them up. Like a thunderstorm, women can wreak havoc—they have a terrible beauty—when men commit the same crimes, they look ugly since it is tainted by the pangs of Reason. One thing, Nikhil, is for sure—in these times, it is women who will salvage our nation. This is not the time for us to differentiate between good and evil, right and wrong; today unscrupulously and indifferently we have to be ruthless and unfettered; we have to anoint sin with holy markers and let the women of the nation receive it cordially. Don't you remember what the poet has said?—

Welcome sin, welcome oh beauty!
Let the flaming tonic of your kiss

Inflame my blood.
Sound the trumpet of malevolence,
Anoint my brow with infamy,
Fill my heart with tumultuous,
Dark, sinful murk, shameless.

Shame on that piety which is incapable of being callously ruthless.'

Having said this, he stamped his foot twice very loudly. Startled, a lot of drowsy dust rose off the carpet and into the air. He stood straight with such pride after having scorned in an instant the very values, which are treasured across lands over the ages, that a shiver went down my spine as I looked at him.

Suddenly he roared again, 'I can clearly see that you are the beautiful goddess of that fire which reduces the home to ashes and burns down the world; today you must give us that inconquerable strength to destroy ourselves, and you must adorn our transgression.'

It wasn't clear to whom these last words were addressed. One could assume it was to the presence that he venerated with 'Vande Mataram' or to the woman who was present there as a representative of that goddess-motherland. One could assume that just as the poet Valmiki had articulated his first meter when his impious nature was struck by compassion, Sandipbabu also uttered these words suddenly when brutality struck against righteousness—or it was perhaps a habitual display of excellent histrionics, common to the business of impressing an audience.

Perhaps he would have spoken some more. But just then my husband rose and patted him, speaking softly, 'Sandip, Chandranathbabu is here.'

The spell broke and I looked up to find the austere, serene old gentleman hesitating by the door, wondering whether to come in or not. Like the setting sun, his face glowed with the soft light of humility. My husband came up to me and said, 'He is my teacher. I have spoken to you about him many a times; touch his feet.'

I touched his feet reverently. He blessed me, 'Ma, may the lord protect you always.'

Just at that moment I was in great need of that blessing.

## Nikhilesh

All my life I have believed that I have the strength to accept whatever God grants. Till date my faith has never been put to test. But now I believe the time has come.

To test the strength of my belief, I have visualized many kinds of misery—including poverty, imprisonment, humiliation and even death—to the extent that I have even tried to imagine Bimal's death. When I felt I'd be able to deal with all this and still not lose faith in Him, perhaps I wasn't very wrong. But there's just one thing that I had never ever foreseen and today I have mulled over it all day long—can I possibly go through this?

Deep down within me there is a pain. I go about my usual duties, but the hurt lingers. Even as I sleep, the pain gnaws at my ribs. When I wake up at dawn, the light seems to have gone from the day. What is it? What has happened? What is this darkness? From where has it come upon my full moon and cast its dark shadow?

My mind has suddenly become too sensitive and the lie of the past sorrows which masqueraded as joy tears me apart. The more my shame tries to hide its face as the sorrow creeps up on me, the more it lays itself bare before my heart. My heart has gained a new vision—it sits and watches what is not to be seen, what I don't even want to see.

That day has arrived when I am being made to feel every day, every moment, with every word and every glance that I was cheated and for too long; I was a mere beggar amidst all my so-called wealth. In these nine years of my youth the interest that I have paid to 'illusion' will now be exacted to the last penny by 'Truth' for the rest of my life. The weight of the heaviest debt has landed on the shoulders of the man who has lost all means of paying his debts. And yet, I pray that I can say with all my strength, 'Oh Truth, may you win, always.'

Yesterday my cousin Munu's husband came to ask for some help for his daughter's wedding. He must have looked around my house and felt that I was the happiest man in the world. I said, 'Gopal, please tell Munu that I shall come to lunch tomorrow.' Munu has turned her needy home into a haven with the goodness of her heart. On this day my heart cried out for a morsel from the hands of that pious woman. In her home, the hardships have turned into her ornaments. Today I want to go and see her once. Oh Piety, your holy grace has not yet vanished entirely off the face of this earth.

Is there any point in holding onto one's pride? Is it not better to hang my head and admit that I am not good enough? It is possible that I lack that power which women value most in men. But is power only about boasting, about whimsicality and thoughtlessly crushing underfoot—but why all these arguments? Quibbling will not make me a worthier man. Worthless, worthless, worthless. Well, perhaps I am—but love doesn't come with a price-tag and it can turn worthless into worthwhile. For the deserving, there are many prizes in this world; it is for the unworthy that Fate has reserved love alone.

Once I had asked Bimal to come out into the world. Bimal was in my home, she was a mere doll, confined to a small space, caught up in trivial duties. The love that I got from her habitually—did it stem from the deep well of her heart or was it driven by social pressures like the fixed ration of municipal water that one receives daily?

Am I greedy? Rather than being happy with my lot, did I aspire for a lot more? No, I am not greedy, I am a lover. That's why I didn't want something being kept under lock and key in an iron chest; I desired her who can only be had when she wanted to give herself to me. I do not wish to decorate my home with flowers cut out from the pages of the *Smrutisamhita* text. I had a great desire to see Bimal in all her glory, blooming with knowledge, strength and love amidst the world.

At the time I hadn't thought of one thing: that if you really must see a person in her true, free self, then you cannot expect to lay any definite claims on her. Why didn't I think of it then? Was it due to the natural arrogance of possessing one's wife? No, it was not that. It was because I had complete faith in love.

I was conceited enough to believe that I have the strength to bear the complete, stark face of Truth. Today that belief is being tested. I am still vain enough to believe that I will pass the test, even if it kills me.

Till this day, Bimal has failed to understand me in one area. I have always considered coercion to be a form of weakness. The weak man doesn't dare to judge fairly. He will avoid the responsibility of following justice and arrive at his goal quickly through unfair means. Bimal is very impatient about patience. She'd rather see in men the dynamic, the wrathful and even the unjust. In her mind, respect and fear are closely connected.

I had thought that when she came into a larger world and looked at life from a wider perspective she'd outgrow this craze for recklessness. But now I'm beginning to feel that this is a part of Bimal's nature. She has an innate passion for the grotesque. She takes the small and simple pleasures of life, rubs salt and spices into them, burning her tongue and innards all the way; any other kind of taste does not appeal to her.

In the same way, it is my firm resolution that I will not use an excitement like dutch-courage to do my duty for the country. I'd rather tolerate inefficiency than raise my hand against a servant. My very being balks at the thought of doing or saying something to someone in anger. I know that Bimal considers my restraint to be a form of feebleness and disrespects it. Today, for that same reason she is angry with me because I am not yelling 'Vande Mataram' and going around kicking up a ruckus.

Today I have earned everyone's displeasure since I have not sat down with a glass of liquor in my country's honour. People think I'm either scared of the police or I'm angling for a title. The police think I am masquerading as a good soul because I have other hidden agendas. Even so, I continue on this road strewn with scepticism and humiliation.

I believe that when you can't summon up the enthusiasm to serve the country by thinking of her merely as the country and its people as mere human beings, when you need to scream and shout out mantras and call her a goddess and go into a trance, then you love the craze more than you love your motherland. The need to place an obsession above Truth is an indication of our innate servility. When we set our mind free, we are no longer as strong. Unless we place an illusion, or an image or some framework of the establishment upon our listless consciousness as a rider, we cannot function. As long as we don't acquire a taste for the plain Truth, as long as we need such an obsession, it is obvious that we haven't acquired the strength to receive our country in all the glory of its freedom. Until then, whatever state we are in, either an imaginary spectre or a genuine presence will continue to trouble us.

The other day Sandip said to me, 'You may have many qualities, but you lack an imagination and that's why you can't perceive the divine form of the country as the Truth.' I noticed Bimal agreed with him. I didn't care to retaliate. There was no joy in winning this argument. This wasn't about a difference of opinion—it was about the difference in nature between Bimal and me. Within the limits of domestic trivia this disparity appears rather small; so it doesn't strike a discord in a harmonious union. In a larger space such differences resonate louder. There, the waves of discord don't just ricochet, they mutilate.

Lacking an imagination? So I guess the lamp within me holds the oil but the flame is missing. I'd say the lack is in you. Like a flint, you are the ones who lack the light. Hence, you need to be struck and make a lot of noise and then a few sparks fly—those disruptive sparks merely enhance the conceit and don't add to the vision.

Lately, I have noticed that there's a palpable sense of greed in Sandip's nature. It's this arrant addiction that made him weave myths around religion and go into a frenzy over serving the country. Since his mind is sharp, he calls his inclinations grandiose names although he is coarse by nature. He needs an expression of his hatred as badly as he needs the fulfilment of his desires. Bimal has often cautioned me that Sandip has an appetite for money. I wasn't unaware of it myself, but when it came to Sandip, I couldn't be tight-fisted. I'd be reluctant to even consider that he was cheating me. I refrained from ever taking up the issue with him, in the fear that the fact of my helping him financially could turn nasty and ugly. But today, it would be difficult to convince Bimal that a large part of Sandip's feelings for the country are a variation of this covetousness. Bimal has begun to worship Sandip in her heart. So, I hate to say anything about Sandip to her, in case it is influenced by my own insecurities and I say something that is not entirely true. Perhaps the image of Sandip that comes to my mind now is warped by the searing heat of anguish. And yet, it's better to put my thoughts down on paper than to bottle them up inside.

I have known Chandranathbabu, my mentor, for all of the thirty years of my life. He fears neither criticism, nor injury and not even death. No amount of advice could have saved my life in the house where I was born. But this person, with his calm, sincere and unsullied presence, placed his life squarely in the service of mine—in him I have perceived benevolence in its truest and most tangible form.

The same Chandranathbabu came to me the other day and asked, 'Does Sandip have to stay here much longer?'

The slightest whiff of misfortune goes straight to his heart; he senses it immediately. He is not one to be disturbed easily, but on that day he could foresee the dark shadow of some great danger. I know just how much he loves me.

Over tea I said to Sandip, 'Won't you go to Rangpur? They have written to me; they think I am the one who's holding you back.'

Bimal was pouring tea. Instantly her face paled. She simply glanced at Sandip's face once.

Sandip said, 'I have thought it over and come to the conclusion that the way we go around spreading the word about swadeshi only leads to a waste of our resources. I believe that if we work from one central base, the results would be much more long-lasting.'

He looked at Bimal and said, 'Don't you think so?'

At first Bimal didn't know what to say. A little later she said, 'One can serve the country in both ways. Whether one should roam about or stay in one place is a choice that depends on one's wish or nature. Of the two, the one that you feel like doing is the best way for you.'

Sandip said, 'Then let me be frank. All these days I thought that my duty was to go from place to place and stir up enough fervour. But I was wrong. The reason for this misunderstanding was that so far I have never found a source of energy or power that can keep me fulfilled at all times. Hence, I needed to gather the vital force for my life by travelling and whipping up excitement in others and then drawing from it to sustain myself. Today you are the motherland's message to me. Till this day I have not seen such a fire in anyone. Shame on me, that I was proud of my own strength. But now, I don't aim to be a hero for this country anymore. I am audacious enough to claim that I'll be a mere instrument and stay put here, setting the country ablaze with the help of your burning fervour; no, no, please don't feel embarrassed. Your place is far above such sham coyness, qualms and humility. You are the Queen Bee of our beehive. We will stay around you and do our work, but the strength for that has to come from you and hence, if we leave your side our work will suffer. Please accept our homage unhesitatingly.'

Bimal blushed with awkwardness and pride and her hands shook as she poured the tea.

Another day Chandranathbabu came and said, 'Why don't the two of you take a trip to Darjeeling; you don't look too well these days. Are you getting enough sleep?'

The same evening I asked Bimal, 'Shall we go to Darjeeling?'

I knew she was very keen to go to Darjeeling and see the Himalayas. But that day she replied, 'No, not now.'

I guess she feared that the country's work would suffer.

I shall not lose faith; I will wait. The road that leads from narrow confines to vaster plains is a stormy one. When Bimal has left the home behind, the rules binding her to those boundaries no longer operate. Once she reconciles with the unfamiliar world and comes to an agreement with it, I shall see where my place lies. If I find that amidst the workings of this vast life, there is no room for me, then I'll know that everything I lived with for all these years was a lie. I have no use for that falsehood. If that day comes, I will not protest; slowly and silently I'll move away. Force and coercion? Whatever for! Can Truth ever be defied?

# Sandip

Only the powerless claim that whatever has been given to them is all that truly belongs to them, and the feeble ones assent. This world teaches you that only whatever I can snatch and grab is rightfully mine.

Just because I was born in this country doesn't make it mine. The day I'll be able to seize the land and make it mine forcefully, is the day it'll truly be mine.

Since we have the natural right to acquire, the inclination to aspire is also natural. Nowhere does Nature claim that one has to be deprived of anything on any account. Whatever the heart desires, the body has to acquire—this is the only decree that Nature accepts. The rules that do not let you accept this Truth is what we call morality and that's why, till date, man hasn't been able to come to terms with morality.

There are a handful of weak souls in the world who do not know how to seize, cannot hold on to what they have, their fists come loose at the drop of a hat—morality is the consolation prize for these souls. But those who can desire with all their heart, savour with all their soul, those who don't suffer from hesitation and reluctance, they are the favourite sons of Nature. It is for them that Nature has set forth all that's beautiful, all that's valuable. They're the ones who'll swim across the rivers, scale the walls, kick the doors open and seize all that is worth taking. This is true pleasure, and the true measure of a valuable thing dwells in this. Nature will surrender, but only to the brigand, because she values the power to desire, to snatch and to receive. Hence, she wouldn't like to grace the bony neck of the half-dead mendicant with the garland of her favourite spring flowers. The band is playing in the ballroom—the hours drift away and the heart grows sad. Who is the groom? I am. The one who can grab the groom's seat, blazing torch in hand, is the rightful owner of that seat. Nature's groom comes without an invitation.

Shame? No, I am not ashamed. I ask for whatever I need and sometimes I take without asking. Those who feel shy and don't take the things that are worth taking, give great names to that misery that stems from their denial. This world that we have come into, is a world of reality—why has man come into this hard world only to deceive himself with a few noble thoughts and to go away from this materialistic market, empty-handed and starved? Did he come here on the request of a bunch of 'pious' babus who spend their time playing sweet, set tunes on their flutes in the fool's paradise up there in the sky? I don't need the tunes of that flute and that fool's paradise won't fill my stomach. When I want something, I want it with all my heart. I'd like to mash it with my hands, crush it under my feet, wear it all over my body and devour it. I am not ashamed to ask and I do not falter in receiving. The feeble criticism of those who have chewed on the famine of morality for too long and have grown thin and pale like the bed-bugs in a long-forsaken cot, won't even reach my ears.

I don't like to deceive because that's a sign of cowardice. But if I'm unable to deceive even when required, that is also a form of cowardice. If you raise walls around that which you want, I'll have to break in to get what I want. You raise walls because you covet and I break in because I crave. If you play tricks I resort to capers. This is the whole truth of Nature. All the states and kingdoms on this earth and all things that happen here, work on this same principle. And when some godly creature comes from the heavens and speaks in the language of that kingdom, it is unreal. Hence, after much shouting and screaming, those words find a place only in the corner of the weak man's home. The ones who are resilient and have taken to ruling the world cannot accept those words because that leads to loss of power and strength. That's because the words are not true in themselves. Those who don't hesitate to admit this, don't feel ashamed to accept this, are the ones who are successful; and those hapless ones who straddle both the boats of the real and the unreal, torn between Nature and the godly creature, can neither move ahead nor live.

A bunch of people are born in this world having vowed that they will not live life. There is a beauty in the sky when the sun is setting and those people are floored by that faint beauty. Our Nikhilesh belongs to that category; he seems almost lifeless. Almost four years ago, he and I had a great verbal battle on this issue. He said to me, 'I accept that you can't achieve something without power. But the debate is about what is called power and achievement. My power is more inclined towards sacrifice.'

'Meaning, you are addicted to the passion for loss.'

'Yes, just as the bird within the egg gets restless to lose the shell. The shell is very real indeed but in its stead it achieves air and light. In your opinion perhaps the bird is cheated.'

Nikhilesh talks like this, in metaphors. Thereafter it is difficult to get him to understand that those metaphors are still mere words and not the truth. Well, if he is happy with these metaphors, let him be—we are the carnivores of this earth. We have teeth and nails, we can run, catch and rip things apart—we cannot spend the entire day romanticizing about the grass we chewed in the morning. Hence, we are not ready to accept it if you, the group of metaphor-people, stand guard at the door to the feast that's laid out for us on this earth. We will either steal or rob or we will die. We are not ready to lie around on lotus leaves, in love with death, and draw our last breath in the tenth chapter, however much it offends my Vaishnava friends!

People dismiss my thoughts with, 'Oh, it's just something you say.' That's because those people live by the same rules as I do in this world, but they spout something else. Hence, they do not know that these rules are what constitute morality. I know. It has been tested through my life that my words are not mere opinions. The rules I live by make it easy for me to win the hearts of women. They are the ones who are beings of this real world and they don't wander the clouds on balloons of vacant 'Ideas' like men. In my eyes and face, my body and soul, they can sense a tremendous desire—that desire isn't dried up by some penance, turned the other way by some logic, it is just pure and full desire—which growls away like a juggernaut: 'I want, I want, I'll have, I'll have.' From deep within, women know that this desire is the life force of this world. That life force wins out everywhere only because it refuses to acknowledge anyone other than itself. Many a time I have seen that women just let themselves go on the face of my desire, irrespective of whether they'll live or die. The power that lets you win these women is the power of the true brave, the power to win the real world. The ones who imagine they'll achieve some other world are most welcome to elevate their desire from its place on the earth and lift it skywards. Let me see how high their fountain rises and how long it lasts. Women haven't been created for these subtle beings, who rove the world of 'Ideas'.

Affinity! God has paired men and women as couples in a special way and sent them into this world; their union is truer than the harmony of the chants—I have said this several times when required, on different occasions. The problem is that people want to accept Nature, but they need to hide behind the veil of words. That's why the world is now full of lies. Why should there be one affinity? There should be thousands. No one has given it to Nature in writing that we'll have to dismiss all other affinities for the sake of just one of them. I have enjoyed several affinities in my life and that wouldn't stop me from pursuing one more. I can see her quite clearly and she has felt my affinity as well. Then? Then if I fail to win her over, I am not a man.

## Bimala

Where had my sense of shame disappeared, I now wonder. I had no time to look at myself—my days and nights were swirling me around like a tornado. Hence, shame found no way to enter my soul.

One day in my presence, my second sister-in-law laughingly remarked to my husband, 'Dear brother-in-law, until today in this household only the women have cried their heart out; now it's the men's turn. From now on, we'll make you cry. Isn't that so, little princess? You've already donned the armour and now you need to just assail the hearts of men.' She looked me over from head to toe. The shades of hue that radiated from me, through my dress and manner, my every gesture, did not escape her eyes in the least. Today I feel ashamed to write this, but that day I felt no shame whatsoever. That day my very Nature was working from within, I was not thinking or understanding any of this.

Those days I know I used to dress up specially. But it was unconscious to an extent. I could clearly sense which outfit of mine pleased Sandipbabu the most. Besides, there was no need for any guesswork. Sandipbabu discussed it openly in front of everybody. In my presence, one day he said to my husband, 'Nikhil, the day I saw our Queen Bee for the first time—sitting silently, dressed in a zari-bordered sari, her eyes looking through eternity like stars that have lost their way, as if for thousands of years she has waited thus, on the banks of darkness, in search of something, waiting for someone—my heart trembled. I felt the fire in her heart was wrapped around her in the borders of her sari. This fire is what we need, these palpable flames. Queen Bee, I request you—once more, could you appear before us dressed like the fiery flame?'

Up until then I had been a nameless river in a village—I had a certain rhythm, a language. But suddenly, with no warning, the ocean flooded me and my breast swelled and heaved, my banks overflowed and on their own, my waves pulsated to the rhythm of the ocean's drumbeat. I could never really fathom the true meaning of the throbbing in my veins. Where was the old me? Suddenly, from where did these waves of beauty come lapping at my shores? Sandipbabu's famished eyes lit up like a pair of lamps to worship my beauty. Through his glances and words, he declared it like the cymbals and bells of the temple: I was awe-inspiring in my beauty and power. At that moment that sound drowned out all other sounds on this earth.

Did God create me anew today? Did He make up for his neglect of so many years? The one who was plain suddenly blossomed into a beauty. The one who was ordinary suddenly perceived the glory of the entire land within herself. Sandipbabu wasn't just one man. He alone symbolized the overflowing hearts of millions in the nation. Hence when he designated me as the Queen Bee of the beehive, I was crowned that very day amidst the whispered hymns of praise by all those who served the country. After that, in one corner of our home, my elder sister-in-law's silent disregard and my second sister-in-law's strident mockery didn't affect me at all. My relationship with the whole world changed.

Sandipbabu had successfully convinced me that the entire nation needed me badly. That day I had no trouble believing those words. I have the ability—the ability to do anything as I am now blessed by a divine strength. It was something that I'd never experienced before. There was no time for me to stop and try to comprehend the nature of this colossal wave of emotions that rose in my heart; it was as if it was mine always and yet not quite my own; as if it were somewhere beyond me, belonging to the entire nation. It was like a deluge and no backyard pond was answerable for it.

Sandipbabu consulted me about every little matter pertaining to the country. At first I was very hesitant, but that soon disappeared. Whatever I said, Sandipbabu's reaction was amazement. He'd always say, 'We, men, can only think but you can plumb the depths of Truth and so you don't need to think anymore. God created women from inspiration but the men, He beat into shape with a hammer in hand.' Listening to him, I'd begun to feel that both natural intellect and power were innate parts of me in a way that I myself hadn't realized before.

Many letters came to Sandipbabu from different parts of the country regarding various matters. I read each and every one of them and none was answered without a consultation with me. On some days, Sandipbabu and I would disagree over something. I never argued with him. But a couple of days later, he'd have a realization as it were and calling me out from the inner chambers he'd say, 'Look, what you said the other day was absolutely right and all my arguments were wrong.' Sometimes he'd say, 'I'm really sorry I didn't take your advice then. Really, can you explain to me the mystery behind this?'

Gradually I began to feel more and more that at the time all that was happening in the country had Sandipbabu at its root and behind him lay the common sense of an ordinary woman. My heart was filled to the brim with the sense of a glorious duty.

My husband had no place in all these discussions that we had. Sandipbabu's manner towards my husband was like that of an older brother who loved his younger brother very much but didn't really trust his judgement on important matters. He'd often laugh patronizingly and imply that in these matters my husband was quite childish and his opinions were really quite contrary. He made it clear that he loved my husband all the more because there was a quaint humour in these strange opinions and erroneous beliefs that he held. Hence, out of this exceptional fondness for my husband, Sandipbabu kept him out of doing any work for the country.

Nature, the physician, has several ways of dulling one's pain. When a profound relationship gradually starts slipping away, one doesn't even know when those antidotes start working within oneself. Suddenly one day we wake up and realize a great chasm has opened up. When the scalpel was cutting away at the most important relationship of my life, my mind was thus shrouded by the vapours of emotion and I didn't even know about the cruel turn of events. Perhaps this is a woman's nature. When our heart is involved in one arena, we lose all our senses of other spaces. This is why we are devastating; we cause havoc through our innate nature and not through logic. We are like flowing water—when we flow between two shores, we nurture with all our might and when we overflow the banks, we destroy with equal vehemence.

## Sandip

I could feel that something was amiss. The other day I got a whiff of it.

Since my arrival, the drawing room in Nikhilesh's home had turned into an ambiguous space, neither indoors nor outdoors. From the outside I had access to it and from within, the Queen Bee did. If we had used this privilege in some moderation, perhaps people would soon have got used to it. But when the dam bursts, the flow of the water is at its highest. Our meetings in the drawing room continued with such gusto that neither of us was aware of anything else.

Whenever the Bee came into the drawing room, I could somehow sense it from my room. There'd be some sounds of tinkling bangles and some other noises. She opened the door perhaps a little too loudly, needlessly. Then the door of the bookshelf, which was a little stiff, made a lot of noise when it was opened. As I came into the room, I'd find the Bee intently picking a book from the shelf, her back to the doorway. When I'd offer to help her in this arduous task, she'd be startled and protest, and then some other topic would come up.

The other day, on a Thursday afternoon, I started from my room after hearing some of the usual noises. On the way, in the corridor I found a guard standing duty. I proceeded without glancing at him. But he stood in my way and said, 'Babu, please don't go that way.'

'Don't go! But why!'

'The mistress is in the drawing room.'

'Fine. Tell the mistress that Sandipbabu would like to see her.'

'No, that's not possible. Those are the orders.'

I was very angry. I raised my voice a little and said, 'I am ordering you to go and ask her.'

The guard was a little daunted by all this. So I pushed him aside and proceeded towards the room. When I was almost at the door, he ran up to me and grabbed me by the hands, 'Babu, please don't go.'

What was this! How dare he touch me! I snatched my hand away and slapped him hard on the cheek. At this point, the Bee came out of the room and found the guard on the verge of retaliating.

I'll never forget the look on her face. It was I who discovered the beauty of the Bee. In our country most people wouldn't look at her twice. She was tall and lissome, a quality which connoisseurs of beauty would mock as 'lanky'. It was this litheness of hers that I admired the most, as if in making her a fountain of life had emanated from the cavernous heart of the maker and shot upwards animatedly. Her colour was dark, but it was the dark of a sword of steel—powerful and razor-sharp. That power blazed in her eyes and face that day. Standing on the threshold, she raised her index finger and said, 'Nanku, go away.'

I said, 'Please don't be angry. Since there are orders, I'd better leave.'

In a trembling voice, the Bee said, 'No, please don't leave. Come inside.'

This wasn't a request, it was an order. I came into the room, sat down and began to fan myself with a hand-held fan. The Bee wrote something on a piece of paper with a pencil and handed it to the bearer saying, 'Give this to the master.'

I said, 'Please forgive me, I was impatient and I hit the guard.'

The Bee said, 'Serves him right.'

'But that poor man did nothing wrong. He was following orders.'

At this point Nikhil came into the room. Hastily I got up, turned my back to him and went and stood by the window.

The Bee said to Nikhil, 'Today Nanku, the guard, has insulted Sandipbabu.'

Nikhil pretended to be such a simpleton as he said, 'Why?' that I could no longer control myself. I turned around and looked at his face steadily and thought, 'So the truthful person does lie to his wife, if she is the right sort.'

The Bee said, 'Sandipbabu was coming this way and he stopped him saying that he has orders.'

Nikhil asked, 'Whose orders?'

The Bee retorted, 'How should I know that?'

Anger and frustration almost brought tears to her eyes.

Nikhil sent for the guard. He said, 'Sire, I am not at fault. I was following orders.'

'Whose orders?'

'The elder and second mistresses called me and gave me instructions.'

For a few moments all of us were silent.

After he left, the Bee said, 'Nanku has to be sacked.'

Nikhil was silent. I knew his moral and ethical senses were strained. He was under great stress. But the problem was a difficult one. The Bee was no simple woman. On the pretext of sacking Nanku, she wanted to take revenge on her sisters-in-law.

Nikhil continued to be silent. The Bee's eyes were showering sparks of fire. Her hatred towards Nikhil's good-heartedness knew no bounds.

Without saying another word, Nikhil left the room.

From the next day, that guard was not to be seen anywhere. Upon inquiry I learnt that Nikhil had transferred him to a position in some village—the guard's losses were compensated amply.

Over this small matter, I could tell, that a few storms had blown over the house. At every point I couldn't help feeling one thing—Nikhil is strange, an absolutely insane person.

The upshot of this incident was that for the next few days the Bee started coming into the drawing room daily and sending the bearer for me to spend some time chatting with me; she didn't even bother to use any excuse of coincidence or necessity.

In this fashion the friendship, through words and gestures, spoken and unspoken, progressed. This was the lady of a household who is usually like a star in a sky, beyond an outsider's reach. There were no trodden paths here. Through this nameless vacuum we navigated our way: the gradual tension, knowing and awareness, each veil of inhibition ripping away into a formless sky and suddenly exposing nature in its naked form—this was a strange, victorious journey of Truth!

Of course this is Truth! The force of attraction between a man and a woman is a very tangible one. From the dust particle on the ground to the stars in the sky, all material things support it. And man would like to keep it shrouded by a few words, to make it his domestic property by some rules and regulations! As if it's a demand to fashion a watch-chain for one's son-in-law out of the solar system. Then, when reality awakens to the call of matter, and in an instant, brushes aside all pretense of man's words and takes its own place, neither faith nor morality can stop its progress. So many charges, regrets and commands come forth! But you need more than mere words to grapple with a storm. It doesn't answer to you, it only shakes you up—it is reality.

Hence, I am really enjoying this palpable revelation of Truth before my eyes. So much shame and fear, so many dilemmas! But without that what's the charm of Truth? This tremble in one's step, this turning away every now and then—it's all very sweet. And the deception is more against oneself than others. When reality wages war on the artificial, deception is its primary weapon because the enemies of matter mock it by calling it coarse. Hence, it needs to either keep itself hidden or use a masquerade. The way things are, it can't say boldly, 'Yes I am coarse, because I am Truth, I am corporeal, I am instinct, I am hunger, shameless and heartless—just as shameless and heartless as the gigantic boulder that's dislodged from the mountainside by the rains and comes rolling onto the heads of human habitation, irrespective of lives lost or saved.'

I can clearly see everything. There, the curtain is drifting in the wind and preparations are being made to set off on a journey of destruction. That tiny flash of red ribbon peeping from the masses of dark hair, washed and cleaned: it's the greedy tongue of the nor'wester, scarlet with the secret zeal of lust! I can clearly perceive the heat off that slight gesture of the sari-border, the little hint of the blouse. Yet, all this groundwork is taking place in a clandestine matter, unknown even to the one who is doing it.

Why doesn't she know? Because, man has destroyed with his own hands the capacity to know and understand reality fully, by always covering it up. Man is ashamed of reality. Hence, it has to work surreptitiously, from beneath the piles and swathes of wrapping that man has constructed; that's why we never come to know of its workings and then when it comes upon us suddenly, there is no way of denying it. Man wanted to evict it and called it Satan, which is why it entered Eden masquerading as a snake and made woman rebel by just whispering into her ears and opening her eyes to the Truth. Since then, there has been no time to rest, there has been only death and nothing else!

I am materialistic. The naked reality has broken free of the prison of sentimentality today and come into the open. My joy stalks every footstep. Whatever I desire should come very close to me, I'll receive it fully, I'll hold it tight and not let it go at all; all that comes in-between will shatter into little pieces, roll in the dust, flutter in the wind—this is joy, this is pleasure, this is the destructive-dance of reality; after this life and death, good and bad, joy and sorrow, all is vain—mere trifles! Trifles!

My Queen Bee is walking in a trance and she doesn't know which way she's headed. It wouldn't be safe to let her know and wake her suddenly, before the time is right. It's better to let her feel that I haven't noticed anything at all. The other day as I was eating, Queen Bee stared at my face fixedly, totally unaware of what that look can possibly imply. When I looked up suddenly and met her eyes, she blushed and looked away. I said, 'You must be really surprised by the way I eat. I can conceal many traits, this greed isn't one of them. But look here, since I am not ashamed of myself, please don't feel embarrassed for my sake.'

She turned her head, blushed some more and began to say, 'No, oh no, you—'

I said, 'I know women adore greedy people because that's the way they win their hearts. I am a glutton and that's why, I've always received so much care from women that today I am in this state, where I don't feel the least bit of shame. So, please feel free to stare your eyes out as I am eating; it doesn't bother me one bit. I will chew up every one of these drumsticks and leave nothing to them—that's my nature.'

A few days ago I was reading a contemporary English book, which contained explicit details of the union between a man and a woman. I'd left it behind in the drawing room. One afternoon I walked into the room for some reason and found Queen Bee reading the book; as she heard footsteps she covered it with another book and stood up. The book she used to cover the first one was a collection of Longfellow's poems.

I said, 'Look here, it beats me why you feel embarrassed about reading poetry. It should be the men who feel shy because some of us are lawyers and some engineers. If we must read poetry, it has to be late at night behind closed doors. You, women, are the closest to poetry. The God who created you is the poet of all poets and it is at His feet that Jaidev has composed his *Lalitalabangalata*.'

The Queen Bee didn't reply; she just laughed and blushed and made as if to leave. I said, 'No, no, that won't do. Please sit and read. I'd left behind a book; I'll just take that and clear out.'

I picked up my book off the table and said, 'Thank goodness this book didn't fall into your hands, or you might have beaten me up.'

The Bee asked, 'Why?'

I replied, 'Because, this isn't poetry. What this contains is the most basic facts about human beings, spoken quite bluntly too, without any artifice. I really wanted Nikhil to read this book.'

With a slight frown, the Bee asked, 'And why is that?'

I said, 'Since he is a man and he's one of us. He loves to see this raw world through a blur and that's why he and I argue so often. You can see, that's the reason why he has taken our swadeshi issue to be like Longfellow's poetry—he'd rather we tread gently on the rhythm for every little topic. We are more prosaic than prose, we're the destroyers of rhythm.'

The Bee asked, 'How is this linked to swadeshi?'

I said, 'You'll know if you read it. Whether it's swadeshi or any other matter, Nikhil would rather go with illusory views; hence, at every step he collides with human nature and then he resorts to calling nature all sorts of names. He refuses to accept that long before views and opinions, our natures were created and they will continue to be, long after all beliefs die.'

The Bee was silent for a while; then she asked solemnly, 'Isn't it in our nature to want to rise above our innate nature?'

I laughed to myself and thought, 'Oh princess, dear one, this isn't you speaking. You've learnt this from Nikhilesh. You are a hale and hearty person, bursting with the juices of Nature; the moment you've heard the clarion call of Nature, your flesh and blood has responded to it—why would the illusory web of all that they've preached to you be enough to hold you back? Don't I know that your veins are alive with the powers of life's fire? How much longer can the wet towel of moral lectures keep you cold?'

I said, 'In this world, there are more weak people than strong; in order to save their lives, they chant those refrains into the ears of the world and drive the strong ones crazy. Only those who have been deprived by Nature and weakened, tend towards enervating other people's nature.'

The Bee said, 'We, the women, are weak too. So we should join the conspiracy of the weak.'

I laughed and said, 'Who says you're weak? Men have cajoled you into thinking that you are helpless and weakened you with shame. I believe that you are the strongest. I can give it to you in writing that women will break free of the fort of chants, take on a devastating form and gain their freedom. Men only show off their strength, but deep down they are caged beings. Until today they have bound themselves by writing their own commandments. They've huffed and puffed and turned womankind into golden chains and wrapped themselves within and without. If man didn't have this amazing capacity to trap himself with his own snares, he'd be far ahead today. The traps built by his own hands are the biggest deities for him. Man has adorned them variously, painted them in different hues and worshipped them with varied names. But women? You have desired reality in this world with your heart, soul and body, given birth to reality and nurtured it.'

The Bee was an educated woman and she didn't give up easily. She said, 'If that were the truth, would it be possible for man to love woman?'

I said, 'Women are well aware of that; they know that men, by nature, appreciate deceit. Hence they borrow words from men, mask themselves and try to entice men. They know that the naturally inebriated menfolk are more inclined towards drink than food; hence, through devious means and tricks and gestures, they try to pass themselves off as liquor and desperately hide the fact that they are actually victuals. Women are materialists and they do not need any accessory illusions; those are set out only for the benefit of men. Women have become enchantresses under duress.'

The Bee said, 'Then why do you wish to shatter the illusion?'

I said, 'Because, I want freedom. I want freedom for my country as well as for relationships between human beings. My nation is very real to me and hence I simply cannot look at her through the misty veils of moral ethics. I am very real to me, you are very real to me and hence I do not condone the business of making two people mysterious and enigmatic to one another simply by scattering a few words between us.'

I had to keep in mind that startling a sleepwalker suddenly wasn't desirable. But my nature is so aggressive that it was impossible to tread softly. I know that my words that day were a little too strong; I know that the first impact of those words could be a little harsh. But women welcome the brave. Men love the ethereal; women adore the tangible. That's why men rush to worship the avatars of their own Idea and women gather their heart's prayers at the feet of the powerful.

Just as our conversation showed signs of warming up, Nikhil's childhood teacher Chandranathbabu came into the room. On the whole, the world was a fairly nice place but the havoc caused by these teachers made one want to quit it. People like Nikhilesh would rather his world remained a school till the end of his life. We were old enough, and yet the school has to tag along; even when we've started living adult lives, the school won't let us go. It'd be quite right to drag the teacher to the pyre with us when we die. That day, the symbol of school interrupted our conversation at an ill-timed juncture. I suppose there's a student-mentality embedded deep inside all of us. Bold as I am, even I was a little taken aback. And our Bee—from her face it was apparent that in an instant she'd turned into the best student in the class and solemnly taken her place in the front bench. It's as if she had remembered suddenly that she had a responsibility to do well in her exams. Some people sit by the roadside like the points-men of the railways; they switch the train of thoughts from one track to another for no good reason whatsoever.

As soon as he entered the room, Chandranathbabu was embarrassed and was about to leave, 'I'm sorry, I—.' Even before he finished the sentence, the Bee knelt down and touched his feet and said, 'Sir, please don't leave; do have a seat.' She spoke like she was drowning in mid-sea and needed his help. Coward! Or perhaps I am wrong. Maybe there was a ploy here—a way of increasing her worth. Perhaps the Bee wanted to let me know in an elaborate fashion that, 'You may think you've overwhelmed me, but I have far greater respect for Chandranathbabu.' So, go ahead. After all, one has to respect one's teachers. I am not a teacher and so I do not want empty respect. I've already made it clear that unsubstantial things do not satiate me—I need matter.

Chandranathbabu brought up swadeshi. I decided I'd let him babble non-stop and not reply to a single comment. It's good to let old people talk; it makes them feel that they're running the world and the poor souls never find out how distanced they are from the actual running of the world. At first, I held my tongue; but even his worst enemies wouldn't accuse Sandipchandra of being a patient man. When Chandranathbabu said, 'Look, we have never done any farming and if we expect we'll reap a harvest so soon after sowing the seeds, we—'

I couldn't help it; I said, 'We don't want a harvest; we say, *Ma phaleshu kadachana*—work without expectation of the result.'

Chandranathbabu was stunned, 'Then, what do you all want?'

I said, 'Poisoned weeds—it costs nothing to grow them.'

The teacher said, 'Poisoned weeds don't just hinder others, it's an encumbrance to itself too.'

I said, 'That's the moral value meant for schools. We're not writing out maxims on a board. Chalk in hand, our hearts are burning and for now that's the most important thing. Right now we'll scatter thorns on the path, keeping the soles of other people in mind. Later, when it'll hurt our own feet, there's enough time to repent at leisure. Is that too much?

When we're old enough to die, the fires will have died down and now that we're young they're burning furiously, as they should.'

Chandranathbabu laughed a little and said, 'If you want to rave and rant, I guess you will. But please don't pat yourself on the back saying that it's the brave thing or the best thing to do. On this earth, only those civilizations have saved themselves that have worked hard—not the ones that have raved and ranted. Those who have always feared hard work like the devil are the only ones who wake up suddenly and believe that they'll get somewhere through the blind alley of wrongdoings.'

I was just getting ready to furnish a severe reply when Nikhil entered. Chandranathbabu rose, looked at the Bee and said, 'I'll take leave today, Ma. I have work to do.'

After he left, I showed my English novel to Nikhil and said, 'I was telling Queen Bee about this book.'

Ninety nine per cent of the people on this earth have to be fooled by lies, but this perpetual student of the schoolteacher is most easily fooled by the truth. He is best deceived when you do it openly, telling all. It's better to play the game of truth with him.

Nikhil looked at the name of the book and kept quiet. I said, 'Man has cluttered up this earth, where he lives, with many unwieldy words and thoughts. So, writers such as this one have set forth, broom in hand, to remove the cobwebs and clearly expose the substance beneath it all. So, I was telling the Bee that you should read this book.'

Nikhil said, 'I have read it.'

I asked, 'What do you think of it?'

Nikhil said, 'For those who learn a lesson from such books, it's good; for those who want to use it for escape, it's like poison.'

I asked, 'What does that mean?'

Nikhil said, 'Look, in this day and age if someone says nobody has any right over his own property, it makes sense only if the speaker is a totally selfless man; but if he's a greedy thief, the words are a lie on his lips. If one's appetites are strong, he wouldn't really be able to make sense of this book.'

I said, 'But appetite is that gas-lamp of Nature which guides us on these roads. Those who deny the appetite wish to achieve a third eye by plucking out both their eyes.'

Nikhil said, 'I accept appetite or proclivity only when I accept renunciation at the same time. If I try to see something by stuffing it right into my eyes, I hurt my eyes and also fail to see it. When people try to realize everything through their appetite, they distort their desires without realizing the truth.'

I said, 'Look Nikhil, it is self-indulgence to see the world through glasses framed by moral ethics; that's why in a crisis you cannot see reality clearly and you cannot complete any task with vigour.'

Nikhil said, 'I don't think a job is successful only if it's done vigorously.'

'Then?'

'What's the use of arguing in vain? These matters lose their charm if they're discussed to no avail.'

I really wanted the Bee to join our discussion. Till this point she sat there without saying a word. Perhaps today I'd really shaken her mind quite deeply and so she was unsure, wanting to revalidate her lessons from the schoolteacher.

Was the dose too strong today? But the jolt was important. At the outset one must realize that something which the mind always accepted as fixed can be shaken.

I said to Nikhil, 'It's a good thing I spoke to you. I was about to let Queen Bee read this book.'

Nikhil said, 'What's the harm in that? Bimal should read any book that I've read. I'd just like to clarify one matter though; nowadays Europe is intent on analysing all things human in terms of science and all discussions rest upon premises like man is merely physiology or biology or psychology or at best, sociology. But, please, I beg you to remember that man is not just a logos, he's made up of all sciences and he goes beyond them all, stretching himself towards eternity. You accuse me that I am the schoolteacher's student; I'm not, but you are. You wish to find man through your science teachers and not through your inner beings.'

I said, 'Nikhil, why are you so excitable these days?'

He said, 'It's because I can see quite clearly that you are denigrating man, humiliating him.'

'Why do you say that?'

'I see it in the environment, through my own pain. You are intent on tortuously killing Him who is the noblest in man, the Beautiful, the Ascetic.'

'This is some mad rambling of yours!'

Abruptly Nikhil stood up and said, 'Look Sandip, I firmly believe that man can suffer endless agony and he'll still be alive; hence I'm prepared to tolerate everything knowingly.'

He finished speaking and walked out of the room.

I watched this display in amazement. Then I heard a sudden sound and turned to see that some books had dropped noisily to the floor, and Queen Bee was walking away hurriedly, keeping a distance from me.

Strange man, that Nikhilesh! He can feel distinctly that dark clouds have gathered over his home. Yet, why doesn't he just throw me out? I know he is waiting to see what Bimala does. If Bimala tells him, 'You are not the right partner for me,' only then will he lower his head and say, 'I see that there's been a mistake.' He doesn't have the strength to realize that the biggest mistake is in calling a mistake by that name. Nikhil is a perfect example of just how Idea enervates a man. I have never seen another man like him. He is an eccentric product of Nature. It'll be difficult to even construct a story or a play around him, let alone a family.

Then of course the Bee—it was obvious that the spell has broken today. She has understood the force of the tide which had her in its thrall. Now, fully aware, she has to either move forward or turn back. Not really; from now on, she'll go forward and turn back alternately.

I'm not worried about that. When your clothes are on fire, you may run around as much as you please and it'll only serve to stoke the flames some more. The jolts of fear will make her emotions stronger. I have seen so many of them by now. That widow, Kusum, finally came and surrendered to me, trembling with fear. And the foreign girl who lived near our hostel—on some days when she was upset with me I felt she'd tear me to pieces. I remember that day very well, when she screamed, 'Go, go' and threw me out of her room; the moment I stepped over the threshold, she came running back, fell at my feet, cried and banged her head on the floor and fainted. I know these ones very well—call it anger, fear, shame or hatred, these only act as firewood within their heart and burn to cinder after stoking the fire in it. The only thing that can contain this fire is Idea. But women don't possess an ounce of it. They do their good deeds, go to pilgrimages, bow piously before the holy man, just as we men go to office—but they stay far away from Idea.

I won't say much to her myself; but I'll offer her some contemporary English books. Let her gradually realize that it's 'modern' to admire and accept desire as a reality. It's not 'modern' to revere control as the greater and desire as the lesser virtue. If she only takes refuge in the word 'modern' she'd gain a lot of courage, because women need a pilgrimage, a holy man, some set traditions; mere Idea alone is unappealing.

Anyway, let's see this play through till the fifth act. I cannot proclaim that I am a mere spectator sitting on a royal seat in the balcony and clapping occasionally. My heartstrings feel stretched and the veins throb from time to time. At night when I switch off the lights and retire to bed, the slightest touch, the smallest look and the tiniest word resounds in the dark. When I wake up in the morning, my heart sparkles with joy and I feel as if a pleasant refrain is flowing in my veins.

In the photo-frames on this table, there was a photograph of Nikhil and one of the Bee. I'd taken her picture out of it. Yesterday I showed her the empty space and said, 'The miser's stinginess makes the thief steal. Hence, it's only fair that the thief and the miser share the blame for the theft. What do you say?'

The Bee smiled a little and said, 'That picture wasn't a good one.'

I said, 'Can't be helped. A picture cannot improve upon itself. I'll have to be happy with whatever it is.'

The Bee opened a book and began leafing through it. I said, 'If you're upset, I'll fill that empty space somehow.'

Today I've done it. This photo of mine was taken when I was younger; my face was more innocent then, as was my heart. I still believed in life beyond the here and now. Although such beliefs often cheat you, they have one good feature—they cast a soft glow on your soul.

My photo is placed beside Nikhil's—the two friends.

## Nikhilesh

I never used to think of myself before. Nowadays I try to see myself from the outside quite often. I wonder how I look through Bimal's eyes. Too stern, perhaps; I have the bad habit of taking everything too seriously.

It's just that it is better to laugh away your troubles than drown them in buckets of tears. That's what I am trying to do. Only because we brush aside all the sorrows that lie scattered at home and in the world, like a shadow or some illusion, that we can continue to eat and sleep; if we held onto them even for an instant as a reality, could we have swallowed a morsel or slept a wink? But I can't see myself as a part of that brushing aside or flowing away. It feels as though the earth is laden with my sorrows which are accumulating like an eternal burden. Hence the grimness, and hence a close look at myself makes me want to burst into tears.

Well, wretched one, why don't you stand in the world's marketplace and compare yourself with the crores of people collected over centuries and beyond and then decide what Bimal is to you? She is your wife! Whom do you call a wife? You have puffed up that word with your own breath and go around carefully protecting it; do you know that one pinprick from outside and it'll all deflate in a trice?

My wife, and hence she is all mine! If she wants to say, 'No, I am myself', immediately I'd say, 'Impossible; you are *my* wife!' Wife! Is that a reason! Is that a truth! Can you actually bind a person into that one word and lock her into it?

Wife! I have nurtured that word within my heart, lavished all that is gratifying, all that is pure upon it and never set it down upon the dusty earth. So many sacred incense sticks, musical flutes, spring blossoms and autumnal shefalis have gone into that name! If it suddenly drowns into the murky waters of the drain like the paper boats we played with, then along with it all my—

There I go, the same old seriousness! What are you calling the drain and which the murky waters? That was just spoken in anger. Something won't change into something else just because it'd upset me, would it? If Bimal is not mine then she simply isn't mine and all the persuasion and outbursts will only serve to make that clearer. My heart is bursting! Let it. It won't make either the world or me a poor man. Man is far greater than all that he loses in one lifetime; salvation awaits him even at the end of all the oceans of tears; that's why he weeps, otherwise he wouldn't.

But in the eyes of society—oh, let society bother with all that and do what they please. I weep for myself and not for society. If Bimal says she is not my wife, then whether society considers her my wife or not, I must abdicate.

Of course I am sad. But one particular misery will be quite untrue and I'll stop myself from feeling it at all cost. Like a coward, I refuse to feel that rejection has reduced the value of my life. My life is valuable;

I wasn't born to use up that worth to merely buy up the inner chambers of my home. A time has come for me to realize that a business venture the size of mine will never run short of funds.

Today, as I look at myself, I should also look at Bimal as an outsider. Until now, I had adorned her with some ideals of my own imagination. My ideal woman didn't quite match with the Bimal of real life at all points; but still I have worshipped her through my fantasy.

It's not my greatness, it's my biggest drawback. I am greedy; I wanted to romance my perfect fantasy image in my mind and the actual Bimal only became an excuse. Bimal has always been what she is. She never really had to turn into the image of perfection for my sake. Obviously, the Maker does not work to meet my demands.

In that case, today I need to take clear stock of several things; I must firmly erase all the colourful doodles I have splattered with the colours of illusion. Until today, I have willingly turned a blind eye towards many things. Today it is obvious to me, that in Bimal's life I am incidental; the person whom Bimal's entire being can truly complement, is Sandip. Knowing this alone is enough for me.

This is not a day when I can be modest even to my own self. Sandip has many great qualities, which are attractive and they used to attract me too until recently; but, even on a modest scale, I'll have to admit that on the whole he is in no way greater than me. If a swayamvara is held and the garland goes to Sandip and not to me, then through this rejection the gods would've judged the one who made the choice and not me. I say this today, not out of pride. Now, if I do not realize my own worth truly within myself, if I think this injury is the ultimate humiliation, then I'll end up in the world's garbage-dump like a piece of trash; I'll be truly fit for nothing else.

Let the joy of freedom raise its head within me in spite of all the unbearable misery of this day. It's good that I understood; I got to know the inner and the outer. After all the debit and credit, whatever remains is all of me. It's not a physically handicapped me or an indigent me or even a feeble me raised on a convalescent's diet in the inner chambers of the home; it is the I who has been fashioned by the strong hand of Fate. Whatever had to happen has happened and nothing worse could be in the offing.

Just now my teacher came up to me, placed his hand on my shoulder and said, 'Nikhil, go to sleep, it is one o'clock.'

It's rather difficult for me to go to bed until Bimal is fast asleep, very late in the night. During the day I see her and even speak to her, but alone in the stillness of night in our bed, what can I say to her? My entire being shrinks in discomfiture.

I asked my teacher, 'Why haven't you gone to bed yet?'

He laughed ever so slightly and said, 'My days of sleep are over, now it's time to stay awake.'

I'd written thus far and was about to retire to bed when suddenly the thick clouds seen through my window parted a little and a lone star glimmered brightly through them. I felt it was saying to me, 'So many relationships sever and tear, but I still remain; I am the eternal flame of the wedding night's lamp, the everlasting kiss of a lovers' night.'

At that moment my heart was full and I felt that behind the curtain of this worldly life, my perpetual lover sat still. In so many lives, in so many mirrors I have seen her face—so many broken, distorted, dusty mirrors. The moment I say, 'Let me possess the mirror and put it inside a box,' the face disappears. Let it be—how does my mirror or that reflection matter! Dear heart, your faith stays intact, your smile will never fade; the sindoor with which you've covered your hairline, glows bright every day with the sun's rays.

A devil stood in a corner in the dark and said, 'Your imagination is fooling the child in you!' So be it, a child needs to be fooled—one lakh children, one crore children, one child after another—children cry so hard! Is it possible to fool so many children with anything but the truth? My love will not betray me—she's Truth, the Truth—that's why I see her again and again and will continue to see her always; I've seen her through my mistakes and through the mist of tears. In the midst of the marketplace of life I've seen her, lost her and found her again and when I slip through death's jaws, I'll see her again. Oh heartless one, don't mock me anymore. If I have lost the way to the path on which you have walked, the breeze with the scent of your hair, please don't punish me forever for that single blunder. That star whose veil has slipped, is telling me, 'No, oh no, don't be afraid. Whatever is eternal will always be there.'

Now let me go and take a look at my Bimal; she's sprawled on the bed, in deep slumber. Let me place a kiss on her forehead without waking her. That kiss is my offering of devotion. I believe after death I'll forget everything—all mistakes, all tears—but the evocative resonance of this kiss will stay somewhere, because through life after life these kisses are being strung into a garland to be thrown around my lover's neck.

At this time my second sister-in-law entered my room. The clock in our hall chimed two o' clock in strident tones.

'Thakurpo, what are you up to? Please, dear brother, go to sleep—don't torment yourself like this. I cannot bear to look at the state you are in.'

As she spoke, tears trickled down her cheeks.

Silently, I bent down, touched her feet and proceeded to my room.

## Bimala

Initially, I didn't suspect anything or feel any apprehension; I thought I was surrendering myself to the work of the country. There's such terrible exultation in total surrender! That day I discovered for the first time that the greatest pleasure lay in wrecking one's own self.

I don't know if this obsession would have evaporated amidst some vague emotions. But Sandipbabu couldn't wait, he made himself very clear. His tone of voice seemed to caress me like a touch, his glances seemed to fall at my feet, pleading. Yet, it held such furious desire, as if it wanted to drag me by my hair and tear me away like a heartless brigand.

I'll be honest: the destructive image of this rampant desire attracted me day and night. I began to feel there'd be a strange thrill in ruining myself totally. It'd bring such shame, such fear and yet, it was a bittersweet treat.

There was also unbridled curiosity—the mystery of his livid lust, of a person whom I don't know very well, a person whom I wasn't sure of having, a person whose powers were immense, whose youth burned in a thousand flames—it was great, it was immense! I had never ever dreamed of this. The ocean, which was far away and of which I'd only read in books, suddenly swelled up in a ravenous flood, overcame all barriers and laid itself down in all its timelessness, foaming at my feet in the backyard pond where I wash utensils and draw water.

To start with, I'd begun to revere Sandipbabu. But that reverence soon washed away. I don't even respect him—in fact I disrespect him. I have understood very clearly that he cannot compare with my husband. And gradually, if not at the very outset, I have even come to believe that the quality which one tends to mistake for manliness in Sandip is nothing but flightiness.

Yet, this veena of mine made of flesh and blood, thoughts and ideas, began to play in Sandip's hands alone. I'd like to hate those hands and this veena—but yet, it has sung for him! And when those tunes filled my days and nights, I didn't have any mercy anymore. Each throb of my veins and each surge in my blood repeated to me, 'You and all that you possess should now sink to the nadir of that tune and revel in it.'

There is no denying it anymore: I have something that—what should I say? Something for which, it's best for me to die.

Whenever the teacher has some time to spare, he comes and sits by me. He has a strength: in an instant he can take your mind to such a great height that you can clearly see the entire range of your life spread out before your eyes—what I've always considered to be the limit suddenly doesn't appear to be the limit any longer.

But what's the use! I don't want to see things that way. I can't even say that I want to be free of the seduction that has me in its grip. Let the home suffer, let the Truth within me grow darker by the minute and die, but I can't stop myself from wishing that my addiction should continue forever. When my cousin Munu's husband got drunk, he beat her and later repented for it and wailed and vowed never to touch that stuff again; he'd reach for the liquor the very next day and I used to seethe with rage. Today I find that my liquor is far more dangerous than his—this alcohol doesn't need to be bought from the store or poured into a glass—it spawns by itself in my blood. What should I do! Is this how I'll spend my whole life?

At times, startled, I look at myself and feel that all of this is a nightmare; this me isn't the real one. This is a terrible contradiction; there is no connection between the beginning and the end; this is dark disgrace painted in the shades of a rainbow by an illusory magician. I can't understand what happened and how it all happened.

One day my second sister-in-law came in, laughed and said, 'Our Chhotorani is very hospitable. She takes such good care of her guest that he doesn't want to budge from the house. In our times too, there were guests coming and going, but they never got so much care. In those times there were some customs, husbands needed some care as well. Just because Thakurpo was born in these times, he's been swindled. He should have come to this house as a guest—then perhaps he'd have stayed awhile—now, one wonders. Little brute, don't you even have the heart to glance at his face once and see what he's become?'

There was a time when these accusations didn't bother me in the least. I used to think they didn't have the capacity to understand the vow that I'd taken. There was a shield of emotion around me then; I'd thought that since I was giving up my life for my country, I had no room for shame and dishonour.

For some days now, there's been no talk of the country. Now the discussion revolves around the relationship between men and women in the modern times and other varied subjects. Under that pretext, there's also an exchange of English and Vaishnav poetry. The tenor of those poems is a very coarse one. I'd never had a taste of this tune in my home; I began to feel, this was the strain of manliness, of the powerful.

But today there are no shields anymore. I have no answer for queries like why Sandipbabu is staying on thus for days on end and why I hold forth with him for no reason whatsoever. So, that day, I was very angry with myself, my second sister-in-law and the entire establishment and I said, 'No, I'll not go into the sitting room again; not even if I die.'

For two days I didn't step out. In those two days it became clear to me just how far I'd gone. I felt all the joy had gone from my life. I felt like throwing away everything that came my way, within my reach. My entire being seemed to wait for someone; the blood in my veins seemed to be waiting for a response from out there.

I tried working very hard. The floor of my room was clean enough; yet, I personally supervised it and had it scrubbed clean with pots and pots of water. Everything was arranged in one way in the almirah; I took it all out, needlessly, dusted it and rearranged everything. That day it was nearly two in the afternoon when I had my bath. That evening I didn't tie my hair. I just put it up in a bun and managed to hassle everyone into reorganizing the pantry. I found that a lot has been stolen from there in this time. But I didn't dare scold anyone for it, in case someone, even in their mind, retorted, 'Where were your eyes all these days?'

I went through the hustle-bustle of the day like one possessed. The next day I tried reading. I don't remember what I read, but suddenly I found myself, absent-minded and book in hand, standing in the corridor leading outside and silently peering through the blinds. Through it, a row of rooms outside on the north side of our yard was visible. Of those, I felt one room had slipped far away from the ocean of my life and ships couldn't ply there anymore. I looked and looked! I felt I was a ghost of the day before yesterday, there in all the places and yet not there.

At one point Sandip stepped out into the balcony, newspaper in hand. I could clearly see the impatience stamped on his face. It felt as though he was getting angry at the yard, at the railings of the balcony. He hurled the newspaper away. If he could, he'd perhaps have torn away a bit of the sky. My vow almost broke down. Just as I was about to turn towards the sitting room, I found my second sister-in-law standing behind me.

'Well, well, quite a show!' She threw the comment in the air and walked away. I didn't go outside.

The next day Gobinda's mother came and said, 'Chhotoranima, it's time you handed out the food that'll be cooked today.'

I said, 'Ask Harimati to do it.' I threw down the bunch of keys and continued with the needlework that I was doing. At this time, the bearer came and handed me a letter and said, 'Sandipbabu gave it.' Look at his nerve: just imagine what the bearer must have thought! My heart was fluttering. I opened the note and found there was no greeting; just these words: 'Urgent need. Country's work. Sandip.'

Forget sewing! Hurriedly I checked my hair before the mirror. I changed my jacket and not the sari. I knew that in his eyes this jacket of mine had a special identity.

My second sister-in-law was sitting and cracking betel nuts on the balcony, which I had to cross on my way out. Today I didn't hesitate in the least. She asked, 'Where to?'

I said, 'To the sitting room.'

'So early? Morning games, is it?'

I went my way without replying. She started singing:

*My Radha keels over as she walks,*
*Like the crab of the deep sea,*
*And oh, she doesn't know of the sticky sugar.*

When I walked into the sitting room, I found Sandip lost in a book listing the paintings exhibited at the British Academy, his back to the door. Sandip considered himself quite a connoisseur of art. One day my husband said to him, 'If artists are in need of a tutor, they won't have a problem finding a suitable one as long as you are alive.'

It was unlike my husband to speak so derisively; but these days his temperament had changed. He never missed a chance to hurt Sandip's ego.

Sandip said, 'Are you of the opinion that artists don't need any further instruction?'

'People like us will always have to learn new lessons from the artists themselves because there are no fixed rules in art.'

Sandip scoffed at my husband's humility and laughed heartily; he said, 'Nikhil, you believe that indigence is the biggest wealth and the more you invest it, the richer you grow. I claim that if someone doesn't have an ego, he's like moss in the rapids, floating about aimlessly.'

My state of mind was a strange one. On the one hand I wished that my husband would win the argument and Sandip's ego would get a jolt, yet it was this same aggressive ego in him that attracted me—like the sparkle of an expensive diamond which nothing could put to shame. Even the sun couldn't outshine it—instead, it seemed to gain a surge of defiance from every challenge.

I entered the room. I knew Sandip had heard my footsteps but he pretended he hadn't heard it and continued reading. I was afraid he'd broach the topic of art. I still felt shy about the kinds of pictures and the kinds of things Sandip liked to discuss with me on the pretext of art. To overcome that shyness I had to pretend that there was nothing to be shy about.

So, for an instant I was tempted to just go back when suddenly Sandip heaved a great sigh, looked up and seemed startled to see me. He said, 'Oh, there you are!'

There was a covert censure in his words, both in his eyes and his tone of voice. I was in such a state that I even accepted this censure. Thanks to the claims that Sandip had acquired over me, it was as if my absence of two or three days was also a crime. I knew that Sandip's resentment was an insult to me; but I was too weak to be incensed.

I didn't respond and just stood there silently. Although my eyes were elsewhere, I was aware that Sandip's accusing eyes laid siege to my face and refused to budge. What was this all about! If he spoke something, I could at least hide behind those words and gain some respite. When my embarrassment became unbearable I said, 'Why did you send for me?'

Startled, Sandip said, 'Does there have to be a purpose? Is it wrong to be friends? Why this disregard for that which is the greatest in this world? Queen Bee, must you drive away the heart's adulation from the door, like a stray dog?'

My heart was fluttering. Dark clouds seemed to gather around me and there was no way to stop them. Fear and excitement struggled equally for mastery. Will I be able to bear the weight of this catastrophe or will it break my back? Perhaps I'd fall flat on my face on the dusty wayside.

My hands and legs were trembling. I stood very firmly and said to him, 'Sandipbabu, you sent for me saying there's some urgent work of the country and hence I dropped my household chores and came here.'

He smiled a little and said, 'My point exactly. Do you know that I have come here to worship? Haven't I told you that I clearly perceive the power of my country in you? Geography is not a Truth. One can't lay down one's life for a map. Only when I see you before me I realize how beautiful the country is, how dear, how full of power and life. I will know that I've received my country's command only when you anoint my brow yourself and wish me luck. When I'll fall to the ground, mortally wounded as I fight bravely, I'll remember this and never think I've fallen on a piece of land in geographical terms, but instead on an anchal—do you know which kind? It's the anchal of the sari you wore the other day, red as the earth and its border as red as a stream of blood. Can I ever forget it! This is what makes life dynamic and death attractive.'

As he spoke, Sandip's eyes burnt bright. I couldn't figure out if it was the fire of reverence or hunger that burnt in his eyes. I remembered the day when I first heard his speech. That day, I'd forgotten if he was a live flame or a human being. It's possible to behave humanly with ordinary humans—there are rules and codes in place for that. But fire belongs to a different genre altogether. In an instant it can dazzle your eyes, turn destruction into an object of beauty. You begin to feel that the truth that lay hidden among the neglected driftwood of everyday life, has taken up its radiant form, rushing to scorch the reserves stashed away by the misers everywhere.

After this, I didn't have the power to speak. I was afraid that at any moment Sandip would run to me and grab my hand, because his hands were shaking just like the trembling flames and his gaze rested on me like sparks of fire.

'Are you determined to privilege the trivial domestic rules and codes?' Sandip spoke up. 'You women have so much energy, the very whiff of which can make life or death a trifling matter to us; is that to be wrapped in a veil and kept indoors? Today, please don't hesitate, don't listen to the wagging tongues around you; today you must snap your fingers at mores and margins and come rushing into freedom.'

When the adulation for the country mingled thus with the adulation for me in Sandipbabu's words and the cords of reticence were sorely strained, then did my blood throb and dance! The discussions of art and Vaishnav poetry, of the relations between man and woman and various other real and intangible subjects, clouded my heart with guilt. But today the gloom of the embers caught fire again and the blaze of light from it veiled my shame. I felt that it was a wondrous, divine marvel to be a woman.

Alas, why didn't that marvel in all its visible brilliance flash through my mass of hair at that very instant! Why didn't a word come forth from my lips, which could, like a chant, instantly take the nation through a fiery initiation!

At that moment, the maid Khemadasi appeared, wailing and screaming loudly. She said, 'Please settle my accounts and let me go. Never in my entire life have I been—' The rest of her words was drowned in sobs.

'What is it? What's the matter?'

Apparently my second sister-in-law's maid, Thako, had unnecessarily quarrelled with Khema and called her unmentionable names.

I tried to pacify her saying that I would look into it and she would get justice but it was impossible to get her to stop wailing.

It was as if someone had poured a bucket of dirty water on the musical piece that was moving towards a crescendo that morning. The muck that was inherent in woman, beneath the budding lotus, was dredged up. In order to cover that up in front of Sandip, I had to rush indoors immediately. I found my second sister-in-law sitting in the balcony, as before, cracking betel nuts with her head lowered; a small smile lingered on her lips and she hummed, 'My Radha keels over as she walks'—nothing about her indicated that anything had gone wrong anywhere.

I said, 'Mejorani, why does your Thako abuse Khema for no reason thus?'

She raised her brows and said, 'Oh really, is that true? I'll take the broom to that vixen's back and throw her out. Just look at that: so early in the day she has gone and spoilt your session in the sitting room. And I'd say, Khema is also quite a fool—can't she see that her mistress is chatting with a babu outside? She just landed up there with her tales—I see she's lost all sense of shame and decorum! But, Chhotorani, you don't have to trouble yourself over these domestic issues. Why don't you go on outside and I'll resolve the matter as best I can.'

The human mind is a strange thing; how suddenly the wind changes and the sail turns around. I felt it was so out of place in my usual domestic routine for me to go and converse with Sandip in the morning, leaving all my domestic duties undone, that I just walked back to my room without a word.

I knew for a fact that at the right time my second sister-in-law must have urged Thako to pick a fight with Khema. But I stood on such unstable grounds myself that I couldn't say anything on these matters. Just the other day, in the heat of the moment I'd fought so defiantly with my husband to sack Nanku, the guard, but I couldn't sustain it till the end. Gradually my own agitation made me feel embarrassed. To add to that, my sister-in-law came and said to my husband, 'Thakurpo, I am to blame. Look here, we are traditional women and your Sandipbabu's ways don't really seem very proper to us—so, I thought it was for the best and I instructed the guard—but I didn't ever think that this would be an insult to Chhotorani; in fact I thought the opposite—alas for my Fate, more fool I!'

Thus, whenever I tried to look at something in glorious terms, from the perspective of the country or worship, and it curdled from the bottom in this way, my initial reaction would be anger, followed by guilt.

Today I came into my room, shut the door, sat by the window and began to think, if only one stayed within the bounds of the preordained rules, life could be so simple. Looking at my sister-in-law sitting cheerfully on the balcony, cracking betel nuts, made me realize how inaccessible the task of sitting on a simple seat and doing everyday chores had become to me. Every day I asked myself, where will it all end! Shall I die, will Sandip leave, will I recover one day and forget all this like a febrile delirium—or will I break my neck and sink into such a disaster that I'll never be able to recoup from it in my lifetime? If I couldn't effortlessly accept the good fortune that Fate had sent my way, how could I tear it to shreds thus?

The walls, ceiling, floor of this room, which I'd stepped into as a new bride nine years ago, were all gazing at me in amazement on this day. When my husband passed his MA and returned from Calcutta, he had bought a vine of some island in the Indian Ocean for me. It had just a few leaves, but the long bunch of flowers that bloomed in it were so beautiful, as if a rainbow was born in the lap of those few leaves and swung in its cradle. The two of us took that vine and hung it up by the window here, in our bedroom. The flowers bloomed just that once and never again; I have the hope that it'll bloom again. It is amazing that I still water the plant routinely; it is strange that the thick twine binding the vine hasn't loosened one bit—the leaves are still as green.

About four years ago, I framed a photo of my husband in an ivory frame and put it up on the mantlepiece. Occasionally when my gaze rests upon it, I can't look away. Till six days ago I used to bow before that picture, place flowers around it after my morning bath. So many days my husband had argued with me about this.

One day he said, 'In worshipping me you make me bigger than I am and this embarrasses me.'

I said, 'Why should you feel embarrassed?'

He said, 'I'm not just embarrassed, I'm also envious.'

I said, 'Listen to you! Who are you jealous of?'

He said, 'That fake me. This makes me feel that you aren't satisfied with the ordinary me and you want an extraordinary someone who'll overwhelm your senses. That's why your imagination has created an ideal me and you're playing a game of make-believe.'

I said, 'I feel so angry when you say such things.'

He said, 'No point getting angry with me, instead you should be mad at your destiny. You didn't really pick me out in a swayamvara; you had to take whatever you got with your eyes shut. Hence you're trying to rectify as much of me as you can, with spirituality. Since Damayanti had a swayamvara she could pick out the man over the god and since all of you haven't had a swayamvara, every day you ignore the man and garland the god.'

That day I was so angry with what he said, tears sprang to my eyes. The memory of it stops me from raising my eyes and looking at the picture on the mantlepiece.

There's another picture inside my jewel box. The other day I pretended to dust and clean the sitting room and picked up the photo-stand in which Sandip's photo is right beside my husband's, and brought it inside. I don't worship that photo and there's no question of bowing before it either; it stays covered up amidst my precious stones and jewellery and it brings such a thrill only because it is a secret. I shut all the doors of the room before I open the box and look at it. At night, I slowly enhance the light of the kerosene lamp and hold the photo before it and look at it silently. Every day I think that I should just consign him to that flame, turn him to ashes and finish it off for all times; and again, every day, I heave a sigh, slowly cover him up with my precious stones and jewellery and keep the photo under lock and key. But wretched, hapless soul: who was it that gave you these precious gems and jewels? So many caresses are intertwined with these. Where will they hide their face now? I'd be happy to just die.

Once Sandip said to me, 'It's not the inherent nature of women to vacillate. They don't have a left or right, they can only go ahead.' He always says, 'When the women of the country will rise, they'll speak much more lucidly than its men: "I want"—on the face of that want, no good or bad, no possible or impossible will be able to stand its ground. They'll just have that one claim: "We want", "I want". These words are the core chant of creation. This chant burns tempestuously in the fire of the sun and the stars. Its predilection of love is extreme; since it has desired man, for ages untold it has been sacrificing thousands of living things to that desire. That terrible chant of "I want", of the devastation of creation, is alive only in the women today. That's why the cowardly men are trying to raise dams on the way of that primitive flood of creation, so that it doesn't wash away their frail-as-pumpkin-creeper-frames as it roars with laughter and dances on its way. Men think they have raised these dams for all times to come. It's collecting, the water is collecting—today the body of water in the lake is quiet and sombre; today it neither moves nor speaks; silently it fills the pots and pans in man's kitchen. But the pressure will mount and the dam will burst; then the dumbstruck powers of all this time will roar "I want, I want" and rush forth.'

These words of Sandip strike up a drumming in my head. So, whenever there's a conflict with my self within me, when shame swears at me, I think of his words. Then I realize that this shame I feel stems from the fear of social repercussions, which takes the form of my second sister-in-law who sits on the balcony cracking betel nuts looking at me mockingly. Do I even care about her! My complete fulfilment is in being able to say 'I want' promptly, unwavering, with all the strength I possess. Failure lies in not being able to say it. What's with that vine or the mantle—do they have the power to insult or mock the radiant 'I'?

I had a strong desire to throw the vine out the window and bring the photo down from the mantle: let the shameless nudity of the destructive forces unfold. My hand did go up, but my heart ached and tears came to my eyes—I threw myself on the floor and began to weep. What, oh what will become of me? What is in store for me!

## Sandip

When I read my own words I find myself asking, is this Sandip? Am I made of words? Am I a book with covers of flesh and blood?

The earth is not a dead creature like the moon; it breathes and its rivers and oceans send up vapours—it's enveloped by that vapour and dust rises all around it. It is covered by this film of dust. If someone looked at this earth from the outside, he'd only see the reflection of this vapour and dust; would he catch a clear glimpse of the countries and continents?

The same way, when a person is alive the sighs of Idea rise from within him and so he becomes misty through that haze. The spots where he is clear, with land and water, where he is peculiar, cannot be seen: it feels as though he is a sphere of light and shade.

I have begun to feel that like the living planet, I too am tracing that sphere of Ideas in me. But I am not entirely just what I desire, what I think or what I decide. I am also that which I *don't* like, which I *don't* desire. I was created even before I was born; I haven't been able to select myself. I have to make do with whatever fell into my hands.

I know this very well that the mightier one is also the cruel one. The law is for the commoners and the extraordinary ones are above it. The earth is a level ground and the volcanic mountain prods through it with its horns of fire and rises up above it. It doesn't mete out justice to others around; it only looks to its own self. It's only by successful malevolence and unfeigned brutality that anyone has ever become rich or powerful, be it a man or a race. Only by blithely swallowing one, will 'two' be able to come into its own or the unbroken line drawn by 'one' would have continued unscathed.

Hence, I preach the practice of the unlawful. I tell everyone, crime is moksha, crime is the burning flame; when it doesn't burn it turns to ashes. Whether race or man, crimes must be committed to get somewhere in this world.

But still, this is only my Idea and not the entire me. However much I extol crime, there're some holes, some gaps in the cloak of Ideas and some things slip out through it, which are indeed naive and gentle. It is because most of me was already created even before I became myself.

Sometimes I put my followers to the test of heartlessness. Once we went to a garden for a picnic. A goat was grazing there and I asked who'd be able to cut off its hind leg with a machete. When everyone faltered, I went and did it myself. The man who was the most merciless in the entire group, fainted when he saw this sight. My calm, serene face made everyone bow down and pay homage to me as a great man, above mortal feelings. That day everyone glimpsed only the vaporous sphere of my Idea. But it was best to hide those spots where I was weak and merciful—whether this was my own doing or that of Fate—and where my heart was weeping within me.

Many things have also been covered up regarding this chapter in my life that has evolved around Bimala–Nikhil. It wouldn't have been hidden if I didn't have anything to do with Ideas. My Idea is moulding my life in its own fashion, but there's a lot of my life that is outside of it. My desires and those other bits of my life don't coincide entirely; hence I like to keep them stashed away, hidden in a corner, or else they would end up spoiling everything.

This thing called 'life' is abstract; it is made up of such diversity. We, men with Ideas, wish to pour it into distinct moulds and view it clearly in perceptible forms; the success of life depends on that clarity. From the famous conqueror Alexander the Great to the contemporary billionaire of America, Rockefeller, each has poured himself into a precise mould, be it of the sword or of money, and only then has he been able to call himself a success.

This is the point on which Nikhil and I start arguing. Both he and I claim that one should know oneself. But from what he says, all that becomes apparent is that not knowing oneself is all that's there to knowing oneself. He said, 'What you call "getting the results" is actually a result that excludes one's own self. The soul is greater than results.'

I said, 'That is an ambiguous one.'

Nikhil said, 'I have no choice. Life is more obscure than a machine; if you take life to be a machine, that won't help you to know life. Similarly, the soul is more nebulous than results; but I wouldn't say you are really seeing the soul for what it is, if you see it realized fully in results.'

I asked, 'So, where do you see the soul? Under which nose or between which brow?'

He replied, 'At the point where the soul knows itself to be eternal, where it leaves results far behind and goes beyond it.'

'So what would you say of your country?'

'The same thing. When the country says, "I'll only look to myself", it may well get results, but it loses its soul; but when it can see Truth as greater than itself, it can perhaps lose all results and yet achieve its own self.'

'Where in history have you seen that happen?'

'Man is so great that he can dispense with examples as much as he can overlook results. Perhaps there are no instances, just like there are no traces of a flower inside the seed; but still the seed does contain the flower. Yet, are there no instances at all? Was it a desire for results that made Buddha inspire India for so many centuries with his aspirations?'

It's not that I can't make any sense of what Nikhil says. That perhaps, is precisely my problem. I have been born in India; the toxin of religiosity permeates my blood. I may loudly assert that the path of denunciation is a crazy one. But I'm not able to brush it aside absolutely. That's why, today, such strange things are happening in our country. The chant of religion and patriotism, both are being sung heartily—we want the Bhagavad Gita as well as Vande Mataram—not recognizing that this makes both equally obscure, the result being like a clash between the ill-matched drums and the shehnai. The task of my life is to put an end to this discordant cacophony. I'll keep the drums intact, but the shehnai has been our ruin. We will uphold the flags of want and desire, which has been handed to us by Mother Nature, Mother Shakti and Mother Mahamaya when they sent us into the battlefield. Desire is beautiful and as pure as the fresh blossom, which doesn't run to the powder-room at the drop of a hat to scrub itself with Vinoliya soap.

One question has been bothering me for a few days: why am I letting my life get entangled with Bimala's? My life isn't just a banana-boat drifting around hitting the shore where it wishes. This is what I meant when I said that I wish I could mould my life on the lines of one Idea, but it spills over. From time to time, people slip and slide. This time I've slipped away a bit too far.

I am not ashamed of the fact that Bimala has become the object of my desires. I can see quite clearly that she desires me: she is my very own. The fruit hangs on the tree by its stem, but does that mean we'll have to accept that stem's rights on it as eternal! All the thirst, all the sweetness that she has was meant to fall into my hands alone; her triumph lies in submitting herself to that. That is her religion and that is her integrity. I will pluck her and bring her there, I won't let her life go in vain.

However, I am worried that I'm getting entangled and I feel that Bimal may become a huge burden on my life. I have come into this world to be a leader; I shall lead people with my words and in their work. Those masses are the horse for my crusade. My seat is on its back, its reins in my hands; it doesn't know its destination—only I know it. I will not let it pause and think when thorns will make its feet bleed or mud will splatter it all over, I'll only make it gallop.

That horse of mine is at the door today, impatiently pawing the earth with its hooves; the skies tremble with its neighing and what am I doing? What am I doing with my time? My auspicious moments are almost slipping away.

I had the impression I could run like the storm; I could pluck a flower, throw it away and it wouldn't slow down my pace one bit. But now I seem to be hovering around the flower like the honeybee and not like the storm.

Obviously when I colour myself with my own Ideas, the colour isn't as fast at all the spots and suddenly I can glimpse that ordinary mortal. If some omniscient God were to pen down the story of my life, I'm sure it'd be seen that there isn't much difference between me and that Harry there—or even Nikhilesh for that matter. Last night I was leafing through my diary written at the time when I'd just passed my BA and my head was fairly bursting with philosophy. Ever since then I'd vowed that I wouldn't allow any illusions, other people's or mine, into my life, and I'd make my life entirely real. But from then until now, what do I see in the story of my life? Where is that tightly woven fabric? This is more like a net; the threads are all there, but there are as many gaps. I have tried to fight those weaknesses, but failed to conquer them. For a while now I was surely moving at a good pace; today again I find a large gap in myself.

It hurts. 'I want it, it's near my fingers and I'll pluck it'—this is a clear declaration, the shortest route. I have always said that those who can walk this path vehemently are the ones who succeed. But Lord Indra didn't allow this penance to be a simple one; from somewhere, he sent the angel to cause suffering and blur the ascetic's vision with the vaporous mesh.

I see Bimala thrashing about like a trapped deer; such fear, so much pathos in those large eyes, her body lacerated by her attempts to free herself—the hunter should be happy at this sight. I do feel joy, but I also feel pain. That's why I'm not able to tighten the noose properly while time flies past.

There have been moments when, had I rushed up to Bimala, pressed her hand and drawn her into my bosom, she wouldn't have been able to protest; she too felt that any moment now something was about to happen, which will change the significance of her entire world—standing before that elemental ambiguity, her face was pale, her eyes filled with fear as well as excitement as if the heavens and the world were holding their breath and standing still, waiting for a decision to be made. But I let those moments pass; I didn't allow the imminent to become definitive, with unabashed strength. From this I can tell that those constraints that were innate to my nature have now come out and stand there blocking my way.

Ravana, whom I respect as the primary protagonist of the *Ramayana*, also died in this fashion. Instead of bringing Sita into his chamber, he kept her in Ashokavana. Thanks to that tiny bit of naive quandary that persisted in that great hero, the burning of Lanka was in vain. If he didn't have the dilemma, Sita would have given up her chaste airs and worshipped Ravana! In the same way, this hesitation always made him pity and disregard Vibhishana whom he should have killed; instead he himself lost his life.

This is the tragedy of life. It hides in a corner of the heart, curled up into a little ball and then in an instant it overcomes the giant. Man is not what he knows himself to be and that is why so many unpleasant things happen.

Although Nikhil is so weird and I laugh at him so often, deep down I can't squash the knowledge that he's my friend. In the beginning I didn't think of him at all. But as the days go by, I feel shame before him, and pain too. Some days, as always, I venture into an argument with him in the course of our conversation, but the enthusiasm flags suddenly—so much so, that I even do what I've never done before, that is, pretend to agree with him on some things. But this hypocrisy doesn't go down well with me and it doesn't suit Nikhil either—here too, we have something in common.

So, these days I try to avoid Nikhil and my day is made if I don't bump into him. These are signs of weakness. The moment one acknowledges the spectre of culpability, it turns into something very real; then, even if you do not believe in it, it catches hold of you. I simply want to let Nikhil know this very frankly, that we must look at these things in larger, more realistic perspectives. A genuine friendship shouldn't get messed up when faced with the Truth.

But I can't deny the fact that this time I have been weak. This weakness hasn't impressed Bimala one bit; she is the moth that singed her wings in the flame of my unreserved masculinity. When the haze of emotions sways me, Bimala is also swayed by it, but she feels revulsion; at that moment, although she cannot take back the garland she has thrown around my neck, the sight of it makes her feel like closing her eyes.

For both of us there is no turning back. I don't have the strength to leave Bimala now. But neither will I let go of my own path. My way is that of throngs of people, not this backdoor to the inner chambers. I'll not be able to abandon my own country now, especially not in these times; at present I'll merge Bimala with my country. The same westward storm that has snatched away the veil of right and wrong from the face of the motherland, will raise the bridal veil off Bimala's face—there is no disregard for her in that nakedness. The ship will sway on the waves of the ocean of people, the victory flag of Vande Mataram will flutter at its helm, roars and foaming waters all around—that ship will be our vessel of strength as well as that of love. There, Bimala will perceive such immense freedom that on its face, all her inhibitions will drop away without shame, unknown to her. Fascinated by this visage of destruction she won't hesitate to turn cruel. In Bimala I have seen the face of that gorgeous ruthless, which is the natural strength of Nature. If women could free themselves of the phony binds placed on them by men, I'd have truly witnessed Kali on this earth—she is the brazen goddess, she is heartless. I am a devotee of the same Kali; one day I'll drag Bimala amidst that devastation and invoke Kali. Let me make preparations for that.

## Nikhilesh

Every corner is flooded by the monsoon torrents; the glow off the young rice stalks is like that from the body of a child. There was water all the way up till the gardens in our house. The morning sun poured down on this earth unimpeded, matching the passion of the blue sky.

If only I had music in my voice! The water in the streams shimmered, the leaves on the trees glistened and ever so often, the paddy fields trembled and sparkled—in the morning music struck up on this July day, I alone was dumb! The tunes are locked within me; all the brightness of this world coming at me gets imprisoned within and cannot go back. When I look at this lacklustre, gloomy self I can understand why I am deprived. No one can endure my company day and night.

Bimal is so full of life. That's why, in all of these nine years, she has never ever seemed boring to me. But if there's anything in me, it is just mute profundity and not rippling surges. I am only capable of receiving but I cannot stir. My company is like starvation; when I see Bimal today I can understand what a famine she has survived all these years. Who is to blame?

Alas,

*Monsoon floods, July and August,*
*My temple lies vacant!*

My temple is built to stay empty; its doors are closed. I failed to understand all these years, that my idol was waiting outside the door. I'd thought he had accepted the prayers and also granted the boons—but, my temple lies vacant, my temple lies vacant.

Every year in the month of July when the earth was in all its glory, we toured the lake in Shyamaldaha in our barge. When the moonlight of the Krishnapanchami waned and hit rock bottom, we returned home. I used to tell Bimal that a song always had to return to its refrain; the refrain of union in life lay here amidst open nature; on these swelling waters where the wind blew gently, where the dusky earth drew the veil of shadows over her head and eavesdropped all night from one bank to another in the silent moonlight—this was where man and woman first united, and not within four walls. So, we returned here to the refrain of that first primal union, the union between Shiva and Parvati in the lotus gardens of Manasarovar in Kailash. After my marriage, two years were wasted in the hassle of examinations in Calcutta; since then for seven years now, every July, the moon has played its silent conch in our watery haven beside the blooming lotus garden. The first seven years of that life went thus; now the second phase begins.

I cannot possibly forget the fact that the full moon of July is here. The first three days have passed; I don't know if Bimal remembers, but she hasn't reminded me. Everything is quiet and the song has stopped.

*Monsoon floods, July and August,*
*My temple lies vacant!*

When a temple falls vacant from absence, the flute plays even in that vacuum. But the temple that falls vacant from parting lies very still and even the sound of weeping is discordant there.

Today my sobs are out of tune. I have got to stop this weeping. I shouldn't be cowardly enough to restrain Bimal with these tears. Where love has turned into a lie, tears shouldn't try and bind it. As long as my pain expresses itself, Bimal will not be totally free.

But I have to free her completely or I will not be free of the lie. Today, keeping her tied to my side is the same as shrouding myself in illusions. It doesn't help anyone, let alone bring any joy. Let me go, let me go—grief will be a jewel in the heart if only you can free yourself from lies.

I feel I have come close to grasping something. People have exaggerated the love between a man and a woman to such an extent that now I'm unable to bring it under control even for the sake of humanity. We've turned the lamp of the room into the fire on the hearth. Now the day has come when it should no longer be pampered but instead, disregarded. Having received the invocations of desire, it has taken the form of a goddess; but we won't accept the kind of prayers that require that a man sacrifice his manliness and have her drink his blood. We must rip apart the mesh of illusions that she has woven through looks and adornment, songs and tales, laughter and tears.

I have always felt a sort of revulsion for Kalidasa's poem *Ritusamhar*. How can man bring himself to thus belittle the joyous rhythm of Nature? All the flowers and fruits of this world simply lie at his lover's feet as objects of the veneration of desire. What was this intoxicant that clouded the poet's vision? The one that I was drunk on for all these years may not be so red in colour, but its effect was just as strong. It was this intoxication that made me hum that strain all day today—

*Monsoon floods, July and August,*
*My temple lies vacant!*

Vacant temple! I should be ashamed of myself. What has made this colossal temple of yours so empty all of a sudden? I have known a lie for what it is and that has taken all the meaning out of every truth I've ever known?

This morning I'd gone in to pick up a book from the shelf in the bedroom. It's been so long since I entered my room in the day. Seeing the room in daylight, I felt very strange. Bimal's sari lay crinkled up on that same rack and her discarded blouse and jacket lay in a corner waiting to be washed. Her hair pin, hair oil, brush, perfume bottles and even the sindoor box lay on the dressing table. Her tiny, zari embroidered slippers stood under the table—in the days when Bimal firmly refused to wear shoes, I'd had this made with the help of a Muslim friend of mine from Lucknow. She nearly died of shame just walking from the bedroom to that corridor there, in these slippers. Since then Bimal has gone through several slippers but she has kept this aside with special care. I'd joked with her and said, 'Every day you worship me by touching my feet when I sleep and today I have come to revere my living goddess by keeping the dust off her feet.' Bimal had said, 'Please don't say such things or I'll never wear those shoes.' This was my familiar bedroom. This room has a fragrance, which my heart knows intrinsically and which is perhaps not known to anyone else. My lovelorn heart has spread so many fine roots into these little and insignificant things: I have perceived this today in a way in which I never did before. The heart isn't free if the core root alone is destroyed. Even those slippers tend to draw him back. Even if Lakshmi deserts you, the mind hovers around the strewn petals of her lotus-seat. Suddenly my glance rested on the mantle. I saw that my picture stood on it as before and some dried, blackened flowers lay before it. The face in the photo was unchanged although the veneration was distorted. Today, from this room, these dry, black flowers were all I deserved. The reason they were still here was that even the need to discard them was gone. Anyway, I have accepted Truth in this stark and dreary form of it—when will I be able to achieve the indifference of that picture on the mantle?

At this point suddenly, Bimal entered the room from behind me. Quickly I looked away and walked towards the shelf, saying, 'I've come to take *Amiel's Journal*.' I don't know why this explanation was necessary. But I felt as if I was an offender here, as if I had no rights and had come in here to steal a look at something that was hidden, something that should stay hidden. I couldn't look her in the eye and quickly left the room.

When it became impossible to sit and read the book in the sitting room, everything in life began to seem difficult—I didn't have the slightest wish to see or hear anything, to say or do anything—exactly when all the days of my future had congealed into that one single moment and weighed down on my heart like a colossal weight, Panchu brought some ripe coconuts in a basket, kept them before me and touched my feet.

I asked, 'What's this, Panchu? Why this?'

Panchu was a subject of my neighbouring landlord, Harish Kundu; I knew him through my teacher. Firstly, I wasn't his landlord and then he was extremely poor—I had no right to accept any gifts from him. I thought, the poor fellow must be desperate and has thought of this novel manner to gain a few rupees' tip to take him through the day.

I dipped into the moneybag in my pocket, took out two rupees and was about to give it to him when he folded his hands and said, 'No sire, I can't take that.'

'Why, Panchu?'

'No sire, let me come clean. At a time when I was very hard up, I'd stolen some coconuts from your private gardens. I don't know when I'll die, and so I've come to repay the debt.'

Today, *Amiel's Journal* wouldn't have served me in any way, but these words from Panchu cleared up my mind in a trice. This world extended far beyond the sorrows and pleasures of unity and separation with one woman. Human life was substantial; I should take stock of my own mirth and tears only as I stand amidst that immensity.

Panchu was a devotee of my teacher. I know how his home runs itself. Every morning he wakes at dawn and takes a basket filled with paan, tobacco, coloured strings, mirrors, combs etc. which appeal to the farmer women, wades through the knee-deep pond and goes to the area where the lower castes live. Over there, he trades his wares for paddy, which fetches him a little more than a purely monetary exchange. On the days he can return early, he finishes his meal quickly and goes to make sweetmeats at the sweet shop. When he returns from there, it's late at night. Even after working so very hard, he and his family get two square meals a day only a few months of the year. His manner of eating is thus: at the very outset he'll fill his stomach with a jug of water and a large portion of his meal consists of the cheap variety of banana. At least four months in a year, he only gets to have one meal a day.

There was a time when I wanted to give him some financial aid. My teacher said, 'You may spoil people with your charity, but you can't end their misery. In Bengal, Panchu is not alone. The breasts of the entire land are dry. You will never be able to pour in money from the outside and make up for the milk which isn't there.'

It was food for thought. I'd decided to sacrifice my life to this kind of thinking. The other day I'd gone to Bimala and said, 'Bimal, let's devote our lives to banishing misery from our land.'

Bimal laughed and said, 'You seem to be my prince Siddhartha. See that you don't walk away one day and leave me stranded.'

I said, 'Siddhartha's penance didn't include his wife. I need my wife's presence.'

Thus the conversation ended in jokes and banter. Actually, by nature Bimal is what they mean by a 'gentlewoman'. Although she comes from a poor family, she's a princess. She believes that the standard of measuring the joys and sorrows in the lives of the people from the lower classes is also lower. They will obviously be needy but it is of no consequence. They are protected by the confines of their inferiority just as the waters in a tiny pond are contained within its shores. If one were to dig and extend those bounds, the water would run out and the muck below would rise up. Bimal had more than her fair share of that pride in her class, which is present in small sections circling independent seats of pride, within which resides, in spite of one's inferiority, a sense of pedigree and class befitting one's individual status. She is indeed a descendant of Manu. I suppose the blood of Guhak and Eklavya flows stronger in my veins. I'm not able to push away those who are below me as someone who is beneath me. My India doesn't belong to gentlemen alone. I'm fully aware that the further the lower classes slide down, it's India that is deteriorating and the more they die, it's India that is dying.

Bimal hasn't joined me in my struggle. In my life, I have given her such a large place that my cause has become smaller in comparison. I have pushed aside the goals of my life in order to make room for Bimal. The consequence of that is that I have only decked her up and adorned her day and night; my life is revolving only around her. I failed to keep in mind just how vast is man and how noble is life.

Yet, amidst all this, my teacher has protected me; as far as possible, he is the one who has guided me towards all that is great. Without him, I'd be sunk in the depths of despair on this day. He is an amazing human being. I call him amazing because there is a great difference between him and the age and times in which we live. He has been able to perceive God within him, and so nothing can distract him anymore. Today when I sit down to balance the books of my life, I can see a gross error, a great loss on one side; but I should always be able to add that there is also a reward that outweighs all losses.

I had already lost my father and come into my own by the time my master finished educating me. I said to him, 'Please stay here with me and don't seek work elsewhere.'

He said, 'Look here, I have already received my wages for what I have given you. If I charge you for the extra that I gave you, it'll be like cheating my God.'

Rain or shine, Chandranathbabu has come to teach me from his house. I've never been able to make him use our cars or vehicles. He said, 'My father always walked to work from Bot tulla to Lal dighi and he never even rode a shared car. Walking to work runs in our family.'

I said, 'Fine, then take up a job with us handling our business or something.'

He said, 'Oh no, my boy, don't trap me in these rich folks' business. Let me remain free.'

His son has now completed his MA and is looking for a job. I said that there's a possibility of working for me. His son too wants the same. At first he'd mentioned this to his father. But when he received no response there, he dropped some hints to me in his father's absence. That's when I mentioned it to Chandranathbabu. He said, 'No, he will not work here.' His son was very angry that his father deprived him of such an opportunity. In response, he left his widower father alone and took a job and left for Rangoon.

My master always said to me, 'Look Nikhil, you are not indebted to me and I am not obligated to you—that is our relationship. If a beneficial relation is bound in terms of money, it is an insult to greater powers.'

Now he is the headmaster of the Entrance School here. Until now, he wasn't even staying at my place. For a while now, I would go over to his house in the evenings and spend time there until late at night. Perhaps he thought that his tiny, damp room was not good for me in the heat of summer and so he has taken up residence at my home. It is amazing how he feels as compassionately for the rich as for the poor—he doesn't ignore the troubles and sorrows of the rich man or those of the poor.

Why is it that the closer you look at reality, the more it affects you? When we see Truth as formless, we can be free. Today Bimal has made the reality of my life so glaring that the Truth seems obscure. Hence, I am not able to hide my misery in this entire world. And so I have spread my tiny bit of despair amidst the people of this earth and sat down to hum:

*Monsoon floods, July and August,*
*My temple lies vacant!*

When I can glimpse the Truth from the window of Chandranathbabu's life, the meaning of the song is transformed into:

*Vidyapati says how will you spend*
*Your days and nights without Hari?*

All misery, all mistakes come from eluding that Truth: If I don't fill my life with the Truth, how will my days and nights pass? I can't take this anymore; Truth, fill my vacant temple now.

## Bimala

I can't explain what happened suddenly to the hearts and minds of the people of Bengal in those days. It was as if the waters of the Bhagirathi came and instantly initiated the sixty thousand sons of Sagar. The ashes of many centuries lay hidden beneath; no spark would light them up, no feelings could stir them and then, on this day, they suddenly woke up and said: 'Here I am.'

I've read in books that in Greece a sculptor brought his sculpture to life by the grace of some gods. There was a gradual evolution from beauty into life there, a quest. But in the ashes of this crematorium of a country, where was that exquisite harmony? I'd have understood it if the ashes were a hard, stone-like object—the petrified Ahalya had also turned into a human being one day. But this was all scattered, they constantly slipped through the fist of the Maker, fluttered around in the wind, sat in a pile but never became one. Yet, all of a sudden, that thing came into our yard and growled in a thunderous voice: 'Ayamaham Bhoh!'

On that day we felt all this was magical. The present moment fell into our palms like a solitaire from the crown of an inebriated god; there was no logical connection between our past and this present. This day was like being on medication which we didn't seek out, didn't buy, didn't receive from a doctor but instead brought on through a dream.

That is why we felt all our sorrows and problems would dissolve by themselves in this mantra. The boundaries of the possible and impossible vanished. We kept feeling that at any moment now, it's about to happen.

That day we felt history has no conduit, it arrives on its own heavenly chariot. At least its mahout didn't have to be paid, there were no costs for its upkeep; its champagne glass needed to be topped up from time to time and then, it was straight to heaven with this mortal body.

It wasn't as if my husband was indifferent. But it seemed like an anguish burned within him through all the excitement, as if he could see something beyond all that lay before him. I remember, one day while arguing with Sandip he'd said, 'Good fortune arrives suddenly and yells out before our door only to show us that we don't have the strength to welcome him and we haven't made any arrangements to invite him in.'

Sandip said, 'Look Nikhil, you don't believe in God and so you speak like an atheist. We can clearly see that the goddess has come to grant us a boon and you are doubting it?'

My husband said, 'I believe in God and that's why I know deep in my heart that we haven't been able to arrange for His puja. God has the power to grant us a boon, but we must have the strength to receive it.'

Such words from my husband always made me angry. I said to him, 'You think this fervour in the land is only an intoxication. But isn't there a power in inebriety?'

He said, 'There's power, but no weapons.'

I said, 'God grants power and that is hard to come by. Weapons—even an ordinary blacksmith can provide those.'

My husband laughed and said, 'The blacksmith won't give it for free, he'll charge you.'

Sandip proudly thrust out his chest and said, 'We'll pay, my dear, we'll pay him.'

My husband said, 'When you do, I'll call in the musicians for the festivity.'

Sandip said, 'We're not waiting for you to call them. There's no need to buy our priceless festivity for a price.' He started singing in his hoarse, intense voice:

*My penniless admirer wanders in the garden*
*And plays the penniless flute most melodiously.*

He looked at me, laughed and said, 'Queen Bee, this was just to prove that when a tune throbs in your throat, you sing even if you are totally out of tune. If you sing heartily, it doesn't matter if the song is perfect or not. Now a tune has taken our country by storm. Let Nikhil sit and practise the notes. Meanwhile, we will sing ourselves hoarse and set everything on fire.

*My home says where will you go,*
*You'll lose everything when you venture out.*
*My heart says, let all that you have,*
*Burn and perish quite merrily.*

'What is the worst that can happen to us—we'll be destroyed, right? Fine, I'm ready for it.

*If it has to go, do let it go,*
*I'll lose everything with a smile,*
*I'm on my way to drink*
*From the fountain of death.*

'The truth, Nikhil, is that we are energized. We can no longer stay within the bounds of all that is right and smooth. We have to set off on the path that is difficult and impossible.

*The dear ones who draw us close*
*Know naught of this nectar.*
*The friend of the wild path*
*Has called out to me.*
*Now let the straight bend to the wild*
*And fall apart in pieces.*

I felt that my husband had something to say. But instead he just walked away.

This tumultuous emotion that was crashing on the shores of the country, came into my life on a different note. The juggernaut of my Fate was approaching and the distant sound of its wheels was making my heart beat louder and faster. Every second I felt a strange and sublime phenomenon was almost upon me, and I wasn't at all responsible for it. Sin? The path that moved away from the spaces of sin and chastity, fair and legitimate, pity and sympathy had already opened up on its own. I had never desired this, never waited expectantly for this; if you look at my entire life, I was in no way answerable for this. All my life I had devoutly prayed and when it was time to grant the boon, a different God had come and stood in front of me! Just as the nation suddenly woke up, looked ahead and said 'Vande Mataram', my heart and soul and every nerve in my body today woke up to say 'Vande' to some unknown, exotic—something that defied explanation!

This was the peculiar similarity between the song in the heart of the country and in my own heart! Many a days I crept out of my bed silently, and went and stood on the terrace. Just beyond the boundary of our house lay the half-ripe paddy fields. To the north, the glistening river could be seen through the thick cover of trees in the village. Beyond that lay the forest. It was formless like the foetus of impending creation, sleeping nestled in the womb of the immense night. I looked ahead and saw my country standing there—a girl just like me. She used to be content in her own corner of the house. But suddenly she heard the call of the wild. She didn't have time to think. She just walked blindly into the dark. She didn't wait to light a little lamp. I knew, on that slumberous night, just how her breast heaved and fell. I knew that the distant flute called her thus, that she felt she was there already, she had found it and now she could even walk with her eyes closed and not be afraid anymore. This wasn't the mother who would remember that the house had to be swept, the lamps lit and the child fed. Today she was the lover. This was our nation in the days of the *Vaishnava Padabalis*. She had left her home and forgotten her duties. All she had was endless passion; fired by that passion she walked on, heedless of the road. I too was a traveller on the same tryst. I too had lost my home and my way. The goal and the means were both misty before me—all I knew was the passion and the journey. Oh nocturnal one, when the night would melt into the crimson dawn, you wouldn't even see a sign of the road back home. But why should I return—I'd rather die. If the darkness that summoned me with its flute destroyed me totally and left me with nothing, all my worries would be over. Everything would be destroyed; not a trace of me would remain. All my sins would mingle in the darkness; after that—what mattered laughter or sorrow, good or bad?

In those days, the time machine was in full steam in Bengal. Hence, even the impossible was becoming a reality in the blink of an eye. It began to feel as if even in that corner of Bengal where we lived, nothing could be stopped anymore. Until then, in those parts, the speed of events was a little slower than in the rest of Bengal. The main reason for that was that my husband didn't like to put any pressure on anyone. He used to say, 'Those who sacrificed for the country, are the great souls. But those who troubled others in the name of the nation, are the enemies. They want to hack away at the roots of freedom and nourish its trunk and leaves.'

But when Sandipbabu came and settled here, his followers began to move around and sometimes there were speeches in the marketplace and in public. The waves began to sway these parts too. A group of local youths joined up with Sandip. Many of them were notorious in the village for deeds best untold. But the flame of enthusiasm ignited from within and without and they glowed. It became clear that when there was elation in the nation's air, people's foibles disappeared on their own. If there was no joy in the country it was difficult for people to be healthy, straight and strong.

At this time, everyone noticed that imported salt, sugar and cloth were not yet banned from my husband's land. So much so, that even my husband's employees began to grow restless and mortified on this account. But, a few months ago when my husband had brought in the home-grown goods into this area, everyone here had laughed at him, either to themselves or openly. We had scoffed at them when the indigenous goods had no link with our heroism. Till date, my husband sharpened his home-grown pencil with the indigenous knife, wrote with the quill pen, drank from the brass pot and in the evening he read by lamplight. But this colourless brand of swadeshi didn't inspire us. On the contrary, I always felt ashamed of the lacklustre furniture in his living room, especially when the magistrate or any other foreigner came to visit. He always laughed and said, 'Why do you let such little things get to you?'

I said, 'But, they'll go away thinking we are uncouth and uncultured.'

He said, 'If they think that, I am free to think that their culture extends only till the polish of the fair skin and doesn't reach the red bloodstream of the world's humanity.'

There was a common brass pot on his desk which he used as a vase. Often, when a British visitor was expected, I hid that pot and replaced it with a colourful ceramic vase and placed flowers in it.

My husband would say, 'Bimal, my brass pot is as un-selfconscious as these flowers. But your foreign flower vase doggedly lets you know that it is a vase. I'd rather keep artificial flowers in it than real ones.'

My second sister-in-law gave my husband a lot of encouragement on this matter. Once she came up to him in a real rush and said, 'Thakurpo, I've heard that they've come out with an indigenous soap—of course, our days of using soap are over. But if it doesn't have animal fat, I'd like to use it. This is one bad habit I have picked up after coming to this house—I gave it up long ago, but still a bath doesn't feel complete without soap.'

That was enough to cheer up my husband. Crates of home-made soap began to arrive. Was that soap or lumps of clay? It was obvious that the foreign soaps that Mejorani used earlier, were still in use. These home-made soaps were just for washing her clothes.

Another day she came and said, 'Thakurpo, I believe they've come out with locally made pens. I really must have some. Please, I beg of you, get me a bunch of those—'

Thakurpo was thrilled to bits. All the sticks that were being passed off as pens in those days began to gather themselves in Mejorani's room. But that didn't matter to her because she was hardly into any form of writing. The daily accounts could have been written with a breadstick for all she cared. I noticed that the ancient ivory pen was still in her writing box and on the rare occasion when she wanted to write something, that was what she reached for. As a matter of fact, she used to enjoy these antics only to highlight the fact that I did not encourage my husband's whims. But there was no way I could explain this to my husband. If I tried, his face became so sullen and thunderous that I realized it was having the opposite effect. Trying to protect such people from being fooled only resulted in getting cheated yourself.

Mejorani loved sewing; one day when she was sewing, I spoke my mind to her, 'What is this! On one hand you drool when your Thakurpo mentions some locally made scissors; but when you sew, you have to have the foreign ones?'

Mejorani said, 'What's wrong with that? See how happy it makes him! I have grown up with him and I cannot hurt him as cheerfully as you can. He's a man and he doesn't have any other passion—one of them is playing around with all these indigenous things and the other deadly passion is you—that'll be the end of him!'

I said, 'All said and done, I don't think it's a good thing to say one thing and believe in something else.'

Mejorani laughed and said, 'Oh my simpleton, you seem to be as straight as a headmaster's cane. Women can't be that straight—simply because they are soft, they bend a little and there is no harm in that.'

I will never forget what she said—one of his deadly passions is you and that'll be the end of him.

Now I firmly believe that a man needs a passion, but it's best if it isn't a woman.

The market in Sukhsayar was the largest in our district. Every day there was a market on this side of the river and on the other side a big marketplace was set up every Saturday. This marketplace began to grow really busy only after the rains. The waters of the pond merged with the river and made the crossing easy. At that time the import of thread and warm clothes stepped up.

In those days there was a wave of revolt against foreign clothes, salt and sugar in the markets of Bengal. All of us were up in arms. Sandip came to me and said, 'Since we have this huge marketplace within our jurisdiction, we should turn it into a totally home-grown one. We must exorcise the foreign evil from this region.'

I agreed vehemently and said, 'Yes, we must.'

Sandip said, 'I have had many arguments with Nikhil on this score—I simply couldn't convince him. He says speeches are fine, but there should be no coercion.'

With a trace of self-importance, I said, 'Fine, leave that to me.'

I knew just how deep my husband's love was for me. If I had the least bit of sense, I'd have died of shame rather than go to him on that day and make demands on that love. But I had to prove to Sandip how powerful I was. In his eyes I was Shakti—the goddess of power! With his powers of articulation, he had explained to me time and again that the supreme Shakti revealed itself to different people in the form of a special person. He said, 'We are all wandering fervently in search of the "Radha" of the Vaishnava Idea. Only when we truly find her do we understand clearly the meaning of the flute that plays in our heart.' As he spoke, sometimes he began to sing:

*When you didn't show yourself, Radha, the flute did play.*
*Now that I have looked into your eyes, my tune has washed away.*
*Then, in many beats and tunes*
*I had cried for you all over the place.*
*Now, all my tears have taken Radha's form and turned into smiles.*

As I heard all this constantly, I forgot that I was Bimala. I was Shakti, I was rasa, I had no ties and all was possible for me; whatever I touched was recreated by me—my whole world was created anew by me. The autumn sky was not so golden before my heart touched it. Every single moment I rejuvenated that brave, that mystic—my devotee—that remarkable genius enlightened by knowledge, fired by courage and blessed with passion. I could palpably feel that I was infusing new life into him every moment; he was my creation. One day Sandip brought one of his favourite followers, Amulyacharan, to me after much persuasion. Within a second I saw his eyes lit by a different light; I realized he had glimpsed Mother Shakti and I knew that my creation had begun its process in his bloodstream. The next day Sandip came to me and said, 'What kind of a mantra is this—that boy is not the same anymore. Within minutes the flame within him has lit up. No one will be able to keep this fire of yours under a bushel. One by one they will come and light their lamps until the country will be ablaze in a festival of lights.'

I was intoxicated by this sense of my own glory and I decided to grant my disciple a boon. I also knew very well that no one could stop me from doing what I wanted to do.

That day I loosened my hair, combed it afresh and tied it again. My British teacher had taught me to draw the hair from around my neck and pile it high up into a knot, which was a favourite with my husband. He would say, 'God has chosen to reveal to me, a non-poet, instead of to Kalidasa, just how beautiful are a woman's neck and shoulders. Perhaps the poet would have likened it to the lotus stem. But I feel it is a burning torch with your dark knot raising its black flame upwards.' And he would reach for my naked shoulder—but alas, why bring that up now.

Then I sent for him. Long ago I used to send for him thus on many pretexts, true or false. Lately all such excuses had come to a stop and I had run out of fresh ideas.

## Nikhilesh

Panchu's wife was stricken by tuberculosis and she died. Panchu would have to atone for it. The society did its calculations and came up with a cost of twenty-three and a half rupees.

I was angry and I said, 'So what if you don't atone for it—what are you afraid of?'

He raised his patience-laden eyes, tired as a cow's, and said, 'I have a daughter; she has to be married off. Besides, my wife's last rites will also have to be done.'

I said, 'If there has been a sin, there has also been enough atonement in the last few months.'

He said, 'Well sir, that there has been! Some of my land had to be sold and some mortgaged to pay the doctor's bills. But if I don't give the necessary alms, and feed the Brahmins, there is no release.'

There was no point in arguing. I said to myself, 'When will those Brahmins, who are being fed, atone for their sins?'

Panchu had always lived on the edge of starvation. But his wife's illness and the subsequent expenses for the rituals threw him in at the deep end. He became a follower of a local hermit perhaps for some consolation. This offered him a new drug to dull the pain of his children being unfed and starving. He realized that life was nothing. Just as there was no joy, the sorrows were also mere dreams. Eventually, one night, he left his four children in the hovel and renounced his material aspirations.

I had no knowledge of any of this. My mind was fraught with the combat between accord and discord. My teacher didn't even tell me that he had taken in Panchu's children and was raising them alone. At the time his own son and daughter-in-law were in Rangoon. He was alone at home and all day he had to be at the school.

When a month had passed thus, one morning suddenly Panchu appeared. His 'renunciation' was a thing of the past. When his two elder children squatted at his lap, on the floor, and asked, 'Father, where did you go?', his youngest took over his lap and the third child, a girl, hugged him from behind and rested her cheeks on his back, he broke down. They just wouldn't stop. He said, 'Master-babu, I don't have the strength to feed them two square meals a day, and I don't have the strength to leave them and walk away. Why do I get beaten like this? What have I done to deserve this?'

Meanwhile his trade, the faint thread on which his survival depended, had gone to pieces. The first few days that he took refuge in the professor's home, turned into a permanent arrangement. He began to while away his time there and never mentioned going back to his own home. Finally Chandranathbabu said to him one day, 'Panchu, why don't you go on home? Your house will soon fall apart. Let me lend you some money. You can start a clothing business and pay me back gradually over a period of time.'

At first Panchu was a little upset. He felt the world was a place devoid of human sympathy, and when the professor made him sign a handnote before giving the money, he felt, 'What's the point of such help when I have to return the money in the end?'

The professor hated the idea of giving alms to someone and making them feel encumbered. He always said, 'Loss of dignity is equal to a loss of pedigree.'

After taking the money thus, Panchu couldn't really bring himself to really bow down low at the professor's feet. The professor smiled to himself. He always wanted a short greeting anyway. He says, 'I would like to respect and be respected in turn. That is my ideal relationship with others. I do not deserve any veneration.'

Panchu bought some clothes and winter-wear and began to sell it to the farmers. He got his payment in instalments. But similarly, the rice, jute or other crops that he got when he made the exchange, were a bonus. Within two months he was able to pay back the professor one instalment of the interest and also a part of the principal. This payback obviously also affected the length of the greeting once again. Panchu began to feel that it was a mistake to take the teacher for a great soul. He actually had his eye on the good old silver.

Thus Panchu's days passed. At this point, the wave of swadeshi swept through the countryside. The young boys from our village or the neighbouring ones, who went to school or college in Calcutta, came back for the holidays, some of them already having abandoned their studies. They appointed Sandip as their chief and wholeheartedly lent themselves to the task of spreading the swadeshi-message. Many of these boys had passed out of the free school run by me; a lot of them had scholarships borne by me. One day they came up to me in one big group and said, 'You'll have to ban foreign threads and clothes from the Sukhsayar market.'

I said, 'That is impossible.'

They said, 'Why? Will it affect your profits?'

I realized the barb was meant to hit home. I was about to retort, 'Not mine, but certainly the poor people's.'

My teacher was present. He exclaimed, 'Of course it will; that will never be your loss.'

They said, 'For the sake of the country—'

Chandranathbabu overrode what they were saying by exclaiming, 'The country is not just this land and soil, it is also the people. Have you ever bothered to spare these people a second glance? Today, suddenly you have woken up to the fact that you must decide what they'd eat and what they'd wear. Why should they tolerate that and why should we let them tolerate that?'

They replied, 'But we ourselves have also taken to indigenous salt, sugar and cloth.'

He said, 'You are all angry on a whim and that has given you the strength to do all this happily. You have the money and if you use a few paise more to buy homespun goods, they don't come and stop you. But what you want them to do is sheer abuse of power. They are caught in the fray of life every single day of their lives, struggling to just stay afloat—you cannot even imagine the value of a few paise to them—you have nothing in common with them. You spend your days in a different section of the palace of life; today you want to transfer your burden onto their shoulders, you want to use them to take the edge off your anger? I believe this is cowardice. You are free to take it as far as you wish, as far as you can go, even till death. I am an old man. I am ready to salute you as the leaders and follow in your footsteps. But if you trample on these poor people's freedom and sing songs in praise of liberty, I will personally stand in your way, even if it kills me.'

They were, nearly all of them, ex-students of the professor and so they couldn't retort to his face. But their blood was on the boil. They looked at me and said, 'Look, are you going to be the only one resisting the vow that the entire nation has taken today?'

I said, 'It is not my place to resist. On the contrary, I'll do my best to encourage it.'

An MA student smiled slyly and asked, 'How are you encouraging it?'

I said, 'I have stocked the homespun cloth and threads in our markets; we also send these out to other markets in the area—'

The student shouted, 'But we went to your market and saw that no one is buying these.'

I replied, 'For that, neither I nor the market is to blame. The only reason for that is that the whole country has not yet taken the same vow as you.'

Chandranathbabu said, 'Moreover, even those who have taken the vow seem more intent on causing havoc. You would like to force the uninitiated to buy the thread, weave the cloth and also buy the fabric. By what means? By force and the use of the zamindar's henchmen and their lathis. In other words, the vow is yours, but the ordinary people are the ones who'll fast and you will celebrate that fasting.'

A student of science asked, 'Fine, then go ahead and explain which part of the fasting have you yourselves undertaken?'

My teacher said, 'Do you want to know? Fine then, hear this: it is Nikhil who has to buy that thread from the indigenous mills. He sponsors the weavers who weave the cloth and conducts classes to train them. Given his business sense, by the time a towel is woven from those threads, it'll be worth the same as a piece of expensive silk. So he will buy that towel himself and hang it up as drapes in his drawing room; it wouldn't even cover the half of it. By that time if you are through with your vow, you'd be the first to laugh at the rustic designs on his curtains. If at all that coloured fabric is appreciated anywhere, it is by the British.'

I had been with him for so long, but never had I seen my teacher quite so upset. I realized that the grievance had been collecting in his soul over the past months, simply because he loved me so much. It was that pain that had chipped away at the dam of his patience, and finally given way.

A student of medicine spoke up, 'You are all elders and so we shan't argue with you. So, in a word you are saying that you will not ban the foreign goods from your markets?'

I said, 'No, I will not do that, because it is not mine to ban.'

The MA student smiled derisively and said, 'You won't because that'll cut into your profits.'

My teacher confirmed, 'Yes it will, and so it is entirely his business.'

Thereafter all the students shouted 'Vande Mataram' and walked out.

A few days later, Chandranathbabu brought Panchu to me. What was up?

'His landlord, zamindar Harish Kundu had fined Panchu a hundred rupees.'

'Why, what did he do?'

'He sold foreign cloth. He went to the zamindar and fell at his feet saying that he had bought this cloth with money taken on loan and once these were sold off, he would never do such a thing again. The zamindar said, "Impossible. Burn the cloth in front of me and only then will I let you go." Panchu couldn't take it. He shouted, "I cannot afford it, I am poor; you have enough. Why don't you buy the cloth and then burn it?" At this the zamindar flared up and said, "You bastard, your tongue wags too much—give him the shoe." One round of humiliation followed and then he was fined a hundred rupees. These are the kind that follow Sandip around, shouting Vande Mataram. These are the so-called servants of the land.'

'What happened to the cloth?'

'Burnt.'

'Who else was there?'

'Hordes of people. They began to shout Vande Mataram. Sandip was also there. He picked up a handful of ash and said, "Brothers, this is the first time the pyre of foreign commerce has been lit in your village. These ashes are sacred. You will have to smear these ashes on yourselves in order to work towards ripping away the shroud of Manchester and turning into naked saints."'

I said to Panchu, 'Panchu, you'll have to go to court.'

Panchu said, 'No one will bear witness.'

'No one—Sandip, Sandip, come here.'

Sandip came out of his room and said, 'What is the matter?'

'This man's bag of cloth was burnt by his zamindar in front of your eyes. Won't you bear witness?'

'Of course I will,' Sandip laughed, 'But I am a witness for his zamindar.'

I said, 'How can you be a witness *for* someone? You'll be a witness for the Truth.'

Sandip said, 'And the Truth is merely what has taken place, is it?'

I asked, 'What is the other Truth?'

Sandip said, 'That which *should* take place. The Truth that we need to formulate. Many lies are needed to make the Truth just as many illusions are needed to make the world. Those who have come into this world solely to create, they do not accept Truth, they formulate it.'

'Hence—'

'Hence, I will be a witness for that which you call a lie. Such false witness has been proudly presented at the courtroom of your Truth by those that have colonized, built empires, formed societies and framed religions. Those who will rule need not fear lies. The iron shackles of Truth are meant for those who will be ruled. Haven't you read history? Don't you know that in the largest kitchens of the world where the mishmash of politics and civics is cooked up, the ingredients are all lies?'

'That may be true of history, but—'

'Oh no, why should you cook that mishmash, instead you'll be forced to gobble it, right? They'll split up Bengal and claim it is for you; they'll close down the doors of education and claim that it is with every good intention towards you; you will be saintly and shed tears and we shall be evil and build fortresses out of lies. Your tears won't stay, but our forts will.'

Chandranathbabu said to me, 'Don't argue over this, Nikhil. If a man is incapable of comprehending that the great Truth within us all is the root of everything, he cannot ever comprehend that man is finally meant to unveil that Truth from all its shrouds and not to create a debris outside oneself.'

Sandip laughed and said, 'You have spoken like a true teacher. These words are fit for the pages of a book. But my eyes tell me that it is man's aim to make a huge pile of things outside oneself. And the people who have achieved that aim successfully are telling lies in bold letters on commercial advertisements every day. They fill in fake figures in the ledgers of civic management, their newspapers are full of lies and just as flies are carriers of the dengue fever, these people's followers spread the message of deception. I am their disciple. When I was with the Congress, I didn't hesitate to to add ninety per cent water to the ten per cent Truth, in accordance with the market conditions. Today I have left the party and I still believe in the principle that it is success and not Truth that is the goal of mankind.'

Chandranathbabu said, 'The fruit of Truth.'

Sandip said, 'Yes, it takes many a lie to grow that fruit. The ground beneath one's feet has to be mashed into a pulp before that fruit can grow. And the Truth, that which grows by itself, is the weed, the wild flower. Those who expect fruits from that plant are the biggest fools of all.'

Sandip finished speaking and stormed out of the room. Chandranathbabu smiled a little, looked at me and said, 'Do you know something, Nikhil? Sandip is not a-religious, he is anti-religion. He is the new moon; no doubt, he is the moon, but circumstances have forced him to rise opposite the full moon.'

I said, 'That is why he and I have never agreed on anything. He has harmed me a lot and will do more harm to me. But I cannot bring myself to disrespect him.'

He said, 'I am beginning to understand that. I have often wondered how you have tolerated Sandip for so long. In fact, at times I have suspected that you are weak in doing so. But now I can see that the two of you may not speak the same words, but you have the same rhythm.'

I spoke in jest, 'Friends in amity have caused enmity. Perhaps Fate has in store another epic in blank verse for our lives.'

Chandranathbabu said, 'Now what should we do about Panchu?'

I said, 'You had once told me that the land on which Panchu's house stands, is ancestral property and has come to belong to him. His zamindar has been trying to get him off that land for a while. Why don't I buy that land and make him my subject?'

'And the hundred rupees' fine?'

'How can they realize that? The land belongs to me now.'

'And the bag of cloth?'

'I will send for more. As my subject he will be allowed to sell whatever he wants, wherever he wants.'

Panchu folded his hands and said, 'Sire, in the battle of kings there'll be a crowd of policemen, lawyers and many such vultures, watching the fun. But I'll be the only one to die.'

'Why, what will they do to you?'

'They'll set my house on fire and I'll die, along with the children.'

Chandranathbabu said, 'All right, let your children stay with me for the next few weeks. Don't be afraid. You are free to do business from your own home, no one will lay a finger on you. I will not allow you to run away, defeated by a wrong done to you. The more you bear, the more the burden grows.'

That same day I bought Panchu's land, registered it and laid my claims on it. Then the squabble started.

Panchu's property belonged to his maternal grandfather. Everyone knew that Panchu was his sole heir. But suddenly a maternal uncle's wife materialized, laying claims to the inheritance, and settled down in his house with her bags, bundles, sacred books and a young widowed daughter. Surprised, Panchu said, 'But my aunt died long ago.'

Her reply was, 'Your uncle's first wife may have died, but the second one came soon enough.'

'But my aunt died long after my uncle's death and so there really wouldn't have been time for a second wife.'

The woman admitted that the second marriage had taken place before and not after death. She didn't want to share space with her co-wife and so she'd stayed in her father's house. When her husband died, she renounced the material world and went to Vrindavan. Some of the officers of the zamindar, Kundu, were aware of all this and perhaps some of the subjects knew about it too; if the zamindar hollered loud enough, then even some of the people who had eaten the wedding feast would surely crawl out of the woodwork.

That afternoon, when I was thoroughly preoccupied with this new hassle in Panchu's life, suddenly Bimala sent for me from her chambers.

I was startled. I asked, 'Who has called?'

The bearer said, 'Ranima.'

'The eldest one?'

'No, the youngest.'

The youngest one—I felt as if a hundred years had passed since she had last sent for me.

I left everyone sitting in the drawing room and went into the inner chambers. In the bedroom I was even more surprised to see Bimala had cared to dress up a little. For a while now this room had begun to look quite untidy; everything was so cluttered up that it felt like the room was also preoccupied. Today, I noticed that the room looked a little like its old self.

I stood silently looking at Bimala. She blushed a little, twisted the bangles on her left wrist with her right hand and said, 'Listen, in all of Bengal our market is the only one stocking foreign cloth; does it look good?'

I asked, 'What will be the best thing to do?'

'Why don't you tell them to throw those things away?'

'But those things do not belong to me.'

'But the market is yours.'

'It belongs much more to those people who come there to buy and sell.'

'Why can't they buy indigenous goods?'

'I'd be happy if they do buy it, but if they don't?'

'What? How can they dare to? You are after all—'

'I don't have much time; what is the point of arguing over this? I cannot bring myself to exploit people.'

'The exploitation is not for your gain, it is for the sake of the country—'

'I suppose you won't understand that torturing for the sake of the country is the same as torturing the country itself.' I left. Suddenly, I felt the whole world was alight in front of my eyes. The weight of the earthly world lifted from my shoulders. Suddenly I perceived how, for an eternity, the earth hurtled through the skies by a strange force, turning night and day like a sacred chant in spite of nurturing the life forms placed on her and maintaining a balance between all the changes and evolution that she undergoes. Responsibilities were endless, but so was freedom. No one, but no one, will ever tie me down. Suddenly, a deep fount of joy sprang from my mind like a swollen wave from the ocean's breast, and reached for the clouds.

I asked myself again and again, what was the matter with me? At first there was no clear answer. And then it became quite clear: the impasse that had tortured me all these days had suddenly ended. As clearly as the glass on a photograph, I could see all of Bimala's actions in my mind's eye. It became obvious that Bimala had dressed herself up to get something from me. Until this day, I had never learnt to see Bimala's dressing up as separate from her. But today her western-styled chignon seemed a mere pile of hair; moreover, there was a time when this chignon was priceless to me and today I realized it was ready to be sold for a lot less.

Sandip and I argued about patriotism every step of the way. Those were real differences. But the words that Bimala spoke in the name of the country, were coming from Sandip's mouth and not from a greater Idea. If Sandip changed his words, so would Bimala. I could see all this very clearly—all traces of the fog had lifted.

As I left the broken nest of my bedroom and emerged into the open air of the autumn noon, I saw a bunch of mynahs chattering in great excitement in my garden. To the south of the garden lay the cobbled path, lined by rows of kanchan trees that overwhelmed the skies with the scent of their pink blossoms which were in abundance. In the distance, by the winding village road the empty bullock cart lay upturned and the two cows, no longer yoked, were roaming free. One was chewing grass and the other basked in the sun while a crow sat on its back, pecking away at its hide as the cow closed its eyes in sheer bliss. At this moment I felt I had suddenly come very close to the soul of this universe which was very simple and yet so profound; its warm breath fanned my heart as the fragrance of those kanchan flowers. I felt that I did exist, and so did everything else; this created a feeling—deep, munificent and indescribably beautiful within me.

The next moment I remembered Panchu, stuck in the mire of poverty and cunning. I thought I saw Panchu amidst that pensive grassland in the autumn noon, lying with his eyes closed, just like the cow—not from bliss but from sheer exhaustion, weariness and starvation. He seemed to personify all the poor farmers of Bengal. I caught a glimpse of the severely religious Harish Kundu, forehead marked with sacred sandal paste. He was no mean feat. He was huge too. He was like a layer of oily green floating on the ancient, rotting pond beneath the bamboo clump, covering it entirely and giving out toxic vapours by the second.

Eventually I would have to fight with those shadows that lay emaciated, tired and blinded by ignorance on the one hand, and on the other hand those that had thrived on the blood of the poor and was crushing the earth under its own immovable weight. This task had been kept aside for many hundred years. Let my trance break, my daze disappear and my manhood be freed from the ineffective mesh of the inner chambers. We are men, freedom is our goal, we shall hark the call of the Ideal and rush forth, we must scale the walls of the demon king and rescue the goddess trapped within. The girl who makes the victory badge for us with her deft fingers is our true partner. We must see through the masquerade of the girl who sits by the door and weaves her spells on us, we must see her true form without illusions—we shouldn't dress her up in the colours of our own dreams and desires and send her out to distract us. Today I felt I shall be a winner. I stand on the straight road; I can see everything clearly. I have been freed and I have also freed—my salvation lies where my work is.

I know there will come a day when my heart will be wracked by pain again. But now I am familiar with that pain. I can no longer respect it. I know it is mine and mine alone—does it really have any value? The pain of the world will grace my brow. Oh Truth, save me, help me. Don't let me go back to that fake world of illusion and artifice. If you must make me a lone traveller on a solitary journey, let the road lead to you. Today I have heard your drums within my soul.

## Sandip

That day the dam of tears was on the verge of giving way. Bimala sent for me, but she was silent for a while, her eyes glistening with unshed tears. I knew she had failed with Nikhil. She had been certain that she would somehow get the results, though I had no such hopes. Women know the weak spots of men, but sometimes find it hard to fathom their strengths. In reality, men are a mystery to women and vice versa. If that wasn't the case, the difference between the two sexes would have been a superfluous creation of Nature.

Indignation! It was not about the important task not being fulfilled. The indignation was all about not being granted what she asked for so plainly. There is no end to the shades of gestures, tears, games over this demand of the 'I' that women have. That is what makes them so sweet. They are much greater egoists than we are. When the Maker made us, He was the schoolteacher, His tools were theories and notes. But when their time came, He had resigned from his job and become an artist; His tools were a brush and paints.

Hence, when Bimala stood there on the edge of the setting sun like a tearful, fiery red cloud coloured by that melancholy distress, I found her very sweet. I went close to her and took her hand. She trembled but didn't take her hand away. I said, 'Bee, we are co-workers, we have the same goals. Now sit down.'

I sat her down on a stool. Wonderful. All that emotion and it took just this to clamp it shut. The monsoon-floods of the Padma that were rushing forth, seemingly not prepared to stop for anything or anyone, suddenly appeared to change its course and began to flow smoothly between its banks again. I took her hand in mine and pressed them, every nerve end in my body playing like the strings of a bow; but why did it have to stop at the first two notes, why couldn't it complete the aria? I realized that the bottomless depths of the flow of life are formed by many years of conduct. When the flood of desire gushed briskly enough, in places it was strong enough to erode that course and in places it met its match. There was a deep-rooted restraint within me, what *was* it? It was not just one thing, but many things tangled together. So I could never figure it out, but I knew it was an impediment. What I really was would never stand a court inquisition and be a writ of law. I was a mystery to myself and that's why I loved myself so much; if I knew that 'I' completely, it would be so easy to root it out, discard it and reach a state of nirvana.

As Bimala sat on the stool watching me, her face paled. She knew in her heart that one of her problems no longer existed. The comet had zoomed past her, but the whiplash of its tail left her feeling enervated for a while. In order to get her out of the stupor, I said, 'There are obstacles, but we shouldn't regret them. We will fight, won't we, Queen?'

Bimala coughed a little to clear her throat and then just said, 'Yes.'

I said, 'Let us work out the details of the plan for our actions in the future.'

I took out a pencil and paper from my pocket and began to discuss how I would delegate work amongst the boys who had come to join us from Calcutta. Suddenly Bimala said, 'Not now, Sandipbabu, I'll come again at five o'clock; we can talk then.' She got up and quickly left the room.

I realized that she simply couldn't bring herself to concentrate on what I was saying; she needed to be alone with herself for a while. Perhaps she'd have to throw herself on the bed and weep for some time.

When Bimala left, the atmosphere in the room became headier. My mood seemed to get tipsier just as the sky is tinged with more pink after the sun actually sets. I began to feel I had let the moment pass. What kind of weakness was this? Perhaps Bimala went away disgusted with my inexplicable hesitation. Possible.

At this time, when my blood was throbbing with the effects of this inebriation, a bearer came and informed me that Amulya wanted to see me. For a moment I wanted to send him on his way, but before I could make up my mind, he came into the room.

Then it was back to news of the battle of salt-sugar-cloth. The heady feeling evaporated. I felt like the dream had snapped. I got ready for battle and off to the battlefield it was.

The news was this: Kundu's subjects who used to bring stuff to the market had finally come around. The officers in Nikhil's employ were all secretly on our side. They were supplying the inside information. The Marwaris were begging to be allowed to sell the foreign cloth in exchange for a fine, or they'd go bankrupt. The Muslims were refusing to give in.

A farmer had bought some cheap German shawls for his children. Some of our boys from the local villages had grabbed the shawls from him and burnt them. That had caused a furore. We offered to buy him some desi warm clothes. But there were no cheap desi warm clothes to be found. Obviously we couldn't buy him Kashmiri shawls. He came and put his case before Nikhil. He ordered him to lodge a complaint against the boys. The local officers had taken the responsibility of seeing to it that the complaint didn't go through smoothly; their chief was also on our side.

The point was, if we had to buy desi cloth for those whose things we burnt, and then also pay for the court case, where were we supposed to get that kind of funds from? And all this burning would hot up the market for foreign fabrics. When the nawab was so taken with the sound of breaking glass that he went around smashing all his chandeliers, the glassblowers had the time of their lives.

The second question was: there weren't any cheap desi warm clothes to be had. Now in winter, should we allow the foreign shawls, wrappers and merino to stay or not?

I said, 'We will not gift desi clothes to the man who wants to buy foreign clothes. He is the one to be punished, not us. If they went to court, we would set their crops on fire; the gentle approach wouldn't work. Hey Amulya, don't look so shocked. I don't get my kicks out of setting the farmer's crops on fire. But this is war. If you are afraid to hurt, go and have fun, be genteel and keel over with love.'

And the foreign warm clothes? Whatever the inconvenience, those will not be allowed to stay. We cannot have a compromise with the foreign stuff under any circumstances, in any condition. When there were no foreign wrappers to be had, the farmer's children double-wrapped their cloth and kept themselves warm. That's what they'd have to do again. I know that wouldn't satisfy them, but this wasn't the time for satisfaction.

We had somehow, by hook or by crook, managed to bring around some of those who brought the shipments to the markets by boat. Mirjan, the most powerful of them all, refused to give an inch. We asked Kulada, the chief-clerk here, if Mirjan's boat could be sunk. He said, of course it could, but the blame would eventually come to rest at his door. I said the blame shouldn't be kept so loose that it could come to rest anywhere; but if at all it came to that, I'd come forward and take it.

At the end of the market-day, Mirjan's empty boat was docked at the pier. There were no boatmen in it. The chief-clerk had cleverly invited them to a show nearby. That night the boat was set adrift with a hole in it and bags of rubbish piled into it.

Mirjan understood. He came to me, weeping and with folded hands, 'Sire, I was wrong. Now—'

I said, 'How did you come to figure it out so clearly just now?'

He didn't answer that, but said, 'Sire, that boat was worth two thousand rupees, if not more. Now I have come to my senses, if you please forgive me this one time—'

He fell at my feet. I told him to come again in another ten days or so. I could buy his loyalty for two thousand rupees. We needed to have people like this on our side. I needed to get hold of some money quickly.

That evening when Bimala came into the room, I stood up and said, 'Queen, the work is almost done; now we need money.'

Bimala said, 'Money? How much?'

I said, 'Not much, but I need the money somehow.'

Bimala asked, 'Tell me how much money you need.'

I said, 'Right now, about fifty thousand would do.'

Bimala was shaken to hear the amount, but she hid it well. How could she say she wasn't up to it, again and again?

I said, 'Queen, you can make the impossible happen. You have done it too. If I could show you what you have achieved, you'd have seen it too. But this is not the time for it; perhaps another day. Now we need the money.'

Bimala said, 'I'll get it.'

I knew that she had decided to sell her ornaments. I said, 'Don't touch your ornaments now. You never know what might come up in future.'

Bimala stood there staring at me.

'You'll have to get this money from your husband's funds.'

Bimala was struck speechless. A little later she said, 'How can I take his money?'

'But isn't his money yours too?'

With anguished emotion she said, 'No.'

I said, 'In that case it isn't his either; it belongs to the country. When the country is in need of it, Nikhil has kept it away from her, stolen it from her.'

Bimala asked, 'How will I get that money?'

'By hook or by crook; you can do it. You will bring the money back to its rightful owner. Vande Mataram. Today this chant of "Vande Mataram" will break open the iron chest, bring down the walls of the store room and it would pierce the hearts of those who, in the name of faith, refuse to bow down to its power. Bee, say it with me: Vande Mataram.'

'Vande Mataram.'

We are men, we are kings, we have the right to collect tax. Ever since we have stepped onto this earth, we have been looting it. The more we have demanded from her, the more homage she has paid us. We are men: since the beginning of time we have plucked and plundered, chopped down trees, dug up the soil, killed animals, birds and fish. From the depths of the ocean, the womb of the earth and from the jaws of death, we have only ever seized. We are the male species. We have not spared a single iron chest ordained by God; we have pillaged and seized.

The earth takes pleasure in satisfying the male of the species. Day in and day out, the earth has met our demands and thus grown greener, more beautiful and more fulfilled; or else, she would have stayed shrouded in woods and forests and never found her true self. All the doors to her heart would have been locked, her diamonds would have stayed buried in mines and the pearls of the oyster would never have seen the light of day.

By the sheer force of our demands, we the men, have discovered the women today. In the process of giving themselves to us constantly, they have found themselves more fully, more completely. Only when they come to submit the solitaires of their joy and the pearls of their sorrow to our treasury do they get a true sense of those jewels. Thus, for men to take is the best charity and for women to give is most profitable.

I have placed a tall order before Bimala. At first I had a doubt: was this in my nature or was it just a petty squabble with my own self? I felt this was a bit harsh. Just once I thought of calling her back and saying forget it, don't go into all this. Why should I stir up your life like this? For that moment I forgot that this was the reason why the male species was an active one: we are meant to stir up the lives of the passive ones and make it a life worth living. If we hadn't made the women weep for so many years, the door to the vast treasury of their grief would have stayed shut forever. The male was meant to make the universe weep and gratify it thus. Why else would his hands be so strong, his fist so powerful?

Bimala's very self desired that I, Sandip, should make a heavy demand on her, call upon her to stake her life. She wouldn't be fulfilled otherwise. She had been waiting for me only because she hadn't been able to express her emotions through tears all these years. She had been so happy for so long that the moment she looked at me, the blue clouds of grief moved over her horizon. If I took pity on her and tried to dry her tears, then I would not be doing my duty.

Actually the reason for my slight hesitation was that this was a demand for money. Money belonged to men. Asking for it brought an element of beggary into it all. Hence I had to make the amount a hefty one. If it were a few thousand, there'd be a strong stench of pilfering. But fifty thousand was a veritable raid.

Moreover, I should really have been very rich. All these years I have had to stifle many desires for the sheer lack of money. This was something that didn't sit well on me of all people. If this was a fault of my Fate, I'd have let it pass; but this was indecent, tasteless. If I have to scrounge to pay my rent and dip into my moneybag only to come up with the fare for an intermediate class when I travel by train, it was not just pathetic but ludicrous. It was clear to me that for someone like Nikhil the ancestral property was quite superfluous. Poverty would have suited him just as well. He would have, quite easily, kept his Chandranathbabu company in a decrepit old buggy.

Just once, I want to have fifty thousand rupees in my hands and blow it in two days, on my own comforts and a few deeds for the country. I want to shed this poor man's disguise and look at the real me, the rich me, in the mirror just once.

But I don't think Bimala would be able to procure the money easily. Perhaps eventually it'll come down to the few thousand after all. Well, so be it. 'It is wise to forego half'—so they say. But since the sacrifice is not by my choice, the wisdom lies in foregoing eighty or even ninety nine per cent.

All that I have written so far are vital matters; I will go back to it in detail again later when I have the time. Now there is none. The chief-clerk of this place has asked me to meet him immediately; I've heard something has gone wrong.

The chief-clerk said that the police suspect the man who drowned the boat. The man was a veteran and he was now in custody. It would be difficult getting him to talk. But it was a matter of time and since Nikhil was upset, the clerk couldn't do anything too obvious. He said, 'Look, if I get into trouble, I'll drag you with me.'

I asked him, 'Where are the ropes by which you'll hang me?'

The clerk said, 'I have one letter written by you and three written by Amulyababu.'

Now I understood why the clerk had written to me and got me to send a reply; it served no other purpose. These wiles were new to me. The clerk had enough respect for me to know that I could drown my friend as easily as I did my foe. The respect would have increased if I had answered the letter verbally rather than given a written reply.

Now the point was, the police had to be bribed. If the matter worsened, then we'd have to settle out of court and offer compensation to the man whose boat we drowned. It was also clear to me that in this vile mesh being woven, the clerk would come by his fair share of the profits. But I couldn't say any of this. On the face of it, I was saying 'Vande Mataram' and he was also saying 'Vandę Mataram'.

The fixtures that one has to deal with to do this work are often below par. I suppose a conscience is so ingrained within us, that at first I felt very angry with the chief-clerk. I was about to write some very harsh words in this diary regarding the fraudulence of our countrymen. But if there is a God, I owe him this debt of gratitude: he has given me a clear mind. Nothing, both within and without, ever remains unclear to me. I may fool others but never could I fool myself. And that's why I couldn't stay angry for too long. The truth is never good or bad, it is merely the truth and that is empirical. Water bodies are formed only by the water that remains after the earth has sucked up as much water as it wants to. The layer of soil below our 'Vande Mataram' was bound to absorb some water and both the clerk and I were a part of that process. What will remain after that absorption, will be the true Vande Mataram. We may curse it and call it deceit, but this is the Truth and it has to be accepted. At the bottom of every noble deed in this world, there is a layer of pure filth, even at the bottom of the ocean. Hence, in doing noble deeds, one must take into account this filth and its demands. So, the clerk would grab some and so would I: it was all a part of the greater need. Feeding the horse some grains wasn't enough, the wheels also have to be oiled.

Anyway, money was sorely needed. I couldn't wait for the fifty thousand. I'd have to collect whatever I could, right now. I know that on the face of such pressing needs one has to let go of the larger goals of the future. A bird in hand is worth two in the bush after all. That's why I tell Nikhil that those who walk the road of surrender never have to curb their greed; but those who choose the path of greed have to surrender it every step of the way. I had to forego my fifty thousand—this was something Nikhil's Chandranathbabu never had to do. Of the seven deadly sins, the first three and the last two are common to man and the two in the middle are for cowards. Lust is fine, but there should be no greed and no envy. Otherwise lust turns to dust. Envy clings to the past and the future. It can waylay the present with ease. Those who cannot concentrate on the immediate present, those who dance to a different drummer's beat, they are like the sad lover, Shakuntala: they fail to attend to the guest at hand and the curse makes them lose the distant one for whom they yearn.

Today I had held Bimala's hand and she was still under that spell. I too was bound by that spell. This echo had to be kept alive. If I were to repeat it often and bring it down to the level of the mundane, then today's symphony would turn into a cacophony tomorrow. Now Bimala was incapable of questioning any of my demands. Some people need illusions to survive—why cut down on it? Right now I have a lot of work; so for now, let this cup of love skim the mere surface. Drinking the last dregs now would only stir up trouble. When the right time comes, I shall not gainsay it either. Oh lustful one, forfeit your greed and master the instrument of envy, playing it like the maestro.

Meanwhile, our work was on a roll. Our group had infiltrated deep inside and set up a stronghold. A lot of cajoling and sweet talk made me realize one thing: the Muslims were not going to come round by coaxing. They'd have to be subdued and shown who was the boss in no uncertain terms. Today they bare their fangs at us; but one day we'll make them dance to our tune.

Nikhil says, 'If India is a true entity, then Muslims are a part of it.'

I say, 'That may be so. But we need to know which part of it they are and then squash them right there, or they'd be bound to revolt.'

Nikhil says, 'Do you think you can quell the revolt by stepping it up?'

I say, 'What is your plan?'

Nikhil says, 'There is only one way to resolve the difference.'

I know that every one of Nikhil's arguments is bound to end in a moral, just like the didactic writings of a philosopher. The strange thing is that even after fiddling around with these maxims for so many years, he still actually believes in them. No wonder I say that Nikhil is a born pupil. Fortunately, he is made of genuine stuff. Like Chand-saudagar of the *Manasamangal*, he has initiated himself into the mantra of fantasy; the bite of reality may kill him but he won't accept it. The problem is that for people like this, death is no final proof. They have closed their eyes and decided that there is something beyond it.

For a while now, I have formulated a plan. If I can bring it to fruition, the entire country will be ablaze. The people of our land won't wake up to her unless they can actually see her. They need a goddess with a form to denote the country. My friends liked the idea. They said, 'Fine, let us build an idol.' I said, 'Our building it won't work. We'll have to use the idol that has always been in worship and make her the symbol of the country. The channels of devotion run deep in our land and we'll have to use the same to channelize the devotion towards the country.'

Nikhil and I had an argument over this a while back. He said, 'If I consider a task to be true and genuine, I cannot use illusions as a means.'

I said, 'Yes, but sweetmeats do win you friends; the common man has to have his illusions and three-fourths of this world is made up of common men. It is to keep these illusions alive that every country has formulated its own gods. Man knows himself.'

Nikhil said, 'Gods are for breaking illusions; only demons keep them in place.'

Fair enough, let them be demons, but they are essential to get the work done. The problem is, in our land, all the illusions are in their place. We pay homage to them and yet, do not put them to good use. Take the Brahmins for example: we bow to them, give them alms and yet we never utilize them. If we used their superiority to the fullest, we could take the world by storm because there is a bunch of people in this world who are doormats and they are the largest in number. They cannot accomplish much in life unless they get trod upon. Illusion is a means to make these people work. All this while we have sharpened these people as weapons and now the time has come to put them to use—I can't put them away now.

But it was impossible to get Nikhil to see this point. Truth was lodged in his mind as firmly as a prejudice, as though Truth was an absolute, empirical given. I have told him many a time, in situations where falsehood was the Truth, it *was* the Truth. It was because our country knew this for a fact that it was said in olden days that for the ignorant the lie was the Truth. If he moved away from it, he would be deflecting the Truth. The man who could accept an idol as the symbol of the country would actually be working on that as the Truth. Given our nature and culture, it wasn't easy for us to accept the nation in its abstraction, but we could easily accept the symbol. Since this was a fact, the ones who wanted results would work on this premise and work effectively.

Nikhil got very agitated and exclaimed, 'Just because you have lost the capacity to strive for the Truth, you want an instant reward to fall into your lap. That's why for hundreds of years, when all the work is left undone, you have turned the nation into a goddess and sat in front of her praying for a boon.'

I said, 'The impossible must be achieved and that's why the nation has to be a goddess.'

Nikhil said, 'In other words, you are not interested in achieving that which is attainable but must be striven for. Everything should stay as it is and the consequences alone should be miraculous.'

I said, 'Nikhil, your words are mere advice. It may be a good thing at a certain age, but not when a man's teeth are itching to bite. I can see it right before my eyes: the harvest that I have never sown is flourishing and growing. On what basis? It is because I can see my nation as a goddess. Turning this into an eternal symbol is the need of the day. A genius doesn't argue, he creates. I will give shape to what the nation thinks today. I will go from one house to another saying the goddess has appeared in my dreams and she wants homage. We will go to the Brahmins and say you are the true priests of the goddess and since you're not giving her her dues, you have lost your status. You'd say I am lying. No, this is the truth. Millions of people all over the country are waiting to hear these words from my lips and that is why it is the truth. If I can successfully spread my own message, you'd see the miraculous results for yourself.'

Nikhil said, 'But how long would I live? Even after the results you would hand to the nation now there may be other far-reaching consequences, which may not be so apparent now.'

I said, 'I want the consequences of here and now, only those are mine.'

Nikhil said, 'I want the consequences of tomorrow, only those belong to everybody.'

Fact of the matter is, perhaps Nikhil had his fair share of that gift so common to Bengalis: imagination. But a parasite of a plant called morality grew around and over it and nearly crushed the life out of it. The worship of Durga or Jagatdhatri that the Bengali had initiated in India was an amazing display of his true nature. I am very certain that this goddess is a political being. These two goddesses are different forms of that spirit of the nation to whom people prayed at the time of the Mughal rule, asking for strength to overthrow the enemy. No other people of India have been able to come up with such external manifestations of their enterprise. It was apparent that Nikhil's imagination had died entirely when he said to me, 'At least when the Muslims took up arms against the Marathas or the Sikhs, they held their own weapons and wanted victory. Bengalis placed the weapons in the hands of the goddess, mumbled some mantras and hoped for victory; but the nation is not a goddess and the only victory was the sacrifice of some goats and of bulls. The day we will work for the welfare of the nation, is the day we will get our reward from the true deity.'

The problem is that on paper Nikhil's words sound very nice. But my words are not meant for paper; they are to be engraved on the nation's heart with a branding iron. It is not the kind of farming the pundit theorizes about in books but the kind of dreams the farmer etches out on the earth's bosom with his plough.

When I met Bimala I said, 'Is it possible to realize that deity, the one for whose homage we have come into this world after a thousand births, until She appears before me in tangible form? How many times have I told you that if I hadn't seen you, I would never have visualized my nation as one entity? I don't know if you understand me. It is very difficult to explain that gods may stay hidden in the heavens, but they are visible on this earth.'

Bimala looked at me strangely and said, 'I have understood you very well.' For the first time, she addressed me with the informal 'you' as opposed to the formal equivalent.

I said, 'Krishna was not just Arjun's charioteer; he had a more colossal form and when Arjun perceived that, he realized the whole Truth. In this entire land I have perceived that colossal form of yours. Ganga-Brahmaputra are the strands of pearls gracing your neck; in the line of forest on the distant banks of the blue river I have glimpsed the lashes of your kohl-black eyes; the young rice fields undulate with the shadow of your striped sari rippling through them; I have glimpsed your cruelty in that raging summer sky, panting like a desert lion with its red tongue lolling. When the goddess has deigned to grant her devotee such a miraculous vision, I have decided to spread the word of her homage in the entire land and only then will my countrymen come alive. "It is your form that I build in every temple." But everyone hasn't quite understood it yet. So I have decided to create the statue of my deity with my own hands, before all the people of this land and worship her in a way that will help everybody believe in her. Grant me that boon, give me that strength.'

Bimala's eyes were half closed. She sat still like a statue, almost one with her seat. Had I spoken some more, she would have fainted. A little later she opened her eyes and said, 'Oh voyager of destruction, you have set out on the road and there is no one who can stop you. I can see that no one can come in the way of your desires. The king would come to lay down his sceptre before you, the rich would come to donate all his wealth to you and even those who do not have anything, would be gratified to lay down their lives at your feet. Ethics and principles, morals and values would all fly away. Oh my Lord, my God, I do not know what you have seen in me, but I have just glimpsed your colossal form in the midst of my heart. It reduces me to nothing. Lord, oh Lord, what a tremendous force it is. It will not rest until it has destroyed me completely; I cannot take it anymore, I cannot bear this pain.' She fell to the ground, reached for my feet and lay there sobbing, sobbing and sobbing.

This *was* hypnotism! This was the way to win the world. This magic spell was better than any other method. Who said Truth wins the day? Victory to illusion! Bengalis have realized that and hence they started worshipping the goddess with ten hands and placed her astride a lion. The same Bengali will build another goddess today and win the world with mesmerism. Vande Mataram!

I picked her up gently and made her sit on the stool. Before the weariness hit her after all this excitement, I quickly said, 'The goddess has assigned me to reinstate her in this land, but I am a poor man.'

Bimala's face was still red, her eyes misted with tears. She spoke in an emotion-laden voice, 'You and poor. Everything that anyone has belongs to you. Why do I have a box full of jewellery? Please seize all my jewels and gems for your work—I don't need any of them.'

Once before too, Bimala had offered me her jewellery. I baulk at nothing but this was my limit. It bothered me because traditionally it was the man who decked the woman with jewellery and hence, taking it from a woman would feel like a blow to my manhood.

But I had to get beyond myself. I wasn't the one taking it. It was for the worship of the Mother and all of it would go for that. The puja would be so glamorous that no one ever would have seen anything like it. In the history of the new Bengal, this would be enshrined for all times to come. It would be my greatest gift to the country. The fools of the land worship the deity; Sandip *creates* the deity.

So much for the big talk. The small talk was also required. As of now I had to have at least three thousand, five thousand would be even better. But could I possibly broach the topic of money at an emotional time like this? Time was running out. I trampled upon my hesitations and spoke up, 'Queen, the treasury is almost empty and the work is grinding to a halt.'

Immediately Bimala's face crumpled in pain. I realized that she thought I was demanding the fifty thousand. It was probably weighing on her mind; perhaps she had worried about it all night and yet had found no solution. After all, she had no other way to show her love—she couldn't possibly give her heart to me overtly and so she wanted to bring this money to me as a mark of all her covert caresses and desires. But the lack of a way to do so was stifling her. Her pain struck me to the quick.

She was now all mine. There was no need to worry about uprooting her; now I needed to tend to her and keep her alive.

I said, 'Queen, that fifty thousand won't be needed right now. I have worked it out and just five thousand, or even three will do for now.'

Bimala was overwhelmed by the pressure lifting so suddenly. Like a song she sang, 'I will bring you five thousand.'

This was the tune to which Krishna's lover Radha had sung:

*For my love I'll don flowers in my hair,*
*The likes of which has never been seen in all the world,*
*The notes of the flute played in the wind,*
*Not for every ear is it meant,*
*Oh look at that, Yamuna has overflowed her banks.*

It was the same tune, the same song and the same words: 'I will bring you five thousand.' 'For my love I'll don flowers in my hair.' The flute played so sweetly *because* the wind had a narrow passage, there were so many restrictions in its way. If my greed had forced me to break the flute and flatten it, I would have heard, 'Why? What do you need this money for? I am a woman, where shall I get so much money, etc. etc.' It wouldn't have a single syllable in common with Radha's song. That's why I say, illusion is the king, it is the flute and without illusion, it is the flute cracked open—I think Nikhil has got a taste of that pure emptiness these days. I feel sorry for him. But Nikhil boasts that he wants the Truth and I boast that I'd never let illusion slip through my fingers. 'Jadrishi bhabana jasya siddhirbhabati tadrishi.' One must act on one's own desires. So there was no point regretting it.

In order to keep Bimala soaring in those lofty heights, I finished the matter of the five thousand quickly and got back to the adulation of that fierce goddess. When and where would we have the puja? The fair in Hosaingaji that was held in September at Ruimari under Nikhil's jurisdiction, had thousands attending it and that would serve as a good locale. Bimala was excited. She felt this wasn't about burning foreign cloth or burning down homes; Nikhil would surely not object to this. I laughed to myself—how little did they know each other, even after nine years spent together. Their knowledge was limited to the bounds of the home. The moment the world came into it, they were all at sea. For nine years they sat and believed that the home and the world matched in spirit. Today they are beginning to feel that some things that have never been coordinated could not suddenly complement harmoniously.

Anyway, let the ones who do not understand one another gradually stumble and find their way around; I don't have to waste too much time on it. But I couldn't leave Bimala in this heightened state, like a flying kite for too long and so I had to get my work done as quickly as possible. When she rose and walked towards the door, I asked, quite nonchalantly, 'Queen, about the money—'

Bimala turned around and said, 'At the end of this month, when the monthly revenue comes in—'

I said, 'No, that would be too late.'

'When do you want it?'

'Tomorrow.'

'Tomorrow you'll have it.'

## Nikhilesh

The dailies have started running a column about me and letters are pouring in; I believe a limerick and cartoons are also in the pipeline. The channels of mockery have opened up, as have the floodgates of lies and everyone is delighted. They know that in this game of mudslinging, the slings are all in their hands. I am just a gentleman walking by the road, my clothes will be mud-stained.

They write, in my area every single individual is eager to participate in swadeshi and all that holds them back is the fear of retribution from me. The handful who dare to sell desi goods are harassed by me in true zamindari style. I am in cahoots with the police, I correspond with the magistrate regularly and the daily had been informed by reliable sources that all this was aimed at earning myself some titles in addition to the ones inherited by me. They have written: 'A man should earn his own name, but we also know that his own fellowmen have demanded that he be dethroned.' Although my name isn't mentioned, it is quite obvious from all they have said. On the other hand, the paper is also flooded by letters in praise of the patriotic Harish Kundu. They write that if there were more such diehard patriots in this land, then by now the factory chimneys of Manchester would also have taken to singing Vande Mataram in tuneful submission.

Meanwhile, I have received a letter written in red ink detailing the number of zamindars whose offices have been burnt down because their loyalties lay with Liverpool. It says that the fire of God has now embarked on this mission of cleansing; steps will be taken to evict those from the mother's lap, who were never her children in the first place.

It is signed, 'A humble claimant to the mother's love, Ambikacharan Gupta.'

I knew that all this was the handiwork of local students. I called a few of them and showed them the letter. Solemnly, the BA said, 'We have also come to know that there is a group of desperados in the land who would do anything to rid the land of the enemies of swadeshi.'

I said, 'If even a single person buckles down under their unfair pressure tactics, it is a shame for the entire nation.'

The MA in history said, 'I don't understand.'

I said, 'Our country quakes under every gaze, be it God's or the constable's. Now, in the name of freedom, if you bring back that terror with a new name to it, if you want to plant your victory flag through oppression, then the ones who love the country would never bow down to that rule of terror.'

The history MA said, 'Is there a country where the law of the land is not one of terror?'

I said, 'The limit of that terror determines how free the people of that land are. If it is used solely to curb violence on others then it's obviously there to protect every individual from the cruelty of another individual. But if the reign of terror determines what one should wear, where he should buy his goods, what he should eat, with whom he should have his meal, then it denies the basics of individual freedom. And that is tantamount to denying man his human rights.'

The history MA asked, 'Isn't there such a system of denying the individual's freedom from the roots in other countries as well?'

I said, 'Of course there is. The existence of slavery in any country is proof of that.'

He said, 'In that case slavery is also a part of man's objective and that is also humanism.'

The BA said, 'We have really appreciated the example raised by Sandipbabu the other day: if you were to sweep up the entire estate of Harish Kundu or the Chakravartys of Sankibhanga, you wouldn't find an ounce of foreign salt. Why? Because they have always ruled with an iron hand. For the masses, who are meek by nature, the greatest danger is in not having a ruler.'

The young man who had failed his FA piped up, 'I've heard this from someone: the Chakravartys had a Kayasth tenant. He refused to obey them over an issue and it went to the courts. The situation came to this that he had hardly enough to eat. After two days of starvation, he set off to sell his wife's jewellery. It was his last resort. But no one bought them from him, fearing retribution from the zamindar. The chief-clerk offered to buy them for five rupees. They must have been worth nearly thirty. Desperate, he agreed to five rupees. The clerk took the bundle of ornaments from him and informed him that the five rupees would go towards paying off his tax arrears. When we heard this, we told Sandipbabu that we should boycott Chakravarty. But he said, if you boycott such vibrant people, who would you work with—the dead ones? They are the masters because they desire with a passion. Those who cannot crave so passionately, would either go along with others' wishes, or die for others. He drew a comparison with you and said, today there isn't a single person in Chakravarty's area who would dare to oppose swadeshi. But Nikhilesh wouldn't be able to do that, however hard he tried.'

I said, 'Of course I wouldn't, because I want greater things than swadeshi. I do not want a lifeless post, I want a live tree. My work will take time.'

The historian laughed and said, 'You'll get neither, because, I agree with Sandipbabu: to have is to seize. It took us a while to learn this lesson, because these are the antithesis of textbook wisdom. I have seen with my own eyes: Gurucharan Bhaduri, the Kundu family's clerk, went out to collect taxes. A Muslim subject had nothing to sell or give. He only had his young wife. Bhaduri said you'll have to marry off your wife and raise the money. A candidate for this nikaah soon turned up and the debt was paid off. I can tell you, that husband's tears almost robbed me of my sleep; but whatever the misery, I have learnt this, that when it comes to collecting money, the man who can make the debtor marry off his wife and raise the debt is a greater human being than I am. I cannot do it, tears come to my eyes and so all is lost. If anyone can save my country, it'll be people like this clerk, this Kundu and this Chakravarty.'

I was dumbfounded. I said, 'If that is so, then it is my job to save the land from these clerks, these Kundus and Chakravartys. Look here, when the poison of slavery that runs in the blood begins to come out, it take horrible shapes. The one who is tortured as the daughter-in-law, turns into the greatest tormentor when she is the mother-in-law. A man may walk with his eyes lowered but when he goes as the groom's party, the bride's household is hard pressed to meet his random demands. You have unequivocally accepted the rule of fear, known that as the right path, and so now you choose to terrorize everyone and bend them to your will. My battle is with this brutality inherent in weakness.'

My thoughts are very simple and any common man would understand them in a minute. But for these MAs who were flexing their historians' brains in this land, the point was to trounce out Truth.

Meanwhile, I was bothered about Panchu's fake aunt. It would be difficult to prove. It was difficult, and almost next to impossible, getting witnesses for the truth. But for something that hasn't happened, one could easily rally forth a whole host of witnesses. This was a ploy to spoil my purchase of the original deeds from Panchu. I was cornered and I even considered giving Panchu some land in my own area and setting him up. But Chandranathbabu said he wasn't keen on letting evil defeat him so easily. He wanted to try himself.

'You will try?'

'Yes, I.'

I couldn't understand what a teacher hoped to achieve in these matters of legal twists and turns. That evening he failed to keep our daily appointment. I went looking and found that he had left with his clothes and things; he had left a message with the servants that he'd be back in a few days. I figured he may have gone to Panchu's uncle's home in the hope of rounding up some witnesses. If that was the case, I knew nothing would come of it. His school was closed for a few days on account of Jagatdhatri Puja and Muharram. So there was no news of him there either.

When the autumn evenings draw to a close, turning the light into a muted yellow, the shades in one's mind also turn colour. Many people live their mental lives indoors—they can totally ignore the 'outside'. My mind seems to reside under a tree, exposed to every nuance, every gust of wind from the outside, resonating every single aria of the sunlight. When the sun was high in the sky and a host of chores jostled for space all around me, I felt I needed nothing more from life. But when the sky grew dimmer, my heart seemed to feel that dusk came upon this world only to draw a curtain over life; at this time solitude would fill up the endless darkness. The life that blossomed amidst others in the day was supposed to withdraw within itself at dusk and that was the true essence of light and shade. I could scarcely turn my back on this profound truth. Hence, when dusk began to glow on this earth, like the glittering dark eyes of a lover, my heart kept repeating, 'It's untrue, the true meaning, the true purpose of a man's life is not work; man is not merely a labourer, be it the labour of Truth, or the labour of life. Nikhilesh, have you lost sight of that man, who lives and rests in the starlight, away from all his work? The man who is completely alone in that space where all the world's multitude cannot give him company, must be so truly alone.'

That day, when the evening had just reached the crossroads of dusk, I had no work; neither did I feel like working. Chandranathbabu wasn't there either. When my empty heart yearned to cling to something, I went to the garden indoors. I love chrysanthemums. I had planted many of them in clay pots and when they all bloomed together, it looked like waves of colour in a sea of green. It was a while since I'd visited the garden. So I smiled to myself, 'Let me lighten up the mood of my bereaved chrysanthemums today.'

When I stepped into the garden the sickle moon just peeped over the walls of our house. Dark shadows lay pooled at the base of the wall and the moonlight arched over it to cast its radiance on the western side of the garden. I suddenly felt the moon had tiptoed up from behind, covered the eyes of darkness and was smiling mischievously.

When I approached the gallery-like steps on which rows and rows of chrysanthemum plants rested, I spotted someone lying quietly beneath the steps, on the grass. My heart missed a beat. She also stood up, startled.

I was in a quandary. I wondered if I should go back; perhaps Bimala also considered leaving. But staying and leaving, both were equally difficult. Before I could come to a decision, Bimala stood up, covered her head with her sari and started walking back to the house. In that one instant, Bimala's unbearable grief stood before me, personified. My own grief and grievances vanished in a second. I called out, 'Bimala.'

She stopped, startled. But she didn't turn towards me. I came and stood in front of her. She stood in the shadow, the moonlight fell on my face. She stood there, hands bunched in fists, eyes shut tight. I said, 'Bimala, my cage here is walled from all sides—how can I keep you here? You cannot live like this.'

Bimala kept her eyes closed and didn't say a word.

I said, 'If I keep you here like this, my life will turn into iron shackles. That's hardly likely to bring me any joy.'

She was silent.

I said, 'I speak the truth, here and now—I release you. If I can be nothing else to you, at least I won't be the handcuffs on your wrists.'

I walked away towards the house. No, this wasn't my magnanimity and hardly my indifference. It's just that if I didn't let go, I wouldn't be free myself. The garland of my heart could not be a burden on it forever. I only pray to the Omnipotent One, that if He doesn't give me any joy, or only saddle me with grief, I would take it all, but never should he keep me shackled, bound and tied. Trying to hold onto the lie as a Truth was like strangling your own self. Please, spare me from killing myself thus.

I came into the living room and found Chandranathbabu sitting there. My heart was swelling with emotion at that point. The moment I spotted him, I burst out saying, 'Professor, freedom is man's greatest possession. Nothing else can compare, nothing at all.'

He was surprised at this excited outburst. He just stared at me.

I said, 'Books don't tell you anything. I have read in the shastras that desires bind you; it binds itself and also others. But they were empty words. The day I truly let the bird fly from the cage, I felt that the bird has really left me and not the other way round. When I keep something chained, I am actually chained by my own desires, stronger than iron shackles. I tell you, this is the Truth people fail to understand. Everyone thinks the cure lies elsewhere; nowhere, nowhere else—just set your desires free.'

Chandranathbabu said, 'We think that freedom lies in getting in your hands whatever you have wished for. But in reality, freedom comes from giving up within yourself whatever you have desired.'

I said, 'Professor, if you put it in mere words it sounds so bald, like a moral. But when I get even a glimpse of it, I feel this is the elixir of life. This is what the gods drink, and conquer death forever. We fail to perceive beauty until we set it free. If I claim that it was Buddha who conquered the world and not Alexander, it sounds like a lie. When will I be able to sing these words? When will these truths of the universe leap out of printed textbooks and flow like the eternal spring of Truth?'

Suddenly, I remembered that the professor had been gone some days and I didn't know where he had been. A trifle embarrassed, I asked, 'Where did you go?'

He said, 'To Panchu's house.'

'Panchu's house? You were there all these days?'

'Yes. I figured I would talk to the woman who is posing as his aunt. She was surprised to see me at first. This was unexpected behaviour from a gentleman. But then I stayed on. So finally, she began to feel a little ashamed. I told her, "Ma, you won't be able to insult me and send me away. And if I stay, so does Panchu. I won't allow him and his motherless children to be thrown out into the streets." For two days she heard me quietly, neither concurring nor disagreeing. Eventually, today I found her packing her bags. She said, "We will go to Vrindavan; give us some money." I know she won't go to Vrindavan, but she'll have to be given a big amount as a sendoff. So I have come to you.'

'Certainly, I'll give whatever is needed.'

'The old lady isn't all bad. Panchu wouldn't let her touch the water jug and always kicked up a ruckus if she so much as walked into the room; but when she heard that I don't mind eating food cooked by her, she took very good care of me. She's a good cook. The little respect that Panchu had for me, vanished altogether. Earlier he thought I was at least a simple man. But now he believes the reason I ate food cooked by this woman was simply to manipulate her. Manipulation may have its place in life—but to compromise your caste over it? If I could have outwitted her as a false witness, he may have understood. Anyway, I'll have to stand guard over Panchu's house for a while even after the old woman leaves, or Harish Kundu may cook up more mischief. I believe he has said to his subjects, "I got him a fake aunt and he has gone one up on me and got himself a fake father. Let's see how his father saves his skin."'

I said, 'His skin may or may not be saved. But if we even lose our lives fighting these various traps these people are designing for our countrymen, in the shape of religion, society, business, etc., I would be a happy man.'

## Bimala

It's hard to believe so much can happen in one lifetime. I feel I have lived seven times over, as if a thousand years have lapsed in these few months. Time was galloping so fast that I scarcely felt it moving. That day I got a jolt and came to my senses.

When I went to speak to my husband about abolishing foreign goods from our markets, I knew we'd have an argument. But I somehow believed that I would have no need of dissembling dissent. There was magic in the very air around me. The fact that an immense ocean of maleness like Sandip came and crashed at my feet like waves, when I had not called out to him, was proof of the fact that this magic existed. And the other day I saw Amulya—young and simple as the tender bamboo reed—come and stand before me, gradually a colour emerging from within him like the river at dawn. That day, a glance at Amulya's face told me just how impressed the goddess could be when she looked upon her devotee. Thus, I had already seen how my magic wand worked.

So, that day, I went to my husband like a bolt of lightning, heading an army of clouds with immense faith in my powers. But what happened? In all of these nine years, I had never seen such indifference in his eyes. It was like the desert sky without a drop of moisture, draining all colour from the object it chanced to look upon. I'd have been happier if he had at least shown some anger. I couldn't touch him anywhere. I felt I was a lie, a dream: and when the dream ended, I was just the dark night.

All these years I had envied my beautiful sisters-in-law their beauty. I knew in my heart that Fate had deprived me of powers and all my power lay in my husband's love for me. Today, I had drained the cup of power to the dregs and I was inebriated. Suddenly, the cup fell to the ground and shattered. How was I to live?

Quickly, I sat down to tie up my hair. Shame. Oh the shame. As I walked passed Mejorani's room, she called out, 'Hey there, little princess, the topknot is leaping out over your head; is your head still in the right place?'

The other day, my husband told me so easily in the garden: I release you. Is it so simple: giving release or being released? Is freedom tangible? It's empty. Like the fish, I had always swum in the waters of love. All of a sudden if I am held up to the sky and told, here is your freedom, I cannot survive.

Today, when I came into my bedroom, I found mere furniture—racks, mirrors, bed. The heart was missing. There was only release, freedom, emptiness. The water had dried up, exposing the rocks and pebbles. No love, just furniture.

When I was so badly hit by doubts about where exactly Truth resided in this world for me, I ran into Sandip again. As the heart slammed into another heart, the fires burned the same as before. Where was the lie? This was Truth brimming over. These people walking around, talking, laughing, Bororani counting her beads, Mejorani laughing with her maids, singing songs—the awakening within me was a far greater Truth than all of this.

Sandip said, 'I need fifty thousand.'

My drunken soul sang out, 'That's nothing. I'll get it for you.' It didn't matter how, and from where. Here I was, rising above everything from the depths of nothing in a matter of seconds. Just like that, things would happen with just one gesture. I can, I can, I can. No doubts about it.

So I walked away. But then I looked around me—where was the money? Where was that magic tree showering currency? Why did the world shame the heart so? But I had to have the money. By hook or by crook—there was no shame in it. Crime stalked guilt. True power was exempt from all fault. The thief steals, but the victorious king loots. I began to look into where the treasury was, who guarded the money and whose hands it came into. At night I stood on the veranda gazing fixedly at the office room. How was I to snatch away fifty thousand from within these iron bars? I had no mercy. If a spell could make the guards of the room drop dead in that instant, I would have rushed in like a crazed soul. Within the heart of this family's queen, a gang of robbers, rapiers in hand, began to dance before their goddess, begging for a boon. But the world remained silent, the guards changed every few hours and the clock chimed every hour—the huge mansion slept on, fearless and undaunted.

Finally, one day, I called Amulya. I said, 'The country needs money. Won't you be able to get it from the treasurer somehow?'

His chest swelled with pride and he said, 'Why not?'

Alas, I too had spoken thus to Sandip, 'Why not?' Amulya's confidence didn't give me the slightest hope.

I asked, 'Tell me what you'll do?'

He began to lay out such outlandish plans that they were only fit for the monthly magazines and nothing else.

I said, 'No Amulya, don't be so naive.'

He said, 'Fine, I'll bribe the guards.'

'Where is the money for that?'

He replied nonchalantly, 'I'll loot the market.'

I said, 'There's no need for that, I have my jewels and that will do.'

Amulya said, 'But the treasurer can't be bribed. There's a simpler plan.'

I asked, 'What?'

'You don't have to hear that. It's very simple.'

'Tell me still.'

First he fished out a small edition of the Gita from his shirt pocket, kept it on the table and then placed a pistol on it; he didn't say anything.

Oh my God—he didn't blink twice before contemplating the murder of our old treasurer. His face was so cherubic that it was hard to imagine him even harming a fly; but appearances are so deceptive. The fact of the matter was, that the old treasurer wasn't real to him—in his place there was a blankness: it held no life, no pain, just a sloka, 'Na hanyatey hanyamane sharirey'. The soul does not die, only the body does.

I exclaimed, 'No, Amulya. Our treasurer has a wife, children, he is—'

'Where in this country would you find a man who doesn't have a wife and children? Look here, what we call mercy is only a kind of self-indulgence: so that our weak minds are not hurt, we refrain from hurting others. This is the depth of cowardice.'

Sandip's words coming from the lips of this child sent a chill down my spine. He is a so raw, so young, he should still believe that goodness exists. Poor thing, this was his time to live, time to grow. The mother in me awakened. For me, there was neither good nor evil—there was only death in alluring shapes; but when this eighteen-year-old could so easily decide that killing an innocent old man was the right thing, I shuddered in terror. When I realized that he had no sense of sin, the sin hidden in his words took a fierce shape before my eyes, as if the sins of the 'father' were visiting the child.

As I looked at those large, ingenuous eyes, brimming with faith and fervour, my heart wept. He was on his way to hell—who could save him? Why wasn't my country taking the form of a true mother and drawing this boy to her bosom? Why didn't she tell him, 'Do not lose yourself in the process of saving me'?

I know that the greatest powers on earth have reached their summit only by selling their soul to the devil; but the mother stands alone, only to lock horns with this very devil. The mother doesn't want results, however glorious; she only wants to save. Today my heart cried out to reach out and draw this boy into safety.

Just a few minutes ago I had asked him to steal. Now whatever I said to the contrary, he was bound to laugh it off as female weakness. That is something they give in to only when it entertains or ruins the world.

I said to Amulya, 'Go on, you don't have to do anything. It's my job to get the money.'

When he was at the door, I called him back and said, 'Amulya, I am your elder sister. I bless you and pray that God keeps you safe and sound.' He was taken aback at these words of mine. But then he bent low and touched my feet. When he stood up, his eyes were moist.

'Dear brother, I am headed for disaster; let me take on all your troubles—let me never plant fresh thorns on your path.' I said to him, 'You'll have to gift your pistol to me.'

'What will you do with it, Didi?'

'I'll practise death.'

'That's what is needed—women too have to die and kill.' Amulya handed me the pistol.

Amulya's youthful face and the glow on it left a trail in my heart like the first streak of light at dawn. I held the pistol to my heart and said, 'This here is my last resort to salvation, a gift from a brother to his sister.'

The window in the heart that guarded the tender spot of maternal feelings flew open just this once. I thought it would stay open from now on. But good always loses out. The lover-woman came and obstructed the mother's way to liberation. The next day I ran into Sandip again. A crazy madness gripped my heart and began its wild dance all over again. But what was all this—was this my true self? Never. Never before had I set my eyes upon this brazen, this audacious self. The snake charmer came suddenly and unwrapped this snake within me. But this snake had never been within me—it was brought by the snake charmer himself. The devil seemed to have me in his thrall. Whatever I did now, was not my doing, but all his.

That same devil came to me one day, blazing torch in hand, and said, 'I am your country, I am your Sandip, you have nothing that matters more than me, Vande Mataram.' I folded my hands and said, 'You are my religion, you are my heaven, I will sacrifice my all for the love of you, Vande Mataram.'

You want five thousand? Fine, you shall have it. Tomorrow? I'll bring it tomorrow. The scandalous insolence of the act will make that five thousand froth and foam, like heady liquor. Then there would be the inebriated dance. The motionless earth would sway beneath the feet, the eyes would burn with hidden fire, a fiery wind would blow past the ears and everything before my eyes would seem blurred; tottering, I shall stumble to my death; in a moment, the fire would extinguish, ashes would fly in the wind—nothing would be left.

I was totally at a loss as to where the money could come from. Then, the other day, in the throes of extreme excitement, I saw the money right before my eyes.

Every year, for the Durga Puja, my husband gifted his sisters-in-law three thousand rupees each. That money lay in the bank, gathering interest. This year too, the money had been gifted. But I knew that it hadn't gone into the bank yet. I also knew where the money was. There was an iron chest in the ante-room adjoining my bedroom where I changed my clothes. The money was in that chest.

Every year my husband went to Calcutta to deposit this money in the bank there. But this year he couldn't make the trip. This is why I believe in Fate. The country needed this money and that's why it was still there. Who would dare to take this money to the bank? And would I dare *not* take this money? The death-goddess has reached out her begging bowl, she says I am hungry, feed me. I would bleed myself to death, for that five thousand rupees—oh Mother, the one who has lost this money hasn't lost much. But you have drained me of all virtues.

So many times have I called Bororani and Mejorani thieves in my heart; they were looting my trusting husband, only taking money from him—this was my grievance. Many times have I told my husband that after their husbands' death they had stolen many things that didn't belong to them. He always held his peace and never answered me back. This irked me; I would say, 'If you wish to donate, do so openly. Why would you allow them to steal?' The Fates must have heard my allegations and smiled to themselves; today I was about to steal money belonging to my sisters-in-law.

At night my husband changed his clothes in that same ante-room. The keys to the chest were in his pocket. I took them and opened the chest. The slightest sound seemed loud enough to wake the whole world. A sudden chill stole over me, petrified me from head to toe, giving me the shivers.

Inside the chest, there was a drawer. I pulled it open and found that there were no notes, only guineas wrapped in paper. There was no time to count how many there were in each wrapping, how much I needed, etc. There were twenty in all and I piled them all into my anchal and tied the knot. It was no mean weight. The burden of guilt dragged me down to the earth. If they'd been wads of notes instead, I may have felt less guilty. This was all gold.

That night, when I had to enter my own room feeling like a thief, the room no longer seemed my own. I had the strongest claim on this room. But my fraud had made me forfeit it.

I muttered to myself, 'Vande Mataram, Vande Mataram. Country, my motherland, my golden land—all this gold belongs to her and to nobody else.'

But in the dark of night the heart is weak. My husband slept in the next room. I closed my eyes and passed through his room. I went straight to the open terrace in the inner courtyard, placed that bundle of guilt under my heart and lay on the floor—the packets of coins hurt my soul. The silent night sat near my head, pointing fingers at me. I had failed to separate my home from the world. Today I have robbed my home, and therefore robbed the land; for this sin, my home was lost to me in the same instant that my land slipped away from me. Had I gone begging in order to serve the country, and even lost my life before completing my service, that incomplete service would have been accepted by God as obeisance. But theft was no worship—how would I hand this to my country? The boat would sink with the weight of this burden. Just because I was headed for death, I didn't have to drag my motherland into the muck, did I?

There was no way of returning this money into the chest. I did not have the strength to go back into that room, open the chest and put the money back this very night. If I tried, I would surely faint at the threshold of my husband's room. Now there was only the road ahead and no other.

I was too ashamed to even sit and count how much money there was. Let it stay hidden, the way it was. I could not possibly calculate the value of theft.

In that dark winter night, the sky didn't hold a single drop of moisture. The stars glittered blindingly. I lay on the terrace thinking: if I had to steal those stars, one by one, in the name of the country, pluck them from the heart of the sky, then the following night the sky would be a widow; the dark sky would go blind and the theft would be from the entire universe. This theft of mine, today, was not merely about money: it was also like stealing the light from the sky, stealing Truth and faith from the entire universe.

The night crept away as I lay on the terrace. In the morning, when I realized my husband must have left the room by then, I got up slowly, wrapped myself in a shawl and walked towards my room. At that time, Mejorani was watering her plants in the corridor. The moment she spotted me, she said, 'Hey there, little one, have you heard?'

I stopped short; my heart quaked within me. I felt the guineas tied in my anchal were sticking out a mile. I felt any moment now that my sari would give way and the gold coins would clatter to the floor all around me; today, the thief who has stolen her own wealth would stand exposed before all and sundry in this house.

Mejorani said, 'That gang of robbers has written to Thakurpo, warning him that they'd raid his treasury.'

I stood there silent as a thief.

'I told Thakurpo he should go to you; goddess, smile upon us and save us from your vengeful followers. We will dutifully chant your mishmash Vande Mataram. So much has been happening lately; now for God's sake, don't let them break into the house.'

I walked to my room quickly without another word. Once you step onto the quicksand there is no way out—the more you struggle, the deeper you drown. I would be so glad to take this money from my anchal and drop it into Sandip's hands. I cannot bear this weight any more, it's breaking my back.

Early in the day I got the message that Sandip was waiting for me. Today I didn't bother decking up; just wrapped the shawl tight around me and walked out quickly.

I stepped into the room and found Amulya sitting there with Sandip. The little self-respect I had remaining seemed to shudder through my entire frame like a lightning bolt and drained out through my feet, straight into the earth. Today, in front of that youth, I would have to unmask the woman in her ugliest form. My crime was being discussed in the group today—they didn't spare me the thinnest of veils.

We will never understand men. When they decide to pave the way to their goals, they never hesitate to break the heart of the whole universe and scatter it as pebbles all along the way. When they are drunk on the pleasure of creating with their own hands, they take great joy in shattering His creations. They wouldn't spare my terrible shame a second glance, their hearts know no mercy, they only have eyes for the Ideal. Alas, who am I to them? I am a mere wildflower in the path of a turbulent deluge.

But what did Sandip gain by snuffing me out thus? Just the five thousand rupees? Did I have no greater value than that? Surely I did. I had heard all about it from Sandip himself and that is what made me ride roughshod over everything in my world. I would give light, I would give life, I would give strength and elixir—the sheer exultation made me overflow my own shores. If someone had fulfilled those promises, I would have been happy even in death; I'd have felt it was worth losing everything.

But did they mean to tell me today that all of it was a lie? The goddess in me didn't have the power to set her devotees' fears at rest? The eulogy I heard, the one that brought me from heaven unto this dust: wasn't it meant to turn this dust to heaven? Was it meant just to turn heaven into earth and soil?

Sandip cast a sharp glance at me and said, 'We need the money, Queen.'

Amulya stared at my face, that boy who wasn't born from my mother's womb, but came forth from *his* mother's womb—that mother, oh it was the same mother. What a youthful face, such serene eyes, oh the sheer youth of the boy. I am a woman, the same as his mother. If he says to me, hand me some poison, would I do it?

'We need money, Queen.'

Anger and shame made me feel like hurling that bundle of gold coins straight at Sandip's head. I simply couldn't untie the knot of my anchal. My fingers trembled. And when the paper wrapped bundles rolled onto the table, Sandip's face grew dark. He must have thought those wrappers held copper coins. What hatred. His face reflected such crude disdain for failure. He looked as if he would hit me. Sandip thought I was here to bargain with him, that I would try to palm off a few hundred rupees against his demand for five thousand. For a moment he looked as if he'd throw those bundles out of the window. He was no beggar—he was the king.

Amulya asked, 'Is that all, Ranididi?'

His voice dripped sympathy. I felt like bursting into tears. I gripped my heart and slowly nodded. Sandip was silent; he didn't touch the bundles or say a single word.

I wanted to leave, but my feet wouldn't move. If only the earth had split into two and sucked me in, this lump of clay would have been so happy to return to dust. The young boy felt my terrible mortification. He pretended to be greatly thrilled and said, 'Well, this is a lot too. This would be enough. You have really saved us, Ranididi.'

He unwrapped one of the bundles and the gold coins sparkled!

In an instant Sandip's face came out of the shadow. He glowed with joy. Scarcely able to control this sudden emotional turnaround of his heart, he jumped off the seat and leapt towards me. I do not know what his intentions were. I shot a lightning glance at Amulya's face and saw that it had turned pallid, as if struck quite suddenly. I gathered all my strength and pushed hard at Sandip. He fell and his head hit the corner of the marble table; he didn't stir for a while. After this mammoth effort, I had no strength left in me. I collapsed on the chair. Amulya's face was bright with elation. He didn't spare a second glance for Sandip, but touched my feet and sat on the floor at my feet. Oh dear brother, dear child, this veneration of yours is the last drop in my empty cup today. I could no longer hold back my tears. I buried my face in my anchal and sobbed my heart out. The occasional, sympathetic touch of Amulya's fingers on my feet from time to time only brought forth fresh bouts of tears.

A little later I composed myself, opened my eyes and found Sandip sitting by the table, tying up the guineas in his handkerchief, looking as if nothing had happened! Amulya stood up from his place at my feet; his eyes were bright with unshed tears.

Sandip looked up at our faces without the slightest trace of embarrassment and declared, 'Six thousand.'

Amulya said, 'Sandipbabu, we don't need so much. I have done some calculations and I think three and a half thousand would be enough for us right now.'

Sandip said, 'Our work is not just the here and now. There is no limit to how much we need.'

Amulya said, 'Whatever. In future, I take responsibility for gathering funds. For now, please return the two and a half thousand to Ranididi.'

Sandip looked at me. I said, 'No, no, I don't even want to touch that money. Go and use it as you please.'

Sandip looked at Amulya and said, 'Men can never give the way women can.'

Amulya was enchanted, 'Woman is the goddess herself.'

Sandip said, 'We, men, can at the most give our strength, but women give themselves. They nurture a child in their body, give birth, and raise him, all from within. This is the true gift.' He now looked at me and said, 'Queen, if your gift today had been mere money, I wouldn't have touched it—but you have given me something greater than life itself.'

Perhaps we have two minds. One of my minds told me I was being fooled, but the other one was happy to be fooled. Sandip lacked integrity, but he had power. Hence, he nourished life and destroyed it at the same instant. He had the divine scabbard, but the weapon in it was the devil's. Sandip's handkerchief was too small to hold all the guineas; he asked, 'Queen, could I borrow one of your handkerchiefs?'

I handed it to him and he immediately raised it to his brow in a salute. Then he dropped down at my feet and touched my feet devoutly, 'Goddess, I had rushed towards you to offer you this very salute. But you pushed me away; I shall take that as my blessing—I have anointed my brow with it.' He pointed to the scar on his temple.

Was I wrong then? Did he really rush towards me, arms outstretched, just to touch my feet? But I thought even Amulya had winced at the sudden inebriated lust that had glistened on his face. But Sandip had fine-tuned the art of eulogizing so well that I could never argue; the eyes seeking Truth always drifted shut, as if drugged. Sandip returned the wound inflicted by me twice over and my heart wept. When I received his obeisance, my act of theft was raised to glorified heights. The guineas lying on the table could then overlook all the shame, the ethical violation, the pain, and sparkle in their laughter.

Just like me, Amulya was also waylaid. The slight loss of respect that he had felt for Sandip in that one instant, seemed to have been replaced by renewed veneration and his eyes glowed with respect for both Sandip and me. It filled the room with a sense of innocent trust as pure as the lone star at dawn. I paid homage, I received homage and my sins glowed bright as embers. Amulya gazed at me, folded his hands and said, 'Vande Mataram.'

But the strains of eulogy fade as time passes. I had no ways and means to salvage some self-respect from within myself. I couldn't enter my bedroom. That iron chest frowned upon me, our bed seemed to raise an accusing finger. I wanted to run away from this deep humiliation that rose from within. All I wanted to do was rush to Sandip and listen to him sing my praise. From the nadir of guilt that ran deep inside, that was the one shrine that was alive. Beyond that, wherever I turned there was only oblivion. So I wanted to cling to that shrine day and night. Applause, applause, my soul thirsts for applause. If the level in that wine glass went down by a notch, I gasped for breath. And so, all day long I yearned to go to Sandip and talk to him; I needed Sandip so desperately today, if only to perceive my own worth on this earth.

When my husband came home for lunch, I couldn't go and stand before him; but not to go would be so much more shameful, that I couldn't do that either. So I sat at an angle from him, such that I wouldn't have to meet his eyes. The other day, I sat in that same fashion as he was eating, when Mejorani came and sat down. She said, 'Thakurpo, you are always laughing off all those dares and anonymous letters about a raid, but I feel very scared. Have you sent our gift-money to the bank yet?'

My husband said, 'No, I haven't had the time.'

Mejorani said, 'Be careful, you are so callous sometimes; that money—'

My husband smiled and said, 'But it is safe in the iron chest in the ante-room next to my bedroom.'

'If they get their hands on it? You never know.'

'If burglars can get all the way into my room, then they can even steal you away one day.'

'Oh dear, no one would take me, don't worry. Whatever is worth taking is in your room, not mine. But seriously, don't keep cash in the house.'

'In about five days or so the estate-taxes would be sent to the bank and I will send that money along with it to the bank in Calcutta.'

'Make sure it doesn't slip your mind—you can be so absent-minded sometimes . . .'

'If the money gets stolen from my room, it will be my loss, Bourani; your money will be safe.'

'Thakurpo, when you talk like this, I feel so angry. Am I making a distinction between mine and yours? Would your loss be any less painful for me? Vicious Fate may have taken everything from me and left me with just a devout brother—but I do know his value. Look here, I cannot stay lost in all those prayers like the eldest queen. I value what God has given me more than God himself. What is it, little princess, you look stiff as a board. Know something, Thakurpo, the little one thinks I curry favour with you. I guess if it came to that, I *would* have too. But you aren't that kind of brother, whose ego one has to pander to. If you were like Madhav Chakravarty, even the eldest queen would have forgotten her gods and hung onto him like a leech, begging for the odd half penny. But I do believe that would have been for the good, because then she wouldn't have had so much time to go making up stories about you.'

Mejorani babbled on, interspersed with her attempts to draw her Thakurpo's attention to the curry or the fish. My head was spinning. There was no time. Something had to be done, and soon. As I was frantically trying to figure out what could be done, Mejorani's incessant babble seemed intolerable to me. Especially when I knew that her eyes missed nothing. Her glance was flicking at me from time to time—I didn't know what she saw, but I felt the whole truth was writ large on my face for all to read.

Audacity can be unbounded. I forced a seemingly amused laugh to my lips and said, 'The fact of the matter is that Mejorani doesn't trust *me*—all that prattle about thieves and burglars is an eyewash.'

Mejorani gave a snide smile and said, 'You've got it right there—a woman burglar is deadly. But of course, I will catch you out—I am not a man. How would you fool me?'

I said, 'If you are so afraid, then let me keep all my belongings in your care as a deposit; if I ever cause you to lose anything, you can deduct it from there.'

Mejorani laughed and said, 'Just listen to the little one talk. There are losses that can't be retrieved through deposits in this life or another.'

My husband didn't say a single word in this whole exchange. He went out as soon as he finished his lunch; these days he never went into the room to rest.

Most of my expensive jewellery was entrusted to the treasurer. Still, the price of whatever little I had with me would be no less than thirty to thirty-five thousand rupees. I took the box of jewellery and opened it up in front of Mejorani and said, 'Here's my jewellery; let it be with you. From now on you can breathe easy.'

Mejorani's brows rose in surprise, 'Oh dear, you really amaze me sometimes. Do you think I can't sleep at night worrying about you stealing my jewellery?'

I said, 'There's no stopping the worries. Besides, what do we ever know about our fellow beings?'

She said, 'And so you have come to teach me a lesson by trusting me so much? Please, I can barely keep track of my own jewellery, what with all this hired help swarming the place. Keep your own jewels with you.'

I left Mejorani's room, went into the living room and sent for Amulya. But Sandip came in along with Amulya. I had little time to lose; so I said to Sandip, 'I need to speak to Amulya about something, could you please—'

Sandip gave a crooked smile and said, 'Do you see Amulya as different from me? If you want to take him away from me, I guess I won't be able to stop it.'

I just stood there silently. Sandip said, 'Okay fine, once you have finished your special discussion with Amulya, do spare some time for a talk with me too, or I would stand defeated. I can take anything except defeat. I have to have the lion's share. I have always fought with Fate over this—I'll conquer Fate and never be defeated.'

Hurling Amulya a fierce glance, he walked out of the room. I said to Amulya, 'Dear child, you'll have to do something for me.'

He said, 'Didi, I will do your every bidding with all my heart.'

I drew out the jewellery box from the folds of my shawl and placed it before him, 'Either by pawning or selling these jewels, you have to bring me six thousand rupees as quickly as you can.'

Amulya was pained, 'No Didi, no, not pawn or sell your jewellery—I will get you six thousand rupees.'

Exasperated, I said, 'Oh, forget all that—I have no time. Take this box and leave for Calcutta by the train tonight; by day after tomorrow you must get me the six thousand rupees.'

Amulya took out the diamond necklace from the box, held it up to the light and put it back with a pained expression. I said, 'All these diamond pieces won't sell easily. That's why I have given you jewellery worth nearly thirty-five thousand rupees; I don't mind if all of it goes, but I have to have the six thousand rupees.'

Amulya said, 'Look here, Didi, I have fought bitterly with Sandipbabu for taking the six thousand rupees from you. Oh, the unbearable shame of it. Sandipbabu says for the motherland you have to sacrifice all sense of shame. Perhaps that is so. But this is a little different. I am not afraid to die for my country and I have the strength to show no mercy while killing; but I cannot get over the shame of taking this money from you. In this, Sandipbabu is far stronger—he suffers no such shame. He says one has to transcend the illusion that money belonged to the person whose purse it was in, or the mantra of Vande Mataram is in vain.' Amulya was inspired as he spoke. With me as an audience, his fervour always doubled. He continued to speak, 'According to the Gita, Lord Krishna has said that the soul cannot be killed. Killing someone is a mere phrase. Stealing money is the same. Whose money is it? No one creates money, no one carries it in death, it is not linked to anyone's souls. It belongs to me today, to my son tomorrow and to the moneylender the day after. If this whimsical money theoretically belongs to nobody, then if it goes towards serving the country instead of falling in the hands of my worthless son, what is the harm in it?'

Every time I heard Sandip's words from the mouth of this innocent boy, my heart quaked. Let the snake charmer play his tune and fiddle with snakes; he is aware of the dangers. But for pity's sake, these are the youth—all the world's blessings should go in keeping them safe; when they, in all ignorance of the snake's venom, reach for it with a smile, I realize just how poisonous a curse this snake is. Sandip was right in thinking that—I may be killed by him but I must snatch this boy away from his grip and save his soul.

I laughed and said, 'So, the money is also needed to serve those who are serving the country, right?'

Amulya raised his head proudly and said, 'Of course. They are our kings, and poverty would only take away their strength. Do you know, we never let Sandipbabu travel in anything less than first class. He never feels embarrassed to have lavish meals. He has to maintain his status, not for his sake, but for ours. Sandipbabu says, that the greatest weapon in the hands of the rulers of this world is the lure of lucre. If they welcome poverty, it won't just be a sacrifice, it'll be suicidal.'

At this point, Sandip slipped into the room silently. Hurriedly I dropped my shawl on the jewellery box. Sandip's voice dripped sarcasm as he asked, 'You still haven't finished your special business with Amulya?'

A trifle embarrassed, Amulya said, 'Oh, we have finished talking. It's not much, really.'

I interrupted, 'No Amulya, we aren't done yet.'

Sandip said, 'So it's exit Sandip once again?'

I said, 'Yes.'

'But what about the re-entry of Sandipkumar?'

'Not today, I don't have the time.'

Sandip's eyes flashed; he said, 'So you only have time for special work and no time to waste, eh?'

Jealousy. Where the mighty have exposed themselves, the weak can hardly resist a jaunty swagger. So, in a firm voice I said, 'No, I don't have the time.'

Sandip went away with a glum face. Amulya was a little disturbed, 'Ranididi, I think Sandipbabu is upset.'

I spoke vehemently, 'He has no reason, or the right, to be upset. Let me tell you one thing Amulya, you are not to mention the job I have trusted you with, to Sandipbabu, even if it costs you your life.'

Amulya said, 'I won't tell him.'

'Then why wait? Leave by the night train.' I left the room along with him. But outside, on the veranda, I found Sandip waiting. I knew he would catch hold of Amulya. In order to stop him doing that, I had to intervene, 'Sandipbabu, what did you want to talk about?'

'Oh, my chatter is not important, it's mere idle talk, and since you don't have any time to spare—'

I said, 'I have the time.'

Amulya left. Sandip stepped into the room and said, 'I saw a box in Amulya's hand, what was it?'

So it hadn't escaped his eyes. I spoke a trifle harshly, 'If I wanted to tell you about it, I'd have given it to him in front of you.'

'Do you think Amulya won't tell me?'

'No, he won't.'

Sandip's anger was palpable now. He burst out saying, 'You think you will score over me. You can't. That Amulya—If I crushed him underfoot and killed him he'd think it was heaven. And you think you can take him away from me? Over my dead body.'

The anger of weakness—at last Sandip had understood that his power failed when compared to me. Hence the untrammelled outburst. He knew that his force wouldn't work against my strength and one condemning glance from me could shatter the walls of his citadel. Hence this show of power today. I smiled silently. At long last I was in the rung above him; I hope to God I never lose it or come down from it. I hope that even amidst my greatest misfortune, I am left with a modicum of self-respect.

Sandip said, 'I know that was your jewellery box.'

I said, 'You may guess as you like, but I won't tell you.'

'You trust Amulya more than me? Do you know that he is the shadow of my shadow, the echo of my echo, and without me at his side, he is nothing?'

'In that space where he is not your echo, he is Amulya and there I trust him more than I trust you.'

'Don't forget that you have promised me all your jewellery for the initiation of the Mother's puja. You have already donated your jewels.'

'If the gods spare me any jewellery I will give it to them willingly. But how can I promise to give the jewellery that has been stolen?'

'Look here, don't think you can give me the slip. Right now I am busy; let me finish the work first and then there'll be time for all your elaborate feminine wiles and games. I may even join in them myself.'

The moment I had stolen my husband's money and handed it to Sandip, the last bit of melody had gone out of our relationship. I had certainly cheapened myself and reduced my worth but Sandip too had lost his powers over me. You can't shoot arrows at something that is already within your fist. So, today Sandip lacked his brave warrior charm. His words held the despicable, harsh echoes of squabbling.

Sandip went on staring at me with his bright eyes and gradually they grew as dark and thirsty as the afternoon sky. His feet moved restlessly. I realized he was about to rise and any moment now he would rush forward and take me in his arms. My heart lurched, my nerves jangled and ears buzzed—I knew that if I continued to sit a moment longer, I would never be able to get up. I called on my entire reserve of strength, tore myself from the seat and ran towards the door. Sandip's choked voice vibrated dully, 'Queen, where do you run?'

The next moment he jumped up after me but the sound of footsteps outside made him return to his seat. I turned towards the bookshelf and stared at the names of books.

As soon as my husband entered the room, Sandip said, 'Hey Nikhil, don't you have Browning in your collection? I was telling Queen Bee about our college-club—you do remember the row amongst the four of us over translating that poem by Browning? What, you don't remember? You know, it went—

*She should never have looked at me*
*If she meant I should not love her!*
*There are plenty . . . men you call such.*
*I suppose . . . she may discover*
*All her soul to, if she pleases,*
*And yet leave much as she found them:*
*But I'm not so, and she knew it*
*When she fixed me, glancing round them.*

'I had somehow managed a Bengali translation, but it was quite unreadable. There was a time when I'd thought of being a poet—any moment the inspiration would grip me. But God was kind enough to let that whim pass. But our Dakhinacharan, if only he wasn't an inspector with the British today, would surely have made an excellent poet; he did a brilliant translation—it read like it was written originally in Bengali, and not in the language of a country that doesn't exist geographically:

*If she had known that she would never love me*
*Was it right that she'd cast her eyes upon me?*
*Many are the men that walk this earth*
*(Though I don't know what they are worth)*
*To whom if she had laid her soul bare*
*They'd still have stood straight and bare.*
*But she knew that I am not of that class*
*So why did she pierce me with her glance?*

'Oh no, Queen Bee, you search in vain; Nikhil gave up reading poetry when he got married. Perhaps he had no need of it anymore. I had also given it up from too much work, but I do feel that crazy fever is about to grip me once again.'

My husband said, 'Sandip, I have come to give you a warning.'

Sandip said, 'About the crazy fever of poetry?'

My husband didn't join in the joke and continued, 'For some time now, maulavis from Dacca have started visiting regularly, trying to provoke the Muslims in this area. They are not too happy with you and something may happen if you don't watch out.'

'Are you advising me to escape?'

'I have come to inform you, not to advise you.'

'If I was the zamindar here, the Muslims would have to worry, not I. It would be better for both you and me if you put some pressure on them instead of coming and getting me apprehensive. Do you know that your weakness has even robbed the neighbouring zamindars of their true powers?'

'Sandip, I didn't offer you advise and it would be nice if you returned the favour. It's pointless. There's one more thing: for some time now your followers have been ganging up and terrorizing my subjects. This has to stop; you'll have to leave my territory.'

'For fear of the Muslims or are there other threats too?'

'Sandip, there are such threats that it'd be cowardly *not* to be scared, and being aware of those threats I am asking you to leave. I am headed for Calcutta in another five days or so. I want you to leave with me. You could stay in our house in Calcutta, that's not a problem.'

'Good, at least I get five days to think. Meanwhile, Queen Bee, let me start humming songs about having to leave your beehive. Oh poet of this day, unlock your doors, let me loot your songs—actually you are the thief, you stole my words and made them yours—the name may be yours but the songs are mine,' he started singing in his slightly off-tune, baritone voice a song set in Bhairavi:

*The sweet season is here to stay in your land of honey,*
*The smiles and tears of coming and going drift in the air.*
*The one who leaves is all that goes, the flowers still bloom and thrive,*
*The ones meant to go, droop at the day's end.*
*When I was close, so many songs I gave:*
*Now I go away, is there a reward to have?*
*In the shade of the flowery grove I leave behind this hope—*
*That the rains would drench in tears this fiery spring of yours.*

His unbounded audacity had no veils, naked as the flames. It didn't wait to be stopped; trying to do so was like denying the thunder, which the lightning laughed and brushed aside. I left the room. As I was heading towards the inner sanctum, suddenly Amulya appeared before me, 'Ranididi, don't worry at all. I'm leaving now. I won't come back empty-handed.'

I looked upon his sincere, young face and said, 'Amulya, I don't worry about myself—but let me always worry for you all.'

As he was leaving, I called him back and asked, 'Amulya, is your mother alive?'

'Yes.'

'Sisters?'

'No. I am my mother's only son. My father died when I was very young.'

'Go Amulya, go back to your mother.'

'Didi, here I see my mother as well as my sister in the same person.'

I said, 'Amulya, before you leave tonight, have your dinner over here.'

He said, 'No time, Ranididi. Give me your blessing to carry with me.'

'What do you like to eat, Amulya?'

'If I was with my mother, I'd have gorged myself on sweetmeats this time of the year. When I come back, Ranididi, I'll have sweets made by you.'

## Nikhilesh

I woke up suddenly at three in the night and felt that my long-familiar world had died and was sitting like a spectre, guarding my bed, my room, all my things. I understood now why people were afraid of ghosts, even those of their close ones. When the eternally familiar turned unfamiliar in an instant, it was a nightmare. When your entire life was running along a certain track and you had to change tracks and make it run a course that wasn't even marked, the task was a difficult one. Even being yourself became a challenge; one felt that he himself was also perhaps a changed being.

For a while now it was clear that Sandip and his gang were terrorizing people. If I'd been my normal self, I would have firmly told him to leave the area. But all this trouble had made me lose my footing; my path was no longer straight and narrow. I felt ashamed to ask Sandip to leave—something else cropped up between us. And that made me feel very small.

Marriage was private and personal; it wasn't merely a duty or about a structured family life. It was the expression of my life. And that was why I couldn't put any pressure on it from without. If I did, I would be insulting the God within. I cannot explain this to anyone. Perhaps I am different and that's why I've been cheated. But how could I cheat everything within me to stop being cheated from without?

I am initiated into the mantra of Truth—that which creates the world outside through the heart. That is why today I had to rip apart all the mesh of the world like this. My inner deity would release me from the slavery, the bondage of the world. I would gain that freedom by bruising my heart. But when I gained it, the kingdom of the heart would be all mine.

I could already taste that freedom. Every now and then, the sound of the birds chirping at dawn burst through the all-permeating darkness of my heart. The man within me reiterated from time to time: there is no harm in letting go of the dream that was Bimala, the illusion.

Chandranathbabu informed me that Sandip had joined up with Harish Kundu and they were preparing to host a puja of Mahishamardini Durga, with great pomp and grandeur. Harish Kundu had already begun to raise the cost for this puja from his subjects. Our court poet and pundit were employed to write an eulogy that could be read in two ways. Sandip and Chandranathbabu had also had a debate over this. Sandip claimed that God has an evolution: if we do not modify the God constructed by our forefathers to suit our needs, it would be an act of atheism. It was

Sandip's mission to give the old gods new colours, release them from the shackles of the past: he was the salvation for the gods.

I have seen this from our childhood days—Sandip was the magician of Ideas; he was never interested in discovering the Truth, because juggling with it gave him greater pleasure. If he had been born in central Africa, he would have taken great pleasure in proving that human sacrifice and feeding on human flesh was the best way to bring human beings close to one another. The one who truly thrived on illusion, could scarcely escape being deluded himself. I believe that every time Sandip created a novel web of illusion with his words, he himself believed 'I have found Truth', however disparate his one Truth was from another.

Anyway, I was loath to offer any assistance in building up this tavern of illusion over my motherland. I would rather not have a hand in getting the young lads, who wanted to serve the country, into the addictive habit right from the beginning. To those who want to cast a spell on young minds and get some results, it is the end that justifies all and those spellbound minds have no intrinsic value. If I could not save the country from frenzied intoxication, then her puja would lay the foundation of her downfall and every action meant to serve her would return back to her bosom to wound her.

I ordered Sandip to leave my house in front of Bimala. I suppose both Sandip and Bimala would read my intentions wrong. But I need to be free of this fear of being misunderstood. Let Bimala misunderstand me too.

The maulavis from Dacca were swarming the place. The Muslims in our area bore as much hatred for cow-slaughter as the Hindus did. But now there had been a few instances of cow-slaughter here and there. I heard about it first from a Muslim subject and he too, voiced his dissent. I realized that it'd be difficult holding them back. There was a false sense of obduracy at the root of the matter. Resistance would only give it credence. That was precisely what the opposition wanted to achieve.

I sent for some of my influential Hindu subjects and tried to talk to them. I said, 'We are free to practice our own religion but others' religion is out of bounds. Just because I am a Vaishnav doesn't mean the Kali worshipper should give up bloodshed. There is no choice. The Muslims should be allowed to practice their religion in their way. Don't create a problem over this.'

They said, 'Raja, all these demonstrations were not there before.'

I said, 'They weren't, but that was their wish. Try to find ways to desist them of their own free will. That is not the violent way.'

They said, 'No Raja, those days are gone. Now you have to snub them or you cannot control them.'

I said, 'Snubbing will not put an end to cow-slaughter, but only increase a desire to kill humans as well.'

One of them had studied English and learnt to chant the language of modern times. He said, 'Look here, this is not only about a tradition; our country is primarily agricultural and for us the cow—'

I said, 'In this country, buffalo-milk is also drunk and that animal also ploughs the land. But when we all slaughter it and dance about with its head, it looks strange if we fight the Muslims over this, using religion as our excuse. Religion ridicules us and violence increases. If it's only the cow that shouldn't be killed and not the buffalo, then it isn't about religion, it's about superstition.'

The British-educated said, 'Can't you see who is behind this? The Muslims now know that they won't be taken to task. Have you heard what they have done in Pachurey?'

I said, 'That a day has come when the Muslims can become weapons against us, is a result of what we have fashioned with our hands. This is how Fate brings justice. What we have heaped over the ages, is now going to be wreaked on us.'

The British-educated said, 'Fine, then let it be wreaked. But there's a joy in it for us—we have won a victory. The law that they held so dear to themselves has been razed to the ground by us: so long, they have ruled but now we will make them robbers. This will not be recorded in history, but we will remember this forever.'

Meanwhile, I became notorious through the many mentions in newspapers. I came to know that 'patriots' had made my effigy and burned it with great pomp in a cremation ground by the river, in Chakravarty's area. There were plans for more humiliation. They had come to me, to get me to buy shares into a joint enterprise in opening a cloth-mill. I said, 'If it was just my money that would go, I wouldn't hesitate. But along with it several poor people would lose money and so I won't buy the shares.'

'Why, pray? Don't you want the country to progress?'

'A business may eventually benefit the country, but setting off to serve the country doesn't make for good business sense. When we were all calm and peaceful, no business took off and now that we are excited, do you think business would suddenly boom?'

'Why don't you simply say that you won't buy the shares?'

'I'll invest when I truly feel your business is worth its salt. The fires in your heart may or may not light up your hearths—I don't know that yet.'

They think I am a calculating miser. Sometimes I feel like showing them my books with the accounts of my work for the country. I suppose they are ignorant of the fact that I once tried to improve the quality of crops harvested in our motherland. I tried to get the farmers to grow sugarcane by importing seeds from Java and Mauritius; I left no stone unturned, as per the advice of the agriculture department of the government. But finally, what was the result? Just the sneaky snigger of the farmers in my area. To this day it has remained sneaky and covert. Later when I tried to translate the governmental agro-journals and went to speak to them about growing Japanese beans or foreign cotton, I realized that the covert snigger was in danger of becoming overt. At the time there was no support from the 'patriots' and the Vande Mataram mantra was silent. And my shipping business—oh, what's the point of harking back to all that? The fires they have lit in order to serve the country, should hopefully be banked by burning my effigy and spread no further.

What is this I hear? Our treasury in Chakua has been looted. Last night the estate taxes worth seven and a half thousand rupees were deposited there and it was supposed to leave for this office by boat at dawn today. The clerk, in order to facilitate sending it, had changed the money into tens and twenties and kept them in bundles. Late in the night a gang of robbers looted it with guns and pistols. Quasim Sardar had taken a bullet and was wounded. The strange thing was that the robbers only took six thousand rupees and left the remainder strewn on the floor. They could easily have taken all the money. Anyway, the robbers have left and now the police processes would start. The money has already gone, but there won't be any peace either.

I went indoors and found they had all heard the news. Mejorani came and said, 'Thakurpo, how terrible.'

I tried to make light of it, 'Terrible is still a long way off. There's still enough to clothe and feed us for a few more years.'

'Oh no, don't joke about this: why are you their sole target always? Thakurpo, why don't you try to appease them a little? How can you fight all the people—'

'For the sake of the people, I cannot let the country go to hell.'

'Just the other day I heard they've done something by the river—it's an insult to you. Shame on them. I am so scared. The little princess has studied with a British woman—she is quite fearless. I can only rest if you let me call the priest and do some pujas to ward off the evil. For God's sake, Thakurpo, go away to Calcutta; if you stay here, they may do something any day now—'

Mejorani's fears and concern were like a balm on my soul. Fair mother, your kindness will always be upon us.

'Thakurpo, keeping that money next to your bedroom is not a good idea. Lord knows, they may hear of it somehow and eventually—I am not worried about the money, but who knows—'

I tried to calm her fears, 'Okay, I'll take out that money right now and send it away to our treasury. Day after tomorrow I'll go and deposit it in the bank in Calcutta.'

I went into the bedroom and found the ante-room locked from within. When I knocked on it, Bimala answered from within, 'I am changing.'

Mejorani said, 'Early in the morning the little one has started her toilette—strange, that one. I guess today there'll be one of those Vande Mataram meetings of theirs. Ahoy there, Devi Choudhurani, are you busy gathering the loot?'

'I'll come back later and straighten it all out,' I came outside and found the police inspector waiting for me. I asked him, 'Did you find anything?'

'We have our suspicions.'

'On?'

'Quasim Sardar.'

'What? But he has been wounded?'

'No real wound that one: just a grazed foot, slight bleeding, he could have done it himself.'

'I cannot suspect Quasim, he is trustworthy.'

'Perhaps, but that doesn't mean he cannot steal. I have seen such things like an employee of twenty-five years, totally faithful, has suddenly one day—'

'If that is the case, I cannot send him to prison.'

'Why should you send? It'll be done by those in charge of the job.'

'Why would Quasim take six thousand and leave the rest behind?'

'Just so that you don't suspect him. Whatever you may say, that man is shrewd. He guards your treasury, but I'm sure he's behind all the looting and raids on the treasuries in this area.' The inspector quoted many instances of how robbers can loot treasuries twenty to thirty miles away and come back the same night to report to the master's office.

I asked him, 'Have you brought Quasim here?'

He said, 'No, he is at the police station; the deputy would be here any moment to investigate.'

I said, 'I want to see him.'

The moment he saw me, Quasim fell at my feet, weeping, 'I swear on my God, sir, I haven't done this.'

I said, 'Quasim, I do not suspect you. Don't be afraid, I won't let them punish you if you are innocent.'

Quasim couldn't describe the robbers very well; he simply muttered away, 'Four-five hundred people, such huge guns, swords, etc.' I realized this was all rubbish. Either fear lent wings to his imagination, or the shame of defeat made him exaggerate. He was of the opinion that since there was bad blood between Harish Kundu and me, this was done by him. In fact, he believed that he had clearly heard the voice of Ikram Sardar, one of Kundu's men.

I said, 'Look Quasim, don't you dare drag someone else's name into this just on the basis of conjecture. You are not responsible for fabricating proofs of whether Harish Kundu is involved or not.'

At home, I sent for Chandranathbabu. He shook his head and said, 'Now there is no peaceful way. We have moved aside ethics and placed the country on that pedestal; now all that is bad in the land would shamelessly raise its ugly head and reveal itself.'

'Do you think this was done by—'

'I don't know. But crime is on the rise. Go ahead, send them all away from your area.'

'I have given them another day's time. Day after tomorrow they will all leave.'

'Listen, let me tell you just one thing: you take Bimala with you to Calcutta. From here, she is getting a narrow vision of the world, she cannot place every person, every object in their right perspectives. Let her truly see the world; let her, for once, see man and his space of work in its true magnitude.'

'I was thinking the same thing myself.'

'But don't wait any longer. Look Nikhil, human history has evolved along with all the races and all the countries and that's why even politics shouldn't sell out on ethics to establish itself or the country. I know that Europe doesn't truly believe this, but neither can I accept that we have to look to Europe for our guidelines. Man dies for Truth and gains immortal fame and if the same is done by a country or a race, it will have the same results. We must strive to let that perception of Truth become all-important and the ultimate in this India of ours, amidst the roaring laughter of the devil himself. What is this foreign failing that has taken the whole nation by storm?'

The whole day passed in taking care of all these problems. Exhausted, I went to bed at night. I decided to take out that money from the iron chest the next day.

At some point in the night I woke up. The room was pitch dark. I could hear a noise, like someone weeping. Every now and then, a tearful sigh floated in the room, like gusts of wind on a cloudy night. I felt the room was sobbing its heart out. There was no one else in my room. For some time now, Bimala slept in another room. I left the bed. Outside, on the veranda, I found Bimala lying on the floor.

These things are difficult to write. It is known and felt only by Him, who sits amidst the kernel of the universe and absorbs all the pain of the earth. The sky was mute, the stars silent, the night was still—and in the midst of it all, this sleepless weeping.

I could perhaps take all my joys and sorrows, compare and contrast them to the world at large, to the written word, and give it a fancy name, thereby ending the matter. But could I give a name to this source of pain welling up and flooding the bosom of this darkness? That solitary night, when I stood in the midst of those millions of silent stars and gazed upon her, a voice fearfully asked me, 'Who am I to stand judgement?' Oh life, oh death, endless creation and the Lord of it all—I salute the mystery contained within you.

For a moment I thought I should go back. But I couldn't. Silently I sat near her and gently stroked her hair. At first her entire body stiffened up and the next instant it began to break apart and disintegrate into sobs. I could scarcely comprehend how the human heart could hold so many tears.

I stroked her head gently for a while. And then, at some point she groped around and took my feet in her hands. She pressed it so hard to her heart that I felt it would break from the burden of my feet.

## Bimala

Amulya was expected back in the morning. I instructed the bearer to inform me the minute he arrived. But I couldn't sit still. Finally I went and waited in the living room.

When I sent Amulya to Calcutta to sell my jewellery, I had no thought for anyone but myself. It never occurred to me that he was so young and if he went to sell such expensive jewellery anywhere, he'd be under suspicion. Women are so helpless that we seem to have no other option than to pass our problems on to someone else. When we die, we drag five other people with us.

I had said with great pride, 'I shall save Amulya.' But how could one drowning person save another? Oh Lord, perhaps I have already pushed him into hell—little brother of mine, I am such an unfortunate sister that the day I prayed for you in my heart must have been the day Yama smiled to himself. Today, I was a burden of ill omens.

I feel sometimes a plague of crime grips people and its sudden arrival brings death that much closer. At these times isn't it possible to keep it far, far away from the world? I could clearly see how damaging its claws were. It was like the torch of danger, burning away merrily only to set the world alight.

The clock struck nine. I began to feel Amulya was in trouble, he was in police custody: my jewellery box was raising a storm of questions, whose was it, how did he get it, questions which eventually I alone could answer. What would I say in front of the whole world? Mejorani, I had really held you in very low esteem all these years. Now it's your turn. Today, you'll take the form of the whole wide world, and have your revenge. Dear God, please help me now, I'll quit all my pride and lay it willingly at Mejorani's feet.

I couldn't be still. I rushed indoors and went towards Mejorani's room. She was fixing herself some betel leaves, sitting in the veranda with Thako beside her. At the sight of the maid, I hesitated for a moment; but I brushed it aside and bent down to touch Mejorani's feet. She exclaimed, 'Hey there, little one, what's the matter with you? Why the sudden surfeit of respect?'

I said, 'Didi, it's my birthday today. I may have done you many wrongs—please bless me, that I may never hurt you again. I am so mean-minded.'

I quickly touched her feet again and left. She started saying, 'Listen, little one, if it's your birthday why didn't you tell us earlier? You're invited to lunch in my room. Sweet sister, don't forget.'

God, please do something so that it really becomes my birthday today. Can I not be born anew? Wipe the slate clean and test me afresh, oh Lord.

As I was about to enter the living room again, Sandip appeared. Hatred burned acrid in my soul. The face that I saw in the bright light of day today, didn't hold an ounce of genius. I said, 'Please go away from here.'

Sandip laughed and said, 'Amulya is not here. Now it's my turn to talk business.'

Hell and damnation. How could I refute the very rights that I once granted him? I said, 'I need to be alone.'

'Queen, the presence of another person doesn't get in the way of being alone. Don't push me into the throngs of other people. I am Sandip, alone even in a crowd.'

'Please come another day; today I am—'

'Waiting for Amulya?'

Irritated, I was about to leave the room when Sandip fished out my jewellery box from the folds of his shawl and placed it on the table.

I was startled, 'So Amulya didn't go?'

'Go where?'

'To Calcutta?'

Sandip smiled a little, 'No.'

Thank God for small mercies. I am a thief and the punishment should stop at me—let it not harm Amulya.

Sandip saw my expression and mocked it, 'So thrilled, Queen? Is the jewellery box worth that much? Then how did you promise all of this to the goddess? You have already given it away—are you going to take it back from the deity's feet?'

Pride doesn't quit, even when you're gasping for breath. I felt like showing him how little those jewels were worth to me. I said, 'If you have your eyes on these jewels, you're welcome to take them.'

Sandip said, 'I have my eyes on all the wealth in the whole of Bengal. There is no greater virtue than greed. For the lords of this earth, greed is the vehicle. So then, all this jewellery is mine?'

Sandip picked up the box and covered it with his shawl. At this point Amulya rushed into the room: his eyes were bloodshot, face pallid and hair dishevelled. He seemed to have shed his youthful innocence in a single day. My heart was stricken at the sight of him. Amulya didn't spare me a second glance, walked up to Sandip and said, 'You have taken that jewellery box from my valise?'

'Does the jewellery box belong to you?'

'No, but the valise does.'

Sandip laughed out loud. He said, 'I can see you have a strong sense of possession where your valise is concerned, Amulya. I guess you will also turn a moralist before you die.'

Amulya dropped down on the chair, covered his face and rested his head on the table. I went up to him, stroked his hair gently and asked, 'Amulya, what's the matter?'

He shot up on his feet and said, 'Didi, I wanted to bring this jewellery box to you myself and Sandipbabu knew that; so he quickly—'

I said, 'What use is that box of jewellery to me? Let it go, who cares?'

Stunned, Amulya said, 'Why should it go?'

Sandip said, 'These jewels are mine—it's a gift from the Queen.'

Amulya went crazy, 'No, no, never. Didi, I have brought it back for you—you cannot give it away to anyone.'

I said, 'Dear child, your generosity will stay in my heart forever, but let the jewels go to those who lust after it.'

Amulya looked at Sandip as a wild animal surveys its prey, 'Look here Sandipbabu, you know that I'm not afraid of capital punishment. If you take this box of jewellery—'

Sandip tried to give a mocking smile, 'Amulya, you should also know by now that your threats do not scare me. Queen Bee, I have not come here today to take these jewels. I came to give them to you. But I couldn't tolerate the injustice of your accepting something that belonged to me, from Amulya's hands and hence I made sure you accepted they were mine first. Now I am gifting my possession to you—here it is. You may sort things out with that child, I am going. For some days now you two have been discussing special matters and I want no part in it. If something "special" happens, do not blame me. Amulya, I have sent your valise, books and all other belongings to your rooms in the market. You may no longer keep your things in my room.'

Sandip rushed out.

I said, 'Amulya, ever since I gave my jewellery to you for selling, I have lost my peace of mind.'

'Why, Didi?'

'I was scared you may be in trouble because of this, they may suspect you of stealing it and take you away. I do not need the six thousand rupees. Now, you must obey this one instruction: go home, go back to your mother.'

Amulya brought out a bundle from under his shawl and said, 'Didi, I have brought the six thousand rupees.'

I said, 'Where did you get it?'

He didn't answer me. Instead he said, 'I tried and tried to get guineas but I couldn't. So I brought notes instead.'

'Amulya, for pity's sake, tell me where you got the money.'

'I cannot tell you.'

I felt the world was drained of all light. I said, 'What have you done Amulya? Is this money—'

Quickly Amulya broke in, 'I know you will say I have got this money by crime—all right, I'll accept that. But you pay the price of your crime and I have paid that price. Now this money belongs to me.'

I had no wish to hear all the details about getting the money. My nerves were cringing and my entire body felt as if it was wilting under pressure. I said, 'Take it back, Amulya, put it back wherever you got this money from.'

'That is very difficult.'

'No, child, it's not difficult. Cursed is that moment when you came to me. I have done you more harm than even Sandip did you.'

Sandip's name seemed to set something off in him. He said, 'Sandip. It's because I came to you that I could recognize him for what he is. Do you know, he hasn't spent a single paise of the six thousand rupees that he took from you the other day? He went from here, locked his room, poured out all the guineas on to the floor and stared at them in bemused wonder. He said, "This isn't money, it is heavenly wealth, notes from the eternal flute that hardened as they fell to earth—these cannot be changed into banknotes. They desire to adorn the throat of a nymph—oh Amulya, don't you boys cast your visceral eyes on these—the smile of the goddess, the grace of the deity; no, oh no, these weren't meant to fall into the uncouth hands of that head-clerk. Look Amulya, he has been lying, the police have no news of any boats being stolen and he wants to use it to his own purposes. We must get hold of those three letters from that man." I asked him, "How?" Sandip said, "By force, by threats." I said, "I'm game. But these guineas must be returned." Sandip said, "We'll see about that." How I threatened the clerk and got those letters from him and burnt them is a long story. That same night I came to Sandip and said, "The danger is past. Now give me the guineas, I'll return them to Didi tomorrow." Sandip said, "What is this foolishness that has gripped you? I suppose now your motherland is shrouded under Didi's anchal. Say Vande Mataram, let your illusions go." You know Didi, how Sandip works his magic. The guineas stayed with him. I spent the dark night sitting by the pond and chanting Vande Mataram. Yesterday, when you gave me the jewellery to sell, I went to him again in the evening. I could tell he was furious with me. But he didn't show it. He said, "Look, if I have those guineas anywhere in my belongings, you are free to take them." He hurled his bunch of keys at me. They weren't there. I asked, "Tell me where you have kept them?" Sandip said, "I'll tell you only when you are free of your trance. Not now." I realized he wouldn't give in and so I had to take another way. Even so, I tried to give him these six thousand rupees in banknotes and get back the guineas. He said he's getting them, kept me waiting, went to his room, broke into my valise and brought the jewellery box to you. He didn't let me bring this box to you. And he claims these jewels are his gift to you? How can I say how much he has cheated me? I will never forgive him. Didi, I am totally free of the hold he had over me. You have done it.'

I said, 'Child, that gives me great joy. But there's more. Freeing yourself isn't enough, you have to wash your guilt away. Don't wait Amulya, go now—put this money back where it came from. Can you do that, dear brother?'

'With your blessings I can, Didi.'

'This is not only your success; it is mine too. I am a woman and the way to the world is closed to me, or I would never let you go—I'd go myself. This is the greatest punishment for me, that you are having to pay for my sins.'

'Don't say that, Didi. The path that I took was not your way. It was challenging and so it seemed alluring. Now you have called me to your path—even if this is a thousand times more difficult, I shall win with your blessings; I'm not afraid. So you would like me to return this money where it came from, right?'

'It's not what *I'd* like, child, but what *He'd* like.'

'I don't know all that: it's enough for me that His wishes have come from your mouth. But Didi, you owe me a meal. I'll go only after you have fed me. Then I'll try and finish the work by tonight.'

I tried to smile and my eyes brimmed over; I said, 'All right.'

The moment Amulya left, my heat sank. I felt I had pushed him into murky waters. Dear God, why do my sins have to be expiated so elaborately, with others' blood? Wasn't my own enough? Must you lay the burden on so many shoulders? Oh, why should that poor soul suffer for it? I called him back, 'Amulya.' But he had left, 'Bearer, bearer,' I called.

'Yes, Ranima?'

'Send Amulyababu in.'

Perhaps the bearer wasn't familiar with Amulya's name; so a little later he brought in Sandip. He stepped into the room and said, 'When you sent me away, I knew you'd call me back. The high and the low tide are both caused by the same moon. I was so certain you'd call me that I was waiting right by the door. The minute I saw your bearer I spoke before he could say anything, "Fine, fine, I'm coming right now." The rustic fool stood openmouthed, certain that I knew magic. Queen Bee, the greatest power in this world is of this mantra. Hypnosis can conquer anything. It works by sound alone, and often even soundlessly. At long last Sandip has met his match in this duel. Your quiver holds many arrows, my dear. In this whole wide world, you are the only one who has been able to turn Sandip away at your will and call him back the same way. So now your prey is here. Now what would you like to do to it—finish it off or keep it caged? But let me warn you, Queen, killing this being is as difficult as holding it captive. So don't hesitate to use whatever celestial weapons that are within your powers to use.'

Sandip rambled away in this manner only because today he was plagued by a fear of defeat. I believe he was well aware that I had sent for Amulya; the bearer must have given his name. But he cheated and came over himself instead. He didn't even give me the time to set him right. But now I had glimpsed the weak and the swagger was in vain. Now I wasn't ready to give up even an inch of my hard-won ground.

I said, 'Sandipbabu, how can you jabber so much so fast? Do you come prepared?'

Sandip's face turned crimson with rage. I said, 'I have heard that raconteurs have a ready stock of long, descriptive paragraphs that they use whenever the occasion arises. Do you also have a notebook full of these?'

Sandip chewed over each word as he spat it out, 'The Fates have blessed you women with enough graces and then the tailor, the jeweller, are all in league with you; why should we, men, be without our own weapons—'

I said, 'Sandipbabu, go and look up your notebook—these are not the right words. I have noticed that you get mixed up sometimes. That is the problem of learning by rote.'

Sandip lost his temper and roared in outrage, 'You! How dare you insult me? Just think how much I know about you. You are—' He was lost for words. Sandip was a seller of spells and the minute his spells failed, he was left with nothing—from a king he turned into a beggar in an instant. Weak, oh so weak. The more he turned nasty and spoke rudely, my heart danced with joy. He was done with tying me up in his spells; I was free. Oh thank God, thank God. Insult me, abuse me, that is your true form. Don't raise me on a pedestal—that's a lie.

At this moment my husband came into the room. Today Sandip didn't have the strength to control himself, as he did on other days. My husband saw his expression and looked a little surprised. Earlier this would have caused me embarrassment. But today I was glad. I wanted to take a good look at this weakling.

Since we were both silent, my husband sat on the stool after some hesitation. He said, 'Sandip, I was looking for you and heard that you are here.'

Sandip spoke with extra vigour, 'Yes, the Queen Bee sent for me early in the day and since I am a mere working bee in the hive, I had to drop everything and rush at her command.'

My husband said, 'I am leaving for Calcutta tomorrow, you'll have to come with me.'

Sandip said, 'But why? Am I your valet?'

'All right then, you go to Calcutta and I'll come along as your valet.'

'I have no work in Calcutta.'

'Which is why you have to go there—you have too much work here.'

'I am not budging.'

'Then you'll be made to budge.'

'By force?'

'Yes, by force.'

'Fine, I'll budge. But the world doesn't consist of two poles—Calcutta and your area. There are other places on the map.'

'Looking at you one would think there is no other place in the world besides my area.'

Sandip stood up and said, 'There comes a time for every man when the whole world shrinks into a tiny space. I have perceived my world amidst this living room of yours and that's why I wasn't moving. Queen Bee, these people won't understand what I say and perhaps you wouldn't either. I worship you and I will continue to do so. Ever since I have seen you, my mantra has changed; no longer Vande Mataram, it's now Vande Priyam, Vande Mohinim. The mother protects us, the lover destroys—and there is beauty in this destruction. You have raised a storm of tinkling anklets—the death-dance—in my heart. The image of this land of mine used to be 'komala sujala malayajashitala'; you have changed this in the eyes of your devotee. You have no mercy; you have come, oh temptress, with the cup of poison in your hands; I shall drink that poison, be ripped apart by it and either die or conquer death. The days of the mother are gone. Lover, oh lover—gods, heavens, ethics, Truth: you have turned them to dust. All else are mere shadows, all bonds of control, order all torn away. Lover, oh lover—I can set fire to the rest of the world and dance exultantly on the ashes at the very spot where you have laid your feet. These are good men, they are very good, they want what is good for all—as if it is the Truth. Never, there is no other Truth in the whole world; this is my only Truth. I worship you. My loyalty for you has made me ruthless. My devotion for you has lit the fires of hell within me. I am not good, I am not devout, I do not accept anything in this world—all I accept is the one whom I have perceived tangibly.'

Strange, surprising. A short while ago I had hated him with all my being. What seemed like ashes suddenly blazed into life. This was true fire. Why does God make us such mixed beings? Was it just to show off his magical prowess? A half hour ago I was quite certain that the man I had once taken for a king was nothing but a mere actor in a play. But no—sometimes a true king may lurk in the guise of an actor. He has much lust, much greed and much that is fake, that he hides within layers of flesh; but yet—it's best to accept that we do not know, we never know the whole truth, not even our own selves. Man is a strange being; only the omnipotent one knew the sublime mysteries that are woven around man. In the process, I am scalded, scarred. Storm. Shiva is the Lord of storms, He is the Lord of joy and he'll set me free of my ties.

I have been feeling for quite some time now, that I have two minds. One is fully aware of the destructive powers of Sandip; the other finds it ever so sweet. When a ship sinks, it drags with it all those who were swimming close to it; Sandip was like that deadly ship. Even before fear gripped me, his magic pulled at me—in the blink of an eye it wanted to swallow me whole, drag me away from all light, everything good, the freedom of the sky, the waft of breath, away from a lifetime's reserves, every day's little thoughts. He was like the spirit of the dreaded piper, walking the streets with his unholy chants, pulling all the youths of the land to him like a magnet. The mother at the heart of the land wailed aloud. Desecrating her stash of nectar, they drink on sinful liquor. I understand it all, but magic can't be kept at bay. This was the test of Truth—drunken brazenness danced before the ascetic and said: 'You are a fool; penance wouldn't set you free, it's a long and hard road to travel. The heavens have sent me, I am the temptress, I am the madness, in my embrace you will achieve moksha in an instant.'

After a moment's pause, Sandip spoke to me again, 'Goddess, the time has come for me to say goodbye. This is for the best. My purpose for coming to you has been fulfilled. If I overstay, all the good will be undone gradually. If you are greedy and cheapen the greatest thing in this world, it can be disastrous. That which is endless in the space of an instant should not be dragged over time or it will be constrained. We were about to destroy that eternal, and at that point you raised your warning hand, saved your own worship as well as that of your devotee. Today, this parting is the greatest proof of my devotion for you. Goddess, on this day, I too set you free. In my earthen temple your formless form was hardly contained; it threatened to fall apart every moment; I take your leave to worship you in your greater form in the midst of greatness—I shall truly perceive you when I am away from you. Here I got your indulgence, but there I shall have your boon.'

My jewellery box was on the table. I held it out to him and said, 'I have given these jewels to the country. Please reach these to the feet of the goddess where they belong.'

My husband stood there silently. Sandip left the room.

I was making some sweets for Amulya, when suddenly Mejorani came in: 'Well hello, little one, are you cooking up a feast for yourself on your own birthday?'

I said, 'Can't I be cooking for someone else?'

Mejorani said, 'Today we will cook for you. I was all set to enter the kitchen when the news all but threw me; apparently some five or six hundred burglars raided one of our treasuries and looted six thousand rupees. Rumours are that they are now headed this way, towards the estate.'

This piece of news set my mind at ease. So it was *our* money then. I wanted to call Amulya immediately and tell him to return the money to my husband right here and now. Later I would give him my explanations.

Mejorani saw the play of emotions on my face and exclaimed, 'You surprise me—aren't you even the least bit scared?'

I said, 'I can't believe they'd actually come to loot our home.'

'And why not? Who could ever imagine they'd actually loot a treasury?'

I didn't answer her. Instead I bent my head and continued to fill the stuffing into the sweetmeats. She gazed at my face a little longer and finally said, 'Let me send for Thakurpo—our six thousand rupees must be sent off to Calcutta immediately, without further ado.'

The minute she left, I dropped my shawl on the floor and rushed into the ante-room which had the iron chest. My husband was so absent-minded that his shirt with the keys to the chest still hung on the rack in that room. I took the bunch from the pocket, extracted the keys to the chest and hid it in my clothes.

At this point there were knocks on the door. I said that I was changing. I heard Mejorani say, 'Just now she was making sweets and now suddenly she's getting dressed. The things I have to see. I guess they'll be having one of those Vande Mataram meetings today. Ahoy there, Devi Choudhurani, are you busy gathering the loot?'

Something made me open the iron chest slowly. Perhaps I was wishing the whole thing would be a dream and I'd open the tiny drawer and find the paper wrapped bundles right there. But alas, it was as empty as the trust betrayed by the traitor.

Without any reason, I had to change my clothes. I tied my hair anew. When I ran into Mejorani and she asked why I was so dolled up, I said, 'Birthday.'

She laughed and said, 'You need the smallest excuse to go and dress up. I've never seen another creature as whimsical as you.'

I was looking for the bearer to go and fetch Amulya, when he came and handed me a piece of paper with a note scribbled in pencil. Amulya had written, 'Didi, you'd invited me, but I couldn't wait. I am off to do your bidding first and then I'll have the meal. I'll be back by dusk.'

Where had Amulya gone, to what new traps? I could only always shoot him like an arrow, but if I missed my mark, I couldn't ever bring him back. This was the right moment for me to go and own up my own part in this whole fiasco. But in this world, women survived on trust—it was their whole world. It would be very difficult for me to live in this world after revealing how I had cheated that same trust. I'd have to keep standing on the very thing I'd broken—the jagged pieces would poke and stab me every now and then. It wasn't difficult to err. But nothing was more difficult than to atone for one's sins, especially for women.

For a while now, the channels of normal conversation with my husband were closed to me. Hence, I simply couldn't figure out when and how to suddenly broach such a big issue to him. Today he was late for lunch; it was nearly two o'clock. He was so preoccupied that he hardly ate anything. I had lost my right to plead with him to eat some more. I turned away and brushed away the tears.

For a moment I wanted to overcome my hesitation and say to him, 'Go and rest in the room—you are looking very tired.' I cleared my throat and was about to say it when the bearer came with the news that the police inspector was here with Quasim Sardar. My husband looked worried as he got up and left.

Soon after he left, Mejorani came and said, 'Why didn't you let me know when Thakurpo came to eat? Today he was late and so I went for my bath. But in the meantime—'

'Why, what's the matter?'

'I heard you are all leaving for Calcutta tomorrow? In that case I cannot stay on here. The elder queen won't leave her idols and deities. But what with all these burglaries I refuse to guard this empty house of yours and keep jumping out of my skin at the slightest sound. Is it fixed for tomorrow?'

I said, 'Yes.' I thought to myself: Lord knows what events and intrigues will transpire in this short while between now and then. After all that, whether I go to Calcutta or stay here, it won't matter to me. Who knows after that what the world would look like, how life would seem. It was all bleary, a dream.

Couldn't someone drag out, by the day, these few hours that were left before my Fate became a reality? I could use the time to tie up the loose ends. At least I could prepare myself and my world for the forthcoming pain. As long as the seeds of destruction stayed underground, they took so much time that one's fears can be lulled. But the moment the tiny shoot shot up above the ground, it grew rapidly and it was impossible to cover it with your heart, your life or your soul. I wanted to blank out, lie in a stupor and wait for whatever tumbled on my head. It would all be over before the day after tomorrow—the knowing, the mockery, the tears, questions and answers—all of it.

But Amulya's face, that innocence that glowed with the light of sacrifice, would not let me rest. He didn't wait around for his Fate—he rushed into the thick of things. I, unworthy even of womanhood, saluted him. For me he was God in the form of a child; he'd come to take my burden of sins quite playfully on to his own shoulders. How could I possibly tolerate this terrible mercy of God, that Amulya would take the punishment for my sins? Oh my child, I salute you. Oh brother dear, I salute you. You are pure, beautiful, brave, fearless and I salute you. I pray with all my heart that in the next life I have you on my lap as my son.

In the meantime, rumour was rife, policemen swarmed the place and the maids and servants were anxious. Khema, the maid, came to me and said, 'Chhotoranima, please put my gold chain and armlet away in your iron chest.' How could I tell her that it was I who had kicked up this storm of anxiety in the entire household and was now stuck in its eye? Like a good little mistress I had to take Khema's jewellery, Thako's savings. Our milkman's wife left a Benarasi sari and some other precious valuables with me in a tin box. She said, 'Ranima, this sari was given to me on your wedding.'

Tomorrow, when the iron chest will be opened, this Khema, Thako, milkman's wife—anyway, what's the point of dwelling on that? Instead let me think that a year has passed after tomorrow, another 3 January was here—would the sores and wounds of my family still be as raw?

Amulya had written that he'd be back by tonight. Meanwhile, I could hardly sit alone in my room, doing nothing. So I went to make sweets again. What I had made earlier was actually enough, but I made some more. Who would eat all this? I'll feed all the maids and servants in the house. I must do that tonight. My days were numbered. Tomorrow was no longer in my hands.

One after another I made the sweets, tirelessly. Every now and then I felt there was some commotion in the general direction of my rooms. Perhaps my husband had come to open the iron chest and found the keys missing. So Mejorani was summoning all the maids and raising hell over it. No, I wouldn't hear it, I'd keep the door firmly closed. I was about to shut the door when I saw Thako rushing towards me. Out of breath, she panted, 'Chhotoranima—'

I said, 'Go away, don't disturb me now.'

Thako said, 'Mejoranima's nephew Nanda has brought a weird machine from Calcutta—it sings like a person. So Mejoranima sent me to fetch you.'

I didn't know whether to laugh or to cry. A gramophone in the middle of all this. Every time it was wound up, it emitted the nasal tones of theatrical songs. It had no worries. When machine imitated life, it resulted in this terrible irony.

The sun set and dusk crept in. I knew whenever Amulya arrived he'd send for me. But I couldn't be at peace. I called the bearer and said, 'Send word to Amulyababu.'

The bearer came back a little later and said, 'Amulyababu is not there.'

It was just a few words, but my heart heaved with fear. Amulyababu is not there—in the melancholy dusk the words rang out like a wail. Not there—he's not there. He appeared like the golden ray of the sunset and then he's not there. I began to imagine many scenarios, both possible and impossible. It was I who pushed him to his death. That he didn't think twice was his greatness, but how would I live with this?

I didn't have a single memento of his; all I had was his loving gift to his sister—the pistol. It seemed like a divine intervention. My own personal God, in the shape of a child, had placed the tool to wipe out the blot that soiled the roots of my life and then vanished into thin air. What a loving gift—what an overtly pure signal.

I opened the box, took the pistol out and touched it to my forehead reverently. At that very moment, the bells and cymbals from our temple courtyard rang out to signal the evening arati. I bowed low on the ground and prayed.

That night I fed the sweets to everyone. Mejorani came and said, 'You went to all this trouble for your own birthday—why didn't you leave something for us to do?' She began to play a host of stage artistes on her gramophone, raising high voices in stretched decibels. To me it sounded like the neighing of the horses from the stables.

The meal took a while. I wanted to touch my husband's feet tonight. I went into the bedroom and found him fast asleep. The whole day he had been roaming around, plagued by endless troubles. I moved aside the mosquito net very carefully and softly lay my face on his feet. As my hair touched his feet, unconsciously he pushed my head away with his feet.

I went and sat in the veranda. In the distance a silk-cotton tree stood in the dark like a skeleton; it had shed all its leaves and the sickle moon gradually sank out of sight behind it. Suddenly I felt all the stars in the sky were afraid of me and the huge nocturnal world looked at me askance, because I was all alone. A lonely human is perhaps the biggest anomaly of Nature. Even the person who has lost every relation to death is not truly alone—he has company from beyond the grave. But when a person has everyone near and yet far away, who has simply fallen away from the daily rhythm of life, a glance at her face in the depth of night would send a chill down the spine of the universe. I am not present at the spot where I stand, I am far away from the people in whose company I stand. I walk, talk and live right on the face of a fissure, like the dewdrops on a lotus leaf.

But, when a person changes, why doesn't everything about her change? When I look to my heart I find everything there as before, only the positions altered. What was once neatly kept is now a muddle, what was once strung on a thread now lies scattered in the dust. That's why my heart was breaking and I wanted to die. But all of it still lived in my heart and so death didn't seem to be an end. I felt death would bring a more terrible sorrow. I would have to clear the accounts by living—

there was no other way.

Oh my Lord, please forgive me this once. All that you had once handed to me as the fortune of my life, I have now turned into a burden. Today I can neither bear it nor relinquish it. Just once more, play the tune on the flute that you once played by the pink sky of my dawn and all this will be resolved; only that tune from your flute can possibly join all that is broken, turn the sullied into pure again. Play the flute and recreate my life all over again. I do not see any other way open to me.

I lay face down on the floor and wept my heart out; some pity was needed, some refuge, a hint of mercy, some consolation that all this may yet be resolved. I said to myself, 'I'll lie like this night and day, oh Lord, I'll fast, I won't drink water until your blessings reach me.'

At this point I heard footsteps. My heart swayed. Who says gods never show themselves? I did not look up, in case he found my gaze repulsive. Come, come, come—let your feet touch my head, come, stand on my swaying heart, oh Lord—let me die this very instant.

He came and sat near my head. Who? My husband. In my husband's heart that Lord of mine was touched, who could no longer bear my pain. I felt I'd faint. And then the floodgates of tears opened, my nerve ends burst and let loose a storm of sorrow. I pressed his feet to my heart—wouldn't they get imprinted there for all eternity?

Now I could have easily confessed everything. But after this, could there be any words? Let my confessions be.

Gently, he stroked my head. I was blessed. I would be able to take my cup of hemlock and humbly touch my Lord's feet on the face of the humiliation that lay before me the next day.

But it broke my heart when I realized that the shehnai that had played nine years ago will never be played again, in my entire life. I came into this room, a new bride. Which gods do I have to pray to, so that the bride could come back, dressed in red and stand on that ceremonial threshold once again? How much longer, how many aeons, before I could go back to that day nine years ago? The gods may be able to create anew, but did they have the power to recreate a broken piece of creation?

## Nikhilesh

Today we are leaving for Calcutta. A meaningless accumulation of joys and sorrows only increases one's burdens. Sitting idle is pointless and accumulation is a futile activity. It is a mere construction that I am the lord of this house; my true identity is of a traveller on the journey of life. Therefore, the lord of the house would be repeatedly injured until the final injury—death. My union with you was along the way—as far as we could go together, it was for the good; beyond that, stretching and pulling would only make a noose of it. Let that noose be, I am setting off today. As we walk along, the little shared glances, the brush of the hand is all very well. And then? Then there is the way of the eternal, the unbounded force of life—how much can you cheat me of, my beloved? If I pay heed to the tune playing ahead of me, I can hear the sweetness dripping through every crevice of our parting. The goddess's infinite cup would never run dry and so she sometimes shatters our cup, makes us cry and laughs at our misery. I shall not go about picking up the broken pieces. I shall carry my regrets in my heart and carry on.

Mejorani came and said, 'Thakurpo, your books have all been packed into cases, loaded on to bullock carts and sent off. What does that mean?'

'It means that I still haven't been able to give them up.'

'It's good to be attached to some things. But are you planning not to return?'

'There will be visits and trips, but no dwelling here anymore.'

'Is that so? In that case come with me once and take a look at all the things I am unable to give up.'

I went to her room and found bundles and bags of all sizes. She opened one box and said, 'Look here, Thakurpo, the things I need to make my paan. I have powdered the dry lime and stored it in a bottle. These jars here each contain a masala. Here are the cards, I haven't forgotten those—even if you don't play with me, I'll find people. This comb here is the homegrown one that you gave me, and this—'

'What is all this, Mejorani? Why have you packed your things into boxes?'

'Because I am coming to Calcutta with you two.'

'What?'

'Don't worry, dear brother—I shan't try to be friends with you or squabble with the little princess. Death is inevitable and so the sooner one reaches the Ganges the better. When I think of the barren banyan tree under which you'll cremate me here, I shudder to even die—why do you think I'm troubling you all for so long?'

It was as if this house of mine had spoken up at long last. Mejorani came to this house when she was nine and I was six years old. I have sat in the shade of the high walls of the terrace and played with her. I have climbed mango trees, plucked the raw fruit and hurled them down as she gathered them from below, chopped them up, mixed them with salt and chilly and made tasty tidbits. I was entrusted with the grave duty of stealing all those things from the pantry that were necessary for the wedding of the dolls, because in Grandma's eyes I could do no wrong. Later, when she wanted my brother to indulge her fancies, I was the messenger boy; I always badgered Dada until he gave in and she got her way. I also remember: in those days the local doctor had strict orders for a fever—three days on a diet of lukewarm water and cardamom seeds. Mejorani couldn't bear my predicament and she often smuggled food into my room; many a times she was caught and severely reprimanded. As we grew older, our joys and sorrows plumbed deeper shades; so often we fought. The issues of property and finance also caused some rifts, jealousy and bitterness. Then Bimal came into it all, and sometimes it felt like the rifts would never heal. But then it was always obvious that the bonds of childhood surpassed the superficial wounds. Thus, a genuine relationship had been nurtured from those early days into the present times. This relationship spread out its branches into this huge mansion, into the rooms, courtyards, verandas, gardens and its shadows lurked all over. When I found Mejorani had packed all her belongings and was ready to leave the house with us, this eternal relationship in my heart was shaken down to its very roots. It became apparent to me why Mejorani, who had never stepped out of this house since the day she was nine, was actually prepared to let go of her familiar world and surrender to the unfamiliar. But she simply couldn't utter those words, and made so many other trivial excuses. This woman, betrayed by Fate, without a husband or a child, had nurtured just this one relationship with her heart and soul. As I stood that day, amidst all her possessions strewn around the room in various stages of packing, I felt her pain in a way I had never felt it before. I realized that the many petty squabbles that Bimal and I had with her, together or individually, were not really about materialism. It was because she had never been able to establish her claim over this one relationship. Bimal appeared from nowhere and she paled into insignificance—it pained her ever so often but she had no grounds for complaint. Bimal had also understood that Mejorani's claims over me went beyond mere social norms, and that's why she was so resentful of this childhood bond of mine. Today, my heart stood shocked with a realization; I sat down on a trunk. I said, 'Mejoranididi, I feel like going back to those days when you and I first met in this house.'

Mejorani sighed heavily and said, 'Oh no, this time not as a woman, not again. All that I have borne is enough for one lifetime, never to be repeated.'

I said, 'The liberation that comes through sorrow is greater than the sorrow itself.'

She said, 'That's possible, Thakurpo. Liberation is for you men. We women want to bind, we want bondage—you won't get your liberation from us so easily. If you want to spread your wings, you'll have to take us with you; you can't throw us away. Why do you think I have set out this medley of baggage? You men shouldn't be left light and airy.'

I laughed, 'That is obvious. It's easy to see what a burden it is. But since you tip us generously for carrying this burden, we don't complain half as much.'

Mejorani said, 'Our burdens are of trivia; whatever you want to leave out will protest "I am trivial, I don't really weigh much"—and thus with trivial weights we load your back. What time are we leaving, Thakurpo?'

'Eleven thirty at night—there's still a lot of time.'

'Thakurpo, please promise me one thing—you'll have an early lunch and take a nap this afternoon. You won't get much sleep in the train at night. Your health is in such bad shape that you look just about ready to collapse any time. Come now, go and have your bath.'

At this point Khema came forth and murmured, 'The inspector has brought someone with him and he wants to see his majesty.'

Mejorani flared up, 'His majesty is not a thief or burglar that the inspector is always after him. Tell him he has gone to have his bath.'

I said, 'Let me go and have a look—it may be something urgent.'

Mejorani said, 'Not on your life. I will send some of the sweets that the little one made yesterday and that ought to keep him busy for a while.' She dragged me by the hand, pushed me into the bathroom and bolted the door from outside.

From inside I said, 'But my clean clothes—'

She said, 'I'll see to that. You finish your bath.'

I did not have the strength to go against such indulgent torture. It was one of the precious things of life. Let the inspector have sweets, let there be a slight neglect of my duties. In the last few days, the inspector had been routinely rounding up suspects in connection with the robbery. Every so often he'd drag an innocent man to the estate and have a circus. Today was probably a repeat performance. But would the inspector have all the sweets himself? No! I banged loudly on the door from inside.

Mejorani spoke up, 'Pour some water on your head, quick, your temper is shooting up.'

I said, 'Send enough sweets for two people. The man whom the inspector has dragged in as a suspect deserves them more—tell the bearer to give him the bigger share.'

I finished my bath as quickly as possible and came out. At the door I found Bimal sitting on the floor. Was this the same Bimal, my Bimal—proud, arrogant, stubborn? With what prayer in mind could she have come to *my* door? As I stalled in surprise, she stood up, bent her head down and spoke softly, 'I need to speak to you.'

I said, 'Come into our room.'

'Are you going somewhere for some urgent work?'

'Yes, but let that be. First let's talk—'

'Oh no, you finish your work. We can have our talk after you've had your meal.'

Out in the living room, I found the inspector's plate was empty and the suspect whom he had brought in was still eating the sweets.

I was amazed, 'What's this—Amulya?'

He looked up with a mouth full of sweets and said, 'Yes, sir. I have eaten my fill and if you don't mind, I'll take the rest with me.' He bundled the remaining sweets into his handkerchief.

I looked at the inspector, 'What is going on?'

The inspector laughed and said, 'Your majesty, the mystery of the thief still remains unsolved and now I am puzzling my head about the mystery of the stolen loot.' He spread out a torn bundle that held a bunch of notes, 'Here is your majesty's six thousand rupees.'

'Where did it come from?'

'Right now, from Amulyababu's hands. Last night he went to the head clerk of your treasury in Chakua and said to him that the stolen loot had been recovered. The clerk was more frightened at this development than when the actual robbery took place. He was afraid that everyone would suspect him of hiding the money and now when the noose was tightening, he'd cooked up this improbable story to return it. He made an excuse of bringing something for Amulyababu to eat and rushed to the police station. I went there on horseback and since dawn I have been with him. He says he won't tell me where he got the money. I said then he wouldn't be allowed to go. He said he'd lie. I said, fine, give it to me. He said he found it hidden in the bushes. I said lying is not so easy—you have to give me all the details of where the bush is and what you were doing there. He said he'd have plenty of time to make up all those stories.'

I said, 'Haricharanbabu, what's the point of dragging this gentleman's name in the mud?'

He said, 'Not just any gentleman, he's the son of Nibaran Ghoshal who was my class-friend. Sire, let me tell you the real story. Amulya came to know who has stolen the money. He knows him well through this Vande Mataram nonsense. He wants to take the blame on himself and spare this other person. Herein lies his bravado. Son, we too were once eighteen years old, just like you; I was studying in Ripon College. Once, on the Strand, I wanted to save a bullock-cart driver from the wrath of a policeman and nearly landed up in jail myself. It was a narrow escape. Sire, now it's almost impossible to catch the thief, but I can tell you who it is.'

I asked, 'Who is it?'

'Your head-clerk Tinkori Dutta and that Quasim Sardar.'

The inspector left, after giving many justifications to support his conclusion. I asked Amulya, 'If you tell me who had taken this money, no harm will come to anyone.'

He said, 'I took it.'

'But—they said a gang of robbers—'

'I was alone.'

Amulya's tale was a strange one. After finishing his dinner, the head-clerk was rinsing his mouth outside, where it was dark. Amulya had a pistol in each pocket. One was loaded with bullets and the other with blanks. Half his face was covered by a black mask. He held up a lantern to the clerk's face and fired a shot from the pistol with blanks. The clerk screamed in terror and fainted. A few of the guards came running and he fired shots over their heads. They ran into rooms and slammed shut the doors. Quasim Sardar came forward with his lathi. Amulya shot him in the leg and he fell down. He then got the clerk to open the iron chest, grabbed six thousand rupees and borrowed a horse from our estate. He rode all night long, left the horse somewhere in the night and was back here at dawn.

I asked, 'Amulya, why did you do this?'

He said, 'I had a great need.'

'Then why are you giving it back?'

'If you send for the person who has ordered me to return it, I'll confess everything.'

'Who is that person?'

'Chhotoranididi.'

I sent for Bimala. She had draped a white shawl around her head and she walked into the room slowly. Her feet were bare. I felt I had never seen her quite like this before. Like the moon at dawn, she seemed to have hid herself in the morning light.

Amulya bent down low at Bimala's feet and took her blessings. He stood up and said, 'I have obeyed you, Didi. I've returned the money.'

Bimala said, 'Thank you, my child.'

Amulya said, 'I had you in mind and so I didn't tell a single lie. My Vande Mataram chants lie here at your feet. The minute I entered this house, I have also received food blessed by you.'

Bimala didn't quite get the last part. Amulya took the handkerchief from his pocket, untied the knot and showed her the sweets, 'I didn't eat them all—I wanted you to put them on my plate with your own hands and so I saved these.'

I realized I was no longer needed here; I left the room silently. I said to myself, I could only talk and make speeches and they in turn made my effigy and burnt it by the river. But could I really pull someone back from the clutches of death? The one who *can*, did it without words. My words did not hold that flawless signal. We are not flames, we are embers, dying ones. We would never be able to light a lamp. The story of my life is living proof of that—I failed to light the lamp I wanted to light.

Slowly, I walked back to the inner chambers. Perhaps my heart raced towards Mejorani's rooms once again, because I needed to feel that my life too has been able to strike a true and pure note in another life. The quest for one's identity seldom led inwards—it lay somewhere out in the world.

The moment I came before Mejorani's room, she came out and said, 'There you are, Thakurpo, I wondered how much longer you will be. Your lunch will soon be here, so hurry up.'

I said, 'Let me just go and take that money out.'

As I walked towards my room, Mejorani asked, 'So what happened about the inspector—has that matter been resolved?'

I somehow didn't feel like talking to Mejorani about the recovery of the six thousand rupees. So I said, 'Still going on.'

I went into the ante-room, took out the bunch of keys from my pocket and found the one to the iron chest missing. I am so careless—all day long I've been opening so many boxes and doors with the same bunch of keys and I never noticed that one is missing.

Mejorani asked, 'Where's the key?'

Without answering her, I groped around in each pocket, looked high and low and gradually it became obvious that the key wasn't lost, but someone had slipped it off the ring. Who could it be? In this room—

Mejorani said, 'Relax and have your lunch first. I believe Chhotorani must have put it away safely since you are so careless.'

The whole thing confused me. It wasn't like Bimala to take a key from my key ring without telling me first. Today Bimala wasn't present when I ate. At the time she had sent for rice from the kitchen and supervised Amulya's lunch as he ate it. Mejorani was about to send for her, but I stopped her.

I was almost done when Bimala came there. I hadn't wanted to discuss the matter of the missing key in front of Mejorani. But that was a lost cause. As soon as she saw her, Mejorani asked, 'Do you know where the key to Thakurpo's iron chest is?'

Bimala said, 'It's with me.'

Mejorani said, 'That's what I said. In these troubled times, Chhotorani wears a brave face but she is careful nonetheless.'

Something in Bimala's face made me doubt that remark. I said, 'Fine, let the key be with you for now. I'll take the money out in the evening.'

Mejorani exclaimed, 'Why wait till evening, Thakurpo, take that money now and hand it to the treasurer.'

Bimala said, 'I have taken that money.'

I was startled.

Mejorani asked, 'And where did you keep it?'

Bimala said, 'I spent it.'

Mejorani said, 'Oh lord, listen to her talk. Where did you spend so much money?'

Bimala didn't answer her. I did not ask her anything either. I just stood at the door quietly. Mejorani was about to say something to her, but she stopped. She looked at my face and said, 'Fair enough; whenever I could, I too stole all of my husband's money that I could lay my hands on. I knew it'd be wasted in the wrong places. Thakurpo, you are in the same boat. So many whims and fancies. Your money will be safe only when we steal it away. Now go and rest a little.'

Mejorani dragged me towards my room. I wasn't conscious of where I was or of anything around me. She perched on the side of my bed and said, 'Hey there, little one, can you give me a paan? You youngsters are so lazy these days—don't you have any here? Why don't you send someone to get me some from my room?'

I said, 'Mejorani, you haven't even eaten yet.'

She said, 'Of course I have.'

This was a blatant lie. She sat beside me and began to prattle about this and that. The maid came and spoke from the door. She said Bimala's lunch was getting cold. Bimala was silent. Mejorani said, 'Oh dear, haven't you had lunch yet? It's way past time.' She pulled her by the hand and dragged her away.

I understood that there was a link between the six thousand rupees that was robbed from the treasury and this money that was in the iron chest. I didn't even feel like delving into it. Never, ever would I ask that question.

The Almighty sketched the lines of our Fate with a blurred pen—He wanted us to make some changes here and there, draw some afresh and realize it in our own ways. I have always felt the ache to take His signal and make my way myself, to pour all of me into expressing one larger Idea.

I have spent my life attempting that. Only the God within me knows how much I have curbed natural impulses, suppressed my baser instincts. The difficult part was that one's life wasn't entirely one's own. If the creator does not include all that is around him, his creation is in vain. Hence, my innermost desires were to draw Bimala into this creative process. I strongly held that since I loved her with all my heart, it was more than possible.

At this point it became apparent to me that I was not the kind of person who could recreate oneself and others around him with ease. I had initiated myself, but I couldn't initiate another person. The ones to whom I laid my soul bare had taken everything from me except this one cherished detail. My test had been hard. Where I had really needed the most support I was most alone. But I vowed to succeed even in this test. Until the last breath I draw, my way would be mine alone.

Today I began to feel that there was coercion deeply ingrained in me. I was hell bent on moulding my relationship with Bimala in one set, perfect mould. But life is not to be poured into moulds. And goodness, if mistaken for an inanimate object, dies on you and takes a cruel revenge. I never knew it, but this oppression gradually took us away from one another. Bimala could have been someone else, but my pressure suppressed her effervescence and forced her to remain at the bottom—the harsh cement of life tore away at her person. Today she had to steal this six thousand rupees. She could not be frank with me because she sensed that somewhere I stood apart from her. The ones who matched with stubborn idealists like us, harmonized with us, and the ones who didn't cheated us. We corrupt the innocent. In creating a partner we destroy the woman.

Was it possible to go back and begin at the beginning? Then I could walk the simple way. This time I wouldn't want to bind my fellow traveller in the chains of idealism. I would merely play the flute of my love and say, 'Just love me. In the light of that love, may you blossom in your truest form, let my demands disappear, may the Almighty's desires in you win the day—let my desires be shamed into oblivion.'

But would it be possible for Nature to work its healing balm on the wound that has manifested itself today, festering in our severance from one another? The veil that shields the workings of healing Nature has been ripped to shreds. Wounds need salves and I shall soothe this one with my love. I shall wrap the pain with all my heart and shield it from the eyes of the world. A day will come when there won't be a sign of this wound. But is there time? It took me so long to learn my mistake, today I have understood it, how much longer will it take until I can correct it? And then? The wound may heal, but will there be any recompense?

There was a sound at the door. I turned and found Bimala leaving. Perhaps she had stood at the door all this while wondering whether to come in or not, and now she was going. I got up quickly and called, 'Bimal.'

She stopped, her back towards me. I held her hand and pulled her into the room.

In the room she fell to the floor, pressed a pillow to her face and wept. Without a word, I held on to her hand and sat by her side. When her tears dried and she tried to sit up, I tried to pull her into my arms. She forced my hands away, knelt before me and repeatedly touched her forehead to my feet. As I made to move my feet, she pulled them back with both hands and spoke with emotion, 'No, no, no, don't take your feet away, let me offer homage.'

I was silent. Who was I to stop this reverence? If the puja was true, so was the deity—why should I be hesitant when I was not that deity?

## Bimala

Come now, let's leave for that holy shrine where universal love joins the ocean of devotion. In the depths of that untainted blue, all murky patches will disappear. I am no longer afraid, of myself or anyone else. I have walked through fire; whatever had to burn has burnt to ashes and what remains is eternal. I have bestowed myself at his feet—of he who has absorbed all my crimes deep within his own sorrow.

Tonight we leave for Calcutta. So long I was absorbed with such turmoil, within and without, that I could hardly concentrate on packing our things. Now I pulled out the boxes and began to pack. A little later I found my husband had joined me. I said, 'No, no, that won't do. You promised you'd take a little nap.'

He said, 'I may have promised, but sleep did not. There is no sign of it yet.'

I said, 'Oh no, you go and rest.'

He said, 'How will you manage all alone?'

'I'll manage very well.'

'You may want to show off how well you can do without me, but I can't do without you and so sleep eluded me in that room all by myself.' He began to sort through things with me. At this time, the bearer came and said, 'Sandipbabu is here. He sent me to inform you.' Neither of us could ask who the information was for. In an instant the light went out of the sky for me and I turned into a shrivelled vine.

My husband said, 'Come Bimal, let's go and hear what Sandip has to say. He had bid goodbye and left. If he has come back, it must be something urgent.'

Since it would be more embarrassing not to go, I went with him. In the living room Sandip stood gazing at a portrait. The minute we entered he said, 'You must be wondering why this man has come back. Until the last rites are duly completed the spirit cannot leave in peace.' He fished out a bundle from under his shawl and placed it on the table—it held those guineas. He said, 'Nikhil, don't get me wrong; I haven't turned ethical in your company. Sandip is not such a wimp that he'd weep tears of regret as he returns these guineas worth six thousand rupees. But—'

Sandip didn't finish the sentence. After a brief pause he looked at me and said, 'Queen Bee, after all these years a "but" has entered Sandip's immaculate life. Every night I have woken up at three and tussled with it; finally I realize that it isn't an empty sound; Sandip isn't free until his debt has been paid off. So, in the hands of my terminator "but" I lay these guineas as a final mark of respect. I thought long and hard and realized that this "but" is the only being in this world from whom I cannot accept wealth—I can only bid you goodbye if I am penniless before you, oh goddess. Here, take it.'

He took out the jewellery box as well and placed it on the table and tried to rush out of the room. My husband called out to him, 'Come here, Sandip.'

Sandip spoke from the door, 'I don't have time, Nikhil. I've come to know that the Muslims want to loot me like the Kohinoor and bury me deep in their burial grounds. But I must live. The train bound northwards leaves in twenty-five minutes and so, for the time being, I say goodbye. Later, if I have a chance, I'll finish the rest of our conversation. If you take my advice, you'll not waste any time either. Queen Bee, hail the queen of hearts, the harbinger of storms.'

Sandip almost ran out of the room. I stood there, turned to stone. Never before had I felt just how meaningless the guineas and the jewellery were. Just a little while ago I had been thinking how much I'd take with me, how to fit it all in and now I felt nothing was important, except just walking out.

My husband rose from the chair, came up to me, held my hands and said, 'There isn't much time left; we should get the work done now.'

At that moment Chandranathbabu walked in. My presence threw him in a bit of a quandary. He said, 'Ma, forgive me, I didn't give notice before coming in. Nikhil, the Muslims are enraged. They have looted Harish Kundu's treasury. That is not so fearful by itself. But the way they are treating the women—it is unbearable.'

My husband said, 'I'll be off then.'

I grasped his hands and said, 'What can you do there? Professor, please stop him.'

Chandranathbabu said, 'My dear, this isn't the time to stop him.'

My husband said, 'Don't worry, Bimal.'

I rushed to the window and saw him galloping away on horseback. He wasn't carrying a single weapon.

Mejorani ran into the room and said, 'What have you done, little one, what crazy calamity have you brought on? Why did you let Thakurpo go?' She ordered the bearer, 'Go, quickly, call the estate manager.'

Mejorani had never appeared before the estate manager. But today she had no shame. She said, 'Quick, send out forces to bring back his majesty.'

The manager said, 'We have all tried to stop him; he wouldn't listen.'

Mejorani said, 'Go and tell him Mejorani has collapsed, she is dying.'

Once the manager left, Mejorani began to curse me, 'You witch, you siren. You sent Thakurpo to his death.'

The daylight waned. Standing at the window I saw the sun set behind the flowering tree in the west, near the milkmen's colony. Till this day, every line of that setting sun is engraved on my heart. With the setting sun in the centre, a rush of clouds had spread their wings to the north and south like the wings of a huge bird. Its flame-coloured feathers unfurled in layers. I felt the day was flying swiftly to cross the ocean of the night. Gradually darkness crept in. Intermittent sounds of hubbub rent the air, just as the occasional flames would lick the dark sky if there was a fire in a distant village. The temple bells sounded for the evening arati. I knew Mejorani was there with folded hands, praying. I couldn't take a step away from the window by the street. My eyes blurred over the road ahead, the village, the distant field empty of crops and the line of trees further afield. The huge lake of the estate stared at the sky like a sightless eye. The ballroom to the left stood on its toes as if peering at something.

There was no end to the masquerades that nighttime sounds indulged in. If a twig swayed close by, it felt like someone running away in the distance. The sudden noise of a door banging shut felt like the entire sky missing a heartbeat. Sometimes I spotted lights beneath the row of trees by the roadside. Then there was nothing. I heard the sound of horses' hooves, only to find the rider galloping out of the estate gates and vanishing in the distance.

All the time I felt if I died, all troubles would cease. As long as I lived, the world would be plagued by my sins. I remembered the pistol that lay nestled in the box. But my feet wouldn't budge from this window, even to go and fetch the pistol—you see, I awaited my Fate.

The clock tower of the estate gonged away—ten o'clock.

A little later, there were many lights on the streets, a big crowd had gathered. In the darkness, the throng of people seemed like a huge black snake slithering in through the estate gates.

The manager heard the noise and rushed towards the gate. At that moment, a rider came up and the manager asked him nervously, 'Jatadhar, what's the news?'

He said, 'Not too good.'

I could hear every syllable clearly from up here.

Then there were some whispers, which I couldn't hear very well.

A palanquin and a doolie drew into the gates. Doctor Mathur walked beside the palanquin. The estate manager asked, 'Doctor, what do you think?'

The doctor said, 'Can't say for sure. Serious head injury.'

'And Amulyababu?'

'He took a bullet in the chest. He is no more.'

# NEXUS

# (Yogayog)

*Translated by Hiten Bhaya*

# 1

Today is the 7th of Ashada. Abinash's birthday. He has turned thirty-two today. Greetings, telegrams and bouquets have kept coming all morning.

This is where the story begins. But there's something before the beginning too, like the rolling of cotton wicks in the morning to light lamps in the evening.

The prehistoric stage of this story finds the Ghoshals on the fringes of the Sunderbans and later at Noornagar in the Hooghly district. It is not very clear if these migrations were caused by the external force of Portuguese advancement or internal social pressures. Often, those who are able to leave their homesteads in desperation also have the resoluteness to set up new homes. So we find the Ghoshals at the dawn of history, in possession of expansive landed properties, many heads of cattle and farmhands, and celebrating all the festivals in the calendar with pomp and grandeur. There was much transaction of money coming in and going out. Even today a ten-acre pond testifies to their past glory—though in a voice choked with mud from behind a veil of hyacinths. Today the pond may still bear their name but its water belongs to the Chatterjees.

Let us now recount the decline of the Ghoshal family glory.

In the middle period of their history, one finds them scrapping with the other zamindar family—the Chatterjees. The dispute was not over property but over the worship of gods. The Ghoshals had dared the Chatterjees by making the image of their goddess two cubits higher than the Chatterjees', who retaliated by erecting arches along the route such that the Ghoshals' image would not be able to clear. The High-Imagers then set out to break the arches and the Low-Archers to break their rivals' heads. The result: the goddess had more than her fair share of human blood that year. Murder and mayhem led to criminal suits. By the time the litigations ended, the Ghoshals were on the brink of ruin.

The fire went out but so did the firewood. All turned to ash. Ashen was the face of the patron goddess of the Chatterjee household. Treaties were concluded but they did not bring peace. The one who was still up and the one who was down, both began to boil inside. The Chatterjees dealt their coup-de-grace by wielding the social scimitar. They spread the rumour that the Ghoshals were in reality, fallen Brahmins, a fact they suppressed on coming to Noornagar. Earthworms cloaked as cobras!

The defamers had a louder voice because their pockets were deeper. So it was not difficult to find drummers for their false campaign from amongst the priestly scholars with their incomprehensible incantations. The Ghoshals lacked both wealth and strong evidence to clear themselves.

So for a second time they had to move to a humble location here in Rajabpur, harassed by a society under the thumb of the temple-crawlers.

Strikers have a short memory, but those who are hit do not find it easy to forget. Because they are disarmed physically, they continue to wield their clubs mentally. This mental game had been running in the family for ages, ever since their striking arm was benumbed. Stories, tissues of truth and untruth, of how they worsted the Chatterjees, was still their stock-in-trade.

On a rainy evening, under a thatched roof, the children would listen to these tales open-mouthed. How scores of their musclemen captured the notorious Dashu Sardar of the Chatterjees, brought him to the Ghoshal court and did him in, was a story running in this family for over a century. As the story went, when the police came to inquire, Bhuban Biswas the Ghoshals' naib, had no hesitation in declaring, 'Yes, he came here on some business of his own, and yes I did take the opportunity to snub him a bit. I gather he could not bear the humiliation and has made himself scarce since then.'

The magistrate was not convinced. So Bhuban added, 'Sir, as sure as my name is Bhuban Biswas, I promise to run him to ground before the year ends.' He then got hold of another scoundrel of Dashu's size and sent him straight to Dacca, the district headquarters. He was put to commit some petty thievery. The police booked him as Dasharathi Mandal and duly sentenced him to a month's imprisonment. The day he was to be let out Bhuban sent word to the magistrate that Dashu Sardar had been located in the Dacca jail. Enquiry confirmed that there was indeed one Dashu in the jail. Whilst leaving, Dashu dropped his shawl in a field across the jail. The shawl was duly identified as belonging to Dashu Sardar. From then on, his whereabouts ceased to be Bhuban's responsibility.

Such stories were rather like cheques from the past on an insolvent present. The days of glory were gone; its history like an empty vessel made a lot of noise. Anyway, just as the lamp goes out when the oil is finished, so does the night end in daybreak. The fortune of the Ghoshals dawned with the extraordinary luck of Madhusudan, the father of Abinash.

## 2

Madhusudan's father Ananda was a stores clerk in Rajabpur. The family barely managed to make ends meet. The women wore simple conch-bangles and the men carried brass amulets at the end of a thick sacred thread, well plastered with the gum of bael. The thickness of the sacred thread counterbalanced the thinning pride of a dubious Brahminism.

Madhusudan's primary education was received in this moffusil school.

But his informal training ran parallel along the riverside, in the grain yards and atop bales of jute. His holidays were spent among buyers and sellers and the throng of bullock cart drivers in the market place. He took pleasure in walking round a garden, rambling amidst rows of claypots filled with jaggery, bundles of tobacco leaf, bales of imported shawls, tins of kerosene oil, heaps of mustard seed, sackfuls of lentils and huge balances and weighing devices.

The father reckoned that this boy would go places. He had only to somehow clear a few exams and land himself a berth in any of the havens of the gentlemanly class—anything from a schoolmaster to a lawyer in the lower courts. The fateline of the other three sons seemed as if they would be limited to nothing more than book-keeping. So they hied forth with quills behind their ears, to be apprenticed with stockists or in a zamindar's office. Madhusudan, however, moved to a dormitory in Kolkata, straining the slender means of his father Ananda.

His professors had hopes of the boy bringing credit to their college.

But it so happened that Ananda passed away rather suddenly. Madhusudan sold all his earthly possessions, his books and even his class notes. He was determined to earn his living. He started with buying and selling second-hand books to the students. His mother cried her heart out. She had great hopes that the exam-passing route would lead her son into the charmed circle of the gentlefolk. And that the family flagstaff of the Ghoshals would then proudly fly the standard of triumphant clerkship.

Right from his childhood Madhusudan had the knack of choosing the right goods. His choice of friends was likewise; none of them ever let him down. His best friend in school was one Kanai Gupta. His forbears were agents of large commercial houses and his father Rajani Babu was well ensconced in a reputed firm dealing in kerosene oil.

As luck would have it, the occasion of Rajani Babu's daughter's wedding came up. Madhusudan did not spare himself. He put up the marquee, decorated it with flowers, supervised the printing of the wedding invitation in gold letters, hired carpets and chairs, received the guests and cried himself hoarse looking after their entertainment—nothing escaped his attention. Rajani Babu was very pleased with this demonstration of prudence and practical sense in matters mundane. He could sense a man of worth and felt that this boy would do well. He helped Madhusudan set up an agency for supply of kerosene in Rajabpur and paid the deposit himself.

From then on, Mudhusudan's race towards prosperity began; and the kerosene depot was left behind as a dot on the horizon. His business rapidly crossed over from the by-lanes to the main street. Large entries to his credit account served as stepping stones in his rise from a retailer to a wholesaler. It was like our great epic starting from an introductory chapter and ending in the chapter on an ascent to paradise. People said 'it is all a turn of luck'. That was to suggest that the train of the present prosperity was running on the steam of past merit. But Madhusudan knew that Fate would spare nothing to trick him out. It was only because his calculations were always right that the examiners could not fail him in the arithmetic of life. It is only those who get their sums wrong who use the excuse of bias on the part of a strict examiner.

Madhusudan was a man of great reserve. He never talked about his own affairs. But one could easily see that the once dry riverbed was again swollen with the flood of good fortune for the Ghoshals. In the domestic milieu of Bengal one's thoughts turn to marriage in such circumstances. The desire to extend the enjoyment of property along the family line into the future beyond death, becomes very strong. Fathers of nubile daughters did everything to encourage Madhusudan in this direction. Madhusudan's reaction was, 'One should feed oneself fully before taking on the responsibility of feeding another mouth.' From this one could guess that whatever the size of his heart, Madhusudan's stomach was of no mean dimension.

By this time, Rajabpur jute had earned a name for itself in the market, thanks to Madhusudan's prudence. He was quick to grab all the land on the riverside. It was going cheap. He put up a number of brick kilns, bought huge timbers of teak from Nepal, limestone from Sylhet and wagonloads of corrugated iron from Kolkata. People were flabbergasted. They said, 'Look at this. Couldn't wait to spend the little he had saved! It is nothing but indigestion of wealth. His business will soon come to an end.'

But this time too Madhusudan's calculations proved right. Soon there was a boom in the market in Rajabpur. Under its spell came brokers and Marwari traders. Coolies were imported, factories were set up and their chimney stacks belched spirals of smoke darkening the skies.

It did not need any great research into his books; his glory was plain to the naked eye. Sole owner of the market place, his two-storied walled mansion carried the apellation 'Madhuchakra' engraved in stone. The name was suggested by his old Sanskrit teacher whose affection for Madhusudan had suddenly become more pronounced than in the past.

His widowed mother at last summoned up the courage to say, 'My son, my days are numbered. Do you think I shall be able to see my daughter-in-law before I go?'

Madhu's brief reply, gravely delivered, was, 'It is a waste of time getting married and so is marriage itself. Where do I have the time to spare?' Even his mother knew better than to insist. Time was money and everyone knew that Madhusudan never minced his words.

Days passed. The floodtide of prosperity swept the suburban office up to Kolkata. Despairing of ever seeing the faces of grandchildren, Madhusudan's mother passed away. Ghoshal & Co. was now known both at home and abroad. Their business ran close to established British business houses and they even had English managers in charge of divisions.

Establishing himself in this manner, Madhusudan himself announced that he was free to marry now. His was the highest credit in the marriage market. Proposals poured in from all sides for brides—beautiful, well-bred, accomplished, rich and highly educated. Madhusudan rolled his eyes at all these proposals and pronounced, 'I must have a daughter of that Chatterjee family.'

A family nursing wounded pride is rather like a wounded hyena—ferocious in the extreme.

## 3

Now the bride's story . . .

The Chatterjees of Noornagar had fallen on bad days. The branch of the family which held a third of the share broke away and were picking at the fringes of the other two-thirds. The more the two parties tried to finely divide the benefice for looking after the family deity, Radhakanta Jeeu, the more their share of crops found its way to the courtyards of their lawyers. The functionaries had their shares too. The Noornagar family had lost its power—there was no income but the expenses had risen fourfold. Nine tentacles of a nine percent interest on loans had spread round the zamindari. It was a family of two brothers and five sisters. The penalty for the crime of having an overpopulation of daughters was still to be paid. Four sisters were married into kuleen families whilst the head of the family was still alive. The Chatterjees' past reputation was vast but their current wealth was slim. So the dowries had to be large enough to match the prestige of their high caste and the extent of their wide reputation. It was this which added another knot of a twelve percent interest to the already existing noose of nine percent interest. The younger brother took a stand. He desired to go to England, be called to the bar and start earning a living. The elder brother Bipradas was left to bear the family burden. At about this time the fates of the Chatterjees and the Ghoshals locked horns once more.

Let me narrate that story.

The Chatterjees owed a large sum to Tansukdas, a confectioner in Burrabazar. Interests were paid regularly and no words were ever exchanged. During the puja holidays Bipradas's classmate, one Amulyadhan, arrived apparently to renew his close ties with the family. He was an articled headclerk in a big house of attorneys. One sidelong glance was enough for this bespectacled young man to gauge the predicament of this Noornagar family. He went back to Kolkata and soon enough Tansukdas demanded his loan back. He said he wanted the money to get into the sugar business.

Bipradas was struck dumb.

This crisis brought the two family names into unfriendly conjunction. Madhusudan had just been conferred the title of Raja by the Hon'ble Government. Our old schoolfriend appeared again in Noornagar at this juncture and said, 'The new Raja must be in a generous mood and may even agree to a loan on easy terms.' And that is exactly how it happened.

The diverse borrowings of the Chatterjees totalled eleven lakh rupees, and a loan for this sum was had from Madhusudan Ghoshal at only seven per cent interest.

Bipradas heaved a sigh of relief.

Kumudini was his youngest sister; and their fortune was on its last legs. The thought of finding a match for her and a dowry to match, was chilling. She was beautiful, tall and slim like the stalk of a tuberose. Her eyes though not very large were intensely dark, and her nose, perfectly straight, was delicate as if fashioned out of the petals of a flower. Her skin was fair and glowing. To be served by her perfectly rounded hands was to receive with gratefulness the favours of Goddess Kamala herself. Patience and compassion lit her entire face with a dolorous sadness.

Kumudini felt embarrassed for herself. She believed she brought ill luck. She believed that men ran the family with their own prowess and the women brought prosperity with their luck. But that was not to be her lot. From the time she could follow things, she had only seen the evil eye of misfortune all around. And the burden of her spinsterhood was like a millstone round the neck of the family. The pain of it and the shame! But nothing could be done except to blame one's own fate. The gods did not find a way out for them except to endow them with the strength to bear hurt. 'Can't there be a miracle? A godsend? A treasure trove? Or the sudden settlement of a loan given in a previous life?' she prayed. Some nights as she lay awake looking over the top of the murmuring casuarina trees, she spoke to herself.

'Where are you, my prince? Where are your sparkling jewels? Come and save my brothers. I shall be your slave for life.'

The more she blamed herself for the misfortunes of her family the more she poured out her heart full of love to her brothers—a love wrung out of deep unhappiness. The brothers also, conscious of their inability to do their duty by Kumu, enveloped her in their affection. They were ever eager to compensate this orphan girl for what the gods had deprived her of. She was like a bit of moonlight cheering the darkness of their poverty. Sometimes when she blamed herself as the vehicle of misfortune, Bipradas would smile and say, 'But Kumu, you yourself are our fortune—there would be no light in this house but for you.'

Kumudini had her education at home, hardly aware of the world outside. She lived in the twilight zone between the old and the new. Her world was dimly lit, ruled by obscure goddessess like Siddheswari, Gandheswari, and Ghentu, a world where one must not look at the moon on certain days, where the evil eye of an eclipse had to be dismissed with conch-blowing, where you would be rid of the dread of snakes if you sipped milk on the holy day of ambubachi. It was a world where one dealt with good and evil by incantations, by promising a sacrificial goat or a simpler propitiation with betel nuts, raw rice and a five-pice measure of shirni, or by wearing amulets of all descriptions. A hope of averting ill luck through propitiation; a hope dashed a thousand times. One often sees for oneself that the branch of auspicious timings does not necessarily bear the fruit of good fortune. Yet reality has no power to dispel by reasoning, the illusions created in dreams. In this dreamland there was no place for logic, there was only the observance of rules and taboos. Perhaps it is this total rejection of the harmony of reason, of the supremacy of intellect and the universality of ethics in this world of fatality, which cast a pall of pathos over her face. Because she knew she had been sentenced without cause, for the last eight years she had accepted this humiliation as her wont. It had something to do with the death of her father.

## 4

The old is well entrenched in the fortress of wealthy families. The new has to cross many halls and courtyards to gain entrance. The inmates take ages to arrive at the new times. Bipradas's father too could not catch up with the changing times.

Tall, fair, with a shock of hair, his large and long eyes reflected unchallenged authority. His booming voice struck terror into the hearts of his followers and retainers. He was strong, used to wrestling with the pros regularly, yet his delicate physique did not bear any sign of toil. Dressed in a well laundered muslin kurta over the flowing folds of a farashdanga or a dacca dhoti, the master's arrival was heralded by the scent of Istambul attar in the air. The khansama followed with a golden paan box, and a liveried orderly was always at the door. At the main entrance, the old jamadar was busy combing his long beard into two plaits and tying them behind his ears after finishing the chore of blending the tobacco and crushing the bhang leaves. Darwans, the next in rank, were on guard with their swords. The walls of the guardroom displayed many types of shields, scimitars and very old muskets and spears.

In the drawing room, Mukundalal sat on the floor on a mattress with a bolster at his back. The courtiers sat a step below in two rows on either side.

The hookah servers were well versed in their relative ranks, and the kind of hookah to be offered befitting the rank—gilded or plain or a simple hubble-bubble. The master had a huge one filled with rosewater.

In another part of the mansion there was a western-type drawing room filled with eighteenth-century English furniture. A huge mirror, slightly pitted, faced the entrance. Two winged fairies held aloft two candlesticks on either side of its gilt-edged frame. On a table underneath was a clock in blackstone, decorated in gold, and a few English glass dolls. The straight-backed chairs, the sofas and the chandelier hanging from the beam were all draped in holland cloth. The walls carried oil paintings of the ancestors and of some British civil servants who were patrons of the family. The entire room was carpeted with English carpets embroidered with large flowers in vivid colours. This room was unveiled only on special occasions when the officials of the district were invited. This, the only modern room in this house, appeared to be cut off from daily living. Old and haunted, a stifling mustiness of disuse hung about it.

Mukundalal's luxury was an essential part of the mores of the day. The abandon of spending was a proud measure of true wealth. In other words, their wealth was not a burden but a slave grovelling under their feet. The display of their charities in public or their indulgence in private were both on a grand scale. They were as impatient in dealing with insolence as they were generous with their dependants. Once a nouveau riche neighbour merely boxed the ears of their gardener's son for a rather grave offence. The money that was spent on teaching this rich neighbour a lesson, was more than what one would spend on seeing a son through the University. Nor was the gardener's boy spared. He was caned mercilessly. The degree of chastisement matched the height of anger: but it did the boy good. He won scholarships and is currently established as a mukhtiyar.

In the tradition of the rich of those days, Mukundalal's life also ran in two compartments. One was devoted to serious duties to the family and the other to merrymaking with friends. If one could be said to be the home of ten sacred rites then the other could be the home of eleven profanities.

The inner compartment housed the family deity and the housewife. Here pleasing gods and guests, observing festivals, fasts and feasts, feeding the poor and the brahmins, neighbours and priests filled the space all the year round. Right outside was the world of nabobs, the splendour of courtly pleasures, women on the fringe of society came and went. The rich of those times sought their company as a way of cultivating courtly manners. The wives had a difficult time caught between the pull of two planets in opposing orbits.

Nandarani, Mukundalal's wife, had her pride. She could not quite get used to accepting the way things were. There was a reason for it. She was sure that her husband was anchored to her, however far his fancy might roam. So her tolerance broke down whenever he hurt his own love. And that is exactly what happened.

## 5

Raslila was a time of great festivity. Plays depicting the life of Lord Krishna were staged on the open courtyard: some evenings were devoted to kirtans sung in praise of the young god. This was where the neighbours and the women of the house crowded. Usually the more profane entertainments were held in the outer court. The women, anguished and sleepless, could only get a glimpse of the goings on, through cracks in the door. This year the men decided to have dancing girls perform on a boat on the river.

With no way of knowing what was happening out there, Nandarani's heart was bleeding in the dark. One had to carry on the daily chores at home, looking after and feeding the household with a smiling face. But no one knew how the heart ached, how one was being stifled inside. Outside, the grateful subjects sang loudly the praise of their Rani-Ma.

The festivities were over at last. The house was now empty. Only the crows and the dogs were left raucously bickering over the torn banana leaves and broken shards of pots. The lampmen took down the chandeliers and dismantled the marquee. The neighbourhood children fought over the broken bits of the chandelier and the floral hangings made out of pith. Occasionally in that crowd, bursts of slapping and screaming shot out like rockets rending the sky. The breeze from the courtyard was sour with the smell of leftover foodstuff, overcast with a sense of fatigue, weariness and gloom. This emptiness became unbearable for Nandarani when Mukundalal failed to come home. Because there was no way of getting at him, her patience was at its end.

She called the dewan and spoke to him from behind the curtains, 'Please tell your master that I have to go immediately to Brindaban where my mother is unwell.'

Dewanjee stroked his bald pate and said softly, 'Wouldn't it have been better to meet the master before you went? News has reached me that he is due home any time.'

'No, I cannot wait,' was her answer.

She had also heard of his impending return. Hence the haste.

She knew for certain that a little persuasion and some tears would settle everything. It had always been so. A proper punishment was thus adjourned forever. But she did not want the same to happen this time as well. So the judge had to flee as soon as the sentence was awarded. It was a wrench. She threw herself on her bed and cried her heart out, just before leaving. But it did not stop her from embarking on the journey.

It was two in the afternoon at the end of the rains. The air was hot under the blazing sun. Amidst the murmur of the litte trees lined on the roadside one could hear occasionally the voice of a koel crying itself hoarse. The road which her palanquin took, offered a view of the river beyond the green fields of paddy. Nandarani could not help sliding the door open a little and looking outside. She could make out a large boat lying at anchor on the other bank of the river, flying a pennant atop the mast. Even at that distance the familiar outline of Goopi, their old runner, met her eyes as did the flash of sunlight on his badge. She banged the door close, as her heart froze inside her.

## 6

Mukundalal landed at his jetty like a ship battered in a storm with broken masts and torn sails: his heart heavy with the weight of guilt. The memory of the revelry was as distasteful as the leftovers of a heavy repast. If the promoters and organizers of the revelry were present he would have whipped them. He had resolved not to let this happen ever again. Looking at his dishevelled hair, bloodshot eyes and drained face, no one dared tell him about the mistress's departure. Mukundalal entered the house in trepidation: rehearsing to himself, 'Please dear wife, forgive me. This will never happen again.' He paused for a moment before his bedroom door and then tiptoed in. He was sure in his mind that she was in bed, sulking. He had decided to fall straight at her feet, but he found the room empty. His heart sank. If he had found her in bed he could be sure that she was halfway down the road to forgiveness. But as she was not in, he knew that expiation would be hard and long. It might have to wait till tonight or even longer. He had made up his mind to accept the punishment in full and not to eat or drink till he had earned her pardon. No devoted wife could bear to see the husband without bath or food till a late hour. He came out of the bedroom and found the maid Pyaree standing in a corner with her head veiled in her sari. He asked her, 'Where is your mistress?'

She answered, 'She left for Brindaban day before yesterday to see her mother.'

He did not quite get the sense and asked in a choked voice, 'Where did you say she went?'

'To Brindaban. Mother's illness.'

Mukundalal gripped the railing of the veranda once and then ran to the drawing room outside, to sit there all by himself. No one dared come near him.

Dewanjee came and said timidly, 'Shall we send someone to fetch the mistress?'

He did not utter a word; simply moved his finger to say 'no'.

When the dewan left, he sent for Radhu the khansama and ordered him to bring some brandy.

The whole household was stunned. When an earthquake rears its ugly head from deep within the earth it is useless to try and suppress it. It was somewhat like that.

He lived on neat brandy for days on end with hardly any food. Such abuse of an already ravaged body led to delirium and spitting of blood.

Doctors arrived from Kolkata and treated him with ice-packs.

Mukundalal would flare up at the sight of anyone. He suspected that the entire household was plotting against him. Perhaps he was nursing a secret grievance against the family which let his wife leave the house.

The only one who could approach him was Kumudini. She sat by his bedside and he stared at her trying to find something of her mother in her. Sometimes he would pull her head down on his chest and lie quietly with his eyes closed, tears rolling down the corners of his eyes. Never did he ask about her mother. Meanwhile a telegram was sent to the mistress of the house and she was due to arrive the next day. But it was rumoured that there was a break in the rail track somewhere on the way.

## 7

It was the third phase of the moon; there was a storm in the evening.

The branches of the trees in the garden crackled and broke. From time to time there was an angry, impatient splash of rain. The corrugated roof of the shed erected for feeding people was blown into the pond. The wind lashed the sky like the tail of a wounded tiger groaning angrily. Suddenly a gust of wind rattled the doors and windows. Mukundalal gripped Kumudini's hand and said, 'There is nothing to fear, Kumu. You have done no wrong. Listen to them grinding their teeth. They are out to get me.'

Kumudini, gently pressing the ice-bag on his head, said, 'No, Father; why should anyone be after you? It is just the storm outside. It will be over soon.' Mukunda continued in his delirium, 'Brindaban? Brindaban. Chandra Chakrabarty, the priest in my father's time. He is dead and gone—a ghost now in Brindaban. Did someone say he is coming?'

'Please do not talk. Try to sleep a little, Father,' said Kumu.

'Out there someone is warning somebody. Beware. Beware!'

'That's nothing, Father. The wind is shaking the trees.'

'Why is she so angry with me? Have I been so amiss? Do tell me Kumu?'

'You have done no wrong, Father. Please try and sleep a little.'

'Remember Madhu Adhikari? Used to act in plays as Bindey the go-between for Radha and Krishna.'

And he began to hum Radha's lines.

*Michhey karo keno nindey*
*Ogo Bindey Sri Gobindey*

(O Bindey why do you blame my Krishna, for nothing?)

*Kaar baanshi oi bajey Brindabaney*
*Soi lo soi*
*Gharey ami roibo kemoney?*

(Who is that playing the flute in Brindaban?

Tell me my friend, how can I stay indoors?)

'Radhu, get me my glass of brandy.'

'What are you saying, Father?' Kumudini asked, leaning close to his face.

Mukundalal opened his eyes, bit his tongue in shame and fell silent. Even when his senses were in disarray, he did not forget that he didn't ever drink in presence of Kumudini. A little later he started humming again:

*I've got to snatch his wretched flute away*
*Or I have to leave Brindaban . . .*

These rambling tunes broke Kumu's heart. She was upset with her mother and laid her head on her father's feet, as if seeking forgiveness on her mother's behalf.

Suddenly, Mukundalal shouted 'Dewanjee!' and when the dewan came, told him 'Can't you hear the stamping of their sticks?'

'It's only the wind hitting the door,' said Dewanjee.

'No, the old man Brindabanchandra has come with his bald pate, stick in hand and a silk scarf on his shoulder. He is going on stomping. Is it his stick or his clogs?'

All this time there was a respite from the vomitting of blood; but it started again around three in the morning. Mukundalal felt about the bed and said indistinctly 'Borrobou, the room is dark. Isn't it time you lit the lamps?' This was the first time he had addressed his wife, after his return from the boat—and the last.

Nandarani fainted at the doorstep when she came back from Brindaban. They picked her up and put her to bed. She lost all interest in her household. Her tears dried up and even the children brought her no solace. The family guru recited many slokas from the holy books but she didn't even look at him. She would not take off her iron bangles, as was the custom for widows to do. Because, she claimed, 'I was told by our palmist that I shall never face widowhood. This has to be true.'

Kshema, a distant relation, pleaded with tears in her eyes, 'Whatever had to happen has happened. Now you should take a look at your household. Remember the last words of the karta—Borrobou won't you light the lamps?'

Nandarani sat up on her bed, and with a faraway look said, 'Sure I will light the lamps. This time there will be no delay on my part.' As she said this her pale face suddenly lit up as if she had just started on her journey with a lamp in her hand.

The sun had started on its journey northwards. It was nearly full moon on that Magh night. Nandarani dressed herself in a red bridal saree, put a big dot of sindur on her forehead and with a smile on her face, passed away without ever looking at her household.

## 8

After his father's death Bipradas discovered that the giant tree that had given them shelter so far was rotting at the roots. All their properties were slowly sinking in the quicksand of debt. There was no option but to curtail their scale of social commitments and their own lifestyle. The issue of Kumu's marriage also raised many questions which he avoided answering. In the end the Chatterjees had to give up the Noornagar mansions and move to a rented house in the Bagbazar area of Kolkata.

In her old house Kumudini's world had been vibrant with life all around—trees and flowers, the cowshed, the puja room, paddyfields and of course, people. There, she had picked flowers to fill her basket, relished the forbidden green plums with salt, mustard and coriander leaves, plucked sour chaalta and gathered green mangoes felled by summer storms in the months of Boishakh and Jaistha. Her favourite spot was the walled pond at the back of the house, framed in green moss and enveloped in dark, comforting shadows. She had swum here every day, plucked lotus stalks, knitted or just sat on the steps all by herself, lost in thought.

The festivities of men were tied with those of Nature, with the change of seasons, month after month—from Akshay Tritiya to Doljatra, to Basanti Puja, so many of them. Man and Nature together had made the whole year into a work of art.

Not that all was happy and pleasant. There was a fair amount of silent envy, or screaming accusations, whispered gossip and expressed denouncement—all over the share of fish or on taking sides in children's quarrels. Worst of all was the undertone of anxiety in the midst of the daily chores, about the troubles that could brew from the whims of the master in his quarters. If something untoward happened it would go on for days on end disturbing everyone's peace—Kumudini would be at the mercy of a trembling heart, her mother would be crying silently in her room and the boys would be going about with long faces. This household was always disturbed by these swings between joy and sorrow, between spells of good and bad luck.

In the midst of all this, Kumudini came to Kolkata. It was like a vast ocean without a drop to quench one's thirst. At home in Noornagar, there was something familiar in the air, in the skies. The village horizon variegated with thick forests somewhere, sand dunes elsewhere, the silver streak of the river water, the temple steeple, empty expanses, wild clumps of casuarina, the towpath on the banks—all these with their many lines and many hues, bonded the skies in a very special way, making it Kumudini's very own. Even the sunlight there was of a special kind. It had acquired a very familiar tinge by the way it blended with everything that it spread over—the pond, the paddyfields, the cane shrubs, the brown sails of the fishing boats, the delicate new leaves of the bamboo trees, the smooth dark green of the jackfruit tree, or the pale yellow of the sand bank on the distant shore. But here in Kolkata, this all too familiar light was splintered by the hard lines of the unfamiliar roofs and walls, and looked askance at her as at a strange intruder.

Bipradas drew her close to his chair and asked, 'Kumu, are you fretting?' Kumudini answered with a smile, 'Not a bit, Dada.'

'Will you come with me to the Museum?'

'Yes, of course.'

She said it with such eagerness, that were he not a man, Bipradas would have realized that it was not a very natural response. As a matter of fact, she would have been greatly relieved if she were excused from visiting the Museum. As she was not used to crowds she had no end of hesitation in going out. Her hands and feet got cold and she could hardly see clearly.

Bipradas taught her chess. An extraordinary player himself, he was amused at her beginner's game. But after many days of practice, she learnt it well enough for Bipradas to be careful when playing with her. Because Kumu had no girl companion of her own age, the brother and sister grew closer, more like two brothers. He adored Sanskrit literature and Kumu took lessons in grammar diligently. As she read Kalidas' *Kumarsambhabam*, she visualized Shiva in her daily prayers, Shiva the great ascetic who was the desired one of Uma's own prayers. In her maiden thoughts Kumu's future husband appeared bathed in divine light.

Photography was one of his hobbies, so Kumu learnt this as well. If one took a picture the other would give it meaning. Bipradas was also an ace shot. Whenever he was at the village home for some festival or the other he would indulge in target practice by floating walnuts on the pond in the backyard. He called out to her, 'Come, why not have a try?'

Whatever was dear to her brother Kumu took care to make it her own. She learnt to play the esraj from him so well that he had to admit that he was no match for her.

Thus, coming to Kolkata she came closer to the brother whom she worshipped from her childhood. The move was worthwhile for her. Kumu was naturally lonesome. Rather like Uma of the hills who lived by the shores of the Manas Sarovar in an imaginary world of her own. One born so lonely, needed open skies and a diffused solitude; and in the midst of that she also needed at least one person whom she could revere with all her heart and soul. This distancing from the world at hand was not viewed as natural by the women around her: in fact, they thoroughly despised such an attitude. They thought it was either conceit or sheer heartlessness. So Kumudini never developed any close friendship among her companions back home.

Bipradas's marriage was fixed when his father was alive, but the bride-to-be died of malignant fever only a couple of days before the formal rituals were to begin. The priests at Bhatpara then discovered from his horoscope that there was a long wait before the evil conjuctions in the astral house for marriage were to end. So all talk of his marriage was forgotten. Meanwhile his father died. And after that there was never any time for matchmaking in Bipradas's home. A matchmaker came tempting them with the prospect of a huge dowry. The result was quite the contrary. The matchmaker had to leave his hookah in a hurry and beat a retreat.

## 9

Subodh the younger brother used to write regularly from abroad. But lately there were long gaps. Kumu waited eagerly for the mail. This time the bearer brought the letter straight to her. Bipradas was busy shaving in front of the mirror. Kumu ran to him, 'Dada, a letter from Chhorda!'

He finished shaving and opened the letter with some apprehension. After he finished reading it, he crushed it hard, as if it was a source of sharp pain.

Kumudini was alarmed, 'Hope Chhorda has not taken ill.'

'No, he is all right.'

'Please tell me, what does he say in this letter?'

'All about his studies.'

For some time now, he had not let Kumu read Subodh's letters; instead, he used to just read out bits. This time there was not even that. And Kumu did not have the courage to ask. She fretted.

In the beginning Subodh used to be quite frugal. The sorrows of the family were still fresh in his mind. As that memory began to fade, his expenses rose. He now wrote, 'Unless you spend generously you cannot reach the top layers of the society here, and if you cannot the whole point of having come to this country is lost.'

Bipradas had no option but to send him money telegraphically once or twice in the past. This time the demand was for a thousand pounds sterling—urgently needed.

Bipradas was stupefied. 'How am I to get so much money! We are straining every limb only to save enough for Kumu's wedding. Do I have to break into those funds? What use is Subodh's barristership if we have to sacrifice Kumu's future for it!' So ran his thoughts.

He was pacing up and down the balcony that night, unaware that Kumudini was also having a sleepless night. When it became unbearable, she ran to Bipradas, held his hand and said, 'I beg of you, please tell me what is wrong with Chhorda. Do not keep me in the dark.'

Bipradas realized that if he suppressed the truth she would fear the worst. So he said, 'Subodh has asked for more money and to send him any is beyond my means.'

Kumu pleaded with him, 'May I say something if you don't take it amiss?'

'If it is something unreasonable I may lose my temper.'

'No Dada, listen to me seriously . . . my mother's ornaments . . . they are for me aren't they . . . if that can be used.'

'Stop it. We can't touch your ornaments!'

'But I can.'

'No, you can't, either. No more of this talk. Please go to sleep.'

The morning dawned in the city of Kolkata with the cawing of crows and the rumble of the scavenger carts. In the distance one heard the whistle of steamers or the siren of the oil mills. In front of their house a man passed by with a ladder, sticking up posters for some anti-fever pills. Two bullocks goaded heavily by the driver were running away with an empty cart and the row between a up-country woman and an Oriya Brahmin was constantly rising in pitch, over who should have the priority for taking water from the municipal hydrant. Bipradas was sitting on the balcony with the tube of the hubble-bubble in his hand. The morning papers were lying on the floor, unread.

Kumu came up and said, 'Please don't say "no" to me Dada.'

'What, do you wish to interfere with my independent opinion? Do I have to say "yes" instead of "no", call night day if you say so?'

'No, I am only asking you to take my ornaments and put an end to your worries.'

'This is why I call you an old woman. How could you ever think that I could take your jewellery to solve my problems?'

'I don't know about that, but I can't bear to see you worrying yourself to death.'

'My dear, the only way to end a worry is to think it through. If you try to suppress it, it will recoil on you. Be patient for a while, I shall manage something.'

The only way he could send money by the next mail was to dip into Kumu's dowry: and that was unthinkable.

In due course Subodh's reply came. No, he would not touch Kumu's dowry but would suggest selling off his share of the ancestral property. He had even sent a document regarding his power of attorney in order to execute the partition and sale.

The letter stung Bipradas to the quick. How could Subodh bring himself to write such a cruel letter? Bipradas sent for his old dewanjee.

'Didn't the Bhushan Rais want to take the Karimhati property on lease?' he asked dewanjee. 'How much were they willing to offer?'

'Maybe up to twenty thousand,' said the dewan.

'Send for him. I want to settle it with him,' said Bipradas.

His grandfather had bequeathed this property solely to him, for Bipradas was his eldest grandson. Bhushan Rai had a thriving moneylending business of over twenty-to-twenty-five lakhs. He was born in Karimhati, this is why he had been trying for quite some time to take a lease on his birthplace. Bipradas has been on the point of yielding in moments of financial crises. But the tenants pleaded with him saying that they could never accept Bhushan Rai as their landlord. So the proposal was aborted many times. This time Bipradas had made up his mind. He knew for certain that this was not the end of Subodh's demands. Still he said to himself, 'Let this lease-money be for Subodh, we will face the future when it comes.'

Dewanjee dared not address Bipradas directly. He went to Kumu and said, 'Didi, Dada listens to you. Please ask him not to do this. It will be very wrong to go through with this.'

The entire household was very fond of Bipradas and could not bear the thought that he should give up his own rights.

It was getting late. Bipradas was engrossed in the deed documents. He had not had his bath nor eaten anything. Kumu had sent for him many times. At last he came into the house, his face drained and worn. Kumu's heart bled at the sight of him.

After lunch he stretched out on his bed, the long pipe of the hubble-bubble in hand. Kumu sat stroking his hair and said, 'Dada, you must not lease your property.'

Bipradas said lightly, 'It seems you are possessed by the ghost of Siraj-ud-daulah, the last Nawab of Bengal. Must you impose your will always?'

'Don't try to avoid the issue,' she said. Bipradas then sat up straight and Kumu had to face him. He cleared his throat choked with emotion, and said, 'Do you know what Subodh has written? Read this.' Kumu read the letter and covered her face with both hands and whispered, 'My God, how could Chhorda write this.'

Bipradas said, 'Now that he can see his property as distinct from mine, can I treat my own legacy separately? Poor boy, he lost his father early, to whom should he turn for help but me?'

Kumu could say nothing more. Silent tears flowed down her cheeks. Bipradas leaned on his bolster and closed his eyes.

Kumu stroked his feet for a while and then added, 'But my mother's jewellery is still there, why don't you . . .?'

Bipradas sat up again and said, 'Kumu darling, you have not understood the real dilemma. If Subodh now squanders your share on theatres and concerts, will I be able to forgive him ever, and will he be able to face up to anyone? Why do you inflict this punishment on him?'

## 10

It was a cloudy day. Bipradas was not well. He was browsing through the morning papers, wrapped in a thin quilt. Kumu's pet cat had found itself an extra bit of the quilt and was curled up in deep sleep. Bipradas's own impudent terrier slept near the master's feet, occasionally grunting in its sleep.

Just then one of the matchmakers turned up.

'Namaskar.'

'And who may you be?'

'Sir the masters knew me well (a lie!). You were only a child then. I am Nilmani Ghatak, the son of Gangamani Ghatak.'

'What brings you here?'

'I know about a good bridegroom. Worthy of your family.'

Bipradas sat up. The matchmaker named Rai Bahadur Madhusudan Ghoshal.

'Has he a son?'

The man bit his tongue in embarrassment, 'No sir, he is unmarried. He has amassed an enormous fortune, and now that he does not have to look after the business himself, he has turned his thoughts to matrimony.'

Bipradas silently puffed at his hubble-bubble for a while, and suddenly spoke aloud, 'We don't have a girl in this family to match a man of his age.'

But the man would not give up. He went on dwelling at length on the wealth of the prospective match, his comings and goings at the Governor's court.

Bipradas remained quiet and then burst out, 'Their ages do not tally!'

The man said, 'Do give it a thought. I shall be back in a few days.'

Bipradas went to sleep with a deep sigh.

Kumu was about to enter the room with a cup of hot tea for her brother but stopped on finding outside the door a tattered wet umbrella and a muddy pair of crude leather sandals like the ones sold in the Taltolla market. But much of the conversation reached her ears. The matchmaker was saying, 'Before the year is out Rai Bahadur will become a Maharaja. This is straight from the Lieutenant Governor himself. That is why he is worried that the place for the Maharani can no longer be kept vacant. Your family astrologer is a distant relative of mine and we have seen the girl's horoscope. It is a perfect match. There is not one girl in town whose horoscope has escaped my scrutiny. But I have yet to come across any like this. Take my word for it. This match is as good as fixed, ordained by Prajapati, the god of marriage.'

Just then Kumu's left eyelid flickered! How mysterious are the ways of lucky omens! Kinu Acharya who read her palm on many an occasion, had predicted that one day she would be a Rajrani. The consequences of her palmcast had presented themselves on her doorstep on their own. Their family planetologist had come recently for his annual dues and he had said that in the coming month of Ashadh, the Taureans would be awarded court honours, gain income through the ladies and overcome enemies. On the adverse side it indicated illness or even the death of the spouse. Bipradas was a Taurus.

There was also some talk of occasional ill health. Last night's cold was a clear proof. The month of Ashadh had just begun. There was no immediate worry about the illness of the spouse. So, all in all, good times were ahead.

Kumu came and sat next to him. 'Do you have a headache?' she asked.

'No, of course not.'

'Has your tea gone cold? I could not come in as you had some visitor.'

Bipradas stared at Kumu and let out a deep sigh. Fate is at its cruellest when it offers a golden chariot with wheels which do not move. Kumu was hurt at this pained look of perplexity on his face. Why was he apprehensive about this godsend? The thought that marriage has also a complication by way of personal liking, never entered her head. From her childhood she had seen her four sisters married one after the other. Theirs was a kuleen family and nothing mattered but the kul—the family credentials. They lived on, day in and day out, engrossed in their children and the rest of the family. When they were hurt they did not protest, they could never imagine that things could be different. Did a mother choose her son? He might turn out to be a good or a bad son. It was the same with husbands. God had not opened a shop for people to choose what they wanted. No one could override Fate.

At long last, her prince had arrived in disguise, having crossed the empty expanse of her bad days. Her heart echoed the sound of his chariot wheels and she was not even prepared to look beyond his mask.

She quickly went to her room and opened the almanac. It was Manorath Dwitiya—a day for the fulfilment of wishes. She called a few Brahmins among the household staff, fed them well and gave them small gifts as well. All of them blessed her and wished her to be a Rajrani with plenty of wealth and many sons.

The matchmaker came into Bipradas's drawing room a second time. The old man entered, chanting 'Shiva, Shiva,' as he yawned to the snapping of fingers. This time Bipradas thought better than to dismiss him with a straight no. How could he take up this great responsibility on himself? How could he be so sure that this was not the best thing for Kumudini? He promised to give his final word the day after.

## 11

Kumu hardly had any furniture in her room. A small cot on one side, a clothes horse with a couple of twisted sarees, and a light yellow towel. Her clothes were kept in a chest made of jackwood. Under the bed, in a green painted tin box were all her toiletries for dressing up, betel nut leaves and in another box things for dressing her hair. A few books, a pen and ink and some letter paper along with a pair of her father's slippers knitted in wool by her mother, rested on wooden racks in a niche in the wall. At the head of the bed hung a picture of Radha and Krishna together. An esraj lay propped up against the corner wall.

The evening was thick with heavy rain clouds. She had not lit the lamps yet. She sat on the wooden chest and looked out of the window. Through the rain was dimly outlined the brick-filled carcass of Kolkata like a prehistoric animal in thick armour. Some lights flickered now and then on this body. Kumu's mind dwelt on her destined future domain, where people, houses and everything else were going to be according to her own ideals. And in the midst of it all, she herself would be established as the satilakshmi—the ideal wife and goddess, full of reverence, adoration and welfare all around. Like her own mother—who had but one deep scar in her otherwise saintly life. She lost her patience for a while at her husband's lapse. Kumu was determined to never make that mistake herself.

She was startled out of her reverie at the sound of Bipradas's steps. 'Shall I light the lamp?' she asked. 'No, Kumu, I don't think so,' said Bipradas as he sat down next to her. Kumu got down to the floor and started to massage his feet gently.

He said softly, 'I didn't send for you as I had a visitor. How long have you been sitting like this all by yourself?'

Kumu was embarrassed. 'No, I was not alone, Aunt Kshema was here for ages.' And to get back to the topic she asked, 'Who was it, Dada?'

'That is what I have come to tell you. You completed eighteen last month and are now going on to nineteen, isn't that so?'

'Yes, but what's wrong with that?'

'Nothing at all. Nilmani Ghatak the matchmaker had come. Please, my dear girl, do not be shy. When our father was alive you were only ten—and a match was almost settled for you. It would have gone through and no one would have bothered about your views. But today I simply can't do so. You must have heard of Raja Madhusudan Ghoshal. Their family is no less than ours in social standing. But he is much older. I could not agree to this match. A word from you and I can put an end to it. Please do not be shy to tell me what you think.'

'No, I won't.'

She was quiet for a while, and then spoke again, 'My match must have been already fixed with him of whom you speak.' She was echoing the matchmaker's very words which must have made a deep impression in her mind unknown to her.

'How ever did it get fixed?' asked Bipradas greatly surprised.

She remained silent.

Bipradas stroked her hair and said, 'Don't be childish, Kumu . . .'

'You won't understand, Dada, I am not being childish in the least.'

She worshipped her brother. But alas, he did not believe in oracles. Kumudini was well aware of this shortcoming in her brother's discernment.

Bipradas continued, 'But you've never even seen him!'

'Maybe, but I know it for certain,' she said.

This one dark corner of her mind was altogether outside his sphere of influence. Still he tried to reason once more, 'Look Kumu, this is a matter of your whole life. Do not commit to anything on a whim.'

'It is not a whim Dada, not a whim at all. I swear to you, I cannot marry anyone else'.

Bipradas was startled. It was useless to argue where there was no logic, no link between cause and effect. One cannot wrestle with the obscurity of the New Moon. He could sense that she had made up some divine message in her own mind. This was indeed so. Only this morning she had prayed to her deity for a sign—'If this bunch of flowers is paired off one by one and the remaining one is blue in colour then I shall conclude that this match is willed by Him.' And the last flower so remaining was in fact a blue morning glory.

Bells were ringing in the Mallik household in the distance, announcing the evening rituals. Kumu folded her hands in prayer. Bipradas sat silently for a long time. With the unceasing rain there were frequent flashes of lightning.

## 12

Bipradas tried a few times more to reason with her, but Kumu just sat quiet with her head bent, intent on picking at the end of her sari.

So the match was fixed and all details were settled except the venue for the wedding. Bipradas would like to have the wedding in Kolkata itself but Madhusudan was determined to have it in Noornagar. The groom's side won, of course.

They had to come to Noornagar a few days ahead to make all the necessary arrangements. There was a new breath of life in Kumu's mind and behaviour, in the same way as the earth turns green after the rains following the dry summer months. She was often ecstatic with the idea of her union with someone who existed only in her imagination until then. The golden light of the autumn days whispered to her eternal words of endearment. She threw puffed rice onto the balcony in front of her bedroom for the birds to come and eat. She also kept bits of bread for the frisky squirrels who looked around, came rushing, stood on their tails, held themselves up on their two hind legs and nibbled away at the bread. Kumudini watched them delightedly.

She was now full of compassion for the entire universe. In the evenings she stood still in the pond, immersed up to her chin. The water seemed to speak to her whole body. The curved rays of the setting sun came through the grapefruit trees on the western end of the pool and shone like gold on the dark stretch of water. Kumudini watched the light and shade play upon her body and she tingled with rapture. In the afternoons she sat on the rooftop all by herself, listening to the dove cooing on the jamun tree next door. The image installed in the temple of her youth was sculpted in deep emotion touched by the romance of the divine lovers, Krishna and Radhika.

She went up to the roof with her esraj and played her brother's favourite tune in Raag Bhupali—

*Aaju mor gharey ayilo piyaraowa*
*Romey romey harakhila.*

(Today my beloved has come to me; every pore in my body is in raptures.)

Every night she bowed in reverence and every morning she did the same before she left her bed. It was not very clear who the object of this veneration was—perhaps just the spontaneous expression of a disembodied adoration.

But an imaginary idol cannot be kept within the closed doors of a temple for ever. It is a sad day for the devotee when the fair image of this deity begins to be smudged by hot blasts of gossip from outside.

In fact one day the old woman from Telenipara, Tinkari, blurted out in front of Kumu, 'What sort of Raja has fallen to the lot of our Kumu? Isn't it more like the gypsy song that goes like this—

*Once upon a time there was a stretch of thorny bush licked by dogs. Our little king cut it and made his throne out of it . . .*

This Raja is more like that. After all, isn't this fellow Modho, the son of the clerk Ando who made his pile by importing rice from Burma, and yet made his mother slog till her dying day?'

The women were curious. 'Did you really know the bridegroom-to be?' 'Did I not indeed? His mother lived in our neighbourhood, the daughter of Chakraborty, the priest. (And then lowering her voice) To tell you the truth, they are not acceptable in marriage by any good Brahmin family. However, Lakshmi the goddess of wealth is no respecter of caste.'

As we had pointed out, Kumudini's mind was not cast in the modern mould. The sanctity of caste and family were realities for her. So the more doubts assailed her, the more she got angry with the maligners. She would suddenly burst into tears and leave them. Others sniggered, 'My, my, such touching concern even before marriage! She outdoes the legendary Sati of Dakshayagna who fell down dead on hearing her husband-to-be denigrated.'

Bipradas was more modern in his outlook, yet this talk of low lineage did get him down. So he tried to suppress it. But the opposite happened; just as fluff which billows out if one presses a torn pillow too much.

Meanwhile, an old tenant, Damodar Biswas, came out with the information that a long time ago the Ghoshals were in fact owners of Sheyalkuli, a village next to their present seat Noornagar. This village was now in the possession of the Chatterjees. Damodar's face flushed with admiration of the Chatterjees as he related how they dispensed with the Ghoshals in the action about the immersion of the images of Durga; and the tactics that succeeded in not only throwing them out of the area but even putting them beyond the pale of society. The fact that at one time the Ghoshals were indeed equal to the Chatterjees in wealth and respectability was good news, but at the same time Bipradas began to wonder if the proposed marriage was also the beginning of a sequel to the old feud.

## 13

The wedding was set for the month of aghran. On the twenty-fifth of Ashwin ended Lakshmipuja and on the twenty-seventh, an overseer from the engineering division of the Ghoshal Company appeared with an army of upcountry labourers. Apparently, the bridegroom and his party had decided to come a few days before the wedding and spend their time in tents to be set up by the pond named after the Ghoshals, here in this village of Sheyalkuli.

'What sort of a proposal is this?' inquired Bipradas. 'Let as many of them come and let them stay as long as they wish to, and we shall make all the arrangements. There is no need for tents. We can vacate our old mansion.'

The overseer said, 'These are the orders of the Rajabahadur. He has also asked for the wild growth around the pond to be cleared. So we need your permission sir, as you are the landlord of the area.'

Bipradas went red in the face. 'Is that fair? We can also clear the jungle ourselves,' he added.

The overseer submitted politely, 'That was the spot where the Rajabahadur's ancestral home existed, so he has taken it into his head to have it cleared himself.'

Bipradas considered this explanation. It was not an unreasonable request altogether. But his relatives were unhappy. The tenants said that this was only an act of one-upmanship over their Babus. The Ghoshals, they alleged, could hardly hide the fact that their treasury was suddenly inflated and they wished to announce it with the beating of drums. If it were the good old days then the bridegroom and his entire gang would have been despatched for good. Even the younger Babu would not have tolerated this and would have seen the last of those visitors and their tents.

They came to Bipradas and pleaded, 'Sir, we cannot yield to them. We are prepared to bear all expenses, whatever they may be.'

A junior share-holder of their property, Nabagopal, said, 'We cannot let our family pride suffer. There was a time when our ancestors made the Ghoshals bite the dust, and now they have the temerity to flaunt their wealth!

'Don't worry, Dada, I shall also pitch in. It maybe true that our property has been divided but the same cannot be said of our family!'

Thus Nabagopal pushed himself to become the self-styled leader of the opposition.

Bipradas had not been able to meet Kumu for the last few days. He could hardly face her. And it was not as if people would spare her feelings and not report the effrontery of the Ghoshals. There were no such social graces left. On the contrary they would perhaps overdo it. The women were angry with her. It was because of her that the family reputation was being compromised. She wanted to be a Rani. And that too to a

Raja who had nothing to recommend him!

Kumu was ready to overlook the matter of caste and rank with her reverence, but the meanness of this attempt to belittle the in-laws by a show of wealth saddened her no end. She avoided meeting people. She was dying to hear from her brother, but he hardly came indoors, not even for his meals.

One afternoon when Bipradas was supervising the setting up of a shed for cooking the wedding feasts, he suddenly noticed Kumu on the steps of the pond staring at the water. She came running up and said, 'Dada, I am at a loss to understand anything,' and started sobbing into the end of her sari.

He gently patted her back and said, 'Don't listen to what people say.'

'But what are they doing? Does it not belittle us?'

'Do think of their sentiments too. They are coming to their ancestral home and may feel like celebrating. Look at it as distinct from the wedding celebrations.'

Kumu kept quiet. Bipradas was desperate. He said, 'Look, Kumu, if you have the slightest reservation, I can cancel it—even now!'

Kumudini shook her head strongly. 'No no. What a shame. That is unthinkable.'

She was already committed in her heart of hearts, the rest was only formality.

Bipradas's modern mind revolted at this blind devotion. He said, 'Marriage ties become real when both parties are honest to themselves. It is no use tuning an instrument if the player is tone-deaf. Look at our mythology—Sita was as great as Rama, Sati matched Mahadeva as did Arundhati and Vashist. The gentlemen of today have no merit in themselves, that is why this one-sided clamour for chastity on the part of the women. They cannot supply the oil but want the wick to give light. And the wick—it simply burns itself to ashes.'

But it was no use telling Kumu this. From now on she repeated her prayer—for better or for worse, he is my lord and master.

*Duhkheshu anudwigna-mana sukheshu bigata-sprihah*
*Beetaraga-bhaya-spriha.*

(Unperturbed in adversity, unconcerned with pleasure, devoid of fear or desire.)

What was true of the ascetic's code was also true of the sati—the dedicated wife. And that transcended joy and sorrow, there was no room for anger or fear. Love? Even that was not essential. Love needs give and take, but devotion was beyond that. There was no appeal, there was only submission.

The concept of sati was disembodied; what is known in English as 'impersonal'. The man Madhusudan may be flawed but the idea called husband is eternal and emotionless. Kumudini dedicated herself to that shadowy being.

## 14

The jungle along the Ghoshaldighi was cleared beyond recognition. The ground was levelled. A brick-red gravelled path, lined with lampposts, ran down the middle. The water hyacinths clogging the pond were cleared. Two brand new English sailing boats were tied to the pond's edge. One had painted on its side 'Madhumati' and the other 'Madhukari'. The tent in which the Rajabahadur was to stay carried a framed sign 'Madhuchakra' in red silk embroidered on yellow baize. The steps to the pond on one side were fully screened with rush mats for the ladies to bathe. On the huge neem tree nearby was a wooden sign 'Madhusagar'. On a small plot of land, in beds of various shapes were displayed sunflowers, tuberoses, marigolds, balsams, cannas and coleas. Small wooden boxes carried English season flowers of many hues. In the middle of this garden there was a shallow brick tank with a cast iron statue of a nude female blowing a conch-shell, which was to serve as a fountain. This area was named 'Madhukunja'. The entrance to the whole place was through an ornamental iron gate on top of which fluttered a flag bearing the legend 'Madhupuri'. The name 'Madhu' was stamped all over.

People came in hordes to see this magic palace that had sprung up, draped in cloth of many kinds, with tents, canopies, festoons, flowers and Chinese lanterns of many colours. Orderlies in bright liveries, yellow turbans with red borders and uniforms in red broadcloth with silver lining, strutted about in patent leather shoes, sounding the gong by the hour and firing blank shots at sunset. Some of them had long swords hanging from belts which spiked the landlord's ground at every step. The old guards of the Chatterjees were ashamed to come out in their shabby old-fashioned clothes. Their whole clan was riled at the goings on. The victory flag of the Ghoshals was flying from a pikestaff thrust deep into the ribs of Noornagar.

Such was the prelude to the wedding!

## 15

Bipradas called Nabagopal and said, 'Nabu, to try to outshine the other in a show of pomp only shows poor breeding.'

Nabagopal replied, 'Brahma, our four-headed creator, has fashioned most people in a fit of disdain. All his four faces are only meant to mouth big words. Ninety percent of men happen to be lowly bred and that is the only way to behave with them.'

'Even then, you may not rival them. It is much better for us to adopt a simple style. That will be more dignified. Let us call a few proper priests and follow the rites as laid down in our revered Sama Veda. They have become Rajas, leave them to their pretentions. We are Brahmins—saintliness is for us.'

Nabagopal replied, 'Dada, you are far behind the times. This is not the good old Golden Age when truth prevailed. You are trying to row a boat in a marsh. You have your tenants like Tinu Sarkar, you have your talukdars—Bhadu Paramanik, Kamaraddi Bishyesh, Panchu Mandal—what do they care for your saintly vegetarian Brahminism. They are not the descendants of Yajnabalka! It will break their hearts to suffer this. You do not have to do anything, just keep quiet.'

Nabagopal joined hands with the tenants. Money was no consideration, they boasted. Everyone from the bailiffs to the lower orders were clad in new uniforms, new red broadcloth wraps and new coloured dhotis. A platform for the musicians was raised, flying gold-fringed pennants which could be seen from afar. Both partners of the Chatterjee clan brought out two pairs of caparisoned elephants who roamed around the Ghoshaldighi now and then ringing loudly the bells round their necks. They slapped their thighs and guffawed at their own dig at the Ghoshals and exclaimed—'After all, you cannot produce elephants out of sacks of rice.'

The date of the wedding was set for the twenty-seventh of Aghran. Still a good ten days ahead. Then the rumour started that the Raja was arriving with his entire retinue. Bipradas's men were in a great quandry. Madhusudan had sent no word to them. Perhaps he thought such civilities were only for the common folk: to be uncivil was the prerogative of the kings. Would it be right then to receive them at the railway station? The right answer to lack of notice was not to take any notice.

But Bipradas could hardly avoid distress by reason alone. His affection for Kumu ran deep. That anything should hurt her was out of question. It was so easy to hurt women, their feelings were so vulnerable. Society had placed the whiphand with the hard-hearted, their rules had no regard for the sensitive backs of the unarmed. Bipradas's people felt it was cowardice to save one's pride by exposing one's dear one to the storm of anger, jealousy and hatred.

Unknown to anyone, Bipradas rode on his horse to the railway station.

The train drew in at five in the evening. The Raja and his retinue got off the saloon car. With a brief acknowledgement he said to Bipradas, 'What a surprise! You need not have taken the trouble of coming yourself.'

'Indeed. You are visiting our place for the first time and should I not welcome you?' said Bipradas.

'You are mistaken. I have not yet come to your place. That will happen only on the day of the wedding,' was the Raja's reply.

Bipradas did not quite get it, but a crowded railway platform was no place for a debate. So he just said, 'The boat is ready at anchor.' The Raja replied, 'There is no need for it. Our own steam launch is ready.'

Bipradas guessed something was amiss. He said, 'But the foodstuff is all ready waiting for you in the boat.'

'Why did you put yourself out to do this? We do not need a thing from you. Please remember that we have landed on our ancestral soil—not on your land. We will be there only on the wedding night.'

Bipradas expected no softening of the mood after this. But he felt deeply distressed inside. He went and stretched himself on the easy chair in the railway waiting room.

It was a winter evening and it was getting dark. The up train was announced and the station was lit up. Bipradas let the horse ride on its own. He reached home fairly late at night. He did not tell anyone where he had been and what had transpired between him and Kumu's groom-to-be.

He caught a chill that night. The cough grew worse. The more he neglected it the worse it got. Kumu had to force him to rest in bed. So all the arrangements were left to Nabagopal.

## 16

A couple of days later Nabagopal turned up and said to Bipradas, 'i need your advice. Please tell me what I should do.' Bipradas got worried. He asked, 'Why? Whatever is the matter?'

'They have brought along with them a few white men, must be touts or vendors of foreign liqour. Yesterday they killed at least a couple of hundred snipes at the Pirpur shoal. As you are well aware, during these winter months birds come in large numbers. I think there is going to be a killing of living creatures on a massive scale by these visitors. Enough to appease all the demons in our mythology like Ahiravana and Mahiravana, Hidimba and Ghatotkach right up to the huge Kumbhakarna. Even in Hell, the ten jaws of the ten-headed Ravana would tire of chewing so much flesh.'

Bipradas was stunned. He could not utter a word.

Nabagopal continued, 'It was your order that no one should hunt in that marshland. You even stopped the District Magistrate from doing so. We had feared that he might shoot you for a swan. He was a gentleman so he went away quietly. But these people do not care if it is a deer, a cow or a Brahmin. Still, if you just say one word . . .'

Bipradas quickly stopped him, 'No! No, don't say anything to them.'

Bipradas had been the best shot at tigers in the whole district, but later once when he shot a bird he was filled with so much revulsion that he stopped all shooting of birds within his territory.

All this while Kumu had been standing behind him, stroking his hair. As soon as Nabagopal left she said sternly, 'Dada, you must stop them.'

'Stop them from doing what?'

'From killing birds.'

'Kumu, they will misunderstand us and then defy us.'

'Let them misunderstand. Pride is not their monopoly.'

Bipradas looked at her and smiled within himself. He knew how scrupulously she was trying to follow the code of the satis—the ideal Hindu wives. *Chhayeb anugata swachchha*—to follow the husband willingly like a shadow. Should there be a split between the shadow and the body over the life of an insignificant bird?

'Don't lose your temper, Kumu. I too killed birds once. I did not realize then that it was wrong. They are still at that stage.'

So the shooting and the picnics went on in full swing. A band played music and there was dancing for the English guests in the evenings, tennis in the afternoons and occasional sailing regattas. The villagers thronged to watch the fun and sights they had never seen before. At night after dinner there was loud singing of 'For he is a jolly good fellow'.

What impressed the people most was that the main players in these festivities were all English men and women. It was a rare sight to see them with their fishing rods and sola hats. The local show put up by the Chatterjees by way of fencing with lathis, wrestling, rowing, jatras and amateur theatre, was nothing in comparison, even when four elephants were thrown in to liven things up.

A couple of days before the wedding was the ritual of the holy turmeric bath. The splendour and range of presents, from heavy jewellery to expensive dolls, from the groom's side, held everyone spellbound. The Chatterjees did their best to tip the carriers handsomely.

This unspoken battle between the Ghoshals and the Chatterjees entered its penultimate round with the feeding of the public. The entire locality was invited by beating of drums to dinner at Madhupuri by the banks of Madhusagar. Nabagopal was livid. 'We are the zamindars. How dare he put up this so-called Madhupuri here!' he fumed.

The arrangements for the public banquet were widely visible. It was no ordinary meal. Fish, cream and curds, sandesh, ghee, flour and sugar were imported to Madhupur with much clamour. Huge fires were lit, cooking utensils of all shapes and sizes from small pans to large pots, water carriers and wide platters were spread out. Rows of bullock carts continued to bring in potatoes, brinjals, raw plantains and vegetables of all kinds. The banquet was to be held in the evening in a blaze of lights.

The Chatterjees, on the other hand, had arranged for lunch. The ryots had come in large numbers and arranged everything. Separate seating arrangements had been made for Hindus and Muslims. The Muslim tenants were in the majority—they had started cooking at the crack of dawn. Regardless of the menu for the feast, the cheering that went on in praise of the Chatterjees was vociferous. Nabagopal personally looked after the guests and did not have his own meal till five in the evening when the last guest left. Then began the feeding of the poor. The senior ryots themselves took charge of this distribution. The air was rent with tumultous cries in favour of their benefactors.

At Madhupuri, cooking went on for the whole day. The tempting aroma of food filled the air. Mountains of earthen plates and cups as well as banana leaves were heaped up. Crows incessantly quarrelled over piles of leftover fish and vegetables, the dogs of the area were engaged in noisy fights. In good time the lights went up. A native orchestra from Metiaburuz played a whole range of ragas—from Imankalyan to Kedara till nightfall. Anxious attendants came from time to time to whisper into the Rajabahadur's ears, that not many guests had turned up till then. It was the day of the weekly fair, so some of the shoppers from distant villages took the opportunity to sit down to a free and generously given meal. There were a few indigent beggars as well.

Madhusudan retired to his solitary tent and let out a growl: 'Hmph.'

A younger brother, Radhu, came and said, 'Enough is enough, Dada, let's go.'

'Where to?'

'Let's go back to Calcutta. These people are not playing fair. There are brides from better families who are only waiting for you to beckon them with your little finger.'

Madhusudan roared, 'Go away!'

A century-old event repeated itself. One party's ostentatiousness was sky high, but the other party waylaid the procession. However the net loss and gain in such matters are never apparent. That domain remains very private.

The tenants of the Chatterjees had a good laugh. Bipradas was lying ill in bed and unaware of all that had happened.

## 17

The raja had forbidden any celebration on the way to the bride's house for the wedding. So, there were no lights, no music—just two of their family priests and a couple of eulogists. The groom arrived quietly in his palanquin. Nobody knew of his arrival until he alighted from his palanquin. But in Madhupuri the groom's party were merrymaking noisily with food and drink. Nabagopal saw it as a retort on their part. Usually the girl's family welcomes the boy's family with folded hands. But Nabagopal did nothing of the sort. He did not even ask about the rest of the groom's party.

Kumudini, dressed for her wedding, came to say goodbye to her brother. She was trembling all over. Bipradas's fever was over hundred and five degrees; he had a balm of mustard and rye on his chest and back. Kumudini put her head down on his feet and broke down, sobbing uncontrollably. Aunt Kshema tried to calm her, 'Please Kumu, you must not cry like this. It is not done.'

Bipradas tried to sit up a little and looked at her face for a long time, tears streaming down his own face. Kshema said, 'It's time to go.'

Bipradas put his hand on Kumu's head and blessed her in a choked voice, 'Let the all-merciful God bless you,' and then fell back on his bed.

All through the wedding ceremony tears rolled down Kumu's face. The hand that she put in the groom's hand was icy cold, and trembling. And when the time came for the two of them to exchange glances, did she look at her husband at all? Maybe she didn't. The behaviour her groom's side had exhibited in the last few days made her somewhat frightened of her husband. Like a bird which feels it had lost its nest for a cage.

Madhusudan was by no means ugly, but his looks were stern. The first thing one noticed in his dark face was a long curved beak-like nose standing guard over his lips. The wide sloping forehead seemed to have swollen till it met the dam of a pair of thick eyebrows. The gaze of the narrow eyes under the shadow of those eyebrows was piercing. The face was clean-shaven, the lips pressed thin and the chin heavy. The hair was thick and curly like an African's, and closely cropped. A stocky build made him look younger than his age, except for the few grey hairs near his temple. He was short-statured, almost of the same height as Kumudini. His hands were hairy and proportionately shorter than the body. Altogether the man seemed to be solid, from head to toe, as if some strong resolve was for ever frozen into his form. Rather like a cannon ball in its relentless trajectory, shot by Destiny. It was plain to see that he had no time for useless talk, trivial issues or small men.

Nobody from Kumu's side was happy at the way the wedding took place. The first meeting between the groom's side and the bride's produced a clangour of dissonance which drowned the festive tune of the wedding. From time to time, Kumu's heart heaved. She tried her best to suppress a doubt. 'Has my Lord let me down?' she wondered. In the solitude of her closed room she often pressed her head on the floor and prayed—'let my mind not weaken.' The hardest task was to keep her doubts hidden from her brother.

Since their mother's death Bipradas had depended totally on Kumudini's care. She looked after all the matters that concerned the family—clothing, the daily expenses, the book cases, grain to feed the horses, the cleaning of the guns, the tending of the dogs, maintaining the camera, the musical instruments and the bedrooms. The last few days before the wedding, she nursed her brother during his illness, taking utmost care not to let any of her own worries cloud her face. Bipradas was very proud of her skill with the esraj, but Kumu was too shy to play often. But these two days she played for him, the ragas Kanada and Malkauns on her own, for him. Into that rendering, she poured all her adoration, her prayers, her doubts and her dedication. Bipradas listened to her music with his eyes closed and asked from time to time for his favourite ragas—Sindhu, Behag, Bhairabi—ragas filled with tears and the sadness of separation. The sorrows that the two of them harboured in their hearts mingled with those tunes. Brother and sister did not exchange any words, nor did they condole or console each other.

Bipradas's fever, cough and chest pain showed no improvement; on the contrary, his condition worsened. Doctors cautioned that this influenza might even turn to pneumonia. Kumu was worried to death. It was agreed that the normal custom of spending the night after the wedding in her own home would be followed and that she would return to Kolkata the day after. But it was rumoured that Madhusudan had suddenly decided to take her back to Kolkata the day after the wedding itself. It was made clear that this was not to meet the demands of their family custom, nor for any 'special need', certainly not for love but only just to discipline her. To ask for a favour, in such circumstances, was unthinkable for a sensitive woman like her. Yet she swallowed her pride and asked her husband, in a trembling voice, to let her stay on for a couple of days more so that she could see her brother on the way to recovery. Madhusudan's curt reply was, 'It's all settled.' There was no room for Kumu's deep anguish in such unilateral rigidity. That night Madhusudan tried his best to make her talk, but she turned her face away and slept on the other side of the bed, without a word. She left her bed at the first sound of birds.

It was still dark. Bipradas had spent a sleepless night. Despite his fever, he desperately wanted to attend the wedding reception, but the doctor prevented him, with great difficulty. So he sent a messenger every now and then to bring him the latest news; and like all news in the time of war, most of it was made up. Bipradas asked, 'When did the groom arrive? I didn't hear the band.' Shibu the reporter said, 'Our groom is very considerate. The moment he heard about the illness in the house he put a stop to everything. It was all so very quiet. You could hardly hear the footsteps of the marriage party.'

'And one more thing, Shibu. Did the food go round? It was one of my big worries. After all, this is not Kolkata.'

'Go round, did you say, sir? So much food was wasted! There is enough left over to feed another lot.'

'Were they pleased?'

'Not a word of complaint. Not a murmur! Many a wedding have I seen, where the groom's party lead the bride's party such a dance! But they were so quiet, you could hardly tell that they were there.'

'After all they are from Kolkata; they know how to behave. They do realize that if the bride's side is humiliated, it is a slur on them as well.'

'Well put, sir. I must repeat it to them. They will be pleased to hear it.'

By the evening Kumu was aware that Bipradas's condition was worse. The thought that she would not be there to look after him, made her feel like a trapped bird. She knew that to her brother, her nursing meant much more than any medicine.

She finished her prayers with a flower at the feet of her idol, and then went into her brother's room. The sun was still to come up. Bipradas's mind was relaxed, with the kind of weariness that overtakes one for a brief spell in the long fight against sickness. Like a harvested field, he was bereft of all the cares of the world and passions of life. The doors and windows of his room remained closed at night. Only now in the morning the doctor allowed the eastern window to be opened. Beyond the dew-drenched leaves of the peepul tree, the orange sky was slowly turning white. In the nearby river, the patchwork sails of the trader boats ballooned out against the red sky. The orchestra was playing the plaintive Ramkeli raga.

Kumu took her brother's fevered hands into her own cool palms. His terrier dog stretched sadly under the bed. As soon as she sat on the bed it put up two paws in her lap, wagging its tail. In its own way, it was trying to ask her something through its doleful eyes.

Bipradas, following the trail of his own thoughts, suddenly said out of context, 'My dearest sister, it is of no consequence as to who is bigger than whom or who is higher and who lower. These are all make-belief. Does it really matter which particular spot a bubble occupies in a mass of foam? Feel free within yourself. No one can ever hurt you then.'

'Do bless me so, Dada, do bless me,' said Kumu, covering her face with both her hands and trying to hold back her tears.

Bipradas raised himself on his pillows, pulled her towards himself and gently kissed her head.

The doctor walked in and said, 'That's all, Kumu Didi. He needs some rest now.'

Kumu settled the pillows, pulled the sheet over her brother, tidied the bedside table and whispered in his ears, 'Come to Kolkata and see me as soon as you get well.'

Bipradas, resting his large gentle eyes on her face, said, 'Kumu, the wind blows the cloud from the east to the west, and from the west to the east as well. We have such winds in our lives too. Accept it easily, my dear sister, as the cloud does its destiny. From now on, try to worry less and less about us. Preside like Lakshmi the goddess of prosperity, over the house you are about to enter. That is all that I wish for you, with all my heart. Nothing more.'

She lay her head on his feet. 'From today,' she said, 'you have nothing to ask of me and I shall have nothing to do with the daily life here. But it is not easy to accept such a big break.' When a storm wrenches a boat from the shore it clings to its anchor; in the same way Kumu held to his feet as her last passionate link. The doctor came in again, and reminded her softly, 'Didi, it is time,' whilst wiping the tears off his own eyes. Kumu came out of the room but sat down on the threshold to weep silently into the loose end of her sari.

She suddenly remembered that she had made some roti with molasses the previous night to feed Bessie, her brother's pet pony. This morning the groom had taken it to the garden at the back of the house. Kumu went there and found the pony grazing under a tree. No sooner had it heard her footsteps, than it pricked up its ears and started neighing. Kumu put her left hand on Bessie's shoulder and started feeding it with her right hand. It glanced at her from time to time, raising its large, soft, dark eyes. When the pony finished the meal, Kumu quickly kissed the wide space between its eyes and ran home.

## 18

Bipradas had expected a visit from Madhusudan since his arrival in Noornagar. But when that did not happen it was clear to him that this marriage would prove to be a sword of separation between the two families. The fatigue of illness made it easier for him to accept this possibility. He asked the doctor if he could play the esraj. The doctor said briefly, 'Not today.'

'Then please ask Kumu to come and play for me. God knows when I shall hear her play again.'

'They have to take the nine o'clock train this morning,' said the doctor, 'otherwise they can't reach Kolkata before sunset. I am afraid Kumu really has no time.'

Bipradas replied with a deep sigh, 'True, she has no time for this place any more. She has spent nineteen long years here, and now even an hour is too long for her.'

The newly-wed couple came to say goodbye. Madhusudan said out of politeness, 'Indeed I do not find you in good health.'

Bipradas merely said, 'God bless you.'

'Do look after yourself, Dada,' Kumu said, as she again touched his feet, sobbing.

Amidst a blast of sounds—ullulation, conch shells and drums—the newly-married couple left.

The spectacle of the two receding into the distance, tied to each other with symbolic knots in the customary wedding scarf, suddenly appeared obscene to Bipradas. History records that Taimur and Chenghis Khan erected victory towers with countless human skeletons. But the edifice of life and death created by those two knots in the holy scarf may reach heights beyond measure. But why such contrary thoughts today, he wondered.

Bipradas was never one for prayers and pujas; but today he prayed with folded hands.

All of a sudden he called out, 'Doctor, please send for diwanjee.'

He recalled that a few days before he had come to Noornagar for the wedding, when he was worried about the money to be sent to Subodh, and worn out from thumbing through the books of account, he had a visitor at about eleven in the morning. It was someone in a state of total disrepair, a pinched face with several days' growth of beard, hands with ropy veins, clad in a short dhoti and chadar and wearing a pair of torn sandals. He greeted Bipradas and said, 'Baro Babu, do you remember me?' Bipradas had looked carefully and then asked, 'Is it Baikuntha?'

In a room next to the school building where he studied in his childhood, this Baikuntha used to sell school texts and exercise books, pens, knives, balls and bats, and tops along with peanuts packed in paper cones. The senior boys used to gather in this room for their adda sessions. No one could beat Baikuntha in the telling of absurd and weird stories.

Bipradas added, 'How have you come to such a pass?'

Baikuntha than narrated his story—a few years back he had married his daughter into a well-to-do household. And because they had really no need for it, their demand for a dowry seemed to be a bit excessive. They settled for twelve hundred rupees in cash and eight kilos of gold in ornaments. Baikuntha had recklessly agreed to it for the sake of his favourite daughter. Because he was unable to gather together all of it at once, they tortured her and bled him dry. He soon went through all his resources but still owed about two hundred and fifty rupees. So now the humiliation of the girl was complete. When it became too unbearable for her, she escaped to her father's home. This was like a breach of the jail regulations by a prisoner, and this compounded her offence. The father could now think of his own escape from this world only if he could save this girl by paying up the remaining amount.

Bipradas could only smile faintly. In his present state, he could not even think of helping out this man all the way. He hesitated a little, then went in, took out his last ten-rupee note and gave it to Baikuntha. 'Try a few more places, I can't do more than this,' he said.

Baikuntha did not believe him one bit. His slippers sounded most disgruntled as he dragged his feet on his way out.

Bipradas had forgotten this incident; but he suddenly recalled it today. He ordered the diwanjee, 'Send two hundred and fifty rupees to Baikuntha right away.' Diwanjee stood silently, scratching his head. The cost of the wedding rivalry had been met somehow, but it would still take quite a while to recover from it. And two hundred and fifty rupees at this point of time was a large sum for them to simply give away in charity!

Bipradas saw the expression on the treasurer's face and took the diamond ring off his finger, 'Take the money from what I have set aside in Chhoto Babu's account, and let this ring be the surety. The two hundred and fifty rupees should be sent on behalf of Kumu,' he said.

## 19

The last explosive episode of the wedding was still to come.

The couple was to leave soon after the final ritual (which was to be held in the bride's house) was over in the morning. Nabagopal had arranged things accordingly. But when they came out of Bipradas's room the Rajabahadur announced that the final ritual—the kushandika—was to be held at his residence in Madhupuri.

The insolence of the proposal was too much for Nabagopal. If it were anyone else, it would surely have lead to a criminal action. As it was, the vehemence of his protest only stopped short of physical violence.

The womenfolk also took this departure from the norm seriously. Relations had gathered from far and wide to participate in the ritual.

Amongst them were some not so friendly or considerate. And all this humiliation had to take place in front of them. Aunt Kshema sulked so much that she could barely utter the usual blessings. Everyone said that it would have been better if the rites were finished in the groom's Kolkata home and not at his Noornagar residence. Kumu felt very small at this insult to her family. She felt as if she herself was guilty of offending her ancestors. In her own mind she remonstrated with her deity, 'My lord, what sin have I committed to deserve this punishment? Did I not accept everything in good faith, as your command?'

The couple boarded the carriage and left her home. In Madhupuri the band that had come from Kolkata played a dance tune loudly. The holy fire was lit underneath a huge canopy. Some of the English guests—men and women—watched the ceremony from the comfort of upholstered sofas, some approached closer and leaned forward to watch the rituals. In between, cakes and biscuits arrived for them. A large wedding-cake adorned a teapoy nearby. At the end of the ceremony, when the guests started congratulating the newly-weds, Kumu was red in the face and hung her head in shame. A portly elderly woman lifted the end of Kumu's Benarasi sari and examined it closely. Her thick gold armlet also attracted the woman's curiosity enough for her to actually turn it round and round. She even had words of praise in English. Some of the English guests went up to Madhusudan and commented about the ceremony, 'How interesting!' and some others echoed, 'Isn't it?'

Kumu had witnessed how he had behaved with her brother and other relatives; now she saw the same Madhusudan with his English friends. Bowing with an effusion of politeness, he wore a perpetual grin of welcome. His character seemed to be like the moon, lit up on one side and perpetually dark on the other. Towards the British it was pleasant like the full moon, bright and soothing. The other side was unapproachable, unfathomable and impenetrable like a mass of frozen ice and this side seemed to be unwaveringly reserved for her brother and relatives.

Madhusudan chose to be with his English friends in the saloon car, leaving Kumu with the ladies in the other reserved compartment. Some of them felt her arms, some lifted her chin and analysed her features. Some said she was too tall and some others found her too thin. Some pretended to ask her naively, 'What make-up do you use? Is it something sent from England by your brother?' They came to the conclusion that her eyes were not large enough and that her stature was a bit too large for a woman. Then they got down to probing each item of her jewellery. Family jewellery it may be, heavy solid gold, but how old-fashioned!

The window in Kumu's compartment opened out on the other side of the railway platform. She kept looking out of it, trying her best not to listen to anything that was being said by her fellow passengers. She saw a lame dog sniffing the ground for some food, hobbling on three legs. She thought it ironical that the loss of just one limb out of the four had made all that was easy for the dog, so very difficult now. Just then she heard a gentleman standing in front of the saloon car and pleading, 'See this peasant girl was being lured away by agents of the tea estates of

Assam. She has escaped from them, but she could only pay her fare up to Goalundo. Her home is in Dumraon in Bihar, if you gentlemen help her a little she can be free.' She also heard a noisy rebuff from the saloon car. Kumu could not contain herself. She emptied her little purse and put a ten-rupee note in the hand of the girl and quickly shut the window. One woman spoke out, 'Our new bride is indeed open-handed,' 'Yes, but it is opening the door to bankruptcy as well,' said another. Yet another one added, 'She has learnt well how to waste money, a little lesson in thrift would have been more useful.' They thought it was a show of arrogance on her part. The menfolk did not spare a pice, but she had to throw ten rupees in their face and outdo them—that's how they perceived it. They thought perhaps this was also a part of the Chatterjee-Ghoshal rivalry.

In the meantime a dark round girl with large eyes filled with tenderness, came and sat beside her. She whispered to Kumu, 'Are you feeling homesick? Don't listen to these women. They will probe and gossip for a few days and when all the venom is out, they will stop on their own.' This girl was the wife of Nabin, Madhusudan's younger brother. Her name was Nistarini but everyone called her Motir-ma, that is, Moti's mother.

She then went on to say, 'The day we arrived in Noornagar we saw your brother at the railway station.'

Kumu was startled. This was the first time she learnt about her brother's visit to receive them at the railway station.

'Oh he is so handsome! I was reminded of the kirtan which sings about the divine beauty of Gora—Sri Chaitanya—who swept the hearts of the housewives of Nadia.'

Kumu's heart softened at that instant. She turned her face towards the window; tears blurring the landscape outside.

It did not take long for Motir-ma to realize that by mentioning Bipradas, she had hit upon the soft spot in Kumu's mind. So she stuck to that topic and asked if he were married. Kumu replied in the negative. 'What a pity!' said Motir-ma. 'No one yet to share the life of such a divinely handsome man! I wonder who that lucky woman will be!'

Meanwhile, Kumu was thinking of other things. 'So he swallowed all his pride and went to meet them only for my sake. Yet these people did not have the courtesy to call on him even once. They dared insult such a person out of sheer money power! Maybe that is why his health broke down.'

Her regret would not leave her. 'Why did Dada go to receive them? Why did he so humiliate himself? Wasn't it all for my sake? I wish I were dead.' Her mind went on torturing itself over all that which could not be undone. She kept recalling his sick and tired but calm face and his deep, gentle eyes full of compassion and blessing.

# 20

The train reached Howrah station at about four in the afternoon. Knotted up in scarves and wraps, the bride and the bridegroom climbed into the waiting Brougham. Kumu shrunk before the myriad eyes of Kolkata in daylight. How could she suddenly drop the extraordinary sense of purity that permeated the very existence of her nineteen years of maidenhood, which protected her like Karna's charmed amulet. There must be a magic word which could take it off in a trice, only it had not yet touched her soul. In her heart of hearts, the man sitting next to her was still an outsider. Any effort by her family to come closer and forge bonds between the two households had only met with resistance on his part. The rudeness in his behaviour and expression pushed Kumu away as well every time.

On his part, Madhusudan felt as if Kumu was a novel discovery. He was a hardworking man who had had little time so far to come to know the female of the species. In the midst of his world of merchandise he had not even come across women of commerce. It is not as if no woman ever disturbed his peace of mind—the earth shook but the building was never damaged. He had very briefly met them in the environs of his household. They did their daily chores, quarrelled and gossiped and cried over trivial things. Contact with them was minimal in his world. He had expected that his wife would also be a part of that banal world, and lead a woman's life, enveloped in trivial household chores, indirectly guided by the whims of menfolk. It had never entered his calculating head that to relate to one's wife was also an art and that the husband-wife relationship was built on a foundation of understanding, trust and give and take. A butterfly is a useless luxury for a big tree, but it accepts the creature all the same. Madhusudan's approach to his future wife was the same.

Then he met Kumu for the first time after the wedding. There is a kind of beauty which is akin to a divine presence, many times rarer than all that is common, and that which is above the usual happenings, exceeding one's expectation every moment. Kumu's beauty was of that kind. She was like the morning star, distinct from the night, yet, not of the day. Madusudan's unconscious mind vaguely perceived her as better than himself. In such a frame of mind he found himself wondering how to behave with her, or what might be the appropriate words to use while addressing her.

At a loss to begin a conversation, he suddenly asked Kumu, 'Is it too sunny on your side?'

Kumu said nothing. Madhusudan pulled the blinds down on the right window.

There was a long silence. He said, as suddenly, again, 'Hope you are not feeling cold.' And without waiting for an answer pulled his English rug over their feet, thus establishing the conjugality of a common cover. It thrilled his body and mind. A startled Kumu was about to remove the blanket but controlled herself and just stuck to the end of the seat.

They remained like this for some time, then Madhusudan suddenly noticed her hand. He took her left hand and said, 'Let me see. What is this that you are wearing in your ring? Is it a blue sapphire?'

She kept quiet.

'Look, you have to give it up. Sapphire is unlucky for me.'

At some point of time he had bought a sapphire, and the same year one of his trading boats full of jute had collided with the Howrah Bridge and sank. Since then he had never forgiven that precious stone.

Kumudini tried slowly to free her hand, but Madhusudan would not let go, 'Let me take this ring off.'

'No,' said Kumu. Once she beat her brother in a game of chess and he had put this ring on her finger, as a prize.

Madhusudan was amused. So she was quite possessive about the ring, he said to himself. He felt more at ease having discovered what he thought to be a common trait between them. He reckoned that the way to win her out of her sulk now and then would be easy, by way of ornaments for her ears, her neck, her arms, or her wrists. Maybe he was a little too old for her but no one could deny his supremacy on this count.

He took off a large diamond ring which he was wearing and said, 'Don't worry, I shall put on another ring in place of this one.'

Kumu could take it no longer. She pulled her hand free. This stung Madhusudan to the quick. He was not one to tolerate defiance of his authority. He said sternly in a dry voice, 'You have got to part with that ring.'

She hung her head, red in the face.

Madhusudan insisted, 'Are you listening? I say it is better taken off. Give it to me,' and he stretched his hand to pull it out.

Kumu waved her hand out of his reach and said, 'I shall take it off.' And she did.

'Give it to me,' he said.

'I shall keep it with me,' she replied.

Madhusudan was annoyed. 'What is the point of keeping it with you? Perhaps you think it is very valuable, but I must make it clear that I shall never let you wear it.'

'I shall not wear it,' she repeated, and put it by in her little bead purse.

'Why are you so attached to this trifle? You seem to be very obstinate as well.'

His voice was abrasive, like sand-paper. Kumu's whole being revolted at his tone.

'Who gave you this ring?'

There was no answer from her.

'Was it your mother?'

There was no avoiding a reply any longer; so she said in an undertone, 'Dada.' Of course it had to be the brother! Madhusudan was well aware of Bipradas's situation. This ring of her Dada itself was the key to disaster and Bipradas's plight. It must not come into this house by any means.

But what irked him most was that the brother was still dearest to her. It is not always easy to accept something only because it is natural. It was something like the annoyance felt by the new landlord who has acquired at an auction an old estate but faces the new tenants sighing for the old times. He had to impress upon his new wife in every way possible, that from now on he and he alone was to be her sole concern. Besides, it was difficult for him to believe that Bipradas was not a party to the humiliation suffered by the groom's party on the day of the feast before the wedding day. This even when Nabagopal had told him the day after the wedding, 'My dear man, let not Dada know about the manners of the rice merchant that you displayed during the wedding. He does not know anything about it, nor is he in good health.'

So the matter of the ring was rested for now but not forgotten.

Apart from her beauty, one other factor suddenly raised Kumu's stock. Whilst still in Noornagar Madhusudan got a telegram to say that he had made a profit of twenty lakhs in his export deals. Doubtless his new bride was lucky. It proved the popular adage that the wife's luck was a man's fortune. So driving with Kumudini by his side he had the supreme satisfaction of coming home with a live guarantee of future gains issued to him by the gods.

Otherwise, this brougham journey might have had an accidental end.

## 21

Soon after he was awarded the title 'raja', the Ghoshal residence in Kolkata had a new name engraved: 'Madhuprasad'—the Madhu Palace. By the iron gate of this palace an Indian orchestra played on one side and an English band played from a tent in the garden. On the top of the gate was a semi-circular sign displaying an invocation to the god of marrriage—'*prajapataye namah*'. In the evening this would be lit up by gaslight. The gravelled driveway from the gate into the house was festooned on both sides with garlands of marigold and deodar leaves. The steps to the first floor were carpeted in red shallon. The bridal carriage arrived at the portico making its way through a crowd of friends and relatives. Conch-shells, ullulations, drums, gongs and the Indian and the English bands blared forth all at once. It seemed as if ten to fifteen differently sounding goods trains had collided at the same place at the same time.

A distant and elderly grandaunt of Madhusudan's came forward to ritually welcome the new bride. She was in a wide red-bordered sari,wearing on her hair the sign of a married woman, the vermillion mark, which was as wide as her receding parting. She wore thick gold bangles and conch-shell bracelets on her stout arms. She sprinkled some water from a silver ewer on the bride's feet, slid on the traditional flat iron bangle on her wrist and a touch of honey. She said, 'How wonderful, at long last the full moon is up in our own blue sky and a golden lotus has bloomed in our blue pond.'

The younger guests had a look of envy in their eyes. One of them remarked, 'The demon has raided paradise and brought home this angel tied in a chain of gold.' Another one said, 'In the olden days kings fought over such damsels. These days export earnings from oilseeds will do the trick. The gods of our kali era lack taste. All the stars presiding over our destiny now seem to belong to the commercial caste.'

Then followed a host of rituals presided over and participated in exclusively by women; these rituals stretched till evening fell. The night that followed was the kaalraatri or the fatal night on which the bridegroom and his bride are required to sleep apart.

The only wedding Kumu had any clear memory of was the one of her elder sister, but she had not seen any new bride come to the house. From her teens she had been in the loving, innocent care of her brother in Kolkata. Her girlish dream world was not moulded by the grossness of a common household. When as a child she was taught to pray for a good husband, her ideal was the great ascetic god, Shiva, the lord of the Himalayas. Her ideal of a devoted wife was none other than her own mother. What serene grace, what patience, how much sorrow, how much prayer and worship, what tireless caring. On the other hand, her father had lapses of behaviour and flaws in his fidelity; even then, his was a character great in generosity, resolute in manliness, totally devoid of any meanness or deceit and with a sense of dignity that gave him the appearance of some classical character. His life was a daily confirmation that honour was above life and real wealth was more than money. Their motto was to preserve their family pride unsullied even if it harmed their petty interests, it was never to propagate the glory of their family fortune.

The day that the broker had brought the proposal and her left eye had twitched signifying a good omen, she had prepared herself with all her devotion and dedication. It had never crossed her mind that anything small or untoward could come in the way. How did the legendary Damayanti know intuitively that she had to choose the king of Vidarbha, Nala, as her husband?

She must have had a definite signal in her mind. Did Kumu not have any such certain indication? She was all ready for a grand reception of her lord and husband. The king did come, but the reality was so different from what her mind had created. Neither his appearance nor his age would have mattered. But where was he—the real king she dreamed of?

And today, when she was being welcomed through the gates of a ritual, into her new home, why was the deep chant of benediction that would have made this new bride sense within herself the blessings of the heavens, missing? Why did not the entire ceremony fulfil itself with the rich paean of praise for the Creator of this universe—who combines in Himself the eternal male and the eternal female—

*Jagatah pitarau bande parbati-parameshwarau!*

## 22

When he had first come to live in Kolkata, Madhusudan had bought an old house, which now served as the ladies' quarters. He had added to the original structure a huge modern building which was now his drawing room and office. The two buildings were joined together but they were, in fact, two different worlds. The floors in the outer building were in marble, covered with English carpets, the walls were papered with designs and all kinds of pictures were hung—engravings, oleographs and oil paintings depicting hounds chasing deer, famous Derby-winning horses, English landscapes or bathing nudes. There were also diverse objects which put together in that room were quite unrelated, irrelevant and ill-placed, such as chinaware displayed along with brassware from Moradabad, Japanese fans alongside Tibetan fly-whisks. The task of acquiring these objets d'art and decorating the room fell on his English assistant. The room was also crowded with chairs and sofas upholstred in silk and velvet. Magnificently bound books were kept in a glass case, never touched except by the room bearer's duster. The teapoys were loaded with albums of family portraits or pictures of English actresses.

The rooms in the interior of the house, on the other hand, were damp, dank and full of soot-covered cobwebs. The courtyard was always dirty. Washing of clothes and utensils seemed to be unending operations and the water tap was always running, even when there was no such activity. Wet saris hung down from the first floor balconies for drying; and parrots' droppings littered the veranda downstairs. The walls bore permanent memories of paan stains and various other marks of decay. Behind the step on the west of the courtyard was the kitchen. From there, the smell of cooking and the smoke pervaded through all the rooms upstairs. Outside the kitchen there was a small walled space heaped with burnt coal, oven ash, broken pots, baskets and ladles full of holes. At the other end a couple of cows and their calves were tied up amidst the piled up straw and cowdung. The whole wall was plastered with cowdung cakes. A solitary neem tree stood at one end, devoid of its bark, lost through constant tying up of cows. It was in a poor shape and mercilessly denuded of its leaves. This was the only piece of land in this part of the house. All the rest was outside and landscaped with creepers, flower beds, mowed lawns, gravelled paths and iron seats.

Kumudini's bedroom was on the second floor in this inner building. There was a huge mahogany bed in it, framed by a mosquito net with silk frills. Towards the foot of the bed hung a picture of a nude woman pretending to hide her shame by pressing both her hands on her breasts. At the head was a portrait in oil of Madhusudan himself, prominently displaying the intricate embroidery of his Kashmiri shawl. On one wall was a mirrored clothes cupboard. There were two ceramic candlestands on either side of the mirror and on a ceramic tray were a box of face powder, a silver comb, several types of perfume and a spray along with a host of other cosmetics all bought by the English assistant. A bouquet was kept in a branched pink flower vase. In another corner there was a writing table with pens, an inkstand made of precious stones, paper-cutters and other writing materials. There were also thickly-cushioned sofas and chairs scattered about. Madhusudan had given special thought to a proper bedroom for the new Maharani. But the result was like a beggar in rags wearing a turban adorned with diamonds and emeralds.

In the night, at the end of a rush of noisy celebrations, Kumu finally reached her room. Motir-ma accompanied her. She was to sleep tonight in this room. A number of women followed them. Their curiosity and craving for fun was insatiable, but Motir-ma got rid of them. As she entered the room she put her arms round Kumu and said, 'I am going to the next room. Do cry as much as you want to. I can see the tears welling up from your heart.'

Kumu sat down on a chair. Tears could wait, her need of the moment was to take hold of herself. What really was eating into her was the humiliation she felt within herself. Her mind was revolting against all that she had carefully cherished all these years. She was not getting any time to control her wayward mind. 'Lord give me strength, do not make my life hollow. I am your maid, make me win over myself. That will be thy own triumph,' she prayed.

A pretty, buxom young widow barged into the room and said, 'I could manage to slip in only now in this little interval Motir-ma has allowed you. She won't let anyone come near you, as if all of us are wanting to kidnap you from her custody. I am Shyamasundari, the widow of your husband's elder brother. All of us thought that he would get married to his books of account in the end. But I must admit that those books do have magical powers. That's how he could get such a pretty bride at his age. Tell me truthfully, have you really liked my old brother-in-law?'

Kumu was taken by surprise. She didn't know what to say.

Quickly drawing her own conclusions, Shyamasundari said, 'I see. Even if you haven't liked him, there is no way out. Now that you have taken with him the seven steps round the sacred fire, twenty-one steps the other way round will not un-knot it.'

'What are you trying to say, sister?'

'Is it an offence to speak out the plain truth? I can read your face. But I shall not blame you. He may be our own man but I am no fool. Let me tell you little sister, you are in tough hands!'

Motir-ma came back. Shyama said, 'Not to worry. I am off. Since you were away, I thought of just looking up our new bride. Truly she is a prize possession to be guarded carefully. I was just thinking, the new wife has got a hold on her husband like half a headache. But if one side of the head brings you fortune, you need to use the rest of your head to keep that luck going. She'll need to get hold of his whole head, otherwise there's no point.'

She rushed out of the room but came back immediately with a case of paan and offered one to Kumu asking if she were used to tobacco flakes as well in her paan. She then took a mouthful of tobacco herself and slowly walked out.

Motir-ma also left, for she had to feed some aunt or the other.

Shyamasundari left Kumu with a bad taste in her mouth. What Kumu needed most at this hour was the comfort of dreams which she was weaving around herself, invoking the help of the supreme artist who endows the universe with beauty and colour of many hues. Shyama had torn into that web of dreams. Deeply affected by Shyamasundari's opinion of her distaste for her new husband, Kumu closed her eyes firmly and tried to tell herself, 'What a shame! To think that I do not love my husband because of his age! It is such a vulgar thought.' She remembered the legend of Sati and how Sati had also faced similar taunts about Shiva, her old husband-to be, and how resolutely she had ignored them.

Any thought about her husband's looks or his age had never crossed Kumu's mind. The love which makes marriage between a man and a woman real is an amalgam of looks and virtues, qualities of body and mind. Kumu never thought of them as necessities. She was trying to dismiss the whole matter of personal choice in marriage.

A boy of about seven dressed in an embroidered shirt and zari-bordered dhoti came in and sidled up to her. He lifted his large gentle eyes and asked in a sweet voice, somewhat timidly, 'Auntie?' Kumu drew him to her lap and asked, 'What is your name, little one?' The boy announced ceremoniously, without omitting the formal Shri, 'Shri Motilal Ghoshal.' Everyone else knew him only as Habloo. That was why on proper occasions he felt it necessary to announce his given name in its full glory, for the sake of his self-pride. Kumu was feeling heavy in her heart and clasping this boy to her bosom gave her much relief. She suddenly felt that the little Gopal Krishna in his boyhood—whom she worshipped every morning with flowers, had himself come to her lap. Just when she was praying to him in her hour of grief, he seemed to have answered, 'Here I am, to console you.' She pressed the boy's chubby cheeks and asked, 'Gopal mine, will you take a flower from me?'

No other name crossed her lips. The sudden transformation of his own name surprised Habloo but Kumu's tone was so set that he could not think of protesting.

Motir-ma heard the voice of her child and came into the room. 'So the monkey is here,' she said, deflating the dignity of the honourable Shri Motilal. Holding the end of the aunt's sari tight, he looked silently at his mother with plaintive eyes. Kumu put her left arm protectively round him and said, 'Ah, let him be.'

'No, my dear. It is quite late, time for bed. It is easy to get hold of him in this house. Perhaps there is no one more easily available.' She took her boy away. This little incident made Kumudini feel a lot lighter. She felt that her prayer had been answered; life's problems would be solved as easily as this child had done.

# 23

Late at night Motir-ma found Kumu sitting up in her bed, her hands clasped in her lap; her eyes though closed seemed to have someone in view. The more she found it difficult within herself to accept her husband, the more she tried to dress him in the image of her personal god. She dedicated herself to her god: the husband was only a token. Her god had made it harder for her; this idol was none too transparent. So it was all the more of an acid test of her faith. A piece of shalgram shila—the sacred black stone—is shapeless, but faith by its own strength, projects the image of the Lord of the Heavens within this formlessness. Her resolve was to see the unseen, to find Him and throw herself at His feet. He would then never escape from her.

She sang to herself a bhajan of Mirabai's which she had learnt from her brother:

*Merey to Giridhar Gopal dusara na koi*

(There is no one for me but my Giridhar Gopal.)

She made light of the rude aspect of Madhusudan which she had come across; it was no more than a bubble to be blown away. There was only one eternal truth in everyone—'no one else'—'no one but the all-embracing one'. There was one other anguish torturing her which she wanted to believe was only an illusion—the emptiness of her life! Parting for ever with all that she had grown up with and the absence of all that which made up her life till now, seemed to make her life devoid of any meaning. But in her resolute mind she tried to convince herself, that this absense was not emptiness but a kind of fulfilment.

She recalled Mira again:

*Baap chharrey, Maaye chharrey, chharrey sagaa sahi*
*Meera prabhu lagan lagi jo na hoye hoyee.*

(All may abandon you, father, mother, friends and playmates but not He who is always within you.)

He has made me forsake all, only to make room for something He will fill me with. Whatever may follow, let me persevere. This song found a voice within her heart, and unknown to herself tears rolled down her face.

Motir-ma watched and listened without a word and left only when Kumu, after a long obeisance, went to sleep with a deep sigh. But a train of thought started in Motir-ma's mind which had never occurred to her before.

It ran like this: 'When we got married we were but little children, unburdened with a mind of our own. Just as a little boy swallows a raw fruit without a thought, the husband's family and household absorbed us without any problem. We did not have to make any effort or wait up, counting days. If they said this was the day of your phulsajjya—flower bed of the nuptial night, so it was. Because it was all a play. But this girl here will have her honeymoon tomorrow night, and what a trial it will be for her! The groom is a stranger to her; it takes time to grow close to one another. How can he touch this girl? How will she bear the humiliation? Our elder brother-in-law took all this time to win wealth, can he not wait a little longer to win a heart? He had to woo Lakshmi the goddess of wealth hard enough, should he not have to beg some more for the favour of this Lakshmi?'

By herself, she was incapable of so much thinking, but somehow she felt for Kumu, heart and soul, as soon as she met her. The sight of Bipradas at the railway station was a prelude to this affection. He looked like the figure of Bhishma straight from the epic Mahabharata. Powerful like a hero, a serene face like that of an ascetic tinged with the humility of sadness. She thought, if no one took it amiss she would have liked to touch his feet in reverence. She still cherished that image. Then, when she saw Kumu, she knew she had met a sister worthy of her brother.

There is a kind of distinction which is not ordered by society but is inborn. Such distinction is likely to hurt a woman mortally; but not the man. Motir-ma had not known this paradox because she married so young; but she realized it now through Kumu. She felt ill as she imagined the horrible picture of a lusty monster crouching inside a dark cavern, licking his chops while Kumudini prayed frantically at the entrance. She said to herself, 'To hell with her god! Isn't he the one who pushed her into this peril? How can he be the one to save her now? What a great pity!'

## 24

Next morning Kumu had a brief telegram from her brother. 'God bless you,' it said. She kept it inside her blouse, close to her heart. The telegram had her brother's touch. But why did it not say anything about his own health? Maybe he was unwell. All these years, never having left his side, she was used to being posted with his news from minute to minute, and now it was all blacked out from her.

Tonight was the phulsajjya, the bridal night—the night of consummation. The house was full of people. The women of the family had been pawing her the whole day. A day when she needed most to be by herself.

Next to her bedroom was the bathroom, fitted with taps as well as showers. She quietly slipped in there, with a framed picture of her divine couple—Radha and Krishna. She put the picture on the marble bathing seat and prayed, 'I belong to you, Lord, you take me today. He is none but you, only you! Let your dual image come true in my own life.'

Meanwhile, at Noornagar, the doctors diagnosed that Bipradas's influenza had turned to pneumonia. So Nabagopal alone came to Kolkata to arrange for the customary gifts for this special night. He did it with great éclat. If Bipradas were himself present, he might not have done it on such a grand scale.

All of Kumu's four elder sisters had been invited to attend Kumu's wedding, but the rumour that the Ghoshals were not high class Brahmins had reached them. So, their families would not let them attend the wedding. The third sister had fought with her husband and reached Kolkata the day after the wedding, but Nabagopal had told her that their prestige would go down if she went to the groom's house. The events of the wedding night were still fresh in his mind.

So he sent only a few young girls who were distantly related to the family, with an old maidservant, to represent them at the reception. Kumu understood that there was no truce as yet; and that perhaps there never would be any.

She was all dressed up for the occasion. The pleasantries and repartee were over. It was time to start feeding the invited guests. Madhusudan had already warned that he had a lot of work the next day and that the feast would have to end early enough. At the stroke of nine, the gong rang loudly. Not a minute more; no one had the courage to exceed the time set by him. The party broke up. Kumu's heart trembled like a dove's at the shadow of an eagle. Her hands were in a cold sweat and her face went pale. She came out of her room and held the hand of Motir-ma, pleading with her to take her away somewhere else. 'Let me be by myself for ten minutes.' Motir-ma took her to her own bedroom and shut the door. She stood outside with tears in her eyes, bemoaning the fate of the bride.

Ten minutes ran to fifteen. People came looking for Kumu. 'The groom is in the bedroom, where is the bride?' they asked. Motir-ma said, 'Don't be so impatient. She has to change and take off her ornaments.' She wanted to give Kumu as much time as possible, and when she realized that no more delay was possible she opened the door to find Kumu in a faint on the floor.

Much noise and confusion followed. She was carried to the bed. Some sprayed water on her face, some fanned her. When she came to, Kumu was unaware of her surroundings. She cried out 'Dada!' Motir-ma quickly bent over her and said, 'Don't worry Didi, I am here.' She helped her up and clasped her to her bosom. She told everyone to make room and added, 'I am taking her to her room just now.' She whispered into Kumu's ears, 'Do not be afraid please, have no fear.' Kumu got up slowly and prayed. Then she walked up to the other end of the room where Habloo was sleeping and kissed his forehead. Motir-ma escorted her up to the bedroom and asked, 'Still afraid?'

Kumu clenched her fists, smiled somehow and said, 'No, not at all.' She thought to herself, 'Such is my tryst, all darkness outside but lit up inside.'

*Merey to Giridhar Gopal dusara na koi.*

## 25

Meanwhile Shyamasundari went panting to Madhusudan and announced, 'Your bride has fainted!' Madhusudan flared up immediately; he asked, 'Why? What is the matter with her?'

'I can't say, except that she is only pining for her Dada. Won't you go and find out for yourself?'

'What's the use? I am not her Dada.'

'You're losing your temper for nothing. They are high-born. It takes time to tame them.'

'I see, she will go into a faint every day and I have to massage her with ayurvedic oil. Is that what I married her for?'

'You make me laugh. In our days women went into a sulk and you had to woo them back, now you have only to nurse them out of a faint.'

Madhusudan sat glumly. Shyama, dissolving with pity, took his hand and said, 'Please don't get upset. I cant bear to see you like this.'

Till now she never had the courage to approach him so closely. The garrulous Shyama used to be unusually quiet with him because she knew Madhusudan was a man of few words. Her feminine intuition told her that it was not the same man tonight. Tonight he was weak and a little vulnerable, not conscious of his dignity. She felt that he had not disliked her touch on his hand. The hurt given by the new bride probably was allayed a little with ministration from someone else. It was no small matter that Shyama never looked down upon him. She was no less attractive than Kumu; maybe a little darker, but her eyes, her hair, her luscious lips!

She spoke out, 'There, she is coming. Let me go. But please do not be angry with her. Poor thing! She is but a child.'

As soon as Kumu set foot into the room Madhusudan lost his patience, 'So you've had a good practice at fainting at your brother's! But that is not in vogue here. You have to get out of your Noornagari style.'

Kumu stood staring in surprise without a word.

Her silence angered him more. Deep inside him was growing a strong desire to win the heart of this girl, hence the frustrated rage. He said, 'Let me make it clear. I am a busy man; I do not have the leisure to wait upon a hysterical woman.'

Kumu answered slowly, 'You want to humiliate me. But you won't succeed. I shall not take your insults to heart.'

Madhusudan was sarcastic, 'I know you are your brother's disciple, but remember, I am his creditor. I can buy and sell him many times over.'

He was a fool to have said this, but he wanted to impress upon her that he was bigger than her brother.

Kumu replied, 'Be as cruel as you like, but do not demean yourself.' And she sat down on the sofa.

He said gruffly, 'What! You mean to say that I am inferior and your brother is better than me?'

Kumu said, 'I have come to your house in the knowledge that you are bigger.'

Madhusudan mocked, 'Bigger, is it? Or is it the greed for money?'

Then Kumu got up, and went and sat down on the floor of the open terrace outside.

It was a mean winter night, dull with smog, the stars were choked under a frowning sky. Kumu's mind was in a daze, without a thought, without any pain; as if she herself was lost in a thick fog.

It was beyond Madhusudan's expectation and comprehension that Kumu could silently walk out of the room as she did. He immediately held her brother responsible for this abject defeat of his. He sat on the bed and punched its emptiness. After a while he lost his patience. He got up in a rush, went out on the terrace and called out to her, 'Borrobou!'

Kumu was startled.

'Why are you standing outside in this dewy cold? Come into the room.'

Kumu stared at his face without any embarrassment. The little authority of ownership he was still nursing within himself vanished. He took her left hand and said gently, 'Please come inside.'

Kumu had the telegram from her brother in her right hand. She pressed it to her bosom. She did not take her hand away but followed her husband quietly into the bedroom.

## 26

The next morning when she woke up her husband was still asleep. She did not look at him lest she felt revolted. She took great care to get up without waking him, touched his feet and went for a bath. When she finished she went into the terrace from the rear door. A faint line of gold was visible in the sky through the fog.

After a while when the sun was up she came back to the bedroom to find her husband gone. She opened the drawer under the mirror to put by the telegram. The sapphire ring was not there.

The serenity that had come over her after her morning prayers vanished. Her eyes were aflame. Motir-ma came to call her for a glass of milk and some sweets. But Kumu was sitting still, hard as a statue of stone.

Motir-ma, a little apprehensive, asked, 'What is the matter, sister?'

Kumu could not utter a word, only her lips trembled.

'Please tell me what has hurt you?'

In a choked voice she answered, 'It is stolen!'

'What is?'

'My ring, my brother's blessing.'

'Who has taken it?'

Kumu stood up and without taking any name, pointed outward.

'Calm down. He must be teasing you. He will give it back to you.'

'I won't take it back. Let me see how much more he can torture me.'

'All right, we shall see about it later. Now please have something to eat.'

'No, I can't swallow a morsel now.'

'Please, my dear, for my sake do!'

'Let me ask you something, sister. Is it true that I can have nothing of my own from now on?'

'No, there is nothing of the sort. All that you may possess depends upon your husband's goodwill. Don't you know we sign our names as dasi—"your obedient servant".'

Servant indeed! Kumu recalled Kalidas's depiction of Indumati's role.

*Grihini sachibah, sakhee mitah*
*priya-shishyaa lalitey kala-bidhau*

—housewife, secretary, companion, friend, and a dear pupil of the fine arts—no mention of a slave! Was Savitri a slave to Satyaban? Or for that matter was Sita of *UttarRamcharit*, a slave maiden?

She asked, 'What sort of men are those who think of their wives as slaves?'

'You have to know him yet,' said Motir-ma. 'He not only makes a slave of others but he is also a slave to himself. The day he is unable to attend office he docks his own pay. Once he was ill and could not go to work for a month, so for the next two or three months he cut down on the household expenses to make up for the loss. So far I have looked after housekeeping and I have a fixed allowance for that. In this house, everyone from the master to the lowest employee, all are slaves.'

Kumu thought for a moment and said, 'All right, I shall also be one of them. I will work for my daily upkeep. I do not want to be an honorary slave here. Do engage me under you, after all you are in charge of housekeeping. I don't want to be mocked by anyone as a "Rani".'

Motir-ma said, 'In that case you have to obey me. I order you now to come for your breakfast.'

As they were going out Kumu said, 'You see, sister, I came here prepared to give myself, but he would not let it happen. Now let him be satisfied with his slave. He will never have me.'

Motir-ma said understandingly, 'The wood-cutter knows how to cut the tree but he only gets the wood, not the tree. The gardener, on the other hand, knows how to tend the tree, so he gets its flower and fruit. You have cast your lot with a lumberjack. He is a trader, there is no room for compassion in his heart.'

After her meal when Kumu came back to her room, she found a box of lozenges. Habloo had deposited a secret gift for her and made himself scarce. So there were cracks even in this stony site for flowers to bloom. The message of these sweets made Kumu feel like crying and laughing at the same time. She stepped outside her room to look for the boy and found him standing quietly behind the door. His mother had warned him not to frequent this room. He was afraid of annoying the master by anything he might do. Everyone in this house was well aware that it was best to keep away from Madhusudan, unless of course he wanted them for something.

Kumu caught hold of Habloo and put him on to her lap. Both of them began to look into everything in her room that could serve as a toy. Kumu noticed that a glass paperweight had caught little Habloo's fancy. The sight of a coloured flower through the glass intrigued him.

Kumu promptly offered it to him.

Habloo was wonderstruck. In all his years he had never heard of such an unthinkable proposition. Could he ever aspire to own such a wonderful object! He looked at her in amazement and hesitation.

Kumu said, 'You can take it.'

Habloo could not contain his joy. He picked up his precious gift and bounded out of the room.

In the afternoon Motir-ma came and said, 'What have you done, my sister? The master has created a rumpus at finding the paperweight in Habloo's hand. Not only has he snatched it away but he also thrashed Habloo, accusing him of stealing. And that strange boy never even mentioned you. I won't be surprised if the word goes round that I am the one teaching him to steal.'

Kumu was frozen to silence.

The crunch of shoes was heard outside. Madhusudan was coming up. Motir-ma hurried away. Madhusudan put the paperweight down in its place with great care and added in a stern voice of calm confidence, 'Habloo had stolen it from your room. You must learn to be more careful with things.'

Kumu said sharply, 'He did not steal it.'

'All right, he misplaced it!'

'No. I gave it to him.'

'So that's how you are spoiling him. You will do well to remember that nothing in this house can be given away to anyone without my approval. I cannot stand disorderliness.'

Kumu stood up and said, 'Did you not take away my sapphire ring?'

'Yes, I did.'

'Didn't that pay for your piece of glass?'

'But I told you, you cannot have it.'

'You can keep your things, only I can't?'

'In this house nothing is exclusively yours.'

'Nothing at all? Then let this house be.' And saying this, Kumu left the room.

As soon as she left, Shyama entered the room busily and asked, 'Where is the bride?'

'Why?'

'I have been waiting with her breakfast the whole morning. Is she going to starve herself in this house?'

'So what? Let the princess of Noornagar not eat! Are you her slaves?'

'Shame on you. One does not lose one's temper with kids. We can't stand her starving like this. No wonder she fainted the other day.'

Madhusudan roared, 'Go away. Nothing needs to be done. She will eat when she feels hungry.'

A dispirited Shyama left the room.

Madhusudan's blood was boiling. He quickly put his head under the shower to cool himself.

## 27

Until evening Kumu could not be found anywhere. Finally Motir-ma found her sitting on a mat in the small corner next to the storeroom where the lamps, oil cans and the like were kept.

Motir-ma said, 'What is all this, Didi?'

Kumu said, 'This is my place in this house; I shall look after the lamps and lights.'

Motir-ma said, 'You have found yourself a nice job. Of course you have come to lighten up this house, but you don't need to look after oil-lamps for that. Now come with me.'

Kumu would not budge.

Motir-ma said, 'In that case, let me also sleep here.'

Kumu firmly said, 'No!' Motir-ma felt that this girl may be good-natured but she certainly had the power of command in her. Motir-ma had no option but to leave.

Madhusudan heard the news when he came to the bedroom at night. His first thought was, 'Let her be in that room. How long can she stick it out? The more we coax her the more stubborn she'll get.'

He put out the light and went to sleep. But sleep would not come easily. Every sound felt like her footfall. Once he felt as if she was standing at the door. He got out of bed and looked towards the door, but there was no one. As the night wore on, his mind was in turmoil. He could not muster up enough resolve to ignore her. Yet it was against his policy to go forward and concede defeat. He splashed cold water on his face, but that too did not help. He tossed around in bed. In the end he could no longer contain his curiosity and restlessness. With a lantern in hand he crossed all the bedrooms till he arrived at the lamproom. He stopped to listen for any sound within, but there was none. He opened the door carefully and saw Kumu sleeping on the floor on a mat, one end of which was rolled up as a pillow. Because he could not sleep, his wife too ought not to have been sleeping, he thought. But he found her deep in sleep, so much so that even when the light from the lantern fell on her face she did not wake up. Just then she turned on her side. Madhusudan fled in the same way as a thief does at the sign of the householder waking up. He was worried that she would see his distress and laugh at him.

As he came out and crossed the veranda he met Shyama with a clay lamp in her hand. 'How come you are here?' she asked. Ignoring the question, he asked back, 'Where are you going, bou?'

'Tomorrow I have a vow to break and have to feed some Brahmins; I am going to the kitchen to make the arrangements. You are also invited. But I have nothing to offer you in return.'

Madhusudan suppressed the reply that readily came to his lips.

In that pre-dawn darkness Shyama's face looked beautiful in the lamplight. She added, with a little smile, 'My day is made, because the first person I met before starting the preparations is a lucky man like you. My vow will be fruitful.'

The slight emphasis she put on the word 'lucky' sounded somewhat embarrassing to him. Shyama could not summon up enough courage to ask him anything about Kumu directly. As she left she said, 'Come to my room tomorrow. I'll give you dinner—that's a promise.'

He went to bed again but kept the lantern outside the door just in case Kumu changed her mind. But as he lay awake, he was unable to dismiss the picture of Kumu's sleeping face. The delicate beauty of her hand relaxed outside the shawl kept tormenting his memory. At the wedding when he had taken that hand into his, he had hardly noticed it. Tonight he could look at it endlessly. When would he be able to win that hand? He got up, lit the lamp and opened Kumu's drawer and saw her bead purse. The first thing that he found in it was her brother's telegram, then a photograph of both her brothers and a small piece of paper with this sloka from the Gita written in Bipradas's own hand.

'Dedicate unto me, O son of Kunti, whatever you do, whatever you breathe, whatever you worship, whatever you gift and whatever you pray for.'

Envy gnawed at Madhusudan's mind. He gnashed his teeth and made short shrift of Bipradas in his own mind. He knew that the end to Bipradas's constant counselling of Kumu was certain, but he had to tighten the screw bit by bit. He would be at peace only if he could snatch away at that very minute all of Kumu's nineteen years which lay beyond his control. He knew of no other way than force. Today he was unable to throw the bead purse away. He was bolder the day he stole the ring. Till then he was under the impression that Kumudini was like any other girl easily disciplined, in fact they liked to be ordered around. But he realized today that Kumu's reactions were completely unpredictable.

There was only one way to bind her life with his firmly, by giving her the experience of motherhood. This was his one consoling thought.

The clock struck five, but the winter night was still in darkness. In a while it would be daybreak and if he didn't act now, this would be another night wasted. He quickly left the bedroom and reached the lamproom with a deliberate clatter. He opened the door noisily, only to find Kumu missing. Where could she be?

He heard the noise of running water in the courtyard. He saw from the veranda that Kumu was scouring with tamarind paste a whole lot of old unused rusty lamps. This was nothing but an attempt, on her part, to wilfully find work, to prolong the sleepless misery of a winter morning.

Madhusudan watched in stunned surprise. He was turning over in his mind possible ways to overcome such strength in the weaker sex. 'When the household gets up and sees her sculling old lamps what would they make of it? What would the servant whose job it is, think? There could be no better way of ridiculing me in front of the whole world,' thought Madhusudan.

A sudden impulse to have it out with her then and there ran through his mind, but the spectacle of the entire family leaving their beds and coming out to watch the farce of the two of them sparring, held him back. Instead, he went back to the main house and spoke to his younger brother Nabin, 'Do you ever notice what is going on in this house?'

Nabin was the manager of the household. He was frightened at this stern question from his brother, quite out of the blue, and hastened to ask, 'Why Dada, whatever is the matter?'

Nabin was well aware that whenever his brother had cause to be angry, he had to find someone to punish. If the guilty managed to escape even an innocent person would do, otherwise his idea of discipline could not be maintained and the prestige of his state would be undermined.

Madhusudan said, 'Do you think I am unaware of the reason for this insane behaviour on the part of Borrobou?'

Nabin dared not ask what madness he was referring to, in case his not knowing got counted as an offence.

Madhusudan went on, 'I have no doubt that your wife is putting ideas into her head and spoiling her.'

With the utmost hesitation Nabin tried to stammer, 'No, but Mejobou . . .'

'But I have seen it myself.'

His had to be the last word. The eyewitness account no doubt included the episode of the glass paperweight.

## 28

Nabin knew that his wife's sincere affection for the new bride would not go down well with the rest of the household. There was bound to be tale carrying of all sorts. He thought something of the kind must have happened. It was no use protesting against Madhusudan's allegations; that would only make him more stubborn. He felt a bit confused about the current situation, for his elder brother had not made it clear as to what really had gone wrong, and what was to be done also remained vague. The only thing that was clear was that the entire responsibility of his anger and displeasure went to Motir-ma. And as the relative importance of a couple demanded, the greater share would be his.

Nabin went and told Motir-ma, 'There is trouble ahead.'

'Why, what is it?'

'God only knows—and Dada. Perhaps you also do. But the pressure is on me.'

'But why?'

'There is pressure on me so that I may correct you before you commit any more follies, and do the same to his new acquisition from his latest deal.'

'All right, so you start with me, let us see if you are better at it than your brother,' said Motir-ma.

Nabin was distressed. 'You remember the time Dada's Oriya servant broke a plate from his expensive dinner set, how I had to pay most of the fine, because it was supposed to be in my charge? But should his new treasure be also my charge? Anyway, Dada is of the opinion that the compensation for her actions or mistakes has to be shared by you and me. Do something about it, don't torture me, Mejobou!'

'What could be the fine?'

'Sending us back to Rajabpur. That is what he threatens us with often.'

'That is because you get bullied. Remember, he did send us out once but had to send across the train fare to bring us back. Even when he is angry, your brother knows his accounts well. He knows it would cost him dear to run this household without me. And he cannot bear to lose a pie anyhow.'

'So what should I do now?'

'Tell your brother that he may be a big Raja, but he cannot win back his Rani with the help of a paid maidservant. The weight of her huge sulk has to be borne by him and by no one else. Ask him not to hire a porter to carry the burden of his honeymoon.'

'Mejobou, he does not need my advice. He will come to his senses on his own. In the meantime you do your job of a go-between, whatever comes of it. At least we will prove to him that we are not ungrateful parasites.'

Motir-ma went to look for Kumu. She knew she was likely to be on the terrace in the mornings. High walls with a few bay-windows covered the terrace. A few empty pots were strewn around. In one corner was a square cage with wire-netting, the wooden bottom rotting. Sometime in the past it used to house rabbits and pigeons, but its only use now was to sun-dry pickles and preserves which had to be protected from the sneaking crows. You got a glimpse of the sky overhead but not of the horizon. On the western sky one could see the chimney-stack of an iron-works factory. Kumu sat here often for the last two days. The only sight was that of the smoke curling up, as if it was the only living thing in the whole sky, swelling and swirling upwards, driven by some strange impulse.

Kumu had finished cleaning the lamps, had her bath and come up here. She sat facing the eastern sky, her wet hair streaming down her back. She was most plainly dressed in a narrow black-bordered thick cotton sari. For warmth she had only a wrap of rough raw silk.

For sometime now this young woman had nursed the longing in her heart by installing in her mind an ideal image of the beloved to be. All her prayers, her rituals and myths were to keep this image alive. In the Brindaban of her mind she was Radha waiting for a tryst with Krishna. She used to sing early in the morning in Raga Ramkeli,

*Hamarey tumharey sampriti lagi hai*
*Suno Manmohan pyarey.*

(Listen, O my beloved, we are in love with each other!)

It was as if, the one on whom she had bestowed all her offerings had been sending her a daily inkling of her beloved-to-be long before his appearance. On a rainy night when the leaves of the trees in the garden were in a tumult because of the incessant impact of the raindrops, she remembered the song in Raga Kanara:

*Bajey jhananana payeriya*
*Kaise karo jaun gharoyarey.*

(How shall I come home to you? My anklets are making such a din.)

The anklets round her own pensive mind were tinkling away, she was out on an unknown assignment, wondering how should she ever go back home! Long before she saw Him, she heard His melody. If someone came close to her on days when she was filled with deep joy and sorrow, all her music would have found a form. But no traveller ever stopped her way. In the secret garden of her imagination, she was all alone. That was why all these days, the flowers she offered at the feet of her little dark god, Shyamsundar, were really meant for her unknown beloved. So when the matchmaker arrived, she asked her god, 'Shall I have you now?' The answer came in that flower—the blue morning glory—which slipped into her hand from the feet of the idol.

But now it seemed as if all the preparations in her mind over all these years had come to nought. Her boat had struck a hard rock and sank in a moment. Her aching youth was today looking for an object for her offerings, now too heavy to bear. The recurrent refrain in her heart was:

*Merey to Giridhar Gopal dusara na koi.*

But today her song drifted into a void, reaching nowhere. This emptiness frightened her. Would the deep yearning within her end like that spiral of smoke, lonely till the end of her days?

Motir-ma sat behind her, at a distance. She was astonished at the dignity of this beautiful girl unadorned. She wondered how this girl would ever fit into this kind of household. The women of this house seemed to belong to a different class altogether. Naturally, they felt alienated from her, angry at her—but did not dare to make friends with her.

As she sat there, Motir-ma saw Kumu suddenly hide her face in her sari and break into a sob. She could not but come up to her, put her arms round her and say, 'My sweet sister, please tell me what is wrong?'

After a long silence, she replied, 'No letter from Dada even today. I wonder what is wrong with him.'

'Is it time for a letter from him?'

'Of course. I left him ill and he knows well how I shall fret for his news.'

'Do not worry. I shall find a way of getting his news.'

Kumu had thought of sending a wire, but who would do it for her? From the time Madhusudan called himself her brother's creditor, she could not bring herself to utter her brother's name in his presence. Today she asked Motir-ma, 'I shall be greatly relieved if you send a telegram to my brother, from me.'

'Of course I will do it. There is nothing to fear.'

'But you know, I have not a single rupee with me.'

'What nonsense. I shall take the money from my household budget. All that money belongs to you. I am now in your employ.'

Kumu protested strongly, 'No no! not a single pie in this house belongs to me.'

'All right, I may not spend for you. But surely I can spend some money on my own? Why are you silent? Is there anything wrong with it? If I had flaunted this offer, you could have refused with pride, but when I give this with love why can't you accept it lovingly?'

'I do,' responded Kumu.

Motir-ma then asked, 'Will your bedroom be without you tonight also?'

'I have no place there.'

Motir-ma did not insist. It was not for her to do so. Let the one who must, do it. She only asked gently, 'May I get you some milk?'

'Not now. A little later.' She still had to have it out with her deity. She was yet to get a signal from within herself.

Motir-ma went back to her own room and asked Nabin, 'Can you do something? Go to your brother's office and see if there is any letter for her lying on his table. Try the drawers as well.'

'That would be calamitous,' Nabin said.

'If you can't, I shall go myself.'

'It is like looking for a bear cub in its den!'

'The boss is in his office. He won't be back before one. In the meantime . . .'

'Look Mejobou, it is impossible for me to do this job in broad daylight. I may only be able to get you some news tonight.'

'All right, that will have to do, but you must send a wire right away and find out how Bipradas Babu is.'

'Fine, but shouldn't Dada be told?'

'No.'

'You seem to be desperate. You know in this house even a lizard can't catch a fly without his permission, and you expect me to . .?'

'It will be from Didi, how are you involved?'

'But it will pass through my hands.'

'Many telegrams are sent daily from his office by hand of the messenger, put this one in among the lot. Here is the money. Didi gave it.'

Nabin would never have agreed to do this daring deed had he not already felt pity for Kumu in his heart.

## 29

As a routine, Madhusudan used to come into the house for his lunch at one, and as a routine, the women fluttered round him, some serving food, others fanning him and whisking away flies. I have already described how the arrangements within his household lacked any show of wealth. His food habits continued to be the same as always—he had taste for rice alone, not of fine quality but good enough to fill his stomach. The utensils laid on the table were expensive. The plates, cups and glasses—all were made of silver. Usually the menu consisted of plain dal, fish curry, a sour and sweet tamarind dish and greens with fishbone. Madhusudan ended his meal by drinking to the last drop a big bowl of sugared milk. Finally he would put a betel-leaf in his mouth and a couple of them in a case. He then pulled at the hookah for about a quarter of an hour and went back to work. From the time when he was relatively poor until today, there was no exception to this routine. He had a good appetite for food but no greed.

Shyamasundari was stirring sugar in the milk. Not too dark, she could not be called fat, but the fullness of her body did make a statement. She was always clad only in a plain white sari, and she always looked neat. She was nearing the end of youth, more like a late summer afternoon when the end of the day is drawing near yet the shadow of dusk has not fallen. Her dark eyes under thick arched eyebrows did not look straight at anyone but took in a lot with a sidelong glance. Her full and ripe lips seemed to have more to say than she cared to. Life had not given her much to savour, yet she seemed to be fulfilled. She knew her worth, she was not mean, but she had a proud disdain of her environs because she felt her value was wasted therein. She had come to this family at the rising tide of Madhusudan's wealth. She had ambitions to be at the top by the power of her youth. One cannot say for certain that Madhusudan was not tempted. But he never surrendered because he was not merely worldly wise but also a genius at it. This talent helped him create his vast wealth in which he was deeply immersed and which gave him great pleasure. His rare instinct warned him that a powerful obstacle had been placed against his goal of amassing wealth, just as how in mythology, Indra the lord of the gods had sent temptresses to distract anyone who threatened to be as powerful by virtue of practising a rigorous asceticism. So, every time such temptation came Madhusudan's way, he had managed to check himself. It was also easy to do so because in the high noon of his business he had no leisure to stray. The occasional glimpse, the casual words he had from Shyama were enough to give him relief in the midst of this hard toil. On occasions of festivals and fairs his partiality towards Shyamasundari was evident. But he never indulged her to the extent that she could afford to be arrogant within the household. Shyama was well aware of his weakness but could not cast off her fear of the man.

She was always present at his meals, today was no exception. She had just come out of her bath wearing a spotless white sari, one end of which was lightly draped over her incredibly black, long and thick hair spread over her back. A mild fragrance of her shampoo wafted from her wet hair.

She did not look up from the milk bowl she was stirring but asked softly, 'Thakurpo, shall I send for her?'

Madhusudan looked at his sister-in-law gravely without a word. The frightened Shyama hastened to explain, 'It is good for her to be present at your mealtime. She can wait on you . . .'

She left her sentence unfinished as she could not make out anything from his expression. He bent his head down and resumed eating. After a little while he asked, without lifting his head, 'Where is she now?'

Shyamasundari quickly responded, 'Let me go and look for her.'

Madhusudan frowned and put up his finger, bidding her not to. He did not want to hear from her the answer he feared most, yet he was very curious. He went up to his bedroom at the end of the meal, with a faint hope in his heart. He even made a round of the terrace. He went into the bathroom and stood still for a while. Then he came back to the bedroom and stretched out on his bed, puffing at the hookah. The routine fifteen minutes went by, twenty minutes passed and at the end of thirty minutes he pulled out his watch and looked at the time. Year in and year out he had never been late in going back to the office even by five minutes. There was an attendance register in his office in which everyone had to record the time of their arrival and departure. Their wages moved up and down according to those records. Of all the employees his had the least deductions. He made no distinction between himself and the others in this matter. In fact, he fined himself at double the rate for others. Today he made up his mind to make up for it, by working overtime. But as the day wore on, he felt less and less like working. Eventually, he came back half an hour earlier than usual, leaving his work unfinished. All the time that he was in the office, he had felt like paying a surprise visit to the bedroom. Maybe someone would be there. He never entered his bedroom in daylight, but today he came inside the house in his office clothes.

Motir-ma was on the terrace, picking up the pieces of mango spread out in the sun for drying. Seeing him enter the bedroom at this unusual hour, she pulled her sari over her head and smiled to herself. Madhusudan was annoyed and ashamed at the same time, at being caught by her, playing truant. His plan was to enter the room very silently, so that the startled deer which might be in the room did not run away. But that plan failed. So he quickly got in just to avoid any more curious eyes. He felt his slipping away from the office had misfired totally. Not only was there nobody in the room, but there was no evidence that anyone ever stepped into the room anytime, even for a short while. He could hold his patience no longer. As the elder brother-in-law he was not supposed to talk to Motir-ma directly. Nor had he ever done it, but today he was dying to call her and ask her about Kumu. Once he even went out to look for her but she had left by then.

In order to save himself from the ignominy of being in his bedroom, abandoned by his new bride, at this odd hour all by himself, he stalked out of the room quickly. In his office room, he leaned over his desk intently, pretending to do some very important work. He opened the first register he saw lying about. Normally he never looked at it, his head clerk did. But to keep up his pretence in front of others he opened it. This register kept record of all letters and telegrams that were sent out with their dates and times. The first entry was a telegram addressed to Bipradas. The sender was the mistress of the house herself.

'Call the darwan!' shouted Madhusudan.

The messenger came.

'Who sent you to despatch this telegram?'

'Mejobabu, sir.'

'Call him.'

Nabin arrived, pale in the face.

'Who ordered this telegram to be sent, without my permission?' It was not easy to name the one who did it, in front of the master disciplinarian. At a loss to answer, Nabin started sweating even on that winter afternoon.

Nabin's silence provoked Madhusudan to ask, 'Was it Mejobou?'

The answer was clear from the way Nabin hung his head in silence. Blood rushed to Madhusudan's head and he was red in the face. He was so angry that he could not bring himself to speak. He dismissed Nabin from the room with a vigorous movement of the hand, and began to pace up and down from one end of the room to the other.

## 30

A crestfallen Nabin came and told Motir-ma, 'That's it, Mejobou. Start packing.'

'Why? What's up?'

'Now you may put by all the stuff in the trunks.'

'If I do as you say, I may have to unpack them again the next day. Is your boss in a temper?'

'I know him well. This time it is our home here that seems to be in danger.'

'So what? Let's go. We won't be stranded wherever we have to move.'

'Who is asking me to go? The order is likely to be "Send Mejobou packing home".'

'I know you can't follow such an order,' said Motir-ma.

'How do you know I can't?'

'Don't think it's me alone; the whole house knows you to be a uxorious man. Till today your elder brother wondered how a man can become a slave to his wife. Now the time has come for him to find out how.'

'What are you saying?'

'I am beginning to see it as your family weakness. Until now this trait was not obvious in your brother's case. Mark my words, it will be far more pungent because it was bottled up so long. The ardour with which he held to his purse, oblivious of the world around, will now be exercised over his wife.'

'So be it. Let the senior uxorious man take the floor, but how will his junior carry on?'

'That's my lookout. Now you do as I tell you. You have to search his drawers.'

Nabin implored with folded hands, 'I shall willingly put my hand into a snake-pit if you ask me, but I beg of you Mejobou, don't ask me to put them into his office drawers.'

'If it were the snake-pit I would have done it myself; but the drawers are your job. You know very well that no letter can be delivered to anyone without first showing it to him. I have a strong feeling that a letter from her brother has actually reached him.'

'I too feel the same way, but at the same time I also feel that if I so much as touch that letter, no punishment will be enough as far he is concerned. Maybe the death penalty along with seven years of rigorous imprisonment will just about do.'

'You don't have to do anything, not even touch the letter, just check if it is there.'

Nabin had great regard for his wife, in fact sometimes he felt that he was undeserving of her. So he welcomed any opportunity to accomplish some difficult task for her, even if he were a little frightened.

The same night she learnt from Nabin that indeed there was a letter and a telegram, in Madhusudan's drawer, for Kumu, from her brother.

The excitement which drove Kumu from her bedroom to a maid's job was waning. Her heart was now heavy with the pall of sadness which was replacing the annoyance at her own humiliation. She knew this could not be a permanent arrangement, yet how would she carry on without some such solution? You couldn't possibly live in a household forever, with such forced detachment.

So ran her thoughts in her closed room which was in one corner of the veranda, screened by a wooden fencing. Except for the entrance, it had no openings. There were wooden racks all along the walls up to the ceiling. All kinds of lighting equipment and accessories were kept on those shelves. The room was thick with soot. Some servant had satisfied his aesthetic sense by sticking on the wall near the door pictures cut out from the wrapping of the lamps. In one corner, some powdered chalk was kept in a tin box. Next to it was a basket of dry tamarind and a few dirty dusters. There was also a row of kerosene tins, mostly empty, except for two or three tins.

Kumu started her day's chore in her amateur fashion. After finishing her job in the store room, Motir-ma peeped in to witness Kumu's predicament in trying to accomplish the impossible. She watched for a while and feared the end nearing for some of the fragile objects. In this house, the slightest loss of things did not go unnoticed.

So she did not wait any longer but volunteered with, 'My hands are free, so I thought I could help in Didi's work and earn some merit.' And she pulled the basket of glass globes and chimneys to herself and started cleaning them.

There was not much force in Kumu's protest because by now she had nearly completed the discovery of her own incompetence. Motir-ma was a godsend. But there was a limit even to Motir-ma's native talent. She found it beyond her to fix the wick in a kerosene lamp to the right length. The entire job was done always under her supervision and she herself measured out the kerosene, but she had never got down to adjusting wicks with her own hands. So she proposed to seek the help of Banku, the old lampman.

The two women had to concede defeat. Banku the farash came and finished the job in no time. By the evening the lamps had to be distributed properly in their respective rooms. Banku asked if he were needed for that job as usual. He was a simple fellow but still there was perhaps a touch of sarcasm in his query. Kumu felt her ears reddening.

Before Kumu could say anything, Motir-ma said firmly, 'Of course you should come.' It was clear to Kumu that her effort to help with the work was nothing but an impediment.

## 31

After lunch, behind her closed door she began to resolve seriously, not to let the flame of anger flash in her mind any more. She said to herself, 'Let me be calm and prepare my mind the whole of today. Then from tomorrow, with the blessings of my deity I shall tread the true path of a housewife.' In this task of resolving the strife within herself, her biggest weapon was the memory of her brother. She had seen the amazing depth of patience in him. The sadness in his face mirrored the greatness of his heart. Her Dada, who embraced the current belief amongst the educated class, of Positivism, who did not have the outward show of saluting the gods but whose life itself was filled with divinity, he would be her role model for the future now.

In the afternoon Banku farash knocked and she opened the door and went out. She told Motir-ma that she would not need any dinner that night. This fast on her part was to cleanse her own mind. Observing her face Motir-ma felt surprise. No longer was Kumu's face flushed crimson with the fire in her heart. Instead, her eyes and her forehead were radiant with a calm tenderness, as if she had just emerged from a holy dip. Her deity seemed to have soothed all her anguish. She appeared to be enveloped in the fragrance of a flower-offering in her heart. And because she knew that Kumu's decision to fast was not for self-torture or out of pique, she did not raise any objection.

Kumu went and sat on the terrace, with the image of her deity in her mind. She realized clearly now that had it not been for this cruel blow, she would never have come so close to her god. She folded her hands in prayer, in the glow of the setting sun, and said, 'My lord, do not desert me ever, make me cry as much as you wish to, but hold me close to you.'

The winter day faded out. Dust, smog and smoke from the factories combined to throw a pall of grey over the clear and sombre majesty of eventide. The sky seemed to be coming down with the burden of spreading grime and likewise Kumu's mind was pulled down with the unbearable burden of worry for her brother.

So she entered her den with mixed feelings of relief at being free of the bondage of resentment and a misgiving on her brother's account. She wished she could also put this burden of worry (regarding her brother's health) faithfully upon her god. But as she herself kept telling herself not to worry she could not feel confident. The question kept on tormenting her—why was there no reply to her wire?

Madhusudan was unable to put his finger on the subtle obstacle in the way of a woman surrendering herself. Even the approach to his own wife over whose body and mind he had full rights, was proving inaccessible. He was at a loss to find a strategy to combat this unexpected conspiracy of fate.

There had never been an occasion for him to neglect his business. But now even that grave symptom was in evidence. Everyone knew how he never slackened in his work even when his mother was ill and dying. In fact they admired his resoluteness. But to discover this new identity of his—that he could give something else, that too a woman, priority over his work—was a stunning experience. He was not sure as to where this strange external force was leading him.

He came to the bedroom after dinner, hoping against hope to find his wife there. So he came in a little later than usual. He was used to going to sleep by the clock. As soon as he lay down, like any normal healthy person he fell asleep. But now, he did not go to bed at all; what if he fell asleep and Kumu came into the room? She would, no doubt, return. He sat on the sofa for a while, then paced up and down the terrace. His time for bed was nine o'clock; suddenly he heard the bell at the main gate sound eleven. He felt ashamed. Twice or thrice he got up and stood in front of his bed but could not bring himself to lie down. Then he decided to go and have it out with Nabin, that very night.

When he reached the front veranda he found a light in Nabin's room. As he was about to enter it, he met Nabin coming out with a lantern in his hand. If it were daylight, he would have seen how Nabin's face went pale in a second.

He asked, 'What are you doing here so late at night?'

Nabin was quick to think up an answer, 'Every night at this time I go to the main hall to wind the clock and change the date card before I turn in.'

'All right. But right now, listen to what I have to say.'

Nabin stood to attention like an accused in the dock. Madhusudan said, 'I don't like anyone else to fill Borobou's head with ideas. My wife will abide by my wishes. That is how it must be.'

Nabin agreed gravely, 'Sure. That is how it should be.'

'So I think, Mejobou should go back to her village home.' Nabin pretended to be greatly relieved.

'It is just as well, Dada. I was also wondering about how to approach you, for you may not have approved.'

Madhusudan was surprised. 'What do you mean?' he asked.

'Well, for the last few days she has been pestering me to let her go home. In fact she has already packed. Just waiting for a suitable day to start.'

Needless to say it was all made up. Madhusudan could order anybody out of his house, but he could not tolerate the idea that anyone should want to leave on their own. He was annoyed. 'Why, what is the hurry?'

'No, now that the mistress of the house is here, it is only appropriate that she takes charge of the household. Mejobou felt that there might be some loose talk if she continued here.'

'Is she the sole judge of such matters?'

Nabin pretended to be naïve, and said, 'You know women and their whims! Somehow it has got into her head that one day you would sack her over something or the other and that would be too insulting for her. So she is determined to go now. A couple of days before the night of the auspicious full moon, she wants to hand over the accounts and leave by that date.'

Madhusudan said, 'Look Nabin, you have spoiled her. Tell her sternly that she cannot go now. You are a man. I can't bear to see you unable to rule your own house.'

Nabin scratched his head and said, 'I shall try. But . . .'

'All right, tell her it is my decision. When the time comes, I shall arrange it myself.'

'But you said you wanted to send her home. That is why I thought . . .'

Madhusudan got agitated.

'Did I say that she had to leave this very moment?'

Nabin crept out of the room. Madhusudan lit a gas lamp and lay down on a chaise-longue. The guard did a round in front of the rooms at night; Madhusudan dozed off for a while and suddenly woke up to find the chowkidar holding a lantern and staring at his face. Maybe he was wondering whether the Maharaj had just fainted or passed away. Embarrassed, Madhusudan got up in a hurry. It struck him in a moment that the pathetic sight of the newly-married Rajabahadur would be quite demeaning in the guard's eyes. He told the guard in a huff, 'Shut the room,' as if it was the guard's fault that it was not shut. The gong at the main gate struck two in the morning.

Before leaving the room, he opened the drawer, dithered a little, put Kumu's telegram in his pocket and walked into the house.

One is not in command of all one's strength as one gets up from a sleep. Maybe that is why one's character during the day is somewhat different from what it is in the night. At this hour of the night when no one was looking and he was answerable to no one but himself, Madhusudan found it easy in his mind to concede defeat to Kumu.

## 32

He turned at the bottom of the stairs. His heart was in a tumult. There was a lighted lantern in front of a closed door. He picked it up and walked up to the lamproom. He found the door ajar and it opened easily. Kumu was asleep on the same mat, covered in a sheet, her left hand resting on her breast. He put down the lantern in a corner of the wall and came and sat down on her left. The reason why this face attracted him with such compulsion was its indescribable serenity. Kumu never had any conflict within herself. In her brother's home, she had suffered from want but that concerned her external environment; it never affected her inner nature. Her household was totally in tune with her own temperament. This was why her expression was one of complete innocence; her bearing always dignified. To Madhusudan, who had to constantly struggle for existence and who had to be alert against daily uncertainty, this grandeur of her unperturbed tranquillity was a matter of great wonder. He himself was never at ease, but there she was—as simple as a divinity. This polarity in their characters drew him strongly towards her. When he looked back on the events that took place when Kumu arrived at his house as a new bride, he found his own helpless anger at the failure of his overlordship a direct contrast to her easy but firm expression of self-respect. Never did her behaviour betray any lack of decency common in saucy females. If she had been like all the other women, then he would have had no hesitation in imposing a husband's rights. But he hadn't been able to really break the ice as far as she was concerned; he could never make out what went wrong, nor could he fathom what strange reason kept her beyond his reach.

He decided to stay up next to her, without waking her up. After a while he got impatient and slowly he moved her hand from her breast and took it in his own. She stirred in her sleep, pulled her hand in and turned on the other side.

He could wait no longer. He bent down and whispered into her ears, 'Borrobou, there is a telegram from your brother.'

She sat up instantly and stared at him in amazement. Madhusudan held up the telegram and said, 'See, it has come from your brother,' and then he fetched the lantern from the corner.

She read it. It was in English, 'Do not worry about me. I am getting better day by day. My blessings for you.' It was such a relief after the agonizing worry, that her eyes were filled with tears. She wiped her eyes and carefully folded the telegram and tied it in the corner of her sari. This made him squirm in pain. They were both at a loss for words. Then it was Kumu who spoke, 'No letters from Dada?'

Madhusudan could not bring himself to tell the truth. He just blurted out, 'No, there is no letter.'

Kumu felt awkward to sit by in such a manner with her husband in that room. She was about to get up when he said abruptly, 'Do not be angry with me, Borrobou!'

This did not sound like a master's voice but more like a lover's entreaty. Kumu was surprised beyond belief. She thought it could only be divine intervention, because during the day she had been telling herself, 'Do not be angry,' and now who had brought the same words to Madhusudan's lips?

Madhusudan asked her again, 'Are you still sore with me?'

She said, 'Not one bit. Not at all.'

It was his turn to be surprised. He stared at her face. It seemed she was talking to herself, or with someone unseen.

He said, 'In that case, leave this room and come to your own room.'

Kumu was not ready to be with Madhusudan, not that night. It is difficult to steel your heart as soon as you get up from your sleep. After her morning prayers she had resolved to enter the married woman's world from the next day. But, her deity had not given her any time. He called her now, in the middle of the night! She was afraid that the immense distaste she felt would count as an offence. So she snapped out of this revulsion and forced herself to stand up and say, 'Let us go.'

Upstairs, she stopped in front of her bedroom and said, 'I shall not be long, I'll be back soon.'

She went to her room, and stepped into the terrace. She sat there and looked up—a sliver of moon, in its dark fortnight, was up in the sky.

She went on repeating to herself, 'Lord, you've called me, you've called me because you haven't forsaken me. You have decided to take me along the thorny path and that will be with you alone, none else, my lord.'

She wanted to blot out everything. All the rest were but an illusion. Even if it were thorny all along, it was still only a part of the way—the way to Him. For this prickly journey she had the protection of her brother's blessings—which she had carefully tied in a knot at the end of her sari. She touched her forehead with it and then bent down on the floor in salutation. She was startled to hear Madhusudan's voice behind her, 'It is cold outside, Borrobou, do come inside.' This was not in tune with the voice of her lord which she wanted to hear within herself. This was her test. Today her god would not lure her with his flute, He would remain concealed.

The more her mind, as an individual, was filled with disgust and distaste, and the more her new home forced its rights upon her, the more she drew a shell round herself. A kind of wall that would keep out the reality of likes and dislikes. In other words it would dull her consciousness about her own feelings. But this was not a matter of a few hours, she had to keep at bay her feeling of dislike and aversion, night and day. In such a situation women are usually helped by a guru to forget themselves. But it was not possible in her case. So she could only try to keep alive by chanting her own mantra constantly in her mind.

*Tasmat pranamya pranidhaya kaayam*
*prasadaye twam ahameesham-eedam*
*piteb putrasya sakheb sakhyuh*
*priya priya-yarhasi deb sodhum.*

(O my venerable lord, I bow to thee with my body and soul, to ask of you this benediction—may you bear with me just as the father does his son, the friend his companion, or the lover his beloved.)

'I too can forgive everything out of love for You, this is the only proof that You do love me.' She prayed with her eyes closed, 'You have proclaimed that You will never abandon one who sees You everywhere and in everything and does not ever forget Your presence. Let me not ever slacken in this goal of mine. '

In the morning, she took a long time with her bath and anointed herself with sandal-water. She dedicated her pure, fragrant body to her deity and tried to concentrate on the thought that her hand was always held in His, and her whole being was ever in touch with Him. It was He who truly possessed her; the corporeal body was merely an illusion. It was but dust to be mingled unto dust in no time. As long as she could feel His touch nothing could debase it. The more she dwelt on this, the happier she felt and tears of joy filled her eyes; her body was free of its fleshly bond. In fact she revered her body as the object of a divine union. If she had a garland of white flowers she would have put it round her neck and on her hair. She wore a white sari with a wide red border; and when she came and sat on the terrace she felt as though the sunbeams caressed her body in a warm welcome.

She came to Motir-ma and asked, 'Put me on to some of your work.'

'Come along,' said Motir-ma with a smile.

Ten or fifteen of those special cutting knives fixed on wooden planks upon which one sat and cut vegetables were set out amongst many large wooden platters, brass salvers, and basketfuls of greens and vegetables.

Women and poor relations sat chatting and swiftly cutting and chopping the vegetables in heaps. Kumu took her place among them. One could see through the iron bars, an old tamarind tree scattering the sunlight which splintered on its endlessly quivering leaves.

Motir-ma looked at Kumu occasionally and wondered if she was actually working or just following the movement of her fingers and letting her mind wander towards some pilgrimage. The more she looked at her the more Kumu seemed like a boat in full sail absorbed in the touch of the wind on its sail and oblivious of the water flowing on its sides. Others in the room could not find an easy way to strike up a conversation with Kumu. Shyamasundari once spoke out, 'Bou, if you must have a bath early in the morning why don't you order some hot water—you may catch a chill?'

Kumu merely said, 'I am used to it.'

The conversation could not proceed any further. A silent incantation was going on in her mind:

*Piteb putrasya sakheb sakhyuh*
*priya priya-yarhasi deb sodhum*

(As a father his son, as a lover his beloved . . .)

When all the vegetables were cut and the work in the storeroom was finished the gaggle of women proceeded for their bath, bustling around the tap.

When she got Motir-ma to herself, Kumu told her, 'I have got the reply to my telegram.'

Motir-ma was surprised. 'When did you get it?' she asked.

'Last night.'

'At night?'

'Yes, it was quite late. He came himself and gave it to me.'

'Then you must have got the letter as well.'

'Which letter?'

'Why, your brother's.'

Kumu was flustered.

'No. I did not get any. Is there a letter from him?'

Motir-ma kept quiet.

Kumu pressed her hand eagerly and pleaded, 'Where is it? Please get my brother's letter to me.'

Motir-ma whispered. 'I can't get that for you. It is in his office drawer.'

'Why can't you get me my own mail?'

'All hell will be let loose if he knows we've opened his drawer.'

Kumu said impatiently, 'You mean to say, I can't read my brother's letter?'

'When he goes out you can have a look and then put it back in the drawer.'

It is never easy to suppress one's anger. Kumu was peeved. She said, 'So I have to read my own letter in stealth?'

'In this house, what belongs to one and what does not, depends entirely on his judgement.'

Kumu was about to forget her resolve, but a voice inside told her, 'Give up anger.' She shut her eyes for a moment. Her lips moved silently, reciting '*priya priyayarhasi deb sodhum*.'

She said, 'If some one steals my letter I cannot stoop to stealing too, just to get even.'

As soon as she uttered those words, she realized they were harsh. She realized that the anger inside oneself does eventually come out without one being aware of it. It has to be uprooted. But you cannot always face it in order to fight it. It hides in a cavern inside a fortress, there is no entry to it. So one needs an avalanche of love to break open the closed door and flood it out. She had one way of forgetting it all—through her music. But she felt shy to play the esraj in this house. She could sing, but her voice was weak. She felt like drowning everything in a stream of songs—songs of deep hurt. A song wherein she could say, 'I have come at your call, then why did you hide yourself? I did not dither a moment, then why have you put me in this dilemma?' She wanted to sing these tunes loudly, perhaps she would then get the answer through music itself.

## 34

There was only one place in this house for her to escape, the terrace. That is where she went. The sun was up and the terrace was bathed in strong sunlight, except for a small shade near the wall. She sat there. One line of a song in Raga Ashawari came to her mind, '*Bansari hamari re, bansari hamare re*,' the rest of the words were always lost in the virtuosity of the maestro. She began to sing that obscure portion with her own variations. Those few words were then filled with meaning, as if trying to say, 'O my dear flute, why are you not full of tune today? Why does it not reach past the darkness, where beyond the closed door there is no awakening yet?—*bansari hamari re, bansari hamari re*.'

When Motir-ma came to call her for breakfast, the little shade on the terrace was gone, but her heart was full of music now, all her grievances against the world had paled into insignificance. The resentment she bore against Madhusudan's meanness with her letter, vanished in this sunlit sky like the buzz of an angry bee. Still she could not help yearning for the affectionate words her brother's letter must have carried.

It was at the back of her mind all the time. So after dinner she informed Motir-ma that she was going to the office room to read the letter.

Motir-ma said, 'Wait till the servants finish work and go for their meals.'

Kumu said, 'No, no, that will be stealthy. I want to go in front of everyone, and I do not care about what they think.'

'Then let me come with you.'

'By no means. You just show me the way.'

Motir-ma pointed at the room through the latticed corridor. Kumu came out. The servants, on the alert, saluted her. She entered the room, opened the drawer and found her letter. She picked it up to find it already opened. No one in her natal house could imagine a greater affront than this. The rush of her sentiment alerted her. She repeated to herself *'priya priyayarhasi deb sodhum'* but the storm within her was already raging. The orderly sitting outside was surprised to see the mistress chanting a mantra to herself. After a while she was able to calm her mind. Then she kept the letter in front of her and sat on the chair with folded hands. She was determined not to have a stolen look at the letter.

Madhusudan came in and was astounded to find her. Kumu ignored him. He went forward to find the letter on his desk. And asked, 'How come you are here?'

She looked at him without a word but also without any trace of complaint. Madhusudan repeated his question, 'Why are you here in this room?'

Her impatient reply to this redundant query was, 'I came to find out if there was any letter for me from my brother.'

His denial last night excluded the obvious reply, 'You could have asked me.' So he said instead, 'I was going to take this letter to you myself. There was no need for you to come here.'

Kumu took a little time to compose herself and said, 'You did not wish me to read this letter, so I shall not read it. I am tearing it up right now. But please do not torture me in this way again. Nothing can be more painful to me.'

She hid her face in her sari and ran out of the room.

Earlier in the day, after lunch, Madhusudan's mind was in a flutter and somehow he could not stop the agitation. He had decided to send for Kumu as soon as she finished her lunch. He took special care to comb his hair. Only this morning, he had ordered from an English hairdresser a fragrant hairoil with spirit in it, and also an expensive perfume. For the first time in his life, he was using such items. He was ready, well dressed and perfumed. It was past three-quarters of an hour beyond his usual time of departure.

He was startled at the sound of footsteps on the stairs. He could not find anything near at hand except an old newspaper, and he pored over it intently, as if it were part of his office work. He even pulled out from his pocket a blue pencil and marked a couple of items.

Shyamasundari came into the room. He frowned at her. She said, 'So you are sitting here when your wife is looking for you everywhere.'

'Looking for me? Where is she?'

'I saw her enter your office room just now.'

He went out quickly. And then followed the whole bitter incident of the letter.

Now Madhusudan's plight was that of a boat whose sail had been torn apart. There was hardly any time. He left for his work. But all through his work the jagged edges of his broken thoughts continued to hurt him. It was impossible for him to concentrate on his work that day after this mental trauma. He informed the office that he had a terrible headache and came home before he had finished his day's work.

## 35

Nabin and his wife could now sense that their foundation in the house was truly shaken and that they had no room for escape. Motir-ma said, 'It won't be difficult for me to find another place where I can work and earn my living, the same way as I do here. My only regret is that when I go, there will be no one to look after Didi.'

Nabin said, 'Look Mejobou, I have suffered a lot in this household and have revolted many times against our living here, but now it is too much to bear. Such a wonderful bride, and Dada did not know how to hold her. He spoilt it all. Misfortune is nothing but broken pieces of good luck.'

'He will soon realize that, but it may be too late to put the broken pieces together again,' said Motir-ma.

'My regret is that I was not fated to become an ideal brother-in-law like Lakshman was to Sita,' said Nabin.

Motir-ma left the room. Nabin could not hold himself any longer. He slowly crept outside Kumu's room and found her lying on the floor. The pain of that torn letter would not go away.

She got up as soon as she saw Nabin. He said, 'Boudidi, I have come to touch your feet and seek your blessings.' This was the first time he spoke to her.

She asked him to sit down. Nabin sat down on the floor and continued, 'I was very happy at the prospect of serving you, but it seems that this poor Nabin is not so lucky after all. We had you with us only for a few days and the regret is that I could do nothing for you.'

She asked, 'Where are you going?'

'Dada will send us away to our village home. Maybe we shall never meet again, that is why I have come to bid you goodbye.'

Just as he bent down to touch Kumu's feet, Motir-ma came running and said, 'Come quickly. The boss is looking for you.' Both of them rushed out of the room.

Madhusudan was at his desk in the office room. Nabin came in and stood there. There was no trace of misgiving on his face; this was quite unlike his usual demeanour in similar circumstances in the past.

Madhusudan asked, 'Who informed Borrobou about the letter?'

'I did.'

'Since when have you become so bold?'

'Borrobourani asked me if there were any letters from her brother, so

I came to look in your desk where all the mail for this house is delivered.'

'You could not wait to ask me?'

'She was very upset, that is why . . .'

'Was that why my orders had to be flouted?'

'She is the mistress of this house, how could I imagine that she has no voice in this place? I haven't got the courage to disobey her. I am telling you, she is not only my employer but also my revered elder and I obey her not out of gratitude but out of respect.'

'Nabin, I have known you since childhood and I know these are not your thoughts. I also know where they come from. Anyway it is too late tonight. You have to leave for the village by the morning train.'

'That is fine by us.'

This short answer was not to Madhusudan's liking at all. He expected Nabin to cry and implore, not that it would have changed his decision. He called Nabin back and said, 'Take your dues and remember from now on you are on your own.'

Nabin said, 'I know that very well, Dada. I shall till the land that is in my share and make a living,' and he left without waiting for Madhusudan to react.

Human nature is a strange mixture of contrary traits. One example is that Madhusudan was extremely fond of Nabin. After their father's death he brought Nabin to stay with him and complete his studies. He continued to keep Nabin who had a natural flair for managing the household, one reason being his sincerity and the other his universal popularity. Wherever there was any dispute Nabin was able to smoothen it out. He could make light of any situation and was not only fair to all but also made each one feel that he was on their side.

A proof of Madhusudan's deep affection for Nabin was that he could not stand Motir-ma. He was totally possessive of anyone he liked. This was the reason why he suspected that she was forever poisoning Nabin's ears. The paternal right he had over his younger brother was constantly being thwarted by a girl from another family. He would have exiled her long ago, were he not so fond of his younger brother.

Madhusudan had planned to go back to work as soon as he finished this little episode with Nabin, but he could not muster enough strength of mind to do so. The picture of Kumu tearing the letter and stalking out was deeply etched in his memory. Such a spectacle was beyond his imagination. For a moment, in his usually suspicious manner, he thought Kumu must have already read the letter. But there was such a glow of pristine honesty on her face that it was impossible to entertain such a thought for long, even for one like Madhusudan.

He felt as if he was fast losing his ability to discipline Kumu firmly and now his own shortcomings began to assail him. He could not forget his age and would have been only too happy to conceal his grey hair. After all these years, the unfairness of fate in ordaining him to be dark-skinned began to irk him. He had no doubt that the reason why Kumu's heart was slipping from his grip was his lack of youth and beauty. In these aspects he was totally vulnerable. He had been set on marrying into the Chatterjee family but he could never imagine that such a girl would fall to his lot who was destined to triumph over him. Yet he did not have the courage to admit to himself that an ordinary girl whom he could control would have suited him better.

He could surpass all others in one thing however. His wealth. So he had a jeweller sent for in the morning, and he bought three rings from him to try out Kumu's choice. He went to his bedroom with those three rings in his pocket. One was an emerald one, the other a ruby and the third a diamond. He imagined that as he opened the first box with the emerald ring in it he would see Kumu's greedy eyes glisten, then he'd open the second box and the ruby would dazzle her and her eyes would widen with delight, and finally the diamond with its precious glow would hold the woman captive. Madhusudan would then say with imperial solemnity, 'Go ahead, take whichever you like.' Then when Kumu chose the diamond, he, amused at the timidity of her desire, would put all the three on her fingers. The curtain would next rise on the nuptial bed.

Madhusudan had planned this event to take place in the night—after dinner. But after the disastrous episode in the morning he could wait no longer. It was late afternoon; he went into the bedroom eager to immediately implement the plan which he had reserved for the night. He found her on the floor of the bedroom busy packing a tin trunk amongst a heap of clothes and stuff.

'What is all this? Are you going somewhere?'

'Yes.'

'Where?'

'Rajabpur, your ancestral home.'

'What do you mean?'

'You have punished Nabin for opening your drawer, but actually, I deserve the punishment.'

It was not in his nature to bend and request, 'Please stay.' His first reaction was, 'Let me see how long she can stick it out.' He turned on his heel and walked out of the room without a second thought.

## 36

Madhusudan called Nabin to his room and said, 'So you two have put her up to it.'

'Dada, since we are off tomorrow I can feel free to talk to you without constraint. I can tell you plainly that no one else need drive her mad, you can do that very well by yourself. If we stayed on, we might have made it a little easier, but you cannot stand that.'

Madhusudan shouted at him.

'Don't be presumptuous! Both of you must have put the idea of Rajabpur in her head.'

'Such an idea did not even cross our minds, let alone reach her.'

'I am warning you not to incite her any more.'

'To whom are you telling all this? Address it to the right quarters.'

'So you did not talk to her?'

'I swear to you, we did not.'

'What will be your stand if she insists on coming with you?'

'We shall come to you. You have your army of men, you can stop it, if you want to. But if your enemies publicize this encounter please do not blame Mejobou for it.'

Madhusudan shut him up. 'Quiet,' he said, 'if Borrobou wishes to go to Rajabpur, let her. I am not going to stop her.'

'But how shall we feed and keep her?'

'Sell your wife's jewellery. Get out. Out of this room, *now*!'

Nabin went out. Madhusudan cooled his forehead with a wet band of cologne water and tried to make up his mind about going back to work.

Motir-ma heard everything from Nabin and hurried to Kumu whom she found folding her clothes for packing.

'What are you doing, Bourani?' she asked.

'I am coming with you.'

'We can't afford to take you with us.'

'Why?'

'Big brother will never see us again.'

'Then he won't see me either.'

'Maybe, but the fact is that we are very poor.'

'So am I. I can manage.'

'People will laugh at him.'

'That is no reason why I should put up with this unfair punishment heaped on you.'

'But Didi, this is not your fault, we have brought it upon ourselves.'

'How?'

'We are the ones who told you about the letter.'

'How is that a crime when it was I who wanted the news?'

'But to tell you without his knowledge was certainly wrong.'

'All right, both of us have been at fault, so let us share the penalty equally also.'

'Right, we shall order a palanquin for you too. The master's orders are not to stop you. Let me now help you pack. You are in a sweat.'

So both of them started to pack. Then there was the squeak of an approaching pair of shoes. Motir-ma made herself scarce.

Madhusudan came in and said straightaway, 'Borrobou, you cannot go.'

'Why?'

'Because I say so.'

'All right then, I shall not go. What more do you wish me to do?'

'Stop packing your things.'

'Very well. I am stopping right now.'

She got up and left the room. He shouted after her, 'Listen to me!' She came back and said, 'I am listening.'

He had nothing to say, yet he thought for a while and said, 'I have bought you a ring.'

'You have forbidden me to wear the ring I really wanted. Now I don't need any other.'

'No harm in looking at it.'

He opened the boxes, one after the other. Kumu sat without a word.

'You may take whichever you like.'

'I shall wear whatever you order me to wear.'

'I think all three will suit your fingers.'

'If you so order me, I shall wear all three.'

'May I put them on you?'

'Do.'

Madhusudan put them on her fingers. She asked, 'Any more orders?'

He said, 'Borrobou, why are you angry with me?'

She replied, 'I am not angry at all,' and left the room.

Madhusudan was upset. He said, 'Where are you off to? Listen to me please.'

Kumu turned back and asked, 'What do you want to say?'

Madhusudan was at a loss for words. His face was red. He said with disgust, 'All right, you may go,' and added angrily, 'Leave the rings here.'

She took off all the three rings and kept them on the teapoy.

Madhusudan barked, 'Go away!'

Kumu left immediately.

He then decided to definitely go back to work, although it was well past office time. The English assistants had left for the tennis court. The senior clerks were about to go home. Madhusudan entered his office at this juncture and plunged himself into work. He worked till it was past six, then seven, till eight at night, when he closed his registers and got up.

## 37

So far, no strand had ever been missed in Madhusudan's daily routine; every moment of the day, every day of the week was predictably regulated. Now, with Kumu's entry into his life, everything was in a chaos of uncertainty. For instance, right now on his way back home he had no idea how the night would turn out to be. He crept into the house in fear, and ate his dinner quietly but did not have the courage to go to his bedroom immediately, as was his wont. For a while he paced up and down in the veranda outside on the south of the house. When it was nine, his usual bedtime, he went in. He was determined to go to bed at the normal time tonight, without fail. He entered the empty bedroom, pulled down the mosquito curtain and fell heavily on the bed; but sleep would not come to him. As the night advanced, the starved being inside him began to emerge slowly. There was no one to chase it away, no sentinel around.

The clock struck one and still he could not get a wink of sleep. He could lie awake no longer; he got up and wondered where Kumu could be. He took off his shoes and walked softly along the corridor downstairs. As he approached Nabin's room he heard voices. Perhaps the husband and the wife were discussing details of the next day's impending departure. He listened carefully at the door. There was a murmur, though one could not make out the words. But it was clearly two female voices talking in whispers. Then it must be Kumu opening her heart to Motir-ma the night before they parted. He was so angry and aggrieved that he felt like kicking the door open and creating a rumpus. But where was Nabin then? He must be somewhere outside, he thought.

A dim light was on in the latticed corridor leading outside. When he reached that spot he noticed Shyama draped in a red shawl. Madhusudan was embarrassed, so he lost his temper. 'What are you doing here so late at night?' he shot at her.

Shyama said, 'I was sleeping, then I heard footsteps outside. So I thought . . .'

Madhusudan roared at her, 'Your audacity is overstepping the limit. Don't you fool me, I warn you! Go to bed.'

Shyamasundari had indeed been taking bolder and bolder steps the last few days. She realized now that she was caught on the wrong foot at the wrong hour. She looked plaintively at him and then turned her face to wipe her tears. She started to go back but turned and said, 'I don't have to fool you, brother. How can we sleep when we see the goings-on? After all, we are not new in this house. How can we bear all this silently?' Then she left.

Madhusudan stood silently for a while and then started to go to the office room outside but ran straight into the night guard. His own iron rules left no way for him to walk about by himself. One was under watchful eyes everywhere. It was unprecedented for the Rajabahadur to come out to the veranda barefoot, like an apparition. The guard could not make him out from a distance; he challenged, 'Who goes there?' As he went near and saw his master, he bit his tongue, bowed low and said, 'Any orders, sir?'

Madhusudan said, 'I just came to see if everything was all right,' words not unexpected of him.

When he went into the office room he found that his hunch was right. There was Nabin fast asleep on the couch, hugging a bolster. Madhusudan lit a gaslamp; but that did not wake up Nabin. He got up in a scare only when Madhusudan pushed him back. Madhusudan did not ask for any explanation but told Nabin, 'Go just now and tell Borrobou that I will see her in the bedroom.' And he left.

In a little while Kumu entered the bedroom. Madhusudan stared at her. She was wearing an ordinary red-bordered sari, the end of which was veiled over her head, but in the dim light of this solitary room she was a stunning presence. She went and sat on the sofa in the corner of the room.

Madhusudan lost no time to go and sit at her feet. She felt embarrassed and tried to get up but he quickly pulled her to her seat and said, 'Don't get up. Just listen to me. Please forgive me, I have been guilty.'

Kumu was taken aback at this unexpected humility on his part. Madhusudan added, 'I shall ask Nabin and Mejobou not to go to Rajabpur. They will stay on in your service.'

Kumu didn't know what to say. Madhusudan had made up his mind to win her back even if he had to swallow his pride. He took her hand and said, 'I shall be back soon. Please promise that you will not go away.'

'No, I won't,' she said.

Madhusudan went downstairs. It was not difficult for Kumudini to deal with Madhusudan when he was mean and rough, but she did not know how to respond to this new politeness, this humbling of himself. The offering she brought with her in her heart when she had been newly married had all gone to dust. She could never pick up those lost feelings again. She began to pray, '*Priya priyayarhasi deb sodhum.*' Madhusudan came back with Nabin and Motir-ma and addressed them in Kumu's presence, 'I asked you yesterday to go back to Rajabpur, but that will not be necessary. I appoint you look after Borrobou from tomorrow onwards.'

They were flabbergasted. Firstly, the order was totally unexpected and secondly, what was the urgency to wake them up and tell them in the middle of the night?

Madhusudan was at the end of his tether. He had made up his mind to stoop to anything to win Kumu's favour that very night. He had never demeaned himself like this in his life ever. And now he was paying the highest price for what he desired most. In his own way, he let her know that he had surrendered to her unconditionally.

She was now facing a great dilemma. How was she to accept this new offer?

What did she have to offer in return? When the challenge comes from outside, one finds within oneself the strength to fight it. God himself comes to one's aid. But if the struggle outside suddenly ceases, there is truce but treaty does not come easily. Then the inner hostility comes out. Now she could no longer take shelter behind petty sulks, nor escape to the lamproom. Praying also was meaningless.

She could be saved if she could keep Motir-ma on some pretext. But Nabin left and a dumbfounded Motir-ma followed suit. Near the doorway she turned and gave Kumu an anxious look. Who would save this girl now from the pleasure of her husband, she wondered.

Madhusudan said, 'Borrobou, won't you change and come to bed?'

Kumu got up slowly and shut herself up in the bathroom, trying to prolong her moments of freedom. She sat on a stool close to the wall.

Her tormented body seemed to be seeking refuge within herself. Madhusudan was looking at the clock from time to time, trying to figure out how long it would take for her to undress. Meanwhile he looked at himself in the mirror, brushed the unruly hair on the top of his head and poured a lot of lavender water on himself.

A quarter of an hour went by, time enough for a change of clothes. He crept up to the bathroom door and tried to listen. But there was no sign of life. Perhaps, he thought, she was doing up her hair. Even Madhusudan was aware that women liked to dress up, so one had to be patient. Half an hour was over. He went again and put his ear to the bathroom door, but still there was not a sound. So he came back, sat on the chair and stared at the painting he had ordered from abroad which hung on the wall facing the bed. Suddenly he got up impatiently, went to the door and said, 'Borrobou, are you still at it?'

The door opened soon and Kumudini came out, as if sleepwalking. She was still in the same clothes. Surely this was not her night dress. Wearing a nearly full sleeved, brown serge blouse, she was leaning hesitantly, with her left hand against one door. An exquisite picture. A perfectly rounded arm wearing an old-fashioned gold bangle with the figure of a two-headed sea animal. Must have belonged to her mother. This heavy thick pair of bangles had endowed her delicate hand with a rich elegance which she carried with such ease that there was no suggestion of ostentation. It was a revelation to Madhusudan. He was struck by her grand elegance. He could not but be convinced that at long last the wealth that he created over the years had acquired class. The picture of this girl standing silently at the door post made him feel that he was not rich enough to deserve her. She would have befitted this place only if he were a King-Emperor. He could see clearly that her nature had been nurtured since her birth in an ambience of a proud family tradition. She seemed to be standing there with the heritage of all the years that preceded her own birth. Not just anyone from outside could enter those precincts where Bipradas reigned supreme. Like Kumudini, he also had around him an aura of unselfconscious pride.

And that is precisely what Madhusudan could not stomach. There was no arrogance in Bipradas—only a great distance, an aura. It was unthinkable, even for a close relation, to come and slap him on the back and ask him familiarly, 'Hey, how are you, my friend?' What irked Madhusudan most was the feeling of inferiority that welled up in him whenever he faced Bipradas. It was the same subtle reason which prevented him from forcing Kumu, that made him withdraw from his own domain where he was the rightful master. But in this case he did not feel anger, instead his strong attraction for Kumu became all the more uncontrollable. He could make out that Kumu was not yet ready for him tonight, that she was standing behind an invisible curtain. But how beautiful! What a white glow of purity! As if a clear dawn was breaking upon a desolate peak of ice.

Madhusudan approached her and said gently, 'Won't you come to bed Borrobou?'

Kumu was taken by surprise. She had expected him to be angry and insulting. Suddenly she recalled a very familiar voice from the past—the way her father sweetly addressed her mother: 'Borrobou'. At the same time she also remembered how her mother had ignored it and gone away. Her eyes filled with tears—she sat down on the floor near Madhusudan's feet and cried out, 'Please forgive me.'

Madhusudan quickly pulled her up and seated her on the sofa and said, 'Why, what have you done that I should forgive you?'

Kumu said, 'I am still not ready in my mind. Do give me some more time.'

Madhusudan stiffened. 'Make yourself clear. What do you want time for?'

'I don't know. It is difficult to explain to anyone.'

Madhusudan's voice was drained of all sweetness. He said, 'It is nothing so difficult. You are trying to say that you do not like me.'

Now she was in a fix. What he said was true, yet not entirely so. She had made up her mind to offer all that she had, only the offering was not at hand yet. Perhaps it would come in time provided there was no hindrance on the way. At the same time she could not deny that she was empty-handed.

She said, 'I am begging for more time because I do not want to cheat you in any way.'

Madhusudan was losing his patience. He said sternly, 'Will time help at all? Or is it that you need to consult your brother before you can start living with your own husband?'

He really believed so. He thought she was only waiting for her brother's word and that she was a puppet in the hands of her brother. He added mockingly, 'Is your Dada your guru?'

Kumudini stood up and said, 'Yes, my Dada is my guru.'

'So it is like that. You won't change or come to bed without his approval.'

Kumudini froze. She tightened her fist stiffly.

'Then let me get his permission by telegram. It is quite late already.'

Kumu started for the terrace without a word.

Madhusudan bawled at her, 'Don't go out. I am ordering you.'

Kumu turned round and said, 'What do you want?'

'Change and come to bed. I give you five minutes only.'

She went into the bathroom, changed her sari and draped herself in a thick sheet, waiting for his next order. Madhusudan recognized the battle dress. He was getting angrier but could not decide on the next course of action. He never lost his practical sense even when he was blind with rage. He said, 'You tell me what you want to do now.'

'Whatever you order me to.'

Madhusudan sat down in despair. That wife of his in a sheet looked like a woman in widow's weeds. It seemed as if there was a silent expanse of the sea of death between her and her husband. You could not cross this ocean by bluster. How did one sail in it? What kind of wind would be favourable? Would such a thing ever happen? He sat quietly as he brooded over such questions. There was no sound in the room except the ticking of the clock. Kumudini did not leave the room but she turned and continued to stare across the terrace, motionless like a picture. The maudlin voice of a drunkard singing could be heard from the crossing of the road ahead. The peace of the night was being disturbed by the incessant moaning of a dog tied up in the neighbour's kennel.

Time stood like an yawning abyss. The whole of Madhusudan's well-oiled machine seemed to have come to a grinding halt. He had a big agenda for the next morning—a meeting of the Board of Directors during which some knotty resolutions had to be cleverly passed without too much opposition. But all those weighty matters were without any substance for him now. Normally he would note down his strategy the night before. But all such thoughts vanished before the stark reality facing him, which was the picture of a woman draped in a white sheet arrested in her tracks on the way out to the darkness of the terrace. After a while he heaved a deep sigh. The whole room seemed to suddenly wake up from its stupor. He quickly got up, went to Kumu and said, 'Borrobou, have you a heart of stone?'

That word worked like magic on her. She suddenly saw a reflection of her mother's life illuminated in her own life. Perhaps it was in her blood to react in the way her mother responded to this address easily, so often in the past. So she turned abruptly, facing him. Madhusudan said plaintively, 'I know I am unworthy of you, but will you not take pity on me?'

Kumudini was flustered. She said, 'Please do not talk that way. What a shame!' She bent down to touch his feet and said, 'I am at your service. You have only to order me.'

Madhusudan picked her up and pressed her to his bosom. Kumudini felt stifled in his embrace but she did not try to free herself. He said in a choked voice, 'No, I shall never order you, but still, do come to me.'

Kumudini blushed scarlet. She lowered her gaze and said, 'It will make my task easier if you ordered me. I am incapable of doing anything on my own.'

'Right. Then you take off that sheet. I can't stand it.'

With much hesitation she took it off.

She had on a plain striped sari. The thin black stripes wound endlessly round her slender figure like a stream, as if some dark, insatiate eyes had left their restless track following her body. Madhusudan was charmed, but at the same time did not fail to notice that the sari was not a gift from this house. It might suit her very well but it was cheap and belonged to her own home. In the dressing room adjoining their bathroom there was a huge mahogany wall cupboard with a mirror set with emeralds and stacked with expensive saris for her, from even before the wedding. But obviously, she was too proud to care for those. He remembered the incident of the three rings—the disdain with which she rejected them in favour of an unlucky sapphire. There was such a vast difference between her concern for him and for Bipradas. All these thoughts hit him like a strong burst of a gale as soon as she took off her wrap. But alas! She was so beautiful, so exquisitely beautiful! Even this spirited disdain became her like an ornament. Only a girl like her could spurn all wealth. She was born magnificently rich in simplicity. She did not have to keep count of her riches.

With what could he possibly tempt her, he wondered.

He said, 'Now you may go to bed.'

Kumu looked at him in silence. The question in her eyes was, 'Won't you go up first?'

He said firmly again, 'Go on. Don't delay any more.'

When she was in bed, he continued to sit on the sofa and said, 'Here I shall sit till you call me to bed. I am prepared to wait till eternity.'

Kumu felt faint. What a trial to face! What was she to do? Her god did not give her an answer. The path she took to arrive up to this point turned out to be all wrong. She sat praying on her bed, 'Lord, You can't fool me, I shall put my trust in You even now. It is You who took Dhruba to the dark forest so that You could reveal yourself to that boy.'

There was not a sound in the silent room. The drunken man's voice was no longer to be heard. Only the neighbour's captive dog, though tired out, was still moaning from time to time.

Even a small span of time appeared to be too long. Was this to be the picture of their conjugal life for eternity—the two of them sitting silently at two ends in an endless night, an unbridgeable silence between them? At long last she summoned up the courage to leave the bed and say, 'Please don't make me the guilty one.'

Madhusudan said gravely, 'Tell me what you want. What must I do now?' He wanted to wring out the last word of consent from her.

Kumu said, 'Come to bed.'

Could it be called a victory for him?

## 38

The next morning when Motir-ma came to the room with a glass of milk for Kumu, she found her eyes red and swollen, her face ashen. She had expected to find Kumu in her usual corner seated at her prayer, facing the rising sun. But she was not there. She was on the floor, leaning against the wall of a shaded spot next to the staircase. Maybe she was sulking against her deity, in much the same way as an innocent child bears the chastisement of his father without protest, out of a deep hurt. Was the call which she expected to be divine going to end in this debasement? In this unfaithfulness of the soul? Has my lord lured me as a prey to his desire for female sacrifice? Did he want his offering to be a mindless lump of flesh? Today she did not feel any devotion.

Till now she had prayed to Him to be tolerant of her, today her rebel mind questioned herself, 'How could I bear with You any longer? With what shame can I come to worship You? Instead of accepting my devotion for You, You sold it in the slave market where women are sold at the same price as animal flesh, where no god waits patiently for a flower offering but feeds it to the goats?'

When Motir-ma asked her to drink up the milk, she simply said, 'Not now.' Motir-ma said, 'But it is no fault of this poor glass of milk.'

Kumu said, 'I haven't had my bath or said my prayers yet.'

'You go and have your bath. I shall wait for you.'

Kumu completed her bath and returned. Motir-ma thought she would now go and sit in her usual corner. She did take a step towards the terrace, out of habit, but came back and sat on the floor again. Her mind was too distracted with doubts, hurt and confusion.

'Is there no letter from Dada?' she asked Motir-ma.

Motir-ma had already thought of Kumu's anxiety to hear from her brother, so she had herself slipped into the office room early in the morning, only to find the drawer locked. The way to rob the robber was closed.

Then Shyama appeared on the scene and said to Kumu, 'Bou, why are you looking so pale? Are you unwell?'

'No, I am not,' answered Kumu.

'Poor thing, you must be fretting for home, that's but natural. But then you will see your brother. He is coming here soon.'

Kumu was startled at the news and looked eagerly at her face.

Motir-ma asked Shyama, 'Where did you gather this bit of news?'

'Look at that! It is but common knowledge. Our kitchen maid Parbati said that he had sent the estate manager to the Rajabahadur, to inquire about his sister and the manager had given the news that he would be coming soon to Kolkata for his treatment.'

'Has his health taken a turn for the worse?' Kumu asked anxiously.

'I don't know, but we would have heard if it were anything serious.'

Shyama knew then that Madhusudan had not told Kumu the news about her brother, lest the bride, whose heart he could not win, got distracted and turned homewards. She teased Kumu further by adding, 'Everyone says there is no one like your Dada. Come Mejobou, let's go down and set out the provisions. If the cooking starts late for the officegoers, there will be hell let loose.'

Motir-ma came to Kumu's room again with the glass of milk and said, 'Please Didi, it is getting cold.' This time Kumu did not protest.

Motir-ma whispered, 'Will you come to the store room with us?'

'Not today,' Kumu said. 'You better send your boy Gopal to me.'

A cruel, dark, senile lust from outside had devoured her, like the legendary monster Rahu eclipsing the moon. This was no calm, comforting dignity of the mature, but unbridled lecherousness where love was akin to craving for material wealth. Its clammy touch was what Kumu found revolting. She did not mind her husband's age but was pained that his age had no dignity left. To give oneself wholly was more like the ripening of a fruit in free air and light, but one could not ripen a raw fruit by crushing it. That this precious time was denied was what she found so hurting and insulting. Where could she possibly escape? Her asking Motir-ma for Gopal was one way of escape from the debasement of age into the innocence of childhood—from the polluted air to the clean breeze of a flower garden.

A somewhat frightened Habloo, wearing a printed cotton quilted jacket, came and stood at the doorway. He had the same large dark eyes as his mother and the same soothing complexion of a rain cloud. His cheeks were round and full and his hair was close cropped.

Kumu got up and pulled him to her breast and said, 'Naughty boy. Why didn't you see me all these days?' The boy put his arms round her neck and whispered, 'Aunty, can you guess what I've got for you?'

She kissed his cheeks and said, 'Must be a jewel.'

'It is in my pocket.'

'Then take it out.'

'So you couldn't guess!'

'You see, I am a fool. I don't even understand what I see, and what I don't see I misunderstand.'

Then Habloo slowly took out a brown paper packet, put it in her lap and was about to run away. Kumu held him back.

Habloo clutched the packet and said, 'Then don't look at it now.'

'Don't worry. I won't, till you go.'

'Well Aunty, have you seen Jatai Burri, the witch?'

'Maybe I have, but it takes time to recognize them.'

'She comes in the evening riding on the back of a bat, to the coal cellar by the side of the veranda downstairs.'

'On the back of a bat?'

'Oh, she can make herself so small that you can hardly see her!'

'Must learn that magic formula from her.'

'Why you?'

'Because if I escape to the coal cellar, as I am, I could still be found.'

Habloo did not quite get it. He went on, 'She has hidden her little box of sindur amongst the coal. Do you know where she got her sindur from?'

'Perhaps I do.'

'Tell me.'

'From the cloud at dawn.'

Habloo was perplexed. He began to think. His special reporter had told him about the land of giants across the seas; but what his Aunty had just said was more likely to be true. So he did not contradict her, but went on to say, 'Any girl who finds it will be a queen—a Rajrani.'

'How awful! Has any luckless girl found it?'

'Shejopishi's daughter Khudi knows. Every morning she accompanies Chhonnu when he goes with his basket to take out the coal. She is not one bit afraid.'

'She is still a child. That is why she is not afraid of being a Raja's wife.'

A cold wind was blowing from the north, so she went into the room, taking Habloo with her, and sat down on the sofa and heaved him up on her lap. On the teapoy next to them there were some season flowers on a silver platter—marigold, balsam, kunda and hibiscus—gathered daily by the gardener. These were waiting to be offered to the god by Kumu as she did every morning, facing the sunrise on the terrace.

Now she held up these flowers, unoffered to the god, in front of Habloo and asked him, 'Will you take some flowers?'

'Yes I will.'

'What will you do with them?'

'Play at puja.'

She took out the kerchief tucked in her sari and tied up the flowers, kissed him and said, 'Here, take them.' She thought to herself, 'I also had my game of worship.' She asked him, 'Which of these do you like best?'

'The hibiscus.'

'Why?'

'You tell me.'

'Because it stole the vermillion before the sun rose.'

Habloo was thoughtful for a while and said, 'Aunty, the colour of this flower is just like the red border on your sari.' In those few words he poured out his little heart.

Suddenly they saw Madhusudan coming. They had not heard his footsteps. His coming inside the house at this hour was quite unprecedented. This was the time when all the remaining bits of the day's work appeared in the office room outside—the agents, the supplicants and his secretary with all tidbits of gossip and some papers. The load of these extra jobs was no less heavy than the main work and Madhusudan was usually engrossed in these affairs at this time.

## 39

That morning Madhusudan had gone out to work with the chafed feelings of a beggar who could gather no grains but only the chaff in his bowl. But the attraction of unfulfilled desire is always as great. It is the obstacle which draws one back to it. The very sight of him made Habloo turn pale. His little heart started pounding and he tried to run away. But Kumu held him tight.

Madhusudan noticed this and scolded Habloo, 'What are you doing here? You should be studying at this hour!'

Habloo did not have the courage to tell his uncle that the tutor had not yet come. He took it silently, got up and walked away, hanging his head down.

Kumu moved to stop him but did not. She only said, 'You've left your flowers behind. Won't you take them with you?'

Madhusudan snatched the bundle and asked, 'Whose kerchief is this?'

Kumu went red in the face and said, 'It is mine.'

It was indeed wholly hers, that is, it belonged to her before her marriage, even the silken border was her own embroidery.

Madhusudan threw out the flowers bundled up in the handkerchief and put the latter in his pocket, and said, 'I am keeping it. What will that youngster do with it? Boy, you may go.'

This act of crudity on his part left Kumu speechless. Habloo left with a pained expression.

Watching the expression on her face Madhusudan remonstrated, 'You are generous with the whole world. Am I the only one to be deprived? This kerchief will be with me, as a reminder that I have something of you at least.'

There was something inherent in his nature which stood in the way of his ever getting what he really wanted. And that was what prevented Kumu from surrendering wholly to him.

She lowered her eyes and continued to sit on the sofa. The red border of her sari flowed down, framing her face on the way, parallel with her mass of wet hair hanging loose. A thin chain of gold encircled her delicate neck. This belonged to her mother and ever since her mother's death Kumu had always worn it. She had not dressed yet and had only a chemise on. Her hands were lying still, open on her lap. The two exceedingly fair and delicate hands carried the message of her whole body. Madhusudan looked at his wife who was slightly upset, from the corner of his eyes and could not turn his gaze away. He sat next to her on the sofa and tried to take her hand in his but felt something hard. Kumu did not want him to hold her hand, because it was holding on to a packet.

Madhusudan asked, 'What is in that packet?'

'I don't know.'

'What do you mean, you don't know?'

'I mean, I don't know.'

He didn't believe her words. He said, 'Give it to me. Let me see it.'

'That is my secret. I can't show it to you.'

As soon as the words were uttered, blood rushed into his head stinging him like a sharp arrow.

'How dare you!' he thundered and wrenched the brown paper packet out of her hand and opened it, only to find a few candied sugar balls. This must have been Habloo's favourite snack which his mother must have packed into his tiffin box for school. So he had carefully packed some of the balls and brought it for Kumu.

Madhusudan was wonderstruck. What a fuss. He then concluded that perhaps she was used to such cheap snacks in her own home and so she sent for these but felt ashamed to show them to him. He laughed to himself, 'After all it takes time to accept the gift of riches.' A plan came to his mind in a flash. He got up quickly and went out.

Kumu put the candies by in a small square box of sandalwood and sat down to write a letter to her brother. She had barely penned a few lines when Madhusudan came back. She quickly covered the letter and sat up stiff. He was carrying a fruit basket whose handle was inlaid with gold and silver work, and which was covered by a scented silk kerchief. He put it on the desk in front of her with a broad smile on his face. And said, 'Do open and take a look.'

She lifted the kerchief. The ornate basket was filled to the brim with the same type of sugar candies. She would have burst into laughter if she were alone. But she managed to maintain a grave expression. It would have been far better for him if she had actually laughed out.

He said, 'There is no need to have them in secret. Nothing to be ashamed of. If you like, I can have them sent for you every day.'

Kumu said, 'But you can't.'

'Can't I? You surprise me.'

'No, you simply can't.'

'Why. Are they so expensive?'

'Yes, money can't buy them.'

A doubt shot through his mind. 'I see. Maybe your brother has parcelled them for you!'

She did not feel like responding to this jibe. She pushed the fruit case aside and got up to go. Madhusudan pushed her back to the seat.

Before he could speak, she asked him, 'Did somebody come from Dada to you enquiring about me?'

He was annoyed that she should have heard about it already. But he said, 'That is precisely why I have come to you in the morning, to give you the news.' Needless to say it was a total lie.

'When is he coming?'

'Within the week.'

He knew for certain that Bipradas was arriving the next day, but he said 'the week' to keep it vague.

'Has his illness taken a turn for the worse?'

'No, I didn't hear anything like that.'

Even this was a way of avoiding the obvious truth that Bipradas was coming to Kolkata for treatment, therefore he must not be in good health.

'Is there a letter from him?'

'I haven't opened the mail box yet. If there is one for you I shall send it.'

Kumu had not yet learnt to disbelieve him, so she accepted this as well. He added, 'If there is one, I shall bring it myself after lunch.'

Kumu curbed her impatience and fell silent. As he was trying to pull her towards him, Shyama suddenly burst on to the scene and said, 'Oh, I am sorry, it is you, brother!' She tried to run away quickly.

Madhusudan said, 'What is it that you came for?'

'I just came to call her to join us at the store room. She may be a Raja's queen, but she has also a home to preside over, like Goddess Lakshmi.' Madhusudan got up and left without a word.

After lunch he lay down as usual, chewing a paan, and sent for Kumu. She came immediately, she knew there would be a letter for her. She came in and stood near the bed.

Madhusudan put down the pipe of his hookah and asked her to sit down. She obeyed him. The letter that Madhusudan gave her had only these few words, formally addressed to her,

> My dearest sister,
>
> I shall soon be going to Kolkata for treatment. As soon as I am well I shall come and see you. I shall be relieved if you let me have news of your welfare, whenever you may find time in the midst of your household duties.

The short letter hurt her at first. She thought, 'So I am now an outsider,' but soon she repented, 'What a small mind I have. He must be unwell.'

Madhusudan could see that she was dying to get up and go. He said, 'Where are you going? Do sit here for a while.'

Having stalled her departure, he was at a loss for conversation. But the ice had to be broken. So the question that was going round his head since the morning spilled out. He said, 'Why did you make such a fuss about those sugar candies? What was there to be shy about?'

'That's my secret.'

'Secret? Even from me?'

'Yes, I can't tell you.'

Madhusudan stiffened, 'This is your Noornagar style! Learnt at your brother's school, I suppose!'

Kumu did not answer back. Madhusudan threw aside his pillow, sat up and said, 'I am not worth my name, if I cannot rid you of that manner of yours.'

'What do you wish me to do?'

'Tell me who gave you that packet?'

'Habloo.'

'Habloo? Then why all this secrecy?'

'I don't know why.'

'Was he carrying it for somebody else?'

'No.'

'Then?'

'That's all. I have nothing more to say.'

'Why this hide and seek?'

'You won't understand.'

He shook her by the hand and said, 'This is too much for me to stand! You are going too far.'

She was red in the face, but still she said calmly, 'I admit I am not used to your ways. You have to tell me what is it that you want me to do.'

The veins on his temple swelled with anger. He could not find an answer. He felt like hitting her. Somebody outside was heard clearing his throat and saying, 'The gentlemen from the office are waiting in the office room.'

Madhusudan remembered it was the day of the meeting of the Board of Directors. He felt ashamed, not to have prepared for it. The whole morning was wasted. He was astonished at this unthinkable lapse from his routine and against his nature.

# 40

As soon as her husband left, Kumu got off the bed and sat on the floor. Was her whole life to be spent like this—trying to swim across an endless ocean? Madhusudan was right. Their ways were totally different. This discord was the worst to bear. Was there a way out?

Suddenly she remembered something and started going down the stairs, to Motir-ma's room. On the stairs, she met Shyamasundari coming up.

'Where are you going? I was coming to you, Bou.'

'Is there something you'd like to tell me?'

'Nothing so important. I saw my brother-in-law in a temper. So I thought I should find out from you what the new hitch in his love affair was. Remember it is we alone who can give you the best advice on how to get along with him. So you are going to Motir-ma. Go, get it off your chest.'

Today it struck her that Madhusudan and Shyamasundari were both cast in the same mould, fashioned by the same potter. It is difficult to say how such a thought came to cross her mind. Not that she arrived at it after any analysis of their characters, nor did they look alike, but there was some resonance in their manners; they breathed the same air in their two worlds. When Shyama approached to make friends with her, Kumu was repelled with the same loathing that she felt for Madhusudan.

Kumu entered their bedroom to find Nabin and his wife both trying to snatch a book. She was about to turn back, when Nabin said, 'Please don't go Boudi, we were about to go to you, with a complaint.'

'What complaint?'

'If you sit down I will tell you our sad story.' So she sat down on the cot. Nabin said, 'This is the height of torture! This lady has hidden my book!'

'Why such a punishment for you?'

'Plain envy! Because she herself cannot read English. I am all for female education but she is against the education of husbands as a class. She resents the growing gulf between my intelligence which is maturing, and her own. I tried my best to argue with her, by quoting the example of our great epic heroine Sita, who chose always to follow her husband. I plead with her not to block my way, even if I happen to leave her behind in the matter of learning and intelligence.'

'Only Saraswati, the goddess of learning, can gauge your learning—but don't boast about your intelligence in front of me,' rejoined Motir-ma.

Kumu burst into a giggle watching Nabin make a face pretending to be in dire distress. This was the first time, in this house, that she laughed like this with an open heart. Her laughter sounded particularly sweet to

Nabin. He said to himself, 'From now on this is my mission. I must make our Bourani laugh.'

Still smiling, Kumu asked Motir-ma, 'Dear sister, why have you hidden his book?'

'Look Didi, do we have to have his tutor waiting for him in our bedroom? After a hard day's work I come in to find a lamp burning and the great pundit at his lessons. The food gets cold but he pays no attention whatsoever.'

'Is that right?' Kumu asked Nabin.

'Bourani, I am not such a saint as not to love food; but what I love better is her sweet urging. That is why I deliberately delay, study is just a pretence on my part.'

'I can't win the battle of words with him,' said his wife.

'And I admit defeat when she stops talking to me,' said Nabin.

'Does that happen too?' Kumu asked.

'May I then give one or two recent instances? They are etched on my mind with indelible tears.'

'That's enough. You don't have to quote any instance. Now you better give me back my keys. See, he has hidden them,' complained the wife.

'I can't go to the police against my own people, so the thief has to be punished by robbing her. First, you give me my book,' said Nabin.

'I won't give it back to you. I shall give it to Didi.' There was a basket of odds and ends of wool and silk pieces, in one corner of the room. Motir-ma picked from the bottom of this basket the second volume of a concise encyclopaedia in English, and put it on Kumu's lap and said, 'Take it to your room. Don't give it to him. Let me see how he fights with you.'

Nabin took out the bunch of keys from the top of the mosquito curtain and gave it to Kumu with instructions not to part with it and added, 'I too want to see how the person in question behaves with you.'

Kumu turned the pages of the book and asked, 'Is this the kind of book he is fond of?'

'There is no book he does not like. The other day I found him engrossed in a book on rearing of cows.'

'That was not meant for tending to my own health, so there is nothing for me to be ashamed about.'

'Didi, do you have something to say to me? Just say so and I shall order this garrulous fellow out of this room.'

'No, there is no need for that. My Dada is coming in a day or two.'

Nabin said, 'Yes, he is coming tomorrow.'

'Tomorrow?' Kumu was surprised at the news. She sat quiet for a while, let out a deep sigh and asked, 'How do I meet him?'

Motir-ma asked, 'Haven't you asked your husband?'

Kumu shook her head.

'Won't you ask him once?'

Kumu remained silent. It was very hard to talk to Madhusudan about her brother. Her husband seemed to be always charged and ready to insult her brother. She had great hesitation to cause the slightest provocation.

Nabin was pained to see the expression on her face. He said, 'Don't worry, Boudi. We shall take care of it. You don't have to say anything.'

From his childhood Nabin was frightened of his big brother, but the advent of his Boudi seemed to have cured him of it.

After Kumu left, Motir-ma asked Nabin, 'Have you thought of any way? The other night when your brother called us to his bedroom and humiliated himself before his wife, in front of us, I knew things would be difficult from then on. In fact, now he turns his face away whenever he runs into you.'

'He has realized that he has lost. Out of a sheer whim, he had emptied his purse and paid in advance for something he has not got yet. Now he can't stand us because we were witnesses to his stupid deal.'

Motir-ma said, 'That may be so, but this rage against Bipradas Babu is like an obsession with him. It is increasing day by day. What a nasty affair!'

Nabin said, 'That is one way of expressing his admiration for Kumu's brother. This type of person flays in public the very person they know in their heart of hearts to be superior to them. Some say that the demon-king Ravana had immense respect for Rama, and that is why he offered him salutation with his ten pairs of hands. I can tell you, it won't be easy at all for Bourani to meet her brother.'

'That won't do. You have to find a way out.'

'Well. I have just thought of one.'

'Please tell me.'

'No, I can't.'

'Why?'

'I feel shy.'

'Even with me?'

'Specially, with you.'

'Let me hear the reason at least.'

'It involves cheating my brother. You better not hear about it.'

'I have not the slightest qualm about cheating for someone I love.'

'Oh, so you have practiced it on me?'

'Where else can I get such an easy victim?' she taunted.

'Right, my ladyship, I give a blank charter to cheat me whenever you wish to.'

'Why do you sound so happy about it?'

'Shall I be frank? God has endowed you women with many ways of deception. But He has topped them all with a touch of honey; and it is this honeyed deception that we call maya—the great illusion.'

'Then the best thing is to avoid it.'

'Good heavens! What will we be left with in this world without illusion? Let the goddesses continue to deceive the fools, cloud their visions, besot their minds and do what they like with them.'

The conversation that followed was utterly useless and has nothing to do whatever with our story.

## 41

For the first time Madhusudan did not get his way at the board meeting. Till now none of his proposals or arrangements had ever been questioned. His immense self-confidence matched the confidence his colleagues had in him. Relying on this he always did his homework in advance before putting forth any proposal to the Board for approval. This time, in furtherance of his indigo business, he was trying to buy the lease for one property, from an old indigo factory owner. Some expenses were also incurred. Everything was ready, only for the stamps to be affixed on the sale—the deed had to be procured and the final payment had to be made. The prospective employees had been promised their jobs. And now this hurdle had come up.

Recently, lobbying was on for a relation's son-in-law, for the post of a treasurer which had fallen vacant in that factory. Madhusudan, who never came to the rescue of the incompetent, paid no heed to all this. This matter which was buried underground had suddenly germinated and sprouted as opposition against him.

There was a loop-hole too. The owner of the property was the nephew-in-law of a distant aunt of Madhusudan's. When she came importuning for the sale, to him, he calculated and found the deal attractive, the price was reasonable and the profit margin was good. There was also the additional reputation of being seen as a great patron of the family. And now the person whose unworthy son-in-law was being deprived of the job was busy exposing Madhusudan's nepotism and carrying tales to the right quarters. He had also taken upon himself to start a whispering campaign about Madhusudan taking a secret cut on all transactions of his company.

Most people do not demand any proof for such false accusations, because the strongest evidence in support of such a possibility is their own innermost greed. It was easy to poison the minds of the people because of Madhusudan's burgeoning prosperity and his insufferable reputation for integrity of character. These greedy people were greatly relieved to learn that even Madhusudan had his secret weaknesses; they were only too eager to do likewise, only they lacked the opportunity.

Madhusudan had given his word to the owner, and he was not the type to go back on his word just because there was a risk of losing money. So he decided to buy the property himself and was determined to prove to the company what a bargain they had missed.

It was late when he came back home. Madhusudan had blind faith in his own good luck, but today he feared that perhaps destiny was pushing the train of his life from one track to another. This first jolt at the Board Meeting gave him a shock. He leaned back in an easy chair in his office room and began to coil his own black thoughts with the dark smoke swirling out of his hookah.

Nabin came in to announce that someone had come from Bipradas for an audience with him. Madhusudan barked, 'Tell him to go. I have no time for him now.'

Nabin could guess from his brother's mood that something had gone awry at the Board Meeting today, and that his mind was weak and distracted at the moment.

Weakness by nature is ungenerous and the self-pride of the weak assumes the mask of merciless cruelty. Nabin had not the slightest doubt that his brother's wounded pride would want to hit Kumu hard. But Nabin was determined to shield her from this blow. The little hesitation he had so far disappeared completely. After a little while he came back to find his brother going through the address book. As soon as he came in Madhusudan asked him rudely, 'What now? Have you come as the advocate of your Bipradas Babu?'

'No, Dada, you need have no fears on that count. Their man got such a rebuke that he will never enter this house, even if you personally send for him.'

Madhusudan could not stand this yet-to-be-faced effrontery either. He said, 'If I move my little finger he will come and fall at my feet. What did he come for?'

'Just to tell you that Bipradas Babu has postponed his trip to Calcutta by a couple of days. He will come as soon as he feels a little better.'

'All right. I am in no hurry either.'

'I want a couple of hours' leave tomorrow.'

'Why?'

'You will be angry if I tell you.'

'I will be angrier if you do not tell me,' said Madhusudan in his typical fashion.

'An astrologer from Kumbhakonam is here. I want my fortune told.'

Madhusudan's heart missed a beat. He felt like running to the astrologer that very instant. But pretending to be supremely unconcerned, he scolded Nabin, 'Do you really believe in all this?'

'Not normally, but whenever I am scared I do.'

'What are you scared about?'

Nabin did not answer. He started scratching his head.

'Tell me who is it that you are scared of?'

'I am not afraid of anyone in this world except you Dada, and I am ill at ease watching you these last few days.'

It always gave Madhusudan great pleasure to know that the rest of the world was in mortal fear of him. He kept looking at Nabin and puffed at his hookah gravely, in silence, savouring his own importance.

Nabin said, 'So I want to know clearly what my stars wish to do with me and when will they let me off.'

Madhusudan said, 'An atheist like you, who does not believe in anything, has at last . . .'

'If I believed in God, I would not trust my stars; those who do not listen to a doctor readily accept the quack,' replied Nabin.

The more Madhusudan was getting interested in probing his own fortune, the more he tried to assume a caustic tone. He said, 'Is this what all your education has taught you, you monkey? You believe whatever anyone tells you!'

'The man has a copy of the *Bhrigu Samhita* which chronicles the horoscopes of everyone born at any time in the past and will be reborn in future, all written in Sanskrit. You can't question that surely. You can test it for yourself.'

'God has taken care to create enough number of fools to feed those who live by fooling them.'

'And he also creates clever people like you to save those fools. He is not only kind to the victors but is equally so to the victims. Why not try your sharp intelligence against the *Bhrigu Samhita* for once?'

'All right, take me there tomorrow morning, let me check up on your Kumbhakonam trickster.'

'But Dada, your disbelief is so strong that it may upset all his calculations. It is the general experience that trust begets trust. It must be the same with the stars. See the example of the foreigners, they don't believe in stars, so the stars have no influence on their lives. I remember a particularly inauspicious conjunction of stars, when your English assistant won at the races. If it were me then, far from winning, the horse would have come and kicked me in my belly! Dada, please do not pitch your logic against that of the stars. Have a modicum of faith when you go there.'

Madhusudan went back to his hookah with a contented smile.

Next morning at seven, the two of them arrived at Venkat Shashtri's house after negotiating the garbage in a narrow lane. It was a dark, dank room on the ground floor; the walls scarred with falling plaster looked like they were afflicted with some terrible skin disease. On the cot was spread an old dirty, torn cotton carpet and at one end some palm-leaf manuscripts lay scattered. A hand-painted picture of Shiva and Parvati hung on one wall. Nabin called aloud, 'Shastrijee!' A dark, short, thin man wrapped in a light cotton shawl entered. The front of his head was shaven, leaving a mop of hair at the back.

Nabin bowed to him with great reverence. The man's appearance did not inspire an iota of respect in Madhusudan, but fearing that a fortune-teller might have some closeness with Destiny, he finished his half-hearted greeting. The Shastri ignored Madhusudan's horoscope which Nabin placed before him but asked to see his palm instead. He took out a pen and ink from a wooden box and drew up some chart. Then he looked at Madhusudan's face and said, '*Pancham Varga*—the fifth group.' Madhusudan could not follow him. So the astrologer recited the Bengali consonant groups, counting on his fingers, 'Ka, cha, ta, twa, pa.' Even then it remained obscure to Madhusudan. The astrologer went on '*Pancham Varna*—the fifth letter!' Madhusudan waited patiently. The man reeled off, 'Pa, pha, ba, bha, ma.' All that Madhusudan concluded from this was that Bhrigumuni must have started the first chapter of his book with grammar. Then Venkat Shastri spoke, '*Panchaksharam*—five letters.'

Nabin suddenly woke up. He whispered into his brother's ears, 'I've got it, Dada.'

'What did you follow?'

'The fifth letter of the fifth group of consonants is "pa" and the fifth letter of that group is "ma" and then your name "Ma-dhu-su-da-n" is spelt with five letters. By a strange grace of your birth stars, there is a remarkable convergence of three fives!'

Madhusudan was stunned. Thousands of years before his parents named him, it was registered in Bhrigumuni's log book What a stellar event! Then he listened dumbfounded to a summary of his own life, written in Sanskrit. The less he understood of the language, the more respectful he became towards Shastri and Bhrigumuni. Life was an embodiment of the words of the sages. He put his hand over his heart and felt that his whole body was like a manuscript compiled in some forest sanctum, with the help of suffixes, case-endings, inflexions and so on. The last words of the astrologer were to the effect that his immense wealth was in preparation of Lakshmi, the goddess of wealth taking up abode in his house. Recently, she had arrived with the new bride. But he had to take extreme care that she was hurt in no way, because if that happened his fortune may be reversed.

Venkat Shastri added, 'Such signs are already appearing. If the person born under these stars does not take heed even now, the danger may become imminent.' Madhusudan was astounded. He remembered the news of his great profit on the day of his wedding, and now this defeat at the Board Meeting! Lakhmi's advent was welcome, but the onus was awesome.

On the way back Madhusudan just sat silent in the carriage. Nabin broke the silence with, 'I don't believe a word of what Venkat Shastri said. He must have heard all about you from someone else.'

'So you consider yourself very clever! Is it so easy to collect information about everyone everywhere?'

'At least it is easier than casting horoscopes of billions of people much before they are born. Where could Bhrigumuni get so much paper and where would Venkat Shastri find the room to keep them?'

'The sages knew how to say a thousand words with one stroke of their pen.'

'Absurd.'

'Whatever is beyond your comprehension becomes absurd? Let your Science be. Stop this debate and go and get hold of the man who came from Bipradas Babu. Don't delay, go today.'

Nabin felt uneasy having deceived his brother. It was such a simple ruse, its success so ridiculous with one like his brother, that Nabin himself felt ashamed and sad at his humiliation. On many occasions he had tricked his brother when in a fix, but he had never felt bad about them. But this time he felt somewhat unclean at so elaborately setting up such a big hoax.

## 42

Madhusudan felt as if a heavy weight had just fallen off his chest—the weight of self-pride, the stony self-esteem which had always suppressed his growing attachment to his wife. A struggle had been going on in his mind against his infatuation with Kumu. The more he found no way but to surrender to her, the more he was angry with her. Now that the stars had clarified that Lakshmi had come to his home in the form of his bride, and that she had to be appeased, all strife was at an end. The thought thrilled him no end. He went on reciting to himself, 'My Lakshmi, my priceless gift of good fortune!' He felt like running to her right away and begging her forgiveness. But there was no time today. He had to rush to work now to mend the breaches in his business affairs. He could not afford to go home even for lunch.

Meanwhile, Kumu's mind was in a turmoil. She was told that her brother was to come the next day and that he was unwell. She was anxious to know for sure, if she would be able to see him. Nabin had gone out on some errand and not come back yet. For some unknown reason, Nabin was certain that Madhusudan would himself come and try to please her in every way, and though she felt that Nabin was expecting too much of his brother, she did not want to deprive him of that pleasure.

It was not possible to sit on the terrace today. It had got cloudy since last night and today since noon, it had started drizzling. Winter rain was like an unwelcome guest. The clouds lost colour, the rain its sound, the wet air was depressing and the earth seemed to shrink away from the poor sunless sky. So Kumu sat on the little shaded place at the top of the stairs leading from her bedroom. Occasionally a spray of rain would come inside. On this dim, monotonous, wet day she felt that her whole life was being swallowed by a python and within the confines of its gullet there was no opening whatsoever. The resentment against her personal god, who had lured her into this helpless morass of hopelessness, flared into a flaming rage today. She sprang into action, took out from her desk the framed picture of Radha and Krishna, wrapped in a piece of printed silk cloth. She wanted to destroy it as a loud protest declaring her loss of faith in Him. Her trembling hands could not open the knots of the wrapper. The more she struggled with these, the tighter they became. In her impatience she tore the string open with her teeth. At the familiar sight of the divine couple she could no longer hold herself back; she pressed them to her bosom. The more the wooden frame hurt her the harder she pressed it close to herself.

Murali, the bearer, entered to make the bed. He was shivering in the cold, wrapped in a dirty old shawl, bald, veins sticking out, sunken cheeks with a salt-and-pepper stubble of many days. He had just recovered from a bout of malaria and was anaemic. The doctor had asked him to give up his job, go back and rest in his village home, but fate was cruel.

'Are you feeling cold, Murali?' asked Kumu.

'Yes ma'am, the rains have made it chilly.'

'Have you no warm clothes?'

'On the day of his investiture the Maharaj gave me a shawl, but on the doctor's advice I gave it to my grandson when he was suffering from cough and cold.'

Kumu took out from the cupboard next to her, a grey shawl, and said, 'Take this shawl of mine.'

Murali bowed low and said, 'Please excuse me. The Maharaj will be very angry.'

Kumu recalled that the path of kindness was very narrow in this house. But she also had to win her lord's reprieve by earning merit with such good deeds. She threw the shawl down on the floor in indignation.

Murali said with folded hands, 'Please Ranima, our own Lakshmi, do not be angry with me. I do not need warm clothes. I stay in the tobacco room with those who tend to the hookahs. They always have those burning pieces of coal in bowls and that keeps me quite warm.'

Kumu said, 'Go and see if brother Nabin is back, and ask him to see me.'

As soon as Nabin came she said, 'You have to do me a favour. Please say yes.'

Nabin said, 'Sure I will, even if it harms me, but never, if it hurts you.'

'What more harm can come to me? I have ceased to care.' She took out her thick golden bangles, gave it to him and said, 'You sell this and arrange a religious service for my brother's recovery from illness.'

'That won't be necessary, Bourani. Your devotion to him is a perpetual service in his favour.'

'Brother, there is nothing else that I can do for my Dada except to offer the gods my service on his behalf.'

'You don't have to do anything. Aren't we there to serve also?'

'What can you do? Tell me.'

'We are sinners; we can sin for him.'

'Do not joke about such matters, please.'

'Not at all. You will agree that it is much more difficult to sin than to do a good deed and when the gods realize it they duly reward the one who does it.'

Normally, she would have been hurt at the disrespect for divinity implied in Nabin's words, but she had to be indulgent towards such lack of reverence as she remembered her brother's equal disbelief in gods. Her tolerance of this offence was rather like the mother's amused and affectionate indulgence to a child's mischief-making.

She said, with a faint smile, 'You men can do as you like on your own right, but we have no way to act on our own. How can we do something for those whom we love but cannot approach? My days seem endless. I see no way out. Is there no one to take pity on me?'

Nabin's eyes were beginning to fill with tears.

She continued, 'I have got to make a token offering on behalf of my brother. This bangle is my mother's. I shall offer it to the gods as from my mother.'

'One does not have to offer anything to a god in person, He takes it on his own. Wait for a couple of days and see if He is pleased with you. If not, I shall certainly do whatever you order me to do. Even take an offering to the god who does not show you any mercy.'

It was getting dark, and familiar steps could be heard on the stairs. Nabin got a start, his brother was coming. He did not run away, but stayed on courageously to face his brother. Kumu's mind, on the other hand, shrank immediately. She was frightened at the severity of the shock to all her nerves from this unseen conflict. Why had this evil got her in its grips?

All of a sudden she asked Nabin, 'Do you know of anyone who can counsel me as a guru?'

'Why, Bourani?'

'I can't cope with my own mind any more.'

'That's not a fault of your mind.'

'I have often heard my brother say that the danger is always from outside but the evil is within your mind.'

'Do not worry, your brother will guide you.'

'Will that day ever come?'

As soon as an understanding was reached in Madhusudan's mind between his worldly wisdom and his feelings of love, the latter began to suffuse all his activity. Kumu's beautiful face was his own fortune.

That it was already turning in his favour was proved today when many of the colleagues who opposed him yesterday wrote to him today changing their tone. The moment Madhusudan had proposed buying the property himself, they thought they were missing a bargain. Some of them even suggested reconsidering the entire proposal.

Also, the peon in the office who had been docked half his month's wages for absence without notice, came and fell at his feet today. Madhusudan at once pardoned him; which meant, of course, that he would compensate the peon from his own pocket. The punishment would however, remain on the books. With him, rules were rules.

It was a day of wonders for Madhusudan. The sky outside was overcast and it was also drizzling a little but this only helped enhance the joy he felt inside. Usually after he returned from work he spent his time in the office room till dinner was announced. Since the day he got married he did break this rule and come inside the house at odd times, but he did that surreptitiously. Today his loud footsteps boldly announced to the whole world that he was indeed going to meet his wife. He had realized today that his extraordinary good fortune could be the envy of the world.

The rain stopped for a while. Some rooms in the house were lit up, others were still in the dark. An ancient woman, with an incense burner, was going round each room, a bat was circling round and round from the sky above the courtyard into the lamp-lit corridors. The maids sitting on the veranda were rolling wicks on their bare thighs. They scampered at the approach of Madhusudan. At the sound of his footsteps

Shyamasundari came out with a box of paan. She always used to send this paan to him when he came back from work. Everyone knew that only Shyama could make the paan to his taste. There was the hint of something more to this common knowledge. It is this extra bit which made her bold enough to hold the box open in front of him and say, 'Brother, your paan is here all ready, do take them with you.' If this were in the past, there would be a few exchanges of pleasantries, with a touch of flirtation. But today, something in his mind made him shun her touch and quickly disappear without the paan. Her large eyes flashed in a sulk but drops of tears soon flooded them. In her heart of hearts, she was in love with him.

As soon as Madhusudan entered the bedroom Nabin got up to go. He touched the feet of Kumu and said, 'I shall remember to look for the guru,' then he turned to his brother and added, 'Bourani wants to listen to the scriptures from a proper guru. We have our family priest but he . . .'

Madhusudan said excitedly, 'Scriptures! All right, I shall take care of it. You don't have to do anything.'

Nabin left.

All the way home Madhusudan had recited to himself how he was going to address Kumu, 'Borrobou, you have come and my whole house is lit up.' He was never used to such sentimental utterances. That is why he had decided to speak them out as soon as he entered the room, without dithering. But the sight of Nabin halted him. And then came the topic of scriptures, which totally silenced him. This little impediment baffled the elaborate preparation that was going on in his mind. Then he saw the fear in her eyes and a shrinking of her mind and body. On other days he would not have noticed these. But today the new light within himself made his vision acute. He was now more sensitive towards Kumu's feelings. Today her apathy seemed to him cruelly unfair. Still he was determined not to be upset. But what promised to be easy and natural was no longer possible.

After a spell of silence Madhusudan said, 'Borrobou, you want to get away? Can't you wait for a minute?'

She was surprised at his tone and voice. She said, 'No, why should I want to go?'

'I have brought something for you, please open it and look.' He put a small golden casket in her hand.

She opened it and saw her brother's gift—the sapphire ring inside. Her heart was in a tumult, she did not know what to do.

'Will you let me put this on your finger?'

She stretched out her hand. He took her hand in his lap and started to put it on very gently, deliberately taking a little longer time than necessary. The he lifted her hand to his lips, kissed it and said, 'It was my mistake to take it off your hand. No precious stone can be harmful in your hands.'

Kumu would have been less astonished had he hit her instead. Madhusudan liked the childlike wonder in her face. He had something more for her in reserve, and now he revealed it. 'Kalu Mukhujjey from your home is here. Do you want to meet him?'

Her face brightened. She exclaimed, 'Kaluda!'

'Let me send for him. While you two talk, I shall finish my dinner.'

Kumudini's eyes brimmed over with tears of gratitude.

## 43

Kalu's relationship with the house of the Chatterjees had lasted for generations. He was their most trusted man. One of his ancestors even went to jail for the Chatterjees. Kalu had come to Madhusudan's office to pay an instalment of the loan interest and take a receipt. He was short, fair, well-rounded, with bulging light eyes overhung with thick bushy eyebrows that were partly grey. His thick moustache was white but the thatch of hair on his head was still mostly black. He was wearing a carefully pleated Santipur dhoti and an old expensive jamawar appropriate to the prestige of his employer. The stone on his ring was not of inconsiderable value.

Kumu bowed as soon as Kalu came. They sat on the carpet. Kalu said, 'Little one, it was only the other day you left us, but it seems years ago.'

'First, you tell me how Dada is . . .'

'Yes, we had some anxious times with him. The day after you left it was critical. But he has an unusually strong constitution and he weathered it. The doctors were surprised.'

'Is he coming tomorrow?'

'That was the plan but it may be delayed by a couple of days. The full moon is due and everyone warned him of the danger of a relapse. How are *you* keeping?'

'I am fine.'

Kalu did not wish to comment, but he wondered nevertheless. Whatever had happened to her graceful beauty? Why were there dark rings under her eyes? Why had her fair skin lost its glow?

Kumu also wanted to ask a question which was bothering her. 'Hasn't he sent anything for me?' As if in answer to her unspoken question Kalu said, 'He has sent something for you with me.'

Kumu was eager to know. 'What is it? Where is it?'

'I have left it outside.'

'Why didn't you bring it in?'

'Don't be impatient Didi, Maharaj said he will bring it himself.'

'What is it, do tell me.'

'But he swore me to secrecy.' Kalu looked around, changed the topic and said, 'They have kept you in great comfort. When I go back and report to Boro Babu how happy he will be. The first two days he fretted for your news. Must have been something wrong with the post, then he got three of your letters all together.'

Kumu could easily guess where the post had gone wrong.

She wanted to ask him to stay to dinner, but did not have the courage to do so. She asked a little hesitatingly, 'Kaluda, you haven't had your dinner yet?'

'I've noticed that in Calcutta late meals do not agree with me. So I've started on Ramdas Kabiraj's makaradhwaja. But it does not seem to have made much difference,' Kalu anwered.

He had guessed that as a new bride Kumu was not yet fully in command of the household and so she must not be able to ask him for dinner directly and would only be sorry for herself.

Just then, Motir-ma signalled to her from behind the door and when Kumu went to her Motir-ma said, 'Please bring Mr Mukherjee, from your home, to the room downstairs and sit with him. His dinner is ready.'

Kumu came back and told him, 'Let your Kabiraj be. You have to come for your dinner right now.'

'What a fuss. It's torture! Not now, maybe some other time.'

'None of that! Just come with me.'

It was obvious that the Kabiraj's medicine had been very effective, for there was no lack of appetite on Kalu's part.

As soon as her Kaludada's dinner was over Kumu returned to her bedroom. His visit had left her mind full of memories of her childhood home. The mango tree in the backyard of her Noornagar home must have blossomed by now. How many quiet afternoons had she spent lying down with her head resting on her arm, in the courtyard near the pond, under the flowering jamrul tree. Those afternoons filled with the murmur of bees, brilliant with light and shade. She used to feel an unknown aching in her heart, which she failed to understand then. That ache coloured her dreams like the dust-laden evening glow in Brajabhumi—the land of Radha and Krishna. She was unaware then, that the yet unmet love of her youth had already spread His enchantment everywhere in the air. It was He who had been playing hide and seek with her when she worshipped the Radha-Krishna duo, it was He whom she had invited in the unseen recesses of her heart as she played Raag Multani on her esraj.

That old home of hers was full of intimations of the dream person of her first youth, that attic from where she could see the winding village road flanked by flaming fields of mustard, the small knoll near the wall of the backyard from the top of which you could make out pictures in green and black from some forgotten times sketched on the mossy wall. On waking up every morning, she could see from her bedroom window on the first floor the white sails against the red sky, receding into the distant horizon, just like her aimless desires. That mirage of her first youth had accompanied her to Kolkata, to find itself in her prayers, in her gardening. That is what had lured her blindly into the noose of marriage, with the pretence of an oracle. But it disappeared in the strong light of the day.

Meanwhile Madhusudan had crept up behind her and stared into her image on the mirror on the wall. He knew that the unknown and unseen realm where Kumu's mind was lost, was certainly out of his reach. Her unmindfulness would have infuriated him on any other day. But today he sat by her side with a quiet sadness, and said, 'What are you thinking of, Borrobou?'

Kumu was startled. She turned pale. Madhusudan caught her hand, shook it and said, 'Will you never give yourself up to me?'

She had no answer. It was a question she had been asking herself, 'What indeed is holding me back?' When he was rough with her the answer was simple, but when he was pliant then there was no one but herself to blame. Kumu had no doubt that it was a great sin not to surrender herself body and soul to her husband, but then why had she come to this pass? Women had only one goal in life, to become an ideal wife—a sati. She wanted to save herself from the great disgrace of losing sight of that goal. So today she told him in all earnestness, 'Please have pity on me!'

'Whatever for?'

'Make me your own, order me, punish me. I feel I am not worthy of you!'

Madhusudan was greatly amused. Kumu wanted to be a dutiful sati. If she were an ordinary housewife that would have been enough. But Kumu was much more to him than just a duly wedded wife. The more he was prepared to offer for that extra bit, the more he found himself short.

His own smallness was exposed to himself. He was getting more and more distressed at the unbridgeable inequality between himself and Kumu.

He heaved a sigh and said, 'If I give you something, what will you give me in return?'

Kumu guessed that what her husband would give her would be the item her Dada had sent her.

'I shall certainly demand the right price for the gift,' he continued, and delved under the bed and opened a packet wrapped in silk. It was her familiar ivory-worked esraj. She had left it at home when she came here.

'Are you happy? Now pay my price,' Madhusudan demanded.

She had no idea as to what he might be wanting.

'Play something for me,' he said.

It was not much to ask but very hard to give. She had realized this much that Madhusudan had no taste for music. It was difficult for her to get over the embarrassment of even thinking of playing for such a person. She started toying with the instrument. Madhusudan repeated, 'Go on, play, you needn't be shy with me.'

She said, 'The instrument is yet to be tuned.'

'Why don't you say frankly that your own mind is not in tune with mine?'

The truth of the statement stung her to the quick. She said, 'Let me tune it and I shall play for you another day.'

'When will that be? Tell me definitely. Tomorrow?'

'All right, tomorrow.'

'In the evening when I come back from work.'

'Sure.'

'You are very pleased with the esraj. Isn't that so?'

'Yes, I am very happy indeed.'

He took out a leather case from under his shawl and said, 'And this pearl necklace that I have bought for you? Will you be equally pleased with it?'

Why ask such an awkward question! She started playing with the bow.

'I get it. Request not granted.'

Kumu did not understand what he was trying to convey.

Madhusudan said, 'I was very keen to place this plea of mine close to your heart, but my case was dismissed long before it could even be heard.'

The jewel case remained open on the table in front of Kumu. Neither of them spoke a word. She sat in a daze as she often did these days. After a while she came to her senses, put the necklace round her neck and touched his feet. She asked, 'Do you want to hear me play?'

Madhusudan agreed readily.

'I will play just now,' she said, tuned the esraj and started with Raag Kedara. From Kedara she worked up to Raag Chhayanat, oblivious of the presence of anyone else. Then she started singing her favourite song,

*Tharri raho meri aankhana-key aagey.*

(Stay in front of my eyes, my love.)

That exquisite presence appeared in the firmament of her music, the very same one whom she had always felt in her heart, in her song. Only the craving to see Him with her own eyes remained unfulfilled forever, hence the eternal yearning in her song—*Tharri raho meri aankhahna-key aagey* . . .

Madhusudan had no understanding of music, but the tune playing on her ethereal countenance, the rhythm that vibrated with every note played by the touch of her delicate fingers, felt like a heavenly benediction showered on him. She was playing unmindful of her surroundings, but at one point she suddenly noticed Madhusudan staring at her face and her hands froze. Shyness overcame her, she stopped playing.

Madhusudan was in an expansive mood after hearing all that she sang. He asked generously, 'Borrobou, what do you wish for? Just name it.' Even if she had asked to go and nurse her brother for a few days he might have agreed. Because today as he looked at her face absorbed in music, he could hardly believe in his good fortune. He was telling himself, 'She is here indeed in my own house, how wonderfully true!'

Kumu put the esraj and the bow down and sat quietly.

Madhusudan pleaded once more, 'Borrobou, please ask for something from me. I shall meet your wishes.'

Kumu said, 'I want to give Murli the bearer some winter clothing.'

It would have been better if she had asked for nothing at all. But a blanket for Murli bearer! It was like asking for shoe laces from one who was prepared to lay down one's crown at your feet.

Madhusudan was astonished. He was annoyed with the bearer and he said, 'So that rascal has been pestering you?'

'No, I tried to give him a shawl but he refused. If you let him have it, then he will have the courage to accept it.'

Madhusudan was struck dumb. After giving the matter some thought he said, 'You want to give it in charity? Let me see that shawl of yours.'

She brought her much-used brown shawl. Madhusudan wrapped it round himself. He rang the small bell kept on the teapoy. An old maidservant appeared and she was told to fetch Murli bearer.

Murli came and stood with folded hands, trembling out of cold and fear.

Madhusudan took out a hundred-rupee note from his wallet and put it in his hand and told Murli, 'This is a gift from the mistress.'

Such unsolicited favour from Madhusudan had never happened in Murli's lifetime. Even more frightened then ever, Murli mumbled, 'But sir . . .'

'What "sir"? You fool, take it from her and buy as many warm clothes as you wish.'

The matter ended there; but so did everything else for the rest of the day. The tide that was carrying Kumu forward towards her husband suddenly ebbed. The wave of self-sacrifice which overflowed the banks of his narrowmindedness went down again at the impact of this trivial plea on behalf of a mere bearer. After this, it was difficult for both of them to speak. He had totally forgotten that someone would be waiting for him in the office about the land lease. He woke up suddenly and blamed himself for this lapse. He quickly got up and left saying, 'I have got some work. I must take leave of you now.'

On the way to the office room he stopped in front of Shyamasundari's room and said loudly enough, 'Are you in?'

It was her day of fasting. She was lying down wrapped cosily in a sheet. At his words she got up and stood near the door and asked, 'Is that you brother?'

'You didn't give me my paan today!'

# 44

Meanwhile, someone was hiding patiently in the dark, behind the door. He could now wait no longer. It was Habloo. He was stiff like a wooden doll because he dreaded Madhusudan. After the last scolding he got from Madhusudan, Habloo did not dare approach his new aunt and was fretting for her. It was not quite safe to come here this evening, but his mother had put him to sleep and left. He had woken up at the sound of the esraj. He didn't know what it was but was sure it was coming from the direction of his aunt's bedroom. He was also certain that Uncle would not be there, because it was unthinkable that anyone should dare play any music in his presence. But when he saw his uncle's shoes in front of the door he wanted to run away, only the glimpse of Auntie herself playing rooted him to the spot. He was listening from behind the door. He knew from the start that this aunt was an amazing person but today his admiration knew no bounds. As soon as Madhusudan left he rushed to Kumu's lap, put his arms round her neck and whispered into her ears, 'Aunty!'

Kumu held him close and said, 'But your hands are cold, were you out in this damp rainy weather?'

He did not answer, afraid that she might send him to bed straight away. Kumu hugged him under her own shawl and asked him why he was up so late.

'I came to listen to your music. How do you play the esraj?'

'You will be able to play as well if you learn it.'

'Will you teach me?'

Motir-ma stormed in. 'So here you are, you thug! I have been looking for him all over. He is afraid of setting foot outside after dark, but when it comes to Auntie's room he seems to have no such fear. Come on, come to bed.'

Habloo clung to Kumu.

'Let him be for a little while,' said Kumu.

'If you encourage him like this, he will run into trouble. Let me put him to bed, then I shall come.'

Kumu was keen on giving Habloo something—some sweets or a toy—but she could not find anything suitable. So she kissed him and said, 'Go to bed tonight sweetheart, I shall play for you tomorrow in the afternoon.'

An unhappy Habloo went with his mother.

Motir-ma came back soon, anxious to find out the results of Nabin's conspiracy. She noticed the sapphire on Kumu's finger as she sat down and knew then that the plot had worked. Just to raise the topic, she asked, 'Didi, how did you come by this instrument?'

'Dada sent it for me,' said Kumu.

'So your husband fetched it for you?'

'Yes,' was Kumu's brief reply.

Motir-ma looked at her face closely but could not find any sign of surprise or excitement there.

'Did he bring any news of your brother?'

'No.'

'He is coming the day after tomorrow. Wasn't there any talk of your visiting him?'

'No, we didn't talk about him at all.'

'Why didn't you ask him yourself?'

'I may ask anything of him but not this.'

'You don't have to ask. Just go and meet your brother. I am sure your husband will not say anything.'

Motir-ma had not realized fully as yet that Madhusudan's kindness was proving to be a problem for Kumu, for she was unable to give in return what he demanded. Her heart was drained out. That was why she was so reluctant to accept anything from him—to be indebted to him in any way. In fact, she went to the extent of wishing that it might be better for her if her brother's arrival was delayed by a few more days.

After an interval Motir-ma spoke up. 'It seems big brother is in a generous mood today.'

Kumu looked at her with troubled eyes and said, 'I can't make out why there is this change of heart. It worries me, I don't know what I should do.'

Motir-ma stroked Kumu's chin and said, 'You don't have to do a thing. Don't you understand this simple fact that he had so far done nothing but business and never come across a girl like you. The more he is beginning to get to know you, the more he prizes you.'

'There is nothing in me, my dear. That he will find by looking closer. I can see myself how empty I am inside. And that is what he will discover gradually. That is why, when I see him so pleased, I think of how he has been cheated. And the day he discovers that, he would be furious. That anger would be for real, so I am not afraid of it.'

'Do you know your own worth, Didi? The day you came to their house you brought with you something for which they should be indebted to you forever. My man is desperate to do something for you. He won't rest until he jumps across the sea for you. If I were not so fond of you, you would have been our bone of contention.'

'It is my great luck to have such a brother-in-law.'

'And what about this sister-in-law? Is she like an evil star for your fortune?'

'If I mention one of you, I don't have to name the other.'

Motir-ma put her arm round Kumu affectionately and asked her, 'I have to ask you for a favour if you agree?'

'Ask then!'

'Let us be each other's confidante.'

'That's already so.'

'Then you can't hide anything from me. Please tell me, why are you so off colour today?'

Kumu looked at her for a long time and then said, 'Shall I be frank? To tell you the truth, I fear myself.'

'What is that? Why should you be afraid of yourself?'

'I have just discovered that I am not the person I believed myself to be. I came with my mind made up and reconciled to everything. Even when my brothers were hesitant, I insisted on treading my new path. But the person who started out so confidently is nowhere to be found.'

'You are unable to love. Is that it? Tell me frankly. Have you been in love with someone else? Do you know what love is?'

'Will you laugh if I say I do know? Yes, love did flood my whole sky with light as the dawn does before sunrise. It always felt as if the sun was just about to come up. I started out in quest of that sunrise like a pilgrim carrying holy water and flowers as offering. I thought I had encouragement from the deity I have worshipped all my life. I came on a tryst. I did not feel the darkness of the night. But now that my eyes are opened in broad daylight what do I see inside and outside of myself? How shall I count my moments, year after year?'

'Do you think you may never bring yourself to love him?'

'I might have been able to love him earlier. I had brought something within me which would have made anything likeable and easy to live with, but your brother-in-law broke it to smithereens, from the start. Today everything hits me hard. It seems I have been skinned raw, everything around me pains me, and I wince at whatever I touch. Maybe time will harden me and I shall become callous. But happiness I shall never taste in my life.'

'You can never tell.'

'Yes, one can very well. I have no illusions left. My life is shamelessly exposed. There is no cover left to console me with. Don't women have any space to themselves till they die? Has God made their world so rigid?'

Motir-ma had never heard Kumu talk at such length and with so much emotion. Specially today when she and Nabin had contrived to soften Madhusudan's mind towards her. She was terrified at the intensity of Kumu's distress. No gardener would now be able to revive this sensitive creeper even with an outpouring of indulgence, she thought.

Kumu spoke again, 'I am well aware that this inability of mine to give myself up honourably to my husband is a great sin on my part. But I am not so disturbed on that count as at the prospect of the degradation of surrender without respect.'

Motir-ma was at a loss to answer.

Kumu went on, 'You, my dear, are so lucky to love your husband with all your heart. I used to think it was the easiest thing to love, all wives naturally loved their husbands. But now I see, to be able to love is the rarest thing. It takes a lifetime of devotion. Tell me honestly, does every wife love her husband?'

Motir-ma said with a smile, 'One can be a good wife even without love. Otherwise the world would be unlivable.'

'Good. Give me that assurance. Let me be a good wife at least, if nothing else. There seems to be more merit in it. It calls for more devotion.'

'Obstacles may come from outside even in that effort on your part.'

'One can overcome such impediments by one's will. I shall succeed. I shall not accept defeat.'

'Of course you will succeed! Who else can but you?'

The rain came in a downpour. The lamp flickered in the wind. A gust of wind rushed into the room suddenly like a wet nightjar flapping its wings. Kumu shuddered. She said, 'I don't feel so strongly the presence of my lord. I recite his name like a mantra mechanically, my mind refuses to respond. That is what is frightening me most.'

Motir-ma did not feel like consoling her with empty words. She just held her close. Someone called from outside, 'Mejobou!'

Kumu was happy to greet Nabin and welcome him in.

'I didn't find any light in my dark room so I came to look for it,' said Nabin.

Motir-ma mocked him.

'My poor thing, like the legendary cobra without the jewel on its head!'

'You can tell the cobra from the jewel easily by its hiss. Isn't that so, Bourani?'

'Don't make me a witness to your quarrel.'

'I know if I did that I'd lose my case.'

'Then you can rescue your lost jewel. I won't keep her in my room.'

Motir-ma said, 'Don't you think he is the least concerned about his lost property? It is only a pretext to come and touch your feet.'

'Do I need any pretext? Those feet are always ready to grace me. Who can try and win that which is most unattainable? When it comes to you, it comes on its own, easily. There are thousands more worthy than me but I was the one lucky enough to touch those beautiful feet, others could not. Nabin's life was blessed—gratis.'

'You dear brother, you don't know what you are saying. Does your encyclopaedia . . .'

'You can't say that to me. What can those English people tell me about the "feet" we worship? They who confine the feet of their own Lakshmis within the narrow high heel shoes can hardly capture the glory of women's feet in the pages of their encyclopaedias. It is said that Lakshman the ideal brother-in-law in our Ramayana, spent the fourteen years of their exile looking at the feet of his sister-in-law Sita. I see you are pulling your sari to cover your feet. You may do so but remember, the lotus folds itself at night but it does not stay shut forever. It opens its petals again in the morning.'

'Is this how he won you, with his flattery?' Kumu asked her confidante.

'Not in the least. He is not one to waste his sweet words on me.'

'Maybe there is no need for it in your case,' said Kumu.

Nabin said, 'The goddesses are insatiable as far as words of praise are concerned. Unfortunately I do not have five heads like Shiva. So the familiar words of praise from this one tongue are now stale for her. She has lost her taste for it.'

Murli the bearer appeared to say that the master wanted Nabin in the office room.

That immediately put Nabin in a bad mood. He had reckoned that Madhusudan would come straight to the bedroom from work today. The boat seemed to have run aground.

After he left, Motir-ma said softly, 'Do remember one thing, our big brother loves you.'

'That's what is so strange to me,' Kumu said.

'Why do you say that? Is he made of stone?'

'I am not worthy of him.'

'There is no man on earth you are not worthy of.'

'He is so powerful, so well-respected, so mature. He is a great man. How little can he get from me? In the few days I have been here, I have realized what a greenhorn I am. That is why I am most frightened when he is in the loving mood. I find myself hollow. How can I serve him with such fraud? Last night I thought of myself as a 'bearing post' mail; if you opened it, there might not even be a letter.'

'You make me laugh, Didi. I know he is a great businessman and no one can match his business acumen. But you have not come to manage his business that you should be worried about your fitness. If he ever speaks to you honestly he will admit that it is he who is not worthy of you.'

'He did say as much to me the other day.'

'And you did not believe him.'

'No. On the contrary I was scared. He had misjudged me and he is bound to realize his mistake some day.'

'Why did you think so?'

'Shall I tell you? This marriage of mine, it is I who made it happen—but out of what a childish illusion! Whatever beguiled me then was entirely false. Yet with what utter conviction, what stubbornness I went into it: nobody could have stopped me. Dada knew that, so he did not stop me, but I was aware that he was extremely worried and apprehensive. Even then I didn't curb myself. I was such a fool. From now on not only do I suffer but I make others suffer too, and curse myself as the sole cause of all this suffering.'

Motir-ma did not have any answer. She asked, 'Tell me, Didi, what made you decide in favour of this marriage?'

'I knew for certain then, that it didn't matter whether the husband was good or bad, he was only a token to prove the glory of the devoted woman. I had not the slightest doubt that whomsoever the god of marriage, Prajapati, chose for me, I was bound to love him. From my childhood I had watched my mother read the puranas, heard the commentators and concluded that it was easy indeed to conform to the holy scriptures.'

'But, Didi, the scriptures were not written for nineteen-year-old maidens.'

'I do realize now that love is a bonus in this world. One has to jettison it and cling to religion to keep afloat in the sea of mundane living. If religion does not bear fruit and flower, its dry stalks at least help you keep afloat.'

Motir-ma let her speak on without interruption.

## 45

Madhusudan reached his office to hear some unpleasant news. A big bank in Madras they had dealings with, had failed. Then the gossip reached him that one of his employees was meddling with the books behind his back. So far no one had dared entertain any doubt about his integrity, but once somebody had given a lead, the charmed protection of no one ever having raised a question regarding it was gone. It was easy to find small lapses in a big job; successful generals win victories in spite of many little reverses. That was how Madhusudan had always won his battles so far, and no one picked on his lapses selectively. Now they had made a selection of those, put the list out in the open and went about saying in self-praise, 'We would never have made these mistakes.' Who was there to remind them that Madhusudan had set sail in a leaky boat and the great thing was that he had reached the shore? And today those very people whom he had safely brought ashore were busy examining the many leaks in the boat and shuddering. It was easy to confuse common men with these isolated criticisms. It was easy because they were only interested in profits, but were not prepared to analyse. And if by any chance they sat in judgment they became deadly. Madhusudan was derisively contemptuous of and angry with these idiots. But where idiots are in the majority there is no way but to compromise with them. The man who climbs a rickety old ladder to the top is threatened from time to time with its creaking and swaying but cannot do away with the prop. If he is incensed and feels ready to kick, it would only make matters worse.

Madhusudan's attitude towards his business was that of a lioness who forgets her own hunger when her cubs are threatened. The company was his own creation. His attachment to it was not just mercenary. Those who have the creative ability find themselves deeply fulfilled in their own creation, and when that is in jeopardy then all other joys, sorrows and desires in life become trivial. In his middle age he had recognized that he felt very intensely the need for love; and this passion having surfaced at the wrong time took a virulent form. The shock was none too small in Madhusudan's case, but now its sting was gone. Kumu's entire being, its magnetism was pulling him with a strong force these few days, but suddenly it lost its grip. Her unattainable love, her mesmerizing personality, all paled into insignificance with the advent of these business problems in Madhusudan's life.

As soon as Nabin entered the office room, Madhusudan asked, 'Do you know if my private book of accounts has been accessed by any outsider?'

Nabin was startled. He said, 'How is that possible?'

'You have to find out if anyone has been frequenting the accountant's room.'

'But our Ratikanta is very reliable. He can't possibly . . .'

'There is reason to suspect that someone has been contacting his office in his absence. Find out very discreetly who are the persons involved.'

A servant announced dinner but Madhusudan ignored him and asked Nabin to send for his carriage right away.

Nabin said, 'Won't you have your dinner? It is getting late.'

'I shall dine out. Have a lot of work in hand.'

Nabin went out with his head down, deep in thought. The plot he had so carefully laid seemed to have gone awry.

Suddenly Madhusudan called him back, handed him a letter and said, 'Give this to Kumu.'

Nabin saw it was from Bipradas. It had arrived that morning and Madhusudan had obviously planned to give it to Kumu himself. His plan must have been to bring a gift like this everytime in an attempt at reconciliation, but the sudden storm in the office had obviously ruined this loving plan of his.

The public must have had enough confidence in the bank that failed in Madras. That Ghoshal & Co. had transactions with the bank was known to the partners and Directors and they had never entertained any doubt whatever. But the moment things went wrong they started saying, 'We had been sceptical all along.'

Madhusudan guessed that as with every crisis, during this critical phase that his company was going through, instead of putting in concerted efforts to save the business, there would surface from all quarters a strong desire to blame someone (especially him) for the failure and that if there were jealous scores to settle, the business would keel over. It was too early to determine the extent of loss arising from the failure of the bank but it was clear that it would help the attempt to tarnish his reputation. Anyway, times were bad, so he had to forget about all else now and concentrate on tackling this issue.

Nabin came back and found his wife still talking to Kumu. He announced, 'Bourani, here is a letter from your brother.'

Kumu got up with a start and took it. Her hands were trembling as she opened it. She feared it would be carrying some bad news. Maybe he was so ill that he couldn't make the trip to Kolkata at all. She opened and read the letter very slowly and then she was silent for a while. Her face showed some hurt somewhere. She told Nabin, 'Dada has been in Kolkata since three this afternoon.'

'He has come only today. He may have . . .'

'He has written to say that he was to have come after a few days but had to come today on some urgent work.'

She did not say anything more. Towards the end of the letter, Bipradas had added that he would himself come to see her as soon as he got better and she need not worry on that count. The earlier letter also had the same direction. But why? What had she done? It was almost clearly asking her not to visit him in his house. She felt like lying down on the floor and crying her heart out. But she stifled her tears and sat in a stony silence.

Nabin gathered that there was something in that letter which had hit her hard. Looking at her face Nabin's heart was filled with pity. He said, 'Bourani, you must go and see him.'

She said, 'No, I shall not go,' and burst into tears. She covered her face in her palms and sobbed. Motir-ma drew her to herself. Kumu added in a choked voice, 'He has asked me not to come.'

Nabin said, 'No, Bourani, you must have misunderstood him.'

Kumu shook her head emphatically to indicate that she had made no mistake in understanding him.

'Shall I tell you where you are mistaken? Bipradas Babu must have anticipated that my brother would not permit you to see him. Lest you try and lest you be humiliated he has made it easier for you this way.'

Kumu felt instant relief. She lifted her wet eyelashes and looked at Nabin tenderly as she realized that Nabin was perfectly right. She blamed herself for doubting her brother even for a brief moment. She felt strong again. She need not rush to him now. She would wait for him to come. It was better that way.

Motir-ma patted her gently and said, 'Look at this, a little crosswind from Dada and her sea of sulk is in full swell.'

Nabin said, 'Then may I arrange for you to go tomorrow?'

'No, there is no need for that.'

'You may have no need. But I have!'

'How does it concern you?'

'Well, your brother may have the wrong impression about my brother. I can't let it pass, I must defend my brother. I won't be stopped by you. You have to go tomorrow.'

Kumu started laughing.

'But Bourani, it is no laughing matter. Any slur on our family also reflects on you. Now wash up and come and have your dinner. My brother is to dine tonight with the Manager. I believe he won't come inside the house tonight. I saw his bed being made in the office room.'

Kumu felt much relief at this news, and immediately felt ashamed to be so greatly relieved.

Later in the night Motir-ma told her husband, 'You have assured Didi already, but what will you do now?'

'Why? What Nabin says he does. Bourani has to go. We shall see what happens then.'

These newly titled Rajas were extremely conscious of their family prestige. They were usually of the opinion that following her marriage into their family the new bride had now acquired a higher status than her maiden home, so there could be no question of her going to her previous home. It was better to let her forget her past. In such a dilemma, if it became impossible to appease both parties, one had to give way. Nabin gave this matter of the silent one-upmanship between Madhusudan and Bipradas some thought and decided who had to step down. Even a few days ago, it was unthinkable on his part to interfere in a domain where his brother had exclusive rights.

The couple discussed all this at length, and decided that Madhusudan should be approached to let Kumu go to see her brother in the morning for a little while. Once she was there it would not be difficult to cook up some reason for her to overstay by a few days.

Madhusudan came home late at night with a bundle of papers. Nabin peeped into the office room and found his brother still awake, at the writing desk with his glasses on and a blue pencil in hand, busy taking notes or marking passages in one document or the other. Boldly, Nabin went in and asked him, 'Dada, can I do anything for you?' 'No' was Madhusudan's brief reply. He wanted to come to grips fully with this crisis in the business—the whole affair had to be crystal clear to himself. Taking help from anyone else would only weaken his position.

Nabin left the room as he could not find any opening to talk. And it did not seem likely to happen soon. But he was determined to send Kumu home the next morning. So he had to get Madhusudan's permission tonight itself.

He came back later carrying a lamp in his hand and said, 'There isn't enough light for you to work.'

Madhusudan felt that the second light helped, but even then gave no further opportunity to Nabin to start a conversation. So Nabin had to beat a retreat.

A little later he appeared again. This time he brought in his brother's favourite hookah which he had lit and placed the long tube on the table by his side. Madhusudan felt that this was also welcome. So he put down the pencil for a while and puffed at his hookah.

This gave Nabin the chance to ask, 'Dada, aren't you going to bed? Bourani may be awake waiting up for you.'

The words 'waiting up for you' went home straight. It was like a small bird settling on the mast of a ship tossing in a storm, which for a moment brought the picture of a quiet peaceful island in the midst of a turbulent sea. But there was no time for such thoughts. The ship had to be steered home.

Madhusudan was perturbed at this weakness of his mind, but he suppressed it and told Nabin, 'Ask Borrobou to go to sleep. I shall sleep here tonight.'

'Shall I bring her here?'

Madhusudan objected violently, 'No! No! No!'

Nabin was undeterred. He said, 'But she is waiting to plead with you.'

Madhusudan said rudely, 'I have no time to listen to pleas.'

'You may have no time, but she too has very little time.'

'Why? What is the matter?'

'News has reached that Bipradas Babu has already arrived in Kolkata so Bourani wishes tomorrow morning to . . .'

'To go tomorrow morning?'

'Not for long, just to . . .'

Madhusudan waved his hand and said, 'All right, let her go, let her. No more words. You may go.'

As soon as he got his orders, Nabin hurried off. But he was hardly out on the veranda when he heard Madhusudan call him back. He was afraid that Dada might rescind his permission. But as soon as he entered Madhusudan said, 'Borrobou will stay with her brother for some time now. You make the arrangements.'

Nabin was careful not to show the slightest enthusiasm about this proposal. On the contrary he began to scratch his head and said hesitatingly, 'But the house will be quite empty without her.'

Madhusudan did not answer. He put the pipe down and started on his work. He knew that the way to temptation was still open, but he blocked it off resolutely.

Nabin left happily. Madhusudan's work proceeded. But he was unaware for a long time of the other stream of consciousness running contrary to the stream of work. At some point of time the blue pencil was dropped and the pipe was on. During the daytime when Madhusudan was free of all thoughts of Kumu, he was happy to be his own master again as before. But as the night advanced he began to suspect that the enemy had not left the fortress, it was still lurking underground.

The rain had stopped and a pale moon up behind a shisum tree overwhelmed the damp night. The cold wind was making demands for the warmth of a human body next to him in bed. He clenched the blue pencil and pored over his books. But in the depth of his mind a thin small voice clearly went on chanting, '*Bourani may be waiting up for you.*'

Madhusudan had resolved to finish some work by the morning; not that it would have made much of a difference if it were done the next day also. But it was a sacred principle of his business to keep to promises made. If he ever slipped up, he could never forgive himself. So far, he had rigidly followed this rule and had been rewarded amply. But recently, Madhusudan by day was slowly turning to be slightly different from the Madhusudan by night—like the two strings of a veena. He had bent over his desk with a firm resolve, but as the night advanced a line began to buzz in his head like a bee, through a chink in that resoluteness. It said, '*Bourani is waiting up for you.*'

He got up and started for his bedroom, leaving the lights on and the books open. One had to cross a veranda to go up to the second floor; Shyamasundari was squatting on the passage near the railing. The moon was half way up the sky and enveloping her in its light. She looked like a picture from a story-book. She seemed to have come a long way out of the hard shell of close familiarity. She knew Madhusudan's way to his bedroom lay through this passage. It was a sight which hurt her deeply and therefore also attracted her strongly. But the waiting was not entirely due to a mad desire to hurt herself with a hopeless pain, there was also a faint trace of hope—just in case something unexpected took place. It was a vigil by the wayside for a miracle to happen.

In his desire to get close to Kumu as fast as possible, Madhusudan looked askance at Shyama and went straight up. She began to hit her head on the rails bemoaning her misfortune.

Madhusudan entered to find the bedroom in darkness and no sign of anyone waiting up. There was a streak of light from the bathroom. For a moment he thought of turning back, but he could not. He put on the gaslight. But this did not wake up Kumu who was fast asleep, wrapped in a blanket. He was annoyed at this picture of comfort. He pulled open the mosquito net impatiently and flopped on the bed. The cot shook with a loud sound. She sat up, startled.

Kumu had been sleeping, secure in the knowledge that her husband would not come tonight. The expression on her face at suddenly facing him was such that it stung him to the quick. Blood rushed to his head and he said, 'So you can't stand the sight of me! Is that it?'

Kumu was at a loss to answer such an interrogation. It was true that her heart sank at the sight of him. Her mind was caught off guard. The feeling that she was always trying to suppress even to herself, had suddenly revealed itself. She was unaware of its strength.

Madhusudan was sarcastic, 'So what about your plea for visiting your brother?'

Kumu was quite prepared to fall at his feet and beg forgiveness but at the mention of her brother she froze and said, 'No.'

'Don't you want to go?'

'No, I don't.'

'Didn't you send Nabin to persuade me?'

'No, I didn't send him.'

'Didn't you tell him about your wish to go?'

'On the contrary, I told him I didn't want to go to see my brother.'

'Why?'

'I can't tell.'

'You can't tell? Again your Noornagar arrogance!'

'I belong to Noornagar.'

'Then you go back to them. You are not fit for this household. I did you a favour, you didn't appreciate it. Now you will have time to regret.'

Kumu sat still. Madhusudan got up, shook her hand in a frenzy and shouted, 'You don't even know how to apologize!'

'Whatever for?'

'For the privilege of sharing my bed!'

Kumu got up instantly and went to the next room.

On his way back Madhusudan found Shyamasundari still in the passage. He bent down and tried to pull her up by her hand, 'What are you up to Shyama?' he asked. Shyama was up immediately and taking his feet in both her hands she said in a maudlin voice, 'Please put an end to my life.'

Madhusudan held her hand and helped her get up. He said, 'You are icy cold. Come, I will put you to bed.' He then covered her with his shawl, held her hand tightly in his right hand and reached her to her bedroom. Shyama asked in a whisper, 'Won't you stay for a while?'

Madhusudan said, 'I have some work to finish.'

Enough of this madness at midnight, no more disruption in my work, he said to himself. At the same time he also realized where his compensation lay for the rebuff he had from Kumu. Tonight he needed to feel loved and wanted. He got a new impetus in his work in the assurance that Shyamasundari waited for him with all her life and love. It softened the pain he suffered from the thorn of rejection he carried in his heart.

Kumu on her part also had some consolation from the trauma she had that night. Every time Madhusudan had been loving to her she had been thrown into the throes of a dilemma. She was distressed by a sense of duty which demanded that she paid for it by loving in return. She had not a chance to win this battle. But the defeat would be ugly; and she tried constantly to suppress the thought of it. Now the suppressed sense of defeat was fully exposed. In her unguarded moment it was totally clear to Madhusudan that her whole being was contrary to his own nature. It was in a way good that both knew the truth for certain and henceforth they would be able to do their duty by each other without any pretence. The reality was that he desired her; and he wanted to cast her out from sheer frustration. It was indeed true that she had no right to share his bed. So far, she had only cheated him. Her place in this house was an embarrassment.

One question had been bothering her throughout the night. Why was he so concerned with her? He was always snubbing her about her Noornagar style, which meant that it was clear to him that they belonged to two different worlds, different cultures. Then why did he still insist on declaring his love for her? Could this ever be true love?

She was convinced that whatever Madhusudan thought now, she could never fully satisfy him. The sooner he realized this the better it would be for all concerned.

Nothing was left the next morning of the joy Nabin felt when he went to bed, having got his brother's consent. It was two in the morning when Madhusudan sent for Nabin after he had finished his work. His order was to send Kumudini to Bipradas's house and not to bring her back till he, Madhusudan, sent for her. Nabin understood it as an order of banishment.

Nabin's bedroom was opposite the covered square yard where Madhusudan met Shyama last night. In fact, Nabin and his wife were talking about Kumu when they heard voices. Motir-ma came out and could see in the moonlight the meeting of Shyama and Madhusudan. She thought to herself, yet another tough knot is being tied tonight in Kumu's string of fortune.

She asked her husband, 'Is it wise for Didi to leave at this critical juncture?'

Nabin said, 'Matters had not gone this far when Bourani was not on the scene. It is because of her that this is happening.'

'How ridiculous!'

'Bourani could not feed the hunger she aroused and that is what is going to cause havoc. In my opinion it is better that she stays away for some time now. At least she will be at peace.'

'So should things drift like this?'

'There is nothing to do but to watch the fire you can't extinguish burn itself out to ashes.'

The whole of next morning Habloo would not leave Kumu's side. When the tutor came and he was sent for, he looked to her. If she had asked him to go for his studies he would have obeyed, but Kumu told the bearer that it was a holiday for Habloo.

The tender tone that prevails when a new bride is about to go to her own place was missing in Kumu's case. It felt as if this house was losing her for good, as though the bird which was caged all this time had found an opening. It would fly away never to return to her cage ever.

Nabin said, 'I would have been happy to ask you not to be away too long, but I am unable to utter those words. You better be with them who respect you. If you ever need anything, just think of Nabin.'

Motir-ma filled an earthen jar with mango preserves and pickles of all sorts she had made herself, and put it in Kumu's palanquin. She did not say anything; she had her own reservations. As long as the barrier was gross and as long as Madhusudan insulted her palpably, all her sympathies were with Kumu. But the fact that internal impediments, which are delicate, emotional, and beyond analysis, are also the strongest, was not easily comprehensible to Motir-ma. To her the natural thing for a wife was to feel fortunate whenever the husband was inclined to be pleased. Not to think so was, to her, going too far. So much so that she did not take it kindly that Nabin should still be sympathetic towards his Bourani. It was indeed difficult ordinarily for a woman to realize that the natural repulsion Kumu felt was only too real and that it was not her pride but a matter of great mental struggle within herself. If a Chinese woman who had submitted to the customary binding of her feet heard of another woman who considered submitting to this torture degrading, then she would surely laugh and dismiss such objection as mere affectation. That which was intrinsically natural would appear to her as abnormal. Motir-ma was the most hurt at Kumu's suffering. Maybe that was why she was now hardening in her attitude towards her. It was impossible for Motir-ma to sympathize with, much less forgive, a woman who did not accept gratefully when fortune turned to offer her a gift.

## 46

As she reached her home, Kumu opened the door of the palanquin a little and looked up. At this time of the day it was usual for Bipradas to sit on the balcony with his newspaper. Today there was no one. Her house had not been informed about her arrival today. The sight of the liveried peon accompanying the palanquin alerted the gateman. He guessed the mistress had come. The palanquin crossed the front courtyard and was proceeding inside, but Kumu stopped it, got out and quickly climbed the outside staircase to the first floor. She wanted to be the first to meet her Dada. She was sure that as a patient he would be assigned the front drawing room. From the window here one could see the grove of gulmohur, kanchan and peepul trees. It was this room that first received the light of the sun filtered through the branches. It was Bipradas's favourite room.

Tom the terrier saw her at the top of the stairs, and rushed and jumped on her, wagging his tail and creating a commotion. He went on barking, trotting ahead of Kumu. Bipradas was leaning on a folded couch, half prone with a light printed quilt on his feet. His right hand was resting on the bed holding a book. It seemed he was tired and had just stopped reading. Next to him on the floor there was an empty tea-cup and the crumbs of bread on a plate. The books on the shelf on the wall near his head were in disarray. The night lamp, full of soot, was still there in a corner.

Kumu was startled looking at his face. She had never seen him so sad, wan and sickly ever. This Bipradas was ages away from the one she knew. She put her head on his feet and broke into tears.

'Is that you, Kumu? So you've come. Come sit here near me.' He drew her close. In his letter he had practically told her not to come, yet there was a faint hope that she might turn up. The fact that she could come made him feel at ease; perhaps there was nothing in the way of her smoothly running her new household. Normally he was expected to propose, arrange conveyance and send an escort to bring her home. But since she came on her own, it led him to believe that she enjoyed much more freedom than he expected her to have in Madhusudan's house.

Kumu was running her fingers through his dishevelled hair, settling it somewhat. She said, 'Dada, how terrible you look!'

'Nothing has happened lately to make me look brighter, but why have *you* lost your looks? Why have you become so pale?'

By then news of Kumu's arrival had reached all the others in the house and everyone came crowding around her. Kumu saluted Aunt Kshema who embraced her and kissed her forehead. All the servants came and bowed to her. When the greetings were over Kumu told Kshema, 'Aunty, Dada is looking poorly.'

'How can he get better without your nursing? He has been used to it for such a long time.'

Bipradas reminded her, 'Aren't you going to offer Kumu anything?'

'Sure. That goes without saying. The palanquin bearers have been served already. Let me go and check up. You two can gossip in the meantime.'

Bipradas called Kshema and whispered something into her ears. Kumu guessed it was about the way the attendants from her in-laws' house were to be taken care of. She was an outsider to this consultation. She had no say in this matter. She did not like this at all. Kumu began her effort to regain her old position in this house.

First she whispered some orders to the khansama and then started to rearrange the room in her own way. She moved out the glasses, cups and plates, the lamps and empty soda-water bottles to the outside veranda; also one broken cane-chair, a few dirty towels and a torn undervest. Then she arranged the books on the shelf, brought a teapoy within her brother's reach and placed on it some reading material, an inkstand, a glass carafe and a tumbler for drinking water, a small mirror, comb and a hairbrush.

Meanwhile Gokul brought hot water in a brass jug and also a brass basin and a clean towel and kept all this on a low cane seat. Without waiting for his permission, Kumu wet a towel in the hot water and sponged Bipradas's face and hands and combed his hair. Bipradas sat quietly like a small child. Then she informed herself about the timing and dosage of his medicines, the diet to be administered, and took over charge in such a manner that it seemed she had no other responsibility in her life.

Bipradas began to wonder what all this added up to. He had presumed that she had come for a short visit and would go back, but this did not seem to be the case at all. He was curious about her relationship with her in-laws but hesitated to ask her directly. He waited for her to tell him herself. Once he asked her in a low voice, 'When do you have to get back?'

'Not now,' she said. 'I shall be with you for some time.'

Tom was trying to go to sleep quietly under the master's couch. Kumu petted him so much that he became effusive in his affection. He jumped up and placed his paws on her lap and started a voluble conversation in his own tongue. Bipradas understood that Kumu sought to take refuge from any further discussion behind this commotion which she created herself.

After a while she stopped playing with Tom and said, 'Dada, it is time for your barley-water. Shall I go and fetch it for you?'

'No, it isn't time yet,' he said and motioned her to sit on the chair close to him. Then he took her hand in his and asked, 'Kumu, tell me frankly how are you two getting on?'

Kumu could not say anything right then. She sat with her head down, her face went red, and then as she used to do in her childhood, she hid her face on his chest and started to cry. She said, 'Dada, I misunderstood everything. I was so ignorant!'

Bipradas stroked her head gently and said after an interval of time, 'I failed to bring you up properly. If Mother were alive, she would have prepared you well for marriage and in-laws.'

Kumu said, 'So far I had only known you. I could never imagine that another household could be so radically different. From my childhood my thoughts had been moulded by yours. So I never feared anything. I have seen Father hurt Mother on many occasions, but that was a kind of wildness, the wound was outside, not internal. Here my humiliation is all deep within me.'

Bipradas sighed silently and began to brood. That Madhusudan belonged to a different world was apparent to him from the preliminaries to this marriage. Anxiety on this count was one reason why he was unable to recover fully. There was no way to save Kumu from this gross elephantine embrace. To make matters worse, his entire property was mortaged to this very person. This humiliating relationship was now affecting Kumu too. During his illness all these days, his constant thought was about escaping from the shackles of this loan. He did not want to come to Kolkata lest it became difficult to maintain a normal relationship with Kumu's in-laws. He had decided to live in Noornagar for fear that his natural claim of affection on Kumu might be outraged at every step in Kolkata. But he was eventually compelled to come here in search of some other moneylender. He knew this was next to impossible and this worry was sitting like a boulder on his chest.

After a while Kumu turned her shoulder a little away from him, and asked, 'Tell me, Dada, is it a sin on my part that I cannot endear my husband to myself?'

'You know very well, Kumu, that my views on what is sinful and what is meritorious are quite contrary to the scriptures.'

Absent-mindedly she began to turn the pages of an illustrated English magazine. Bipradas continued, 'The events and circumstances in every person's life are so different from each other that to lay down firmly a general rule about good and evil will remain merely a rule, it will not be practical ethics.'

Kumu kept her eyes lowered on the magazine and said, 'Mirabai's life, for instance . . .'

Whenever the struggle between what is to be done and what is not to be done raged fierce in her mind she thought of Mirabai. She wished fervently for someone to explain to her the ideals of Mirabai.

With some effort she overcame her hesitation and said, 'Mira found her real beloved within herself, so she could sincerely give up her social husband. But have I got such a major right to relinquish my mundane household?'

'But, Kumu, I thought you already had your deity fully within yourself.'

'So I used to think. But when I was in a crisis I found myself bereft of feelings. I tried my best but was somehow unable to make Him real in my heart of hearts. This is my greatest regret.'

'The mind has its ebb and flow too. Night descends every now and then but that does not stop the day from dawning. Whatever you have achieved is one with you.'

'Bless me so that I do not lose my faith in Him. He tortures one in order to give Himself in the end. But, Dada, I have made you ill worrying about me!'

'Kumu dear, I am used to worrying about you since your childhood. If I stop getting your news or am not allowed to worry about you there will be a big void in my life. Groping in that emptiness is what has tired me out.'

Kumu was stroking his feet. She said, 'You must not think too much about me. My protector is within me. I have nothing to fear.'

'All right. Let that be. Right now I feel like teaching you some music as I used to.'

'Thank God for the music you taught me. That is what keeps me alive. But do not teach me today, when you get stronger, then. Today let me sing to you instead.'

She sat near his head and began to sing softly,

*Piya ghar aaye, so hi pitam piya pyaar re.*
*Mira ke prabhu Giridhar naagar*

*Charana-kamal balihar re.*

(My beloved has come home. He is my true love. Mira is thrilled to be at the feet of her lord Giridhari.)

Bipradas was listening with his eyes closed. As she sang she had an extraordinary vision. Her inner world was filled with light. The beloved had come and she could feel the touch of his feet in her heart. As she embraced her beloved that world turned into her reality. Her singing had transported her to that world. The last lines of the song filled her whole existence with endless ecstasy. There was no room for the petty afflictions and insults of the everyday world. 'The beloved had come home.' What more did one want? If this song never ended it could be her escape for life.

Gokul came and put some pieces of toast and a glass of barley-water on the teapoy. Kumu stopped singing and said, 'Dada, sometime back I was looking for a guru, but do I need one? You have given me the mantra of music.'

'Don't put me to shame. Gurus like me are a dime a dozen. They themselves are ignorant of the mantras they impart to their disciples. Now tell me how long exactly can you stay here?'

'Till I am sent for.'

'Did you ask to come here?'

'No, I didn't.'

'Then what is the meaning of all this?'

'It's no use trying to get the meaning. You won't get it even if you tried. It is enough that I am here close to you. The longer I can stay here, so much the better. You are not eating, Dada. Please finish your food.'

A servant came and announced the arrival of Kalu Mukherjee. Bipradas seemed to be somewhat concerned at this news. He said, 'Send him in.'

## 47

Kumu bowed to him as soon as Kalu came in. he said, 'So, little one, you've come! Now Dada will soon be well.'

Her eyes were filled with tears. She said, 'Dada, won't you have some lemon juice in your barley-water?'

Bipradas waved his hand casually indicating that it really didn't matter. Kumu knew he hated barley-water so she always put some lemon juice and rose-water and made a sherbet out of it. None of that was available today for Bipradas never told anyone else about his own taste; he took whatever came with equal distaste.

Kumu went in to make the drink properly.

Bipradas asked anxiously, 'Tell me the news, Kaluda.'

'No one is willing to lend money on your signature alone. They want Subodh's as well. Some rich Marwaris may be willing but that would be speculative, and the exorbitant interest demanded would be beyond us to pay.'

'Kaluda, maybe we should wire Subodh to come. Time is running out.'

'I too am uneasy. The other day when I went to Madhusudan with the money from the sale of your ring, in part payment of the loan, he refused to accept it. I knew then that things were not going to be smooth. One day, at his own convenience, he will suddenly tighten the noose.'

Bipradas started thinking seriously.

Kalu said, 'How did our Little Sister come home suddenly? Hope it is not out of pique with Madhusudan. We must remember that we are in no position to annoy him.'

'She says she has got his permission.'

'I won't rest till we know the nature of this so-called permission. I can't tell you Dada, how careful I have to be in dealing with him. Even when my blood boiled I bore everything coolly, like the Everest where the ice does not melt even at high noon. He is not only our creditor but also a brother-in-law. To manage him is no mean task.'

Bipradas continued to be deep in his thoughts.

Kumu came in with the barley-water, held the cup close to his lips and ordered him to drink up.

Bipradas woke up from his reverie. Kumu realized that he was immersed in some deep problem.

She followed Kalu out to the veranda and said, 'Kaluda, you must tell me everything.'

'What do I have to tell you, Didi?'

'Something is bothering you two. What is it?'

'If you have property, you can't escape problems, Little Sister. It is like a fruit on a tree full of thorns, when you are hungry you have to pluck the fruit but you also scratch yourself all over.'

'Cut it out and tell me whatever is happening.'

'One does not share business details with women.'

'I know for certain what you've been talking about. Shall I tell you?'

'All right, tell me.'

'It was about the loan Dada has taken from my husband.'

Kalu did not reply but looked at her with an amused smile, his big eyes wide in amazement.

'You must tell me if I am right.'

'Like brother like sister, quick on the uptake!'

On the first day after the wedding, when Madhusudan had flaunted being Bipradas's creditor it had become clear to Kumu that their relationship was not honourable. She had wished every day for it to end. She had no doubt that Bipradas was deeply wounded. When Nabin explained her brother's letter that night she knew immediately that at the root of all this there was this relationship between the creditor and the debtor. It was clear to her now why her brother was not able shake off his illness and what the urgent work was that had brought him to Kolkata.

'Kaluda, please don't hide anything from me. Dada has come to raise another loan.'

'Well, one has to borrow in order to repay. Money does not fall from the skies. In any case it is not a good thing to have in-laws as creditors.'

'That's right, but have you been able to arrange it?'

'I am going round looking for it. Something will turn up. Not to worry.'

'I can see you have not been successful.'

'So Little One, if you know so much then why ask me? When you were small you pulled my moustache once and asked me how it grew. I said I sowed seeds of it in time. The matter ended there. But if I had to answer that same question now I'd have to get hold of a medical man. It is nowhere laid down that you have to be told everything in full.'

'I am telling you Kaluda, I have to know everything about my Dada.'

'Including how he grew his moustache?'

'You can't change the topic in this manner. I could tell from his face that you could not arrange the money.'

'Even if that be so, what good is that knowledge to you?'

'I can't tell, but I must know. You have not got a loan?'

'No, I have not.'

'It won't be easy?'

'I shall get it no doubt but yes, it won't be easy. But it might be more useful for me to go in search of money than try to answer all your questions. So long then.'

He then retraced his few steps and said, 'Little One, tell me frankly, there is no ugly hitch behind you coming here today?'

'I don't know for certain if there is or not.'

'Did you get your husband's consent?'

'He gave it without my asking for it.'

'Out of anger?'

'I am not sure of that either. He has said that I need not go back till I am sent for.'

'That is neither here nor there. You go back before that. On your own.'

'But that will be going against his orders.'

'We will take care of that.'

Kumu could not help thinking that she was the cause of all this trouble her brother was facing. She felt like hitting herself; hitting hrself very hard. She had heard of sadhus who could lie on a bed of nails. She was willing to do that if it helped in any way. If some holy person showed her the right path she would be his slave for life. There must be such a person, but how to trace him? Were she not a woman she was sure to have found a way out. But what was the other brother—Mejdada—doing? How could he live in peace in England leaving all the burden on Dada's shoulders?

Kumu came back to the room to find Bipradas lying down quietly, looking at the ceiling. How could he ever get well like this? She felt like banging her head at the door of their hostile Fate.

She sat on his bed stroking his hair and asked, 'When will Mejdada come?'

'I really don't know.'

'Why don't you write and ask him to come?'

'Tell me why I should.'

'How can you carry all the burden of this household on your own?'

'The world consists of two sets of people, one has all the demands and the other all the responsibilities. I have chosen the latter as my role, I don't want to give it to anyone else.'

'If I were a man, I'd have forced it off you.'

'Then you admit there is some attraction for taking on the onus, and because you can't do it yourself you want to have the vicarious pleasure of having your Mejdada taking it on. Why should I not be the one?'

'Dada, are you here to raise a loan?'

'How did you guess?'

'From the look on your face. Can I be of no help whatever?'

'How?'

'Such as putting my signature on some documents. Is my signature of no value at all?'

'It is of great value but only to us, not to the banker.'

'I beg of you, please tell me something that I can do.'

'Darling sister, be calm, wait patiently, remember that is also of great importance in the world. To keep your head cool in a crisis is as important as it is to keep your boat steady in the face of a storm. Go bring my esraj and play for me a little.'

'Dada, I am dying to do something.'

'Does playing this instrument count for nothing?'

'I wish to do something challenging.'

'I think it is harder playing the esraj than signing your name on a legal document. Go and get the instrument.'

## 48

Like everyone else in the house, Shyamasundari too was afraid of Madhusudan. But she sensed that there were occasions when he softened towards her. However, she could not figure out where and when to cross the fence and get closer to him. For so long she had groped in the dark and tried but had so far always met with a rebuff. Madhusudan was then building up his business assiduously. Women to him were trivial compared to the pursuit of wealth. His dismissal of their species made women particularly frightened of him. But even such fear has its own attraction. Shyama always hovered around him with a trembling heart and a thin veil of hesitancy. In some unguarded moments he had indulged her; but those were the most dangerous moments. Because, these would be soon followed by contrary behaviour on his part in an effort to prove that the place of women in his life was beneath contempt. That is why Shyama had kept herself in check so far.

After his marriage she could bear it no longer. If Madhusudan had spurned Kumu like he did the other women she could have borne it. Somehow. But when she saw that he could also lower his defences and go blindly frantic about a woman, it then became difficult for her to observe restraint. The last few days she tried to advance every now and then and found that it was permitted. Sometimes there were some obstacles but those also could be overcome. Madhusudan's weakness was now exposed, so Shyama could no longer contain her patience. He had never been so close to her as he was the night before Kumu left. She was afraid of the usual backlash; but she was wise to the fact that if she were not diffident herself there was nothing to fear.

Madhusudan had left the house in the morning and came home after one in the night. For a long time he had never had this kind of disorder in his daily routine. Today he came home extremely tired and the first thing that came to his mind was that Kumu had left for her home—and willingly. So far he had been sufficient in himself, but somewhere he had let himself go and the desire for a woman's love in times of distress, which lay dormant in him, was awakened now. That is why he was so upset at Kumu's absence. Tonight Shyama had deliberately not come to attend his meal as she usually did. Madhusudan came to his empty bedroom, and sat quietly for a while. Then he sent for Shyama. She came wrapped in a red English woollen shawl and stood looking at the floor. Madhusudan called her, 'Come and sit here by my side.'

She sat near his head and said, stroking his head, 'You look very tired today.' He said, 'Ah, your touch is so cool.'

At night, when he went to bed, Shyama entered the room unasked and said, 'Poor you! All by yourself!'

Shyamasundari was now bold enough to do away with any more pretence. She was anxious to establish her claim with everyone as witness. There was no time to waste. Kumu might come back any day. Her possession must be complete before that happened. If the possession was public it would be more compelling, therefore there was no room for coyness.

Very soon, even the servants became aware of the situation. The long- suppressed fire of passion in Madhusudan came out in the open with vehemence without caring for anybody. Concupiscence had made its appearance rather crudely in this household.

Nabin and Motir-ma knew that once this floodgate was opened it could not be dammed.

'Should we not call Didi back? It is not safe to wait too long,' said Motir-ma.

'I was thinking on the same lines, but we can't move without Dada's orders. Let me try.'

When he came to see Madhusudan and find a pretext to broach the topic, he found him ready to start out and the carriage waiting for him.

He asked, 'Are you going somewhere?'

Madhusudan answered a bit sheepishly, 'Yes, to that astrologer Venkat Swami.'

He wanted to hide his weakness from Nabin but thought it might be useful to take him along. He said to Nabin, 'Do come with me.'

Nabin was scared. He said carefully, 'Let me first find out if he is at home. He was supposed to have gone to his village.'

'Let us go and find out then.'

As soon as they reached the astrologer's house, Nabin got off, peeped into the house and said, 'There does not seem to be anybody at home.'

But that very moment Venkat Swami came out of the door chewing a stick of neem commonly used as a toothbrush. Nabin quickly went and touched his feet whispering, 'Be very careful in what you say.'

They went and sat in that same dingy room. Nabin sat behind Madhusudan and spoke out before Madhusudan could say anything.

'Shashtriji, the Maharaj is going through very bad times, please tell us how to propitiate his stars.'

Madhusudan was annoyed at Nabin's blurting out of his affairs. He pinched Nabin's thigh hard.

Venkat Swami cast Madhusudan's horoscope and showed him clearly that Saturn was casting evil eyes at his house of wealth.

Knowing the name of the star was of little help because it was difficult to contend with them. Of more use would be the identity of the people who were bringing him misfortune. Their names had to be found to whichever letter of the alphabet they might belong. The problem with Nabin was that he was totally in the dark about Madhusudan's office affairs so he was unable give signals to the man.

Venkat Swami meanwhile was reciting some verses from the Sanskrit primer *Mugdhabodh* and stealing furtive looks at his client. The old Bhrigu manuscripts must have been totally silent about modern-day names. Suddenly the Shashtri said loudly, 'The enmity comes from a woman.'

Nabin heaved a sigh of relief. If he could now somehow establish that the woman in question was none other than Shyamasundari there would be nothing to worry about Madhusudan, who was hankering after a name. The Shashtri then started with the alphabets serially, the first series started with 'ka'. As he uttered it he pretended to listen intently to the invisible sage Bhrigumuni, keeping an eye on Madhusudan at the same time. The letter 'ka' startled Madhusudan a little. Nabin was shaking his head vigorously to indicate that it was wrong. But the poor fellow was totally unaware that such shaking of the head both ways meant exactly the opposite of dissent in the south of India—where Shashtri came from. Venkat Swami was now certain. He raised his voice to say 'ka' once more. He had also guessed as much from Madhusudan's facial reaction. So he elaborated it by way of explanation that all his misfortune lay in the letter 'ka' which also starts the Sanskrit prefix 'ku' which is used to qualify all things evil.

After this explanation Madhusudan did not insist on knowing the full name (he had probably made up his mind that Kumu was the person concerned) but asked, 'What is the remedy?'

Venkat Swami gravely repeated a Sanskrit adage '*kantake-naiba kantakam*' (a thorn must be taken out with another sharp one)—that was to say another woman would come to the rescue.

Madhusudan was taken aback. Venkat Swami was a good student of human psychology.

Nabin intervened, 'Swamiji, please let us know if Maharaj's horse won in the races.'

Venkat Swami knew as a rule that most horses lost. So he pretended to do some calculations and declared, 'I see only losses.'

It so happened that Madhusudan's horse had actually won a big event only recently. Before he could say anything, Nabin with a long face asked again, 'Swamiji, what is the future for my daughter?' Needless to say Nabin had no daughter.

Venkat Swami guessed that Nabin must be looking for a match, and judging from Nabin's looks knew her to be no beauteous damsel. So he said, 'It won't be easy to find a match for her. Dowry will cost a lot.'

Without giving Madhusudan any chance to intervene, Nabin fielded ten or twelve random questions and elicited strange answers to them. Then he got up and announced, 'Dada, we have had enough. Let us go.'

In the carriage he said, 'Dada, it's all a hoax. The charlatan!'

'But the other day he . . .'

'He must have had prior information.'

'But how could he know about my visit?'

'It is all my fault. I am sorry I brought you to him.'

Despite all the evidence of the astrologer's cheating, the affair of the letter 'ka' stuck in Madhusudan's mind. He concluded that stars may give random answers to odd questions but were perhaps right about the major one. Madhusudan never expected a reverse turn in his fortunes, but it did happen at the same time as his marriage. What more evidence was needed?

Nabin slowly spoke, 'Dada, it is already about a couple of weeks, shall we get Bourani back home?'

'Why, what's the hurry? Let me tell you once and for all, do not raise this topic with me ever. I shall ask for her whenever I so wish.'

Nabin took it as the final word on the subject. Still he took courage to ask, 'May Motir-ma go and see her?'

Madhusudan gave this no importance and briefly said, 'Let her.'

## 49

Bipradas was all attention; he pushed a chair forward and welcomed Nabin to sit.

Nabin said, 'Maybe you have not placed me. You take me to be a spoilt child of the Raja's family; but I am the humblest servant of one who happens to be your younger sister. If you show me so much respect you will only deprive me of my blessings. But what have you done to yourself, you are a shadow of your old self!'

'It is good to be reminded sometimes that our body is but a shadow without substance. It helps one to be prepared for the last lesson,' said Bipradas.

Kumu entered and asked Nabin to go with her and have something to eat.

Nabin said, 'I shall come with you on one condition, and until that is fulfilled this Brahmin will fast on your doorstep.'

'May I know what the condition is?'

'I had made this request once before when you were in our house, but I could not find much encouragement there. You must let your admirer have a portrait of yours. You had said then that you did not have one with you, but you can't have that excuse here. I see one right in front, in your brother's room.'

It is rarely that a good portrait is achieved. This picture of Kumu's was composed in one of those rare moments. It had the right light on her forehead which reflected the quality of her mind on her face. There was the glow of clear intelligence on her temple and her eyes had the deep tenderness of innocence. Her beautiful right hand was resting on the arm of an empty chair. It seemed she had stopped in her tracks, staring at a glimpse of her own future.

She had not noticed this photograph of hers. The day before her wedding her brother had called a professional from Kolkata and had this picture taken. Her heart melted at the thought that he had put it up in his own bedroom. There would be copies available with the photographer. Kumu looked at her brother for confirmation. Nabin said, 'You see Bipradas Babu, Bourani is agreeable. Look at her eyes. She has a soft corner for me precisely because I am so worthless.'

Bipradas smiled and said, 'Kumu, look into that leather case of mine—you will find some more photos. If you wish to grant a favour to your devotee you will have no difficulty.'

Soon after Kumu took Nabin in, Kalu entered Bipradas's room. He said, 'I have sent a telegram to Mejo Babu to come soon.'

'From me?'

'Yes, in our name, Dada; I knew you would dither till the last, meanwhile time is running short. According to the doctors you can't bear so much strain.'

The doctors had said that there was some problem with his heart and he needed both physical and mental rest. At one time he had overindulged in his wrestling act: that combined with the present mental stress and anxiety had led to this situation.

Bipradas was not sure that forcing Subodh to return like this was such a good idea. He was deep in thought. Kalu said, 'Borrobabu, it is no use thinking so much. We have to take some final decision right now about the property, and it can't be done without Subodh. We can't mortgage our lives to the Marwaris at twelve percent rate of interest. They also demand a deduction of two lakh rupees in advance. On top of this, there is also brokerage to be paid.'

'All right, let Subodh come, but do you think he will?'

'He may be a big English gentleman now, but he cannot ignore your wire. You needn't worry on that count. But you must send Khuki back to her in-laws without delay.'

Bipradas remained silent for a while and then said, 'There is some problem about sending her until Madhusudan says so.'

'Why? She is not his hired labour for cutting the jute crop. She does not have to wait for anyone's orders to go to her rightful home.'

Nabin had his meal and came to Bipradas alone. Bipradas asked him, 'Kumu is fond of you. Isn't that so?'

'Yes she is, because I am so undeserving.'

'I want to ask you a few things about her. Please be frank with me.'

'I have nothing to hide from you, sir.'

'I feel there is something not so straight about Kumu's coming here.'

'You are right. Even those whom one knows to be above reproach do get unfairly treated in this world.'

'So she has been insulted.'

'It is the shame that brings me here, since I can't do anything about it but touch your feet and beg forgiveness.'

'Is there any harm if she goes back to her husband tonight itself?'

'To tell you the truth, I dare not advise you to do it.'

Bipradas did not press Nabin for the exact details. He thought it would not be fair to ask him. Nor did he feel like questioning Kumu. So he fretted within himself. He called Kalu and questioned him, 'Kaluda, you have been to their house, perhaps you may know something about Madhusudan's frame of mind?'

'I have got some inkling, but I don't want to tell you anything unless I have the whole picture. Just wait for a couple of days and I shall be able to get you some information.'

Bipradas was sick with apprehension and since there was no remedy at hand, his heart was torn in agony.

## 50

Kumu's closest wish was fulfilled. She was back in her familiar room embraced by her brother's affection, but she missed her easy natural place. Sometimes she sulked and felt that she should go back, because she could clearly sense the question on everyone's lips, 'Why doesn't she go back? What is the matter with her?' In the midst of her brother's deep affection, there was this one anxiety, which could not be discussed openly because she herself was the subject, yet it was a closed book to her.

The afternoon sun was fading. Kumu sat near the bedroom window. The crows were noisy, carriages could be heard along the road and a variety of noises came from the neighbourhood. The air of spring however failed to bring colour to the bricks and stones of the houses around. A restless wind scattered the afternoon light by playing on the thick green leaves of an almond tree which nearly screened the house in front. It is in times like this that a tame deer wants to rush into the unknown forest ahead. It is when the wind has the touch of spring and the whole earth seems to eagerly look towards the blue sky beyond the horizon. In such a time everything around appears unreal and only that appears real whose abode is unknown, and when you try to paint its portrait the palette of colours spills all over the sky; its figure flickers everywhere in land and water like a beacon and disappears in a flash.

She was restless today, wishing to get away from it all, including herself. But how fenced in she was! Even here, in her own house. In her thoughts even death appeared desirable. She imagined herself trudging to her tryst with her dark god, beyond the banks of the dark Yamuna, day after day on an endless road, full of suffering. She recalled that she had come here to nurse her brother's illness and now she was only aggravating it. Whatever she did would have a contrary effect. She covered her face in her palms and sobbed to her heart's content. When she was calmer she decided to go back. She would cope with whatever happened—after all there was always the final release—cool, dark and delectable. The more she thought about death the more she felt that life would not be totally unbearable. She began to hum—

*Pathapar rayani andheri*
*kunjapar deep ujiyari.*

(The night is dark on the road but the lamp burns bright in the grove at the end.)

She had put her brother to sleep in the afternoon. It was time now for his medicine and food. When she came to his room she found Bipradas with a portfolio on his lap writing a long letter to Subodh, in English. She scolded him a little, 'Dada, you haven't had your full sleep today.'

Bipradas said, 'You are convinced that one rests if one sleeps. But when one feels like writing a letter, then that is what gives one rest.'

Kumu guessed that the letter concerned her. What a lucky sister to kill one brother with anxiety on this side of the sea and worry the other at the other end of the ocean! After she finished serving tea she put it to her brother gently, 'I have been here long enough, now I should go back home.'

Bipradas tried to guess from her look what she really meant. The clear understanding that the brother and sister had between them so far, seemed to have changed. Now each had to grope about to reach the other's mind. He stopped writing, made her sit by his side and stroked her hand, without a word. Kumu could follow that language. The worldly knots in their relationship had hardened but the affection they had for each other had not. Her eyes filled with tears but she made an effort to hold them back. Kumu thought to herself that she should not overburden this love so she repeated her plea, 'Dada, I have decided to go back.'

Bipradas did not know what to say, because it was better that she go, it was also her duty. He sat quietly. The dog woke up and put his paws on her lap, begging for a leftover piece of Bipradas's toast.

Bearer Ramswarup came and announced that Mukherjee Babu had come. Kumu was worried. She said, 'Dada, you have not slept well today, you will only tire yourself arguing with Kaluda. Let me go instead and listen to what he has to say and I shall report to you in due time.'

'You feel you are a great doctor! Do you think the patient is at ease if someone else listens to what is meant for him?'

'All right, I won't, but neither should you, at least not today.'

'Kumu, an English poet has said that an unheard song is sweeter than the one heard. A piece of news may be tedious but the unheard one may be more tiring, so it is better to get it over with right away.'

'All right, but I shall be back within a quarter of an hour, and if I find you two still talking, I shall start playing my esraj—Raag Bhimpalashi!'

'I agree.'

In half an hour she entered the room with the instrument in her hand but she put it by in a corner when she noticed the look on her brother's face. She sat next to him, held his hand firmly, and asked, 'What is the matter, Dada?'

A deep sorrow was rooted in the restlessness that Kumu noticed in her brother these days. Bipradas had suffered much in his life but no one had ever seen him perturbed. He had never allowed his troubles to gather within himself, by being interested in many things such as reading, music, watching stars through a telescope, horse-riding, or collecting unknown plants from all over, and planting them in his garden. This time because of his illness he had closely confined himself to limited activities. Now he yearned for company, got upset if he did not get his letters regularly and soon his thoughts turned dark. That was also why Kumu's affection for her brother had turned more maternal—how did her serious and self-possessed brother come to present a childlike aspect—such unconcern, such restlessness and such obstinacy? At the same time such grave unhappiness and anxiety.

But when she entered the room she found that her brother was no longer in that daze. There was a fire in his eyes like the third eye of Shiva the destroyer. It had nothing to do with his personal sorrow, but he must have confronted some evil which he wanted to extinguish. Bipradas did not offer any reply but sat gazing intently at the wall opposite.

Kumu repeated her question, 'Tell me, Dada, what is wrong?'

Bipradas kept looking in the distance and said, 'When you try to avoid pain it only gets hold of you more strongly. It has to be accepted and faced squarely.'

'If you advise me how, I shall certainly be able to accept it.'

'I can see clearly that dishonouring women is at the heart of our society. It is not just a personal problem of a particular woman.'

Kumu could not quite follow him.

He continued, 'So far, I felt the pain as solely ours, now I understand it is to be fought as a common cause.'

Bipradas's pale face was suffused with red. He threw aside the silk embroidered pillow from his lap and was about to get up and sit on the seat next to his bed. Kumu caught his hand and said, 'Be calm, Dada, do not get up, it will make you ill.' And she practically forced him to lean on the pile of pillows behind him.

Bipradas clutched the end of his cover and said, 'Just because women have no other way but to bear all this, they are being outraged all the time. The time has come for them to say we shall no longer tolerate this. Kumu, can you consider this as your permanent home and stay here? You certainly cannot go back to that house.'

Bipradas had gathered a lot from Kalu today.

The relationship that had developed between Madhusudan and Shyamasundari was out in the open. Both parties were equally unabashed. The very thought that people may find them guilty made them bolder. Because there was nothing delicate in this relationship they did not find it necessary to hide anything from each other or care for public opinion. It was rumoured that sometimes Madhusudan had even hit Shyamasundari and when she quarrelled loudly he was heard calling her names and telling her to get out of his house. But that made little difference. Madhusudan had maintained his full control over Shyama. If ever she tried to grab anything more than what Madhusudan let her have, she was rebuffed. Shyama coveted and wanted to get into the position that Motir-ma held and she wanted to run the house, but she was thwarted there as well. Madhusudan trusted Motir-ma completely but he didn't trust Shyama. Shyama had not touched his fancy, he had only developed a crude addiction to her. More like a much-used, coarse and soiled winter quilt, lacking in any fancywork, and not worth picking up even if it slipped onto the floor from the bed. But it offered warm comfort. Shyama did not need any managing. Besides, the certain knowledge that she sincerely thought him superior in every respect and was prepared to do anything for him, was soothing to his pride, something which got a daily jolt during Kumu's stay.

Kalu did not have to probe much to discover Madhusudan's recent history. Everyone in that household had discussed it—so much so that they had stopped gossiping about it.

The news stung Bipradas like a flaming arrow. Madhusudan had made no attempt to conceal his shameless affair! It was so easy to insult one's wife in public; there was so little outside protest against anyone torturing his wife! Society has devised a thousand instruments of torment to compel a helpless wife to obey her husband but no mandate to save her from his tortures. The way this cruel shame and anguish were being perpetuated in every home, through the ages, came clearly to him in a flash. There was the attempt to stifle this pain with the glorious plaster of satihood but none to uproot it altogether. Women in their world were so cheap, so trivial!

To his sister who was blissfully unaware of the state of her own marriage, Bipradas continued, 'Kumu, it is not difficult to bear an insult but it is wrong to do so. You have to demand the respect due to you, on behalf of all the women. If society chooses to chastise you for it, let it.'

Kumu said, 'What disrespect are you referring to? I can't quite follow you.'

'So you do not know all that is going on?'

'No, I don't.'

Bipradas was silent for a while. Then he said, 'I am carrying within me the anguish of dishonour to all women. Do you know why?'

Kumu kept looking at him. He went on, 'I can never forget what my mother suffered her whole life because of our amoral society.'

Brother and sister differed slightly on this point. Kumu was specially fond of her father. She knew how soft and kind he was at heart. She would always remember that his was a great personality in spite of all his faults. In fact she secretly held her mother responsible for the tragic end to his life.

Bipradas also respected his father's greatness, but he could never forgive him for the fact that he never checked himself from repeated lapses which were a public insult to their mother. In fact, he was proud of the fact that their mother did not condone them.

He said, 'The disrespect to my mother was disrespect to all women. You must forget your personal sorrow, and stand up against this insult. You must never surrender.'

Kumu lowered her face and said softly, 'But, Dada, don't forget that Father loved Mother very dearly. That kind of love can cover many sins.'

'I agree, but in spite of his love how easily he could shame Mother! His sin was a social evil. I can never forgive society for this. Society has no love, it has only rulings.'

'Dada, have you heard something?'

'Yes, I have. I will tell you by and by.'

'That's better, because I feel this kind of talk today will only make you feel worse.'

'On the contrary, Kumu. All these days my health was giving way under sorrow and sadness. Now, when my mind is prepared for a lifelong battle I feel stronger from within.'

'What battle, Dada?'

'Against the society which has so grossly cheated women of their dues.'

'What can you do to society?'

'I can defy it. I have to think out what else I can do. The struggle begins from today. You have your place in this house, not by anyone's favour. You will stay on here in your own right.'

'All right, be that as it may. You stop talking now.'

Somebody came and announced that Motir-ma had come.

# 51

Kumu took Motir-ma to her own bedroom. as they talked, it became dark. The bearer came to light the lamp but Kumu asked him not to.

Kumu heard everything from Motir-ma and kept quiet.

'It is like a haunted house,' said Motir-ma, 'It is impossible to live there. Aren't you coming back?'

'Have I been asked?'

'No, it may have escaped him altogether. But you have to come.'

'What can I do? I cannot satisfy him. In a way it is all due to me, but there was no help. What I could offer him was unacceptable to him. Now what is the point of my going empty-handed?'

'What are you saying, Bourani? The household belongs to you! You can't let it go by default.'

'What do you mean by "household"? A house, things, people? I feel ashamed to claim them as my own. Does one crave for outward things when one has lost rights over the interior?'

'Do you mean to say you are never coming back?'

'I am at a loss to understand anything. Earlier I would have prayed to my deity, asked for an omen, or I'd have consulted a soothsayer. But all those things have been washed away. In the beginning everything seemed to bode well, but none of it came to pass. It has occurred to me many times today that had I depended on my brother's judgement rather than on my god I'd not have faced this calamity. There may be room for doubt in my mind but even then my heart belongs to my Lord. I come back again and again and throw myself at His feet.'

'Your words scare me. Have you given up the idea of coming home?'

'It is difficult to imagine that I shall never get back, at the same time it is not easy to promise that I will.'

'Well, let me talk to your Dada. Let us hear what he thinks. I hope I can meet him.'

'Come, I will take you right away.'

As she entered his room Motir-ma stopped in her tracks. He reminded her of a dark ruined temple after an earthquake where silence and darkness reigned. She touched his feet and sat down on the floor.

Bipradas rushed to offer her a chair.

Motir-ma shook her head to mean she was all right where she was. Her eyes were aglow under her veil. She realized that his condition was causing Kumu great pain.

In order to make things light, Kumu said, 'Dada, she has come specially to get your opinion.'

Motir-ma protested, 'No no, taking his advice is only secondary. I have really come to pay my respects.'

Kumu continued, 'She wanted to know if you thought it proper for me to go back.'

Bipradas sat up and said, 'That is someone else's house. How can

Kumu go and live there?' The fire contained in those words might not have raged so fiercely had he uttered them in anger, and though his voice was even and his face showed no excitement, his dark anger came across quite clearly.

Motir-ma whispered something. She wanted Kumu to sit by her side and convey her words to her brother. But Kumu did not agree. She said, 'You better raise your voice and say what you have to say yourself.'

So Motir-ma became a little more articulate and said, 'Please tell him that what is yours can never be made over to anyone else, whosoever may try to take over.'

Bipradas said, 'That is not true. She is only a dependant there. She has no right of her own. If she were turned out, some may criticize, but they would do nothing to stop it. All the penalty is only meant for her. One could still accept dependency, if it were at least magnanimous.'

Motir-ma had no answer to this. She believed that when her husband's protection was threatened, it was the wife's people who had to be the supplicants. Here it seemed to be the reverse!

After a pause, she added, 'But women can't live outside the shelter of her own home. Men can float about, but women need stability.'

'Where is this stability? In the midst of dishonour? Take it from me, whoever created Kumu created her with utmost respect. No one is so superior that he can ignore her, not even the King-Emperor.'

Motir-ma was genuinely fond of Kumu, respected her too, but it did not sound right to her ears that a woman's worth could be such that her pride should surpass her husband's. Let there be quarrels with the husband, let there even be much insult and suffering on the part of the wife, it was even understandable that some wives may hang themselves to escape it, but to be totally independent of the husband and stand on her own was, according to Motir-ma, a kind of arrogance. Why should women have so much vanity? Madhusudan may be absolutely unworthy of her, he may have been grievously wrong, but still he was a man. By virtue of being a man he was somewhere naturally superior to his wife—a fact that was unarguable. Could one win a case against the Maker?

She said finally, 'Some day or the other, she has to go back. There does not seem to be any way out for her.'

'"Has to go" is a phrase meant for a slave, not for a human being.'

'The wife does become a property in a sacramental marriage. The day you go round the sacred fire seven times with the groom, your body and mind are bound to him for ever. There is no escape. It is worse than death. Once you are born a woman you may not reverse the course of a woman's fate.'

Bipradas then realized that women themselves valued women the least. They were not even aware that this was the reason why it was so easy for men to dishonour women in every home. The women themselves had put out their own light. And then they lived in perpetual fear and anxiety, oppressed by unworthy men, and accepted that the highest attainment in a woman's life was to bear all of this silently, without protest. So much violation of human rights could not be allowed any longer. Those whom society had degraded so much were now pulling the society down with them.

Kumu was sitting next to his bed with her head down. Bipradas did not answer Motir-ma but put his hand on Kumu's head and said, 'Try and understand what I am trying to tell you. Wherever power comes to one without effort, where it is never tested, and where one does not have to prove worthy of retaining it, there, power only leads to degradation. I have explained this to you often enough, but you would not give up your traditional beliefs, and in the end it is you who is suffering. When you used to feed Brahmins to earn merit I did not stop you but tried to explain to you time and again that taking someone's superiority for granted without question does harm not only to that person but lowers the standard of superiority in the entire society. Why does not one ever pause to think that by such blind reverence we only show disrespect for our own humanity? You are somewhat familiar with writings in English—can't you see that the world is up in arms against this kind of sectarian, fundamentalist, insensitive exercise of power? The time has come to smash the cosy retreat of deliberate, blind slavery, which men have long preserved under the cloak of high-sounding words.'

Kumu said, with her head still held down, 'Dada, is it your view that the wife may surpass her husband?'

'I am against any transgression, Kumu. But my view is that the husband too must not suppress the wife.'

'Even if he does, should the wife also . . .'

Bipradas did not let her finish. He went on, 'If the wife tolerates that wrongdoing then she is accepting injustice to all women. This is how every individual adds to the sum of misery and paves the way for oppression.'

Motir-ma added impatiently, 'Our Bourani is a sati, she is like Lakshmi, no amount of insult can touch her.'

Bipradas now raised his voice in excitement. 'You are concerned only with your idea of satilakshmi, why don't you ever think of the plight of the bully who daily exercises the license you are giving him, to oppress her?'

Kumu got up, began stroking his hair and said, 'Dada, you have talked much today, you should stop now. What you call freedom, comes through knowledge and that is just not in our blood. We cling to men, and we also cling to our beliefs and we are unable to untie the knot. The more we are hurt, the more we go round and round and get enmeshed. You men know a lot and that liberates your mind, we women believe a lot and that fills the emptiness in our lives. When you explain things to me, maybe I can see my mistake. But to know your weaknesses is not the same as giving them up. Like the tendrils of a creeper, our possessiveness clings to everything, good and bad alike, and then we can not let go of them.'

Bipradas said, 'That is precisely why the cowards and bullies of this world do not lack in women devotees. They recognize the evil as evil all right, yet they follow them as the holiest of the holy.'

Kumu said, 'What can we do, Dada, we have been created to embrace the mundane with both our hands. We hold on to a big tree as well as to a straw. It takes us as much time to accept a guru as to yield to a charlatan. No one can save us from a life of suffering. So I often think, if suffering is our inescapable lot, then we have to accept it and find a way of transcending it. That is why women stick to religion so desperately.'

Bipradas kept quiet.

His silence hurt her, because she knew it weighed more heavily than all his talk.

As they came out, Motir-ma asked her, 'What have you decided, Bourani?'

Kumu said, 'I can't come. Besides, I have no permission to get back.'

Motir-ma was somewhat peeved with her. Not that she herself was a great admirer of her in-laws' family, but, long years of belonging had won that family her loyalty. She could not bear the thought that any daughter-in-law of that house should transgress its bounds. The sense of what she then told Kumu was like this, 'It has to be accepted from the start that men by nature lack compassion and self-control. We are not the creators of the world, we have to make do with what we get. We have to run households by taking for granted that "they are like that". Because, a household belongs to the woman. It does not matter whether the husband is good or bad. If one does not accept this truth, death is the only way out.'

Kumu said with a smile, 'Maybe that is so, but what is wrong with death?'

Motir-ma anxiously responded, 'Don't say such things!'

Kumu did not know that recently in their neighbourhood, a seventeen-year old bride had committed suicide by swallowing some acid. Her husband had a Master's degree and held a good post in a Government office. His mother had complained to him that the wife had lost a silver hair comb and so he went and kicked his wife. Motir-ma remembered the incident and shuddered.

Nabin arrived on the scene. Kumu was delighted to see him. She said, 'I knew that we would see you soon.'

Nabin laughed and said, 'Bourani is well versed in logic. She first saw Mrs Smoke and did not find it difficult to infer that Mr Fire would follow suit.'

Motir-ma said, 'Bourani, you have spoilt him. He knows that you like to see him and he is so proud of that.'

Nabin rejoined, 'The one who may also be glad to see me is no less powerful. My creator may be regretting his own handiwork but neither the gods nor men know what my spouse thinks of me.'

'The two of you may bandy words. I do not wish to be a third person to spoil the fun. I am off now,' said Kumu.

Motir-ma said, 'My dear, who is the third person here? Do you think he spent money in hiring a carriage just to come and see me?'

'No, I don't think so. But let me order something for him to eat.' Kumu left.

## 52

Motir-ma asked him, 'Is there any news?'

'Yes, there is. That is why I came post-haste to consult you. After you left for this house, Dada came suddenly into my room—exceptionally bad-tempered. A cheap gilt ash-tray had disappeared from his desk. Its present owner must have thought it to be made of gold, otherwise why should he or she risk retribution in the next life? You know how Dada cannot bear the loss of the most trivial item—it is as if the very foundation of his huge property is being shaken. This morning, before leaving for his office, he ordered me to send Shyama back home. I had started on that sacred task with great enthusiasm. My plan was to complete my job before he came back from office. But around half-past one he suddenly barged into my room and said, "Hold it for now." As he was going out his glance fell on the portrait of Bourani on my desk. He stopped. I knew he was feeling shy to straighten his gaze and look directly at the photograph. So I said, "Dada, wait here for a while, I shall bring and show you a Dacca sari. It is a present for Motir-ma's sister-in-law, who is expecting a baby. But I have a feeling Ganeshram is cheating me. I want to check it with you. In my estimate it should not be as much as thirteen rupees. At best it could be nine or nine and a half."'

Motir-ma was surprised. She said, 'How did you ever think of it? My sister-in-law has no chance of having another baby in the near future. Her youngest is only a month and a half old. I find you these days capable of making up any story. Where did you learn this art?'

'The same place from where our great poet Kalidas got it. Direct from the Muse, our goddess of learning, Bani Binapani.'

'It will be difficult to live with you, so long as the Muse does not leave you alone.'

'It is my vow to visit hell before I go to Paradise, like Yudhistir in our epic. That would be my gift to Bourani.'

'But tell me how did you get hold of your nine-and-a-half rupee sari that very moment?'

'Nowhere. After about twenty minutes I came back and reported that Ganeshram had taken back the sari without waiting for my approval. From Dada's face it was apparent that the portrait had by now entered his head and taken the shape of a dream. I don't know why, but I am the only one in the whole world with whom Dada has some feeling of delicacy. If it were anyone else in front of Dada he would have grabbed the picture without a moment's thought about who was watching him.'

'You are no less greedy. You could have presented it to him.'

'In fact, I have given it to him but not with an easy mind. I told him, "Dada, how about making an oil-painting from this photograph to hang in your bedroom?" He pretended to be disinterested and said, "We'll see," and went up with the picture. I am not sure what followed. Maybe he didn't go back to work, nor do I have any hope of getting back the photo.'

'Since you are willing to give up paradise for the sake of your Bourani, the loss of a photograph shouldn't matter,' said Motir-ma teasingly.

'Paradise may be doubtful, but the picture was real to me. It was rarely that such a picture happens. It had captured that very rare moment when the grace of heavens was fully reflected on her face. On some nights I have got up and lit a lamp to look at it. It seemed that the inner beauty was more apparent in the light of a lamp.'

'Aren't you a little afraid of being so effusive in front of me?'

'If I were afraid then you would have real cause to worry. The truth is that I am amazed at her sight. I wonder how her presence became possible in our family. I am thrilled that I call her our Bourani and that she sits down and feeds an inconsequential chap like me. How on earth did all this happen with such ease? My brother is the least fortunate in our family. What he got so easily, he lost by trying to possess it too closely.'

'Good heavens, there is no stopping you once you start on your Bourani!'

'Mejobou, I know it hurts you slightly.'

'Never.'

'Yes, a little bit. In this context let me remind you that all that you said when you saw Bourani's brother for the first time at the Noornagar railway station could be called in plain language "gushing".'

'All right, let us stop that debate. Now tell me what you came to tell me.'

'I believe Dada will send for her any day now. That she came here eagerly and never talked of going back has also hurt his pride greatly. Poor Dada is unable to understand that the bird has no fascination for a golden cage. The foolish bird! The ungrateful bird!'

'Good. Let him send for her. That was the understanding.'

'I think she should go before she is sent for. Let that little margin of pride be with Dada. Besides Bipradas Babu also wanted her to go. It is I who advised him against it then.'

Motir-ma gave no indication of the conversation that she had earlier with Bipradas about this. She merely said, 'Go and find out from him.'

'That's what I will do. He will be pleased to hear of the developments.'

Kumu asked from outside the door, 'May I come in?'

Motir-ma said, 'Your brother-in-law is anxiously waiting for you.'

'Yes, I have been waiting for ages and ages, and now I am blessed with your presence.'

'My goodness, how you can go on and on spinning out words!'

'True, it surprises me too.'

'Come on for dinner now.'

'I would like to have a word with your brother before we sit down to eat.'

'No. That's not possible.'

'Why?'

'He has talked enough for the day.'

'But I've got some good news for him.'

'Maybe, but in that case why not come tomorrow? No more conversation for him today.'

'Maybe tomorrow I won't be free, something else may turn up. Please let me have just five minutes with him. I am sure he will be happy and no harm will be done.'

'All right, first you finish your food, and then we'll see.'

At the end of the meal Kumu took him to Bipradas and found him still awake. The room was almost in darkness and the light was dim. Stars could be seen through the open window and the south wind was blowing freely. The curtains, the bedcovers and his clothes were tossing about, throwing strange shadows around. A loose sheet of newspaper was flying around aimlessly. Bipradas remained still, in the midst of this, half reclining. The shadow of the dusk and the pallor of his illness had shrouded him in such a manner that he seemed to be very far away—in another distant world altogether. He looked the loneliest man on earth.

Nabin touched his feet and said, 'I don't want to disturb your rest. I have just come to say that it is time for Bourani to come back. We are all waiting for her.'

Bipradas did not reply. He just sat still.

Nabin said again, 'We shall arrange to take her back as soon as you permit.'

Meanwhile Kumu had come and sat near her brother's feet. Bipradas looked at her and said, 'If you think the time has come for you to go back, then you may do so, Kumu.'

Kumu said, 'No, Dada, I shall not go back,' and threw herself upon his knees.

The room was silent, but from time to time a gust of wind rattled a loose window. Outside, the leaves of the trees in the garden rustled in the breeze.

Kumu soon got up and told Nabin, 'It is time to go. Dada, you try to sleep.'

Motir-ma came home and said, 'This is going a bit too far.'

'You mean to say that it is all right to be poked in the eyes but it is quite improper for the eyes to get red.'

'No, my dear, it is all their conceit. They find nothing in this world to match their worth. They are above everyone.'

'It is true that such pride does not become most people, but they are indeed a class by themselves.'

'But that does not mean one can disown all relationships.'

'One can't claim a relationship by merely announcing it. We must admit that they belong to a class quite different from ours. In fact, I feel hesitant to be familiar with them only by virtue of our recent relationship.'

'You must remember that however high a person may be in society, relationships have a compulsion of their own.'

Nabin could sense a sting of envy on the part of Motir-ma in relation to Kumu. It was also true that family ties were very precious to women.

So he cut short the debate and said, 'Let's watch for a few days. No harm in sharpening his interest a little more.'

## 53

Shyamasundari had every reason to hope that her position in this household was now firm; but she could not feel so yet. In the beginning she thought she had acquired the right to boss over the domestic staff, but now she was made to realize at every step that they were unwilling to accept her as the mistress. It was as if, given a chance, they would be happy to defy her. This was why Shyama would scold them without reason, send them on unnecessary errands, constantly find fault with them, nag them and abuse them. She was trying very hard to wipe out her earlier image of a nobody in this house but found that it would not wash with any of the servants. One old servant could not bear her badgering any longer and resigned from his job. Shyama had to eat humble pie on that score. The reason was that Madhusudan had some blind superstitions concerning his fortune. He took it as an ill omen if any of the employees associated with his good times died or resigned. For a similar reason an old ink-stained desk from those times was incongruously but firmly established in the midst of the expensive modern furniture in his office room. On top of it was placed an old zinc ink-pot and a cheap English wooden pen, the same one with which he had signed his first big contract in the early days of his business. Dadhi, the Oriya employee who had resigned, belonged to those times. So Madhusudan not only ignored his resignation but even rewarded him handsomely. Shyama had to endure Dadhi's smiling face thereafter.

The problem with Shyama was that she really loved Madhusudan; so she was afraid of putting too much strain on his temper. She had to gauge timidly if the limits of her pettishness were reaching the border of transgression. Madhusudan was also quite certain that he need not waste time or thought over Shyama. Even if her demand for love or her expenses were curtailed there was no danger. He undoubtedly had a crude attraction for her, and he was encouraged by the thought that even if he indulged in it to his heart's content, he could still manage to keep it within restraint. If it were not so, this tie would have broken much earlier. Nothing counted for him more than work. And for his work what he needed most was control over self. Shyama's hold could not extend to that domain. Every time she tried to take a small step towards it, she stumbled badly. So it had been her lot only to give; she lost whenever she tried to take.

Shyama had always been deprived of money and things and she had no end of craving for them. But even in this she had to move with care. What should have been easy to expect of such a rich man, was beyond her dreams. Madhusudan had sometimes bought her clothes and jewellery but that hardly brought her gratification. So she always nursed an impulse to pick up small objects of desire. But even that was not easy. It was a small incident like this which earned her an order of banishment. Even then, Shyama's service and her company had become an addiction with Madhusudan as cheap and strong as the habit of chewing paan or tobacco. If he denied himself these pleasures, it might affect his work, he realized. So she got a reprieve. But it hung over her head like Damocles's sword.

Because of her weak hold, she was also forever apprehensive of Kumu coming back to her throne. This pang of jealousy gave her no peace of mind. She knew she could not compete with Kumu, they were not in the same playing field. Kumu's great strength was that she was beyond Madhusudan's control, whilst his control over Shyama was so complete that she was certainly of use to him but of no value. Shyama had cried over this situation a great deal and often wished she were dead. She beat her breast and lamented, 'Why did I become so cheap to him,' but later consoled herself with the thought that the reason she could get a place at all, was because she was cheap; the dearer ones may be more desired, but the cheap ones won in the end.

All the while that Madhusudan had not accepted her, she had not been so unhappy. She had been reconciled to her deprivation. The little that she got from time to time from the brief conversations with him seemed enough for her. But now she could not compromise between the right to have and not have. She was frightened of losing all the time. The track of her fortune was laid on such shaky ground that derailment was imminent every moment. She tried to unburden herself and get some consolation from Motir-ma, but the way she was dismissed with a violent shrug made her want to retaliate severely then and there. She knew that in the management of the household Madhusudan regarded Motir-ma as most useful, and would not tolerate any disruption there. From then on the two women had stopped talking to, and even avoided, each other. Thus Shyama's space in the house had shrunk even more. She was comfortable nowhere.

Then one evening, as she entered Madhusudan's bedroom, she saw Kumu's photograph resting on the wall. The lightning from the thunder that threatened to strike her, blinded her eyes. Her heart was a-flutter like a hooked fish. Much as she wanted she could not take her eyes off the picture. She continued to stare at it with an ashen face and clenched fists, with fire in her eyes. She wanted desperately to break or tear something apart. She feared that she might damage something in the room if she stayed in it any longer. She rushed out, threw herself on her own bed and tore the sheet into shreds.

Night fell. The bearer announced from outside her door that the master had sent for her in his bedroom. She did not have the power to say no. She quickly got up, washed her face, put on an embroidered Dacca sari and perfumed herself. All this was in an attempt to distract him from that portrait on the wall. But unfortunately for her, the lamp was lit right in front of the picture and it seemed someone's glowing gaze was illuminating the entire picture. That photo was the most visible object in the room. Shyama gave Madhusudan the usual pack of paan and began to press his feet. For some reason he was in a good mood that evening. He had also bought a silver photo-frame from an English shop. He gravely presented it to Shyama, merely saying, 'Take this.' Even when he was being nice to her he was miserly in the matter of displaying soft emotions. Because he knew that if Shyama was indulged slightly, she lost her dignity. The frame was packed in brown paper. She opened it slowly and asked, 'What is it for?'

'Don't you know? It is for framing photographs inside.'

Shyama felt as if she was being lashed. She asked, 'Whose photo do you intend to put there?'

'Why, yours. The one that was taken the other day.'

'I don't need such a show of affection,' she said and flung the frame on the floor.

Madhusudan was taken aback. He asked, 'What does this mean?'

'Nothing,' she said and started crying. Then she got off the bed and began to hit her head on the floor. Madhusudan thought she was upset because the present was cheap and she had expected some expensive ornament. After a tiring and long day, he did not like this fuss. It was like an attack of hysteria—the one thing he hated most. He scolded her sternly, 'Get up! Get up right now.'

Shyama got up and ran out of the room. Madhusudan swore to himself. 'This will never do,' he muttered.

He knew her only too well. He expected that in a little while she would come and fall at his feet and beg forgiveness. That would be the best time to firmly tell her a few home truths.

It was ten at night, but Shyama did not turn up. Once again there were summons outside her door, 'Maharaj is calling you.'

Shyama said to the bearer, 'Tell Maharaj that I am not well.'

Madhusudan fumed. 'How audacious! She dares disobey my orders.'

Still he expected her to turn up later. But she didn't come. At a quarter to eleven he got up and quickly went to her room to find it in darkness. But he could make out Shyama lying on the floor. He thought it was only a ploy to demand some petting from him.

He roared. 'Get up and come with me. Now! None of this fussing.'

Shyama got up without a word.

## 54

The next day as he came up for a little rest after lunch and before going back to work, Madhusudan found Kumu's photograph missing. Shyama was not ready with her paan to serve him like other days. In fact, she was not around at all. She was sent for. It was evident that she was hesitating to appear before him. Madhusudan asked her, 'Where is the photograph that used to be on my table?'

Shyama pretended ignorance, 'Photo? Whose photo?'

Women generally have little regard for male intelligence, hence her pretence was a shade too obvious.

Madhusudan said angrily, 'Haven't you seen it?'

Shyama was innocence herself. She said, 'No, I don't seem to have.'

Madhusudan roared again, 'You are lying!'

'Why should I lie? What use is a photo to me?'

'I am warning you. Wherever you may have hidden it, go and get it!'

'What a bother! How can I get a picture of yours?'

Madhu called the bearer and ordered him to get Nabin.

Nabin came. Madhusudan said, 'Arrange for Borrobou to come back.'

Shyama made a face and sat stiff like a wooden doll.

Nabin scratched his head and said after some time, 'Isn't it proper for you to call on them once? If you go and ask yourself, Bourani will be very pleased.'

Madhusudan puffed on his hookah solemnly for a while and then said, 'All right, tomorrow is Sunday. I shall go.'

Nabin rushed to his room and told his wife with suppressed excitement, 'I have done something.'

'Without consulting me?'

'There was no time.'

'Then you are sure to be in trouble.'

'Possible. In my horoscope there is no star in the house of intelligence, only my wife. That is why I always keep you at hand. It happened like this: Dada ordered today that Bourani had to be brought back. I blurted out, "Dada, it would be much better if you went personally and raised the topic." I didn't know what his mood was, but he readily agreed. Since then I have been wondering what the consequences might be.'

'Not at all good. From the little I saw of Bipradas Babu, I am worried about his reaction. What he might say could lead to a royal battle. Why did you get into this?'

'The main reason was that my intelligence was at level zero, because you were somewhere else then. Secondly, when the other day Bourani declined to come, I guessed the real reason. Her brother had been lying ill in Kolkata all these days and her husband had not come even once to find out how he was. This hurt her deeply.'

Motir-ma understood this in a flash and wondered why it had not struck her in the first place. She had probably, unknown to herself, some pride in her in-laws' family. It had never occurred to her that, like everyone else, Madhusudan also had obligations towards his own in-laws.

Nabin brought up the old debate and said sarcastically, 'I would have never thought about it on my own had you not reminded me the other day.'

'How?'

'You said that the obligations of relationships had priority over family pride. That gave me courage to think that even a great fellow like the Maharaj owed a visit to Bipradas Babu.'

Motir-ma was not disposed to accept defeat. She dismissed this with, 'How can you indulge in such useless banter at a critical time? You should now think seriously of the next step.'

'You are likely to lose if you start thinking of the end at the very beginning. We should think first of the immediate step. And that is for Dada to call on Bipradas Babu. If we start thinking of the consequences from now then that may be a tribute to your power of thinking, but it would be overdoing it.'

'I don't know. I feel there will be trouble.'

## 55

The next morning Kumu spent a long time practising music with her brother. Our morning ragas help one's personal sorrows to merge with eternity and become universal and through that music we escape from our bondage. Just as the mythical serpents in the matted locks of Mahadeva become his adornments, the rivers of sorrow flow into their final resting place, the ocean of sorrows. They change their features, and their restlessness is stilled in the great deep.

Bipradas heaved a deep sigh and said, 'In our world the immediate present is the only reality, the eternal remains always in the background. In music, the eternal comes to the fore and the trivial recedes. That is how the mind is liberated.'

At this point the servant announced, 'Maharaj Madhusudan is here.'

Kumu's face went pale in a second. Bipradas was pained at this sight and said, 'Kumu, you go in. We may not need you after all.'

Kumu disappeared quickly.

Madhusudan had deliberately come without notice. He was keen not to allow them any time to hide their poverty of reception. Madhusudan believed that Bipradas secretly nursed a great sense of pride in his aristocratic descent. And Madhusudan could not bear such a thought. That was why he had come today as if it was not a visit he was paying but more like an audience he was granting them.

Madhusudan's strange attire was such as would overwhelm the servants. He had on a coloured floral silk waistcoat on top of a striped English shirt. A folded shawl hung over his shoulder. He wore a carefully pleated black-bordered Santipur dhoti and a pair of burnished black court shoes. His fingers were resplendent with rings bearing large diamonds and other precious stones. Encircling his spacious girth was a gold watch-chain and he held in his hand a fancy stick with a gold top shaped like an elephant's head and decorated with precious stones.

After some quick and half-expressed greetings he sat himself on the chair next to Bipradas's bed and said, 'How are you, Bipradas Babu? You look none too good.'

Bipradas made no reply but said, 'You seem to be keeping well.'

'Can't say I really am, I have a slight headache towards the evening and my appetite is not good either. The slightest change in diet upsets me. But what pains me most is my insomnia.'

An introduction to a case for whole-time care!

Bipradas said, 'Must be too much pressure of office work.'

'Nothing unusual. Office work takes care of itself. Mr McNaughton bears most of the burden and Sir Arthur Peabody also helps me a lot.'

The hookah and the paan came. Madhusudan picked only one cardamom and puffed the pipe a couple of times, after which he continued to hold it in his left hand. It was never used again. Snacks arrived from inside the house. He quickly protested, 'You have to excuse me. As I told you, I have to be very particular about my food.'

Bipradas did not ask him again. He told the servant, 'Go and tell Pishima that our guest is not well. He will not eat.'

Then he fell silent. Madhusudan expected that the topic of Kumu would naturally come up. So many days had gone by that Bipradas should be now showing some anxiety on his own. But he was not even mentioning Kumu. Madhusudan began to rage inside. He thought it was a mistake to have come. All this was Nabin's doing. He wanted to go back quickly and think of some heavy punishment for his misdeed.

Kumu entered then, dressed in a plain black-bordered sari, veiled properly like a married woman. Bipradas had never expected this. He was most surprised. She touched first her husband's feet, then her brother's and told Madhusudan, 'Dada is very tired and the doctor has advised him not to talk much. You better come with me into the next room.'

Madhusudan was red in the face. He got up quickly. The pipe slipped from his hand. He said, without even looking at Bipradas, 'So long, I am going.'

His first impulse was to stalk out and step into the carriage to go back home. But his heart was in a bind. He was seeing Kumu after many days. This was the first time he saw her in homely attire. She had never looked so beautiful. So cool, so easy. In his own house she was a formal person, here she belonged. Today he saw her from very close. How soothing was her presence. He wanted to take her away without any delay. He turned over in his mind again and again these words, 'She is mine, she is mine alone, she belongs to my home, she is my treasure, she is my heart and soul.'

So when she showed him to a sofa in the next room and asked him to sit down, he had to. If it were not so open, he would have pulled her down to sit by his side. But Kumu did not sit, she stood behind a chair with her hands resting on its arms. She asked, 'Do you wish to say something to me?'

He did not quite like the tone of her question. He asked, 'Aren't you coming home?'

'No, I am not.'

Madhusudan was startled. 'What do you mean?' he asked.

'You have no need for me.'

He guessed that the Shyamasundari affair had reached her ears and assumed that his wife was sulking. He liked the idea, and said, 'How absurd! Of course I need you. Who likes an empty house?'

She did not feel like arguing with him but briefly reiterated, 'I am not going back.'

'How do you mean? Can a woman refuse to go to her husband's home?'

Her brief reply again was, 'No, I am not going.'

Madhusudan jumped up from the sofa and said, 'What! You dare refuse to come? You will have to!'

Kumu said nothing. Madhusudan shouted at her, 'Do you know I can call the police and drag you home by the scruff of your neck? You think you can say "no" that easily?'

Kumu continued to remain silent. Madhusudan raved, 'So the tutoring has started afresh in your brother's Noornagar school?'

Kumu glanced once at her brother's room and said, 'Be quiet, do not talk so loudly.'

'Do I have to care for your brother's wishes? Do you know I can throw him out on the streets this very moment?'

Next moment, Kumu found her brother standing at the door, tall, frail, pale in the face, his large eyes burning in indignation. A thick white sheet covered his body and trailed on the ground. He said, 'Kumu, come to my room.'

Madhusudan screamed, 'I shall remember this arrogance of yours. I shall smash your Noornagar pride, or I shall not call myself Madhusudan.'

Bipradas took to bed straightaway. He closed his eyes, not to sleep but out of tiredness and anxiety. Kumu sat at his head and started fanning him. After a long time, Aunt Kshema came and asked, 'Aren't you coming for your lunch? It is quite late in the day, Kumu.'

Bipradas opened his eyes and said, 'Kumu, go for your lunch and send Kaluda to me.'

Kumu said, 'I beg of you, Dada. No Kaluda now. Try and sleep a little.'

Bipradas did not say anything, looked at her with deeply pained eyes, let out a long sigh and then closed his eyes again. Kumu went out softly, leaving the door ajar.

Soon Kalu sent word that he wanted to come. Bipradas sat up leaning on a bolster. Kalu said, 'Our son-in-law came and left in no time. What happened? Didn't he say anything about taking Kumu back?'

'Yes he did, but Kumu said "no".'

Kalu was dismayed. He said, 'What are you saying? This is disastrous for us.'

'We have never been afraid of disasters. We fear dishonour.'

'Then get ready. There is not much time to lose. I knew it was in your blood, and that you can't escape it. I remember how your father lost about a couple of lakhs in defying the magistrate. It is your family hobby to march forward and bravely court disaster. At least my family does not suffer from this disability. That is why I can not bear to watch it silently. But how shall we survive?'

Bipradas put his right leg over the raised left one, leaned back on the bolster, closed his eyes and was deep in thought for quite a while. At last he opened his eyes and said, 'According to the clauses of the loan agreement Madhusudan cannot claim repayment from us without six months' notice in advance. Meanwhile Subodh will be here by the month of Ashadh and we shall find a solution then.'

Kalu said with some irritation, 'Sure you will find a solution. Instead of all the lights going out at the same time, they will be turned off at decent intervals.'

'In any case the light is in its last throes, now it matters little as to which bearer comes in and how he blows it out. I am sick of looking after the end piece of that light. A complete darkness will give me greater relief.'

Kalu was hurt at this response from Bipradas. He understood that it was the reaction of a sick person. Normally Bipradas was not a person to give up so easily. Kalu knew he was planning a lot to avoid the final disaster and he also believed that he would get over it. It was hard for him to think that after today there was no room even for such a belief.

Kalu looked at Bipradas gently and said, 'Brother, you don't have to think any more. I shall do whatever is necessary. Let me go and meet the brokers.'

The next day Bipradas had a letter from Madhusudan written in English. The language was legalistic, probably drafted by his attorney. It demanded to know for certain if and when Kumu was coming back, and that appropriate action would be taken depending on the reply to his letter.

Bipradas asked Kumu if she had considered all sides carefully.

Kumu said, 'I have given up thinking about it totally. And that is why today my mind is at rest. I have a feeling that for me, everything was just as it used to be; and whatever had happened in between was nothing but a dream.'

'If they try to force you to go, will you be able to resist it?'

'If they leave you out of it, I shall certainly be able to manage.'

'I am asking you because, if you have to go back in the end, then the more you delay the nastier it will be. Have you developed any soft corner anywhere in your mind for your in-laws?'

'Not in the least. I like only Nabin, Motir-ma and Habloo but more like an outsider.'

'You see, they are going to torture you. They have the power of money and the society to torture you. That is why we have to defy it. And to do that you have to stand up in public without shame, fear or hesitation. There will be a storm of criticism at home and outside, yet you have to keep your head in the midst of all that.'

'Won't it bring you harm and disquiet?'

'What do you call harm and disquiet, Kumu? What could cause me greater harm than you leading a life of dishonour? And nothing could cause me more disquiet than the knowledge that the home where you lived had not become your own and the person who should have been closest to you was the farthest from you. Father loved you very much, but in those days the heads of families were distant entities, and the thought that you also needed some education, never crossed his mind. I have taught you and brought you up right from the beginning. I am no less than your parents. Today I realize the onus of that task. If you were like any other girl you would have had no problems. But today, any place where there is no recognition, no respect for your own distinct identity would be hell to you. Can I have the heart to banish you to such a place? Why not stay with me forever as any younger brother of mine might have?'

Kumu rested her head on the bed close to her brother's chest but turned her face away and said, 'But won't I be a burden on you? Tell me frankly.'

Bipradas stroked her head and said, 'My dear sister, how can you be a burden? I will make you work your feet off! You will look after all my jobs. No private secretary could do all that. On top of it you will have to play music for me and my horse will be in your charge too. You know that I love to teach, and I could not hope for a better pupil than you. Let's do something I always wanted to do—learn Persian. We will study together. You are bound to excel me, but I assure you I won't be jealous!'

Kumu was enthralled listening to him. Nothing could be more pleasurable in life.

Bipradas said then, 'Let me tell you something more, Kumu. The times will change and with it our mores too. We have to live like poor people and you will be the poor man's treasure.'

Tears welled up in her eyes. She said, 'If that happens, I shall be the luckiest girl in the world.'

Bipradas held Madhusudan's letter in his hand. He did not reply to it.

## 56

Within a couple of days Nabin came with Motir-ma and Habloo. the little boy climbed up on Kumu's lap and hid his face in her breast and started crying. It was difficult to guess what the crying was for, was it a sulk for the past, a childish demand of the present or a concern for the future?

Kumu embraced him and said, 'It is a cruel world, Gopal—there is no end to tears. What do I have that I can offer to wipe your tears? Can I try and stop the crying with mine? That's about all I can do. The love that gives oneself and nothing more, is the kind of love you children have. Your Auntie will not be there forever, but remember her words and remember her—do remember.' She kissed his cheeks.

Nabin said, 'Bourani, we are off to our ancestral home in Rajabpur. This chapter is closed.'

Kumu said in distress, 'I am the unlucky one who brought you this misery.'

Nabin said, 'On the contrary. We have been toying with the idea for quite a while. In fact, we were ready and packed to leave, when you appeared in our lives. We were so happy—but the gods did not let it be.'

It was clear that Madhusudan on his return the other night must have raised Cain.

Whatever Nabin might say, Motir-ma had no doubt that Kumu's advent had turned their household topsy-turvy and she had no intention of pardoning her on that score. In her opinion Kumu should have gone back with her head hanging in shame and accepted whatever torment was in store for her. She asked Kumu somewhat harshly, 'So you have decided never to set foot in your in-law's house?'

Kumu was equally firm. 'No, I shall not.'

Motir-ma asked, 'Where will you be then?'

Kumu said, 'There will be some space for me in this wide world. One loses much in life, but something is always left.'

Kumu understood that Motir-ma had mentally distanced herself from her a lot. She turned to Nabin and asked, 'So what will you be doing now?'

'We have some land by the riverside. That will be enough for our living, plus there will be plenty of pure air.'

Motir-ma said with some hauteur, 'No, my dear, you don't have to worry about that. No one can take away our rightful earnings from the Mirzapur household. We are not such honourable people that we shall walk out just because the big brother had chased us out. He will call us back sooner or later. We can hold out till then. Take it from me!'

Nabin was a bit disappointed and embarassed at her outburst. He said, 'I am well aware of that, Mejobou, and I have no pride on that account. If there is rebirth as they say, then my only wish is to be born an honourable man, even it means starving.'

In fact Nabin had often made up his mind to leave his brother's shelter and take up farming on his own in their village home. Motir-ma also fumed a lot, but when push came to shove, she could never bring herself to move. She had stopped her husband every time. To her way of thinking, she had full claim over her elder brother-in-law. He was almost like her father-in-law. He might do something wrong but that could never be taken as an insult. It appeared totally outlandish to her that Kumu should refuse to live with her husband, whatever his behaviour towards her might have been.

The doctor was announced. Kumu said, 'Do wait till I find out what the doctor has to say.'

The doctor said, 'His pulse is no better. He is not sleeping enough at night. The patient needs more rest.'

Kumu was getting back to her visitors when Kalu met her and said, 'I must tell you something. The matter is getting very complicated. If you do not go back it will become worse. Frankly, I see no way out.'

Kumu stood silently. Kalu continued, 'Summons have come from your husband. Do we have the strength to resist it? We are well within his grip.'

Kumu held on tightly to the railing and said, 'I am at a loss to understand anything. I feel stifled. It seems there is no way out for me but death,' and quickly ran inside.

Motir-ma was exchanging news with Aunt Kshema, whilst Kumu was with her brother. Comparing notes about her symptoms, both suspected that Kumu was pregnant. Motir-ma was happy and prayed to goddess Kali that this was true. Now she was trapped good and proper! The proud woman wanted to ignore her in-laws but now it was a knot in the cord of life, not a mere ritual marriage tie. There was no escape for her this time!

She took Kumu aside and told her about what she suspected. Kumu's face was drained of all colour. She clenched her fists and said, 'No, no, this cannot be, must not be!'

Motir-ma said testily, 'Why not? You may belong to the highest in the land but the laws of life won't be changed for your sake. You belong to the Ghoshal clan now and the family god of the Ghoshals won't let you off easily. He is guarding your escape route.'

The fear of pregnancy brought clearly to Kumu's mind the distorted image that was taking shape out of her brief encounter with her husband. The differences between one person and another that are insurmountable are often very tenuous in their elements. There may be nothing apparently clashing in language, bearing and small hints of behaviour, but they are spread over unspoken gestures, tone of voice, manners and ideals of living. There was something in Madhusudan that not only hurt her but deeply shamed her. He was desperately poor at the start of his life, so the opinions he expressed now and then, boastfully, about the supremacy of 'money' was the reflection of an inherent inferiority within himself. He had raised this topic of worshipping the god of wealth as a barb against her own family. His natural vulgarity, harshness of speech, arrogant incivility and his mental and physical personality as well as the intrinsic ugliness of his household had repelled her body and mind every day she spent there. The more she tried to overlook these and not to think about them, the more they heaped up around her like a gigantic garbage dump. Kumu had fought valiantly against this feeling of hatred within herself. She spared no effort on her part to keep up the tradition of husband-worship. She had not realized until now how pitifully she had lost her battle. Now she was linked by flesh and blood with Madhusudan; the horror of it began to torment her. She asked Motir-ma anxiously, 'How can you know for certain?'

Motir-ma was incensed, but she controlled herself and said, 'I am the mother of a child. Who will know better than me? The time has not come to be absolutely sure. You had better get yourself examined by a qualified midwife.'

It was time for Nabin, Motir-ma and Habloo to leave. But Kumu could not put her mind to anything but this grave unfair blow fate had dealt her. So her leave-taking from her friendly in-laws was perfunctory. Nabin said, 'All good things must end sometime. I was so lucky to be of service to you. But I could hardly imagine it should end so abruptly.' Nabin touched her feet. Habloo was crying silently. Motir-ma kept a stern exterior and did not utter a word.

# 57

The news reached Bipradas. The midwife came and put an end to all doubts about Kumu's pregnancy. The news also reached Madhusudan's ears. He had wanted wealth and amassed enough of it. He had wanted a title worthy of his status—he had got that too. And now the final goal of his wordly duties would be attained if he could perpetuate his own glory through family succession. The more he was pleased at the thought, the more he transferred the burden of all guilt from Kumu to her brother Bipradas.

He wrote him a second letter starting with 'Whereas' and ending with 'Your obedient servant' and appended his own signature in full—Madhusudan Ghoshal. In between there were clauses like, 'I shall have the painful necessity' etc. Usually these kind of threatening letters had the contrary effect on the Chatterjees. Bipradas showed the letter to Kalu who turned red in the face. 'This kind of letter provokes even a cool fellow like me to get into the Badshahi mood, call the Kotwal—the chief of police—and order him to cut off the head of the writer and bring it to me instantly.'

Because he had a lot of paper-work to finish during the day, Bipradas could send for Kumu only in the evening. Kumu had not met her brother the whole day. She was avoiding him carefully.

Bipradas got up from his bed and sat on a chair. Lying down made his mind weak. He had also reserved a seat for Kumu in front of him. The lamp was kept shaded in a corner of the room. A large hanging fan was being pulled from outside with great gusto. The air was still hot, it was the end of Boishakh. Short spurts of breeze from the south offered scant respite. The leaves of the trees were still, as if listening—all ears. The darkness of the evening was somewhat like the blue of the sea at the mouth of the Ganga, toned down by the river as it ran into the ocean. In between, there were flickers of the last light of the lengthening eventide. The pond in the garden was usually in the shadows, but the reflection of a very bright star in it tonight was like a beckoning finger. The owls hooted as the servants passed to and from under the trees with lanterns in hand.

Kumu came into the room a little late, still hesitant. As soon as she sat down near Bipradas, she said, 'Dada, I don't like the look of things at all. I feel like going away somewhere.'

Bipradas said, 'You are mistaken, Kumu. You are going to like it. In a little while you will be fulfilled in body and mind as well.'

'But then . . .' Kumu stopped halfway.

'I know, but who can release you from your bondage now?'

'Does it mean I have to go?'

'I don't have the right to tell you not to. I dare not rob your child of its rightful home.'

'When do I have to go?' she asked in a low voice.

'Tomorrow. It brooks no delay.'

'Dada, I am sure it is clear to you that they will never let me come to you again.'

'Yes, I am well aware of it.'

'Then let it be so. But I do not want you ever to call on them. I know I will die of longing to see, you but I do not wish to see you in that house ever. I just could not bear the thought.'

'No, Kumu, you don't have to worry on that score.'

'But they will also try to create trouble for you?'

'When they finish doing with me what they will, they will also lose all hold on me. I shall be free that very moment. Why do you call that trouble?'

'Make me free too at the same time. By then I would have been able to deliver their child to them. There are things one cannot give up even for a child's sake.'

'Have your baby first and then we shall see how you feel.'

'You may not believe me. But do you remember Mother? I believe, she chose her own time and place of death. The day she lost her rightful place in the family she could leave her children easily. When one desires freedom intensely, nothing can hold one back. I am your sister, I too want freedom. Take it from me, the day I renounce my ties, my mother will bless me.'

Both of them sat quietly again for some time. Suddenly there was a gust of wind, the leaves of the book on the teapoy started fluttering. The fragrance of bael flowers blew in from the garden to fill the room.

Kumu said, 'Don't think, Dada, that they wilfully caused me pain. I am built in such a way that they could not make me happy. I too cannot please them. There will always be a problem with those who cannot please them easily. Then why all this torment. I shall have to bear all the calumny from the society, they will go unscathed. But mark my words, Dada, one day I shall be rid of them and I shall be free to come back to you. There is no point in being the Borrobou of that family if I can't be Kumu, my own self. I know, Dada, you don't believe in God, but I do. Even more now, than I did three months ago. I have been thinking the whole of today—why with so much anomaly, such chaos everywhere, the world is still not overwhelmed by dirt? There lies beyond all this a space where the sun, moon and the universe are still turning—that is where paradise lies, that is where my god resides. I feel shy to talk to you like this, but there may never be another opportunity. I poured out my thoughts so that you may not be consumed with worry unnecessarily on my account. I have realized that there is a residue of your own even after you've lost all. And that is inexhaustible, that is my god. If I hadn't realized this truth, then I'd have clung to you till my death and never entered that prison-house again.'

When she finished she lay her head on his feet. For a long time Bipradas looked out of the window, lost in endless brooding.

## 58

Early next morning he sent for Kumu. She found one esraj stretched on his lap and another lying on the bed. He said, 'Pick up the instrument, let's play together.' It was still somewhat dark. After the whole night, the breeze had cooled down and was lightly blowing through the peepul leaves, and the crows had started cawing. The two of them started with a slow alaap in Raag Bhairon—sombre, quiet and plaintive. It recalled the mood of Mahadev in the morning after he had reconciled himself to the loss of Sati. As they played, the rays of the sun shone brighter through the flowering branches of gulmohar; the sun came up beyond the garden wall. Servants came, stood near the door and went away. They could not do the room. Sunlight filled the room, the orderly came and kept the newspaper on the side-table and left silently.

When they finished Bipradas said, 'Kumu, you think I have no religion. I don't talk about it because then there wouldn't be an end to it. I see its form in music where deep sorrow and ecstasy mingle together. I am unable to give it a name. You are leaving today, perhaps for good. So this morning I thought I would see you off beyond the pale of all discord and disharmony. You have read Kalidas's *Shakuntala*. Remember when Shakuntala was starting out to join her husband Dushyanta, the sage Kanva travelled some distance with her. Much sorrow and humiliation lay on the way to the destination he was leading her to. But she did not stop even there, but crossed over to eternal peace. This morning's Raag Bhairon captures the same peace, and my heartfelt blessings may reach you towards your entire fulfilment—a fulfilment which may inundate your inner and outer being and flush all your sorrows away.'

Kumu said nothing. She rested her head on his feet. Then she stood near the window looking out into the light. She said after a while, 'Let me go and get your tea and toast.'

Madhusudan had called the astrologer who fixed any time after ten that day as auspicious. At the appointed hour, a covered palanquin with red velveteen and gold embroidered interior arrived, escorted by men with pikestaffs, and carried Kumu to the palace in Mirzapur where an orchestra was playing and Brahmins were being fed with great éclat.

Manik brought a glass of barley water for Bipradas who was not in his bed today but sat still on a chair by the window. He did not even notice the barley water. The servant went back. Then Kshema auntie came with his food. She put her hand on his shoulder and gently reminded him, 'Bipu dear, it is getting late.'

He slowly got up and lay down on his bed. Kshema very much wished to describe to him at length the great fanfare with which Kumu was taken back to her husband's house, but she could not say anything in the face of his grave silence. It seemed he was looking into a yawning abyss.

When Bipradas spoke out, 'Pishi, please send Kalu to me,' those simple words seemed to come through a thick pall of silence. Pishi shuddered.

Bipradas gave Kalu a letter. It was Subodh's letter from England. He wrote to say that if he returned to India now without finishing the quota of bar dinners then he would have to come back to England again. It would be more convenient if he returned after the last bar dinner towards the end of winter. That would also save some expense. He believed the property matters could well wait till then.

Kalu did not wish to bother Bipradas with mundane crises, today of all days. He said, 'Dada, there has been no talk as yet about the return of the loan. If we keep quiet for some time and don't provoke anyone, maybe there will be no trouble. Anyway, you shouldn't worry.'

Bipradas said, 'I have no worries, Kalu. Not in the least.'

Kalu did not like him to worry, but such total indifference caused him more concern.

Bipradas picked up the newspaper and started reading. Kalu took it as a hint that Bipradas had not the slightest desire to discuss the matter. Usually Kalu left as soon as business was over, but today he sat quietly for some more time, wishing to raise some other topic or be of some use in some way.

He asked, 'Shall I close the front window? The sun is streaming through.'

Bipradas shook his head to indicate that there was no need for him to do anything.

Still Kalu continued to sit. The emptiness of the room without Kumu by the side of her brother made his heart sink. He suddenly heard Tom the terrier sobbing under the bed. The dog had seen Kumu leave, felt that something amiss had happened, but he was unable to communicate what he felt.

# NOTES AND GLOSSARY

**The Bengali Calendar:**

The Bengali New Year starts with *Boishakh*, around 15th April. The Bengali calendar starts from around 593 AD. So 1900 is Bengali San 1307 and year 2000 is BS 1407.

*Summer: Boishakh* (mid-April to mid-May)
*Jaistha* (May-June)
*Rains: Ashadh* (June-July)
*Shraban* (July-August)
*Early Autumn: Bhadra* (August-September)
*Ashwin* (September-October)
*Late Autumn: Kartik* (October-November)
*Aghran* (November-December)
*Winter: Poush* (December-January)
*Magh* (January-February)
*Spring: Falgun* (February-March)
*Chaitra* (March-April)

**Bengali Kinship Terms:**

Bengali families, being mostly joint families, abound in uncles, aunts, sons, daughters, cousins, their wives and so on, necessitating extra-specific kinship terms to indicate the exact relationship in the hierarchy of the extended family, rather than do with generalized terms like uncles, aunts and cousins. Some of those used in this translation are explained:

**Grandparents**

*Thakurda* Father's father
*Thakurma* Father's mother
*Dadu* Mother's father
*Didima* Mother's mother

**Paternal Relations**

*Jyatha* Father's elder brother (from Sanskrit *Jyeshtha*—elder)
*Kaka, Khuro* Father's younger brother
*Kakima, Khurrima* His wife
*Pishima* Father's sister
*Pisha-moshai* Her husband

**Maternal relations**

*Mama* Mother's brother
*Mamima* His wife
*Mashima* Mother's sister
*Mesho-moshai* Her husband
*Relations by marriage*:

**Same generation**

*Dada* Elder brother (short suffix-*da*)
*Didi* Elder sister (short sufix-*di*)
*Khoka* A young boy
*Khuki* A young girl

*Bhashur* Husband's elder brother—never to be addressed directly
*Deor* Husband's younger brother, addresed as *Thakurpo*
*Nanad* Husband's sister
*Nandai* Her husband
*Bhaaj* Brother's wife—to a sister
*Boudi* Elder brother's wife—to a brother
*Bou* Wife, any married woman in the family
*Bou-ma* Form of address for a married woman in the family by any elder member

Prefixes like *Borro, Sejo, Mejo and Chhoto* (eldest, next to the eldest, middle one and the youngest respectively) are added to indicate relative positions age-wise. All the above terms and addresses are also used socially amongst non-relatives alike. Short suffixes like—*da* (from *Dada),* or—*di* (from *Didi)* are added as appropriate.

Most of the Indian words used are now familiar in Indo–English writing. Many have even found acceptance in the new OED.

**Ashram** A kind of residential school in a forest where a sage teaches young boys the scriptures and other arts and skills for over a decade in preparation of their role as householder.
**Adda** A distinctive cultural feature of life in Kolkata. It means an idle gossip, or bull session amongst peer groups—students, unemployed youth or retired elderly people—any time, anywhere, discussing kings and cabbages.
**Badshah** An imperial and imperious personality. From Badshah, Persian for Emperor.
**Bhajan** A popular devotional song.
**Dewan** Estate manager.
**Esraj** A many-stringed instrument played with a bow.
**Hookah** A portable hubble-bubble for smoking tobacco which is lit on top in a clay pot and puffed through water contained in an empty coconut shell.
**Karta** The head of a joint family.
**Khansama** A man-servant waiting at the table.
**Kirtan** A devotional song wherein the audience also takes part in the refrain.
**Kuleen** The highest pedigreed among the Brahmins.
**Mukhtiyar** A local lawyer in a lower court—as opposed to a Law Graduate.
**Naib** A functionary in the zamindar's office, a bailiff.
**Paan** Betel-leaf, commonly chewed, with lime and spices.
**Roti** Indian unleavened bread.
**Ryot** A tiller tennant.
**Sindoor** Vermillion. Used for applying a dot in the forehead and in the parting of hair, by Hindu married women.
**Zamindar** A rich landlord.

# Farewell Song
## (Shesher Kabita)

*Translated by Radha Chakravarty*

# 1

# Speaking of Amit

Amit Rai is a barrister. Recast in the English mould, his surname, if transformed to 'Roy' and 'Ray,' would lose its charm but gain many subscribers. Instead, seeking a touch of the unusual, Amit spelt his name so his English friends would pronounce it 'Amit Raye'.

Amit's father was a barrister of formidable repute. The fortune he had amassed was sufficient to ensure the moral downfall of the next three generations. But Amit managed to survive the terrible impact of his paternal legacy, emerging unscathed.

Before he was ready for graduate studies at Kolkata University, Amit entered Oxford. There, he spent seven years intermittently attempting his examinations, or abstaining from them. Because he was intelligent, he did not study very hard; yet it did not appear that he lacked learning. His father had no extraordinary expectations of him. He had only wanted his son to be so thoroughly steeped in the Oxford dye that it would not fade in the desi wash even after his return.

I like Amit. He's a fine fellow. I am a new writer with very few readers, of whom Amit is the worthiest. He is dazzled by the brilliance of my writing. He believes that in our literary marketplace, writers of repute have no style. Like the camel in the animal kingdom, their writings are ill-proportioned and awkward in gait, traversing only the bleak, barren desert of Bengali literature. Let me hasten to assure critics that this opinion is not mine.

Amit likens fashion to a mask, and style to beauty of countenance. Style, he feels, belongs to the literary elite, who live by their own wishes. And fashion is for the ordinary lot, who make it their business to please other people. The Bankim style may be seen in his own *Bishabriksha*; for in it, Bankim has found his métier. The Bankim fashion may be seen in Nasiram's *Manomohan's Mohanbagan*; for in it, Nasiram has reduced the original Bankim to dust. You may view a professional dancing girl beneath the awning of a public marquee; but for the first glimpse of the bride's face during the shubhodrishti ritual, a veil of Benarasi fabric is required. The marquee belongs to fashion, the Benarasi veil—which reveals the special one's countenance shaded by a special hue—to style. Amit says it's because we're afraid to venture beyond the beaten track that style is held in such low esteem in our country. A scriptural elaboration of this idea may be found in the Dakshayajna story in the Puranas. Indra, Chandra and Varun, the fashionable deities in the celestial world, would be invited to events in the yajna circuit. But Shiva had style; he was so original that the prayer-chanting priests who performed these sacrificial ceremonies thought it improper to offer him oblations. I like hearing such words from someone with a BA degree from Oxford. For I believe my writing has style. That is why all my books attain moksha in single editions, liberated from the cycle of rebirth, never to appear again.

My wife's brother, my shala Nabakrishna, couldn't stand Amit's talk. 'To hell with his Oxford degree!' he'd protest. A prodigiously impressive MA in English literature, he had studied a lot, and understood little.

'Amit always lionizes minor writers, only to belittle major ones,' he observed to me the other day. 'It suits his fancy to drum up a show of contempt, and you serve as his drumstick.'

Sad to say, my wife, his very own sister, was present at this discussion. But it's supremely gratifying to note that she didn't like my shala's words at all. Her taste matched Amit's, I observed, although she wasn't highly educated. How amazing is the natural intelligence of women!

Sometimes, I, too, have some doubts, seeing that Amit has no compunctions even about denigrating many well-known English writers. These are writers of the mass market, branded with the label of greatness. You need not read these writers in order to admire them, for in order to pass your examinations you need only sing their praises blindly. Amit, too, does not need to read their works, for he has no hesitation in criticizing them blindly. Actually, he finds the most famous writers too publicly official, like the waiting room at Burdhwan station; while the authors he has himself discovered are his own exclusive territory, like the saloon compartment of a special train.

Style is Amit's passion. Not just in his literary taste but also in his dress and manners. His very appearance is cast in a special mould. He is not one of a crowd but one who stands out among many. You'd notice him in a crowd. A rounded countenance, clean-shaven and gleaming, with a dark, glowing complexion; a lively manner, restless eyes, restless smile, restless gait and gestures, quick at repartee; his mind a flint that emits sparks if tapped ever so slightly. He often wears homespun fabric, because members of his social set don't. He sports a dhoti of white cotton yardage, carefully pleated, because this style is not fashionable among his peers. The buttons on his kurta run diagonally from the left shoulder down to the right side of his midriff. The sleeve is slit right to the elbow. On his left hip, from a broad, brown, zari-trimmed waistband, hangs a small printed pouch containing his pocket-watch. His feet are shod in Cuttack-style white leather shoes with red leather trimming. When he ventures out, a folded Madras scarf, embellished with a border, is draped over his left shoulder, down to his knees. When invited to friends' homes, he wears a Muslim-style Lucknow cap, embroidered white on white. I wouldn't quite describe this as dressing up: it's more like a loud burst of laughter. I don't comprehend his Western garb, but those in the know tell me it's somewhat dishevelled, yet *distinguished*, as they say in English. He feels no urge to beautify himself but has boundless relish for mocking at fashion. Those who claim to be young by virtue of their age and birth-chart are a dime a dozen; but Amit's rare youthfulness is the result of his pure immaturity, utterly heedless, flighty, like a flood-tide carrying all in its wake as it rushes out, holding nothing back.

Meanwhile, his two sisters, nicknamed Sissy and Lissy, are like the latest merchandise in the market, carefully packaged from head to toe according to the reigning vogue. High-heeled shoes, low-cut lace-trimmed jacket revealing necklaces of coral and amber, sari draped aslant, wrapped tightly around the body. They walk with a tripping gait, speak in loud voices, and modulate their peals of shrill laughter. Head tilted slightly, they glance obliquely upwards with a faint smile; they know the art of a meaningful look. Every now and then, they flutter a pink silk fan close to their cheeks, and perched on the arm of their menfriends' chairs, they rap their admirers with the fan in feigned protest against the men's feigned impertinence.

Within his social circle, Amit's male friends are envious of his way with women. Amit is not particularly indifferent to women, nor does he seem particularly attracted by anyone; yet, he never lacks romantic charm. In a word, what he feels for women is not passion but enthusiasm. Amit attends parties, plays card-games, loses wagers on purpose, urges tone-deaf women to sing and if someone wears an unsuitable colour, inquires where such fabric may be bought. He adopts a tone of special partiality when addressing any female acquaintance; yet everyone knows that his show of favouritism masks total indifference. He who worships many gods secretly hails each deity as superior to the others; though perfectly aware of this, the gods can't help feeling flattered, all the same. The mothers of marriageable daughters refuse to give up hope, but the brides-to-be realize that Amit is a golden, ever-receding horizon, always available, yet never to be captured. About women, his mind is in perpetual debate, never reaching a conclusion. This explains his daring in plunging into intimacies that are blind alleys, leading nowhere. That is why he gets along with everyone so easily; for even in the presence of inflammatory substances, he is safely insulated from catching fire.

Once, at a riverside picnic, when the moon rose above the deep, dark, intense silence on the opposite shore of the Ganga, Lily Ganguly was by his side.

'The new moon across the river, and you and me together, on this shore,' he murmured to her in a low voice. 'Such a conjugation will never occur again in all eternity.'

For an instant, Lily Ganguly's heart had lurched with brimming emotion; but she knew these words only as true as the style of their utterance. To claim anything more would be like reaching for the rainbow above the bubbles. So, jerking herself out of her momentary trance, Lily laughed: 'Amit, what you say is so obviously true that you need not have said it at all. Even that frog leaping into the water, is an event never to recur in all eternity.'

'There's a difference, Lily,' smiled Amit, 'a vast difference. Tonight, the leap of that frog is a disjointed, fragmented event. But taken together, you and I, the flow of the Ganga, and the stars in the sky, have created a complete harmony—like Beethoven's Moonlight Sonata. I think there's an insane goldsmith in the celestial workshop of Viswakarma, maker of the world. Having carved these three hours into a perfect golden ring set with sapphires, diamonds and emeralds, he has instantly cast it into the ocean, never to be found again.'

'All the better, Amit, for now you need not worry about settling accounts with Viswakarma's goldsmith.'

'But Lily, after a million ages, beside some thousand-mile long canal, in the red forest-shadows of Mars, should you and I perchance come face to face, and if that fisherman in the Shakuntala story should slit the catfish's belly to retrieve for us this exquisite golden moment, we would gaze at each other, startled. But imagine what would happen thereafter.'

'Thereafter, the golden moment would sink unnoticed into the sea,' retorted Lily, rapping Amit with her fan. 'Never to be found again. We've lost count of all those other moments, crafted by the insane goldsmith and discarded by you, because you have forgotten them.'

With these words, Lily hastened away to join her female friends. This episode is an example of many other such events in Amit's life.

'Ami, why don't you get married?' Amit's sisters Sissy and Lissy asked him, once.

'For marriage, a paatri—a prospective bride—is the first requirement,' replied Amit, 'and after that, the paatra—the prospective groom.'

'You surprise me,' exclaimed Sissy. 'There are so many women!'

'Women were sought in marriage in olden times, when horoscopes were matched,' declared Amit. 'I want a paatri worthy of the role, whose own self is her identity, second to none.'

'Once she enters your home, you will take precedence, and she will occupy second place,' Sissy pointed out. 'Her identity will be defined by yours.'

'The woman I secretly await in vain as the right match for me has no fixed address,' replied Amit. 'She usually doesn't make it to my threshold. A falling star, she bursts into flames as soon as she enters my heart's atmosphere and vanishes into thin air, without ever reaching my earthly abode.'

'Meaning, she's a far cry from your sisters,' retorted Sissy.

'Meaning, if she were to join our household, she would be more than an addition to the family,' answered Amit.

'Tell me, dear Sissy,' interrupted Lissy, 'why doesn't Ami fancy Bimi Bose, who waits so eagerly, and would come running at the slightest signal from him? She lacks culture, he says. Why, my dear, she stood first in MA Botany! Education is culture, after all.'

'The stone of the *kamal*-diamond is education, and the light that radiates from it is culture,' explained Amit. 'The stone has weight, and the light, brilliance.'

'Oh, he has no time for Bimi Bose!' cried Lissy, enraged. 'If ever Ami has a mad desire to marry her, I'll warn Bimi Bose not to spare him a second glance.'

'Why would I want to marry Bimi Bose unless I was indeed mad?' demanded Amit. 'If that ever happens, please consider medical treatment, rather than marriage, for me.'

Their relatives had given up hoping that Amit would ever marry. They had concluded that, being unfit for the responsibilities of married life, he dreamt of the impossible and went about trying to impress people with his perverse talk. His heart was a will-o'-the wisp, dazzling if seen outdoors but impossible to capture and bring home.

Meanwhile, Amit socialized with abandon, treating stray acquaintances to tea at Firpo's, taking friends on unnecessary motor-car drives whenever the fancy took him, buying odd items from here and there and giving them away to all and sundry, leaving newly purchased English books in friends' homes and forgetting to retrieve them.

His sisters were particularly annoyed by his habit of airing contrary views. He was always sure to contradict the ideas approved by civilized society.

Once, when some political theorist waxed eloquent about the virtues of democracy; Amit exclaimed: 'When Vishnu dismembered Sati's body, more than a hundred scattered places of pilgrimage sprang up across the country. Today, democracy has produced a host of sites for the worship of small, fragmented aristocracies. The world has been taken over by minor aristocrats—in politics, literature and society. They lack seriousness, all of them, for they have no faith in themselves.'

On another occasion, a philanthropist, championing the cause of helpless women, blamed men for the oppression of women under patriarchy. Suddenly, Amit removed the cigarette from his lips and blurted out: 'If men surrender their authority, women will at once begin to dominate. The dominance of the weak is a fearsome thing.'

'What's that supposed to mean?' angrily demanded the helpless women and all their champions present at the gathering.

'One with shackles at his disposal would tame the bird with them,' replied Amit. 'In other words, he would use force. One who owns no shackles must subdue the bird with opium—in other words, with charm. The user of shackles can exercise control but no charm; the user of opium can exercise control as well as charm. A woman's pill-box is full of opium, and wicked Nature keeps up the supply.'

One day, at a literary gathering in Baliganj, the poetry of Rabindranath Tagore was the subject of discussion. For the first time in his life, Amit had agreed to preside over the discussion. He had arrived mentally armed for battle. The speaker was a very simple, old-fashioned man. His aim was to prove that Robi Thakur's verse was indeed real poetry. Barring a couple of college professors, most members of the audience acknowledged that the proof he offered was more or less satisfactory.

'Every poet should enjoy a five-year term for writing verse, from the age of twenty-five to thirty,' declared the chairperson, rising to his feet. 'What we expect from the next generation is not something better but something different. When the season for fazli mangoes is over, we wouldn't clamour for a better variety of the same fruit. We'd say, "Fetch us some good-sized custard-apples from New Market, sir." A green coconut has a brief shelf-life, as long as it has juice; a ripe coconut lasts much longer, for it's the substance that counts. Poets are short-lived, but philosophers outlive trees and stones. . . . The greatest complaint against Robi Thakur is that, in imitation of old man Wordsworth, this gentleman has lived unfairly long. Yama, god of death, repeatedly sends his henchmen to extinguish his life, but the man still stands, clutching the arm of his chair for support. If he doesn't voluntarily make a dignified exit, it would be our collective duty to withdraw from his literary circle. His successor, too, will declaim, in rhythmic metre, that the sun doesn't set on his empire, for he holds the celestial city Amaravati chained to his threshold, here on earth. For a while, devotees will offer him garlands and sandalwood paste, keep him well-fed, prostrate themselves at his feet. Then will come the holy date for his ritual slaughter, the auspicious moment of his devotees' release from their bondage to him. In Africa, four-footed deities are worshipped in the same way. The worship of two-footed, three-footed, four-footed and fourteen-footed gods of verse also follows the same rule. There can be nothing more impure and corrupt than to render the ritual of worship monotonous. . . . Taste is subject to evolution. If taste remains static where it was five years ago, it becomes painfully evident that it's unaware of its own demise. At the slightest nudge, the deceased must confront the fact that his sentimental kinfolk have postponed his last rites, perhaps to permanently delude his worthy successors. I have vowed to publicly expose this illicit conspiracy of the Robi Thakur faction.'

'Do you want to remove loyalty from the world of literature?' asked our friend Manibhushan, his spectacles flashing.

'Absolutely. Here begins the age of the short-lived poet-president. The second thing I want to say about Robi Thakur is, that his literary works are like his handwriting: rounded or undulating, like a rose or a woman's face, or the moon. This is primitive, an imitation of Nature's script. From the new President, we require lines that are sharp and straight—like arrows, like spearheads, like thorns. Not like flowers but like streaks of lightning. Like the pain of neuralgia. Cast in the mould of a Gothic church with sharp angles and corners, not like the mandap or prayer-pavilion in a temple. No harm, indeed, if its shape resembles a jute-mill or a secretariat building. . . .From now on, discard the artistry of rhyme and metre designed to charm the reader's heart; we must seize the reader's heart by force, as Ravana had abducted Sita. The heart may weep and protest when dragged away, but go along it must. Jatayu, that ancient creature, will appear on the scene to remonstrate, and lose his life in the process. Soon after, Kiskindhya will be stirred to action, and suddenly, some Hanuman will leap into Lanka, setting it ablaze, in order to rescue the heart and bring it back home. A reunion with Tennyson will follow; we'll cling to Byron, weeping profusely; we'll beg Dickens's forgiveness for having cursed him in our urge to cure ourselves of enchantment. . . . If all the enchanted workmen of India, from Mughal times to the present day, were to build domed marble bubbles across the country, then every bhadralok or gentleman would hasten to renounce the world the day he crossed twenty, to live like a hermit in the woods.

We must destroy the magic of the Taj Mahal precisely in order to restore the Taj Mahal's attraction.'

(At this juncture, it must be added that, unable to cope with the flood of words, the raporteur at the gathering had grown dizzy. His report proved even more unintelligible than Amit's lecture. We have presented above the few fragments of it that we could retrieve.)

At the mention of the revival of interest in the Taj Mahal, a devotee of Robi Thakur exclaimed, 'We can never have too much of a good thing.'

'Quite the contrary,' declared Amit. 'In this world, good things are valued because they are rare, or else overabundance would render them mediocre. . . . Poets who are not ashamed of surviving to be sixty or seventy invite punishment by cheapening themselves. Ultimately, they find themselves trapped, hemmed in by the mimicry of their band of imitators. Their writing becomes warped; beginning to steal from their own earlier works, they become receivers of stolen goods. In such situations, for the general public good, it is the duty of readers to ensure at all costs that such overage poets are not allowed to survive; I speak of survival in the poetic, not the physical sense. Let their longevity be transferred instead to elderly professors, politicians and critics.'

'Who would you like for president, may I know?' demanded the speaker of the day. 'Please name the candidate.'

'Nibaran Chakrabarti,' replied Amit, in a flash.

There was a murmur of surprise from different segments of the audience: 'Nibaran Chakrabarti? Who's that?'

'Today's question is a mere seedling, the answer to which will rear its head tomorrow, like a giant tree.'

'Meanwhile, we'd like a sample of his work.'

'Listen, then.' He produced a long, slim, canvas-bound notebook from his pocket and began to read aloud from it:

I herald the advent
Of the Unknown One, announcing
His name to the world,
To known faces in public streets.
A newcomer, I deride
The ways of the ordinary rabble.
Open your doors!
For I bear heaven's message,
In script inscrutable,
Inscribed by Time.
Say, who dares reply,
Who dares to stake his life
On the difficult answer?
They will not listen;
Folly's army
Blocks my path.
Cry of fruitless anger,

Crashing upon my breast,
Like the futile waves
That beat their heads in vain
Against the rocky shore,
In self-destructive pride.

I wear no flower-garlands; no armour
Shields the bareness of my breast.
On my forehead's empty page is drawn
A deep mark of victory,
A tattered wrap my poor man's garb.
I'll deplete your treasure-house.
Open, open your doors!
Suddenly,
I extend my hand:
Delay not, give me what you will.
Your heart flutters, the door-latch trembles,
Your world is in turmoil,

The horizon rent
With fearful screams:
'Away at once,
Unquiet beggar!
Time and time again
Your voice assails
Our deep nocturnal slumber.'

Where are your weapons?
Rattle your sabres, stab me in the side!
Let death destroy death; let my immortal life
Be my legacy.
Enchain me, then!
Tie me down! At once, I'll break my bonds,
And claiming liberty, set you free.

Where are your scriptures?
Attack me with them.
In learned dispute
Let's loudly defy
The divine decree.
I know for sure, the arrows of debate
Will be shattered. Our eyes,
With worn words long befogged,
Shall see the light again.

Ignite the fire!
If what's good today
Should tomorrow be charred,

Burnt to ashes
Worldwide,
So let it be.
Feel no sorrow.
Let my ordeal by fire
Bring glory to the world.

My obscure words
Will deal a stunning blow,
To subdue the obdurate
With shock and fear.
My wild rhymes
Will alike perplex
Seekers after salvation,
And creatures of appetite.
They'll beat their brows, and one by one,
In anger, pain or fear,
They'll accept the public victory
Of the Unknown One.
The Unknown One!
Who rocks the world
With fiery Baisakh storms;
Smashes the cloud-banks with a mighty blow
To unleash their hidden hoard of rain.
And tears the world apart, to set it free.

On that occasion, Robi Thakur's supporters were silenced. They departed, threatening to respond in writing.

'You must have created Nibaran Chakrabarti in advance, and carried him in your pocket, just to fool all the simpletons,' observed Sissy to Amit as he drove home, after having dumbfounded his audience.

'He who promotes someone yet to arrive, is known as god of the unarrived,' replied Amit. 'That's what I am. Today, Nibaran Chakrabarti has arrived in this world; there's no stopping him now.'

Sissy was secretly very proud of Amit. 'Tell me, Amit,' she asked, 'Do you prepare all your well-honed speeches, just like the latest one, as soon as you get up in the morning?'

'It is the essence of civilization to be ready for all eventualities,' declared Amit. 'Barbarity is unprepared for everything in this world. This thought is also recorded in my notebook.'

'But you have no opinion of your own, blurting out whatever sounds good in a particular situation.'

'My mind is a mirror. If I were to leave it forever smeared with my own fixed views, it would cease to reflect the image of every passing moment.'

'Ami, you will spend your life chasing images in a mirror,' warned Sissy.

# 2

# Encounter

Amit chose to visit the hills of Shillong. Because members of his social circle didn't frequent the place. Also because the flood of marriage proposals would be less overwhelming there. The deity with the love-bow who constantly hovered over Amit's heart preferred to haunt only fashionable areas. Of all the hill-resorts in the region, Shillong offered him the most restricted scope for target-practice.

Amit's sisters shook their heads. 'Go alone if you must,' they said. 'We're not coming with you.'

Carrying folding parasols of the latest style in their left hand and tennis racquets in their right, cloaked in fake-Parisian shawls, off went the sisters, to Darjeeling. Bimi Bose had already reached the place. When the sisters arrived minus their brother, she cast her eyes about and discovered that Darjeeling had people but no real men.

Amit had informed everyone in parting that he was going to Shillong to savour the solitude. Within a couple of days, he realized that in the absence of people, solitude lost its flavour. Amit had no taste for roaming with a camera in search of scenic beauty. I'm not a tourist, he'd say; I like to taste things with my mind, not swallow them with my eyes.

He spent a few days reading in the shade of deodar trees on the hill-slopes. He didn't touch fiction, for reading fiction while on holiday smacked of ordinariness. He began to read Suniti Chatterjee's philology of the Bengali language, hoping intensely that he would disagree with the author. From time to time, at intervals between his study of grammar and his spells of indolence, the hills and forests of this place would suddenly strike him as beautiful, but it stirred no intense emotion in his heart. It was like a monotonous alaap, the prelude to a performance of classical music, with no refrain, no taal or rhythm, and no sam to emphasize the recurring main beat in a rhythmic cycle. In other words, his outlook was wide-ranging but lacked focus; to his eyes, everything seemed diffuse and scattered, failing to coalesce. In the universe of his own self, this lack of internal coherence caused Amit to constantly and restlessly disperse his identity. He found this as distressing in Shillong, as in the city. But in an urban setting, he managed to expend this restlessness in many ways; here, it persisted, and accumulated, like the pool that forms when a waterfall's path is obstructed. He had begun to contemplate escaping downhill on foot, wandering at will through Shillong and Shilchar. Just then the Ashadh rains descended, across the hills and through the woods, spreading their shadowy cloak of moisture-laden clouds. News arrived that the mountain-peaks of Cherrapunji had faced the onslaught of the gathering early monsoon clouds. Now, heavy showers would incite the mountain waterfalls to madness, urging them to break their bounds. He decided that the occasion demanded a visit to the dak-bungalow of

Cherrapunji, where the spirit of *Meghdoot* must be invoked. There, his powerful rendering of the Cloud-Messenger's invisible thunder would impel the heroine to streak across his mental skyline like disembodied lightning, leaving behind neither her signature, nor any address.

On that day, he donned thick highland socks, sturdy, thick-soled leather boots, a khaki Norfolk tunic, knee-length shorts, and on his head, a sola hat. He didn't quite resemble a Yaksha in an Abani Thakur illustration, but he could have been taken for a district engineer out to inspect the roads. In his pocket, though, were three or four slim volumes of poetry in different languages.

The path was narrow and tortuous, a forest-covered precipice on his right. This was the way to Amit's lodgings. There was no likelihood of encountering traffic here, so he drove rashly, without sounding the horn. At that very moment, he was thinking that the motor car, in modern times, is the appropriate messenger for a distant beloved; for it combines elements of smoke and fire, desert and sea, in the right proportions, and a letter sent through the driver can get one's message across, in no uncertain terms. In the coming year, he decided, at the very onset of the Ashadh rains, he would drive down the path described in *Meghdoot*. For perhaps fate would spare him a kind glance to ensure that the beloved—Avantika or Malavika, or some wanderer in the deodar forests—would appear before him, to fulfil some unthinkable destiny. At this moment, he suddenly arrived at a bend in the road to see another car making its way upwards. There was no space for the vehicles to pass each other. Stepping on the brakes, he drove right up to the car; they collided, but there was no mishap. The other car rolled a little way down to stop at the edge of the hillside.

A young woman alighted from the vehicle. Against the dark backdrop of their narrow escape from death, she stood out like a clear picture drawn in streaks of lightning, independent of everything around her. Like Lakshmi arising from the foaming sea when it was churned by the Mandar mountain, the woman was above all the turmoil, although the waves of the great ocean continued to heave and swell. Amit took this rare opportunity to observe her. In a drawing-room, in company, he would not have perceived this woman in all her uniqueness. In this world, one may sometimes find a person worth gazing at; but a suitable location for the viewing is rarely to be found.

The woman was dressed in a white, narrow-bordered sari, a jacket made of the same warm fabric, and white shoes of a desi pattern. She was tall, with a dark, glowing complexion; her large eyes, shaded by heavy eyelashes, had a tender intensity; her hair was tied back, swept away from her broad forehead; her beautifully rounded face and chin had the charm of an unripe fruit. The sleeves of her jacket came up to her elbows; on her wrists, she wore a pair of slim, plain bangles. The end of her sari, not confined by a brooch at her shoulder, was draped over her head, held in place with a silver filigree hairpin.

Leaving his hat in the car, Amit came and stood silently before her, as if awaiting some punishment that was his due. At this, the young woman showed some signs of pity, mingled with amusement.

'I am at fault,' apologized Amit, in a low voice.

'No fault but an error,' smiled the woman. 'The error began with me.'

Her voice was pure, like the water bubbling forth from a spring. Smooth and full, like the voice of a young boy. When he returned home that day, Amit spent a long time trying to conjure up words to describe the music of this voice, its taste and texture. Opening his notebook, he wrote: 'It's like the light, hazy smoke of ambergris-scented tobacco as it spirals through water, not with the pungency of nicotine but with the tender fragrance of rose-water.'

'I had gone out in search of a friend after receiving news of her arrival,' said the woman, to explain her error. 'As soon as we'd climbed a little way up this road, the chauffeur pointed out that we were on the wrong route. By then it was too late to turn back without driving all the way to the top. That's why we were on our way up, when higher powers assaulted us.'

'There is a power beyond the higher powers—a hideous, evil planet, whose adverse influence has brought this about.'

'There's not much damage done,' the driver of the other vehicle informed them, 'but it will take a while to fix the car.'

'If you forgive my car for the offence just committed, I could drive you wherever you permit,' offered Amit.

'There's no need, I'm used to walking in the hills.'

'The need is mine, as proof that I am forgiven.'

The woman remained silent, seeming a little hesitant.

'I have something more to say,' declared Amit. 'I drive fast—not a worthy thing to do, for I can't drive this vehicle into the realm of posterity. Yet, that is your first and only impression of me. But even that is caught in a snag, worse luck. As an epilogue to this drama, please let me demonstrate that, in this realm, at least, I am not inferior to your chauffeur.'

When they first meet a stranger, women are reluctant to relinquish their reserve, fearing unknown dangers. But the trauma of imminent danger had broken down her fences in a single blow, rendering preliminaries unnecessary. Some unknown divinity, lacking patience, had brought the two of them face to face on a solitary mountain road, and fused their hearts together. The lightning-flash of this sudden revelation would haunt them often at night, etching itself against the darkness. Like the flaming imprint of sun and stars on the azure of the sky during some great cosmic collision, it left a deep impression within their consciousness.

Without a word, she entered his car. Following her directions, they arrived at her destination.

'Please drop in tomorrow, if you have the time,' she suggested, stepping out of the car. 'I'll introduce you to the lady of the house.'

'I have all the time in the world; I could drop in right away,' Amit felt like blurting out. But he was too embarrassed to utter the words.

Back home, he wrote in his notebook: 'What madness awaited us on the road I took today! It wrenched the two of us from our different moorings, and set us on the same track, perhaps. The astronomer was wrong. From some unknown galaxy, the moon had descended into the earth's orbit. Like vehicles, they collided, and ever since that near-death experience, they move together through the ages, the two of them, their radiance illuminating each other's countenance. Their mutual bond keeps them together as they travel. My heart tells me, here begins our journey together. As we travel, we shall string together, moment by moment, a garland of the bright instants garnered along our way. We can no longer depend upon fate, hoping for a safe, predictable life, with a fixed salary and a fixed livelihood; all our exchanges will be sudden and unexpected.'

Outside, it was raining. 'Nibaran Chakrabarti, where are you?' exclaimed Amit to himself, as he paced the verandah. 'Come, possess me now. Give me words, give me words.' Out came the long, slim notebook, and Nibaran Chakrabarti declaimed:

We travel on the drifting breeze, bound
By our journey's invisible ties.
  In our hearts, a festival of colour, wrought
By this bright-hued moment, darling of the dust,
  The horizon dances, flashing
    Its veil across the rainclouds.
Its sudden radiance
  Dazzles the mind.

Not for us the kanak-champa groves,
Nor forest-arbours full of bakul clusters.
  At dusk, some unknown flower
  Spreads its sudden fragrance
    At dawn, as if mocking
  The rosy clouds,
On the treetops bloom
  Bunches of rhododendron.

Not for us the wealth of hoarded treasure,
Not for us the love and care of home.
  We seek not to encage
The bird that flutters past,
  Content to hear the song
    Of that winged freedom-lover.
Irradiated are we, by the rare glory
  Of the unimaginable.

At this point, we must pause for retrospection. Once we have disposed of the past, our narrative can proceed unhindered.

# 3

# A Backward Glance

During the first phase of English education in Bengal, a storm had erupted over the disparity between chandimandaps for the worship of Durga, and educational institutions like schools and colleges. Gyanadashankar had surrendered to the turbulence of that social revolution. He belonged to the older generation but had been suddenly catapulted into the modern age. He was born ahead of his time. In intelligence, speech and behaviour, he was unlike his contemporaries. Like a bird that loves to ride the sea-waves, he took pleasure in baring his breast to onslaughts of public blame.

When the grandchildren of such forefathers try to make amends for such reversals of date and time, they rush to the opposite extreme, the terminus at the other end of the almanac. So it was in this case, as well. After his father's demise, Gyanadashankar's grandson Baradashankar regressed almost to the era of his grandfather's early ancestors. He would worship Manasa, goddess of snakes, and simultaneously try to appease Sheetala, the deity of small-pox, by addressing her as Ma. He began to drink water in which amulets had been rinsed, and spent entire mornings inscribing the thousand names of Durga. The Vaishyas in his locality, who were out to prove their scriptural erudition, were harassed in public and private. To preserve the customs intended to protect Hinduism from the corrupting touch of science, he lavishly showered free words of wisdom upon the modern mind, through countless pamphlets printed with the assistance of the Bhat community, people of mixed caste. In a very short time, through holy rituals, meditation and penance, baths, incense, and devoted service of cows and Brahmins, he ensured that his immovable fortress of religious purity became completely impregnable. At twenty-seven, he ultimately left for his heavenly abode, carrying with him the blessings of countless Brahmins in exchange for having donated cows, gold and land, in the name of his father, mother and daughters.

Barada had been married to Yogamaya, daughter of Ramlochan Bannerji, his father's close friend, college-mate and companion from the days when they frequented restaurants for chops-and-cutlets. At that particular time, there was no class-difference in the lifestyles of Yogamaya's parental and marital homes. The women in her family were educated. They appeared in society, and some had even published travelogues in illustrated monthly magazines. Coming from such a family, she found herself married to a man who strove to prevent the slightest lapse in her adherence to the rituals of purity. Yogamaya's movements were restricted by various passport procedures designed to safeguard the boundaries of religious orthodoxy, fixed by unshakable moral law. A veil descended over her eyes, and over her mind. If Saraswati, goddess of learning, ever found the time to pay them a visit, even she had to undergo a security check before being allowed into the private quarters of their house. The English books she carried were confiscated at the outer gate itself; if detected, Bengali writings published after the pre-Bankim era could not cross the inner threshold. For a long time, a beautifully bound edition of the *Yogabashishtha Ramayana* in Bengali translation lay on Yogamaya's shelf, awaiting her attention. That she would one day take it up by way of pastime, was a wish the master of the house had cherished to his dying day. It was not easy for Yogamaya to fold herself into the iron safe of antiquity like a safe deposit, but she had reined in her rebellious mind. In this mental prison, her only refuge was Deenasharan Vedantaratna, the family priest. He appreciated Yogamaya's clear, natural intelligence.

'Ma, all these wasteful religious rituals are not for you,' he would succinctly declare. 'The foolish not only delude themselves but are deceived by everything under the sun. Do you think we believe in any of these things? Don't you see how it pains me to distort the scriptures by twisting the syntax as occasion demands? In other words, we reject these restrictions in private, but must outwardly pretend to be fools to please those who are foolish. If you are unwilling to be deluded, I cannot undertake to deceive you. Please send for me whenever you wish, Ma; I shall read to you from the scriptures only what I believe to be true.'

Sometimes, he would visit Yogamaya and explicate passages from the *Gita* or the *Brahmabhashya*. Vedantaratna was delighted at Yogamaya's intelligent questions and had boundless enthusiasm for discussions with her. For the hangers-on—important or otherwise—who surrounded Baradashankar, Vedantaratna had immense contempt.

'Ma, yours is the only house in this entire city, where I find pleasure in conversation,' he would assure Yogamaya. 'You have saved me from self-contempt.'

In this way, amidst a relentless routine of rituals and fasts, days passed by, chained to the dictates of the holy almanac. Her whole life became a matter of 'fulfilling her obligations,' as they say in the bizarre language of today's newspapers. Immediately after her husband's demise, she took to travelling, accompanied by her son Jatishankar and daughter Suroma. She would spend the winter in Kolkata, and the summer in some mountain resort. Jatishankar was now a college-student; but unable to locate a girls' school suitable for Suroma's education, she managed to find, after much searching, a teacher called Labanyalata. This was the woman Amit had suddenly encountered, early this morning.

# 4

# All About Labanya

Labanya's father Abanish Dutta was principal of a college in the western region. He had brought up his motherless daughter in such a way that even the struggle to pass numerous examinations had not diminished her intellectual powers. In fact, she still retained an intense love of learning.

Learning, the father's only passion, had found complete vicarious fulfilment through his daughter. She was dearer to him than his own library. He believed that a mind honed in the pursuit of learning was like an impermeable slab of concrete through which the gases of frivolous emotions could never penetrate from below. Hence, a person with such a mind had no need for marriage. He was firmly convinced that the portion of his daughter's heart which could have provided tender, fertile soil for marriage and motherhood had been hardened to cement by mathematics and history—a heart extremely strong and firm, scratch-resistant, immune to external assaults. He had even imagined that, if Labanya did not marry, she could remain forever wedded to learning.

There was someone else he doted on. The young man's name was Shobhanlal. One rarely encountered such a deep interest in studies from such an early age. With his broad forehead, clear gaze, pleasant set of the lips, simple smile and handsome countenance, his appearance was instantly attractive to the viewer's eye. He was extremely self-effacing, flustered if anyone paid him the slightest attention.

He was a poor man's son. Step by step, aided by scholarships, he cleared the insurmountable peaks of numerous examinations. His professor anticipated with pride that Shobhan would one day be famous, and that Abanish's own name would head the list of those who had chiefly engineered this success. Shobhan came to his house to receive instruction; he had free access to the library. He would cringe in embarrassment if he saw Labanya. This embarrassment created a distance between them, leaving Labanya free to imagine herself his superior. Women don't notice a hesitant man who does not assertively draw attention to himself.

Meanwhile, Shobhanlal's father Nonigopal arrived one day at Abanish's residence and cursed him roundly. He complained that, on the pretext of offering tuition at home, Abanish hoped to trap the boy into marriage with his daughter, to satisfy his urge for social reform by ruining the caste-purity of Shobhanlal, a Vaidya's son. As proof of his accusations, he submitted a pencil-sketch of Labanyalata. The drawing, covered in rose-petals, had been discovered inside Shobhanlal's tin trunk. Nonigopal had no doubt that the picture was a love-token gifted by Labanya herself. In his calculating mind, Nonigopal had worked out, to the last detail, Shobhanlal's current value in the marriage market, and how much it was likely to increase if one waited patiently for a short while. Abanish's ploy for seizing this valuable property free of cost amounted to nothing less than a stealthy act of burglary. How was it different in any way from stealing money?

Until then, Labanya had been completely unaware that her image was being worshipped at some secret shrine, away from the public gaze. In a corner of Abanish's library, amidst a cluttered heap of pamphlets and magazines, Shobhan had chanced upon Labanya's photograph, faded from neglect. Having persuaded an artist friend to reproduce the portrait as a drawing, he had returned the photograph to its original place. Like his own shy, secret love, the roses, too, had blossomed in his friend's garden with a natural simplicity; they carried no trace of unlawful presumption. Yet, he had to be punished. With lowered head and scarlet face, wiping away a secret tear, the shy young man took his leave from the house. From afar, Shobhanlal had offered one last instance of self-sacrifice, known only to the Maker. In the BA examinations, he had secured the first place and Labanya, the third. That had been a major blow to Labanya's self-esteem. The reasons were twofold: first, that Labanya was often stung by Abanish's deep respect for Shobhan's intellect. The fact that Abanish's respect was combined with special affection only aggravated her suffering. She had tried very hard to surpass Shobhan in their examination results. When Shobhan outshone her nevertheless, it became very difficult for her to forgive him. In her mind remained a lingering suspicion that the difference in marks was the result of Abanish's special tutelage, although Shobhanlal had never sought Abanish's help in preparing for the examinations. For a few days, Labanya would avert her face if Shobhanlal crossed her path. There was no likelihood of her surpassing Shobhan in the MA examinations, either. Yet, she defeated him. Abanish himself was surprised. Had Shobhanlal been a poet, he could perhaps have dedicated pages of verse to Labanya; instead, he had sacrificed a large number of examination-marks as an offering to her.

After this, their student days were over. At this juncture, Abanish discovered within himself the agonizing truth that even if the heart is stuffed full of learning, the god of love can somehow intrude, and find no dearth of space. Abanish was then forty-seven. At that extremely vulnerable, helpless age, a widow entered his heart, penetrating the protective shield of books in his library, surmounting the high walls of his scholarship. There was no obstacle to their marriage, save Abanish's affection for Labanya. He faced a terrible conflict of desires. He would will himself to study, only to be overpowered by thoughts that were stronger, and more extraordinary. *The Modern Review* would commission a critical article and send him an attractive volume on the history of Buddhist ruins, but he would meditate upon the unpublished book like a Buddhist stupa, weighed down by centuries of silence. The editor would grow impatient, but such is usually the state of a learned man when his scholarship is challenged. When an elephant steps into the quicksand, what chance that it will survive?

At long last, Abanish was troubled by a painful regret. Never having found the time to look beyond his books, he suspected he had failed to notice that his daughter was in love with Shobhanlal, for it would be unnatural for anyone to not love this young man. He grew annoyed with all fathers in general, with himself, and with Nonigopal.

Then came a letter from Shobhanlal. He wanted to borrow a few books from Abanish's library, to write an essay on the history of the Gupta Kingdom, for the Premchand Raichand scholarship examination. 'Have no hesitation,' was Abanish's prompt and affectionate reply. 'You shall read in my library, as before.'

Shobhanlal was agitated. He assumed that the eager tone of the letter indicated Labanya's covert consent. He began to frequent the library. On his way in and out of the house, he would sometimes chance upon Labanya, very briefly. Shobhan would then slow his pace. It was his utmost desire that Labanya should say something to him; that she would ask after him, or express some curiosity about the article he was busy writing. If she had, he would have found great relief in opening his notebook to discuss his ideas with Labanya, sometime. He was very eager to know her views on some of his cherished original ideas. But no such conversation took place, nor did he have the courage to force a discussion on her.

Several days passed, in this fashion. It was a Sunday. Shobhanlal had arranged his notebooks on a table, and was turning the pages of a book, taking notes every now and then. The room was deserted, for it was afternoon. Taking advantage of the holiday, Abanish was going somewhere on a visit, he didn't say where. He left instructions that he would not be home for tea.

Suddenly, the door, which had been ajar, was flung open. Shobhanlal's heart gave a sudden jolt. Labanya entered the room. Flustered, Shobhanlal didn't know what to do.

'Why do you come to this house?' demanded Labanya, blazing with fury.

Shobhanlal was too stunned to speak.

'Do you know what your father has said about your visits? Aren't you ashamed of bringing such humiliation upon me?'

'Please forgive me,' pleaded Shobhanlal, with downcast eyes. 'I shall leave at once.'

Without retorting that he was there on Labanya's father's personal invitation, he gathered his books and belongings. His hands trembled violently, a dumb pain beating against his rib-cage. Hanging his head, he left the house.

If one is deprived by some obstacle of the chance to love someone truly loveable, it leads, not to indifference but to blind hate, the very obverse of love. Perhaps Labanya, unbeknownst to her, had once awaited a chance to grant Shobhanlal the boon of her love. But Shobhanlal had not approached her in the appropriate way. All subsequent developments went against him. He hurt her most deeply on this last occasion. In her anguish, Labanya utterly misjudged her father. She concluded that it was from a desire to free himself of all obligations that he had summoned

Shobhanlal again, hoping to arrange a match between the two of them. This explained her terrible rage against the blameless Shobhanlal.

Labanya now seemed stubbornly determined to ensure that Ábanish's marriage took place. Abanish had put aside almost half his savings for his daughter. But after his marriage, Labanya insisted that she would have no part of her patrimony, for she wished to earn her own livelihood.

'I was not keen to marry at all,' protested Abinash, wounded to the quick. 'It was you who obdurately insisted on my marriage. Why do you abandon me now, in this way?'

'I have taken this resolve so that our relationship never deteriorates,' replied Labanya. 'Don't worry, Baba! Grant me your blessings, always, that I may find the path to true happiness.'

She found a job. The entire responsibility for Suroma's education was hers. She could easily have tutored Jati as well, but he would not accept the ignominy of being trained by a female teacher.

Days passed by, in a routine, everyday fashion. Her spare time was stuffed full of English literature, from ancient times to the recent works of Bernard Shaw, and especially the history of ancient Greece and Rome, and the works of Groat, Gibbon, Gilbert and Marr. Whether or not her heart was sometimes ruffled by a restless breeze, I can't say; but her lifestyle left no loophole for any major disruption. At this juncture, disruption arrived in a motor car, driven soundlessly down the middle of the road. Suddenly, the monumental history of Greece and Rome appeared very light; sweeping all else aside, the intensity of the immediate present jolted her consciousness, forcing her awake. Instantly aroused, Labanya at last saw herself as she really was—immersed not in learning but in pain.

## 5
## Introductions

From the ruins of the past, let us now return to the new constructions of the present.

Leaving Amit in the study, Labanya went in search of Yogamaya. Like a bee at the heart of a lotus blossom, Amit settled into the room. Glancing around, he felt in everything a touch of wistfulness. On the shelves, and on the study table, he saw volumes of English literature. The books seemed to come alive. They had been read by Labanya, their pages turned by her fingers, bearing the trace of her daylong thoughts as her curious eyes travelled over them, books that would lie neglected on her lap on days when she was distracted. He started when he saw the works of John Donne on her table. In his Oxford days, Amit had specialized in the lyrics of Donne and his contemporaries. Today, by a quirk of fate, these same lyrics became the meeting-ground for their hearts.

Like a schoolmaster's textbook, its cover hanging loose from years of use, Amit's life had grown dim, rusted by the prolonged dullness of his days and nights. He had no curiosity about the coming day, and felt no need to greet the present with whole-hearted enthusiasm. But now, he seemed to have landed on a new planet. Here, the pull of gravity was so mild that there was a weightless feeling, like floating above the ground; every moment reached eagerly for the inconceivable; at the touch of the breeze, the body yearned to be a flute; the radiance of the sky suffused his blood, and his innermost being was filled with an excitement like the sap of life that makes a tree blossom. The dusty screen that had veiled his heart was blown away, revealing the extraordinary even in the ordinary. Hence, when Yogamaya slowly entered the room, even this simple act filled Amit with wonder. 'Ah! An apparition, not a mere entrance!' he said to himself.

She was almost forty, but age, instead of slackening her form, had only imparted added dignity. Her fair countenance was full and firm. Her hair was trimmed short, as customary for widows; her benign eyes were full of motherly feeling; her smile was tender. A length of plain, coarse fabric was draped over her head and wrapped around her body. Her bare feet were exquisitely pure. When Amit touched her feet in respectful greeting, he felt as if the blessings of a goddess were coursing through every vein in his body.

'Your kaka Amaresh, your father's younger brother, was the most prominent lawyer in our district,' Yogamaya informed him, once introductions were over. 'He had come to our rescue once, when some disastrous litigation had brought us to the brink of bankruptcy. He used to call me Boudidi.'

'I am his unworthy nephew,' acknowledged Amit. 'Kaka saved you from bankruptcy, but I have brought you loss. As his Boudidi you gained benefits, but as my maternal aunt—my Mashima—you will suffer losses.'

'Is your mother still living?' asked Yogamaya.

'She was, once,' replied Amit. 'I should have had a mashi, too.'

'Why such longing for a mashi, baba?'

'Just think: if I had crashed my mother's car today, there would have been no end to all the scoldings; she would have called it rascally conduct. But if the car were my mashi's, she would laugh at my lack of expertise, taking it for immature behaviour.'

'So let it be your mashi's car, then,' laughed Yogamaya.

Amit sprang up to touch Yogamaya's feet. 'This is why we must believe that we reap the fruit of our deeds from past lives. Born into my mother's lap, I have never striven for the favour of a mashi. Crashing a car can't be called a good deed, yet, in a flash, mashi descends into my life like a divine boon. Think how many centuries of karma must be behind this occurrence.'

'I wonder whose karma this involves, baba,' laughed Yogamaya. 'Yours, mine, or the motor-mechanic's?'

'Tough question,' acknowledged Amit, running his fingers through his thick locks. 'Karma is not one person's but the whole world's. The stream of karma, flowing from planet to planet through the ages, carrying all their combined influences, has culminated in a collision today, at exactly nine forty-eight on Friday morning. What will happen next?'

Yogamaya smiled, casting a sidelong glance at Labanya. She had decided upon a match between these two as soon as she was introduced to Amit. With this in mind, she suggested: 'Baba, the two of you could have a chat while I go and attend to your meal.'

Amit could establish a quick rapport with people. 'Mashima has ordered us to get to know each other,' he began, without any ado. 'Introductions begin with names. Let's get those straight first. You know my name, don't you? My "proper name", as English grammar would call it?'

'I know you as Amitbabu,' replied Labanya.

'That doesn't work in all situations.'

'Situations may vary, but the subject's name should surely remain the same,' smiled Labanya.

'What you're saying doesn't apply to modern times. If place, time and people can vary, it's unscientific to imagine that names would remain unchanged. I have decided to stake my claim to fame on promoting the "Relativity of Names". I would like to inform you at the very outset that for you, my name is not Amitbabu.'

'Do you fancy a Western style of address? Mister Roy?'

'That's a remote, overseas sort of name. When determining the distance signified by a name, one should measure the time it takes to travel from the threshold of the ear to the inner chambers of the heart.'

'So, what's this name that travels so swiftly?'

'To increase speed, we must shed some weight. Drop the 'babu' from Amitbabu.'

'Not so easy! It will take some time,' answered Labanya.

'The time taken shouldn't be the same for everybody. There's no such thing as uniform time; the pace of a pocket-watch depends on the pocket. That's Einstein's view.'

Labanya rose to her feet. 'Your bath water is turning cold, I'm afraid.'

'I shall accept the cold water with reverence, if you will allow a little more time for introductions.'

'There's no time, I have work to do,' insisted Labanya, and quickly disappeared.

Amit did not proceed immediately for his bath. He savoured in his mind the form of every word as it had taken shape on Labanya's lips, uttered with faint amusement. Amit had seen many beautiful women, but their beauty had the veiled brightness of a full-moon night. Labanya's beauty was like the morning; instead of the allure of mystery, it was suffused with radiant intelligence. While making her a woman, the Creator had added a masculine element to her nature. It was clear at first sight that she had not only the strength to endure suffering but also the power of intellect. This, for Amit, was her chief attraction. For in Amit's nature, there was intellect but no mercy; judgement but no patience; a great deal of knowledge and learning but no inner peace. In Labanya's countenance, he had glimpsed a peace that did not arise from the contentment of the heart but rested, motionless, in the depths of her intellect.

## 6
## Getting Acquainted

Amit was a gregarious person. He could not dwell for long on the beauties of nature. He was accustomed to the sound of his own voice. One couldn't laugh and joke with trees and mountains; any attempt to take liberties with them would boomerang on oneself. Trees and mountains followed their own routine, and expected others to be equally disciplined. In a word, they were humourless. So, away from the city, Amit felt bored and fretful.

But suddenly, the hills of Shillong all around him seemed to fill Amit's heart with zest. Today, he was up before sunrise, quite contrary to his personal religion. From his window, he saw the needles shivering on the deodar trees, against a backdrop of light clouds, upon which the sun, hidden by mountains, had drawn his sweeping, golden brush-strokes. The fiery glow of all these colours left him speechless.

After a quick cup of tea, Amit set out. At that hour, the path was empty. He chose a space under an ancient, mossy pine, and stretched out on the fragrant carpet of pine needles. He lit a cigarette, holding it between his fingers for a long time, without remembering to take a puff.

This forest was on the way to Yogamaya's house. From here, Amit savoured the fragrance of the house, as one breathes in the aroma wafting from the kitchen just before a meal. As soon as his watch signalled a civilized hour, he would go there and demand a cup of tea. At first, evening was the appointed time for his visits there. On the strength of his reputation as a litterateur, he had a standing invitation to join them for discussions. For the first few days, Yogamaya had expressed her enthusiasm for these discussions, until she sensed that Amit's own eagerness was waning as a result. It was not hard to guess that this was due to the use of the plural in place of the dual number. Since then, Yogamaya found frequent reasons to stay away. The slightest probing would have revealed that these occasions for absence were neither unavoidable, nor heaven-decreed but invented by Yogamaya herself. Evidently, Yogamaya had noticed that these two discussants felt an affection for each other that was considerably deeper than their affection for books. Amit realized that, despite her advanced age, Mashi was sharp-eyed, yet tender-hearted. This intensified his enthusiasm for discussion. With the intention of extending the appointed time, he made a mutual arrangement with Jatishankar to help with his English lessons for an hour in the morning and two hours every evening. The help he offered was so excessive, that morning would frequently advance into afternoon, and tutelage would slide into aimless talk, until the pressures of civility, coupled with Yogamaya's requests, made it obligatory for him to stay on for lunch. In this way, it became apparent that the call of duty was increasing by the hour.

He was supposed to assist with Jatishankar's lessons at eight in the morning. Normally, he would have considered this an unearthly hour. He used to insist that, for a creature that spends ten months in the womb, the hours of sleep required cannot be measured by the habits of animals and birds. Until now, Amit's nights had encroached upon several hours of his mornings. These stolen hours were best suited for sleep precisely because they were forbidden, he would argue.

But nowadays, he no longer slept soundly. In his heart was an intense eagerness to wake up early. He would awaken needlessly early, and dared not turn over on his side, for fear of oversleeping. Sometimes, he would advance the hands of his watch, something not to be repeated too often, for fear of being caught in the criminal act of stealing time. Today, he glanced at his watch once, and found it was not yet seven. It seemed his watch must have stopped. He held it to his ear to listen to its ticking.

Suddenly, he was startled to see Labanya walking down the road, swinging an umbrella in her right hand. She was dressed in a white sari, with a black, triangular, fringed shawl draped across her back. Amit was sure that Labanya, having glimpsed him from the corner of her eye, was nevertheless unwilling to acknowledge his presence by turning her full gaze upon him. As she reached the bend in the road, Amit ran to her side, unable to restrain himself any longer.

'You knew you couldn't avoid me, but still you made me run after you in hot pursuit!' he protested. 'Don't you how difficult it becomes when you move far away?'

'Difficult? In what way?'

'The unfortunate wretch you've left behind yearns with all his heart to call out to you. But by what name should I call you? With gods and goddesses, it's easy, because they're happy to be addressed by name. Even if you bellow "Durga! Durga!" the ten-armed deity doesn't take offence. But with people like yourself, there's a problem.'

'If you don't call me, there will be no problem.'

'When you are near, I manage without any form of address. Therefore I plead, please don't move far away. There is no sorrow greater than being unable to call you even when I yearn to.'

'Why, you're used to English ways.'

'Miss Dutt? That's for the tea-table. Look, the vision of beauty created at the auspicious moment when land and sky came together in the light of dawn, contained within it the name by which heaven and earth call out to each other. Don't you hear that call, resounding in the heavens above, and here below, on earth? In the lives of mortals, too, isn't there a moment for the creation of such a name? Imagine that I have just called out to you, a full-throated cry from the depths of my heart; the name resounds in the forests, and ascends to those brilliant clouds; at the sound of that name, this mountain before us stands lost in thought, its head covered in clouds. Can you ever imagine that name to be Miss Dutt?'

'The naming ritual takes time; meanwhile, let's take a walk,' proposed Labanya, evading the question.

'Human beings take long to learn how to walk, but with me it was just the opposite,' replied Amit, taking the cue from her. 'Since I came here, I have finally learned how to rest. A rolling stone gathers no moss, as they say in English. That's why I was waiting by the wayside before daybreak. So I could glimpse the light of dawn.'

'Do you know the name of that green-winged bird?' asked Labanya, quickly changing the subject.

'Until now, I knew in a general way that the created world includes birds; but I never had the time to discover the special significance of this fact. Strangely enough, since I came to this place, I have clearly understood that birds indeed exist, and that they even sing.'

'How extraordinary!' laughed Labanya.

'You're laughing at me! I can't remain serious even when I'm being profound. That's a congenital bad habit. The moon, the celestial body that dominates my birth-chart, can never fade away without the flicker of a smile, not even on the dark, deadly night of Krishnachaturdashi.'

'Please don't blame me for feeling amused,' begged Labanya. 'Even the birds would probably burst into laughter if they heard you.'

'Look, people laugh because they fail to grasp my words at first; if they understood my meaning, they'd ponder in silence. It seems a laughing matter that I have learnt to see birds in a new light today. But my words imply a hidden meaning: that today, I see everything in a new light—including myself. That's no laughing matter! Take yourself, for instance: I'm repeating the same idea, but this time, you are speechless.'

'You are not an ancient person, after all,' smiled Labanya. 'You're of very new vintage. Where do you find such enthusiasm to seek out something even newer?'

'In reply to that, I must say something very profound, not suitable for the tea-table. The new element that has entered me is timeless, older than time, ancient as the light of dawn; like the newly blossomed bhuichampa flower, it is the fresh discovery of something eternal.'

Labanya smiled. She didn't say anything.

'This smile of yours is like the watchman's lantern, meant for spotting thieves,' remarked Amit. 'I realize that my ideas strike you as familiar, for you have encountered them already in your favourite poet's works. I beg you not to brand me a thief. At times my heart, like Sankaracharya, insists that the difference between my writings and someone else's is maya, mere illusion. This morning, for instance, it suddenly occurred to me that I should extract from my knowledge of literature a line that would appear to be my own fresh composition, something no other poet could have written.'

'Could you find such a line?' Labanya couldn't help asking.

'Yes.'

'What was it? Please tell me!' begged Labanya, unable to contain her curiosity any longer.

'For God's sake, hold your tongue
  and let me love!'

There was a tremor in her heart.

'You must know who wrote that line?' asked Amit, after a long pause.

Labanya slightly inclined her head to indicate assent.

'This line would not have occurred to me if I hadn't discovered the works of John Donne on your table, the other day.'

'You discovered them?'

'It was a discovery, indeed. In bookshops, we glance at books; but on your table, books appear in a new light. When I view the tables in the public library, they seem burdened with books; but when I saw your table, I found it a nesting-place for books. That day, I was able to view the poetry of Donne through the eyes of the spirit. Like paupers at a rich man's funeral, a great crowd of people seem to press against the gates of other poets, But the palace of Donne's verse is solitary, with space enough only for two. That is why I could clearly hear the words that came to me this morning:

'For God's sake, hold your tongue
  and let me love!'

He had recited these words in Bengali.

'Do you write poetry in Bengali, then?' asked Labanya in surprise.

'I may begin from today, I fear. The old Amit Raye has no idea what the new Amit Raye might do. Perhaps he'll go out to wage war, at this very moment.'

'Wage war? Against whom?'

'That I can't decide. I feel a blind urge to surrender my life to some great cause; the time for regret can follow later.'

'If you must surrender your life, please be cautious,' smiled Labanya.

'Needless to warn me. I'm not willing to step into communal riots. I shall avoid Muslims and Englishmen. If I came across a non-violent, pious-looking elderly person, sounding his motor-horn and driving somewhere in a hurry, I would stand before him, obstruct his path, and demand: "Grant me the gift of war!" I'm referring to the kind of people who visit the hills instead of the hospital to cure their indigestion, shamelessly setting out to savour the air in order to improve their appetite.'

'What if the man drives away, disregarding you?' smiled Labanya.

'Then, I shall raise my hands to the sky and call out after him: "I forgive you this time, for you are my brother; we are children of the same mother—our nation, Mother India, Bharatmata." You see, when we become magnanimous, we can fight but also forgive.'

'I was frightened when you spoke of waging war, but after your discourse on forgiveness, I feel reassured that I have nothing to fear,' smiled Labanya.

'Will you honour a request of mine?' asked Amit.

'Please tell me what it is.'

'Please don't stay out much longer to improve your appetite, today.'

'Very well, but what next?'

'Let's rest under that tree, where the water trickles by, beneath that rock covered in many-coloured moss.'

'But there's not much time,' protested Labanya, glancing at her watch.

'It is the tragedy of life, Labanya Devi, that time is short. On the desert track, we have with us only half a leather-bag of water. We must ensure that it doesn't spill over to be wasted in the dry dust. Punctuality is for those who have plenty of time to spare. God has limitless time at his disposal, hence the sun rises and sets exactly on time. Our tenure is short; it would be prodigal of us to waste time on punctuality. If, at the gates of the celestial city Amaravati, someone were to ask: "What did you accomplish, on earth?" it would be embarrassing to reply, "As I went about my work, I was too busy watching the clock, to find time for the contemplation of all those things which transcend the limits of time." That is why I was impelled to invite you to that spot.'

Amit spoke as if there was no possibility of anyone objecting to something to which he himself had no objection. Hence, it was difficult to resist his proposal.

'Let's go,' said Labanya.

In the deep forest shadow, the narrow path descended towards a tribal village. Halfway down, the path was crossed by a small mountain stream, flowing from a waterfall, spreading pebbles to mark its right of way, following its own course in seeming oblivion of the public thoroughfare. Here, the two of them found a place on the rocks. At that spot, water had collected in a hollow crevice, like a green-veiled maiden too timid to appear in public. The very solitude of this spot embarrassed Labanya, for it made her feel exposed. To hide this feeling, she felt like making some trifling remark but could think of nothing to say. It was like choking in a dream.

'Look, my wise lady,' observed Amit, realizing the need to break the silence, 'there are two languages in our country: one formal, the other colloquial. But there should have been yet another language: not the language of society, or of business, but the language of seclusion, meant for places such as this. Like the song of birds and the verse of poets, this language should rise to the throat as readily as sobbing. What a shame that people must rush to bookshops to fulfil this need. Imagine what would happen if we had to rush to the dentist every time we wanted to laugh. Tell me truly, Labanya Devi, don't you feel the urge to voice your thoughts in melody, at this moment?'

Labanya remained silent, her head bent low.

'In the language of the tea-table, there's no end to nice determinations of what's civilized and what isn't. But here, there is nothing either civilized or uncivilized. So what's the solution? It has become necessary to recite a poem. Prose takes very long, but we don't have so much time to spare. If you permit me, I shall begin.'

She had to permit him, for it would be embarrassing to refuse.

'Perhaps you like the poems of Robi Thakur,' said Amit, by way of introduction.

'Yes, I do.'

'I don't. So, please forgive me. I have a favourite poet. His writings are of such high quality that very few people read them. In fact, nobody even considers him significant enough to be condemned. I would like to recite his poems.'

'Why are you so scared?'

'My experience in this matter has been distressing. To criticize the great poet is to be shunned as an outcaste by all of you; to ignore him would also invite harsh words. All the bloodshed in this world has to do with my fancying what others may dislike.'

'Have no fear. I'll cause no bloodshed. I don't seek the approval of others in support of my own taste.'

'Well said. So let us fearlessly begin:

O unknown! How can you evade my grasp
Until I come to know you?

'Do you notice the subject? The bondage of not knowing. It is the harshest bond. Imprisoned in an unknown world, one must get to know it in order to find release: that's the philosophy of liberation.

At what blind moment,
Between sleep and wakefulness,
As night gave way to dawn,
Did I glimpse your face?
I met your gaze, and asked:
In what corner of self-forgetting
Do you hide?

'There's no corner more obscure than the point where you forget yourself. All the precious things in the world that one could never glimpse have vanished into the corner of self-forgetting. But one can't give up hope for that reason.

Getting to know you
Will not be easy, not like
Whispering sweet nothings.
Your shy, hesitant speech I'll conquer,
Dragging you with rampant force
From fear, shame and doubt,
Into the pitiless light.

'He doesn't give up. What power. Do you see the virility of the writing?

In a flood of tears you'll awaken,
And know yourself at once.

Your shackles will be broken;
In your freedom, I shall find mine.

'You won't detect quite this tenor in your famous writer's work, for it's like a fire-storm in the sun's atmosphere. These are not mere lyrics: they are life's cruel philosophy.' Fixing his gaze on Labanya's face, he recited:

O unknown!
Day's done: 'tis dusk; no time remains.
Let a sudden blow destroy
Our fetters. Let knowledge of you
Set me aflame. To that fire
I yield my life, a prayer offering.

As soon as his recitation came to an end, Amit grasped Labanya's hand. She gazed at him wordlessly, without withdrawing her hand.

Now, there was no need for words. Labanya forgot even to look at her watch.

## 7

## Matchmaking

'Mashima, I'm here to do some matchmaking,' announced Amit to Yogamaya. 'Don't be parsimonious when it's time to pay my dues.'

'Only if I like the proposal. Let's begin with the name, background and physical description of the candidate.'

'The candidate's name doesn't indicate his worth.'

'Then some deductions must be made from the matchmaker's dues, it seems.'

'That's an unfair thing to say. A person with a well-known name spends less time at home, more outside. He's busy keeping up appearances in public, instead of maintaining peace on the domestic front. The wife gets a very tiny share of her husband's attention, not enough for complete fulfilment in marriage. The marriage of a well-known man is a partial, inadequate thing, as much to be condemned as polygamy.'

'Very well, so he is not eminent by name. What about his appearance?'

'I'm reluctant to describe him, lest I exaggerate.'

'Must he be marketed only through hyperbole?'

'When selecting a candidate for marriage, two things must be kept in mind—the groom's name should not outshine the reputation of the bride's family, nor should his beauty exceed the bride's.'

'Very well, let's forget his name and appearance. Tell us the rest.'

'The rest, in a nutshell, could be called substance. Well, the man does not lack substance.'

'What about intelligence?'

'He has intelligence enough to be mistaken for a clever man.'

'Learning?'

'Like Newton himself. He knows that he has merely gathered pebbles at the shore of the sea of knowledge. But unlike Newton, he doesn't have the courage to declare this, lest others take him seriously.'

'I can see that the candidate's list of accomplishments is rather short.'

'It was to reveal the full glory of Annapurna that Shiva assumed the role of a beggar. It's nothing to be ashamed of.'

'Then explain the candidate's identity a little more clearly.'

'The family is known to you. The candidate's name is Amitkumar Ray. Why do you laugh, Mashima? Do you take this for a joke?'

'I do feel anxious, baba, that it may ultimately turn out to be a joke.'

'To harbour such a suspicion is to cast aspersions upon the candidate.'

'Baba, the ability to laugh away the worries of this world is no mean gift.'

'Mashi, the gods have this ability, which is why they are unworthy of marriage. This was something Damayanti had realized.'

'Do you really like my Labanya?'

'How would you like to verify that?'

'The only test would be for you to know for certain that Labanya is entirely in your hands.'

'Please explain a little more clearly.'

'The true jeweller is one who understands the real value of a jewel, even if it is cheaply bought.'

'Mashima, you refine the argument too much. As if you're polishing the psychology of some short story. But the matter itself is extremely coarse: as per the custom of this world, a gentleman is eager to marry a lady. In his personal qualities, the young man would pass muster; as for the young lady, she is beyond description. In such a situation, the ordinary mashimas of this world would naturally be overjoyed, and instantly begin to thresh rice on the dhenki, to prepare celebratory wedding sweets.'

'Have no fear, baba, my foot is already on the dhenki pedal. You may assume that Labanya is yours. If your desire for her remains intense, even after you have her in your possession, only then would I regard you as a worthy match for such a girl.'

'Your words dazzle even an ultra-modern person like me.'

'What signs of modernity do you find in my words?'

'I find that twentieth-century mashimas are afraid even to arrange a marriage.'

'That's because the girls married off by mashimas of earlier centuries were dolls, mere playthings. The marriageable girls of today are not interested in fulfilling their mashimas' game-plans.'

'Have no fear. To have is not to possess completely; rather, it increases one's desire. Amit Raye was born into this world only to demonstrate this truth, by marrying Labanya. Why else would my motor car, an inanimate thing, bring about such a bizarre mishap in the wrong place, at the wrong time?'

'Baba, your words have not yet acquired the ring of maturity expected in a person of marriageable age; I hope this won't turn out to be a case of child-marriage.'

'Mashima, my mind has a specific gravity of its own, causing even the heavy words of my heart to float lightly to my lips. But that doesn't reduce the weight of what I say.'

Yogamaya went away, to supervise kitchen chores. Amit wandered from room to room but failed to glimpse anyone worth seeing. Encountering Jatishankar, he remembered that a lesson on *Antony and Cleopatra* had been scheduled for that morning. From Amit's expression, Jati sensed that it was his duty to take the day off, out of sheer human kindness.

'Amitda,' he pleaded, 'if you don't mind, I'd like the day off to visit Upper Shillong.'

'Those unable to take time off from their studies merely read, without digesting their lessons,' responded Amit, delighted. 'Why harbour such impossible fears? Would I be offended if you wanted the day off?'

'Tomorrow being Sunday, is anyway a holiday. What if you were to imagine . . .'

'I don't have the mentality of a schoolmaster, my friend. I don't count regular holidays as days off, at all. Enjoying a routine holiday is like hunting a chained beast. It dilutes the joy of taking a break.'

Jati was highly amused, for he sensed the real reason for Amitkumar's enthusiasm in his animated elaboration of the doctrine of holidays.

'Of late, your mind has thrown up all kinds of new ideas about the doctrine of holidays,' he said. 'You had offered me advice the other day, as well. A few more days of this, and I'll become an expert at taking time out.'

'What advice had I offered, the other day?'

'You had said, "Truancy is one of the greatest human qualities. We must not waste a second in answering its call." With these words, you immediately closed your book and rushed outside. Perhaps an occasion for truancy had presented itself, somewhere outdoors, though I had failed to notice it.'

Jati was almost twenty. His heart, too, was stirred by the restlessness in Amit's. All along, he had regarded Labanya as a teacher; but today, Amit's behaviour had made him realize that she was a woman.

'That one should be ready for any task that presents itself, is a maxim of high market-value, like a gold sovereign of Akbar's vintage,' laughed Amit. 'But on its obverse, there should be an engraving exhorting us to heroically embrace truancy whenever the occasion arises.'

'These days, your heroism is very much in evidence.'

Amit patted Jati on the back. 'My friend, when your life's almanac announces Ashtami—the sacred date when urgent duties must be sacrificed at one stroke—don't be tardy in your goddess-worship. For Bijoyadashami—when the prayers must end and the goddess' image destroyed—arrives soon after.'

Jati departed. Amit's urge for truancy was acute, but there was no sign of the one who inspired truancy. Amit stepped outside.

The climbing rose was in full bloom, flanked on one side by a host of sunflowers, and on the other, by chrysanthemums in square wooden flowerpots. At the top of a grassy slope was a giant eucalyptus tree. Reclining beneath it, leaning against the tree trunk was Labanya. She was wrapped in a grey shawl, sunning her feet in the morning sun. A handkerchief in her lap held a few scraps of bread and some walnut fragments. She had planned to spend the morning feeding the creatures of this world but had forgotten all about it. Amit came up close; raising her head, Labanya gazed at him in silence, a gentle smile suffusing her countenance. He faced her directly.

'There's good news. I have Mashima's consent.'

Without offering any reply, Labanya cast a walnut fragment at a peach tree that bore no fruit. Instantly, a squirrel ran down the tree trunk. It was one of the creatures awaiting Labanya's charity.

'If you don't mind, I'll shorten your name a bit,' proposed Amit.

'Shorten it, then.'

'I shall call you Banyo, the wild one.'

'Banyo!'

'No, no, this name might ruin your reputation. Such a name is more appropriate for me. I shall call you Banya—the flood. What do you say?'

'Call me by that name, then, but not in your Mashima's presence.'

'Never! Such names are like the root mantra, never to be disclosed to anyone. This name is for my lips and your ears only.'

'Very well.'

'But I, too, need an unofficial name of the same kind. I wonder whether "Brahmaputra" would do. Banya, a sudden flood, bursting the banks of the river to make her entry.'

'The name is too weighty for everyday use.'

'You're quite right. One would need a porter to carry such a name. Why don't you give me a name, then? It will be your creation.'

'Fine. I, too, shall shorten your name. I'll call you Mita, my intimate friend.'

'Wonderful! In the romantic verses of the Padavali, the name has a double—"Bandhu". Banya, I think you could address me by that name in public: what harm in that?'

'What's precious to one person may be cheapened if heard by many. That's my fear'

'That's not untrue. What, between two people, signifies an intact whole becomes fragmented if it reaches the ears of many. Banya!'

'Yes, Mita?'

'If I write verses to you, do you know what word would rhyme with your name? 'Ananya,' the unique!'

'What would that signify?'

'It would signify that you are what you are, and nothing else.'

'That's nothing extraordinary.'

'What do you mean? It's extraordinary, indeed. Rarely do we come across a person who startles us into acknowledging that she is entirely like herself, not like everyone else. In verse, I would put it like this:

'O my Banya, you are Ananya,
Glorified in your own being.'

'Would you write poetry, then?'

'Sure. Who can stem the flow of my verse!'

'Why this desperation?'

'Let me explain. Last night I stayed up till two-thirty, flipping through the pages of *The Oxford Book of Verse*, just like someone tossing and turning sleeplessly. I couldn't locate any love-poems at all, though earlier I used to stumble upon them at every step. The world is clearly waiting, today, for me to take up my pen.'

With these words, he grasped Labanya's left hand in both of his. 'My hands are joined with yours, so how would I hold my pen?' he asked. 'The finest form of union is a meeting of hands. No poet could match in writing the ease with which your fingers communicate with mine.'

'You don't like anything easily; that's why I fear you so much, Mita!'

'But try to understand what I'm saying. Rama tried to test Sita's purity with external fire; that's why he lost her. But the purity of verse is tested by the fire of the heart. If a person lacks this fire in his heart, how would he undergo such an ordeal? He would have to rely on the opinion of others, which very often is abusive. Today, my heart is aflame; when I test all my previous reading in the light of that fire, how little survives! Most of it burns instantly to ashes in the roaring flames. Today, I stand in the midst of all those noisy poets, and find myself forced to plead: Don't shout! Speak the truth quietly:

'For God's sake, hold your tongue
and let me love!'

For a long time, the two of them remained silent. Then, Amit raised Labanya's hand to stroke his face.

'Just think, Banya,' he said, 'today, at this very moment, what countless numbers across the world experience the same sense of yearning, but how few will find fulfilment! I am one of those very few. Only you, of all the people in this world, spotted this fortunate man under this eucalyptus tree in a remote corner of the Shillong hills. It's the extraordinary things of this world that remain extremely understated, elusive to the eye. Yet the hollow noise of crooked politics raises its fist at the great void, and its shout echoes all the way from Goldighi in Kolkata to Noakhali and Chittagong. This utterly worthless news makes headlines all over Bengal. Who knows, perhaps it's for the best!'

'What is?'

'It's best that the things that really matter wander freely in the thoroughfares of everyday life, yet elude the gaze of evil eyes that would hound them to death. They are in tune with the inner pulse of the universe. Tell me, Banya, I've been chattering away, but what are you thinking of, so silently?'

Labanya kept her gaze averted. She made no reply.

'Your silence is like dismissing my words without paying any wages,' protested Amit.

'Your words frighten me, Mita,' answered Labanya, without raising her eyes.

'What are you afraid of?'

'What is it you want from me, and what can I really offer you? I find it hard to figure out.'

'What you offer requires no thought: that is the value of your offering.'

'My heart quailed when you said Korta Ma had given her consent. The day seemed near when I must surrender to captivity.'

'Surrender you must.'

'Your tastes and intellect are far superior to mine, Mita. On our journey together, I may one day fall far behind; then you will never turn back to call me. When that happens, I shall not blame you at all. No, no, don't say anything: listen to me first. I beseech you not to ask for my hand in marriage. If we try to undo the knot after we are married, it will only get more tangled. What I have received from you is enough to last me a lifetime. But you must not delude yourself.'

'Banya, in today's spirit of largesse, why summon up fears of the miserliness that tomorrow might bring?'

'It is you who empower me to utter the truth, Mita. What I say now is something you already know in your heart of hearts. You don't want to admit it, lest it interfere, ever so slightly, with the pleasure of the moment. You are not meant to lead a settled life; taste is a thirst that drives you to a life of wandering. That's why you frolic in different literary fields, and the same urge draws you to me, as well. Shall I tell you the truth? In your innermost heart, you consider marriage to be what you would call vulgar. It's terribly respectable, the cherished favourite of those God-fearing materialists who use their property and their spouse as an enormous bolster to prop them up.'

'You can say extraordinarily harsh things in an extraordinarily gentle tone, Banya.'

'I hope love will always give me the strength to remain firm, Mita; may I never falter ever so slightly from a desire to delude you. May you remain exactly as you are, and may you like me only as much as your taste permits. But I will be satisfied only if you don't assume the slightest responsibility.'

'Let me have my say, Banya. How amazingly you have analysed my nature! I shall not argue about that. But you are wrong on one count. Human character is also subject to change. In the domesticated state, one's identity is static, bound in chains, as it were. Then, by a sudden stroke of fortune, the shackles are broken, and one's character rushes out into the wilderness to assume a different image.'

'What image have you assumed today?'

'One that doesn't match my usual appearance. I have met many women before this, but that was always on the paved banks of man-made channels, by the lantern-light of taste. Such meetings permit you to see but not to know. Tell me yourself, Banya, is my acquaintance with you of the same order?'

Labanya remained silent.

'When two stars circle each other, exchanging greetings from a distance, their style is quite pleasant and safe, a matching of tastes rather than a union of hearts. But if a sudden deadly encounter takes place, their lanterns are extinguished, and the two stars merge in flames. Such a fire is now ignited, and Amit Raye stands transformed. Such is the history of man. What seems like a stream of continuity is really a string of coincidences. The rhythm of the universe is jolted and jostled along by these coincidences; the ages succeed each other to the uneven beat of the jhaptaal. You have altered my rhythm, Banya; a rhythm that binds your music to mine.'

Labanya's eyelashes grew wet. All the same, she couldn't help thinking: 'Amit's mind is of a literary bent, each experience summoning up a fountain of words. This is the harvest of his life, the source of his joy. That's why he needs me. Like a shower of rain, my warmth must melt all the thoughts frozen in his heart, thoughts that weigh him down, though he does not hear them.'

They were silent for a long time.

'Tell me, Mita, don't you think Shah Jahan rejoiced in Mumtaz's death when the Taj Mahal was complete?' asked Labanya, suddenly. 'Her death was necessary for his dream to come true. Death was Mumtaz's greatest gift of love. The Taj Mahal is not an expression of Shah Jahan's grief: it's an image of his joy.'

'At every instant, you startle me with your words!' exclaimed Amit. 'You must be a poet.'

'I don't want to be a poet.'

'Why not?'

'To merely light the lamp of words with the fire of life is not what my heart desires. Words suit those born into this world for the express purpose of decorating the festival of life. But my life's warmth is dedicated solely to work.'

'Do you disown words, Banya? Don't you know how your words awaken my heart? How would you understand the nature and significance of your utterances? I see it is time to summon up Nibaran Chakrabarti again. You are tired of hearing his name repeated so often. But how can I help it, when the man acts as custodian of my heart's innermost thoughts? Nibaran has not yet grown tired of himself; every time he writes a poem, it's his first, a new beginning. The other day, leafing through his notebooks, I chanced upon a piece he wrote not so long ago. It's a poem about a waterfall. How did he discover that I have found my own waterfall here in the Shillong hills? He writes:

O waterfall! In your stream, so pure and clear,
The sun and stars see their image appear.

'Had I been a writer, I could not have described you more clearly. You have a transparent quality that easily mirrors the brightness of the sky. I glimpse that all-suffusing radiance in your countenance, your smile, your words, your stillness when at rest and your movement as you walk down the path.

Today, upon your water's edge,
Let my shadow sometimes play,
And with that shadow, smiling, merge
The cheerful babble of your voice.
Grant me speech, for you possess
The gift of speech eternal.

'You are the waterfall, not merely flowing with the current of life but also matching your speech with your movement. Your flow strikes chords of music even from the hard, immobile rocks of this world.

'My shadow and your laughter
In one image converge,
Arousing within my soul
A wild poetic urge.
Moment by moment, in rhythmic motion,
Your sparkle stirs my soul to words.
O waterfall! I saw myself today
As word made flesh.
In your flow my heart awakens
And I recognize myself.'

'For all my sound and light, your shadow remains but a shadow. I can't hold it captive,' observed Labanya, with a wan smile.

'But you may find, one day, that when all else is gone, I shall remain personified in words,' replied Amit.

'Where?' smiled Labanya. 'In the notebooks of Nibaran Chakrabarti?'

'That wouldn't be surprising. The subterranean stream that flows within my heart somehow emerges into public view as Nibaran's waterfall.'

'Then perhaps, some day, I may find your heart in Nibaran Chakrabarti's fountain, and nowhere else.'

At this moment, they were summoned to the house for their morning repast.

'Labanya wants to see everything clearly by the light of her intellect,' mused Amit, on the way. 'She can't forget herself even at moments when people would naturally wish to forget themselves. I can't refute what Labanya has said, after all. We must express the deepest ideas of one's innermost soul. Some of us achieve this in the way we live our lives, and some of us through creativity—touching life, yet withdrawing from it, just as a river constantly moves away from its shores as it flows. Shall I always move away from life, carried away by the flow of my writings? Is this the difference between men and women? Men devote their entire energy to create something that loses itself at every step in the cause of its own progress. Women devote their whole energy to preserve and protect, blocking the path of new creation only to sustain the past. Innovation is the enemy of the conservative; the conservative obstructs the path of creation. Why should it be so? They are bound to clash at some point. Intense affinity is usually accompanied by great animosity. Which leads me to believe that liberation, not union, is our greatest goal.'

The thought pained Amit, but his heart could not reject the idea.

## 8
## Labanya's Argument

'Labanya, my girl, have you understood the situation correctly?' Yogamaya wanted to know.

'I have understood it correctly, Ma.'

'Amit is very restless, I must admit. That's why I'm so fond of him. Don't you see how disorganized he is? As if he has butter-fingers: things seem to keep slipping from his grasp.'

'If he indeed had to keep a grip on things, if matters didn't keep slipping out of his grasp, he would find it difficult,' smiled Labanya. 'Not to possess what becomes his own, or to lose a thing as soon as he owns it—such is the law of his life. It doesn't suit his nature to keep what he gets.'

'Truth be told, my child, I really enjoy his childish behaviour.'

'That's the way with mothers. When it comes to childish behaviour, the mother takes all the responsibility, while the son's actions are ascribed to mere playfulness. But why do you ask me to become a burden on someone who cannot take responsibility?'

'Don't you see, Labanya, his wayward mind seems to have grown much more tranquil of late. I feel very sorry for him. Whatever you may say, he does love you.'

'He does, indeed.'

'Then why worry?'

'I don't want to wound his nature by inflicting even the slightest torment upon it, Korta Ma.'

'To the best of my knowledge, Labanya, love demands a degree of torment, and inflicts a degree of torment as well.'

'Korta Ma, such forms of torment have their own grounds; but a threat to one's nature is unbearable. The more I read the literature of love, the more strongly I'm convinced that the tragedy of love occurs whenever people fail to accept their mutual independence, when they impose their will unjustly on others, when they imagine that we can change people, re-create them to suit our own desires.'

'Well, my girl, if two people are to set up house together, it's impossible not to re-create each other to some extent. Where there's love, such re-creation is easy; where love is missing, the attempt to hammer people into shape brings about what you describe as tragedy.'

'Forget those who are born for domesticity. They are made of ordinary mortal clay, moulded and beaten into shape by the pressures of everyday life. But those who are not made of mortal clay at all can never relinquish their independence. A woman who fails to understand this feels ever more deprived, the more insistently she asserts her claims upon her partner. The man who fails to understand this increasingly loses touch with the real person, the more he tries to dominate her. I'm convinced that, in most cases, what we call fulfilment is nothing but the touch of handcuffs on the wrist.'

'What do you want to do, Labanya?'

'I don't want my marriage to become a cause for sorrow. Marriage is not for everyone. Do you know, Korta Ma, people with a finicky nature accept others selectively, choosing the qualities they like, rejecting what they dislike in a person. But when trapped in marriage, men and women come too close; in the absence of separate spaces, it becomes necessary to deal with the whole person, from very close quarters. It's no longer possible to conceal any part of oneself.'

'You don't know yourself, Labanya. For you to gain acceptance, no part of your nature need be excluded.'

'But it's not me he wants. I don't think he has ever glimpsed my everyday, home-loving self. At my touch, his heart instantly erupts into a non-stop flood of words. With those words, he has merely constructed an image of me. If his heart grows tired, if he runs out of words, then in the ensuing silence will emerge a very ordinary woman, not of his own creation. Marriage forces one to accept people as they are; there's no room for the creation of imagined forms.'

'Do you feel that Amit can't entirely accept even a woman like yourself?'

'He can, if he changes his nature. But why should he change? I wouldn't want that.'

'What do you want?'

'To remain, as long as possible, a dream that lives in his words, and in the playfulness of his heart. And why call it a dream? It's a special incarnation of my self, a special form, which manifests itself as a reality within a special world. So what if it's a short-lived, many-hued butterfly newly emerged from its cocoon, what harm in that? It's not as if a butterfly is less real than anything else in this world. So what if it appears at sunrise and dies at sunset? We must only ensure that this short life-span should not have been in vain.'

'Let us assume that Amit will only find you a short-lived enchantment. But what about you? Do you not wish to marry? Is Amit, too, a mere infatuation for you?'

Labanya remained silent, offering no reply.

'When you argue, I can see that you are a very well-read young lady,' said Yogamaya. 'I can neither think like you, nor speak like you. What's more, I probably can't act with the same firmness. But I've also observed you through the chinks in your argument, my child. The other night—it was about midnight—I noticed a light in your room. Entering,

I found you bent over your table in tears, your face hidden in your hands. The girl I saw was not a scholar of philosophy. I had a brief urge to comfort you; then I thought: every woman must weep when it's time for tears, no use trying to suppress anything. I know very well that you want to love, not to create. If you can't devote yourself to service with all your heart and soul, how will you live? That's why I insist, you can't do without him. Don't take a sudden vow of spinsterhood. I'm apprehensive because it's hard to change your mind once you've taken a stubborn decision.'

Labanya remained silent, needlessly pleating the end of her sari in her lap.

'I have often thought, looking at you, that your minds have grown too refined, from so much reading and thinking,' continued Yogamaya. 'Our world is unworthy of the ideas that have secretly taken shape in your minds. It seems that you wouldn't spare even the inner light of the mind which remained hidden in our times. This light seems to pierce through the coarse fabric of the body, rendering it invisible. In our times, the simple emotions of the heart were enough to create the joys and sorrows of our world, and even then, the problems we faced were not inconsiderable. Today, you've carried things to such an extreme, all of you, that nothing remains simple anymore.'

Labanya gave a faint smile. Just the other day, Amit had been explaining to Yogamaya about the invisible light of the intellect; that was the source of her argument—and it was a refined argument, too. Mathakrun, Yogamaya's mother, wouldn't have understood such ideas.

'In the course of time, Korta Ma, the more clearly the human mind begins to understand everything, the more staunchly it can withstand the impact of such knowledge. The fear and the sorrow of living in darkness are intolerable, because you can't see clearly in the dark.'

'I feel now that it would have been better if the two of you had never met.'

'No, no, don't say that. I can't even imagine that things could have turned out any differently. It was once my firm conviction that I was utterly dull and uninteresting, that I would spend my life merely reading books and passing examinations. Now I have suddenly realized that I'm capable of love, as well. It's enough for me, that something so impossible should have become a possibility in my life. I feel as if, having remained a shadow all these days, I have now become a real person. What more can I desire? Please don't ask me to marry, Korta Ma.'

With these words, she flung herself on the ground, hid her face in Yogamaya's lap, and burst into tears.

# 9

# Change of Abode

At first, everyone had assumed that Amit would be back in Kolkata in a fortnight. Naren Mitter had laid a heavy wager that he wouldn't stay away longer than a week. A month went by, then two months, but there was no sign of Amit. His stay at the apartment in Shillong was over. Some zamindar from Rangpur had come to occupy it. After much hunting, lodgings were found close to Yogamaya's residence. It was once home to a milkman or a gardener, before it fell into the hands of a clerk, who had given it a touch of shabby gentility. The clerk, too, was now dead; his widow rented out the lodgings. Due to the scarcity of doors and windows, the room offered little scope for the free play of light, air and space, the three elements; but on rainy days, water, the fourth element, descended with unforeseen plenitude, penetrating through unseen openings.

One day, seeing the condition of the room, Yogamaya was shocked. 'Baba, why subject yourself to such an ordeal?' she demanded.

'Uma undertook the penance of starvation, giving up even a diet of leaves in the end. Mine is the penance of dispossession: giving up bed, table, chairs, I am down to the bare walls, almost. That other event took place in the Himalaya mountains; this one has happened in the mountains of Shillong. There, the bride desired a groom; here, the groom longs for a bride. There, Narad played matchmaker, but here, we have Mashima herself. Now, if Kalidasa ultimately fails to make an appearance, I'll have to play his role as well, as best I can.'

Amit spoke these words in jest, but they pained Yogamaya. She was about to say, 'Come and stay with us,' but stopped herself in time. The Maker has brought a crisis into being, she thought; my intervention could cause impossible complications. She sent across a few items from her own house. Meanwhile, her sympathy for this hapless youth grew doubly strong.

'Labanya, my child, don't harden your heart,' she pleaded repeatedly.

One day, after a heavy downpour, Yogamaya went to inquire after Amit, to find him crouching alone on a blanket under a rickety table, reading an English book. Finding that raindrops had unrestricted access to random areas of the room, Amit had ensconced himself in a cave-like shelter under the table. At first he laughed heartily at himself, then turned his attention to literary criticism. His mind raced to Yogamaya's residence, but his body proved an obstacle. For, having bought an expensive raincoat in Kolkata, where such an item was redundant, he had forgotten it when he left for this place where it was a constant necessity. He had brought an umbrella, which he had most probably left behind at his chosen destination, unless it was lying beneath that old deodar tree.

'What's the matter, Amit!' exclaimed Yogamaya, as soon as she entered.

'My room today is struck by a wild, raving lunacy; its condition is not much better than mine,' explained Amit, hurrying out from under the table.

'Raving lunacy?'

'Meaning, the ceiling is almost like the Indian nation. The links between its parts have come loose. So, an onslaught from above causes a random downpour of tears everywhere; and a storm that strikes from without raises the hiss of deep sighs. By way of protest, I have raised a scaffold above my head, an example of peaceful home rule amidst the misgovernment of this entire room. This demonstrates a basic law of politics.'

'What's this basic law, let's hear.'

'Namely, that even the haphazard arrangements of the poor tenant who occupies the house are better than the rule of an absentee landlord, however powerful he might be.'

Yogamaya now felt very annoyed with Labanya. The deeper her affection for Amit became, the higher he rose in her esteem. 'Such learning, such intellect, so many degrees and qualifications, and yet, such a simple heart! What an extraordinary ability to put things neatly in words! And speaking of personal appearance, he is much more beautiful to my eyes than Labanya. It's Labanya's good fortune that, under some special planetary influence, Amit has found her so enchanting. And for Labanya to cause such suffering to this excellent young man! To simply announce, upon a whim, that she will not marry! As if she's some royal empress! As if she's Sita, vowing to marry only the man who can break the fabled bow. Such arrogance will do her no good. The wretched girl is condemned to die of grief.'

Yogamaya thought, once, of driving Amit to her own residence. Then, an idea occurred to her.

'Wait a bit, baba, I'm just coming,' she told him.

Back in her own house, she spotted Labanya reclining on the sofa in her room, her feet wrapped in a shawl, immersed in Gorky's *Mother*. Yogamaya's temper flared at the sight of such comfort.

'Come, let's go for a drive,' she proposed.

'Korta Ma, I don't feel like going out today.'

Yogamaya didn't realize that Labanya had sought refuge in this work of fiction, in an attempt to escape from herself. All afternoon, ever since she finished lunch, she awaited Amit's arrival in a state of restless anticipation. Her heart kept telling her that he would arrive at any moment. The pine trees outside were stirred by the playful breeze from time to time, and in the heavy downpour, the mountain springs that had newly sprung to life were overactive, as if racing breathlessly against the short span of their life. A restless desire grew within Labanya, to break all barriers, discard all hesitation, and grasping Amit's hands in her own, to declare: 'For ever and ever, in this life and the next, I am yours!' Today, it was easy to make such a declaration. The whole sky was full of desperate bravado, calling out some unknown message carried in gusts of wind. The language of the sky had awakened the wilderness to words; covered in torrents of rain, the mountain peaks stood waiting to hear the voice of the sky. If only someone would wait upon Labanya's words in just the same way, enormous, silent, with open-hearted attention! But hour upon hour had passed, and no one appeared. Gone was the auspicious moment for uttering the secrets of her heart! If someone were to approach her afterwards, she would be at a loss for words; her mind, then, would be full of doubt, and the resounding war-cry of god in his dance of destruction would have faded from the sky. The years pass in silence; then one day, at some special hour, speech comes knocking at one's door. If one fails, at that moment, to find the key to unlock the door, never again can one receive the divine power to utter the truth without embarrassment. The day such power of speech arrives, one feels like announcing to the whole world: 'Listen, all of you! I am in love!' 'I am in love!' These words, like some unknown bird flying across the seas, have travelled so far, over such a long time! It was for these words that divinity had waited within my heart, all these days. At the touch of these words, today, my entire life, my whole world, grows pure and true. Her face hidden in her pillow, Labanya cried importunately, to some unknown person: 'Truth, truth, there is no truth greater than this!'

Time passed, but the awaited visitor did not arrive. Labanya's heart ached with the burden of anticipation. She stepped into the veranda to wet her body with splashes of rain. Then a deep languor came over her heart, filling it with intense despair. It seemed as if the spark of life had been ignited in a single flash of fire, only to be extinguished for ever, leaving the future blank. She lost the courage to accept Amit completely on the strength of her inner faith. The strong faith aroused in her heart just a while ago, had now dwindled. After lying in silence for a long time, she reached for the book on her table. It took some time for her to focus on the story; then, without being aware of it, she entered the flow of the narrative and forgot herself.

At this juncture, Yogamaya invited her for a drive, but she felt no enthusiasm.

Yogamaya drew up a chair and fixed her shining eyes on Labanya's face. 'Come, tell me the truth, Labanya. Do you love Amit?'

Labanya started up. 'Why do you ask such things, Korta Ma?'

'If you don't love him, why don't you tell him clearly? It is cruel of you; if you don't want him, then don't hold him captive.'

Labanya's heart was heaving, but no words rose to her lips.

'I just saw him in such a sorry state, my heart breaks for him. For whose sake does he languish here like a beggar? Don't you realize at all, how fortunate is the woman such a boy desires?'

'Do you ask about my love, Korta Ma?' exclaimed Labanya, struggling to overcome the lump in her throat. 'I can't imagine anyone in this world to be more in love than myself. I could die for love. All that I have been, through all these years, has evaporated. For me, this is a new beginning, a beginning without end. How can I explain to anyone how extraordinary is this transformation within myself? Has anyone ever known such a state of mind?'

Yogamaya was astonished. She had always noted a deep tranquillity about Labanya. Where had this intolerable agony concealed itself, all these years?

'Labanya, my child,' she gently coaxed, 'don't suppress your true self. Amit is searching for you in the dark. Reveal yourself fully to him, without any fear. If the light ignited within you could light a spark in him as well, then he would not lack for anything. Come my child, come with me. Let's proceed immediately.'

They headed for Amit's lodgings, the two of them together.

## 10

## The Second Stage

Amit was perched on a stack of newspapers, placed on the damp seat of his chair. He was writing at the table, a pile of foolscap paper by his side. At that very moment, he was embarking on his famous autobiography. When asked the reason why, he would reply that his life, at this moment, had suddenly taken on a many-hued brilliance, like the hills of Shillong when the clouds part at dawn. How could he refrain from expressing his new-found awareness of the value of his own existence? According to Amit, biographies are written after the subject's death for then, though the world takes one for dead, one lives again, intensely, in the minds of men. It was Amit's feeling that, during his stay in Shillong, he had experienced a death of sorts, his past vanishing like a mirage, while in another sense, he had become vibrantly alive. Against the dark backdrop of the past, a radiant vision had appeared. It was necessary to place this revelation on record. For few in the world are fortunate enough to experience such a thing; like a bat nesting in a cave, most people spend their life, from birth to death, in a kind of twilight gloom.

It was drizzling. The stormy wind had died down, the clouds had lightened.

'How unfair, Mashima!' exclaimed Amit, rising to his feet.

'Why, baba, what have I done?'

'I'm completely unprepared for this visit. What will Srimati Labanya think?'

'We need to give Srimati Labanya some food for thought. When we seek to know something, it's best to be acquainted with all the facts. Why should that give Srijukta Amit cause for worry?'

'It's best for the Srimati to be acquainted with facts about the Srijukta's wealth. As for the poverty of the "Sriheen", or the hapless one, knowledge of it is meant for you, my Mashima.'

'Why such discrimination, my child?'

'For my own sake. One must claim riches with riches, and blessings with want. In human civilization, devis, goddesses like Labanya, have given rise to wealth, while the Mashimas have provided blessings.'

'The devi and the mashima may be one and the same, Amit; there is no need to hide your penury.'

'This must be answered in the language of the poet. To explain what I say in prose, the language of rhyme becomes necessary. Matthew Arnold calls poetry a criticism of life. I would like to amend that to "a commentary on life, in verse". Let me inform my special visitor that the lines I am about to recite are not composed by a famous poet:

Seek not your heart's desire
When your hands are empty,
Nor beg at love's threshold with tear-wet eyes.

'Please think about this: love is fulfilment; its desire is not the poverty of the destitute. It is when the Lord loves his devotee that He appears to him in a beggar's guise.

We'll exchange garlands when
You bring a necklace made of gems;
Would you place the deity's shrine
On the empty dust beside the road?

'That's why I asked the goddess to consider before entering my room. What shrine can I devise for you when I have none to offer? These damp newspapers? Nowadays, I am terrified of being stained by editorial ink. As the poet says, I invite the desired one to join me in revelry when the cup of life brims over, not to share my thirst when I'm thirsty.

In the blossoming forests of spring,
Clasp your loved one to your heart
When the lamp of life burns brightly,
A myriad flames shining in the dark.

'In the laps of our mashis, we begin the first stage of life's tapasya or holy endeavour: a meditation on poverty, the naked ascetic's prayer for affection. The hardships of this hut are meant for such devotional pursuits. I've decided to call this hut the Mashtuto Bungalow, named after my mashi.'

'Baba, the second stage of tapasya is the pursuit of wealth, a meditation on love, with the goddess beside you as your partner. Even in this hut, your prayers will not be concealed by damp newspapers. Are you trying to delude yourself that a divine boon has been denied you? In your heart of hearts, you must know that the boon has been granted.'

With these words, she stood the two of them side by side, and placed Labanya's right hand on Amit's. Removing the gold chain from Labanya's neck, she used it to bind their hands together. 'May your union be everlasting!' she proclaimed.

Together, Amit and Labanya touched Yogamaya's feet in obeisance. 'Wait here, both of you,' she instructed them. 'I'll fetch some flowers from the garden.'

She drove off in the car to collect the flowers. For a long while, the pair sat side by side on the cot, in silence. Then, raising her face to

Amit's, Labanya asked, in a low voice: 'Why did you stay away all day?'

'The reason is so trifling,' replied Amit, 'that it would take courage to mention it on a day such as this. History provides no instance of a lover postponing his rendezvous with the beloved on a cloudy day, for lack of a raincoat. Rather, the books decree that the lover must swim across the fathomless waters. But then, we speak of the history of the innermost heart. Do you imagine I'm not swimming in those waters, too? Can I ever make my way across that shoreless deep?' He proceeded to recite, first in English, then in Bengali:

For we are bound where mariner has not yet dared to go,
And we will risk the ship, ourselves and all.

'Did you wait for me today, Banya?'

'Yes, Mita. All day, I seemed to hear your footfall in the sound of the rain. It seemed you were travelling an impossible distance to come to me. But now, at last, you have indeed entered my life.'

'Not knowing you was like a dark abyss at the centre of my life, Banya. That was the most hideous part of my existence. Today, that hollow is full to the brim: the light sparkles on it, the entire sky is mirrored in it. Today, that very spot has become the most beautiful part of my existence. These words, pouring out of me, are the sound of waves in the lake that fills my heart. There is no stopping them now.'

'What were you doing all day, Mita?'

'You reposed, motionless, at the centre of my heart. I wanted to say something to you, but where were the words? The rain came down from the skies, and I kept pleading, give me words, give me words!' He recited, in English and then in Bengali:

'O, what is this?
Mysterious and uncapturable bliss
That I have known, yet seems to be
Simple as breath and easy as a smile,
And older than the earth.

'That is what I do. I take the words of others, and make them my own. If I had the gift of music, I would set Vidyapati's rain-song to a tune, and make it completely my own:

Vidyapati wonders, how shall I pass
My days and nights without Hari?

'How can I pass day after day in the absence of the person I cannot live without? Where can I find the right tune for this particular idea? I gaze heavenwards, pleading, sometimes, "Give me words!" and sometimes, "Give me music!" The deity even descends to earth, bearing words and music, but somewhere along the way, he mistakes someone else for me, and offers his gift randomly to another—perhaps to that Robi Thakur of yours.'

'Even the admirers of Robi Thakur don't remember him as frequently as you do!' laughed Labanya.

'Banya, I'm a little too garrulous today, am I not? A monsoon shower of words has descended upon my heart. If you keep track of the weather-report, you will note the countless inches of madness I've been notching up, each day. Had I been in Kolkata, I would have burned out the tyres of my car to rush you to Moradabad. If you were to ask, "Why Moradabad?" I would have no reason to offer, none whatsoever. When the flood is upon us, it babbles, rushes on, and carries time along with it in frothy tide of laughter.'

At this juncture, Yogamaya brought in a basketful of sunflowers. 'Labanya, my girl, offer these flowers at his feet, today,' she advised.

This was nothing but a womanly attempt to produce, through ritual, an outward, concrete form for what lay concealed in the recesses of the heart. Women have an innate desire to create immanent form by giving things a material, bodily shape.

'Banya, I want to offer you a ring,' whispered Amit to Labanya.

'Why, Mita, what is the need?' she asked.

'I can't begin to fathom the immensity of the gift you have offered me today, in giving me your hand. Poets harp on the beloved's face. But how much of the heart's language is signalled through the hand! All the fondness of love, all its dedication, all the tenderness of the heart, all the unutterable words—the hand conveys all! The ring will encircle your finger, like a tiny little statement from me. What I wish to say is only this: I have found you! Why not let this utterance of mine adorn your hand in the language of gold and gemstones!

'Very well,' said Labanya.

'I'll order it from Kolkata. Tell me, which precious stone do you like?'

'I want no stone, just a single pearl.'

'Fine, that's a good idea. I, too, am fond of pearls.'

# 11

# Love's Philosophy

The wedding was fixed for the month of Agrahayan. Yogamaya would travel to Kolkata to make all the arrangements.

'You were to have left for Kolkata long ago,' Labanya reminded Amit. 'You spent your days in a state of uncertainty, but now you're free. You may depart with a mind free of doubt. We shall not meet again until the time of our wedding.'

'Why such harsh discipline?'

'To sustain the simple joy you spoke of the other day.'

'These are words spoken from deep knowledge. The other day, I suspected you were a poet, but today, I suspect you're a philosopher. Well said, indeed! To keep simple things simple, one must be harsh. If you want your verse to have an easy rhythm, you must fix the caesura firmly in the right place. I am so greedy, my mind resists marking a pause at any point in the poem of my life. The rhythm is broken, and life, lacking pace, becomes bondage. Very well, I shall depart tomorrow, abruptly cutting short these days of fulfilment. It will be like that line in the epic about Meghnad's death, a line that seems to have stopped short in amazement:

When you departed for hell
Untimely!

'I may go away from Shillong, but the month of Agrahayan can't suddenly slip away from the almanac! Do you know what I shall do in Kolkata?'

'What will you do?'

'While Mashima makes arrangements for the wedding, I must prepare for the days that are to follow. People forget that conjugal life is an art, to be created anew each day. Do you remember, Banya, how King Aja had described Indumati in *Raghuvamsha*?'

'"My favourite pupil has artistry in her blood,"' quoted Labanya.

'Such artistry of the blood belongs to conjugal life,' declared Amit. 'Barbarians generally imagine the wedding ceremony to be the real moment of union, which is why the idea of union is often so utterly neglected afterwards.'

'Please explain the art of union as you imagine it in your heart. If you want me to be your disciple, then let today be the first lesson.'

'Very well, then, listen. The poet creates rhythm out of deliberately placed obstructions. Union, too, should be rendered beautiful by means of deliberately placed obstacles. To cheapen a precious thing so that it is to be had for the asking is to cheat your own self. For the pleasure of paying a high price is by no means negligible.'

'Let's hear how the price is to be calculated.'

'Wait! Let me describe what my heart has visualized. Beside the Ganga, there will be a garden-estate on the other side of Diamond Harbour. A small steam-launch would take us to Kolkata and back, within a couple of hours.'

'But why the need to travel to Kolkata?'

'Now there is no need to, please be assured. I do visit the bar-library, not to engage in trade but to play chess. The attorneys have realized that I have no need for work and, therefore, no interest in it. When a case comes up, concerning some mutual dispute, they hand me the brief but nothing more than that. But right after marriage, I'll show you what it means to set to work, not in search of a livelihood but in search of life. At the heart of the mango lies the seed, neither sweet, nor soft, nor edible; yet the entire mango depends on it, takes shape from it. You understand, don't you, why the stony seed of Kolkata is necessary? To keep something hard at the core of all the sweetness of our love.'

'I understand. In that case, I need it, too. I must also visit Kolkata, from ten to five.'

'What's wrong with that? But it should be for work, and not in order to explore the neighbourhood.'

'What work can I take up, tell me? Without any wages?'

'No, no, a job without wages is neither work nor play: it's mostly all about shirking. If you wish, you can easily become a professor in a women's college.'

'Very well, that shall be my wish. What then?'

'I can visualize it clearly: the shore of the Ganga. From the lowest level of the paved bathing area rises an ancient banyan tree, laden with aerial roots. While cruising down the Ganga to Ceylon, Dhanpati may have tethered his boat to this same banyan tree and cooked his dinner under its shade. To the south is the moss-encrusted paved bathing ghat, the stone cracked in many places, eroded in patches. At that ghat is tethered our slim, elegant boat, painted green and white. On its blue flag, inscribed in white lettering, is the name of the boat. Please tell me what the name should be.'

'Should I? Let it be named Mitali, for friendship.'

'Just the right name: Mitali. I had thought of Sagari, in fact I was rather proud of having thought up such a name. But you have defeated me, I must admit. Through the garden flows a narrow channel, bearing the pulsebeat of the Ganga. You live on one side of the channel, and I live just across, on the other side.'

'Would you swim across every evening, and must I await you at my window, with a lighted lamp?'

'I'll swim across in my imagination, crossing a narrow wooden footbridge. Your house is named Manasi, the desired one; and you must give a name to my house.'

'Deepak—the lamp.'

'Just the right name. Atop my house, I shall place a lamp to suit the name. A red light will burn there on the evenings when we meet, and a blue one on nights of separation. When I return from Kolkata, I shall daily expect a letter from you. It should sometimes reach me, sometimes not. If I don't receive it by eight in the evening, I shall curse my ill-fortune and try to read Bertrand Russell's textbook on logic. It will be our rule, that I must never visit you uninvited.'

'And can I visit you?'

'Ideally, both of us should follow the same rule, but if you occasionally break it, I shall not find it intolerable.'

'If the rule is not to be observed in the breaking, what would be the condition of your house! Perhaps I should visit you in a burkha.'

'That's all very well, but I want my letter of invitation. The letter need contain nothing but a few lines of verse, taken from some poem.'

'And will there be no invitations for me? Am I to be discriminated against?'

'You are invited once a month, on the night when the moon is at its full, after fourteen days of fragmented existence.'

'Now offer your favourite pupil an example of the kind of letter to be written.'

'Very well.' He produced a notebook from his pocket and wrote, first in English, then in Bengali:

'Blow gently over my garden
Wind of the southern sea
In the hour my love cometh
And calleth me.'

Labanya did not return the piece of paper to him.

'Now for an example of the kind of letter you would write. Let's see how much you have gained from your lessons.'

Labanya was about to write on a piece of paper. 'No,' insisted Amit, 'you must write in this notebook of mine.'

Labanya wrote, in Sanskrit, and then in English:

*Mita, twamasi mama jivanam, twamasi mama bhushanam,*
*Twamasi mama bhavajaladhiratnam.*

Mita, you are my life, my adornment,
The jewel in the ocean of my world.

'The amazing thing is, I have written the words of a woman, and you the words of a man,' remarked Amit, putting the notebook in his pocket. 'There is nothing incongruous about it. Whether the wood comes from a red silk cotton tree or from a bakul tree, when set alight, the fire looks the same.'

'So, after the invitations, what next?' Labanya wanted to know.

'The evening star has risen,' Amit replied. 'The Ganga is in high tide; a breeze ripples through the rows of fir trees; the waves lap against the roots of the ancient banyan tree. Behind your house is Padmadighi, the large pond; there, you bathe at the secluded ghat and plait your hair. You wear a different colour each day; as I approach, I wonder what colour you would wear this evening. There is no fixed place for our meeting: sometimes, it's the paved area beneath the champa tree, sometimes the rooftop of your house, sometimes the riverside terrace. I shall bathe in the Ganga, and wear a white muslin dhoti and wrap, with ivory-inlaid wooden sandals on my feet. I'll find you reclining on a carpet, waiting for me with a silver platter containing a jasmine garland, a tiny bowl of sandalwood paste, and on the side, some burning incense. During the Durga Puja, we'll go on a holiday, the two of us, for at least a couple of months. But we'll go our separate ways. If you go to the hills, I shall head for the seas. Thus I present to you my formula for our conjugal dual rule. Now tell me your opinion.'

'I am willing to follow the formula.'

'There is a difference between following a formula and embracing something with your whole heart, Banya.'

'Even if I don't require what is necessary for you, I shall still raise no objections.'

'Have you no requirements?'

'No, none. However close, you would still remain at a great distance from me. It would be pointless for me to preserve that distance by means of any formulae. But I know there is nothing in me which can withstand your close scrutiny without causing me shame; hence I would feel safer if the two of us spent our married life in separate palaces, located on opposite shores.'

'I can't let you win, Banya!' exclaimed Amit, rising to his feet. 'Let my garden-estate go. We shall not step outside Kolkata. I shall hire a room on the floor above Niranjan's office, for a rent of seventy-five rupees. There you will live, and so will I. In the heaven of our souls, there is no distinction between distance and proximity. To the left of our five-foot-wide bed will be your palace Manasi, and to the right, my Deepak. On the eastern wall of the room will be a dresser with a mirror, in which we shall see both our faces reflected. To the west will be our bookshelf, its back blocking the sun, its front housing the only circulating library available to its two readers. To the north of the room will be a sofa; I shall occupy a corner of it on the left, leaving some space. You will stand, concealed by the alna, our clothes-rack. Just a couple of feet away, I shall hold up with trembling hands your letter of invitation; it will say:

Blow gently across the terrace,
O southerly breeze,
For in an instant, my eyes
Will meet my beloved's.

'Does this sound awkward, Banya?'

'Not at all, Mita. But what is the source?'

'The notebook of my friend Nilmadhav. His future wife's identity was not known for certain at the time these lines were composed. Addressing her, he had recast the English poem in the Kolkata mould, and I had aided his efforts. Having obtained an MA in Economics, the man brought home his new bride, complete with a dowry of fifteen thousand rupees and eight bharis of gold jewellery. They gazed into each other's eyes, the southerly breeze also blew, but he was unable to make any further use of those lines of verse. Now, his collaborator will not hesitate to lay claim to the complete meaning of that poem.'

'The southerly breeze will blow across your terrace as well, but will your new bride remain forever new?'

'So she will, she will, she will!' proclaimed Amit in a loud voice, thumping the table forcefully.

'What will remain, Amit?' inquired Yogamaya, rushing in from the next room. 'My table, it seems, will not remain much longer.'

'Whatever is durable in this world will remain. A new bride is hard to find in this world, but if by good fortune, one such in a million is discovered, she will remain a new bride forever.'

'Can you offer an example?'

'I shall one day, when the time is ripe.'

'That will take some time, it seems; meanwhile, let's have lunch.'

# 12
# The Final Evening

'I leave for Kolkata tomorrow, Mashima,' Amit informed them after lunch. 'My relatives have begun to suspect that I have adopted tribal ways.'

'How would your relatives know that words could bring about such a transformation in you?'

'They know only too well. Else, what are relatives for? But it's not a matter of words, or of taking to tribal ways. Is my transformation merely a change of caste? It's an epochal transition! Between then and now, a whole era has passed, like a kalpanta—the four-hundred-and-thirty-two million solar years that make up a day and night in the life of Brahma. Prajapati, god of marriage, has awakened in my heart, in a new form. Mashima, please permit me to take Labanya for an outing today. Before my departure, let the two of us offer joint obeisance to the hills of Shillong.'

Yogamaya assented. As they walked, their hands touched, their bodies drew close. From the edge of the secluded path, the deep forests sloped downwards. Somewhere in the forest was a clearing, where a patch of sky, suffused with the fading glow of sunset, could be glimpsed above the watchful mountains. At that spot, the two of them came to a halt and stood, facing west. Drawing Labanya's head to his heart, Amit raised her face. Tears trickled from the corners of her half-closed eyes. Against the golden backdrop of the sky, the light faded in myriad tints, like melting rubies and emeralds. Here and there, through gaps in the clouds, the deep blue of the sky could be seen; it seemed to resonate with the unspoken echoes of that immortal realm where there is no bodily existence, only pure joy. Slowly, the darkness deepened. Like a flower at dusk, the open patch of sky seemed to close its many-hued petals.

'Let's go now,' said Labanya softly, her head resting on his breast. Somehow, at this point, she felt it was best to bring things to an end.

Amit sensed this but said nothing. He clasped Labanya's head to his chest just once, before they turned back and retraced their steps, very slowly.

'I must set out early tomorrow morning,' he told her. 'I shall not visit you again before I leave.'

'Why not?'

'The Shillong chapter of our story has ended at the right place today. Here endeth the first canto, entitled "Our Very Own Paradise".'

Labanya walked on in silence, hand-in-hand with Amit. There was joy in her heart, and mingled with it, a silent grief. Never again in her life, she felt, would she come so intimately close to grasping the unimaginable. After such an auspicious shubhodrishti—the ritual meeting of eyes between bride and groom—was a ceremonial wedding night required? There remained only a last obeisance to be offered, a combined salute to their union and their parting. She felt a strong urge to make that gesture now: to say to Amit, 'You have made me blessed.' But that was not to be.

'Banya, say your last words to me in the form of a poem,' requested Amit, 'so I can easily carry them as a memory. Recite to me some lines that you remember.'

Labanya thought for a while, then recited:

'I did not bring you joy but gave you freedom,
My prayer-offering, when daylight dawned.
Nothing else remains: no prayer, nor the poverty
Of each passing moment, no reproachful words,
No petty tears, nor the laughter of arrogance;
No looking back. I only filled my prayer-basket
With the gift of my death, to offer you liberty.'

'Banya, that was unfair. Never! Such words are not to be uttered on a day like this. Why did you think of these lines? Please take back this poem of yours immediately.'

'Have no fear, Mita. This love, tested by fire, claims no happiness; it liberates because it is free; it does not lead to exhaustion or decline. What more can one offer?'

'But I want to know where you found this poem.'

'It's Robi Thakur's.'

'I have not come across it in any of his books.'

'It has not been published in any book.'

'Then how did you come upon it?'

'There was a young man who respected my father as his guru. My father had fed his appetite for knowledge. The young man, too, was devoted to the pursuit of the sacred. Whenever he had the opportunity, he would approach Robi Thakur and beg for morsels from his notebooks, carrying them back as frugal alms.'

'And he would offer those morsels at your feet.'

'He wouldn't dare. He would leave them around, hoping they would catch my attention, hoping I would pick them up.'

'Did you show him kindness?'

'I did not find the opportunity. I pray in my heart of hearts that the Lord would show him kindness.'

'It is abundantly clear to me, that the poem you recited today actually echoes the private emotions of this unfortunate man.'

'Yes, indeed it does.'

'Then why did you remember this poem today?'

'How can I say? There was another fragment of verse to accompany it; I can't say why that, too, comes to mind on this occasion:

'O beauteous one, you bear the gift
Of tears that fill your eyes.
Clasped to your bosom, you carry
The flame of sacrifice.
It brightens sorrow, breaks the magic spell
That holds the heart enchanted.
In its warmth, our parting blossoms
Like a hundred-petalled lotus.'

'Banya, why has this young man come between us today!' protested Amit, clasping Labanya's hand. 'I'm not jealous, for I detest jealousy. But a strange apprehension troubles my mind. Tell me, why did these poems, his gifts to you, surface in your memory in this fashion, on this very day?'

'The day he bid us farewell and departed from our house, I discovered these two poems on his writing-desk. I found them along with many other unpublished poems by Robi Thakur, almost enough to fill a notebook. Today, it's my turn to bid you farewell. Perhaps that is why I remembered these lines written in parting.'

'Is there no difference between those farewells and this one?'

'How can I tell? But this argument is totally unnecessary. I have simply recited to you the poetry that appeals to me: perhaps that's all there is to it.'

'Banya, until people have completely forgotten Robi Thakur's writings, his best work will not really be recognized. That's why I don't quote his poems at all. The appreciation of partisan readers is like a fog that soils the brightness of the sky with its damp touch.'

'Look, Mita, women's taste regards the object of adoration as an exclusive personal possession, to be cherished in the private chambers of the heart. It takes no account of public opinion, offering the highest price it can afford, without comparing prices with others to ascertain the object's market-value.'

'Then there is hope for me as well, Banya. Concealing the tiny stamp that bears my market-price, I shall proudly sport a large sign stating your estimate of my worth.'

'We are nearing our house, Mita. Let me hear you recite the poem that will mark your journey's end.'

'Don't be annoyed Banya, but I can't recite lines from Robi Thakur.'

'Why would I be annoyed?'

'I have discovered a writer, whose style . . .'

'I regularly hear you speak of him. I've ordered his books from Kolkata.'

'What a disaster! His books! The man may have many other faults, but he never tries to publish a book. It is through me that you must gradually get to know him. Or else . . .'

'Have no fear, Mita, I am convinced that I can learn to understand him exactly as you do. Victory shall be mine.'

'How?'

'What I acquire through my own taste is mine, and what I shall gain through your taste will also be mine. I shall reach out with both hands to receive the joint offering of both our hearts. In your tiny room in Kolkata, on a single shelf of your bookcase, I shall be able to accommodate the works of both the poets of our choice. Now recite your poem.'

'I no longer have the inclination. All these intervening arguments have ruined the atmosphere.'

'It's not ruined at all! The atmosphere is fine.'

Flicking back his hair, Amit began to declaim in a highly emotional tone:

O beauteous morning star!
From beyond the distant mountain-peaks,
Reveal yourself, at night's end,
To the lost wayfarer.

'Do you understand, Banya? The moon beckons the morning star, to be his companion for the night. He is unhappy with the way his own night has turned out.

Where earth meets sky, I linger.
I am the moon, half-awake,
The cleavage, half in shadow,
On the bosom of the dark.

'This half-awake condition of the moon, his faint, glimmering light, makes only a slight dent in the darkness. That's the cause of his anguish. Caught in this web of shallowness, longing to tear it apart, he seems to have simmered with resentment during his nightlong sleep. What an idea! How grand it sounds!

Deep in slumber, the universe waits,
For me to ascend my shrine.
In dreams, I strum my instrument,
To ruffle the surface of its sleep.

'But then, the burden of such a shallow existence is too much to bear; debris collects in the sluggish flow of a dwindling river; a trivial person finds it fatiguing to carry his own weight. Hence, he says:

With slow steps I head for the shore.
My journey is done.
My voice falters as I sing,
My limbs flag in tiredness.

'But is such fatigue to be the end of him? There is hope that his slack strings will be freshly tuned; for, from beyond the horizon, he seems to hear someone's footsteps:

O beauteous morning star!
Come swiftly, before night's end.
Complete, in our waking hours,
The speech that was lost in our dreams.

'There is hope of salvation, for he can hear the immense commotion of awakened universe. The harbinger of that great journey is about to appear, bearing a lamp in her hands:

Retrieve the words from the depths of night,
And offer them to the dawn.
In darkness, speech had lost itself:
Now, let it shine in glory.
Where torpor disappears,
Where celestial music is heard,
There, I offer up my veena:
I, the moon, half-awake.

'I am that unfortunate moon, of course. Tomorrow, I depart. But I don't want to depart in emptiness. Presiding above the event, the beauteous morning star will arise, chanting the song of awakening. At dawn, the beauteous morning star will bring to completion all that had remained indistinct in the dreams of a life filled with darkness. This poem reveals the power of hope, the shining glory of the morning to come: it's not the wilting, despairing lamentation of your Robi Thakur's verse.'

'Why are you so angry, Mita? Robi Thakur can only accomplish what is within his power, no more: why say the same thing over and over again?'

'All of you give him too much . . .'

'Don't say that, Mita. My taste is mine alone; if my likings coincide with someone else's, or fail to coincide with yours, am I to blame for that? Let me promise, then, that if I ever find a place in that seventy-five-rupee abode of yours, then you may recite to me the verses of your favourite poet, but I shall not recite to you the verses of mine.'

'But that would be unjust. To accept with bowed head the torment inflicted by each partner upon the other—that's what marriage is all about.'

'But you can never tolerate the torment inflicted by taste. At the festival of taste, you don't allow any uninvited guest; but I welcome even a passing stranger.'

'I shouldn't have provoked this argument. It has brought a discordant note into the harmony of this, our last evening here together.'

'Not at all! Our harmony is created from the notes that ring true even after we have spoken our minds plainly. In it, there are no limits to forgiveness.'

'I must subdue the bitter taste in my mouth, today. But not with Bengali verse. English poetry helps me keep my cool, to a great extent. After my return to India, I, too, had done a short stint as a professor.'

'Our intellect is like the English bull-dog,' laughed Labanya. 'It barks at the merest sight of swaying dhoti pleats, having no conception of the protocol that obtains among dhoti-wearers. Instead, it wags its tail upon seeing the badge on a cook's livery.'

'I must admit that's true. A bias is not a natural thing. In most cases, it's created on demand. One has developed a habitual bias for English literature, from regular discipline and chastisement during childhood. On account of that habit, one lacks the courage to condemn one party, or to praise the other. Never mind. There shall be no Nibaran Chakrabarti today, only pure English verse, without translation.'

'No, no, Mita, let your English be, leave that for the study table at home. Tonight, our last poem must be one by Nibaran Chakrabarti. No other poet will do.'

'Victory to Nibaran Chakrabarti!' exclaimed Amit, in glee. 'At last, he has become immortal. Banya, I shall make him your court poet. He shall seek favours only at your doorstep, nowhere else.'

'Will that always satisfy him?'

'If not, we shall pull his ears and dismiss him.'

'Well, we shall decide about the ear-pulling later. Now recite the poem.'

Amit began to recite:

How patiently you stayed,
Day and night, by my side!
How frequently your footprints left their mark
On my fortune's dusty path!
Now, when I must depart
For a place far away,
I shall sing to you
Of your own victory.
How often, in our lives,
The fire of sacrifice fails to ignite,
Spirals of smoke rising
Into empty space with a sigh!
How often, a momentary flame
Faintly draws a mark
On the brow of darkness insensate,
Only to vanish without trace!
But now, upon your advent,
The sacred fire burns
In full glory.
Blessed will be my holy sacrifice.
At the day's end, to you I dedicate
My final prayer-offering.
Accept my homage,
The fruits of my life's endeavour.
Bless me with your tender touch,
As I bow at your feet.
Where you reign in splendour,
Upon your glorious throne,
Summon me to you.
There, let my prayer find a place.

## 13

## Apprehensions

Next morning, Labanya found it difficult to concentrate on her work. She had even missed her morning walk. Both she and Amit were responsible for ensuring that he kept his vow not to visit her before leaving Shillong. That morning, Amit would have to take the route along which she usually took her daily walk. So, she was sorely tempted, and had to curb her eagerness with great difficulty. Yogamaya would customarily pluck some flowers for her prayers, after an early bath. Before she emerged outdoors, Labanya left that part of the garden to seek out the shade of the eucalyptus tree. She carried a couple of books, perhaps to delude herself as well as others. A book lay open, but the hours passed, and the page was not turned. In her heart was the persistent feeling that her days of celebration were over. From time to time this morning, she felt the harbinger of separation flash his message across the sky, in the gaps between cloud and sunshine. She felt a deep conviction that Amit was an eternal fugitive, never to be found once he had slipped away. During their journey together, he would begin a narrative. Then, night would descend, and the next morning, it would be discovered that the wayfarer had vanished, leaving his story incomplete, full of loose ends. So Labanya was sure that his narrative would forever remain unfinished. Today, the gloom of that incompleteness could be felt in the morning light, and the mournful breeze was laden with the weariness of an untimely decline.

Meanwhile, at nine in the morning, Amit burst noisily into the house, calling out, 'Mashima! Mashima!' Morning prayers over, Yogamaya was busy sorting daily provisions. Today, she, too, felt troubled. All these days, Amit had filled her loving heart and home with his garrulity, good humour and liveliness. Weighed down by the sorrow of his departure, her morning drooped like a flower cast down by the weight of falling raindrops. Today, in this household racked with the pain of separation, she had not summoned Labanya to assist her with daily chores, realizing that she needed to be alone, away from the public eye.

Labanya jumped to her feet, the book slipping from her lap without her noticing it. Meanwhile, Yogamaya came rushing out of the storeroom.

'What's this, Amit, my boy, is there an earthquake?' she cried.

'An earthquake, indeed. My baggage was dispatched, the car arranged, when I went to the post-office to check for mail. There, I found a telegram.'

'All is well, I hope?' inquired Yogamaya anxiously, watching his expression.

Labanya joined them in the room.

'My sister Sissy is arriving this very evening, along with her friend Katy Mitter, and Katy's elder brother Naren,' Amit informed her, with great agitation.

'So what's there to worry about, my son? There's a vacant house beside the racing track, I'm told. If that's unavailable, can't we offer them accommodation of sorts at my place?'

'I have no worry on that score, Mashima. They have booked themselves into a hotel on their own.'

'Under no circumstances can we let your sisters come here to find you living in that godforsaken cottage, son. They will blame us for the madness of their own kinfolk.'

'No, Mashi, mine is a case of paradise lost. I must bid goodbye to that paradise of bare essentials. My dreams of happiness must fly from their nesting place in that rope-strung cot. I, too, must seek refuge in some ultra-civilized room of that ultra-clean hotel.'

The words were not particularly significant, yet Labanya's face grew pale. It had not occurred to her, all these days, that Amit's social world was a thousand leagues removed from her own. In an instant, this realization dawned on her. Amit's imminent departure for Kolkata had not borne the harsh semblance of separation. But from his compulsion to move into a hotel today, Labanya understood that the home which the two of them had until now been building in their imagination, with various invisible ingredients, would perhaps never materialize.

'Whether I move to a hotel or to hell, this house remains my real home,' declared Amit to Yogamaya, after a brief glance at Labanya.

Amit had realized that the arrival of visitors from the city did not bode well. He was mentally conjuring up many plans, to prevent Sissy and her group from visiting this house. But of late, his mail had been directed to Yogamaya's address, for he had not anticipated then that this could one day become a source of trouble. Amit's inner feelings were not readily repressed; rather, they he tended to overstate them. His extreme anxiety about his sister's visit had struck Yogamaya as excessive. Labanya, too, felt herself a source of embarrassment for Amit where his sisters were concerned. She found this a distasteful, humiliating thought.

'Do you have time to spare?' Amit asked Labanya. 'Would you care to go out with me?'

'No, I have no time,' was Labanya's rather harsh reply.

'Why, my child, why not go out for a while?' Yogamaya urged her, anxiously.

'Korta Ma, I have really neglected Suroma's studies of late. It was remiss of me. I had decided last night itself, that I must not show any slackness today.' With these words, Labanya pursed her lips, her face grim.

Yogamaya was familiar with Labanya's stubbornness. She did not dare pester her.

'I, too, must set out to do my duty,' said Amit, in a listless tone. 'I must see that things are in order for their arrival.'

Before taking his leave, he paused for a moment in the veranda. 'Look, Banya,' he urged. 'Beyond the trees, you can catch a brief glimpse of the thatched roof of my cottage. I haven't told you yet, but I have bought that cottage. The owner is surprised. She probably thinks I've discovered a secret goldmine there. She has substantially raised the price of the property. I had indeed discovered a goldmine there, something known only to me. The wealth of my shabby hovel will remain hidden from everyone's eyes.'

Labanya's face was shadowed with a deep sadness. 'Why do you think so much about what everyone would say?' she demanded. 'So what if everyone got to know? Indeed, they ought to know the truth about us, so nobody would dare to show any disrespect.'

'Banya, I've decided we must spend a few days in that very cottage, after we are married,' Amit informed her, without answering her directly. 'My garden-estate on the shores of the Ganga, that ghat of ours, that banyan tree, they have all merged into that cottage. Mitali, the name of your choice, suits that cottage alone.'

'You have left that cottage today, Mita. If you try to re-enter it on some other occasion, you will find it too small to accommodate you. In today's home, there is no room for tomorrow. You had said, the other day, that in life, a person's first struggle is with poverty, the second with wealth. But you didn't speak of the third phase of the sacred endeavour, which has to do with renunciation.'

'Banya, that's your Robi Thakur's idea. He writes: 'Today, Shah Jahan has even renounced his Taj Mahal. It doesn't occur to your poet that we create only to transcend the created object. In the created world, that's what is known as evolution. A strange demon possesses one, commanding one to create. With the act of creation, the demon is exorcised, and the created item also becomes redundant. But this doesn't imply that moving on, leaving things behind, is the ultimate goal. In the world, the immortal saga of Shah Jahan–Mumtaz Mahal continues unabated. They are not mere individuals, after all. That's why the Taj Mahal could never be rendered vacant. As a concise postcard-reply to your celebrated poet's *Taj Mahal*, Nibaran Chakrabarti has written a poem about the bridal chamber:

When the night grows restless
At the sound of dawn's chariot-wheels,
I must leave you, O bridal chamber!
In the world outside, alas,
Separation lurks like a fiendish robber.
Yet, though he may smash and destroy,
And rip apart our wedding-garlands,
You remain untouched,
*Always;*
Your festive celebrations
Never silenced or disrupted.
Who says the newlyweds have abandoned you,
Leaving your bed desolate?
They have not gone away.
At your call, they return
As new sojourners, knocking
At your welcoming door.
Love is undying, O bridal chamber!
And you, too, are immortal.

'Robi Thakur only speaks of parting, he can't sing of lovers remaining together. Banya, does the poet say that when we, too, knock on that door, it will not open for us?'

'Please Mita, I request you not to invoke the war of the poets today. Do you imagine that I have not realized, from the very first day, that you, yourself, are Nibaran Chakrabarti? But don't immediately begin constructing a poetic monument to our love: at least wait for our love to die.'

Labanya realized that Amit, today, was trying to suppress some inner turmoil by saying all sorts of nonsensical things.

Amit, too, sensed that the battle of the poets, though it had not seemed inappropriate yesterday, had struck a discordant note this morning. All the same, he did not like the idea that Labanya saw this clearly, as well.

'Let me go, then,' he proposed, rather dully. 'I, too, have work to do; at the moment, my task is to conduct a survey of hotels. Meanwhile, it seems that for the unfortunate Nibaran Chakrabarti, the honeymoon is over.'

'Look, Mita,' pleaded Labanya, clasping Amit's hand, 'I hope you will always be able to forgive me. If ever the moment of our parting arrives, I beseech you not to abandon me in anger.' She rushed to the adjoining room, to hide her tears.

For a while, Amit stood stock-still. Then, slowly and absently, he went to stand beneath the eucalyptus tree. There, he saw some scattered walnut-shells. His heart was seized with pain at the sight. The scattered traces we leave behind us in the course of our lives are pathetic in their very triviality. Then he saw a book lying on the grass: it was Robi Thakur's *Balaka*. The back of the book was damp. He thought once of returning the book but placed it in his pocket instead. He almost left for the hotel but again thought the better of it; instead, he reclined beneath the tree. The damp clouds of night had polished the sky sparkling clean. In the breeze, washed free of dust, the picturesque surroundings were clearly visible. The silhouettes of mountains and trees seemed etched against the deep blue sky. The world, seen up close, seemed to directly touch the heart. The day was declining slowly, to the strains of the ragini Bhairavi.

Labanya had vowed she would immediately set about her household chores in real earnest, but espying Amit under the tree, she could restrain herself no longer. Her heart heaved, her eyes swam with tears.

'What are you thinking, Mita?' she asked, coming up to him.

'The very opposite of what I had thought all these days.'

'It's essential for your well-being to turn your mind upside-down and scrutinize it from time to time. So, let's hear what upside-down thoughts are in your mind.'

'All these days, I kept constructing houses for you in my heart, sometimes beside the Ganga, sometimes atop a mountain. Today, in the morning light, my mind casts up the inviting image of a path, stretching across those mountains, shaded by forests. I walk, clutching a long stick topped by a sharp metal blade; strapped to my back is a square bag. You will accompany me. May your name prove true, Banya! Your tide, it seems, has swept me from my enclosed chamber, out onto the open path. In the chamber are all kinds of people, but on the path, only the two of us.'

'The garden-estate at Diamond Harbour was already lost, and now the poor seventy-five-rupee room is gone, as well. Never mind! Let them go. But on our journey, how will you ensure our separation? At the end of the day, will you enter one travellers' inn, and I another?'

'There is no need for that, Banya. The journey makes us new, at every step; there is no time for staleness. Ageing occurs when we remain static.'

'How did this suddenly occur to you, Mita?'

'Very well, let me tell you. I have suddenly received a letter from Shobhanlal. You may have heard of him: he's an expert on the Raichands and Premchands of this world. For some time, he has been out on a journey to discover the ancient travel-routes of Indian history. He wants to retrieve the lost pathways of the past. I want to create pathways for the future.'

Labanya's heart gave a sudden, violent lurch. 'I took the MA examination with Shobhanlal, in the same year,' she interrupted. 'I would like to hear all his news.'

'He had once been excited at the prospect of rediscovering the old route through the ancient Afghan city of Kapish. That was the route of Huen Tsang's pilgrimage to India, and before that, of Alexander's military invasion. He earnestly studied Pushto, and practised Pathan customs. With his handsome appearance, dressed in loose-fitting clothes, he didn't look quite like a Pathan, more like a Persian. He came and begged me for a letter of introduction addressed to the French experts who were working in the same field. Some of them had tutored me when I was in France. I gave him the letter, but he was denied permission by the Indian government. Ever since then, he wanders in search of old routes in the Himalayas, sometimes in Kashmir, sometimes in Kumaon. Now, he feels the urge to explore the eastern sector of the Himalayas as well. He wants to discover the routes through which Buddhism spread in this region. The thought of that compulsive wanderer makes me melancholy, too. Our sight grows dim scanning the books to find our direction in life, but that lunatic has set out to scan the book of the road, written in the Lord's very own script. Do you know what I think?'

'Tell me.'

'In the first flush of youth, Shobhanlal must have received a blow from some bangle-adorned hand, which flung him from his home onto the streets. I am not clearly acquainted with his whole story, but once when the two of us were alone together, we stayed up chatting till the wee hours. Suddenly, from our window, we saw the moon appear behind a flowering jarul tree; at that moment, he tried to tell me about someone. He took no names, nor did he describe her at all; he had barely given me the slightest hint when his voice choked, and he quickly left the room. I could tell that, lodged somewhere in his heart, remains the sting of some extremely cruel experience. That's what he probably tries to erode, step by step, as he travels on his journey.'

Labanya suddenly developed a fascination for botany. She bent low, gazing at a wild flower, yellow-and-white, blossoming in the grass. She felt a sudden, urgent need to count the petals of the flower, with single-minded concentration.

'Do you know, Banya, you have flung me out into the road, today?' Amit asked her.

'How?'

'I had constructed a house. This morning, your words made me feel that you were hesitant to step inside. I have spent two months mentally decorating that house. I called out to you, saying, "Come, my bride, enter my home!" Today, you discarded your bridal finery, and said, "There is no room for us here, my friend. We shall spend our lives walking round the fire." '

The botanical study of wild flowers would not do anymore. Rising to her feet, Labanya pleaded, in anguish, 'Mita! Please say no more! Time is up.'

## 14
## Comet

It took a long time for Amit to realize that his relationship with Labanya was known to all the Bengalis of Shillong. Discussion among clerks in government offices usually centred upon the determination of their own career prospects by the position of ruling planets on their professional horizon. Then, in the astral sphere of human life, they saw a pair of twin stars appear, emitting light of the first magnitude. The star-gazers, as is their wont, propounded many theories about the fiery drama behind the birth of these two new stars.

Having come to Shillong to savour the mountain air, Kumar Mukherjee, the attorney, had found himself drawn into these theoretical speculations. Some called him Kumar Mukho for short, while others nicknamed him Mar Mukho, the One on the Warpath! Though not a member of Sissy's private circle, he could be described as her acquaintance, for he belonged to the group of people she knew. Amit had named him Comet Mukho. For though he did not belong to the coterie, Mukho would occasionally sweep his tail across their orbit. It was everybody's guess that he was especially attracted by the planet named Lissy. This was a source of general amusement, but Lissy herself was annoyed and embarrassed about it. Hence, she would often vigorously wrench his tail in passing, but clearly, this made no difference to the comet, for his head and tail remained intact.

Amit had caught an occasional distant glimpse of Kumar Mukho on the streets of Shillong. It would be hard not to spot him. Because he had not yet been to England, Mukho's English style was flagrantly visible. Between his lips would be a thick, heavy cigar, the main reason for the nickname Comet. Amit tried to avoid him by keeping a safe distance, deluding himself that the Comet had not sensed this. But to see without taking any notice takes immense skill, just like the art of burglary. The proof of its success lies in evading detection. It requires expertise in fixing one's gaze somewhere far beyond the scene before one's eyes.

From the Bengali social circles of Shillong, Kumar Mukho had culled many facts which could be broadly classified under the head: 'The Excesses of Amit Raye.' The persons most vocal in their criticism had secretly derived the greatest relish from the situation. Kumar had planned to spend some time in Shillong to mend a disorder in his liver, but his acute urge for rumour-mongering made him hasten back to Kolkata within five days. Once there, by means of his cigar-smoke-filled exaggerations about Amit, he generated a crisis in the Sissy–Lissy circle, arousing a mixture of mockery and inquisitiveness.

The seasoned reader would have guessed by now that the Katy Mitter's elder brother Naren was the vahana or sacred beast devoted to the service of goddess Sissy. There was a rumour that his prolonged devotion would now culminate in marriage. In her heart of hearts, Sissy was amenable to the idea. But by pretending indifference, she had created a haze of uncertainty. Naren had decided to overcome this obstacle by obtaining Amit's consent, but Amit, the humbug, would neither return to Kolkata, nor answer his letters. Like arrows piercing the sound-barrier, he had already dispatched in Amit's direction all the English expletives at his command, both in public and in private speech. In fact, he had not balked at sending an extremely rude telegram to Shillong; but like a firework missile aimed at an indifferent planet, it vanished without leaving any burn-marks. Ultimately, by general consensus, it was decided that the situation demanded a spot-investigation. In the flood-tide of disaster, if they could but catch the slightest glimpse of Amit's floating head, it was their urgent duty to grab him by the forelock and drag him to the safety of the shore. In this respect, the enthusiasm of Amit's own sister Sissy was far exceeded by that of Katy, sister to someone else. Katy Mitter's attitude closely resembled our own political heartburn at the loss of Indian riches to foreign powers.

Naren Mitter had spent a long time in Europe. Son of a zamindar, he did not have to worry about earning or spending; his urge for learning was proportionately muted. While abroad, he had concentrated mainly on wasting both time and money. One can simultaneously attain freedom from responsibility and undeserved self-esteem by calling oneself an artist. Therefore, he had inhabited the bohemian quarters of various big cities of Europe, in pursuit of the goddess of art. After some initial attempts, he was forced to give up painting upon the insistence of his plain-spoken well-wishers. Now, he introduced himself as an art critic, for that required no credentials. He could not make art blossom but was able to mangle it with gusto. In the Parsian mode, he had lovingly sharpened the pointed ends of his moustache, while remaining carefully careless about his unruly head of hair. His appearance was quite pleasant; but in the holy endeavour to improve it further, his dressing table was weighed down with various Parisian forms of self-indulgence. The paraphernalia arranged beside his wash-basin would be excessive even for the ten-headed Ravana's toilet. There was no doubting his noble birth, from the easy nonchalance with which he discarded his expensive Havana cigar after a couple of puffs, and his regular practice of sending his garments by parcel-post to Parisian laundry houses. The best European tailoring-houses kept a record of his measurements in their registers, where one might encounter the aristocratic names of Patiala and Kapurthala. His slang-ridden enunciation of the English tongue was slurred, drawling, and understated, accompanied by the lazy glance of his half-shut eyes; those in the know opined that such inarticulate intensity was to be found in the voices of many rich, blue-blooded Englishmen. In addition, Naren was a role model among his peers for his command of bad language in the form of racecourse swear-words and English oaths.

Katy Mitter's real name was Ketaki. Her deportment was refined, thrice-distilled in her own elder brother's etiquette factory; it contained the pungent essence of British aristocracy. She had arrogantly scissored the ordinary Bengali woman's pride in her long tresses, shedding her hair-knot like a tadpole's tail, with the new convert's eagerness to imitate. The natural fairness of her countenance was enamelled with layers of paint. In the early stages of her life, Katy's dark eyes bore a gentle expression; now, it appeared, she couldn't even see ordinary people. If she did see them, she failed to notice them, and if she did notice them, her glance had the edge of a knife half-unsheathed. In childhood, her lips had a simple sweetness, but now, from frequent sneering, they had developed a permanent resemblance to a hooked elephant-goad. I am inexperienced at describing women's dress. I don't have the vocabulary. To put it in simply, one noticed her wearing a flimsy outer layer, like cast-off snakeskin, through which was visible a hint of inner garments of some other hue. Much of her bosom was exposed; and she made a careful attempt to arrange her bare arms carelessly, now on the table, now on the arms of a chair, now entwined with each other. And when she smoked a cigarette, holding it between two fingers embellished with well-polished nails, it was more for decorative effect than from a desire to inhale the smoke. Most disturbing of all were the intricate postures of her high-heeled shoes. When the Creator forgot that the human foot should be modelled on the goat-hoof, this evolutionary flaw was rectified by the cobbler's gift, the high-heeled shoe, that bizarre device for tormenting the earth with the distorted gait of artificially elevated feet.

Sissy was still at an in-between stage. She had not yet attained the highest degree but was steadily earning double promotions. In her peals of laughter, excessive cheerfulness and non-stop chatter, there was a constant, bubbling vivacity, highly prized by her admirers. In literary accounts of the adolescent Radha, her manner seems sometimes mature, sometimes naïve; the same was true of Sissy, as well. Her high-heeled shoes were the victory-gate signalling entry into the new era, but in her knot of uncut hair remained traces of the old order. The lower edge of her sari was draped a few inches too high, but in their extent of exposure, her upper garments still conformed to the bounds of modesty. She wore gloves habitually, for no particular reason, yet she still sported balas—thick bangles—on both wrists instead of one. Smoking a cigarette no longer made her dizzy, but she still had a strong addiction to chewing paan, betel leaf. She didn't mind having pickles and mango papad sent to her, camouflaged in biscuit tins; given the choice between Christmas plum-pudding and the pitha served at the Poush-festival, she had a slight preference for the latter. Though trained by a white dancer, she demurred at ballroom dancing.

They had rushed to Shillong, all of them, because the wild rumours about Amit had made them anxious. The point of contention was that, according to their definition of class difference, Labanya was a governess, specially created to destroy the caste purity of the men of their own class. They were convinced that it was out of greed for money and prestige that she had clung to Amit so tenaciously. To rescue him from her clutches, it was necessary for the ladies to intervene, with their purifying touch. Brahma, the four-faced deity, must have simultaneously glanced at and sided with women with his four pairs of eyes; hence, he had created men to be complete idiots where women were concerned. That explained why, unless assisted by women of their own social group, untouched by class ambitions, men found it so hard to escape the webs of enchantment woven by women of a different class.

At present, the two women had agreed upon the procedure to be adopted for this rescue operation. It was decided that Amit must be kept in the dark at first. The enemy and the battle-terrain must first be inspected. Then, they could challenge the powers of the sorceress.

The first thing they noticed upon arrival was that Amit had acquired a strong vein of provincialism. Formerly, too, Amit's attitude had not matched that of his coterie. But still, he was then a keen urbanite, scrubbed, polished, shining. Now, it wasn't as if his complexion had darkened from exposure to the open air; rather, it was as if trees and vines had cast their shade upon him. He seemed to have become raw, and in their opinion, somewhat stupid. His deportment was almost like that of ordinary folk. Formerly, he would treat all subjects with an element of humour, but now, he had virtually lost that urge. They took this for the ultimate danger-signal.

'We had imagined from afar that you were descending into a tribal lifestyle,' Sissy told him bluntly, on one occasion. 'But now we realize that you are ascending into a state of greenness, like the pine trees of this region: healthier, perhaps, than before but not as interesting.'

Borrowing Wordsworth's idea, Amit retorted that living in close proximity to nature, one's body, mind and soul acquire the stamp of 'mute insensate things'.

We have no complaint against mute, insensate things, thought Sissy to herself; we are concerned about those ultra-sensate beings who specialize in fluent sweet-talk.

They had hoped that Amit himself would bring up the subject of Labanya. A day passed, two days, then three, but he was utterly silent on the subject. Only one thing seemed certain: like a wave-tossed boat, Amit's desires were in turmoil. Even before they were up and dressed, Amit would be back from an outing somewhere; his face then would seem ravaged, like banana leaves shredded by the stormy breeze. Even more disturbing was the fact that some people had spotted a copy of Robi Thakur's works on Amit's bed. On the inside leaf, the first syllable of Labanya's name had been crossed out in red ink. Her name was the touchstone that had probably raised the book's value.

Amit would go out every now and then. 'I'm going to appease my hunger,' he would say. The others were not unaware of the source of the hunger, or of the fact that his hunger was acute. But they would feign ignorance, as if it was impossible to imagine that Shillong could offer anything beyond its air, which increased the appetite. Sissy would smile to herself, while Katy would nurse the burning jealousy in her heart. Amit's own problems loomed so large, that he lacked the power to notice any outward signs of trouble. Hence, he would unabashedly say to his female companions: 'I'm setting out in search of a waterfall.' But he failed to realize that others may have some doubts about the nature of the waterfall and the direction of its flow. This morning, he departed claiming he was going to trade orange honey. Meekly, in very simple language, the two ladies expressed a desire to accompany him, as they felt an irrepressible curiosity about this exquisite honey. The route was difficult, Amit informed them, and could not be negotiated by car. Nipping the discussion in the bud, he rushed away. Noting the restlessness of this bee, the two friends decided to delay no further. It had become imperative to make an expedition to the orchard where the oranges grew. Meanwhile, Naren was at the races. He had been very keen to take Sissy with him, but she did not join him. Who but a sympathetic soul would understand how much self-control such abstinence had entailed!

## 15

## Complications

Having crossed the gate into Yogamaya's garden, the two friends could not spot any servants. Entering the porch, they noticed a teacher and her pupil, studying at a small table on the verandah. It was clear to them that the elder of the two was Labanya.

'I'm sorry,' said Katy, high heels clicking as she stepped onto the verandah.

'Who would you like to meet?' asked Labanya, rising to her feet.

'I came to inquire whether Mister Amit Raye is here,' replied Katy, sweeping Labanya with a sharp glance that took in her entire appearance, from head to toe.

At first, Labanya could not figure out what sort of creature 'Amitraye' might be. 'We don't know him,' she answered.

The two friends exchanged a lightning glance, suppressing a secret smile.

'We are aware that he visits this house oftener than is good for him,' Katy flashed back, with a toss of her head.

Startled by her manner, Labanya realized who they were, and what a blunder she had made.

'Let me call Korta Ma, she'll give you news of Amit,' she suggested, flustered.

'Is she your teacher?' Katy inquired curtly of Suroma as soon as Labanya was out of sight.

'Yes.'

'Is Labanya her name?'

'Yes.'

'Got matches?' Katy asked, in English.

Unable to understand this sudden need for matches, Suroma gaped at Katy, mystified.

'Deshlai—matches,' explained Katy.

Suroma fetched a matchbox. Katy lit her cigarette. 'Do you study English?' she asked Suroma, between puffs of smoke.

Suroma nodded in affirmation and immediately rushed from the room. 'Whatever else the girl may have learned from her governess, she certainly hasn't acquired any manners,' remarked Katy.

There followed a discussion between the two friends, much of it in English. 'So this is the famous Labanya! Isn't she delicious! She has turned Shillong into a volcano, splitting Amit's heart, like an earthquake. Silly! Men are funny!'

Sissy laughed out loud. There was generosity in this laughter, for the stupidity of men had not given Sissy cause for complaint. After all, she had created an earthquake even on stony soil, splitting it right apart. But what an unheard of situation! With a woman like Katy pitted against that strangely dressed governess. A wet blanket, looking as if butter wouldn't melt in her mouth. In her company, the mind would grow mouldy, like a biscuit in rainy weather. How could Amit stand her for a single moment!

'Sissy, your brother's heart has always been topsy-turvy. He has taken a sudden, perverse fancy to this woman, convinced that she is an angel.'

With these words, Katy rested her cigarette against the algebra book on the table, and taking out her silver-handled cosmetic bag, she powdered her nose and darkened her eyebrows with the pencil liner. Sissy was not unduly annoyed by her elder brother's lack of propriety; in fact, she secretly felt rather fond of him. All her anger was directed at the false angels who bask in the admiring gaze of men. Katy lost patience at Sissy's amused indifference about her elder brother. She felt like giving Sissy a hard shake.

At this juncture, Yogamaya appeared on the scene, dressed in white spun silk. Labanya was not with her. Accompanying Katy was a tiny dog named Tabby, his eyes virtually hidden behind his shaggy head of hair. He had sniffed at Labanya and Suroma by way of making acquaintance. Seeing Yogamaya, the dog seemed suddenly excited. Rushing up to her in a show of false affection, he raised his forelegs, his soiled paws leaving their scratchy signature on her pure sari. Sissy caught him by the scruff of his neck and dragged him to Katy. 'Naughty dog!' admonished Katy, wagging a finger in front of his nose.

Katy did not leave her chair. Puffing on her cigarette with an air of detachment, she tilted her head slightly to inspect Yogamaya with a sidelong glance. She was perhaps even more resentful of Yogamaya than of Labanya. She believed that there was a flaw in the official version of Labanya's history. Yogamaya herself, disguised as an aunt, must have tried to trick Amit into marrying the girl. It wouldn't take much intelligence to deceive a man, for the Creator had personally fashioned blinkers for men's eyes.

'I am Amit's sister Sissy,' said Sissy, coming forward and making a faint gesture of greeting.

'Amit calls me Mashima, which makes me your mashima, too, my child,' responded Yogamaya with a smile.

Observing Katy's attitude, Yogamaya took no notice of her. 'Come, my child, come inside,' she urged Sissy.

'We have no time. We have simply come to ask whether Ami has come here or not,' replied Sissy.

'He's not here yet,' Yogamaya informed her.

'Do you know when he is expected?'

'I can't say for sure. Well, let me find out.'

'The governess who was conducting lessons here pretended she had never met Amit at all!' Katy interrupted sharply, from her chair.

Yogamaya was confused. She realized there must be a problem somewhere. She also understood that it would be difficult to maintain her dignity with these people. Instantly discarding her aunt-like attitude, she retorted, 'I'm told Amitbabu lives in your own hotel, so you should know his whereabouts.'

Katy gave a menacing laugh. 'You may try to hide, but you can't escape,' her laugh implied.

Truth be told, Katy was in a foul temper right from the start, when she first set her eyes on Labanya and was told that the latter didn't know Amit. But Sissy felt only apprehension, no heartburn; she felt drawn to the profundity of Yogamaya's beautiful countenance. She was therefore embarrassed by Katy's deliberate insolence in not rising from her chair to greet Yogamaya. Yet, she never dared cross Katy in any matter, for Katy was expert at quelling sedition: she wouldn't tolerate the slightest resistance. She had no qualms about being nasty. Most people are cowardly; when confronted with blatant nastiness, they admit defeat. Katy took a certain pride in her own extreme harshness; she would harass any of her friends who showed signs of what she called sweet naivete. She boasted of her own rudeness, which she took for forthrightness; those who cringed at such aggressive behaviour felt relieved if they could somehow keep Katy pacified. Sissy belonged to this category. The more she secretly feared Katy, the more she imitated her ways, to demonstrate that she herself was not weak. She didn't always succeed. Katy had realized, today, that in a corner of her mind, Sissy nursed a secret objection to her behaviour. She had therefore deemed it necessary to forcefully demolish Sissy's resistance, before Yogamaya's eyes. She rose to her feet, and placing a cigarette in Sissy's mouth, offered to ignite it with the lighted cigarette in her own mouth. Sissy did not dare refuse. The tips of her ears turned slightly red. All the same, she forced herself to adopt a dismissive air, as if she would snap her fingers at those who frowned upon their modern, westernized habits: as for their disapproval, she cared 'that much for it!'

Exactly at that moment, Amit arrived on the scene. The women were taken aback. He had left the hotel dressed in a felt hat and a British shirt. Now, he was wearing a dhoti and shawl. The scene of his transformation was that very same cottage of his. There, he kept a bookshelf, a wardrobe and an armchair donated by Yogamaya. After lunch at the hotel, he would take refuge in this place. Of late, Labanya had enforced strict discipline; during her lessons with Suroma, nobody was allowed to intrude in search of waterfalls and oranges. Hence, before teatime at four-thirty in the evening, Amit was denied permission to visit the house to quench his physical or psychological thirst. He would somehow pass the intervening hours, then dress to pay his visit at the appointed hour.

Today, before he left the hotel, the ring had arrived from Kolkata. He had already imagined himself ceremonially placing the ring on Labanya's finger. Today was special. It would not do to keep this day waiting at the threshold. Today, all work must come to a standstill. He had secretly decided to approach Labanya where she was conducting her lessons, to declare: 'One day, the Emperor arrived on an elephant, but the gate was too low. He turned back, lest he be forced to bow his head. This day, for us, is a great occasion, but you have kept the gates of opportunity too low. Break them down, so the Emperor may enter your home with his head held high.'

Amit also meant to point out that punctuality means arriving at the right moment. But the clock cannot determine the right moment, for it merely knows time by numbers, not the value of time.

Glancing outside, Amit saw that the sky was cloudy, its dimness suggesting that the hour might be five or six in the evening. Like a mother afraid to use the thermometer to check her long-ailing child's temperature once his body feels cool to the touch, Amit avoided looking at his watch, lest its rude message contradict the sky. Today, Amit arrived much earlier than the appointed time. For desperate longing knows no shame.

From the road, one could see the corner of the verandah where Labanya conducted her lessons. Today, he found that spot vacant. His heart leapt for joy. At last, he looked at his watch. It was only twenty minutes past three. The other day, he had said to Labanya that rules are for men to obey, and for the gods to violate; we struggle to observe the law on earth, only to savour the nectar of lawlessness in heaven. Such a heaven sometimes appears on earth. When that happens, one must salute its arrival by breaking all laws. He hoped Labanya would understand the glory of breaking the law; perhaps her heart had felt the touch of a special day, breaking down the fences of everyday routine.

Coming close, he found Yogamaya outside her room, looking on in stupefaction as Sissy lit the cigarette in her mouth from the cigarette in Katy's. He was left in no doubt that the insult was deliberate. Tabby, the dog, rebuffed in his maiden attempt at friendship, was trying to go to sleep at Katy's feet. At Amit's approach, he again grew restive at the prospect of greeting him. Sissy again applied discipline to make him understand that such expressions of goodwill were not welcome in this place.

'Mashima!' Amit called out from a distance, and prostrated himself at Yogamaya's feet, without so much as glancing at the two female friends. It was not his custom to touch her feet in this manner. 'Mashima, where is Labanya?' he demanded.

'How would I know, my child? She's somewhere in the house.'

'But it's not yet time for her lessons to have ended.'

'Upon the arrival of these people, she has probably taken leave and retired to her room.'

'Come, let's go and see what she's doing.' Amit dragged Yogamaya indoors. He completely disregarded the presence at the scene of any other form of life.

'This is an insult! Come, Katy, let's go home!' cried Sissy, rather loudly.

Katy was no less incensed. But she didn't want to leave without witnessing the end.

'It's no use,' argued Sissy.

Katy's enormous eyes were dilated. 'A conclusion must be reached,' she insisted.

Some more time elapsed. 'Let's go, my friend,' repeated Sissy. 'I don't feel like staying a moment longer.'

Katy firmly ensconced herself on the verandah. 'He must depart by this route,' she declared.

Ultimately, Amit emerged, accompanied by Labanya. Her face bore an air of tranquil detachment. There was not the slightest hint of anger, arrogance or reproach. Yogamaya was in the room nearby, but she had no wish to step outside. Amit dragged her out. In an instant, the ring on Labanya's finger caught Katy's eye. The blood rushed to her head, her eyes became bloodshot; she wanted to aim a kick at the whole world.

'Mashi, this is my sister Shamita,' Amit said by way of introduction. 'Baba had probably given her a name to rhyme with mine, but there remains the extra syllable. This is my sister's friend Ketaki.'

Meanwhile, there was another disturbance. When Suroma's cat emerged from the room, Tabby's canine logic saw this act of daring as a legitimate reason for declaring war. He would advance from time to time to bark at her, but upon encountering the hissing cat with its claws unsheathed, would retreat again in some doubt about the possible outcome of the battle. In this predicament, deciding that growling mildly from afar was the only safe way of demonstrating his heroism, he began to make an incessant noise. Without responding in any way, the cat arched its back and left the scene. Katy could bear it no more. She pulled the dog's ears with intense rage. Much of this ear-pulling was directed at her own ill-fortune. The dog squealed in shrill protest against such maltreatment. Fortune smiled, in silent amusement.

When the commotion had subsided, Amit addressed his sister: 'Sissy, this is Labanya. You have not heard me mention this name, but you must have heard of it from sundry other people. Our wedding has been fixed for the month of Agrahayan, in Kolkata.'

Katy wasted no time in summoning up a smile. 'I congratulate you,' she declared. 'The orange-honey wasn't hard to access, it appears. The quest was not difficult, for the honey had leapt forth to offer itself to your lips, of its own accord.'

Sissy burst into her customary giggle.

Labanya realized that this was a barbed comment but could not fathom its full meaning.

'When I set forth this morning, they asked me where I was going,' Amit explained to her. 'I told them I was going in search of honey. That's why they are amused. It's my fault, actually; people can't tell when I'm not being facetious.'

'Victory is yours, as far as orange-honey goes,' intervened Katy, calmly enough. 'Now make sure that I don't lose out, either.'

'Tell me what I must do.'

'I have a wager with Naren. He had insisted you would never go to the races, because nobody could persuade you to visit a place frequented by gentlemen. I had wagered this diamond ring on taking you to the races with me. I combed the waterfalls and honey-shops of this area, until I finally ran you to earth here. Sissy, why don't you tell him what a wild-goose chase this has been, if I may borrow an expression from the English!'

Sissy smiled wordlessly.

'Do you remember that story, Amit, the one you told me yourself?' pursued Katy. 'Some Persian philosopher, unable to trace the thief who stole his turban, had ultimately chosen to wait for the culprit at the graveyard. From here, there could be no escape, he had argued. I was temporarily thrown off the scent when Miss Labanya said she didn't know him, but my heart assured me that, sooner or later, he would have to reach this place, his own graveyard.'

Sissy laughed out loud.

'Amit didn't utter your name,' Katy informed Labanya. 'He used honeyed terms to describe you as orange-honey, while you, being too simple to speak in riddles, blurted out that you didn't know Amit at all. Yet, there was no retribution for you in the Sunday-school mode: fate, the divine arbiter, imposed no penalty on the two of you. One of you consumed the hard-won honey in a single gulp, and the other grew familiar with a stranger at a single glance. Now, must I, alone, be condemned to suffer defeat? Sissy, just imagine how unjust this would be!'

Another shrill laugh from Sissy. Tabby the dog, deeming it his social duty to join in this exuberance, showed signs of excitement. For the third time, he had to be restrained.

'You know, Amit, that if I lost this diamond ring, nothing in the world would console me,' pleaded Katy. 'This ring was once your gift to me. It has never left my finger for a moment; it has become part of my body. Must I ultimately part from it here, in the mountains of Shillong, by losing a wager?'

'Why did you have to place a wager, my friend?' inquired Sissy.

'From my secret pride in myself, and faith in other human beings. My pride has been demolished; the race is over, and this time, I stand defeated. I can't persuade Amit anymore, it seems. Well, if you must inflict this strange form of defeat on me, then why did you give me this ring with so much affection? Did that gift not signify any commitment? Didn't it imply a pledge to protect me from humiliation?'

As she spoke, Katy's voice became choked with emotion. She held back her tears with difficulty.

Seven years ago, when Katy was eighteen, Amit had removed the ring from his finger and transferred it to hers. They were both in England at the time. At Oxford, there was a young man infatuated with Katy. On that day, Amit had defeated this Punjabi youth in a friendly rowing competition. In the June moonlight, the sky seemed to speak out loud; the profusion of flowers blossoming in the meadows made the earth restless. At such a moment, Amit had placed his ring on Katy's finger. In his heart were many thoughts, unexpressed; but nothing remained concealed. At that time, Katy's face had not acquired its coat of make-up; her smile was artless, and her countenance did not try to hide its blush in the heat of emotion. Once the ring was on her finger, Amit had whispered to her:

'Tender is the night
And haply the queen moon is on her throne.'

Katy was not yet skilled in the art of conversation. She had simply sighed, as if saying to herself, '*Mon ami*,' the French expression for 'My intimate friend'.

On this present occasion, Amit, too, found himself at a loss for words. He could think of nothing to say.

'If I have lost the wager, then let this permanent token of my defeat remain with you, Amit. I shall not let it sustain a falsehood by keeping it on my finger.'

With these words, Katy removed the ring from her finger, placed it on the table, and hurried away. Tears flowed profusely down her enamelled cheeks.

## 16

# Liberation

Labanya received a brief note from Shobhanlal:

I arrived in Shillong last night. If you grant permission, I shall visit you. If not, I depart tomorrow. You have punished me, but to this day, I have not clearly understood when and how I have given you offence. I come to beg you for an explanation; otherwise, I shall have no peace of mind. Have no fear. I have nothing else to ask of you.

Labanya's eyes filled with tears. She wiped them away. In silence, she reviewed her own past. She recalled the pathetic timidity of the tender seedling of love, which could have blossomed, had she not stifled it and prevented its growth. She could have cherished the seedling and brought it to fruition by now. But at that time, she had been proud of her learning, devoted single-mindedly to the pursuit of knowledge, full of arrogant independence. Observing her father's fascination for learning, she had mentally condemned love as a form of weakness. Today, love had avenged itself, and her pride was forced to bite the dust. What would then have been as easy as breathing or simple laughter, now seemed extremely difficult. Today, she hesitated to welcome with open arms this person who had once been a passing visitor in her life; yet her heart broke at the thought of relinquishing him. She remembered Shobhanlal in his moment of humiliation, the inarticulate anguish on his face. Such a long time had elapsed since then! What nectar had sustained that unrequited love in this young man's heart? It must have been the inner nobility of his own nature.

Labanya wrote:

You are my greatest friend. I do not, now, possess the wealth to repay you adequately for this friendship. You have never demanded a price; this time, too, you offer all you have to give, claiming nothing in return. I have neither the power nor the arrogance to spurn your gift with feigned indifference.

She had dispatched the letter when Amit came to her and proposed: 'Banya, let's go out today, the two of us.'

Amit had made the suggestion rather timidly, fearing that Labanya might now refuse to accompany him.

'Let's go,' agreed Labanya, quite readily.

They set out together, the two of them. With some hesitation, Amit tried taking Labanya's hand in his. Without the slightest hint of resistance, Labanya let him hold her hand. Amit pressed her hand hard, unable to communicate in words anything beyond the emotions this pressure might convey. They walked up to the same clearing in the forest which they had visited the other day. Touching a treeless mountain-top with its declining rays, the sun disappeared from view. The exquisite greenish glow slowly faded to a deep, tender blue. The two of them stopped to gaze in that direction.

'Why did you use me to remove the ring you had once placed on someone else's finger?' asked Labanya, very softly.

'How can I explain everything to you, Banya?' protested Amit, stung by her words. 'The person to whom I had once presented the ring, and the person who today removed it from her finger, are they one and the same?'

'One was the product of the Creator's love, the other of your negligence,' Labanya declared.

'That's not entirely true,' argued Amit. 'I alone am not responsible for the suffering that has produced the Katy we see today.'

'But Mita, when a person had completely surrendered herself to you, why didn't you cherish her as your own? For some reason, you slackened your grip on her before she felt the pressure of sundry other grasping hands, transforming her very image. It's because she lost your love one day that she set about decorating herself in ways that would appeal to others. Today, she appears to me like a doll in an English toyshop; this could never have happened had her heart remained alive. But let such things be. I have one request to make. You must keep it.'

'Sure, just tell me what it is.'

'Take your companions to Cherrapunji on a holiday, for at least a week. You can entertain her, even if you can't bring her happiness.'

'Very well,' agreed Amit, after a short silence.

'Let me tell you something, Mita,' said Labanya, resting her head against his breast. 'I'll never bring up the matter again. You don't bear the slightest responsibility for the inner bond that exists between us. I don't say this in anger; I insist with all my love that you should not offer me your ring, for there is no need for tokens between us. Let my love be immaculate, bearing no mark, no shadow, of the external world.'

With these words, she removed the ring from her finger and slowly placed it on his. Amit did not stop her.

Quietly, glowing with tranquillity, Labanya lifted her countenance towards Amit's, like the earth, at dusk, silently raising its face to a sky suffused with the glow of the setting sun.

As soon as a week had elapsed, Amit returned to Yogamaya's house. The house was locked, everyone was gone. They had left no forwarding address.

Amit stood beneath the same eucalyptus tree, then wandered about for a while, with an empty heart.

The gardener, a familiar face, came up and inquired: 'Should I unlock the house? Would you like to wait inside?'

'Yes,' replied Amit, after some hesitation.

Entering the house, he went into Labanya's sitting room. The chairs, tables, shelves were still there, but the books were gone. Scattered on the floor were a few torn, empty envelopes, bearing Labanya's name and address, inscribed in an unfamiliar hand; on the table, a few used and discarded pen-nibs, and a used-up, tiny pencil stub. He put the pencil in his pocket. In the bedroom immediately adjacent, there was only a mattress on the iron bedstead, and on the dressing table, an empty bottle of oil. Resting his head on his arms, Amit lay down on the mattress, making the bed creak. There was a dumb emptiness about the room. It could answer no questions. It had collapsed into a fainting fit from which it would never again awaken.

Afterwards, Amit returned to his own cottage, a heavy lassitude weighing down his heart and body. Everything was exactly as he had left it. In fact, Yogamaya had not even reclaimed her armchair. He realized that she had left him this chair out of affection; he seemed to hear her quiet, tender voice calling to him—'My boy!' In a gesture of obeisance, Amit prostrated himself before that chair.

The mountains of Shillong had lost all their charm. He could find no solace anywhere.

# 17

# Parting Lines

Jatishankar was a student at Kolkata University. He stayed at the Kalutola Mess in Presidency College. Amit would often invite him home for a meal, read all sorts of books with him, startle him with all kinds of strange conversation, or take him for a drive.

After that, Jatishankar lost touch with Amit for a while, and had no definite news of his whereabouts. Sometimes he would hear that Amit was in Nainital, sometimes in Utakamand. One day, he heard a common friend say jokingly that Amit was now striving to alter Katy Mitter's outer complexion. He had found a task after his own heart: to transform the very colour of a person's identity. All these days, Amit had depended on words to satisfy his urge for constructing images; but now he had found a live model. The person in question was also ready to shed her brightly coloured outer petals one by one, in the hope that her efforts would ultimately bear fruit. Amit's sister Lissy had reportedly commented that Katy had become virtually unrecognizable—in other words, that her appearance now was rather too natural. Katy had instructed her friends to address her as Ketaki, a shameless act for someone like herself; as if a woman usually dressed in flimsy Shantipuri saris were to coyly don a blouse and chemise. Amit was known to call her 'Keya' in private. There was also a whispered rumour that while boating on the lake at Nainital, Katy had taken the rudder, while Amit read to her from Robi Thakur's *Journey to Nowhere*. But rumours were not to be trusted. Jatishankar drew the conclusion that Amit's heart was sailing on the high waters of escapism.

Ultimately, Amit came back. The city was abuzz with talk of his impending marriage with Katy. But Jati had never heard Amit bring up the subject. Amit's manner had also undergone a marked transformation. He would buy Jati English books as before, but he would not discuss those books with him in the evening, as in earlier times. Jati realized that the discussions had now found a different channel. Nowadays, Amit would not invite Jati to join him for a drive. It was not difficult for someone of Jati's age to sense that there was no room for a third person in Amit's celebration of his own 'journey to nowhere'.

Jati could restrain himself no longer. He accosted Amit and demanded: 'Amitda, you are to marry Miss Katy Mitter, I'm told?'

'Has this reached Labanya's ears?' asked Amit, after a short silence.

'No, I haven't written to her. In the absence of direct confirmation from you, I have said nothing.'

'Your information is correct, but Labanya might misunderstand.'

'Where is the room for misunderstanding?' smiled Jati. 'It's quite straightforward: if you are to marry, then that's exactly what you're going to do.'

'Look, Jati, nothing in human life is ever straightforward. Like the Ganga at its estuary, where it enters the sea, a word to which we affix a single dictionary meaning acquires seven different meanings when it enters the field of real life.'

'In other words, you're saying that the word "marriage" doesn't signify marriage at all?'

'I'm saying that marriage can mean a thousand different things, for it acquires meaning from the way it is practised by human beings. If you try to fathom its meaning without taking human subjects into account, you're bound to be confused.'

'Why don't you explain your own special understanding of its meaning?'

'Definitions are useless. One can only explain with reference to real life. If I say the basic meaning of marriage is love, it leads us to an entirely different issue. As a word, "love" is much more alive than "marriage".'

'In that case, Amitda, we should discard words altogether. Why weigh ourselves down with words as we chase their meaning, if meaning keeps eluding us, sliding this way and that, like a fugitive taking a zigzag route of escape.'

'Well said, my brother! Your association with me has given you a way with words. We need words because we must somehow muddle through in this world. Truths that can't be encompassed by words are discarded because they have no practical value, for words are what we must profess. We have no choice! Even if understanding suffers, words can blindly keep things going.'

'Must we then abandon our subject of discussion?'

'If this discussion is for the sake of knowledge rather than life, then there's no harm in dropping it.'

'Let's assume it's for the sake of life.'

'Bravo! Then listen.'

At this point, there's no harm in inserting a footnote. Of late, Jati had been frequently savouring the tea personally served him by Amit's younger sister Lissy. Perhaps this explained why he harboured no grudge against Amit for discontinuing his evening discourses on literature and their twilight drives in the motor car. He had granted Amit his heartfelt forgiveness.

'Oxygen floats invisibly in the atmosphere, for one of its functions is to sustain life. But it also functions in another way, igniting coal to produce fire, which is essential for many everyday tasks. We can't dismiss either function. Now, do you understand?'

'Not entirely, but I do wish to understand.'

'The love that roams free in the sky is for the companion of one's innermost heart; but the love that permeates all aspects of daily life, is for one's partner in worldly matters. I want both.'

'I'm not sure I understand you correctly. Why not explain a little more clearly, Amitda?'

'Once, I had spread my wings to discover the sky; today, I have found my little nest, where I can fold my wings. But my sky remains, as well.'

'But in your marriage, can partnership and companionship not combine?'

'In life, there could be many opportunities that fail to materialize. Fortunate, indeed, is the man who wins the proverbial prize of half a kingdom plus the princess's hand in marriage. The man who does not enjoy this double advantage is no less fortunate, if by a gift of providence he finds a kingdom in one area of his life and the princess in another.'

'But . . .'

'But there is a dearth of what you would call romance? Not at all! Must we fall back on story-book stereotypes for our fixed quota of romance? Never! I shall create my own romance. My heavenly romance will remain, and I shall make romance happen on earth, as well. The people you describe as romantic would outlaw the one to preserve the other. They either swim like fish, or roam the earth like cats, or range across the skies like bats. But when it comes to romance, I am like the swan. I have the power to enjoy romance on land, in water, and also in the sky. The river-banks would remain my permanent property; yet, to satisfy my spiritual desires, I would roam the freeways of the sky. Long live my Labanya, long live my Ketaki, and long live Amit Raye in all his dimensions.'

Jati listened in silence, perhaps because the argument did not ring true to his ears.

'Look, my friend,' smiled Amit, observing his expression. 'All words don't apply to everyone. Perhaps I speak only for myself. If you apply my words to yourself, you are bound to misunderstand, and to curse me. All the violence and bloodshed in this world stems from the attempt to impose one person's meanings upon the words of another. Let me give you my point of view in no uncertain terms. I must speak figuratively, or else such ideas would lose their beauty, for the words would feel constrained. My initial relationship with Ketaki was indeed based on love, but it was like water in a pitcher, to be collected daily, and used up everyday. While my love for Labanya remains a lake, its waters not to be carried home but meant for my consciousness to swim in.'

'But Amitda, must one not choose between the two?' asked Jati, rather awkwardly.

'That may apply to others but not to me.'

'But if Miss Ketaki were to . . .'

'She knows everything. Whether she understands everything, I can't say. But I shall devote my entire life to making her understand that I am not deceiving her in any way. She must also realize that she is indebted to Labanya.'

'That's as may be, but it's necessary to inform Labanya of your wedding plans.'

'I shall certainly inform her. But before that, I wish to send her a letter: would you deliver it?'

'I shall.'

Amit wrote:

The other evening, when I stopped at the end of the road, I concluded my journey with a poem. Today, too, I have halted at the end of a journey. I wish to bequeath a poem to this final moment. It will not bear the weight of any other words. The unfortunate Nibaran Chakrabarti died as soon as he was caught out—just like a delicate freshwater fish. Hence I have no choice but to place upon your favourite poet the responsibility of communicating my last thoughts to you.

I glimpse your image eternal, as you vanish
Forever into the secret chamber of my heart.
    The philosopher's stone, its golden touch, are mine;
You have filled the spaces of my emptiness.
I found you when my life grew dark; your gift,
The lamp in my heart's shrine.
    Love emerged from parting's sacred fire,
In the shape of a prayer, revealed in the glow of sorrow.

Mita

Time passed. One day, Ketaki went to attend the annaprasan—the rice-tasting ceremony—of her sister's infant daughter. Amit did not accompany her. As he lay reading the letters of William James, reclining on an armchair with his feet propped up on a stool, Jatishankar brought him a letter from Labanya. One page bore an announcement of Shobhanlal's marriage to Labanya. The wedding was to take place six months later, in the month of Jaishtha, on the crest of the Ramgarh mountain. On the second page was written:

Do you hear the chariot wheels of Time?
        Ever-unseen, rousing
    The pulse-beats of the universe;
Crushing the heart of darkness, as the stars lament.
            O my friend!
        Time, rushing by,
    Caught me in its net,
        Prisoner of the speeding chariot,
    On a dangerous journey, carried
        Far away from you.
            It seems to me I crossed

A thousand deaths to reach
The pinnacle of this new dawn—
My old name tossed to the winds
By the chariot's rushing speed.
There is no way back;
If you gaze at me from afar,
You will not recognize me.
My friend, farewell.

Sometime, when you are at ease,
When from the shores of the past,
The night-wind sighs, in the spring breeze,
The sky steeped in tears of fallen bakul flowers,
Seek me then, in the corners of your heart,
For traces left behind. In the twilight of forgetting,
Perhaps a glimmer of light will be seen,
The nameless image of a dream.
And yet it is no dream,
For my love, to me, is the truest thing,
Death-defying,
My eternal prayer-offering, which to you
I bequeath.
I float away on a tide of change
In the journey of time.
My friend, farewell.

Nothing have you lost.
Of mortal clay I'm made; if you saw in me
An image eternal, then let it be
Worshipped at dusk,
Your prayer-game unsullied
By the bleakness of my mundane touch,
Prayer-flowers untainted
By the yearnings of desire.
At your soul's celebration, in vessels meant
To receive emotion's nectar, to quench
Your thirst for words, I shall not mingle
My offering of dust, soaked in my tears.
Today, too, perhaps,
You will create from memory
A dream-image of me, in words inscribed,
Free of burden, free of any claims.
My friend, farewell.

Grieve not for me.
For me, there is duty, for me the universe.

My cup of life is not empty;
To fill the void will ever be my pledge.
If there is one who awaits me eagerly,
My glory resides in him.
He who can wrest the fragrant tuberose
From moonlit nights
To adorn his prayer offering
On a dark, moonless night;
Who can view with mercy infinite
All that is good and bad in me,
To him I sacrifice my soul
What I have given you
Is yours forever.
Drop by drop I'll now dispense myself;
The piteous moments drink their fill
As I pour out my heart's oblation.
O incomparable one!
O wealthy one!
All that I gave you was really your gift to me;
For all that you received, you hold me in debt.
My friend, farewell.

Banya

# The Garden
# (Malancha)

*Translated by Malosree Sandel*

# 1

Neerja lay half-reclined on her sick bed, propped up against pillows that were piled high behind her. A white silk sheet covered her legs, like the pale moonlight on the third day of the waxing moon when it is behind a light cloud. She was pale like the conch-shell, her bangles hung loose on her wrists, blue veins lined her thin arms and on her dense eyelashes were the stains of a long-drawn illness.

Quite like its occupant, Neerja's room too seemed to be under a shadow. A picture of Ramakrishna Paramhansa adorned one wall of the marble-floored room; the only pieces of furniture other than the bed were two wicker stools, a small table, and a clothes rack which stood in a corner. In another corner a metal pitcher held a bunch of white rajanigandha sticks, whose mild fragrance pervaded the closed air of the room.

From the east-facing window that lay open, Neerja could observe the garden below: the orchid room, made of mud-plastered bamboo laths, and the blue-flowered aparajita creeper on the fence. Not far off, the water pump throbbed on near the pump, and water ran down the channels to the flower-beds with a trilling sound. In the fragrant mango grove a cuckoo sang fervently, as if in desperation.

The garden porch clock struck twice. It seemed to be matching its tune to the fury of the sun. The gardeners had left for their break; they wouldn't be back before three. The sound of the gong filled Neerja with pain, her mind grew sad. The ayah came to shut the window. 'No, no, let it be,' Neerja protested; she continued to stare at the garden below where the sunlight and shade played hide and seek beneath the trees.

Her husband Aditya had made a name for himself in the floral business. Ever since their wedding, the love that Neerja and Aditya had for each other had come by various channels to mingle together in caring for this garden in all ways possible. In the blossoms and sprouts of their loved garden, their combined joy and love had grown and was expressed in new ways, in new beauty. Just like a person abroad waits eagerly for the day of the special mail delivery, anxious to hear from his friends, so in different seasons Neerja and Aditya would wait earnestly for their plants to greet them in new and novel ways.

Staring unseeingly at her beloved garden now, Neerja could not help recalling images from those days past. It was not very long ago, but the days seemed to lie beyond the endless meadows of time, the history of another age. On the west of the garden was the great ancient neem tree. It used to have a twin, which had decayed and fallen some years ago; the trunk was sawed smooth to make a table. There the two of them would sip tea at dawn, from between the trees the green-bough-strained sunlight would fall at their feet; the garden mynahs and squirrels would arrive to ask favours. After tea, Neerja and Aditya would go about the various chores in the garden. Neerja's head would be sheltered with a silk parasol with floral designs, while Aditya donned a sola hat and carried on his belt a pair of garden shears. When friends dropped in, socialization would blend with the garden chores. Friends could often be heard saying, 'Really, dear, your dahlias make us envious.' Some would ask ignorantly, 'What are those big flowers? Are they sunflowers?' and Neerja would reply gleefully, 'No, no, they're marigolds.' Someone with a bit more gardening sense would say, 'How did you create such huge jasmines, Neerja Devi? There must be magic in your hands. They are as big as togors.' This knowledgeable person would be duly rewarded with five potted jasmine plants to take home, to the abiding dismay of Hola the gardener. On several occasions thrilled friends were taken on a tour of the grounds—the flower garden, the fruit garden, the vegetable garden, and so on. Before they left Neerja would fill their baskets with roses, magnolias, carnations—and along with the flowers there would be papayas, lemons and wood apples. The serving of tender coconut water would signify the finale of this giving away of bounty. The thirsty would exclaim, 'What sweet water!' And they would hear her proud reply, 'It's from my garden.' Everybody would remark, 'Ah, that's why!'

The memory of those early mornings spent beneath the trees with the steaming vapour of the Darjeeling tea mingling with the scents of the seasons brought out a long, deep-drawn sigh from Neerja. She wanted to snatch those golden days back from the thief who had stolen them away. But why could her agonized mind not find someone to blame? She was not a person to accept her fate in silence with bowed head. Who was responsible? What child whose reach was all over the universe? What monstrous lunatic? Who could create such meaningless havoc in her perfectly ordered existence!

The ten years after her marriage had passed in pure bliss. Her friends envied her in secret; they felt that she had been given much more than she was worth. The men called Aditya a 'lucky dog'.

But the boat of Neerja's domestic happiness hit rock bottom one day, and this had to do with their dog Dolly. Before Neerja had entered the household Dolly used to be Aditya's sole companion. But with Aditya's marriage, Dolly's devotion was divided between the couple, and Neerja's portion was decidedly more. As soon as she spied the car approaching to pick up Neerja when she had to go out, the dog would turn uncontrollable. She would continuously wag her tail to convey her vigorous objection to her mistress's departure. Then, she would boldly attempt to leap into the car and would be thwarted by Neerja's raised forefinger. With a deep sigh Dolly would curl up her tail and lie listlessly at the door. If Aditya and Neerja were late in returning, she would sniff the air and roam around and in the inexpressible language of canines excite the heavens with pathetic questions.

Then some disease suddenly struck Dolly; as she lay ill, she stared mournfully at them, and one day, silently resting her head on Neerja's lap, she died.

Neerja's affections were strong and uncompromising. She could not imagine anyone—even God—attempting to intrude on her love. She trusted the world as a support to her. Till the day of Dolly's death nothing had occurred to shake this faith. But on the day the incredible and the seemingly impossible death of Dolly took place, there appeared the first hole in the fortress of her fortitude and convictions. It signified to her distraught mind the first entrance of an ill omen. It seemed as if the Lord of the worldly life was of a disorderly mind—His apparent gifts could not be relied upon to last.

Everyone had given up hope of Neerja bearing a child. While Neerja was wreaking havoc with her repressed affections showered on their manager Ganesh's son who was sheltered by them, and as the boy was finding the onslaught of her restless affections unbearable, she found herself pregnant. Maternal feelings welled up inside her; the horizon of the future turned rosy with her excited anticipation of the child she was going to give birth to. Seated under a tree, Neerja whiled away her hours happily, embroidering new clothes for her soon-to-be-born child.

Then came the birthing time. The midwife had foreseen the impending trouble. Aditya became so restless that the doctor rebuked him and kept him away. Complications necessitated an urgent surgery, which left no scope for the survival of the child if Neerja was to be saved. The baby's death devastated her completely; overcome by shock and trauma, she was unable to get up from bed after the surgery. Like a dried up river lying spent on a bed of sand in summer, her anaemic body lay weary on the bed. The life force that she contained within herself in profusion had suddenly disappeared altogether. Now, as she lay on the bed she could feel the heated breeze bringing in the smell of muchkundo flowers through the open window, or sometimes a breath of the batabi flower—as if her days of spring were softly asking her from the distant past, 'How are you?'

What caused her most hurt and misery was that Aditya's distant cousin, Sarala, had to be called to help in the garden. From the open window whenever she saw Sarala wearing a lofty, embroidered silk toka, ordering the gardeners about their work, Neerja found her useless limbs unbearable. Yet when she used to be healthy she used to invite the same Sarala every season during the festive occasion of seed planting. Work would begin at dawn. Then they would swim and bathe in the pool, and eat off plantain leaves beneath the trees; afterwards the gramophone would play native and foreign music. The gardeners would get curds, sweetened rice grains and sweetmeats. The sounds of their merriment could be heard from the tamarind grove. Slowly the day would wind up and the water in the pool would ripple with the afternoon breeze, the birds would chirp on the bokul branches and the day would end on a contented, happy note.

The sweet sap within her, why had it turned bitter today! Just as her weak body was a stranger to her active, healthy former self, her sharp dry nature too was unfamiliar to herself. There was no charity in this nature. At times when the poverty of her mind and body became visible to her, she'd feel ashamed—but she had no control over herself. She found it frightening to think Aditya might notice her meanness; that some day he might see clearly that her mind at present was like a fruit mauled by a bat's teeth, unfit for decent use.

The gong sounded once again. The garden was desolate. Neerja gazed afar where even the mirage of unrealized longing could not be seen, where in the sunlight without shade the void just follows itself.

## 2

Neerja called out, 'Roshni!'

The ayah came into the room. Elderly, with white streaks in her black hair, thick brass bangles on her hard hands, and the scarf of thin cloth draped on the skirt worn by up-country women—this was Roshni. The posture of her lean body and stern features held the stamp of permanent seriousness; as if in her court of law she was prepared to pronounce judgement against this household. She had reared Neerja—all her affections centred on her. So she viewed with rebellious suspicion anyone who came close to Neerja, even if it was Neerja's husband.

She entered the room now and asked, 'Shall I fetch you water, Khokhi?'

'No, sit.'

The ayah sat on the floor, her knees hunched up.

Whenever Neerja felt the need to talk, to open herself up, she would summon Roshni. The ayah was the audience for her soliloquies.

Neerja began, 'This morning I heard the door open.'

The ayah said nothing but her expression which reflected her annoyance, could be interpreted as, 'And when isn't it heard?'

Neerja asked an unnecessary question, 'Did he go with Sarala to the garden?'

The answer was certainly known to Neerja, yet everyday she made the same query. Turning the palm of her hand once and twisting her lips scornfully, the ayah sat silent.

Neerja gazed out of the window and mused to herself, 'He would wake me too, at dawn, I would also go with him to the garden then. This wasn't too long ago.'

When Neerja rambled on in this manner nobody was expected to join this discussion, but the ayah could not be quiet. 'As if the garden would dry up if she weren't taken along!' she said.

Neerja continued to talk, as if to herself, 'Not a day passed when I didn't arrange for the early morning flowers to be sent to New Market. Those flowers were sent this morning too, I heard the sound of the vehicle. Who sees to this nowadays, Roshni?'

The ayah did not answer what was already known, she sat with her lips tightly pursed.

Neerja told her, 'Whatever happens now, when I was in charge the gardeners could never hoodwink me.'

The ayah spoke in repressed grief, 'Those days are gone now. Now both hands are used to steal openly.'

'Really?'

'Am I lying? How many flowers reach Kolkata's New Market! As soon as Jamaibabu leaves, the gardeners sell the flowers at the back door.'

'Nobody checks this?'

'Who can be bothered?'

'Why don't you tell Jamaibabu?'

'Who am I to say anything! I have to keep my dignity. Why don't you tell him? Everything belongs to you.'

'Let it be, let it be, fine. Let it go on like this for a while, when everything is ruined it will be exposed. One day the time of reckoning will come; the stepmother's love is never greater than the mother's, is it? So say nothing now.'

'But I still say, Khokhi, there's no work to be got from your Hola gardener.'

Hola's indifference to work was not the only thing that perpetually annoyed the ayah. That Neerja's affection for him, to her mind, was growing unreasonably, was the most significant reason for her irritation with Hola.

'I don't blame the gardener. Why should he tolerate the new mistress? He belongs to a family whose profession has been gardening for the last seven generations and your Didimoni's skills are derived from books—to order him about, isn't it unseemly? Hola doesn't like to obey eccentric laws, he complains to me. And I tell him to shut his ears to it.'

'The other day Jamaibabu was going to release him from work.'

'Why, whatever for?'

'He was sitting around smoking a beedi and right in front of him a cow strayed in from outside and was eating the plants. Jamaibabu said, "Why don't you chase away the cow?" and he answered insolently, "Me chase the cow! The cow will chase me. Don't I have fear for my life!"'

Neerja laughed; she said, 'He talks like that. Well, whatever it is, he is what I've created with my own hands.'

'Jamaibabu tolerates him for your sake, whether a cow strays in or a rhino chases him. Being so pricey and haughty isn't good, I tell you.'

'Be quiet, Roshni. Don't I know what grief kept him from chasing that cow? His chest burns in sorrow. There's Hola—going somewhere with a towel on his head. Call him here.'

The ayah called Hola who came into the room. Neerja asked, 'Well, are there new instructions these days?'

'There are, definitely. Hearing them makes me laugh, brings tears to the eyes.'

'Let me hear what.'

'Over there from in front of the Mullicks' old house that is being demolished—I have to get brickbats from there and spread it beneath the trees. This is her order. I said, "The trees will feel hot when the bricks heat up in the sun." But she pays no attention to what I say.'

'Why don't you tell Babu?'

'I told Babu. He scolded me and said, "Be quiet." Boudidi, release me from work, I find this intolerable.'

'That's why I saw you carry in a basket of rubbish.'

'Boudidi, you are my mistress forever. With you still here, they've made me hang my head in shame. I've lost my standing in front of everybody. Am I a common labourer that I should carry bricks?'

'All right, go now. When your Didimoni asks you to carry in brickbats, tell her in my name I forbid this . . . Why do you still stand here?'

'A letter's come from my village. The big ox used for ploughing is dead.' Saying this Hola scratched his head sheepishly.

Neerja said, 'No, he isn't dead, he's hale and hearty. Here, take these two rupees and don't blabber any more.'

She took out the money from the brass box on the table. But Hola continued to stand there.

'Now what?'

'An old garment for my wife. Something that you have no use for. You will be praised all over the place.' Saying this Hola widened his betel-stained black lips and grinned.

Neerja said, 'Roshni, go give him that sari that's on the clothes-stand.'

Roshni shook her head vigorously and exclaimed, 'What talk is this, that is your Dhakai sari!'

'Let it be my Dhakai sari. Now all saris are the same to me. When will I ever wear them?'

Roshni set her face and said stubbornly, 'No, that cannot be. I'll give her the red bordered factory-made sari. Look here, Hola, if you pester Khokhi like this, I shall tell Babu to banish you far away.'

Hola clasped Neerja's feet and wailed, 'I have lost favour with fortune, Boudidi.'

'Why, eh? What's the matter with you?'

'I call Ayahji mashi. I don't have a mother, until now I used to think she loves this wretched Hola. But Boudidi, if you have something for me, then why does she create an obstacle? It's nobody's fault I suppose, it's my fate that's at fault.'

'Don't worry, your mashi loves you, she was praising you before you came. Roshni, give him that garment or he'll lie here obstinately as if he were imploring in front of a deity at the temple.'

With an extremely sullen expression the ayah got the sari and threw it in front of Hola. Hola picked it up and bowing low touched Neerja's feet and saluted her respectfully. Then he stood up and said, 'Let me wrap it in this towel, Boudidi. My hands are dirty and it will get stained.'

Without waiting for permission Hola took a towel from the clothes-stand and vanished rapidly.

Neerja asked the ayah, 'Roshni, do you know for sure if Babu has gone out?'

'I saw him leaving with my own eyes. What hurry! Forgot to take his cap.'

'Today it happened for the first time. The flower he presents to me every morning was forgotten. This forgetfulness will increase daily. Finally I will be kept aside in the dump in this household, where the burnt out coal is stored.'

Seeing Sarala approach the ayah grimaced and left. Sarala entered the room. In her hand was an orchid. It was a spotless flower, the tip of the petal was of a faint purple colour. It looked like a huge butterfly whose wings were spread fully. Sarala was tall and slender, dark complexioned; her large eyes, bright and sad, were what struck everyone at the first glance. She was wearing a coarse hand-spun sari, with her hair carelessly tied up, hanging untidy and loose over her shoulders. Her unadorned form did injustice to her youth.

Neerja refused to look at her. Sarala gently kept the flower on the bed, in front of her. Neerja did not hide her annoyance and asked brusquely, 'Who told you to bring this?'

'Aditda.'

'Why didn't he come himself?'

'He had to leave in a hurry for the New Market shop, as soon as he finished his cup of tea.'

'Why this rush?'

'Last night there was news—the office lock has been tampered with and money stolen.'

'Couldn't he spare five minutes for me?'

'Last night your pain increased. You fell asleep early in the morning. He came to the door and then turned back. He told me before leaving that if he didn't return by the afternoon I was to give you this flower.'

Before beginning his work for the day Aditya would specially select a flower to place on his wife's bed. Neerja waited for this every day. And today he had left that special flower with Sarala. It had not entered his mind that the essential value of giving a flower was to give it personally. Even the holy water of the Ganges loses its significance if it flows out of an ordinary pipe.

Neerja pushed the flower aside scornfully and said, 'Do you know how costly this flower is in the market? Send it there. What is the point of wasting it?'

Saying this, her voice grew heavy.

Sarala understood the situation. She knew that answering Neerja would merely aggravate her grief. So she stood silent. A little while later Neerja asked, 'Do you know the name of this flower?'

Sarala could have said 'I don't know' but perhaps that hurt her pride; she said, 'Amaryllis.'

Neerja snapped at her quite unreasonably, 'So much for your knowledge! The name is Grandiflora.'

Sarala replied mildly, 'Maybe so.'

'What do you mean, maybe so? Of course it is so. Are you trying to say I don't know?'

Sarala realized that Neerja had purposely given the wrong name, to alleviate her own agony by inflicting it on another. In defeat she was about to leave the room slowly; but Neerja called out, 'Listen! What were you doing all morning, where were you?'

'In the orchid room.'

Neerja became agitated, 'Why must you go so often to the orchid room?'

'Aditda had asked me to splice some orchids and graft them anew.'

Neerja said in disapproving tones, 'Like an ignorant person you will ruin them all. I have taught Hola the gardener to make them, couldn't he have done it if instructed?'

There could be no answer to this. The candid answer would be that in Neerja's time Hola the gardener might have worked well, but Sarala could not manage him at all. In fact, he often insulted her by showing indifference.

The gardener had realized that not working well in the present regime would please the mistress of the previous regime. It was a bit like boycotting classes and not passing the examination being of more value than getting the college degree.

Sarala could have got angry with all the pettiness Neerja was displaying, but she did not. She recognized that her Boudidi's heart ached. The garden occupied all of this childless woman's heart and today after ten years it was so near her, all around her, and yet she was banished from it! What a cruel separation!

Neerja said, 'Shut it, shut the window.'

Sarala closed the window and asked, 'Now shall I fetch some orange juice?'

'No, you don't have to get anything.'

Sarala reminded her rather timidly, 'It's time for you to have your makardhvaj.'

'No, no need for makardhvaj. Are there any more instructions for you concerning the garden?'

'I have to plant rose cuttings.'

Neerja said with some spite, 'Oh, and is this the time! Who gave you this idea, let me hear?'

Sarala said softly, 'From the outstation suddenly there are several orders so Aditda resolved somehow to prepare many plants before the monsoons. I had said not to.'

'Said not to, I see! All right, all right, call Hola here.'

Hola came in. Neerja said, 'Have you become a fine gentleman? Do your hands get cramps planting rose cuttings? Is Didimoni your assistant gardener? Before Babu gets back from the city you will plants as many cuttings as possible, no breaks today, I tell you. Mix the sand with the scorched leaves and grass and prepare the ground on the right bank of the pool.'

Neerja decided to lie on the bed and organize the planting of roses from there itself. There was to be no deliverance for Hola the gardener.

Hola smiled indulgently and told Neerja, 'Boudidi, this is a brass water-pot made in Cuttack by Horosundar Maity. Only you can appreciate its finesse. It will look good as a vase for you.'

Neerja asked, 'How much does it cost?'

Pressing the tip of his tongue between his teeth to show abashment, Hola said, 'Don't say such things. As if I can take money for this pot! I am poor but not ungrateful. You have reared me with food and clothes.'

He put the water pot on the table and taking flowers from another vase began to arrange them there. Finally, turning to go, he remarked, 'I have told you of my niece's wedding. Don't forget the armlet, Boudidi. If I give her brass jewellery you will be criticized. I am a gardener in such a prosperous household, a wedding in my family will naturally arouse the curiosity of the whole locality.'

Neerja replied, 'All right, don't worry, now go.'

Hola left. Neerja suddenly turned on her side and placing her head on the pillow, cried out in suppressed grief, 'Roshni, Roshni, how petty I have become, my mind has become like that of Hola gardener's.'

The ayah said, 'Shame, shame, Khokhi, what are you saying?'

Neerja continued to speak absently, 'My misfortune struck me down on the outside, but why is it making me so mean on the inside? Don't I know how Hola regards me now! Standing so close, grinning and taking his tip he left. Call him here. I will rebuke him sternly, get rid of his wickedness once and for all.'

But when the ayah rose to call Hola, Neerja said, 'Let it be, let it be for now.'

## 3

Some time later Neerja's cousin-in-law, Romen, arrived. 'Boudi, dada sent me here,' he said. 'He has plenty of work at the office, he will eat out, since he will be back rather late.'

Neerja chuckled and said, 'Fine excuse to come running here with this message, Thakurpo! Why did you have to trouble yourself, is the office bearer dead?'

'To be near you do I need any other excuse but yourself, Boudi? Can the bearer express the affection that I feel for my Boudi?'

'My dear, you scatter pearls in the wrong place. What error brings you to this room? Your female florist roams alone in the lemon grove, go and see her there.'

'Let me pay homage to the goddess of the garden first and then I shall go in search of the female gardener.' Saying this he brought out a book from his shirt pocket and handed it to Neerja.

Neerja was delighted and said, '*Asru Shikol* (A Chain of Tears)—this is the book I wanted. I bless you, may the florist of your garden be eternally chained to your heart in joy. She whom you call your imagination's partner, the companion of your dreams. What amour my dear!'

Romen said suddenly, 'All right Boudi, I want to ask you something, but answer truthfully.'

'What?'

'Have you quarrelled with Sarala today?'

'Why do you ask?'

'I saw her sitting silently beside the pool. Women are not like men who while away the time daydreaming when they ought to be working. I have never before seen Sarala in such an idle state. When I asked her, "In which direction is your mind wandering?" she retorted, "In that direction where the heated wind blows withered leaves." I said, "That is a riddle. Speak in plain language." She answered, "Does everything have a language?" Again I saw a riddle. A line from that song came to mind then: "Whose words have hurt you today?"'

'Maybe something your Dada said.'

'That cannot be. Dada is a man. He may sternly reprimand your gardeners. But can the fire devastate the beautiful flower?'

'All right, let's not talk any more nonsense. Instead, I want to ask you something important. I entreat you, please marry Sarala. To marry and save a spinster would be great piety.'

'I don't care about piety but I covet that maiden, this I swear to you.'

'Then where is the obstacle? Isn't she agreeable?'

'I haven't even asked her. She is more my fancy's match, not my worldly partner.'

Suddenly, with tremendous eagerness, Neerja clutched Romen's hand. 'Why not, it has to be. Before I die you have to be married or I shall haunt you both, I tell you.'

Neerja's agitation caused Romen to stare at her in amazement. Finally he shook his head and said, 'Boudi, I am younger than you in our relationship by marriage but older than you in years. The flying wind blows the seeds of weeds; if encouraged by suitable conditions the weeds grow roots, and then who can uproot them?'

'You don't have to advise me. I am your elder, and I'm giving you good counsel, marry her. Don't delay. There are good dates in this month of Phalgun.'

'In my almanac all three hundred and sixty-five days are good. There may be good days Boudi, but there is no path leading to such an event taking place. I have been to prison once, even now I'm on the slippery road that heads gaolwards. The minions of Prajapati, the god of marriage, don't tread those paths.'

'Do girls nowadays fear the jail?'

'Maybe they don't but that is not the way to go around the sacred fire seven times. On that road one is stronger keeping his bride in his heart, not by his side. She will always be in my heart.'

Sarala entered the room and placed a tumbler of Horlicks upon the table. She was about to leave when Neerja called her, 'Don't go, listen Sarala, whose photograph is this? Do you recognize her?'

Sarala replied, 'It is mine.'

'Your picture in the early days. When at your Uncle's place Aditya and you used to work in the garden, isn't it? Looking at this photo, it seems you were fifteen. Wore your sari like a loin cloth tucked in between the legs, like the Maharashtrian women.'

'Where did you get this?'

'I saw it in his desk, didn't notice it then. Had it brought from there now. Thakurpo, Sarala looks better now than she did at that time. What do you think?'

Romen replied, 'Was there a Sarala then? At least I did not know her then. For me this is the only true Sarala. Whom should I compare her to?'

Neerja said, 'Now her appearance has a mystery arising from her heart—like the cloud once plainly white is now brimming dark with monsoon showers. This is what you call romantic, eh, Thakurpo?'

Sarala turned to leave; but Neerja stalled her, 'Sarala, sit here a while. Thakurpo, for once let me look at Sarala from a man's perspective. Tell me, what does one notice about her right in the beginning?'

Romen said, 'Everything at once.'

'Definitely her eyes; she knows how to gaze solemnly. No, don't go, Sarala! Sit a while longer. Her form too is well rounded, perfect.'

'Are you set to auction her, Boudi? You know, even otherwise I don't lack enthusiasm.'

Neerja spoke up with an agent's earnestness, 'Thakurpo, look at Sarala's hands, as supple as they are well formed, and so attractive. Have you seen hands such as these?'

Romen laughed and said, 'Whether I have seen hands such as this will not bear saying in front of you.'

'Won't you claim those two hands?'

'If not forever, from time to time I have claimed them. When I come for a cup of tea at your house I get something more served to me by the ingenuity of those two hands. Can I ask more from her hands—by asking for her hand?'

Sarala rose from the stool. When she tried to leave the room once again Romen blocked her way at the door, declaring, 'Promise me something and I shall let you go.'

'Say, what.'

'Today is the fourteenth day of the waxing moon. I, the traveller, shall go to your garden, if there are words still, they need not be uttered. This is a time of famine—I never get to feast my eyes on you the way I would like. This sudden meeting in this room is like a fistful of alms—it leaves me unfulfilled, hungry for more.'

Sarala said calmly, 'All right, I will see you.'

Romen returned to his chair by the bed and told Neerja, 'Then I shall take my leave, Boudi.'

'And what more reason for you to stay! Boudi's purpose has been served.'

Romen left.

## 4

After Romen left, Neerja lay on the bed hiding her face in her hands. She couldn't help reminiscing about the past—such enchanting days had been hers too once. She had made so many spring nights exciting. Had she ever been what seventy-five per cent women were, mere furnishings in the husband's household? Lying on the bed she kept recalling the innumerable times when her husband had clasped her curling tresses and tugging them said in ardent tones: 'You are the wine of my pleasure-house.' Even after ten years the pleasure had not faded, the cup of wine was full. Her husband would tell her, 'In the olden days women's feet would make asoka flowers bloom as they walked the garden, the intoxicating drop of wine from their mouth would make the bakul bloom; in my garden is captured Kalidasa's time. The path where your feet tread every day has come forth with vividly coloured flowers on either side; the spring breeze has showered wine, the rose-bower is intoxicated by it.' He would continue, 'If you weren't here this bower of bliss would be taken over by some merchant, who would rule over it like some senseless demon. It is my good fortune that you are here, like the queen of the gods, to make this garden paradise.'

Alas, her youth had not gone but gone was its glory. That is why the queen of the gods had lost her seat today. Did she have even a trace of fear in those days? Nobody could dare to step where she reigned; in her horizon she was like the rising sun, radiant in her solitude. Today the sight of the slightest shadow made her heart beat faster; she had no faith in herself any longer. Who was this Sarala, what was her worth! But today her presence made Neerja's mind restless with suspicion. Who would have known that such misery was to befall her so soon! For so long God had given her such bountiful joy, such honour, but then like a petty thief He had stolen it all away one day through the back door.

She shook herself from her reverie.

'Roshni, are you there?'

'What, Khokhi?'

'Your Jamaibabu once referred to me as the colourful treasure of his pleasure-house. We have been married ten years, that colour has still not faded, but what about the pleasure-house? Where has it gone?'

'Where will it go, your house is right here. You didn't sleep properly last night, sleep now, let me massage your feet.'

'Roshni, soon there will be a full moon. So many moonlit nights I have spent awake and happy. The two of us would roam the garden. But look how I keep awake now—in pain and loneliness! If only I could sleep now I would be saved, but the wretched sleep does not come.'

'Be quiet, let me see, you will soon be asleep.'

'Tell me, do they wander about the garden on full moon nights?'

'I have seen them pluck flowers at dawn to send to the traders. How will they wander about at night? Where is the time?'

'The gardeners sleep so much these days. Do they deliberately not wake the gardeners?'

'You aren't there, who dares to lay hands on the gardeners now?'

'Was that the sound of the car?'

'Yes, Babu's car has arrived.'

'Pass me that hand-mirror. And get me that large rose from the vase. Let me see, where is the box of safety pins? My face is so pale today. You go from this room.'

'I am going, but the Horlicks lies there, have it, Khokhi.'

'Let it remain there, I won't have it.'

'You haven't had even two doses of your medicine.'

'You don't have to rant. Go now, I tell you, open that window and leave.'

The ayah went away. The clock struck three. The sunlight had taken on a reddish tinge, the shadows were falling eastwards, the southern wind had picked up and the water in the pool rippled restlessly. The gardeners were back at work; Neerja could see them from her window.

Aditya rushed into the room. A bouquet of pale yellow laburnums, locally grown, covered his arms. He put the flowers at Neerja's feet. Sitting on the bed he clasped her hand and said, 'Haven't seen you all of today, Neeru.'

Hearing this, Neerja could not contain herself, she sobbed aloud. Aditya got up from the bed and, kneeling on the floor, hugged Neerja, kissed her wet cheeks and said, 'You know, don't you, that it wasn't my fault?'

'Tell me, how I can know that for sure? Am I what I used to be in those days?'

'What is the point in taking stock of days? You are mine as you always were.'

'Today everything makes me nervous. I don't feel strong in my mind.'

'It feels good to be a little nervous, doesn't it? You want to spur me on with a little jibe, don't you? This cunning is a woman's inborn impulse.'

'And isn't forgetting a man's inborn impulse?'

'Do you ever give me leave to forget?'

'Oh don't say that, by the curse of God what long leave I have been forced to give you.'

'It's the other way round. Even if I were able to forget you in times of joy, I would never be able to forget you in times of strife.'

'Tell me honestly, didn't you forget about me this morning?'

'The things you say! I had to go, and till I returned, my mind, Neeru, was without peace.'

'How you're sitting! Raise yourself to the bed.'

'Do you want to chain me in case I escape?'

'Yes, I want to make a chain. In life and death, without doubt, your feet must be fastened to me.'

'Doubt me a little sometimes, that makes love more charming.'

'No, not a bit of doubt should arise in my mind. Not even a little.

Which woman has a husband like you? To suspect you, that would be to reproach myself.'

'Then I will suspect you, or the drama will not be well arranged.'

'Do that, no worries there. That will be a farce.'

'Whatever you say, you were angry with me today.'

'Why say that again! You don't have to punish me—I am punished already.'

'What need is there for punishment! If the heat of anger doesn't rise at times, I would believe love's pulse is faltering.'

'If I ever make the mistake of being angry with you, know it isn't me but some mischievous spirit possessing me.'

'We all have a mischievous spirit, sometimes manifesting itself unreasonably! If you are sensible and take Rama's name it flees.'

The ayah came in and said, 'Jamaibabu, Khokhi has not had her milk or medicine since the morning, and no massage either. If she continues to do this we won't be able to manage her.'

Saying this she left speedily, swinging her arms.

As soon as Aditya heard this he rose, declaring, 'Now I shall be angry.'

'Yes, be angry, very angry, as angry as you can—but forgive me afterwards.'

Aditya went near the door and called out, 'Sarala! Sarala!'

Neerja's nerves jangled the moment he uttered Sarala's name. She felt as if the thorn embedded in her heart had been shaken to and fro, causing her more agony.

Sarala came in. Aditya asked in annoyed tones, 'You didn't give Neeru her medicine today, not even anything to eat all day?'

Neerja spoke up hastily, 'Why do you scold her? What fault is it of hers? I was obstinate, I didn't take my medicine, scold me instead. Sarala, you go. Why stand here and be rebuked unreasonably?'

'What do you mean by "go"? Let her fetch the medicine. Get that glass of Horlicks here.'

'Aha, the whole day you make her slog in the garden, why pile upon her the duties of a nurse as well? Don't you have some pity? Call the ayah if you need anything.'

'Will the ayah be able to do all this properly?'

'It's hardly any work, she can do it. Do it better even.'

'But . . .'

'What is the "but" now? Ayah! Ayah!'

'Don't get so excited, Neeru. You'll make trouble, I can see.'

'I'll call the ayah,' said Sarala and left the room. Words objecting to Neerja's statements never crossed her lips. Aditya was surprised; he pondered whether it was true that Sarala was being wrongly overworked!

After the medicine was taken, Aditya told the ayah, 'Call Saraladidi here.'

'Always calling for Sarala, you will worry that poor girl,' Neerja interrupted.

'I have something important to ask her.'

'Let important things wait now.'

'Won't take long.'

'Sarala is a woman, how many important things can you have to discuss with her? Better to call Hola the gardener.'

'After marrying you, I've discovered only women work, men are intrinsically lazy. We men slave because we are obliged to, you women work with zest arising from the heart. I am considering writing a thesis on this. There are plenty of examples recorded in my diary.'

'This woman is deprived today of her heart's work by Providence, how shall I dispute that? The towers built by my work have been destroyed by an earthquake, that's why this deserted house is now the haunt of ghosts.'

Sarala came in. Aditya asked, 'Is the orchid room's job done?'

'Yes, done.'

'Everything?'

'Everything.'

'And the rose cuttings?'

'The gardener is preparing the soil.'

'Soil! I had already prepared it. You've put Hola gardener in charge? Now instead of a rose garden, we'll have a harvest of dried-up saplings, which will look like a garden of toothpicks.'

Neerja said hastily, 'Sarala, go and get me some orange juice, put some ginger essence and honey in it.'

Sarala left the room with her head bowed. Neerja asked her husband, 'Did you wake at dawn today like we used to daily?'

'Yes, I did.'

'Was the alarm clock wound up like it used to be?'

'Yes, of course.'

'That tree trunk under the neem tree—the tea arranged on it; did Basu lay it all out properly?'

'He did. Otherwise I would submit an appeal to your court, to claim damages.'

'Were two seats arranged?'

'They were arranged as before. And there was that blue-rimmed cream-coloured tea set, the silver milk jug, the small white stone sugar bowl, and the Japanese tray with dragons painted on it.'

'Why did you leave the other seat empty?'

'I didn't leave it empty on purpose. The stars in the sky numbered the same, only the waxing moon of the fifth night remained out of view. If given a chance I would capture it and bring it there.'

'Why didn't you ask Sarala to join you at the tea table?'

An answer that would have pleased Neerja's mind would be—'My mind rebels against seating somebody else on your throne'. But Aditya being a truthful man said instead, 'I think she does some puja or something in the morning, she's not a godless barbarian like me.'

'After the morning tea it seems you took her to the orchid room?'

'Yes, there was work to do, I explained it to her and then rushed to the shop.'

'Okay, let me ask you something, why don't you arrange for Sarala to wed Romen?'

'Is match-making my profession?'

'No, I'm not joking. She will have to marry, where will you find a groom like Romen?'

'The groom is on one side, the bride on the other, being in the middle I don't have time to investigate whether their hearts are inclined or not. From a distance there seems to be a problem.'

Neerja said with some heat, 'If you were really keen there would be no problem.'

'Somebody else is to get married and I have to be keen? Can anything be done this way? Why don't you try and see?'

'Give the girl's vision a break from those plants and trees, she will eventually look where she should.'

'In the light of the Shubhadrishti—the glance of true love—trees and mountains and everything else become transparent. It's a kind of X-ray vision, actually.'

'Nonsense. The truth is you don't want this wedding.'

'You've got it at last. If Sarala goes what will happen to my garden? We have to think of profit and loss too. What is that, are you suddenly in pain?' he asked anxiously.

Neerja said harshly, 'Nothing is wrong. You don't have to be concerned about me.'

When Aditya was about to get up to go she said, 'It was after we were married that the orchid room was built, you haven't forgotten that? Afterwards every day both of us decorated that room. And now you don't feel a thing about spoiling it!'

Aditya said in shocked tones, 'What is this talk! Where did you see me wanting to spoil it?'

Getting highly agitated Neerja asked, 'What does Sarala know of a flower garden?'

'What are you saying! Sarala does not know! My uncle who adopted and reared me is also Sarala's uncle. You know, it was in his garden that I was first initiated to this kind of work. Uncle used to say jobs in the flower garden should be done by women, that and milking cows. She would accompany him in his work.'

'And you would accompany them.'

'Yes, indeed. But I had to study, go to college, I did not find as much time to work there as she did. Uncle taught her most of what he knew.'

'And that garden was the cause of your uncle's misfortune. Such is the girl's luck. That is what I fear. Unlucky girl. Look at her—her forehead like a field, she gallops like a horse. A woman should not think like a man. That brings misfortune.'

'Tell me, what is the matter with you today, Neeru? What are you saying! Uncle just knew how to make a garden, he knew nothing of trade. He was unrivalled in creating a flower garden; but nobody equalled him in losing money either. He was respected by all but never compensated. When he loaned me the capital to start trading as a florist did I know his treasury fund was on the verge of collapse? My only consolation is this: before he died I had paid back all that I owed him.'

Sarala came in with the orange juice. Neerja instructed her, 'Leave it there and go.'

Sarala put the glass down and left. The glass remained there, Neerja did not touch it.

'Why didn't you marry Sarala?'

'Listen to this! I never even thought of marrying her.'

'Never thought! Is this the poet in you speaking?'

'I first knew poetry when I saw you. Before that Sarala and I—two wild beasts—spent our days in the shady forest. We forgot ourselves. I don't know what would have happened if we had been reared in the current ways of society.'

'Why, what is society's crime?'

'Society now is like a Duhshashan wanting to strip naked the heart. Before we can feel something it tells us what we should feel. For it the fragrance is too subtle, it gathers information by tearing the petals.'

'Sarala isn't bad looking.'

'I knew Sarala as Sarala herself. Whether she was good looking or not was not something I ever thought about.'

'All right, be honest, didn't you love her?'

'Of course I did. Am I an inert object that I wouldn't love her? Uncle's son was a barrister in Rangoon, so Uncle had no worries regarding him. He merely wanted that Sarala care for his garden always. He believed the garden would occupy her heart and soul, and that she would not be interested in marriage. Then he passed away, Sarala was orphaned and the garden went to debtors. That day my heart broke, didn't you see? She is a loveable creature, why wouldn't I love her! I recall, how once Sarala's joyful laughter used to be so spontaneous, it was as if her feet had a bird's wings in them. Today she walks with a heavy heart, yet she is not broken. Not one day has she drawn a deep sigh, neither in my presence, nor alone.'

Neerja interrupted, 'Stop, dear, stop, I've heard all this, you don't have to say anything more. Extraordinary girl. That is why I say, let her be the headmistress in that girls' school in Barasat. They have pleaded so many times.'

'Barasat Girls' School! Why not the Andamans!'

'No, no joking. You can let Sarala work anywhere in the garden but not in that orchid room.'

'Why, what has happened?'

'I tell you, Sarala does not know anything about orchids.'

'I tell you too, Sarala knows about orchids more than I do. Uncle's main passion was orchids. He would send people to Celebes, Java, even China to get orchids; nobody was as involved with orchids as he was.'

Neerja knew all this and that was why she found Sarala's presence in the orchid room so intolerable.

'Oh very well. She may know about orchids better than me or even you. Even then, I still say the orchid room is yours and mine only, Sarala has no place there. Give your whole garden to her if that is what you really desire; but keep away from her just a bit that is absolutely dedicated to me. After all these years I can surely claim at least this little bit. It is my ill fortune that I lie here like this, and so . . .'

Overcome by helplessness and despair, Neerja left her sentence incomplete and turned her face into the pillow and wept restlessly.

Aditya was stunned. It was as if he had been in a dream all these days and was awakened with a start by Neerja's harsh words and the raw display of her grief. He realized that her outburst, her weeping, all of it was the result of an agony of many days. It was as if the cyclonic storm of pain had been building up with increased momentum in Neerja's mind every day, and Aditya had not recognized it even for a moment. So foolish he had been, he had actually thought Neerja was pleased that Sarala was taking care of the garden. Especially so since she was unparalleled in selecting seasonal blossoms to decorate the flower beds. Suddenly he remembered—once when on some occasion he had praised Sarala and said, 'Not even I could prepare the kamini hedges so attractively,' with a sardonic laugh Neerja had retorted, 'My dear sir, if you commend more than one deserves, ultimately you harm the person.' Aditya recalled now that, if Neerja could pick some fault with Sarala's knowledge of botany she would repeat it with relish. He clearly remembered how Neerja would search English books for lesser known flowers with outlandish names and then innocently question Sarala; when Sarala failed to provide the correct answer, Neerja would hardly cease chortling in glee, 'What a great pundit! She doesn't even know it's called *Cassia javanica*! Even my Hola gardener knows that.'

Aditya sat and pondered over the matter for some time. Then he took Neerja's hand and said, 'Don't cry, Neeru, tell me what I should do. Do you want me to ask Sarala to stop working in the garden?'

Neerja snatched away her hand, saying, 'I want nothing, nothing at all. It is your garden. You keep anybody you want there, it's entirely up to you!'

'Neeru, how could you say that—my garden! Is it not yours as well? When did such a division grow between us?'

'From the time you have the run of the entire world and I, just this corner of the room. With my broken self what strength have I to compete with your astonishing Sarala? Where is my strength that I may care for you, or care for the garden?'

'Neeru, so many times you yourself have called Sarala and consulted her on several matters regarding the garden. Don't you remember how, just a few years ago, the two of you grafted a Pomelo and Colombo lime just to surprise me?'

'She was not so arrogant then. Providence chose to throw me into the dark shadows completely which is why suddenly you find that—she knows this, she knows that, she is peerless in her knowledge of orchids. I never had to hear such things in the old days. Then today, in my days of misery, why are you comparing us like this? How can I rival her today? What have I to match her now?'

'Neeru, I never expected such words from you. It seems as if all that you are saying now are not my Neeru's words, they are spoken by somebody else.'

'No, I am just so, the same Neeru. You could not understand her, all this time. That is my greatest grief. When after our marriage I learnt that this garden was as precious as your life, I never let a division grow between it and myself. Otherwise I would have picked a fight with that garden, I wouldn't have been able to bear its closeness to you. It would have become my rival. But you know very well that my constant effort has been to make it one and the same with me. I have become completely inseparable from it.'

'I know that, of course. You are there in everything I have.'

'Leave all that talk. Today I saw an intruder easily enter the garden—that was till now solely ours. Nothing hurt anywhere. Could you think of cutting open my body to let in somebody else's heart? Is not the garden my body? Would I have done this if I was in your place?'

'What would you have done?'

'Shall I tell you what I would have done? The garden may have been ruined; the business might have collapsed; I would have kept ten gardeners instead of one, but I would not have let another woman in—especially one who thinks that she knows more about gardening than me. Why should you use her vanity to insult me every day—that too, when I am disabled and dying, when I have no way to prove my competence? Shall I say why this was possible for you?'

'Tell me.'

'Because you love her more than me! You had hidden this all the time.'

Aditya sat stupefied for a while, his hands clutching his hair. Then he said in dazed tones, 'Neeru, you have known me these ten years, in happiness and grief, in various conditions, in all kinds of work; despite all our years together, if you can say all this then I shall not answer you. I am leaving. If I stay here you will be sick. I shall move to the Japanese room next to the Fernery. Send word if you need me.'

## 5

On the other side of the pool, behind the chalta tree the moon rose, throwing deep shadows across the water. On the near bank the new leaves of the basanti tree were rosy like a the eyes of a babe just awakened, and its flowers were the hue of molten gold. Their deep aroma hung densely like a heavy fog. The fireflies glowed on the boughs of the jarul tree. On the stone-embanked slope, on a platform sat Sarala, absolutely still. There was no breeze, no leaves trembled, the water was framed in black shadow like a mirror of polished silver.

The question came from behind her. 'May I join you?'

Sarala replied in soft tones, 'Come.'

Romen sat down on the flight of stairs leading to the pool, near her feet. Sarala was embarrassed and said, 'Where are you sitting, come up here, Romenda.'

Romen remarked, 'Don't you know the deities are worshipped with eulogies from their feet upwards? If there is a place by your side I shall sit there later. Give me your hand; let me pay my address in the English style.'

He kissed Sarala's hand and said, 'Accept my salutations, empress.'

Then he stood up and smeared some dry red colour on her temple.

'What is this?'

'Don't you know today is Holi? Your trees and boughs are splashed with colour. Spring does not colour people in the same way, but their hearts are coloured. You must express these hues, or, forest goddess, you shall remain banished forever in the asoka grove, away from your beloved.'

'Where do I have the skills to banter with you?'

'Why do we need words! The male bird sings, the female just listens and that itself is response enough. Now let me sit beside you.'

He sat by her. For a long time they sat silently. Suddenly Sarala asked, 'Romenda, how does one go to jail? I need to know.'

'Now there are so many ways of going to jail that it would be difficult to tell you a way of *not* getting there. These days it is the white man's flute that does not let us rest at home.'

'No, I am not joking. After much thought I've realized my liberation lies there.'

'Tell me frankly what you mean.'

'I will tell you everything. You would have understood completely if you had seen Aditda's face.'

'I gathered something, some indirect suggestion.'

'This evening I was alone on the veranda. A catalogue of pictures of flowers had arrived from America; I was glancing through it. Every evening by four-thirty, after tea, Aditda calls me to work in the garden. Today I saw him pacing restlessly; he didn't even look up at the gardeners who were working. It seemed as if he wished to come to my balcony, but he hesitated and went back. That tall well-built man with his powerful stride, his energetic way of speech and of work, always alert, a stern master but with a compassionate smile—today, he was walking differently, he did not look up, staying engrossed in his thoughts. After a long time he came slowly up to me. Any other day he would glance at his watch and say "It's time" and I would rise and go. Today, instead of saying this, he slowly pulled up a chair and remarked, "Looking at the catalogue, eh?" Taking the catalogue from my hands he began turning its pages. It didn't seem to me that he was looking at anything. He glanced up at me suddenly as if he had resolved to express something urgent without any further delay. Then again he looked down and said, "See Sori, what a large nasturtium!" His voice held deep weariness. For a long time nothing more was said, just the pages were turned. Once more he glanced up abruptly at my face and immediately shut the book and threw it on my lap—then rose to go. I asked, "Won't you go to the garden?" Aditda replied, "No, my dear, I have to go out, there's work." And as if tearing himself away, he left.'

'What had Aditda come to tell you? What do you reckon?'

'He had come to say, "You have already ruined one garden, now it's been ordered, it's your fate that you shall ruin another."'

'If that happens, Sori, then I shan't be free to go to jail.'

Sarala smiled sadly and replied, 'Can I block the road to jail? The King Emperor himself shall leave it open.'

'You will lie on the road like a blossom shaken from the boughs and I will triumphantly jangle my chains and march to prison, can that ever be? If this transpires, I'll have to learn to be a decent man at this age.'

'What will you do?'

'I will declare war on your unlucky planets—and drive them away from your birth chart. And then I shall take long leave, maybe even beyond the Kalapani.'

'I cannot hide anything from you, Romenda. One thing has become clear to me recently. Shall I tell you about it, if you don't mind?'

'I shall mind if you don't tell me.'

'From childhood I have been brought up with Aditda. Not like brother and sister but like two brothers; side by side we ploughed the soil, cut down the trees. My aunt and mother died of typhoid within a few days of each other; I was six then. My father died two years later. Uncle wanted so much that I keep his garden blooming with all my heart. He had moulded me in that way. He could never mistrust anyone. He had no doubt that the friends to whom he had loaned money would repay him one day and release the garden from debt. You probably know some of this history, yet today I feel like telling you the whole story from the beginning.'

'Everything seems new to me.'

'Then, as you know, it all sank. When I was pulled ashore Fate brought me to Aditda's side. We were together again, two brothers, two friends. Since then I have been sheltered by Aditda, that is just as true as the fact that I have provided a refuge for him. The effort has not been any less on my part, this I can say with confidence. So I had no reason to be contrite. It was as if I had returned to a younger age, an age when the two of us used to be together. This is how it could have continued forever . . . but what is the use of saying any more.'

'Finish what you were saying.'

'Abruptly I was jolted and made to realize with a shock that I am much older now. The veil covering the past when we used to work together had blown away in a moment. You must know it all, Romenda, nothing about me escapes your sight. Boudidi's antipathy towards me used to puzzle me, I could not understand why she felt the way she did. All this time I never recognized myself; Boudidi's aversion was the flame that lit up my own essence, and I came face to face with a new truth. Do you understand me?'

'The submerged affections of your childhood have been brought to the surface.'

'What can I do, tell me. How can I escape myself?' Saying this, Sarala clutched Romen's hand.

Romen was quiet. Sarala continued, 'As long as I am here, my wrong-doing increases!'

'Wrong-doing towards whom?'

'Towards Boudidi.'

'Look here, Sarala, I don't believe in this conventional wisdom. On what basis are you denying your affections for Aditda? Your feelings for each other are rooted in the togetherness that you both shared so many years ago. How can you judge who has claims over that time? Where was Boudi then?'

'What are you saying, Romenda! How can one indulge oneself at the cost of another! We have to think of Aditda too.'

'We do, certainly. Do you think the jolt that shocked you left him untouched?'

'Is that Romen?' called a voice behind them.

'Yes Dada.' Romen rose.

'Your Boudidi is asking for you. The ayah just told me.'

Romen left. Sarala was about to follow, when Aditya said, 'Don't go, Sori, sit a while.' Sarala's heart ached, looking at Aditya's face. The hardworking, unselfish, absentminded mass of a man seemed to be tossed about now like a rudderless boat amidst the waves.

Aditya said, 'We began this worldly life as one. So simple was our togetherness that it was impossible to imagine that there could ever be a division between us. Is that not so, Sori?'

'What is joined at the shoot is divided as it grows, there is no way not to accept this, Aditda.'

'That is the external separation, the visually perceived division! The inside cannot be broken in the essence. Today you are being pushed away from me. I could never imagine I would be so struck—Sori, do you realize what has come upon us so suddenly?'

'I know. I knew—before you did.'

'Can you bear it, Sori?'

'I will have to bear it.'

'I wonder if women are able to bear more than men.'

'You men battle against suffering; women tolerate sorrow over the ages. Except for tears and tolerance we have no other recourse.'

'You will be torn from me—I cannot let it happen. I will not. This is wrong, cruelly wrong.'

Saying this he clenched his fist towards heaven as if warring with an invisible foe. Sarala took Aditya's hand on her lap and stroked it gently. She spoke softly, as if to herself. 'It's not a question of right and wrong, Aditda. When the ties of a relationship become twisted into a noose it hurts many people at once, for the rope is tugged at from so many directions. Who is to be blamed for that!'

'You can bear it, I know. I remember an occasion. What splendid hair you had then. Even now. You were vain about your hair and everyone indulged this vanity of yours. Once I quarrelled with you. In the afternoon as you slept with your hair spread on the pillow, with a pair of scissors I snipped off an elbow's length of the hair. You woke immediately and stood up; your dark eyes glowed darker. You just said, "You think you can get away with that?" Saying this you snatched the scissors from my hand and cut off your tresses right up to your neck. Uncle was shocked. He exclaimed, "What is this!" You told him calmly, "I feel hot." He just smiled a little and accepted your explanation. He asked no questions, did not scold you, just took the scissors and trimmed your hair evenly. He was *your* uncle after all.'

Sarala laughed, 'You and your brains! Do you think that was me forgiving you? Not at all. That day I tricked you more than you tricked me. Tell me if that isn't true.'

'Absolutely. I could all but weep to see you shorn of your tresses. The next day I could hardly face you for shame. I just sat quietly in my study. You entered and, holding me by the hand, dragged me out to work in the garden, as if nothing had happened. I recall another day: that time when in the month of Phalgun an untimely storm blew away the roof of the room where the paddy seed was spread; you came then and . . .'

'Stop, no need to say more, Aditda.' She sighed. 'Those days can never come back.' She rose hurriedly.

Aditya clutched her hand, 'No, don't go, don't go now, there will be a time to leave, and then . . .'

Getting agitated now, he said, 'A time to leave! Why? What crime has been committed! Jealousy! These ten years I faced the test of domesticity and now this is the result! Jealous of what! In that case I must erase the history of twenty-three years, ever since we met!'

'I cannot speak for all the twenty-three years, Aditda, but at the end of all these years is there no reason for someone to be envious? We must speak the truth. What is the point in deceiving ourselves? Let there be nothing unclear between us.'

Aditya sat still for a while; then said, 'There is nothing unclear any more. In my heart I realize life means nothing without you. He whom I got you from in life's first season, He is the only one who can snatch you away from me.'

'Don't say such things, Aditda, don't increase our grief. Let me think calmly.'

'Thoughts cannot carry us to the past. When we two began life on Uncle's lap we did so without thinking. Today can one use a weeding-tool to uproot those days? I don't know about you, but I at least don't have the capacity to do that.'

'I beg of you, don't make me any weaker. Don't make the road to salvation inaccessible.'

Aditya clasped Sarala's hands and declared, 'There can be no road to salvation, I shall not keep that path open. That I can say I love you so easily and so honestly today fills my heart with happiness. What had been a bud for twenty-three years has, with divine grace, blossomed now. I tell you, to crush that is cowardly, it is a crime.'

'Hush, hush, don't say any more! At least for tonight—forgive, forgive me.'

'Sori, I am the blessed receiver, to the last day of my life I shall be the one deserving your mercy. Why was I blind! Why didn't I recognize you, why did I marry someone else? You didn't; so many men desired you, they wanted to marry you, I know that for a fact.'

'Uncle had dedicated me to caring for his garden, otherwise maybe . . .'

'No, no, in the depths of your mind the truth shone and you were bound to it willingly. Why didn't you make me aware too? Why did we go our separate ways?'

'Let it be, let it be, who can you fight to deny what must be accepted! What is gained by struggling against shadows like this! Tomorrow in the daytime we will decide something.'

'All right, I shall be quiet. But in this moonlight I shall leave something with you that will speak for me.'

While working in the garden Aditya used to carry a small cloth bag fastened to his waist, to hold a few essential things. From that bag he now brought out a small broach made of five nagkeshor flowers, their petals flaring like serpents' hoods. He said, 'I know you love nagkeshor. Shall I fasten it on your sari, on your shoulder? I have the safety pin here.'

Sarala made no objection. Aditya took a long time to fasten the broach. Sarala stood up then; Aditya stood facing her, holding her hands and gazing at her face as if he were gazing at the moon. He said, 'You are wonderful, Sori, so wonderful!'

Sarala snatched away her hands and fled. Aditya did not follow her, he just stared at her retreating figure silently, for as long as he could. Then he sat down on the platform on the embankment. The servant came to say dinner was served.

Aditya replied, 'I shall not eat tonight.'

## 6

From the threshold of the room Romen asked, 'Boudi, did you ask for me?'

Neerja cleared her throat and said, 'Come.'

The room was dark. Through the open window the light of the full moon streamed in, falling on Neerja's face and on the laburnum poesy which Aditya had placed near the head of the bed. Everything else was in darkness. Leaning against the pillows, Neerja was half-sitting, half-supine, staring out of the window. There, beyond the orchid room could be seen the row of betel nut trees. A wind had arisen and the leaves swayed, the fragrance of mango buds wafted in as well. From afar came the sound of the tom-tom and singing from the coachmen's dwellings where they were engrossed in celebrating Holi. On the floor lay some milk cake and coloured powder, a present from the security guard. The whole house was silent, so that the patient's rest was not disturbed. But outside, from one tree to another two koels continued their exchanges, neither willing to let the other bird have the last call. Romen pulled up a stool near the bed. Neerja was silent for a while; she was trying to keep some control over her emotions, for she was afraid she would break down and start crying. Her lips trembled, her throat felt as if her pain was coiled in a knot there. She managed to reign in her feelings; two petals of the laburnum that had fallen were crushed in her grip. Then, without speaking, she handed Romen a letter. It was written by Aditya. It said:

> After all these years, today it became possible for you to question my integrity. I find it shameful to argue about this or to defend myself. In your present state of mind everything I say or do shall appear contrary to your sensibilities. That unreasonable torment will damage your health further every moment! It is better to keep my distance until you feel healthier. I know that you wish for me to send Sarala away. Maybe I shall have to do this. After some reflection, I realize there is no other way. Still, I would say this—my education and my progress owe a great deal to Sarala's uncle's charity; he had shown me the way to live life. The treasure of his affection, Sarala, is now destitute, helpless. If today we send her away it will be a sin. Even for your sake I cannot do this.
>
> After much thought I decided this: I will establish a new branch of our business, to make seeds of fruits and vegetables. In Maniktala we can get a house with grounds attached. I shall send Sarala to work there. I don't have sufficient money in hand to begin this project. I will have to mortgage the garden house to raise the money. Don't be angry at this proposal, this is my earnest request. Remember, Sarala's uncle loaned me funds without any interest for the garden; I heard he had to borrow some of it himself. Not just that, the resources we needed to begin our project—seeds, grafted trees, rare new plants, orchids, lawn mowers and other equipment—he donated without payment. If he had not given me this opportunity, I would have been a mere clerk, renting a house for thirty rupees a month, and I would not have the good fortune to wed you either. After my last conversation with you, the question that recurs in my mind is, have I been a refuge for Sarala or has she provided me a shelter? I forgot this simple truth, you reminded me. Now you must keep it in mind too. Never think Sarala is our dependent. I can never repay their debt, and nor can she ever cease to have claims upon me. That you do not have to see her again is what I shall try for now. But I understand now more than ever that my ties with her can never be broken. I cannot say today

all I wish to, my grief is beyond words. If you can realize what is implicit, you will know, or else for the first time my sorrow remains unexpressed to you.

Romen read the letter twice and fell into silence. Neerja said in anxious tones, 'Say something, Thakurpo!'

But Romen declined to answer.

Neerja fell upon the bed and hitting her head on the pillow repeatedly, said, 'I was wrong, I was wrong. But don't any of you see what made me insane!'

'What are you doing, Boudi! Be calm, you'll hurt yourself.'

'This broken body has caused me this misfortune, why feel for it? I suspected him—where did that suspicion come from? I can only suspect myself, my own disability. Where is that Neeru now whom he would sometimes call the florist, sometimes the goddess of the forest! Who has wrested away her grove now! Did I have just one name! When he would be late and I would wait up for him and watch over his food, he would call me Annapurna, the goddess of plenty. At dusk we would sit by the pool, and I would arrange jasmine flowers and paan on a silver plate, he would chuckle and call me the Betel Bearer. Those days he consulted me in all domestic affairs; he would call me his Home Secretary. I was like the overflowing river reaching out to the sea, my tributaries spread in all directions; but in one fatal moment the water from all my streams evaporated at once, leaving behind only the stony river bed.'

'Boudi, you will be well again, once more you will occupy your throne and you will rule in full power.'

'Don't give me false hope, Thakurpo! I've heard what the doctor says. That is why I cling on this household of so many happy days, with my miserable destitution.'

'Why do you need to, Boudi? So long you have poured yourself out to your domestic world. Can there be anything nobler than that? You received as much as you gave, how many women have got so much? If what the doctor says is true, if it is time to go, then what you have received in abundance, donate it freely. You spent so many days here in such honour, why must you trivialize this honour now, if you have only a short time left with us? Act such that your last days in this house attain new glory.'

'My heart breaks, Thakurpo, my heart breaks! I could have left all these years of happiness behind me and gone smiling if I felt that I would be missed fervently and loved even after death. But I can't help thinking: will there be no void anywhere where a small lamp may burn, even dimly, for me and our separation? Thoughts of this make me resist even death. That woman Sarala will possess everything completely, is this what Fate ordains?'

'I shall be honest, Boudi, but don't be angry. I fail to understand what you're saying. What you are unable to relish, can't you give away to one whom you have already given so much? Will your love be stained with this blame forever? The lamp of respect that you carried in your household is being smashed to bits by yourself. You will escape that agony forever but it will hurt us for all time to come. I beg you, don't let the generosity of your entire life dwindle to meanness in the last moment.'

Neerja wept in spasms. Romen sat quietly, not attempting to console her; when the tears were finished Neerja sat up in bed and spoke, 'I have one prayer, Thakurpo.'

'Instruct me, Boudi.'

'Listen to me. When the heart is swept away with tears, I gaze at Ramakrishna's picture there. Yet, his words fail to reach my heart. My mind is ugly, petty. In whatever way you can, find me the guru. Or else I will not be able to break these ties. My mind is trapped in attachment to the world in which I spent such joyful days. After I die I will be spending age after age weeping in the ethereal plane if I don't attain freedom from this attachment—save me from this, save me!'

'You know, Boudi, I am what is called a heretical creature in the scriptures. I don't believe in anything spiritual. Prabhas Mittir persuaded me to visit his guru once. Before I could get attached to him, I fled. The jail has a fixed term; but there's no end to a spiritual sentence.'

'Thakurpo, your mind is strong, you can never understand my peril. I know that the more I struggle the more I am sinking bottomless waters, I cannot control myself.'

'Boudi, listen to me. As long as you think somebody is set to capture your treasure, your heart will burn in agony. You won't have peace. But sit still and say, "I give it. What is most precious I give it to him whom I love most." Then the entire burden shall be lifted in a moment. Your heart will be filled with joy. You don't need a guru; say now, "I give, give all, keeping nothing, I give up everything I own, I am ready to depart unencumbered and in purity, not leaving behind any sorrowful bondage in this worldly life."'

'Ah, go on Thakurpo, repeat those words to me again and again. So long whatever I have done for him has given me great joy, and now because I cannot give any more, it hurts so much. I will give, give, give—give everything I have—no more delay now. Bring him here.'

'Not tonight, Boudi, take a few days to convince yourself. Strengthen your resolve.'

'No, no, I can't bear to hold back any more. From the time he said he would leave this house to stay in the Japanese room, this bed seems to be my funeral pyre. If he does not return now, this night will never end for me and I shall die of a broken heart. Call Sarala here too, I shall weed out this thorn from my heart; I shall not be afraid, that I can tell you for certain.'

'It is not the right time yet, Boudi, leave it for now.'

'I fear the passage of time. Call them now.'

Looking at the picture of Paramhansadeb, she said, folding her hands, 'Give me strength, give me strength, Lord, save this foolish, fallen woman. My grief has kept God from me, all acts of worship are ruined! Thakurpo, let me say something, don't stop me.'

'What?'

'Let me go to the prayer room just for ten minutes, I will be strong then, my fear will leave me.'

'All right, go then, I shall not stop you.'

'Ayah!'

'What, Khokhi?'

'Take me to the prayer room.'

'What! The doctor . . .'

'The doctor cannot keep death away from me; then, should he keep me away from the Lord?'

'Ayah, take her. Don't worry, it will only be for her good.'

Holding on to the ayah, Neerja left the room. Soon after, Aditya came in. He asked, 'What is this, where is Neeru?'

'She has gone to the prayer room. She will be back soon.'

'Prayer room! That's not close by. The doctor has specifically forbidden her to exert herself too much.'

'Don't heed that, Dada. This will work better than the doctor's medicine. She will be back after offering flowers and her salutations just once.'

When he had written that letter to Neerja, Aditya was not fully aware that the script that Destiny had written on the canvas of his life would be touched by the heat outside and suddenly burn so bright. At first he had decided to send Sarala away, and had come to the garden to tell her this—that there was no other way, they would have to separate. But when it was time to say it, his tongue had uttered the exact opposite. Afterwards he sat in the moonlit night, on the embankment, and said repeatedly to himself—the truth of life had been discovered late but that did not mean it could be denied. He was not at fault, so he had nothing to be ashamed of. It would be wrong to hide the truth. He would not hide it—come what may. This Aditya realized with certainty, that if, from his life and his work, he removed Sarala, then loneliness and apathy would destroy him—his work too would stop forever.

Now, as he waited for Neerja to return, he said to Romen, 'Romen, you know about us, I know that.'

'Yes, I do.'

'Today I shall settle everything, lift the screen.'

'You are not alone, Dada! You cannot just shrug the burden off your shoulders and be done with it. Boudi's feelings also have to be considered. The ties of life are complex.'

'I cannot let a lie stand between your Boudi and me. From childhood the relationship between Sarala and myself has carried no guilt, you understand that, don't you?'

'Certainly.'

'This simple relationship contained great love. We did not realize it then; but was that our fault?'

'Who says it was a fault?'

'If I hide this fact it will be the crime of hypocrisy. Instead, I will declare it boldly.'

'Why should you hide it, or even declare it loudly? What Boudidi has to know she has already discovered by herself. In a few days the knots of this dreadful sorrow will loosen themselves naturally. Don't tug at them needlessly. Listen to what Boudi wants to say, you will know how to give the appropriate answers without any effort.'

Seeing Neerja enter the room, Romen went out. Seeing Aditya, Neerja sank to the floor and laying her head at his feet, spoke in weeping tones, 'Forgive me, forgive me, I have sinned. After this long don't reject me, don't cast me away.'

Aditya helped her up with both hands and clasping her to his breast led her slowly to the bed and helped her lie down. 'Neeru, don't I understand your pain!' he said.

Neerja could not stem the flow of her tears. Aditya stroked her head gently. Neerja tugged at Aditya's hand and clutching it to her breast, she asked, 'Tell me honestly that you forgive me. If you aren't pleased I will not be happy, even after death.'

'You know, Neeru, at times there has been dissent between us, but has our mental harmony ever been shattered?'

'Before this you have never left the house. Why did you go now? What made you so cruel?'

'I was wrong, Neeru, you must condone this.'

'What unreasonable things you say. From you I get all my punishments, all my rewards. In hurtful resentment I tried to judge you, that is why I am in this state. I told Thakurpo to call Sarala, why isn't she here now?'

The prospect of having Sarala in the room struck a discordant note in Aditya's mind. He didn't want to face up to the situation regarding her at least for some time. So he said, 'It is late tonight, let it be for now.'

But Neerja spoke up, 'There, listen, I think they are waiting outside the door. Thakurpo, come in, both of you.'

Romen came in with Sarala. Neerja stood up from the bed. Sarala bent down to touch Neerja's feet. 'Come, sister, come to me,' said Neerja.

She took Sarala by the hand and seated her on the bed. She took out a jewellery case from under her pillow and taking out a pearl necklace, she put it around Sarala's neck. She said, 'I once wished that when I am burnt at the pyre this necklace would be around my neck. But this is better. You wear this for me, right to the end. On special days I have worn this necklace so many times, your Dada knows. If you wear it around your neck he will remember those days.'

'I am not worthy of this, Didi, why do you shame me!'

Neerja had figured that in this all-sacrificing act of charity Sarala too would play her part and raise some objections. But that her heartache in announcing this sacrifice would manifest so clearly in the act was not known fully even to herself. Aditya, on the other hand, sensed how the whole scene hurt Sarala; he said, 'Give me the necklace, Sarala! Its value to me is more than it can be to anybody else; I cannot give it to another person.'

Neerja exclaimed, 'My luck! After all this I still can't make you understand! Sarala, I heard there was talk of making you leave the garden. I will never allow that. I will bind you to everything I own in this earthly life; my giving you the necklace symbolizes this. Here, I hand you the binding chain, so I can die in peace.'

'You're making a mistake, Didi, it is better not to chain me, no good will come of it.'

'What kind of talk is this!'

'I shall speak the truth. Until now you could trust me. But now don't ever trust me, I tell you this in front of all of you here. What gifts Fate has cheated me of, I shall not acquire by cheating someone else. Here, I touch your feet and leave my salutations. I am going. The fault is not mine; it is His, the God to whom I prayed twice a day. This too ceases as of now.'

Uttering these words, Sarala left the room in haste. Aditya could not contain himself, and followed her out.

'Thakurpo, what is this that has happened, tell me, Thakurpo.'

'This is why I told you not to call them tonight, Boudi.'

'Why, I poured out my heart and donated all I have. Did he not realize this?'

'He did, without doubt. But he also realized that your heart held something back. Something was out of tune.'

'Nothing makes my heart pure! Even after so much grief! Who will make me pure? Oh, sanyasi, save me—please. Thakurpo, who is there for me, who will I go to?'

'I am here for you, Boudi. I will take responsibility for you. Now sleep.'

'How can I sleep! If he leaves the house again only death will have the power to put me to sleep.'

'He cannot leave; he does not wish to, nor will he be able to. Here, take some sleeping tablets, I want to see you asleep before I go.'

'Go, Thakurpo, you go, see where those two are and tell me. Or I shall go myself; let my body fall to bits if it will.'

'All right, all right, I am going.'

## 7

When she saw Aditya following her, Sarala said, 'Why have you come! it's not right for you to leave Didi alone. Go back. I will not let you get entangled with me like this.'

'Whether you will or not is hardly the point; my life is already entangled with yours. It may be good or it may be bad but I have no say in the matter.'

'We will discuss this later; go back now, and tend to the patient.'

'I want to open a new branch of the garden, I wanted to tell you …'

'Not today, please. Let me think over things for a day or two; I have no energy for thought now.'

Romen came and said, 'Go, Dada, give Boudi her medicine and help her sleep, don't delay. Don't let her talk in any circumstance. It is very late.'

After Aditya left Sarala asked Romen, 'Don't you have a meeting at Shraddhananda Park tomorrow?'

'We do.'

'Won't you be there?'

'I was supposed to. But this time I shan't be there.'

'Why?'

'What is the point in telling you all this?'

'People will criticize you, saying you're a coward.'

'Those who dislike me will certainly criticize me.'

'Then listen to me. I will release you. You must attend the meeting.'

'Make yourself a little more clear.'

'I will go to the meeting as well, with a flag in my hand.'

'I see.'

'The police may stop me, I'll accept that, but if you stop me I won't obey.'

'Well, I won't stop you.'

'It's a deal then?'

'A deal it is.'

'Both of us will go together then, at five in the evening.'

'Yes, we'll go; but these wicked people will not let us be together afterwards.'

Just then, Aditya joined them. Sarala asked, 'What, you came away so soon?'

'After saying a few words Neerja grew exhausted and fell asleep, so I slipped away slowly.'

Romen said, 'I have work, I have to go.'

Sarala smiled, saying, 'Keep the place ready, don't forget.'

'Don't worry—it's a known place,' saying which he went away.

## 8

Now Sarala stood up and said to Aditya, 'What you aren't supposed to say, don't tell me tonight, I beg of you.'

'I won't say anything, don't be afraid.'

'But I have to tell you something. Promise me you will do as I say.'

'If it is not impossible, I shall, you know that.'

'It's very clear to me that I should not stay here any longer. I would have been happy to tend to Didi, but it isn't my fate to do so. I have to go away—wait, let me finish. You heard the doctor say she doesn't have much longer. In this short time you must pluck away the thorn from her mind. At least for these few days don't let my shadow fall over her life.'

'If the shadow is cast from my mind over hers, what can I do?'

'No, don't belittle yourself, talking like that. Is your mind like the ordinary Bengali boy's, cloying and unstable like wet mud? Not at all, I know that.'

She took Aditya's hand and said, 'Keep this vow for me. Fill Didi's last days with your generosity and caring. Make her forget that I ever came into her life to shatter the vessel brimming with her good fortune.'

Aditya stood silent.

'Give me your word.'

'I will, but you must also promise me something, say you will.'

'The difference between us is that if I ask you to do something it is always possible, but when you ask for a promise, it may be something quite impossible for me to do.'

'No, it won't be.'

'All right, tell me.'

'The words I utter aloud reflect what I feel in my heart and that cannot be a crime. I will obey you and do what you want without fail, if I know for certain that one day you will fill my emptiness. Why are you silent?'

'I don't know, there may be all kinds of obstacles in our way.'

'Are there any obstacles in your mind? Tell me that first.'

'Why do you give me grief? Don't you know that there are some things which when uttered lose their lustre?'

'All right, I have got my answer. Now I shall leave for work.'

'And you won't look back now?'

'No, but I want to stamp the seal of this unexpressed promise, on your face.'

'What is simple need not be forced. Let it be for now.'

'All right, but let me ask something. Where will you live now?'

'Romenda has taken that responsibility.'

'Romen will give you refuge? Has that vagabond have anything to call his own?'

'Don't worry ... he will provide me with a good enough refuge. It's not his own, but there won't be any problems.'

'Will I know where you are?'

'Indeed you will, I promise you that. But you will not try to come and see me, promise me this.'

'Won't you feel worried?'

'If I am, nobody except my inner self will know.'

'All right, but will you say goodbye leaving my begging bowl entirely empty?'

Aditya's eyes brimmed over. Sarala drew near him and raised her face.

## 9

'Roshni!'

'What, Khokhi?'

'Why haven't I seen Sarala since yesterday?'

'What are you saying! Don't you know she's been sent to jail?'

'Why, what did she do?'

'She plotted with the guard and stole into the viceroy's wife's room.'

'To do what?'

'To steal the Queen's seal from the box in which it's kept—what a nerve!'

'And what would that achieve?'

'Listen to that! You can do anything with that seal. She could have sent the viceroy himself to the gallows. That seal runs the country.'

'And Thakurpo?'

'They found a tool to cut a hole through a wall in his turban, so he's been sentenced to rigorous imprisonment, and will be made to break stones for fifty years. Khokhi, let me ask you something. Before leaving the house Saraladidi gave me her saffron-coloured sari. She said, 'Give it to your son's wife.' My eyes filled with tears. I have given her so much grief. If I keep the sari do you think the police will catch me?'

'Don't you worry. But I want the newspaper; it's in the drawing room, go get it, hurry.'

Neerja read all about what had happened. She was surprised that Aditya had not told her this news. 'See her arrogance! That girl won by going to jail! If I were well, could I have not gone? I could go laughing to the gallows.'

'Roshni, did you see your Saraladidi's doing?' she said. 'In front of a crowd of commoners, a girl from a decent household ...'

The ayah said, 'I get gooseflesh thinking of that den of thieves and bandits she will have to live in! Shame, shame!'

'She has to show off in everything she does. No sense of decorum, whether she's in the garden or in jail. Arrogant even while she's being crushed.'

The ayah recalled the saffron-coloured sari.

'But Khokhi, Didimoni has a generous heart.'

This gave Neerja a severe jolt. She seemed to wake abruptly and said, 'You are right, Roshni, you are right. I had forgotten. If the body is ailing the mind ails too. I have become so mean. I am so ashamed, I feel like hitting myself. Sarala is a pure woman, she does not lie. You won't find another one like her. She is much better than I am. Quick, call our manager Ganesh.'

When the ayah left Neerja found a pencil and composed a letter. Ganesh came in. She asked him, 'Can you deliver this letter to Saraladidi in jail?'

Ganesh Ganguly took pride in being able to manage things. He said, 'I can. I will just need some money. But let me hear what have you written, Ma, because it will be checked by the police.'

Neerja read aloud, 'You have been noble. Now, when you are released from jail, you shall see my path has merged with yours.'

Ganesh remarked, 'That path business doesn't sound all right. I'll have to ask our lawyer to check it out.'

Ganesh went away. Neerja silently saluted Romen and said, 'Thakurpo, you are my guru.'

## 10

Aditya came into the room with a cup of medicine.

Neerja asked, 'What is this, now?'

Aditya answered, 'The doctor says you must have this every hour.'

'And is there no other person in the house to give me my medicine? You can keep a nurse for me during the day if you are so anxious.'

'In the pretext of taking care of you if I can get close to you, why should I let go of the opportunity?'

'Better if you take the opportunity to work in your garden. I lie here and with every day that passes the garden is going to weed.'

'Let it. Get well first, then we'll work together in the garden the way we used to.'

'I know, Sarala is away, you are alone and you don't feel like working anymore. What can be done? But don't run into losses because of that.'

'I am not thinking of losses, Neeru. You had made me forget that the garden is also my source of income. I was happy to work. Now I'm just not able to concentrate.'

'Why do you lament like this? You worked well until the other day. For a while if there is an obstacle don't get so agitated.'

'Shall I turn on the fan?'

'Don't overdo your bedside manners; it doesn't suit you, and it disturbs me all the more. If you just want to pass the time, you have your Horticulturists' Club.'

'I searched the garden for the colourful lilies that you love but could not find any. It didn't rain well this time, the plants don't have that lustre.'

'What are you going on about? Why don't you call Hola, I shall lie here and organize the garden. Are you saying because I am bedridden the garden shall be bedridden too! Listen to me. Uproot the withered seasonal flowers and tend the soil there. The room below the banisters has sacks full of mustard skins. Hola has the key.'

'Really? Hola never mentioned it at all.'

'Why should he? Haven't you insulted him enough? Just as a new sahib comes and ignores an old and experienced clerk.'

'If I wanted to speak the truth about Hola it would turn unpleasant.'

'All right, I will lie on my bed and supervise his work; you'll see the garden get back its glory in two days. Give me the map of the garden. And my garden diary. I will mark the spots with a pencil on the map.'

'I won't have a say in it?'

'No. Before I go I shall impress my personality on this garden. I tell you, I am not keeping any of those bottle palms bordering the road. I will plant a cluster of casuarinas trees there. Don't shake your head like that. Look at it after it's done. I shall not keep that lawn of yours either; I shall have a marble patio there.'

'Will the patio look right there? A bit like—nouveau riche.'

'Be quiet. It will look absolutely right there. You will say nothing. For a few days the garden shall be mine, only mine. Then I shall bestow my garden on you before I go. You thought my strength had left me, didn't you? I will show you what I can do. I need three more gardeners and about six labourers. You said I hadn't learnt to decorate the garden. Whether I can or not shall be proved to you before I go. You will have to remember this is my garden, my personality can never be separated from it.'

'Very well then, but what will I do meanwhile?'

'You can be in your shop; there's plenty of office-work for you there.'

'I am forbidden then to be at your side?'

'Yes, for I am no longer the one who is worth being occupied with always—now I can only remind you of someone else—what is the use of that?'

'Well, fine. When you are able to tolerate me, I shall come then. Today I have some wonderful white gondhoraj in the flower basket, let me put them on your bed. Don't mind me.' Saying this, Aditya rose.

Neerja caught his hand and pleaded, 'No, don't go, sit awhile.'

She pointed to a flower in the vase and said, 'Do you know the name of this flower?'

Aditya knew what answer would please her, so he replied, 'No, I don't know.'

'I know. Shall I tell you? Petunia. You think I know nothing, that I'm ignorant.'

Aditya laughed and said, 'You are my life partner; if you are ignorant then you are my equal in ignorance as well. The affair of ignorance in our lives is divided equally in two.'

'That affair for me is fated to end now. That guard there chopping tobacco, he will be there in the porch, but after a few days I shall not be here. That cowcart that's returning after delivering its load of coal, its journey will carry on every day, but my heart will not carry on.'

She suddenly gripped Aditya's hand and said, 'Won't I really be here? Not in any way? Tell me, you have read so many books, tell me honestly.'

'The wisdom of the authors I have read is the same as my own. I reached a standstill in my mind on the question of death, and could not venture further.'

'Tell me, what do you think? Will I not exist in any way at all? Not even a tiny bit?'

'If it is possible that we exist now, then our existence later is also possible.'

'Definitely possible. That garden is possible and I won't be possible—that cannot be, never. In the twilight hour, when the crows return to their nests, the branches of the betel-nut tree will sway in the breeze, even as I see them doing now. Think then that I am there, I am there occupying the entire garden. Think, as the wind lifts your hair, those are my fingers that caress your face. Tell me, will you remember?'

Aditya had to say, 'Yes, I will remember.'

But he could not say it in a tone that was convincing.

Neerja caught the forced note in his voice and grew restless, 'The people who write your books are hardly wise, they know nothing. I know for certain, trust my words. I *will* exist, I will exist here, I will be by your side, I can see that clearly. I tell you, give you my word before going, I shall take care of your trees and plants better than I used to earlier. You won't need anybody else. Not any one.'

All this while Neerja was lying on the bed but now she sat up and propped herself against the pillow, saying, 'Have mercy on me, have mercy. Recall how much I love you and have mercy. The loving place you gave me in your home, keep me there always. In every season as our flowers bloom, put them in my hands in your mind. I will not be able to stay if you are cruel. If you wrest my garden away I shall wander unfulfilled in the void and never find rest.' Tears flowed down Neerja's cheeks.

Aditya rose from the stool and sat on the bed. He held Neerja's head to his chest and stroked her hair gently. He said, 'Neeru, don't wreck your body.'

'Let my body go. I just want you with everything that is here. Listen to me, let me say something, don't be angry.'

Saying this her voice choked. Calming herself a little she spoke, 'I have wronged Sarala. I touch your feet and promise, I will not do any more wrong. Forgive me for what has happened. But love me, love me please, I will do whatever you want.'

'Your mind was ill, the same as your body, Neeru, which is why you were tormenting yourself with wild fantasies.'

'Listen to me. Since last night I resolved over and over that when we meet this time, with a pure heart I would embrace her like a sister. Help me fulfil this last vow of mine. Tell me that I shall not be deprived of your love, and then I shall leave my own love here for everybody else.'

Instead of replying, Aditya kissed her on the lips and on her forehead. Neerja's eyes closed slowly. After some time she asked, 'When will Sarala be released? I am counting the days. I am afraid of dying before that; what if I cannot tell her this before going, that today my mind is pure? Turn on the light now. Read to me from Akshay Boral's *Esha*.'

She took out the book from under her pillow. Aditya read aloud.

Listening to him read, she was dozing off when the ayah came in and said, 'There's a letter.' Neerja awoke with a start. Her heart pounded. A friend had written to Aditya saying that due to lack of space in the jail, some prisoners would be released before their term ended; Sarala was among them. Aditya's heart leaped in joy. With great effort he supressed his ecstasy. Neerja asked, 'Whose letter is it, what news?'

In case his voice trembled while reading out loud, he handed the letter to Neerja. She glanced at Aditya's face. He was silent but there was no need for words—she read his mind in his silence. Neerja too could not speak for a while. Then she forced herself to say resolutely, 'Then there's not much time left. She will be here today—bring her to me.'

'What! What happened! Neeru! Ayah! Is the doctor here?'

'He is in the outer room.'

'Get him immediately. Here, doctor. She was talking quite easily just now, and then she fainted suddenly.'

The doctor felt Neerja's pulse and did not say anything.

A while later Neerja opened her eyes and said, 'Doctor, you must save me. I cannot go without seeing Sarala. That would not be right. I want to bless her. Give her my final blessings.'

Again, her eyes closed. But her fists were clenched; she muttered, 'Thakurpo, I will keep my word, I will not die a miser.'

Sometimes her consciousness faded and the world turned hazy, but then, like a dying earthen lamp, the flame of life flared up again. She kept asking her husband, 'When will Sarala be here?'

From time to time she called out, 'Roshni!'

'What, Khokhi?'

'Call Thakurpo right now.'

Sometimes she spoke to herself, 'What will happen to me, Thakurpo! I will give, give, give, give my all.'

It was nine at night. In the corner of Neerja's room flickered the dim light from a candle. The breeze carried the fragrance of dolon champa from the garden. Through the open window could be seen the outline of the trees plunged in darkness, and above them, in the sky, the constellation of Orion. Thinking that Neerja was asleep, Aditya left Sarala standing at the door and slowly approached her bed.

He saw her lips moving. As if she were praying silently. Between consciousness and unconsciousness, her face was strained. Aditya bent to whisper in her ear, 'Sarala is here.'

Opening her eyes slowly, Neerja said, 'You go.' Aditya obeyed. Then she called out, 'Thakurpo'—but there was no response.

As soon as Sarala touched her feet in salutation, Neerja's body seemed to vibrate, as if electrified. Her feet retreated swiftly. In broken tones she cried, 'I cannot—I cannot, I won't be able to give.'

As she uttered these words, an unnatural power seemed to grip her body. Her eyes dilated and blazed. She gripped Sarala's hand, her voice grew shrill; she screamed, 'You will have no place here, you witch, no place! I will stay, stay, stay!'

Suddenly the loose chemise-clad pale, shrivelled figure left the bed and stood up erect. In a strange voice she said, 'Run, run, run away now, while you can! Otherwise every day of your life I will drive a stake through your heart—I will drain your blood away!'

Saying this she collapsed on the floor.

Hearing her voice Aditya came running into the room. Having spent all her life force, Neerja had breathed her last by then.

# GLOSSARY

| | |
|---|---|
| **Aparajita** | A common creeper with blue flowers. |
| **Asoka** | A tree with red flowers. In the Ramayana, Sita was held captive by Ravana in an asoka grove. |
| **Babu** | Respectful term of address for male head of the family. |
| **Basanti** | A tree bearing light orange blossoms. |
| **Batabi** | The shaddock. |
| **Beedi** | A kind of cheap cigarette rolled up in a tobacco-leaf. |
| **Bokul** | Large evergreen tree with sweet scented flowers. |
| **Boudi/Boudidi** | An elder brother's wife, also term of respect for the mistress of the household. |
| **Britrashur** | A demon who was slain by Indra and is the symbol of darkness. |
| **Chalta** | A tree bearing edible acrid fruit. |
| **Dada** | Elder brother, also respectful address. |
| **Didi** | Elder sister. |
| **Didimoni** | Respectful address for younger female member of the family. |
| **Dolon champa** | Tree of the magnolia family, with pretty champak flowers. |
| **Duhshashan** | Kaurava prince, Duryodhan's brother, who tried to strip Draupadi naked in the royal court in the Mahabharata |
| **Gondhoraj** | The gardenia, a fragrant white flower. |
| **Indra** | The king of the gods. |
| **Jarul** | Oak-like tree whose timber is used to make furniture. |
| **Kalidasa** | One of India's greatest poets and dramatists, who lived between the fourth and the fifth century AD and wrote in Sanskrit. |
| **Kamini** | A variety of sweet scented white flower. |
| **Khokhi** | Equivalent of 'my girl', endearing term for a daughter or little girl. |
| **Makardhvaj** | Medicinal sublimate of mercury, sulphur and gold. |
| **Mashi** | Mother's sister, respectful address for an older woman. |
| **Muchkundo** | A variety of champak flower. |
| **Nagkeshor** | A local flowering plant. |
| **Neem** | The margosa tree. |
| **Paan** | Betel leaves prepared with lime, catechu etc. |
| **Prajapati** | Brahma, the creator and protector of all living creatures. |
| **Rajanigandha** | The tuberose. |
| **Rama** | The seventh incarnation of Vishnu, the hero of the Ramayana. |
| **Ramakrishna Paramhansa** | A mystic saint and seer from Bengal, who lived in the nineteenth century. |
| **Sanyasi** | An ascetic. |

| | |
|---|---|
| **Shubhodrishti** | Auspicious look exchanged between bride and bridegroom during the wedding ceremony. |
| **Thakurpo** | Husband's younger brother. |
| **Togor** | A kind of larger white flower. |
| **Toka** | A large straw hat to protect the head from the sun, generally used by farmers. |

# Four Chapters
## (Char Adhyay)

*Translated by Sunanda Krishnamurty*

# Prologue

Ela found self-expression first through revolt. Her mother Mayamoyee was neurotic, guided by neither reason nor discretion. Her unrestrained temper distressed her family; her suspicions were unfounded, and her punishments unjustified. Whenever Ela pleaded innocence, she would snap at her saying, 'You are lying.' Yet, Ela's truthfulness was like an addiction, so she was punished most severely. So Ela began intolerant towards all forms of injustice. Her mother felt that it offended the norms of femininity.

It was clear to Ela from her childhood that oppression thrived on weakness. There were many relatives in their house who were dependent for food and shelter. They were confined within the narrow boundaries drawn by favours and repression, and because of them the family environment was vitiated and her mother's tyranny went unchallenged. In reaction to this unhealthy environment Ela developed an irrepressible desire to be free.

Ela's father Naresh Dasgupta had a degree in psychology from an English university. He had a sharp, analytical and scientific mind, and was well known as a professor. He chose to work in a private provincial college because it was his birthplace, and also because he had neither the desire nor the skill necessary for material advancement. He was too trusting and his misplaced trust harmed him; yet he did not change. Those who manage to get favours easily or by cheating are the cruellest in their ingratitude. Naresh accepted it as an important feature of human psychology; he did not complain. But his wife never forgave him his lack of practical sense, and made spiteful remarks all the time. Even when the reason for her complaint was well in the past, she could not forget it, and her biting comments did not allow the hurt to heal. Since Ela saw her father being cheated repeatedly because of his trusting and kind nature, her love for him was mingled with compassion, like a mother's love for her foolish son. Her mother's sharp jibes, that she was more intelligent and sensible than her husband, hurt Ela most. Ela saw her father being humiliated by her mother under various pretexts, and at night tears of helpless anger soaked her pillow. Yet she felt that her father's excessive patience was wrong, and in her heart she could not help holding him culpable.

Once, in extreme distress she said to her father, 'It is wrong to tolerate so much injustice so quietly.'

Naresh replied, 'Protesting against someone's nature is like trying to cool a hot iron by stroking it. It might be an act of bravery, but there is no comfort in it.'

'There is even less comfort in keeping quiet,' she retorted and left quickly.

Ela observed that those who flattered her mother conspired and caused cruel injustice to the innocent. She couldn't bear it and brought proofs of innocence to the arbitrator, her mother. But authority in its conceit regards irrefutable logic as impertinence, and cannot tolerate it. It doesn't push the boat of justice forward but instead overturns it.

Ela was also disturbed by her mother's mania for 'purity'. Ela had once spread out a mat for a Muslim guest to sit on; her mother threw away the mat when he left. Had she spread a carpet, it would have been acceptable! Ela had a logical mind, she couldn't help arguing. She asked her father, 'This obsession with purity—whose touch pollutes, and all this fuss about food and bath—why does it take hold of women especially? It is heartless; it is following something blindly, like a machine.' Her psychologist father replied, 'For thousands of years, women's minds have been shackled; they have been rewarded for accepting, and not questioning. So the more blindly they accept, the more important seems the act of acceptance. Some men too have the same mindset.' Ela couldn't help asking her mother about the uselessness of rituals, but each time she was rebuked. These rebukes pushed her towards disobedience.

Naresh realized that the conflict within the family was taking its toll on his daughter's health, and it hurt him deeply. One day Ela came to him, terribly distressed by a particular injustice and said, 'Father, send me to a boarding school in Kolkata.' The suggestion was sad for both of them, yet he understood her, and despite strong opposition from his wife, he sent Ela away. He immersed himself in his studies and in his teaching, amidst his unsympathetic family.

Her mother said, 'If you wish to turn your daughter into a memsahib by sending her to the city, by all means do so, but your spoilt daughter will have a very difficult time in her in-laws's house after marriage. Don't blame *me* then.' Detecting a trait of independence in her daughter, she expressed this worry again and again. She was sure that Ela would be a source of great trouble to her future mother-in-law, and she expressed at great length her pity for that imaginary woman. From all this the daughter was convinced that women must prepare for marriage by crippling their self-esteem and by numbing their sense of right and wrong.

When Ela completed her matriculation and joined college, her mother died. Once in a while Naresh tried to persuade her to consider proposals of marriage. Ela was beautiful, and there was no shortage of suitors, but aversion to marriage had taken a deep root in her. Ela got through all her examinations, and her father passed away leaving her unmarried.

Naresh had brought up his younger brother Suresh, and had paid for his education. To send his brother to England to study for two years, he had to borrow money from the moneylenders, and also face his wife's anger. Suresh was now a high-ranking officer in the postal department, and he earnestly accepted Ela's responsibility.

Suresh's wife's name was Madhavi. In her family, girls were allowed a moderate level of education. After returning from England, her husband obtained an important position, travelled to distant places, and socialized with many outsiders. With practice, she got used to observing the customs and manners of foreigners at parties and gatherings. Even in the British Club, she could manage to cover up for her imperfect English by laughing, sometimes without reason.

Around this time, when Suresh was posted in a large provincial town, Ela came to live with them. Her uncle was proud of her beauty, her personality and learning. He was keen to present Ela to his superiors, colleagues, and to his Indian and foreign acquaintances. Ela's feminine instinct told her that the result would not be good. Madhavi, pretending to feel relieved that Ela could take over some of her social responsibilities, kept saying, 'What a relief—I am neither intelligent, nor educated; why burden me with English-style socializing?' Sensing her aunt's resentment, Ela built a wall of seclusion around herself. She took the responsibility of teaching Suresh's daughter Surama with excessive zeal, and used her spare time to write her dissertation. The subject was a comparative study of Bengali *Mangalkavya* and the verses of Chaucer. Suresh was very proud and he told everyone about it. Madhavi commented that this was going too far.

She asked her husband, 'Why did you ask Ela to teach Surama, what is wrong with Adhar as a teacher? Say what you will, I . . .'

Suresh was surprised: 'What are you saying! Can there be any comparison between Ela and Adhar?'

'Passing examinations by memorizing a few notebooks does not make one learned.' Saying this Madhavi turned away and left the room.

She could not bring herself to talk about one particular matter to her husband: 'Surama has crossed thirteen, and soon we must search far and wide for a suitable match for her; but if Ela is near her—young men are fascinated by pale light skin—what do they know of beauty?' She sighed and decided that it was no use saying this to her husband, men have no sense.

Then she set out in earnest to get Ela married as soon as possible. She didn't have to make much of an effort as eligible young men turned up voluntarily: extremely desirable parties, whom Madhavi was tempted to secure for her own daughter. Yet Ela repeatedly turned them away.

Suresh was concerned about the stubborn and unreasonable behaviour of his niece, and his wife was extremely displeased. She believed that for a Bengali girl of marriageable age, it was an offence to spurn eligible men. She worried about the pitfalls common to the young, and felt overwhelmed by her responsibility. It was clear to Ela that she was about to cause a conflict between her uncle's love for her and his relationship with his family.

Then Indranath came to this town. The students followed him around as though he were an emperor. He had an unusually strong personality, and was well known for his scholarship. Suresh invited him home. Although Ela didn't know him, she took the opportunity to ask him, 'Could you find some work for me in your organization?' The request was not surprising, but he was struck by her spiritedness. He replied, 'Recently a new school for girls has opened in Kolkata called the Narayani High School. I can offer you the principal's position. Are you prepared to accept it?'

'If you have faith in me, I am ready to accept it.'

Indranath's bright gaze was on Ela, and he said, 'I am a good judge of character, I placed my faith in you the moment I met you. I felt that you are the herald of a new age.'

Ela felt a tremor in her heart at the unexpected words of Indranath. She said, 'You make me apprehensive. Please don't overestimate me. If I try too hard to be worthy of your esteem, it would break me. I will follow your ideals to the best of my ability, but I can't pretend to be what I'm not.'

Indranath replied, 'You must promise never to get caught in family ties. You belong to the country, not to your community.'

Ela raised her head and replied, 'I promise.'

As Ela was leaving, her uncle intervened, 'I won't bring up the topic of your marriage again. Please stay with us. Why don't you start a class here and give lessons to the girls in the neighbourhood?'

Annoyed at the imprudence of her soft-hearted husband, Ela's aunt commented, 'She is an adult, and it is good that she wants to be responsible for herself. Why do you oppose it? No matter what you say, I can't be concerned with her any longer.'

Ela said firmly, 'I have found work, and I intend to take it up.' She left home to begin her work.

Since then five years have passed, the story has progressed quite far.

# 1

Scene: A tea shop. In a small room next to it some school and college textbooks—many of them second hand—were kept for sale. There were also English translations of modern European stories and plays. Young men of limited means browse through them but didn't buy any. The shopkeeper didn't mind. The owner—Kanai Gupta—was a sub-inspector once and now he was a pensioner of the police department.

The main road was in front, and a lane was on the left. A part of the room was separated by a frayed jute curtain for those who wanted their tea in privacy. Today there were special arrangements in that section of the room. The lack of chairs was compensated by packing boxes labelled 'Darjeeling Tea Company'. The crockery was unmatched. Some were of blue enamel, some, of white China. A bouquet of flowers was placed in a broken-handled milk jug. It was almost three in the afternoon. The young men had invited Elalata at two-thirty because the shop was empty at that hour. They had said that she must not be late even by a minute. The tea rush started from four-thirty. Ela was on time, but there was no sign of the young men. Sitting there alone she was wondering whether she had mistaken the date, when she was startled to see Indranath entering. One certainly did not expect to see him in such a place.

Indranath had spent many years in Europe, and had received special recognition in science. He had earned the right to a prestigious post and had recommendations from several European professors who praised his work to the skies. While in Europe, he had met a corrupt Indian politician, and after returning to India he was hindered at his work by that man. Ultimately, on the recommendation of a famous British scientist he did get a teaching post, but under an incompetent boss. Incompetence is associated with jealousy, so his attempts at scientific research were hampered at every step by his boss. Finally he was transferred to an institute which had no laboratory. Indranath realized that he could not pursue his highest goal in this country. Nor could he accept the misery of just repetitive teaching without the scope of advanced research that would end in retirement on a small pension. He knew that his ability would have been recognized in any other country.

He started giving French and German lessons, and also started coaching college students in geology and botany. Slowly and invisibly, from this small group, the complex roots of a covert ideology spread out far.

Indranath asked, 'Ela, how come you are here?'

'Since you have forbidden them to come to my house, the boys have invited me here.'

'I heard about it, and sent them away on an errand. I have come to apologize on their behalf, and also to pay the bill.'

'Why did you spoil the party?'

'To suppress the talk about your sympathy for the boys. Tomorrow you will see that I have sent an article to the newspaper in your name.'

'Have you written it? Your writing style will not allow it to pass as another's. Nobody will believe that it isn't genuine.'

'It is written as though left-handed, unpolished; doesn't indicate much intelligence but contains good advice.'

'Such as?'

'You have written that the misguided young men are ruining the country. You have appealed to the women of Bengal to bring them back to sanity. Since they won't hear rebukes from far, the women must join at the centre of their gatherings; no matter if it comes to the notice of the authorities. You have said that women are mothers; if women have to sacrifice themselves to save the young men, it would be worthwhile. I have soaked the article with maternal sentiments; it will bring tears to the readers' eyes. If you were a man, you might have received the title of "Raibahadur" on the strength of this article.'

'I can't deny that those words could have been mine. I am fond of these reckless young men; where would one find the likes of them? I was in college with them. In the beginning they wrote silly things about me on the blackboard. They would shout "small cardamom" from the back, and then innocently stare at the sky. My friend Indrani was in the final year, and they referred to her as "large cardamom". She was rather large, and her skin was dark. Many of the girls were upset but I used to take the boys' side. I knew that unfamiliarity led to this silly or sometimes even ugly behaviour, but it was not natural to them. Familiarity brought an easy note. "Small cardamom" became "Eladi". Sometimes there was a touch of romance, and why not? I never worried about it. I know from my own experience that it is easy to get along with young men, unless women knowingly or unknowingly try to make a conquest of them. Then I saw that the best of these young men, those who are not mean or vulgar, who hold women in respect as is worthy of men . . .'

'You mean those who are unlike the young men of Kolkata whose humour has turned vulgar?'

'Yes, they are the ones who desperately run after the messenger of death. They are simple-minded, like me. When they are determined to die, I don't wish to live secure in a corner of my room. But sir, I must speak out the truth—what was once our purpose is gradually becoming an addiction. Our method of work is erratic and doesn't stand up to reason. I don't like it. These young men are being sacrificed to a blind faith! It breaks my heart.'

'Your distress is also the prelude to the battle of Kurukshetra in Mahabharata. Arjuna too was mortified. Initially, when I was studying medicine, I almost fainted with disgust when I had to dissect a dead body. That disgust is itself disgusting. To attain power, one must learn to be merciless; forgiveness might come later, in the end. You people say that women are mothers by their very nature, but that is not something to be proud of. Nature has designed motherhood, even animals can be mothers. What is much more important is that women are the embodiment of energy, and you must prove it by overcoming mushy compassion, and reaching the firm ground of power. Bestow energy to the men.'

'You are distracting us by these big words. You are claiming much more for us than what we are. It is too much.'

'A strong claim is realized. You will become what we believe you to be. You too must believe in us so that ours becomes a true endeavour.'

'I like to provoke you to talk, but this isn't the time for it. I would like to say something.'

'Not here; let us go to the room at the back.'

They entered a darkish room with drawn curtains. It had an old table, two benches, and a large map of India on the wall.

Ela said, 'What you are doing is wrong. I can't help saying this.'

Ela alone could talk this way to Indranath. Yet, even for her it wasn't easy. Hence her voice was unnaturally forceful.

It was not enough to say that Indranath was handsome; he had a hard attractiveness: as though thunder was tied up in his innermost self, one could not hear its roar, yet sometimes its harsh light burst out. His expression was refined and polite, like a well-sharpened knife. He did not hesitate to say harsh words, but he said it with a smile; he never raised his voice in anger but instead expressed it through a smile. He took just enough care of his appearance to maintain his dignity but no more. His hair was close-cropped and it looked neat without requiring much care, and his brown skin had a tinge of red. He had a broad forehead, sharply intelligent eyes and lips that indicated determination and the pride of authority. He could make extraordinary demands that were hard to meet, and yet he knew that they could not be easily ignored. Some knew that his intelligence was extraordinary; some believed that he had superhuman powers. Some had boundless respect for him; some had unreasonable fear.

Indranath asked with a smile, 'What wrong have I done?'

'You have ordered Uma to get married, even though she doesn't wish to.'

'Who says that she doesn't?'

'She says so herself.'

'Perhaps she doesn't really know, or doesn't speak the truth.'

'You know that she took a vow to stay single.'

'It was the truth then but not now. Truth can be created by words. She would have broken the vow herself. By asking her to break it I have saved her from guilt.'

'Only she is responsible for her promises, and for the guilt of breaking them. Why not let her take that responsibility?'

'It would have disrupted our organization; it would have harmed all of us.'

'But she is distraught and weeping.'

'Then I must not let it continue, I must organize the wedding by tomorrow or the day after.'

'What of the rest of her life, beyond tomorrow or the day after?'

'When women weep before their wedding, it is like the roar of thunder at dawn, it doesn't last.'

'You are heartless.'

'God, who loves human beings, is also cruel; he is kinder to animals.'

'You know that Uma loves Sukumar.'

'That is why I want to keep them apart.'

'Is it a punishment for loving?'

'That has no meaning. One wouldn't punish someone for catching small pox but send him to the hospital to be treated.'

'Why not marry her to Sukumar?'

'Sukumar has done no wrong; there is hardly anyone of his calibre in our organization.'

'What if he himself wishes to marry Uma?'

'It is possible, and that is the reason for the hurry. It is easy for women to distract a high-minded man such as him. He can be persuaded by a few drops of tears to mistake common courtesy for indulgence. Does this upset you?'

'Why should I be upset? I have seen many instances when women quietly and expertly indulge men and the men bear the obligation. For the sake of truth one must be fair, and that is why women don't like me. What does Bhogilal, the man you have ordered Uma to marry, say about it?'

'That good soul is unencumbered by opinions. He holds all Bengali women to be God's wonderful creation. A doting nature like his must be taken out of the group, and marriage is the best method of disposing garbage.'

'Why have you brought men and women together in the organization then, in spite of the risk of such possibilities?'

'Because the work can't be done by the unmanly, the ascetics who have overcome the needs of the flesh, and have burnt all desire. Yet, when I find that someone of the group has been careless and set his own house on fire, I remove him. We have set the whole country aflame. The work can't be done by those whose minds are not stirred, nor can it be done by those who don't know how to extinguish fire.'

Ela was grave. After a while, with downcast eyes she said, 'In that case, please let me go.'

'Why do you wish to inflict such a loss on us?'

'Don't you know?'

'Who says that I don't? I noticed a touch of colour in your khadi clothes, and I knew that it reflected the touch of colour in your heart. I know whose footsteps you wait for. Last Friday, when I visited you, you were expecting someone else. I noticed that you took time to compose yourself. Don't feel embarrassed, there is nothing wrong.'

Ela blushed and remained quiet.

Indranath asked, 'You love someone, don't you? You are not made of stone. I know who he is. There is no cause for regret.'

'You said that one must do the work single-mindedly. There might be circumstances when it isn't possible.'

'May not be possible for everyone; but love won't divert you from your mission.'

'But . . .'

'There is no place for any doubt. We can't let you go.'

'I am not of any use in your work, and you know that.'

'We don't want any work from you, nor have I fully informed you about our work. When you apply the mark of sandalwood paste on the foreheads of these young men, it inspires them. Even you don't realize it fully. You wouldn't be as effective even if we employed you on a salary. We don't believe in renunciation. When money can help, we use it; when a woman can influence, we place her on a pedestal.'

'I don't wish to deceive you. I know that this love is overshadowing all other love.'

'Have no fear. Love as much as you wish. The immature address the country as "mother". The country is not a mother, it is *ardhanarishvara*—half man and half woman—its realization is in the union of man and woman. Don't weaken it by confining it in the cage of domesticity.'

'Yet you have asked Uma . . .'

'Uma! Kalu! They are incapable of facing the harsh and terrible side of love. Before it is too late I want them to marry, because conjugality marks the death of all endeavours. Let that be. I heard that the night before last a burglar entered your room.'

'Yes.'

'Did your training in Judo come handy?'

'I must have broken his wrist.'

'Your conscience didn't trouble you?'

'It would have, but I feared that he would dishonour me. Had he acknowledged defeat, I wouldn't have broken his wrist.'

'Did you recognize him?'

'I couldn't make out in the dark.'

'It was Anadi.'

'Our Anadi! But he is so young.'

'I sent him.'

'You sent him! Why did you?'

'It was a test for both him and you.'

'You are cruel.'

'I was waiting downstairs, and reset his wrist immediately. You consider yourself to be compassionate. I wanted you to realize that it is not natural when confronted with danger. The other day I asked you to shoot a goat cub, and you said that you could never do it. Your cousin, in a show of bravado, shot it. When the animal was hit on the leg and fell down, she pretended not to care and laughed aloud. It was a hysterical laugh; she didn't sleep that night. If you were faced with a tiger and were unafraid, you would not hesitate to kill it. We see that tiger clearly in our mind, and relinquish pity and love; otherwise I would loath myself as sentimental. Krishna had explained this to Arjuna. Do not be cruel, but be relentless in performing your duty. Do you follow me?'

'Yes.'

'In that case, I have a question: do you love Atin?'

Ela did not answer.

'If he ever betrays us, will you be able to kill him?'

'Since it is impossible for him to do so, it would be easy for me to say yes.'

'And if, by some chance it were possible?'

'I might have an answer for now, but do I know myself fully?'

'You must know yourself. You must think of all eventualities and be prepared.'

'I am convinced that you made a mistake in selecting me.'

'I am sure that it wasn't a mistake.'

'Sir, I entreat you to let go of Atin.'

'Who am I to let go of him? He is caught in the bond of his own resolution. He will always have doubts, it would seem distasteful to him, yet his self-esteem will take him till the end.'

'Do you never make mistakes in judging the character of a person?'

'I do. There are some whose mental make up consists of two opposing characteristics, yet both are real. They misjudge themselves.'

A deep voice from outside the room inquired, 'How are things?'

Indranath asked, 'Is it Kanai? Come in, come in.'

Kanai Gupta entered the room. He was short, fat, looked old, and had a week's growth of hair on his face. The front of his head was bald; he wore a dhoti and a chaddar, which had not been laundered, and he wore no shirt. His arms were short in proportion to his body, giving the appearance of being ever ready for work. His tea shop was really to provide sustenance to the members of the group.

Kanai said to Indranath in his normal hoarse voice, 'You are reputed to be a man of few words, like an ascetic. But Ela didi seems to have ruined that reputation.'

Indranath said with a smile, 'We endeavour to be silent, but exception proves the rule. This girl doesn't talk much, but she allows others to talk, offering invaluable hospitality to speech.'

'How can you say that Ela didi doesn't talk? With you she might be quiet, but elsewhere she is a flood of words. When I hear her voice, I leave my account books and listen from behind the partition. Now you must pay some attention to me. My voice might not be like Ela didi's, but what I have to say is important.'

Quickly Ela stood up to leave. Indranath said, 'Before you leave I must tell you that I often speak ill of you to others in the group. I have even said that a time might come when we will need to remove you without a trace. I have said that you are trying to make Atin break away from the group, leading to its further disintegration.'

'By saying this repeatedly you are making it the truth. But why? Who knows, perhaps I *am* a misfit here.'

'In spite of that I don't distrust you, yet I speak ill of you to them. The view is that you have no enemy. But three-fourths of your admirers, with their Bengali mentality are keen to believe ill of you. They have no integrity. I make a note of their names, filling many pages of my notebook!'

'They speak ill because they like to do so, not because they have a grudge against me.'

'You have heard of Ajatashatru; such people are *jatashatru*. People like them have, from the very beginning, hindered Bengal's development.'

Kanai interrupted, 'Enough for today, we can complete the discussion next time. Ela didi, if I have spoiled your tea party, please don't take it amiss. The time has come to close down my tea shop. I might have to open a barbershop a few hundred miles away. I have already prepared five barrels of Alakananda hair oil. You must give a certificate saying that after applying the oil, tying your hair has become a chore, and that even the ten-armed goddess Durga would find it difficult to manage such a long plait.'

Seeing that it was time to leave, Ela went to the door but turned around to say, 'Sir, I will remember your words and be prepared. When the time comes to remove me, I will silently delete myself.'

When Ela left, Indranath asked, 'Kanai, you seem disturbed.'

'The other day a few young men were preaching violence sitting at the table facing the road. I reported them to the police with evidence of sedition.'

'I hope you were not mistaken in your suspicion.'

'It is better to err by suspecting than to err by not suspecting. If they are fools, no one can save them, but if they are the enemy then no one can harm them. My report will only help. They were proposing a bloodbath of the evil administration loudly. I was balancing my accounts one evening when suddenly a young man wearing dirty torn clothes came in and whispered that he needed twenty-five rupees to go to Dinajpur. He mentioned our Mathur Uncle. I jumped up and screamed at him, "How dare you! I will call the police immediately." Had I more time I would have ended the farce by taking him to the police station. The young men of your group who were drinking tea in the next room didn't know what was at stake, and were angry with me. They tried to collect money for him, but between them they had only thirteen annas. Seeing my reaction the boy left quickly.'

'It appears that the smell of food has escaped through the hole in the lid and is attracting flies.'

'Undoubtedly. Send your boys away to distant places soon. Not one of them should appear to be unemployed. Each of them must have an ostensible means of livelihood.'

'They must. Have you thought of a way?'

'Yes, long back. I wasn't free to do anything, but I have thought and I have collected the means slowly. Madhav Kaviraj sells fever reducing pills, 75 per cent of which is quinine. I will buy them from him and change the label to malaria pills. Pratul Sen can carry a canvas bag and advertize it. Nibaran got a first in M.Sc. chemistry. He shouldn't feel embarrassed to take up protective amulets as a subject of research. By adding the names of a few new metals to the seven metals of the amulets he can work on the hitherto unknown connection between the ancient holy men and modern science. Jagabandhu can use Sanskrit verses and grammar to prove that Chanakya was born in Netrakona in Bengal. In fact my birthplace is in the same subdivision. Let there be a lot of discussion in literature on this, until we celebrate Chanakya's birth anniversary in my great grandfather's dilapidated house! Your Tarini Sanyal, a doctor from Campbell Medical College, can go round the neighbourhood asking for contribution for a temple of goddess Sheetala. The point is that your proud grenadiers must hide behind some useless occupations, no matter if some call them fools and others call them clever and worldly.'

'Listening to you I feel like taking up some business, if for no other reason than to learn the ways to bankruptcy and lessons in psychology.'

'The business you are engaged in is on the verge of bankruptcy for sure, if not today then tomorrow. People become bankrupt not because they don't understand, but because they just cannot reject the path of loss. It is a sublimely attractive death-wish. But now is no time to discuss that. Let me ask you something. Do you agree that it is rare to find a woman as beautiful as Ela?'

'Of course I do.'

'Then how do you dare to keep her amongst you?'

'Kanai, you should know me by now. One who is afraid of fire doesn't know how to use it. I don't wish to exclude fire from my work.'

'In other words you don't care if the work is spoilt.'

'The creator plays with fire. Creation isn't possible on the basis of assured result; great creation is inspired by uncertainty. I am not interested in cold clay dolls. That young man Atin has joined us, attracted by Ela, but he has in him the dynamite that can bring danger; that is why I am so interested in him.'

'My friend, we are just orderlies in your dangerous laboratory. If a gas explodes, if equipment shatters, then our lives too will be shattered. We are not strong-minded enough to boast about it.'

'Why don't you give notice and quit?'

'Because we covet the result, even if you don't. Your agents had once talked about the elixir of life. We poor people have got caught in the plot of your ruinous project in the hope of a definite outcome, not the mist of uncertainty. You look at it as a gambler, we as clear-sighted businessmen. Don't play a cruel trick by setting our account books on fire. Every penny in it is earned with our blood.'

'I don't have blind faith, nor think of victory or defeat. I lead a vast organization because I am best-suited to do so. Here victory as well as defeat is important. They had shut all the doors around me and had tried to prove that I was insignificant. I wish to prove my greatness even if it means death. So many worthy men have ignored death and joined us on hearing my call. Why have they? Because I know how to call. I know it and I will have it known, no matter what happens later. Once you seemed ordinary, I brought out the extraordinary in you. What more do I need?

An epic poem may end in the great cremation ground of defeat, but it still remains an epic. In this country, suppressed under slavery and lacking in humanity, an opportunity for a glorious death is also an opportunity.'

'You have brought an unimaginative, practical man like me into your frenzied dance floor. I can't fathom the mystery.'

'I have influence over you because I don't beg like a destitute. I have never beguiled or offered a reward to anyone. I beckon them to the unachievable, not for the outcome but to prove themselves. My nature is impersonal; I accept the inevitable calmly. I have studied history and seen how so many empires had climbed the height of greatness, then turned into dust. They had a debt which they did not redeem. I don't foolishly claim that this country will enjoy good fortune forever and have a permanent position of greatness in history in spite of all the reasons to the contrary just because it is mine. With my illusion-free scientific mind I accept that when the time comes, death is certain.'

'Then why . . .?'

'The wretched state of my country won't force me to bow my head, I am above all that, even when death is near I won't allow my spirit to fail.'

'What about us?'

'You are not children! Can you save a ship sinking in mid-ocean by weeping or chanting mantras or by appealing to God?'

'If we can't, what then?'

'You have knowingly and fearlessly raised the sail of that sinking ship in the face of storm. With a few like you, even while drowning we shall be victorious. You have flown the flag of victory on the mast of a country blindly prepared for ruin, without false hopes, without begging, without crying in disappointment. You haven't given up when the ship's deck is flooded. Giving up is cowardly. My work is done with the few of you. After that? Work for the sake of work, not for the result.'

'You have omitted something important.'

'What is that?'

'Are you so impersonal that you don't even bear any anger?'

'Against whom?'

'Against the British.'

'I loath a man who can't fight unless he drinks till his eyes are red. If one sets out on a mission in anger, one is likely to make mistakes.'

'Even so, when there is cause for anger, it is only natural to be angry.'

'I am familiar with Europe, and I know the British. They are the greatest of all the western races. They can strike, but they are restrained by shame from destroying totally. They are most afraid of answering to the best among them; they deceive both themselves and their superiors. I can't muster the anger required for full steam.'

'You are strange.'

'They could have broken our back for ever had they wished but they didn't. I salute their humanity. Ruling another country is eroding that humanity and ruining them. No other nation has such a heavy load of colonies, and it is spoiling their nature.'

'It is their lookout. But you are making your endeavour sound meaningless; I find that somewhat excessive.'

'You are wrong. I won't be unjust or impassioned, I won't shed tears addressing my country as "Mother"; yet I shall work, and there lies my strength.'

'How will you raise you hand against an enemy you don't hate?'

'With calm intellect, just as I would hit a stone lying on my way. The debate is not about whether or not they are good or evil. Theirs is a foreign rule which is eroding our self-esteem from within. In attempting to confound this unnatural state of affairs I acknowledge my humanity.'

'Yet you don't really expect success.'

'Even so, I won't insult my nature, although death might be the most likely outcome. On the face of probable defeat I must preserve my self-esteem by audaciously ignoring it. I believe this is our ultimate duty now.'

'Here comes the one who propagated a bloodbath. I'll go and offer him some tea and tell him clearly that he has been reported to the police. I hope the fools in your group don't lynch me!'

## 2

Scene: Ela was seated cross-legged in an armchair with a pillow supporting her head. She held a notebook with Deshabandhu's picture fixed on a clipboard on her lap, and she wrote in it with rapt attention. Although it was getting dark, she had not tied her hair. She wore a purple khadi sari—shabby home-wear—a couple of red bangles and a gold chain. She was slim, and her complexion was like ivory. Although she looked very young, her face showed the gravity of mature intelligence. In a corner of the room against a wall there was a narrow bed covered in green khadi. A flat-weave rug woven on the loom of Narayani School was spread on the floor. On one side stood a small desk with a blotting pad, an inkwell, pencils, pens and a brass flower vase with white fragrant flowers. An old photograph hung on the wall—yellow and faded. She thought of getting up and switching on the lights when Atindra pushed the curtains aside, entered the room like a gush of wind, and called, 'Eli!'

Ela was startled yet pleased. She said, 'Uncivil! How dare you enter without permission?'

Atin sat down on the floor at Ela's feet and said, 'Life is too short and the rules of social etiquette too long. The kings of ancient times had the longevity to observe those rules. In kaliyug time is at a premium.'

'I haven't changed yet.'

'Good. We shall blend well: you riding in a carriage and I a pedestrian doesn't hold with Manu's laws. Once I was a perfect gentleman, you removed that guise. Have you noticed my present garments?'

'The dictionary wouldn't define it as garment.'

'What is it then?'

'I can't find the right words; perhaps words can't describe it. That long crooked mark on your shirt, is it an advertisement of your own brand of stitching?'

'It shows that I accept my fate. I don't dare give this shirt for mending; after all, the tailor has some self-respect!'

'Why didn't you give it to me?'

'You have taken the responsibility of reforming the new age; how could I burden you with an old shirt?'

'Why must you wear it?'

'Out of the same need that makes a man tolerate his wife!'

'Meaning?'

'Meaning that there is no other.'

'What are you saying, Antu, you have no other shirt?'

'Since it is wrong to exaggerate, let me cut the story short. In his previous incarnation Atindra possessed numerous clothes of several varieties. Then the country was hit by floods. You said in your speech that in this tear-drenched disaster many lack the bare minimum clothes. Those who have clothes in surplus should be ashamed. You said it well. I smiled inwardly, although I didn't dare to laugh. I knew for sure that your box contained more clothes than necessary. But if women have fifty garments of fifty different colours, all are essential! That day the patriotic women were competing as to who could collect more clothes. I placed my box full of clothes at your feet; you clapped your hands in joy.'

'How was I to know that you would give away everything?'

'Why does it surprise you? Who has inspired me to have the strength to bear insurmountable loss? If our Ganesh Majumdar was collecting clothes instead of you, it would have made only a small dent in my box.'

'For shame, Antu, why didn't you tell me then?'

'Don't distress yourself, it isn't all that sad. I have dyed two shirts for daily use. I wear one and wash the other. Two more are put away for emergencies. Just in case one day I need to prove that I am a gentleman, those two shirts have the certificates of the tailor and the washerman.'

'Your looks bear the certificate from the creator, you don't need any witness.'

'Flatterer! It has always been the man's role to flatter the woman. You wish to change the roles?'

'Yes, I do. I wish to spread the word that women have more and more rights these days. They may now speak the truth about men. I find that in modern literature women are full of praise for themselves. They make themselves out as though they are goddesses, and pass off eulogies on themselves as literature. It is like their make-up, applied by themselves, not by God. I am ashamed of it. Antu, let us go to the living room.'

'There is room enough here; I am not an assembly all by myself.'

'All right. What is the important thing you wanted to say?'

'I have suddenly remembered two lines of a poem but can't remember where I read it, so I came to ask you.'

'That is important! Say the lines.'

'Think and tell me who wrote it.

'I looked into your eyes
And saw my undoing.'

'Surely not a famous poet.'

'Doesn't it sound familiar?'

'I find the hint of a familiar voice. What happened to the next line?'

'I had hoped that you would recall it.'

'If I hear from you once, I might recall.'

'Then listen:

In the glow of the setting sun
On that Chaitra evening
I looked into your eyes
And saw my undoing.

Ela touched Atin's head and said, 'What new lunacy is this?'

'My lunacy began on that Chaitra afternoon. Days that get lost before reaching the end take on a shadowy form and hover in the imagination. My meeting with you is in that bridal chamber of illusion. I have come to beckon you there. It will hinder your work.'

Ela dropped the clipboard and the notebook on the floor and said, 'Never mind my work. Shall I switch on the light?'

'No, don't. Light shows only the visible; let us turn instead to the lightless invisible. Almost five years ago I was on a steamer ferry crossing the river to Mokama. I was clinging on to my inheritance even then, although the dues were many. I was still given to niceties, both outwardly and inwardly, like the lingering cloud of a spent day. I was wearing a silk kurta, and had a neatly folded muga scarf on my shoulder. I was sitting all alone in a cane deckchair on the first class deck. It was fun to watch the pages of the discarded newspaper flying around, as though it were a haphazard dance of embodied hearsay. You were among the masses, a deck passenger. All of a sudden you appeared in front of me. I can still see your brown sari; the sari edge tied to your hair was swaying in the breeze. Making an effort at pretending to seem unabashed you asked me, "Why don't you wear khadi?" Do you remember?'

'Very clearly. You are able to verbalize the picture that is in your mind's eye, my picture is mute.'

'I will recount the events of that day. You must listen.'

'Of course I will. That day gave the indication of a new life for me; my mind wants to go back to it.'

'Your voice thrilled me. Its tone touched me like an unexpected light beam, as though a wonderful bird snatched away my everyday life. Had your impudence angered me, the ferry wouldn't have brought me to this strange mooring; I would have walked the usual path and lived a respectable life. But my mind was like a damp matchstick, the fire of anger didn't light. Since vanity is my main virtue, I thought that unless the girl liked me particularly, she wouldn't have come especially to rebuke me. Preaching khadi was just a ruse. Was I right?'

'I have said it so often: sitting in a corner of the deck I was looking at you for a long time. I didn't know if others noticed it. That was the most wonderful moment of eternal acquaintance. I wondered where you came from—a man of a different breed, not of ordinary dimensions; a thousand-petal lotus blooming in the moss. There and then I vowed to pull in that rare man not only to me but into our group.'

'It is my misfortune that your need in the singular got suppressed under the need in the plural.'

'Antu, there was no other way. Before she saw Draupadi, Kunti asked her sons to share whatever they had brought. Much before I knew you I had vowed to keep nothing for only myself. I am promised to my country.'

'You are going against your nature to keep your vow. If you could break it, truth would have been served. You are sacrificing for the group a need that is pure and comes from one's conscience and you will suffer for it.'

'Antu, my punishment is endless; it flogs me all the time. That wonderful good fortune which is beyond all endeavour was before my eyes, yet I could not accept it. Our hearts are united, yet I am like a widow and no woman should undergo my unbearable grief. I was confined within a barrier, but when I saw you I became eager to break away. I had never imagined such an upheaval was possible. It would be untrue to say that no one had touched my heart before, but by controlling my feelings I felt proud of my strength. Now I have no pride in overcoming my emotions, nor do I wish to. Don't go by what you see outwardly; look into my heart, I am defeated. You are my valiant hero, and I am your prisoner.'

'I too have lost to that prisoner. My defeat is not over; I am losing every battle every moment.'

'Antu, when I first saw you from a distance you appeared like a wonderful revelation. Until then I used to believe that my ticket for third-class travel was a shining example of modern aristocracy. Then you travelled second class on the train. Your coach pulled me towards it inexorably. I even thought of a trick. I thought that I would get into your coach moments before the train started and I would say that in my hurry I had made a mistake. In poetry, women go for trysts; perhaps poets feel sorry for them because they are bound by social rules. The haphazard wishes of their restless hearts hit against the walls of their inner dark chambers. Women don't like to admit to such thoughts; you have made me admit it.'

'Why did you?'

'I could offer you only that admission, nothing more.'

Atin suddenly gripped Ela's hands and asked, 'Why couldn't you? What stood in the way of your accepting me? Society? The difference in our castes?'

'For shame, don't entertain such ideas. The impediment is not from outside, it is internal.'

'You didn't love me enough?'

'Enough has no meaning, Antu. I had vowed to remain unmarried. Even otherwise it might not have been possible.'

'Why not?'

'Don't misunderstand me, Antu; I hesitate because I love you. I have nothing. I have little to offer you.'

'Speak plainly.'

'I have, often.'

'Say again, I want to finish saying all that we have to say to each other. After today I won't ask you again.'

Someone called from outside, 'Didimoni.'

'Is it Akhil? Come inside.'

Akhil was about sixteen or eighteen. He had a pleasant countenance, and a mischievous and obstinate expression. He had ruffled curly hair, a darkish complexion, bright and restless eyes. He wore khaki shorts, a short shirt of the same colour with the buttons opened, showing his chest; his pockets were bulging with useless items of property, and a knife with an ornate handle made of deer horn was in his breast pocket. He made models of boats and planes. Recently, in the ayurvedic garden of Mullick and Co., he had seen a wind-powered machine for pumping up water, and he was trying to copy that with biscuit tins and other discarded objects. He had cut his finger and had wound a piece of cloth around it. He took no notice when Ela inquired about his wound. Ela was distantly related to this orphan boy, and she tolerated a lot from him. Akhil had bought a small monkey from someone very cheaply. It stole food from the kitchen, and was a terrible nuisance in Ela's small household.

Akhil entered shyly and quickly touched Ela's feet. Ela knew that there was a motive behind this because showing respect wasn't natural to Akhil.

Ela asked, 'Aren't you going to touch the feet of your Antu dada?'

Akhil didn't reply but stood erect with his back to Atin. Atin laughed at that. He patted Akhil on the back and said, 'Bravo! If you must bow, bow to one god. I too bow to that one and only goddess! Please don't fight over her favour; there is enough to go round.'

Ela asked Akhil, 'Is there anything in particular that you want to tell me?'

'My mother's death anniversary is tomorrow.'

'Oh yes, I forgot. You wish to call anyone for the ceremony?'

'No one.'

'Then?'

'I want three days off from studies.'

'Why do you need the holidays?'

'I will make a rabbit cage.'

'You don't have a single rabbit, who will you make it for?'

Atin laughed and said, 'One can imagine the rabbit, but the important thing is to make the cage. Human beings are impermanent, but many—from Manu to his present-day incarnations—have tried to build strong and permanent cages for them. They enjoy the task.'

'All right, Akhil, you may have your holiday.'

Akhil ran out without another word.

Atin said, 'I couldn't tame him. I had an old wristwatch, one of an assortment of objects from earlier days. Today's youngsters would greatly value it. I offered him the watch, but he shook his head and left. This shows that we aren't on good terms, a sign of a likely Antu–Akhil riot.'

'You are good at making friends with youngsters, how come you failed with this one?'

'Because a third party is in the middle, otherwise we would have been close pals. Never mind all that. Tell me, what was your excuse, why did you keep yourself away from me?'

'Why do you forget that I am older than you?'

'Because I remember that you are twenty-eight and I am twenty-eight plus a few months. It is easy to prove because the document, unlike archaeological finds, isn't written in the Brahmi script on a copperplate.'

'But my twenty-eight has left yours far behind. In yours all the lamps of youth still burn. Your window is still open to those who are yet to come, to those who are yet unexpected.'

'Eli, you don't understand because you don't want to. You are trying to fool yourself and me with arguments because you have taken a vow against truth to your group. Please don't say that in my life the future one, the unexpected one, is far away. She has come, she is you. Yet she is unattainable. Should my window remain open for her forever? Through that void my voice will cry out in longing, "I want you". Will it never be answered?'

'Ungrateful! How can you say that it is unanswered? I want you; I want you above everything in this world. But we didn't meet at the auspicious moment which could have united us. Yet, it is fortunate that we didn't.'

'Why so? What harm could come of it?'

'I would have been blessed, but that is of little importance. You are not like others, you are special. I could see that light in you because I kept away. I dare not think of binding you to someone ordinary like me. I would not confine you to the insignificant pursuits of my little world! How can I explain how much I look up to you? Perhaps there are women who wouldn't hesitate to bury even a man like you under the nitty-gritty of life—that is all that women have. I know of the tragic consequences. I have seen how the embrace of the creeper stunts the growth of the tree; these women think that the embrace is enough.'

'Only the receiver knows what is enough.'

'I don't wish to fool myself, Antu. We women have always suffered indignity from nature. We are intended to fulfil a biological purpose, and are equipped with the weapons and spells given by nature. If we know how to use them, we can win our throne cheaply. Men have to prove their worth through endeavour. I have been fortunate to realize that worth. Men are much greater than us.'

'Taller too!'

'Certainly so, and with potential of greatness that can overcome the limitations set by nature. I may not be very clever, but I have offered myself in humility to that greatness.'

'Have you never been bothered by anyone indecent?'

'Yes, I have. Men who stoop down to the lowest physical level in our attraction get warped. We women—in our ways, dress, and words—seem to have joined in a conspiracy to pull men down, even when there is no personal wish or need.'

'To tempt the naïve?'

'Yes, you are all naïve! We are vain because you can be enticed so easily. We have loved the fools, yet, in their foolishness perceived the potential of greatness. I have seen many who are indecent, dirty, who vilify; many who are mean and nasty. Yet there are many more who are not, and I have seen them in their brightness. Some of them will be forgotten, yet they are great.'

'Eli, I am embarrassed, and I know that I should protest, yet I like what you said. But I must speak the truth. I must speak about the cowardice of my countrymen that I have seen from my childhood, and have been concerned about. For instance, the intolerable dominance of mothers-in-law in families I know, and even in my family. Cruelty of mothers-in-law is legendary in our country.'

'Yes, I know. The weak are the enemies of the weak. No one else can be as cruel.'

'Ela, don't make this a prologue to the reputation of your future mother-in-law! We often hear of extreme cruelty to a new daughter-in-law, and the main protagonist of that drama is the mother-in-law. But who has given her unrestrained rights to do wrong? It is the son. A man who can't protect his wife from such an abuser is not mature enough to marry. When he is mature enough to protect her, he goes to the other extreme of childlike dependence on his wife. When men lack manliness, women are diminished in stature and they bring the men down. As a result, in our country men who have a mission renounce women; those cowards are afraid of them. In this country of cowards, you have vowed to remain single just in case a young soul is led astray by your womanly influence! The real man finds his fulfilment with the strength of the true women—this is God's ruling, which flows in our bloodstream. Those who make it naught are not real men. You could have put me to that test; why didn't you?'

'I could argue with you, Antu, but I won't. You are using these false arguments because of your frustration. You are just not able to forget about my vow.'

'No, I can't forget. You said that men are greater than women and that you fear that women would bring them down. But women don't need to be great; they are complete in what they are. Man, unfortunately, is incomplete. He shames the creator.'

'Antu, we can see the creator's wish even in that incompleteness. That wish itself is important.'

'I don't know if that wish alone is important, his imagination is no less so. The touch of that imagination brings magic to the woman's nature; they bring an artist's endeavour to our homes, they express the inexpressible in their body, mind and heart through colour and music. Just because it is natural to them, it isn't necessarily easy. The effect of that gold chain round your smooth, shell-like neck . . . you didn't have to study books to do that. Perhaps there are the unfortunate women who don't add to the beauty of life. They are the talkative, domineering women displaying their jewellery and wealth; or else the servants who spend their lives cleaning courtyards. They might be numerous but they don't signify.'

'I blame the creator for not giving women the strength to fight. Why must they take recourse to deception to protect themselves? When I read in books that women do better than men in the most despicable profession in the world—spying—I wish that I am never reborn as a woman. I have seen men from a woman's perception, and I have seen what is good in them and their potential for greatness. When I think of my country, I think of them, they are my country. When they make mistakes, those are big mistakes. It breaks my heart to think that there is no place for them in their homes. So I am their mother, their sister and their daughter and it makes me proud. English-educated women hesitate to serve others, but my fulfilment is in that. The ultimate expression of our love is in this devotion.'

'You can offer your devotion to other men, why not me? Is it because I can do without it? It is my bad luck that in your list of women's roles—mother, sister, and daughter—you left out the most important one.'

'I know you better than you know yourself. Your wings would have been restless in the small world of my love, and my trifling offering would have seemed like dregs. Then you would have realized my inadequacy. That is why I haven't claimed you but instead given you up wholeheartedly to my country. There your abilities will not be constricted by lack of space.'

Atin's eyes blazed; it was a blow on his wound. He paced up and down and then stood in front of Ela. He said, 'It is time for some harsh words. Who are you to offer me to the country or to anything else? You could have offered the gift of your charm, your grace, your love—which are truly your own; call it what you will: serving or blessing. I can come to your door with humility, or with vanity. But you see your gift as unimportant. In the glory of womanhood, you could have gifted the wealth of your heart; but you withdrew that and said that you bestowed me to the country. You can't do that, no one can. The country can't be passed from one hand to another.'

Ela's face had paled. She said, 'I don't understand.'

'I am trying to say that a woman's gift of love might appear to be small, but the depth of it is unfathomable; it is not a cage. On the other hand the country, which you designated to be my true place, is a construct of your group; it is like a cage for my true self, whatever it might be for others. Because my own strength does not find expression there, it gets warped. When I try to give expression to what is not genuinely my own, the madness of it shames me; but there is no exit. You don't realize that my wings are clipped and my legs are shackled. I had the ability to take my rightful place in my country. Why did you make me forget it?'

Ela asked wearily, 'Why did you allow yourself to forget?'

'Because you women have the infallible weapon of persuasion, or else I would be ashamed of being persuaded. I admit that you have that power. Yet, had I not been persuaded, I would have doubted my manhood.'

'Then why do you rebuke me?'

'Why?! Let me explain. You could have led me to your own space which is rightfully yours. Instead, you echoed the words of your group and said that you are all bound to one common mission. My life is in turmoil revolving in that hard, officious and tortuous path of duty.'

'Officious path of duty?'

'Yes. It is like the chariot of Jagannath. The leader asks you to close your eyes and pull a thick rope, and thousands of young men start pulling. Many come under the wheels, many lose their limbs. Then suddenly the mantra commands you to reverse, and the chariot turns back. But the broken bones are not set, the handicapped are swept aside. The self-esteem of these young men was crushed at the very beginning in such a way that they proudly agreed to mould themselves into puppets. When they begin dancing at the pull of the leader's string, they are amazed, believing it to be a display of power. But when the puppeteer lets go, thousands of human puppets are eliminated.'

'But many of them took wrong steps; they couldn't step to the beat.'

'Human puppets can't dance for long. Perhaps human nature can be changed, but it takes time. It is a mistake to think that by destroying human nature and making puppets of human beings, the work would be easier. One must recognize the power of the human spirit. If you had respect for my spirit, you would have drawn me to yourself, not to your group.'

'Antu, why didn't you rebuke me and push me away right at the beginning? Why did you make me feel guilty?'

'I have answered that often. The simple truth is that I wanted you. That desire was insurmountable. Since the conventional route was barred, I pledged my life to the devious route. You were fascinated. Now I know that I will die on this route. After that you will call me with your arms outstretched to your empty heart day after day, night after night.'

'I beg of you, don't say that.'

'It sounds foolish, romantic, doesn't it? As though a formless, substanceless possessing can be called that! As though your pain of separation then could compensate for the union rejected today.'

'Antu, you are caught up in words today.'

'Only today? Always! When in infancy speech first came from dark silence, there were so many random words; later, when I entered the world of literature, I found the dust of destroyed empires, the broken armours of the brave knights, trees taking root in the cracked monuments of victory, and the efforts of centuries silent in heaps of dust. But, at the summit of the ruin I saw the unshakable throne of speech. The waves of different ages sweep the foot of that throne. I dreamt that I too was born to add to the ornamentation of that throne. Your Antu loves words. But there is no hope of your knowing him; you have got him inducted into the chess game of your organization!'

Ela got up from her chair and sat at Atin's feet. Atin pulled her up to sit next to him. He said, 'Mentally I have decorated your slim form with words, you are my evanescent, flowering creeper; my joy and my sorrow. There is an invisible curtain of speech around me, the words come down to me from the heaven of literature and keep the crowd out. I have an independent spirit, and your guru is aware of that, yet he trusts me; I wonder why.'

'Because of that spirit. To be one of them, you would have to climb down to their level, which you could never do. That is the basis of my faith in you. No other woman has ever trusted a man so much. Had you been an ordinary man, I would have feared you the way ordinary women do. Your company is safe.'

'Had you been afraid you would have perceived the man. You demand daring for your country, why not for yourself? I am a coward; why couldn't I, in spite of your refusal, claim you when there was still time? I was civilized! But love is barbaric; it turns stones to make way; it is a waterfall, not the tame tap water of the so-called civilized city.'

Ela rose quickly and said, 'Come, Antu, come inside.'

Antu stood up and exclaimed, 'Fear! Fear at last! I have won. In my first blush of youth I didn't know women. I had imagined them to be distant, inaccessible. The time to prove that I am what you want has passed. In my essence I am a man, barbaric and reckless. If I could have that time, I would hold you in a tight embrace, until your ribs hurt. I wouldn't give you time to think, or allow you to cry; I would drag you into my orbit. But now I am walking a road that is narrow like the edge of a knife, there isn't room enough to walk together.'

'You don't need to rob; it is yours for the taking.' Saying this Ela walked up to Atin with outstretched arms, embraced him, and lifted up her face to him.

Suddenly she glanced towards the street through the window and exclaimed, 'How awful! See over there.'

'What is it?'

'There, at the street crossing. It must be Batu, he is coming here.'

'He knows his way to a worthwhile place.'

'I am disgusted by him. His nature is crude and indecent. No matter how much I try to avoid him and keep him at a distance, he comes close. The man is unclean.'

'I can't stand him either.'

'I try to calm myself by thinking that it is all in my imagination, but I can't. The look in his bulging eyes insults me as though it were a lecherous touch.'

'Don't pay any attention to him, Ela. Can't you ignore his existence?'

'I can't because I'm afraid of him. His inner nature is like a disgusting octopus. I fear that he would engulf me in shame with his sticky tentacles; he is plotting for that day. You might laugh it off as an irrational female fear, but this fear has gripped me. I fear not just for myself, but even more for you. I know that his jealousy is hissing at you like a snake.'

'Ela, beasts like him have no courage, only an odour. That is why no one wants to be mixed up with him. But he is terrified of me, not because I am terrifying but because I am different.'

'Antu, I have thought of many possible kinds of sorrow and danger, and I am prepared for them. But I would prefer to die rather than be in his power.' She gripped Antu's hands, as though asking to be saved. She continued, 'You know, Antu, when I imagine being attacked by a wild animal I pray that I shouldn't be dragged into muck by a crocodile. Tigers or bears would be preferable.'

'Am I in the category of tigers and bears?'

'No, you, my dear, are my narasimha, man-lion. Death by your hands would be my salvation. Listen, he is coming up.'

Atin came out of the room and said firmly, 'Batu, not here, come to the sitting room downstairs.'

Batu asked, 'Ela didi?'

'Ela didi is changing her clothes. Come downstairs.'

'Changing? So late? It is eight-thirty . . .'

'Yes. I caused the delay.'

'I need just five minutes.'

'She has gone for her bath, and doesn't want anyone to come in here.'

'Except you!'

Batu gave a knowing smile. He said, 'We have always remained within the common rules of grammar, but you have quickly become an exception to the rules. But remember, an exception is on slippery ground, and may not last.' Saying this he quickly climbed down the stairs and left.

Akhil came in holding a small saw and handed him a letter. Obviously he had been engaged in some creative work. Atin asked, 'Is it for your Ela didi?'

'No, for you. He asked me to give it to you.'

'Who asked you?'

'I don't know him.' Akhil walked away.

Atin knew from the red colour of the paper that it was a danger signal. He read the coded message: 'Leave immediately without saying anything to Ela.'

Atin accepted the discipline of his work and defying it would be demeaning his self-respect. He tore the letter to pieces as was customary. He stood still for a moment outside the locked door of the bathroom. The next instant he rushed out. From the street he looked up once at the upstairs window. The window was open; he could see a corner of the armchair, and the red-and-yellow striped square cushion on it. Then he jumped on to a moving tram.

## 3

Scene: Dense vegetation of light green, dark green and yellow-green shrubs and trees; a pond covered with rotted bamboo leaves; by its side wound a crooked lane marked by the wheels of bullock carts. Fences were covered by various creepers. From the gaps one could see water-filled fields of young paddy demarcated by mud walls. The lane ended near the Ganges. The old landing stage, constructed with small bricks, was broken and bent; under it the river had silted and the water course had shifted away. Further, beyond the wharf and in the jungle there was an ancient dilapidated building. They say that 150 years ago a man killed his mother, and his ghost inhabited the accursed building still. So far no heir to the property had tried to claim his rights from the ghost.

The scene was the abandoned courtyard, large and moss-covered. Nearer the river there were the ruins of a temple, a platform where the *raas* festival used to be held, parts of a wall, and a broken boat in the darkness under a banyan tree.

This was Atin's current home, and towards the end of the day Kanai Gupta entered its large, shadowy courtyard. Atin was startled because even Kanai was not supposed to know this address. He asked, 'What brings you here?'

'I am on a spying mission.'

'Is it a joke? If so, could you explain?'

'It isn't a joke. I am an insignificant shopkeeper. One day the devil entered my tea shop, and I left. But its evil eye followed me, so in the end I had to join its cadre of spies. For those of us who face only the road to the cremation ground, this is as safe as the Grand Trunk Road spanning the country from east to west.'

'So, instead of concocting tea, you are concocting news?'

'This business can't run on concoction, it demands undiluted genuine news. When someone is caught in the net, I tighten the string. When they received the necessary information about your Haren, I supplied the remaining superfluous information. He is now in a jail in Jalpaigudi.'

'Now is it my turn?'

'Yes, almost. Batu has supplied most of the information. My role in this allows you some time. Do you remember that you had lost your diary while you were living in your ancestral home?'

'Of course I remember.'

'The police would have found it, so I had to steal it.'

'You took it!'

'God helps the one with good intentions. Once when you were writing in it, I tricked you into leaving the room for a few minutes and I removed it.'

Atin held his head in despair and asked, 'You have read the entire diary?'

'Yes, indeed. When I finished reading it was past one-thirty at night. I didn't know that the Bengali language could be so powerful and so sweet. It contains secrets, but not about the British empire!'

'Was it decent to read it?'

'I don't know. You are a good writer, you didn't go into details, didn't mention any names, but you expressed such disgust, such contempt. Had a politically ambitious retiree penned it, he would have been rewarded by the government. If Batu were not in your pursuit, the diary would have exonerated you.'

'You read every word?'

'I did. If I had a daughter and if she had inspired you to write like that, I would have gloried in my fatherhood. To tell you the truth, Professor Indranath has harmed the country by involving you in his mission.'

'Do the others know about your latest business?'

'No one knows.'

'The professor?'

'He is sharp. He might have guessed, but he has neither asked me, nor heard from me.'

'Why did you tell me?'

'It is surprising indeed! I have a suspicious nature, but if I can't trust someone, I feel suffocated. I am neither a thinker nor a fool; nor do I write a diary, but if I did, I would have felt relieved to show it to you.'

'Why don't you confide in the professor?'

'One can give him information but not confide in him. I am his principal aide; yet don't imagine that I know all about him, and I don't even dare to guess some of it. I believe that he, like myself, sends those who drop out of our group to the police. It might be heinous, but I am not a sinner. I must warn you that one day—either with his help or with mine—you will be handcuffed. But please don't misunderstand me. Batu was the one who informed the police about your hideout; so, to outdo him, I took some photos of this place and gave them. Let me talk business now. I can give you twenty-four hours to clear out. If you don't then I will have to lead you to the police station. On this paper I have written down the address and the details of a place. You read the code, memorize it and then tear the paper. See this map; you will stay in the corner room of the school building on this side of the street. You have been appointed a teacher of Bengali language in that school. The police station is across the street. A relative of mine is only a constable there, but he is powerful. His family has lived in that area for many generations. He will certainly search your bags and your pockets; take it as a favour. He refers to Bengalis in abusive terms, but don't try to protest. Don't attempt to return. There is a cycle outside, as soon as you get the signal ride away. Come, this might be our last meeting, let me embrace you.' Kanai left.

Atin sat quietly. He looked inwards. The last act was upon him, too soon in his life; the curtains were about to close, the lights were fading.

His journey began in the pure light of dawn; he had moved very far away from that point. There was nothing left of what he had had with him at the start of that journey; in the last leg of the journey he survived by deceiving himself. Once, all of a sudden at a turn in the road, fate brought a wonderful gift of beauty. He had never imagined that he would experience that unfathomable bounty; he had only read about it. He felt that Dante and Beatrice were reborn in the two of them. It inspired him; like Dante, he too jumped into the whirl of a national revolution. But where was its truth, its heroism, its glory? With an inevitable force it pulled him down into muck, into the darkness of theft, robbery and murder, all hidden behind a mask. History would not hold it in the light of glory. By destroying his soul, he now realized that there was no genuine outcome possible; without doubt it was defeat that lay ahead. Defeat too had a value but not the defeat of the soul, a defeat that brought surreptitious, abominable horror, which had no meaning and no end.

Daylight was fading, the sound of crickets wafted from the fields, and bullock carts rolled by on their screechy wheels.

All of a sudden Ela rushed into the room with a dishevelled, blind force, like someone jumping into water intending to commit suicide. As Atin stood up she threw herself at him, and in a voice choked with tears exclaimed, 'Atin, I couldn't stay away.'

Atin slowly detached himself and holding her in front of him looked at her tear-stained face. He asked, 'Eli, why have you come here?'

'I don't know why.'

'How did you get this address?'

Ela replied sadly, 'You didn't leave me your address.'

'But whoever informed you can't be your friend.'

'I am aware of that too; but when I don't know your whereabouts, the void is unbearable. I am not in a condition to judge who is a foe and who is a friend. I haven't seen you for so very long.'

'You are admirable!'

'Antu, you are admirable. When you were forbidden to visit me, you could accept it.'

'It was part of my natural pride. A tremendous desire to see you was choking me like the grip of a python, but I couldn't give in. They say I am sentimental, and they believe that in a crisis I would turn out to be pulpy as wet soil. They can't imagine that sentimentality is my unfailing weapon.'

'The professor knows.'

'Eli, since this uncanny neighbourhood was first created, no Bengali lady has come here.'

'It is because no other Bengali lady was ill-fated to have such an unbearable need.'

'But Eli, what you have done is illicit.'

'I know. I accept my weakness, yet I would break the rules not only for myself but also for you. Every day I felt that you were calling me. I couldn't return your call and it was killing me. Tell me that you are happy to see me.'

'I am so happy that I am willing to face any danger to prove it.'

'No, no. Why should you be in danger; whatever the danger might be, may it come to me. Now I should leave, Antu.'

'No, don't leave. You have broken a rule to come to me, so I shall break the rule and keep you with me. Let us be equally guilty. I first saw your face in the light of spring; that was another era. Let me invoke that meeting now in this dilapidated room. Come, come closer.'

'Wait, let me first tidy the room.'

'Alas! It would be an attempt to use a comb on a bald patch!'

Ela looked around her. There was a blanket on the floor, and a mat on it; a canvas bag full of books passed for a pillow, and a packing case for a desk. In a corner stood a water pot covered with an earthenware lid. In a tattered basket there were a few bananas, and a chipped enamel bowl was used for tea when there was a chance occasion. On the other end there was a large chest with an image of Ganesha on it. It proved that Atin had a companion here. A string was tied from one pillar to another with many stained and dirty towels hanging from it. The room was damp and humid.

Ela had seen such surroundings before. She hadn't felt sad but had silently congratulated the brave, self-sacrificing young men. Once she had seen the burnt remains of an attempt to cook rice by a novice; it had seemed like the romance of revolution witnessed in a painting in ashes. Yet now she was overcome with sadness. She normally looked down on young men brought up in luxury, but she couldn't reconcile to Atin being in this shabby, indigent state.

Noting her expression, Atin laughed and said, 'You are stunned by my wealth, the part of it that is invisible. You see, we must be free so that when we run, neither people nor things call us back. There is a jute factory nearby; the workers call me "Master babu". They ask me to read out their letters, write the addresses, and explain accounts of their credits and liabilities. A few of them dream that their sons would rise from the working class to the bourgeoisie. They want my help, they bring fruit and snacks; those who have cows at home, bring milk.'

'Antu, whose property is that chest in the corner?'

'Living alone in an odd place like this, I become conspicuous. Somehow, a Marwari man, bankrupt for the third time, has come here. I fear that his main business is to go bankrupt! The dilapidated courtyard is a training school for his two nephews. They come early in the morning, dye cheap saris which they sell to the slum women, and from the income pay interest on the money borrowed, and also pay back part of the capital. Those large earthenware pots are not for my cooking but for making the dyes. They keep the dyed saris, glass bangles, combs, small mirrors and brass amulets in that box. The resident ghost and I guard these. They leave at three in the afternoon with the wares to sell, and don't return here. I don't know what the Marwari's business is in Kolkata. He wanted me as a partner because I know English, but I—in my kindness—declined. He tried to inquire about my financial standing, but I explained that the wealth of my forefathers is now with their families.'

'How long will you be here?'

'I guess for twenty-four hours. Colour dyeing will continue day after day in that courtyard, but Atindra will disappear in the distant, pale horizon. I hope the Marwari doesn't get caught because of his association with me.'

'What is your future address?'

'I am not allowed to reveal that.'

'Can't I be allowed to even imagine the place where you would be?'

'Why not? Imagination is a good thing.'

Ela took out the books from the sack and looked at them: poetry books, some in English and a few in Bengali.

Atin said, 'All this time I carried them around so that I shouldn't forget where I belong. My original habitat was in that world of words. If you turn the pages you will find passages marked in pencil—the lanes and bylanes to my home. And see where I am today.'

Ela fell at his feet and entreated, 'Forgive me, Antu, please forgive me.'

'There is nothing to forgive. If there is a God with infinite kindness, I hope he forgives me.'

'I brought you to this road before I really knew you.'

Atin laughed and said, 'Won't you give me even the credit for reaching this state in my own madness? If you try to treat me like a juvenile and act like my guardian, I won't tolerate it. It would be better for you to come down from your pedestal, look into my eyes and say, "Come, my beloved; come, be with me."'

'Perhaps I would. But why are you so upset?'

'I am upset. You claim that you brought me to this path.'

'Why does the truth upset you?'

'Truth? You were only an excuse. The urge was my own. Had it been a woman from a different background rather than you, I would be playing bridge in the Anglo–Indian club by now, or climbing up towards the governor's box at the racecourse. If it is foolishness, then I proudly proclaim that it is my own foolishness, a God-given talent.'

'Please, Antu, don't go on talking in that manner. I can never forget that I ruined your career and now your life is uprooted.'

'At last the real woman in you has come out! It is obvious that in the theatre of national struggle you are a romantic. You imagine yourself to be at the centre of the organization, taking care of its members like a housewife cares for her family. It is temporary derangement, rather than clear thinking that has brought you to the dangerous arena of politics.'

'Antu, no one can beat you in words, not even women.'

'Do women really say anything? They only jabber. I had hoped to uproot ignorance with the power of words. You people want to exploit that ignorance and forcibly erect your monument of victory on it.'

'I entreat you, please explain why you allowed yourself to be led by my mistake? Why did you accept the pain of giving up your career?'

'It was a gesture. If I hadn't accepted that pain, you wouldn't have realized how much I love you. You would have walked away from me.

Please don't take it lightly and say that it was for the love of the country.'

'Doesn't the country figure in this?'

'It does because the endeavour to regain the country and the endeavour to win you have become one. Once, a man had to prove his valour to win a woman. Today I have the opportunity to prove myself by sacrificing my life. Instead of realizing that you are mourning for my ruined career!'

'You must accept one request. We women are worldly, and can't bear indigence. I have inherited a house and have some money. Please listen to me; please don't hesitate to take some money. I know that you need it.'

'If I am really in need, I have the choice of many jobs, from writing books for cramming for the exams, to being a porter.'

'I know that I should have put all my money into our work for the country. But because we women have fewer avenues of earning, we cling to our savings. We are wary.'

'That is only common sense. Women lose their grace if they are dispossessed.'

'In our small nests we gather many little things. It isn't just for the need to live but also for the need to love. If only I could make you understand that whatever I have is for you.'

'I can't accept that. So far women have provided the care, and men, the income. The reverse is humiliating. You refused the gift that I unhesitatingly asked of you; instead you built the barrier of your vow. That day when you were checking the accounts of your Narayani School, I came to you like a bird hit by a storm. I had come with a wounded soul. But it is difficult to shake women's allegiance to anything labelled duty, just like their devotion to priests. You didn't see me. I sat gazing at you, wishing for the pleasure of a touch of those delicate fingers on my body and mind. But you remained unmoved; you couldn't give even that much. I said to myself that a greater sacrifice is required of me. One day I will be felled, with skull cracked and body cut up, then you will hold me in your lap.'

Ela's eyes were damp. She said, 'Antu, why couldn't you ask? Why didn't you snatch my book away? Don't you know that your reticence makes me hesitate? In a way your nature is similar to women's. You might long for something, yet you can't claim it impetuously; it is distasteful to you.'

'It is ingrained in our blood for generations. I have always respected the purity of a woman's body and mind. We have inherited from our forefathers the notion that women's honour must be protected. If ever your heart softens and you wish to indulge me, please don't wait for me to ask you. I have never learnt to ask that way. I have infinite hunger, but I can't be greedy; it is not in my nature. I can't degrade my desire.'

Ela sat close to Atin, drew his head to her chest and rested her head on his. She passed her fingers through his hair. After a while, Atin lifted his head and held her hands. He said, 'That day when I boarded the boat at Mokama, I didn't know that fate would box my ears with her invisible fingers! From then on my mind wanders down memory lane in search of the unattainable. Are you bored with the story?'

'No, not at all.'

'Then listen. My servant had taken my heavy luggage from the deck into the car. I had a small leather case with me, and I was looking around for a porter. You came and asked very innocently, "You need a porter? I can carry it for you." Before I could stop you, you picked it up. Seeing my embarrassment you added a postscript, "If you feel embarrassed, you may carry my suitcase, then you won't be indebted to me." So I had to pick it up. It was much heavier than mine, and I carried it with difficulty, transferring it from one hand to the other, and finally managed to drag it into the third class compartment. By then my silk shirt was soaked with perspiration, and I was out of breath. You were laughing silently. Perhaps you did feel pity but preferred not to show it. You had the noble task of reforming me.'

'Please don't go on! I am ashamed of my behaviour; I was so foolish and so peculiar! I became more audacious because you didn't laugh at me. How could you tolerate it? Didn't you expect a woman to have some intelligence?'

'It didn't matter. The ambience in which we met had nothing to do with higher mathematics or logic; it was an enchantment, it was illusory; something that had withstood even the teaching of Shankaracharya. The day was drawing to a close; there were clouds in the twilight sky. The water of the river was shimmering in the evening light. Your slim form against that light is etched in my mind forever. What happened after that? You called. But where I am now is so far away from you. You don't know the details.'

'Why don't you let me know, Antu?'

'I must obey the rules, but that is not all. Anyway, there is no use of saying more. The light has dimmed; come, come nearer. I want a holiday, which is only possible with you. My holiday is of small dimensions, like a gold-washed frame. Let me frame a picture in it. The picture of you as a lock of hair falls over your eyes and you push it away quickly; your black-bordered tassar sari, the sari edge pinned to your hair; your tired and sad eyes; your lips entreating. The daylight is fading into obscurity. What I see now is wonderfully true; I can't explain what it means. In its unexpressed sweetness lies a deep sorrow because it couldn't be captured in verse. This wondrous completeness is threatened by something that is corrupt, something with a long name and a long shadow.'

'What are you saying, Antu!'

'A whole pack of lies. I remember that you had asked me to live in a slum among labourers, intending to destroy my arrogance of birth. I was amused by your determination, and I joined in the democratic picnic. I frequented the neighbourhoods of horse-cart drivers and milkmen; they called me "brother", "uncle". But both they and I knew that such relationships couldn't last. Some gifted people might be able to play music on any instrument; but if we try to copy, we can't get the right note. Haven't you noticed your neighbour, the clergyman who calls everyone "brother" and embraces them as a part of his ritual? It actually ridicules Christ.'

'Antu, what frustration is making you say such things? Are you saying that duty can't be accepted as duty, even if it isn't distasteful?'

'It isn't a matter of taste, Eli; it is a matter of one's temperament. Krishna asked Arjuna to do the duty of the brave, in spite of it being distasteful; he didn't advise him to study agricultural economics to plough the soil of Kurukshetra!'

'What would Krishna have asked you to do?'

'He had whispered in my ear long ago. I had the responsibility of saying it out loud. There is so much artificiality because we are taught that we all have the same duties. I must say bluntly that you too have no place in the arena which you approach with pretentious humility. You are all goddesses! Like the others, you are a fake goddess in fake garb which, like all other garbs of women, is a male construct.'

'I still don't understand why you didn't turn away from a path that was not yours.'

'Let me explain. I didn't know, didn't think about many things before I took this path. I met many young men who were worthy of respect. The unbearable truth of what they saw and suffered would never be known. That pain was my driving force. I vowed that I would not be defeated by fear, or by torture. If I died breaking my head against a stone wall, I would still disregard the heartless wall.'

'Then your view changed?'

'Hear me out. He who fights the powerful, despite being weak himself, becomes equal to the powerful. It preserves his honour. I had imagined that honour for myself. But in time I saw men of exceptional nature lose their humanity. No loss can be greater. Although I knew that they would laugh at me, or taunt me in anger, I told them that if we do as much wrong as the wrongdoers, it is defeat. Before we lose, before we die, we must show them that we are superior in our humanity, otherwise why are we fighting a battle that we are sure to lose? Some of them did see my point, but they were very few.'

'Why didn't you leave them then?'

'How could I? I knew by then that the net was closing in on them. I understood their heart-wrenching pain, so in spite of my anger and aversion I couldn't abandon them. I have learnt for sure that if we use force against the powerful in this unequal battle, we can't win. Illness is bad for everyone but fatal for the weak. Those who are in power can abandon humanity and continue by the use of force, but we who are in a weaker position can't do so. We shall be tainted, totally defeated, and then disappear into the darkness of disgrace.'

'I too clearly see the image of this terrible tragedy. I was beckoned by glory, but each day brings more shame. What should we do now?'

'Everyone has a chance of fighting a just war, where death might bring salvation. But for a handful of us, that route is closed. The consequences of our karma here must be faced here.'

'I understand, yet I am hurt by the way you talk disparagingly about our work for the country.'

'The time to explain the reason for that has passed.'

'But still, please tell me why.'

'I admit that I am not what you call a patriot. There is something greater than patriotism. Those who don't agree use patriotism only as a vehicle, like crossing a river on the back of an alligator. I see clearly that their lies, meanness, distrust of one another, intrigue for power and spying on others will pull them down under slime. I can't guard my honour and do anything worthwhile in this ugly hole, in this polluted air of lies.'

'Antu, what you call self-destruction, does it happen only in our country?'

'I can't say that. Nationalists the world over are declaring with brute force the terrible lie that by destroying the soul of a country, the country can be saved. My protest against it churns in my mind. I could have said it aloud truthfully, and it would have been much more worthwhile and enduring than this covert, underground attempt to free the country. But I don't have much time left. That is why my pain has turned me cruel.'

Ela sighed and said, 'Antu, come back.'

'That is not possible.'

'Why not?'

'Even if I am in the wrong place, I still have responsibilities.'

Ela wound her arms around his neck and pleaded, 'Come back, Antu. You have shaken the foundation of my belief. Today I am hanging on to a broken boat to stay afloat. Please rescue me and take me with you. Don't stay quiet like that, say something! Order me to break my vow, and I will do it. I made a mistake, forgive me.'

'There is no way now.'

'Why not? There must be a way.'

'An arrow can miss its aim, but it can't return to the quiver.'

'Marry me, Antu. Let us not waste any more time, take me with you as your wife and companion in your journey.'

'If it were only a dangerous journey, I would. But I can't take you on this journey of dishonour. Let that be. At the end of it all there is still some truth left. Let me hear that from you. '

'What would you like me to say?'

'Say that you love me.'

'Yes, I love you.

'Say that even when I am not there you will remember that I loved you.'

Ela was quiet, tears streaming down her face. After a long time she said in a voice choked with tears, 'Antu, I entreat you, please take something from me. Take this gold chain.' She placed the chain at his feet.

'No. I can't accept that.'

'Why not? Is it your pride?'

'Yes, my pride. There was a time when I would have placed it round my neck. But now you are giving it to relieve my want. I can't accept charity from you.'

Ela fell at his feet and pleaded, 'Please take me with you.'

'Don't tempt me, Ela. I have said again and again that this road is not for you.'

'Then it is not yours either. Come back.'

'The road is not mine, but it owns me. A noose is not a necklace.'

'Antu, you must know that I can't live without you. I have no one but you. If you doubt it now, I hope that after death the doubt will be removed.'

Suddenly Atin jumped up. The sharp sound of a whistle came from afar like an arrow. He was startled and said, 'I am leaving.'

Ela clung to him and pleaded, 'Stay a little longer.'

'No, I can't.'

'Where are you going?'

'I don't know.'

Ela entreated, 'Don't leave me behind.'

Atin halted for a second, but the whistle blew again. He shouted at her, 'Let me go,' and dashed out of the room.

The evening got darker. Ela lay on the floor. Her pain had left her drained of tears. All of a sudden she heard someone call her in a deep voice. She sat up to find Indranath, holding a flashlight. She stood up quickly and said, 'Bring Antu back.'

Indranath asked, 'Why did you come here?'

'I knew there was danger'

Indranath snapped at her, 'Nobody is concerned about your danger. Who gave you this address?'

'Batu.'

'Didn't you understand his motive?'

'I didn't care. I couldn't bear to be away.'

'I would kill you now if I could. Go back home; a taxi is waiting outside.'

# 4

'Akhil, you have run away from the hostel again! I have repeatedly told you not to come here. You might die!'

Akhil didn't answer her but whispered instead, 'A bearded stranger has climbed over the wall and entered the garden. I have locked the door of this room. Listen, his footsteps!' Akhil drew out a knife with the longest blade.

Ela snatched it from him saying, 'There is no need for bravado, give that to me.'

They heard someone speak from the staircase. 'Don't be scared, it is me, Antu.'

Ela paled and asked Akhil to open the door. Akhil opened it and asked Atin, 'Where is the bearded man?'

'You will find the beard in the garden, but the man is here. Go, look for the beard.' Akhil left.

Ela stood still staring like a statue for a few minutes and then she said, 'Antu, you look dreadful.'

'Unattractive?'

'Then it is true.'

'What is true?'

'That you are suffering from a terrible disease.'

'Different doctors have different opinions, you needn't believe them.'

'Have you eaten?'

'It isn't important. Let us not waste time.'

'Why have you come here, Antu? They are waiting to catch you.'

'I don't want to disappoint them.'

Ela gripped his hands and asked, 'Why have you come here knowing that it would be dangerous? What shall we do now?'

'Before I leave I shall tell you why. Now I want to forget it for as long as possible. I'll go and lock the door downstairs.'

He returned a little later and said, 'Let us go to the terrace. I have removed all the light bulbs downstairs, don't be afraid.' They entered the terrace and locked the door behind them. Atin sat with his back against the door, Ela sat facing him.

'Ela, try to relax as though nothing has happened, as though we two are at ease, not expecting any danger, like Rama and Sita in the Ramayana, living in peace in the forest, unaware of the dangers ahead. Your hands are ice cold and shaking! Let me warm them.' Atin placed her hands on his bare chest under his shirt. The sound of the shehnai wafted in from a house where wedding celebrations were going on.

'Eli, are you afraid?'

'Afraid of what?'

'Of everything, of every second that passes.'

'I am only afraid for you, nothing else.'

'Eli, imagine that we are in a similar, still evening fifty or hundred years later. The present has small dimensions; within that fear, worry, sorrow and pain seem enormous. It wears a mask to scare us as though we are babes in arms. Death removes that mask, it doesn't exaggerate. What one longed for, mistaking fake for valuable, what one lost and was heartbroken for something that was transient. Life cheats; it pretends to be endless. Death smiles at it; not a cruel smile, not a smile of ridicule but the serene and beautiful smile of Shiva at the end of illusion. Eli, when you are alone at night, have you ever tried to feel the pleasant and deep freedom of death, which brings infinite forgiveness?'

'I don't have your vision, Antu, but in my overwhelming concern for you I feel with certainty that it is easy to die.'

'Coward! Why do you think of death as an escape route? Death is the most certain of all, the ocean where all life flows, the ultimate synthesis of all truth and untruth, good and evil. Tonight, at this moment we are enclosed within the arms of that greatness. Remember the lines of Ibsen:

Upwards
Towards the peaks,
Towards the stars,
Towards the vast silence.

Ela sat holding Atin's hands on her lap silently. He laughed suddenly. He said, 'The comedy of life plays on to the last act against the still, black backdrop of death. Observe a picture of that tonight. Three years ago on this day on this same terrace you celebrated my birthday, remember?'

'I do indeed.'

'Your adoring young men were all present. The feast was not elaborate. Fried *chida*, boiled peas with pepper sprinkled on top, and egg cutlets. They enjoyed the food. Suddenly Motilal began a speech: "In this new era, on the birthday of Atin babu . . ." I stopped him saying if he tried to give a speech, it would be his end. Batu accused me of abortion of speech. I hate phrases such as new era, new life, the gate of death, and so on. They tried hard to colour my thinking, but the colour didn't stick.'

'Antu, I was a fool. I thought that by putting the same uniform on you we could assimilate you with us pedestrians.'

'That is why you made a show of acting as their elder sister, for my benefit. You believed that a touch of envy was necessary to reform me. You displayed many things in your basket of goods such as care, bonhomie, advice, and unnecessary concern, like goods displayed in a variety store. I can hear you saying, "Nandalal, your face looks flushed." Before the poor fellow could deny it you brought a damp cloth to cool his fever. I was fascinated, yet I knew that your playacting—the role of an ideal, home-grown elder sister—was at the behest of your holy country.'

'Antu, please say no more about it.'

'You must admit that you did much that was superfluous, unnecessary and silly showing off in those days.'

'I do admit it. You put an end to all that. Why then do you recount it so cruelly now?'

'Hear the reason. The other day you asked for my forgiveness for making me deviate from my vocation. I have strayed from truth, yet what I could have claimed against it was not given to me. I went against my nature, yet you in your blind faith could not break your vow which was untrue. It wouldn't have been superfluous to ask to be forgiven for that. I know what you are thinking: "How could this happen?" '

'Yes, Antu, my wonder does not cease, I can't understand how I had such power.'

'How would you know? Women get their strength from nature. The wonder of your voice creates a galaxy in the infinite sky of my mind. And your hand—those fingers—can work like a touchstone on truth and untruth. I don't know what fascination made me accept the shame of this aberration of a life. I have read such examples in history but never imagined that it could happen to me, so proud of my intellect was I. My time has come, so I must tell you the truth no matter how harsh.'

'Tell me what you must, don't be kind. I am cruel, insensitive and foolish. I never had the ability to understand you. The incomparable reached out for me, but I—undeserving—didn't appreciate its worth. It was my good fortune to be offered such treasure, but I lost it forever. If there is a punishment harsher than that, punish me.'

'Why talk of punishments? I will forgive; the same infinite forgiveness that death brings. That is why I have come today.'

'That was the reason?'

'Yes, only that.'

'You need not have come to this dangerous place to say that you forgive me. I know that you don't wish to live. If so, then please allow me a few days to look after you.'

'What is the use? I have unbearable regrets, how can you help me when I have lost the way of truth?'

'You haven't lost it; it is still intact in yourself.'

'You would shudder if you only knew what I really am.'

'Antu, you are imagining things. What you have done selflessly can't taint your nature.'

'I have killed my nature, the most sinful of all killings. I couldn't destroy any evil, only destroyed myself. For that sin, even though I have the opportunity, I can't unite with you. How can I accept your hand in marriage with my tainted hands? But let that be. I have come to the bank of the dark waters of death that removes all stains. Let us say what we want to with a smile. Let me complete the story of that birthday.'

'Antu, I can't concentrate.'

'Only those few carefree days deserve our attention now. There were very many difficult days that we needn't recall.'

'All right, Antu, go on.'

'The feast was over. Suddenly Nirad decided to recite from "Palashir Juddha". He stood up, waved his arms about, and recited like Girish

Ghosh. Nirad is good-natured and simple, but his memory is so good that it is merciless. When I was desperate to break up the party, they asked Bhabesh to sing. He said that he couldn't sing without a harmonium. Thankfully you didn't have one, and I breathed a sigh of relief. All of a sudden Satu raised a question: which is the real birthday, the English calendar date, or the star birthday following the Indian almanac? He just wouldn't stop. Then patriotism came into the discussion, voices were raised, and friendships were in jeopardy. I was cross with you. My birthday was just an excuse to bring your fellow patriots together.'

'From the outside you can't judge what is the goal and what is a pretext. I deserve to be punished but not unjustly. Don't you remember that on that birthday I started calling you Antu, rather than Atin babu? Is that a small matter? But tell me how you got that name.'

'When I was four or five, I was short for my age, hardly talked and had a foolish expression on my face. My uncle came from another part of the country and saw me for the first time. He picked me up, and asked, "Who has named this little person Atindra? He should be called Anatindra". So, Anati got abbreviated to Antu. Later, for you too Ati lost its dignity and become Anati.'

Atin suddenly stopped in alarm, and said, 'I can hear footsteps.'

Ela called Akhil, and Akhil answered. She opened the door to the terrace. Akhil informed them that dinner was ready. They had no cooking arrangement and got a nearby restaurant to deliver food. Ela said, 'Antu, come and have your dinner.'

'Don't talk about food. It takes a long time to die of hunger; otherwise there would be no India! Akhil, take my share too, and then run away as far as you can.'

Akhil left. Ela and Atin sat on the floor of the terrace and Atin resumed his recounting of that birthday. 'The birthday party went on and on, no one showed any sign of leaving. I kept looking at my watch, to remind them that it was late. Ultimately I had to say to you that you shouldn't stay up late since you had just recovered from influenza. Someone asked what the time was; I said ten-thirty. Some yawns and movements indicated that the party was about to break up. Batu said, "Why are we waiting, let us leave together." When I asked where we were supposed to go, he answered that we were to pay a surprise visit to the sweepers' colony to stop them from drinking. I was furious and said, "You might stop them from drinking, but what will you offer instead?" Perhaps I overreacted. Those who were about to leave, stopped. They challenged me, "Are you saying that . . ." I interrupted harshly, "I don't wish to say anything." But such harshness was also inappropriate. I lowered my voice, and said goodbye to you. But when I stood outside your room on the first floor, I couldn't go any further. Then I had a brainwave. I touched my breast pocket and said, "I have left my fountain pen behind." Batu said that he would find it and quickly went to the terrace. I followed him. After a pretence of search he smiled and said, "Look in your pocket." I knew that I had left it behind at home, so I had to say, "I have something important to discuss with Ela di." Batu offered to wait for me, but I asked him to leave. With a sly smile Batu asked me not to be angry, and then left.'

Hearing footsteps again, Atin stopped. Akhil came and said, 'Someone has given this piece of paper for Atin babu. I have asked him to wait outside on the street.'

Ela was frightened. She asked, 'Who can it be?'

Atin asked Akhil to let the man enter. Akhil firmly refused.

Atin said, 'There is no reason to be afraid, you know the man, you have seen him often.'

'No, I don't know him.'

'Of course you do. Don't be afraid, I am here.'

Ela said, 'Akhil, don't be scared, go.' Akhil left.

Ela asked, 'Is it Batu?'

'No, it isn't him.'

'Tell me who it is, I feel uneasy.'

'Let me resume my story.'

'Antu, I just can't concentrate.'

'Ela, let me conclude the story, there isn't much left. You came back to the terrace; I could smell the fragrance of rajnigandha. You had kept the bouquet hidden to give it to me when we were alone. For me that welcome in privacy with the shy flowers was the real starting point in our relationship. After that Atindra's education, intellect and reserve gradually sank into a fathomless self-oblivion. That day for the first time you put your arms around me and said, "Take your birthday present." It was our first kiss. Today I have come to claim the last kiss.'

Akhil entered again and said, 'The man is banging on the door, he might break it. He says he has an important message.'

'Akhil, I will tackle him before he breaks the door. You must go away from here. I will be here for your Ela di.'

Ela drew Akhil to herself, kissed his forehead and said, 'Akhil, my dear little brother, you must leave. Here is some money for you with my blessing. Promise me that you will leave immediately and not delay.'

Atin said, 'Akhil, if anyone asks you, you must tell the truth. You must say that at eleven o'clock at night I forced you out of the house. Come, let us make it true.'

Ela drew Akhil to herself once more and entreated, 'Please don't worry about me. Antu is here, there is no reason for fear.'

When Atin was leaving with Akhil, Ela said, 'Let me come too.' But Atin did not let her.

Ela leaned against the terrace wall, overcome with grief. She knew that Akhil had left forever.

Atin returned and said, 'Akhil has left, and I have locked the door from inside.'

'And that man?'

'I made him leave. He thought that I was neglecting my assignment and just chatting; as though a new Arabian Nights had begun. Arabian Nights indeed! The whole thing is a story, a fantasy. Ela, are you afraid?

Aren't you afraid of me?'

'Afraid of you?'

'I am capable of anything. The other day our gang looted the home of an elderly widow. Manmatha knew her and led the others to her house. When the old woman recognized him in spite of his disguise and asked him how he could do such a thing, they killed her. Ostensibly the money is for the country, but it has come to me, and I have broken my fast with that money. I am a thief; I have touched and used stolen money. Batu has betrayed me to the police. In case due to lack of evidence I am let off, or get a light punishment, Batu has conspired through the police superintendent to have the commissioner issue an order to have my case heard by the Bengali judge Jayanta Haldar, rather than be heard at the English magistrate's court. He knows that I will be caught tomorrow. You should be afraid of me; I fear the dark ghost of my dead soul. There is no one else in your room.'

'You are here.'

'Who will save you from me?'

'I don't need to be saved.'

'In your group, all your brothers in the same cause—those foreheads you anointed on brothers' day each year—the same heads are now saying that you should not be allowed to live.'

'Is my offence more than theirs?'

'You have a lot of information about them. Under torture you might disclose everything.'

'Never!'

'How can I say that the man who was here today didn't carry that order? You know the power of orders.'

Ela was startled, 'Is it true, Antu?'

'We have heard that the police will come at dawn to arrest you.'

'I was sure that the police would come to arrest me.'

'How did you come to know that?'

'Yesterday I received a letter from Batu. He says that I will be arrested, but he can save me.'

'How?'

'If I marry him he would stand surety for me and take my responsibility.'

Atin looked grave. He asked, 'What was your answer?'

'I wrote one word on his letter: "vile", nothing else.'

'I am informed that Batu himself will come with the police tomorrow. If you agree, he will make a compromise with the tiger and drag you to the shelter of a crocodile pit. He is kind!'

Ela held Atin's hands and pleaded, 'Antu, please kill me with your own hands. It would be a blessing.' Kissing him again and again she said, 'Kill me, kill me.' She tore off her blouse.

Atin stood still as a statue.

Ela said, 'Don't hesitate, Antu. I am yours, entirely yours even in death. Don't let soiled hands touch me. Take me, I am yours.'

Atin said harshly, 'Go to bed immediately. It is my order.'

Holding on to Atin, Ela entreated, 'Antu, my love, my king, my god, I could not fully express how much I have loved you. For the sake of that love, kill me.'

Atin held her hands firmly and took her to the bedroom. 'Lie down and sleep,' he ordered.

'I can't sleep.'

'I have a sleeping pill with me.'

'There is no need for it, Antu. Do you have chloroform? Throw it away. I am not a coward; help me stay awake till I die in your lap. Let our last kiss be endless, Antu. Antu!'

A whistle sounded from far.